soulmates by FATE

BREYSON & KINZLEIGH

CHARISSE SPIERS

2nd Edition for Fate 1-4, 2018

Cover Art by Clarise Tan
Editing by Nikkita McDuffle
Formatting by Nancy Henderson

GIVING SOMEONE A PIECE OF YOUR SOUL IS BETTER THAN
GIVING A PIECE OF YOUR HEART. BECAUSE SOULS ARE ETERNAL.

— Helen Boswell

accepted
FATE
FATE SERIES BOOK ONE

ONE

Kinzleigh

It's Friday, the week following junior year and the start to a perfect summer. I can't wait for two whole months of shopping, no schedule, and lying on the beach. Everything in my life is going the way I want it to. Making squad captain was just the cherry on top.

Mom left a couple hours ago since she's due in court on some big case, Dad is always gone before sunup, and I haven't seen my brother, Konnor, since his high school graduation last Saturday. I have the house to myself again. I'm starting to sense this is going to become a normal thing this summer.

I put my arms above my head to stretch. I look over at the clock on my bedside table—eight thirty—the perfect time to get up and head to the gym. And I do mean *cheer* gym not fitness.

I need to be practicing, so I can keep my body limber. We already cut down on squad practice over the summer months, so it's up to me to make my own schedule. I need to call my coach before someone else books his schedule solid.

Sitting up and getting ready to get out of bed, my phone starts ringing. Looking at the screen all lit up, I see Presley's name and her photo. Touching the green answer button, I wait for it to connect. "Hello?"

Still somewhat half asleep, a noise comes through the phone. *Is that a treadmill? What on earth is she doing?*

"Please tell me you're not still in bed, Kinzleigh Baker. We only have a couple short months of fun before we're back to being slaves in high school and you're not going to waste it away sleeping. I will form an intervention if I need to," she says sarcastically, with a smile in her tone.

I smile to myself and roll my eyes, because Presley knows me a little too well. *She cannot possibly be running while she's talking on the phone, can she?* She doesn't even sound out of breath. "Presley, I get up early ten months of the year, so why would I get up early during my summer vacation? How do you expect me to enjoy freedom from school if I can't sleep in? What are you doing anyway? Did you call me while you're exercising?"

She sighs playfully. "Okay for one, what's with the twenty questions? Two, you're a lost cause, Kinzleigh. How many times do I have to tell you, if it's Monday through Friday, the hot guys work out early or late at the gym and not midday? Most people actually have a life to get to. Don't you want some of that amazing muscle for yourself? Don't you want to watch the sweat bead up on the skin of a hot guy standing mere steps away? So close that you can smell it . . ." *Eww.* "You don't want to go with the old and ugly people, do you?"

Presley has always been a little too crazy about the male population if you ask me, but what do I know? I'm single and intend to stay that way. I have seen the recurring cycle of love and loss. Heartbreak is something I intend to avoid at all costs. I'd rather take precautions up front and steer clear than to deal with the consequences after the fact. "No thanks, I'll leave that for you. I'm fine having my precious sleep time . . . *alone.*"

My brother, Konnor, is only a year older than me, and my only sibling, so we have always been close. He was with the same girl for three years, and a month before graduation he walked in on her at a senior party with his best friend buried between her legs. The bitch didn't even have the decency to act upset.

Instead, she blamed it on the fact they were about to head off to colleges on opposite ends of our great big state—California—when she should have been the adult she's supposed to be at eighteen and broke things off if she wanted to fool around. He beat the crap out of his best friend, Logan, putting him in the hospital for almost a week.

The month following, Konnor went off the deep end, started experimenting with drugs, and stayed drunk. If it hadn't been so close to the end of the year and his GPA not already high, he might not have graduated.

He almost lost his football scholarship to the University of California at Los Angeles—UCLA. My parents freaked out, of course, and made him start talking to a therapist.

Since my dad is alumnus and donates a lot of money to the football program, the coach gave him until startup of summer training to deal with his issues. He was the best quarterback at our school and was offered scholarships from several schools across the country, but is barely holding onto a good thing because of love. He is one of so many people that end up hurt.

No, thank you, I'll pass.

"Oh, right, I forgot I'm dealing with a prude." She laughs back at me, before becoming serious again. "You need to venture out and meet a guy. It's unhealthy to completely cut guys out of your life. We're going to be seniors in the fall. One day you're going to regret missing out on things like dating. It's fun. Don't you want to go to prom and homecoming at least once? You shouldn't miss out on everything in high school just because you're afraid of getting hurt. No one said you have to fall in love, but please, let me set you up one time."

"How many times do I have to tell you dating is your thing, Presley? This conversation is pointless; you know this. We've had it like a thousand times already," I whine through the phone, falling back down onto my pillow. "I don't have to date to enjoy my life. Besides, I have too much to do to work toward my future without having some guy requiring more of my time than I have to give. A career, and even school, is more important to me. Now, you know that I love you, but what do you want?"

She sighs. "Fine, have it your way, but don't think we won't revisit this conversation later. I'm not giving up. For now, get your skinny butt out of bed and meet me down at the beach in an hour. We have to work on your pale skin before Cabo. You know we leave in a week. Don't make me come get you, Kinzleigh, you know I will."

She's so bossy when she wants to be, but that's one of the things I love about her. Presley has been my best friend since I can even remember. It's a typical story from growing up in Laguna Beach, California, but second generation. Our moms were best friends growing up and still are. They went to law school together and even made partners at the same law firm, not to mention we're the same age. You know they're close when they planned pregnancies together. We were destined to be with each other from the beginning.

Presley and I are completely different; although, maybe that's what has kept us together since we were in diapers. We seem to balance each other out. Where she's outgoing, I'm shy. She is tall and slender with long, cascading brown hair and sapphire blue eyes, whereas I'm short and petite with platinum blonde curls and bright green eyes.

I twirl my hair around my finger and sit quietly, just to make her wait a little. She's a very impatient person. I can already tell she is becoming irritated by the huffs coming from her mouth. "I was going to call Andy and set up a practice. What about after?"

"Getting my keys ready, babe. What's it going to be?" I laugh, imagining her really driving over here just so she can prove a point.

"Okay, fine, but you owe me a practice and I'm going to work you hard, so you better get those muscles ready. I'll see you in an hour." I disconnect the call and head for the shower.

Standing in the shower, my hands covered in a thick layer of coconut-scented suds from washing my hair with my favorite shampoo, I start thinking about our trip to Cabo San Lucas next week. There is no telling what Presley is going to try dragging me into. I'm not sure if I should be excited or scared.

My parents take us, and one friend each, on a weeklong vacation every summer. Usually, Presley and Logan tag along, but I'm not sure who Konnor is bringing now that Logan is out of the equation. That's one thing that makes me nervous—the unknown.

Presley has always had a thing for my brother, but she can't seem to get him to look past the *little sister's best friend* issue. Plus, he has always had the Sophia blinders on until now, so I'm not sure if or what she will try now that he's a single man. That probably means a shopping trip this week, knowing Presley. Not that I'm complaining. Retail therapy is a girl's best friend.

Twenty minutes later, now washed and shaved, I'm running around my room in a towel, throwing various items into my pink beach bag sitting on my bed. Digging through my drawer I finally find what I'm looking for; my new turquoise and peach swirled bandeau bikini top and matching bottoms. I fell in love with it the moment I laid eyes on it last week and had to have it.

Since my parents work long hours, Dad gave me my own Amex when I got my driver's license. As long as I stay out of trouble and keep my grades at A's, I'm able to spend as I please—using good judgment, of course.

I pull on my swimsuit and black, lace cover-up, before I walk to my closet in search of my flip-flops. Combing my fingers through my wet hair on the way out, I then throw my head forward and tousle the blonde strands to rid of extra water until they curl up. It should be dry by the time I reach the beach.

Standing back up, I dab on my gloss and throw it in my small makeup bag along with my hair tie. Finally, I perform my routine mental checklist before I go.

Towel, check, sunscreen, check, tanning oil, check, shades, check.

I grab my purse from my desk and slide it on my shoulder, shoving my beach bag on the other, and head for my bedroom door. Having almost everything I need for a day in the sun, I turn off my light and close the door.

Running downstairs into the large kitchen, I grab some supplies for the day. I take a few granola bars from the food pantry and a couple bottles of water from the refrigerator, tossing them in my tote to reside with the rest of my stuff. I walk through the house, making sure everything is off before I leave for the day.

Once finished, I set the alarm and close the front door. Digging my keys from my purse, I turn to my beautiful, black, Range Rover sitting in the drive and unlock the doors with the remote. It's normally kept in the garage, but the detailer came by and cleaned it this morning.

Mom and Dad surprised me with it on the morning of my sixteenth birthday. Mom kept telling me I wouldn't be getting a car until later, since Konnor and I are so close in age; however, I was depressed, because Grams had died earlier that year. Grams was my dad's mom and was as close to me as Mom. My parents were gone a lot with work; therefore, I was with Grams almost daily for fifteen years. She fought a three-year battle with cancer before it defeated her.

I felt shattered and lost, losing all hope for happiness. I stayed in my room for months after she died, with the exception of being at school. Right then, I learned, never allow yourself to love anyone other than family, no exceptions.

The pain of losing someone you love hurts too much to risk it when it's avoidable. The day I felt that kind of pain, I knew then, I would never allow myself to feel it again if I could control it. Loving a man is controllable; family is not.

Friends became a distant memory that year. Needless to say, I guess Mom and Dad felt badly for me.

The morning of my sixteenth birthday, I stepped out of the front door, ready for school, and headed for Konnor's silver BMW parked out front. That's when I saw it sitting in the driveway, glistening, with a big, red bow. That car is my baby. It marks a turning point for me. One chapter closed and on to new beginnings.

I shake off my thoughts and pull down my aviator shades, walking toward my car. Time to hit the beach . . .

Pulling into the beach, I recognize Presley's White Mercedes almost instantly. It takes me a while to find a place to park, because apparently, everyone else had the same idea today. The beach is packed, and I consider turning around and going home.

Contemplating what I'm going to do, I glance over and see Presley making her way toward my car. How does she even know I'm here? The girl has to have ESP—so much for making a run for it . . .

I grab my cell phone from my purse with one hand and stow my purse beneath my seat with the other. As she moves in closer, I remove my keys from the ignition. Lifting my bag off the seat, I toss my cell and keys inside and then open the door and step out.

"I was starting to wonder if I was going to have to come and pick you up," she says. A smile begins, along with a mischievous look in her eyes that tells me she's up to something. Nothing good ever follows that look. I place my bag on my shoulder and hold onto my door in case I need to make a dash for it.

"What are you up to, Presley?" I ask nervously, fidgeting with my cover up. She moves faster, as if I'm about to take off running, and then grabs my hand and shuts the door.

"What makes you think I'm up to something?" She loops her arm through mine and continues. "Don't you trust me?"

The tone in her voice alone says it all. *No, I shouldn't, and I should get back in my car right now before I go any farther.*

She must see the hesitation on my face, because she pulls me down the sidewalk, toward the beach. I concentrate on the rays from the sun bearing down on my skin, the heat enveloping me. The seagulls are screaming overhead, drowning out the sounds of the beachgoers. The salty sea air calms me, but only for a moment.

As the water comes into view, I begin to understand that look on Presley's face. Some of the girls from the cheerleading squad have plastered themselves right in front of a group of guys playing volleyball. I recognize some of them from the football team at school, but the rest of the boys don't look familiar.

Great, this is going to be awkward.

I've never been one of the flirty girls at school, because I really don't see the point. I get a front row seat to Presley's show every day and that is enough for both of us. Flirting serves one of two purposes—looking for love or trying to get laid—and I do not want either.

Love stands in the way of dreams and aspirations, cripples you, and makes you dependent on someone else. It sets you up for failure, because you're always going to get hurt. If you don't get cheated on, you get left behind. I have worked too hard for my dreams to get shattered over something completely preventable. Since you can't control who you fall for, I just avoid it all together.

Look at my brother, wallowing in pity, because he let someone else take priority over everything else in his life. He gave away his heart and mapped his whole life out according to the wants of another with the expectation it would last forever. Now, here he is, brokenhearted and settling for his second-choice school, as well as the possibility of losing his dream to play college football if he doesn't get his crap together before season. What did he do all that for? Absolutely nothing.

I look over to Presley standing behind her towel, adjusting her perky C-cups, as if her breasts aren't hanging out enough already. Shaking my head, I pull my towel from my bag and spread it flat beside hers.

In a way, Presley doesn't date either; at least not one person. After her breakup with Corey last fall, she swore off men, in the emotional sense anyway. Her heart will and always be made of ice because of him, or so she says. I think it's because secretly she's keeping her options open in hopes of attaining Konnor.

Her and Corey were similar to throwing fire to gasoline, his jealousy leading to constant fights, so for now she enjoys being an upper-class slut. I only call her that in love and because she's my best friend, no judgment. She would agree if you asked her. She's always careful, and it works for her.

"Do you have to do that? Adjust that top any more and they're going to fall out." Taking a seat on my towel, I pull my hair back in a loose bun on top of my head and grab for my bag. Digging through its contents, I pull out my iPhone and earbuds, along with my water and tanning essentials. Pulling off my cover-up and flip-flops, I toss them in the bag and set it to the side.

The waves crashing against the shoreline makes for a peaceful day. The sound could take anyone's stress away. There is a reason it's used for white noise. It's calming. Even with the high-pitched squeals and laughter that accompany it from the kids screaming in the distance, running back and forth as the water rolls onto the sand.

There's a slight breeze out, making the heat welcome. The gritty specks of sand are already covering my feet. I begin spreading the sunscreen on my face and shoulders, before applying the tanning oil to the remainder of my body.

Presley sits beside me on her towel and begins coating her legs with tanning oil as well. "Hey, just because you're celibate and hate male attention doesn't mean the rest of us do. Maybe you should try something new. You're becoming a bit of a grump these days. All of that built-up sexual frustration is starting to show." She laughs, swirling her finger in front of my face. "You never know, you might like having the girls played with." She winks as her eyes trail down to my chest.

Rolling my eyes, I turn to acknowledge some of the other girls from the squad. "Hey, you guys. What's up? It's nice out today, right?"

Lexi and Madison are sprawled out in their beach loungers on rental. I still haven't figured out what they have against the sand. What's the point in coming to the beach if you aren't going to enjoy it to its fullest? They always were the prissy two of the group.

I'm starting to think they can't hear me, when finally, Lexi pulls her eyes from the volleyball game and slides her shades down her nose, lifting a brow. "You really have to ask with all of that man-candy right in front of your face?" She smirks, as if I just asked her what two plus two is.

I scrunch my nose, causing my eyebrows to wrinkle. "You too? All of you are hopeless," I say, and lay down to work on my tan. At least one of us is going to leave with some dignity intact. It looks like that person is going to be me, since I'm the only one that's not practically drooling over the shirtless guys in front of us.

I plug my earbuds into my iPhone and start my music. The softness of the voice mixed with the heat blanketing my bare skin, my breathing evens out and I grow tired.

Almost asleep from listening to the sweet voice of Colbie Caillat—

adding an island vibe—something smacks me right in the center of my face. Startled, I scream—more like an elevated squeak—and jump to my feet. "What the heck?!"

I look down at the sand and see a volleyball lying beside my towel. I bend over and reach down to pick it up, so I can toss it back to the guys playing. "You could be a little more careful!" I yell, grabbing the ball in my hands as I stand up.

When I turn around I'm staring right at a chest—a sweaty, smooth, tan, and muscular chest. My face is so close I can feel the heat radiating off his body. My eyes widen and trail upward to see who is standing in front of me. They lock with a pair of dark blue eyes, deep and rich, like staring into the midnight sky. For a second, I forgot where I am and what I was doing, at a loss for words.

As my eyes scan his face, Mister Beautiful Blue Eyes swallows, his Adam's apple bobbing up and down, and then his mouth opens. "I'm really sorry about that. I guess I got caught up in the game and stopped paying attention. Are you okay?"

Dang, that voice; it's so deep and raspy. Is that an accent? Southern, maybe? Great, I'm still staring at him. I probably look like an idiot. What is wrong with me?

Now would be a great time to speak, Kinzleigh.

"Yes, I'm fine. Here is your ball back." I extend my arm, palm side up, supporting the ball.

He takes the ball with one hand, pulling it against his hip. Wow, his hands are big, and clearly controlled to be able to do it one-handed without dropping it. He extends the other hand out, a wide smile spreading across the bottom half of his face, revealing straight white teeth. "Forgive my manners. I'm Breyson, and you are?"

I look down at his hand, staring like he's grown an extra limb. My eyes wander. First, to his navy and orange swim trunks, covering a nice set of tanned, muscular legs. He must play some type of sport to have a body like that. His abs are defined, tightening each time he breathes. He has a V of muscle that disappears into the waistband of his shorts. His hips are narrow, widening into a pronounced chest, defined and smooth.

My eyes won't stop the embarrassing stroll up his body.

His arms are built, slightly flexed before me from his stance, and I wonder how they would feel wrapped around me. His jaw is long, his lips perfect and pouty, barely open. His eyes are thickly lined with dark lashes, despite his hair being lighter—the shade of dirty blond, and short mostly, but long enough on the top it could hold gel. It looks shiny and thick, perfect for running fingers through, grabbing ahold of, and holding on for dear life. Wow. In my entire seventeen years, I've never witnessed something so beautiful.

Suddenly, he looks unsure of what to say, and that's when I realize what's going on. I'm standing here as if it's my first encounter with a human after being locked up in a room my entire life.

Good job, Kinzleigh. Now, not only will he think you're a stuck-up brat, but also ignorant and weird.

Presley clears her throat. "Are you just going to stand there or are you going to introduce yourself sometime today?" she asks, removing her shades as she looks up from where she's lying on her towel. "Not that I mind the view from down here, but you're going to give California girls a bad rep."

Judging by the look on her face, she is pleased with the sight before her as well. She stands and glances over at me, a smile forming on her face, and then looks back at him. "Please excuse my friend. She must have gotten hit a little too hard. I'm Presley." She knows I was staring. I'm never going to hear the end of this. She's always trying to set me up with people. Now that she's seen a break in my armor, she's never going to stop. She closes in and elbows me in the ribs.

I pull my sunglasses up to rest on my head. Placing my hands on my hips, I try to clear my mind. "My name is Kinzleigh. Sorry for being rude, you caught me off guard."

He's staring at me with a smirk on his face, as if he's really amused by me. *Awesome!* Based on the cocky grin, he knows I find him attractive.

"Well, Kinzleigh, it's nice to meet you. Y'all wanna play? There's room for a few more. As an apology, you can be on my team. It's a guaranteed win," he says playfully, winking at me. His smile comes back full force and my stomach flutters like I've just started down the drop of a rollercoaster.

All of a sudden, I'm hot and I feel dizzy. Maybe I'm hungry. It's been a while since I've eaten, and I never usually skip breakfast. That has to be the explanation for this weird feeling I have. Where in the world is this guy from? I wonder if all guys there look like this. "Y'all? Come again. You're not from around here, are you?"

Please say no.

I really don't need this right now. I've got too much going for me to be interested in some boy. It's the heat. It has to be the sun frying my brain.

He shrugs, bouncing the ball from hand to hand. "Nah, just visiting some family. You going to play or what?"

I've got to do something to make up for my weird behavior earlier. "Yeah, okay, sure."

The girls quickly jump in and volunteer to play, as if they've been waiting for the opportunity. I guess if you put ten attractive, half-naked men in front of them, they have the motivation for anything. Thank goodness I don't have to do this alone.

Breyson hands me the ball back, appearing happy with my answer. "Ladies first."

He needs to stop smiling at me like that. Every time he does, I start to shake, and my breathing becomes heavier. He's sexy, and I don't think I have ever looked at a guy like this.

Why, oh why, didn't I stay home today?

This is the last thing I need right now. I haven't worked twenty hours a week in the gym for the last twelve years—cheering and stunting and perfecting routines—to suddenly get distracted by some guy. I don't care how sexy that accent is.

I take the ball and smile. "As long as you don't get in my way." Growing up close to the beach, everyone knows how to play volleyball, and well. He smirks, as if that is exactly the opposite of what he is going to do, and backs up to give me some space.

About an hour later, we're up three points. I'm waiting for Lexi to serve, and suddenly, I feel like he's watching me. Now feeling paranoid, I glance at him underneath my shades, from the corner of my eye. He's looking right at me, as if there is something he wants to say.

Maybe there is something on me. I start discretely doing a self-check to make sure my swimsuit is still in place, when I hear him chuckle.

I glance back across the net and see the ball sailing through the air. Not even thinking, I take off running to hit it back. Before I can stop myself, I collide with Breyson midair and land flat on my back in the sand beneath him. Electricity shoots through my body and I feel like I can't breathe. His body is lying perfectly aligned with mine, pressed against me. "Oh my gosh, I'm so sorry." My voice comes out strained.

His eyes are staring straight into mine, as if he's trying to read into my soul, to discover all of the secrets that lie inside. He puts his weight on his forearm in the sand, next to my head, while his other brushes up my leg, stopping on my hip.

A moan slips from my lips at the contact, causing me to close my eyes. When I open them, he bites his lip as his eyes move down to mine. My face starts to flush.

He's so close his breath tickles my face, and I find myself wishing he'd kiss me. Everything else has faded away, except him. We could have been here, staring at each other, for five minutes or five hours. I don't have a clue. It seems I can't think looking into those deep blue pools. Presley clears her throat, breaking me from my somewhat frozen state. "Guys, are we going to play or just stand here and watch you two all but hump each other on the beach?"

Embarrassed, I place my hands on his muscular chest and try to push him back, not having any effect at all. "Can you please get off me?" I say, irritated I act so stupid around him.

This is not like me at all. I should know better. How could I allow myself to be sidetracked by some guy? I don't even know him! How can someone I just met put me in a state of bliss in front of all my friends? I've never acted like this. I'm humiliated.

He stands and offers out his hand to help me up. I take it and stand to my feet, quickly brushing the sand from my body, and trying to gain control of the emotions that are obviously in a state of panic. I'm in uncharted waters, a foreign state of mind.

Knocking the remaining sand off, I realize I have to get out of here. "Thanks, I just remembered my parents needed me home early. I have to go. It was nice to meet you." He looks as if there's something he wants to say or do, but doesn't, and I find myself slightly disappointed, though I don't know why. I'm the one leaving. I rush over to my towel, shove everything in my bag in a hurry and take off toward my car.

Hands shaking, I unlock my door and climb inside. In the past, I would always change in the bathhouse, because I take really good care of my car and would never allow sand inside. This time, though, I'm going to have to make an exception.

I don't know what has come over me suddenly, but I never get stupid around a guy. Frankly, I just don't care. I'm not that kind of girl; never have been. I can admire a hot guy and then move on without acting. To this point it's never been an issue. I've seen too many girls put their dreams on hold to chase after a boy and I will not be one of them. When he's gone, there may not be any chances left.

Pulling into my driveway, I notice Mom and Dad's vehicle parked in the open garage. That's strange. It's still reasonably early and they are never home before seven during the week, at least never together. I'm not sure if I should be excited to spend some time with my parents or nervous something bad has happened.

The first thing running through my mind is that something bad has happened to Konnor. Ever since he walked in on Logan and Sophia, his ex, I'm terrified I'm going to come home to find he has done something stupid like take his life. I love my brother and he's never been a depressed guy, but when he loves something he gives it everything he has. He's passionate. That's what makes him a good athlete. Every time I think of what that witch did to him, I could kill her. I still may. No one messes with my family; especially not some stupid whore.

Trying to calm my nerves for what I'm about to walk into, I inhale deeply. I've been known to be a worrier over people I care about. After Grams died, I was on medication for anxiety, but have had it under control recently.

Come on, Kinzleigh, they would have called if something had happened to Konnor.

It could even be nothing. Maybe they just had a light day at work. Getting out of my car, I walk toward the front door and place my hand on the doorknob.

You can do this, calm down.

Opening the door, Dad is sitting in his recliner reading today's paper and Mom is flipping through a magazine on the couch. Nothing looks wrong, but maybe they are just trying to break it to me gently. Dad speaks first, lowering his newspaper. "Hi, sweetie, did you have fun at the beach?"

Now I'm really confused. They look like they are in a good mood. "Mom, Dad, the two of you are home early, and how did you know I was at the beach?"

Mom looks up from her magazine and smiles as if that was the silliest thing she's heard. "Your swimsuit would be the first clue." Then it dawns on me; I was in such a hurry to get away from *him*, that I forgot to even put my cover-up back on.

Suddenly, feeling very naked, I cradle my beach bag in front of my chest. Mom and Dad are more of the conservative type and they always instilled that in us. They wouldn't be too happy with me running around in only swimwear. "Oh, right, sorry. Why are you home so early? Is everything okay?"

She laughs as if I'm the one she should be worried about. "Of course, sweetie, everything is fine. You're not starting to get anxious again are you? I won that big case I've been working on, so your dad and I thought we would all go out and eat to celebrate. Plus, we have some news to discuss with you and your brother. Konnor should be getting home soon and then we'll go. I called him about an hour ago and he said he's been training and working out with Kyle."

I wonder what could be so important that they can't discuss now. My parents have never been able to hide anything, and something tells me I'm not going to like what they have to say. I let out a breath, trying to relieve some of this tension I've built up. "Okay then, I'll head upstairs and get ready."

TWO

Breyson

I remain standing here, watching her walk away, and though I know I should go after her, I can't. She's just a girl. I've never been one to chase after a girl—I've never had to.

But this may be one of the times I really want to say screw it and go. That girl is the most beautiful thing I've ever seen. There is no way she's single, or is she? Something about her stirs primal instincts that need to remain at bay. Going after her wouldn't be fair for several reasons.

First is the fact that I sort of have a girlfriend back home. Secondly, I'm only here for a week and then it's back to Mississippi for me. I know I could be selfish, enjoy a week with a gorgeous girl, then head home with no strings attached except for a great memory, but something about her says it wouldn't be enough. Her eyes tell me I would want more, but that's something I can't give myself.

We wrapped up the game shortly after Kinzleigh took off. As soon as she left, the girls with her went back to lying on the beach to 'tan' as they call it. I've never understood why any woman would want to sit in the sun and bake for fun. Maybe that's just the football player coming out in me. When you run outside five days a week, hours on end with shoulder pads strapped to you, cooking in the sun is not something I consider fun.

I usually come down for a week every summer to stay with my cousin

Ryland. We're the same age and he was my next-door neighbor and best friend back home, until they moved here when he was fourteen. I flew in this morning for my annual week in the California sun. We usually just chill on my first day here, because I'm jetlagged, but he said today was supposed to be a pretty good day for surfing.

Since I'm from the south—where the only waves are from the tide rolling in and definitely not big enough to surf, thanks to the barrier islands—I usually just sit out and watch or find something to do. Ryland has attempted to teach me a few times, but he gave up my second summer here. Some of us are just designed for land sports.

I just now realize I'm still staring at the street where Kinzleigh left when I hear Ryland in the background. I turn around and he is talking to that Presley chick as if he knows her. I wonder if he knows the blonde. This girl has her breasts practically in his face.

It looks like someone is getting laid tonight. Wish it were me . . . Wait, what am I saying? You have a girlfriend, dumbass. It's going to be a long week.

I shake off my thoughts. He grabs the swimsuit string between her breasts, pulling her closer.

"Where's the party at tonight?" he asks, grabbing her ass and pressing her against him. I have to admit, it's times like these I wonder what the hell I was thinking when I agreed to date Natalie.

It seemed like a good idea at the time, because we've been friends since freshman year. She's always flirted with me, as most girls from school do at one point or another, but it was mostly platonic. I usually ignored it, until about four months ago.

She stepped up her game and practically raped me at a school party when I was drunk. I was hammered, and I don't even remember having that much to drink. I'm still not sure how she managed to get me so drunk that I slept with her. I couldn't have stopped it if I wanted to, though. I was horny as hell and she was practically naked, rubbing against me. Besides, what high school guy turns down offered sex with a hot girl?

None.

I felt bad, since we were friends, and realized there were some perks. Anytime I wanted sex, she gave it up freely. No work was required and that worked for me . . . or so I thought. Now, I'm not so sure.

I made sure she understood I could give her sex and the title she was looking for, but nothing more. I was game for fun, but that's about it. It works for us, because she's okay with not getting the emotional, romantic, and bubbly shit like letters between classes, date nights and talking on the phone for hours. Definitely no *I love you's.* I don't do it, ever. There are no exceptions.

Presley is running her finger down his arm, looking as if she can't wait to get him alone. "Logan's graduation party is tonight. You should come." As she says the word come, she places her lips to his ear, saying something only he can hear. His face takes on a look I understand, causing him to squeeze her ass. "I promise I'll make it worth your time," she says, running her finger underneath the band of his shorts.

Ah hell, I guess tonight I'm flying solo. This is too complicated. I don't like restrictions. Maybe I should just call Natalie and break if off, have a week of parties and sex with no commitments and deal with her when I get home. The more I think about it, the better it sounds. It's an asshole move, but she knows how I am. I do what I want, and I don't care what anyone else thinks.

They aren't anywhere close to finishing this up it seems, so I take it upon myself to get everything moving along. "Yo, Ry, what's the plan?"

I'm getting tired of watching them eye-fuck each other. I have other things I could be doing and watching someone else isn't one of them. Voyeurism isn't my thing. A pair of green eyes comes to mind, though. I rub my hand through my sweaty hair, waiting for him to answer.

He tosses me his keys. "We're hitting up Logan's tonight. Wait for me at the truck, yeah?"

Catching the key ring midair, I nod my head. "Aight, but hurry up. You can pick that up later."

I've been sitting in the truck for about twenty minutes now. I have no idea what's taking Ryland so long. What could he possibly be doing with a girl at a public beach, surrounded by hundreds of people? I get it, the bastard is horny, but I'm pretty sure he isn't lacking.

Ryland has always had a string of girls following him everywhere he goes. The guy has a tan and a set of dimples and he knows how to use them; not to mention that whole surfing thing he has going on.

He finally gets in the truck with a smile that was not present the last time I saw him—a post orgasmic smile. Well, shit. Kinky bastard. Didn't know the little freak had it in him.

Tapping at my wrist sarcastically, I look at him. "Would you care to explain what took you so long?" I can tell by the look on his face he won't be in such a hurry to get to that party now.

"Hey, if I get offered a pre-party surprise by a hot girl without doing any of the work to get it, I'm not turning it down. Besides, I've been trying to get with Presley for a while, and now that she doesn't have Corey following her around like a freaking puppy, I'm hittin' that. I just needed to give her a little motivation for what she'll have inside her later. A little oral representation . . ."

That's information I would have been perfectly fine without. "Do I even want to know where you had the guts to pull that off?" I can't imagine where on a public beach that's possible without him getting arrested for indecency.

He smirks at me and raises his brow. "Don't ask questions you don't want the answers to, because you know I won't spare any details. Modesty has never been my thing. I'm proud of what I got." I nod, understanding exactly what he means as he pulls out of the parking area.

We pull into Ryland's drive and he parks his truck. One thing I like about Ryland is that even though he moved across the country, he hasn't conformed to the ways of all the other rich kids here. When he got his license, his parents offered him a fancy little sports car. Instead, all he wanted was a lifted-up GMC Sierra with mud grip tires and rims. His reason—he had to have a place to haul his surfboard and his parents couldn't argue that valid point.

That's probably the only reason we've remained friends throughout the years. He's family, but distance complicates things. But he's down-to-earth and doesn't care what other people think. He was raised in the south, so, like me he has that deep southern drawl. Somehow, though, he makes it work for him here. I think it's part of his appeal.

Dinner took longer than usual. It often does on my visits here from the lengthy conversation that comes with catching up. His parents ask a lot of questions, and because I rarely see them, I happily answer. It always ends talking about football—a rehash of the last season. My uncle still keeps up with my games, even all these miles away. After Ryland and I finished dinner with his parents, we both slept through our food coma the twelve-ounce rib eyes induced, and finally started getting ready for the party a couple hours later.

I stand in the shower underneath the rain of water, the steam swirling from the heat and fogging the glass. I let the hot water rain down my face and I blow out, before wiping it with my hands to remove the salt stuck to me. My fingers comb through my hair, standing it up on the top.

She pops in my head. *Kinzleigh.* I saw her coming from a mile away. I could tell before she got to the beach she was going to be attractive, but I didn't expect her to take my breath away. No other girl ever has.

Once my eyes caught sight of those bouncy, blonde curls and emerald green eyes, I could barely look away. I wanted to meet her then. It was all I could do to continue playing ball with the guys I'd met before Ryland went to surf.

I wasn't doing too good of a job, obviously, because instead of paying attention I sent the ball sailing in her direction. I couldn't help it, though. Every time I looked over at her, my eyes held, because she was doing something else that was turning me on.

When she was rubbing oil all over her firm little body, in my head, those hands rubbing down her inner thighs were mine. Every time she adjusted her bikini top, making sure she was covered, those perfect breasts bounced slightly, as if they were begging to be touched.

I probably looked like a total asshole when the ball hit her in the forehead. What I won't admit to anyone was the reason I wasn't paying attention was because I was adjusting myself to hide my arousal from watching her.

I place my hand on the shower wall, trying to clear the thoughts of her from my head, but it seems my mind has ideas of its own. All I can think about is how cute she was when she jumped up, startled. I tried hard not to laugh, so she wouldn't take it the wrong way.

Her hair was pulled in a bun of loose curls on top of her head, begging to be pulled free. She was trying not to scream, but failed, and what came out was more of a squeak. The sound was similar to a mouse. I wonder how she sounds when she's turned on instead of startled.

Great, now I have thoughts of that voice panting and moaning in my head.

I look down to my soldier standing tall. *Dammit.* I rub my hands up and down my face, trying to stop thinking about this girl, but instead my mind starts to reel some more. I'm going nowhere fast.

What the hell . . . No one will know.

I squirt some conditioner in my hand and start to stroke myself to the memory, spreading it around as my mind takes me back. I was standing at her towel with a legitimate reason to be talking to her, so I didn't look like a creep. She had no clue I was behind her. I had to clench my fists to keep my hands to myself. I bit my tongue to avoid verbal outbreaks.

She was bent over instead of squatting like most girls do, her plump, round ass staring me in the face. Her swimsuit had slightly shifted over her right cheek. It would take barely any effort to slide it over, grab her hips, and slip inside. And in my mind, it takes even less effort to picture it.

That's exactly what happened.

Small thighs that don't touch, a perky ass with enough grip, and height short enough that moving her would be so easy. *God, I bet she's tight.* And no straps on her top. Perfect for just pulling it down to take a peek and mouthful of her nipples. Pink, hard, appetizing little buds I could bite and lick.

I clench my shaft harder to indicate the grip I think her body would have on me if I were between her legs, and quicken my strokes, thrusting inside her from behind.

She turns her head, those bright green eyes hooded from the feel of me. Her cheeks are flushed with a light shade of pink. She likes what she sees. That's one look that remains the same, no matter the girl. My mouth pulls into a smirk on one side. I guess my dad's nutrition and exercise obsession really paid off.

Her neck glistens from sweat as the sun hammers down on her skin. Her lips open, her soft voice expelling with, *Breyson, make me come.*

Shit. This isn't going to take long.

Our eyes meet, the pleading of her request in them, and every time they locked before it was as if gravity was holding them together.

The hot water runs down my sensitized body. I want her muscular legs wrapped around me as I inch inside her. I want to look at her. I turn her around and shove her down on her towel, following until I'm holding myself off of her.

My breath catches in my throat and all I can see is a pool of green that shimmers in the sun, her head rolling back in ecstasy as I slide back inside. The conditioner adding a slick layer makes it easier to imagine what the inside of her feels like.

I study her face as I move, pushing in and pulling out. She has the cutest little button nose. Her sun-kissed skin is blemish free and she has the most beautiful full lips. Lips made to kiss, to suck, and to be sucked.

Damn.

Mentally exploring that beautiful little body, my movements pick up, stroking faster, clenching harder. I kiss her full breasts, her top now sitting around her flat and toned stomach.

She wraps her legs around me, her heels digging in. She had the cutest little feet, toenails painted pink and her ankle wrapped in a small, silver chain holding some kind of charm, a heart maybe. I can't be sure.

Her body feels warm, her breasts full. I pull her closer and kiss her, rubbing my hands along her body as I continuously dive into her. She moans against my lips, her back arching and pushing her chest into me. Her chin tips up until her neck is longer and her veins are more prominent, and she finally clenches around me.

That thought and I'm done, a growl tearing through my throat with my balls clenching, heat ripping through my dick as the hot, white cum releases into the shower, mixing with the water as it runs toward the drain. I watch it disappear, my dick jerking in my hand until I'm finished, my breathing labored as I press my forehead against the shower wall, letting the water soak my back.

I'm broken from my thoughts of her body pressed against mine with Ryland beating on the door. "Dude, are you going to stay in there all night? Girls don't even take this long. I still have to shower too, you know."

Crap, how long have I been in here? Standing slumped, hands against the wall, underneath the shower, I look down and realize I'm still aroused. *You've got to be kidding me.* How can I still have a boner? I've got to get this chick out of my head. I have a feeling it's not going to be that easy.

Jerking off. If it weren't so ludicrous it'd be laughable. I rarely have to anymore now that we're all driving. And here I am, strokin' it to a girl I just met—and not the one titled as my girlfriend—in my best friend's shower. This is a new low for me.

I have to come up with something quick—something believable between two guys. Ryland knows it doesn't take me this long to shower, and I sure as hell am not telling him I just busted a nut in the next room. "I'll be right out. I had to take a shit." I yell back, so maybe he will move away from the door.

"Make sure you spray, dick."

Relieved he bought it, I hurry through the rest of my shower and emerge from the bathroom, towel wrapped around my waist.

Ryland is laying across his bed, flipping through the channels on the television. He looks over, a smile forming on his face, as if he knows my dirty little secret. "If you needed some quality time with your little buddy, all you had to do was say so and I could've used the shower downstairs," he says, shaking his head at me as he laughs.

Well this is embarrassing, no matter how close we are. It makes me look like a loser that never gets laid. "Shut up, asshole! That's not what I was doing and there is nothing *little* about my 'buddy' as you call it. How do you know I wasn't taking a shit?"

"Because you always go in the guest bathroom to shit and I heard your grand finale in there. Must have been a good spank bank. Tell me, who was it starring? The hot little blonde at the beach you scared the shit out of by almost dry humping in the sand?"

I bite back a laugh, remembering the look on her face when she realized we were in the middle of everyone before she ran off like her house was on fire, my jaw flexing from the act.

"Go to hell. The shower is all yours." The laugh comes anyway. Pleading the fifth may be equivalent to agreeing, but the words will never come out of my mouth. There is no way I'm admitting what just happened because of a chick I only saw one time.

"Enjoy her in your head, because you'll never touch her. Trust me, we've all tried," he says in passing, before disappearing into the bathroom. And then it replays.

The hot little blonde at the beach you scared the shit out of by almost dry humping in the sand? Experienced girls don't get scared. Shy. She's just shy. I head over to my suitcase to grab my clothes, shoving any other thoughts out of my mind before I get my ass in trouble.

I'm standing in front of the mirror, spraying some cologne, when I hear *Crazy Bitch* by Buckcherry playing on my phone. This is the last thing I need right now.

Waiting on Ryland still, I grab my phone and walk outside onto the balcony for some privacy. "Hey, Nat, what's up?" It's silent, as if the call has been disconnected. I look down to see if she hung up, but the timer is still clocking the call. Placing it back to my ear, I hear her sniffle like she's crying. "Natalie? What's wrong?"

She sighs. "Were you even going to call me while you were there?"

What?

When did she turn into the needy, emotional type? We rarely talk on the phone. Usually, it's just text messaging. Now, suddenly, I'm more confused than ever.

Scrunching my brows, I begin rubbing my forehead. "Was I supposed to call you, Natalie? Because I must have missed that message when I texted you from the airport. I'm visiting family."

Based on the silence you would think I slapped her.

Finally, she sighs again, sounding hurt this time, "All I'm saying, is it would have been nice to hear from you. We usually see each other at least every other day and now you're gone for a week. You are my boyfriend, you know. Is it so wrong to want to hear from you? We used to talk on the phone every day before we started dating and now you only text me."

Obviously, she rehearsed this before she called from the sound of it. This is exactly what I was afraid of when I agreed to date her. Girls can't handle emotionless relationships. At least if it's just hooking up there is a mutual understanding. No matter what they say, the second you say you're exclusive they get attached. Next, it's pledges of love and jealousy.

She's always been good with giving me my space. I don't know why she's suddenly being a pain, but it's not going to work out in her favor if she keeps it up. I never should have agreed to date her, because it's probably going to ruin a perfectly good friendship.

Starting to feel guilty, I sit down on one of the chairs. Closing my eyes, I try to think of the best way to handle this. Before I can even say anything, she blurts out, "Breyson, I love you."

My eyes go wide in shock. Surely, I didn't hear that right. "Natalie . . ."

I don't even get the chance to finish before she starts to panic. "I'm sorry. You don't have to say it back. I just thought you should know. I didn't mean for it to happen, it just did. It's true, though, Breyson. I love you and I miss you."

Yep, I heard that right. Damn. Damn. Damn. We've been friends for three years—good friends—and everything is about to turn to shit. This is my fault entirely.

I'm about to be the biggest dick in the universe to someone important to me. What else can I do, though? I don't love her. She knew this going in. I exhale the breath I didn't realize I was holding. "You know I can't give you that, Natalie. I told you this in the beginning. Look, maybe this wasn't the best idea. I care about you and I always will. You were my friend before my girlfriend. We crossed that line and now we have to deal with it. I thought you wanted the same things, to have a good time. I can't and won't do love, Natalie. I'm not interested in cuddles, kisses, and romantic gestures. I will never be a member of the sappy love society. The risks outweigh the benefits. This was supposed to be about two friends that like to hang out, but also like sex. I thought you needed the title so you didn't feel like a slut. I can be faithful to you physically. Sex with one is the same as sex with many, but emotionally, I have nothing to give. Ever."

I sit, waiting for a string of cursing or crying, but something other than silence. I hear a door close in the background. I hope she didn't say all that in front of a friend or have me on speaker.

I'm starting to wonder if she is going to speak, when she finally barks out, "Don't you dare break up with me, Breyson. You may not see it now, but we're good together. I can give you what you need. I only told you so you would know how I feel, but I'll never mention it again until you feel the same. I wasn't looking for anything in return. I'll let you go for now, but text me later."

She really doesn't get it. I will never feel that way about her. You can't force yourself to feel that way about someone. It's there or it's not. To be honest, the thought of loving someone freaks me out. With her it's just not there, but I'm mentally spent from this conversation and it just started. I'll have to deal with this when I get back home. For now, I need a drink. I need to forget—about this conversation, about Natalie, and about a certain someone with blonde hair and green eyes. "Bye, Natalie."

Feeling frustrated, I walk back inside in search of Ryland. He has to be ready by now. For him to have something to say about the time I spent in the shower is insane. The boy has changed clothes like ten times in the last thirty minutes. If I didn't know he had something swinging between his legs, I would think he was a girl. I don't even want to know what he does standing in the mirror that long.

I've looked in like three different places already with no Ryland in sight. "Ry, you ready?" I call out across the house.

I finally find him sitting on the couch, putting on his Puma shoes. Looking up at me, he must sense my sudden change in mood. "Are you all right? You look a little pissy," he says, leaning back against the couch, before throwing his arms up on the backing.

I lean against the doorframe, crossing my arms over my chest, because thinking about it again, I am a little pissed. "It's nothing, just dealing with some of Natalie's shit. I need to have some fun. You ready to go?"

He stands up and grabs his keys from the coffee table. "Yeah, let's go. I have just what you need."

A huge house on the beach comes into view. We park across the street, because of all the cars already here. The stone driveway leads to a four-car garage of a massive brick home. About halfway down, the driveway loops to the left, forming a circle drive that wraps around a large fountain. The steps lead to a high porch, covered in brown wicker furniture with bright cushions, in front of a large front door. Each corner is decorated with tall palms.

It's hard to imagine this is where someone lives, but then again, many houses here are enormous. Houses like these put Mississippi mansions to shame. I open the door and step outside, as does Ryland. He starts up the walk and I just stand here, staring.

When he notices I'm not right behind him, he turns toward me. "Are you coming? Logan is cool; his parties are usually packed. It shouldn't be hard to find something, or *someone* to get into," he says with a grin. It's only nine o'clock and from the cars parked everywhere I would say the place is already at maximum capacity. Here we go.

Walking through the door, the house is packed from wall to wall and we haven't even made it out back. Music is blaring from speakers built into the ceiling and a DJ is setup by the door. I'm assuming that leads to the pool. Ryland said after a while everyone usually ends up in the pool at the back of the house.

He nudges me in the arm. "You good? We'll go find the bar and then I may take off and find Presley in a bit." He looks at me, a cocky smile spreading across his face.

Even if I were uncomfortable, I wouldn't admit it. I have never seen him into a girl like this before. Plus, I've never really had a problem making friends before. I nod at him. "Yeah, man. I'm cool. I'll find something to get into. Let's go find that bar."

We get to the bar and there is a guy running the keg. Ryland slaps his hand and looks back at me. "Logan, this is my boy, Breyson. Show him a good time, yeah? He needs to see how Cali people party."

I look toward the guy and he extends his hand. "I'm Logan, and this is my crib. I'll show you around and introduce you to some people. What's your beverage of choice?"

I shake his hand. Usually, I stick to beer, but today I need something stronger. "Have any whiskey?" I really hope he has something worth drinking. I can't do girly drinks.

His lips tip. "Ah, finally. Someone is ready for some real fun." He turns and places his hands around his mouth to enhance the loudness of his voice and yells. "Who's ready for some games?" The crowd goes wild with excitement. What have I gotten myself into?

I turn to Ryland, who is looking around the room. I guess he's hunting that Presley girl. The boy has it bad. "Ry, what you want to drink?" He must've spotted her, because he starts to move in the other direction.

"Just give me a Miller Lite. Actually, make it two." He reaches in his pocket and pulls out his keys, handing them to me. "If you get ready to go, just head to the house. I doubt I'll be home tonight. I think Presley's parents are out of town for the weekend. I'll probably just crash there and get a ride home in the morning. You cool with that?"

"Yeah, man, I'm good. Just give me a call if you need a ride." He bumps his fist with mine and takes off in the direction of the pool. I turn back around and Logan has a table set up, pouring shots.

After three rounds of quarters, I'm slightly past the point of intoxication. I stand, cutting myself off, because I have to drive home. Quarters is my favorite drinking game and I'm good at it, so I never get very drunk. I walk into the living room that has been transformed into a dance floor.

Upon entry, I see the back of a head covered in platinum blonde hair, grinding on some guy. Jealousy and rage course through my body. Before I can stop myself, I rush across the room and grab the girl's arm. When she looks at me with a look of disgust, I realize my mistake. I'm staring at a pair of hazel eyes. Wrong girl. I don't have the chance to apologize before a fist connects with my jaw.

Stunned, I come to and realize everyone has stopped dancing. *What in the hell is wrong with me?* I'm normally laid back. This is completely out of character for my normal behavior. I've got to get out of here. If I can't control myself, I may be cutting this trip short as well.

I stand and look at the girl, wide-eyed and hidden behind the guy. Rubbing my hands over my face, I look at them. "Look, I'm really sorry. I'm a little drunk and thought she was someone else. I meant no disrespect."

The guy almost looks like he feels bad and the anger fades from his face. "It's cool, man, but you may want to double check before doing some shit like that again. You'll get yourself killed messing with someone's girl around here."

I nod my head in understanding. I deserved that hit, but I have to get out of here and clear my head. I've been here barely any time and I'm already doing stupid shit. Only one place comes to mind. The place that started all this shit. The beach.

But I can't drive just yet. I'm not one of those idiots that get behind the wheel drunk. Too many people get killed over self-absorbed idiocy. My older cousin Beau, Ryland's brother, was one of them. He went off to college and joined a fraternity. One night he got drunk and got a call from another frat brother that his girl was out with another guy. He was drunk and not thinking, so he took off after her and was speeding on a curvy road. He came around a curve going about sixty and wrapped his mustang around a tree. He was killed on impact and that was three years ago.

I take off, not saying anything else. I head outside toward the pool to sober up a bit. There are several people in and around the pool. I'm not sure what I want to do until I can drive, but I'd rather be alone to sort this mess out.

I turn to head toward the front when I feel a tug on the band of my jeans, then a body plastered to my back, rubbing her arms up my torso. "Hey, gorgeous, I remember you from earlier today at the beach."

I turn around and see a petite girl with short, black hair and a tan. Apparently, this girl lives in the tanning bed. She's cute, but not my type. She has now stuck herself against my front side, wrapping her arms around my neck. I grab her hands, pulling them from around me. "I'm sorry, who are you?"

"You're cute. I'm Lexi. I was with Presley and Kinzleigh at the beach this morning." Ah, Kinzleigh. Exactly who I would rather be stuck to right now. "We should go upstairs. I could show you a good time, California style."

She licks her lips and brushes her fingers down my stomach, stopping on my buckle, trying to unfasten my belt. *Whoa, not happening, sweetie,* I think, grabbing her hands and removing them.

"Look, you're cute and all, but I'm not interested. Actually, I was just leaving." I've got to get out of here. I think I am sober now.

She begins to pout. "What's wrong? Do you have a girlfriend or something? I'm sure what she doesn't know won't hurt her." She smiles and winks at me, going for my belt again. I'm pretty sure if I gave her the go-ahead, she wouldn't even be able to make it to a room.

Public foreplay is not my thing. Call me a douche, but I don't want my temporary girl or myself left out for the eyes of someone else's enjoyment. I also don't believe in sleeping with a girl that's clearly intoxicated. It's not my style. That's usually the guys that can't get any when the girl is sober.

"You seem like a nice girl and you look decent enough, if I wanted to go there, but I'm really not interested." *In you anyway.* I hate to be rude to the girl, but begging is not going to make me change my mind.

"Fine, you're a jerk. See you around, I guess." She turns on her heels and stomps away toward the next contender. With that crap out of the way, I head for Ryland's truck. If I wasn't sober before, I am now.

I make my way through the scattered couples, some making out and some doing things I really don't want to witness, and get in the truck. Putting the keys in the ignition, I crank the truck and head for the beach.

THREE

Kinzleigh

I stand in front of the mirror, putting on the finishing touches of my makeup, trying to decide what to wear. Mom told me we were going to one of the nicer restaurants in town that requires a semi-formal dress code.

I walk over to my closet, fingering through my wardrobe, until I stop on my floor length, black satin halter dress with a sweetheart neckline. Mom bought it for me when she was in LA on a case a few months ago, but I've never had anywhere to wear it until now. I don't dress like this much. I pull the hanger from my closet and walk over to my bed. Removing it from the hanger, I step in and pull it up my body, securing the clasp behind my neck.

I take in my reflection. The dress does look perfect with my platinum blonde hair. I add my black strappy heels and pin the front of my freshly straightened hair back, securing it with the diamond-encrusted clip I received on my birthday. For the finishing touch, I add my diamond stud earrings that once belonged to Grams.

I used to constantly look at them, sitting perfectly nestled in the Tiffany Blue box each time I visited. Gramps gave them to her on their fiftieth anniversary. The Christmas before she died, she wrapped them and gave them to me. She said she had cared for them long enough and they deserve to get out of that old box, plus gramps would want me to have them. He passed away from a heart attack five years before grams died.

I really miss them.

After dabbing on my gloss, I sit on the bed to change out my purse when I hear a knock at my door. "Come in, I'm dressed." I call out, my voice carrying across the room. I expected it to be mom, but when the door opens Konnor is standing on the other side. He's wearing a baby blue button-down shirt and black slacks. The blue in the shirt really stands out with his short, inky-black hair and ice-blue eyes. He really is a handsome guy.

He comes in and shuts the door, placing his hands in his pockets. "Hey, Sis. You look beautiful, as always." He smiles a sad smile, but it doesn't reach his eyes. I could kill Sophia for what she did to him. If anyone deserves a happy ending, it's Konnor. He is the best guy I know, and I don't say that because he's my brother. He has a heart full of love and would give a stranger the shirt off his back.

I walk over to him, wrapping my arms around his waist to give him a hug, trying to hold back the tears attempting to fall free. My heart aches for him. I place my cheek against his chest. "I love you. You know that, right?" Looking up at him, he nods, answering my question.

My voice is barely above a whisper; scared he will break at any moment. I guess it would be worse to actually find someone cheating than to be told. Something about seeing it with your own eyes would make it more real and unforgettable, I would imagine. "How are you holding up?" We haven't gotten a chance to really talk since it all happened.

He clears his throat, as if he's holding back tears as well. "I've been better, but I'm okay. Stop worrying about me, Sis, it makes me feel worse. I'll be fine. I don't know when, but I have to deal with my own shit. It's mine to bear and mine alone. Now that I don't have to see her anymore, it should get easier. Maybe now I can finally get the image out of my head."

I can't stand this anymore. I hate seeing him in this much pain. I see it in his eyes—he's holding on by a thread. We have always been close. I can feel when he's hurting as can he with me.

I pull away and notice him staring at the wall behind me, checked out mentally. Grabbing each side of his face, I pull it down for his eyes to meet mine. "Konnor, look at me."

When he finally does, I can't help but to spill my heart out. "I hate her for what she's done to you. She doesn't deserve you. You're too good for her. I swear, Konnor, you better listen to me and listen to me good."

He's staring at me and nods so I know he's listening. Tears begin to fall, no longer controllable. "We all love you and I know you're in pain, but don't you dare do something stupid. Don't let that heartless bitch win. She's the one that screwed up. Show her what she's missing. She will regret what she's done one day when she ends up with a loser that will likely do the same thing to her. You know what else? When it happens, you will have already found someone that deserves your heart, someone worthy of your love. Sophia isn't it. She isn't the one for you. Bring my Konnor back. I want the real you, not the shell of a man you're becoming. This doesn't have to ruin you. One day, when you find that perfect someone, this will be just a bump in the road. I see how much this is breaking you. If you do something stupid, I will kill her. That is a promise. I will kill for you, Konnor. It's blood for blood in my book. Do you understand?"

A tear escapes his eye. The first I've seen since he was a kid. He pulls me in his arms and squeezes me tight. "You always did have my back, Sis. You're right, about everything. Just give me time, okay? I know you think love is just a crutch, but one day you'll change your mind. You may think you can control it by avoiding it, but you can't. When you meet that person, it just happens. You can't stop it like you think you can. One day, you're going to fall; just promise me you'll enjoy the ride down. You will make some lucky guy happy. I love you, baby girl; now stop blubbering before you get makeup on my clean shirt. Let's go. Mom and Dad are waiting downstairs."

He releases me and turns for the door. He's wrong about one thing. I will not allow myself to fall in love with some guy; the cost is too high. But for the first time in over a month I see a genuine smile. There is no way I'm killing it. Maybe I'm getting through to him after all.

We walk downstairs where Mom and Dad are waiting. I walk to my mom first, giving her a hug. "You look pretty tonight, Mom."

She's wearing a sleeveless, red, knee-length dress, pencil style that accents her small figure. Her long, black hair is pulled back in a neat twist, looking like perfection, as it always does. She has lightly coated makeup and glimmering green eyes, similar to mine. Every time she smiles, her dimples are deep set in her cheeks and she is wearing her favorite black pumps. She is a beautiful woman—one that has aged gracefully. Konnor looks like Mom, but with Dad's eyes.

Dad comes over shortly after, scooping me into his arms, giving me his usual bear hug and twirls in a circle. I always have been his little princess. Kissing me on the cheek, he smiles that heart-wrenching smile. "You look amazing, baby girl. Are you ready to do some celebrating?" He always could make me smile, no matter what mood I was in. Him and Konnor have called me 'baby girl' since I was old enough to talk, and it stuck.

I'm an exact replica of my dad, although, I received Mom's eyes. It's funny how genetics work, really. Dad is handsome, athletic, and tall. He is dressed in gray slacks, a black Giorgio Armani button-down, and the watch we got him for Christmas when I was seven. He never leaves home without it. He says, every time he misses home, he just looks at the time. He's quite the philosophical one, I must say. He's got the same blond hair as me, short, and gels it up in the front.

I was blessed with the greatest parents on earth. Not many kids can say that, but I can, because they have earned the credit. They have always been a part of mine and Konnor's life, no matter how hectic work got for them.

They never missed a game, cheer competition or school activity. They always tried to bring home a positive attitude. Dad always said that work should be left at work and home left at home. Never mix business with pleasure and you'll go further in life. I've rarely heard my parents fight, because they chose to be role models for us. My mom always told me to never go to bed angry with someone you care about in case a new day never comes. Live as if today is your last day. She has lived by that motto my entire life.

I've always looked up to my parents. They are completely and passionately in love—a once in a lifetime love. When you're granted a love like that, you're never given it a second time. I figure if you don't get it to begin with, then you don't have to worry about losing it. I smile at my dad as he sets me back down on my feet. "Ready as I'll ever be."

We pull up at valet and exit the car. We're seated at our table almost instantly. The restaurant is beautiful with high ceilings, low lighting, and candlelight dancing from every table.

Once we're seated, Mom and Dad order a glass of white wine as we glance at the menu. The waiter soon takes our order and the four of us enjoy a bit of small talk as we wait for our food. We're having a really good time, but I feel like my parents are avoiding something. My mom mentioned having to discuss some important news that they have yet to bring up since we've been here. I'm starting to wonder if it's something bad.

Now nervous, I pick up the crystal glass and take a sip of my water, trying to calm down. I look up and find my parents staring at each other with this look, as if they are talking in some code. Yes, I know that look. It always comes when they are preparing to tell us something we're not going to like. I look over at Konnor, but he just shrugs, knowing exactly what I'm asking him.

The waiter sets our food down just as it looked like Dad was about to speak, breaking the moment. Dad must sense my nervousness, because he smiles as if nothing just happened and starts eating, along with Mom, and Konnor following suit.

I'm seventeen years old and my parents still act as if we can't read them like a book. They never were good at hiding things, maybe because they are such honest people.

I'm picking at my food, when finally, I can't take the suspense any longer. My stomach is a ball of knots, no longer allowing me to eat anything. Clearing my throat, I look to my parents. "Mom, Dad, what was the big news you wanted to talk to us about?"

Dad finishes chewing the mouthful of food he was working on, looks to my mom, and nods. Okay, this is really starting to get weird.

Dad lets out a breath and then puts down his fork. "As a family, we're about to make some big changes. I signed a contract that will extend over the next five to ten years. It's going to change the face of the company your grandfather has built from the ground up."

I'm starting to feel relieved, because that wasn't near as bad as I was expecting, but then I realize there is something else. "Dad, how is this going to require us to change? You have new contracts all the time."

This is when my dad starts to look nervous, because he begins rubbing the back of his neck. "The contract is for us to build strip malls across the southern region."

My brows come together as he's still not making this clear. "Meaning, what?"

Mom jumps in to relieve Dad as she usually does when he's afraid of upsetting us. "We're moving."

I sit here, wide-eyed and in shock. There is no way I just heard that correctly. My parents would not do this to me right before senior year— the most important year for me. I have always done the right thing; never made them worry, never stayed out late, and worked my butt off in school. I just made cheerleading captain and have been checking out various cheerleading programs at colleges across the country. Our squad is the best in the state and top five in the country, which pretty much guarantees me a spot on any college squad of my choice. They cannot be doing this to me.

"I'm sorry, what did you say?"

Mom begins rubbing her temples—a habit she developed when her anxiety starts—and then looks back at me. "Honey, I know this is unexpected, but this is a great opportunity for your dad. He has always supported us, as will we for him. We are a family."

Now she is going to play the guilt card? Because I of all people know my dad deserves it. I close my eyes, trying to process this.

Okay, Kinzleigh, think this through. Maybe this is all just a dream, and you're going to wake up, with everything completely normal. Think, think, think.

I look back up at Dad. "Who is going to run the company here?" He starts to look a little relieved. "Uncle Danny is going to run the company here. I will build up the southern offices, while getting the first project off the ground."

This makes no sense, whatsoever. Uncle Danny's kids are grown. Why do we have to uproot our lives and start over? I'm really starting to get angry, something I never do with my parents. "I don't understand. Why can't Uncle Danny move and start up the company there? His kids are grown and self-sufficient."

My dad is back to rubbing his neck again, turning it red. "Uncle Danny doesn't have the experience to expand the company into an entire new region. It's too much for him to handle. He will serve me better here. Stop letting the negative in. This could be a good thing for you. You've always been good at making friends. You will adjust in no time at all."

I feel like I'm in a nightmare I can't wake up from. Like the ones where someone is trying to kill you and you try really hard to escape, but can't? This feels like one of those times. "Mom, what about your job, my cheerleading dream, or Konnor's football scholarship? We can't just change our whole lives when we have everything planned out. This isn't fair. I've always done everything you guys have asked of me. I've never been in trouble. I make straight A's at school and I work hard in the gym. I don't even date for goodness sakes. I never cause strife. This is going to destroy all of my plans. Where are we even moving?" I'm starting to raise my voice at this point, causing the surrounding tables to glance in our direction.

I can see the defeat in Dad's eyes. He always did hate to upset me. Maybe I should calm down some. I'm about to apologize, when Mom holds up her hand, stopping me. "Kinzleigh, I know this is a lot to take in, but you will not take that tone with us again. I think we can all agree that Dad has only ever had our best interests at heart, but regardless, we are a family and we will continue to live that way. Are we clear?" I nod, because when Mom gets frustrated the best thing to do is remain quiet.

I take a deep breath, trying to process everything they are saying, and Mom begins again. "This is going to affect all of our lives, not just yours, and we understand that. I'm not all that thrilled with leaving my job and friends either, but family supports each other, and this is what Dad needs right now. We are not going to be selfish with all that he's done for us. You have until the end of June to spend time with your friends and say your goodbyes. If, after your senior year, you decide you want to go to college back here, then we will evaluate at that time. We are not trying to crush your dreams, Kinzleigh. It's just one year of high school. You can cheer anywhere. I know you are my little planner and can't seem to function in chaos, but sometimes the unexpected happens and you just have to roll with it."

She then turns to look at Konnor, who is just sitting there, as if nothing abnormal is even happening. "Konnor, as for you, you are eighteen now and ready to start college. Dad and I understand you have made a commitment to UCLA for football. You have two options. If you want to continue with that commitment, that's fine. You'll be in the football dorms anyway. If you want to be closer to us, Dad will do everything in his power to get you set up at your first-choice school. It's your decision, but you need to think about it before it's no longer an option. You have a week to decide. Dad has already contacted the coach at Alabama and pulled some strings. There are walk-on opportunities. If you choose that option, then we will absorb the cost of your school and provide you with housing as we've always planned. I know the SEC conference was your original choice for football, because they have some of the best football programs in the country, but you chose to stay in California for Sophia. Since that is no longer the case, maybe you need a change too, sweetie."

I'm sitting there in complete shock. This is actually happening. Before I can stop myself, I blurt out, "Where are we moving?"

Dad finally appears to be calming down. He looks at me, placing his hands in front of him on the table. "We're moving to Mississippi." My mouth drops and my eyes go wide. I'm speechless. This is not just my worst nightmare, but also Hell on earth.

Tears begin to fall. I can't hold them back any longer. I look from Mom to Dad, mouth quivering, trying not to cry hysterically. "You're sending us to live in a place with a bunch of red-neck hillbillies? Do they even know what cheerleaders are? Dad, you've seen on television the kind of people that live there. Please tell me this is a joke."

He is beginning to look angry, as if I've offended him. "Kinzleigh, I'm very disappointed in you right now. You know your mother and I have always taught you to never judge anything or anyone by hearsay or appearance. Things are rarely as they seem. Do you really think I would move my family somewhere unfit? I should have earned more respect than that."

I feel like I'm going to be sick. I've had enough bad news for one night. I need to get out of here, to think all this through. Usually, I work out my stress and frustration in the gym practicing, but it's too late. I'll have to go to the one place I always find peace and serenity—the beach.

I wipe the tears from my face as best as I can and place my napkin on my plate. Scooting my chair back, I stand. Looking at my parents—the two people I adore the most other than my brother—who have just hurt me worse than ever imaginable, I ask, "May I be excused? I really need to be alone right now."

Both parents nod their heads, excusing me from dinner, before Mom says, "You can go for now, but we need to finish this conversation later."

I can't imagine it being anytime soon. "I'll be home later. Don't wait up, okay? I'll get a cab." I grab my purse, turn, and walk as fast as possible until I get to the door of the lobby.

I reach the outside of the restaurant before my breaths become short and quick. I bend forward, placing a hand on each knee, trying to breathe. I'm on the verge of a panic attack; one I haven't had since Grams died.

Breathe Kinzleigh, breathe, I repeat to myself over and over, trying to calm down. I finally catch my breath enough to stand upright. I walk to the curb and hold up my arm, trying to hail a cab. Thankfully, it's late enough I don't have to wait long.

Getting in the cab, an elderly, white-haired man wearing a beret turns to me, tipping his hat. "Miss, where would you like to go?"

I probably look like a hot mess. I pull out my compact mirror to try and fix myself and look back at him. "The pier please."

FOUR

Kinzleigh

The cab pulls in about a half-mile from the pier. The driver turns to me, placing his arm over the back of the seat. "Is this okay, Miss?"

I nod and hand him a twenty. "This is fine. Thank you. Keep the change."

I open the door, placing my right foot outside, when I hear the driver clear his throat. "You look like you've had one of those days. I hope things get better for you."

I step out of the car, before sticking my head back inside. "It isn't looking that way, but thank you for your kindness. It's a rare quality these days."

I shut the door and watch the driver pull back onto the street, before turning around to face the sand, luminescent in the moonlight. Holding onto the rail that leads down the steps to the beach, I pull off one shoe, followed by the other. I have enjoyed the tranquility of the beach since I was a kid. The waves crashing against the shore always had a way of melting the stress away.

I walk down the steps toward the shoreline, my silver clutch hanging from my wrist with my shoes in one hand, holding my dress up with the other. The sand, squishing between my toes, is still warm from the hot day. I make it to the water's edge and stop.

Placing my shoes down in the sand, I release my dress and look up at the sky. It's a beautiful night. The stars are twinkling as if they know I'm here, enjoying their beauty. My hair and dress begin dancing in the breeze. For a summer night, the temperature is perfect. It's dark being so far away from the street lamps, but I welcome it.

As I look out across the water, the Pacific Ocean looks black, with just the reflection of the moonlight sitting on top. I close my eyes, enjoying the sound and the feel of the water crashing against my ankles, completely at peace. The bottom of my dress gets soaked from the waves washing ashore, but I don't care. I begin walking out farther into the ocean as if it's calling to me, but decide against it. I still have to get home and I don't have a change of clothes.

The half-mile strip from here to the pier is usually free from locals or tourists, aside from the occasional fisherman. That's why I love it here. I can come here and enjoy being free from worry or stress or heartache. It's an escape for me. The only person that knows I come here is Konnor.

The night I found out Grams died, I took off and came here. He was worried and ended up finding me here when I didn't come home or answer my phone. That's the last time I had to come here at night—my safe haven. I'm really going to miss this place.

I pick up my shoes from where they're sitting in the sand and start to walk toward the pier. I don't understand why I have worked so hard to be good and yet somehow, fate has turned against me. I walk the half-mile along the shoreline when I reach the pier.

I climb the steps and begin walking toward the end, along the worn wood planks that are suspended and run about a mile out into the water. The pier is enclosed with side rails and a roof overhead, perfect for whatever the weather has planned. At the end, there is a bench on the right and a bench on the left, followed by a section that is uncovered, but continuous railing for fishing.

I finally reach the end and sit, placing my legs over the side, but because of my height they do not reach the water. The night begins to replay through my mind. I can't believe my life is crashing down around me. Everything I've worked so hard for is being taken from me.

Being squad captain is something I've dreamed of since I started cheerleading. Even if this Hicksville town, Mississippi has a cheerleading squad, will they have room for an additional cheerleader this close to the start of another school year? Do they even compete or is football games it? Now, I'm going to have to work harder just to get a tryout at the colleges

I'm interested in.

Why would my parents just pick up and move us across the country when I have one year of high school left? How do they expect me to just leave everything I know behind and start over? I have friends and family here. That has to mean something to them. This isn't fair. Maybe I can think of a way to stay behind. I have to. My parents have to understand what this will do to me. It will crush me. I so desperately want to wake up and realize this is all a bad dream. All I can do is stare out at the ocean, lost in thought.

All of my emotions finally catch up to me and the tears start to fall, heavier this time. I can't stop them anymore. I don't know what to do. Everything was going great in my life and now the misery is about to begin. I don't even try to wipe the tears away anymore. I just let them flow.

I don't understand why, out of all the states in the continental U.S., my parents have to choose some po-dunk town in Mississippi. I can't imagine the kind of people that reside there. After that big hurricane—Katrina I think—they had people on television walking around barefooted and missing teeth. Do they even have shopping malls and designer clothes, I wonder, or is it full of trailer parks and cow fields? My stomach turns at the thought.

I'm not sure how long I've been sitting there, staring at the water, but my back is beginning to hurt from my position and I'm growing tired from crying. I can't stop the constant draining tears that continue to fall.

I should go home and go to bed, but I'm not ready to face my parents yet. I know they will still be up and wanting me to talk. That I cannot do yet.

I lay back against the pier, arms outstretched to my side, looking up into the sky. It's dark, but the sky is clear; the perfect shade of onyx marked by the speckled pattern of stars, glittering across the horizon. The moon glows like a spotlight, lighting up the pier. It's beautiful glancing out at all the stars, shining brightly as if each holds a story of their own. It's also a full moon tonight.

I remain flat against the warm wood and allow myself to enjoy the starry night. I wonder, if you were to talk, would there be someone to listen up there? Maybe there is a keeper of the sky, assigned to keep the stars in perfect order and change the days to night. Maybe he gets lonely and just wants to listen. At least then, all my secrets would be safe.

Listen to yourself, Kinzleigh. A sky keeper? Really? You're becoming quite the delusional one.

A strange peacefulness washes over me, causing me to close my eyes. Clearly, my mind is not in normal territory, because I would never close my eyes late at night on a public beach. There are too many creeps out there, but I suddenly just feel the need to sleep, like someone or something is watching over me.

I couldn't have been lying here but what seems like a few minutes, in the midst of a new dream, when I hear footsteps along the pier. I must've dozed off, but instead of my eyes bolting open at the sound, I just incorporated it into my dream. That is, until, "Mind if I join you?" flows through my ears in a deep, raspy, southern voice. My eyes pop open and a tall familiar face is standing over me, looking down with a smile on his face.

I panic and sit up in a hurry, embarrassed at being caught sleeping on a pier. Embarrassment is a rare trait for me, and this guy has brought it out twice in one day. "I'm sorry. I don't usually do this, but it's been a bad night. I'm a little more tired than usual."

I look back out at the water, gripping the side of the pier as if the most beautiful boy isn't standing behind me. He stuns me. Right then, I can feel his breathing on the back of my neck, quickening my heart rate. In the short time of his presence, he has managed to squat behind me, placing the inside of each knee resting against my sides. I don't even think he's trying to touch me, but the contact is making my body do things I don't understand.

He whispers in my ear. "May I keep you company for a while? I'll be quiet if that's what you need." His breath is so light it tickles my ear. I can barely breathe, let alone speak, so I just nod. Would I even be able to tell him no if I wanted to? My head is fuzzy and I can't think when he's this close.

He pulls up his pants legs and sits beside me. He removes his shoes, placing his feet in the water. I'm finally able to exhale the breath I've been holding. "How long have you been here?"

I turn and glance at him to find he's staring at me. I don't know where this guy is from and I don't really care, but he's gorgeous. I never take an interest in a guy. It's one of my few rules to avoid falling into the never-ending cycle of the love-struck patrons, but following rules have gotten me nowhere, obviously. I'm not thinking clearly anyway, so I guess I can break my rule and enjoy his company for a while. He's fun to look at; especially those lips. He's leaving soon anyway, and right now I need a distraction from all this bad news.

He reaches out slowly as if he's afraid I'll run away, placing his hand over my cheek. He begins rubbing his thumb underneath my eye, freeing it from the wetness of my tears. I fall into his touch like a cat being petted. Great, I have no idea what I look like right now. "I needed to clear my head and came to the beach. I saw you standing by the water earlier and didn't want to leave you out here alone. Are you okay?"

My eyes close at the warmth from his hand. I should be mad he followed me, but I'm not. I just want him near me. His voice soothes me, but no personal questions are allowed. I don't need him to know me or what makes me tick. I don't need any complications.

I open my eyes to him staring at my lips. "Can we just exist together without trying to exchange personal information? Let's enjoy casual company—two people needing nothing from each other. Clearly, you're not from here, meaning you'll be gone soon. I'm not one of those girls that needs or wants to know everything about you, nor do I want to spill my entire life to you. We don't have to pretend with each other. Let's call this what it is—a moment to avoid being alone. Can we do that?"

He stares at me as if he's trying to figure me out; like I'm a book full of secrets in another language. He seems lost in my eyes—amused, confused, I don't know. We sit there staring at each other as if we can't pull away. As if we don't want to.

He doesn't say anything; just bites his lip as if he's trying to answer his own question, or to decide. I'm about to get up and walk away when his other hand reaches behind my neck, pulling me closer as he closes in. His lips stop in front of mine, close enough to touch, when he whispers, "Beautiful girl," and crashes his lips to mine.

His lips are soft and full, but needy. I don't know what I'm doing, but for some reason the act comes natural with him. Our lips fit together as if they were molded for the connection. His warm tongue slips through the opening of my lips barely, requesting entry. I open up to him, granting his request. Our tongues touch, taste, and dance together. He tastes as good as he smells. I always thought it was kind of nasty to imagine exchanging spit, but with him, I want more. The senses coming at me are overwhelming.

A moan, barely more than a whisper, escapes my lips. I run my hands across his arms and up his neck, into the back of his hair. My heart is beating wildly. Foreign emotions are running through my body. I have entered into the depths of the unknown. I've never felt this need before, but it's as if my body needs more. Suddenly, I feel like I need to cross my legs from the spasms down below. What is he doing to me? What does this mean?

He turns, laying me against the pier. He has one hand on my waist and the other beside my head, holding his weight above me, like when we were at the beach. He continues to kiss me, taking my bottom lip into his mouth, lightly sucking. His hand slips down, brushing against my butt. When it does, he makes a low growling sound from his throat. I'm not sure why until I feel his need pressed against the bottom of my belly, making my eyes go wide from surprise. I tense. Oh no, I can't go there. As if he can sense my panic, he stops. He kisses me one last time softly and releases my lips.

He looks me in the eyes, a smile growing across his face. He brushes his fingers through my hair, down my arm and grabs me by the hand, interlacing his fingers with mine. "Nothing personal, huh? I think I can do that."

His lips brush mine quickly once again, before he moves back to his place on the pier, pulling me by my hand to sit between his legs. "I promise I'll be good for the rest of the night. I've just wanted to do that all day. Since the second I laid eyes on you actually."

I'm completely and utterly speechless. I have no idea what I'm even doing. I never do reckless or unplanned things like this. I have no idea who this guy is, really, and now I'm sitting on the pier making out with him for the entire world to see. I need to get my head back in the game. I always think everything through before I make a decision. Like mom said, I'm a planner. It's my quirk, I guess, but it's what keeps me sane. I need it like I need cheerleading. Being around him takes away my ability to process. Right now, there are so many unknowns, but what I do know is that I'm not ready for it to end just yet.

I sit here between his legs, staring out at the ocean, completely at peace and trying to replay what just happened. I would have never imagined a first kiss like that. At Presley's thirteenth birthday party, we played spin the bottle and I was forced to kiss Brantley Cooper. It was awkward and over in a second. We didn't even touch inside each other's mouths. Since then, I haven't been the least bit interested in boys nor kissing.

Presley thinks there is something wrong with my girly parts. Maybe it's because of all the risk involved. In Family Dynamics class, we had to listen to nurses present a slide show and talk about sexually transmitted diseases and teen pregnancy. I was utterly grossed out. Who wants to deal with that scary mess? Not me. After that, my immature sex drive took a hiatus and never returned.

That, though, was worthy of locking away in my memory bank and never forgetting. That kiss set me up for all future kisses. Nothing will ever be able to compare. My body feels like it's housing an electrical current. My heart feels like it's on some kind of speed.

I lay my head against his chest and realize his heart is beating fast as well. Maybe he has the same reaction to me as I to him, but what does that mean? Whatever it means, though, right now I'm content to just exist, no words or thinking required.

He lays his chin on my head and places his arms around me, nestling me in the cocoon of his curled-up body. I feel so small and protected like this. The water is completely still and calm. This has been the strangest day. It has gone from bad to worse to a little bit better. If someone would have told me when I woke up this morning that I would be in the arms of a sexy, southern boy by midnight, I would have laughed, yet here I am. I begin to shiver, but it's not from being cold. Actually, it's pretty warm outside, being it's June.

He holds me tighter, the rhythm of his breathing soothing me, melting away all of the built-up tension from earlier. He rests his cheek behind my ear and whispers against it. "Are you cold? I can take off my shirt."

"No. Thank you, though. I'm okay," I say. He really needs to keep that shirt in place. I'm in no kind of place to be seeing the muscles I remember from earlier. Having them pressed against me in this state of mind is dangerous. "The kind of day I've had is still surreal. I'm just upset."

"Want to talk about it? I'm a pretty good listener." He brings his head down to rest on top of my shoulder, cheek to cheek.

Should I talk about it? I wonder if it's a good idea. Maybe it would help to get some of this built-up anger and frustration off my chest. I still don't want to talk about anything personal. A friend wouldn't hurt, though. I suppose it would be best to talk to someone I will never see again.

I exhale. Here goes. "My parents told me tonight that we're moving at the end of June. It may not seem like a big deal, but I've spent my entire life chasing after a dream. One I've wanted since I was a kid. My brother has always loved football. From the time he was old enough to throw a ball, he would drag Dad or me outside to throw with him. He was always trying to be like the big boys—the pros."

I breathe and continue. "When I was eight my parents asked him what he wanted to do for his birthday. He didn't even have to think about it. He wanted to go see the San Diego Chargers play. It was October and my parents made a whole weekend out of it. Everything was so big and exciting. We got in the stands and took our seats between Mom and Dad. I looked down at the field and saw the cheerleaders taking their place on the sidelines in their amazing showy outfits. They were beautiful. The entire game I couldn't look away. I sat there and watched them cheer and do amazing stunts the entire time. From then on, I knew what I wanted to be when I grew up—a professional cheerleader. My mom, being the amazing woman that she is, noticed me in complete awe the entire game. When it was over, she somehow managed to get a meet and greet with one. There was this girl that had blonde hair like me. I remember asking her how I could become like her when I grew up."

I start to cry again, thinking how my life is about to change. I love everything about California. "She bent down in front of me, so we could be the same height. She looked at me and placed her finger to my chest and said, *always follow your heart and work hard. You'll find your way, but don't let anything or anyone stop you. When you think you're working hard, work harder.* See, that's what I have always done. I have always been the good girl. I hung the picture I took with that cheerleader on my mirror and always remembered what she said. I've worked extremely hard for years on the best squad around. You don't just up and move your senior year. Squad tryouts are always held at the end of the previous year. I don't know what I'm supposed to do now. My heart has always been with California."

He sits here rubbing my arms. "I don't know anything about you, but from what I've seen so far, you'll find a way to make it happen. If you have worked this hard, then continue to work hard like she said. Make it happen. My dad used to always tell me the best things in life never come easy. If you want something bad enough, there is always a way to obtain it, no matter how out of reach it seems. I understand why you're upset. We work for years to be seniors. We're supposed to have seniority, not be brand-new. But there are always some pros with starting over in a new place where you don't know anyone. You can be anybody you want to be. Even if you think the door has closed for you, there is always a way to burst through. We have the power to control our outcome, no matter what problems arise before we get there."

I turn around, now kneeling on bent knees between his legs, placing my arms around his neck. "Aren't you just Mister Insightful tonight . . ." I tease. "Are you always this deep?"

He holds me by the waist, rubbing my ribs with his thumbs, a smile taking place. "Only when I'm trying to cheer up a beautiful girl." He reaches up, removing the tears from underneath my eyes. "I meant it, though, Kinzleigh."

"Maybe I just needed to hear it from someone else. I was rude to my parents when they told me. Oh, crap, what time is it? They are probably worried. I never stay out late. When I told them not to wait up they probably took it as a joke." I start to stand so I can go get my phone from my purse on the bench to check the time, but he grabs my waist, stopping me.

Breyson has his eyebrow cocked. "You've never stayed out this late?" He pulls his cell from his pocket and unlocks the screen. "Kinzleigh, it's only eleven o'clock. You can't be serious." He laughs, as if he thinks I'm lying.

"What is so funny? I don't drink and that's usually all that goes on around this time. I have to keep my body at its best if I want to have a chance. Alcohol is not going to do anything for me. I've seen the stupid things people do while intoxicated. I only go to parties on very rare occasion if Presley drags me out, and I'm always home by now, if not before, because hanging around drunk people sober isn't fun to me."

I take a breath, before driving my point home. "I don't date, ever, so I don't have to worry about someone else occupying my time with other activities. Like I said, I'm always home by now. Plus, my brother threatens his friends with life or death when they come over. If I'm not at school or cheerleading, I'm with girlfriends. I only hang out with male friends on the rare occasion when we all have a group trip. But usually, I hang out with friends during the day or early evening and practice at night, unless I go to a concert or something."

Something different has replaced the look that was previously on his face, but I'm not sure what. I have never been good with reading people.

"Don't go yet, in case I don't get to see you again before I have to go back home." He brushes my long hair over my shoulder. I know I should go, but how can I tell him no? He has the most handsome face and he has been nothing but nice to me.

"What do you want to do?" The breeze is picking up and with the bottom of my dress still damp, I'm starting to get cold. Goose bumps take place along my arms.

"I don't care. We'll find something. Come on, let's get you warm. I have Ryland's truck." He slides back to stand, never letting go of me. When he gets to his feet, he helps me to mine and wraps his arm around me. We start back toward the beach, picking up my shoes and clutch along the way. Something tells me that as much as I'm trying to avoid complications, I'm already headed for trouble.

"Okay. I guess I can stay out a little bit longer, but I need to text my mom once I get to the truck." What on earth am I going to tell her? I can't exactly tell her I'm with a boy she's never met. I have to be on the verge of a mental breakdown, because I can't believe I am about to get in the truck of a guy I just met earlier today. He could be a rapist or serial killer for all I know. I have never even been on a date before, so how can I tell my mom I'm going out with a guy this late at night. She'll think I'm losing it.

We get to the beginning of the pier and he gets to the bottom of the steps first, holding out his hand to help me. "So, what's there to do around here for fun at night?" I take his hand, trying not to be rude, but quickly release it once I get to the bottom. I don't want him to think he's going to get any more of what happened earlier.

I fold my arms over my chest, shrugging my shoulders. "Just depends; mostly parties or concerts at night, and sometimes bonfires on the beach. Other than that, whatever is open." I'm not sure what to do honestly. I rarely stay out this late. I wasn't kidding.

"I just came from this guy named Logan's house party. We could go there if you want," he says nonchalantly as we make our way down the beach.

"I can't go to Logan's," I say quickly, hoping he won't ask any further questions. I absolutely will not have anything to do with Logan after what he put Konnor through. He has pretty much been a member of our family since elementary school, and to know he ruined a long-term friendship over meaningless sex is enough to steer clear of him for good. Don't guys have some kind of stupid motto, 'bros before hoes?' Obviously, their head reigns over their heart and I don't mean the one with the brain.

He furrows his brow as if he wants to ask, but doesn't. "Are you hungry?" I feel relieved, because I won't explain my reasons for not going to Logan's. It's not my place to tell Konnor's business.

As if on cue, my stomach growls. I guess I am hungry. I didn't get a chance to finish dinner with my parents. "I could eat. I didn't have much of an appetite earlier," I say, trying to smile.

We finally make it back to the parking lot. What I see when I get there is a huge, silver GMC truck with blackout tinted windows, a pair of matching black running boards and a black front grill guard. Complete with big tires and black rims. Wow. From what I remember Ryland has a southern accent too. I've never really hung out with him. And our school is big. This must be a country boy thing, because most guys around here like their sports cars or luxury vehicles. "So, this is it?" I ask, looking around the parking lot, thinking there is going to be something else around.

A smile begins to take place on his mouth. "You have been in a truck before, haven't you?" He unlocks the doors with the remote and opens the passenger door.

"Only my dad's company truck, because he is a contractor and needs the bed to haul supplies. There aren't exactly a lot of these around here." I laugh nervously, wondering how I'm supposed to get in this thing. It's so high off the ground I'm not sure I can. I am on the shorter side. I go to grab the door handle with both hands, trying to step on the bar. My body weight is offset, causing me to slip. "Crap," I say, and begin looking to see if there is another way.

He places one hand on my left side, cupping my waist, and grabs my right hand. He is now completely touching my entire backside with his body, causing my heart to race. His voice comes out low and deep beside my ear. "Try it this way."

He places my hand in the handle above the dashboard beside the doorframe. "Now place your foot on the bar."

I do as I'm told, and he runs his hand down my right arm, causing me to shiver. He places it on my right side, mirroring the left, and lifts me, helping me into the truck.

My stomach is in knots. I sit down after he releases my waist, turning toward him. "Thanks," I say, not sure what else to say at this point. He is staring at me, clenching his jaw with a predatory look in his eyes. He stands there for a good while, not turning away from me, before he finally shuts the door and walks around the truck.

He gets in and shuts his door. Putting the key in the ignition, he looks over at me. "Where to? Lady's choice."

I'm not sure what the look on his face means. He looks guilty, as if he's doing something he shouldn't, but wants to anyway. Maybe I should just go home. "We don't have to go anywhere. You can just take me home or I can call a cab. I don't live that far."

"No way. You need to eat. I wouldn't have asked if I didn't want to." Now he acts like he's scared I'm going to back out. He is confusing the heck out of me by his sudden change in facial expressions. I feel like it's giving me whiplash.

"Okay, what about *BJ's Restaurant & Brewhouse*? I think it stays open until midnight." Everything should be closing down soon, leaving not much but partying and late-night movies.

"Lead the way," he says and turns the key, firing up the engine. The truck roars to life. I jump. I didn't even know trucks could sound like that. He chuckles in amusement.

"What's so funny? Do all trucks sound like this where you're from?" I look at him in wonder. I don't know why anyone would want to listen to all that noise while they drive.

He shakes his head, still silently laughing. "No, all trucks don't sound like this. Ryland has *Flowmaster* pipes installed. It's a country boy thing, I guess."

This southern thing, I have to admit, does have my interest piqued. I roll my eyes, teasingly, as he finally backs out of the parking lot and heads for the restaurant. I pull out my phone and quickly send Mom a text.

Kinzleigh: Just letting you know I'm fine. Heading to BJ's to eat with a friend. Be home in a little while.

Within five minutes I get a response.

Mom: Okay sweetie. Thank you for letting me know. I'll leave the front light on for you. We will talk tomorrow. Love you.

Kinzleigh: Love you too. Goodnight.

I place my phone back into my clutch and put on my seatbelt. We're heading down South Coast Highway when we pull into the restaurant. BJ's is still pretty busy for being so late. I look down, just now remembering I'm a little overdressed for this type of restaurant. "Maybe we should just order something to go. I'm not really dressed for this place."

He smiles and takes my hand, looking me over. He shakes his head. "You look perfect. Let's go."

He steps out of the truck before coming around the front to open my door. I put my heels back on my feet and turn toward the door, carefully placing my feet on the step bar. He is standing in the doorway. I place my hands on his shoulders and he picks me up by the waist to help me down, not straining at all.

He starts to close the door when I realize my purse is inside on the seat. "Wait, I need my purse."

I start to reach for it, but he takes my hand, shaking his head. "I invited you. Why would you need your purse?"

"Why would you pay for my food? This isn't a date." I begin twirling my finger in my hair, staring at him in curiosity. Usually when we go out as friends, whether a group or just a couple of us, we pick up our own tab, except for the people in relationships.

He begins running his hand through the back of his hair, looking lost in thought. He then shuts the door. "Date or not, where I come from girls don't pay for their food when a man is around. If my parents knew I took a girl to eat and didn't pay they would have a heart attack, and my dad is a cardiologist, so he's a health nut."

By the look on his face there is no point in arguing. He seems pretty sure of his stance on this subject. "If you insist, but it's really not necessary," I say. He sounds the alarm, locking the doors.

His smile comes back. "I insist," he teases. "Come on. Let's go eat. I'm pretty hungry myself." We begin toward the door of the restaurant, side by side.

He opens the door, allowing me to enter first. "Welcome to *BJ's Restaurant and Brewhouse*. Is it just the two of you dining tonight?"

We come to a stop at a podium and see a tall slender girl with short, blonde, pixie-like hair. She looks from me to Breyson, stopping on him, and she bites her lip when her eyes look him over. For some reason the look she has toward him bothers me. I look at her and narrow my eyes.

I'm not jealous, but it's rude to look at a guy that way when he's with a girl. She has no idea I'm not his girlfriend. I did just kiss him, so that has to give me dibs for the night.

She is still staring at him and doesn't seem ashamed of it at all. I'm starting to get angry and I can feel the look on my facing showing it. "It's just the two of us. Can we get a seat somewhere private please?" Breyson asks beside me.

HA! Time to get a move on it, sweetie. The stare fest is over.

I start twirling my hair again as a competitive smile begins on my lips. It's a nervous habit I developed years ago. I turn to look at Breyson and he is staring at me, barely acknowledging the hostess, with that cocky grin on his face.

Dang it!

I really need to pay more attention to who's watching if I'm going to stare daggers at another girl enjoying the view of the man in my presence. He always seems to notice my stupidity. I can't even blame the girl; he's gorgeous and available. Come to think if it, he's probably a man-slut, so

I'm better off not even thinking about it. The thought of him with another girl begins eating away at my thoughts. I have to think of something else.

The hostess quickly grabs the flatware and menus, suddenly seeming embarrassed by her behavior. "Of course, right this way." She then leads us to a booth in the back and sets the table. "Your server will be right with you."

We haven't been seated longer than about five minutes when a server appears. "Hi, I'm Anna, what can I get you kids to drink tonight?"

She's a little older, probably mid-thirties. Her brown hair is pulled back in a low ponytail. She has dark brown eyes and a set of dimples when she smiles. "I'll have a tropical tea, please," I say, glancing up at the server.

"Iced tea for me, please," Breyson adds, glancing over the menu.

"Tropical tea and iced tea," she repeats as she writes it down. "I'll be right back."

"Did your parents tell you where you're moving?" I look away from my menu at Breyson, who now has his hands crossed over his closed menu as if he knows what he wants.

Before I can answer, the waitress returns, setting down our drinks. "Are you guys ready to order or would you like another minute?"

"I think I'll have the seared Ahi salad, dressing on the side."

She writes it down on her notepad and looks to Breyson. "What'll it be for you, sweetie?"

"I'll have the grilled chicken club, light on the mayonnaise." The server takes our menus and leaves the table.

Breyson is looking at me, waiting on an answer as he adds sugar packets to his tea. I turn my nose up in disgust. He is going to end up in a diabetic coma doing that. I look back up and I shake my head. "No specifics."

"Oh, come on. Are we still at that? I just want to know a little bit about you besides your name and that you're a cheerleader with a brother." He raises his hands in surrender. "I promise I'm not a stalker."

He smiles at me. That smile I can't deny that makes me feel things I know I shouldn't.

Contemplating what I can give him to satisfy his desire for more information and my desire to keep it to myself, I sit in silence. I'm not one of those people that volunteers endless, meaningless details about myself to other people. There are some things even my best friend of seventeen years doesn't know. "Fine, if you must know. We are moving to the . . . south at the end of June. My father is a contractor and CEO of the family business my grandfather started right out of high school. He just signed a major contract to build strip malls across the entire southern region of the country. I guess this could change the face of the company, making it a multi-million-dollar enterprise. So now, Daddy dearest is moving my mother and me across the country and I'm not happy about it. Happy now?" I ask teasingly, hoping that is enough.

"All jokes aside, it might not be that bad. You might like the south." He winks playfully.

Of course, me, earning a D minus in the subject of Flirting 101, just sits here stupefied. Maybe it wouldn't hurt to get a few training tips from Presley. Oh no, what am I saying? That will never happen. "I'm guessing telling me the state in question would violate your confidentiality rule?" He raises a brow as he takes a sip of his tea.

"You catch on quickly." I laugh. Ask me what my reasons are, and to be honest, I'm not sure. Since I will never see him again after tonight, I don't really know what it would hurt to answer his personal questions, but if I don't answer his questions then I can't ask. The less I know about this sexy, southern boy, the better.

The server brings out our food and places it before us, along with the check. "Let me know if you need anything else. I'll keep a watch on your drinks. You kids have a good night and be safe."

We enjoy our meal mostly in silence since it's almost closing time. Once Breyson pays for the food we stand to leave. I'm starting to feel the fatigue setting in. It's been a long day. "Is it okay if we call it a night? I'm really tired from today's string of events."

He looks disappointed, but nods in understanding. "Sure, just tell me where you live and I'll take you home." We get to the truck and he opens my door, helping me in.

Once in the truck, he starts the ignition. "How long are you here visiting Ryland?" I'm not sure why I asked since I don't plan on seeing him again. It just slipped out.

"I'm only here until next Friday, then I fly back." He pulls out of the parking lot and heads in the direction I instruct him.

We spend the remaining twenty minutes with casual small talk before pulling into my driveway. The censored lights come on at the garage. Pulling to a stop, he kills the headlights. I'm assuming, because there is something he wants to say. I gather my clutch in my hand and grab for the handle of the door. Turning to him I say, "Dinner was good, thank you. It was nice having some company aside from my friends."

When I start to open the door, he pulls on my left hand, stopping me. "Kinzleigh, wait. Is it okay if I see you again before I leave?" I get nervous. What am I going to say? I'm not sure I want to see him again. It's just going to further complicate things.

"I don't know . . ." I exhale, thinking. "I'll tell you what. If it's meant for you to see me again, you will. Obviously, we know some of the same people now, so we will see how things play out."

It's the only answer I can come up with. "You're not going to make this easy for me, are you?"

"The best things in life are never easy." I smile, repeating his quote from earlier, and open the door. "Goodnight, Breyson."

I reach the paved driveway and head for the front door, slipping inside and shutting it behind me. Placing my back against the cool wood of the door, I take a deep breath. After a few minutes, I hear him pull away.

Everything is dark but the spotlights over the fireplace, meaning my parents are in bed. Trying to avoid any questions tonight, I walk quietly to my room and shut the door. I am finally able to breathe easily for the first time tonight.

I walk into my bathroom and wash off my makeup, before changing into my favorite pink tank and a pair of short boxer shorts. I climb in my high king size bed, placing my phone on the bedside table to charge. As I slide underneath my pink satin sheets and comforter, my eyes grow heavy. I smile, remembering how much fun it was to do something out of the ordinary for once.

The last image I remember before falling into a peaceful slumber is two beautiful blue eyes and a smile to die for.

FIVE

Breyson

I pull away from Kinzleigh's house, heading back to Ryland's. My mind is in a cloud, running crazy. I doubt I'll get to sleep anytime soon and it's only twelve thirty in the morning. I would call Ryland, because I want more information on Kinzleigh, but I don't want to be a dick knowing he's probably at Presley's.

Surprisingly, Ryland only lives about five blocks from Kinzleigh. As I pull into the driveway I turn off the headlights—trying not to wake his parents—and park outside of the closed garage.

After killing the engine, I step out of the truck and walk through the fence to the backyard where the pool is located. It's a large infinity pool looking over a drop off. The house is set in the hills surrounding Laguna Beach. I love coming here, because it's so different than back home.

I stand in front of the pool, enjoying the view below and admiring the different lights gleaming throughout the hills. Most of the lights are off at his house, aside from the security lights.

Continuing across the edge of the pool toward the pool house, the door comes into view. I unlock it and open the door, stepping inside. His parents insisted this year that I sleep out here, so I can have my own space now that I'm seventeen and we're allowed to go out. Before, I always took the guest room down the hall from Ryland.

I didn't get a chance to come in here earlier, since we went straight to the beach as soon as I got here. And once we got back, I was busy catching up with Ryland and his parents before getting dressed in the main house.

Shutting the door, though, I realize his mom has already put my suitcase inside the door. I'm surprised Ryland hasn't called permanent dibs on this place as nice as it is. It's like having your own house.

The spotlights are dim over the fireplace wall, giving enough light to comfortably see. In the center of the large, mostly open room sits a black, leather sectional surrounding a rug and coffee table. Straight ahead on the center wall is an electric fireplace topped with a mantle and large, wall-mounted television.

The floors are all wood and to be what looks like bamboo, giving it an island oasis vibe. On the right-hand side of the room is a small kitchen behind a bar with stools, housing a stainless-steel refrigerator, some cabinetry, and a built-in cooktop, as well as a wine cooler fully stocked. Built into the bar is a sink and dishwasher, hidden by the bar top until you walk around it.

To the left-hand side of the furniture, there is a door leading to the back half of the pool house. There are small touches of decor all around that resembles the style of the main house.

I pick up my suitcase and head toward the bedroom after locking the entry door. When I walk in, a bedside lamp is lit on the nightstand next to a king size bed. It's covered in a white, down-filled comforter and made up with satin turquoise sheets and matching decorative pillows of different shapes and sizes; a few coral-colored ones thrown in.

I walk over to the right and place my suitcase on the bench at the foot of the bed. The room smells like lavender and chamomile. I only know the scent, because I asked his mom when the smell had spread throughout the bedrooms of the house earlier. On the left wall there are two doors separated by a dresser. I assume one leads to a closet and the other into the bathroom.

I grab my shower bag from my suitcase and head into the left-hand door. If I'm not going to be sleeping anytime soon, I might as well get the sand and feel of the beach off of me by showering again. I hate going to bed dirty. The sand leaves you feeling grimy and gritty.

The bathroom has a long counter top with double sinks, ornamenting a basket filled with hand towels. Instead of the same bamboo floors throughout the rest of the house, they have tile in here. In one corner, cradled in a nook, is a Jacuzzi tub and a standing shower in the other corner, with a linen closet in the center. Across from the sink is a small closed in space containing the toilet.

I remove a towel from the closet and throw it over the towel bar, then discard my clothes in front of the shower door, before turning on the water to begin warming it up. Getting in, I stand beneath the hot water, letting it run down my body, relaxing any tense muscles.

My mind is running nonstop. I can't quit thinking about Kinzleigh. I don't know what it is about her that draws my attention. Maybe it's the mystery of her; the fact that I know nothing about her. Most girls practically throw themselves at me, dishing out any useless information they think I may grasp onto. It's no secret that girls like athletes, and if you're any good, that gives you an advantage.

She's different.

Most of the time I get bored with girls quickly, because most are all pretty much the same. I usually don't date seriously. I like to have fun. Go out with who I want. Natalie is the exception, because in high school it's frowned upon to sleep with a girl and ditch her, but after her behavior earlier today I remember why I avoided relationships in the past. I don't like restrictions. I like to be in control of myself and don't want to answer to a girl.

"Ugh!" I growl, aggravated, rubbing my hands over my face and through my wet hair. That's another issue I have to deal with. I want to spend more time with Kinzleigh before I leave, but it's not right to do that to Natalie no matter what the situation is. How much of a jerk would I be, though, to break up with her halfway across the country? And over the phone at that . . .

Do I really care? No, not really.

I *do* care enough I don't want to hurt her, but as a friend she deserves more than anything I will ever give her. I can't help that she thinks she loves me. In my defense, I tried to prevent it from happening by not getting close. She has never been around my family and vice versa. I don't call her and talk for hours at a time and we don't go on dates, not really anyway. Parties or places with a bunch of other friends, yes, but intimate dates like what I did with Kinzleigh tonight, no.

Personally, I have no idea how this happened. I don't give the girl much of anything besides my body. We have sex. That's about it. I know I'm going to be the biggest ass in the world, because as much of a friend as Natalie is, I want to see Kinzleigh again. It takes priority since my time is limited.

I shampoo my hair, trying to decide how I'm going to find Kinzleigh again now that I've decided I'm breaking it off with Natalie. The girl confuses the hell out of me. She seems attracted to me but refuses to release any information about herself. She is making this harder than it has to be.

Maybe I can get some information out of Ryland about her. I'm out of my league with her, because I've never had to chase after a girl's attention. Most of the time they are shoving their number at me or tracking mine down from someone else. That doesn't include the Facebook stalkers. I go to a large school, so it's not uncommon to go to school with people you don't know.

The most work I've ever had to put in is a little flirting or complimenting her looks, and just like that, I make it to at least second base, but mostly third. Some let me round the field and bring it home.

My dad has had me in sports since I was old enough to walk, particularly football. I've been the starting running back since my freshman year, and Dad has me on a strict workout program that keeps my body fitter than most guys my age. He's more hardcore than my coach.

I'm coming up blank on how to get to her. Maybe I just need to sleep on it and figure it out in the morning. I finish my shower and shut off the water. Securing my towel around my waist, I step out and dry off, before pulling on my black boxer briefs. Quickly towel drying my hair, I toss the towel and run my fingers through the damp strands.

As I'm getting ready to brush my teeth, Natalie's ringtone plays on my phone. My shoulders fall. I was hoping to get some sleep before dealing with this, but I guess it's better to do it sooner than later. I put down my toothbrush, about to walk into the bedroom to get my phone when the ringing stops. I guess I missed it. No reason to rush then. I quickly brush my teeth and head to the bed to get my phone.

Sitting on the bed, I grab my phone and unlock the screen. Pulling up the missed call from Natalie, I hit the call button and put it to my ear. It only rings once before she answers. "Hey."

"Hey, Nat, what's up?"

"Are you having a good trip?"

"I am. Look, Nat, we need to talk."

She sighs, her voice coming out a little off beat from before. "Okay . . . About what?"

This blows. I've never wanted to do this. It's easier to stay single. She is going to get hurt either way. I need to do this and get it over with. "Natalie, I feel like a dick to do this over the phone, but this relationship isn't working out anymore. The truth is we want different things. You've been a good friend for three years now, but I can't do this. We're stalling the inevitable and that's going to make it worse later. Next year we'll be going off to college . . . separately. I'm not looking to get married. You deserve to have what I can't give you, and there are plenty of guys willing to give it. But that guy isn't me."

She starts sniffling and I can tell she's crying. Dammit! Please don't do this to me. Just make it easy. "Breyson, please don't do this. If it's about earlier today, I'm sorry. Just forget I ever mentioned it."

"It doesn't have anything to do with . . . *that*; although, it did make me realize I will never give you what you want. It's okay to want love, Natalie, and to be loved, but that's not something I want. The feelings aren't there."

I can tell she's starting to panic at this point and the crying is getting heavier. "I don't need those things. Maybe I was just confused. I can be whatever you need, Breyson. You know we should be together. I won't let you throw it away. Whatever brought this on, we can fix it."

"Maybe not what you need right now, but it's what you want . . ." I wipe my hand down my face in frustration. "So stop lying to me, Natalie. You seem to forget I've known you for years. Stop settling for less than you could have to hold onto this relationship. I'm not even sure why you want to be with me when you know I don't feel that way for you. I never have. Our relationship is no different than friends with benefits but with an added title. I let you call me your boyfriend and don't sleep with anyone else."

"Oh, my god." The crying suddenly shuts off. "You've met someone, haven't you? Who is she?"

That wasn't part of the plan. I don't want to make matters worse, but I've always tried to be an honest person, even if it comes back to bite me in the end. "Yes and no. I did meet someone, but it's not like you think. Who she is isn't any of your business."

"Did you sleep with her?" Her tone is laced with venom. "That home-wrecking whore. Why would you allow some tramp to ruin our relationship?" She takes a breath. "You know what? Never mind. I forgive you. I know I'm not there to meet your needs. It's okay. Just please tell me you used a condom." I just sit here, eyes wide and in shock. She has lost her damn mind. Am I even hearing this correctly? No woman—unless she is a gold-digging whore—would be okay with that, and we are still in high school, so that can't be it.

Then my mind repeats what she said. A surge of anger shoots through my body at how she talked about Kinzleigh when she doesn't even know her. "Natalie, I'm going to say this one time, and you better listen closely, because I won't repeat myself. Don't ever talk about her or any other girl I may or may not take interest in that way again. You have no idea who she is or what she's like."

"But—"

"First of all, no, I didn't sleep with her. She isn't that kind of girl. But to be fair, I did kiss her. *I* kissed *her*. I admit it was wrong to do so before having this conversation. There, I said it. The rest was friendly. Secondly, what we will or won't do from here on out is none of your business, because you and I are no longer together. Lastly, my dick and whether or not I wear a condom is also none of your business unless I'm having sex with you. And I won't be anymore. You were my friend first, and I'd like for you to remain that way, but your behavior is borderline crazy."

"Ugh!" she growls out. "Fine, Breyson, go have your week of fun. Screw her and get it out of your system. I know I wasn't your first girl. I'm more worried about being your last. What happens in between doesn't matter. Don't think this is over for good. I didn't get you by giving up easily and I won't lose you that easily either. You're in a different place and she may seem like a new toy, but when you get home you'll come back where you belong. I'll grant you a pass this time and overlook your temporary stupidity. I'll even be faithful to you, because I want you to have the best. Just remember me when you're banging her."

What? It's almost insane enough to laugh. My maturity takes priority. I have officially had enough. If I had any doubts I would regret my decision, right now would confirm I don't. "Goodnight, Natalie."

I couldn't end the call fast enough. Throwing my phone at the end of the bed, I fall back on the pillow. Now I wonder if she's always been this crazy and I've somehow overlooked it because she's hot and I thought she was cool or if something just snapped.

Rolling over, I hug my pillow and close my eyes. All of a sudden, I'm exhausted.

SIX

Breyson

A beating sound occurs, waking me up. It must be the door. I rub my eyes with the palms of my hands. Who in the world could that be? It gets louder. "I'm coming. Hold on."

Throwing the covers off my body, I sit up, placing my feet on the floor beside the bed. Standing too fast, I sway a little, trying to regain my balance. I adjust my morning wood and walk toward the front door.

When I get to the living room and make it to the door, I pull it open. Ryland is standing on the other side, fully dressed in a yellow, nylon, button-down fishing shirt, khaki cargo shorts and boating shoes, topped off with a visor hat. He has a really big smile on his face. One that is not usually present on anyone this early in the morning. "Looks like someone had a good night," I say sarcastically, rubbing my stomach.

"Get dressed. We're going deep-sea fishing with Dad. Not even your smartass mouth can kill my mood," he says, that smile getting bigger. I don't even want to know what put it there, because I have a feeling I already know. Damn tail-chasing girl-loving boy.

"What time is it?" The sun isn't even over the clouds yet, so it can't be past like six or seven. "And how did you get home?" I run my hand through my messy hair, attempting to comb it.

"It's six fifteen. We have to be at the charter boat by seven." Jeez, how can he go out and party all night then be up ready to go strong at six o'clock?

"All right give me a few minutes. By the way, you owe me coffee for this."

He raises his brow in sarcasm. "Fine, I guess I'll take coffee duty, but hurry up Dad already has the truck loaded."

He pushes the door open and heads for the kitchen. Okay . . . I didn't think this kitchen was fully stocked too. I guess his mom thinks of everything.

Shutting the door, I head back to the bedroom in search of some clothes. It's been a while since I've been deep-sea fishing anyway. Fishing is one thing that has always relaxed me. Dad and me used to go back when I was a kid if he wasn't on call with the hospital.

Some of my fondest memories are just Dad and I sitting in a bass boat on one of our nearby lakes, making small talk and catching brim or bass mostly. Occasionally, he would take my brothers and I down to the coast and charter a boat for deep-sea fishing, but he doesn't have much time for that between clinic and call unless he requests off.

Even though Dad is a successful cardiologist, he always prided himself on raising active boys that had a love for anything and everything outdoors. He said even though he could comfortably provide for us, no kids of his were going to act like spoilt rich brats. He hated entitlement by association.

He wanted us to learn responsibility and to know what it meant to earn money by sweat and hard work, so throughout the year but mostly during the summer, I help my grandfather on his cattle ranch. Fishing, hunting, work, and sports are things I know well.

I get to my suitcase and pull out my favorite khaki shorts and navy fishing shirt similar to Ryland's, along with my sneakers. I love these shirts. The material is thin to keep you cool, dries quickly when wet, and is vented at the back shoulders with a breathable mesh lining. Ten minutes tops and I'm dressed, all the way down to brushed teeth and deodorant—perks of being a guy.

Removing my polarized sunglasses from my bag, I pull the eyewear tether over my head, securing them around my neck, followed by sliding on my favorite ball cap. After losing several pairs between the river and ocean, I learned the hard way to buy a sunglasses strap.

I push my wallet into my shorts pocket. I remember I forgot to charge my phone, so I plug it in with the charger and leave it on the table. Now that Natalie is out of the picture, no one should need me. My parents and brothers know I made it. Grabbing up Ryland's keys from the nightstand, I head back in search of a highly needed caffeine fix.

Just as I'm walking toward the kitchen, Ryland meets me at the door, two to-go cups of coffee in hand. "You ready?" he asks, handing me a cup.

Taking one, I hand him his keys. "Yeah, I'm ready. Let's go."

"Keep them while you're here. There's a pool house key on them and I have an extra set. Mom is weird about keeping the doors locked, so you'll need them. I'll get them before you go home." He holds the door open, waiting on me to pass.

We get to his dad's brand-new Toyota Tundra to see him standing against the hood with his arms crossed. As soon as he sees us coming he smiles. "You boys ready for some fishing?"

Ryland's parents are like second parents to me. Since we were next-door neighbors back home, we were also best friends, until he moved here three years ago, right after Beau died. Ryland is my cousin, as well as Beau's younger brother. Our moms are sisters. After he died they needed a change, a different place to grieve, I guess. Being around constant reminders of him was too hard for my aunt, so when Uncle Joe got a job opportunity they packed up and moved here.

"Yes, Sir. How's the fishing here?" I place my free hand in my pocket once I'm standing in front of him. Uncle Joe stands about five-foot-eleven with short brown hair and light blue eyes. He is a little heavier set, but not overweight, and wearing brown shorts with a red angler's shirt identical to ours, a straw hat topping it off. Uncle Joe is the fun, free-spirited one. He lives life to its fullest; always has. This move was good for them, because Beau dying sent a plague of depression for everyone around.

He wraps his arm around my shoulders, giving me a sideways hug. "I have to admit, it's not like Mississippi fishing, but California can hold its own." He winks and smiles playfully. "Let's go before we're late. I already put down a non-refundable deposit."

I walk toward the back of the truck and climb in the back seat, Uncle Joe and Ryland following closely behind. We start off toward the harbor where we are supposed to meet up with the charter crew.

Staring out the window, while watching everything pass by, I start to wonder what Kinzleigh is doing right now. She's probably sleeping with it being this early in the day. I want to ask Ryland about her, but now doesn't seem like the best time. I don't need the teasing from Uncle Joe that I've developed a crush.

I can't seem to get those beautiful green eyes out of my head. I don't know what it is about her, but I want to know her, even if just for a short time. She seems so closed off, though. I don't know how to go about it. Whatever it takes, I'm prepared to do. I have to hang out with her again before I head back home. If I don't, I know I'll regret it.

Lost in my thoughts, I didn't realize we were already at our destination. We pull into *Dana Point Harbor* and park in the mostly vacant lot. We must be the first trip scheduled. There are several boats still docked in the harbor, the water at a peaceful calm, standing still.

We get out and grab the things we brought for the day, starting with the cooler of drinks. We make it to the boat and meet the crew that's taking us out today. "Hello, it's good to have you all this morning. My name is Jeff and I'm going to be your guide today," he says, extending his hand to Uncle Joe. "You guys ready to get started?"

Jeff looks to be around his mid-thirties, taller and leaner around the middle than Uncle Joe. He has a tan that's only obtained by daily hours beneath the sun, his teeth whiter against the dark contrast of his skin. His jaw is long, his eyes bright, and his hair is the color of chestnuts, peeking out of his khaki fishing hat. Sea foam green tee shirt with the logo of his tour company and swim trunks reflect his easygoing personality.

"Absolutely, I've been waiting for this all week. I'm Joe Reeves. My nephew, Breyson, is visiting from Mississippi, so I want to show him how fishing is done in the Pacific Ocean." Uncle Joe says it with a smile on his face, looking at me. He then looks at Ryland and squeezes him on the shoulder. "This is my son, Ryland."

"I think we can handle that." the guy returns, shaking his hand. He looks at me and winks. "Well, let's get started while it's still cool outside."

We walk onto the boat and the guide starts discussing the day's events as well as going over standard safety information for liability purposes. He hands each of us a life jacket and shows us to our spot, along with getting our gear in order for the day.

The boat pulls away from the harbor, so I utilize the time it takes to get to our first anchor to ask Ryland about some wanted information. We're standing on the deck, elbows resting on the railing, looking out at the ocean as the boat begins churning through the water. "Hey, Ry, can I ask you a question?"

He looks at me, studying me with curious eyes. "Sure, what's up?"

"You know a girl named Kinzleigh?" Ryland was out surfing during the time Kinzleigh was at the beach, so I'm not sure if he knows who I'm referring to or not, but I am hoping he does.

"Kinzleigh Baker?"

Ahh . . . finally, a little more information on Miss Secretive.

"I don't know," I say. "I never caught her last name. She has light, curly blonde hair and bright green eyes. Perfect body . . ." I trail off at the memory of her.

"Yep, that's her. Why do you ask?" He now has his eyebrows pulled together as if he's honestly curious. He takes hold of his visor bill and begins moving it up and down across his forehead.

"Just curious I guess. I had a run in with her on the beach yesterday while you were out on the water. Then, last night I did something stupid at that party, so I took off to the beach to clear my head and found her crying . . ."

I don't even have the chance to finish before Ryland cuts in. "What the hell, dude? Are you holding out on me now? What happened at the party? All you had to do was call me, bro. Now I feel like shit for leaving you alone."

"It's not important. Besides, I handled it. I wasn't going to call you when you were clearly . . . busy. You never chase after a girl, so I know she must be something."

A smile takes form on his face before he turns serious again. "Wait, did you say she was crying? I have never, and I mean ever, seen Kinzleigh cry. The girl comes across about as emotionally breakable as a cement wall. She's a sweet girl but doesn't take crap off anyone. Is she okay? Presley didn't mention her being upset. The two are normally glued at the hip. The only reason she wasn't at Logan's was because of her brother."

What happened with her brother? "She said her parents told her at dinner they are moving at the end of June. She doesn't really like to give out information about herself, apparently. I couldn't get much out of her. What happened with her brother that would keep her from going to a party? Did someone do something to her?"

A flash of rage floods my body at the thought of someone trying to hurt her. I begin clenching my fists unconsciously. "Calm down, Rambo. If you just met her, what's up with the caveman act?" he asks raising his brows.

"Shut up."

"Moving, huh? That sucks. I wonder if Presley knows? That's going to be interesting to watch. If you didn't know any better, you would think they were twins separated at birth."

He laughs. "Anyway, about Konnor and Logan . . . I don't like putting people's business out there, but since you're leaving I don't see how keeping it a secret is relevant, just keep it to yourself. Konnor, her brother, and

Logan, the guy you met at the party, were best friends until about a month ago. Konnor dated this girl Sophia for three years. He was obviously pretty crazy about her from the way he acted. In my opinion, the girl was a whore in training by the way she flirted with *everyone* when he wasn't around, but what do I know? The guy is way better than her anyway. He's too nice and everyone loves him. She was a classic spoiled rich girl that always made sure she got what she wanted, regardless of what it did to anyone else. Not to mention, he's the best quarterback around these parts. He's a football star, kind of like you and Braxton."

"He dominated the rankings all four years he played. I'm really not sure how they lasted as long as they did, thinking about it now. She was like two different people. The perfect little girlfriend when he was with her and always flirting behind his back when he was away. And I mean like bent over, tits hanging out cleavage or rubbing on a guy's thigh in class under the table, even with his friends and teammates. But no one had the heart to tell him. Sophia could do no wrong. He was sickly in love with her."

He pauses. "God, some girls can manipulate . . ." I know where he's going, but he continues. "It wasn't because he couldn't get anyone else either, because the guy could get any girl he wanted. I overheard conversations at parties when he walked into the room and saw the stares. They were all lined up waiting for them to break up. Long story short, someone, names shall not be called, finally got tired of her whoring around behind his back and tipped him off. He came to Logan's in an angry panic. I guess he thought it was a joke at first, but after seeing the look on everyone's shocked faces he burst through Logan's locked bedroom door and found them going at it. Logan was trashed, so I don't even know how he was able to get it up, but Sophia didn't seem all that drunk at all. I'm telling you, she's a bitch. He freaked out and went all ape shit, put the guy in the hospital. I still wouldn't be surprised if that wasn't even the first time she cheated. No one would say after they saw what he did to Logan. It was brutal. They haven't spoken since. The asshole hasn't even tried to apologize. He just keeps telling people he doesn't remember anything until Konnor walked in. Maybe him not pressing charges was his fucked-up apology. I actually like Logan. He's cool as shit and throws good parties, and I get it. I've been that drunk before, but fucking your best friend's girl, whether accidentally or purposely deserves an apology. Could you imagine that shit? Walking in on your girl riding another guy's cock . . . That shit is messed up. Kinzleigh and her brother are really close, so she cut her ties with anything Logan related."

Great, now I feel like a dipshit for going. *Sounds like a charming guy,* I think sarcastically. *That's going against all bro code.* "I want you to help me see her again. We went and ate at BJ's last night after we talked on the pier for a while. The girl is harder to crack than embedded code."

He's shaking his head, trying to hold back laughter. I don't see what is so funny. "Dude, there is no way you're getting anywhere with Kinzleigh Baker. Do you know how many guys have tried, me included? The girl doesn't date. She doesn't even flirt. I'm pretty sure she is still a virgin. She's a really nice girl, but all she does is cheer and practice flips or whatever it is that cheerleaders do. I actually think she despises guys, with the exception of her brother. If she didn't before Logan screwed up, she does now."

"Well, considering I kissed her last night, maybe I can knock down some of those man-hater walls. If her tongue in my mouth was any indication of how she felt about guys there is hope, for one, at least. I don't usually kiss and tell, but I'm getting aggravated. Are you going to help me or not?" I don't want to hear about all the guys that have tried to seduce her or get with her, and some that possibly slept with her. I can feel my veins popping out of my neck.

Ryland is staring at me with his mouth wide open, as if he's in shock. *My interest in her isn't so funny now, is it?* "Are you joking? You kissed Kinzleigh Baker? How the hell did you pull that off? I'm pretty sure she hasn't ever kissed anyone; none that I've heard about anyway. No one would keep that a secret. How did *you* manage to be the one to get to her?"

He seems genuinely curious, but I have given him way too much information already. I am a very private person. I don't get into the gossip ring of sharing worthless information just to showboat with other guys. Most of the guys that sit around talking about their conquests are lying anyway. I've seen too many girls' reputations get ruined because of a stupid guy running his mouth. "Ryland, you're my cousin and best friend, but *how* is really irrelevant at this point, don't you think?"

"You're really serious about this? If Konnor gets word, he will be at my doorstep the second he can get to you. He knows she's a good girl and her virtue is still intact, so he takes his protection of her overboard. I've seen the guy in action. Do you really want to deal with that over some girl? Wait, don't you have a girlfriend?" I'm getting tired of all his questions, but he's my only option at getting anywhere with this topic.

"Yes, I'm serious. I wouldn't be having this conversation if I weren't. I'm not trying to sleep with her. I just want you to help me get to the same place as her. If her brother needs to discuss anything, you can send him my way. I have a little sister, so I can handle a man-to-man conversation. Not that it's any of your business, but I broke up with Natalie last night."

"No joke? Why? I thought that was a sure thing. Plus, you're only here until Friday and then you'll be thousands of miles away from Kinzleigh." I am really starting to wonder about the questions. He seems awfully persistent in trying to sway me away from this subject, almost as if he wants her himself. He did say he tried. Now, I'm getting pissed, but he's my cousin.

"It was coming and needed to be done, regardless of Kinzleigh or not. So, you going to help me, or do I need to go another route?" I raise my brow questioningly as a smirk takes place, mirroring his earlier.

"Bro, you know I will help you; just getting the facts down. Presley is having an end of the year pool party tomorrow. She should be there. I think Presley said they leave for Cabo in a few days or a week. I can't remember."

"Are we invited?" I really hope we are, because I may crash it regardless.

"To the pool party? You know it," he says with his cocky grin in place.

"Okay, awesome. Let's catch some fish." I need to pass the time until this party.

We head back over to the rest of the group to bait up our lines and get everything ready for a day of fishing. I usually do well at anything I try, given my competitive nature. Today we're fishing for Blue Marlin, my favorite. Since it's heavier fish and bait than normal small game fishing, the charter provides all the fishing rods and bait.

I'm standing on the deck and I cast out my line beside Ryland. Uncle Joe and the rest of the charter crew are on the other side. The sun is coming up, so I pull my sunglasses over my eyes from where they are dangling around my neck. Looking across the water, I try to formulate a plan for this pool party.

I want to get Kinzleigh alone. She doesn't seem to open up at all around other people. She acts like she has some kind of phobia against males. Remembering her perfect body and the things Ryland said about guys trying to get with her, I know it's probably going to be a challenge. I can't stand the thought of another guy putting his hands on her. I barely know her and I already feel protective.

My knuckles turn white, grasping the pole. The thought of another man putting his lips on her and touching her in intimate places is like toxic venom running through my blood. I can't breathe and I feel weak. I don't even notice the tug on my reel.

"Breyson."

My eyes see nothing but the reels in my thoughts of her biting her soft lips and her big, beautiful eyes closing in pure ecstasy at the pleasure of someone else. How many guys have tried to sleep with her?

"Breyson!"

My vision turns red and blurred. My fists hurt from how hard I'm grasping the rod in them.

"Breyson, what the hell? Sink your line before the fish gets off!" I finally realize where I am and what is going on. Dammit, I've got to get a grip. This has never once in my entire life happened to me. I don't know what is wrong with me. I prop the bottom of the pole into my lower abdomen for support and jerk the line to sink the hook into the mouth of the fish.

Quickly, I begin reeling in my line. I can feel the fish playing tug-o-war as I use all of my strength to get it to the boat. From the weight on the other end and the amount of strength it is taking, I can tell it's going to be a good size catch—a prize.

I finally get the fish close to the boat and Ryland scoops it into the net. He cuts the line from the fish and places it in the storage compartment of the boat, not even wanting to measure it. Placing his hands on his hips, he narrows his eyes at me, as if trying to figure something out. "Mind telling me what is going on with you? I've never seen you spaced out like that and you looked like you were seconds away from breaking that rod in half and ready to stab someone."

I lock the rod into the pole lock on the deck of the vessel until I re-bait my line. I rub my hands over my face in aggravation. "Dude, I don't know. I can't get this girl out of my head. It's driving me crazy. You know me. I never get this way. Maybe it's because she's not easy like the rest of the girls I usually mess around with. I don't know, but I've got to fix it. I can't handle all this shit in my head."

He looks at me and a knowing smirk takes place over his face. He grabs me by the shoulders. "You, my friend, have the hots for Kinzleigh Baker. The one thing every guy that has crossed paths with her has had, but never actually been able to obtain. She's every man's dream, but that's all it's ever been for the rest of us—a dream. I'm going to be honest, so you don't get your hopes up. Several have tried and gotten nowhere. I'll help you get on her radar, but man, I'm not going to lie. You're going to need a lot of luck, because I've seen many crash and burn when it comes to her. Maybe you'll be different for her. For your sake, I hope you are."

He is not helping the situation any. The last thing I want to hear is the many failed attempts of men trying to make her theirs. "Man, would you shut up? That is the last thing I want to know." I pull my cap off and throw it down the deck.

He watches me act like an idiot, not saying a word. I've been known to have anger problems. "Be realistic, bro. Even if she gave you the time of day, what are you going to do when you have to leave six days from now? Kinzleigh is not the kind of girl you screw and run back to Mississippi with another notch in your belt. She's the kind of girl you take home to meet your parents; the kind of girl you marry. She is a rare find; a diamond in the rough. Once you get a girl like her, you try everything in your power not to screw it up, because chances are you won't find another one like her in your lifetime. Don't think about yourself, think about her. It wouldn't be fair. You know every girl in your clutch falls for you. Am I wrong? Look at the way things turned out with Natalie. If you want to have a good time, I'll introduce you to the right girls, but she's not it."

I pull away from his grasp and cross my fingers behind my head, exhaling for relief. If I really think about it, he makes sense. I didn't think this through. What am I going to do when I go back home? Most grown adults don't keep up anything long distance, much less high school kids. I'm definitely not anywhere in the realm of marriage.

Running my hand through my hair, pulling it in different directions, I sigh. "You're right. I guess I haven't really thought about it. We'll just go to the party and have fun. There was a cute girl last night that came on to me. Maybe I can revisit that offer." I try to smile, but it isn't real.

"Nice, who was it?" He crosses his arms over his chest.

"Lexi, I think. I wasn't really into it then."

He bites his lip a little, trying to hide a smile. "Now we're talking something that can be done. Piece of cake."

"Aight, cool. I guess it's settled then." I try to get in a good mood, but it was just slaughtered. "Let's get this done. You know I can't go home until I beat you." My competitive smile takes place.

Ryland stands there and studies me a few more seconds. He seems to be contemplating something by the way he is rubbing his chin with his fingers. "Let's do this."

We spent the rest of the day fishing. Once I got my head back in the game, I did pretty well. Ryland ended up with a catch of five at the day's end and me with seven. Uncle Joe had four. We're headed back to the house and it's about four forty-five in the afternoon. I'm staring out the window, index finger propped over my lip and thumb resting under my chin with my elbow on the door, lost in thought.

"You boys have fun?" Uncle Joe asks while looking in the rearview mirror.

"Sure did, Uncle Joe. Thanks again," I say, never looking his way. I can feel Ryland staring at me, but I can't bring myself to look away from the window. I can't concentrate on anything, nothing but her. It's starting to anger me at this point. I feel like hitting something. I tap my knuckles against the window, trying to relieve the tension before I actually do hit something.

Everything Ryland said was true, though. I have to figure out a way to forget about her. I can tell she isn't just a hook-up kind of girl and that seems to make forgetting her more difficult. Maybe we can just be friends.

Friends are better than nothing at all; although, I don't know how I'm supposed to do that after getting a taste of those sweet lips. I have never been much of a kisser before. Personally, I think it's too intimate for what I'm generally interested in. It screams commitment. It's just an easier way for a girl to develop feelings. Girls at my school know by now relationships aren't my thing. Natalie is the closest I came to one and it was evident what that was.

With Kinzleigh it was different. It was like I couldn't control myself around her. The first thing I wanted to do and the last was to kiss her. Getting a taste had to be the smartest and stupidest thing I've ever done. Like a drug addict thinking he can be done after one taste of his potent poison.

Maybe Ryland is right. Maybe I just need to find the closest hot girl and get her out of my system. That's exactly what I'm going to do. I've made up my mind. The problem is trying to get my mind to actually believe it'll work.

We pull into the drive and start walking to the pool house when Ryland breaks me from my thoughts. "Hey, cuz, you want to go out tonight? I know a few things going on."

We get to get door and unlock it. "I'm kind of beat. Mind if we just stay in tonight? Watch some movies maybe . . ." I say. His mouth drops a little. I guess I do sound like a total douche. I'm usually the first one to be up for a party, especially on Saturday night. Walking in the pool house, I head toward the couch and grab the remote as I sit down.

"You're really bummed about her, aren't you? I thought you were just hot on her, dude. I didn't know it was like *that*. Crap, man," he says, removing his visor and running his fingers through his longer, messy hair, curled in all the right places to add to his whole surf boy vibe.

"Nah, you're right. It wouldn't be right. She's just different from any girl I've come across. I don't know, maybe I do just need to hook-up with someone. Maybe it's all this Natalie crap coming at me. I just don't feel like partying tonight."

He grips the back of the couch with both hands. He's staring at me as I browse through the channels. I can see him through the corner of my eye. "I'm about to head to *Redbox* and get some DVDs. Any requests? I'll get a pizza on the way back. Drinks should be in the fridge."

"Okay, cool. Just no chick flick and I'm good." I go to grab for my wallet, but he starts shaking his head.

"Keep it. I got it this time." He pulls out his phone and starts touching the screen before holding it to his ear. "I'll be back shortly." He turns and heads for the door, but right before he shuts it I make out the first few words of his conversation. "Presley, I need a favor."

I wonder if he's making a stop on his way. Didn't the guy just get some last night?

SEVEN

Kinzleigh

I've been hard at work since ten o'clock this morning with my cheerleading coach. I didn't even take a break for lunch. I have too much on my mind. For starters, the images that my traitorous brain decided to play like a movie during what could have been a peaceful night's sleep. I woke up in a complete sweat, scared to go back to sleep at the thought of returning to one beautiful half-naked body on top of mine, kissing me senseless. The best way to control its wandering abilities are to focus on my stunting.

Coach Andy grabs me by the waist and throws me into a liberty. My knee shakes as I try to lock my right leg into position. "Stick it, Kinzleigh!" he yells as he struggles to hold me steady. I'm always the flyer, because of my size, and I'm really good at it. I rarely have problems sticking and for the first time I feel like an amateur. As I'm pulling in my left foot toward my knee to finish, I lose my balance and fall, Coach catching me on the way down. "Where's your head at today, girl? You're never this clumsy, and I've worked with you for seven years now."

Those are words I never hear from my coach and it infuriates me. Nothing ever gets in my way of cheerleading. "Just a slip up, Coach. My center was off a little. I must have gone up unbalanced. Easy fix. Let's go again."

He repositions on the mat behind me, placing his hands around my waist again. "One man stunt this time. Are you ready?" he asks into my ear.

Andy has been my coach since I was ten. He's about an average height at five-foot-ten and has light blond hair and honey colored eyes. He's the strongest person I know. He is about thirty now and takes coaching very seriously. He has the body to prove it. He also coaches the university squad nearby. Once Mom realized the cheerleading dream was not going away, she looked up the best coach around. She told me if I was serious then I was going to be trained by a professional. I think most of it was to keep her baby safe from trying to do my own stunts, but turns out I love him.

I nod, slightly squatting to give me some extra height in my jump and place my hands on his wrists. "What kind?"

"Just go into a tuck once you're in the air, but don't forget to lock on your way down. I want it clean and flawless. Got it? One, two . . ." He lifts me by the waist and throws me high into the air. I perform the perfect tuck before he grabs me by the middle of each foot at chest level and extends his arms high above his head. "Tighten your form, Kinzleigh," he says, looking up at my arms wavering slightly in the 'V' position. "That would be a deduction on your score at competition. You need to pay closer attention. You're really off today. Get ready to de-mount." He lowers me back down to chest level and tosses me just high enough to cradle me in his arms.

He sets me on my feet. Crap! This freaking sucks, and I won't allow myself to screw up. I can't remember the last time Coach had to correct me, especially not more than once in a matter of twenty minutes. "I want to go again."

"Maybe we need to call it a day or work on something else. I think your mind is elsewhere and it's showing in your form."

"No, Coach, I'm good. Let's go again." I refuse to show weakness, especially in front my coach. "What about the scorpion? You up for it? I need the practice now more than ever. You know I have tryouts coming up in a few weeks for the national all-star squad. I cannot fail. I've been working for this too long."

This is one of the things I have been waiting on for several years now. This is the one thing I have trained and shed sweat and blood for. My parents will not take this away from me. I don't care where they move me. I have been waiting for my tryout invitation since I applied freshman year and I have only had my acceptance invitation since last December. They send out invitations six months before tryouts to give you ample time to train. I was so excited, because it came the week before Christmas.

There are four divisions across the country. Usually, it's based on the territory that you live in; however, it is not a rule. Trust me, I have seared them to my memory bank. To even try out you have to apply and then after extensive review of your application and credentials, wait on an invitation. The board of judges only picks the best girls in the country and there are only a limited number of open spots each year. They only invite high school seniors and college age applicants for tryouts and they compete all over the world.

To even get a tryout says a lot about your skill level and talent. If I make the team, I will have experiences most people only dream about. Plus, every win, members get a bonus of cash and prizes. Before, I wasn't really worried about the money, but now that my parents are trying to shatter my dreams, I need every penny if I want to move back to California after senior year.

"Kinzleigh, I've known you for years, so why don't you just tell me what's going on in that head of yours. It may help you practice getting it off your chest." Coach knows I never talk about my problems, so I don't know why he is even asking. Heart-to-heart chats make things awkward for everyone involved since no one really understands except oneself. Some things are better left locked away.

"Can we just practice? I don't want to talk about it. You know me, Coach. This is how I deal with my crap." I'm hoping this can be the end of this conversation. I never deal with problematic conversation well. It makes me nervous.

"Very well then. I guess we can do a few more mounts," he says, looking at his watch. "It's almost six. We've been at this since this morning. Are you sure you don't want to call it a day?"

He smiles, because he knows me better than anyone. Even covered in sweat, as I am, and feeling the soreness in my muscles, I could do this well into the night. The right side of my lip pulls up into a slight smile as I shake my head in response. "I didn't think so."

He winks and turns to walk to the trampoline. "Come on. We're done with lifts for the day. We can practice on your tucks and back handsprings for a while. You may be small, but I've been lifting you since you warmed up this morning. My arms need a rest," he says teasingly.

I follow him to the trampoline and hop on. I begin securing the halter from the bungee cords that hang from the ceiling beams. We always practice on the trampoline if we're tired or learning something we haven't done very much and then take it to the ground once we're ready. I'm securing the last strap when I hear shuffling feet behind me.

"There's my favorite bi-atch!" That's a voice I would know anywhere—the one and only Presley Dunagin. Why is she here? I have a hard-enough time getting Presley here when she has to practice for the team, much less during her summer vacation.

I turn around to face her. By the looks of her wardrobe she isn't here to practice. She has her hair curled in big waves down her back and her makeup is heavier, as if she's going out. She's wearing white denim shorts and a black low cut, three-quarter sleeve top with tan wedges. Her cleavage is peeping out of her neckline. I shouldn't be surprised. Ever since she came to school freshman year bearing full C-cups, she has them on display whenever possible.

"What are you doing here? I thought I was supposed to meet you at your house tomorrow morning to help get everything ready for the pool party." I quickly scan my memory, trying to remember if there was something I forgot I was supposed to do. My mind has been on overload lately, so it's definitely a possibility, but nothing comes to mind.

She walks right past me with her eyes set on Coach Andy like she's a woman on a mission. On top of Coach being the best around, he's also young, attractive, and a hunk of muscle. I'm used to the drool plastered on females when in his presence. Even with Presley in all her promiscuity, this is a new one for her. She is not even eighteen yet and Coach is thirty.

I turn back to face Coach in complete confusion. The look on his face is as if he just saw a ghost. He looks nervous, and knowing Presley's reputation for getting what she wants, I can understand why. Poor guy. He has always been nothing but professional. She stops in front of him, barely leaving a space between them. "Presley, do you mind telling me what's going on?"

She turns back to look at me with a guilty gleam in her eye. Oh no, what has she done? "I just came to borrow you for the rest of the evening. Something suddenly came up." A seductive smirk takes form on her face, before looking back to Coach Andy. She places her index finger right over his navel and begins lightly trailing it up his torso. "You wouldn't have a problem with cutting this practice session a little early, now would you, Coach?"

He looks over to me, turning a little pale. "We'll pick this up in a couple of days, Kinzleigh. Just give me a call to set up the details, okay?" He starts backing away from Presley, looking side to side. I imagine he is terrified of another parent seeing a seventeen-year-old rubbing up on a grown man. Rumors can ruin a perfectly innocent person now days, and I don't have a problem admitting that Presley is jailbait.

I sigh, defeated. I might as well see what Presley is up to. She always gets her way. I know this by now. I look to Coach apologetically. "Okay, Coach. I guess we'll call it a day."

As he turns and walks rather quickly toward the office, stopping only long enough to gather his belongings, I start to unstrap myself from the harness that I'm still standing in. I think I was in such shock by the series of events taking place that I couldn't remove myself from the confinement of the trampoline.

Presley is making her way toward the entry of the trampoline. Her face now appears totally serious, as if nothing out of the ordinary just happened. What did just happen? I have no idea, but I'm going to find out. "Presley, what the heck was that? Do you want Coach to stop training you? It isn't like he needs the money with the mile-long waiting list of other girls wanting to train with him. What are you doing here? I was a little busy. You could have called."

She's smiling, setting me off further. My small, five-foot-two body comes flying off the trampoline, arms wailing in every direction as I yell at her. "If you need me to be backup for you to get with some guy, fine, but ask. Some of us have actual important things going on in our lives," I say harshly, sounding a little angrier than I meant.

"Are you done yet?" she asks sarcastically, as if daring me to continue. "This right here," she says, waving her finger in my direction, up and down my body, "is exactly why I'm here. Look at you, Kinzleigh. Do I really need to elaborate?"

Now calming down from my earlier burst of anger, I look myself over, trying to figure out what is wrong with my clothes or body. I wouldn't think workout clothing is anything outside of the realm of normal. I'm wearing black yoga shorts and a neon pink sports bra.

The only place I dress this way is practice or training with Coach, because it is easier to stunt and flip in fitted clothing. My hair is pinned up in a tight bun on my head to keep it out of my face and I'm barefooted with my black ankle sleeves on to keep from twisting an ankle. I'm glistening with sweat, but I've been practicing all day, for goodness' sake.

Now I'm confused, which isn't uncommon around Presley. After seventeen years of friendship, I still am not sure what all goes on in that head of hers. Her thinking is unlike anyone else. Her brain should be left to science one day. "What's wrong with my clothes? I always dress like this for practice," I say, walking to my gym bag to grab a towel. Presley is following closely behind, making a loud noise on the floor with her shoes. I grab my hand towel and begin wiping the sweat from my forehead and the rest of my face, then around my neck. I throw the now damp cotton back in the bag and grab my bottle of water.

Taking a refreshing sip, coating my dry mouth, I sit on the small set of bleachers utilized for family watching practice. Standing in front of me, Presley crosses her arms over her chest and narrows her eyes at me. "You really don't get it, do you? Look around, Kinzleigh. It's Saturday night and we're on summer vacation. Look where you are. You're wearing gym clothes, no makeup, and covered in sweat from head to toe. I get that you have the national tryouts coming up and you want to make the squad, but come on, Kinzleigh, you know you're going to make it. You're the best cheerleader around. The most driven. You don't have to have sex and drink alcohol if you don't want to, but you need to get out more. You need to experience life while you're young. I try my best to leave you alone, but it's time I put my foot down. You're my best friend, and it's my duty to keep you from wasting away like an old maid. This is supposed to be the best time of our lives, and I'm not letting you waste it away by practicing and staying at home with dear ole Mommy and Daddy. You won't get a do-over of your senior year."

She comes to sit beside me and grabs my hand. I look down at our hands fitted together. This is definitely awkward. That's one reason Presley and me get along so well. We are not emotional people. We don't entangle our hearts to men or anyone else like the rest of the girls do.

It's easier to keep your heart to yourself, to worry about one heart instead of two. If it makes me seem like a heartless person then so be it, but at least I know it will forever be intact and completely mine. Maybe when I'm older and have accomplished all of my dreams I will consider sharing it. Call me selfish. I don't really care.

She sighs as she stares off across the building. It's a large warehouse packed with mats, trampolines, harnesses and swings. There is a small lobby up front and an office. "What are you afraid of, Kinzleigh? I get that you want to keep your heart out of the equation, because you and I are one and the same, but you don't have to fall in love to have fun, you know."

Presley, of all people, should understand. Corey was as close as she has ever come to giving her heart away, and I am quite positive she wasn't in love with him. It was more so *we've been friends since kindergarten kind of I love you.*

Besides, look how that turned out. She ripped his heart out and stomped it to pieces, because they didn't share the same type of love. He has loved her since childhood. He finally got her to notice him in a way other than friends sophomore year. He unintentionally smothered her and became overly jealous and controlling. No man will ever control Presley. The girl has a mind of her own and isn't afraid to use it. She's beautiful and bold and turns guys' heads everywhere she goes.

If he were smart, he would have embraced her qualities. In return for his behavior, she ruined him for all other females while she carries on unaffected. It's sad really, how one person can forever change the life of another.

Love is cruel that way. Two people passionately and completely in love are the minority in a pool of people who love one they can't have. The best thing to do is avoid it at all costs. Protect your heart from heartache by caging it up and keeping it hidden from anyone else.

From anything I have ever seen, getting involved with someone does nothing but emotionally drain you, so why lead someone on when you have no intention of putting your heart out there for the taking.

So many indulge in love, hoping to get the fairy tale they read in books and see in movies, but that's not reality. Reality is hard, ugly, and painful. It doesn't take one with an experienced broken heart to know that's the way it is. Just look around you. You will see pain-stricken and brokenhearted people everywhere. I just think it's easier to avoid it than try to pick up the pieces after it's said and done.

She snaps her fingers in front of my face. I guess I was lost in thought. I turn toward her and straddle the bench. I shrug my shoulder at her. "I don't know what you want me to say, Presley. I just have other priorities in my life right now. I get that you're worried, but my parents have put a lot on me and I need to remain focused. You're just like me, but instead of focusing on cheerleading you focus on guys, in the plural form, to keep from giving your heart away. That's okay, but that's you, not me. I don't need a guy to make me happy."

I reach into my bag to pull out my pink *Fudpuckers* t-shirt. In the bottom of my bag lies a brochure size BJ's menu. How did that get in there? I wonder, my brows coming together before I am reminded of last night?

Suddenly, I imagine what Breyson is doing. The boy has a gorgeous smile and body from what I saw that day at the beach. I have never seen a guy my age that built and defined. Maybe he is as involved in something as I am with cheerleading. My lips tingle like they did after he kissed me. I begin fanning myself. Gosh, it's really hot in here. I guess Coach forgot to turn down the air.

"I call bullshit," she says, a little snippy.

"Excuse me?" Now what is she talking about? She still hasn't told me why she is actually here. I slip on my shirt and designer flip-flops, before removing my keys from my bag, zipping it up.

"You may have everyone fooled, Kinzleigh, including yourself, but I know you better than anyone and I know you were affected by a certain southern charm. Get up, you're coming out with me. I'm not taking no for an answer."

I drop my head down, resting my forehead into the heel of my hand. "Presley, I'm not even dressed to go anywhere. I've been sweating, and I would imagine I don't smell pleasant, even with deodorant. Can I please just go home?"

Her mischievous look comes on and she shakes her head. "I thought you might say that, so I grabbed some clothes and your makeup bag from your room. The bag is in my car. You can shower in the locker room."

She must have planned all this out. I stand, as does she. "When did you go to my house?" She throws her arm around my neck, towing me toward the door.

"Now, now, how did you think I knew to come here? If you don't want to be found, you should become less predictable." I roll my eyes as we walk closer to her white Mercedes convertible.

She bends over into the car to retrieve my bag from the passenger seat. The top is down. As she reaches over the driver's seat, her pelvis resting on the rolled down window, her feet lift slightly off the ground, leaving her rear in the air. I chuckle lightly. Presley can't do anything the easy way. Could she not have just walked to the passenger side? "Where are we going, anyway, that is so important? Some big summer party you forgot to mention? A concert?"

She pulls the bag across the seat and lifts it from the car, turning around. Extending her hand toward me with the handles resting in her palm she says, "Uh uh uh. A girl never tells her secrets. You go get fabulous and leave the rest to me. I will be right beside you to keep you company, so don't even think about bailing on me," she says, and pops a piece of gum in her mouth.

"Oh, heavens, what would I ever do without you?" I roll on the sarcasm thick, before grabbing the bag and turning on my heels, walking back inside toward the locker room.

She skips up beside me, slapping me playfully on the butt like baseball players do, catching me off guard. I yelp. "Lucky for you you'll never have to find out. Get a move on it, sister. We have places to be and people to see."

Walking into the locker room, I set my duffle bag on the countertop. There is no telling what Presley packed. The girl doesn't have conservative in her vocabulary. I exhale and begin sifting through the bag. I pull out necessities for showering, my makeup bag, the folded bundle of clothing, and my shoes.

Surprisingly, it isn't as bad as I expected. She packed white denim capris, a coral and salmon candy-striped, open shoulder sleeveless that meets at the neckline, front and back, and my favorite coral sandals. "Not bad, huh?" she says, leaning over behind me, directly beside my ear.

I jump. "Crap! You scared me. Do you have to do that?"

She moves beside me and turns her back to the countertop, gripping the side with her hands and jumping slightly to sit on top. "Oh, don't be such a baby. I may be dealing with the socially impaired, but I know how you like to dress, doll. You know I take care of my girl. Baby steps. One of these days I'll bring out the sex goddess I know is in there, but for now, getting you out of that pretty little shell is top priority."

She smiles, kicking her dangling legs back and forth. As much as I hate to admit it, I'm really going to miss her when I'm gone. I don't know how I'm supposed to leave her behind, or any of it for that matter. Why couldn't this wait one more year? One thing about Presley that only I know is that she acts all tough, but deep down she has a heart of gold. Everyone thinks she is this outgoing, emotionally disabled heartbreaker, but most of it's just an act.

What she doesn't know is I know the one thing that can break down her barriers. I guess the one person is more appropriate. I've watched her pine after my brother, hopelessly, for years. He is the real reason she could never fall for Corey. It's kind of depressing, to be honest.

She is only promiscuous to take her mind off the one person she wants but can't have. It's why I don't judge her. I think some of it is to even try and get his attention; to show him she isn't the little girl that follows him around anymore. He never gives her a second glance, though; not really anyway. I'm sure like many guys he thinks she's hot. I see him glance her way occasionally, but that's all it is.

The truth is, Konnor and me made a pact a long time ago. When I was becoming a teenager, he made me promise not to date any of his friends and in return he wouldn't date any of mine. I think he only did it trying to play the big brother role and protect me from being used and thrown away, as so many girls are, but the thing is, Konnor never breaks a promise. He never has.

At the time, I was selfish and didn't want him dating my friends, but after watching her all these years and seeing how Sophia treated him, maybe they deserve each other. Maybe that's why she is letting out this emotional side to her I've never really seen. Maybe it's because of Konnor being single. I wonder if she is allowing herself to feel in hopes that he will notice her and make a move.

I don't know how or when I'm supposed to tell her I'm moving. Thinking about everything, maybe I need to lighten up on Presley some. I'm sure I'll wish I did when I no longer have her around nagging me all the time. "Babe, are you going to shower or stand there looking at me all night? I know I'm a sight to see, but we really need to get going," she says, a smirk turning up on one side of her face.

And she's back.

One good thing about having curly hair is less prep time when you're in a hurry or being rushed by one impatient but charming best friend. Thirty minutes later, I'm dressed and putting the finishing touches on my makeup. "You look gorgeous, baby girl, as always. Now let's go. I'm tired of waiting."

I'm putting my stuff in my bag and I turn to gaze at Presley. She is looking at her phone again. She has been texting nonstop since I got out of the shower. "So, who are you texting? They have been blowing up your phone for thirty minutes." I pick up my bags and start for the locker room door, where she is standing against the doorframe.

She looks up, locking her phone, as I get closer. "Just Corey being Corey," she says, as if it's a normal thing. I can tell she is lying. Presley is the worst liar for two reasons. One, she is blatantly honest, so when she tries to 'lie' it is obvious. Two, Corey doesn't text her anymore. He gave up when rumors started flying of her random hooks-ups over Christmas break. I guess the guy figured groveling wasn't getting him very far. If she were a good liar, she would have known not to use that excuse. I would have actually believed it was Konnor first. They've always been friends, just nothing more.

"Uh huh," I say, not believing a word she just said. "You ready to go?"

She links her arm with mine in the way she always does. "I thought you'd never ask." The rest of the walk to the car is silent.

When we get to the parking lot, I remember we both drove. "I need to take my car home and let my parents know I'm going out."

"We'll drop it off at my house. It's on the way. I've already talked to your mom. You're staying with me." The little vixen has thought of everything to keep me from backing out.

"Fine, let's go before I regain my sanity and change my mind. I'm sure I'll regret this later." I get into my car, tossing my bags into the passenger seat.

She sits in her car, waiting for me to leave. I roll down the window. "Are you really going to follow me there?"

She nods her head. "I know your little games, Kinzleigh Baker. Get a move on it." I roll my eyes. I guess we're going to act like we're five. I pull out first and head for Presley's house.

Approximately ten minutes later, I pull into Presley's driveway. She lives in a large, three-story house with a four-car garage, the exterior walls all cream stucco with lots of windows, because there is one thing you don't block in Laguna Beach, and that's the views. All four doors are closed, so I park my Range Rover in front of Presley's garage door. As I'm getting out of the car, Presley pulls behind me, pressing on the horn. "I'm coming! Could you be a little more patient?" I ask, opening the passenger door and getting in.

"I've been waiting on you long enough. I'm starting to feel gray hair coming through," she says sarcastically. Always the dramatic one . . .

"Are you ever going to tell me where it is we're going?" She pulls away, staring straight ahead, never once glancing back at me.

"You'll find out soon enough. Don't get your panties in a bunch." She smiles, but continues to watch the road. "It wouldn't be a surprise if I told you, now would it? Let's just say it's a much-needed outing."

She reaches in her console and pulls out a small makeup bag; her emergency kit, nonetheless. Driving with her knee holding the wheel, she unzips the pouch and pulls out her famous pink lip polish. She never leaves the house without it. I'm more of a natural girl myself, but I guess the vibrant, shimmery pink does fit her personality.

Looking in the mirror, she smears on a coat and tosses it back in her makeup pouch. She then takes out a small bottle of perfume, the sweet but clean smell permeating the air as she applies a spritz to her neck and wrist. She then hands it to me. "Put this on. It's amazing and my favorite."

One of the things Presley and I have in common is our need and obsession for girly things, designer brands even more.

I spray myself, and as I'm handing it back to her she pulls into a gated driveway. She stops at the keypad and enters some random code. The gates slowly open. I raise my brows, looking at her. "Been here much?"

I don't even know whose house this is and she knows the gate code. That's pretty personal if you ask me. It's a gorgeous house, as most are around here, but I don't recognize it from any of the people we hang around. The garage doors are closed, so I can't scope out the vehicle.

She pulls up behind the garage door, closest to the fence that leads to the back of the house. Before killing the ignition, she presses the button to raise the top of her convertible, turning to me. She bites her bottom lip, trying to hold back a smile. "Maybe a time or two. Come on."

I step out of the car, leaving my purse in the passenger seat, but first remove my iPhone and slide it into my back pocket. I'm a little uneasy about this whole situation. I've never been the extroverted one in new places or when meeting new people. I've always been shy. I've gotten a little better over the last two years, because Presley is usually dragging me along on all her spontaneous endeavors, but I'm nowhere close to outgoing. I look up at the entryway and exhale, shutting the car door. "Okay, let's go."

Instead of walking to the front door, Presley cuts to the right and opens the gate of the privacy fence. It leads into a fairly large backyard with a huge pool. That says a lot considering we live in California. You pay a hefty price tag for outdoor living.

You can see for miles over the hills. I stop briefly, admiring the view. It's beautiful up here. I'm dying to know who lives here. "You coming, girlie?"

I turn around and Presley is standing at the door to what I assume is a guesthouse. I nod and begin making my way to the door beside her.

She knocks. It's only been a few seconds and I can hear footsteps getting closer. I begin fidgeting with my top—stupid nervous habit. I don't know why I'm shaking. Presley is standing against the doorframe looking down at her phone.

I'm about to ask what she is doing when the door opens. Turning toward it, everything begins to make sense. Oh . . . my . . . Every thought has completely left my brain. All I can see is six feet of solid muscle, standing in all its half-naked glory. It's . . . *him.*

He's barefooted, wearing nothing but gray cotton sweatpants. The elastic band of his underwear is sticking just above the top of his pants. I nervously bite my nails as my eyes adjust to the magnificent sight before me.

His chest rises and falls to the rhythm of his breathing. His stomach is like a piece of artwork, smooth but solid, revealing each abdominal perfectly, as if they are sculpted from stone. He has the slightest trail of blond hair that travels from his belly button downward, disappearing into . . .

My eyes follow it, landing on his . . . Oh gosh, am I staring at his crotch? I slap my hand over my eyes, trying to contain them from wandering. This is humiliating. "I'm going to let you two catch up." I can hear the laughter in her voice. Great, I probably look like an infantile schoolgirl.

Presley passes by him, walking inside the house, most likely with a big smile on her face. She loves to humiliate me. "Let's get this party started," she says. "What are we watching? Please tell me you got *Pacific Rim.* Charlie Hunnam is so sexy, and I heard there is a shirtless scene. I wouldn't mind having dreams about that sexy piece of man-candy tonight."

I can hear the sound of the leather moving as she plops down on the couch.

I separate my middle and ring fingers to peek and see if the coast is clear. That's a negative, ghost rider. Now he is standing in the middle of the doorframe with both arms raised, gripping the top in his hands, causing his muscles to flex. His hair is damp as if he just got out of the shower and he has a rather large smirk on his face. I'm such an idiot. I will not let his cockiness affect me. I'm around good-looking guys all the time and it never fazes me. Why he is different I have no idea. That is the million-dollar question.

I drop my hand and try to look into the house. I give myself a second to calm my heart rate before attempting to speak. "Hi," I say, giving him a slight wave. "So . . . I take it this must be Ryland's house?"

I slide my hands in my back pockets, not knowing what else to do with them.

He begins walking toward me with that same cocky grin still in place. It may even be bigger. I back up. He is looking straight into my eyes, as if he is on the prowl. "I guess I found you," he says in a low, sexy tone. He has one hand in a fist and the other flat, swinging them together in front of him, kind of like a pendulum swing, as he continues forward. He is already completely out the door, having shut it behind him.

"I guess you could say that," I say, smiling nervously. My stomach feels like it's full of butterflies fluttering around. I keep backing up until I can feel the edge of the pool. I look down and I'm one step from falling in. I'm trapped. Now what am I supposed to do? "Presley mentioned we're watching movies? What are we watching?"

He grabs the thin fabric of my shirt in between his thumb and index fingers, slightly pulling me toward him. "Come in and I'll show you what we've got. I promise I won't bite, unless you ask."

He winks, taking hold of my hand and turning back to the house. He has a tattoo between his shoulder blades. It's script in another language. I wonder what it says or what it means. Most people our age don't have tattoos, unless it's significant or you have parents that don't care about anything. You can't even get one unless your parents sign a consent form or you get by with a fake ID.

Tonight should be interesting. I don't usually hang around with guys, except in a large group. Sure, I get asked out on dates, but I've never had a problem declining . . . until now.

Somehow, though, I have to stay strong. I have to find a way to keep my distance from him. He could potentially ruin *everything*.

EIGHT

Breyson

At first, I thought I was seeing things. That surely my mind was deceiving me. The girl who's taken residence in my mind is standing before me. I had watched TV for a while, mindlessly flipping through the channels but not really paying much attention to what was on. Ryland came back a little while later with two large pizzas and a handful of DVDs.

I had finally decided Ryland was right. In a few short days, I was going to be heading back to Mississippi and I would likely never see her again. No matter how much it sucks, that's the way it is.

Ryland ran to the main house to get some more blankets and pillows. He said he had a couple of girls coming over to hang out and watch movies. He never did tell me who, so I just figured it was that girl from the party.

I had just gotten out of the shower when I heard a knock at the door. The first thing I found was my sweatpants, so I quickly pulled them on and went to answer the door. I definitely wasn't expecting to find what I did on the other side of that door.

I owe Ryland for this. I'll gladly do whatever he wants after tonight, because standing on the other side of that door is the most beautiful sight I've ever seen. Each time I see her she gets more beautiful. Honestly, I never knew that was possible. I was temporarily at a loss for words when I saw her standing there.

I quickly recovered when I saw how shocked she was that it was me who opened the door. I guess she was as surprised to see me as I was her. She's so shy that I can't help but to smile every time I'm around her. Presley just scored one of the top five spots in my book of the best girls for bringing her here. What makes her even better—she left us alone, no questions asked.

I can tell Kinzleigh is attracted to me too, but also how much she fights it. I've got my work cut out for me if I'm going to get anywhere with her, and I have a short time to do it. But she's here tonight, and that's a start.

This girl is becoming like a drug to me. Comparable to that first high you always hear about. She's my gateway drug. I may go back to Mississippi and spend the rest of my life searching for that same first high, but right now I'm going to savor the real deal, and that's her.

God, I love it when she gets embarrassed. I can't help but to play with her. The way she blushed when she realized she was looking at my crotch will forever be engrained in my memory.

I pull her into the house and shut the door. "Do you want anything to drink or eat? Ryland picked up some pizzas." She's standing beside the door, looking around the room as if she is afraid to go any farther. She's twirling a lock of hair around her fingers. I've noticed she does it a lot when she seems uncomfortable.

She looks at me, her cheeks a shade of pink. "Pizza sounds good. I accidentally skipped lunch today." How does someone forget to eat? I'm always thinking about food. Girls are weird about eating, especially around guys. That's not something I wanted to hear. She has a beautiful body, but she is small enough. She doesn't need to be missing meals. I walk over to the kitchen and take a few plates from the cabinet. I nod my head for her to come to where I am.

She walks over to the edge of the bar and pulls out a stool, sitting down. "Do you do that often?" Her eyes are focused on the place setting in front of her like she is afraid to look at me. I don't know why a girl as hot as her is so shy. "Kinzleigh, look at me."

She looks up at me slowly, her cheeks changing to a more prominent shade of red as she scans up my naked stomach. "I was training with my coach all day. It slips my mind sometimes when I'm at it for hours at a time." Her voice comes out just above a whisper, as if she is having trouble catching her breath.

I put a slice of pizza on each plate when Ryland comes barreling through the door, arms full of blankets and pillows. He looks at Presley lying on her belly on the floor, digging through the DVD collection. Kinzleigh turns around on her stool. "Hey Ryland. How's it going? I haven't seen you in a while." She smiles. Ryland looks at her and up at me with that knowing grin rising from his lips. I can't help it that I'm grinning ear to ear knowing the hottest girl in all of California is sitting right in front of me. He knows I owe him one for this. I can see it written all over his face.

"Kinzleigh." He nods. "I'm glad Presley got you to come. You guys up for some movies?"

"Sure, what are we watching? Nothing scary, right?" I take some glasses from the cabinet. When I turn back around Ryland is looking at me with a guilty expression. I know exactly what he's thinking and for once I like where his thoughts are going.

"I think one or two of them are horror. Is that okay? I've been dying to see that new movie *The Conjuring*. I missed it in theater. Presley and I can take the floor and you guys can have the couch. Will that work for you?" Only I know that tone is Ryland's form of sarcasm. To everyone else it sounds genuine. If I didn't like the idea of getting her close to me I'd slap him in the back of the head for doing her that way.

Her eyes widen, and she looks unsure. Ah hell, I can't do this to her. I'm about to tell him to put on *Pacific Rim* when Presley rolls onto her back, props up on her elbows with a big smile on her face, and says, "You'll be fine, Kinzleigh. You're staying at my house tonight, so you shouldn't have any nightmares. I haven't made you watch one since *The Ring*. A little fear is good for everyone every once and a while."

"Okay then. I guess it's settled." She turns back toward me and I set her plate in front of her, as well as a glass of ice.

"What do you want to drink? Soda or water?" I set my plate down beside hers and start to walk toward the refrigerator.

"Water, please." She suddenly looks a little embarrassed. "Do you have a fork?"

Grabbing a water and soda, I shut the door and set them down, my brows coming together, a little puzzled. "A fork?"

She smiles. "I don't like getting the grease on my hands. It makes me feel gross. Sorry, it's a little strange, I know."

Her embarrassment is such a turn-on. Usually, girls that look like she does ends up being a complete bitch, but not her. "I have to admit, I don't usually witness someone eating pizza with a fork, but I'm always game for something new." A smile spreads across my face. Ryland comes over and grabs a plate for him and Presley while she gets their drinks.

Presley stops before returning to the sitting area. "You have ten minutes to get over here or I'm coming to get you, whether you're finished eating or not," she says, a goofy grin on her face to show she's joking with her.

I look at Kinzleigh. "We can watch something else if you don't want to watch a scary movie. Don't listen to Ryland. He can watch it later. We did get other movies."

She begins cutting up her pizza, making me smile. She looks like she has to put some muscle behind it to get through the crust. "It's okay. I'll never hear the end of it if I don't. Plus, I'd rather watch it first and get it over with. That way, by the time I go to bed I'm thinking of something else. If you stick around long enough, you'll learn there is no use in arguing with Presley."

I'd love to stick around long enough, but there is no way I'm going there with this conversation. I may have the hots for this girl, but I'm not a pussy. I don't like to sit around and talk about my feelings to a girl; trying to fill her head with garbage in hopes of getting laid. It's not my style. We finish eating and head over to the couch, just as Presley is skipping through the commercials.

I finally remember I'm not wearing a shirt. I'm not used to having to cover up after a shower unless I'm going somewhere. Ninety percent of the time this is how I'm dressed around the house, because I never have girls over. When girls are around, I'm at a party or in my truck and the night usually ends with me removing clothes, not putting them on. Her pattern of barely looking at me and constantly blushing now makes sense.

I walk to the back bedroom to grab a black sleeveless shirt and pull it on. When I return to the living area, Kinzleigh is sitting on the couch, barefooted, with her legs crisscrossed. I grab a couple of pillows and a blanket from the stack Ryland brought in, placing them on the couch beside her.

As she notices my shirt a smile occurs. She takes a pillow and places it in her lap. "Thank you . . . on both counts."

I pull the bottom of my shirt back up my stomach, toying with her. That smile quickly fades and her eyes go wide. I laugh, because I can't help myself. She almost acts younger, and with girls, I'm generally used to the opposite. Between the well-matured body and the clothing and makeup adding to it, you can't tell who's your age and who's older anymore. Her cheeks turn a soft shade of pink. I'm about to sit down when she smacks me in the face with the pillow she's holding.

She laughs softly at the startled look on my face. I love her laugh. "Behave yourself or you can sit on the hard floor," she says with a playful look in her eyes, pointing to the floor. She's finally relaxing. I knew she had a feisty side. It just needed to come out.

I hold up my hand, index and middle finger pointed upward in unison. "Scouts honor," I say in return. "Is this seat taken?" I point beside her, only joking, because I'm sitting there whether she invites me or not. She looks down the vacant couch and back to me, sucking her bottom lip between her teeth, shaking her head. "Good, because I was prepared to vacate it if necessary."

I take a seat beside her and Ryland pops his head up from the bed he made with blankets on the floor that him and Presley are sharing. "Dude, are you going to turn out the lights? Last one standing gets the job and you know it. Hurry up, we're waiting on you two to start the film."

"Could you not have told me sometime in the last ten minutes I've been standing here?" I get up and turn off the lights. As I sit back down the opening credits come on. It has that creepy music always used in horror films. I look over at Kinzleigh and she has pulled her knees to her chest and spread a blanket over her body, the top clutched in her hands right below her nose. She is staring at the television with one eye open and one eye closed. I have to bite my tongue to keep from laughing.

I grab the side of the blanket and lift it, scooting underneath it closer to her. "You really don't like scary movies, do you?" I talk low, trying not to be too loud. She looks at me, shaking her head. I scoot close enough to her that our sides are touching and put my arm around her shoulder, pulling her toward me. "I promise I'm not going to try anything," I whisper against her ear. "It makes it less scary feeling another body close to you."

She looks up at me and raises a brow questioningly. "Who told you that?" She doesn't believe me. I can tell by her tone.

"I used to have nightmares when I was a kid. My mom would come and sit beside me when I woke up in a sweat screaming. I think she called them night terrors. She used to sing and pull me close enough I could touch her. She said as long as I could feel her near, the nightmares would go away. Maybe it was a load of crap, but it always worked." I shrug nonchalantly.

Her face softens. She grabs her hair in the fist of her hand and pulls it to the opposite side, laying it to rest over her shoulder. She places her head on the top of my shoulder. "Okay, I'll give it a try. I just have really colorful dreams; always have. That's why I avoid scary movies."

I can't describe the feeling I have with her body touching against mine—peacefulness maybe. I've never wanted to be this close to a girl before, aside from sex, and that's just long enough to get off and get her dressed. For the first time in my entire life, I just want to be near her and do nothing but talk to her. Don't get me wrong, I'd love nothing more than to experience all of her, but it's not a priority with her, which surprises me. I feel the need to make her mine in every way possible, somehow, some way. Only thing wrong with that picture is come Friday we'll be on two different coastlines. Maybe I can somehow get out of her where she is moving. Anywhere in the south is closer than we are currently.

We are about forty-five minutes through the movie with nothing major happening at this very moment. Kinzleigh is still buried beneath the blanket, folded into my arms. Out of nowhere, an image jumps on the screen, causing Kinzleigh to scream and bury her head into my side. I bite my tongue in an effort not to laugh out loud at her burst of terror. I bite down so hard I can taste blood. I love her nestling into my side. It makes me feel like I'm protecting her.

Ryland and Presley didn't even budge. They haven't come up for air the entire movie. From the sounds and the movement under the cover they won't be anytime soon.

I look over at Kinzleigh, barely peeking out of the blanket. I can tell she is really bothered by the movie. "You want to go to the other room? There is another television in there. We can put on *Pacific Rim* or *We're the Millers.*" She looks like she is about to decline when a moan comes from Presley's mouth, causing her eyes to widen as big as saucers.

I don't know what it says about me that I like she is uncomfortable in sexual situations. The thought of her making sounds like Presley from another guy sends my blood boiling. "Okay, will you grab the movie?" She keeps eying the mound of blankets moving in different directions and the doorway to the other room.

I nod, and before I can get up from the couch she grabs the pillow and bolts in the direction of the bedroom door. I shake my head in laughter and get up to grab the DVDs.

When I walk in the bedroom she is laying on her stomach with her legs crossed behind her in the air. She has her phone in front of her and doing what appears to be texting. I wonder if she is texting a guy. The thought plagues my mind and embarrassingly I want to grab it and find out. I want her for myself.

I rub my hand through my hair. I need to get a grip. *What the hell is wrong with me? Is this what jealousy feels like?*

I have never cared who a girl talks to, not even Natalie. We basically had a 'don't ask don't tell' policy as far as talking goes. I like to have fun. Since I started driving, I only needed them for one thing, and the type of girls I usually hung around it was understood they liked the same kind of fun—easy to give it up too. I don't like this at all.

"What will it be?" I hold up the movies from where I stand in front of the bed. She lays her phone down in front of her, looking up at me. She props her chin on the heel of her hand, wiggling her fingers above her upper lip as if she's thinking. "I think *Pacific Rim* is the better option of the two. Konnor said it was really good and we usually like the same movies."

"Great choice," I say, putting down the other DVD, so I can open the case and put it in the Blu-ray player. "Will you see if the remote is in the drawer by the bed?"

She sits up on her knees and turns toward the drawer. She bends over, resting on her right palm, rummaging through the drawer of the nightstand. Her shirt comes up slightly, revealing the bottom of her back. Just above the band of her jeans sits two perfect dimples. My eyes lower, lingering on her perfect round bottom. I need something to take my mind off of her before I start undressing her in my mind. Knowing that it's there, I look down and confirm my hard-on. Quickly adjusting myself, I try to think of something to calm my raging thoughts. "So Konnor is your brother?" If talking about another guy isn't an erection kill, I don't know what is.

She pulls out the remote and turns around, sitting crisscrossed on the bed. She points the remote at the television, turning it on. "Yeah," she sighs and pulls her knees against her chest to wrap her arms around them, dropping the remote on the bed. "He's going through a lot right now. He just told me he's at a tattoo shop picking out a new tattoo. He asked if I wanted to come and watch."

I remember Ryland telling me about his ordeal, but I don't want her to be mad at Ryland for telling me, so for now I'll keep it to myself. "You don't like tattoos?"

She is a little spaced out as she stares down at her knees, lost in thought. "It's not that." She shrugs. "I don't know. It's his second one in a month. At this pace he's going to be covered in a year from head to toe. They aren't small ones either. He's never been the 'bad boy' type. He's just becoming very . . . different, and fast. Each tattoo represents something different and it's not the happy reason to get a tattoo. He and his girlfriend recently broke up after three years of dating. What's going to be next? He turns into the rest of the jocks at school and sleeps with everything that walks? Breaking hearts along the way or becomes the bad-boy rocker man-slut seducing women with his voice? I'm scared he's going to regret it when he finally gets over all of this. He really loved her, I guess." Her nose scrunches in disgust.

Point one—she obviously doesn't condone sleeping around. Point two—it's making me want her all the more. I don't know what to say, because I've never been in that situation. I learned years back not to trust a woman with your heart. It will only kill you in the end, Beau being the example in that lesson. I have no idea what that feels like, and from the looks of her she doesn't want to go into any further detail. I finally got her laughing and having a good time, so I'm perfectly fine with steering away from this conversation.

I nod in understanding and turn to put the DVD in the player and then return to the bed after turning the lights off. "Do y'all have a curfew?" It really isn't that late, but according to what she said last night she's never out late.

She shakes her head. Her smile is slowly coming back. "As long as Presley's mom knows where she is and it's someone's house she can stay out until two in the morning. Anywhere else she has to be home by twelve." She leans back against the pillow and starts to shiver. Ryland keeps it cold. Last I checked the thermostat was set on sixty-five.

"You can get under the cover. I promise I'll keep it PG-13." I grin. I like messing with her.

She raises her brow at me and plays with her curly hair as a smirk forms. "I think you better keep it G-rated or I'm kicking you off the bed. I know how to fight."

Oh, would I love to see that.

I might give it a go for that very reason. "I'd like to see you try," I say playfully. I can't imagine her tiny body being able to do much damage.

"My parents wanted me to learn self-defense, so I had to take classes when I was fourteen. I'm quite experienced in taking down an attacker. Don't let my size fool you." She pauses and then smiles. "Didn't your mom teach you not to judge a book by its cover?" She is getting more comfortable around me and I like the sassy side that seems to be trying to break through.

I place one knee on the bed, followed by the other. Feeling playful, I grab her by the ankles and pull her across the bed to meet me. Kneeling between her legs, I release her ankles and grab her hands in mine, pinning them to the bed. "Is that a challenge?"

I lean forward, getting closer to her face. I can feel her breaths coming out short and quick. I can tell I'm having an effect on her. She brings her knees up beside me, the bottom of her feet flat on the bed, opening her spread wider. Her eyes are slightly hooded. I place my mouth right beside her ear. "One point for me."

With a big grin on my face, I release her hands and sit back up, grabbing the remote and pressing the play button. She quickly sits up and moves back to the head of the bed. I'm starting to worry she's mad, but then she smiles. "Not a chance. Payback's a bitch."

We lay here watching the movie. It's mostly quiet with occasional small talk. Things are easier now than when she first got here. The more I talk to her, the more I realize how down-to-earth and likable she is. We seem to have a lot more in common than I originally thought.

I look at her, lying back on a pillow watching the movie. Her hair is fanned out behind her head. She has one leg bent in the air, the bottom of her foot flat against the mattress with her hand resting on the thigh of her bent leg while the other is lying flat against the bed. I notice the same anklet she was wearing at the beach. It must be her favorite piece of jewelry or either something meaningful. She's beautiful. I wish I could take a picture with my phone without it seeming creepy, so I'll have something to remember her by when I go back home.

"Ryland said something about a pool party Presley is having tomorrow. Are you going?" She rolls onto her side and turns toward me, propping her upper body onto her elbow.

"Yeah, I have to help setup. She has one at the beginning of every summer. Her parents go all out and have it catered. It's kind of become a tradition. Pretty much everyone from school will be there. Presley has me running around picking things up while she sets up at the house. I guess you could say I'm the chauffeur for all the supplies."

"Do you need some help? I don't have any plans tomorrow. I think Ryland said he had some stuff to take care of for school before the party anyway, so I'll just be stuck here or following him around."

She's looking me in the eyes. She doesn't answer for a moment. I wish I knew what was going through her mind right now. She finally answers, smiling. "Yeah, okay. I could use some of your muscle."

We haven't heard much out of Presley and Ryland since they changed the movie in the other room. I assumed they finally finished taking care of business until we start hearing Presley calling out his name. Kinzleigh looks at the door. "You have got to be kidding me." She looks back at me. "Does it take everyone that long?"

Her face flushes at the question.

I glance at her lips being sucked between her teeth. Her innocence shows more and more as I get to know her. I like it more than I care to admit.

I meet her eyes with my own. "Depends on the guy . . . If you're dealing with a man it does. A man cares about the pleasure of his girl before his own. A man waits on his girl to be satisfied first. A man holds out as long as necessary, regardless of what he has to do. And on the occasional slip, he goes again. Only a boy lets himself get off first and then he's done."

I notice the slightest moan escape her lips. It's so low I wasn't even sure I heard it. Presley starts up again, louder this time. I can tell Kinzleigh is getting really uncomfortable. Me—I'm not bothered by it. Being on the football team you hear and see so much it doesn't even faze you after a while.

There is a door in the bedroom that leads outside. "Come on," I say. "Let's get some fresh air."

We get up at the same time and she follows me outside the door. The door comes out on the side of the house so, we walk back to the pool. "It must be nice to have views like this every day," I say, standing at the edge of the pool.

"It is," she replies. "I love it here. I'm going to miss this place. I plan to try to come back after senior year for college." She stops behind me. My tattoo must be slightly showing from the neckline of my shirt, because she starts tracing the outline. The light caressing of her finger sends chills down my arms. "People our age don't usually have tattoos. What does it mean?"

I don't talk about my tattoo, because it's mine and mine alone. Something I don't want shared with the world. I've never told anyone what it means; not even Ryland. That's the reason it's in Latin. She whispers, "Infragilis."

For some reason, though, I want to tell her. "Unbreakable. It's Latin." I expect her to ask a lot of questions, to quiz me on the meaning, but she surprises me when I hear nothing at all.

Only a sigh of contentment.

She runs her finger down my back. She then clasps her small hands around my waist. The feel of her so close makes me close my eyes. I try to turn around when she shoves me off the side, causing me to fall into the pool.

I come up for air—completely soaked—to her bent over laughing. "What was that for?" I'm trying hard to sound mad, but her laughter is contagious and before I know it I'm laughing along with her.

She stands upright, placing her hands on her hips. "That's for earlier." She winks. "I don't get mad, I get even."

I come to the edge, placing my palms flat on the cement, pulling myself up. She doesn't realize she just made this a game. I can do this all night. It's in my competitive nature. I'm trailing water as I stalk toward her. She is still laughing a little until she looks me in the eyes. Her eyes widen as she realizes what I'm doing and takes off running.

I chase after her around the yard. She's pretty quick to be so short and dainty, but no match for me. Back home, I play baseball and football to be close to each of my brothers and I'm one of the fastest guys on the team. I'm not even breaking a sweat and I'm on her heels. I'm giving her a few minutes lead just to toy with her, allowing her to think she's won. Right before she gets to the gate, I increase my stride and wrap my arm around her waist, causing her to scream out. When she realizes it was a little loud, she slaps her hand over her mouth, trying not to cause commotion with Ryland's parents.

I pull her backward toward me and scoop her into my arms, cradling her. She places her arms around my neck for stability, but begins kicking her legs, trying to break free from my grasp. "There's not a chance I'm letting you get away now, sweetheart. I love a good challenge."

She looks at the pool getting closer with each step and turns back to me. "You wouldn't dare." She narrows her eyes. "Breyson, no!"

"Oh, but I would," I say, and take off running toward the pool. I jump off the deep end with her in my arms. Breaking through the water, I release her, so we can each come back up for air.

She breaks the surface, brushing her hair back out of her face, laughing. "The water is freezing," she says, teeth clattering. "I can't believe you did that!" She splashes water at me. "I didn't bring any extra clothes."

Her thin, satin top is clinging to her body, revealing the outline of her bra and cleavage. For the top to be so conservative—reaching all the way to her neck in which it connects with the back fabric—this is by far the sexiest view I've ever had. There is something to be said about a girl that leaves a little to the imagination. When it's all out there for the world to see, for some reason it's less appealing.

"I wouldn't worry about clothes. I'm sure we can find you something." She is wading in the middle of the pool and I am closer to the farther side. I begin making my way toward her, my eyes never leaving hers. She has the slightest smile on her face. When she sees me coming toward her, she begins swimming backward, slowly. "You trying to run from me?"

I grin, because she is getting closer to the side, leaving less room for her to go.

"You trying to catch me?" she counters sarcastically. You got to love a girl with a little spunk. Her back finally reaches the corner of the pool, not far from the diving board. She turns around, noticing she is now trapped and I have her right where I want her. She bites the corner of her lip.

I stop right in front of her, grabbing the edge of the pool on each side of her. "Maybe I am. I know a good catch when I see one."

Her eyes are slightly hooded like earlier, giving me the answer to the question in my head. She is giving me confirmation that she feels the way I feel right now. I close the distance between us, the warmth from our bodies mingling around us. The water isn't so cold anymore. I wrap one leg at a time around me to support her against the wall. I remain holding one edge of the pool and place the other hand on her neck.

I lean in closer, our lips just a breath apart. "Stop running, Kinzleigh." Her eyes close as she releases a sigh. I can't stop myself anymore. I don't want to. I don't care if I have to go back home in a few days. I would rather have a few days I'll never forget than spend the rest of my life in regret.

I softly kiss her lips, before sucking the droplets of water from them slowly, savoring her taste. They are full and soft. She slowly relaxes, letting me suck and pull at her bottom lip. I can feel her inexperience with every movement. She allows me to lead her lips where I want them. I lightly lick her lips, requesting entry, in which she grants. As I slide my tongue inside her mouth, I seek out hers. It's warm and moist, entangling with mine.

I run my hand from her neck down the seam of her body, stopping at her waist, just before testing the water and cupping her bottom. It feels as good as I envisioned it would feel and it's covered in denim. I can't imagine how it would feel bare.

I continue to kiss and suck her lip, guiding her tongue in the perfect rhythm with mine. As she slides her tongue inside my mouth, I clench it with my lips and suck it, then release. The lowest moan escapes her perfect lips, as if she's afraid I'll hear her.

My hormones are raging. It's unavoidable. Holding her by the butt, I pull her closer at the waist. My erection is pressing between her legs. Even in this pool of cool water, I can feel the heat radiating from inside the opening at her thighs. A growl comes from within my chest, causing her to slightly bite my bottom lip. Oh damn, for the first time in my entire life I feel like I could come, and she hasn't even touched me. She brings her arms up around my neck, interlocking her fingers at the back.

I lightly rub my erection over the material separating us. She rolls her head to the side, giving me access to her neck. I kiss just below the lobe of her ear and run my tongue lightly down her neck, stopping at the top of her exposed shoulder.

She gets a little bold and sways her hips from side to side. "If you keep doing that, I'm going to lose my control, and this will end up going further than you likely want."

She lifts her head and looks at me, smiling mischievously, and kisses the area on the front of my neck between my collarbones. She lightly trails kisses higher up my neck. "Kinzleigh, you're playing with fire." I warn. She clamps her legs tighter behind my back and clenches the muscles between her legs that are pressed against my sides.

I can't take it anymore. Without thinking, my hand goes for the button of her pants as I take her lips, more roughly this time. I finally pull away to look her in the eyes. I rest my forehead against hers. "I'll have to go inside and get a condom from my wallet if you want to go any further."

I look into her eyes and her breathing is quickening. She looks like she is thinking about it, which only tells me one thing. "Kinzleigh, you have had sex before, right?"

I thought Ryland was blowing smoke up my ass when he was talking about her being inexperienced with guys, but I didn't think he meant literally none. I will not be the one to take her virginity. That's a connection and attachment I stay away from. Plus, she doesn't deserve that. Her first time should be with someone who has a warm beating heart, someone who'll take his time, make it memorable. Mine turned to ice a long time ago.

She isn't looking at me. As a matter of fact, she is staring at the water. She releases my neck. "No, I haven't. Does it really matter whether I have or not? Since when do guys care about that sort of thing? It's just sex, right? Maybe it's time I stop trying to be so perfect. Look at where it's getting me. Nothing is going the way I planned. A few weeks from now my life will be over as I know it. Maybe I should just live for myself and have fun like everyone else. It's perfect really, if you think about it. You can help me get it out of the way and then we won't ever see each other again once you leave. No lies, no expectations; just fun."

Dammit! Why in the hell does she have to be a virgin? I run my fingers through my wet hair. I want her; so bad I can't stand it. I've never turned down a girl that looks even half as beautiful as her and I'll probably hate myself for this.

She may not want any attachments, but I can't do it to her. She deserves better. I want to claim her as my own, to mark her in the most absolute way, but at what cost? "Let's go inside and change clothes and we'll continue this there." I kiss her softly and lift her to sit on the side of the pool. I lift myself out of the water, and once standing, I reach for her hand. "Come on, beautiful."

Walking into the bedroom, I grab two towels from the linen closet. I hand her a towel, along with a pair of boxers and a t-shirt. "Thanks. I'll be right back," she says as she turns and disappears into the bathroom. I remove my wet clothes and put on a pair of dry boxers. I sit on the edge of the bed, leaning forward, resting my forearms on my thighs. How fucked-up is it that I can't stand the thought of someone else being her first? But for once, sex alone isn't enough; at least not with her. This time, I can't be selfish. I have to think about her and not me.

The door to the bathroom opens. She saunters toward the bed. She tied her wet hair up on top of her head. As she gets into bed, she yawns. I pull back the comforter for her to lie down. Crawling in, she lays down on her side, facing away from me. I wrap my arm around her waist, placing my hand against her belly, and I pull her toward me until our bodies are aligned. "What time is it? I should probably check on Presley, so we don't miss curfew."

Pulling the blanket over our bodies, I nestle her in the nook of my curled body. She fits like a glove, like we were cut from the same cloth and now coming back together. "Just lay with me for a while, please." She doesn't say another word; just relaxes beside me. If I were breakable, this girl is possibly the only thing that could do it. That scares the hell out of me. That's my last thought before falling asleep with her in my arms.

NINE

Kinzleigh

I'm having the most peaceful night's sleep until I'm jolted awake by someone shaking my shoulder. I rub my eyes, trying to wake up. "What time is it?"

Presley is standing over me beside the bed, talking in a hushed whisper. "It's almost two in the morning. We have to get going or my parents are going to ground me before my pool party."

I then realize there is an arm wrapped around my waist, holding me tightly, as if to keep me from going anywhere. I can't see the look on Presley's face, because it's dark, but I'm sure I'll hear about this later.

I lift his arm carefully, slipping out of the bed as quietly as possible to avoid waking him. Tonight was probably one of the best nights of my life. I'm not quite ready for it to be over yet.

Maybe I can spend a few days with him and then everything will go back to normal. He makes me feel things I never knew you could feel, and I haven't decided if that's good or bad. I want to feel him out some more. He's easy to talk to and I'm myself around him. I don't have to pretend to be someone I'm not.

Maybe it wouldn't be so bad to be friends with a guy. I can't deny I'm attracted to him. It sounds like neither of us want to pursue anything more after hanging around each other for the time he's here, so maybe having a little fun won't ruin everything. At least when I have to leave this place, I'll have something to take with me. "Can you grab my clothes from the bathroom?" I continue her charade of whispering in hopes we can ease out of here without being caught.

"Yeah, but hurry up," she whispers, walking to the bathroom. I walk around the bed to Breyson's side. I only have one thing to give to someone and that's my body. My heart will never be owned. That's the way it is and the way it has to be. I will forever hold my own heart in the palm of my hand.

But if I'm going to give a piece of myself away to someone else, I want it to be him. I've made up my mind. It may be stupid to lose my virginity without my heart involved, but that's the way I want it. I won't risk everything in my life for something that will never last. It's time I do something for me instead of making everyone else happy.

I'm standing over him, looking down. He looks so peaceful. I bend over and whisper in his ear. "Thank you for tonight." I kiss him on the cheek and he stirs in his sleep. I still until he stops moving and head for the door, following behind Presley.

We quietly walk out of the door and tiptoe in a running fashion toward Presley's car. I can finally see her with the sensor operated floodlight shining from the edge of the house. She looks at me, examining my clothes with a big smile on her face. "Shut up," I say, smiling back at her. "I don't want to hear what is about to come out of your mouth. By the way, next time you want to rendezvous with a guy, can you at least be more private?"

She unlocks her car and we get in. She starts the engine before saying anything in return. As she pulls out of the drive she decides to respond. "If what I think is about to happen, happens, you'll find out being less vocal is not always possible. That boy is one good piece of ass." She looks at me with a smirk in place.

"Do you have to be so crude about it? It's really awkward." The smell of Breyson's clothes passes through my nasal passages. It smells so good. It's a really clean smell of laundry detergent mixed with only his smell, like when you walk in someone's house and there is a distinct scent to each one that can't be replicated. I think I may keep this shirt.

"It's only awkward for you, love, but by the looks of you smelling that shirt, that may change soon." Crap, I've been busted. I didn't even realize I smelled it noticeably.

We pass through the mostly dark streets in silence. "Presley, can I ask you a question without getting a bunch of crap from you about it?"

She glances between the road and me. "Sure, babe, what's up? You know I only give you heck because you're my bestie, right? I'm always here if you need to talk. No judgment."

"What's it like?" She scrunches her brows, showing she is clearly confused as to what I'm talking about. "Sex, I mean. Is it worth it? Losing your virginity."

"Whoa, Kinzleigh, are you thinking about giving him your V-card?"

I shrug my shoulders. "I don't know. I'm just starting to wonder why I'm still hanging onto it is all. Most people with it still intact are saving it for the person they intend to give their heart to, but I don't plan on giving mine to anyone. He's just . . . different, and maybe after tonight I'm a little curious. I've never been interested in anyone before. What better person than that to give it to? He's leaving in a few days, Presley. It could be one of those awesome weeks you have and then remember it forever."

She is watching the road, deep in thought. "I don't know, Kinzleigh. Your first time hurts if the guy is even average in size. If he's big you can count on it. It isn't really enjoyable when you first start out, which is why most people do it in a relationship. It sucks until your body gets used to it and that can take a few tries. Are you sure you can give something like that away without any emotion involved? It's harder than you think to go that far with someone and not develop an attachment. Even with my experience, I have to set myself in the right mind frame to not let emotions get in the way. It's human nature. What if you regret it? One day you may decide love is not your worst enemy."

I look at her, pulling my mouth up in disgust. "Um, no thanks. If I do this, it's for the point of avoiding that stuff."

We pull into Presley's house with a minute to spare. Parked behind my car is a white Porsche 911. As Presley kills the engine, I grab my wet clothes and walk toward the porch with her by my side. "Whose car is that?"

"Preston's. He just got home for summer vacation. He made the dean's list third year in a row at UC Berkeley. Since he's Dad's clone and will soon take his place in the Dunagin Empire under Dad after graduation, I guess Dad is bribing him—or motivating as he calls it—to finish his business degree at the top of his class. Granddad is really on Dad's case about stepping up as CEO, so he can retire. We all know that means Preston will become CFO in Dad's place. It was set in motion when he was born." She shakes her head. "He doesn't shut up about that hefty bonus Preston will get when he joins them. I think he's terrified Preston will go his own way."

We get to the door and stop. Before Presley turns the knob, she looks at me. "Be quiet, because I don't want my parents to see you dressed like that, not to mention Preston. Definitely not Preston. All I'll hear is how bad of an example I am for you. You know he's had a killer crush on you for years. If he could ever take the Kinzleigh goggles off, he might actually stop sleeping around with every hot unattached girl that walks in that frat house of his and settle down. He seems to think if he just has fun and stays single you'll come to your senses and see that he's the best guy for you. I'm pretty sure if you gave him the go ahead, he'd have a massive diamond picked out and purchased the day he graduates college."

I roll my eyes. Presley is always giving Preston crap about having a crush on me. I think she is one severed string away from insanity, but what do I know? What I do know is there is no way Preston Dunagin is waiting around to date me. He's gorgeous with the same brown hair and blue eyes as Presley.

He reminds me of an *Abercrombie* model the way he's built. He's attractive and he knows it, making him cocky. He's sitting really high on the preppy scale—a pretty boy. He has that rich-boy persona down pat. He also tends to whore around a little too much for me. Plus, I've known Preston all my life.

I'm not ever settling down, most likely, and nothing good comes from dating a friend of the family. It would ruin everything, because it's destined for failure. Our families are too entwined for that to happen. I'm not interested in screwing things up for my parents and will not pretend that I am, no matter how happy it would make our moms.

We walk inside and quietly shut the door. All the lights are off, so obviously everyone is asleep. We tiptoe across the marble floor to the large staircase in the center of the even bigger room. Presley is already halfway up the staircase to the second floor when I step on the bottom step. I grab the rail and make my way to the second floor. When I get to the top, we turn right and walk down the hallway to Presley's bedroom.

When we get inside, Presley shuts the door and turns on the light, letting out a sigh of relief. She looks at me, and smiles. "So . . . I want details, and lots of them. How did you end up dressed in his clothes, asleep in his bed with him wrapped around you, and still holding onto your V-card?"

I knew I wasn't going to get away with keeping it to myself. She is always ready for the latest juicy gossip. "I'll tell you, but first I have to pee, so you're going to have to wait." I walk into the bathroom and take care of my business.

I'm standing at the sink, bent over, washing the smeared makeup off my face when I feel two hands wrap around me from behind. I have soap all over my face and my eyes are closed, so I can't see who it is, but I have an idea.

Presley and Preston's bedrooms are connected by a bathroom they share. They have their own counter space, though, making it ideal. Since he lives on campus Presley has taken over the space, but they share when he's home for holidays and summer. As I'm trying to rinse the soap off my face, a body aligns to the backside of mine. "I'm glad you're here," he says in a low whisper into my ear.

I grab a hand towel near the sink and stand upright, drying the water from my face. When I open my eyes, staring into the mirror in front of me, I see Preston towering over my short body in a pair of blue and gray plaid pajama pants and a gray shirt with the college logo on the front. I turn around, standing against the counter. "Preston, what are you doing?"

"Something I should have done a long time ago." He leans forward, placing each palm on the counter, entrapping me, making us eye level. He is really close to my face, making me slightly uncomfortable.

I look off to the side to put some distance between us. "Are you going to make me chase after you forever? Stop being difficult and give me a chance? You know we'd be good together. Our moms are dying to find a way to combine our families. I graduate in a year and I'll take my dad's place. I could take care of you and give you everything you want."

Is he on something? He has always been flirty, even throws lines out there that make me wonder sometimes, but never all this. Maybe Presley isn't crazy after all. I never considered the fact that they may talk like Konnor and I do. Preston has always been a busy guy between school and social events, parties, the like.

I turn my head back to him, but try to lean back so he's not practically kissing me. "What are you talking about, Preston? Where is this coming from? Are you drunk and scheming to get in my pants, because it's not happening? You have plenty of other girls willing to give it up trailing after you that you don't have to lie to."

It doesn't work. He grabs me by the waist, picks me up, and sets me on the counter, continuing this debauchery. "You've known me your entire life, Kinzleigh. Quit pretending you don't know how I feel about you. Do you really think I'd tell you this to get laid? I would never do that to you. That's not even my style with other girls. I want to be with you, Kinzleigh."

He scoots me to the edge of the countertop. "I have wanted you since

I was twelve and you were nine and you came barreling into my fort demanding to be included. I've never wanted anything the way I want you."

I'm sitting here, blinking as if my brain stopped working. He looks dead serious. "That's never going to happen, Preston."

He looks agitated. "Why the hell not? Just give us a chance. I could make you happy. I know you better than anyone."

"That's a disaster waiting to happen. I'm young. I have goals and dreams. None of them entail being a trophy wife and bearing sons to carry the family name. I highly doubt I'll get married at all. I don't even date. And it's only going to get easier to avoid the older I get."

His eyes are roaming over my body. He must just now realize I'm wearing male clothing—clothing that does not belong to him. He clenches his jaw. "Whose clothes are you wearing, Kinzleigh? Was this Presley's idea? One of her schemes to practically pimp out your body? Is she trying to drag you into shit again? Are you sleeping with him? You're better than that."

Now I'm starting to get angry. "How is any of that your business? What if I am? I'm not yours to have and control, first of all. Secondly, you sleep with everything walking that's female, pretty much, so how dare you question my sexual activity."

He stands upright, closes his eyes, and rubs his hands over his face, releasing a breath in aggravation. "You're right. I just care about you. She's always trying to get you to do stuff you don't want to do. It frustrates me. But I won't give up until I convince you. We belong together. And I know you'd want to take it slow. You may not think so now, but I'll show you. I've waited for so long for this. I know about your cheerleading dream and I can help give that to you. I will make you mine. I don't stop when there is something I want, and you, Kinzleigh, are what I want. You don't want me to sleep around . . ." He walks closer, cupping my face in his hands, and lifts my head to look at him. "Consider it done. I don't need another girl to satisfy me. I was just biding my time until I could have you. They aren't satisfying me anymore anyway. You're almost eighteen now." He lines my body with his. "I will claim you as mine sooner or later. You deserve the best and I have the means to give it to you. The sooner you realize that, the sooner we can stop playing these games and I can start giving it to you."

I'm stunned. Speechless may be a better word. He brings his head in closely, tilting his head. "I want you to be mine. I always have." He touches his lips to mine and I try to pull away, but I can't even move. His lips aren't as soft as Breyson's. He kisses a little rougher and faster. He slides his tongue inside the opening of my lips.

I can't bring myself to kiss him back. It doesn't feel right. None of this feels right. He nibbles on my lower lip and then releases my lips from his. "It may come as a shock to you now, but one day you will kiss me back. I will wait. I won't try to kiss you again until then, but know that I will never stop trying until you're mine."

Good luck with that.

Presley walks in the door. "Babe, what on earth is taking you so long? Did you fall . . . Oh." She looks the way a person would look who just walked in on her parents going at it, terrified and freaked out. "Am I interrupting?"

She is standing with one hand on the doorframe and the other on the doorknob. "No, I was just finishing up in here."

I push Preston by the chest so he will take the hint and move. As he backs up, I jump off the counter and take off toward Presley's room, almost knocking her over to get through the door. "Think about what I said!" he calls out as I come barreling through the door.

Presley peeks into her bedroom before she walks in the bathroom door saying, "I'll be right out. Find something to watch okay?"

I nod, and the door clicks shut. I have no idea what she's up to, because all I hear are hushed whispers. I can only imagine what that looked like with him standing between my legs, holding my face in his hands.

I sit on the edge of the bed and place my hands over my face, shaking my head. What just happened? Is he insane? He can't possibly think I'm going to change my mind. Could he? Somehow, I need to rectify this, or our family gatherings are going to be really awkward.

After all that the first thing that passes through my mind is Breyson. His kiss was perfect, not rushed. My lips tingle at the memory of his touching mine. I'm really tired. I need to go to bed and maybe I'll wake up and none of this Preston stuff will be real. Maybe I'm asleep and just dreaming it all up. The subconscious can be a deceiving thing.

What time is it anyway? I get up to charge my phone and realize I don't have it. Maybe I left it in Presley's car. Thinking about it, though, I know exactly where it is; on the bedside table next to one hot country boy that's gotten my attention.

I'll just have to go get it tomorrow. I crawl up to the head of the bed, turning back the covers and nestling beneath them. As I close my eyes a smile forms. I get to see him again after all. Falling asleep comes much easier as the memory of tonight all comes flooding back.

TEN

Kinzleigh

The tide rolls in, crashing against the shoreline, birds migrating overhead. Their calls echo against the perfect, clear blue sky. I'm standing on the beach, sand particles covering my damp feet, wearing a white monokini swimsuit that gives an extra glow to my sun-kissed skin. My blonde hair is blowing in the breeze, but it's cut shorter—just below my shoulders.

I stare out at the water, enjoying the warm sunny day. I don't recognize this place. It's absolutely beautiful. The sand is bright-white and the water is crystal-blue, swirls of aqua mixed in, revealing the ocean floor at a glance from the shoreline. Coral and seashells litter the sea floor.

Two arms wrap around my waist, resting on my stomach. "You make this place even more beautiful than it already is." I love the sound of his voice. It's so soothing. I close my eyes and rest my head against his chest, placing my hands over his.

"You're too good to me." I sigh in contentment. He picks me up, cradling me in his arms. I interlock my hands at the back of his neck, sunlight reflecting off my left hand with movement, making the diamond attached to my ring finger sparkle. Wrapped around my third finger lies a beautiful, large square cut diamond surrounded by small, round diamonds embedded in an antique style white gold band. It's has a vintage *yet still modern design.*

I look around us. There isn't another person in sight, just a small hut on the vacant private beach. He walks me over to a wood frame canopy bed covered in white linens, sitting in the sand. The almost black knots in the dark-stained wood tell its story and the uneven planes give it a hand carved feel. Hanging from the canopy are sheer white sheets, blowing in the breeze. He lays me down gently in the center of the bed, before removing his shorts, and then kneels on the bed over me. "You're the most beautiful woman I've ever seen."

He pulls the straps of my swimsuit down my arms, slowly freeing them, before peeling the rest of it from my body. He lays over me, holding his weight with his arms beside my head. Without me having to make a move, he spreads my legs apart with his knees. He kisses me gently, not getting in a hurry. "I'm going to make love to you; today, tomorrow, and forever. Today has been the best day of my life. Here's to forever. I love you, Kinzleigh Abercrombie. Promise me you'll never leave me; until death do us part."

He slowly thrusts inside of me, and stops, knowing I'd be ready without question. I'm always ready for him. "Promise me."

"I promise," I say. "I'm yours forever."

He moves slowly, thrusting in and out. This moment—it's beautiful and it's ours, the first day of our forever. I bite my lip, trying to hold onto the tightening taking place in my body. "Let it go, baby." And just like that, I fall into an orgasm, contracting around him.

He picks up pace and a few thrusts later, releases his semen inside my womb. He leans down and kisses me, a smile across his face as he pulls my left ring finger to his lips. I love seeing him this happy. "I love you, Breyson, my husband."

My eyes pop open. The sounds of my heavy breathing are all that fills the silent room and I'm covered in sweat. I look around. The beams from the sun are peeping through the curtains. Everything in the house is completely quiet, meaning it's early.

I'm still tired from being up late, but after a dream like that I'm scared to go back to sleep. Why on earth I would dream something so horrifying? I can't even say the 'M' word, let alone image it for myself. Talk about your subconscious going haywire.

I look beside me and Presley is still sleeping peacefully, not a single limb moving; only the steady rise and fall of her chest signifying she's very much alive. I sit up and throw my legs over the side of the bed. Only one thing is going to make me feel better right now—to run.

I get up and walk to Presley's dresser. I know she keeps her yoga clothes in the third drawer. Pulling the handles toward me at a snail's pace, I slide it out slowly to keep noise down, and grab a pair of black yoga pants and a lavender racer-back tank. I fold the clothes I'm wearing and neatly place them on her dresser to take them home later. I tiptoe into her closet and grab a pair of running shoes and some socks. Thank God we wear the same size in everything.

Dressed, I walk to the door as lightly as possible since we're on the second floor, directly above her parents' bedroom. Opening the door, I peek out into the hallway, hoping Preston isn't anywhere to be seen. Everything is still dark and quiet.

Tip toeing down the steps, I make it to the front door. I look around one last time to make sure no one is up. Finally making it out the door, I relax a little as I take off running through the neighborhood. This is the best way to clear my head, because it's just the pavement and me. The sun hasn't fully risen yet, so the heat is still hibernating along with most of the residents.

I don't know how long I've been running and I don't care, because it's far better than my thoughts running into places it has no business wandering to. Just a few more days and a certain someone consuming my thoughts will be long gone and across the country. I'll enjoy having some fun and then everything will go back to normal . . . I hope.

The sun is now exposing itself fully and attacking my delicate skin with its rays. The heat is dry but torrid. My clothes are drenched in sweat. I finally stop running, my lungs working overtime to pull in air. I look around and realize I ran about ten miles from Presley's house. My stomach lashes out at me with a growl. I have no idea what time it is, and I still have to shower and pick up some of the stuff for the party.

I'm now realizing how long it's going to take me to get back and summer is showing its hand today. Crap! Leave it to me to end up ten miles from my car. I better get started if I want to keep a good time. I turn around and begin running back toward Presley's house when I hear a truck slowing to a stop. I don't think much about it until a door shuts, followed by shuffling of feet on the pavement. "Kinzleigh, wait up."

I stop abruptly, turning toward the familiar voice. He is walking around the truck with his hands in his pockets. He's wearing a pair of shorts, a polo, and a pair of boating shoes. Just when I get him out of my thoughts he waltzes right back in and takes them over. "What are you doing here?"

"Presley woke up and you were gone. When she called your phone to see where you were it started ringing and woke me up." He pulls my phone from his pocket. "I saw it was her, so I answered it. She panicked since you were supposed to be picking stuff up for the party. I told her I'd come find you, so she could finish up there. She figured you wouldn't be far since your car is still parked out front."

Of course, she did. She knew good and well if my car was parked out front I wouldn't be far, unless I was kidnapped, and I highly doubt someone would take me and leave her if that were the case. There is only one street in front of her house. She could have looked herself. She knows I run to keep my body fat percentage down since I'm always a flyer in cheerleading, but instead, she sends him after me when I look awful, sweaty, and in need of a shower. "Will you just run me to Presley's to pick up my car? I can go home, shower, and meet you in town."

"There is no need for two vehicles. Ryland took the family Jeep and left his truck with me. I can come by and pick you up. Is that okay?" Whatever is fine as long as I can clean myself up. I don't usually argue with people; I never win. This is a tad bit embarrassing. I hope my deodorant holds up; although, it's Sunday and my parents will be home, so I'm not sure how to explain him. I better be figuring it out fast.

I place my hands on my hips. "That really isn't necessary. My parents will be home and possibly my brother. Unless you want to go through an interview, I can just meet you there." I can't even imagine how my parents would respond to me bringing someone home, because it has never happened.

He stands there, looking back and forth between the truck and me. He interlocks his hands behind his neck. I'm hoping he is going to make this less complicated and meet me there. "Nah, that's okay. I'll just come pick you up." I sigh, defeated. Well, this will be interesting. "Come on, get in."

It takes about five minutes to get back to Presley's. I hurry to my car, because Preston's car is still in the drive. I guess he is partaking in the party festivities today. After last night, I really don't need any drama from him.

I've known Preston all my life. Other than the age difference, I'm as close to him as I am Presley. With our parents being such good friends, we were constantly around each other growing up, so it comes with the territory. If it had been anyone else last night, I would have been thoroughly creeped out, but I know that's not how he meant it, so I will let it go. He is spoiled and a bit of a control freak, in the non-psychotic way, so when he is losing something he's after or it's not going his way, he tends to panic. And well, then he's kind of an asshole.

I pull out of the driveway with Breyson following behind. It took some maneuvering to get out, since Preston's car was behind mine, but I managed. I would hope that my parents are gone, but that's not going to be the case.

If I were one of those kids always sneaking out and getting into trouble, it would be easy, because my parents are predictable. They are always home on Sunday and we always go to church. They are conservative. My dad has always said that he's pulled the company this far, because he doesn't work on Sunday and he reserves it for a day of rest, as it was intended.

Pulling in my driveway, I glance in the rearview mirror. Breyson is pulling in behind me. I press the remote on my visor, raising the garage door. I might as well get this over with. I feel nauseous from the nerves when I hear him shut the truck door at my rear. My hands are sweating and my breathing is becoming impaired. I've never once in my life introduced my parents to a boy. I have no idea what to expect.

Closing my eyes and resting my forehead on the steering wheel, I breathe deeply, trying to calm down. A moment later, I hear tapping on the window. Opening the door for me to get out, Breyson is standing there with a cocky grin on his face. "What's the matter? Are you scared your mom and dad won't like me?" he asks, teasingly.

Walking toward the garage door and twisting the knob, I stop. "They may be a little shocked, since I've never . . . uh . . . brought a guy home before. I really hope Konnor isn't here," I say, opening the door.

Konnor is in a bad place right now and bringing a guy home for the first time, knowing he is going to think the worst, scares the crap out of me. The garage door leads into the mudroom and from there into the kitchen.

Opening the opposing door, Mom looks up at me from the kitchen island. She is standing over the cook top, stirring something inside a pot with one hand on her hip. She is wearing her glasses, which means she has been reading—probably case files or a book. "Hey, baby girl. Did you and Presley have a good time? You missed Sunday Mass." She gives me that look. I nod, knowing she's displeased. Breyson comes through the door, making himself known, and her jaw falls slightly.

She quickly recovers, placing a smile on her face. Yep, my absence at Mass is quickly forgotten. Wait for it . . . Here it goes. She places the spoon down on the counter and heads toward us. Looking straight at me, but closing in on Breyson, she says, "Who is your friend, honey?" Breyson is slightly behind me, off to the side.

I look at him apologetically, mouthing 'sorry', as she opens her arms to give him a hug. "It's so good to meet you, dear. Kinzleigh has lost her manners. I'm Leigh Baker, Kinzleigh's mom."

I stand here, speechless, watching the interaction. This is really awkward, to say the least. What am I supposed to say? I didn't think this through. How am I supposed to introduce him? *Hey, Mom, this is the guy I just met and may let de-flower me before he heads back home to . . . wherever he's from.* Not going to happen. But what are my other options? He's not my boyfriend and he's not really a friend either, so I'm at a loss. Nothing is coming to mind.

Breyson is looking at my mom with a grin on his face. "I think she may just be a little caught off guard. It's nice to meet you, Mrs. Baker. I'm Breyson Abercrombie, Ryland Reeves' cousin. I'm here visiting like I do every summer and met Kinzleigh at the beach Friday. I'm just helping her get everything ready for this pool party of Presley's that I keep hearing so much about."

She releases him and looks at me with a big smile on her face. "I do believe I know Ryland. He's a sweet kid and comes from a good family too. It's great to have you here, Breyson. I'm glad Kinzleigh is meeting new people. I'm cooking some lunch if either of you are hungry."

She releases him from her grasp and looks at me. "By the looks of you, you still need to shower. The food should be ready before you leave." No way am I sitting around the table having a family meal with him here. I need to hurry up and get showered, so we can be out of here.

"Mom, we're in a hurry. Rain check? We can just grab something in town." I look over at Breyson. "Right?" He doesn't even look uncomfortable. He should be very uncomfortable. Am I the only one freaking out right now?

He shakes his head at me, smiling, as if he knows what I'm trying to get out of. "Where I come from, you don't turn down home cooking for fast-food. Presley told me what time we need to be back and gave me the rundown on what your duties are. I think we have time to eat before we go."

He looks back at my mom, and I can tell he's laying the charm on thick. "We'd love to eat, Mrs. Baker, thank you."

My mom wraps her arm over my shoulders, steering me toward the living room. I can hear the golf announcer coming from the television. "You go on and get dressed. I'll introduce Breyson to your dad and brother."

I bite my nails. "Konnor is here?"

Great. This is just what I need. Not.

I should have just showered at Presley's and borrowed some clothes. My mom looks at me as if I'm being ridiculous. "Of course, he's here. It's Sunday. Normally, you are too. We always hang around here on Sundays together. We haven't been home from Mass long. Everyone missed you this morning."

She stops in the doorway and turns back to Breyson, who's still standing at the dining room table. She waves him over toward the living room. He walks over and she wraps her other arm around his shoulders, towing us together. "Ken, we have company. Turn that television volume down."

Breyson looks over at me with a smirk on his face, raising his brow questioningly. I guess he figured out where I got my name. Dad always wanted a little girl and when they got pregnant so soon after having Konnor, they thought it would be fitting to combine their names—Kinzleigh being the result. Ever the sentimental ones, those two are. Konnor was named after Gramps. George Konnor Baker was my dad's father, also founder of G. Baker and Sons Contracting, L.L.C.

Dad is sitting in his recliner, hidden behind the Sunday paper that is spread across his lap. He lowers the page, raising his brows as his eyes lock on Breyson. He looks at Mom. "Who do we have here, Leigh?"

Oh brother, he has that tone. He's not too thrilled. *Awesome.* Konnor turns around from the couch he's sitting on. One look at Breyson and I can tell he isn't pleased either. How am I supposed to leave him down here with these two vultures?

"Ken, this is Kinzleigh's friend, Breyson." She pats him on the back. "You know Joe and Susan Reeves. This is their nephew."

Konnor looks at him, his eyes slightly narrowed. "You're Ryland's cousin? I don't recall seeing you around here before."

Why do they have to make this a big deal? I've never brought home a guy before. So what? At the rate they're going, this will be the last time as well. Breyson walks toward my dad and brother. He stops at my dad first, holding out his hand. "Breyson Abercrombie, Sir. It's nice to meet you. I'm here visiting family for a week. Third summer now and I love it here."

I inch forward, but Mom grabs my shoulder, halting me. I look at her, but she shakes her head at me. "Go get dressed, honey. Time is wasting. He will be fine. This is something that every dad looks forward to. Don't take that away."

She smiles at me. "Run along. I'll supervise. I've been where you are. It'll be fine." No, she hasn't been here before, because Dad is the only man she's ever been with. I, however, have no intention of taking this further than a week and then I'm sending him on his way. Him meeting my family will just further complicate things, because Mom is already making it sound like he is a prospective boyfriend.

"Breyson, what are your intentions with my daughter since you will be gone in a week?" Dad speaks out, breaking me from my stare off with Mom.

"Dad!" I yell out, completely humiliated that this is happening. Why can't they just be normal and talk about football or something?

Konnor looks at me with a smirk on his face. "What's the matter, Kinzleigh? You know we have to keep your best interests at heart."

Breyson looks at me, giving me a reassuring smile. "It's okay, Kinzleigh, go get ready. I'll get to know your family a little." I don't feel good about this. As a matter of fact, I tried to avoid it, but what other choice do I have now? I can't go to the party like this.

I move toward the stairs, dragging my feet. "Dad, please don't embarrass me. Behave," I say, pointing my finger at him.

"Kinzleigh, I believe you have a shower calling for you. We'll be fine down here. I don't need tips on how to parent, but thank you for your concern."

Sighing, I run upstairs to get ready, quickly, so we can get out of here before he tries to give him the *Daddy with the shotgun speech* or something else completely crazy. Dinner with the fam was just crossed off the to-do list. I don't care what he says. Manners went out the window when words like *intentions* went flying through the air.

I'm standing in the middle of my room, staring at the clothes spread across my bed, showered and wearing my bra and panties. What do I wear? I already know I have to take my swimwear, but what do I wear until then? Now that I may want to go through with this *losing my virginity* thing at some point in the very near future, I should probably put forth a little effort in getting ready; as in what a guy would like versus what I like.

My two choices, as I stand here pondering, are my black one shoulder mini-dress that stops halfway to my knee and is fitted, but not tight, with a butterfly style sleeve opening as it falls. I usually pair it with my beige canvas wedges and gold hoops. The other choice is my chevron shift dress in mint green and white with three-quarter length sleeves that I usually pair with my white gladiator sandals topped off with a splash of red in my jewelry.

"Hmm . . . What to wear?" I say, tapping my index finger to my lips.

Mom slips inside my door. "You always look beautiful in the mint green one. It does wonders with your blonde hair and makes your eyes stand out. Plus, the flats will be more comfortable. All that walking may be hard on your feet in those heels. You don't want to try too hard. The black one says, *take me to dinner,* and the other says, *I'm cute but comfy.*"

I always did love my mom's eye for good fashion. Send us shopping and we always put a dent in Dad's wallet. He has limited our mother-daughter shopping outings to a minimum. Really, he just jokes, since Mom is a big shot lawyer and all, contributing a large portion of what's there. "You really think so? What should I do to my hair?"

"I know so." She smiles and comes to my side, brushing my curls off my shoulder. "It makes the green in your eyes pop. You always were my little princess. You're growing up so fast. At least you've waited this long to bring boys around. You're making me feel old, you know." She winks at me playfully and sits on the bed. "Now put on that dress and bring me that comb and some bobby pins and I'll do your hair."

It's been a long time since Mom has done my hair. It makes me feel like a little girl again. I pull the dress over my white, lace bra and panty set with baby pink trim. Grabbing the container of bobby pins and the comb, I sit between her legs on the floor. "What are you going to do to it?"

"You just sit still and let me worry about that. I will make sure that boy's jaw drops when he sees you." My hair is parted down the left side of my head, the biggest portion of hair laying over to the right. She begins to braid loosely from my part down the right hairline, beside my face. Just behind my right ear, she ties the braid with a small hair band.

I close my eyes, as the light tugging of my hair makes me want to go to sleep. She used to brush my hair each night when I was little. "What are they doing to him down there? Is Dad behaving himself? Is Konnor freaking out?"

She chuckles as she swoops all of my hair to the right side. She piles all of my curly hair, including the loose braid in one hand and ties it with a pony tail holder at the bottom of my hairline, below my right ear. She begins forming a messy bun with the ponytail. "Honey, every man dreads the day he has to share his little girl with another man. You'll see one day when you have a daughter. I would say Dad is doing pretty well considering he had no warning. Usually, it's when you're sixteen and come home asking to go to the prom, months in advance, and he has a chance to get used to the idea before a boy shows up at the front door. You've always surprised us, though, never going by the book on anything. As relieving as it is that you never give us an ounce of trouble, I was beginning to wonder if I was ever going to get to take you prom dress shopping and other mother-daughter things I have been waiting to do with you."

She almost sounds sad. I suppose this isn't the time for me to announce I don't plan on having kids, ever. Kids are a blessing from above and everything, but it's just not for me. I don't see that ever changing. I would think it's a desire you have at an early age if you're going to have it. I have too many dreams for myself than to be tied down to children or marriage. Traveling would be one.

She puts the last of the bobby pins around the bun to hold it loosely and gets up to grab the hairspray. "Come here. Let me finish you off."

I stand up and walk to the mirror. I have to admit my mom is one awesome fashionista to be a mother with two nearly grown kids. It's a loose bun of curls on the lower right side of my head, beneath my ear. "I have something for you." She pulls a handkerchief from her pocket, holding it in her hand. She unwraps the cloth, revealing a small pair of diamond hoops.

My eyes widen as they lay perfectly still, glimmering in the light. "Your father gave these to me one year from the day we started dating. I had them cleaned and put up for you for this occasion. The first day my little girl became a woman. To me, that day is today. You have blossomed and have shown your maturity, so I think you're ready."

I really feel bad that I have no intention of becoming serious about dating. "Mom, you don't have to do this. You know we're not serious, right? I just met him. I'm only showing him a good time and taking him around while he's visiting, nothing more."

She holds up her hand to stop me. "Honey, I know you're not holding out your hand waiting on a diamond ring, but this is a big step for you. Take them. They will look beautiful on you."

I give her a hug. "Thank you. I love them." She releases me and watches me put the earrings on, one by one.

"You're welcome. Now, let's get you finished. You have one handsome boy down there waiting on you. You know how to pick a cute one. Hurry up or your brother may not let him leave with you in hand. He seems a little on edge." She winks again and sprays my hair. Just like that I pick up pace. I know Konnor and I've seen him in protection mode when his friends used to show an interest in me. I don't want to rehash those times.

Putting on my gladiator sandals, I grab my mint green clutch purse I bought to go with this dress and put my necessities inside. Handbags and shoes are my personal weakness among fashion. I have a bag for everything.

I run to my closet and pull my mint green and gold tote from the shelf. I place my black monokini swimsuit and matching sheer cover-up skirt in the bag, as well as my black shimmery flip-flops. Walking into my bathroom, I grab my black and pink beach towel.

As I come back out, Mom is standing at the doorway, holding onto the knob. "You look beautiful. He isn't going to let you out of his sight. You ready to go?"

Smiling, I nod and start for the door, trailing behind my mom. As we're coming down the stairs, everyone looks my way, standing to their feet. I feel like a princess being announced at a ball. It's strange. I don't usually like being the focal point, but right now, knowing I'm the focal point to a guy that looks like that, really isn't all that bad.

A big smile spreads across Breyson's face at the same time a scowl crosses Konnor's. I walk beside my dad and he puts an arm over my shoulder. "You're gorgeous, just like your mother," he says, kissing my cheek. He then turns to Breyson. "I expect you to take special care of my baby girl. You do that and we won't have any problems. Understood?"

Breyson nods. "Yes, Sir. That won't be a problem." He looks over to me. "You ready to go?"

I can tell Konnor wants to say something the way he is looking at me. I look him in the eyes, telling him I'll be fine. We've always had a way of communicating without actually speaking. He nods his head in response to my silent message.

I look back at Breyson, excitement fueling my response. "As ready as I'll ever be."

ELEVEN

Breyson

I wasn't prepared for what came walking down the stairs. Sure, I've seen her dressed in several different ways at this point, but what she looks like now barely allowed me to breathe. If I thought it was hard to contain myself before, it just got harder. This girl puts any other girl to shame, and today she's mine. Legs to die for. It brings back the memory of them wrapped around me in the pool.

I can't believe I'm at a girl's house, meeting her family. I'm not sure what that says about me when it comes to her. It's too intimate and gives off messages I don't want made, but this girl has a way of making me want to do things I never usually do without even trying. I have to admit that now I know why I never do this.

After sitting in the living area with her family, listening to the *I've got a shotgun and I'm not afraid to use it* speech, I wasn't all that disappointed to leave without eating. Not to forget her brother staring daggers at me like he wanted to kick my ass. I can't say that I blame him, though, because I have a fourteen-year-old sister. I imagine if a guy like me were thinking about her in the same way that I'm thinking about Kinzleigh, I'd want to beat his ass too.

We walk outside and get in the truck. "Do you realize how beautiful you are?" I'm not much for compliments, but if this girl doesn't realize how gorgeous she is, she needs to be told. It blows me away that someone hasn't tried harder to claim her. If I lived here, I wouldn't let her out of my sight.

The fact that she actually wants to give me her virginity gives me chills. Instead of it freaking me out, as it should be, I'm imagining how much I want to be her first, to go where no other guy has gone.

I've never been with a virgin before. I've always stayed far away from them; it's an unspoken rule of mine. A girl that loses her virginity is looking for love and I am not the place to find it. Apparently, she is one person that could make me change my mind. The thought of being her first is consuming my mind, and probably more much than it should. Is it normal for it to thrill me; give me an adrenaline rush?

She blushes as I sit here staring at her. I can't help it. I can't take my eyes off of her. "Thanks, I guess. Where to first? You said Presley gave you the rundown, so I'm assuming I don't have to?"

"Yeah, I got everything covered. Let's go." We pull out of her driveway and head toward town. According to Presley, we really don't have much to get. A catering company is delivering the food and a rental company is setting up all of the tents and tables. A DJ will setup his own equipment as well. I think it was mostly just extras and stuff for her. Presley said there was a party planner in charge of the decorations and making sure everything ran smoothly.

Personally, this is all a little new to me. Where I'm from, party planners don't put a party together. Most people just get together and do their own thing. I wish I could take her back home and show her how it's done in the south. The guys would be falling all over her.

Wait, what the hell am I thinking? That's exactly why I wouldn't want her back at home. I like not having to share her. I'm going to enjoy the extra hour with her alone before we head back to Presley's and I no longer have her all to myself. "I have to run to the mall and pick up Presley a new swimsuit," she says, breaking the silence.

"Knowing what Presley's house and car look like, I find it hard to believe she doesn't have a swimsuit," I say teasingly.

"Girl rule number one. Always have a new outfit for every occasion," she replies sarcastically with a smile on her face.

"You're telling me she hasn't already picked it out? Don't girls do that stuff weeks in advance?" I don't know much about girls other than physical anatomy, but I know enough from girls at school that those things are topics for weeks on end, prior to the event.

"Presley is a little . . . different, I guess. She knows the new swimwear line comes in today. She refuses to have on the same swimsuit as anyone else since it's her party. Don't ask me why, because I have no idea."

I shake my head. Girls are a species from an alien planet. You can't live with them and you can't seem to live without them either. "I'm just the driver; tell me where to go."

We come to a stoplight. Take a few right turns and Laguna Hills mall isn't far on the left. "You remember how to get to BJ's, right? It's in that same location." I nod and follow her directions.

It really doesn't take as long as I thought to get here. Pulling in the parking lot, I find a spot and kill the engine. "What all do we have to get again?"

She hops down off the side step, upon getting out of the truck. "Just pick up the party favors and Presley's stuff. That's all, unless something calls to me," she says with a smile on her face. "She called ahead for the party favors, so we just have to pick them up. It may be several trips, though, because the party favors alone will be three or four different stores. I think for the girls it's candles and cosmetics, and for the guys, I don't even know. I may have to call her. Probably sports memorabilia or watches or something."

"She puts a lot of money into this, doesn't she?" I don't know why it has to be so extravagant for a pool party. I'm out of my realm on this one.

We begin walking to the huge mall standing before us. "Well, her birthday is during the holiday season and cooler weather, so it's never a big deal. This is her way to make up for it. She's had one every year since she was fifteen. It's just become a tradition now. I don't know what everyone will do when she graduates. I guess her little sister Paxtyn will take over. By the time we graduate she will be in high school," she says, shrugging her shoulders.

As we walk into the mall, I notice just how busy it is. Making our way through the crowded interior I ask, "Where to first?"

She looks at me as she weaves through the mass of people. "I don't know. I guess *Victoria's Secret* is the best place to start."

I stop abruptly, before realizing there are several people following me. A woman pushing a stroller almost slams into the back of me. I walk quickly to catch up with Kinzleigh. "You did not say anything about *Victoria's Secret*. Victoria can keep her secrets, because there is no way I'm walking in that store."

"I don't know where you're from, but here you better keep pace or you'll become a floor mat." She laughs and keeps walking, not even fazed by the fact I'm silently, as well as outwardly, freaking out about walking in a lingerie store.

For such short legs she sure can walk fast. When I catch up to her she is at the edge of the store, about to walk in. "Well, are you coming?"

I stand here looking into the store filled with racks upon racks of lingerie and underwear. I have no experience underwear shopping; only removing the already purchased product. I run my fingers through my hair. I have never in my life been to a woman's lingerie store. Do men even go in these types of stores if they aren't married? She raises a brow at me. "Scared something is going to jump out and bite you?"

It baffles me that I'm so hung up over a hot girl I'm about to walk in this place. It's a little intimidating. Sighing, I say, "You owe me for this and once I decide what it is, I will collect."

She rolls her eyes at me. "Whatever you say, lover boy, now come on," she says sarcastically.

Funny, I actually like the sound of that. She is halfway through the store when I realize I'm still standing here at the entry. Putting my hands in my pockets, I walk quickly in her direction. Bypassing the store associates and other shoppers—all female—smiles turn up on each of them and multiple ask me, "Is there something I can help you with?"

Smiling politely, I pick up pace to catch up with her. Shaking my head, I reply, "No, thank you. I'm just along for the ride." The awkwardness is evident in my tone as I point at Kinzleigh flipping through the neatly arranged swimsuits on a table in the back.

I walk up beside her, smiling. "Now you owe me two things. Shall we continue to add favors?"

She looks at me, scrunching her nose. "Uh, how do you arrive at that assessment?"

"You just left me to fend for myself in a woman's lingerie store. The associates are eying me like flying vultures over road kill, waiting to swoop down and pick at me."

"Oh, don't be so dramatic. Your uneasiness makes you stick out like a sore thumb. They sense your nervousness. Just play it cool and watch," she says, holding up a swimsuit top. I eye it stupidly. How is this supposed to help? "Hey, babe, hold this for me, okay?" She says it loud enough that the store associate closest to us hears.

I awkwardly take the swimsuit, looking her in the eyes. She turns up one side of her mouth and has a mischievous look in her eye. "Okay . . ."

Sure enough, as I take the swimsuit, the girl closest to us wrinkles her nose in a look of disgust and stomps off like someone just stole her toy.

"You can thank me later," she says teasingly and goes back to rummaging through the pile of swimsuits. Thirty minutes later we're checking out with two armfuls—one for Kinzleigh and one for Presley.

This is not motivating me to want to do this again. I think I'll leave shopping to females. Usually, I just let my mom buy my clothes or run in one of a couple stores and have an entire new wardrobe in thirty minutes tops. The amount of money a girl can spend on underwear and swimsuits is insane to me. Five hundred dollars later, we're leaving the store, ready to finish getting everything for the party.

Two hours went by in a bit of a blur. Between hauling out hundreds of candles and other meaningless items, I'm ready to get to this party. If it wasn't for Kinzleigh being so freakin' hot, I would have never agreed to this. The girl has me doing all kinds of random things I would never in a million years do, without even asking me to do it; I volunteer. From all the constant trips back and forth to the truck, I'm sweating. We stopped about an hour ago and grabbed something to eat from the food court to replenish some of this lost energy.

Finally in the truck, I turn to Kinzleigh. "Please tell me we're done." At this point, I'll tell Presley personally that she can do it herself.

Kinzleigh shyly smiles over at me. "Yes, I'm sorry. I shouldn't have let you tag along. It was a lot of work." What she doesn't know is there was no way I wasn't coming along. Any excuse to spend more time with her, I'll take.

"Nah, it's okay, but Presley can do the rest herself. I'm not used to parties entailing so much work. Y'all do things a lot different around here. I didn't have anything better to do; I'm just giving you a hard time."

"We still have a little while until the party starts if you want to just drop me off at Presley's and come back later. She always times it to start in the afternoon and continue into the night, where she can turn on the pool lights and light up the tents." There is no way I'm letting her go this early. I can only imagine what dickweeds I'll have to go through to get her attention once everyone shows up. If what Ryland said was true, every male with something swinging between his legs will want to get close to her in a swimsuit.

The thought of someone else trying to touch her is starting to get to me.

I let out a deep breath, trying to get a grip. "How about we drop this stuff off and you can come with me? I have to go by Ryland's and get my swim trunks anyway. I didn't think about it when I left this morning. Ryland's parents were going to some company BBQ, so it'll just be us most likely. We can hang out for a bit and change, then head over to Presley's a little before it starts to make sure she doesn't need help. I think Ryland said he was helping her."

"Are you sure? I don't want to take up your entire week here. I know there are probably other things you'd rather be doing. You don't have to occupy your time with the likes of me." The fact that she is humble enough to think she's keeping me from something better than being with her makes me like her all the more. The girl could likely have any guy she wants and she really doesn't see it.

"I'm sure," I say, pulling into Presley's driveway. That same Porsche is sitting in the drive from earlier, but now in the open garage. I wonder whose car that is. Just as I pull up, a guy walks to the driver's side door and opens it. He looks about twenty or twenty-one. When he looks at the truck his eyes focus on the passenger's side, clearly recognizing Kinzleigh. A snarling expression comes across his face. "Who is that?"

She sighs, as if not wanting to enter into this discussion. "That's Preston, Presley's older brother. He's home for the summer from UC Berkeley."

Hell no. She stayed the night with that guy in the same house? I know that look he's wearing. He wants her, and he is willing to do whatever it takes to get her. I've seen that look before. I want to hurry up and get her out of here. The way he is staring at her is pissing me off.

Ryland's yellow Jeep is sitting in the driveway beside me. "Will you be okay long enough for me to switch keys with Ryland?"

She nods, looking slightly confused. "Why wouldn't I be?"

"Well, for starters, that guy is still standing there staring at you, looking like he wants to tear my head off every time he glances in my direction." I look back over and see him standing with the door open, his fists clenched. I don't like to fight or start trouble, at least not over a girl, but if he wants to start anything over this one, I'm all in.

We seem to be having one of those man-to-man stare-offs. The one where you both understand what the other is after and she is the prize.

May the best man win.

My hands tighten around the steering wheel, my knuckles turning white. I may have to leave her to him in a few days, but right now she's mine. I will stake my claim if he doesn't back off. I hope this clown doesn't intend to hang around the party, trying to get her attention. He may be older and taller, but not by much and I'm twice his size.

"Preston won't hurt me; we just have some . . . unfinished business. It's fine. I'll go ahead and take my bags to the Jeep. Let Presley know her stuff is here, will you?" She looks at Preston and opens the door. Great, now I don't want to leave her side. The faster I go get those keys, the faster I can get back.

"I'll let her know when I tell Ryland to come unload everything. I'll be right back." I jump out and head for the backyard, where the pool is, in the opposite direction of the garage. I get to the back and see Ryland almost immediately. "Hey, Ry, come here, man," I say, waving him over in a sprint toward him.

"What's up? You okay? You look pissed."

"It's nothing; me and Kinzleigh are running by the pool house and we'll be back in about an hour. I need your Jeep keys. I'm going to let you unload everything from the truck."

Handing me the keys, he runs his other hand through his curly hair. "What's up with you? You cool?"

I keep looking back toward the front of the house, as if I could actually see what was going on with the two of them if I tried. "Yeah, man, I've got to go. I'll be back."

I grab the keys and take off toward the driveway. When I round the house, I see Kinzleigh leaned up against the Jeep with her arms crossed over her chest and that Preston guy has a hand on each side of her head, against the door of the Jeep. They seem to be having some kind of conversation. Seeing him that close to her has me raging to hit something. I close my eyes and pop my neck to the side, trying to calm down before I lay him out on the ground and freak her out.

As I approach the Jeep, I grab her bags from the ground beside her feet and look at her. "You ready to go?"

He pushes off the Jeep, but doesn't put any more distance between them. "Where are you going? You're not missing the party, are you?" His voice is deep, but he sounds a little panicky.

That's right, she's going with me.

She rolls her eyes as if she's slightly aggravated. "Preston, this is Ryland's cousin, Breyson. Stop being rude; it's not like you. He's visiting for a while." She looks over at me. "Breyson, this is Presley's older brother, Preston. I'm sorry, he's not usually like this," she says, crinkling her brows in confusion.

In a split second, his face relaxes, and he holds out his hand. "Kinzleigh is right. My apologies." He has a cocky grin and I know why. In all of that information he heard one thing—I'm visiting. He knows he has the lead, because I'm leaving soon, and he's not stupid enough to piss her off. Well, two can play that game.

I hold out my hand, grasping his. "Nice to meet you." His handshake says it all. My dad gave me a lesson on a man's handshake and what it means. He's overbearing in his grip. He's telling me she's as good as his. Well, assume away, because we will see who she ends up with. I tighten my jaw, looking him in the eyes.

Kinzleigh clears her throat. "I hate to break up this little bromance that's brewing, but we need to go if we're going to get back in time."

I can't help but to smirk, standing before him. I feel like a fighter that's just won his match. Yeah, she's coming with me. I drop my hand and open her door.

"I'll be waiting for you," he calls out as I shut the door, backing toward the garage, and just like that my temporary victory was shattered. I should have known better. Of course, he's going to hang around a bunch of high schoolers in order to be around her.

"I wouldn't count on it," I mumble after closing the door. I get in and start the ignition, backing out of the driveway.

The drive to Ryland's was short and silent. I was mad and trying to sort through all these emotions pumping through my body. I've never dealt with jealousy and rage when it comes to a girl and I sure as hell never had to compete.

As I park and kill the engine, she looks at me from the passenger seat. "Are you okay? You haven't said anything since we left."

I need to get my crap together. "Yeah, I was just thinking about some things. Come on and grab your stuff."

As we walk into the door, she sets her bag down. "We need to get going in about thirty minutes," she says, walking around to the front of the couch.

Awesome! I can't wait to get back to the spoiled little rich boy trying to one-up me. "We'll be ready." I sit down and reach for her hand, pulling her into the opening of my legs. "I just want to sit with you for a while. Will you do that?" She nods her head and I notice the slightest blush appear on her cheeks.

I grab her waist, pulling her closer to me. She places her hands on my shoulders, looking down at me. "What do you want to talk about?"

"Tell me where you're moving," I say. She starts to open her mouth, but then closes it again. Clearly it caught her off guard.

She shakes her head. "No specifics. Remember? That was the deal to hang out."

She is so stubborn. "What will it hurt? Maybe it's close enough to me that we can meet up some. It can't be too far from . . ." She slaps her hand over my mouth before I can say Mississippi.

"I don't want to know. Look, this can't go further than the time you're here. I can't afford any complications in my life. I've worked too hard for everything to let anything get in the way now. Me moving doesn't change anything. A year from now I'll be back in California. Nothing or no one, my parents included, will change that. My heart will always be in California. I won't give it away. I can give you my body and a few days while you're here and that's it. There is no reason to kid ourselves with some illusion that'll create an attachment that isn't necessary. I've thought about it a lot. I want to give my virginity to you, and not because I want anything from you, but because it's what *I* want, and the fact that you'll leave shortly after makes it less complicated. I always do the right thing. I'm doing this for me."

Well I'll be damned. I'm staring at the female version of myself. Of course, the one time I find someone exactly like me she has to be across the country. There are too many people blinded by the illusion of love. I know that, even at a young age.

I have finally found someone that doesn't care one thing about it. Someone who actually wants to live and go after the things she wants. I love that about her. I, on the other hand, have lived under my father's shadow all my life. He pushes my brothers and me to be doctors just like him and my mom, but I would rather play sports. It's something I'm good at. The one day of the year I wait around for is the NFL draft. During the fall I live, breathe, and sweat football.

To Dad, sports are just a part of high school and college—a way to keep you occupied—but nothing more. He is always riding me about keeping perfect grades. He loves sports just like the next person, but to him, professional sports are meant for the people that cannot excel academically, giving them a means to success. None of us stands up to him on how he believes. We all just go along with it. Since my mom is an OBGYN at the largest women's clinic in town, she's pretty much just like Dad.

To me, being drafted in the NFL my senior year of college would be a dream come true. It's an accomplishment only a small percentage of athletes attain. The main reason I'm Dad's lab rat when it comes to training and cardiovascular health is because I want to be recruited by one of the best colleges in the country.

I keep straight A's in case he has to pay for school at the college of my choice. Out of state tuition is expensive. It's among the many reasons a serious relationship isn't in the cards for me. I'll even major in biology like he wants as long as I can play football. All I have to do to keep dad happy is choose the major of his picking, then hopefully I'll get drafted before I have to worry with medical school.

I'm the fastest running back in our district and started getting college scouts last year. I've been first-string running back since freshman year. I haven't been benched a single game either. I have my list of top picks, but it's all about the offers. One more year and I'll be that much closer to my dream.

I just now realize I haven't said anything back, because I'm still shocked we're having this conversation. It's like someone handing you money and telling you not to worry about paying it back; no strings attached. "I don't know, Kinzleigh. As much as I want you, and believe me, the thought of having you before any other guy is appealing, but I'm not a virgin. I haven't been one for a while. In fact, I've been with enough girls you probably wouldn't want your first time to be with me. Isn't that supposed to be a special moment to share with someone else that's never done it before either?"

I can't believe I am actually trying to talk her out of this. Maybe I should check and make sure my dick is still down there. What red-blooded male turns down an opportunity like this? I lay my head against the back of the couch, looking her in the eyes, trying to read her emotions. She almost looks annoyed. "Are you done rambling yet? If you haven't noticed already, I don't usually follow what everyone else does. I would actually prefer this way, because I don't need it to be a gateway for anything, like dating. This is perfect," she says, as she straddles me on the couch, getting bolder. "You can teach me what I don't know and then you'll be free to go back home without worrying of me forming an attachment to you; to do whatever you want with whomever you please."

My breathing becomes ragged as I place my hands on each side of her waist. She grabs my hair in her fists, causing me to close my eyes. She lowers herself closer to my lap. A girl has never turned me on so hard and fast. I'm trying to calm myself down. I haven't even touched her yet.

My jeans are becoming so tight the seams could separate with one quick movement. The compression against my genitals is painful; it needs room. She lightly rubs against the zipper back and forth. She is experimenting, and I like it. A lot of people bitch about being used, but I can handle this.

A wave of heat radiates from between her legs, making it worse. She presses a cheek against mine, her lips barely touching my ear. "So, you up for it, or are you going to leave the job to someone else?"

She is playing with fire, as if she knows I can't stand the thought of another guy touching her. One specific guy comes to mind. It doesn't matter. I can't take it anymore. To hell with everything. I press her tight against my jeans, allowing her to feel what she's doing to me.

She is breathing hard, acknowledging that I'm having the same effect on her as she is on me. I take her face in my hands, looking her directly in the eyes. "Are you sure you want to do this? You have one chance to change your mind and I'll never bring it up again or attempt to kiss you."

I'm shaking and my voice is deeper than it usually is. I feel like I'm about to combust with need. "If you don't change your mind right now, this will happen before I leave. I will have your body. This is your one chance to back out and me forget this ever happened. You're making me crazy. After this, I will not be able to stop anymore."

I can't read her thoughts. She can hide them like a professional poker player. "I've never been surer of anything. I want you. I've never been interested in sex before," she says as her face flushes, her cheeks becoming a mild shade of red. "I don't know what these feelings mean or what to do with them. I may not be any good at . . . it, but I can learn if you will teach me."

That was the last straw. She hasn't even touched me there yet and she has me wound up so tight I feel like I can't breathe. I can't fathom her being bad at anything, especially sex. It then dawns on me. "Kinzleigh, have you ever had an orgasm?"

Her cheeks brighten in color. "I told you I've never been with a guy like that; that meant as in nothing at all."

It's appealing that she doesn't fully get what I'm asking. "I remember you saying that, but that's not the only way to orgasm. You have never given yourself one? You know, to learn your likes and dislikes." Her eyes widen and she bites her lip, shaking her head.

"I've never wanted to do that. It's weird to think of touching myself."

I thought this conversation would calm these raging, Kinzleigh-induced hormones, but it's not. It's having the reverse effect.

"Kinzleigh, had you ever kissed someone before the night on the pier?" That conversation with Ryland is playing back loud and clear. I can't believe he was actually right.

She closes her eyes as I pull her closer to me. She is holding onto my wrists. When she opens her eyes, I have the answer to my question. I can see it all over her face. "Not since I played spin the bottle at Presley's thirteenth birthday party. I'm a quick learner, though; just teach me."

What she doesn't know is, I haven't kissed a girl since I lost my virginity at the age of fourteen. I haven't wanted to until her, and it was damn near perfect. I'm not interested in emotional attachments or acts so intimate it ties you to a person. I watched Beau lose his life over a girl. Me, him, and Ryland were really close. I saw how one girl could destroy an entire family, because she didn't have the decency to break up with him before she gave herself to another man. The day we laid him in the ground was the day I promised I would never let a woman break me.

I pull her in for a kiss. She will be mine—maybe only for a week, but a week nonetheless. Her lips are full and moist. I suck in her bottom lip. She tightens her grip in my hair. Slightly parting her lips, I slip my tongue inside. The menthol in her gum cools my tongue as it connects with hers. She twirls her tongue around mine, only plunging it slightly into my mouth.

I place my hand on the back of her neck and then run my hands down her spine, before stopping at the bottom hem of her dress that is resting on top of my legs. Taking ahold of her thighs, I trail my callused hand up her legs, beneath her dress.

Her skin is as smooth as molasses with a sun-kissed glow. I get to her perfect, round bottom covered in lace. She lightly bites my bottom lip, causing me to pull her closer to me in need. I run my tongue along hers. I kiss her chin and trail my tongue along her jaw line. When I reach the end of her jaw, I suck in her ear lobe, causing her to roll her head back, revealing her neck in full.

Her breathing picks up and she begins to rock back and forth in my lap. I continue kissing down her jugular vein as my fingers lightly brush up her body, continuing along the skin of her back. She arches, and her breasts press into my chest. Her bra must be made only of the same lace as her panties, because her excitement is noticeable through the thin fabric. Her dress travels upward, along with my hands.

I would not be doing this if Ryland's parents were home, but they aren't. She raises her arms, knowing what I want. I release my lips from her neck and I pull the dress over her head, revealing her body to me. Throwing it on the couch beside me, I pull back to admire the sight before me. "You really are beautiful."

She links her hands behind my neck, playing with the bottom of my hairline. "Shut up and kiss me," she says, closing in for more.

I minimize the space between us, lining my body with hers. She kisses me hungrily, as if she's just discovered something she likes and needs more. I unclasp her lacy bra, pulling it down her arms and off.

She nervously tries to cover herself by crossing her arms over her chest. Looking her in the eyes, I grab her wrists and pull them back around my neck. "Don't hide from me. You're the most beautiful girl I've ever seen. I mean it." I do mean it. She is just as beautiful naked as she is clothed. I'm lying. She's more beautiful naked.

I know she's inexperienced, so I want to go slow. I'm ignoring my own wants to make it memorable for her. I may be emotionally numb, but a girl like her doesn't come around often. She deserves to be treated with respect. She is different than all the other girls I entertain this way. I have four days to be different for her, and that's what I'm going to do. I'm going to drag this out.

I grasp her hips and rock her back and forth against the hardness that lies under the fabric of my jeans, rubbing the spot I know she needs stimulated. I continue kissing her with everything in me.

She begins to make little noises against my lips, but I can tell she's holding back, because she is shy and embarrassed. She doesn't know that as a guy, I need to hear it. I want to hear her confirm how good it feels.

Releasing her lips, I tell her, "Don't hold back, baby. It's okay to show me you like it. I want to hear you." She bites her lip and her eyes begin rolling back. "Do you feel that?" She nods in response. "Don't tense up. Let it go, baby."

I continue to rub her against the roughness of my jeans. I can't believe I feel like I could actually get off like this—just rubbing her against me and watching her get off. Her heart rate quickens and her breathing becomes heavier. After a few moments, she pulls tightly on my hair and stops moving, taking my lips in hers, moaning against them. I can tell she got her release by the feel of her underwear pressed against me.

She pulls away and lays her forehead on my shoulder, trying to calm her breathing. When her heart rate slows down she looks up at me. She has a nervous look on her face and I realize it's because I'm still hard beneath her. "Tell me what you like. I may suck at it, but I'll try my best."

I shake my head. I may be in misery the rest of the day, but it's totally worth it. This is about her. Just the fact that she is concerned with me having an orgasm is enough. "Don't worry about me. We still have four days. My plane leaves Friday morning. Let's go get changed for that pool party."

I grab her bottom and stand to my feet. She wraps her legs around my waist and locks her feet behind me. On the way to the bedroom, I grab her bag by the door.

Walking in, I make my way to the bathroom door and set her down. My eyes scan her body now that I have a full-frontal view. "I'll change out here in the bedroom. When you get *cleaned up* and changed," I say with a smirk on my face, "we'll be on our way."

Her cheeks redden, and she places one arm across her chest to cover up. I love how shy she is. It makes me smile. "Thanks," she says, closing the door.

This girl is going to be the death of me, and there is no way to stop it, I think to myself as I walk to my bag in search of my swim-trunks.

TWELVE

Kinzleigh

I place my back against the door and slide down to the floor. Wow. Is that what I've been missing? No wonder Presley has turned slutty and loving it. Don't get me wrong, I have no intention of being promiscuous, but dang it if that wasn't better than I ever thought it would be. I wonder if actual sex feels like that. Presley said it hurts, but I've worn tampons since my mom allowed me to at the age of fourteen, since my menstrual cycle can be rather heavy.

I've always been scared to go all the way or even think about it. Mom gave me the *birds and the bees* speech at the age of twelve. It was really awkward and scary. She had it drilled in my head that my dad would go to jail for murder if a boy ever tried to take that from me before walking me down the aisle like a lady. She said I had too much class to be loved and left or to whore around.

She also said the only purpose for sex was reproducing or making memories with my husband and I had no business making her a grandmother until I was married. To mom, reputation is everything. She came from a very traditional, Catholic family. She always took pride in telling me she waited until her wedding night to be intimate with a man—that man being my father. Birth control was an absolute no.

I have always followed my mother's advice and done as she instructed.

Maybe it's time to make my own decision for once. Who knows, I may regret it and I may not, but at least it will be at my own risk. Besides, I have no intention of conceiving a child, ever, or getting married. My parents will have to rely on Konnor for grandkids.

I place my face in the palm of my hands, trying to calm down. I need to get it together before Presley starts calling my phone.

Standing up, I pick up my bag from the floor and place it on the countertop. Ryland's mom really has great taste. This place is decorated beautifully. I pull out the swimsuit I brought from home. Discarding my underwear into my bag, I step in my swimsuit and pull it up my body.

This is one of my favorite swimsuits. Mom doesn't care for it, because it's slightly revealing for her taste, but she tries to let me make my own judgment with my clothes within reason. It's a black monokini. The bottom is basically a standard black bikini bottom, but the top connects with the bottom by two gold hoops on my hips and it forms an infinity symbol from my neck to where it connects at the bottoms, covering only my breasts. I bought it to fit snug, because all it takes to reveal my chest is a pull too hard on the banded top.

I look in the mirror to make sure all my secret spots are covered. This should be perfect. I pull out my sheer, black cover-up wrap and tie it around my waist. My hair is still perfectly in place from when Mom fixed it earlier. I slip on my black, leather flip-flops with a matching gold metal piece that lies on top of my foot. I finish off with my clear gloss by applying it to my lips.

I exhale, hoping to get a reaction from Breyson. Shoving my things back into my bag, I make a mental note to pick up my dress and bra on the way out. I definitely don't want that left lying around. I open the door to him lying on his back across the bed with his feet planted on the floor.

As I walk out, he sits up and takes me in. His eyes widen as they sweep down my body. "Is that what you're wearing?"

Okay, so that wasn't exactly the reaction I was looking for. Maybe I don't look as good as I thought I did. Now unsure, I look down at the floor. "Yes, what's wrong with it? This is a designer swimsuit."

He places his hands together against each side of his nose, forming a line down the center of his face, as if he's frustrated. "Kinzleigh, will you please change? Don't take this the wrong way, because your body is sexy as hell, and I want nothing more than to undress you wearing that, but if we're going to hang out while I'm here, I don't want to have to break someone's jaw because they are ogling your body right in front of me. I guess it's a guy thing."

I smile. Ah, so he doesn't want someone else looking at me. Well, too bad. A little jealousy never hurt anyone. If he can rattle my thoughts all hours of the day, then he can deal with someone looking at my body. I'm not his property. I'll show him who the boss is. "This swimsuit is fine. Besides, it's the only one I brought. I only bought underwear in the mall today. Are you ready to go?"

"You're killing me. Maybe we should just stay here and I'll keep your body to myself." He raises his brows at me and I feel my face flush. Why does he embarrass me so easily?

I will not be weak.

I strut over to the door, my bag in tow, passing him in the direction of the couch when I hear a growl behind me. I smile brighter, knowing he can't see my face. It doesn't take long before I hear him walking behind me. I reach over the back of the couch to grab my dress and bra, quickly tossing it in my bag.

His hands take hold of my waist and he presses himself against my backside. Snaking his hands up my sides, under my arms and beside my breasts, he cups my shoulders, standing me upright in alignment with the front of his body. "Do you like torturing me, Kinzleigh?" His voice sounds husky and deep. My breathing picks up. At this rate we're never going to make it to the party.

I shake my head. "We need to get going. We're going to be late." The way my voice is coming out I'm not very convincing. Darn him. He runs his fingers lightly down my sternum, between my breasts, giving me chills.

He flattens his hand over my belly and pulls me closer, poking me from behind. "Now do you see what you're doing to me? A guy can only take so much. If you want to make it to that party, stop teasing me. And remember, two can play that game," he says and nips at my earlobe. "Now get your cute little butt in that truck. I'm giving you a five-second head start. If you aren't out that door, we're skipping the party."

He releases me and steps back, giving me room. One little tidbit of information about me—I don't have to be told twice. I turn and take off for the door. As I round the corner and cut through the gate, I can hear his laughter. I have to become immune to him and his flirtatious behavior. I need tips from Presley. I will not succumb to his seduction tactics.

Now sitting in the passenger seat of Ryland's Jeep, Breyson saunters through the gate in yellow swim trunks the same color as the Jeep and a t-shirt. He gets in and gives me that full on, breath-consuming grin. "You ready?"

I nod and bite my tongue, trying not to smile.

He will not win. He will not win.

The drive to Presley's was just casual small talk, thank goodness. I don't know why he gets under my skin so badly. It's driving me crazy and I feel like a weakling. Nothing ever affects me this way.

When we pull into the driveway, it's already packed full of cars. He has to park close to the road in the grass. As I look from side to side, people are consecutively piling in through the entryway gate. Opening the door, I grab my towel and step outside to walk to the front of the vehicle where I wait on Breyson.

He reaches for my hand. I'm not sure what to do. Holding hands is a little too intimate for what we are, and I don't want anyone to get the wrong idea. Instead of taking his hand, I wrap my arm around his and cup his large bicep in my hand. As our skin touches, he flexes beneath my hand. He must spend a lot of time in the gym with a trainer to have a body like this. Most guys our age don't have bodies this cut. Is it weird that I want to rub my hands down his torso, along the ridges of his stomach?

We come into the backyard, and it looks exactly as I expected. There are tents everywhere and tables full of food. The pool is packed with kids from school and the outer edge is lined with girls tanning. The first person I notice is Lexi with a scowl on her face. "Hey, Lex."

She narrows her eyes at Breyson before looking back at me. "Hey girl, what did you drag in?" Her voice feigns sarcasm.

What's up with her? Lexi is usually so bubbly and hyper. I don't think I've ever heard her sound this way, come to think of it. "Lexi, this is Breyson. He's Ryland's cousin."

She looks at him with a smirk on her face like she has an ulterior motive. "From the party right? At Logan's?"

Logan's? When did he go to Logan's? I look over at him, confused. He looks slightly nervous. "Yeah," he says, and looks at me. "You ready to go find Presley?"

What is up with these two? They act like there is something between them that they aren't telling me; like everyone is in on the same joke, but I missed the punch line. "I guess. I'll find you later, Lex."

We walk through the tents filled with people. I grab a bottle of water from one of the ice-filled tubs. In passing, I notice all of the single guys are staring at me. Some have their mouths hanging open and some look downright angry. What in the world is up with everyone at this party? I'm starting to get paranoid I have a boob showing or something and begin looking myself over.

I finally realize I am still holding onto Breyson's bicep. To make matters worse, his arm is wrapped around my waist and his hand is resting on my hip. Of course, everyone is staring. I've never been seen hanging on a guy, because I've never been with one.

Now that I look around a second time, every guy that looks angry is someone I've declined to go out with in the past. I drop my arm and Breyson tightens his hold.

How did I not even notice I was wrapped in his arm? I'm really weird about public displays of affection, which is why I'm always so awkward around Presley with her boy-toys. Feeling uncomfortable, I shimmy out of his arm and speed up my pace.

As I come to the end of the tent, I see Presley lying in a leaf shaped lounger inside the edge of the pool. Ryland is in the pool in front of her playing water volleyball. Madison and Amber—two of the cheerleaders from my squad—are on a lounger at each side of Presley.

As I close in behind them, Madison is at Presley's ear whispering. I can't hear what she is saying, but the way Presley turns around, I know it had to do with me. Great, now I'm going to have the entire high school population of Laguna talking. This is so not what I need. "Hey, sweetie, it's about time you got here. Everyone has been asking about you." She scans my body and then Breyson's. She smiles, but bites her lip, trying to refrain. "Amber, sweetie, why don't you be a gem and scoot over to the next lounger. I need some Kinzleigh time."

If I ever thought I could hide anything from Presley, I was wrong. I swear the girl has some kind of weird sixth sense. "Don't be silly. Amber, you don't have to move. You were there first. I can sit in the next one."

Maybe I can dodge the conversation I know is coming. She won't say anything if I'm not beside her. She knows I'm a private person.

"Kinzleigh Berlyn Baker! Get your skinny little butt over here and sit down! Amber, scoot." She starts waving her hand at her as if she's shooing a fly, and then turns and points at Breyson. "Breyson. Pool. Now. I need girl time."

When Presley gets like this she is scary, and everyone knows she can be dangerous with her tantrums. She comes from money and her parents spoil her. I hate, with a special emphasis on the word hate, when she uses my middle name.

My parents have a strange sense of humor. Not only did they combine their first names to name me, but also, they chose to assign my middle name after the city in which I was conceived. Mom spelled it different, because she thought my spelling was more feminine than the spelling of the place.

Really, Mom, who is going to even get to the way it's spelled when they find out you're named after a city in Germany? The one in which you have to hear about your parents getting busy. That's gross. If I didn't know my parents have never tried a drug in their lives, I would think they were high the entire time my mom was pregnant.

Breyson shakes his head in laughter and turns to me, removing his shirt—slowly, might I add, each abdominal being revealed one at a time.

The guy has the best body I've ever seen, hands down. His shorts sit low on his waist, revealing the V of muscle. This view is better than the one at the beach. Why? Well, because he is standing before me doing his version of a male striptease. As his arms move up his body, each muscle flexes in front of me.

"Share the view with the rest of us!" I'm broken from the frozen state I didn't even know I was in by Amber's outburst. I turn to look at them and realize they are all staring, along with one angry Preston. The girls are looking between us as if something big is about to happen.

I turn to Breyson, smiling like a champion. He knew Preston was standing there and I'm gawking like an idiot. Kill me now. Could this get any worse? Why, oh why, do I feel like I'm unwillingly being tugged into a lo—lust triangle?

Breyson walks toward me, closing the space between us, and hands me his shirt. "Will you hold this for me?" His naked torso brushes against mine, goose bumps forming along my arms. I grab his shirt in my hand, but before he releases it, he whispers in my ear, "I told you things would happen if you wore that swimsuit and I caught another guy undressing you with his eyes. Don't say I didn't warn you."

With that, he turns and heads toward the pool where Ryland is watching, as if he's got front row seats to a big fight.

I turn, ignoring them, and Presley has a rather large smile on her face behind Preston. He is blocking my lounger with his exposed body. Preston isn't lacking in the muscle department; he just does nothing for me. No fireworks are shooting off and my girly bits are in check.

Whereas Breyson has more bulk of muscle and definition, Preston is more of a lean muscularity and tone. What am I supposed to do with him now? I am outside of my element here. It's not a good idea to go from no intimate contact with the male species to two in the matter of a day. Sighing, I walk toward my seat next to Presley in hopes that he will just move aside.

He watches me the entire time I walk toward him, not moving one. Not. One. Single. Inch. I stop, leaving distance between us. Everyone finally went back to what they were doing. I guess Preston having a thing for me is just as obvious as Presley always makes it seem. How was I the only one blind to this? Was I really that sucked into my own life? "Preston. Do you mind if I sit down in my seat?"

He's being annoying. I've never given him the impression there was something between us. He's just standing there with the vein in his neck still bulging. I can see the muscle in his jaw moving back and forth. "Preston! Did you not hear the girl? Are we going to have to have another heart-to-heart?" Presley is now standing to my right, facing the sides of us as we stare at each other.

He releases a deep breath and his face relaxes. I wonder what it was they talked about last night. "Hey, Kinz, you look gorgeous, as always."

Preston has always called me that. Hearing it calms me down. I need to figure out a way to deal with all this without getting angry with him. At one time, I was closer to him than Presley. Some nights when I stayed over at night, he would sit up with me until daylight watching funny movies when I was scared from Presley making me watch a horror film.

"Thanks, Preston. Look, can we talk later, just you and me? Right now is a bad time. I promise I'll give you my undivided attention." At this point, I don't know what else to do. How did I get myself into all this mess? I guess I was crazy to think I could totally avoid men forever.

Presley is still standing here, listening to everything we're saying. If they weren't brother and sister it would be awkward. "Okay, Kinzleigh, I can do that. I really need us to talk, though. Last night didn't go exactly as I planned, and then when I got up this morning you were gone."

His voice has a disappointed tone that usually isn't present where Preston is concerned. I've never seen Preston this way. He's usually arrogant face to face, with a different girl on his arm every time I see him.

I look at Presley, trying to hint for her to leave for a minute, so I can make sure he's okay. She, of course, doesn't get the memo, because she is the leader of all things related to drama and gossip. "Okay, Preston. I promise I'll come find you later."

He nods and walks off. I notice he looks at Breyson on the way to the house. To actually think boys call us impossible to figure out is just crazy. I've been close to Preston since I was a kid and still thought boys had cooties. In all those years, he's never once acted like we were anything more than friends. Now, suddenly, he's throwing things at me like dating and forever. The thought of settling down forever makes me physically ill, especially at my age. If more women would be worried about making themselves happy instead of being at every beck and call of a man, there would be less heartache in the world.

I have my life planned out. I want to travel the world and spend my younger days cheerleading in the NFL, maybe do some coaching on the side. I don't know in terms of a career yet when it comes to a college major. I have plenty of time to decide.

When I'm older and have lived a little, I want to start a cheerleading company and be known across the country for training the best cheerleaders around. No one got to the top with a baby on her hip, doting on a man.

I start toward my lounger and Presley is keeping pace. "You, missy, have some explaining to do," she says with a devious grin on her face.

I lay down the towel I've been carrying and sit down. Presley really does have the coolest pool around for pool parties. It's a full-sized pool, but the difference is, there is a platform completely surrounding the inner edge of the pool that rests a couple inches below the water. It is lined all the way around with leaf shaped loungers made for the water. I love it in the summer, because you can lie barely submerged in the water while you tan.

In one corner there is a rock formation wall, suspended in the air for a waterfall that harbors a small cave like opening behind it. Diagonally across the pool is a water slide formed into the same kind of rock. Between the pool and outdoor kitchen and fire pit, Presley's house is known for her backyard. Her parents had it built for this sole purpose—to entertain. In California, residents pay a lot for outdoor entertaining. We are always at Presley's, with and without parents present.

"What is it that you want me to explain to you? Did I leave my sunglasses here?" There is no way she knows I was slightly naughty earlier. That is my secret.

She dangles a pair of black Versace sunglasses in the air with an evil gleam in her eye. "Oh, you mean these sunglasses?" I reach for them and she pulls them back out of my reach. I hate that she is shaped like a model—tall and thin with arms and legs for days. "Tsk, tsk, tsk, you know what you have to do to get them back. I want information and I want it now."

My four hundred-dollar sunglasses are my favorite accessory and she knows this. I'm very particular about my things. My parents work hard to give me the things that I have. "There is nothing to tell you," I whine, reaching for my sunglasses again. She pulls them higher than before.

I huff and look out at the pool. The boys and some of the girls have a volleyball game set up in the middle of the pool. My eyes land on Breyson as he jumps in the air to spike the ball back over the net. Water beads trickle down his back as his muscles flex.

His tattoo waves as his shoulder muscles protrude with the rotation of his right shoulder as he smacks the ball with the palm of his hand. I bite my lip as I think of being wrapped in those strong arms. "Uh huh, someone got some action. It's written all over your face. You must really think I'm stupid. I know you better than you know yourself. I could see it when you got here and now you just confirmed it. Spill."

I look over to Presley, now that I've been caught gazing at his body. I can't help but to smile, thinking about earlier. "Why must you know everything? One of these days your brain is going to explode from all of the information that lies in there."

I look around to see who all is listening, not wanting anyone to overhear. When I turn back to Presley, Lexi is standing behind her. "Hey, girls. What have I missed?" She has a malicious look on her face. I wish I knew what was wrong with her.

"Hey, Lex. Are you okay? You don't seem like yourself today." She looks out at the pool. Her eyes glass over. When I turn to see what she is looking at, it's Breyson. They did act like they knew each other earlier. Maybe I'm missing something.

"So, he's trying to screw you now too, huh?"

I whip my head back toward her. I couldn't have heard her right. "Excuse me? What do you mean?"

"Awe, that's so sweet. You really thought he liked you," she says sarcastically sweet. "Poor thing, we really need to teach you a thing or two about boys. It's not your fault; you aren't used to the dating thing. They can be hellacious creatures. Always after one thing and not thinking of the destruction it causes in its path."

"Lexi, what are you talking about?" I'm starting to panic at this point. I hate being out of the loop on things.

"I met him the other night at Logan's. He was drunk and all over me. I was about to go upstairs with him until he accidentally mentioned he had a girlfriend. It's sad, really. She's probably sitting at home all alone, waiting on his return, and he's out here hooking up with other girls. I don't really care, but sloppy seconds aren't my style."

Presley has her eyes narrowed at Lexi. "You're lying. I know you, Lexi Callahan. What I can't figure out is why. Kinzleigh has never done anything to you. Why would you be such a conniving little bitch?"

She pulls her sunglasses down from their resting place on top of her head as a smirk forms on her lips. "Don't take my word for it, just ask him." She looks out at the pool one last time and prances off.

How could I be so stupid? I feel sick. I think I'm about to have a panic attack. There is one thing I will not tolerate and that is cheating. I may not be the relationship type, but I will not be the floozy either. My brother has been shattered over a cheating little harlot and I will not be the cause of someone else's pain.

"I need to go. Presley, I'm sorry." I am staring down at my feet, trying to breathe.

"Okay, sweetie. Do you need me to give you a ride? Don't let her get to you, Kinzleigh. She probably isn't telling the whole truth. You know she is a spoiled little brat and will do anything to get her way."

I look out in the pool and see Breyson. The color drains from his face. That was all the answer I needed. It said enough. It doesn't matter if some of what Lexi said was a lie, because he just answered the one part I'm interested in. "That's okay. Stay here with your party guests. I'll find Preston and get a ride. Call me later, 'kay?" Breyson is making his way across the pool. I've got to get out of here.

I stand quickly and step out of the pool. "Kinzleigh, hold up," he calls out. I run. I can feel a meltdown coming. I've been having panic attacks since the day Grams died but have had them under control for the last year. I don't even have to take medication anymore, and over the last few days they are starting up again.

I make it to the patio door when I feel a hand on mine. "Kinzleigh, stop. What's wrong? What did she say to you?"

I'm angry, and it all starts to set in. Turning around to face him, he steps back. "Why didn't you tell me you had a girlfriend? Do I look stupid to you? Did you think I wouldn't find out? I may be inexperienced, but I have boundaries. I am not a cheap whore you can just use and run back to your girlfriend in a week. I didn't care that you've been with several girls, but this crosses the line. I should have known. People like you are all the same. You should all stick together—cheaters and liars. I am not one to judge, usually, but my brother was destroyed over a girl just like you." I'm yelling at this point, but I can't help it. This is a very sensitive issue with me. I've watched what's left of my brother day in and day out, trying to piece himself back together.

Preston opens the sliding glass door. "Kinzleigh, are you all right?"

"I need a ride home. Can you take me?" My heart is pounding in my chest and I feel like I'm going to pass out.

"Of course, let me grab my keys." He turns and disappears out of sight.

Breyson is tightening his fists by his sides. "So that's it then? You're not even going to let me explain? You won't even hear the story from both sides before just believing someone else? I thought you were different than that, Kinzleigh."

"What is there to hear, Breyson? Lexi told me you were all over her at Logan's until she found out you had a girlfriend. Did you think you were just going to move on to me next since she wouldn't give you what you wanted?" My voice is starting to break. The stress is taking over my body and I can feel tears stinging my eyes, trying to break free.

I only cry when I'm severely angry. I guess it's my body's way of releasing the toxins roaming through my veins. "I broke rules for you, because I thought you were different. I was okay with a casual fling, but I will not be the cause of someone else's heartache and I will not be used against my will."

"I don't have a girlfriend, Kinzleigh. I did, but it's not what you think." He starts pulling at his hair. "Can we please talk and I'll explain?"

"Did you or did you not have a girlfriend any of the times you kissed me?" It's a simple question and the only one I'm interested in. He stares at me as Preston appears back in the doorway and the look on Breyson's face gives me my answer. "Goodbye, Breyson. Have a nice life."

I turn and walk inside, behind Preston, leaving him standing in the doorway. When Preston gets to the garage door, he turns toward me as he grabs the doorknob. "Are you sure you're okay? I can make him leave if you want to stay. This is just as much your house as it is mine."

Preston has always thought of me first, especially now that I stop and think about it. I feel kind of like the story I learned in church of Adam and Eve in the Garden of Eden. I've gone all this time blinded to everything around me and now that I've tasted the fruit, my eyes are open. I want to go back to being blissfully unaware and it's impossible. It's too bad that I am not one of those girls that want to be in a relationship, because Preston honestly would be perfect.

He's sexy and our families are really close. We've been friends since we were kids, so there are no surprises. Him and Konnor have always been and are still close friends when he's home from school, so he knows what he's going through and how I feel about it. I don't know, but it's not enough.

If I were going to give my virginity to anyone else, I might consider Preston since I'm moving, but with him bringing up some of that crazy talk I don't think he can handle it without wanting more. I can't risk messing up our tight knit family circle. Plus, I don't get the butterflies when I'm around him like I do with Breyson. He doesn't make me weak in the knees or short of breath. Maybe it's stupid to compare, but I don't know, I liked the way being around Breyson affected me.

"That's okay, Preston, just take me home. I don't really feel well, and I promised you we would talk anyway. We can knock out two things at once." He nods his head and walks out the door.

"Nice car," I say, taking a seat in the sleek white Porsche with black, leather interior. Even though it's a luxury car, Preston has made it his own with black star like rims and a spoiler on the back. He backs out of the garage with a smile on his face.

"You could have one, you know. All you have to do is say the word the day I graduate. I get a big bonus when I walk across that stage and receive my business degree." I roll my eyes. He is not helping calm me down by trying to buy me. It freaks me out more.

"Preston, you know this conversation is having the opposite of the desired effect, right? I'm not that kind of girl and I never will be. You know that if you know me. I don't want to live off someone else. I want to be my own person. If I wanted a new car I would buy it myself. Are you forgetting I'm only seventeen? I still have to graduate high school and go to college. You act like we're on the same page and we're reading two different books. Where is this coming from? I'm pretty sure there are plenty of girls that would love to be your trophy and spend your money."

He's deep in thought as we drive down the road, listening to the purr of the engine. It really is a beautiful car. He passes my house and I wonder where we are going, but I keep quiet. Obviously, he has things he wants to say, and I promised I'd listen. I owe him that much. He has always been there for me, no questions asked.

He pulls in the harbor and I know where we are. The yacht our parents bought together is anchored here. He kills the engine and looks at me, resting his left hand on the door handle. "I know you don't feel well, but I wanted to talk. This is one place we can do that."

We exit the car and walk down the dock, passing a string of boats in various shapes and sizes. We finally reach the end of the dock where ours sits at port. We haven't been on it in a while, since summer vacation just started. We pretty much live on this boat during the summer, because our parents use most of their vacation time then. It's been a tradition since we were kids.

Preston steps across the space between the dock and the vessel, planting both feet on the other side. He turns around and holds out his hand. This part always scares me a little, no matter how many times I've been thrown or suspended in the air with cheerleading. Something about the boat being so high and rocking as you're trying to get a good balance with the possibility of falling in freaks me out. I take his hand and cross the barrier, but he doesn't release my hand.

As we walk across the deck of the yacht and down the stairs, I take in its beauty. I love it here. It's decorated in reds and browns and is so homey. I should take advantage of my last month to come here. He sits down on the couch and pulls me down beside him. "What's on your mind, pretty girl?" He was always so much easier to talk to than Presley; maybe, because he's a lot like Konnor and me. He's laid back and can talk forever or just listen. He's probably the only person aside from my brother I really would go to if I had a problem.

"Just thinking of how much I'm going to miss this place." I guess I might as well let the cat out of the bag. Then he will realize anything he is about to say is probably a waste of breath. "Mom and Dad are moving us across the country. I don't want to go, but I have no choice. As much as I want to kick and scream in a tantrum, they are pretty set that it's a done deal." Just thinking about this all over again is depressing. "I have no idea what I'm supposed to do about cheerleading and my national all-star tryouts are the same week we move I think."

He sits there looking at me, waiting to be sure I'm finished before he talks. Typical Preston. He's a very patient person, which will make him a good businessman. Him following in his dad's footsteps is exactly where he should be. "Dad mentioned that the other night. They are freaking out about it too. He left telling Presley up to Mom, so I don't know if she knows yet. By her behavior, I would say probably not. She will most likely have a meltdown since you two are like twins separated at birth."

"So, you already knew? Then where is all this nonsense coming from about you and me? You've never once made any attempt at a relationship becoming more than friendship, and now you act like you're planning our wedding." We are sitting sideways on the couch, facing each other.

He has his right leg resting against the cushion and his left leg planted on the floor, mirroring my opposite. His right side is leaning against the back of the couch with his elbow propped on the top of the backrest. His hand is resting just below his nose, index finger against his lips, and knuckles facing the ceiling. He is smiling as if he is amused. "Are you done yet? You always were headstrong about everything. If you would give me the floor I will explain everything, but I need you to promise not to say anything until you've heard me out and keep an open mind."

I have to give him credit where credit is due. He seems to have this all planned out. "Okay, I promise; although, I'm not sure what I'm getting myself into."

He turns his body to the left, facing frontward, with both feet now pressed against the floor. He leans forward and rests his elbows right above his knees, looking at the floor. "Kinzleigh, you've known me a long time. You know I would never lie to you. I think I've had plenty of moments to prove myself worthy of your trust, wouldn't you agree?" He looks up at me for a response. I nod for him to continue.

"I know you're seventeen and I know you still have to finish high school and college. I know everything there is to know about you. I've spent a lot of time learning what makes you, you." He looks back down at the floor, as if he's nervous. "I've wanted you, Kinzleigh, since we were little. I want you to listen to what I have to say before you freak out or say anything in return. I've loved you since we were kids. I will always love you, Kinzleigh. You're it for me. I've waited around, silently, because of our age difference. I know you don't want to fall in love because you have dreams; I get it. I have been buying time by being with other girls, but they don't satisfy me anymore. You will be eighteen in the next several months. I know how you are and I know you won't be in a long distance relationship. That's not what I'm asking you; today, anyway."

He takes a deep breath. I cannot believe I'm hearing any of this correctly. I have to be mentally unstable. "All I'm doing is planting a seed. I want you to think about it this year, while you're gone—think about us. I know you're not the kind of girl to make a hasty decision. I know you have your certain views in regard to dating. I've seen many guys crash and burn in an attempt to capture your heart. And I can't say that it hasn't made me happy. But regardless, I want you to know how I feel. No regrets. It's always been you,

Kinzleigh. You're the only girl that's ever stolen my heart. I'm not telling you this in hopes of getting a response today or anytime soon. You won't hear me tell you I love you after today unless you choose to be with me. I'm only telling you now, because you deserve to know. I don't want to lose my chance to someone else, because I was too scared to tell you how I felt."

He scans my face before he goes on. I know it's to make sure I'm not about to bolt out the door. "Before you jump to any conclusions, I know you don't want kids and that's why you don't want to get serious with someone, and one day married. I've been around you long enough to know that you don't want to be held back. I'm okay with not having kids if it means having you. Not much would even change. I will never make you give up cheerleading. I will never pressure you to marry me unless I know it's what you want. It's not a contract that takes away your freedom. It would just be a life together. We could go wherever you want, live wherever you want to live. We have businesses all over this country and Dad wants to expand globally. I have the means to make you happy. Everything is within reach. I just need you to trust me. To choose me."

I rub my forehead, trying to process all this information. I'm not used to someone knowing me like their favorite movie, reciting every line as I would say it. It's a little intimidating. I didn't know I was so obvious. "What exactly are you proposing?"

"Nothing as well as everything. I don't want you to take this for more than it is. When I come to your senior graduation, I would like an answer to a question I've wanted to ask you for years. Can we be more than friends? That's it. I know you want to be in California. If your answer is yes, then you will move back here with me and we will see how things go. I just want you for myself. I know you're not like many girls and that's one of the things I love about you. I learned a long time ago, if I wanted a chance, it had to be on terms you could handle. Don't overthink it. Live the way you would if I never mentioned it. I do want you to know, though, I won't touch another woman until then. I know I can't expect the same of you, but I can't pretend with other girls anymore when the one I want is right here."

I can't even begin to think about all this. At least I'm not completely freaked out. I guess when it's all laid out in front of you there isn't a whole lot to freak out about. Maybe it's that I can't fathom what next year will be like much less after. He does make some good points. The curiosity wins. "Why have I never noticed you felt this way?"

He smiles a genuine smile for the first time since we arrived. "You tend to only notice the things in the world of Kinzleigh."

"I don't really know what to say, but I'll think it over. I'm still a little shocked, to be honest."

He stands, reaching for my hand, and pulls me to my feet. He cups my face in his hands, like in the bathroom last night. "Don't be sorry, Kinzleigh. You're reacting better than I expected. I was prepared for a slap, screams, red cheeks."

He smiles, pretending he knows my little fits better than me. "I know I'm throwing a lot on you. You panic under pressure. I thought you would be in California senior year. That I would have more time to push you slowly. I've been thinking about all this since Dad mentioned you moving. It made me really think about my future and where I want it to go."

"Your future is bright, Preston, regardless of who is on your arm. She will be lucky to be loved by you, whoever she is."

He looks me in my eyes. "Can I kiss you? For real this time?"

What am I supposed to do? I'm not one for kissing multiple people in one day; it's rather trashy to me, and low class. But he's waiting for my response and I can see the hope in his eyes. One time wouldn't hurt. I won't be seeing Breyson anymore anyway. "Okay."

He pulls me in slowly, touching his lips to mine. He kisses my bottom lip and then my top. He sucks my lips between his. He kisses me as if he's trying to cherish this moment, memorize it. He lightly licks my bottom lip, asking for entry. If I'm going to do this I might as well make it count. I slip my tongue into the opening of his lips. He entwines his tongue with mine. It's warm and mingles with need.

He walks me backward until my back presses against something hard. He picks up pace, kissing me as if he's a dying man.

He runs his hands down my body and stops just below my butt, picking me up. I wrap my legs around his narrow waist, somewhat lost in what we're doing.

He continues to kiss and suck and nibble. I'm not sure how much time goes by, but he finally moans and releases me, setting me down onto the floor.

He cups my cheek in his right hand and brushes his thumb across my bottom lip. "You have no idea how long I've wanted to do that. And nothing could have prepared me for how it'd make me feel. This will be what gets me through my last year of school. I'll just have to make it last until I come back for you. I will come back for you, Kinzleigh."

The conviction in his voice both excites me and scares the crap out of me.

THIRTEEN

Breyson

I'm a pretty laidback guy in my opinion, but there is one thing I hate—to be judged. I'll be the first to admit when I've done wrong. In this case, I have. Even though I know the true situation with Natalie, I shouldn't have kissed Kinzleigh while I was technically dating her. I even understand her anger, because cheating is wrong to any degree. It hurts people. I have a dead cousin to prove it.

I attempted to fix the error of my ways by breaking up with Natalie and I even came clean that I had taken interest in someone else. What pisses me off is that she didn't even give me a chance to explain. We live in a country that prides itself on being innocent until proven guilty, so what was that exactly? If she doesn't want to speak to me once she's heard me out, fine, but I deserve a chance to explain what I'm being accused of. And that shit about Lexi? That's a damn lie. I'm the one that turned her down.

I'm so mad right now I want to hit someone. I want to hit someone hard and repetitively. I need to blow off some steam. I have been called a playboy, a jerk, and manwhore, along with everything else out there, but I will not be called a liar. I have always told the truth. We could both be termed being in the wrong. Not one time did she ask me if I was dating someone.

Some may say that omission is a form of lying, but I don't exactly think clearly when I'm around her. That has to count for something. I have been with my fair share of girls for a seventeen-year-old. Some my age, some older, and I'll own up to every accusation that is true, but I will not stand around while someone believes a lying, deceitful bitch over me.

I never once was all over that slut at the party. To lie on someone that way is low, even for a girl. Girls like her are what give guys a bad rep. I don't know if she's mad she got turned down, or jealous, but I will find out.

Right now, though, what bothers me more is that I just had to watch Kinzleigh leave with that little rich playboy just waiting to get his hands on her. I know his type. They sit around playing the best friend role until they can swoop in and take her when someone else takes an interest. What does it matter? She was pretty clear she didn't want to see me again. I sit down on the steps, trying to ponder my next move. What is it about this girl I can't let go?

Back home, I would just go find a random, willing, attractive girl, and take her somewhere private. The vast majority of the female high school population is so ready to be older, rebellion is high, and every chance they can act older, they do. Most of us *are* out partying and screwing around. Parents overlook it so they don't have to acknowledge and deal with it.

The problem is, I've now tasted something better than a hookup. Anything else would be like shooting cheap, student-budget whiskey after being offered a shot of Johnnie Walker, Black Label—my dad's favorite drink.

I'm sitting here, lost in my own head, when red toenails come into view. I know it's not Kinzleigh, because there is no anklet surrounding the left ankle that is always there, it seems.

My eyes travel upward, along the seams of long, tan legs. She's wearing a black and red polka dot bikini, a flat stomach between fabric pieces, and a metal bar through her navel. Skinny with a nice sized rack. Maybe this is my answer to all this frustration, I think, until I reach her face.

Lexi.

Well, she does have some balls; I'll give her that. "What the fuck do you want?"

She smiles, but it has motive behind it. "What a shame. It's such a waste when a man chases after a girl that is better than him. We owe it to ourselves to stick with our own kind. By the looks of you, I'd guess you have plenty of experience in bed, and I bet you don't disappoint. I don't mind you being a man-slut; personally, it works in my favor, but Kinzleigh is different. Every guy wants her and every girl wants to be her. She's the closest thing to perfection any girl will ever be. Sweet, innocent, good, hot as hell. Ask any guy here at this party. Preston Dunagin has had his eyes set on her for years, and I'd say it appears he's pretty close to finally getting her."

She walks over and sits next to me. "If she were going to be with someone, it'll be him. Trust me. Those two were cultivated to be together by those parents of theirs. Everyone here knows it. Accepts it even. What makes you think you're different? I've watched so many guys like you attempt and fail; only to end up with a girl like me. I'm doing you a favor, you know. No other guy will lasso her heart. Isn't that a term you southern people use? I'm not saying he's innocent, because a boy like that is hard to turn down and he knows it. He has the looks, the personality, and the money, but he's done the one thing you haven't—put in the time with her. Been in the friend zone for years."

She laughs. "It's twisted, really. Every girl he hooks up with is a physical replica of Kinzleigh—blonde hair, nice body. One girl even mentioned he made her get on all fours and called out her name when he came. Once he gets her, he isn't letting her go. Just thought you should know. He'll get her when he gets out of school. That's always been the plan. He makes it obvious, so it's hard to miss."

I'm so mad I can't speak. I pop my knuckles in frustration, unable to look at her, because I'm afraid I'll hit her. "Awe, don't be upset, sweetie. You aren't the first and you won't be the last."

She runs her fingertip up my arm and down my front. "You want a girl with some experience anyway. All guys do. What fun is a girl that doesn't know what she's doing? Just lies there like a corpse. I know what a guy like you wants to hold your attention," she purrs in my ear, brushing her breasts against my upper arm.

She's not done. I can tell. "Come on, sexy. I'll even let you pretend I'm her, just like *Preston* likes to do. Would you like that? Makes a better lay, because then you can show me just how much you want her . . ."

God, she has issues. That's what this is about—jealousy. It's a poisonous emotion, and deadly in the wrong person. I guarantee she's used to getting her way. And she's little bit fucking crazy. She knows exactly what she's doing. Two can play that game. "You're probably right. I need a girl that can keep up with me," I seethe. She stands up and struts, thinking she's won.

"I'm glad you understand," she says, smiling. I trail after her in the direction of the side of the house. We enter through the mudroom door. As she walks through, she glances around, as if making sure she's unnoticed. I think Presley's parents were in the outdoor kitchen with a game on the television if that's who she's looking for.

We walk to a small set of service stairs. She ascends them quietly. When we reach the top, she walks to the end of the hallway and stops at the farthest room. Looking back at me, she smiles. "I can't wait for this. I've wanted you since I saw you at the beach. I can only imagine what's under those shorts," she says looking at my crotch.

We walk in what appears to be a guest room. In the center of the room sits a queen size bed. The walls are a light yellow and the bedding a bright print.

I walk to the center and stop not far from the bed. She circles around me like an animal circling its prey. "You sure you're ready for this, Lexi? I don't go slow. Slow is boring. I like it hard and rough is what I'll give. And you just took away the one thing I wanted. I have a lot of aggression to take out on you."

She licks her lips. "That's what I'm counting on," she says seductively. She closes the space between us. Wrapping her arms around my neck, she pulls in for a kiss.

I allow her to kiss me, but I will not touch her tongue. I don't want to taint my mouth with her bitterness after experiencing the sweetness that is Kinzleigh. I grab her thighs and pick her up roughly, hoping like hell it hurts.

She wraps her slender legs around my waist. I slip my hands underneath her bottoms, close to her sweet spot but not touching—only to tease.

She moans against my mouth. "I need more." She begins rubbing herself against me, clearly ready for me. I release her lips. I can't stand her touching my mouth any longer. I hate kissing—except with Kinzleigh. I kiss down her neck to distract her.

Walking her backward to the bed, I throw her down roughly on the mattress. She spreads her legs automatically. Girls like her require no effort at all. They are all the same. There is no chase and it's boring. All they are good for is a quick lay—an easy dick lubricant. No one ever takes this girl home to meet Mama. I pin her arms above her head and straddle her. She rubs her foot between my legs in search of what she wants. "You want it?"

"You know I do. Get a condom and hurry up already." Her eyes are hooded, and she is begging. I got her right where I want her. I lower my bottom half, resting between her legs, allowing her to get a feel of what she could have. I've always been well endowed. It's not showboating, it's the truth. I don't have to brag about it. When I want someone to know about it, she will.

When she feels it against her, she arches off the bed and wraps her legs tightly around my waist. "Oh, damn. I need you inside me; fill every inch of me."

I lean closer to her, next to her ear so she can feel my body against hers. Whispering into her ear, I ram myself against her swimsuit; the hardness under my shorts prodding between her legs.

Guys aren't like girls. It doesn't take feelings to arouse a man. Guys are physical creatures of habit. The right stimulation and physical attraction and it's ready to go. She can get me hard, and if I wanted to, I could screw her without going soft, even if I practically hate her right now. The funny thing is—I don't want her. I'd rather get myself off than get off for her.

With all my anger backing it I say, "That's too bad, isn't it? You'll never get this. I've been with plenty of girls like you. It's not fun anymore. I'd rather spend the rest of my life chasing after a girl like Kinzleigh and never get her than to settle for second best. The truth is, guys that sleep with you really are imaging a girl like her. It's sad that you know it and don't care to change it."

I grind against her. "This is all you'll ever be to a guy. Cheap pussy. You may get other guys by conning them into sleeping with you, but I'm not one of them. Just a word of advice—if you ever want to be more than a nice piece of ass, I suggest you stop being such a bitch and stop when you're not wanted."

I distance myself from her. She is laying there with her eyes wide open in a daze. She goes limp. I'm not an asshole, but she had it coming when she lied about me and then pissed me off. Someone needs to snap her back into reality from the warped self-absorbed world she lives in. I've done what I came here to do. I stand up and turn for the door. Moving quickly, I slam it behind me.

I'm going after Kinzleigh.

FOURTEEN

Breyson

I will make her hear me out, because the truth is, I'm already in too deep. I need a few more days with her. Rushing down the stairs, I dash to the front door.

I'm in a full-fledged sprint out the door, headed to the Jeep. When I get to the driver door, I realize the keys are back at the party. Linking my hands on top of my head, I'm trying to decide what in the heck I'm going to do. I don't want to go back to that party. From the corner of my eye, I notice Ryland's truck. Maybe he left the keys in it since it's close to the house.

I make my way back to the truck and open the door. The keys are in it. One problem down, but one problem remains. It is among several other vehicles crowded together in the driveway. There is a path I could get it out, but it's going to be a tight squeeze. I get in the truck and start the ignition. Pulling out my phone, I notice a text from Ryland.

Ryland: Dude, where did you go?

Me: Taking the truck. I need to find Kinzleigh. I'll explain later.

Ryland: Presley is freaking out about you having a girlfriend. Care to explain what happened in the five fucking minutes I had my back turned?

Me: Lexi started a bunch of crap and lied. Kinzleigh ran off with that Preston guy and didn't let me explain. I broke up with Natalie Friday night right after I kissed Kinzleigh. I was honest with her about meeting someone.

No one cared to hear my side. Just handle it. I have to go, man.

Ryland: Aight, bro. I got you covered. Next time keep me in the loop, so I know what's going on and don't look like a dick.

Me: K

Looking around, I back out. I have to back up and pull forward a few times, maneuvering the truck, but I manage to get out. As I'm pulling out of the entryway gate, I realize I'm still in swim trunks. If her parents are home, this isn't the best way to show up. Headed to her house, I spot a thrift store on the way. This is better than the alternative.

Pulling in, I kill the engine and exit the truck. It doesn't seem busy, but it is open according to the flashing neon sign over the door. I walk inside to racks upon racks of clothing. There is an older lady about mid to late sixties with fully grayed hair sitting at the front counter, to the left of the door, reading a magazine. She looks up as the bell dings above the door. "Can I help you, son?"

The darkness is taking over as the sun goes down. I'm not sure if Kinzleigh's parents are weird about houseguests at night. Since I'm in a shortage of time, maybe she can help. "Yes, ma'am. I left a pool party in a hurry, and where I'm going I need some clothes. I don't have time to run by the place I'm staying. Do you have anything for me?"

She lights up as if I've just made her day. She must not get very many customers in here. "Oh, wonderful! I think we can find you something, dear. Come on and follow me," she says, smiling a grandmotherly smile and walks out from behind the counter toward the back of the store.

Come to think of it, she kind of reminds me of my maternal grandmother. She's warm and welcoming with excitement every time I see her and she always has something baked, such as cookies or cake. She doesn't get many visitors. I should go see her when I get home. Mom keeps telling me she won't always be here, but I never seem to listen. I'm closer to my dad's parents.

I trail after the older woman in the direction of the rack in the back of the store. On it hangs several t-shirts in all colors and sizes. She shuffles through the hangers but stops to look at me. "Hmm, let's see," she says, rubbing her chin. "Are you trying to impress a young lady?"

I smile at her sweet personality as she inquiries about my personal life. "Yes, ma'am, actually I am. She is a little angry with me right now, so I'll have to do some groveling."

She stares off at me for a moment and I wonder what she's thinking.

"Ah, yes, I think I may can help with that too. My Henry used to be the champion at groveling. That's one reason it was so hard to stay mad at him for long," she sighs, making it clear he's no longer around. "You remind me of him. That sandy blond hair and those beautiful blue eyes. You have quite the smile too. I think I can give you a few tips and you're sure to have her back in no time." She winks and goes back to strumming through the hangers.

Stopping briefly, she looks me over. This should be perfect. "Come here, son; let me see if this will fit. Looks like we have a lot of muscle to cover."

I walk over and stop before her. She holds out the shirt, close to my body. It's a vintage, clover-green Jimmy Hendrix t-shirt. "I think this will work." She releases the hanger to me, and heads toward the sidewall. "I think I got some shoes in the other day that look your size; brand new too. I tell you, things just aren't the same as when I was young. Generations now are spoiled and wasteful. Back when I was a kid, we didn't get a new pair of shoes until our current pair was no longer wearable."

Yep, she is just like my grandmother—always on her soapbox comparing then and now. I can't help but to smile. I come to a stop behind her as she pulls down a pair of black and neon-yellow Nike sneakers. "What size are you, honey?"

"Eleven."

"I may be old, but I still got it. I knew they would fit. Now, let's talk about this special girl. I'll tell you a little something about women, but it's our secret. Got it?"

I nod, curious where she is going with this. "We don't know what the hell we want. We like to pretend we do, and sometimes even convince ourselves we do, but we don't. There are two things you need to remember, and you'll get far with the lucky lady. One—she is always right. It doesn't matter if she really is or not, just let her think so regardless. Two—compliments are better than candy is what I always say. You can't buy a woman's heart, but you sure can sweet-talk your way there. Romance her, woo her, and sweep her off her feet. You do that, and she'll forever be yours."

I have discovered one thing about the elderly—they tend to be wise. It's best to listen, even if I don't have the heart to tell her I have no intention on falling in love. They don't really care about the ways of the up-and-coming generations. They just like to give advice and keep the old ways alive. "I'll definitely keep that in mind, thank you. I need to get going before I miss my chance. How much do I owe you?"

"You're a cute kid. I'll tell you what, since you listened to an old woman ramble, it's on the house. You go make up with that girl. I have a feeling she's special."

"No, ma'am, I'd like to pay for the stuff." She holds up her hand to stop me as I put on the shirt and shoes. My shorts are now dry.

"I insist. This is my store and I can do as I please," she says, grinning. "Go on now. Flash one of those smiles of yours and I'm sure all will be forgotten."

"Yes, ma'am. Thank you." I turn to head for the door.

"My pleasure," she says, beating me to it and opening the door for me.

I get in the truck and back into the street. The old woman is still standing in the door, waving goodbye. I return the gesture and begin on my way. I have no idea what I'm going to say when I get there. Why I never thought to get her number when she left it at the pool house, I have no idea. I wish I could just get her alone. The thought of her family being there freaks me out a little. Maybe because I don't have that much experience with parents and the ones I do are because they are my friends' parents.

It doesn't take long before Kinzleigh's house comes into view. I pull in and park off to the side. I'm not even sure if Kinzleigh is home. I'd like to hope she is, because the alternative drives me crazy to even consider. My hands are slightly sweaty. In attempt to dry them off, I wipe my hands on the sides of my shorts.

I walk up to the front porch. Well, I guess what I would compare to a front porch. It's more of a tall entryway in front of the door with tall columns and a covering. I knock on the door. After a few seconds I hear feet trekking on the hardwood floor.

When the door opens, standing in the doorway is her brother. He doesn't say anything. This should be fun. "Hey, is Kinzleigh here? I was hoping I could talk to her."

He looks behind him and steps outside, shutting the door. "What do you want with her? Preston brought her home a few minutes ago, meaning, she obviously doesn't want to talk to you. If she did, you would have been the one to drop her off."

I guess I had that one coming. "Look, man, I know you don't know me, but it's all a big misunderstanding. If I could talk to her, I could explain."

Her brother is beefy like me. We're about the same height and both full of lean muscle. "I don't think so. Look, I'm not saying you're a bad guy, but you're only here visiting. Kinzleigh is . . . she isn't like most girls. She's headstrong and beautiful and has these twisted views when it comes to relationships. Right now, she's really on it, because of all my shit. I wish that wasn't the case, but it is. We're close, so my issues affect her and vice versa. If you've already screwed up, unfortunately, you're wasting your time. Trust me."

If the guy weren't so damn nice, I'd punch him in the face. Why can't he just let her decide for herself? "Are you saying you won't even tell her I'm here?"

He nods. "If I thought it would change the outcome I would, but she's already messed up over moving. She doesn't need more confusion. If she's upset, I won't further upset her. I'm sorry, man, but I think you should go and enjoy the rest of your time here, then head back home and forget about her." He turns and opens the door, disappearing inside.

If I can't get anywhere with him, it's pointless trying. I'm not really feeling the California sun anymore. Knowing what I'd be missing by staying here without seeing her, I'd rather just go back home.

I pull up at Ryland's shortly after leaving her house and walk into the pool house. As I come into the back bedroom, I pull out my phone and call a number from the Google search I made to get it. A female answers after the first couple of rings. "Los Angeles International Airport, Dana speaking, how can I help you?"

"I need to know when the next flight out from LAX to New Orleans is please."

"I can help you with that. Please hold while I check the system." I hear clicking of the keyboard before she comes back on the line. "The next available flight is scheduled for nine tomorrow morning with United Airlines."

"I'll take it."

"Your name?"

"Breyson Abercrombie."

"Okay, I show you had a ticket for Friday morning, will you be exchanging?"

"Yes, please."

"Okay, I have you booked on flight UA 504. I'll email your flight confirmation."

"Thanks," I say ending the call.

I begin shoving all of my things into my suitcase, with the exception of a change of clothes and my shower bag. It's now completely dark outside.

Since I have nothing else to do, I might as well go to bed. Before charging my phone, I send a text to Ryland to inform him of the change in my plans.

Me: Can you take me to the airport in the morning?

Ryland: What the hell for?

Me: I'm just not feeling it anymore. There hasn't been anything but drama since I've been here. I think I'm going to head back home.

Ryland: Things go bad with Kinzleigh?

Me: I never got past her brother.

Ryland: Shit, dude, that's what I was afraid of. I'm sure Preston didn't hesitate to fill him in on the details. He can be a little bitch when it comes to her. What time is your flight?

Me: 9 a.m. is take off. I need to leave early.

Ryland: I got you covered.

Me: Thanks. I'll see you then. I'm going to bed.

I plug the charger into my phone and place it on the bedside table. I didn't even bother to read the last text from Ryland. I'm not in the mood anymore. I know he will try to talk me out of it, but I don't really feel like hanging around the easy girls while he hangs out with Presley. Nothing is going the way it usually does when I stay here. It's always Ryland and me doing stuff, but we're older now, and right now he's occupied. I don't want to be a little whiny bitch that demands boy time. This is best for everyone, so I grab my shower bag and head for the shower. I still can feel the chlorine from the pool like a film over my skin.

Ten minutes later, I emerge from the steam-filled bathroom, showered and in a clean pair of boxers. Lying down in the bed, it doesn't take long before I drift off to sleep.

FIFTEEN

Kinzleigh

It's midnight and I just crawled into bed. Preston dropped me off around seven and insisted he needed to talk to Konnor. After a day like today, I didn't want to argue. I ate a ham and cheese sub leftover from dinner earlier and took a shower. After that, I walked into the den upstairs and found Dad watching old home movies. He does it from time to time, reminiscing in the memories. He said it ensures he never forgets the details. If I catch him watching them, I sit on the arm of his leather recliner and lay my head on his shoulder, watching them alongside him.

I get underneath my oversized fluffy comforter and turn out my bedside light. Just as I'm getting comfortable, my door bursts open, shining the light from the hallway into my dark room. I sit up, realizing it's Presley. She waltzes in wearing pajama shorts and a tank. "Presley, what are you doing here?"

She jumps on my bed beside me, landing on her knees and palms. "You know I need bestie time after what happened earlier today. Plus, I need to talk some sense into you. I got the scoop and I'm going to have Lexi's ass on a platter when I see her. We will see what she thinks when I forget to catch her sorry butt next time she goes up in the air."

Now I'm really confused. "Mind telling me what you're rambling about?"

She sighs and places her keys and phone on the table, before moving to the other side of me, farthest from the door. She slides under the covers and turns on her side, facing me. "You know come hell or high water I'm always on your side, but I will always be honest and tell you when you're being a royal pain in my ass." She has such a potty mouth sometimes, but that is one thing that makes Presley, Presley. She is so sassy.

I roll my eyes and turn toward her. "How exactly am I being a pain in your butt? I can't wait to hear this."

"For starters, I get that you jump to conclusions because of what happened to Konnor, but would it have killed you to hear the boy out before you stomped off in a rage?" Weird, I thought she'd be pulling for her brother on this one. Back when we were kids we used to plot ways to become sisters. Ninety percent of the time the solution was she would marry Konnor; imagine that.

"He kissed me with a girlfriend after hitting on Lexi the same night. What do you want me to do? Maybe it was doing me a favor. I will not do to someone else what was done to Konnor."

"You always were the stubborn one. Kinzleigh, I talked to Ryland. He didn't hit on Lexi. As a matter of fact, it was the opposite. I knew she was lying when she said it to begin with, that's why I called her out on it. I can smell a lie from a mile away, regardless of the fact that she's horrible at it. She's such an obvious liar. The little jealous tramp just wanted him for herself." She is right; she's always been good about calling bullcrap.

"It still doesn't change the fact that he kissed me with a girlfriend," I say, needing to reiterate how wrong that is.

She sighs, clearly annoyed, though I don't exactly know why she's taking up for him in the first place. "Kinzleigh, when are you going to take off those rose-colored glasses you wear? When are you going to see the world for the bullshit that it is? Things happen, and people make mistakes, but you know what? We shouldn't be defined for those mistakes. You go to church every Sunday, but when it comes time to practice what you preach, you fall short every time. We can't all be as perfect as you are."

"So, what are you saying? I should just forget that he purposely omitted having a girlfriend, or *had* a girlfriend, and just go along like that's okay? I can't do that, Presley. Not only is it wrong to do that to his girlfriend, but also to me. I deserve to know something like that before I kiss someone. It goes against everything I believe. You know how strongly I feel about that. If you don't want to be faithful to someone, you shouldn't date them."

She exhales impatiently. "This is the part I was referring to about being a pain in my ass. Did you ever ask him if he had or has a girlfriend when you were thinking about losing your virginity to him? Hmm? Or what about when you were kissing him back?"

"Well, Presley, excuse me, but I would think it's an unspoken rule that you should mention that before you try and kiss someone. When he kissed me, I assumed that meant he was single. I may not know much about dating, but why would you kiss someone if you have a girlfriend?"

"Kinzleigh, I'm not saying that it wasn't wrong of him to kiss you on Friday with a girlfriend. What I'm saying is you should have given him the chance to explain his actions. If you had, you would have learned that he was only dating her because they were friends with benefits and he didn't want her to be a termed a slut." She pauses, as if thinking. "That sounds so dumb repeating it. I don't know, maybe it's a southern thing. Personally, I don't know why it matters. Anyway, he broke it off with her that night on the phone, because he wanted to spend more time with you, but didn't feel right about doing that to her. He even explained to her that he met someone he was interested in getting to know. I'm not excusing his initial screw-up, but at least he tried to make it right. Would you cut the boy some slack? You can deny it all you want, but I know you like him and want to see more of him too."

I roll onto my back and look up at the ceiling. I don't know what I'm supposed to do. I know she's right, but at the same time, this is becoming very complicated already and he is supposed to leave in like four days. "I don't know. It just seems like too much of a headache already. Could you have not told me all of this tomorrow? I've had enough for one day. First Preston and now this—it's too much to absorb."

"Preston? Jeez. What now?"

"Nothing." I lie. "Continue."

"I could have waited until tomorrow, but then he wouldn't be here. He scheduled a flight out tomorrow morning, because he came over to talk to you and Konnor wouldn't let him through the door. He decided he would rather go back home than to stay here with you not speaking to him. Ryland is freaking out about it, because he only sees him twice a year."

All I can do is blink. He came here to talk to me? Konnor didn't even tell me? That's not like him at all. "What exactly are you proposing I do?"

"I could take you to the airport in the morning. I know which gate he's at. You could easily clear up all this miscommunication." That sly grin comes over her face, but then it disappears. Sadness appears in her voice. "Mom told me about you moving."

"Why didn't you tell me you knew?"

"I don't know. I guess I was waiting around for you to tell me yourself, hoping it wasn't real when you didn't. I want you to do something for me and I'm completely serious. This isn't a joke to me. You have to promise, and you know me and you never break promises."

"Okay, what is it?"

A tear rolls down her nose. "I want you to live this year. Get out there and do something you wouldn't normally do. I know I won't be there to push you, but I want you to venture out and have fun. You're such a likable person when you let yourself go; free the inner spirit that I know you keep buried deep inside." I've never seen Presley cry; not since we were little, anyway. It's a little overwhelming.

Before I know it, tears are falling down my face too. "Hey, you know you'll always be my best friend, right? I know I can be difficult sometimes, but I love you. You're the only sister I've ever had. It's only for a year and I'm coming back. This won't change anything between us. We'll still go to the same college, right? Be dormies like we always planned? Pinky promise me."

I hold out my hand, extending my pinky. When we were kids we saw on a movie where two people made a blood promise and thought it would be neat, so we made a blood promise we would go to the same college. It's silly, I know, but she's always been my sister, blood or not, and we always do everything big together.

A smile breaks free in the midst of her tears. "You're damn right," she says, linking her pinky with mine. "I wish you didn't have to go. Senior year is going to suck without my partner in crime. What about cheerleading captain? What about cheerleading in general?"

"Come on, you know I'm usually just holding you back. You're the co-captain, so that automatically makes you captain and Madison had the third highest score at tryouts; she will become co-captain. As for cheerleading, well, I guess I'm hoping this school has a decent squad and an extra spot."

This is so much harder than I thought now that it's real. "Will you visit on Christmas break?"

She wipes her eyes. "Of course I will. You can show me around and introduce me to some southern boys. I've always wanted to meet a real cowboy, and if any are like Breyson, I can't wait. That boy is hot, Kinzleigh."

Leave it to Presley to turn this into something about guys. I push her shoulder lightly, laughing. "Count on it. Let's call it a night if I've got to be up at the butt crack of dawn to go to the airport."

Her face lights up like a kid on Christmas morning. "I knew you'd see it my way. Night, sweetness," she says and kisses my cheek, before turning over to go to sleep. Always the one to have a glutton for punishment . . .

SIXTEEN

We pull into LAX at 8AM sharp. "You owe me a white chocolate mocha after this," I say groggily. "Extra-large."

I am not a morning person. I like my sleep, unlike a certain perky brunette I know. I don't think the girl ever sleeps more than five hours a night. She was up, showered, and dressed in a pair of my clothes when I was just stirring from my slumber. It's a tragedy we weren't sisters, a universal mishap. We do everything together and can wear all the same clothes except for jeans, because I'm short and she's tall.

She reaches over and squeezes my hand in an endearing way. "You do this and I'll buy you as many mochas as your heart desires. I'm proud of you, because I know this is hard for you. Ryland said they are sitting outside the gate."

We step out of her white Mercedes in the parking garage. "Let's just get this over with." Heading for the main entrance of the airport, we catch a ride to the door. "What terminal is it, Presley?"

She looks down at her phone, scrolling through a text message. "Terminal seven, flight UA 504 to New Orleans. Departure is 9 AM." I head in the direction of the terminal before I remember they won't let you through without a security check and boarding pass. Crap!

I stop mid step and turn toward Presley. "I can't get back there without a ticket, and we're already pushing for time."

A smirk comes across her face as she holds up a printout. "I have the ticket confirmation. We just need to get the boarding pass, so come on."

My amusement shows. "You spent money on a flight ticket? Isn't that a little pricey for this?"

She waves me off. "Do you know how many air miles we have on the credit card? Flying to Dad is no different than driving a car. He does it multiple times a week. Sometimes daily."

This is true. If Mr. Dunagin gets wind of a deal that will make him money, he's gone within the hour. Buying property for cheap and building on it is something he does all over the place.

We get to the cashier window. Presley slaps the piece of paper down on the countertop. The attendant looks at the printout. "Good morning, Miss Baker. Do you have some identification?"

"Sure," I say, and dig through my purse for my wallet. Pulling it out, I remove my license and hand it to the woman in front of me.

She clicks away on the keyboard in front of her and then hands my license back to me. "I have your seats confirmed. Here is your boarding pass. You will be in terminal seven. Enjoy your flight."

She smiles and hands me my pass. "Thank you."

We hurry to airport security and wait impatiently until I've been checked. It's almost boarding time and I'm running full speed. I cannot believe I'm doing this over a guy. A guy I'm not even serious with! If I didn't feel so bad about jumping to conclusions I wouldn't be.

As I come into the seating area, I stop to catch my breath. I spot Ryland standing next to the terminal looking nervous. He's talking to Breyson, who has his back turned toward me. As Ryland catches sight of me, a smile spreads across his face. I don't think I've ever seen him smile so big.

I'm not sure what he said, but Breyson turns around, staring me down. I can't move. Maybe I should have planned what I was going to say. Which is what, exactly? I always seem to be at a disadvantage around him.

He looks a little surprised, but he smiles. I'm not sure I'll ever be immune to him. I've heard the term *panty-dropping smile* and it never made sense until now. It makes me slightly weak in the knees seeing him smile.

He drops his bag next to Ryland and begins walking toward me, never breaking eye contact. He stops inches away from me. When he looks me in the eyes like this, I can't look away, as if he's forcing me.

"Hi," I say nervously.

"Hi," he quips back, his smile brightening.

"Why are you leaving early?"

"I didn't have a reason to stay."

"What reason do you need? I thought you were here to visit your cousin."

"I just figured if I couldn't hang around with you, I didn't have a reason to be here. You've kind of grown on me," he says teasingly, but then he shrugs. "And besides, he's having fun with Presley right now."

I can't help but to smile. "I guess you've kind of grown on me too."

"Look, I'm sorry about Friday. I shouldn't have done that to you. I did end things as soon as it happened, though. I swear. I should have told you about her. And about what happened at the party . . ."

I place my hand over his mouth, stopping him. "It doesn't matter. The only thing that matters is that you're upfront with me from here on out. No more omitting the truth. Honesty is a make or break with me."

He nods and steps closer. I remove my hand from his mouth, but he grabs my wrist and kisses my palm. Releasing it moments later, he cups my neck in his hands, tilting my head back for me to look up at him. "You have my word."

He then tilts his head slightly to the side and leans in, pressing his soft lips to mine. Each time our lips touch, tingles spread all over my body. Our tongues meld together, his commencing the flicking and twisting with mine in a playful jousting match. Our mouths fit together perfectly and his breath tastes of fresh mint, barely numbing my tongue.

The world fades away, and for a moment it's just us—two people becoming lost in each other. I may be young, and I may be headstrong, but even I know saying goodbye in four days is going to be the hardest thing I'll ever do.

SEVENTEEN

Kinzleigh

As the sun beams in through the windows, my eyes pop open. Glancing at my phone, I notice it's still early. I have too much to do to sleep. It's my last day with Breyson and I'm determined to make it count. I still haven't figured out the best way to tell him goodbye.

Sitting up, I rub my hands over my eyes, trying to wake up.

Swinging my body to place my feet on the floor, I stand from the bed and walk toward my balcony door. The large, panel windows are covered in sheer curtains the same hot pink as my satin sheets.

I love my room.

It's decorated in a black, pink, and gray color palette with Eiffel towers scattered about and a few black and white photos framed on the wall of the city. My parents always take us on a family vacation every year and the year we went to Paris I completely fell in love. I must admit; it's weird that I don't want anything to do with love, but my favorite place is known for the very thing I want nothing to do with—the city of love.

I open my balcony door and walk outside. From my balcony I can see the beach in the distance. I love sitting out here, people watching and staring at the palm trees and the ocean. If I wake up early enough, sometimes I can even hear the surf.

Leaning against the railing, I close my eyes and bask in the sunlight warming my face and shoulders. It's hard to believe four days have passed since that day in the airport. It's all been very surreal. There is only one word to describe the emotions I've experienced—magical.

Breyson and I have been together the entire four days with the exception of sleeping. We've done just about everything time would allow.

Monday, when we left the airport, I took him around Los Angeles. He said this is his third year in Laguna, but I wanted this year to be special. I wanted him to experience the beauty and the personality of California the way it's meant to be experienced. I wanted him to see what I love about this place. I didn't only do it for him. Since I'm about to be gone for a year, it was a little for myself too. To date, it was one of best days of my life.

Tuesday, we hung around Ryland's pool house. The four of us swam for most of the day, playing pool games, and his parents grilled lunch for us. They are really nice people and a lot like my parents. We even played board games inside. I felt like a kid again.

Last night, though, was the best night yet. Breyson picked me up from my house when the sun was going down. He had told me earlier that day to dress comfortable. I had no idea what he had planned, but I was full of excitement. Once we got in the truck, we headed over to the beach. I didn't think much of it until we got there and I saw he had a picnic planned. I didn't know people even did that anymore, other than in the movies.

I couldn't help but smile when he pulled out that big picnic basket from the backseat. He slipped up and said his Aunt Susan helped put it together. We walked down to the beach hand-in-hand. He spread out a blanket and we ate fruit and sandwiches. Then we laid underneath the stars, snuggled up next to each other, and talked for hours.

It's amazing how much alike we are. He is as devoted to football as I am with cheerleading. He gets it—to want something so bad you'd do anything to obtain it. And I think that's what makes setting aside my fears for a little fun easier.

He has been nothing but a gentleman; quite the contrary to what I thought mere days ago. We have had quite a few heated make out sessions, but nothing more. Those times were absolutely amazing. No words will ever be enough to explain the way kissing him makes me feel.

So, I've decided that tonight—the fifteenth of June—I will give myself to him. At least in every way I am willing. I may not give my heart away, but I will give him my body. I realized throughout the week there really isn't a reason to hang onto my virginity anymore. If I had any intention of getting married I might save it, but that isn't the case with me.

With that thought, I don't want to be a slut either. I love Presley and she is always really picky and safe with whom she hooks up with, but all that is a job in itself. The only reason I have made this decision is because come tomorrow morning, Breyson will be hundreds of miles away. It will be special, but not permanent.

Tonight, I even have the house to myself. The timing couldn't be more perfect. Mom and Dad left this morning for Turks and Caicos, to celebrate their twenty-fifth anniversary. They won't be back until Sunday night.

Konnor is with Kyle in LA for the night at some event that has several bands playing. They decided to get a hotel to avoid a late drive, they said, but I know it's really to party.

I have all day to prepare for Breyson coming over. Today he promised Ryland they could do guy things since he's spent so much time with me. I told him we could just watch movies and hang out since he has to get up so early for his flight. He is supposed to come over this evening.

I need to put together a mental list of what all I need to do. Isabella, the housekeeper, has already cleaned the house for the week, so everything is tidy for tonight. I thought about making a trip to the mall to pick out some lingerie and candles, maybe even a new outfit. I get one chance to do this. I'm determined to get it right.

I told him not to eat dinner, because I was going to attempt cooking. I'm not really sure why, because there are only a few things I can cook from watching Mom in the kitchen. If I fail, there is always take-out.

Walking into my bedroom, I make up my bed and pick up what I messed up since Isabella cleaned. I'm a neat freak and well-organized person, but I haven't been home much over the past few days. Karate chopping the middle of the decorative pillows to make a homey crease just like they do on staging shows, my bed is finished. I remove my favorite Lavender and Vanilla spray from my bedside table and spray my bed, so it will smell nice later.

Since I showered last night, I am going to wait until right before he comes over to shower, so I'll be freshly cleaned and shaved. I am nervous about having sex, since obviously, I've never done it before. Opening my dresser drawer, I pull out a pair of white denim shorts and a t-shirt, pulling them on. I tousle my curly hair and pull it into a low side ponytail to stay cool, before putting on my sneakers.

I imagine it will probably be busy at the mall, so I need to get started if

I'm going to get back in time and have everything ready by the time Breyson gets here. I put on a pair of simple hoop earrings for the finishing touch and reach for my purse.

Standing in my doorway, I turn and look at my room one last time before I go. Next time I see it everything will change. I may only get to stay in the house I love another couple of weeks, but I will always have something to remember it by.

I plan the menu on the descent down the stairs. I think I am going to put salmon steaks on the grill with asparagus wrapped in bacon. It's easy and I know it will be edible. Excitement bubbles under my skin. After seventeen years, I'm finally going to do this. I close my eyes. I just hope I can make it memorable for him too . . .

I pull into the mall parking lot in record time. I lock my doors and head for the entrance. First stop on my list is the bath and body store. I usually keep a stock of everything scent related, but I haven't done much shopping lately with my busy schedule for cheerleading.

Walking in the store, I immediately notice the signage advertising a big sale they run a few times a year. Perfect. I grab a mesh shopping bag and begin loading it down with a little bit of everything; from scented plug-in refills to candles and sprays and body products in all different scents.

It doesn't take me long to make my purchase and head toward the lingerie store. Every time I go in this store now, I will think of the day Breyson was in here with me. It's the funniest thing; all it takes to embarrass a guy is to bring him to a women's store.

As I walk into the store with my bags in tow, a store associate immediately greets me. "Hello, I'm Heather. Is there anything in particular you're looking for?"

"Maybe. I'm trying to buy something for someone, but I'm not sure what to buy." Personally, it embarrasses me to be in here buying this type of clothing—undergarment might be a better word, or swatch of fabric. I've never bought actual 'lingerie' before. My mother would kill me.

The associate looks to be in her mid-twenties and can obviously sense my discomfort. "I see. Is this someone a special guy in your life?" I nod, because really, I don't know what else to say. The truth of what we are is irrelevant to the purchase. "I think we can find something for you."

She smiles, discretely moving to the other side of the store. "Follow me, sweetie."

She heads toward the back of the store with me on her heels, stopping in the center of all the frilly and sexy lingerie. I'm getting more nervous the more I see, taking in fabric hanging from hangers that become scantier as the store deepens.

She walks me into the dressing room area, unlocking a door for me. "Tell me what you're looking for. Do you want something you can wear under clothes or something to change into?"

She makes a valid point; one in which I have not thought of. Maybe I should have chosen the outfit before I came here. I shrug my shoulders. "I'm not sure. I never got that far in the thought process. I'm not even sure what I'm wearing. I'm sorry I'm not much help. I've never really bought anything like this before."

"You don't have to be sorry, hun. That's why I'm here. Luckily for you, I'm a pro," she says, winking at me with a grin spread across her face.

She stands there looking me over. "Let's see. We probably want to stay sexy, but simple, considering your age." She pauses, and then taps her index finger over her pursed lips. "You have a killer body and gorgeous hair. What if we go for something under the clothes, so you can knock his socks off and it be unexpected?"

Clearly, I am out of my league here. "Whatever you think. I'm your model, so you can do as you please." Her face takes on a mischievous look. Apparently, I just made her day.

She opens the dressing room door she previously unlocked and leads me inside. "Stay here and I'll be right back with some things for you to try." Disappearing into the store, she comes back about fifteen minutes later with an armful of items. Oh my . . .

As I'm leaving the store, much later than I'd hoped, I have concluded I never want to go through this experience ever again. I have tried on more lingerie than I care to see again in my lifetime. Some of which was flattering and others that even make a slim person feel overweight.

I have no idea what time it is, because I've been stuck in a dressing room for what seems like forever, with different items being shoved at me. Now I know why people just hire personal shoppers for this sort of thing, or even better, order online and hope it fits.

I ended up leaving with a matching set that consists of some really sexy black and pink underwear, a skimpy bra, a garter belt, and stockings to go under my clothing.

I'll admit, with my natural skin tone pink is one of my favorite colors to wear. I'm comfortable in what she chose. It's sexy yet simple, just like she said.

The push-up bra is a black undertone covered in a lace design of dark pink with a small bow between the breasts. The panties are the matching design, a thong, with the same bow in the center of the back, sitting right above the beginning of my bottom. I didn't try on the bottoms, but I know it will look really good all put together.

The last stop is a boutique close by and then home to get ready. Looking at the time on my cell phone, I realize it's going to have to be a quick stop. I only have another hour or so before I need to be back at home, and traffic will take up a good portion of that time allotment.

I've gotten a few texts from Presley asking if she could give Breyson my number and he has asked each time we're together, but my answer remains the same. I don't want any complications. As much as I would love to talk to him more, it's not plausible living in different states. And he's also leaving tomorrow. There is no reason to continue talking once he's gone. It will only make things worse. When he leaves here I want him to take away a fond memory and that be that.

There are a few popular boutiques in town. They all have really cute clothing. I pick the closest one to me and pull in. As I walk inside, I notice a few people, but it's mostly quiet. I can already tell I'm going to do some damage today just by the things in the window. Presley would have a fit if she found out I came in here without her. We rarely shop separately. If I weren't in such a cramp for time, I would have told her to meet me here.

I walk through the store grabbing everything that catches my eye in my size. One thing I've learned when trying to find *the outfit* is to grab a few contenders and choose later. An outfit always looks different the second time you put it on, sometimes better and sometimes worse. The first time your mind is always too overwhelmed to judge how you really feel about it.

Once I've filled my arms, I leave them at the counter and continue on my shopping escapade to the shoes and jewelry. Of course, I can't omit my most precious accessory—handbags.

I finally make it out of the store with just enough time to get home and get myself ready before Breyson is supposed to be at my door. My backseat is loaded down with bags from my shopping spree. Presley and I always end up buying way more than we intend. It's an addiction I never want to break. As long as I can cheer and shop I don't need anything else.

I pull into my garage with absolutely no time to spare. If I'm going to get everything ready, I need to get a move on it. I unload all the bags from my car, but it takes a few trips. I remove all the candles from the bag and begin lighting them sporadically throughout the first floor of the house, saving my favorite for my bedroom and bathroom. Next comes plugging in the oil scents and spritzing the linens and furniture with the matching room spray.

As I finish everything downstairs, I grab the rest of my bags and run up the stairs toward my room. I toss them onto the bed and finish setting out and lighting the candles around my room.

Breathing heavily from rushing, I turn on the string lights that hang from the canopy over my bed. Sheer charcoal gray curtains hang from the canopy rail to the floor on each of the four corners of my king-sized bed. By the time he gets here, it should be dark outside. The wall directly across from my bed has my dresser as well as a wall-mounted television we can stream movies on.

I look around the room. Everything should be set. I can already smell the fragrance filling the room. It's a light and soothing smell from the sleep line. I walk into the bathroom and start the shower. One thing I love about this house is that I have my own connecting bathroom, as does Konnor.

Freshly showered thirty minutes later, I grab my new underwear and put them on. I'm now in the negative for time, because I had to shave everything, including places I don't normally shave. Tuesday night when Presley and I left Ryland's house, she insisted that we have a little talk. If I've never thought before that having a friend know everything about you is awkward, I do now.

In this little girl talk 101, she informed me that girls having sex no longer have hair down there. I have always groomed with a trimmer, but never totally rid the area, in mild terms. According to her, if I am going to go through with this, then I need to be up to speed with everyone else. I have never done it, because for obvious reasons, I have never had to.

And well, it took longer than I thought in my effort to not cut myself with the razor right before a guy has his business and eyes down there. I look down at myself, taking in the sudden bareness of my pelvis. Bald. It's a sight that makes me feel like a little girl waiting on puberty. Maybe it's something I'll quickly get used to.

I exhale, trying to rid the nerves that have decided to go haywire in my stomach. I look out over the bed at everything I bought today. I finally decide on a pair of bright palazzo pants in a paisley pattern. The top I bought with it is a solid aqua boat neck cotton shirt with three-quarter length sleeves. I move it to the side and grab up the remaining clothes in handfuls and toss them into my closet. I will have to put them up later.

Shutting the closet door, I walk back over to the bed. I have to put on the garter belt and stockings before I can put on my clothes. Staring down at the contraption in front of me, I'm a little intimidated. The store associate gave me instructions on how to put them on, but because you never try on panties or stockings, I don't have hands-on experience. Linking the garter belt around my waist, sadly, is the easiest part.

Removing the stockings from the pack, I sit on the bed, holding them out in front of me. They are a black sheer in color and look complicated. Mom has tried to get me to wear stockings to church, but I'm usually bare or covered with leggings. I pull one foot onto the bed and pull the stocking over my foot. I manage to maneuver it up my leg close to the clasp that hangs from the garter belt. Standing up, I try to figure out this whole mechanism.

After a few tries I get the front done, but now I have to get the back hooked. People put forth a lot of effort just to have it taken off. It takes longer to get the back one connected, but I manage. The second leg doesn't take as long as the first. I look myself over in the full-length mirror attached to my closet door. Turning around and seeing the finished product has me excited. Maybe it's worth it to feel this sexy.

I pull on my clothes and a pair of flats to cover up my stockings for later. After drying my hair, I decided to straighten it instead of wearing it in my usual curls. As I'm putting on my gloss—the last of my makeup—the doorbell rings.

Shoot! I was hoping to have a head start on dinner, but I guess I can cook while we talk. I pop a piece of gum in my mouth and start for the door.

When I get there, I open it to Breyson looking sexier than ever. He is wearing a pair of faded denim jeans, hanging low on his hips and a pair of brown leather shoes, as well as a fitted dark-pink polo that looks amazing against his tanned arms. His hair is gelled in the front and he's holding a bouquet of pink Gerber daisies. I smile at the gesture, because he remembered they are my favorite from our conversation last night. He holds them out for me to grab. "You remembered."

"Of course, I remembered," he replies. "I remember everything you say. I thought it might brighten your day." I go to grab the flowers and he pulls me in for a hug, sending my face directly into his broad chest.

He smells so good. I'm not sure what scent he wears, but if I ever find a bottle I'm buying it, though I'll never admit that to anyone. "What's this for?" I turn my head to the side, resting my cheek against the center of his chest.

"Me," he says. One little word and I'm already shaking. This boy is dangerous to me; like kryptonite. I love the feel of being wrapped in his strong arms. He walks me backward, inside the house, but never releases me. Once inside the door, he pushes it shut with the bottom of his foot. "I've missed you, beautiful girl. You're hell on my ego." His voice makes me close my eyes. The sound is hypnotic.

He grabs my chin and turns it up to face him. I know what's coming next. Will I ever be ready for the havoc it reaps on my body? Probably not. Do I still want it? Heck yes!

My heart starts palpitating in my chest the closer he gets to my lips. As his lips touch mine, my blood starts racing throughout my body. I can hear my pulse boom in my ears and I feel like I'm frozen in time.

His tongue lightly brushes mine, playing and teasing. He sucks my bottom lip into his mouth and his teeth graze the skin. My stomach starts clenching, and a need I've never had, until him, begins forming down below, making me want to be touched in response.

I wrap my arms around his waist and continue to kiss him. I could kiss him for hours. I get lost in an array of emotions that I can't stop. I hate what he's doing to me, but I love it all the same. He runs his fingers through my hair, cupping the back of my head with one hand and trails the other down to my waist. At this rate we won't make it to dinner, or to my room for that matter.

Reluctantly, I break the kiss. "It's good to see you too." I smile. Grabbing his hand, I tow him toward the kitchen. "Come on, I have plans for you."

As we make it into the kitchen, I stop next to the refrigerator, opening the door. "Can you cook?" He raises a brow as if he's really not sure.

I pretend to be offended. I may be well taken care of and my parents may have money, but they are still practical people. Mom has a housekeeper that comes once or twice a week and that is as dependent on someone else as she gets. My parents are very family-oriented people. Cooking and eating together is a big deal in our house. We always eat at the table with the exception of Super Bowl Sunday. Football is a big sport in this family and my parents always have a big party for Super Bowl.

"Are you scared I might poison you?" Reaching into the refrigerator, I pull out the wrapped salmon and set it on the island behind me. From the corner of my eye, I can see him watching me, but purposely I don't acknowledge him. I carry on as if he isn't standing beside me. I remove the asparagus and bacon next and place them beside the salmon.

"I didn't mean anything by it. I've just never known anyone my age that could cook. I guess you're a little more down-to-earth than I realized. I kind of took you for a high- maintenance girl." It's really cute that he thinks I'm upset. I think I may let him sweat a little more. It may be cruel, but it's amusing. A little fun never hurt anyone.

I make my way around the island to get out the dishes I need. "Can you start a grill?" I look into the cabinet as I speak, because if I look at him I am going to break. I grab a glass baking dish.

As I stand up, I place the baking dish down and grab the salmon, opening the wrapper. "Of course, I can start a grill. I have been man-handling the grill since I was tall enough to reach it."

"Good. If you walk outside the patio door, you'll see the grill on the left. I should be done seasoning this by the time you get back." Turning around, I begin searching through the spice rack for the seasonings I need.

As I'm standing against the countertop, a hand takes residence on top of the counter to each side of me. His body becomes flush with my backside. My heart rate quickens and my breathing becomes uneven.

He brushes my hair over my right shoulder. I can feel his warm breath tickle the back of my neck. On reflex my eyes close. He makes me weak and I need to be strong.

He kisses the top of my bare left shoulder and trails kisses up the side of my neck. He stops just below my ear. "Are you mad at me?"

His voice is low and seductive. How am I supposed to compete with this? He is playing in the major leagues and I'm still on a high school team. It's unfair how good he is at this. Oh, gracious, like now. He lightly licks the outline of my ear with the tip of his tongue. That feels . . . euphoric.

I turn around, trying to get some distance before I come unglued. Wrong move. He has a huge grin on his face, which is maybe an inch from mine. "Why would I be mad?" My voice breaks as it comes out, barely above a whisper.

Great, Kinzleigh, you're doing a swell job of being convincing.

He runs the tip of his index finger along my jaw line. "You're going to be the death of me, Kinzleigh Baker."

He continues his exploration down my neck and body, stopping at the small of my back. Resting his forehead against mine, he looks me in the eyes. It doesn't take a genius to know what he is doing. He is asking my permission to continue with his hands. In response, I place my hands over his, gliding them downward until they are perfectly covering my bottom.

His breathing becomes ragged and he closes his eyes as he squeezes his hands. He closes in for a kiss. It's much different this time. He is needy and choppy with his movements, twirling his tongue with mine. It's bittersweet. He picks me up, rubbing me against his front on the way, before setting me on top of the counter.

I wrap my arms around his neck, running my fingers through his hair. This is my last night to see Breyson Abercrombie and I'm going to cherish it. I return his kiss at full force, giving him everything I have. I kiss him for everything that tonight is. It's an end to something beautiful; something I will remember every day for the rest of my life.

Wrapping my legs around his waist, I pull him closer. He is a good bit taller than me. With me sitting on the counter, he is at eye level with me. He pulls me to the edge of the countertop, pressing me against him, allowing me to feel the effect of our little tryst in the kitchen. "I can't control myself around you. We are never going to make it through dinner. Why don't we just do something quick and go watch a movie?"

I will not let him get out of it that easily. I have been planning this all day. "No way. Get your butt outside and man the grill," I tease authoritatively, releasing him from my hold and then push on his chest for emphasis.

He backs away, holding his hands up in surrender. "Okay, okay. I'll be right back." He adjusts himself and turns as he walks toward the patio, stepping outside. I hurry back to the food—now sitting idle on the counter—to begin seasoning and preparing it for the grill. Heaven help me, because my nerves are taking a turn for the worst.

EIGHTEEN

Kinzleigh

The rest of dinner passed by uneventful. Mostly just small talk and glances between the two of us. Standing from the table, I walk to the sink, placing my plate inside. Breyson follows close behind me, doing the same.

I turn to face him as he grabs me by the waist. From behind, he grabs me by the inside of my legs, lifting me. I wrap my legs around him, interlocking my feet behind his waist and grab a hold of him by the shoulders. "What are you doing?"

"I can't take it anymore. I want to cuddle and kiss you until I have to leave." He walks to the living room, carrying me. "Where to?"

He stops in the living area where he met my parents a few short days ago. If only there was a button to make time stand still in those frames of life worth repeating. If someone asked me what moment in time I would want to hold onto, I'd say this week.

"My room. We have to go up the stairs, though, so you can put me down." He looks at me as if he would rather die than put me down.

He moves toward the stairs, but never looks away. I'm not sure how he can even see where he is going, but he climbs the stairs one step at a time. Something about that look leaves me wanting more. If I were interested in giving my heart away, it would be for him. It would never work, though.

When he stops at the top of the staircase, I know he is waiting for further instructions. "It's the room at the end of the hall."

Nerves are starting to take their toll on me. It's getting closer to the time I've spent all day preparing for. He opens my door and stops in the doorway. For the first time since he picked me up, he breaks eye contact to look around the room. He smiles and looks back at me. "This room is fitting for you."

Walking me inside, he lays me down carefully on the bed. He is so gentle with me, like he could break me if too rough. "It smells good in here. I feel like I could go to sleep."

I smile, because sleeping is not on the agenda for tonight. I have the rest of my life to sleep. I don't have the rest of my life to spend in his arms. And the fact that he's acting like he's not getting in my pants tonight makes me want to do this all the more. He hasn't tried anything since the couch before the pool party. I have a feeling when this almost ended early he cut out the possibility that he was still getting my virginity. He definitely is.

I seductively scoot backward on the bed. He watches me in amusement before getting on the bed himself, knees first. "Just so you know, we won't be sleeping anytime soon."

He crawls on his hands and knees until he is straddling me at the head of the bed. "What did you have in mind?"

"A little of this and a little of that." I tease, grabbing a fistful of his shirt and pulling him toward me. "I guess you'll just have to wait and see." I kiss his lips, hungry for his taste. I don't know what has gotten into me. I have gone from never kissing a boy to craving it, or him, in a matter of days.

I'm not sure how long we have been kissing, but a low growl radiates from his throat as he rubs himself against me, picking up pace. I can feel his need pressing between my legs as he lowers himself closer to me. I had a movie planned, but it can wait. I don't care about the movie anymore. I just want to feel him in every way possible. I am ready to move forward—more so than I'll ever be.

I sit up, pushing him back slightly so he is holding his weight on his knees, resting his butt on his heels. He rubs his hands over his face. I can tell he thinks he's gone too far. "Kinzleigh, I'm sorry. I'm really trying not to maul you like a bear. You're too damn sexy. I can't help myself," he says in frustration.

I press my index finger over his lips to stop him from talking. I raise my arms above my head to get my point across. His eyes widen in response as he bites his lower lip. "Kinzleigh, don't feel pressured to do anything. I'm okay with just kissing or doing nothing at all."

"Would you shut up already? You can lay the good boy act to rest for a while. I need the sexy Breyson to come out and play. Are you going to undress me or continue talking?" That was all it took and he moans. That voice does things to me that should be illegal. I still am not used to all these emotions and feelings roaming free throughout my mind and body. It leaves me feeling frustrated each time we stop kissing.

He grabs the bottom of my shirt and slowly pulls it up my body and over my head. It's dark outside, and the only lighting in here is the soft flicker of candlelight around the room and the dim glow from my string lights above my bed. It accentuates him, making him sexier than in the full light, if that's even possible. Tossing my shirt onto the floor beside my bed, he leans in and kisses me. His taste is like an aphrodisiac, making me deepen the kiss.

I run my hands along the band of his jeans, unsure of what to do next. Do I tell him what I want or just unbutton his jeans? He has the slightest trail of hair starting from his navel and running downward where it disappears into his jeans, tickling the back of my hand. His body is so hard and defined against the knuckles of my fingers.

I lightly caress my fingertips around to his back and up the seam of his spine, underneath his shirt, dragging it with me. I can feel goose bumps form beneath my touch. Once I reach underneath his arms, he breaks free from my lips and grabs it by the back collar, pulling it over his head and throwing it aside. He is the most beautiful thing I have ever seen. I know it's not the most masculine way to describe a man, but other words fail me.

He looks down at my bra-covered breasts. "Damn," he says, bending down and kissing my cleavage. He runs his tongue over my perky breast and down the crevice between the two, leaving a thin film of saliva in its wake. Thank you, Heather, at the lingerie store!

He presses kisses in a line down my center, stopping at the band of my pants. Grabbing my ankle in his hand, he pulls off my shoe, dropping it, and does the same with the other foot.

Sliding his fingers beneath the waistband of my pants, he begins inching them down slowly. I slightly lift my butt, so he can work them over my hips and down my legs. His breath hitches when he notices the rest of my hidden underwear. He sits back on his heels and raises my legs removing the remainder of my pants.

Disposing of them, he releases my legs to the bed. His eyes travel up my body and stop once our eyes meet. "You're absolutely stunning and I haven't even gotten you naked yet."

He backs up to the foot of the bed and stands before me. He really makes those jeans look good. I cross my legs from the increased pressure and sensitivity going on. The damp feeling makes me uncomfortable.

I prop up on my elbows, taking him in. When he notices what I'm doing he smirks and unbuttons his pants, revealing the top band of his boxers. He removes his shoes and slides his pants down with his thumbs, stepping out of them. "Are you sure your parents won't come home?"

"Yes. They called me when they landed."

"Your brother?"

I bite my bottom lip, trying not to laugh at the nervous undertone in his voice where Konnor is concerned. "He's been posting photos on Instagram. He's exactly where he's supposed to be, and drinking, so he's not going anywhere."

He nods, instantly relaxing. After removing his socks, he bends over toward the floor. My brows come together. "What are you doing?"

He stands up, holding out a condom. Now I feel stupid, because that never crossed my mind. I just nod.

He comes across the bed at record speed. Grabbing my waist, he pulls me down so that I'm lying flat. "Hey, stop it. I know that look and there is no reason for you to feel embarrassed. I love your innocence. Stop thinking it's a bad thing. Okay?"

"Are you always this perceptive? I'm not sure if I like being read like a book."

He shakes his head. "Only with you."

He leans down and presses his lips to mine. In one swift move he turns, pulling me on top to straddle him. The feel of his body beneath mine only turns me on more. He makes me feel small, and the way he looks at me sends an electrical sensation through my body that reminds me of the way a battery feels against your tongue.

Reaching behind me, he unclasps my bra and slides it off without ever breaking the kiss. He sits up, holding me in his lap. The closer we get to full nudity, the more nervous I become. I don't know what to expect. He places his palm against my cheek, rubbing his thumb lightly across my bottom lip. "Are you sure you want to do this? It's not too late to back out. You know I'll be gone tomorrow, and we'll never see each other again."

I don't even have to think it over. I nod my head, looking him in the eyes so he can tell it's the truth. "I know the facts. I want you, and I want to give to you the only thing I have to offer. I don't need to worry about tomorrow, because all I need is tonight. You don't need to worry about me clinging to you; it's why I don't want to exchange numbers. All we need is right now. We're alike, you know. I will never let someone break me, so yes, this is what I want. I've thought about it all week."

He smiles, pressing his forehead to mine. "Where have you been all my life, Kinzleigh Baker? It figures I would meet a girl version of myself and then never see her again." When he kisses me again, the emotion behind that kiss is overwhelming.

Wrapping his arm around my back to hold me against him, he turns, laying me back down against the bed. He unhooks the stockings from the garter and rolls each one, individually, down my legs.

He throws them over his shoulder and hooks each index finger inside the belt and my thong, pulling them down my legs in unison, until they are completely removed. I feel like I'm about to pass out from the nervousness. I've never been naked like this in front of anyone.

I press my legs together, feeling vulnerable. He shakes his head at me, opening them at the knees. "I want to see you; all of you."

I'm shaking now, and it's not from being cold. I can barely breathe. I'm afraid of it turning into a panic attack. I look up at the ceiling in an attempt to calm down. He touches his hand under my breast where my heart is pounding excessively. My breaths are coming out in short bursts.

He comes to rest between my legs and kisses me softly. "Damn, baby, you're shaking. Look at me." I do as he asked. He is directly above me looking down, holding himself off of me. "I won't do anything you don't want to do, okay? Just say the word and we'll stop."

His voice is already calming me down. "I'm okay. I'm just nervous." He leans to the side, holding his body on his left forearm and removes his boxers with his right hand.

I look down at him as he searches for the condom on the bed. My eyes widen at the sight before me. Oh gosh. I start to panic all over again. I try to calm myself before he notices. I will not do this again. It's humiliating. I have never seen one before, except a few times when Presley showed me a photo of one to tease me. I'm not sure what would be classified as big or small, but I'm pretty sure what I just witnessed is every boy's dream size. The pain that Presley mentioned comes to the forefront of my mind.

He pulls the condom wrapper between his teeth, tearing it at the edge. The word *Magnum* across the wrapper answers my question. Maybe it works like a needle—out of sight out of mind. I try to concentrate on him instead.

He removes the condom from the wrapper and slightly unrolls it on the tip of his thumb. His hand disappears from my direct line of vision. Moments later, he spreads my legs with his knee and rubs his finger down below; touching me in my most private spot. I can't even describe the way it feels when he slips a finger inside. "Damn, you're tight. It's snug on my finger and I'm a lot bigger. Are you sure you want to do this, baby?"

I nod and grab him behind the head, pulling him down to kiss me. I never thought I would like to be called baby, but something about it being from him makes it okay. "I've come too far to chicken out. Just go slow. I don't know what I'm doing, so it may not be that great for you."

I always hear girl talks about guys favoring girls that know what they are doing in bed. "Are you really worried about it not being good for me?"

"Maybe, don't guys like the girl to be on top and all?"

He settles back directly above me, looking me straight in the eyes. Grabbing my chin in his fingers, he angles my face to look at him. "Anything you have heard from a girl about what guys like, forget it. Girls that get around are only used for one thing—convenience. A girl like you is what every guy dreams of."

He kisses me from my forehead to my nose and down to my lips. I will never get used to the way I feel around him. It's a powerful emotion and a scary one. He kisses me soft and slow, marking me his.

No other kiss will ever come close in comparison. He moves one hand down my neck and over my breast, leaving excitement visibly behind. Once his hand is no longer visible, I feel a round tip swirl in the area down below, being rubbed up and down against me. This is it. It's hard to enjoy the kissing with all these stupid nerves.

Just then he pushes in slightly and releases my lips. That wasn't so bad. "You ready, baby?"

Ready? Ready for what?

"What do you mean? What did you just do?" He smiles and places a chaste kiss on my lips.

"That was just the tip, baby. Do you want me to stop?" I shake my head for him to continue. He grabs my lips with his in a hurry, and before I have time to think he thrusts forward. I feel a tear. One word enters my mind: pain. A searing, burning pain. I want to cry and scream out, but I will not let myself. I've never been great about enduring physical pain; just blocking out the emotional.

Once he has filled me to capacity, he stops and looks down at me. A tear trickles down each side of my face. "I'm so sorry. Are you okay? Do you want me to pull out?"

He looks truly concerned, but I can't think of anything but the pain. Oh the pain. It throbs with my pulse. He begins rubbing my hair. "Baby, talk to me. Hell, I'll stop."

Before he moves I grab his face and look him in the eyes. "No, just give me a minute. Okay?" He nods and wipes a tear from my face.

"I don't like seeing you in pain, Kinzleigh. This is messing with my head. It's not worth it if you're in pain. I can pull out." My body must be over the initial shock, because the pain has worn down to a dull ache and has been replaced with desire to continue.

I grab his waist and hold him between my legs, spreading them wider to accommodate his size. "I'm fine. Breyson. I just wasn't prepared for that amount of pain. I was warned, but I didn't listen. It's not so bad now, but I need you to move. Sitting here isn't enough. I need friction." He scans my face, obviously trying to read my emotions. When he can tell that I'm serious, he starts to smile.

As he begins to thrust in and out, slowly, it starts to feel blissful. His eyes never stray from mine the entire time. "You feel so good. It's not going to take me long."

I begin kissing him, memorizing the way his lips feel against mine. I'll never forget this day as long as I live. The sight before me will be forever branded in the banks of my memory.

He places his hand between us as he continues; touching another private area with the tip of his thumb that I've heard of, but never felt. "You remember the pool house, baby?"

He picks up pace, causing me to close my eyes. So that's how he did that? I nod. "Baby, look at me. Please. I want to see your face when you come."

I open my eyes at the feel of his finger making circular motions alongside him penetrating me. The different types of feelings working together have me lost in a sense of euphoria. It's taking over my body and consuming my mind. "When you feel like that again, baby, relax."

His voice is mesmerizing, and just like that the feeling from the pool house returns. I arch off the bed as it takes over. It pulsates through my body, consuming every part of me.

I begin moaning uncontrollably. "Breyson." Everything is tightening and my body shudders. It's like everything is going in slow motion.

"That's it, baby. God, bless. I can't hold out any longer. You're too tight. Shit." His voice comes out raspy and low. He thrusts inside me once more and stills. "Fuck, you feel amazing."

I run my fingers through his hair. He's breathing hard. I'm not ready for it to be over. For once, I'm terrified I'll never be the same after this. Maybe I'm not as strong as I think I am. I just want to feel his lips on mine. I always hide my emotions or block them out completely, but this once I'm going to let him feel all of me.

This is it. This is the end of something beautiful. He expects me to come pick him up and drive him to the airport in the morning, but I can't do it. Call me a coward, but I can't tell him goodbye. I know I will break down and give him my number, but I can't. We don't live in the same place; making anything more virtually impossible. I'll have to write it in a letter and send it with Presley. I will remember this blond-haired blue-eyed boy for the rest of my life.

His breathing calms and he looks down at me. We just stare at each other for I don't know how long. He has a look on his face that I imagine mirrors mine. It's one of those bittersweet things. One where it's been more of a dream than reality, but all good things must come to an end.

I could never tell him how I feel, but I can show him. Pulling him in, I kiss him with everything in me. For the first time in my entire life and the last, I put myself out there for a guy. I put everything into this kiss, telling him that even though the universe isn't on our side, and distance isn't our friend, that I'll remember him forever.

And from his panicked return of his kiss, he knows this is goodbye.

NINETEEN

Breyson

I can't get last night out of my head, and I'm afraid getting it out is going to be harder than I imagine. What I wouldn't give to be right back with her in my arms or buried inside her. She was supposed to be taking me to the airport, but I knew from the look when we said goodbye, that was it.

She's not coming, but why? I wish I knew. I'm standing in the driveway of Ryland's house with all my bags, ready to head to the airport. I have already said my goodbyes to my aunt and uncle. Ryland is on standby to give me a ride, but I told him to give me a few minutes to see if Kinzleigh shows up.

After a night like last night, I know my head is going to be forever fucked-up. My mind continuously replays the entire scene—in great detail—in my head, as if it's stuck on repeat. It makes me want to pull out a bottle of Jack and blast rock music to manually override the thoughts running around up there, and I may do just that when my brothers pick me up at the airport.

How do I go back to sleeping with easy girls after a taste of perfection? The thought alone disgusts me. I knew better than to let myself have her. One taste and I'm hooked. Something about her has me on edge constantly.

I didn't sleep at all last night. I kept staring at my phone like it would make her text me. Before I left her house, I gave her my number. She insisted she didn't want it, but I left it in her hand—physically balling her hand into a fist around the torn piece of paper. The ball is in her court since she refuses to give me hers.

I'm about to go inside after Ryland when Presley's white Mercedes pulls in the driveway. She isn't who I expected to see, but I find myself searching the passenger seat in hopes to see one beautiful blonde. "She's not here," she sighs as she steps out of the vehicle. "I know that's who you're looking for."

"Where is she?" It's the first time I've noticed Presley looking bummed since I met her a week ago today. She bends over into her car, reaching in the center console. When she stands to face me, she has a folded piece of paper in her hand. She begins walking toward me, not giving anything away.

"She's not coming. Kinzleigh is not one to get emotionally involved with anyone. I don't know what you've done to her, but I got a call this morning from her in a panic that she needed a favor. I haven't seen her this strung out since her grandmother died. I was afraid this was going to happen, but I pushed it anyway." She stops before me and grabs my suitcase by the handle. Handing me the piece of paper, she begins rolling my bag toward her car. "Come on. Let's go."

"I don't need a girl to get my bag. Ryland can drive me." I'm aggravated, because I'm not a damn charity case. If Kinzleigh wants to coward away instead of telling me she doesn't want to drive me, fine, but I don't need any favors. After all, she is the one that told me this was nothing but a fling, so why can't she just drive me to the airport and say goodbye.

"I know you don't, but from the looks of her this morning, I have a feeling when you read that letter you may have some questions. I'll be the one that knows the answers if anyone does, so let's go." One thing I've learned from my mom is to never argue with a woman. You're a fool if you do and you'll surrender in the end, so you may as well save the energy. She places my bag in the back seat and shuts the door.

She pulls out of the driveway in a hurry, obviously not worried about speed limits. With a car like this, I can't say I blame her. "She went through with it, didn't she? She slept with you." That's a way to rip off the Band-Aid.

"It's none of your business. I don't kiss and tell. I have more respect for girls than that. It's one reason Lexi was able to lie on me so easily." I look over at her and she raises a brow at me.

I should have known that wouldn't work with her. The two of them are too close. I nod silently and turn to look out the windshield as the images of touching her and filling her replay through my mind.

I've got to get a freakin' grip. What is wrong with me? She's just a girl—

one that I'll never see again. This kind of thing happens all the time. That's part of the appeal to vacation when you're single. I need to release all this pent-up frustration when I get home.

"I thought so," she voices in a low tone. She says nothing more; just watches the road in front of her. I'm not sure what is going on in that head of hers. Girls are the most complicated creatures on the planet. They say they want one thing and mean another. I guess now is as good a time as any to read this letter. I unfold it carefully to avoid it tearing.

Breyson,

I know you must hate me for sending Presley in my place, and for that I'm sorry. I really did want to drive you to the airport. I tried to talk myself into it so many different times, which is why I didn't forewarn you of the change in plans, but the truth is—I can't do it.

I can't look you in the eyes and tell you goodbye. Please don't misunderstand; it's not because of last night, and yet it is. I really don't know how to explain, so I'll give it my best shot.

I knew you would be leaving today, which is one reason I let last night happen. What I didn't realize was the way I have come to feel about you. Last night made it clear for me. I can't explain these emotions and I don't want them in my life.

I cannot let something we knew was ending interfere with all my plans. I've worked too hard to block out any emotional contact to change now. This is just a setback I can overcome. With that said, I know seeing you will make it harder on me and I will cave by giving you my number.

I hope you can understand how hard that has been for me. I've thought it over so many times, but it will only make things worse. I will not be that girl, Breyson. The one that follows a guy around like a little lost puppy. You don't have to worry; I shred yours, so I won't be contacting you.

You are a weakness to me I can't explain. A lethal dose of poison injected straight into my heart. I will not allow myself to be vulnerable to that kind of pain. I am terrified of what might happen if I allowed myself more of you; like an addiction you can't fight or a drug you can't live without.

I am writing this to you so you will know you are the closest I've come to feeling something for someone and you will also be the last. Last night I wanted to show you what you do to me. How you make me feel. I wanted you to be able to hold onto that forever, knowing we had one spectacular week we can hold close.

This week has been beautiful and I will forever cherish every memory and moment. I will always remember your touch to my body and your lips on mine. My virginity was a gift to you. You have forever marked me and ruined me for anyone else's touch. You set the bar high on how sex should be when you could have been selfish. You will make one lucky girl happy someday. I wish you the best.

With love,

Kinzleigh

Without thought, I punch the dash. This is the last thing I need. Not because of what she said, because for the first time I actually feel the same way. Dropping the letter to the floor, I place the heels of my hands against my eyes. I'm so angry my eyes gloss over, burning my eyes begging for release. What the hell did I get myself into? The one time I have feelings for a girl other than sex, she has to be just as stubborn as me or worse. Long distance can work. People do it all the time.

"Are you done trying to break my car?" she asks sarcastically. I had forgotten for a second Presley was in here.

"Sorry. I wasn't prepared for that and it pisses me off." I have to find a way to forget her. I have no idea how, but she has left me no choice. "Why is she so damn hardheaded?"

She takes a deep breath, as if the answer to that question will take a while to explain. "How to explain Kinzleigh Baker is like trying to explain advanced algebra to a toddler. It's impossible. I've been trying to get her to take a chance on someone since we started high school. She somewhere down the line developed this warped view of love, or hell, even just dating. I've even talked to Konnor about it and we can't figure it out. She has parents that have been hopelessly in love since college and her grandparents since high school on both sides. She has it set in her head that if she allows herself to like a guy, she won't get to fulfill her dreams. It's like she's afraid if she loves someone, or even just likes someone, that has to be it. That she can't do anything else. I have to say, though, that you are the only person that's actually been given a shot. Whatever you're doing, you're doing right. I just wish you both weren't so far apart. You two would likely be together if you lived here."

I can tell from the look on her face it's genuine. "Did she tell you where she is moving? I have asked her over and over, but she refuses to tell me."

She shakes her head. "Well, she told me the state, but not exactly what city it will be. She's been so upset, I'm not even sure she knows. My mom told me, I think, but I doubt I was listening past the point of 'moving'. Because I don't remember. Come to think of it, I haven't even asked where you're from. That's rude of me."

She smiles. I can see why Ryland likes this girl. She doesn't take crap off anyone, but she is still cool to hang out with and she has a sweet side I don't think she shows much.

We pull in the airport and it's getting closer to time to go. This week has flown by. She parks the car and stares at me. "Where are you from, Breyson?"

I reach for the door handle about to get out. "Mississippi." Her eyes widen slightly, but then they retract. She clearly doesn't want to give anything away. When her lips part, she forces them back together, as if she's refusing what she wants to say. I have a weird feeling I know why.

"Where is she moving, Presley?" She looks out the window, and at this point, I'm getting aggravated. She knows something she isn't telling me. Something that could help me. I don't know why girls have this code amongst themselves. "Presley!" The boom of my voice surprises even me. "Is she moving to Mississippi?"

I glance at my phone, checking the time. I'm getting impatient, because I don't have much time before takeoff and I still have to go through security.

"Look, I can't say without her consent. She's made her decision about this. If she wouldn't tell you herself, then I can't tell you, no matter how much I want to." She starts to smile and then stops.

I narrow my eyes at her, clearly displeased. "I'll tell you what; give me your number and I'll feel her out after I talk to her. She was bordering on a panic attack this morning when I rode by and she shoved the letter in my hand. I think she even has to take her medicine for it again after this all coming at her at once, so I don't want to make it worse. If I can, I'll text the information to you. If you don't hear from me, you know how to find me."

As much as I want the information, the thought of Kinzleigh having anxiety issues stops me from saying anything further. Once I'm out of the car, I pick up the letter and fold it into a neat square and place it in my wallet. "Give me your hand."

I pull a pen from my pocket. It's habit to keep one from school. I write down my number on her hand and I remove my luggage from the back seat. This is probably the one and only time in my life I'm waiting and hoping I get a text or call from a girl.

As I walk through the tunnel of the New Orleans airport, I look around for my brothers. They are supposed to be picking me up. I texted them all the flight details in a group message, so they better be here.

I am one in a set of triplets. Braxton and I are identical twins—split from the same egg—and then there is Briar, who would be considered my fraternal twin if Braxton weren't part of the equation. Two eggs fertilized and one split in two. We are a rare freak of nature to say the least.

Briar looks and acts completely different than Braxton and me. If we hadn't all three been males, my parents probably wouldn't have tried for Brylee, but Mom was determined have a girl, fertility problems be damned. Brylee is the one that will be in misery her entire existence—three older brothers. Every male within five counties is considered an enemy.

As I come into the baggage area, I see Braxton, but not Briar. He spots me and smiles. As I get closer he slaps me on the back. "How was your trip, little bro? Score any hot California girls?"

"Why do you call me that? Being one minute younger than you does not make me your little brother. Besides, I am physically bigger than you and better looking. You look like you've been slacking in the weight room. I'm surprised Dad let you leave the house." I tease, punching him in the arm.

We are really about the same size, but it drives him crazy to be called small. He is the egotistical one of the three of us. I guess being a prized player does that to you. He is the starting quarterback and I am the star running back, so we usually dominate the games at our school.

Briar plays baseball exclusively. He's definitely more laidback and toned down in comparison to Braxton and me; more content with less words.

He's not into the hitting and violence that comes with the territory of football. Braxton and I thrive on it, and we're much more extroverted. If we weren't born at the same time you would never believe Briar was our triplet. "Where is Briar?"

He looks at me with an ugly scoff on his face. "Dude, you are not bigger than me. We are physically identical, so shut the hell up. Briar is tailing around after Londyn. It makes me sick. She finally gave him the time of day and he goes and gives the Abercrombie boys a bad rep with the way he acts love-struck around her. You need to help me knock some sense into him. Her girl parts can't be any better than the other hot girls at school. He must be spellbound by her exotic features."

Braxton and I are pretty much identical in everything down to personality; it's why we're so much closer to each other than to Briar. And by exotic features I know exactly what he means. Londyn is mixed—Asian American. Her Dad met her Mom when he was in the military stationed overseas. I've met her Mom a time or two. She's fluent in English, but when she starts talking fast it gets harder to understand her. Londyn, however— the girl is hot. She got just the right amount of each feature.

"Londyn? When did Londyn show an interest in Briar? Wasn't she just trying to hook up with you like the week before I left?"

"Yeah and I shut her down, because Briar is so damn obvious with his lusting over her or I would've taken some for myself. The girl is hot. I'd love to see some of those dance moves off the field, but it's bros before hoes. Last week at the creek she went for Briar. You know no girl turns down an Abercrombie boy." He laughs and grabs my neck in the crook of his arm. "Let's go. I want some details about your trip. Don't hold out on me either."

I laugh back on the walk to baggage claim. I have missed my family. "It was boring. Ryland got more action than me."

He rubs his knuckles over the top of my head, roughly. "You're full of shit. I know your dick just as good as you do. You forget, we were wombies for nine months."

I can see baggage claim. I shove into him, trying to knock him off, my laughs becoming more frequent. "You're a damn idiot. Take me home."

New Orleans is about an hour and a half to two hours from our house, so I'm sure Braxton will grill me the entire way. The entire school probably knows by now that Natalie and I broke up. There is likely some ridiculous story floating around. That's the bad thing about living in towns where everybody stays in everybody's business. And generally, it's a twisted version of the truth.

We're headed down Interstate fifty-nine and not much has been said to this point as we've been stuck driving through New Orleans traffic. "Anything interesting happen since I've been gone?" It's easier to talk now since it's nothing but open road ahead.

He looks over at me from the driver's seat with the beginning of a grin on his face. "Well, aside from Briar's . . . whatever it is, I'm curious to know what you did to Natalie. Rumors are flying, my brother. It's about time, though. If you're just going to use someone for sex, why limit yourself to one chick? I'm glad you finally came to your senses. Plus, no one likes Natalie. She's a bitch."

This is what I was afraid of. Gossip ruins people's lives. If I had to name one good quality about myself, it would be that I never believe any bullshit that comes out of someone's mouth about another person. If I want to know something, I go straight to the source. "Well, if you must know, I met someone and didn't think it was right to pursue it with Natalie in the background."

"Sweet! Who is she? Did you hit it? Is she hot? Where is the picture? I know you have one, so don't even try to deny it." I did get a picture the night she was sleeping in my arms at Ryland's pool house, but that is mine to enjoy and no one else; not even my brother. I also got a picture before I left her house last night when we were goofing off in bed, after the most perfect night of my existence.

"Her name is Kinzleigh and she is gorgeous. What we did is none of your business. What's with the twenty questions? I don't like it." He rolls his eyes at me. I ignore him. It's the best way to get him to shut up. "What is going on back home tonight? I need to get my mind off some things."

He continues to look between the road and me. "There is a party tonight at Simon's house. I think his parents are out of town or something for the weekend. He is trying to keep it on the down low, but you know that's never going to happen. He always throws the best parties, because his brother can score the alcohol. I think he's home from Ole Miss for the summer anyway."

He smiles as he looks over at me. "You know you'll have your pick of any girl in school now that you ditched Natalie, but I'm sure she will have her claws out regardless. Who will be the lucky lady tonight?"

"Well it definitely won't be Natalie, because I'm not going down that road again. Several nights ago, I got a dose of her crazy side apparently, so that's over." I rub my hands over my face.

Hooking up with another girl is not appealing to me like it normally does, but I've got to get her out of my head. I voice my frustration out loud. "I don't know, dude, this girl is messing with my head. I'm in the dark here. I have never had this problem. I don't know how to get her out of my head. How do you downgrade when you've had the best there is?"

When I move my hands from my face and look at him, he has a knowing look on his face—one that I've never seen present before when referring to girls. "She's one of those? Shit, man. You better get ready, because she isn't going to just disappear. That type of girl is unforgettable."

"You know what I'm talking about? When did you ever feel that way about a girl? I didn't know you actually saw past a girl's physical appearance and the nearest place to strip her naked," I say jokingly.

He places his hand over his heart, pretending to be offended. "Ouch. Don't hate the game when you're one of the main players, Breyson. But for your information, yes, I know what you're talking about. Do you remember that girl that lived here for two years freshman and sophomore year? Her name was Madileigh Carlisle."

He raises his brow as if I should know this information without giving it much thought. Running my fingers through my hair, I try and remember who he's talking about. We do go to a pretty big school. "Wait, isn't that the girl you lost your virginity to? The army brat that moved when her dad got reassigned? Did y'all even date?"

His eyes zone out as he stares straight ahead at the road, lost in thought. "Yeah . . . we dated. We would have kept dating had she not moved. I had never seen a girl like her and haven't since. If this girl messes with your head like that, I'm sorry, man; it doesn't go away. You can numb it, but never get rid of it. I haven't dated anyone since her. Hooking up with other girls is a temporary distraction and a lot of fun, but that's it. It's mental torture."

I just nod, because there isn't much else to say. We don't really ever have these deep conversations and it's a little overwhelming. We're usually emotionally incompetent. That's why our lives are generally easy.

The rest of the ride home is pretty quiet. We pull into the driveway of our house. Looks like Mom and Dad are both gone, as well as Briar by the lack of vehicles in the driveway, but overall, I'm glad to be home.

Mom and dad are probably at the clinic. I'm not sure what their call schedule is for the weekend since I've been gone all week. I am tired from having to change time zones, but I need to somehow find a way to get these images of her out of my head.

Leaving the cab of the truck, I make my way to the house robotically. After entering the front door, I continue to my room without stopping. Braxton stops by my bedroom door on his way to his. "Be ready at nine."

TWENTY

Kinzleigh

I walk into my room with my protein smoothie, my hair sweaty and up, pulling my earbuds from my ears. My entire body is damp from my midafternoon run. I barely got any sleep. I tossed and turned until lunch. Truth is, I've thought about last night so much I'm tired of thinking about it. The memory of every touch, every whisper, and every kiss is making me crazy.

The first thing that halts me is my unmade bed. I walk over to it and place my shaker bottle on my nightstand, and the second I sit down I can smell his cologne. I know I should wash my bedding, so my parents don't find out I had a boy in my room, but I still have some time to breathe it in before they'll be home. I'm not sure what I envisioned my first time being like, but that wasn't it. For something to be casual, he worshiped my body.

The condom wrapper on my nightstand draws my attention. I grab it up quickly. I can't believe I left that there. Konnor could have come home early. Not like him after a night of drinking, but anything is possible. I don't need him to find out about this. I know the condom is gone. Breyson told me he disposed of it in my bathroom garbage and I took that out this morning.

But it was . . .

Words fail me. I almost wish we had done it again. I mentally chastise myself for that very thought. He's gone. That would have made things harder. Which is the exact reason I asked Presley to take him to the airport.

It's best to have cut our losses last night when both of us expected to see each other today before things could be awkward. I need to take last night with me and use it for what it was—an experience.

I sit on my bed, running my empty hand over the place we laid and watched a movie after it was done. Only we didn't just watch the movie. We kissed, touched, groped, and cuddled, but we didn't have sex again. I exhale the scent I've come to love.

I slide off and fall to my knees, lifting my bed skirt. The box immediately comes into view. I pull it toward me, grabbing the notebook off the top labeled 'Firsts'.

I pivot my body, placing my back flush against the side of my bed, and then run my hand over the sparkly design on the front I created with markers and glue and glitter several years ago. No one knows about this book, not even Presley. "You're worthy," I whisper, and then open the front.

I navigate through the pages, briefly scanning each one—first sip of alcohol, first time to try a cigarette, first crush, first kiss, first boy-girl party. Each page has an item from that time, and each page has a diary-like entry, so I'll always remember. Just because I didn't want to be like everyone else and continue to do those things, doesn't mean I didn't want to *try* those things.

I stop at a blank page and place the notebook on my lap to free my hands, and then pull the tape from the box. I place the condom wrapper on the page and secure it with two small strips of the clear tape.

I look at it, trading the roll of tape out with a marker I keep in the box. Then I uncap it and place the tip at the page, just below the wrapper, and I write everything I feel about the moment, letting myself keep it forever.

Summer of 2014
June . . .

I met this boy on the beach. <3 Breyson Abercrombie <3 He was unlike anything I've ever seen. Blue eyes that could make you tell the truth. Blond hair that makes his tan skin appear darker. And a smile that makes me question being single. When he speaks, I get lost in him. He has this accent that is like a time warp. I tried to avoid him. His ability to make me feel things I normally try to avoid scares me.

Mom and Dad told me we're moving at the end of the summer. In ways I feel like they're ruining my life. But then he found me, on the pier, and he just makes me feel . . . better. He kissed me, and I let him. It may not have been my first encounter with a kiss, but it was the first time I felt things before, during, and after it happened.

I tried to run from him on so many occasions. I tried. And I failed. So, I stopped fighting it, and I'm glad I did. I had one week with him. One blissful, perfect, memorable week this summer. We had some highs and lows, but I wouldn't change anything if given the chance.

He cared about me, and didn't push me, and so, I gave him my virginity. If anyone was worthy, it was him. I wanted it to be him. It was more than I ever imagined it to be. He looked at me as if he was scared to close his eyes. He touched me like I was a mirage. And he kissed me like I was a dream.

Then he pushed inside me, and everything in my world circled, and all I could see was him.

My eyes well up and I let it spill over.

I was a coward today. I couldn't say goodbye. A truth I will take to my grave—I miss him like I would miss breathing should someone take away the ability. I couldn't tell those eyes I'd never look in them again. I couldn't kiss him and know it's the last. I couldn't watch him leave without the smile on his face I love. I couldn't tell the boy goodbye that I know should he stay . . . I'd keep him. I couldn't let myself tell him—he's the boy that changed me, when no one else could.

So I didn't. And it'll probably be my only regret.

I cap the marker pen and close the book holding all of my secrets, placing it inside the box and returning it to its hiding place where it'll stay until I have another first that deserves to be a memory. I wipe my face and stand, returning to my bed. My phone sits in the middle. I grab it, pulling up Facebook instantly. The temptation is well on its way to killing me. One part of me screams to do it, but the other part of me says I'll regret it. I have today . . .

I touch the search bar and type in the words, letter by letter. Breyson

Abercrombie. The profiles pull up in a list, the top hit stealing my breath. *One mutual friend.* I don't even have to look at the friend to know it's Ryland. Breyson's face is on the thumbnail. I know it's him. His hair is messy and all over his head, his face is layered with sweat, and he's wearing a football uniform. Black jersey with gold lettering. It must have been taken after a game. God, he's beautiful.

My pulse is racing as I go to his profile. I sigh in relief when his location isn't part of his 'about' section. And his profile is public, which is why his personal info is kept to a minimum, I'm assuming. I can't help but smile, though, when I notice the relationship status: 'single'.

My thumb robotically flicks up on the screen, scrolling down his profile. He updated his profile ten minutes ago:

California. I want to come back to you.

I swallow hard. Is he talking about the state or . . . My thumb hovers over the like button, questioning if I should open that door, but my eyes are more interested in the comments that are steadily increasing in number. And not the comments from obvious male friends, but the other ones. The bigger percentage of the comments are from girls. One in particular makes my heart plummet to my stomach.

Natalie: *So glad you're home, babe! Celebrations are in order! Whoop-whoop.*

I force myself past it by going to his photos. I stop on one of three guys. One looks identical to Breyson while the other is totally different with his dark hair and darker skin. It's weird seeing two of him. Then there is one of a girl, younger, but looks more like the guy with brown hair than Breyson and his twin. That must be his sister.

Every photo and every status update makes me miss him more. It gives me a look into his life and I don't know if that's a good thing. Because I find myself wanting him more. One thing that puts me at ease—the only photos with him and that Natalie girl are the ones she posted and tagged him in. Looking at his uploads, it's like she doesn't even exist. Relief washes over me, and I'm not sure why. I should feel sorry for her, because it seems one-sided.

Something I don't understand overcomes me, and I go back to his status without thinking and hit the comment button. Before I can think, my fingers type.

Kinzleigh Baker: *California won't be the same without you.*

And like the adolescent I am, I post it and turn my phone off. I don't know why I did that. It opens us up for conversation. It's a jealous move. And I'm not entitled to make it. I refused him my phone number. I didn't show up this morning. He may very well hate me.

And he has every right to.

Breyson

I leave my luggage somewhere between the door and the bed, before falling face first across my mattress. I want to sleep, but my mind is processing about a million different thoughts all at once, making me restless.

I roll over and reach into my pocket, pulling out my phone. When I look at the lock screen, Facebook notifications cover most of it. I scroll through them and stop, doing a double take on one.

Kinzleigh Baker commented on your post.

Why *the fuck* didn't I think of Facebook? God, I'm a tool sometimes. I touch it and unlock my phone, waiting for it to go straight for the comments. My heart is pounding, and the gears in my mind are turning quickly. She sought me out. That has to mean something. I cringe seeing Natalie's comment. I'm going to have to deal with her at some point and I don't want to.

Kinzleigh Baker*: California won't be the same without you.*

I click on her name to go to her profile, immediately sending her a friend request. Her profile is private. Thank God mine isn't. I've never cared who sees my stuff. I don't post overly personal stuff anyway. I just keep my demographics to a minimum and usually don't post anything with a location.

I click on the message option and wait for the app to switch me to Messenger. I attempt the call option, but it's unsuccessful. I type a message.

Please call me here. Message back. Something. If Facebook is all I have with you I'll take it.

I stare at the screen, waiting for the 'delivered' notification to pop up, but it doesn't. I growl out. Then it occurs to me. If we aren't friends she may not even see the damn message. I go back to the comment to reply.

Check your messages please.

I turn my ringer on so I don't miss a notification. It never leaves vibrate, but she could call. She would call, right? I'm pathetic. What the hell is wrong with me? I growl out, frustrated.

But she looked me up. That has to be a sign.

TWENTY-ONE

Breyson

Still no response from Kinzleigh. I've checked it all damn evening. The fact that she did it and won't respond pisses me off. The friend request is still showing as sent, so she hasn't declined it. And the message isn't showing as delivered. I'm starting to think maybe her phone is off, but why I don't know.

We pull up at the party right as everything is getting rowdy. There is already a crowd of people here. As we walk through the door, I can smell the beer from the red plastic cups speckled throughout the room. Some people are sitting and some dancing or standing. It's packed to capacity.

As I walk toward the kitchen, I can see a beer pong table set up with the majority of the football team gathered around. "Brey-son!" I look around as my name is screamed in a slurred unison around the table. "Get over here, son. I need actual competition. I'm getting bored," Jared says with more remaining cups than the other player."

"You sure you're ready to get beat, Jared? Looks like you're on a roll so far." Jared is one of the linebackers. He is a big grizzly looking guy with short, reddish-brown hair and a beard. When puberty hit him, it came all at once. He's got more hair than anyone I know. He's also stocky and funny as hell, but one damn good linebacker.

"Dude, everyone is getting trashed but me. I need someone that can hold their own. It's about time you finally decided to come back home and quit running around with those California girls. Tell me, are they a good lay?"

"I don't know what you're talking about," I say, trying to smother the laugh.

"Shit, I ain't stupid. Fess up. We've already heard there is a special someone and based on that comment on your Facebook post that Natalie has been ranting about around here, I think we know who." He holds his hand up and whispers not so quietly. "She's fuckin' hot. How was it?"

"None of your business, asshole." I laugh.

"Okay, fine. I get it. You don't want to add drama where drama is due. You've been a hot topic of conversation among the ladies. Natalie is pissed, boy. Speaking of, you mind if I try to tap that since you're finished?"

"Have at it. You'd be doing me a favor. We're done." Gossip—something you can count on around here, and something I don't need.

Right now, I really wish I could turn back the hands of time and go back to last night. I want to be back in Kinzleigh's bed, holding her in my arms. I want to be able to look down at her as I enter her, making her mine. The look on her face when I kissed her goodbye will haunt me for the rest of my life.

She's beautiful and smart and knows what she wants. I'm well past pissed off. She is the one that chose not to have any more communication, and then she makes me aware of her, giving me an ounce of hope this isn't over, but won't answer any more, so why am I the one suffering from all these jumbled thoughts in my head?

I stood there and told her I wanted more; even gave her my number. I need to think about someone else. I need to forget her. I hope that Braxton was wrong earlier. I can't focus on anything like this. I grab the Ping-Pong ball from Adam, who's holding it beside me and drinking from his cups anyway, listening to the conversation. "Set me up. Let's play."

An hour in and the alcohol is taking effect, leaving me in a relaxed and peaceful state. I'm about to throw the ball into a cup when an arm snakes up my back, underneath my shirt, causing me to drop the ball into my own cup in surprise. "I'm really glad you're back, babe. Why don't we go somewhere and talk? I can give you the welcome home you deserve."

From the purr of her voice alone I can tell it's Natalie and she's drunk, which makes her difficult to deal with. As a matter of fact, I hate when she drinks. She's nothing but drama and I usually regret being around her.

All of the guys have smirks on their faces. You can never get away from the high school drama. Placing my hands around her wrists, I turn around and remove her hands from my body. "What do you want, Natalie?"

"Oh, come on, don't pretend you didn't miss me, Breyson. I know you did." I can smell the coconut rum and Diet Coke on her breath—her signature drinking choice. She's making a fool of herself. I'm starting to wonder if she's always been this way and I just looked over it because she is hot, or if she's grasping at straws because she's really in love with me. Either way, Kinzleigh or no Kinzleigh, I'm not into it.

"Natalie, you're drunk. I told you we're over. I meant it. Just because I'm home doesn't mean that's going to change. I think you should go home or go back to your friends before you embarrass yourself." She goes for my pants before I can stop her, trying to grab my dick. "Fucking quit. I'm not kidding, Natalie. We can do this here or you can take my advice and we hash out the details later privately."

"What happened to you? You used to be fun before you ran off to California and met that stupid little bitch. I saw her comment. It was all I could do not to message the slut that stole my boyfriend. News flash, Breyson, you're back now. You're not stupid enough to actually think that'll work. Are you going to let her ruin your life? She's not here. She's halfway across the country. I mean, what did you think was going to happen? That you were going to come back here and continue whatever it was you two had over there?" She laughs. "Right. I bet she's already moved on to someone else."

She's treading on thin ice with me. I can barely even look at her right now without wanting to hurt her. I don't believe in laying a hand on a woman and the thought runs through my mind as I'm listening to her call Kinzleigh name after name. She'll never be half of what Kinzleigh is. I need to get out of here. "Fuck you, Natalie. I was trying not to hurt your feelings, because we've been friends for a lot longer than fuck buddies, but you're getting brave with the way you talk to me. You need to remember your place. You don't even know her. Slut? Bitch?" I laugh. "Might wanna check yourself, sweetheart. You're just pissed I don't want you like that anymore."

I hold out my index finger and thumb for emphasis on how close she is coming. "See this? This is how close you are to me washing my hands with you. We can go back to being just friends or I can drop you all together. It's your choice. Don't follow me."

I notice her eyes widen as I storm off in a fury. I walk out the back door to the patio that is only a few feet from where the game is set up. Simon's house sits on Lake Serene. I walk out to the pier and connecting boathouse. Taking a seat at the end of the short pier, I clench the edge as anger consumes my body.

She may have some good points, but she has no right to voice her opinion; her and I are over. She needs to accept it and move on. It was bound to happen even if I had never met Kinzleigh. We weren't together for the right reasons.

"Breyson? Are you okay?" I turn around at the soft voice behind me. It's Adalynn, one of the cheerleaders. She's hot with her long red hair, green eyes, and tanned skin. She doesn't fit the typical description for a redhead. She is sweet instead of that fiery attitude you usually see. Instead of an orange shade, her hair is more of a dark red, and no freckles on her skin are present. She has a certain sex appeal about her.

"Hey, Adalynn, what's up?" She continues to walk toward me until she reaches the edge and sits beside me.

"Natalie being a pain?" She even has a sweet voice. She has legs for days and a nice rack. I'm not sure why I've never noticed how hot she is before.

"You could say that." She looks almost shy, but keeps looking at my lips as if she wants me to kiss her. I know that look all too well. Maybe this is the distraction from Kinzleigh I need. Grabbing her by the waist, I pull her closer to me. "What are you doing here, Adalynn?"

The rhythm of her breathing changes. "I just thought you could use a change of scenery, and maybe some company. Do you want me to leave?"

"You can stay, as long as you're good with it being nothing but a hook-up. I'm not in a talkative mood. I'm also not looking for a girlfriend. Dating Natalie was a disaster and a one-time deal. You should know up front what my intentions are."

"I'm okay with that. Friends with benefits, right?" She licks her lips.

Nodding, I say, "Something like that. Come on and let's go in the boathouse. I'm not one for groping you out in the open just to give everyone something to talk about."

Standing up, I hold out my hand to help her up. "I like that idea," she says.

As we enter the boathouse, I lock the door. It's pretty bare, with just a twin-size bed and supplies, such as life jackets, fishing gear, and skiing equipment. Turning around, I grab her by the fabric of her tiny dress and pull her toward me.

Grabbing the bottom hem of the tight material, I pull it up her body and over her head. I love hooking-up with cheerleaders. They have tight little bodies and they're limber. It makes for a better lay; one that I need desperately. I want her to ride me like I know she knows how. The perks of sleeping with someone that's already broken in.

She comes closer to kiss me and I dodge, causing her lips to press against the corner of my mouth. We can do this without kissing. It may be one of the easiest ways to get them ready, but not the only. I can find other ways to make them wet.

Kinzleigh is the only girl I have willingly kissed since the day I lost my virginity on a family vacation years ago. We had a cabin next to a family with all daughters. We had been hanging out with them a little since we arrived, and one night their parents left and so did ours for a few hours. We were all old enough to stay by ourselves for a while. The one I had taken an interest in was a couple years older than me, and more than willing to show me how.

I back her toward the bed, pulling her bra down and kissing down her neck along the way. She moans in response when I grab her breasts in my hands, clearly ready to go. When the backs of her knees touch the bed, I unclasp her bra to remove it all the way, letting it drop to the floor. Pushing her backward, she sits and reclines her back across the bed. Grabbing her panties in my hands, I pull them down her legs, baring her completely.

Coming down on top of her, she spreads her legs, wrapping them around my waist. "You're so sexy. Take off your clothes. I want to see your body."

Grabbing my collar, I pull my shirt over my head, tossing it aside. My jeans tighten around my groin as I take in her naked body. I look up at her and Kinzleigh's face flashes through my mind, blurring Adalynn's face.

Shaking my head in an attempt to clear my thoughts, I flip her over on her knees. "You like it like this, babe? I like where this is going."

Grabbing her breast in my hand, I squeeze, tugging at the hard nipple, trailing down the front side of her body with the other hand until I make it to between her legs. I push into her wetness, before pulling my middle finger back up, immediately circling the spot. She moans, and I swear I hear Kinzleigh's voice. What the hell?

Pushing her head into the pillow, trying to smother the sound, I increase movements to make her orgasm, so I can come quickly. Seconds in and she's backing against my hand, riding out her orgasm. When I know she's done, I speed things up before my thoughts get out of hand.

Unbuckling my belt, I grab a condom from my pocket, tearing it at the edge, and then push my jeans down my legs. When I look down as I roll the condom on, Kinzleigh's blonde curls and perfect body flashes through my mind, but I know it's Adalynn laying there.

Dammit! What is wrong with me? I pull my hair in frustration, trying to change the direction of my thoughts, but it only makes it worse. Every time I look at her it's Kinzleigh's face I see. Maybe I should just go with it instead of fighting it. I align the tip at her center and grab her hip, about to push in, but I stall.

I'm doing exactly what Lexi tried to get me to do. It's not fair to Adalynn. I'm not that guy. She deserves a guy that's thinking about her. "Breyson? Are you okay?"

Her breathing is heavy still from her orgasm. She's looking at me, concern clearly present. I swear she looks just like Kinzleigh, but I know that's not possible. Kinzleigh is in California. It makes no sense. Can my mind really be altering my eyesight?

"Kinzleigh," I whisper. Backing away from the bed I fall to the floor, landing on my knees. Covering my face, I voice my frustration out loud. I feel like I'm going crazy. "Adalynn, I'm sorry, but I can't do this. Trust me, I want to. You're hot . . . but I can't. I'm an asshole for this. It's not fair to you, though. Every time I look at you, I see someone else, and I'm not trying to. I don't know how to stop."

She moves off the bed and kneels in front of me. "Hey," she says, removing my hands from my face. "You don't have to be sorry. I can relate, believe it or not. She's a special girl to get your attention like this. She should feel lucky. She's the first, right?" I nod and look at how beautiful her body and face is. It's a damn shame my head is this messed up.

"I hate this. You're a cool girl, Adalynn. I'm sorry. You deserve so much better than this. When a guy looks at you he should see you for how sexy you are. He should see you for you." I hang my head in shame. I've never thought of a different girl while hooking-up with one. This is a new low for me. It seems I'm having a lot of those lately.

"Breyson, look at me. I swear I'm not mad or upset. Yes, it sucks we don't get to go further, because I think you're really hot and I needed the mental release too. It sounds like for the same reason as you, but I'm glad to see someone this torn over a girl still exists with guys. It says a lot that you can't go through with it. You're a good guy, Breyson. This can be our secret. Okay? Drama isn't my thing. I hope things work out for you with this girl."

She reaches for her clothes and begins dressing. I feel like the biggest douche right now. I fasten my pants and put my shirt back on, standing to my feet. "Where did you meet her? I hope you don't mind me asking."

"California, but she refuses to go any further than we have, so it's best to move on." I reach in and pull her to me, giving her a hug. "Thank you for understanding."

"No problem, babe. Don't stress over it. These things have a way of working out when it's meant to be." She kisses me on the cheek. "Come on, let's get out of here and you can take me home. You owe me that much." She winks at me, and for the first time in a while, I actually smile.

I pull in the drive from dropping Adalynn off and head straight for the pool house. Mom and Dad are both home, but I don't feel like talking. I told Braxton to get a ride with one of the guys from the team, so I could take the truck. There is only one thing I can do when I'm this stressed out and that is to beat it out of me.

Walking over to the punching bag that hangs in the corner, I pull my shirt off and grab the boxing gloves. Once I get them on, I swing my arms a few times to loosen up.

After a few seconds, I begin punching with everything I have, not letting up once. Each time her face scrolls through my mind, I hit the bag harder. I hit it until I can't feel my arms and then some. Once my arms give out completely, I begin kicking. Every sound, every tear, and every emotion on her face from that night is brought back full force.

I'm pouring wet with sweat when Dad walks in and grabs me by the shoulders. "Son, stop. You're exhausted. Don't overexert yourself. Want to tell me what's on your mind? I don't see you like this often. What's got you so worked up?"

Placing my back against the wall, I slide to the floor, barely able to catch my breath. Resting my limp arms over my folded knees, I rest my head against the wall. "Just a girl I met in California."

He doesn't say anything; just grabs a bottle of water from the refrigerator and sits next to me. "Here, drink this before you get dehydrated. I smell the alcohol in your sweat. What have I told you about driving when you've been drinking? I don't care if you're not drunk. You can still lack proper judgment and cause a wreck. Don't make me ground you when all you have to do is call. A DUI could ruin your chance of playing college football and I know that's not what you want. I'm disappointed you'd make such a poor decision."

"I'm sorry, Dad. I wasn't thinking clearly. It won't happen again."

We both sit silent for a moment, my chest still heaving. He breathes out, letting the tension roll off him. It's something he does often when he's mad at any of us. "Breyson, do you want to end up like Beau? I sure as hell don't want to get that call as a parent. I've always been honest with the three of you. You're about to be seniors. I know there will be drinking whether I let you or not. Teenagers always find a way. I'd rather teach you safety than you sneaking off and lying to me to do it. Call me next time. I'll come pick you up. It's not realistic to think you'll never drink, but I'll be damned if you're going to be stupid about it."

I drink the bottle of water in its entirety and throw it across the room, still frustrated. He's right. I should have called. I knew better. "Yes, Sir."

"Tell me about this girl." Even though my dad pushes me about being a doctor, he's still the coolest dad. I think he's seen too much bad in his medical profession to let us slide. I can talk to him about anything and he doesn't judge me. Even football he respects as far as college. It's professional he thinks is a waste of mind space.

A girl, though, is something I don't know how to talk to him about. I've never been this bent out of shape from a girl before. I don't know how to get her out of my head. I figured once we slept together that would take care of it, but it seems to have had the opposite effect. "How do you forget a girl that consumes your thoughts, but wants nothing from you; not even phone contact? I look at another girl and see her. I jump at every whim to talk to her. This is ruining everything. I tried to get her number, but she refuses to make things *complicated*."

"Did you sleep with her?"

"Uh . . ." I'm not having this conversation with my dad. It was awkward enough having 'the talk'. Living with two doctors—one being a gynecologist—you get STD photos, CDC statistics on shit like the percentage of teens walking around with HPV that carry no symptoms, and teen pregnancy stories. I don't want to know what he'd say hearing his seventeen-year-old son is sleeping around. I'd rather him just live in a state of ignorance when it comes to my sex life.

A laugh slips from his lips and he shakes his head. "What's so funny?"

"Son, you may think I'm old and my generation knows nothing, but I've known the three of you are sexually active for a while now. I'm not stupid. I'm a doctor for Christ's sakes. Plus, when I go to put up clothes for your mother and find boxes of condoms in each of your rooms, it blows my ignorance to shit and back, don't you think? But before you try to lie, I'll applaud you for using safe sex. That's all I can ask."

I cover my eyes. I cannot believe I'm about to tell my dad this. Maybe he'll call me a lunatic and help matters some. Or maybe he'll raise hell for doing that to a girl and make me feel better that she doesn't want anything to do with me. "She was a virgin."

He clears his throat. Yes, I feel the awkward elephant now in the room. "And by was I'm taking it you fixed that for her?"

"Call me an asshole. I can handle it. I'm ready for your wrath. It was stupid when I was going to be leaving. I can see how you'd think it was disrespectful."

"I'm not going to do any of those things."

I look at him like he's grown a second head. "What?"

"You're old enough to make those decisions. I presented you with the facts years ago. I explained safe sex. You know right from wrong. We've raised all of you in church. We give you limits on freedom with curfews and knowing where you are at all times. Your mother and I have done our part. I'm not going to keep you boys on a tight leash and you end up going crazy the second you get a little freedom. We are perfectly aware that high school kids drink and have sex and experiment. It happened when we were in school. I'm not going to pretend your mother and I didn't do some of those things."

"I feel a *but* coming on."

"And you're right. But, you shouldn't have taken that girl's virginity if you didn't really care about her. There are consequences for every action. You're dealing with your conscience. Respect isn't earned for the man that gives in to every desire, but for the man that can turn away. Have sex in a relationship if you're going to have sex."

"That's what I was doing with Natalie. It meant more to me that one time with that girl than a lot of times with her." I'm on a confession roll now, why quit . . .

"Because you realized she respected herself enough to hang on to something most don't. Am I right?"

I shrug. "Maybe. Maybe it was something else entirely. Maybe it was just her."

"Maybe your heart was telling you she's different for you. Love still exists regardless of what you think. I will never understand having a relationship that resembles polygamy. There is something to be said about monogamy and romancing your partner. You and the kids your age may think it's stupid, but it's so much better than whoring around. You're still young. Maybe it's love, maybe it's not, but you obviously feel something for this girl. Keep trying until you know it's time to move on. If it's meant to be, things tend to fall into place."

There is no way I love her. We've known each other a week. It has to be because she cut things off before I did, or maybe because I didn't get her out of my system. It has to be lust. Why is it that I feel like I'm having to convince myself?

I was a fool to think I could handle one night with her and nothing. I need more. I need to talk to her. Why is it that the thought of never seeing her again gives me chest pain? Dad stands and makes his way to the door. "Dad."

"Yeah, Son."

"How do you know when it's time to move on?"

"You meet someone else and suddenly you wonder why you spent so much time trying." He grabs the door handle as I stare straight ahead. "Oh, Breyson."

"Sir."

"Right now I'm going to tell you this as your doctor and not your dad. A condom is ninety-eight percent effective in a perfect situation. People aren't perfect. Cut that percentage down to eighty-five percent effective due to normal human error. Look out for you. Make sure she's on birth control if you're going to 'sleep around'. Even then, I've seen the situations where he 'thought' she was on birth control and she stopped taking it. Unfortunately, some girls will do crazy things to hang on to a guy. Be one hundred percent sure you love her before you take the risk of waking up one day with a child you didn't plan. Food for thought. Don't tell your mother."

He walks out the door, shutting it behind him. Fuck. Natalie was never on birth control. I just pulled out. With a condom.

TWENTY-TWO

Breyson

I walk out to the pool and sit on the lounger, staring out at the water. The pool lights are on, slowly changing colors. It's hypnotic to stare at. The red has always been my favorite. It adds a warm tone to an already cool hue.

A slight breeze is out, making the southern heat bearable. Humidity here is so much different than the west coast. Here, it's like constantly breathing in steam. It makes your lungs feel heavy and your heart is constantly working harder.

I look out across the yard at the lake that our house sits on, along with so many others. Most have their own boathouse and dock just like at Simon's; we do. The water is calm; all the boats from the day anchored or housed. I like it best like this—peaceful. I can hear a few kids from school yelling out not too far away—some guys with a few girls' laughs tossed in.

People may not admit it, but you're tagged socially by where you live here. I suppose it's that way everywhere. Everyone who's anyone chooses their residence by the name, and their kids reap the benefits. A vast percentage of Oak Grove is split between three major subdivisions; the kids that come from money anyway.

My phone vibrates in my pocket. I pull it out, my heart already pounding. I glance at the screen and freeze.

Kinzleigh Baker accepted your friend request.

I close my eyes, trying to calm the hell down. That's not the reason for the vibration. It's the message. She responded. I open it.

I do want to be friends, but give me time. I need a little distance. Give me the summer. Then we'll go from there.

I blink, rereading it over and over. It's a start, right? It's better than nothing. Summer. That I can do. I usually work at Pops' ranch anyway, so that'll keep me busy. I quickly respond while she's at her phone.

Ok, Kinzleigh. I'll give you the summer, but then, I want to figure this out. I'll take what I can get.

Another message comes through. *If it means anything, I meant every word of my comment. Goodnight, Breyson.*

So did I . . . Goodnight, Kinzleigh.

I stare at my phone again, but it never shows she's typing. That's probably all I'm going to get out of her. Before I can stop it, I smile. "Breyson, we need to talk."

I close my eyes, hoping I'm hearing things. I glance up at Natalie, standing maybe ten feet away. "What do you want?"

"I saw you with Adalynn earlier. I didn't want to do it this way, but . . ." She holds up some white stick. "I'm pregnant."

My phone slips from my hand and the corner of the rubber cover bounces off the cement and it hits the water, quickly sinking to the bottom. My mouth falls and bile rises to my throat. A wave of nausea hits. That fucking bitch. There's no way. Then everything Dad said hits me. And for the first time since I was a kid, my eyes sting with unshed tears.

No. Please, God. No.

changing
FATE
FATE SERIES BOOK TWO

ONE

Breyson

It's been three days since Natalie dropped that bomb on me. Two words—I'm pregnant. I saw red. I knew I had to get away from her before I did something I'd forever regret. That's a new low, even for her.

I couldn't talk to her. I couldn't calm down. And I couldn't even look at her. So I told her to get out of my sight and don't breathe a word to anyone until I called her.

Three days I've cried. Three days I've slung cuss words like baseballs. Three days I've prayed. And three days I've thought about just how damn crazy she is lately. I know the statistics. But I also know me. I've never nut inside of her. Not even with a condom on.

I've always bought my own condoms, brand name, never borrowing from someone else. I check them before and as I roll them on for tears or noticeable defects. I check the expiration date. I *always* buy them with spermicide. It doesn't add up. There is no way she's that small percentage.

I pull up the message box.

Me: Come the fuck on.

Nat: I'm coming. Give me a sec.

I sit in my truck, idling in her driveway. This is going to go my way. My eyes are homed in on her front door, everything around me colored in brown from my shades. It finally opens, and she saunters out all made up with a goddamn smile on her face. If she knew the thoughts swimming around in my head right now she'd wipe that grin off. I'm pretty sure at this point murder isn't so farfetched.

She opens the truck and grabs the handle, pulling herself up. "Hey, babe. Where are we going?"

"My house."

She shuts the door. "Finally! I get to see your room."

"No."

She crinkles her brows. "Then where are we going?"

"Pool house. I don't want you in my room."

"I don't understand. I thought we were back together, because . . . you know."

I pull out of her driveway and step on the gas, throwing her into the door. "You thought wrong. Buckle up."

I stare straight ahead at the road, fists clamped around the steering wheel, listening to her annoying as hell voice as she talks about absolutely nothing I want to hear. I don't understand my sudden hatred for her, but I'm going to guess it has to do with that fucking piss stick.

Fifteen minutes. The longest fifteen minutes of my damn life. And I'm about to add to it. I pull into the driveway and throw it into park, killing it and quickly getting out, grabbing the Wal-Mart bag on the way.

She follows me in my trek to the pool house. Clouds are gray—exactly the way I feel. Ninety percent chance of rain, so Pops told me to stay home. My brothers are fishing on the lake before the rain comes in. My parents are at work. Brylee is at home, though, and I don't want her getting wind of this.

I open the door and storm to the back of the room. I hear her on my heels. "Breyson. Are you going to talk to me?"

I turn around as I reach the bathroom door, my hand in the plastic bag. I pull out the Clearblue digital pregnancy test box and shove it into her chest. "There are three. I'm going to watch you take every fucking one."

Her eyes widen, but then she narrows them and grabs the box, looking it over. "I already took one. I showed it to you. I peed before I left home. Guess we'll have to wait 'til I have to go."

I stomp over to the refrigerator and grab a bottle of water. She walks up behind me and grabs my dick, cornering me in. I immediately get hard. Memory is all it is. A guy's dick prefers to be wet, and it remembers hers always was. Plus, my shorts are thin and she knows how I like it. Even hatred doesn't change that. It's why I ended up with her ass in the first place.

My eyes close. I silently curse myself. When I don't make an effort to move, she ascends to my waistband and slips her hand beneath it, gripping me palm to dick, her fist tight enough to jerk me. And then jerk me she does. I can't see her. If she doesn't open her damn mouth I can pretend it's—

"You know this is what we do best. I know how to get you off. Don't deny me. We don't even have to use a condom anymore."

And just like that I turn and grab her neck, slamming her into the wall. "You think I'm stupid, bitch? You think I'm going to buy into your little game and nut inside of you, so you can trap me? Go take the fucking test, Natalie, and then, if it's positive, I might consider touching you again. Might being the keyword."

She shoves at my chest with all her might. "I wish you had never gone to California. I hate her for doing this to us."

"Maybe you should, because her pussy was a hell of a lot tighter than yours. And she didn't have to throw this shit on me to get my attention."

She screams, grabbing the bottle of water from my hand, and storms to the bathroom in a tantrum. The second the door slams I open it. "I thought you wanted me to pee on the stick."

I grab a small cup from the stack on the sink and flip it over. "And I'm going to watch you. You have nothing to hide. I've seen it."

"Fine." She drops her shorts and sits, placing the cup between her legs in the bowl, and then I hear it filling the cup. "You're such an asshole sometimes."

"I have to be to deal with you. You couldn't just let it go, could you? Instead of us ending on good terms you had to make me hate you."

"And what if it's really positive, huh? Then how will you feel for treating me this way?"

"Something tells me it won't be."

She pulls the cup up and places it on the counter. "There."

She stands after she's finished and pulls her shorts up. I hand her one package and keep the other two. She stalls, before finally opening it and dipping it in the cup of urine. I follow suit, watching it climb the pad as it's absorbed, praying every second that I count. I read how to do it online before I got them.

Snapping the cap back on, I lay it flat and I recite mentally, *please be negative. I will do anything. Don't stick me with her forever.*

Then, I continue with the third test. When they're all lying flat, I watch the little blinking hourglass on the display panel, before finally counting with the timer on my phone. Three minutes. Ninety seconds that will define my future. Every second feels like an eternity.

And it finally ends. With two words on the screen instead of one. *Not pregnant.*

And I can finally breathe. My chest no longer feels like I'm lying under a concrete wall and the tears of anger well up in my eyes. My fists close at my sides. And I finally look at her. "I must have miscarried. I've worried nonstop for three days."

She has the audacity to keep going with her lies. "Get out."

"It's fairly common with stress."

"Get the fuck out!"

She jumps.

"I don't want to see you. I don't want to talk to you. I don't even want to breathe the same air. If you see me walking in the hall, walk a different way. If we're at the same party, stay far away from me. For three days I haven't eaten. This could have ruined my entire life. And for what? Because I found someone else? You may think this is a game, but you're gambling with my future, and I was careful." The tears spill over, relief coming at me so hard I can't catch my breath. "You mean *nothing* to me. So get out."

She pushes past me and slams the door the second she's out. I press my thumb and index finger into my eyes, trying not to break down from the onslaught of emotions. I've gotta get out of here for a while. I'm going to stay at Pops' 'til I can get my head back on straight.

And calling Kinzleigh over Facebook is consuming my every thought. I told her I'd give her the summer. I'm not going to screw that up. Not now. Not ever.

TWO

Kinzleigh

It's hard to believe today is moving day. So much has happened since school let out for summer that I have whiplash thinking about it. Writing Breyson that letter was one of the hardest things I've ever done. I've never been good with the emotional parts of life; it's why I avoid it. Life is easier that way.

I love my friends and family, but that's all my heart can stand to let in. Something about that boy, though, has my insides trying to do damage control on the tornado that came through while he was here. And now this 'friendship' is lingering in the air. What do I do?

After he left, Presley came by that night trying to get me to talk to him. I didn't tell her what I'd already done. Those things are better left unsaid. I had a weak moment, I'm not going to lie, but I'm still in turmoil about how far I can or will go.

I figured by now he'd be long forgotten and just a memory, but that's wishful thinking. The only way to ensure I didn't cave more than I already did was to burn his number in a candle.

Cabo came and went in a blur. What can I say—I wasn't feeling it. Our annual vacation is usually my favorite time of the year. Presley had her fun and Preston stayed by my side. I'm sure I wasn't much fun to be around, though.

I stayed glued to my iPod at the beach or pool and locked in my room at night. Somehow, Breyson burned himself in the depths of my memory and lit a fire in my heart that I can't seem to smother; no matter how hard I try.

The last night I saw him we took photos together to remember each other by. I'll never admit to anyone that I saved it as my background and stare at it constantly in a twelve-hour period. The only reason it's not twenty-four is because I have to sleep. What is it about those beautiful blue eyes that won't let go of the hold they have on my soul?

I stare into my empty room, numb inside. The movers already picked up everything and are on their way to the new house. Mom and Dad went house hunting and bought a house as soon as we got back from Cabo.

Cheerleading tryouts came and went a few days ago. I hope and pray that I receive that letter of acceptance, because I've worked my butt off for it. Yesterday I said goodbye to my cheerleading coach, Andy, and the rest of the girls from my squad. It's the first time I've seen Andy tear up in the seven years I've known him. Through all this I've learned goodbyes aren't my thing.

The hardest part, though, was saying goodbye to Presley. I never realized how much she truly means to me until it was time to let her go. She stayed the night with me last night and we reminisced about old times. We did a little laughing and a lot of crying. I'm going to miss that girl a lot more than I thought. She has been my best friend since I developed memories, always barging through the walls of my heart, demanding to be loved. There are photos of us in diapers together.

Tears fall down my face as I look into the empty room of the house I love. I walk over to the wall my mom has measured my height on since I was a small child and run my fingers along the pen marks etched in the sheetrock.

There are so many memories here. I say a silent prayer, asking to be brought back home. Pulling out my phone, I snap a photo of the wall art in front of me. I can never get this back. If I could cut it off and take it I would. "Baby girl, it's time to get on the road if we're going to make that stop you wanted to make before we have to be at the airport. I know it's hard to leave this house, but we will make memories in our new home. I told you we're not going to sell right away."

I blow out a breath. I guess it is time to let it go. "Is Konnor already gone?"

What to say about Konnor. He is clearly still distraught over the whole Sophia incident. I'm really hoping that Alabama is good for him.

He started writing music, and the tattoo shop is becoming a second home for him. I'm starting to worry, as are my parents, but he's eighteen now. At least he's channeling the pain with the lyrics he writes in his notebook instead of trying to drown it by putting toxins in his body.

He chose to walk on the football team at Alabama instead of accepting the scholarship at UCLA. Most may think it's stupid, but my parents support it and agree that he needs some distance from home, even if it costs them tuition. I have to admit I was surprised, but maybe this is what he needs. I want him to be happy again, and he clearly isn't going to be here.

"Yes," Dad says. "He left this morning while you were still asleep. He had to be there for summer training. He said you guys had your goodbyes last night and he didn't want to wake you. He is going to let us know his schedule and we'll figure out when to see him again."

He comes over and stands behind me, resting his hands over my shoulders. "I know it's hard to leave behind, sweetheart, but everything will be okay. You will see. Come on if you want to make that pit stop on the way."

We pull up at the one place I can't leave without saying goodbye—the cemetery where my dad's parents are buried. "I'll be right back," I say to Mom and Dad as I open the door. "And I'd like to do this alone if that's all right."

"Take your time, sweetie. We made time for this." Mom looks at me with a small smile on her face as I step out of the car. Making my way through the various rows of headstones, I come to the one I'm in search of.

I lay the bouquet of daisies on the grass in front of the headstone that I had Mom pick up this morning. They were Grams' favorite, so I never come here without a fresh bundle. She always had a vase of them laying around her house if she could get her hands on them. The memory makes me smile. I glance at her headstone.

ALMA LOUISE BAKER

Beloved wife, mother, sister, and grandmother

FEBRUARY 4, 1946 - JANUARY 8, 2011

Forever in our hearts you will stay

The day we lost you, heaven gained an angel

I kneel on my knees, resting on my heels in front of the headstone. "Hey, Grams. It's been a while since I've come to visit. I'm sorry about that. I wanted you to know that we're moving today. I couldn't leave without telling you goodbye. I don't know when I will be able to come back. Don't miss me too much . . ."

I attempt to laugh but fail. Tears fall instead—hard. I didn't wear makeup today. It was no use. I knew I'd be coming here and it always does this to me. Goodbyes aren't my thing and that will never change. It's too hard to say goodbye to someone.

I sniffle to keep my nose from running. "I really miss you, Grams. I wish you were still here. You were always good at giving me advice when I feel lost. It's only been two years and I feel like it's been forever. I miss our talks. I really need you right now. I didn't have enough time with you. I know I'm just being selfish, because you're in a better place, but I would give anything to have you back. I know I can talk to Mom, but I was always more like you. I can't hear your laugh anymore, Grams."

I change positions, resting on my right butt cheek, placing my legs side-by-side, folded behind me. I drape my arms over the top of the headstone, laying my cheek on the limestone, picturing it as her shoulder.

The floodgate breaks and I let it out. I set free all of the emotions I've been holding hostage. Grams was the one person I would let see the ugly. "I met a boy, Grams. I don't want him to be, but he's special. He's different than anyone I've ever met. He makes my heart beat off rhythm and when he smiles I get shaky and short of breath. It reminds me of when you used to tell me stories of when you met Gramps. That terrifies me. I'll never see him again, though. I had to end it. I knew in my gut he would be the one thing that could ruin me. He could tear down the walls I've spent so long building. I can't go through this again, Grams. My heart won't survive this kind of pain another time. I barely came out of the internal pain caused when God called you home."

My face is soaked, but I continue, leaving them for the sun to dry. "I would rather spend a life alone than to be destroyed over the loss of the one that held my heart. It will always come; it's just a matter of when. I don't want to see the girl I would be if my heart shattered again. I barely picked up the pieces when you left me."

My sight is blurred from the overload of tears trying to escape through the small ducts. The limestone is wet from my hysterics. "I need you, Grams. How do I live without you? I was supposed to have you at graduation or my wedding or at the birth of a child. Now that you're not here to see any of that, I don't want it at all. It's not fair. I just want you back."

My emotions are running wild. I can't breathe. My chest spasms, and I gasp for breath that will not come. I panic, feeling like a fish out of water. I can't move as I fight to breathe.

I ball up in a fetal position, trying to find relief, and I wheeze. I need my emergency inhaler, but I can't stop crying. I guess it's like the saying— *when it rains it pours*. It's been a long time coming. I haven't had an attack like this since my first one when I found out Grams passed away.

Dad kneels down and picks me up, cradling me in his arms. "Shh. Shh. It's okay, baby girl. Calm down. You need to breathe. Take long deep breaths."

Mom holds my inhaler out for me to grab. Holding it to my mouth, I release the mist and inhale into my lungs. My airway opens, and I can finally breathe, but the tears continue to pour down my face. Dad's soothing voice coats my mind. "It's okay to let it out sometimes, baby. It's not healthy to keep it all bottled up inside. I know you miss her. We all do. But she will always be in your heart. Anytime you need her, she'll be listening. You can't stop living because she is gone. She wouldn't want that for you."

Wrapping my arms around his neck, I lay my head on Dad's shoulder as my heart rate calms. My limbs are numb and tingling, and suddenly walking requires too much effort, so I let him carry me to the car. When he turns around to walk back to the car, I look over his shoulder. "Goodbye Grams."

The moment the words escape my lips a small bird lands on the headstone in my puddle of tears. When our eyes meet, it chirps. It may be silly, but I believe it's a sign she heard me. Suddenly exhausted from my emotional free fall, my eyes drift closed to the beautiful face of one charming southern boy.

THREE

Kinzleigh

Mom gave me my anxiety medicine once we got to the car, because of my panic attack this morning. It usually puts me out of it for a while. From the car ride to the flight is all a big blur. The plane just landed at the New Orleans airport. Mom and Dad are having all our vehicles transported, so we will have to get a rental until everything arrives.

Since the movers took care of everything, all we have with us are our personal belongings, which makes arriving that much easier, since we can skip baggage claim.

I'm officially in the south for the first time in my life. I'm not sure what to expect once we get to Mississippi, but I'm ready to get it over with. I just want to go to sleep. Dad said we have a bit of a drive ahead, so I think I'll do just that. Sleep always takes care of an overworked mind, allowing you to temporarily forget.

My eyes flutter open to a big green exit sign overhead that reads Highway 98 West Hattiesburg/Columbia. Dad takes the exit, and what looks like a main strip of town comes into view. I have to admit by the traffic and all the businesses, maybe I exaggerated on how bad it was here. I will find out soon enough. We pass by several shops and restaurants—many I recognize by their chain names—and I even notice a shopping mall as we drive down the highway.

Just as I'm about to complain about the lengthy drive, Dad turns onto a road marking a subdivision. He drives down the road, weaving through the houses lined on each side. Some are big and some are average, but most nice. He finally pulls in a house with a sold marker staked in the grass of the front yard. I have to give my parents props on house shopping, because it's beautiful. I'm guessing by the looks of my surroundings, this is the more prosperous people of the area that live here.

Dad kills the engine to the car and we all get out. Walking in front of the vehicle, Dad stops beside me, wrapping his arm around me and pulling me close to him. "Does this beat cow fields and trailer parks?"

The memory of dinner that night and how rude I was over that span of days plays back through my mind. I'm embarrassed remembering how I acted. "About that . . . I'm sorry Dad. I was a brat and I didn't mean any of it. I was shocked and the whole thing caught me off guard. You were right. I shouldn't be judgmental."

"I know, baby girl. It's going to be a big change for everyone. What's important is that we remain a tightknit family. There will be an adjustment for all of us. We all left something behind. Now, come on, you still have to see your room. I'm sure your mother is dying to decorate. My credit card is already dreading it," he teases.

Walking inside, the house is massive. The exterior didn't do the interior justice. The ceilings have to be twelve foot and everything is so open downstairs. Boxes and furniture are scattered everywhere throughout the room.

Mom didn't want the hassle of transporting a houseful of furniture, so she sold it and bought new. She said a new house deserves a new look. Personally, I couldn't care less what kind of furniture we have.

Mom has really good taste, though. It's crazy she is a lawyer and not an interior decorator or designer. The woman has mad skills, so I gave her free reign with my room. I'm standing in the middle of the foyer, unable to move, trying to take everything in.

"Sweetie, I had the furniture guys put your furniture in one of the rooms upstairs. If you don't like it, we can move it to the room of your choice. I thought you would want the bigger one since Konnor is away at school." Following her voice, I look over and Mom is coming in the door with an armful of bags.

"That's fine, Mom. I'll look around in a bit. I think I'm going to check out the patio and pool." I can see the glass doors that lead outside across the room.

If it stays as hot as it is outside right now, I'm sure the pool is going to be where I'm at when I'm home and not sleeping. The heat here is ridiculous. It's thick and muggy. I feel sticky and already sweating with no effort. It's also harder to breathe here compared to the California heat. It can be upward of a hundred back home and still bearable.

Walking outside, I stop on the patio in front of the pool. Well, it definitely doesn't have the view of the California hills, but I guess it isn't so bad. I scan the area. Outdoor kitchen with top of the line amenities including a big screen TV. Built-in Jacuzzi that flows into the pool. Iron lanterns outside of the door that look to be gas. And a privacy fence with lighting running along it. I wonder if it's a heated pool.

Yeah . . . It could have been way worse from the things my mind had imagined. I seat myself on the soft beige cushion lined in black that covers the dark wicker lounger beside the edge of the pool. Hands to each side of me, I bounce, getting a feel of the quality. Seems to be of thick material; definitely not cheap. I swing my legs up and lay back, pulling my shades over my eyes. Maybe I should go find my box of swimsuits. I'm sweating profusely.

"You must be my new neighbor." The words in a feminine voice are yelled across the pool. Definitely female. "Is it okay if I come through the gate?"

Turning my head toward the gate to the backyard, I see a girl that looks about my age standing in the opening of the now open gate. She has long, dark red, freshly curled hair bouncing as she walks. She is tall with slender arms and legs, but she still has curves.

Some girls get all the good genes—height plus the perks of a curvy figure. She is tan too, and it doesn't look like fake and bake tan, but natural. She is definitely the most gorgeous redhead I've ever seen, hands down.

"Sure. I'm not doing anything. We just arrived a little bit ago." She picks up pace and sits in the lounger beside me. Turning toward her, I lean my side against the back of the chair. "I'm Kinzleigh, what's your name?"

She holds out her perfectly manicured hand toward me. "Aren't you the prettiest thing . . . And here I was worried my new neighbor was going to be knocking on senior citizens' door and no fun. Name is Adalynn. Nice to meet you."

Yep, I'm definitely not in California anymore. It's going to take a while to get used to that accent. It was sexy on Breyson, but I guess it's going to be different on everyone else.

I grab her hand. Apparently, this is a common thing amongst southerners, because I remember Breyson doing the same thing, but this time I'll try not to look like an idiot.

"It's nice to meet you too, Adalynn. Don't take this the wrong way, but you're different than the type of girl I expected to meet. You're gorgeous."

"That's okay, hun. Trust me. Being from the south, you get used to the stereotypes that come our way. Where are y'all from? I have to admit, I've been dying to see who's moving in since the house sold." You can tell she is high maintenance. Maybe a friendship is in the works. I need something to keep me busy.

"I'm from California. My dad moved here to expand his business." Her brows dip in between her eyes and she looks like she is thinking something over. "What's wrong? Did I say something bad?"

"What did you say your name was?"

"Kinzleigh. It's Kinzleigh Baker. Why?" Her eyes light up and a small smile forms on her face.

"Do you know anyone around here, Kinzleigh?" Why on earth would I know anyone around here? I shake my head at her. "What part of California are you from? I've always wanted to go there, but my parents don't like to travel much. Workaholics mostly."

"Ever heard of Laguna Beach? Like the MTV show." Her eyes widen, and she has a mischievous gleam in her eyes. If she is anything like Presley I am in trouble. Then again, maybe it'll be easier to be away from her with someone like her.

She nods. "Well, the boys are going to love you; a few particular ones especially. You're beautiful and we don't get new girls that often; especially that look the way you do." She grins. "Are you going to be at Oak Grove in August?"

"I think so? Honestly, I've been so upset about this move I haven't asked that many questions, but the name sounds familiar." *I swear I've seen that somewhere. But where?* "Is that where you go to school?" Please say yes. I need to know someone, and I think I like this girl.

Nodding, she asks, "Are you a cheerleader? I can usually pinpoint them pretty far away."

"I am actually. I just tried out for a national squad and was supposed to be captain at my school senior year. Now everything is getting pulled out from under me. I feel like a freshman all over again, without the benefit of knowing any of my classmates."

"Well, Kinzleigh Baker, it's your lucky day, because I happen to be the squad captain and I think we have room for another person. What do you say; you up for it?"

I'm grinning so hard I can't even speak. Is this really happening? I can continue cheering. Maybe everything will work out after all. Without much thought, I grab her up and give her a big bear hug. "YES!"

I release her and cover my mouth, not meaning to scream so loud. "Sorry, you don't realize how much you just made my day. You don't need me to show you anything or try out, though?"

"Nope, I'm feeling generous today. I also get the vibe you know more stuff than some of the girls on the squad. We need someone else to whip them into shape. I have a good feeling about you; a feeling you and I will be best friends. Actually, I am sure of it."

"Adalynn! Let's go."

We both turn toward the sound of a female voice echoing through the backyard. "I've got to go to some family thing, but I'm picking you up in the morning to show you around a little bit. Have your measurements when I get here, so we can put in a rush order for your cheerleading uniform. Wear a swimsuit. A bunch of us are going to the creek."

She stands to leave. A what? Did she just say a creek? Ew. She notices the look of disgust on my face and laughs. "Don't worry, I'll have you broken in before long. You'll be a southern girl in no time." She curtsies, holding out the imaginary gown, thickening her accent some more. "A southern *belle* to be exact."

Then she winks and makes her way in the direction she previously came. She gets to the gate and stops. Turning back to me, now with a serious demeanor on her face, she says, "Oh, and Kinzleigh. I think you'll like it here. Give it some time and you'll see."

She leaves without another word. Maybe, just maybe, I will like it here. If everyone else is like her, it can't be that bad.

FOUR

Kinzleigh

I stayed up late last night unpacking. I was also slightly nervous about meeting new people today. I've been in my own little bubble with people I've known all my life, and now I have to start over.

It won't be long now until school starts back, and senior year will be in full swing, which means classes will commence and football season will follow. It's crazy to me that I am going to be a senior. I will finally be at the top of the totem pole. The thought of everything being so new scares me, but all I care about is cheerleading. At least I have the opportunity.

It's almost time for Adalynn to show up. The thought of swimming in mucky, snake-infested water keeps running through my mind, setting off red flags. I can't believe people actually swim in creeks. The only time I have ever seen one is on country music videos, which I rarely watch.

Digging through my box of swimsuits, I'm not sure what to wear. I will not be wearing white or designer, because there is no telling what it will look like after being in a dirty, murky creek. I'm not even sure that I'm getting in the water.

I settle on a basic bright blue and mint green bikini. At least it's not one of my expensive ones, but the thought of ruining it still bothers me, because I take care of my things. What do you even take to a creek? Surely, we're not lying in the dirt. Should I buy a lounge chair?

Playing twenty questions in my head, I hear the doorbell chime throughout the house. Running in the bathroom, I change into my swimsuit quickly. "Kinzleigh, you have company!" Mom yells up the stairs from the bottom.

"I'll be right down. Give me a few minutes," I yell in return. Moments later, a knock sounds at my door just as I'm coming back into my room. "Come in."

The door opens and Adalynn is standing on the other side, looking just as gorgeous as ever. The girl could be a model, and it makes me feel plain and ordinary. "Hey, girlie. You about ready?"

She looks me over and whistles. "Dang, girl, check out that body. You're nothing but muscle and curves. I can't wait to show you off," she says playfully.

"What are you talking about? Look at you. You're beautiful. I don't even compare to you."

Her face is clearly amused by my comment. "I feel honored that you see me that way but stop it. You really don't see it, do you?"

Did I miss something? "What do you mean?"

"Girl, you are hot. I have no idea why you are so humble, but it makes me like you more. The guys are going to be drooling at your feet. You're a likable girl, but we need to bring you out of that shell. You gotta use what you've got to your advantage. This modest, shy vibe you give off has got to go," she teases as she steers me to stand in the mirror and begins talking at our reflections. "You're wasting that gorgeous figure. Own it and show it off, because it rocks."

I swear the girl could be Presley's long-lost twin; at least from the aspect of her personality. I don't know how I attract this type of friend. It's like I have a flashing sign stamped on my forehead.

I roll my eyes. "What exactly are we supposed to take to a creek?" Every time I say it, I have the same reaction.

She looks at me and bursts out laughing. I don't know what I said that was apparently funny. "I love this. I can't wait to teach you the ways of the country kids. You take the same thing you take to the beach, silly. Go put some shorts and a tank top on and let's go."

When we walk outside there is a Chevrolet Avalanche sitting in my driveway. Looking at Adalynn, I raise my brow. "I wouldn't have taken you for a truck kind of girl.

"Hey, never judge a book by its cover, but this," she points at the truck, "is not mine. This is my dad's. Where we're going my car might not be able to handle it. Come on, California. Time's a wastin', and you have people to meet." I'm guessing that's supposed to be my nickname.

Original.

We pass over a bridge—on what road I have no clue—before turning down the grass-worn path just after it ends. The trail was clearly made by cars driving on it repetitively over time. It goes down a slight hill and curves around to the left, continuing underneath the bridge. It reminds me of something that should be in a scary movie.

There is graffiti painted on the bridge, and if you look down another slope you can see running brown water. If it weren't the middle of the day, I would be looking for someone to pop out of the bushes with a knife. What if this is a body dump?

As I stumble out of the truck and shut the door, a black lifted truck pulls in behind us. My thoughts instantly sway to the night in Ryland's truck.

The bed of the truck is filled with shirtless guys wearing ball caps. I going to assume they're part of the football team by the solid muscle on each one of them. Once parked, three other girls exit the cab of the truck. Great, I already get awkward around people I don't know. Last time I was around *one* unfamiliar body it didn't go so well, and now I am graced with a whole slew of them.

Guys start jumping from the high truck bed like a group of gorillas, whistling as they take us in. "Who's your new friend, Adalynn?" I seek out the voice, my head following the guy that was driving as he stops in front of us. "I don't think I've seen you around here," he says, scanning my body. "I know most people our age within a fifty-mile radius."

He's cute enough with his ash-blond hair that has a natural cowlick in the front. He has honey-brown eyes and his dimples do his smile wonders. He appears to be about five-foot-ten with defined muscles.

Hello six pack.

He's no Breyson, but he's definitely sexy. I never imagined southern guys would be so hot. One of the girls moves closer to him, clearly staking her claim.

Adalynn comes up beside me, putting her arm over my shoulders. "Simon, this is Kinzleigh. She just moved here from California and has the pleasure of being my new neighbor. I'm showing her how we have fun around here."

She looks at me, but then points as she introduces everyone. "Kinzleigh, this is Simon, along with half of the football team and some of your new squad members." Pointing to the girl with the scowl on her face next to Simon first, she begins naming them off. "This is Dallas, Layne, and Kristen."

Looking at each of them, I attempt to smile and be polite. The Simon guy keeps looking me over with a big grin on his face, making me slightly uncomfortable. "Oh, we can show her some fun," he says, and when he does that Dallas girl narrows her eyes at him and begins to pout.

I am going to assume she has claimed a boy that is not claimable. That's exactly the type of girl I will never be. Look at her puppy face and love-struck eyes. It's sad more than anything else and clearly it doesn't work on him anyway, because he is still staring at me.

I continue to look between everyone, wondering if we're going to just stand here or actually do something. This is awkward, and I'm not trying to become enemies with the girls I'm about to be surrounded by daily over a guy that doesn't mean anything to me. Simon grabs my hand and pulls me toward the creek bank before I can even respond.

As I'm being pulled away, I look back at Adalynn, pleading with her not to leave me with him. She is saying something to Dallas in hushed tones. Before I get too far away, I hear, "Pull the claws back in, Dallas. She's not after Simon, even though you don't have a say if she were. He's not yours. I warned you about hooking up with him. He only uses you for convenience."

Then she pulls Dallas in and whispers something in her ear that seems to smooth the frown off her face, and she nods. We reach the edge of the water and I stop, trying to pull my hand free from Simon's. Standing ankle deep in water, he turns to me with a smirk on his face. "What's wrong? You can swim, right?"

I nod but scrunch my nose as I take in my surroundings. The stench is awful—like dead fish or some small animal. There are empty beer bottles and random pieces of trash lying in various spots on the edge of the creek. I can see pieces of wood poking up through the surface of running water throughout, making me wonder what all there is down there that could be stepped on—a breeding farm for tetanus. "Yes, I can swim. I lived across from a beach all my life, but do you guys really swim in this kind of water? It makes me feel dirty just looking at it. It's brown."

He smiles and looks from me to the water. When he returns the glance, his dimples are deep-set in his cheeks from the grin on his face. Wow. He really is attractive. His bottom lip is pouty with a thin upper lip. He could be a good distraction from *him.*

My chest tightens at the small remembrance I allowed passage into my thoughts. I will not think about him. I had decided if things got easier as the summer went on that I wouldn't contact him again. It'll only be more upsetting when life steps in the way and we're too busy to talk. It's better to remember what little bit of time we had.

"This is cleaner than ocean water, believe it or not, because it's running water. So, you coming, girl, or do I need to help you out?" He winks, as if that's going to make the decision easier. It might, if I looked at those dimples long enough.

I refocus on his eyes instead. I've clearly amused him. I'm glad someone finds this funny, because I am really freaking out about this cloudy, brown water. What if I see a snake? Or something worse. What would actually be worse? What if I don't see it, because of the color of the water? "I don't know if I want to. Maybe I can just sit out and watch you guys. I don't have to get in."

I back away from the water. His eyes never leave mine, but a smirk pulls up at the corner of his mouth. I'm not sure what he is making that face for until I run into a hard, bare chest, causing me to squeal in surprise. "Where you going, sweetheart? We haven't even started having fun yet."

I turn around to a guy that is a little more of a stocky build, and shorter, but still has a nice body just lacks the definition. He's probably a lineman. He is scruffier looking thanks to his facial hair; making it obvious he hasn't had an appointment lately with a razor. He has reddish-brown hair and brown eyes. "I don't think we've been properly introduced. My name is Jared."

"Hi." I hold up my hand and slightly wave. I could hit myself. This always happens. I get awkward and act weird around guys. Maybe I shouldn't have acted so dumb when it came to hanging around guys back home, because it shows now. I need to make friends being in a new place or this year is going to suck.

Adalynn finally appears with the other girls following behind, loaded down with floats and towels. Some of the other guys set down a cooler; cooling who knows what, but I can only guess it's probably beer. I don't know where they would get alcohol at our age, but I hope they have some water in there.

It's scorching hot out here. The gross brown water is starting to sound pretty good with this beam of heat boring into my skin, leaving a rosy color in its wake. I can't even remember the last time being in the sun left me burnt. Normally I tan. The sun here is brutal. The funny part—it's the same darn sun!

"Jared, stop harassing my new friend. You're going to run her off and I need her for my squad," she says, giving him a light shove. She then links her arm with mine, towing me toward the water, but I stop at the same edge I can't seem to get past. "Come on, hun. I swear it's not as bad as you think. If you don't like it, you can have one of the floats.

Before I have time to respond, Simon picks me up from behind, cradling me. He takes off running into the water until we are submerged almost completely and lets go. It happened so fast I didn't even have a chance to fight it. I splash water in his face as I stand. "You butthole!" I try to act mad, but then he flashes that set of dimples and I end up laughing instead.

He raises his brow and takes a step toward me. "Hey, someone had to get you in the water. Did you just call me a butthole? I don't think I've been called that in years. Not old enough to cuss?" He laughs. It's not that I have never said a curse word or have anything against those that use them, but I choose to only use them on rare occurrences. My mother was never fond of curse words. She thought they devalued an individual when used in excess. I guess we pick up a lot of the things that we're taught throughout the years.

"Ha-ha. I just think of other synonyms faster," I say as everyone else joins us in the water. He runs at me, and dives, as he grabs me by the thighs. Then he shoves his head between my legs, catching me off guard, and stands up with me on his shoulders. My balance is thrown off. I Grab his hair in my hands to avoid falling off and lock my feet around his waist. Jeez, he is strong. "What are you doing?"

I look around and Dallas is staring daggers at me. I thought we were past that. That was short-lived. Great. I'm in a new place and I've already got someone that looks like she wants to rip me to shreds. "Chicken fight!" Jared yells into the air with his hands formed around his mouth to portray a megaphone. "Do we have any challengers?"

"I'll do it," Dallas calls out as she wades through the waist-deep water. This should be interesting. She is about my size and I'm good at sports, so I should be able to take her, but I learned a long time ago not to judge someone by their size.

I've pissed her off without even trying, so she is most likely going to try and make me look stupid. Jared looks like he is about twice Simon's size, so I'm going to have to try and knock her off. I don't see him going down easily. "Squat down, Jared, and let me on."

Simon grips my thighs above my knees, but it's close enough to my hips it makes my stomach flutter. How am I supposed to concentrate with his hands right there? "You ready?"

He looks up at me and winks with that dang smile glued to his face again. "Don't let her intimidate you," he says low so only I can hear. "She is only doing this because of me. It's not your fault she thinks we're in a relationship. I have never given her reason to think she has a claim on me. Show her what you got."

I'm not sure why he felt the need to give me that tidbit of information, because if they really were dating, I'd hope he wouldn't be doing this in front of her, or at all, but it does make me feel more comfortable. I don't want to be classified as a boyfriend thief when I have only been here a day. So far, I like the people I've met.

Simon makes me feel at ease around him. I feel like I've known him for years versus thirty minutes. I think Adalynn was right. Maybe I am going to like it here. At least, I hope so. And then the count begins, signaling it's time, and the brawl begins.

Once I beat Dallas at shoulder wars, not once but twice, she stopped acting like a brat and actually was pretty likable. We stayed at the creek most of the day, relaxing and floating along the current. The guys and some of the girls drank beer that came from the cooler the guys brought. They never mentioned where they got it since most of us are only seventeen. I graciously declined when it was offered to me, and thankfully Adalynn had brought a small cooler with water.

The only times I've had alcohol was wine at communion, on special occasions at dinner, and it was a minimal amount. I am not into drinking. I've seen it make people do stupid things. Nothing good ever comes out of it, that's for sure. High school kids only drink for one reason—to get drunk. I would rather hold down a decent reputation.

Adalynn pulls into my driveway just as the sun is going down. I can feel the heat radiating from my sun-kissed skin. "Thanks for today. It was nice," I say as I step down from the truck and shut the door.

She cracks the window. "No problem, hun. See you later!" And then she pulls off toward her house a few feet away.

I stand in my driveway, my thoughts consuming me. I couldn't have asked for a more perfect day. New friends in a new place that isn't as bad as I thought it would be.

One chapter of my life has ended, and another began. I am almost excited to see what this year holds for me. There is only one thing that would secretly make it better, or one person, I guess, would be a more appropriate word.

Just the thought of those soul-quenching deep blue eyes makes my heart go pitter-patter in my chest. "As usual, beautiful boy, I'll meet you in my dreams," I mumble and make my way toward my house.

FIVE

Breyson

I wake up to the sound of my alarm clock going off on the table by my bed. Rolling over onto my stomach, I cover my head with the pillow, trying to drown out the sound. I'm about to doze back off when my door creaks open. "Breyson, get up. It's the first day of school and my first day of high school. I want to get there early enough to find my classes. I don't know the building like you do."

The first day of school always sucks; more so now that I am all out of whack over a girl I'll never see again. She won't answer anymore. I've tried several times over the last week—end of summer.

But, now it's here—senior year. I should stay in bed. It's pointless to go the first day, because all the teachers do is go over rules in the handbook that haven't changed from the year prior.

I used to like the first day of school. It was a day to see which girls got hotter over the summer. All of them put forth their best effort the first day of school. But now, the desire is gone. What does it say when I can't even hook up with another girl because of her? The last two weeks have been filled with end of summer parties and I've tried, on a few different occasions—mostly from the relief of the Natalie situation—but my mojo was left in Kinzleigh's bed.

The farthest I've made it with a girl was with Adalynn. I can't even make it to a bedroom with a girl now before her face flashes through my mind, blurring my vision. After the third time, I stopped going to parties all together.

I haven't been playing football as good as I usually do. Last practice I got tackled four of the times I could've easily made a touchdown, because when I was supposed to be running the ball I was lost in thought, and that doesn't include the interceptions.

Coach is pissed and said if I don't get my head out of my ass by this week, he is benching me. No field time equals no recruiters, and this is the year that counts.

I've become a hermit; not hanging out with any of my friends. The last week I have been in the gym more than I have my entire life trying to work out this frustration, since obviously, I can't release it the way I prefer. I don't know what Kinzleigh did to me, but I want my life back. I need my life back. This is more than I bargained for.

The desperation even got so bad that I called Ryland a few days ago and got Presley's number. It was a dead end, though, because she said Kinzleigh's family changed cellphone companies just recently and hasn't given them the new numbers yet. It's like she's a ghost—only alive in the essence of my memory.

The sooner I get to school, the sooner I'll be preoccupied with whatever girls follow me around between classes. That's the plan, at least. I may not be able to have sex but talking will keep my mind from wandering into the never-ending maze known as Kinzleigh Baker.

My sister stealing my pillow and hitting me in the head with it breaks me from my thoughts. "Breyson! Did you hear what I said? You're the only one left in the house."

I roll over. "I'm up, I'm up. Stop hitting me with the pillow, Brylee. Where is Braxton and Briar?" Throwing off the covers, I get out of bed and stretch my still sore muscles.

"Ew, would you put some clothes on? I don't want to see you in your boxers. To answer your question, they both left to go pick up someone for school. The buttholes wouldn't wait on me." She covers her eyes with her hand for emphasis.

She's in that dramatic *I'm starting to like boys* stage. She wants their attention. It's obvious. It's full on. Makeup. Primping. Taking more time picking out clothes. Here lately, it always seems like she's wearing something I've never seen before. Her cellphone stays glued to her hand.

Thank god we don't share a bathroom. She only lasted this long because she has three older brothers who would beat a boy's ass for messing with their sister.

This summer there have been more girls in my house than there have ever been with the three of us and girls. Eighth grade girls annoy me. The little flirty looks and the giggling is a constant. They've taken over the pool, and a lot of times the game room too. The nights she has her friends over, I stay far, far away.

"Nope. You're in my room, Brylee. This is how I sleep. If you don't want to see me in my boxers, then stay out of my room. You have your own. It's that simple." I walk past her and out the door, heading for the shower.

"Whatever, grumpy," she says, following me. "What's wrong with you? Some girl shut you down?"

"No," I say, pushing the door shut when she looks down at her blue nails. It's a strange color to wear on your fingers. What was probably considered trashy a decade ago is now in style. Makes no sense.

She shoves her palm into the door, stopping it. "Are you going to follow me into the bathroom or let me shower?"

"Just hurry up, okay? I don't want to be late for class. I have to find my locker, figure out the code, and find my classroom for first block all before the tardy bell."

"Meet me at the truck in fifteen minutes." I don't give her the chance to say anything else before I shut the bathroom door, locking her out.

Pulling into the school parking lot. I search for my assigned parking spot and shut off the engine to my truck. Grabbing my book bag and schedule, I step down out of my truck and lock the doors.

Other students are making their way toward the sidewalk, backpacks attached to their backs. It's sunny, but since it's early it's not unbearable. By lunch it'll feel like Hell on earth. August in the south is no joke. The humidity here is much worse than any other place I've been.

I hold out my arms to my side, stretching. It feels good when my spine pops. Brylee shuts the passenger side door, looking at a sheet of paper with her purse hanging in the bend of her arm. "Where is English I?"

I start walking, taking her schedule when she falls in line beside me as I pass the tailgate. I glance at the teacher's name—Mr. Woodson. I give it back to her. "He's in the main hall, all the way at the end in the corner. Pay attention. He can be a bit of an ass and loves to call on the people not listening for embarrassment. If you study the stuff he goes over in class his tests are easy. Might as well get ready for all the writing you're going to have to do. Essays are his favorite things to assign. It takes most people half the course to figure out his method, but he never just pulls from the textbook. You can pass with an A without even opening it. It's always what he goes over in class. Why you should pay attention."

"Great. Of course I get that class first block when I'm still half asleep. Just my luck."

"Brylee, wait up." We both turn around at the same time. Melody, her best friend, is well on her way to being right beside us. "Walk with me."

I start back walking. "I'm gonna go. Text me if you have a question." She nods, already in excited, girl conversation before I've made it five feet.

Students are scattered all over the place. I walk down the hall in the direction of the lockers. When I get to my locker, there are already a few girls waiting on me. It never ceases to amaze me how they get information. It's the first day of school and locker assignments change every year, but somehow, they know where mine is.

They are so predictable, unlike Kinzleigh. Dammit! I've done it again. Everything ends up comparing to her. I can't deny it, though; it's one thing that drew me to her. She is spontaneous and does the complete opposite of what you think she is going to do. I feel like banging my head against the metal to escape the constant thoughts of her.

"What's up, ladies? Need something?" What I thought would be a nice diversion from the nuisance of my thoughts, ends up having the opposite effect.

"We were just wondering if you had first period with any of us," Lacy says.

"So we can sit together before the teacher locks in the seating arrangement," Kelly adds.

They all smile sweetly, batting their mascara-caked eyelashes, aggravating me further. I need to come up with some way to get a grip on all of these feelings or I'm going to be in a permanent bad mood all year. At this rate, I'll end up an alcoholic by graduation. "What class are you headed to?" Jennifer asks, stepping closer to me.

"Physics." I open my locker and shove everything inside, except my pen, slipping it in the pocket of my khaki pants. All the schools went to uniforms a few years ago, leaving the halls dotted with multicolored polos and slacks. Usually, the only people that take physics are the smart kids or the ones that have taken everything else. I'm the lucky one that has to get my schedule approved by my dad, as do my brothers, and I'm sure Brylee too, so here I am stuck with advanced courses. They all put on their fake puppy faces and scatter off toward their classes.

By lunch, I'm in no better mood than I was this morning. After physics I went straight to calculus. All of my classes are hard, so maybe by the time assignments start, homework and football will consume my thoughts and time. Once I get through the cafeteria line with my tray, I head in the direction of the football table. We sit at the same table every year.

Sitting in my claimed seat, I notice everyone in some kind of serious conversation. Something must be pretty big to have all of their attention. I look across the table to one of the second-string players. "What's got them so focused?"

His face lights up, as if me talking to him made his day. He's one of the sophomores if I remember correctly and doesn't see any playing time unless we're up by double the points, at least, in the fourth quarter on the scoreboard. Coach never gets bigheaded about being ahead unless it's a for sure win. I think it's a superstitious thing.

He swallows his mouthful of food. "Some new girl. She's been hanging around with Adalynn and Simon all morning. Word in the halls is she's Adalynn's neighbor, meaning she must come from money if I remember what that house next-door looks like. I think they have been hanging out since she moved here a couple of weeks ago."

He picks up his water and untwists the cap, continuing before taking a sip. "One of the girls on the cheerleading squad said she is one of the cheerleaders now. She's hot as hell, though. I saw her this morning. Seems kind of quiet. Too bad she's a senior or I'd be trying to talk to her. Probably wouldn't matter if she wasn't. I think Simon has called dibs on her judging by the way he walks her to all of her classes, not giving anyone else a chance to get near her. After first block he was already traipsing after her. The boy moves in quick." He laughs. "Dallas is pissed."

New girl? Why am I just now hearing about a new girl at lunch? News like that usually travels quickly around here. People can't wait to stir up the latest gossip and drama. I would think a new girl qualifies as an important topic of conversation. If half of the football team is talking about it, then it has to be. "What new girl?"

"I don't remember her name. Kinley maybe? She moved here from . . ." He scratches the back of his head, trying to gather his thoughts. "Oh yeah. California."

My heart skips a beat and my eyes go wide. No way. I jump to my feet. The sudden commotion draws a crowd of stares across the cafeteria, but I don't care. It can't be her, can it? A tidal wave of emotion courses through my body. There is no way I would be this lucky. It has to be a coincidence. The entire football table stopped talking and is staring at me like I've lost my mind, the kid across from me especially. Devin—his name just dawned on me. I place my hands together down the center of my face. "Kinzleigh," slips from my lips before I can stop it.

"Hey, that's her name. Have you met her? She's one of the hottest girls I've ever seen." He is still rattling off worthless information that I care nothing about. One thing does stick out, though—Simon. He just said Simon is trying to get his grubby little whoring hands on her.

Over my dead body.

That stupid prick.

He uses enough of the girls in this school, along with others. He damn sure isn't getting mine. He doesn't have lunch this block.

He will not get her.

If I recite it to myself enough times, it's bound to stick. All this time I've been going mentally insane and she's been under my nose—about ten freaking minutes down the highway. This is the kind of shit that happens when I stay cooped up in the house.

For weeks she has possibly been hanging out with Simon—the dickhead probably trying to sleep with her. My hands clench by my sides. I have the twitch in my arms, ready to swing. Everything visible is behind a red filter. I have to find her. Once I get to her, I will not let her go. She can fight it or not. I storm off in a rage, determined to look in every corridor of this school until I find her.

I know she can't be with Adalynn right now, because she is on my lunch block and sitting at the cheerleaders' table. That can only mean one thing. Kinzleigh is with Simon somewhere. I hope and pray that when I talk to Adalynn she didn't know who Kinzleigh was and purposefully keep it from me, or may God help her. After we had that little heart-to-heart in the boathouse at Simon's, she should know better. I know she wouldn't do this to me. I've never pegged her for that kind of girl.

When I get to the table the cheerleaders sit at, Dallas takes me in, eyes wide, and mumbles something I can't hear. Adalynn turns around, confused by the look on her face. "Breyson? What's wrong?"

"One question. I swear to God, Adalynn, if you lie to me, I am going to be pissed." I have almost lost my sanity over this girl and Adalynn knew her name. To know it could have been avoided with a text from her makes me so angry I can't think. "Did you know?"

Her breath catches as she realizes what I'm referring to. "I didn't know your number, Breyson. I knew you would be at school. What did you want me to do?"

"We don't live in the fucking nineties, Adalynn. The internet is readily available on everyone's cellphones. We're Facebook friends. There is a little thing called 'messenger' or posting on someone's timeline—*I need to tell you something important.* There's even a 'DM' option on Instagram. A little effort and my life would have been less complicated!" She looks up and down my face, starting to panic. I have been known to have a temper, and when I do it shows.

I slap my palms down on the table, causing a ruckus in the cafeteria. Stepping back slightly with my left leg, I bend over, trying to clear my raging thoughts. I bury my face in the bend of my arm, trying to calm myself down before I completely snap.

One, two, three, four, five, six, seven . . .

I count to myself, but it doesn't help. Looking around the table at the rest of the girls in shock, I stop on Adalynn directly to my left. "Where is she, Adalynn?"

"Breyson, I'm sorry. I thought it would be a nice surprise. Don't be a dick. Jeez, I didn't think it was this bad. I've never seen you this worked-up over a girl before." Standing here listening to her ramble is just making it worse, and deep down, I know she didn't do it maliciously.

"Tell me where she is, Adalynn." I've wasted enough time in misery to continue on.

She looks at her cellphone. "She should be coming out of chemistry in about five minutes. Do you want me to text her?"

"No! I'll handle it." I'm becoming more and more of an ass, but all this stored frustration seems to come out in waves. Taking off in a sprint toward the glass doors, I push them open a little harder than I meant to. I'm sure everyone will be talking about all this activity next period.

I come into the main hall right as the bell rings. Doors open and kids start filing out of classrooms one after the other. About halfway to the chemistry classroom I see those blonde curls and my heart stops. All I want to do is run up to her and pick her up in my arms. I didn't realize I could miss someone so much.

She doesn't see me right off, because she has her head turned talking to Simon. Jealousy floods my mind, drowning every rational thought, causing me to stop mid-step. Maybe I should just lay him out right here in the middle of the hall. He may get any girl he wants, but he isn't getting this one. I'll kill him first.

She is walking directly toward me. When she gets within hearing distance it feels like my heart starts up again; pounding so hard I can feel it all over my body. She is more beautiful than the last time I saw her. The old saying goes—*absence makes the heart grow fonder.* I'm starting to believe it's true.

"Kinzleigh." A name that falls from my lips so easily—reverently.

She turns her head at the sound of my voice and her eyes connect with mine. I'm drawn to her like a magnet is to metal. She freezes in the middle of the hall, clutching her books in her arms. I move forward, slowly, as her eyes search mine.

"Breyson?" My name comes out in a whisper. I can hear the confusion in her voice, as if she's not sure I'm real and maybe a figment of her imagination.

"Yeah. . . It's me, baby." In this moment, no one else exists but her. I feel like I've been walking around with half of my heart, not beating, and now I've found the missing half. Like the pull of gravity, they collide, intertwining with each other and begin to beat again as one. Her eyes gloss over. I can tell she's attempting to hold back tears. She drops her books to the floor.

When I get close enough to touch her, a solemn expression forms, but her eyes never turn away. "I didn't think you were going to talk to me again. I kept trying. I've missed you." One sole tear escapes the corner of her eye, trickling down her cheek. Reaching up, I catch it with the back of my index finger. "Don't cry, baby."

"What are you doing here? How did you find me? This has to be circumstance. Stuff like this doesn't just happen." I can't stand it anymore. It's been too long since I've touched and tasted those lips. We have a no PDA—public display of affection—rule at school, but sometimes rules are meant to be broken.

I smile. "This is where I live, Kinzleigh. Where I go to school. And now you go here too. I can't explain it. I don't know how we got this lucky, but I'm scared to question it. Maybe serendipity is real. What I do know—I've left you once and it almost drove me insane. Don't ask me to do it again. Come hell or high water, I'm staying."

Placing my palm against her cheek, I cup my fingers around her neck, pulling her to me carefully, her lips mere inches from mine. "I just have one question. Did you miss me too?"

Her eyes scan mine for a moment before she closes her eyes and exhales. "More than you'll ever know."

That's all I needed to know before my lips crash with hers.

SIX

Kinzleigh

I have missed these lips. More than I should, I know. I've dreamed about them every night since the last time I got to experience them in reality. I can't stop kissing him and I don't want to. He doesn't seem to want to stop either. His kiss is like my inhaler. I don't want to need it, but I do. His kiss speaks where words aren't needed. He lets me feel his emotions, opening himself up to me. Misery. Torment. Aggravation. It's all in his kiss.

I can't imagine anything ever being perfect, because nothing ever is, but that kiss is as close to perfection as I will ever get.

Now that I'm here, surrounded by him for at least a year, there is no use in fighting it. It's only going to wear me down. I want him. I just have to be careful not to get my heart involved or all will be lost.

I can't let that happen.

One year is what I can give and then I have to set him free—for good. I *have* to. What scares me is that something makes me think I've already set myself up for failure. Something tells me I'm already in too deep. One word comes to mind when I think of him: quicksand.

Reluctantly, I pull away from his lips. Looking around, everyone is standing in the hall with their mouths wide open, gaping at us. This should be good. Not only am I the new girl, but also standing in the middle of the hall making out like a tramp. For all everyone knows I don't even know Breyson.

"Breyson, how do you know Kinzleigh?" Simon asks, clenching his jaw.

I forgot he was even standing there. I'm being rude. Simon has been a really good friend since I met him at the creek. I've hung out with him a few times but nothing serious. He flirts, but I pretend not to notice like I have all my life.

Well, until . . . *him*. The boy standing in front of me. He changes everything. A prime example would be right now, making out in the middle of a huge school hallway packed full of kids from class change. Breyson never breaks eye contact with me. "I'll make sure she gets to where she needs to be, Simon."

"Why don't you let her decide? She's not one of the girls that follows you around like a little pet." A look washes over his face I've never seen. It's scary. A little bit crazed.

Most of the other kids finally scattered off to their classes. It's just us three. I look over at Simon, trying to cool him down a little. "It's okay, Simon. I need to talk to Breyson anyway. I'll catch up with you later, okay?"

He looks between the two of us for a moment before he finally turns to leave. He gets a few steps and turns back around with a smirk on his face. "Oh yeah. Kinzleigh, don't forget our study date tonight. My place. Calculus teacher is hardcore. I'm going to need all the help I can get," he says, looking at Breyson before he scampers off. That was dirty.

When I gaze at Breyson, he looks like he's about to kill someone. He turns around and punches the closest locker, leaving a small dent. I don't like seeing him all worked up like this.

I lean against the row of lockers in front of him, still trying to process all of this. I grab a fistful of his shirt and pull him toward me, kissing the edge of his mouth. "Hey, don't let him get to you. He's just a friend I met with Adalynn at the creek a while back."

He has his arms raised above his head, resting on the facing of the locker, looking down at me. He has the most serious expression, and I can't tell what he's thinking. "He wants you, Kinzleigh. I know him better than you. He'll—"

"So what." I can't tell if he's mad at me or just mad. "I don't want him; not like that." I can see the muscles in his jaw twitching as he stares into my eyes. He's so sexy. Will I ever get used to what he does to me?

I clamp my hand over his wrist and pull down his hand, placing it where my heart should be. "He doesn't do this to me." My heart is racing. I feel like I just ran a 5k marathon.

He takes the hand holding onto his shirt and moves it to the position that mirrors mine. "You do it to me too, beautiful girl. Come with me? We need to talk. That's not something we can do here. Let's leave. Missing half of a day won't hurt anything."

He never lets go of my hand as he walks toward the doors leading outside. Lord, help me, because I don't think I can help myself.

We sprint toward the parking lot, hand-in-hand, careful not to get caught by the parking lot cameras. As we come closer to a candy apple red Ford F-150, he presses a button on the remote, causing the lights to flash and the locks to sound. The truck is lifted with big tires and black rims that accent well with the dark tint and black accessories.

As he opens the passenger door for me, I look at him questioningly. "What?" He grins from ear to ear as he gives me a boost by wrapping his arm around my waist.

His touch does things to me that should be off limits to any woman wanting to keep her sanity. It makes me needy; something I've never been and refuse to become. Taking a seat, I look at him, but I break. I laugh, shaking my head. "Southern boys and their big trucks."

"Real men drive trucks," he says, winking at me, revealing that beautiful smile. My heart feels like it is going to run away and burst through my chest. Closing my eyes, I rub my palm over my heart. If only I had a way to stop it from soaring, because I'm afraid of the fall.

When I open them, he is watching me, saying nothing at all. He places his hand over mine, grasping it, and then brings it toward his mouth. He kisses my palm. "I'm scared too. Just don't run from me. We can be scared together."

How does he do that? With one look it's like he can see into my mind, reading my most intimate thoughts. I feel bare and I don't like it. I've always hidden my emotions. "I'll certainly try."

And I meant it. Because running leads me right back to him.

We drive down the highway in silence, alone in our thoughts. Looking out my window, the trees pass by one by one. Sunlight beams down on them, creating a magical glow between the leaves. I love this time of year. It's so open here.

He turns down a few different roads, and halfway down the most recent the road changes from pavement to dirt. Nothing exists here but woods. "Where are we going?"

He looks over at me, no emotions present on his face. "Just somewhere that we can talk where I know we won't be bothered. I would have taken you to my house, but I didn't want you to think this was about sex; it's not. You'll hear rumors about me, but I am asking you to promise that you will ask me before you listen to anything, okay?"

What kind of rumors? For some reason, it doesn't matter to me. I trust him more than I've ever trusted anyone. "Okay."

He pulls over to the side of the dirt road. Killing the engine, he points his head over to the other side of the road. "Come on."

When we get to the other side, you can see running water at the bottom of the slope, filled with rocks and broken limbs. "What is this place?"

He sits down in the grass and pulls me between his legs to sit, my back facing his chest. The ground is warm against my hands as I get into a comfortable position, as if it's been under a warming lamp all morning. The smell of freshly cut grass wafts through the air from somewhere. "It's private land, which is why it's dirt, but I think it's public right-of-way. If you keep going it turns into a paved road again."

He wraps his arms around my waist, pulling me as close as he can get me. Resting his chin over my shoulder, his cheek pressed against mine, I can barely breathe. "I've missed this."

His voice sounds pained and weak, but why I'm not sure. "Why?" It may be a dumb question, but it's one I want to know the answer to. All we both talked about was that it was nothing serious.

"I don't know. I've tried not to, but I can't stop it. You're all I think about. Ever since that day on the beach, I can't forget you, no matter how hard I try. I'm sorry, Kinzleigh. I know you just wanted a fling. Hell, that's what I wanted, but now you're here and it's so much more to me than that." My heart squeezes the more miserable he sounds.

I turn around, kneeling on my knees between his legs. I grab his face between my hands and kiss his lips. "Hey, stop it. I'd be lying if I said I didn't miss this too. You kind of became my best friend back home."

He extends his legs out in front of him to rest on the grass and pulls me on his lap to straddle him. "I don't deserve to have you, though. I'll never lie to you, Kinzleigh. I've been with a lot of girls for my age. I shouldn't have let that night happen, but I was selfish and wanted you for myself, and for some reason I can't tell you no."

His breath tickles my face and I find myself running my fingers through the back of his hair. It's short, but just long enough to grab ahold of.

I don't want to think of him with other girls. It sends a negative energy though my body I don't want, making me bitter. "You don't have to tell me about your history with other girls, Breyson. We have never been a couple. We're not a couple now. I have no claim to you or reason to be mad about your sexual endeavors. We haven't known each other long. I may be naïve, but I know most people our age are having sex, unlike me. I've hung around Presley long enough to know better. I didn't think that you were abstinent when I decided to sleep with you."

Something flashes in his eyes, but he quickly recovers. He shakes his head. "Let me finish, please. I need to get all of this out. I need to tell you what I want, but in order to have it I need you to know what you're getting. Will you listen? I know you're stubborn and have to always have the last damn word and be in control, but do this for me."

Well, when he puts it like that how can I tell him no? He always makes me do the opposite of what I intend to do anyway, so why try and fight it now? "Okay."

A flapping sound in the trees draws my attention. Birds are playing with each other on a tree branch. Then a rustling pulls me in the other direction. A squirrel took off running up the trunk of a different tree, causing the leaves to shake. He takes my chin and pulls me back to him, smiling. "Yes, things are a little different here."

Everything is peaceful as he searches my eyes. I focus on the rhythm of our breathing and the water flowing over the rocks down below. "My interest with girls went as far as sex and that's it. I made it clear, upfront, that's all it was ever going to be. I never promised anything more. I only dated Natalie because we've been friends for a long time and she came on to me one night, but I never gave her anything more than a title and a good time. I was monogamous with her for the time we dated . . . until you."

A fearful look takes hold of his features before he is able to smooth it out. "I've since learned the bitch is crazy when it comes to me. She may be difficult, but she means nothing. And she lies."

He pauses for a minute. "I'm getting off track. As soon as I kissed you on that pier, I broke it off with her. I don't care about her that way. It was more of a convenience. My feelings for you showed me I didn't need to be with her. You're all I can think about. I know you don't want anything serious, and to be honest, neither do I. When we graduate, we will most likely part ways for college, but for now, I can't let you go—this go."

He rubs his fingertips over the skin exposed from my shirt riding up. It gives me chills on a warm day. "I've tried several times and several ways. I want you in whatever way I can have you. You have one chance to tell me no. If I'm not what you want, I'll try my best to leave you alone and deal with my feelings. I'll figure out a way to see you every day without beating some guy's ass."

His eyes sway to my lips and back up again. "But should you choose me, you will be mine and only mine. Fuck Simon or any other guy in school."

I lean down and kiss his neck, but he pulls away, confusing me. "Kinzleigh," he says, now sounding a little worried. "I need to tell you something before you hear from it someone else."

"Okay . . . You're freaking me out. What is it, Breyson?"

"I hooked up with Adalynn right after I came back from California. Since she's your friend, you should know.

Hurt ensues. I have no right to feel upset, but she is my friend, and I can't help but to be bothered that he barely left my bed before jumping into someone else's. There has been no one else since him and jumping in Preston's bed would have been as easy as looking at him a certain way, especially in Cabo. But I didn't.

I start to move off of him, trying to think. He stops me. "I couldn't go through with it."

I'm confused. "But you just said—"

"I didn't sleep with her. We did some things. I was upset you didn't take me to the airport. I was angry you were pushing me away. I was trying to prove you didn't change me. But all I proved was that you did. It was weird. All I could see was your body and your beautiful face."

I blink over and over. What do I say to that? Am I pissed he hooked up with Adalynn? Yes! Do I have a right to be? No. Is this what I want? Do I want to be tied down with a girlfriend title? I don't like the idea of being anyone's property, and that's what that sounds like to me. "I don't know, Breyson. My head is spinning from everything. I'm getting a headache. I don't like possession over someone. I'm my own person. I will not succumb to someone else's wants or demands. That's usually what comes from having a *boyfriend*. I've worked too hard to establish being my own self."

He shakes his head. "I don't care whether you call yourself my girlfriend or not. Titles don't matter to me, but if you hook up with me from this point forward, you hook up with *only* me. I will give you the same respect in return. I can't handle the thought of you being with someone else. I want you all to myself."

I twirl my hair in my fingers, staring at him. He does this to me. Every.

Single. Time. Each time our eyes meet, he holds me to him, not allowing me to look away. If he's being truthful, and that's all it is, then maybe I can handle it. As long as he doesn't plan on ordering me around.

I don't want to give myself to anyone else that way anyway. I never planned to hook up with someone else. Once you've had a first time like me, it ruins you for anything less. "So, to make sure we're on the same page, you're suggesting we hang out just like we did in Cali? The two of us hooking up with each other and no one else? No expectations otherwise? No trying to control what I do or me, right? No trying to tell me who I can be *platonic* friends with, male or female? Just making the best out of senior year and getting each other out of our systems, right?"

He nods. "You can title us if you want to or not. I don't care as long as I know in here," he points to his temple, "and in here," he lays his hand over his heart, "that you're mine."

Why do I feel like this will change everything? That this is going to be so much more than what is being said? I feel like this will be the end of my control over my heart. Will this ruin me? Make me regret this decision? He's dangerous for me.

Something tells me, after this, there is no going back to before. Warnings fire off in my brain. Do I wish I could tell him no? Yes. Am I going to? Never. He is my drug of choice—my poison.

I'm going to ride the high, but what scares me is coming down. Will I hit rock bottom? Will I survive? I'm not sure, but the high keeps me coming back for more. I may never come back from this, but the addiction has me jumping off the cliff.

Looking at him, he's silent, waiting for me to answer. I know I'm about change the course of my entire life. It scares me and excites me. When I'm around him there is a force that dominates all rational thought and my decision-making ability. I could fight tooth and nail, but I could still lose everything.

Moving only a breath apart, I let the adrenaline flood my system. I open myself up to something more. Sometimes life is better with no words. Sometimes it's necessary to let raw emotion consume you and take the bull by the horns. These are mottos my grandmother used to live by.

Grams, this is for you. Please don't let me fall, because heartbreak is too hard to bounce back from.

Crushing my lips to his, I give him my answer. I pour my heart out to him, no-holds-barred.

Please don't make me love you.

SEVEN

It's the first weekend since school started. It feels weird to be the new kid in school—having to learn new friends, new teachers, and a new town all at the same time. No one wants to completely start over the final year of high school. But at least I know there is a light in all of this. I have a familiar face. And it's one I'm not at all upset to look at.

Because this past summer with him was unforgettable. It was life changing. And now I get more of it for a little while.

"What if they don't like me?" I stare at the large house in front of me, my eyes immediately setting on the windows of the upper floor, knowing deep down I've never had to do this before. I wonder if Breyson felt this way when he met my parents.

He takes my hand from where I sit in the front passenger seat of his truck and pulls it over the console, before he rubs his thumb up and down the back of it. "It's impossible for anyone not to like you."

I roll my eyes at him. "I think the girls at school who have stared me down all week with dirty looks would disagree with you."

"Haters will hate when they're jealous. Look at you." He winks at me, the smile already spreading across his face, giving me butterflies. "I was probably giving Simon the same looks on the first day of school, because for a moment, he had you. Don't let them get to you."

I take a deep breath, trying to prepare for this. My anxiety is lurking around the corner. I look out in front of me, my fingers rubbing up and down my skirt from my nerves. The door to the garage is now open, a truck and an SUV filling the two-car garage. "Who all is going to be here?"

"Hey." I look at him. "Stop freaking out. I promise they're not like that. My brothers are both going to that field party. We can go after or stay here. It's up to you. I just wanted you to meet them since they're here together. Both being doctors, that's not always the case. My sister may be here too, but that's it."

My shoulders drop. "Okay. I'll try. This isn't easy for me."

"Come here," he says, and I push off the seat to lean toward him. Our lips meet, each falling between the other's, and for a moment, my nerves calm. Our foreheads pressed together, our lips barely apart, he says, "Just give me fifteen minutes and then I'll take you upstairs for a movie or we can go to that party."

"Okay," I whisper, trying to seem unaffected by the thought of us being alone. We've had sex once. He hasn't tried to touch me aside from kissing here and there at all since we found each other on the first day of school. And I want him too, but I don't know how to tell him. "But I don't want to go to the party. I want to spend time with you alone."

His teeth show through his smile, and then he pulls back as he cuts the engine to his truck and opens the door, his cologne lingering in the cab as he gets out. I follow suit, trying to get out before he can open my door.

We meet at the front and I don't miss the look on his face, as if he knows what I'm doing. "Might as well get used to it."

I smother the smile trying to form. "I don't know what you're talking about." I lie.

He takes my hand, locking the two together. It's almost dark out, the sun quickly fading. I look over as the sprinklers pop up out of their hiding place close to the ground, drawing my attention because of the sound cutting through the silence, and then they start spraying, watering the lawn.

He tugs at my hand and my feet start to move, the nerves back. We make our way up the paved driveway toward the garage. I follow him between the two vehicles all the way to the garage door.

There is a light shining through the glass, confirming what we already knew—someone is home. He places his hand on the doorknob, about to open it. "Wait."

He kisses me, calming we once again. "It'll be fine. They'd be crazy not to love you. They already know about you anyway."

I nod, trying to stop being such a baby. I've been around the same people my entire life. I haven't had to meet anyone new.

He makes his way inside, me following closely behind. It leads into a laundry room. A familiar scent envelops me—the smell of Breyson's clothes. It's a scent I've memorized, and missed terribly, even though I wouldn't admit that part.

The sound of the dryer tumbling is relaxing for some reason. Maybe because it makes them seem like normal people. When he reminded me both of his parents are doctors, it was unsettling, knowing he came from so much prestige in his family. Sure, my mom is an attorney, and a good one, but my dad being a contractor makes us appear more down-to-earth, even though his business is successful. He doesn't sit in an office all day. He's constantly on a job site.

We move farther inside, passing through an expansion of the laundry room that appears to be a walk-in pantry, no sounds of televisions or appliances ringing in the air. But the smell is still here. It lingers all around, coating the entire house. I breathe it in. My nerves slowly unravel with each inhalation.

"Mom, is this healthy?" The voice of a female carries throughout the large, open space, swaying my attention to the kitchen as we approach. It's a girl, and she's digging in a large plastic bag filled with disposable containers of what I'm assuming is food since it has a restaurant logo on it.

I recognize her immediately as Breyson's sister. But with her being a freshman, I haven't been around her. I've been meeting Breyson at school every morning, lucky to make it to class before the tardy bell rings, and she rotates who she rides with, I think.

"It's *Panera Bread*, Brylee. Their whole slogan is 'clean eating'. That's a dumb question." I nudge him in the side with the back of my hand he's holding, chastising him for being rude.

She looks up at him, before taking me in, and then her palm waves in a single motion toward me, revealing the turquoise Fitbit around her wrist. "Hey. Brylee. You must be the famous Kinzleigh he won't shut up about."

I line my lips, trying not to laugh. It does warm my heart a little that she knows who I am before we've properly been introduced. "That would be me."

Her thick, silky, shoulder-length hair is cut in razored layers, the front angled toward her face, and it's dark in color, but she has streaks of blonde weaved in. I finally get a good look at her face. Her features are more similar to Briar's, but she still has her own look.

She's pretty; her face blemish free to be in the middle of an acne-prone age group, but her body seems to still be maturing. She's petite, on the taller side compared to me, and her slim legs are covered with leggings and she's wearing an oversized t-shirt. Her gaze returns to Breyson. "Don't showoff just because your *girlfriend* is here," she says, giving it right back to him. "It's annoying."

She then lifts a container out of the bag, flipping the top back to open it, and then extends the box out to where I can see what's in it, putting a smile on her face as she ignores Breyson altogether. A familiar set of dimples emerge. "Would you like something to eat, Kinzleigh? So far, I've found soup, salad, and sandwiches."

"Thank you, but I ate before I left."

"Okay. More for me," she says, grabbing a set of plastic cutlery and taking the salad with her as she walks toward the living space. "If he gets on your nerves come find me. He's good at that."

"I think you're mixing up our roles, Brylee," Breyson shouts after her, and when he looks back at me, I smile. "What?"

"I like her. She has some spunk to have three older brothers. Poor girl."

Breyson smiles, a little pride showing through behind it. "Poor guy is more like it."

Something sparks my interest. "You don't have to eat at the table together?"

His brows fold in. "No. Not often. Why?"

I shrug. "Mom doesn't allow us to eat anywhere but the table. We almost always eat together as a family."

"Probably not a bad thing. It's just not really feasible with three teenagers in high school sports. Brylee made the high school dance team before school let out for summer, so that will add basketball season to football and baseball. And Mom and Dad have hospital rotations thrown in the mix with their clinic schedules. We're lucky to eat at the table together once or twice a week, but that's not guaranteed."

"I see. Could have its perks."

"One down. Two to go. Ready to go find my parents? You have my brain stuck on *alone time*."

I squeeze his hand. "Let's do this."

Breyson

"I can't believe you have a media room," she whispers from the recliner next to me as the movie plays. The previous owners put it in, and I guess it appealed to my parents with multiple kids when they were looking for a bigger house years ago.

The recliners are identical to the ones in the movie theater with the automatic reclining option. They even have remote-controlled back massagers included, as well as a heating and cooling option. There are eight reclining chairs—four per row—all facing a large projector screen that covers the entire front wall. The projector is mounted on the ceiling. "Why?" I whisper back, finding humor in the fact that she's whispering when we aren't at the theater. "It's a fairly common thing."

"Well, I don't have one." Her whispers continue close to my ear. She's leaning over the armrest, her legs folded back in the seat so that we're close enough to touch without our hands hanging in the middle. I didn't have to ask her to do it. I started talking and she moved over.

"Mom sent me to bring this to you," Brylee says, before walking into the room with a bowl of popcorn and two bottles of water. Kinzleigh pulls herself back into her own chair at the sound of Brylee's voice, as if she's going to get in trouble for sitting too close to me, causing me to laugh out loud.

My parents were out on the patio drinking a glass of wine when we got here—something they do often. They've always enjoyed the view of the lake at sunset when it's cooling down outside. They spend a lot of time out there. I think it's something they like to do to spend time together with hectic schedules. It's why they purchased an entire outdoor furniture collection and put out there. In the winter they turn on the fire pit table.

We sat across from them and talked for about fifteen minutes. It was more like a game of twenty-one questions. Them asking and Kinzleigh answering. You could see her nervousness written all over her face. Body language said even more. She would barely make eye contact.

I don't think Mom believed me when I told her Kinzleigh was extremely shy, but after an awkward, mostly quiet encounter, Mom suggested a movie in the media room with a look that said *don't even try to go to your room.* She's not stupid. She knows a beautiful girl when she sees one, and three teenage boys later, she's picked up on things.

And that is most definitely the reason she sent Brylee in here with popcorn—her way of spying on us without actually doing the spying. It's a good thing the first girl I brought home is a shy one and terrified of a parental shadow. Me, on the other hand—I may find motivation in this.

I take the bowl, a smirk in place, because I know the expression Brylee is wearing, and it's one of boredom. She was forced to come in here when she was probably more content glued to her cellphone or tablet. "You can tell Mom we're behaving."

"Perfect," she returns in a singsong voice, and with her lingering presence after turning the waters over to Kinzleigh, I know something else is coming.

"What?"

"So, wanna make a deal?"

"What kind of deal?"

She smiles, and then looks at Kinzleigh before returning her gaze to me. "I'll watch for you if you do something for me."

"Why would I need you to watch?"

She raises a brow. "I may be fifteen, but I'm not stupid. And my room is closest to the stairs . . ." she taunts.

I remember all the kissing we've done here and there since we got together over this past week. And with that comes the memory of that day in her bed. When I had her all to myself . . . Something I've dreamed of having again since the day I left. But I don't want our next time to be in the backseat of my truck. That's tacky. I've had other girls in there. She deserves more. And neither of us have had an opportunity like we did this past summer. The downfall of being in high school.

"What do you want?"

"I want you to tell Mom you'll double with me and this guy if she'll let me go. She won't let me ride with a guy or date until I turn sixteen. It's stupid. He's only a year older. He's a sophomore."

I narrow my eyes, not liking this tradeoff. She is my sister, and I'm positive she still has her v-card, despite the fact that kids are giving it away younger and younger every year. God, I can't even imagine my sister with a guy that way. Gross. And hell no. I'll rearrange his face first.

I also remember being a high school sophomore. We were more confident than when we were as freshman, no longer at the bottom of the totem pole. It was easier to flirt with girls, especially the new freshman girls. You're also able to park at school, and with a vehicle you get cocky. Parents start letting you do more, and then you end up with girls in your truck with no chaperones. Sex becomes easy and that's your single target with whatever girl is sitting shotgun. "What guy?"

"I'll tell you when you agree . . . As in, when he picks me up. Remember that little thing I said? I'm not stupid."

"I don't like it. I can find out."

She grins. "No you can't. We haven't been seen together," she says, thinking she's outsmarting me.

"Why didn't you ask Briar? He's your favorite." Briar is everyone's favorite. He's the *nice* one, because he's laidback. He's labeled the more caring one out of our trio.

"Jealous much?" she says, getting more confident in the one week she's been considered a high schooler. She then rolls her eyes when I don't say anything, waiting for her response. "I don't have a favorite. I use each of you for different things, and you're *Mom's* favorite."

"Am not."

"In terms of getting what you want, yeah you are. Braxton is the troublemaker. He's sloppy. Mom is always watching him. She'd never let me go out with him this young. Briar is the responsible one—the rule follower. He'll never go for it. Mom knows that and will shut me down before I get anywhere. And you, you're the sly one. You know exactly how to kiss Mom's ass to get what you want without her knowing that's what you're doing. It's sickening to watch," she smiles bigger, "I'm still taking notes for when you graduate."

I stare at her blankly. She finally huffs and grabs a handful of popcorn from the bowl I'm still holding, but her mischievous smile returns. "And if you want *alone time,* you'll go along with it. I've been bribed with Mom's credit card to be the annoying little sister tonight to keep an eye on you, so that you're not taking advantage of a nice girl. I do like to shop with little restriction, and I'm not granted that option often, but there's no reason we can't both get what we want. I want to go out and do stuff. My birthday is forever away."

"Is this an actual double or are you trying to con me into lying so you can be left alone with a perverted sophomore that has one thing on his mind, because I'm not doing that. You're my little sister."

She shoves a kernel into her mouth. "It can be an actual double . . . if you keep your distance."

"It could be fun," Kinzleigh says, breaking her own silence. When I look at her, she's biting her bottom lip, her top teeth pressed into the skin just barely, and this whole bullcrap plan sounds a little more appealing. Suddenly parts of me that were previously in sleep mode are waking. I need to get rid of Brylee.

"Fine. Go away. If Mom comes in here the deal is off."

She grabs another handful of popcorn, the last already gone, before pivoting on her feet and heading for the door. "I'll keep Mom busy. Pleasure doing business with you, big brother. Love you . . ." And with her exit, the door softly closes for the first time since we came in here.

I lean over and place the bowl of popcorn on the floor by the wall, careful not to spill it. When I look back at Kinzleigh, her cheeks are red. "Come sit with me," I say.

"I'm embarrassed."

"Why?"

"Because. Your parents are downstairs. What if we get caught?"

"We won't. Trust me."

"Okay." She stands, before coming to stop in front of my chair. I scoot to the edge, placing my hands on her hips and pulling her between my legs. I slowly lower them, making it to the hem of her skirt but stop myself before I cross over to the other side.

"Do you want to wait? We can wait. I don't want to pressure you just because we have done it already. You still have a choice. I'll respect it."

She leans down, coming in for a kiss, but before she finishes, she says, "No. I don't want to wait. I've waited long enough."

When we kiss it's with a new-driven hunger. With every tongue and lip movement flashbacks of that day in her room come back, making my heart pound in my chest. She's here. She's mine. And nothing or no one is standing in my way.

Thank God Natalie is just freaking crazy.

My hands run up the outside of her thighs, under her skirt, before grabbing ahold of the fabric hugging her hips. I pull her panties down, letting them fall in a pile at her feet. She steps out of them, hard breaths being exchanged between us. Her leg bends and she places her knee on the leather of the recliner, her hands going for the button on my jeans.

I lean back, making it easier for her to undo them. My hand makes a move for her center when the two sides of my jeans release, pulling apart. My finger becomes drenched as soon as I insert it inside her. Two pumps in and I'm completely hard. I slide back. She slips her fingertips under the waistband of my boxers and rubs along the head, making me crazy. When a quiet moan sounds in my ears I pull away, my chest heaving and breathing labored. I pull my finger out. "What's wrong?" she asks in a hushed tone.

I smile at her, now realizing how much I've missed her innocence. "Nothing," I say, before lifting one side off the chair and pulling out my wallet. I open it and slip the condom out of the hidden compartment, handing it to her and dropping my wallet to the floor. "Want to put it on?"

"Will you show me how?"

"Open it."

As she does, I shove my jeans down low enough that my dick is out in the open but close enough I can easily pull them back up if someone tries to walk in. She takes it out of the foil, inspecting both sides to see which way it unrolls. I grab her wrist in one hand and the base of my shaft in the other, guiding her hand to my head. When the latex tip is pressed against my skin, I change the position of her hand and layer mine on top of hers, before instructing it downward in a quick but even stroke, the condom rolling open as it sheathes me at the same time.

She casts her eyes to my pelvis, studying it, her breathing uneven. And then, she places her other knee on the chair, both now stationed on the outside of my thighs. I grip my hands around her legs, pulling her closer. "Are you sure you want to do this?"

She pulls at the bottom of my shirt, moving it up as she lowers herself to get it out of the way. I hold myself straight, waiting for her to get close enough I can press inside. "Yes. I've thought about this since the last time we had sex."

My eyes briefly close. *Me too.* "Okay. Push down."

She does. I fight to keep quiet as her body wraps around me, causing a tight fit. I let go before she's completely seated in my lap, my hands tracing up her thighs until they're cupped firmly on her ass. "It feels better this time," she says, killing me slowly.

I sit up and kiss her, then lift her up and pull her back down before I come out of her. About to do so for the third time, she pushes me back in the chair and begins pumping up and down on her own accord, getting more comfortable. The movie playing in the background keeps the sound of her muscle rubbing against the latex from hugging my dick tight hushed from anyone but us.

I shove a hand up her shirt, forcing my fingers beneath her bra until I can feel her nipple. Her pace quickens, driving me wild. I can already tell I'm getting close. Dammit. She feels too good, even wearing a condom. I force our lips apart, trying hard to hold on. "Rock. Can you do that?"

She stops when I'm as deep as I can be, and then changes direction. I know she's done it right when her lips come down on my shoulder to muffle her moans that are now uncontrollable. One hand on her breast and the other on her ass, I'm about to force her off until I can finish and change condoms, unable to last, when her long rocks become shallow and her nails dig into my skin. I clamp down on every muscle I can, trying to wait a few more seconds.

She sits up, her eyes hooded and her cheeks red, trying to control her erratic breathing. But before I can even go back to forcing her body up and down on me, she does it automatically. She doesn't even make it to five before I push her off my dick at the first spurt into the condom, spots clouding my vision.

My head falls back against the chair, eyes closed and swallowing hard, waiting as I finish. When my eyes open, she's smiling at me. "Does it get better like that every time?"

Shit. I can't catch my breath.

I pull my hand out of her shirt. "I don't know. Sex with you is different. I can't explain it, but if it does, you're going to think I'm a perv, because I'll be trying to get you in every corner with no gazing eyes to experience it."

"Different good or bad?"

"Different good. I thought I was going to come before you could. I got scared for a second."

She laughs, before standing to grab her panties from the floor, immediately stepping back in them to pull them up. "I would have forgiven you."

"Breyson," Dad shouts from a distance.

"Shit," I say, quickly pulling my jeans up and shoving my dick inside, fastening them so fast I can only pray I don't catch anything in the zipper. Footsteps sound down the hall. I grab my wallet and the condom wrapper, shoving both in my pocket as the door opens.

Kinzleigh is sitting on the edge of her chair, her nails in her mouth. I glance at Dad. He stares at me a little too long, and for a second, I think he's going to call me out of the room, but whatever look he's wearing disappears. "Your mother and I are running to town. Do you need anything?"

"Protein mix," I return, hoping he leaves quickly.

He nods. "I'll be on my cell if you need me."

When he turns to walk out, he surprisingly shuts the door back. Mom wouldn't allow it. She'd question why it was closed to begin with. The credits on the movie start to roll, and when I look down at Kinzleigh, she looks horrified. "What if he knows?"

"How would he?"

She covers her face with her hands. "Your hair is messed up, your cheeks are flushed, and there is a wet spot on the front of your pants. They're going to think I'm a slut."

I look down, realizing I'm soft with a cum-filled condom on in my effort to quickly put it away before discarding it. Yep, he knows. He's either going to let it go or this is going to be a conversation later, when we're alone. He won't tell Mom. That much I know.

I lean down and kiss her lips. "No he won't. My dad is a lot laxer than he appears." *And he already knows we've had sex.* "But I do need to go take care of this and change pants before Mom sees me. Find us another movie?"

She nods. "But hurry back."

I smile. "Why? Want to try my bed out before they get back?"

She shoves at me. "No! One scare is enough for tonight."

I laugh as I make my way to the door. When you live with your parents, no risk equals no reward. If it comes to her, I'll chance getting caught . . . every time.

EIGHT

Kinzleigh

Today is game day. It's the first game of the season and it's a home game. I'm excited, because we have been making signs all week to post all over the school and the field fencing. I am flowing with positive energy for the pep rally to come later.

Standing in the mirror, I look at myself in my uniform. Black and gold are my new school's colors. It doesn't look half bad. "There. Finished," I say out loud as I finish drying the warrior head tattoo on my cheek by fanning it.

Coating my lips with my clear gloss, I rub them together and make a smacking sound in the mirror to ensure it's dispersed evenly. I reach down to pick up my pink backpack when my door opens.

I smile, because I know who it is without looking. He's never late. Since that weekend at his parents' house, he picks me up for school every morning. I'm not sure what the point in having a car is if he's going to drive me everywhere. My parents should be happy, I guess, because it's saving them gas.

Since that first day of school, we have been together every chance we've had when we don't have prior commitments. We've been a public couple since the second day of school. It's been a month and people are still talking about it. Apparently, everyone was shocked over the sudden three-sixty

Breyson made so suddenly. I guess he *was* telling me the truth. It makes me smile to know I'm different.

We even have an English Literature class together after lunch. I can't explain the way he makes me feel. It's still surreal to me and hard to imagine this is my life compared to what it was such a short time ago. "I have a car, you know."

Turning around, I lock my arms around his neck. "I could meet you in the parking lot at school like we did the first week." We have this conversation at least once a week and it always ends the same. I just like to give him a hard time, because the truth is, I like the attention he gives me.

"Yeah, but that means I would see you less. Besides, I like to show you off. You are the hottest girl in school now," he teases, and then kisses the tip of my nose.

I roll my eyes, still not used to the constant compliments. I would hardly agree. There are lots of beautiful girls at school, and plenty prettier than me.

He rubs his fingers up my arms, stopping on the back of my hand behind his neck. Unlocking them, he grabs one hand and holds it in the air for me to twirl. "Let me see you."

To make him happy, I participate and twirl in a three-hundred-and-sixty-degree turn. "Happy now?"

He smiles without revealing his teeth, before pulling a marker out of his pocket. "Not quite. You fit in perfectly, as if you belonged here all along, but you're missing one thing."

Placing my hands on my hips, I narrow my eyes at him. "Oh really? What's that?"

"Come here, beautiful. If you're going to walk around like that all day with me knowing what every guy is thinking, I at least want you representing my number." I shake my head at him and smile. Why boys have to stake their claim on everything, I will never know.

He grabs my chin between his thumb and index finger, carefully turning it so the blank cheek is facing him. Uncapping the marker between his teeth, he begins drawing on my face. The wet ink is slightly cold as it transfers from the marker head to my skin. After a few seconds of feeling a tickle across my cheek, he blows and then caps the marker. "There. Now we can go."

I look in the mirror at a backward four that matches his jersey. I can't help the grin that follows. My man. I love how that sounds. He wraps his arms around my waist from behind, pulling me to him as we stare at each other in the mirror. "You know, we have some time before we really have to leave, and we're all alone," I say seductively while smiling at his reflection.

He bites his lip and his eyes become hooded. Just the effect I wanted to have. I turn in his arms and pull his shirt free from his pants. He begins breathing heavily as I lightly run my fingertips over his skin. Right when I stop on his pants button, he stops me. "No, Kinzleigh. You know the deal. That's not all I want with you."

We haven't done anything but make out since that night at his house and I'm starting to become frustrated. I thought it was going to get easier after that—me being able to tell him when I want it. I want him. I want *all* of him.

Looking up at him, I give him my best pouty face. Since we've been a couple, I've used it a few times and it's worked. "Come on, babe. It's not like we haven't done it before. It was easy enough at your house . . . with your parents downstairs. I want you that way again. What's the problem? It wasn't good last time, despite what you said, was it? Is that why you don't want to do it again?"

I know it's a low blow, but he's driving me crazy. I don't see what the big deal is. He used to hook up with girls all the time before me. Knowing he did then while refusing me now is making me angry. What's the point in giving someone your virginity after waiting seventeen years if they're not going to continue to sleep with you after?

He grabs my face in his hands, tilting it up to look at him. He lightly kisses me on the lips and then looks me in the eyes, making my heart weaken just a little bit more. "You know I want to. I already told you that it's different with you . . . in a *good* way. Last time was amazing, and so was the first time, so don't you ever think it was anything less than perfect."

He pauses, still studying me. "But that's the thing. You're different than any other girl to me. I don't want to cheapen what we have with parking lot sex and quickies before school. I told you I want us to get to know each other more and then it will come. As much as I liked it the last two times, and as freaking good as it felt, I shouldn't have made you that kind of girl when I know you're better. You barely knew me the first time. And the second time was in a damn chair instead of in a bed right after you met my parents, and only a week after we started seeing each other again. Next time we do it, I want it to be because I'm different to you. I've never felt this way about anyone, Kinzleigh. I know it doesn't make sense to you, but could you do this for me?"

Now I feel like a brat. Boy, what are you doing to me? He doesn't know, but he is different. I just won't tell him, because I'm trying to deny it myself. I'm trying to keep a safe distance. If my heart refuses to listen, then I'll have to keep it to myself.

My beautiful, blue-eyed boy—will I ever be able to tell you no? Slowly, but surely, I feel the cage around my heart beginning to disintegrate. How do I stop it? What happens when it's no longer protecting me? Will my heart still be mine or will it slip away completely?

I can feel the pull already, every time he touches me or looks me in the eyes. He has this power over me that I can't explain. *Please stop. It's all I have left. I don't want to give my heart away.*

I huff, trying to sound frustrated. "Fine. Your loss. I just thought you might like to see my new underwear. I must say, they are sexy."

I slip from his arms and walk toward the door, strutting for emphasis. As I do, I hear a growl come from him in a low rumble. I smile internally.

That's right. I'm not the only one that's going to be frustrated today . . .

NINE

It's finally nightfall and minutes away from kickoff of the first game of the season. The stands are filling up quickly and I'm getting nervous. I haven't seen Breyson since the pep rally at the end of the school day.

The cheerleaders have been busy as well, getting ready for tonight. "I see someone branded you like cattle," Adalynn teases as she joins me on the sidelines while we wait to welcome the team at the field goal.

"Ha. Ha. Very funny," I say sarcastically as we watch the stands fill up with the opposite team's fans. We are playing Petal High tonight. According to the cheerleaders, this is one of the biggest rivalry games of the season.

"It's cute, though. Breyson has never, and I mean ever been this type of guy. You must have some serious voodoo, girlie. Every girl with a brain in this school has attempted to get his attention and all have failed miserably, except you. Whatever you're doing, you could bottle that shit up and sell it. You'd make a fortune."

Rolling my eyes at her, she laughs. "Are you ready to head to the field goal? It's about that time. The opposing team's cheerleaders are already in place."

It's still awkward to know that Adalynn has been intimate with Breyson, along with other girls at school, but it's something I'm working through. It was before me and I can't be mad. I knew he wasn't a virgin when I gave him my virginity.

"Yep, me and you have back handsprings to get to. I'm glad I have someone that takes tumbling as serious as me. You know Braxton and Breyson are captain and co-captain, so we'll have quite the audience," she teases, nudging me in the arm. I still can't believe he has an exact replica of him. That was an interesting day—seeing the two of them side by side for the first time. I haven't been around them together enough to be able to instantly tell them apart if I didn't see Breyson first, since they don't dress the same, unless they both speak. I hope I don't get them confused and embarrass myself.

"Thanks for that added pressure," I say as we take our position in front of the sign the rest of the cheerleaders are holding for the football players to break through. I hear cleats traipsing along the pavement, making me more nervous knowing Breyson will be in the front. I have never worried over someone watching me before.

Calm down, you can do this. You've done this a million times. It's second nature to you.

The opposing team breaks through first since they are the visitors on our field. As they're announced over the speakers a heard of red, black, and white come barreling through the sign behind their cheerleaders, running toward the sidelines. The guys begin chanting and yelling behind our sign, already revved up to play. "You ready for this?" Adalynn asks, stretching slightly to loosen up.

"As I'll ever be," I respond. "On three?" She nods and I begin to count. "One, two, three . . ."

We take off running, leading into our roundoff back handsprings across the field. Three back handsprings in and the team tears through the barricade, running across the field behind us. Once we reach centerfield, we finish off and mount. The stands are echoing loudly with feet banging against the metal and shouts welcoming the team.

Turning around to make my way to the sidelines next to the football players, I'm blocked by shoulder pads and tight pants. My eyes skim their way up from cleats to tight, yellow pants painted on one amazing pair of legs, all the way up to a black jersey with the number four across the front.

My breathing picks up as I take in the sight before me. My favorite view is now a football uniform; at least on one specific person. Once I reach his face a knowing smirk appears on one side of his mouth. "If I have to watch you do that again, I may take you back to the locker room and have my way with you."

I bite my lip as the dirty thoughts enter my once pure mind. The things he does to me. I'm trying to come up with something to say when Adalynn begins tugging me backward. "Leave my cheerleader alone, Breyson. You already hog her enough. Learn to share."

He never breaks eye contact as I walk backward. "Kinzleigh Baker is someone I'll never share. You better get used to it."

It finally occurs to me where we are. I hate when he does this to me. The way he makes me forget there are other people around besides the two of us. It's like we're in the middle of a time tunnel, just me looking at him, and everything around is blurred.

"Breyson, get your ass on the field and leave the cheerleaders alone. You can do that when you win us a ballgame," Coach calls out across the field, and I run to where I'm supposed to be. Great, first game of the season and we're already causing a scene.

"Sure thing, Coach," Breyson says as he sprints backward, taking his place in the center of the field for the coin toss. He turns around, breaking the hold he has on me and I can finally concentrate on what I'm doing.

With one minute left in the game we are down by seven points. The team looks worn out. I'm on edge at how close the game is. Both teams are playing hard. We have the ball, and if we don't run it down the field, we will lose the game. The team is huddled at the sixty-yard line.

"Come on, Breyson, run the ball, babe!" I didn't think he could hear me until he pops up from the huddle.

Even from here I can see that he is sporting a major grin. He kisses his index and middle fingers together, his helmet in the way, and then he holds it up at me. I've learned that everyone has a weak spot. My weak spot is said blue-eyed boy, marked with a number four and Abercrombie across the back.

Braxton takes the hike, and as he acts like he is going to run with it, he passes to Breyson in the opening. Everyone is screaming for him to run the ball as he receives the pass. Cradling it in the crook of his arm, hunkered over to protect it, he takes off down the field, weaving in and out of bodies wearing white and red jerseys.

Right as he gets to the fifteen-yard line, a player from the other team grabs his waist, but he never lets up, dragging the player along with him. He has some amazing legs. The other player finally weakens him. As he comes down to the ground, he extends his right hand out with the ball in hand, touching it in the end zone. "Touchdown, Warriors!" the announcer calls, foghorns sounding off in the stadium.

Fans all over the home side jump up and down cheering. All we need now is an extra point to tie the game and go into overtime. The crowd huddles around him in joy, some patting him on the helmet and others shaking him in excitement.

The team lines up and the kicker kicks the ball. At the exact second the ball flies through the goal, the buzzer sounds. We're now tied at twenty-eight. We have one chance to win this.

We were able to hold the other team from getting any points on the board, and at the end, Braxton faked a pass and scored the winning touchdown. Jumping up and down, I lean in to hug Adalynn when I feel arms wrap around my waist, turning me around.

Breyson, sweaty and all male, picks me up and kisses me. "We won," he says, elated. He wears nothing but happiness as he twirls me in a circle. I don't even care that he is dripping in sweat with his hair standing up all over the place. This is the sexiest I have ever seen him. He kisses me again, and everything around me fades away—the crowd, the players, and the cheerleaders. Nothing exists but the two of us.

On reflex, I wrap my legs around him and deepen the kiss. If this is what it feels like when two hearts beat as one, I want more; to exist completely and irrevocably intertwined with another.

His kiss is slowly becoming the air my lungs need to breathe, the blood my heart needs to pump, and the food my body needs to survive. He is becoming my lifeline. What scares me—when you cut off your lifeline everything dies, piece by piece, and leaves you a lifeless corpse; a vegetative form of human life, no longer able to function in the world as it did before.

He breaks the kiss, placing his forehead to mine. "You're my entire world, girl. I don't know what you're doing to me, but I can no longer survive without it. Get used to me, because you're stuck with me now. Those deep green eyes are the first thing I think about when I wake up and the last thing I see before I go to bed. You've caught the uncatchable."

As he lowers me to the ground, the last bit of the wall around my heart shatters. I can't fight it anymore. I'm falling for Breyson Abercrombie. Like it or not, I might as well accept it. My heart has decided what it wants and is fighting against my brain. My heart is ahead in the battle, but I'm not sure it will win the war.

Grabbing his face in my hands, I close my eyes and softly kiss his lips. "This feeling scares me," I whisper honestly. "I don't want to fall for you. I don't want to be this vulnerable."

"I know, beautiful girl. Meet me at the truck. Don't make any plans, okay?" Nodding, I release him and watch as he picks up his helmet and takes off in a sprint toward the field house.

"Y'all have it bad for each other. You know that, right?" Adalynn comes up behind me and wraps her arms around my neck, linking her arms out in front of me, before resting her chin on her upper arm beside my face.

"That's what scares me. I don't want to love him. I don't want to love anyone, but I don't know how to stop it from happening." I stare off in the direction he disappeared in only moments ago.

"Girl, you better grab ahold of it run, and never let go. Most people aren't that lucky. Trust me. I know this personally. I had something similar once and I'd give anything to have it back. I didn't have the option like you do," she says, exasperated.

I turn around to look at her, suddenly curious. "What happened?"

She zones out as she speaks. "I was stubborn like you; thought I was too young to be in love. I wanted to hold on to myself to avoid getting hurt and he left for college. By the time I realized what an idiot I was, I went after him, only to find out he had moved on with someone else. He replaced me and was happy, so it was too late. That's the thing about guys. Most of them don't hold on as hard as girls do. He got tired of waiting around for me to come to my senses and found someone that gave him what he wanted. Don't make the same mistake I did. You'll regret it someday. It may not be now, but one day you will." She attempts to smile, but I know it's just a cover. "Come on, let's go."

The parking lot is quickly being vacated as I stand beside Breyson's truck, waiting on him to emerge. After what I assume has been fifteen minutes or so, he slowly walks through the parking lot with some of the other players. The closer he gets, the stronger his cologne becomes. I inhale the masculine aroma I've come to memorize. "See you later, man." Breyson says as he bumps fists with a guy I'm not familiar with. I'm still new and it's a big school.

Pinning me to the bed of the truck between his arms, he lays one on me. Even though bodies are dispersed, it feels private out here. The mixture of his taste and smell has me under a spell. Without thought, I roll my head back, exposing my neck for him to continue touching me with his soft lips. I moan, my eyes closing, and he chuckles. "You ready to go, beautiful? What time do I need to have you home?"

"Please don't stop. You're torturing me." I open my eyes to look at him. "I think Mom said no later than two, and that's only if I'm with you. It seems you have impressed them with your parent-wooing ability. If I didn't know any better, I would say you were a professional. Should I be worried?" I raise my brow in question, trying to hide my smile while waiting on his response.

"I'll have you know I've never tried to *woo* anyone's parents but yours. I'm just a likable guy, I guess." He opens the passenger door, helping me inside. "It's time for me to be alone with my woman."

We pull into his parents' subdivision. It's not too far from mine, but I've learned a large percentage of the school lives in one of a handful of different subdivisions. "Where are we going? Is someone having a party?"

"To my house." My eyes go wide, remembering the last time I was there with his parents. He did not say anything about going to his house. I'm not ready to face them again yet.

"Breyson, I don't know. You remember last time. The way your dad looked when he . . . Can we go somewhere else?" I twirl my hair around my finger nervously as he turns down various roads within the subdivision.

Taking my hand, he kisses the back. "Relax. My parents are both on call at the hospital this weekend. I doubt my brothers will be home, and my sister always stays at a friend's house when my parents work overnight on the weekend. What's the big deal? They never said anything after that night. They love you."

I relax considerably over the information that his parents won't be there. I'm not used to this whole dating thing. It's a big adjustment, even still. It freaks me out a little knowing his dad likely knows what we did in that media room. I need a little time to come to terms with it, because my parents wouldn't be as cool about us having sex. He has to understand that. I shrug my shoulders, not sure what to say. I don't want him to be offended and think that it has something to do with him. "I was awkward around them last time. And then I got embarrassed that we almost got caught messing around the first time I met them. I just need to get over it, and that will take a little time."

He drops my hand and stares ahead at the road in thought. I feel like he's mad at me, though I don't know why. It's not like I said I would never be around them again, just not right now. I don't understand why this is a big deal. "Are you mad at me?"

Pulling into his driveway, he shuts off the engine and exhales. "Come here, baby." I make my way over the center console, straddling his lap. Running his fingers through my loose curls, he pulls me down to kiss my forehead, followed by my nose, and then stops on my lips. "I could never be mad at you for something like that. I get it. Going in no pressure, yeah?"

His voice is soft-spoken. If I once had a heart of steel you would never know it, because it's completely mush now. I haven't decided if I like all of these feelings constantly being thrown at me. It has me on emotional overload. "I'm just overwhelmed with everything. You have to remember, I've never dated anyone, let alone felt this way about someone. I've never had to worry about making someone else happy, or what his parents thought of me. This is all new. All I'm asking for is patience."

"I get it, baby. It's new for me too. I've never wanted another girl to interact with my family, so I haven't brought them around. Something is different about you. I always want more and that's new territory for me. We'll work through it together, okay?" I nod. An urge hits me. I want to kiss him; in a way I have never wanted to kiss him before. I can't explain it. My chest feels like it's weighed down with a cement block. I feel like I'm on the verge of a panic attack without the panic.

On impulse, I grab the back of his head and pull him toward me. Clenching his lips in mine, I slip my tongue in the open space. It's like something else has taken over my body. I can't get enough. I'm craving his taste, the feel of his hands on my body, and the passion I feel when we connect. It's a hunger that can't be satiated and a thirst that can't be quenched. He returns the kiss full force and everything within me feels like it is on fire.

I rock slightly when I feel the bulge beneath me harden. He grabs my waist, pressing me against it harder, and then runs his hands up the back of my shirt. As quickly as things get heated, it comes to a screeching halt and he pulls away from me.

His chest heaves up and down and he closes his eyes. "Dammit! We have to stop. I can't control myself around you and I'm trying really hard. You make me so hard I could explode. I want to be deep inside you, but I want to do this right. I've never cared about that before. You're not some quick lay, Kinzleigh. I want it to mean something. I want you to feel different than the girls I used to waste my time on."

"I do feel different, Breyson. Stop putting me on a pedestal. I want this just as much as you do. I'm telling you it's okay."

He shakes his head. "I'm not budging on this, Kinzleigh. I'm not going to fuck you. That night in the media room was a wake-up call. I want to do something I've never done before. I don't just want your body, but also your mind, heart, and soul. I want all of you. I want to make love to you, but I know you're not ready for that yet. When you are, I'll let myself have you again."

He kisses me softly and opens the door of his truck. "To think you call me stubborn is absurd." He sets me on my feet and I align my now twisted cheerleading skirt. I should have brought a change of clothes.

"I'm not stubborn. I know what I want. I had a lot of time away from you to think. I've experienced having you and then leaving you. I will avoid a repeat at all costs. You deserve the best and you're going to get the best—not some guy that can't keep his zipper up. I want to make myself wait. I need to go without sex. I want you to experience with me what I get to experience with you—knowing you've never given yourself to anyone else. I know I can't give you *that,* but I can give you the next best thing." He kisses me on the cheek. "Let's go get a blanket and go out by the lake."

I follow him through the house, only stopping long enough for him to grab a blanket from inside the cabinet in the built-in entertainment center. Then we continue outside, crossing the back patio.

He spreads out the large blanket over a section of grass and sits, motioning for me to sit beside him. The sky is clear, nothing but the water to keep us company and the moonlight and stars shining brightly from above.

He lays back and turns on his side, propping his upper body on his elbow, and then rests his head in his palm. He pats the blanket for me to lay back as well. Without hesitation I do as he asks, mirroring him. "You really are beautiful."

He kisses me softly, not giving me a chance to respond before he lies flat, pulling me in his arm. "I'm glad it worked out the way it did."

Laying my head on his shoulder, I drape my arm across his stomach in complete satisfaction. I could lay like this all night. "Me too." I close my eyes. "You always smell good. What kind of cologne do you wear?"

Definitely a smell I'll never forget.

"*Polo Black* by Ralph Lauren."

Mental note: buy a bottle for pillow snuggling.

My dreams are already consumed with him; my senses might as well be too. He begins lightly rubbing his fingertips up and down my arm, causing goose bumps to rise. I'm comfortable and my eyes are getting heavy because of it. I could go to sleep like this. I've never been interested in sleeping outside beneath the stars, but I think if I were in his arms I could sleep anywhere. He makes me feel protected. "Breyson . . ."

I close my eyes with him looking up at the dark sky. "Yeah?"

"Why did you pick that tattoo? What's the meaning behind it?" Everything goes quiet and he stops rubbing my arm. Maybe I overstepped. Maybe it's too personal. He may not want me to know. I shouldn't have pried.

I open my mouth to tell him to forget I asked when he starts rubbing my arm again. "You remember Ryland is my cousin, right?"

He pauses. "I'd never forget."

"He had an older brother, Beau, that was four years older than us. Even with the age difference we were all close until he went off to college. He was dating this girl he met at orientation his first semester. Her name was Macie. He was completely in love with her. Always talked about her when he was home. I guess you could say it was love at first sight. One Christmas he kept going on and on about how he was going to marry her."

He clears his throat. I can tell it bothers him to talk about it. I know from personal experience when someone is talking about something difficult to listen, because it probably won't happen again.

I remain lying here, in his arms, waiting for him to continue. "We all thought he was crazy, but that's how Beau was. He was full throttle, balls to the wall, all the time. He made a decision and that's how it was from that point forward. He didn't care what anyone thought."

He pauses for a moment, as if he's thinking back. "One night we got a call from my Aunt Susan. She was hysterical on the phone, screaming that he was in a car accident. We all rushed to the hospital, but he had too much internal bleeding. He died shortly after the ambulance brought him in."

"I'm sorry. What happened?"

"One of the guys from his fraternity came forward at the funeral, apologizing from guilt, and said he saw Macie at a restaurant with another guy that night. He didn't know the guy. When he called to tell Beau to give him a heads up, he said Beau went ballistic and ran out of the house party drunk before anyone could stop him. It wasn't like Beau to drive drunk."

He breathes out, his tone different, a little agitation laced in. "He came around a sharp bend in the road in his Mustang going too fast. Wrapped the car around a tree. Macie didn't even come to the funeral. We were supposed to meet her that summer. The girl was practically part of the family already, yet she couldn't even show her face when we buried him. All we wanted were answers. She was the cause of his death and then couldn't own up to it. She's a coward."

His heart is racing. "She's a heartless bitch. If that's what love does to people, I don't want any part of it. I didn't think I did anyway. I promised myself I would never let someone close enough to break me. I'd never care about a girl that much. I was fourteen then, and until I met you, I never have."

He turns on his side and pulls me as close to him as possible. I continue looking at the sky, counting the stars.

I will not cry. I will not cry.

Despite the chanting command in my head, a tear falls free, and then another. I hate how emotional I've become. I feel like a stupid little girl.

He grabs my waist and rolls me over to look at him. I close my eyes, trying to control the tears. If I look at him, I won't be able to hold myself together. "Look at me." Keeping my eyes closed, I shake my head. "Kinzleigh." His voice is stern as he says my name.

Opening my eyes, I can't hold it in anymore. The dam broke and the tears are falling freely. I'm crying for the pain he's been through, because I know how it feels. I am crying because he's scared to let people in after watching someone he cares about get hurt, knowing I have the same fears. We're a lot alike. I'm also crying because we're so undeniably perfect for each other it's terrifying.

"I was wrong, Kinzleigh. Everyone is breakable. I was a kid. I see that now. The best thing we can hope for is that we find someone that *won't* break us. I didn't figure that out until I had to leave you."

Please stop talking.

I can't take anymore.

I don't want him to be right.

But deep down I know that he is.

"My turn to ask a question." I wipe beneath my eyes, knowing my mascara is probably smudged. He swipes away my remaining tears. "What is so special about the heart anklet you never take off your ankle?"

Stunned, I look at him. No one has ever asked that before. I'm sure it's just a piece of jewelry to most. Its irreplaceable value has always been my little secret. Something I cherish and keep to myself. I don't know if I want to give away everything about myself.

Something pushes me to tell him. I don't want to keep anything from him. "My grandmother gave it to me on my thirteenth birthday. She told me I was at the age I would slowly start becoming a woman and my heart was ripening for the special someone that would later pick it. She told me our hearts are only ours to hold for a little while, and when the right person comes along, I would let it go. I wouldn't be able to control it, she said, but I would know when it was time. My anklet was to symbolize that I always have it in my possession until someone is more deserving of it. Kind of like a promise ring, but different. I haven't taken if off since the day I put it on."

Without warning he moves over me, pressing his lips to mine. "One day it's going to be mine. I'm going to earn it. If you don't believe anything else I say, Kinzleigh Baker, believe that. We may only be seventeen, but I've never been surer of anything in my entire life. We can fight it or we can embrace it, but it's meant to be. My heart is meant to beat for you and yours for me. There's a reason we met and there's a reason you're here with me."

"How do you know? What if all this is just a fling? We're moving so fast. I can't risk getting hurt. What if I stop holding back for you and you leave me like I never mattered? Or worse? Someone I loved more than anything in this world was taken from me. I've had my heart broken. That's why I'm so worried about Konnor. I can't keep from loving my family. We're born with that love already there. I can only pray not to lose them. And what about our future? It's always the girl that sacrifices everything. I won't give up my dreams for anyone, including you."

He's staring at me, all of his focus on this conversation. "I would never ask you to do that. All I'm asking is for you to trust me and stop holding back."

This has become my reality—staring into the blue eyes of the most beautiful boy I've ever seen, asking me to trust him. A million different thoughts are running through my head. Some things Grams said, some Presley, or Konnor even, and last but not least, Adalynn.

My mind warns me to protect my heart, but my heart begs to lead. My soul knows my heart is winning. One day I may look back and be lost in a dark realm of heartache and pain, but at least I will have experienced the light for a little while—to love and to be loved.

The one thing I'm sure of is that I'd rather fall with him and wake up at the bottom alone than to have never experienced him at all. "Okay, you can have it your way. I trust you. Now shut up and kiss me."

TEN

Breyson

Today is Kinzleigh's birthday. I've spent days thinking about what I want to do. It's Saturday, October fifth, and if we didn't already have enough in common, our birthdays are only three days apart.

I usually work with my grandfather on his ranch Saturdays and summers for extra money—even though my parents pay for everything—but I haven't helped any since school started. All of my time is split between football and Kinzleigh. Life is pretty damn good right now.

I walk into the kitchen to fix a bowl of cereal. Braxton is already sitting at the bar. His hair is sticking up all over the place and he's sitting in his pajama pants. "Sup. You coming today or what? It's time to break in that sweet little California princess. It's your duty to show her what the country kids do for fun."

Taking a seat on the stool next to him, I grab a bowl and pour it full of cereal, followed by the milk he hasn't put up yet. "Shut up. I like her the way she is. I'm going to pick her up before we load the four-wheelers on the trucks."

I shove a spoon into the middle of the cereal pool. "I think she's with Adalynn right now shopping for a dress for the homecoming court and an outfit for the dance. She said something about Adalynn buying her cowgirl boots for her birthday—which is today. I'm not sure what to get her yet."

I shove a spoonful into my mouth, a moan slipping through while I chew as a result of the hunger in the pit of my stomach. I swallow. "What do you get a girl that has everything? I've never bought a girl a gift and Brylee is too young to ask. That's what I'm choosing to believe anyway."

He turns and his lips curve upward. "You know they say diamonds are a girl's best friend. Hope you've been saving that paycheck from working at Pop's, because you're going to need it."

He's wearing a full grin now.

Lacing my hands on the back of my head, I stretch over the chair back of the stool. "I don't know. She's not that shallow. I don't think we're at that phase in our relationship yet. She's not like most girls. Knowing her, she'd probably get offended over something expensive. Assuming anything about Kinzleigh makes you look like an ass. I've made that mistake already."

His brow rises into his forehead. "Dude, are you kidding? The girl has lived around Hollywood all her life and comes from a rich family. Now she's lost in the south among rednecks. A lot of people talk shit about Mississippi because of the barefooted, toothless hillbillies that somehow *always* end up in the media. This is your chance to give us a good name. Get her some bling. Show her southern boys are better than west coast boys."

I pull at my hair, unsure. "I don't know. We've only been dating two months. I don't want to freak her out. Things are good. We're good. I don't want to mess that up."

He looks down and crosses his arms across his chest. "I know what you mean. You can still do jewelry without going overboard. Go with any colored stone. Stay away from diamonds. What's her favorite color?"

"Pink—pretty much every girl's favorite color."

I go back to eating my cereal before it gets soggy. He cracks his neck to each side. "What about a pink sapphire ring or earrings? That says *Happy Birthday* without going crazy. Probably a better price tag too."

"I'm not worried about the money. I've been saving for years just from working at the ranch. I've been investing most of it. I could likely support myself through college without having to work or dip into my trust fund and I still have at least a year to save more. That could work. Do you want to go to the mall with me? We have plenty of time before we have to load the four-wheelers."

Looking at the clock on the wall while shoveling his cereal into his mouth, he nods at me. We've had it planned for the last couple of weeks to go riding at Red Creek. I think tonight is the night I give in to Kinzleigh.

God knows I want it—sex with her. I think about it every second of every day. We've been together every chance we have since the day I saw her in the hallway, and she hasn't held herself back since I asked her to trust me.

I know it was a big step for her and life couldn't get any more perfect than it is right now. It's her eighteenth birthday. I have the house to myself for the night since my parents are gone. And I've proven I can go without sex. I've invested time to get to know her. Every time I see her she gets more beautiful. I can't stand it anymore.

My control is quickly unraveling.

Yep, tonight it's going to happen. Just me, her, and my bed—a place no other girl has ever been. All I need—a new box of condoms.

Flipping open the top of the little black box I look at my new purchase. I found a pink sapphire ring. The center stone—the largest—is square and sits above a row of smaller pink sapphires in two different shades of pink. There are also tiny round diamonds embedded in the part of the setting that holds the center stone secure.

This is a leap forward for me. A first. It makes me happy that I can give her a first. Kinzleigh is the only girl I have ever wanted a real relationship with. The only girl that has meant anything. We have so much in common too. Makes it all that much better.

The longer I stare at the ring, the more nervous I become. She could hate it. She could refuse to wear it. She could throw all of my confidence away with one meltdown. "Why don't you put that in your pocket? You look like you're about to puke. It's not like you're about to ask her to marry you."

Looking at Braxton, I close the box and slide it in my pocket. "Would you shut up? That'll never happen. Neither of us want to get married. I'm just having second thoughts on my choice. I've never bought anything for a girl before, so cut me some slack. I am allowed a free pass to be freaked out. What do you know about any of this? I don't see you giving girls gifts."

Pulling out my phone, I scroll through the contacts until I reach the one I'm looking for. "Yeah right. That's what they all say," he mumbles under his breath as I press the call option. The phone rings a few times before the line picks up.

"I thought I told you to share. Let us shop in peace. This is not sharing, Breyson. You get the birthday girl later. It's my turn. What do you want?"

"To talk to my girlfriend." Adalynn huffs into the phone, feigning boredom. Who would have thought she had a bitchy side disguised by all that sweetness?

"No. It's getting a little sickly, Brey. You should be enjoying boy time. Take your manhood back before it's lost forever."

Kinzleigh's voice cuts through the line, flinging one question after another, although lower like she's in the background. I assume she's talking to the store associate since Adalynn hasn't shut up long enough for it to be her. All I can make out is something about them rubbing her heels and squeezing her toes too tight.

The boots must be uncomfortable. So much sass in such a small body. It makes me smile. My California girl is getting more southern every day. I can easily picture her stomping around the boot store complaining about her feet hurting. All I ever see her wear are sandals, flip-flops, or sneakers. "What is she doing?"

She pauses for a moment and then continues. "If you must know, she is being complicated. I keep trying to tell her she has to break them in, because the leather is new, but she's not having it. She's throwing a tantrum. I feel bad for the store associate. I hope he gets commission from the sale. There are boot boxes everywhere."

"Are y'all almost done?"

"Shh. Don't rush us. It's been a long morning. We finally got her a dress for homecoming, but not before nearly pulling her hair out over the fact that she is participating in the homecoming court. Do not let her back out. You're going to be picking your jaw up off the floor when you see her. I hate to cut this conversation short, but we still have to get her an outfit for the dance to go with these boots I'm making her buy, so you'll just have to wait longer."

She doesn't sound remorseful at all. My heart speeds up as I remember how she looked dressed up that night on the pier, and suddenly, waiting until tonight seems like an eternity. "Will you give her the phone please?"

Braxton is looking at me with a look of amusement. He knows I'm trying not to get frustrated. "No. You can talk to her when we're done. You'll get her all by yourself on that big comfy four-wheeler of yours, so don't get your boxers in a bunch. Tell Braxton I'm riding with him. I don't do third wheel. We'll meet you at your house when we're done. I'll leave my car there."

I clench my teeth, trying to keep my temper in check. I don't like someone telling me I can't talk to my girlfriend, especially when I called *her* phone. If it wasn't her birthday, I'd have something to say about it, but Adalynn is her best friend.

"Fine. Tell her to text me when y'all are on your way." I lean my head back against the headrest, waiting on her to respond.

"Uh huh. Sure thing. Kinzleigh Baker, put those boots back on!" I jerk the phone away from my ear as she shouts through the phone. "Gotta go. Bye, lover boy." Just as the last syllable comes through the phone, the call disconnects.

ELEVEN

Braxton and I are pushing the four-wheelers out of the garage when I hear a car turn into the driveway. I glance up to Adalynn's Nissan Maxima coming to a halt. Finally. I don't have the patience for girls and shopping.

I'm already sexually frustrated. And I haven't seen Kinzleigh all morning. Even though my frustration is self-induced, patience is not my strong suit. I question my sanity each time I see her and won't give in. She hasn't made it easy on me either. The girl has some serious seduction skills for being so innocent.

Or maybe it's just her.

Hell, I don't know.

I can't stand it any longer.

Walking to the passenger side, I open the door and grab Kinzleigh's hand, pulling her out of the car. Once she's standing on her feet, I slam her body against mine, placing my palms low on her back, right above her ass. "What are you doing?"

"I've missed you, woman. I need some lovin', and tonight I'm going to get it." She leans back and looks up at me with slightly widened eyes, her cheeks already changing colors.

"Does that mean . . ." She bites her lip. I nod. "It's about time. I think you're trying to kill me. You can't give me a taste of the batter and then deny me the cake."

She grabs a handful of my ass in her hand. "I remember how sexy this is bare." The heat in her cheeks deepens the color from pink to red. "You know I'm a sucker for your glutes. That uniform you wear hugs it in all the right places. Every game it has me all worked up, so stop denying me the goods."

Only Kinzleigh is going to reference my dick or our sex life to something sweet. If she wasn't so damn sexy, I might would take offense. I lean in close to her neck, just below her ear. "How bad do you want it? If you want to play, you're going to have to make it sound more appealing than cake."

Slipping my tongue out to taste her skin, she rolls her head, giving me better access to her neck. Trailing my tongue down, I stop and nip the area connecting her neck and shoulder. She smells citrusy but clean. Her skin reminds me of lemons and her hair always smells like coconuts. The combination of the two mixing is intoxicating.

Skimming her fingers beneath my shirt, the rhythm of her breathing changes. The soft tips of her fingers brushing along my skin makes my stomach muscles tighten. "Um, guys, can y'all get a room if you're going to mentally sex each other? The real thing is better and you don't need an audience."

Kinzleigh jumps back at the sound of Adalynn's voice, slapping her palm to her chest. Looking around, she bites her nails as if she's embarrassed that we got caught.

Turning to tell them to shut the hell up, I find Adalynn standing next to Braxton, and both of them have smug looks on their faces with their arms crossed over their chests. They should be the ones embarrassed that they were standing there watching us when they could have easily walked off or turned around.

I grab her hand, lugging her toward the house. Passing them, I leer at Adalynn. "It's not our fault you two don't have anything better to do than watch us. Y'all can get everything ready. I'll be back to load my four-wheeler after I coax my girl into giving me the kiss I've been missing all morning now that you've embarrassed her."

Once inside the garage door, I propel her toward the stairs, making my way to my bedroom. When we reach the top of the stairs, she looks around. Knowing what she's doing, because I've spent so much time with her, I say, "They're not here. It's their rotation at the hospital. They try to get the same schedule now that we are older, so they can see each other more."

Gripping the doorknob, I open the door. She suddenly looks unsure. "What if they find out? You remember last time. If it had taken us a few minutes longer . . . or he came five minutes earlier . . . I don't want to be labeled a slut to your parents like other girls that's been here."

She thinks I've brought other girls in my room. The damn reputation I've made for myself with girls pisses me off now. If only she knew.

Turning around to face her, I cup my hand on the back of her neck, tugging her toward me, inside the room. Shutting the door with my foot, I bring her lips just an inch from mine. "If you don't listen to anything else about me, I want you to hear this . . ."

I lock my eyes with hers. "I would never do anything to make you look like a slut. You've never been like any other girl to me. Even if my parents did come home and find us in here, they wouldn't think anything of you for several reasons. One, if they were mad at anyone it would be at me, because I know better. Two, I've never brought a girl in my house and especially not my room. That's a dead giveaway you're not like other girls."

She closes her eyes as I brush my fingers down her shoulder, tracing her body down to her thighs. Clenching each hind leg in my hands, I pick her up. She wraps her tiny arms and legs around me for support. "I'm the only girl that's been in here?"

I can see the shock all over her face. Nodding my head, I turn around and carry her across the room in the direction of my bed. "You never cease to amaze me. Why would you bring me here and not anyone else? When will the special treatment stop?"

Laying her down on the bed, I move over her, bracing myself on my hands and knees. Her eyes are exquisite. If you look close enough you can see the smallest black dots in the green of her eyes, almost like freckles. They are a narrative of her soul if you read between the lines.

"Because I love you," I say, watching her, scouting for her reaction.

Her breathing stills and she closes her eyes. As her eyelashes meet, a tear falls down the side of her face. Leaning in, I swipe it with my tongue. "I need you to look at me right now."

She opens her eyes, and when she does, it's there. She loves me too. I've spent the past two months learning her emotions. I know exactly when she is blocking them and when she is letting them show. Every day I wake up wanting more. It's only been two months, but I know she's the one for me.

My girl.

We can spend the rest of our lives just dating or not having any titles at all. I don't care. As long as I get to wake up every day knowing I'm a part of her world, that is good enough for me.

We both have the same outlook on life. We have dreams to pursue, not needing marriage or kids to be happy. "I know it's only been two months and seems sudden, but it's one thing I'm sure of. I can't stop thinking about you, I can't get enough of you, and I sure as hell can't bear the thought of losing you. I didn't tell you expecting you to say it back. I will never pressure you. I don't want you to say it back unless you mean it. I just thought you should know—that I do, love you."

She lies there looking up at me, her eyes scanning my face, for what seems like an eternity. "What happens when we graduate? You know I have dreams and so do you. Our lives are only just beginning. You can't love me, Breyson. We can't love each other. It'll only tear us apart in the end."

She starts crying. "You don't want to love someone as selfish as me. I won't give up the things that I want. I won't settle. I would never let you do that either. This was supposed to be simple—a fling. You're not supposed to fall in love with me," she says, her voice so low it's a whisper.

That is exactly why I love her. She doesn't ask me to, doesn't expect me to, nor does she want me to. She wants me to pursue my dreams instead of changing them. And for that reason alone, I would follow her around the world. I would choose any football team in the continental U.S. for her. It's always been my goal to play college ball at Louisiana State University, but for her I'd change.

I'll never love another girl. She's it for me. She's my soul mate. If I can't have her, I'll spend the rest of my life alone. I'd fight hand over fist for her. I'd kill for her. I've found the one that makes me want to live. I will never find another one like her.

How could she ever think she is selfish? She is the most passionate, selfless person I've ever met. "I can, and I do love you. I will. I'm not worried about what happens when we graduate as long as I get to be with you. I would never ask you to settle. I don't believe you're selfish. You may not love me back right now, and that's okay. I still love you anyway. Let's not think about our future. It's okay to live day by day and the rest will work itself out. Happy Birthday, baby."

I lean down and kiss her lips, all while reaching in my pocket for the ring. "I have something for you, but before I give it to you, promise me you won't jump to any conclusions. I am aware that we're only eighteen, so don't freak out."

Her forehead lines in confusion. "Okay . . . should I be scared?" I grin at her as I hold the black box in my hand. Her eyes widen and she reaches out slowly, as if it's going to bite her. "Oh my . . . Breyson, I told you not to buy me anything."

"Would you open it already?"

She grabs the box in her hands. Opening it slowly, she looks at the ring and then at me. "It's beautiful. It's perfect. You shouldn't have, but I love it. This is the best birthday of my life so far." Holding the open box, she grabs my face and pulls me down to kiss her. "You're the best boyfriend a girl could have."

My heart swells at hearing her call me her boyfriend for the first time. It's a big step for her. I know I would be lost without her. This is what I want to be—her man. I'll do anything it takes to make her fall in love with me.

I kiss her over and over, playfully, making her laugh. Grabbing the box from her hand, I remove the ring from the satin slit of the small velvet box. "Let me."

As I take her right hand, she spreads her fingers and waits for me to slide the ring on. I place the pink sapphire ring on the tip of her ring finger with my left hand. She smiles from ear to ear as I slide it up her finger into place, leaving it at the base.

I love to see her smile. I'd pay or do anything to see that smile permanently worn on her face. "This is the best gift I've ever gotten. Thank you."

She looks up at me with love in her eyes. It's evident, and it makes my insides feel like they're on fire. Everything in the world is right when she's around. I can't explain it and I don't want to try. "You're welcome, baby. Anything for you."

I make sure she is looking at me. "I mean it. You know I'd do anything for you, right?" She smiles lightly and looks around as if she is thinking it over.

Grabbing her chin, I turn her back to me, so that I make sure she gets what I am saying. "I would do anything for you, Kinzleigh. I would take a bullet for you. I would walk through Hell for you. I will spend the rest of my life protecting you, whether you ask me to or not. No matter where I am in this world, as long as I'm alive, I will always find my way back to you. You will always be the girl that has possession of my heart."

She closes her eyes, and before she opens them, I lean in to taste her plump lips. They keep me going during the day and occupy my dreams at night. From now on, this is what I live for—her.

It makes me proud to know that no other man has had her like this. Running my hand up her smooth leg, I slip it underneath her shorts and continue until I reach the seam where her leg ends and her torso begins.

Her breathing amplifies the closer I get to the prized possession between her legs. She reaches for the button on my jeans. I back my hand away, trying to control myself. "We don't have to do this right now. This wasn't what I was expecting from you by giving you a gift. I can wait."

Smiling at me, she unbuttons and unzips my jeans. "Would you shut up already? It's my birthday. That means I get a wish. I don't want a cake. I don't want candles. What I want is you. You asked me not to hold back and I expect the same from you."

She blows me away. Who am I to deny a birthday girl what she wants? I would never deny her anything. I couldn't. Grasping the back collar of my shirt, I pull it over my head. She runs her hands up my stomach. "I love your body. I miss feeling it pressed to mine."

I know what you mean . . .

I grab the waistband of her cotton shorts and pull them down her legs. Once off, she wraps her tiny legs around me, pulling me toward her, so I can't look anywhere but her face. Sitting up, she raises her arms above her head, giving me a hint at what she wants.

Not wasting a single second, I remove her t-shirt. She's the most beautiful girl I have seen in all my eighteen years. I still can't believe she's here. She quickly pulls her long camisole down that was underneath her t-shirt after I remove the top shirt. I'm assuming she wants to keep it on. With it being the middle of the day and people downstairs, I'm not going to comment on it. "You leave me speechless."

Her underwear is lavender lace, and judging by the matching colored straps beside her camisole straps, I'm going to say the bra is the same. The color is amazing against her smooth, lightly tanned skin, but nothing compares to her completely bare. I decide against my previous notion to let her leave the camisole on. I'm about to remove it when she stops my hand. "Leave it on this time. I have a surprise for you later when we're alone."

I don't question her even though it makes me curious. Leaning into her, I kiss her and pull the straps of her bra and camisole over her shoulder. "Can I do this?"

She nods, so I continue to pull them down her arms, revealing her breasts. She lets me pull both sides down until the neckline of her camisole and the cups of her bra come to rest on her ribcage. She places her palms against my back and pulls our torsos flush with one another. "Touch me."

I smile at her moment of courage to tell me what she wants. "Tell me what you want from me, baby. Where do you want me to touch you? Here?"

I touch her shirt-covered stomach. She shakes her head and bites her lip. "Here?" I cup her breast in my hand. She closes her eyes and arches underneath my touch. Touching my lips to her skin, she makes the slightest noise as she lays her head against the mattress. I haven't been this turned on by a girl since I first saw one naked. Out of all the ones I've seen, she tops them all.

She shakes her head again. Continuing kisses along her chest, I place my thumb on the outside of her panties, between her legs. I lightly brush my thumb up and down where her folds are. "Right here?"

She nods and tightens her hold around me. "Please stop teasing me. You can do that another day. I've waited long enough. That night in the media room was great, but this—being here in a bed with you—is all I've thought about since that day at my house. Please don't make me wait anymore. I want you in every way I can have you."

Hearing her beg like this turns me on more than it should. Hooking my finger underneath the fabric of her panties, I pull them down her legs in one swift motion.

Pulling a condom from my pocket, I lean in and kiss her. She slides my jeans and boxers down until the waistband is under my ass. She then hooks them between her toes and pushes them the rest of the way down.

She grabs the back of my head and weaves her fingers in my hair, before bringing me to meet her lips. "I'm not ready to say that to you yet but know that I care. I care about you more than you could imagine. I like you so much that it scares me. You're the one that got my attention when no other guy had before. My heart aches for you. I wish I could say it, but I have to be sure. I won't throw that word around. If I say it, you'll know that I mean it with everything inside of me."

She rubs her fingertips up my spine. "My heart wants you right now. I don't know for how long, but I'm following its lead. Just give my brain time to catch up with my heart, okay?"

My heart skips a beat. I've learned she isn't good with verbalizing how she feels. The fact that she is telling me this is epic. I can't stand it any longer. I have to be inside her. I've proven I can date her without sex, but this is where I want to be. The raw, consuming emotions are too much.

Rolling the condom on, I lay above her and stare into her eyes. I can't look away. Rubbing her bottom lip with my thumb now free, I say, "I would wait an eternity for you."

I thrust inside her at the same moment my lips touch hers. I'll never get over the way it feels being inside of her; knowing I'm the only guy she's been with. It's indescribable. I still, giving her a minute to get used to me. "How does it feel?"

She smiles. "The best yet."

I move slowly, inching in and out of the slick opening. "Damn, baby, you feel so good. I love being inside you. You're so tight."

Her legs fall open, widening her spread. When I push inside it feels deeper. I speed up a little. She digs her nails into my back, a moan slipping between her lips. "Breyson."

I can already feel the need to come getting closer. "I don't think I'm going to last long. You're so wet. It's on my skin. You're mine, Kinzleigh."

She moans again and brings her knees in against my sides. I kiss one nipple and then the other. Her breathing is ragged. She's arching off the bed with every touch to her skin, as if her nerve endings are all overly sensitive. "I'll never give you to another guy. I found you first. I need you to say that you're mine."

She opens her mouth, but nothing comes out. And every time I talk dirty to her, I feel another surge of wetness spread farther out from my dick up my pelvis. I speed up again. "Say it. Tell me you're mine. I need to hear it."

"I've always been yours. Since day one."

"You like how it feels when I'm inside you?"

"Yes," she whispers.

She unleashes territorial feelings inside me when we have sex. I'm getting close. I feel like a damn amateur inside her. I don't want to come until she comes.

Rolling over, I pull her on top of me, stopping for a second so that I won't come yet. She's completely bare except for the lower half of her torso covered by her shirt. I continue to kiss her, tasting more of her with every slip of the tongue. She's beautiful above me. Her curly hair falls forward, curtaining our faces as we kiss.

Grasping ahold of her by the hips, I rock her back and forth. She's getting more comfortable on top based on the whimpers and moans. She fists my pectoral muscles and arches, releasing my lips. "Baby, are you about to come? I can't hold on much longer. You're too tight and you keep clenching around me. It feels utterly fucking blissful."

I continue to rock her back and forth, slightly harder and wetting me more. I can tell she's coming when her muscles start to pulsate around my dick. She closes her eyes instantly. Her spine rounds. Her head falls back, her long, blonde hair sweeping against my thighs. Her mouth opens. And then she says, "Oh, my God."

I'm done. I've never seen a girl orgasm like that. I can't hold out anymore. I clamp down on her body, holding her hard and still against me, and spurt-by-spurt my entire body lets go. It feels like nothing I've ever experienced. The first time was gentle. The second time was rushed. But this time, it's something else entirely. Grabbing her by the neck, I pull her down to me. "I love you, baby. I'll never forget that."

She ruined me. In barely any time at all. No other girl will ever compare to her. That I know for sure. A knock sounds at the door and Kinzleigh's eyes bulge. "Dude, are y'all coming? We need to leave. Adalynn is ready to go and everyone is going to be waiting on us at Red Creek."

Braxton.

"We're coming. Give me five minutes." The deepening of my voice makes me obvious, but I try to cover it anyway. Kinzleigh scrambles off of me and goes in search of her clothes. I enjoy the view of her bare ass for a moment as she walks away from me pulling her shirt back up.

Standing up and pulling on my jeans, I walk into the bathroom to discard the condom. When I get to the toilet, about to grab some toilet paper to wrap it in, I realize the condom broke—something that has never happened since I started having sex. "Fuck!"

I quickly remove the condom and conceal it in the toilet paper, before throwing it in the trashcan. Kinzleigh comes up behind me, now dressed, and wraps her arms around my waist. "What's wrong?"

I turn around to a worried expression on her face. I take her face in my hands and kiss her on the lips. "I just noticed the condom broke. It caught me off guard."

I'm internally freaking the fuck out, but I can't let her see it. Her breathing picks up and I remember what Presley said about her having panic attacks. "Has that ever happened before?" she asks, anxiety hugging every word.

"No, it has never happened before. Look at me. Don't freak out. It's fine. Condoms are coated in spermicide for this reason. I never buy them without it. I always buy the best brand and check the dates. I have never had sex without a condom. I've never come inside of another girl with a condom on. You're the only girl I have had sex with and not pulled out."

She starts biting her nails and looks down at the floor. "What do I need to do? Was it something I did wrong?" I wasn't prepared for that response. And she's completely serious. It's not just an act. The girl continues to peel away my layers, one by one.

I kiss her long and hard. I can't get enough. "No, you did not do anything wrong. It just happened. I probably just freaked out over nothing since it's never happened before. Like I said, it was covered in spermicide. I'll just be more careful. Don't worry about it. Trust me, yeah?"

She nods and wraps herself around me, laying her cheek against my bare chest. She is my priority. I won't let anything come between us. I need her like I need water. I want her like I want a lifetime of football. I'll do anything to keep her. "Come on. Let's go have some fun. We have birthdays to celebrate. We're both officially adults. I've been waiting to go riding out at Red Creek. You have to be eighteen without an adult."

We pull up at Red Creek and everyone that has already turned eighteen is already waiting just beyond the entrance. After waiting in line a while, we get to the gate to pay the riding fees. The attendant walks over to the window, and as if rehearsed he says, "Photo IDs, please."

I pull out my wallet and remove my license from behind the clear pocket it resides in. Kinzleigh pulls hers out as well, handing it to me. "You reserving for the day or overnight?" The older gentleman looks down at our licenses as he jots down information on his sheet of paper attached to a clipboard.

"For the day," I say as he looks up and tells me how much I owe. Pulling the money from my wallet, I hand it to him in exchange for our photo IDs.

As he hands me the parking pass, he looks at Kinzleigh and says, "Happy Birthday, Miss. You came to the right place to celebrate. Drive forward and you will see where to park and unload. Have a good day."

He steps back to let us pass.

Once parked, I hop out of the truck and walk to the back, dropping the tailgate down. Sliding the ramps out and placing the edges on the flat surface of the tailgate, I jump up into the bed of the truck to unload the four-wheeler.

I turn around after straddling the seat to make sure Kinzleigh is out of the way before backing it out. She is standing beside Adalynn. "Stay there until I'm unloaded. Sometimes the ramps slip. I don't want you to get hurt."

She nods and backs up a few feet.

I become one hundred percent red-blooded male when the roar of the engine comes to life. I love my four-wheeler. It's a canary yellow Honda Foreman with black rims, mud tires, and a suspension kit, enhanced with a snorkel for mud riding in bodies of water to keep the engine from flooding. Braxton has one to match in bright red and Briar in hunter green. We got them for our fifteenth birthday and our trucks the following year.

I shift into reverse and back up slowly until the tires roll over the top of the ramps. Once the wheels tip over the bend, I let it roll the rest of the way down, clutching the brake every few inches, stopping once I'm on the ground and backed away from my truck. Upshifting to neutral, I get off and throw the ramps into the back of my truck, then shut the tailgate.

I look over at Adalynn, who is bent over into the side of Braxton's truck. "Hey, Adalynn," I call out loudly. She turns to look at me. "Did you bring Kinzleigh a change of clothes?"

Kinzleigh immediately crumples her facial features, looking confused. Adalynn gleams from ear to ear. "Sure did. Let's do this. Kinzleigh, you're going to need these." Kinzleigh looks at her and she tosses her a pink ball cap and ponytail holder, along with a pair of sneakers to replace her flip-flops.

Kinzleigh catches each item one by one. When she looks back over at me, it's evident she has no idea what we're about to do. I told her to dress comfortable, but she has no clue she's going to be drenched in mud from head to toe. Time to southernize my California girl. Where she had crystal clear beaches we have open land with pockets of manmade mud holes. "Why do I need a change of clothes?"

Adalynn walks over to her and takes the ponytail holder. She begins pulling her hair back in the middle of her head. "Do now and ask questions later, darlin'. You'll need the cap. It gets hot out here. You don't want a sun burnt scalp with that pretty blonde hair that hides nothing; they suck."

Pulling the Velcro apart she places the cap in place and refastens it underneath her ponytail. "There we go. One step closer to being a country girl already. When this is over you'll convert. I'm sure of it. Put on those sneakers. You don't want to have to keep up with flip-flops out here."

As Kinzleigh finishes tying the laces, I get back on my four-wheeler that's lined up with Braxton and Briar's, along with the rest of the crew, and pat the seat behind me. Everyone has a girl on the back already. She comes over and I hold out my hand for hers. "Step on with your right foot and throw your leg over."

She takes a seat behind me and Adalynn gets on the back of Braxton's four-wheeler beside us. I grab her hands and wrap them around my waist, cinching them over my stomach. "Don't let go and keep your legs off the motor. It gets hot."

I grin as she nods her head, looking down at the motor to see how close she is from it. Looking over at Braxton, I call out, "Let's ride!"

Taking off, I drive in the direction of the trails and mud holes. As I shift through the gears, increasing speed, she tightens her hold around me. I can see a muddy pathway come into view. Before she notices I drive straight through it, spinning up mud all around us.

She squeals as droplets of mud rain down, settling all over her. "Breyson Patrick Abercrombie!" I love hearing her scream out my name. Standing up, I downshift as the tires sink into the mud, throwing more into the air. Once I make it out of the soggy mud, I stop, waiting on everyone else.

Turning around to enjoy the dirty view, Kinzleigh has mud splattered from head to toe. She is trying to appear angry, but the grin breaking through her tense expression reveals her true mood. I can tell she is biting her tongue to try to keep from smiling and is failing miserably. "Admit it. It's fun."

"If I were being honest, I never thought I'd like being dirty. This is definitely a first. You bring out a lot of firsts in me," she says with a smirk in place.

Briar and Londyn pull up beside us with smiles on their faces. We've spent more time with them and Adalynn and Braxton since school started. I think Adalynn and Braxton are hooking up, but he hasn't admitted it yet. Usually he's open about the girls he hooks up with. My personality has nothing on Braxton. I'm a sweetheart in comparison. He's the egotistical one of the three. The fact that he's said nothing makes me think he has feelings for her.

"How you like it, girlie? Is he making you want to run back to California yet?" Londyn asks, laughing at the site of Kinzleigh covered in mud. All the girls down here are used to dirty recreational fun. Guys like mud. Girls like guys.

Londyn and Adalynn have taken to Kinzleigh naturally. It doesn't feel forced, which makes me like them even more. They've become a trio at school. Anyone who takes care of my girl automatically makes it onto my good list.

"Not yet. I'm starting to like it here. It's growing on me. I have a little bit of guilt going on with my prejudgments. Maybe I was meant to be in the south," she says playfully. Her comment tugs at my heart a little.

Looking at her, I kiss her lips briefly. "You want to drive?"

"What if I get stuck or something?" Her facial expressions are constantly changing and always do something to me. I can't explain it.

"I'll shift. You won't get stuck. I have the biggest mud grips you can buy on here." Grabbing her by the waist, I help her up and move her in front of me, sliding back just enough to give her room.

Man, she feels good against me. It's stirring a fantasy inside. If we were somewhere more private, I'd make it reality. Placing her hands on the handlebars, I explain the throttle. "When I tell you to let off the gas, release it, so I can shift."

I kiss beneath her ear and can feel the goose bumps rise on her skin. "I'm right here. You'll be fine. Let's go."

Briar and Braxton take off ahead of us as she starts to accelerate, driving through the small-scale pond. She stops at the edge and turns the handlebars loose. "I'm going to let you go through there."

Snaking my arms underneath her armpits, I grasp onto the handlebars and place my chin on her shoulder. "You ready to get wet?" I love making her uncomfortable. I always get a spike of testosterone when she squirms over something I do or say. Seeing her blush is my kryptonite.

Nodding, she replies, "It seems like I'm always ready when it comes to you."

Taking off through the large mud hole, muddy water flies all around us, drenching our clothes. Her white t-shirt becomes transparent, revealing the outline of her camisole. I'm glad she's wearing it or everyone would be able to see her bra. It's making me want to take her into the woods and slip inside her, but I refrain. I ripped the Band-Aid off our abstinence. Now, there's no going back.

Hours have passed in the day. Since we got here we've done nothing but ride and bog down in every mud hole and pond like body of water on the property. It's the most fun I've had in a long time. It's going to be hell getting all of this mud off my four-wheeler, but completely worth it. "I have something to show you," she says nervously in my ear.

I stop and let the engine idle as everyone continues to ride off. She turns around to face me, still straddling the seat in front me. "What?"

"It's kind of your birthday present, but I had to wait until today to get it. Adalynn went with me. It's not something you can hold, but I thought you might like it and it means something to me." She looks more nervous with every passing second.

"Show me. Whatever it is I'm sure I'll love it. You know you didn't have to do or get me anything. Spending time with you on my birthday was all I wanted and I got it."

She stands and hooks her thumb underneath her waistband. I look around, making sure no one can see. "Baby, as much as I would love to take you here, I don't think this is a good place. It's packed with four-wheelers and no one else is seeing my woman naked but me. I'd murder someone or get hauled to jail. Whichever comes first."

Playfully slapping my shoulder, she laughs. "Not that, you pervert. Jeez, I'm not a nympho. You may have a magical touch, but I think I can manage going a few hours without it."

I can't help but laugh at her comparing herself to a nymphomaniac. I'm surprised such a word even came from that pretty little mouth. "Okay, okay, show me my present."

She pulls the bottom of her shirt and camisole up, exhales, and pushes down the front of her shorts, slightly revealing a piece of plastic bag taped on all four sides close to her left hip—the same side as her heart. She pulls the top of the adhesive free, showing ink underneath, and slowly removes it completely.

It's a heart made out of words with a date in the middle. The phrase that makes up the shape of the heart is—*The day my heart was compromised.* Inside the heart is the date—*6.5.13.*

My heart temporarily stops beating. She permanently tattooed the date we first slept together on her skin—the date she gave me her virginity. I don't know what anyone else would think, but this turns me on so much that I want to take her right now, over and over, for the rest of the day. It's permanent for crying out loud.

I keep staring at it, speechless. My heart feels like it's about to burst wide open. "You did this for me?"

"I did it for both of us. It's the truth. Do you like it? Or is it too much? You're making me nervous."

When I look at her so much emotion is consuming me that I can barely process what to say. "Like doesn't explain the way I feel right now. I fucking love it. I know you don't like foul language, but I don't know any other word that could explain to you what's going on in my head. I love you, Kinzleigh. I love you so much I can't think straight. This will make my top five life-altering moments. Number one is that day."

She leans forward, and just before kissing me, she whispers against my lips, "It was mine too."

TWELVE

Kinzleigh

Freshly showered, I come out of the bathroom in my underwear. Adalynn is standing in front of the mirror putting on her makeup.

Tonight is homecoming, and for some unknown reason I got nominated for football sweetheart—the new girl. I still can't wrap my head around how this happened. I am part of the homecoming court. I don't like the idea of having to walk centerfield in front of all those people. I tried to get out of it, really I did, but Adalynn is making me participate.

I can't wait until Presley comes to visit over Christmas. She and Adalynn will get along great. I think she would be proud of how far I've come since I've been gone. I've barely talked to her, truthfully, since I've been so busy. I try to make my weekly call to chat, but they are getting sparser and turning into more texts than calls. I miss her like crazy, but Breyson, Adalynn, and Londyn are keeping me busy between cheerleading and everything else.

If Breyson and I aren't alone, we're double or triple dating with Braxton and Adalynn and Briar and Londyn. I've developed a tight-knit circle of friends since I've been here.

Standing beside Adalynn, I reach for the lotion and squirt a small amount in the palm of my hand. Looking down, I begin spreading it out over the freshly inked skin of my tattoo. The guy that tattooed me said it helps to avoid peeling and loss of color until it heals. "I still can't believe you got a love tattoo. I wish I could have seen the look on his face when you showed it to him. What did he say?"

My memory replays that moment and I smile to myself. "He was stunned. It was priceless. But keep your voice down. If my mother finds out she will kill me. I haven't even told Konnor I got one. He told me if I ever wanted one not to go without him, so he may be mad or hurt at first."

"When do I get to meet this mysterious brother of yours? He sounds like a hottie," Adalynn says as she pulls the hanger that holds her dress down from where it hangs on the closet door.

Her dress is emerald green. It's beautiful with her red hair and tanned skin. It's one shoulder and slim fitting until it gets to her thigh, then fans out like the fin of a mermaid tail. It makes her look absolutely breathtaking.

I collect my dress and remove it from the hanger. "Christmas is when he is supposed to be coming home. You get to meet him and Presley. She is coming with her parents. I'm not sure if her brother Preston is coming. I hope not or things are going to get awkward."

One night during one of our girl talks I told Adalynn about the whole Preston situation.

I love my dress. It's a Tiffany Blue strapless with a sweetheart neckline. The top half of the dress has the most beautiful pattern of silver glitter. It gives it the right amount of sparkle as the light hits it without making it look cheap, because cheap it wasn't.

The dress has a satin underlay with sheer chiffon layered over it that flows down into a small train in the back. It's fitted across the bust line and made of a thicker, firmer material to form the breast cups, but then hangs loosely from the sternum to the floor. It flows and the color works well with my bright blonde hair.

"This is going to be fun," she says as she steps into her dress and pulls it up her body. If only she knew that Presley has had her eye on Konnor since we were old enough to know that boys didn't really have cooties.

"I thought you and Braxton were kind of . . . you know." I raise my brow, scolding her. I see the way they look at each other. It's pretty obvious there is something there, even if I don't know what that something is. Some kind of unspoken feelings are swarming in the air each time they're around.

She laughs as she comes to stand before me to zip the back of her dress. "Braxton doesn't get serious about anyone. Even I know that. He dated a girl named Madileigh for a while before she moved away. I guess she was his *Kinzleigh* . . . We're just having fun is all. I'm not over my ex,

Justin. A relationship is the last thing I need, but I've never been into the whole sleeping around with a random guy thing, so Braxton and I have an *arrangement* of sorts. Not all of us get a Breyson," she says and turns to wink at me.

I can't help but smile. He is pretty great. I'm not sure how the queen of solitude landed the sweetest guy on the planet, and he loves me. I feel bad about that, but I don't love him back, or do I? It's a big fat question mark. "What's going on in that head, girlie?"

I realize I'm staring off into space with the debate going on in my head, holding onto her zipper. "Oh, sorry."

I zip it up. "Can I ask you a question? How do you know if you love someone?"

I pick my dress up off the bed and step inside, raising it to cover my body and zip it in the side seam, allowing it to conform to my chest.

"Whoa. Love? We're breaking out the big guns. Wait one minute." She holds out her hand, giving the stop signal. "Did he tell you he loved you?"

She looks like she just saw a ghost. I nod nervously. "Holy shit! Breyson Abercrombie told a girl he loves her? That's a shocker." She plops down on the mattress and fans her face as if she's having a hot flash. "Well I'll be damned. Maybe there is hope after all."

She stares straight ahead for a few moments. I wave my hand in front of her face. "Hello . . . should I be worried?"

She blinks repetitively and then looks up at me. "Sorry, I'm back. I think I just had a mild seizure. Let me think."

She narrows her eyes, pondering over whatever is going through that brain of hers, and then crosses her legs and rests her elbow on her knee, laying her chin in the cup of her palm. "How do I explain what love feels like? Well, it's something that is hard to explain, but I'll try."

She taps her fingers against her upper lip. "Love is a complicated emotion. It propels you to be a better person for yourself and for that person. It makes you weak and strong at the same time. For me, my heart feels like it wants to beat out of my chest when he's around and aches when he's not. When you look into his eyes no one else exists."

She twirls a finger around a lock of red hair. "It's like you're in this little love bubble. You crave his touch, taste, and smell all hours of the day. Keeping him becomes your basic instinct. You can't fathom being with anyone else. You're ruined for all other guys."

Her eyes focus on me. "Love can be different for everyone. That's what makes it beautiful and sought after. At the end of the day, if you would choose that person over anything else you're in love. It's scary, sucks when you lose it, but it's worth every damn second. Call me old fashioned, but I believe in soul mates. Sure, you can love other people, but there is only one that makes you whole. Only one that can see into the deepest corners of your soul. We—as humans—can only hope we're not blinded by lust over the wrong person, so we can find the one we're meant to be with. To go on living without your soul mate would be a tragedy."

I stare at her, stunned. Did that just come from her mouth? I've never heard something so beautiful. So much sadness. It's poetic. Now, I'm terrified. How did I let myself fall in love with Breyson Abercrombie? I'm doomed. "You love him, don't you?"

That's a question I'm not ready to answer . . .

"I don't want to think about it anymore. I never wanted to love anyone, Adalynn. I wasn't cut out to be this kind of girl. A hopeless romantic. A love-struck girl. He changes everything. He makes me wish I wanted a typical relationship full of love. I won't bend my preset plans. Selfish people don't deserve to have someone like him. I can't change who I am. I will pursue college and NFL cheerleading, no matter what I have to let go to do it." I hear the words coming out of my mouth, but for some reason, I'm having trouble convincing myself it's the truth.

"Sit, babe. I need to do your makeup and we're going to talk this out. I need to know what is going on up there."

I look at her and huff, but take a seat on the edge of the bed. "Why are you afraid to let yourself be happy with him? He is freakin' perfect. He loves you. He would probably give you the moon if he could, and he's smokin' hot. I am allowed to say that, because I'm sleeping with his clone."

She winks and one side of her top lip pulls up to her nose, emphasizing she is being funny, and it's making me laugh.

She begins working her magic on my makeup while she waits for me to say something—what, I'm not sure. What am I supposed to tell her? Each time I consider my reasoning for why I am the way I am it sounds silly and immature, but to me, it makes sense. "Were you in love with Justin?"

She is sponging foundation on my cheeks, standing over me. She peers down at me and raises her brow. "This is the last question you get to ask me and then you're spilling your heart out. Am I clear?" She smiles, but continues painting my face. I nod to buy some time.

She picks up the eye shadow brush and plunges it into the silver powder.

I close my eyes and listen as she begins. "Justin is hard to explain to a third party. We were not like most couples. He used to live here actually. We were next-door neighbors until he went off to college. He was two years older than me. We started out as just friends, hanging out when we were bored. He was like the older brother I never had until I hit puberty."

I can feel her breath against my skin as she breathes in and continues. "One day during freshman year I came over after school when his parents were gone. He was acting completely different around me. He started looking at me different and flirting with me. He said that we should lose our virginity to each other since we trusted each other. Long story short, I did, and we just kind of became a couple after that. I didn't love him up front like with you and Breyson. I grew to love him over time."

I can feel the wetness of the eyeliner being lined on my lids. "You need to realize what you found in Breyson is rare. It's like finding a diamond in the rough. You're never going to find someone like him again or feel that kind of love. You're lucky to find it at all. Some people aren't that fortunate. Could you love someone else? Probably. But will it be that heart-wrenching, soul-captivating kind of love? Hell. No. What you have is a blood diamond. Everyone wants to find it and will kill to get it."

The sound of the mascara brush dipping in and out of the tube cuts through the brief silence. "I decided when he graduated that I didn't want to compete with college girls. Being in that atmosphere is too tempting to have someone back home. I broke up with him. He was upset with me. Promised me he didn't want anyone else. That I was throwing everything away over some bullshit theory. Called me for a while. He finally stopped when I wouldn't give in. Then when he was no longer there I regretted it. I lost not only my boyfriend but also my friend, and that made it hurt worse. I went after Justin because he was my comfort. Not because his absence consumed me whole. It was too late. I guess my theory wasn't just a theory after all."

A large brush tickles my face, as if she's ridding my face of excess shadow. "One thing I never admitted to anyone was that I had another reason for breaking up with him. The way we loved each other was different. He wanted something from me I couldn't give him—magnitude. If I ever find the type of sublime love that you and Breyson have for each other, I'm grabbing it and holding on for dear life."

She brushes a goop of mascara on my top lashes. I linger on the story in my mind. What if she's right? Will I regret it if I don't grab ahold of it and live like there's no tomorrow?

When she stops painting my face, I open my eyes, words suddenly itching to come out. "My biggest fear is to lose myself; to love wholeheartedly and be left behind . . . again. A passionate nature runs in my family. Maybe it's my mom's Italian bloodline coming through. I don't know. What I do know is when you love like that being on the receiving end of heartache is deadly."

She starts combing mascara through my lashes from the underside now that my eyes are open. I keep quiet until she's done, and when she finishes, so do I. "When Grams died, I wasn't sure I would survive that kind of pain. I promised once I picked myself back up that I would protect myself from ever being hurt like that again; at least where I can control it. Then a girl hurt my brother. That amplified my craziness. Breyson makes me feel things that terrify me. Loving him could be the death of me, Adalynn. If something were to happen to him or if I got cheated on, the person you see today would be long gone, a memory. A miserable person left in the shadows of humanity. When you enter into that kind of darkness, it's virtually impossible to come out."

She moves along to making my hair into a work of art for tonight's affair, pulling and tugging, twisting and braiding, pinning and spraying. She stays silent as what was said lingers in our minds. "Babe, I understand where you're coming from, but to live that kind of life is the ultimate catastrophe. You're basing happiness on 'what ifs'. You know that saying, *it's better to have loved and lost than never to have loved at all?*"

I nod. "Well, there is so much truth in it. Part of loving someone is taking the risk of eventually losing them. For example, you live for cheerleading right? It's something that you would do no matter what the cost?"

I nod again, not knowing where she is going with this. "If someone told you that you have an eighty percent chance of breaking a bone or becoming paralyzed from a stunt gone wrong would you stop or take the risk doing something you love and hope for the best possible outcome?"

"Of course I would continue. There is always a risk of getting hurt in sports. I wouldn't stop just because of some statistic." Her eyebrows lift up in the mirror as if the light bulb just went off and I solved my own problem. "And you're suggesting that love is the same way? That the benefits of a lasting love outweigh the probability of an unforeseen circumstance?"

"Yes. You can't let the statistics of losing keep you from playing the game. If you asked anyone that had an unfortunate outcome if they would go back and change it given the opportunity, I'd bet the majority of them would say no, because the time they had with the good makes it worth having to live through the bad."

She makes a good argument, I must admit. I'm not sure where she gets all this wisdom. It reminds me of the old talking willow tree on that classic children's movie about the beautiful Indian girl. "Do you sit around and read inspirational books or something? You're quite excelled for an eighteen-year-old. It's a little intimidating."

She smiles and puts in the last bobby pin. "There. All done. You look sensational. Now get up and see for yourself. Breyson is going to be beside himself."

Standing up, I walk over to my dresser mirror. My hair is parted down the middle and pulled back into the loose bun of curls pinned just above my neck. Before she pulled it all back she took a small section of hair on each side of my part and braided it all the way down my length, securing it with a small rubber band at the ends. A thin braid runs along each side, front to back, atop the rest of my hair, and is secured in the ball of curls.

The crown is teased just enough to keep it from being slicked to my head. The hairstyle looks beautiful with the natural flow of the dress. I feel like Kate Hudson in one of her movies—the name escapes me. My breath catches at the sight.

I may be the football sweetheart, but Adalynn is the homecoming queen—a position voted on by the entire student body. We are due at the football field soon to get all of the cars in the lineup. Me, Adalynn, and Londyn all made signs together for our cars since we're all in the court— funny how that worked out. It almost seems rigged. Londyn is one of the senior maids. A knock sounds at my door and a throat clears. "Baby girl, are you almost ready? It's time to go."

Adalynn grabs my chin in her hand and quickly coats my lips with a soft pink matte lipstick. "Come in," she says, ensuring it's even.

Dad opens the door, looking especially handsome in his slacks and crisp button-down, topped with a suit jacket. I grab my perfume and spritz it on myself. "You look beautiful," he says, and the look on his face as he takes me in gives me a surge of confidence. "You're all grown up."

I smile, grabbing a section of dress in my hand to hold it up, my heels now showing. He bends his arm at his side, hinting for me to take it. I walk forward, placing my hand in his elbow bend. "Some have said I look just like you. Pretty daughter, handsome father."

He smiles to the point that it reaches his eyes, and then he kisses my temple, before leading us forward. I can hear Adalynn following behind. "I may have contributed to the making, but you get your beauty from your mother."

A peaceful breath exits, happiness flowing through my body. Passionate in the way we love—definitely a trait that runs in my family.

THIRTEEN

Kinzleigh

The cars are all lined up beginning with the freshmen maid, followed by the sophomore and junior maids, then me and lastly Adalynn. All of the cars are beautiful, some plain, some exotic, and others classic beauties.

I take a seat on the ledge of the back seat, on top of the trunk of my grandfather's white 1929 Duesenberg, fully restored. He loved this car. When he passed away he handed it down to my dad, because he knew he would be the one to enjoy it as he did.

Dad is sitting behind the wheel when he turns to look at me. "Seeing you like this makes me sad that you're no longer my little girl. Time flies." He makes me smile. I've always been close to my dad. Our personalities are so similar it makes it easy.

He winks at me and his eyes trail off behind me. Something caught his attention. I turn to see what it may be and my face smacks into a gold number four, forcing me to lean back.

My eyes clash with his. They're glowing under the field lights like burning embers. There's heat in his stare as he scans my body, slowly, as if he is savoring the sight of me. He is magnificent, like a warrior that our mascot represents, standing in all of his muscled glory. "Hey, big guy," I say nerdily, waving my hand in the air.

He smirks at me and raises his brow in amusement from my awkward greeting. "Beautiful, may I have a word with you?" He looks over at my dad. "Hey, Mr. Baker. I hope you're doing well today. Do you mind if I steal your daughter for a few minutes?"

Dad looks at me and grins from ear to ear. "You're right about one thing. She's definitely beautiful. Since you took notice I think I can share her for a few minutes."

"I'll have her back before you know it." He extends his hand to help me out of the car. As I stand, he hooks one arm around my back and the other behind my knees, scooping me into his arms. I yelp in surprise, grabbing around the back of his neck. "I won't let you go." I have a feeling he means more with that statement than dropping me.

"I do love a man in uniform," I tease as he carries me toward the field house. "Are you trying to swoop me off my feet, handsome? You can't just come and whisk me away. I have certain duties I have to attend to."

He smiles ahead at the darkening horizon, never making eye contact with me. It's so close to dark the stadium lights are already on. "There's a certain blonde that's had my attention for a while. Winning her heart isn't as easy as winning a football game. She's immune to womanizing males."

He looks down at me, capturing my attention, dominating my mind, body, and soul. How much longer until he has my heart as well? Immune. Yeah right. If only I could be immune to him. It would make things much easier. I'm not so lucky. "Do you have any advice on how I could sway her heart in my direction? I promise I'll cherish it if I ever get it."

Oh, beautiful boy, if only you knew how little control I still have over my heart. It feels like it's being summoned each time it's in the presence of yours . . .

After that conversation with Adalynn, I'm afraid I've found my soul mate. I'm slowly realizing that's what he has to be. And now that I have, it's getting harder to fight the pull. I don't know how long I can keep this secret before it finds a way out. I'm completely and irrevocably in love with Breyson Abercrombie.

He stops on the far side of the field house, out of sight for everyone else. He places his index finger just below my ear and traces down my neck and over my bare shoulder, all the way to my hand, where he takes hold and brings the back to his lips. "You take my breath away every time I see you. You are the most beautiful girl I have ever met. That's not a load of bull crap. I mean it."

Pulling my body against his, he clamps down on my bottom lip between the edges of his teeth, lightly skimming my skin. It's just enough to make me want more. "Why do you do this to me? I need you in ways I can't have you right now. Don't tease me."

Cupping my face, he kisses to the left of my mouth and then the right, followed by my lips. The way he tastes and smells is an aphrodisiac to my senses. The overload of pheromones released when we're together is enough to make you lose all modesty. A dying need to feel every inch of him inside me. I can no longer fight my addiction to Breyson Abercrombie. The withdrawal I experience when I do is almost unbearable. "I would never tease you, baby. Everything I have is yours as long as you are mine. Only yours."

He kisses me again, a little longer this time. Thank God it's a lipstick that dries on—smudge resistant, waterproof, and made for kissing. "I need you tonight. We'll find a way. Any place. I want to look deep into those beautiful eyes while you say my name. I want to see our tattoo on your skin as I slide inside you. Do you want me as much as I want you?"

Like he even has to ask . . . "Yes. Always."

He skims the tip of his nose down the length of mine. "You are the love of my life. I keep thinking about how everything happened between us. This is a sign, Kinzleigh. We're supposed to be together. Nothing is ever this coincidental. Me in California. You here. Close down your reservations tonight and just feel."

I kiss him this time, long and hard, frantic. I don't care about my makeup. I want him in the worst way. He pulls back before I'm ready. Something is clearly on his mind. "I want you completely connected to me. Your heart, in time, will be mine, but I need you to open yourself up to me. I'm going to make love to you—mind-blowing, passionate, unforgettable sex that we feel in our hearts too. That is the only way I will have you. I've experienced that high and I can't stop. I will go through any means to keep getting that drug. You are my drug, Kinzleigh."

He touches his lips to mine and slides his tongue in my mouth, on the hunt for mine. Once he finds what he's after they mingle, barely brushing against each other. Kissing him is an escape for me; sucking me into a world that I've never known and want more of.

The loss of him is going to be the end of me . . .

The last of my walls crash down around me. I feel naked and vulnerable. My existence was mapped out for him. I was born to love this boy. Nothing has ever been more obvious.

God, I'm giving in. I'm letting go of my heart. I'm following the pull. Please, oh please, don't rip him from me. I will not survive.

What I am about to do there is no going back. It's irreversible. If he leaves me, my heart goes with him. The body can't survive without a vital organ. Only one thing will happen in its absence: death.

I reach down and pull up the bottom of my dress, revealing my left ankle—the one closest to my heart. This is going to change everything.

Unclasping the anklet that holds a silver heart engraved with my initials, I stand back up and look at him. His eyes take on a new emotion when he discovers what I'm holding. There is something in those midnight-blue eyes I'll spend the rest of my life trying to interpret. They've had me in a trance since day one.

Solid, raw, uninhibited emotion is written on his face. His hands are fisted at his sides. Wrapping my small hand around his fist, I pull it between us, upward facing. I open it. Placing the anklet in his hand, I look him directly in the eyes without even blinking.

And then I close his hand around the anklet, knowing that it means everything to me even though it'd be stupid to anyone else. I breathe slowly, trying to keep from crying and smearing my makeup. "Please don't hurt me, Breyson. I can't promise you forever or happily ever after, but I can promise you right now. I have tried to steer my heart away from you to protect it. It's no use. It reigns over my brain and it wants you."

Talking comes over the loud speaker from the press box, signifying it's getting closer to time to start. Plus the quickly darkening sky confirms it even if the announcer didn't. I don't want Breyson to get in trouble for not being with the team. I'm sure he's not supposed to be out here. When it comes to me he does what he wants. It's nuts.

I need to speed this along. "Listen, I've thought about it. I would rather give my heart to someone that deserves it than to keep it forever being cautious. I don't know what will happen after graduation or in the future, but I know after only a few short months you are different to me. You're the guy that barreled into my life and knocked my walls down. You're the one I'm giving it to. I'm pretty sure it's been yours all along. I can't deny it anymore. I love you, Breyson. I do. The love I feel for you is scary as hell, to be honest. Please don't make me regret this."

He doesn't say a word; just stares at me, as if he's at a loss for words. His eyes gloss over. That shows how much of a momentous moment this is. He holds his right fist over his heart, encapsulating the anklet. "I will spend the rest of my life loving you. This is more than just a high school fling. I can feel it. We will always be together. If it means jumping from an airplane or swimming the width of the ocean, I'll do it. You have no idea what it feels like to hear you say you love me."

Grabbing ahold of my waist, he lifts me off the ground and spins me around in a circle. I feel like Cinderella in the arms of my prince. He grins from ear to ear. "I love you, Kinzleigh Berlyn Baker."

For the first time since my grandmother died that word doesn't scare me. "I love you too, Breyson Patrick Abercrombie. Let's go. You have a football game to win and I'm needed centerfield."

Someone very wise once said—*three things will last forever: faith, hope, and love. The greatest of these is love.* If you don't believe me, read First Corinthians chapter thirteen verse thirteen in the good book.

I'm going to have faith it's the truth, hope I don't get hurt, and love like I'm dying, because the alternative isn't good enough anymore.

The six of us all get out of Breyson's truck. We decided to ride together, because it would be more fun as couples and Breyson is close with his brothers. I can understand that, being as they've been together since they were conceived. I love that family is important to him, because I am close to mine.

I look down at myself and want to laugh. Never have I owned a pair of cowgirl boots. Adalynn does have fabulous taste, though. I give her credit for that. She has me in a navy-blue dress that slides off the shoulders and ends right above the knee. It's comfy but classy. She coupled it with a pair of pointy toe, calf height boots in tan.

Breyson meets me in front of the truck and grabs my hand with a big smile on his face. I guess he's going to be in a superb mood for the rest of the night. "You ready, baby? You owe me the first dance."

He kisses me on my cheek and I flush red. I'm not sure how the most popular guy in school, not to mention the hottest, in my opinion, is so sweet and crazy about me. "As I'll ever be."

We walk hand in hand into the building alongside his brothers and the girls. As we move inside, the door shuts. It's dark with strobe lights swirling around the room, bouncing off the walls. The music is blaring. I can barely hear anything else. In the back of the room is the makeshift dance floor facing the DJ that's setup against the back wall.

Breyson leans down to talk into my ear. "I'm going to request a song and hit the bathroom on the way. You okay until I get back?"

"Sure, babe, go ahead." I swat his butt for emphasis. As he walks off Briar and Londyn head in the direction of the dance floor, leaving the rest of us. A slow song is currently playing.

Braxton turns to Adalynn and grabs her hand, before backing toward the dance floor with a flirty grin. She returns the expression and starts to follow with no hesitation, but then pulls back. "I can't leave her alone. Breyson isn't back yet."

He gives her that face I know she can't deny, because I can't deny it when Breyson uses it on me. A little bit pouty and feigning hurt feelings. She looks between us as he starts pulling her away again. I can tell she's crazy about him. Maybe she'll get her chance at soul-binding, true love after all. "I'll be right back, okay?"

I nod, because I am not going to be a baby.

I'm alone for only a few moments when a girl comes to stand beside me. I don't recognize her with the lack of light, but she's pretty.

That is until she opens her mouth. "I guess it's finally time for me to officially meet the home-wrecking tramp that stole my boyfriend."

I knew it was coming sooner or later. She's been eying me in the halls since the first week of school. My guess is she hasn't caught me alone long enough to make her move. She didn't waste any time with accusations.

Breyson and I have had many conversations about how crazy she's become. A fake pregnancy to keep him comes to mind. It's disturbing to say the least, but I'm glad he was honest with me about it. The infamous Natalie.

"I didn't steal anything, Natalie. I didn't know he had a girlfriend when I met him and I didn't have anything to do with the two of you breaking up. I didn't even know where he was from, so I certainly didn't anticipate living in the same town. Not that I owe you an explanation. You can dislike me if you want, but I won't tolerate being falsely accused of something I did not do. If you've ever been to California, you'd know it's a great big place. You weren't anywhere close to my radar. Move on."

By her stunned expression I'm assuming she didn't expect me to defend myself. Girls like her are bullies. They get their confidence by picking on weaker people. She's spoiled. Used to getting her way. I may not be outspoken, but I will stand up for what I believe in. Every. Single. Time. I've always been nice to everyone unless they personally do something to me. I never judge someone before I know them.

She looks at me with so much hatred in her eyes. I look around for Breyson. This is awkward. I have no idea what else to say to her. "I wouldn't get too attached to him. He's only with you for one thing: to fuck. Breyson Abercrombie doesn't do serious relationships or love. He only cares about when, where, and what position."

Her smile is one of a villain. "He'll tire of you eventually, just like he did me. I see you around school. You're in love with him. I can see it in your eyes. You're not the only one that feels that way about him. I'm not giving up yet. Just remember, we have history. I've known Breyson for years. I know what he likes and what he dislikes."

She runs her fingertips along my hairline, giving me a creepy chill. "You look a little too innocent for him. He'll get tired of playing with you. When he's over the boring sex I imagine you give, he'll come back to the rough and rowdy he had with me. You're just something unfamiliar right now, like a shiny new toy. It's only a matter of time until he gets bored, and I'll be waiting. Watch yourself, *sweetie*." The nickname slides off her tongue, dripping in sarcasm.

She is pissing me off. The thought of her being intimate with him like I have makes me sick, and her arrogant attitude about taking him back makes me want to slap her. I won't let her get to me. I'm going to be the stronger person. I have to be or it'll ruin us. I don't want to be the jealous girlfriend. He asked me to trust him and I said I would. I'm going to stand by my word. "Goodbye, Natalie."

Flipping her hair, she stomps off in a rage. She is acting like a child. I don't know what he saw in her if she always acts this way. It makes her look like a fool.

I take a seat in one of the chairs against the wall, waiting on Breyson. I look around again, wondering where he is. He's been gone a while. I haven't seen any of the others either.

Finally, fifteen minutes later, Breyson comes into view with two cups of punch. "I'm sorry it took so long. I ran into a problem that I had to deal with. You thirsty?"

I nod and take one of the glasses from him. "Thanks." Before I can think about it I drink the whole glass. I was thirstier than I thought, and now frustrated from my unwelcome visitor.

"Let's go dance. I'm tired of sitting here." He sets down his punch, takes my hand, and leads me to the dance floor.

We've been out here for a few songs. I was having a good time, but everything is starting to feel really weird. Dizziness hits me. My head is pounding from the strobe lights. I have no idea what's going on.

Breyson brushes against me. The sensations of it on my skin make me want to take my clothes off right here. Something is wrong. This isn't normal. "Kinzleigh."

I can't concentrate. Everything is blurring together. My anxiety is shooting through the roof. I sway before I can catch myself, unstable on my feet. "Kinzleigh! What's wrong?"

He grabs my face in his hands and looks at me. My heart is pounding wildly. I feel like I'm on some kind of speed, energized and scared all at the same time. All of my senses are amplified, uncontrollable. The longer he stares into my eyes, the more he looks like he wants to kill someone.

He looks back and Natalie is standing in the middle of the dance floor, staring right at us with a smirk spreading maliciously across her face.

"Breyson," I scream, but I feel like I'm barely audible. The heaving of my chest begins, making it difficult to breathe. "Something is wrong with me. I feel like I'm dying. My heart is doing something crazy. I have a headache. Something is wrong."

Tears stream down my face and wheezing follows. Like a stupid girl I didn't bring my inhaler, because I haven't had to use it since I found out Breyson was here. I'm having a panic attack. Trying to inhale, enough air isn't reaching my lungs. It's like someone constricting your airway.

Breyson grabs me by the shoulders, trying to calm me down. "Baby, it's okay. Just breathe. I'm here. I got you."

I blink over and over, trying to focus on his eyes, but my eyes start to roll back in my head, and in an instant, everything goes black.

FOURTEEN

Breyson

I'm going to kill that bitch. I swear on my life I'm going to kill her. I know exactly what that look was. She's done it before with other girls at school. Guys do it. Though I never have. The new thing at parties is for someone to put ecstasy in a drink and give it to someone. It catches them off guard when the high hits. They get away with it by saying it livens up the party and takes away the fear of trying it when you don't know it's there. If you want to be any part of the popular crowd at school, you don't say shit about it. No one has gotten caught.

The night I slept with Natalie for the first time someone put one in my beer. Now that I look back on it, knowing how crazy she is, the dumb bitch was probably the one that did it to get in my pants. I had turned her sly attempts down in the past, because we were friends.

If that was the case, it worked, because I wanted to screw everything that walked and was female. The sensations are crazy, but I'm not into drugs. And she was the first girl to try. God, so much makes sense now.

When I came out of the bathroom I went straight to the punch table. Natalie swooped in the second I got there like a watching vulture. She immediately started apologizing for everything that's happened and wanted to make a truce. She said she missed being friends and wanted to wish me the best with Kinzleigh.

She then handed me the two full cups in her hands as a 'peace offering' since the line was long. I never thought she would stoop to this level of crazy, even after the pregnancy stunt. She is dead to me.

I was too busy talking to Kinzleigh while she was drinking hers to drink my own, and then she wanted to dance, so I never drank from my cup. I feel like shit. Natalie is my fault. I was a dumbass to think she'd really let everything go. I never should have taken that cup from her.

I'm trying to calm Kinzleigh down, to explain it'll wear off if she'd just relax, but it's not working. She is screaming and crying and drawing attention. Everyone has stopped dancing.

Adalynn and Londyn rushed over when they knew something was wrong. As soon as Adalynn gets to us she narrows her eyes, staring into Kinzleigh's eyes. The longer Kinzleigh panics the more Adalynn's expression changes. She looks at me. I know by the look she's giving me that she's put it together, but she doesn't want to freak Kinzleigh out more.

She doesn't touch her, because she knows the drug alters nervous and sensory systems. "Babe, calm down. It's going to be okay. What do you need from me? You need to be able to breathe."

Kinzleigh shakes her head from side to side. She is making a whooping sound each time she breathes. Adalynn turns to Natalie, who now looks nervous. "Natalie, what the hell is wrong with you? You're such a brat! You couldn't stand someone else getting Breyson over you and him actually falling for her over her being a mutual fuck buddy like you were, could you? Get over it. He doesn't want you anymore. If you want someone to blame, blame him. You two can work out this shit. Kinzleigh has done nothing to you! You know why it's immoral to spike someone's drink? You have no idea what that drug will do to a person. Everyone's body reacts differently. There are chaperones scattered around here for God's sake!"

"It was supposed to be a joke. I just wanted to knock her off that high horse she's riding. Push her down a notch from perfect. Tarnish her innocence a little. I'm sorry. If she'd stop freaking the hell out she'd be fine. She's going to get us suspended. No one at parties acts like this." Her voice is low, but menacing, and she's biting her fake nails.

If she weren't a girl I'd beat the shit out of her. We all know she deserves it. If anyone's riding a high horse it's her spoiled ass. Maybe I should get a girl to do it for me. Her eyes widen when she glances back at Kinzleigh and that's when I realize she is convulsing underneath my hands.

I turn back around and Kinzleigh is having a seizure. Her eyes are rolling back in her head and her body is jerking and shaking. Her limbs are limp. The only thing holding her up is me. "Kinzleigh! Oh fuck . . . Someone call an ambulance!" I scream, now in full panic mode.

God, please let her be okay.

Please don't take her from me.

I'll do anything.

Adalynn is in full hysterics, pulling out her cell phone with shaking hands, likely from her adrenaline being on overdrive. Kinzleigh falls backward following a hard jerk of her body, slipping from my grasp.

My knees hit the floor, pain shooting up my thighs, but just before her head hits the tile I cup the back of her head in my palm. What the hell am I supposed to do? My parents are doctors, but they've never prepared me for someone having a seizure before.

My eyes are burning from the tears threatening to spill over seeing her this way. Adalynn is screaming into the phone, trying to get someone out here to get Kinzleigh. I feel so helpless.

I slide my arms under Kinzleigh's legs and neck. Picking her up, I cradle her in my arms and sit on the floor, pulling her into my lap. I have never been more terrified than I am right now. She is breathing, but unconscious. My eyes are full of unshed tears. I'm not a crier. I never have been, but something about seeing her completely unresponsive is breaking me down.

"What the hell happened?" an adult barks out in the background. I don't let her go. My frantic emotions are consuming me. I can't hold them back any longer. Spilling out, the tears run down my cheeks and drop onto hers as I pull her face to mine.

Rocking back and forth, I plead with her. "Kinzleigh, please be okay. I just started loving you. I haven't had enough time with you. I'm begging you, please come back. I need you, Kinzleigh. Dammit, I need you. I've never felt this way about someone before. I'll do anything if you'll just be okay. I'm so sorry I took that drink. I didn't know. I swear on everything I didn't know."

I'm not sure where my brothers are, but Adalynn is kneeling in front of me, staring at Kinzleigh as if she would break should she touch her. Her voice comes out in a faint whisper. "I know you can't touch Natalie, but I can. I will make her pay for this. No one harms my friends or my family and gets away with it. That girl is more of a family to me than my own sister. She's never done anything to anyone to deserve this."

My heart feels like it's being ripped from my chest the more she shakes.

Adalynn stands and walks over to where Natalie is standing by the wall. I can't hear what she is saying, but by the look on Natalie's face as her eyes bulge out of her head, it isn't good.

Before I can process what's happening, Adalynn slaps her across the face, hard. It had to have hurt, because it echoed across the room, and a red handprint is already appearing on her cheek. Overhead lights start to come on one by one in the large space like a domino effect, the fluorescent making the room way too bright.

Natalie looks at me with tears in her eyes and takes off out the door. If she wants sympathy from me she isn't going to get it. We each make our own decisions. I warned her what would happen if she didn't cut the psycho bullshit. She chose to spike the drinks. We have to reap what we sow. I hug Kinzleigh to my chest.

The paramedic runs inside with a stretcher in tow. He kneels in front of me after being pointed in my direction. I look up, my eyes meeting with a pair of dark ones. The guy in uniform is thirty at the oldest. "Hey, man, I need to take her with me. I promise I'll take good care of her, but to do that I need to check her out."

He's talking so fast I can barely process what he's saying, but he continues to rush his words. "The quicker we get started the better off she'll be. I need you to trust me. Let her go. We need to get her to the hospital."

He reaches down trying to take her from me in a hurry. Looking down at her, I lightly kiss her lips and transfer her to him, letting go. "Please help her. I don't know how and it's killing me. I'll follow you to the hospital."

He wastes no time before placing her on the stretcher and securing her. He starts rolling her toward the entrance, but looks back at me before he gets too far. "We'll go to the closest hospital."

I nod as he picks up pace, rolling her out the door. That girl is everything to me. If something happens to her I will get revenge. Natalie will pay for this.

FIFTEEN

Breyson

Something inside of me dies seeing her taken away in an ambulance. I jump in my truck, along with my brothers and the girls. Everyone is silent, the only sounds in the cab coming from the hushed cries of Londyn and Adalynn. I start the engine and tear out of the parking lot as fast as I can.

Pulling out my smartphone, I touch my dad's name from my favorites list on my iPhone. It rings a couple of times before he picks up. "Breyson? Are you all right? You hardly ever call. I thought you were at the homecoming dance."

"Dad, I need your help. Kinzleigh is on the way to the hospital, because Natalie spiked her drink with ecstasy and she panicked over the effects and that somehow spiraled into a seizure. She has anxiety and panic attacks. Dad, help her. Please, help her. I don't know what to do. I love her. You have to do something. Anything." I'm talking so fast I can barely get the words out, short of breath.

And then it hits me that I said the L word out loud for the first time to someone other than Kinzleigh. I'm scared to look at the reaction on my brothers' faces, or the girls'. I completely forgot they were in the truck.

"Calm down, Son," Dad orders. "You're no good to anyone this upset. I'll call the Neurologist on call and meet you at the hospital. She'll be okay.

People have seizures all the time. See you in a bit." He disconnects the call and I drop the phone in my lap, concentrating on the road.

I tighten my grip on the steering wheel and press my foot firmly on the gas pedal to increase my speed, trying to get to her faster. My biggest obstacle is going to be weekend traffic and stoplights.

I look through the rearview mirror at Adalynn. She is still crying. "Will you call Kinzleigh's parents? I'm not sure I can right now, but they need to know what's going on, and I'd prefer them hear it from one of us and not freaking out over getting a call from a hospital."

"Sure, Breyson, I'll call them." I look at the road again when she pulls out her cellphone to call.

We pull into the emergency entrance of the hospital and find a parking spot. As soon as I get the truck parked and shut off, I bail and take off running toward the entrance, leaving everyone else behind, including my keys. My brothers can get them or leave them. Someone can steal the damn thing for all I care. That's what insurance is for. All I care about is getting to her.

When I make it to the registration desk I stop. The lady behind the desk with a name badge is talking on the phone. The privacy window is closed, shutting out her conversation. I tap my fingers on the counter impatiently, waiting for her to hang up. After what feels like an eternity, she returns the phone to the base and looks at me. "Can I help you?"

"I need to know where they took Kinzleigh Baker. She arrived by ambulance a few minutes ago." She types something into the computer and looks up at me.

"Do you know her date of birth?"

"October fifth, nineteen ninety-five." She looks back at the screen and explains what floor Neurology is on and how to get there. I turn and take off down the hall toward the elevator.

Once I get off on the correct floor, I see the nurse's station ahead. I hate not knowing how she is. I stop at it and place my hands on top of the counter. A brunette in scrubs with the same kind of badge as the other lady—only different information—looks up at me from the paperwork she's filling out. She smiles, and then runs her hand through her long ponytail. "Can I help you?"

She can't be that much older than me. She's probably fresh out of school. "I need to know what room Kinzleigh Baker is in."

She gathers information from her computer; adjusting her glasses with one hand as her other clicks repeatedly on the mouse. "I'm sorry, but she hasn't been assigned a room yet. She is in imaging having some tests run. The doctor will give an update soon. Until then you can wait down the hall in the waiting area."

Is she freaking serious? How am I supposed to sit here not knowing how she's doing? My frustration is building. Worry is setting in. Anxiety over what the outcome will be is spreading. I want to hit something to release some of it. "Can you just tell me how she is?"

"Unfortunately, I can't give out any information. You'll have to wait on the doctor." I push off the counter with force and walk to the waiting area they expect me to just sit in as if the love of my life isn't somewhere in the vicinity hurt, maybe even scared.

I sit down in the stagnant neutral chair and bend forward, placing my elbows on my legs just above my knees. Forehead in the palms of my hands, I grip my hair. I pull hard, trying to draw the pain away from my chest. It does little to settle the fear in my mind.

I close my eyes, trying to drown out the bad thoughts. I can hear the material of the chair cushions under strain beside me, telling me someone just sat down. "So, you love her?"

There are few voices I'll remember forever. His I can pick out anywhere. I can hear it in my head even when he doesn't speak. Same with my other brother. I look beside me at Briar sitting down, leaned back in the chair. Braxton is on the other side of him.

For some reason it feels more personal admitting it to someone else. Briar and I have always been close, because the three of us are triplets, but we don't have as many heart-to-hearts as Braxton and I do.

I see the worried expression on his face. "Like crazy; so much that if anything happens to her I don't know what I'd do. She owns my heart. She's different. She gave me everything. Made me see what life could be like for me. I've never felt more whole than when we're together. I can't lose her, Briar. I'm in too deep."

My vision clouds and I rub my hands over my face. I will not let my brothers see me cry again. A guy is only allowed a cry on rare occasion without being considered a wuss.

The girls are across the waiting area consoling each other and Braxton is staring off into space. I don't know what's going on with him lately. I think he went into this thing with Adalynn as a hookup and is starting to have feelings for her. He doesn't talk about girls anymore, but I get the impression he feels guilty having feelings for someone other than Madileigh.

Briar leans forward, mirroring my position. "I can tell. I've never seen you like this over a girl before. It's nice to see you care about someone. She seems like a good girl. Those are harder to find. Be good to her, because if you screw up there is a line of guys waiting to take your place."

He pauses, but I don't think he's finished, because his position doesn't change. "About tonight . . . Now isn't really the time to say this, but then it is. Always play defense if you see this relationship being serious or long-term. Protect her. A girl like her has no chance against girls like Natalie. You have a lot of girls after you and now you see what kind of psychotic jealous bullshit they will do to get to you. Just because Natalie is the first, I doubt she'll be the last. If you get a shot at the NFL it'll get worse."

Sitting here listening to this feels like Déjà vu. It's so similar to that day on the boat deep-sea fishing with Ryland. Do people really think I don't know what I have? Do I come off as that big of a prick? I stopped thinking with my dick the day I met her on the beach. I know she's special. I know other men want her. They will have to pry her from my cold, dead fingers to get her, but I'm not stupid enough to think there aren't people that would kill to replace me.

I could throw up at the thought of some sleazy girl trying to harm her. I feel so stupid for trusting Natalie. I thought she was better than that, but I was way off kilter with her. This is the perfect example of someone being totally different than the person they want you to see.

"I know all that." I growl. "I'm so stupid. Dammit, why did I trust her?" I smash the heel of my hand into my forehead. "I hate Natalie for doing this to her, to me. She better hope Kinzleigh isn't permanently damaged, because I won't be responsible for the aftermath if she is."

"Don't do something stupid, Breyson. Jealousy blinds people. I'm not, in any form, defending Natalie, but remember she's someone's daughter just like Kinzleigh. You're not thinking straight right now, because you're hurt, and I get that. All I'm saying is use your head."

He doesn't get it, because it's not Londyn lying helpless in a hospital. "That's easy for you to say, because it isn't Londyn lying in there helpless and defenseless and scared. Put yourself in my shoes. Are you telling me you wouldn't avenge an act of wrong done to Londyn when she didn't deserve it if it were her? Come on. Don't feed me bullshit. You're the starting pitcher. You have just as many girls after you as I do. An eye for an eye, right? If something happens to her I will not move on like nothing happened. No one made Natalie do what she did."

As he considers what I just said he remains quiet. He acts like he's about to say something, but then shuts his mouth. It seems a little different when you imagine it being your loved one laying there for no good reason. Everyone has a piece of advice to give until they actually put themselves in that place. It changes your perspective.

Kinzleigh's parents come into the waiting area in a rush. They look extremely worried and I don't blame them. As they get closer to me, I stand and rush over to them, placing my hands in my pockets and lower my head to the floor.

Guilt consumes me. This is my fault. I should have waited in line and watched them pour my drinks instead of being in a rush to get back to her. "Mr. and Mrs. Baker, I'm so sorry."

My voice cracks. "I didn't know the drink was spiked, but it's my fault. I take full responsibility for what happened. I should have never accepted a drink from someone that I knew has been acting out in ways she never has." I press my fingers against my eyelids, trying to stop the tears of rage that want to spill over this whole situation.

When we started dating all her dad asked me to do was to respect her, protect her, and love her the way she deserves to be loved or let her go. I made a promise I would do all of those things and I failed tonight. Her mother is crying. Mr. Baker looks at her. "Leigh, why don't you go get us some coffee until we hear from the doctor. I need to talk to Breyson."

He probably wants to kill me. I can't say that I blame him. If I were him I would want to kill me too. What he asked of me was simple. If I can't handle those three small tasks, maybe I don't deserve her.

Kinzleigh's mom nods and walks off in search of the cafeteria. When he looks back at me, I'm surprised. He doesn't look angry like I imagined he would be.

He looks at his watch and then up at me. "Come on, let's go someplace quiet. I imagine it'll be a while before we can see her. They are still running tests." He wraps his arm around me and squeezes my shoulder in his hand, leading me toward the hallway.

We come into a vacant hallway and stop against the wall. I'm nervous, and I'm never nervous. My palms are sweaty. I wipe them on my jeans, trying to dry them off. He stands there zoned out for a few minutes, calculating what he is going to say. "It's not your fault. I don't want you to beat yourself up over this."

I open my mouth to say something and he holds up his hand, stopping me. "Let me finish. I can see the guilt written all over your face. I admire the fact that you're willing to take the fall for someone else's shortcomings, but it's not necessary. You have done more than what I expected of you in regard to my daughter. Every man is terrified of having to trust his little girl to another man. You have earned my trust with her, but sometimes bad things happen and you can't do anything to stop it."

I'm a little shocked, to be honest. You hear about men waiting around with their shotguns all your life, looking for a good reason to pick a guy off over their daughters. And even though I'd take his anger and not say a damn word, I respect him a lot more this way.

He doesn't look like he's finished saying what he needs to say, so I remain quiet. "The world is an ugly place. We all learn that when we bring kids into it. You raise them to the best of your ability and hope everything turns out for the best, but it wouldn't be realistic of me to think we can avoid every bad thing. Kinzleigh has always been an exceptional child. She never parties, never drinks, and I'm going to hope that she doesn't have sex, but I'm not even going there, because I don't want to know."

He takes a deep breath. "She's eighteen and there isn't much I can do about it now if she is, but there are some things a father can't deal with knowing. I'm proud that she chose someone like you. I think you're a good kid, Breyson, and you follow the rules her mother and I set, no questions asked. We never worry when she's with you."

He glances down the hall when a dinging sound goes off, but then focuses back on me. His expression is softer. "Kinzleigh has battled anxiety and depression since my mother died, even though she'd never admit to the depression part. They were close. I need you to be strong for her. When she wakes up she is going to want you there and I don't want you causing her more stress by blaming yourself. I can tell you love her. Most adults think young love is just a teenager blinded by lust, but I disagree. Sometimes love that starts out in the early years is the strongest kind, because you experience more highs and lows together. If you really love her, stop blaming yourself and be the strength she needs when she can't find her own. If you don't do anything else I ask, do that."

I let out a sigh of relief. He's right. I never thought of it like that. "Yes, sir. I can do that. I do love her. I hate seeing her hurt. She's special to me. I'm positive I'd be in a bad place if something happened to her."

He pushes off the wall he was leaning against. "I appreciate your honesty.

Honesty and love will take you far in life. Always remember that. Let's go. We have a sick girl to take care of."

Shortly after we got back to the lobby the doctor came out and gave us an update on her condition. He thinks the anxiety attack came from her panicking about the drug effects since she didn't know what was happening to her body, and in turn overloaded her brain. The drug test confirmed it was ecstasy. Since she already has issues with anxiety—which is a mental illness—the mixture of that and the drug's effects on her brain was too much for her mind to handle. The way it reacted to the stress was through the seizure, trying to shut it all off to protect itself.

He ran extensive tests on her brain and didn't see any permanent damage. *Thank you, God.* He did say because her body has had one seizure, she's at risk for recurring, so he is putting her on an anti-seizure medication to prevent any further.

The doctor gave us permission to see her, but gave us orders—only two at a time and to let her rest. He said she'll be sleepy and shouldn't be doing any excess talking, because she would most likely be out of it for a while from the wear down of the seizure on her brain and body. He is keeping her overnight and then will do another test before he releases her. I'm thankful it isn't worse than it is—like an overdose.

I stare at the door to her room, waiting to enter. Her parents were getting tired since it's past midnight and went in to see her first. Dad came by to check on Kinzleigh and took rounds for another physician since he wanted to be here for me. He said he would stay in touch with the Neurologist on her condition and check back in a little later.

I refuse to leave her alone here. After meeting my dad, her dad agreed to let me stay overnight since a nurse and tech will be in and out all night and plan to be back first thing in the morning once they've had some sleep.

My dad had a pillow and blanket sent up for me to sleep on the couch in the room that lets out into a flat surface for sleeping when he finally got the point that I wasn't leaving until she did. He didn't really force me to. I think he just wanted me to get some rest, but I'm not going to get any more sleep at home than I would here.

Briar, Londyn, Braxton and Adalynn all made their rounds and left to get some sleep as well. Mom came in to make her rounds with patients earlier, but is on the Obstetrics floor and said she would come back down when Kinzleigh was awake to see how she's doing. It wasn't too hard to get dad to switch out with the attending to work considering they weren't on the same shift tonight.

I push the door open and see her lying perfectly still on the hospital bed. She is hooked to all kinds of machines; most of them monitors keeping track of brain activity, heart rate, and vitals.

Her hair is fanned out across the pillow. Her skin is smooth and pale. Her eyes are closed. She is wearing a hospital gown and her bottom half is covered with a blanket. She looks delicate like that. She looks like an angel.

I place my palm over my heart and rub at the pain in my chest. It's dulled a little since I found out she'll be okay, but still present. Even laying in the hospital she's absolutely beautiful. Damn, I love her.

Walking over to the side of the bed farthest from the door, I move the oversized chair from the window to the side of her bed and sit. I lean forward, placing my folded arms on the side of the bed beside her body. Interlocking her fingers with mine, I watch her while she sleeps.

She looks peaceful. You would never think just a few hours ago this happened. I will never be able to remove seeing her like that from my mind. I never want to feel that helpless again.

My hand never leaves hers. I like feeling her pulse with one touch to her wrist. It reminds me she's alive. I feel like I owe her an explanation, an apology. She shouldn't be here. If anyone should be in this hospital bed, it should be me.

She is the best person I know, inside and out. Why someone would want to hurt her dumbfounds me. Natalie may not have done it with the intent to harm her physically, but she was trying to be cruel and that's no better.

I squeeze her hand. "Baby, I'm so sorry. I know I made your dad a promise, but I have to get this out. If I can't do it when you're awake then I'll do it now. I failed you. As a man I am supposed to protect you. I didn't. Please forgive me or I'll never forgive myself. I've never been so scared in my entire life. Seeing you that way is not something I ever want to see again. At one point the thought of you dying passed through my mind."

I pause, trying to calm down. "I have to die before you. I can't handle living in this world without you here. Kinzleigh, after this, I know without a shadow of doubt I can't live without you. It's crazy that I've only known you four months, but now that I do I can't go back to not knowing you. You make me want to be a better man. My love for you runs deep. Loving you knows no bounds. I will do anything for you. Please let me love you forever. From now until my dying day, I will do right by you."

Tears stream down my face, but I don't care. If anyone is going to see the ugly, I'm glad it's her. I don't know what I did to deserve a chance with her, but I'll be forever in gratitude that I was standing on the beach that day.

We don't choose our fate. Our fate chooses us. You might as well just accept it and live your life. We get one chance to make it count. After today, I'm living each day as if it's my last. I'm not going to worry about the future or what it holds.

Truthfully, we can't control it anyway. It's up to the big guy upstairs. I realized something. The people that surround us are important in life, not what college we go to or what team we play for or the things we have. One second they're here and the next they could be gone. I'll never take advantage of her from this point forward. Her life is too precious to me.

"I love you with every ounce of energy inside me. One more day will never be enough with you. You make me want more out of life. I cannot exist without you. If you go, I go. From now on that's the way it will always be."

I bring the back of her hand to my lips and then gently put it back down, careful not to wake her. "What once made me happy no longer does unless you're a part of it. I'd give up everything for you. Wherever you go, I'll happily follow—any school, any state. I can play football anywhere. What I know is I've been walking around with half of my heart for seventeen years. The moment I met you I felt different. Together I feel whole. You enthrall me. I'm begging you not to leave me."

Her hand lightly squeezes mine. I barely felt it, but it was there. Either that or I'm going crazy. I look up, but she is still sleeping. At least I know she heard me, subconsciously or not.

Laying my head on my crossed arms, my eyes become heavy, and before I can think of anything more, I doze off. My mind goes back to a time that was good. The two of us standing on the other side of that field house where she gave me her heart . . .

SIXTEEN

Kinzleigh

My eyes flutter open to an unfamiliar place. White is the palette that surrounds me and it smells of bleach and chemicals. Gross. Where am I? As I look down at myself, I realize exactly where I am by the completely unfashionable gown I'm sporting—a hospital. Why am I in a hospital?

I look down to Breyson sleeping with his arms crossed over the bed and he is holding onto my hand. He doesn't look comfortable. Surely he didn't sleep all night like that. I scan the room. The untouched folded bedding and pillow on the couch confirms he did.

I sit up. I feel like crap. My body is sore and I'm tired. I just want to go home and crawl in my bed; maybe take a hot bath. Anything other than laying here.

My fingers are cramped from being interlaced with Breyson's. I try to slip mine out of his without waking him, but it doesn't work. Instead, it has the opposite effect. He jumps up, dazed and confused, causing his chair to tip over. I look into a set of bloodshot eyes that look swollen like he's been crying. What on earth happened? He looks scared to death. "Breyson," I say slowly, trying not to wind him up more than he apparently already is. "Are you okay?"

He exhales and his shoulders relax. "I am now. I was so scared, baby.

I never want to see you like that again." My forehead scrunches at his admission and he moves closer to me. Leaning over the side of the bed he kisses me on the lips. I keep them closed at the paranoia of morning breath.

Grabbing the edge of the blanket and scooting to the side, against the raised bedrail, I fold back the covers and pat the bed for him to lay beside me. Glancing down, he looks unsure if he should. "Breyson. Come on, lay with me." I pat the mattress harder to reiterate what I want. He shakes his head. I give him my best pouty face. "Please . . . don't make me beg."

He rubs his face and takes off his shoes. Works. Every. Time. I should feel bad, but I don't. A girl has to have a secret weapon for times when she wants something. This is mine—the pouty face.

He sits on the side of the bed with the lowered rail and puts his feet under the blanket. He lays back, his arm extended across the mattress. I lay back down on my side, resting my head on his shoulder, draping my arm across his stomach. "Why am I here, Breyson?"

He takes a deep breath. "Natalie put ecstasy in your punch behind my back. When it took effect you went into a full panic attack. You had a seizure from the mixture of the anxiety and the high."

Pain is weaved through his words as he tells me what happened. I know exactly why. He's blaming himself for this. My hero. Trying to take the fall for the bad seeds of the world. Not this time. That little twit can live with what she did.

He turns so that we're face to face. "I'm sorry, baby. I'll never let anything happen to you again. I swear. Please give me a chance to make this right. Don't let her ruin us. I didn't know. Please believe me. I love you. God as my witness right now, Kinzleigh, I love you more than my life."

He can't actually think I would blame him for her behavior. After all, I knew she was off her rocker from the one-sided conversation she forced me in prior. He couldn't possibly think I would break up with him over this. Would he?

"Breyson." I purse my lips and narrow my eyes to signify my aggravation. "Would you stop trying to be perfect? It's irritating me, and frankly, unnecessary. You have me up on a pedestal and I have no idea why. I am no more special than any other person. As long as you have me up there, this relationship is going to be setup for failure. You will never be perfect and neither will I. Bad things are going to happen, Breyson. There is nothing you can do about it."

His jaws are clenched and I realize I'm probably being a little bitchy—

more so than I intended.

I place my palm on the side of his cheek and rub his jaw with my thumb. "This is coming out wrong. Breyson, I love you. You know I mean it, because I've never said it to another guy. I don't need perfection to be happy. I need perfectly imperfect. The imperfections in life are what make things beautiful. Perfect would be boring. I need you to keep me on my toes. You've already been my saving grace on several occasions. I wouldn't be living life to its fullest if it weren't for you. You have shown me how to love someone. That is all I'll ever need."

Screw morning breath. I need him.

I pull him to me and kiss him. His warm tongue slips in my mouth and a sensation jolts through my body. A moan escapes me. I throw my leg over him, pulling myself to straddle him, which forces him to turn on his back. It doesn't register where we are.

He places a hand on each thigh and moves up my legs, underneath this horrid gown. Our lips part when his tongue trails down my neck. He lingers at the base and sucks the skin into his mouth. "Make love to me, Breyson. I need to feel you; all of you."

Lifting up on my knees, I unbutton and unzip his jeans. I feel needy, already going through withdrawal from the absence of him. I don't need his clothes off for what I want. "Kinzleigh, your parents are supposed to be coming back and I don't really want them walking in on me violating their daughter."

I'm not worried about that. I'm ready, and based on the hard bulge pressed against my entrance, so is he. I've never been brazen enough to take what I want, but something about him has me trying all sorts of things. "This doesn't have to take long."

He grips the sides of his jeans and pushes them down enough that they're out of the way. I grab his shaft. He puts his hand through my hair and tugs to pull me back to him. His breathing is heavy. I have him right where I want him. The noble act is sweet and all, but right now it's not going to work. I know what I want.

I bite his bottom lip and suck it into my mouth, before releasing it. I continue my plan of seduction by kissing him on the chin and down the front of his neck as I lightly rub the body part I have come to love.

I don't really know what I'm doing, but I can pretend. "It's your fault, you know—the reason I can't get enough. You're the one that took my virginity. And now I know what I was missing. *You* made me like sex. It would be wrong of you to turn me down after that. You don't want to be known as *that* guy do you?" I purr against his neck.

He clenches my hips in his hands and jerks me forward until the length of his dick is parallel with my lips, and then he grinds me against him. "I am going to ruin you the way you've ruined me," he growls.

His eyes are blazing. He presses back against the bed and lifts me up enough to position his dick below me. Once in position, I sit down, allowing him to enter me.

I wasn't lying. I can't believe this is what I've been missing. It feels amazing. For some reason it feels different than before. "No one else will ever touch you here. Do you understand? This is mine. You are mine, Kinzleigh."

He forces my body up and down on him, not being gentle. It feels so good. "Say it," he says huskily. "I need to hear it." He places his thumb on my tattoo, as if it's sacred.

This isn't going to take long at all. I love seeing his wild side come out and play. I love this boy. Something so demanding coming from him sends a want and need through my body I can't explain. I want to be his. I need to be his. Always and forever. "It's always been yours, Breyson. I gave it to you. I belong to you. I don't want anyone else."

Pulling me down by my neck, he kisses me greedily. "You feel so good. I love you so much. Go with me?" He rocks me back and forth, hitting against my insides in a way that makes me want to scream.

I nod as the sensation builds in my core. My toes curl and everything feels like it's in slow motion when it takes over. A whimper escapes my lips as they crash against his and we both climax together.

He is my rock. He is my necessity. "I love you too. More than you will ever know." It's the truth, completely and wholeheartedly.

A knock sounds at the door and I scurry to get off of him. Breyson jumps off the bed in a panic and runs to the bathroom to clean up. Throwing the blanket back over me, the door opens and a middle-aged man in a white coat walks through the door. The doctor I presume.

He looks at the screen by my bed and jots something down on his clipboard. Looking at me, he introduces himself and fills me in on information that really makes no sense to me.

Breyson walks out of the bathroom and when the doctor sees him he looks at me with a knowing expression. Maybe it's just my guilt talking. It clicks. Embarrassment flushes my cheeks. The heart rate on the monitor is accelerated from our tryst a few moments ago. It gave me away before he ever came in here. I'm mortified.

"Miss Baker, I hope you're resting. You had a seizure. Your body needs it." He gives me a stern look like my father would. I want to hide under my sheets.

"Yes, sir. I haven't been up long." He watches Breyson take a seat beside the bed. His face is flushed and his hair is messy from my hands being in it. He should have just stayed in the bathroom. Can this be any more humiliating?

What am I supposed to say? The door opens and in walks two more adults in lab coats. Two I recognize. Great. The answer is yes. It can get more humiliating. The two men shake hands and Breyson stands, rubbing his hand through his hair.

The man I've come to know as Breyson's dad is handsome and tall. He's muscular, but lean. He has the same dark blond hair as Breyson and Braxton, but his eyes are a hazel color. The night I met him it was dark out. When he came to the media room it was quick and I was embarrassed, much like now. And since, I've avoided them. Now that I get a good look at him, he resembles Breyson.

His mom is stunning; though a little intimidating. Her hair is Auburn, the red showing more with light, and she has big beautiful blue eyes. These two make pretty babies. Their kids, well, being as one got me to hand over my virginity, confirms that very statement. She takes me in and smiles kindly. Obstetrics and Gynecology is embroidered on her jacket. I remember how hovering she was when I was at his house that night, and considering her specialty, it makes sense. She's much like my mom in that category. I've been scared to death of his parents since.

Breyson takes my hand before looking at his mom and dad. "Mom, Dad, I'm assuming you remember my girlfriend Kinzleigh. I know it's been a while."

He looks back at me with an apologetic smile, given I had no warning to prep for his parents and we just had sex like five seconds ago! Had I known they were coming I wouldn't have been trying to screw their son. "Kinzleigh, I know they look a little different than at the house, but my parents wanted to check on you to make sure you were okay."

He mouths, *I'm sorry*. He's wearing the same embarrassment I am. Much to my embarrassment, I look at her closer, hoping she isn't so good at her job that she knows what we just did. Her and Briar share many of the same features. I was in no way prepared for a visit with his parents. I don't even know what I look like. I probably look awful.

In a panic, I run my fingers through my hair, attempting to make myself presentable. I need a shower and I need to brush my teeth. His mom moves toward me, her perfume wafting through the air. It smells good, but it's subtle. I'm assuming so that it doesn't make patients sick. She extends her arms in front of her.

Please don't let me stink.

She wraps her arms around me, and whispers in my ear. "You look beautiful, sweetie. Stop fiddling with yourself."

Leaning back, she winks, smiling angelically. "I don't think we had time to get to know each other last time. Breyson was telling us a lot about you, leaving out most about us. And maybe that's why you were so uncomfortable. I'm Ava, Breyson's mom, as you already know. He talks about you a lot. I'm glad a good girl finally got his attention. You're leaving a lasting impression."

Already I adore her. She doesn't seem as scary this way. I look at Breyson. He looks like he may hurl. His face has gone pale and he's squeezing my hand. Why is he nervous? Technically, I've already met them. But still, I'm the one that should be nervous over looking like crap and lying in a hospital bed. Maybe he thinks I'm mad at him for not warning me. "Son, we're going to talk about what happened later and why people you associate with are bringing drugs to social activities."

"I know," he says, defeated.

The doctor informs me he is going to schedule one more test before he discharges me and excuses himself from the room.

Breyson's dad walks over beside his mother and gives me a sideways hug. Embroidered in the same black thread as his wife, his coat reads, Cardiology and Cardiothoracic surgery. A family full of doctors is a bit intimidating. I don't think that feeling is going to go away.

I understand how Breyson feels about football now more than I did. It's textbook really. Adults with careers of high stature expect their kids to follow in the same footsteps. Doctors, lawyers, bankers, and successful entrepreneurs like Presley's parents. My mother has hinted at it in the past, but she's also very supportive of letting us choose our own path. Not every parent is the same.

"I'm glad you're okay. You gave Breyson quite a scare," he says, seeming genuinely concerned. "I think our first introduction was a little thrown off for everyone. You haven't been back since. I hope that will stop now. I expect to be called Mr. Brooks, not Dr. Abercrombie. As long as you make my boy happy we're too close for formalities," he teases.

"I'm sorry it seemed like I was avoiding you. That was not my intention. I'm shy and a little socially awkward," I admit. "I haven't had to meet someone's parents in a very long time. I've been friends with the same people since elementary school. There have been lots of changes for me lately."

I feel relieved now that I've admitted the way I feel. I'm slightly overwhelmed and Breyson is standing here speechless, not making things any easier. I look at him and narrow my eyes, trying to break him from his little trance. "Are you okay? You don't look so well."

"I think he's afraid we'll embarrass him. He likes to think we're different when we're in a professional environment versus home. He hasn't made it a habit of bringing girls to meet us. I have to give him a little credit. He has good taste. I feel like we've raised him well," his mom says, looking at him, and just like that he smiles from ear to ear as if he just made a winning touchdown.

I bite my tongue and press my lips together, trying not to laugh. My beautiful boy. I guess he's a mama's boy at heart, needing her approval.

Another knock sounds at the door and in walks my parents. My mom is toting a duffle bag in her hands. Thank goodness. Clean clothes. I've had enough of this hospital getup. But it occurs to me that our parents haven't formally met. They seem close in age.

By the way they are conversing with each other they hardly seem like strangers. How long was I out? It seems like I've missed a lot. What a way to spend a perfectly good weekend.

I need a shower, but I don't want to be rude and kick everyone out. Our parents have been chatty for about an hour now. Breyson is eating every bit of it up. Leaning my head back against the bed, I close my eyes and listen to the different voices around the room. "I think we should let her get some rest, Brooks. I'm sure she's tired."

Opening my eyes, Breyson's parents stand and head toward the door to leave after giving me another hug. Grabbing ahold of the door handle, his mom turns to me and says, "Kinzleigh, while I'm thinking about it, we always have Thanksgiving dinner at our house. Time will fly and things will be forgotten with busy schedules. Most families need time to plan for everyone to make their rounds to all family. I hope to see you there if I don't see you before. You're welcome at our house anytime."

She turns to my parents as well. "Leigh, Ken, you all are welcome to join. I've got some charts to update before heading home." She smiles and exits, closing the door behind them.

My parents left soon after his. My test came back normal and as soon as the nurse goes over my discharge paperwork I'm free to leave. My parents wanted to take me home, but Breyson insisted he was staying 'til the end when they suggested he go home and get some rest, so they gave up trying. It was a lost cause.

"Finally, we're alone again." He kisses me sweetly on the lips and rubs his thumb over my cheek. "My parents love you," he says, and his face gleams. "I can tell."

"Were you worried? Is there something you haven't been telling me?" I love toying with him.

"No. Everyone loves you, Kinzleigh. You are special. You just don't realize it." He's so positive in the way he sees me. I've got to be one of the luckiest girls in the world.

"That's a matter of opinion, don't you think? It's normal for you to like me. You are the one getting the goods." I wink, trying to break his serious demeanor, but it doesn't work.

"It wouldn't matter if we never had sex again. My stance would remain the same. The fact that you don't see it makes you that much more lovable." I roll my eyes at him and throw the covers back in an attempt to get out of bed.

"Whatever you say, babe, but I need a shower." When my feet hit the cold floor, he scoops me into his arms and kisses the tip of my nose. "I can walk to the bathroom, Breyson. I had a seizure. I didn't break my legs."

He starts walking. "That may be so, but I want to take care of you. I've never wanted this with a girl. It makes me happy. Let me take care of you. Okay?"

How does any woman stay independent with a man like this? I have a feeling I'll never be able to deny him anything he wants.

SEVENTEEN

Kinzleigh

I knock on Adalynn's door as the sun is going down. It's Halloween and Simon is having a costume party. I have never been to a costume party, so I am nervous, but excited too. Between everyone's excitement over costumes, I don't think I could get out of it if I wanted to.

The door opens to Adalynn standing on the other side. "How many times do I have to tell you not to knock?" she asks me, as if I should know this already. "My parents worship the ground you walk on. You have become like a third daughter to them. Stop acting like a houseguest. I'm almost positive Mom buys you something every time she buys me something now."

"It still feels rude to just come in, not knowing what everyone is doing. I was raised to be invited before going to someone's house and to be respectful once there. It's second nature. Blame my parents." I walk in, carrying my tote full of everything I need for tonight.

She shuts the door after I come through. "You want anything to drink before we head upstairs?"

"Water, please." Adalynn's house is beautiful on the inside. Everything is done in creams and browns from ceiling to floor. It's cozy, but classy, with a masculine feel and neutral to the gender. Everything is top of the line.

The door bursts open a few minutes later with Londyn waltzing through.

"What's up, bitches?" she says with a smile on her face. "Are y'all ready to drop some jaws? Briar has no idea what we have planned and that says a lot, because I am horrible at keeping secrets."

She looks at me from head to toe. "I can't wait to see Breyson's reaction. This is going to be video worthy. It's about time to show off that gorgeous body."

Adalynn laughs. "I second that. Someone has to record his reaction. It's going to be priceless. Luckily, I don't have to worry about that. Braxton couldn't give two shits what I do or wear."

She is crazy. I see the way they look at each other. Londyn has noticed too. We're waiting for them to notice and do something about it, other than taking the frustration out on each other in bed. Those two are going to end up together. I could almost guarantee it if they would ever stop living in denial.

"Oh, please. Breyson doesn't care about what I wear. Why are you guys making such a big deal about it? You'll see. You're both being overly dramatic." They look at each other and burst out laughing. It angers me. He knows better than to question me. "Come on, let's go."

Once we get to the top of the staircase, we pile through the doorway to Adalynn's room in a single file line. Her room is large and it's done in black, white, and gray, with hints of red thrown in. She has beautiful artwork all over her walls of the New York City skyline, as well as Paris and Rome—the major fashion capitals of the world.

For being almost completely void of color, it's breathtaking. You feel like you're standing in the various places. She mentioned once that she dabbles a little in modeling and wants more opportunities, but hasn't found her opening yet.

Laying my bag on top of her bed, I pull the items out before me. We all decided it would be fun to do couple costumes. Each time I look at my costume, my mind wanders, and I get turned on thinking about what Breyson is going to look like.

We made a pact we wouldn't leak any details of our costumes to the boys. We told them what to wear and that was it. A smile plays out across my face as I look at my Indian costume.

I carry the main pieces into the bathroom to change. I have to strip completely naked to wear it. The top is a nude bandeau with suede fringe covering the entire piece of fabric that wraps around my body. There is a segment of turquoise beading along the top hem. Removing my shirt and bra, I pull it over my head and adjust it into place.

The bottom is a pair of skintight nude leggings accentuating the same fringe as the top. The waistband is a strip of material in a southwestern pattern. There is a flap draped over the front center with beading to match the top. My entire midriff is bare. Once I have both pieces on, I grab my clothes and walk out of the bathroom.

As I come into view Londyn and Adalynn start whistling. "Day-um, girl! You've been keeping that hidden? No wonder Breyson wants to keep you all to himself. Look at those abs. You don't have an ounce of flab. Everything is flat and toned, but you still have a great rack and butt. I'm jealous," Londyn whines.

"What are you talking about? You're tiny." Londyn has silky black hair and big, slightly slanted, chocolate-brown eyes, lined with thick black lashes. She has pouty, full lips, and a small beauty mark above her one. She is petite like me, but she is leaner like Adalynn without the height to be a model. Her skin is naturally bronzed all three hundred and sixty-five days a year. I learned quickly her dad is American and her mom is Asian, so she has the best of both worlds. She's passionate about her mixed heritage and I love that about her. The girl is devastatingly beautiful.

"Yeah, well, I don't have all that hard muscle and hourglass curves." She takes out her costume and pulls her white, skintight dress over her head. She chose a nautical theme. Londyn is a sailor. The bottom hem of her dress and the sleeves are blue and white stripes, outlined in red. Red anchors and bows hang in various places. The collar is also outlined in thick red stripes.

She inches the dress down her body like a second skin. I highly doubt Breyson is going to be the one mad. From what I hear Briar has been after Londyn for over a year. "Okay, hot stuff, look at you. Briar is going to be the one guarding his goods."

She smiles as she sits down to pull on the matching thigh-high tights. "I know, and I can't wait, because that means he's going to peel it off of me later. I don't think I will ever get enough of that boy. I can't believe I didn't give in to him earlier. He is hot." She pants the more she talks about him.

"Save it for later, girl. We still have hair and makeup. This is a once a year thing. I've been waiting impatiently all year. We're going all out." Adalynn decided she was going to be cupid this year. She said it was perfect since she was able to talk some sense into me about Breyson.

She is still convinced she was the factor that brought us together. I let her run with it. Who am I to kill her aspirations of being a matchmaker?

Braxton needs to get his crap together. The girl has a serious overload of passion suppressed inside that needs to be freed. Maybe she will sink her cupid teeth into him tonight and he will have a wakeup call.

Her costume consists of a short piece of white lingerie in a mono-style nightie with the entire right side cut out in front and back. It looks like a two-piece connected on one side. There is a piece of bright red velvet draped across the waist of the bottom and the breasts of the top, tying in a bow on the end that is connected at the hip. Instead of a matching headpiece like Londyn and me, she has a set of red feathery wings that attach to her back.

A burst of adrenaline shoots through my body at the sight of the three of us dressed out and we aren't even finished yet. Sitting on the edge of the bed, I pull on my moccasin calf-height boots and secure my beaded necklace in place.

Once finished straightening my curls out, I part my hair down the middle and braid each side. My makeup consists of earth tones with cream-colored eye shadow, bronzed cheeks, thick black liner, light mascara, and clear gloss. I finish my costume off with the fringe suede arm piece and the headband that matches the band of the pants. Lastly, I insert my feather earrings into my ears.

"Are you nervous?" Londyn paints on bright red lipstick to match her outfit and places her sailor hat on top of her now curled hair, completing the look with her navy-blue pumps.

"I'd be lying if I said I wasn't. No matter how hard I try, I can't picture Breyson dressed up as a cowboy." Breyson and I are the cowboy and Indian, Braxton is wearing a toga, and Briar is the typical sailor.

Adalynn walks up beside me, pulling her wings in place. "Oh, girl… Those boys in Wranglers are unforgettable." She looks at me and grins. "Just wait until they start helping their grandfather again and you get to see him on a tractor! If you ever thought it was impossible to have an orgasm without being touched, it's not." She fans her face and I can't help but to keel over in laughter. I'm laughing so hard my abs are hurting, causing me to place my arm over my stomach.

"Your ass may be laughing now, but just wait. Hottest sight you'll ever see. True story. I swear it," she says, and holds up her hand as if she's about to swear on a bible.

She is towering over me now that she has on bright red pumps to match her wings. Standing side by side in the mirror, we link arms. Already this year is so much different than any of the previous years I've been in high school. This is going to be fun. I can't wait.

The doorbell sounds across the house. "They're here!" Londyn squeals.

"Showtime," Adalynn adds.

I let out a nervous breath. Why do I feel like I'm about to see him for the first time in six months? I've seen him every day for the past two months. "Let's do this."

We walk downstairs and stop in front of the heavy, wooden front door. The glass is frosted. All you can see is the shadowed silhouette of one of the guys. "Here we go."

Adalynn lets out a breath of her own and it looks like she is nervous too. Now why would she be nervous? I thought she didn't have any feelings for Braxton. Ha! She is such a bad liar.

What I see as she opens that door I never expected in all of my eighteen years. Holy guacamole! Now I know the meaning of that country song *Save a Horse (Ride a Cowboy)* by Big and Rich. He is magnificent. I want to lick him and I haven't even seen the rear parts yet. Every one of them washboard abs are glistening in the light. I don't even notice the other two, because my eyes have been glued on Breyson the entire time. I don't think I'm breathing right now.

Breyson is standing before me wearing a pair of dark blue, tight Wrangler jeans covered in chaps and a pair of cowboy boots. He has on a long sleeve western style snap up shirt left unbuttoned and a cowboy hat. As if all of that doesn't already have me drooling, he topped off the look with a red bandana tied around his neck like a western movie and he has a holster with a prop pistol around his waist.

I eye him up and down. The thoughts processing in my mind right now are so wrong. And very immoral. When my eyes meet his and the cocky smirk across his face, it's obvious I'm blushing like a schoolgirl. I don't even care or try to hide it.

His eyes roam over my costume. As they scan every inch of my body, his eyes darken in a lustful gaze. It makes me feel sexy. What I wasn't expecting was what comes out of his mouth. "Hell no, Kinzleigh, you are not wearing that!"

I scoff. Come again? There is one way to truly and royally piss me off. One. What way is that, you may ask? Tell me I'm not going to do something and see what happens. It's downright embarrassing to be talked to that way. It seems Breyson Abercrombie needs to be reminded that I will do what I want.

He comes stalking toward me like a child that didn't get his way. Grabbing me by the waist, he pulls me closer. Just one touch and I feel like Jell-O. I melt against his touch. It's pathetic what he does to me. "I won't watch people gawk at you all night. I know what they will be thinking. No guy is going to undress my girl with his eyes and mentally screw you right in front of me. I need you to go change."

If I weren't as stubborn as I am I might consider it, but I am, so he's about to learn what pushes me too far. There are lines in every relationship, and he just crossed ours. "I will not change. It should be good enough that I'm on your arm. This is what I chose and this is what I'm wearing." I look him in the eyes. "Whether you like it or not."

His face turns bright red and his jaw locks, showing his sudden mood change. Too bad I don't care. I move backward out of his grasp. He follows me. "Then we will just stay here."

I shake my head, quickly making it clear that option isn't on the table. "Breyson, you need to chill the fuck out before you regret it," Braxton says from across the room beside Adalynn. Smart boy.

Breyson turns to face him. "Now would be the time to mind your own damn business, Braxton. Meet me at the truck."

Braxton and Adalynn look back and forth between the two of us, before making their exit, Braxton shaking his head, because this is all completely ridiculous.

Once the door closes, he looks back at me and grabs my hand. The raging waters are starting to calm. "Baby . . . will you please change? You're smokin' hot and your body is to die for, but I don't want others seeing what is mine."

He places his lips against mine and traces my lips with the tip of his tongue. Oh my . . . He cups my breasts, one in each hand. "These are mine." They travel down my body, stopping on my bottom. "This is mine."

I wrap my arms around his waist, pulling him against me. The skin-to-skin contact is fabulous, sending a sudden jolt of heat through my body. The friction of our bodies rubbing together sets off a charge of energy that flows between us. "You know Simon wants you. Seeing you like that is going to make it worse."

Just like that it's like someone dumped a cooler of ice-cold water all over me.

Placing my palms on his chest, I push him back. "That's what this is about, isn't it? Your jealousy over Simon. Your lack of trust in me." I'm furious and the scowl on my face shows it. His eyes widen in realization that he just screwed up. "Simon is just a friend. He's always been *just a friend*. He knows his place, because I've made it clear you are what I want. If you trusted me, this wouldn't be an issue."

"Baby . . ." He begins to speak, but I'm officially done with this conversation.

Holding my hand up to stop him, I finish this once and for all. "I'm done, Breyson. I won't be told what to do or what I can and cannot wear. If my parents are okay with what I'm wearing then you shouldn't even question it. Maybe I haven't made things clear. I'm not one of the pathetic girls that have always followed you around pining for your attention. I don't need my boyfriend's consent for anything. When you realize that we will have a discussion. I'm driving myself to the party. If you know what's good for you, you will leave me alone right now. I need to cool off and I can't think around you. Catch on. This is a make or break with me."

"Baby, please, don't do this. Let's talk it out." He rubs his hands over his face in a panic. The look in his eyes almost makes me cave, but he needs to know I won't be ordered around or this relationship will never work. That's the problem with relationships. One ends up miserable because the other is insecure. And nine times out of ten, the insecure one gets exactly what his behavior stemmed from—left behind while she moves on with someone that is happy to be with her.

I have never done anything to question his trust and I have to worry about just as many girls daydreaming about him. He's the one that's been with other girls, not the other way around. I've only been with him. Still, even knowing girls have seen and been with him in ways I have, not once have I tried to order him around. I haven't given him jealous fits. It's not fair for him to treat me any different than I treat him.

"Bye, Breyson." I turn on my heels and walk out the door, leaving him standing in the living room. My heart cracked a little seeing him almost in tears, but better to learn now than two years down the road. I don't ask for much, but this is one of those things I have to have—freedom. I will not give up my independence. One of the many reasons I wasn't interested in dating.

I get in my car and start the engine. When I do, Adalynn comes running to the car. Opening the door, she gets in the passenger seat. "What are you doing? Aren't you riding with Braxton and Briar? Londyn is going to be left out."

I pull on my seatbelt, as does Adalynn. "I'm not leaving my best friend by herself. I told Braxton I'll meet him at the party. He's a big boy. He'll be okay. It looks like you need some girl talk."

When I see Breyson running out the front door, I quickly back out of the driveway before he can stop me. "I'm fine. I just won't be told what to wear by a guy. Ever. End of discussion. He needs to learn that now or it's going to build until it destroys everything. My mom is very conservative and was okay with my outfit. She trusts me. She's giving me room to make responsible decisions. He should too."

"I think it's just a guy thing, Kinzleigh. They're all territorial at some point. Jealousy is a natural male emotion. If anything it's a compliment. Don't you think you're overreacting a little? Braxton wasn't too thrilled with my outfit either and we're not even dating." I'm not in the mood for lectures right now.

Looking at her, I narrow my eyes. "I didn't see him call you out on it in front of everyone as if you're a child. I will never be the type of girl that's submissive and dependent on some guy micromanaging her every move. He knows how I am and he can take it or leave it. I will not conform."

She holds up her hands in surrender. "You're right. I'm not the enemy in this, Kinzleigh. I'm on your side. I'm just trying to be the mediator. He did take it a little too far. But I also knew the Breyson before you. The guy that *didn't* care what a girl wore. And more times than not, he went for the sluttier the better. I think the guy just has it really bad for you. It makes him go to extremes. You, my sweetness, are the one that changed him, and that can make a guy a little crazy."

If I weren't so mad I would laugh at her and her crazy talk. "I just want to have some fun. You have to understand, Adalynn, I've never wanted to participate in things like this—parties, social events, high school things. Now, I want those things. He's not the only one who's changed. I want to participate in the 'rite of passage' things that make up high school. I'm finally living a little. I shouldn't have to answer to someone over petty things. I think I want to drink tonight."

"Are you sure that's a good idea? You just got out of the hospital for Pete's sake."

I raise my brow as we drive down the road toward Simon's subdivision. "Adalynn…don't do that," I warn. "We just got done with this conversation."

"Stubborn, stubborn girl. Would you chillax? You know I just care about you, Kinzleigh." I need to calm down. Tonight is supposed to be fun. That's not going to happen if I don't let it go.

"I know. I'm just aggravated. Show me a good time, okay? Within moderation . . ." She nods and we turn into the subdivision entrance. "Which house is it?"

"Keep going and I'll show you where to turn."

We pull my Range Rover into an empty space on the lawn and shut off the engine. I move quickly to get out of my car before Breyson gets here. I'm not ready to see him yet. I want to be mad at him for a while before I come to my senses and cave. Because let's face it, he has a way of always making me cave. The vacancy of his touch and presence are already having an affect on me.

As soon as Adalynn and I walk into the house, I feel eyes on us. The room is covered in costumes of various styles and theme—some scary, some sexy, and some just plain silly. "Come on, let's go get a drink," Adalynn says, pulling me off to the side.

We come into the kitchen to a completely stocked bar with different types of liquor and drinks to mix with them. Sitting off to the side are two full size kegs. I don't know how a bunch of high schoolers got their hands on so much alcohol.

Simon greets us at the bar. "Hey, pretty girl. You drinking tonight?" I smile and nod my head. He makes me feel at ease, like a brother would. "What's your poison?"

I shrug my shoulders and look at Adalynn for help. "I've never drunk anything other than wine here and there."

Simon grins from ear to ear and hands me shot of amber liquid. I hold it to my nose. It smells wretched. "Here, let me show you. Simon, hand me the salt and a lime," Adalynn commands.

He reaches behind him and grabs it, handing it to her. I watch her for instruction. "This, my lovely, is one of your four favorite men: Jose. The key to good tequila or vodka is cost. You can't go cheap or you'll hurl."

She licks her wrist to wet it and sprinkles the salt to make it stick. I remember seeing this on one of those wild MTV shows once—Jersey Shore or something similar. "Watch closely."

She holds the lime wedge in one hand and the shot glass in the other. "Rule number one, open the back of your throat and let it slide down. Lick, shoot, lime—in that exact order." She licks the salt, pours the shot back, and then bites the lime, sucking the citrusy liquid into her mouth. Simple enough. "Here, now you try."

Simon hands me another shot glass and a wedge. He grabs my hand, holding my wrist face up. Smiling, he looks me in the eyes and licks my wrist, before sprinkling salt on it. That doesn't seem sexy like if Breyson were doing it.

Kinzleigh, stop it! You're supposed to be mad at him.

Licking the same spot Simon just did, I hold the salt on my tongue and bring the shot glass to my lips. Holding my breath and opening the back of my throat, I pour the glass back, swallow quickly, and bite the lime. The burn in the back of my throat makes me cough. I can feel the warmth run down my esophagus.

It wasn't as bad as I imagined it would be. Once I stop coughing, Simon looks at me. "Another?"

Already starting to relax, I nod.

Just as I'm about to take another shot, the glass is jerked out of my hand. When I turn to see who it is, a very angry Breyson is standing so close I can smell his cologne. He's blood red and looks like he's about to breathe fire. What he doesn't know is I can hold my own. "Stop giving my girlfriend alcohol, Simon! You're real close to getting your ass whooped."

He looks at me. "What are you doing, Kinzleigh? Are you really going to get drunk with him? All you had to do was wait ten more minutes for me."

I pinch the bridge of my nose. He doesn't get it. "I thought we dealt with this earlier. I remember the words *I am done* being said," I seethe. "And yet here you are, still trying to control me. Stop telling me what to do, Breyson! Leave me alone!" My voice is several octaves higher at this point.

He yells right back as if I was ludicrous to think he'd actually back off and tone down his crazy. "I will not leave you alone to be taken advantage of with half your body on display! Not to mention intoxicated when you never drink! Fuck, Kinzleigh, chill out. You know I'm only looking out for you! I love you!"

The problem with this is that I despise yelling. It sets me off like dynamite. Why? I have no idea. I've been that way since I was a kid. Most people slither away like a scolded child, but I on the other hand, have the opposite reaction. It brings out the worst in me.

Also, to make matters worse, that shot just started to take effect in my system, making me brave. Placing my palms on his chest, I push as hard as I can. "If you love me then leave me alone!"

Everyone around us waiting for a drink is staring. A few more bodies gather in to watch the theatrics. Great, we are the focal point of half the party. He bounces back and comes toward me, but Briar grabs him by the arms. "Dude, leave her alone for a while or you're going to do more damage. Don't make her hate you. Let her cool off . . . Trust me."

At least someone gets it. Breyson stands there for a few more minutes staring at me, pleading with me, but I won't budge. He owes me an apology if he wants me to listen. I am not his child. I'm his girlfriend, his equal, and I will get respect one way or another.

He storms off, and before Briar goes after him, he looks at me. "Please think about what you're doing. He may not go about it in the best way, but he really does love you."

Turning back to Simon, he has a smile on his face that I kind of want to slap off. "I want another shot."

"Whatever you want, sweetheart." He winks at me, and for the first time around him, I feel uneasy.

Three shots down and the toxin is flowing through my bloodstream. Adalynn and Braxton have been by my side the entire time. Braxton went after Breyson at first, but came back shortly after. I'm not sure if it was for Adalynn or to watch after me or because Briar was already dealing with Breyson. I'm relaxed and having the best time. I wish I had tried this before.

Pulling on Adalynn's arm, I whine. "Adi, come dance with me. I don't even care that I can't dance worth a crap. I want to anyway. Everyone makes it look like so much fun."

I give her my pouty face and she laughs. "You don't have to use that, silly girl. It doesn't have the same effect on me as it does Breyson."

Speaking of, I haven't seen Breyson since I told him to leave me alone. I'm not sure where he is, but at the given moment I don't care. I just hate that I had to upset him to get my point across.

We move to the middle of the makeshift dance floor. The hip-hop music is blaring—a genre of music that makes you feel alive. Adalynn is in the middle with Braxton behind her and I'm up front. Raising my arms in the air, I let the music take over my mind and body. I think of nothing; just let my body sway to the rhythm of the music. I close my eyes and get lost in the sensuality of the words.

Two hands snake around my waist, pulling me closer to the front of a body. I don't even notice at first that it's a male and not Adalynn. It doesn't matter, because I'm having fun. Holding my waist, the body behind me grinds against my rear, allowing me to feel his excitement through his jeans.

Leaning my head back against his chest, I go along with his rhythm, not even caring that I probably look ridiculous. If it's not a cheerleading routine, I'm actually a horrible dancer. That seems to be the beauty of alcohol—it takes away your paranoia and insecurities.

Time is no longer being calculated. It's just the music and me. Slowly, the world fades away and my mind is blank, exactly as I want it. I can't think of anything. I can barely control my actions much less stop them. Everything feels good, simple, until I'm suddenly unstable on my feet by the absence of the prior body keeping me upright. I fight to keep my balance. I hear a loud thump. What in the heck?

Turning around, I see Breyson punch Simon across the jaw. Simon goes down to the floor before I can process what is happening. Major buzz kill. Breyson straddles him and starts hitting him over and over. "Breyson! Stop! You're going to kill him!"

Blood is flying from Simon's mouth and he is barely putting up a fight. I'm guessing he's too drunk. I've never seen Breyson like this. He looks like he's out to kill. "I told you to fucking leave her alone, Simon. You can't stand it, can you? Knowing there is one girl you can't have. One fight and you're already going after what's mine. I warned you and you didn't listen." He's still hitting him repetitively as he screams out his words. He's not even thinking of what he's doing.

My reflexes react before my thoughts process, compliments of the alcohol in my body. I push Breyson off and get elbowed in the rib, stumbling backward and hitting the floor.

"Breyson. Stop, dammit, you just hit Kinzleigh!" Braxton is shouting, trying to pull him off when he sees me trying to get off the floor.

Rushing over to me, tears are pooling in the corner of his eyes. "Baby, I'm so sorry. Why would you do that? Please forgive me. I would never do anything to hurt you on purpose."

Simon sits up, spitting blood from his mouth. I can't look Breyson in the eyes right now. I don't know what to say. I know he would never hurt me on purpose, but he let his jealousy and rage take over, making him do things he wouldn't normally do. His behavior tonight has been insane. I need a break from here, from him, from everything. He's too much right now; too extreme. I may regret this later, but right now I need some space. "Simon, can you take me home?"

He looks between Breyson and me for a minute before he finally responds. "Sure, Kinzleigh, I'll meet you at my truck." And then he stands and walks out of the room, mumbling cuss words under his breath. I can't say that I blame him.

When I stand to follow after him, Breyson grabs my arm. "Baby, please, don't leave with him. I'm begging you to talk to me. I'll do anything if you'll talk to me."

I hand him my keys, because I know I can't drive right now and there aren't many I trust with them. "I'll talk to you in a little while. I need some space to think, Breyson, alone. Tonight is ruined. All I wanted was a little fun with my friends—people I care about. Can you please just give me that? Someone has to bring my car home. I'll talk to you then if you want. You have my word. I need to be by myself for a bit. My parents are gone for the night on business, so you can stay over if you want to talk."

Hesitantly, he grabs the keys and nods. He looks torn and it's killing me, but I'm not used to all this drama. I've always been the girl to stay away from it. It's screwing with my head. "I love you, Kinzleigh. I'm sorry."

"I know," is all I can say, before I turn around to leave.

EIGHTEEN

Kinzleigh

Simon pulls into my driveway. I'm glad to be home. I'm worn down emotionally after tonight. What was supposed to be fun and laidback turned into a night from Hell.

Simon's face is swollen and he has the beginning of a black eye, along with a busted lip. I feel horrible. Guilt racks my body. This is my fault. I knew Breyson was acting out, but I didn't care, and because of it someone got hurt. "I'm sorry, Simon. It's not right what he did to you. You've been a good friend to me since I moved here. None of this was your fault. We started fighting before we even got to the party. You just ended up in the crossfire."

He reaches across the truck and puts his palm on my cheek. "Shh. It's not your fault either. You don't have to apologize for him. I've had my ass handed to me worse than this. This is nothing." He attempts to lighten the mood by laughing, but it's unsuccessful.

He gets out of the truck and I meet him at the front. We walk side by side to my house. I lead us around back toward the pool, purposely avoiding going inside. Truth is I don't want another guy inside my house. None of this was meant to be wrong.

I take off my boots and pull up my tight pants, before sitting on the edge to place my feet in the cool water. "You can sit if you want."

Taking a seat beside me, he does the same. "Why do you want to be with someone that tries to control you? You deserve better than that, Kinzleigh. Breyson and me, we're a lot alike, but we're different too. What he said— takes one to know one. He's used to getting every girl he wants too, and when one comes along like you, making things harder, night like tonight happens."

"He's not usually like this. He'll learn if he wants us to work. No one will ever control me." I don't feel comfortable having to defend mine and Breyson's relationship to him. It's none of his business.

"You shouldn't have to wait around for him to be the kind of guy you need when you could have it with so many other guys. Guys without insecurities." He is confusing me more. He's always been a friend, but I feel like he's overstepping boundaries.

I stare off into the water, smooth from the lack of airflow, trying to think, but the alcohol is inhibiting me from doing so. "Kinzleigh."

I look over. Simon has moved closer to me. Grabbing my face in his hands, it occurs to me what he's doing. Do I want this? I don't have the same feelings for him as I do for Breyson.

He closes in on me and before his lips touch mine, I whisper, "Please don't."

"Why not? How do you really know you want him if he's been your only option?"

His lips are too close for comfort. I attempt to lean back, but he holds me close. "Because I love him. He's the only one that's ever on my mind. The truth is, I'd rather fight with him every day than never fight with someone else."

Everything just became so clear. My own words woke me up like a light bulb coming on. I'm so stupid. "Simon, I'm sorry. I think you should go."

The tears begin to fall. I've hurt him over my selfishness. Without saying a word, Simon nods. He looks at me briefly, but then speaks low. "Every story has to have a superhero and a villain. He's made me out to be the villain in this one, but sometimes the villain isn't a bad guy. He's just the one that showed up last with a little too much motivation to take what he wants. If he messes up again, you have options. I like you, Kinzleigh, probably more than I should. I don't care if it pisses him off. Maybe it'll remind him what he's got. If you change your mind, you know where to find me."

He stands and walks away.

"I'm the lucky one." The words come out with a reverence to them. Why didn't I realize this before? As soon as Simon is out of sight, I run to my purse in search of my phone.

After digging through it in a hurried fashion, I finally find what I'm looking for. I scroll through my call log and hit the most recent call. After the first ring, the call picks up. "Hey, baby."

His voice hits home. This is everything to me. "Breyson, I'm sorry. Please forgive me for being a selfish brat. This is my fault. All of it. I'm so stupid."

I'm crying hysterically into the phone. I can barely decipher what I'm saying. "Fighting with you every day still beats being with someone else. I know that now. Please don't be mad at me anymore. I can't stand it. Come over."

"Baby, I'm already here. It's okay. Turn around." I turn and he's standing behind me at the gate. Putting his phone in his pocket, he begins walking toward me. I drop mine on my purse and take off running in his direction. Once I reach him, I jump in his arms and he catches me. "You were right, Kinzleigh. I should have never tried to tell you what to do. Yes, I'm jealous. I hated seeing you with him. I swear it'll never happen—"

I stop him mid-sentence with a kiss. His lips feel so good against mine. Now that we're together, my heart doesn't ache anymore. He completes me. I've never been good at explaining my emotions, but I want to show him. Deepening the kiss, I run my fingers through his hair. I could kiss him for hours, but it's not enough. I'll never get enough of him.

Breaking the kiss, I grab his face to look me in the eyes. "No, Breyson, I was in the wrong. I need to say this. I don't like being talked to like I'm a child, but instead of acting the way I did I should have talked to you about it when you asked. All of this could have been avoided with communication. For that I'm sorry. I had an epiphany through all of this. Like I said on the phone, at the end of the day, if I had the choice to fight with you or be perfect with someone else, I would choose to fight with you every single time. Whatever it takes, I'm yours—always have been and always will be. I love you so much. I need you, Breyson. My parents aren't here. Take me to bed."

"I love you too, baby." He is grinning from ear to ear. That beautiful smile makes me melt. "I thought you'd never ask."

NINETEEN

Breyson

This is the path my life has taken. Consumed by a blonde I'd do anything to exist in her world. Two phrases I never want to hear come out of that pretty mouth again. One, *I'm done,* and two, *it's over.* When I heard it, I stopped breathing.

Yeah, that may make me whipped, but she is my life. It doesn't take a rocket scientist to know when you've found something worth cherishing. She is mine.

Tonight has been Hell on earth, but in the end she knows she wants me and no one else. That alone makes everything worth it. And maybe the positive in all of this is that it will lay the question of Simon and her to rest. I'd be lying if I said it didn't cross my mind from time to time.

It almost killed me seeing Simon grinding all over her. No one touches what's mine, especially when they actually *know* it's mine. He knew how I felt about her and that we're a couple. His behavior was disrespectful to any guy, which is why I lost it.

Someone needed to teach Simon a lesson. Hitting him felt so good it scares me. I shouldn't like dishing out that kind of pain on someone else, but I did. In the end I started a fight, and that's something I have to live with. This is what she does to me. She has my emotions running all over the place: love, hate, hurt, and happiness. With her, I've experienced it all.

When she kissed me there was something different there. Something that hasn't been present any of the other times she's kissed me, including the time she told me she loved me: vulnerability, anguish maybe. That kiss was sacred. Something I may never see again. She kissed me as if she was scared I wouldn't want her back—if she only knew.

She could likely commit murder and I wouldn't want her any less. I'm in too deep with her, almost drowning. There is no backing out now. It's full throttle from here on out. I need her as much as I want her. I just need to control my jealousy around her.

One phrase came out of those beautiful lips that I'll remember for the rest of my life. *Fighting with you every day still beats being with someone else.* Damn. What do you even say back to that? She keeps stealing my heart piece by piece.

She asked me to take her to bed and that is what she'll get. Bottom line is we've been fighting. I want her just as much as she wants me. I can barely keep my mouth off of her, much less my hands or any other parts.

She doesn't realize how beautiful she looks. I've been dying the entire night, watching every single guy in school mentally undressing her. As I walk toward the door with her in my arms, I notice a Jacuzzi. I have a better idea. "I need to put you down for a minute, baby."

"Is something wrong?" Nope. I'm about to feel that beautiful body in its entirety against mine in the warm water.

The Jacuzzi is under the covered area in the back of the house not too far from the entrance to the house. It's under a trellis, with cafe lights hanging from above and it's covered in ivy, making it look like it's sitting in a nook made specifically for it. It's out of sight to anyone but those coming out of the house. "No. I just have something I want to do with you."

Setting her flat on her feet, I lift the cover and make sure the heat is turned up as hot as it'll go. The thing about Jacuzzis is that they feel amazing when you first get in, but after time they decrease in temperature significantly from being left uncovered and cooled by the air. The digital thermostat reads one-hundred-and-two degrees Fahrenheit. Perfect.

Discarding the cover, I take her hand and pull her toward me. Removing her headband, I toss it on the patio. Grabbing each braid separately, I slide the ponytail holders down her blonde hair, removing them. "I love your hair down."

Running my fingers through her hair, I clench a fistful and pull, angling her face to me. She closes her eyes at the act. Maybe my beautiful girl likes it a little rough.

She groans as soon as my touch vacates her body. She looks me over, and her eyes hood at the sight of my costume, giving me an idea to be brought up later. Hooking my thumb over her top, on each side of her breasts, I remove her clothes in one swift motion down her body.

Less is more in some cases. Squatting as I slide them down, she rests her hands on my shoulders for support. Picking up one foot at a time, I remove her clothes from her feet, kissing her leg. She is impeccable.

Standing back up, she bites her lip as she takes me in. She brushes her fingers up my abdomen and over my chest, stopping on my shoulders, and then slides off my shirt, pushing it down my arms, letting it fall to the ground.

When she hooks her hand behind the waistband of my jeans, I know where she is headed. Toe to heel, I remove each boot. "You look so sexy like this. I can't keep my eyes off of you. You're mine too, right?"

As if she couldn't get sexier, she just did. Wanting me like I want her, and saying it aloud, is possibly the sexiest thing I've ever heard. I've never wanted to be claimed or clung to by a girl until her.

She works my belt loose until it's unbuckled. "Everything I have is yours. Heart, mind, body, and soul—it's all yours, forever. I don't want anyone else, Kinzleigh. I'll never want anyone but you. This thing between us is real. I've fallen in love with you."

I wait for her reaction, expecting her to freak out. Instead, she places her arms around my neck, leaving my unbuttoned jeans, and jumps in my arms. "You know your way to a girl's heart, Breyson Abercrombie."

A tear falls from the corner of her eye. Our emotions are still on overdrive from our first fight. "How am I supposed to be normal when you say things like that to me? How am I supposed to come back from this when you leave me? One way or another, it's going to happen. It's inevitable. We're so young."

Running my fingertips along her bare back, my heart aches hearing the words coming from her mouth. How could she think I would leave her? Just because we're only eighteen doesn't mean I'll want someone else later. No one would ever compare to her. I would marry her the day we graduated if she wanted to.

Did I really just think that? Marry. Would I marry her? At eighteen? Whoa . . .

I would without a second thought.

"It's okay to change what 'normal' is. This is our normal, Kinzleigh. I want you to look me and listen. Our future will change, develop, and adjust with age and time, but my feelings are permanent. The only way I'm leaving you is if I'm six feet under. As long as I am alive, I will fight for you no matter what the situation is. The only person that has the power to take me from you is God almighty himself. Do you understand?" Her eyes soften and she kisses me hard, harder than she's ever kissed me before.

She starts rubbing herself against my skin at the opening of my jeans. I can tell she's ready from the wet section left behind. Holding her up with one hand, I pull a condom from my pocket before removing my jeans and briefs with the other. I carefully step inside the Jacuzzi.

I sit in the corner by a jet, the warm water hitting our chests. She straddles me and rubs against my dick, telling me what she wants. I've been pretty stupid with her, so there's one thing I have to know. I've been thinking about it off and on, especially after that whole Natalie disaster. With her I wasn't worried. With Kinzleigh I have a reason to be. "Baby, I love you and I'm not trying to kill the mood, but have you had your period?"

She blushes as if she's embarrassed to discuss her menstrual cycle with me. I'm pretty sure I'm not alone when I say that once guys start having sex, a girl's period becomes a good thing and not a bad. I've never really had to think about it much, because I've always been careful, taking extra precautions even, until her.

Before her, birth control was always the first topic, not the last. Girls I slept with were always on birth control and I wanted the proof. With us being young, the girls whose parents weren't oblivious to the fact that high schoolers *do* have sex put them on the pill. Some were on it for their periods alone. Words of a few girls, not mine. Plus, I always had a condom and wore it, and then pulled out before ejaculation . . . until her.

Truthfully, I've been pretty damn careless with her. My parents are doctors. My dad explained the importance of condoms and why they're necessary. "Yes, I have a period every twenty-eight days and I haven't missed one."

I nod, a little relieved. Opening the wrapper with my teeth, I remove the condom and toss the empty package over the side of the Jacuzzi. Standing, I turn us around and place her on the corner seat where I just was.

Leaning in closer, I take her lips in mine. They are so soft. The taste of her saliva mixing with the chlorine in the water from the jet splashing our faces is turning me on more. I stand tall enough that my dick isn't submerged in the water to roll on the condom, and then I drop back down and take hold of her thighs, positioning myself between them.

She has her arms wrapped around my neck, pulling me as close as she can. "I love you, Breyson. I need you. We don't have a house to ourselves often. Don't make me wait. Please."

Is it wrong that every time she begs I feel like beating my hands on my chest like a caveman? Lining the tip up with her entrance, I stop. I want to hear it again. "Say it again."

Her brows scrunch in confusion. "I love you?"

I shake my head and push in, but just barely. "I need you?"

Still not what I'm looking for. I shake my head once more. "Please don't make me wait, Breyson. Please, I need to feel you. I need to connect with you in a way no one else has felt me."

"Show me how much you want it. I need to know that no one else can make you feel the way I do. I need to know you'll never want anyone else to touch you the way I touch you. I want to ruin you in a way no one else can." My lips brush up hers, teasing her and pulling on her bottom lip, then her top. Sliding my tongue inside, I find hers and feel it flutter against mine.

She hooks her legs around my waist, digging her heels into my butt. Clamping down on my waist, she pulls my lower body closer to hers, forcing me to slowly enter her core. I don't know if I will ever get used to how tight of a fit it is. Every. Single. Time. She moans as she inches me into her and it is the hottest thing I've ever watched.

She leans her head back and rests it against the ledge, closing her eyes as she takes all of me. Then she pushes my hips back until I'm out as far as she can reach, before pulling me back, entering her once more. I stare at her in complete fascination. Watching her pleasure herself with my body is the most erotic thing I've ever experienced, hands down. I can't take it anymore.

Resting one knee on the bench for support, I extend the other leg, digging my toes into the floor of the Jacuzzi. Grabbing her hands in mine, I place them along the top of the Jacuzzi to her sides, and I begin thrusting, lifting her by the waist to meet me. The water makes her weightless. Placing one hand between our bodies, I touch her sweet spot, stimulating it the way she likes. "Breyson, I'm close. Will you go with me?"

The fact that I have to control my thoughts to avoid it, she doesn't have to ask. Leaning forward, I continue moving slowly, making love to her. "The second you go, I go. Let me feel you."

As she clenches around me, making the fit tighter, I pick up pace, feeling my own release on the edge with every slide in and out. Gripped tight, eyes closed, and mouth open, she pulsates around me, and then heat shoots through my groin, spurt after spurt filling the tip of the condom.

Holding her around the waist, I change our position so that she is straddling me again, but never break our physical connection. These are the moments that make trusting your heart completely worth it. One time of many when you can look your girl in the eyes and know that you would die before living a single second without her.

Being with her is the ultimate unknown, but it's an unknown I'd take over a life of knowns any day of the week. She makes me crazy, sometimes scared or mad, but isn't that what makes her different than anyone else? To love someone, I'm learning you have to love her through every emotion and not just the good ones.

I may not know what's at the end of this road we call life, but I do know one thing: I want her with me. Every second of every day that she gives in and the ones that she doesn't. I'll do everything in my power to keep her. "Every day I live for you, Kinzleigh. My heart beats for you, my mind thinks for you, and my soul thrives for you. My body longs for you and will never forget your touch. I will love you infinitely. Time will never cease my love for you. I know we're young, but maybe we are one of the lucky ones—the couples that get to experience their entire lives together."

Running my fingers through her now wet curls, I kiss her lips, remembering something her dad told me. "One of the wisest men I've ever met told me that young love was the best kind of love, because you get to experience more highs and lows together. I think he was right, because I want every facet of my life to include you—the good and the bad. You changed me, Kinzleigh. You made me want something I never wanted for myself."

I smile, remembering the first day I met her. "I'll never be the same. All thanks to one hot California day on the beach when the volleyball went sailing through the air and landed next to this beautiful blonde."

Swiping the tear off her cheek with my thumb, I place it in my mouth, sucking the salty wetness from it. "That was beautiful."

She kisses me in various places all over my face and body. "I don't know what I did to deserve someone like you. You're too good to me, Breyson. I've always been pretty selfish. Why do I get a guy like you?"

"I'm good to you, because you're you. You love me for who I am and don't try to change me or change who you are to please me. You don't try to win my love or expect it. It comes naturally. You didn't have to earn me, baby, or deserve me. You were born for me. We were made for each other before we were ever conceived. We had to grow up separately is all. That day on the beach, and now you living here—our destiny fulfilling itself."

"If I ever thought it was impossible to be rendered speechless by a boy, you just proved me wrong. Will you stay with me tonight? I want to sleep with you. We can cuddle. My parents shouldn't be back until tomorrow evening." She starts to push up off of me, but I hold her down for just another few seconds. Moments like these are few and far between.

"I would love nothing more than to hold you while you sleep, but I want you to do something for me too." She scans my face, trying to sense my mood. She'll never guess what I'm about to ask her to do with me, but after seeing her reaction to my cowboy costume, I can't help myself.

"What is it?" She is playing with the short hair at the nape of my neck. That mixed with the warm temperature of the water and the cool night air is placing me on the verge of a sleep-induced coma.

"I promised Pops, my grandfather, I would help him at his ranch tomorrow. He's shorthanded and I haven't helped him as much as I normally do. I haven't been out there since before I left for California. I'm overdue. I want you to come with me. They'd love to meet you. Spend the day with me. Please?" I stroke my hands up and down her arms and kiss her on the lips, prepared to persuade her if necessary.

"Okay." One little word from her is all I needed. "Let's go to bed." She lifts herself off of me. I stand and we both leave the warm water of the Jacuzzi.

I grab my jeans and step into them, slowly working them up my wet legs. She begins picking up the scattered pieces of clothing that remains. "I'll meet you upstairs, okay? I have to run to your car and get my bag."

Looking at me, she fails at holding back her smile. She saunters over toward me and pulls me into her arms. "You brought a bag? You were planning to stay before you got here? Even after the way I acted?"

That smile is what thawed the ice and broke the chains around my heart—the one that still weakens me on contact. "I stopped by my house right after I left Simon's. It's just the next street over. That's the only reason I wasn't here earlier."

Her eyes soften. "I know I offered, but I wasn't expecting you to. I thought you were mad at me. You had every reason to be. I said and did some hateful things. I'm sorry. I can be quick to speak and slow to think instead of the opposite like I should be. It's one of my flaws."

How could I ever stay mad at that face for long? "Beautiful, you would have to do a whole lot more than that to send me packing. I was madder at myself than you. You certainly didn't make things easier, but technically I started it. Some of the things you said were warranted. They made me think. I don't blame you. I let my jealousy to keep you to myself get in the way of rational thinking. I'm just glad something worse didn't happen. Had you hooked up with him I wouldn't be okay."

"I wouldn't have been able to do that to you, Breyson," she says, her voice ridden with guilt.

I kiss her, trying to diminish it. "Hey, this is new to both of us. We'll work through it, but together . . . Okay?"

Closing her eyes, she breathes a sigh of what sounds like relief. "Together is good. I can do that. Just be patient with me."

Kissing her again, I place my hands on her shoulders and turn her around to face the door. "Always, baby. Now, go get dressed before someone sees my woman and her beautiful body. After tonight, I understand compromise. Flaunt what you were given in moderation. Midriff—I'll come to terms with. Thighs—fine. Cleavage—as long as you're with me, I'll deal with it. But for the love of God, please keep nipples, ass, and pussy covered. Those are my zones. I don't want to hit someone else tonight. I'll be up in a minute." Her smile quickly turns into a laugh, and then her arm snakes across her breasts, covering one of said three zones.

As she walks off, I slap her on that perfect, round, bare butt, causing her to squeal. I couldn't resist myself. It was tempting me. I failed the test miserably.

After walking to her Range Rover to retrieve my duffle bag off the passenger seat, I come into the house ready to find my girl. When I enter the backdoor I hear an awful noise. It sounds more like a screeching sound and it's loud, but is drowned out by the distance.

Walking up the stairs quietly, I slip into Kinzleigh's bedroom door unnoticed. What I see when I enter makes me stop dead in my tracks.

Leaning through the doorway, careful not to make any noise, I stand here with my arms above my head, gripping the doorframe. I watch her silently, imprinting this moment on my mind to keep forever. A soon to be readily available memory on record.

Kinzleigh has her ear buds in, facing the opposite direction, and she's dancing her heart out while singing—more like her attempt at rapping—*Work bitch* by Britney Spears. She is singing at the top of her lungs, completely uninhibited.

If you've ever heard someone use the phrase 'sounds like a coyote howling in a metal trashcan' then you can envision it perfectly. There is a reason God gave us ears to hear what we sound like when we sing. Volume control for one, and there is no rhythm or cohesion between the lyrics and the music when you can't hear yourself. It's horrible.

Add in the perfect visual description of *Shake Your Bon-Bon* by Ricky Martin as she dances in a bright pink camisole and a pair of multicolored panties that reveal the bottom of her cheeks and the sight before me is unforgettable. But still, seeing and hearing how horrible it is, I'd still be front row to her concert with a lighter waving back and forth—her biggest fan.

The song must have switched and she still hasn't noticed me standing here. Some may say this is an invasion of privacy, to watch them without them knowing, but who am I to disturb her private concert?

This time she is pelting out the lyrics of *The Heart of Dixie* by Danielle Bradbery. She throws her arms in the air, phone in hand, swaying to the music as she hits the top of the bridge. I know now she wasn't meant to be a singer, but she's still the most beautiful girl I've ever seen, dancing around in her panties, squawking the song lyrics, completely unashamed.

She picks up a brush off the dresser and pretends it's a microphone. I have to bite my tongue to keep from laughing so she won't think I'm making fun of her. She's in her own little bubble. Then she finally mutters, "Where is Breyson? Surely, it doesn't take that long to get a bag."

She turns around and when she sees me her face drains of all color. Her eyes widen, knowing she's been caught. I can't help the smile displayed on my face. "How long have you been standing there?" she asks, yanking her ear buds from her ears.

"Long enough." She spies the brush in her hand and begins brushing her hair as if that's why she was holding it all along. I walk toward her.

"How long is that, exactly?" Her cheeks redden with embarrassment.

"Long enough I got free front row seats to a surprise concert." I smile, hoping she doesn't get upset.

She braids her wet hair to the side. "You weren't supposed to see that. I got a little carried away," she whispers and shrinks into herself, all of her confidence quickly waning.

"Baby, you're no Christina Aguilera, but few are. Don't be embarrassed. I like seeing all sides of you. For the record, I can't sing either." I wink to drive my point home.

She smiles, her posture returning. "Care to give me a sample?"

"Another time. I want to cuddle with you. Let's go to bed."

She lays her brush and phone down and crawls into bed, waiting for me. I slide off my jeans, replacing them with cotton boxer briefs, and then switch off the light, joining her.

When I lay my head on the pillow, she scoots up beside me, laying her head on my chest and her arm across my stomach. "This feels nice. Kind of like that night in Ryland's pool house when we fell asleep watching a movie."

I smile against the dark, remembering all too well. That was the night things started changing. "Except this time you don't have to sneak out."

She giggles, mindlessly rubbing her fingertips along my stomach, making my skin tingle. "Thank goodness for that. I expect morning sex. Might be our only chance for a long time."

I look at her when I feel her head tilt upward. And I kiss her. "Anything for you, beautiful. I love you."

And then she settles back in, breathing a sigh of contentment. "I love you too."

I lift the lower part of my arm to the one she's laying on, spreading my fingers. She aligns the back of her hand with the palm of mine, interlacing our fingers. I've never been big on sleeping away from home. I haven't shared a bed with someone to sleep since my brothers and me were kids. I'm one of those people that like to be in my own bed, but this . . . This feels like home.

TWENTY

Breyson

I wake from the best night's sleep I've ever had. Instead of groggy I feel energized. I look down at Kinzleigh's leg thrown over my pelvis and her arm draped across my chest with her head tucked under my chin, making this very act a little difficult. The side of her face is over my heart.

It surprises me that I never woke up in a position like this. I'm a hot-natured person and usually end up kicking the covers off sometime during the night, even with the air conditioner turned way down. If I sweat I can't sleep, which in turn has me tossing and turning in aggravation. I have to have sleep or I'm an asshole. To my memory, I didn't wake up once with her halfway on top of me, radiating body heat.

I need a shower, but she looks peaceful. In my attempt to slide out of the bed without waking her, she starts talking in her sleep. I still. I can only make out every few words. So far it's something about rope, chocolate syrup, and a blindfold. What the . . .

Trying to process these three words, she laughs, and suddenly starts panting my name. 'It tickles' flies out next. Is she having a sex dream? Innocent Kinzleigh that just kissed for the first time, hooked up, and lost her virginity all in the same week? Which was just months ago. Where would she even learn such dirty thoughts? All I know is I can't move. Screw a shower. I want to hear more.

The longer the dream goes on, the clearer it becomes to hear. "I like it dirty. Mmm, give it to me rough, baby. Spank me." My breath catches in my lungs, refusing to break through.

Please keep going.

This is by far the most sexual thing I've ever heard come from that mouth of hers. Her innocence is quickly fading. Thank God she's a sleep-talker. "That feels so good. Yeah, like that. I'm so ready for you. Don't stop, baby. Breyson . . ."

She trails her hand down my torso and slips her hand under my briefs, grabbing my manhood—full on hand wrapped around my shaft. I can't take this anymore. I am completely aroused. Without saying one word, I stand from the bed and cradle her in my arms, before sprinting toward the shower.

Halfway to the bathroom, she stirs, waking up. "Breyson? What are you doing?" I set her on her feet and turn on the shower.

Quickly discarding my clothes and hers, I have to ask, "Were you having a dirty dream about me?"

As soon as it's out of my mouth her face turns blood red and she looks off. I grab her by the chin to look at me. "It's nothing to be ashamed of, Kinzleigh. Tell me. You have me so turned on right now, I feel like I'm about to combust."

"Promise you won't laugh?" Laughing is not in the vicinity of my mind right now. She has me wound up so tight I feel like I can't breathe.

"You have my word." I run my finger through her center to see if she's as turned on as she appeared in the dream, and when it's confirmed, I crush her against the wall and kiss her greedily, my body pressed firmly against hers. "Tell me."

"Well, Adalynn showed me the Kindle app for my iPad and gave me a list of book recommendations to start with. I've been reading some before I go to bed. I found that it helps wear down my brain when I'm wired. Some of them are erotic. I didn't even know such a thing existed—sexy books. I guess subconsciously I'm curious, because they followed me to dreamland a few times." She hangs her head as if she is ashamed.

"Is this stuff you're interested in trying?" The idea of experimenting with her is only turning me on more.

"Would it make me dirty and slutty if I said yes?" Sweet Jesus! This is every guy's darkest fantasy and she's scared it makes her look slutty.

I rub my hands down her naked body. "Baby, there is nothing slutty about trying things with your partner in a monogamous relationship. Always tell me if there is something you want to try. I'm your man. I want you to be happy with our sex life. It's give and take. Some of what you like and some of what I like. It's only slutty if you're sleeping with a bunch of guys at the same time. Fantasies aren't anything to be ashamed of. Got me?"

She nods and bites her bottom lip. "Will you show me something new?"

My chest swells. My dick jumps. And my hands roam over her body, kneading every soft round place they pass. "I would love nothing more than you bend you over," I say, and then push her into the steamy confinement of the shower.

TWENTY-ONE

Breyson

I turn onto the long dirt road that leads to Pops' ranch. Following every bend along the way, I grab Kinzleigh's hand, interlocking our fingers on top of the center console, enjoying the ride.

I'm breaking her in well. I didn't even have to tell her what to wear before she walked out of her closet in a pair of jeans and a long sleeve, clover-green, button-down over a white tank, with her boots Adalynn got her for her birthday tying it all together. Her long, thick, blonde curls are cascading down her back, stopping mid-center. She's gorgeous.

It's the first day in November. Usually, it's still hot out, but today there is a cool breeze, making it actually feel like fall. I'm missing football games today. It's the perfect day for sitting in front of the television with the air conditioner off and the doors wide open, rooting for your team. I rarely miss it. This is my favorite time of the year. But it's not often that Kinzleigh and I have time together without parents or siblings in the mix, so my sacrifice is worth it.

I drive through the field and pull up to the big red barn out back, killing the engine. "Come on. There is someone I want you to meet. Grab those apples."

I meet her at the front of the truck and wrap my arm around her shoulders, pulling her close to my side. I lead her through the doors and pass the stalls one by one, until I get to the last one on the right. I whistle at the horse facing the back wall. "Hendrix, come here boy."

He turns around at the sound of my voice. He's a chocolate and white paint with a black mane and blue eyes. As he shoves his head over the gate, he huffs. "Yeah, I know it's been a while, don't be mad."

When I hold out my hand he nuzzles my palm. I've had Hendrix since I was just a kid. We've been through a lot together. He's the horse I learned how to ride on. We have a tight-knit relationship, and I suddenly feel bad I haven't come to see him in a while.

I rub up and down his nose, before leaning in. "I have someone for you to meet. She's important to me, so be nice to her, okay?" I whisper, so only he can hear. He responds with a neigh. I look back at where Kinzleigh is standing, watching us. She looks afraid. I take ahold of her hand and pull her toward the gate.

"Kinzleigh, this is Hendrix." She looks at him, unmoving. Apparently she doesn't have much experience with horses.

Pulling her wrist up to his nose, I cover her hand with mine and place it palm down on his coat. "He won't hurt you, but he can sense your nervousness, so relax. He's peculiar about who he lets ride him, but you're with me, so he'd never harm you."

She finally releases some of the tension in her stance by dropping her shoulders. "You got the apple, right?"

She nods and rubs between his eyes, under his hair. "He's beautiful. How'd he get his name?"

"I went through a Jimmy Hendrix phase when I was a kid. It was around the time Pops bought him for me. It fit at the time. He actually likes to listen to it. Sometimes I come out here and play it on my phone through my truck's Sync system. He loves the attention. Want to feed him?"

She smiles. "Sure, what do I do?"

"Hold out your hand flat with the apple sitting on top. He will take it from you. Don't put your fingers around it. I don't want him to accidentally bite you." She does as I say and Hendrix takes the apple.

She looks at me, excitement visible. "Will you teach me to ride?"

"Of course. Come on and I'll show you how to saddle him up." I've already been looking around to buy her a horse for Christmas. She just doesn't know it yet. I have Pops looking around for a gentle mare, so we can ride together. I've already found and paid for the saddle I'm getting her. I just have to go pick it up.

I've been thinking about Christmas since right after her birthday. I haven't been this excited for the holidays since I was a kid. I love spoiling her and I've never wanted that with a girl before. It's ironic.

Walking in the tack room—a small room in a barn used to store horse gear and feed—I pull out all the things I need to saddle him up. Saddling a horse is all about repetition. The more you do it, the faster you get.

It doesn't take long and we're ready to ride. I have to check on all of the cattle around the property, checking for newborns, so we'll be at it a while. I have to watch for tears in the fencing too. "You ready?"

She looks up at the saddle, confirming again that she's short. "How do I get on?"

I walk up behind her and place my hands on her hips. "See the horn on the saddle? Grab it with your left hand and the back lip with your right. Then place your left foot in the stirrup, and when I give you a boost throw your right leg over his back. I'll be right behind you."

When I finish talking, she nods and does as I instructed, mounting the horse. I follow suit until I'm seated behind her. I have to adjust her a little so that we can both fit. I try to ignore her ass so close to my dick. Her entire back is molded to my front.

Placing my lips outside of her ear, I explain some basic steps. "Here are a few key pointers to make things easier. Always stay in the saddle. The area behind it is his. Never walk behind a horse. It spooks them and you're liable to get kicked. It's a defense mechanism."

I lift the reigns in my hands. "This is like the steering wheel. Tug it lightly in the direction you want to go and back for stop, but don't pull too hard. The bit in his mouth hurts him. A little gets the point across. Too hard and he may buck. He knows what to do with a slight stern pull and command— *whoa*. To make him go, tap his girdle—the area beside the stirrups—with your heels and he'll start walking."

She exhales deeply in front of me. "Okay, I think I can do this." She stalls. "What if he hates me? He doesn't know me."

Her breathing picks up. "Kinzleigh, don't freak out. You'll be fine as long as you do what I say. It's controlling a horse not taking the SAT exam. I'm sitting right behind you. All you have to do is steer since this saddle is too big for you and you can't reach the stirrups."

I heel Hendrix and hold onto the horn of the saddle in a protective hold so that she doesn't fall off. "Come on, boy," I call out after I whistle. He takes off in a trot. She leans her head back against me. It's hard not to love this. My girl in front of me, my horse beneath me, and family land extended for miles. Today is going to be a good day . . .

We spent a large percentage of the day riding the property. I wanted to show her around my grandfather's ranch. I love it here. It's so freeing. No subdivisions or rules to follow. Just open land with small rolling hills and hollers. Cattle grazing. Sunshine beaming down on the grass.

I spend a lot of my time here—more than either of my brothers—and it's not just for the money. Sure, it pays to work and beats any other part time job, but there is something to be said about the lay of the land and the country. It's hard to explain. You have to live it to understand.

I've always said if I make it to the NFL I'm going to buy some land from Pops and build a place to come and hide from the world, to relax and enjoy the countryside.

She experimented with the reigns a little, but it wasn't long before she insisted that I take over. We rode for hours. She squealed at the sight of every calf. I laughed when she called our bulls steers, knowing she's probably heard it said on television a time or two, especially where rodeo is concerned. I had to explain to her that we don't have steers, which are castrated male cattle. If they can't produce they're no good to us. All of our male cows are un-castrated—bulls.

She was eager to learn more about it. And I liked teaching her. It was peaceful—just me, her, and Hendrix. Definitely something I could become accustomed to. She seemed to be enjoying herself. She asked a lot of questions and we talked through most of it.

To be honest, I've never been much of a talker, but talking to her is completely different. I like to get insight into her mind; she has a beautiful one. "If you were granted one wish, what would it be?" she asks.

"That's easy. To spend time with you." She rolls her eyes, but it's the truth.

"No, Breyson! You already get that. I'm being serious. Like if someone were going to do something for you or get you a gift and you got to choose what it was without knowing, what would it be?" Hmm. No one has ever asked me that before. I'm a laidback guy. It doesn't take much to make me happy. I'll have to think on it.

Football. It all comes back to football . . . "I would like to go to the Super

Bowl one day. It's something I've always wanted to do, but my parents don't have time to do that kind of stuff. They get very little time off and when they do, it's usually a family vacation or something. Imagine how much it would cost to take a family of six to the Super Bowl. The price of tickets alone is crazy. My dad likes football, as most men do, but he isn't as serious about it as Braxton and me. He thinks it should be a hobby. And I don't see Mom and Brylee spending their yearly family vacation in a football stadium."

She nods at the information. I can tell she's thinking it over. What is she up to? "Your dad doesn't support you wanting to play in the NFL, does he?"

She's very perceptive. I've probably hinted at things here and there, like the fact that he wants me to be a doctor, but we don't talk a whole lot about my family, because I'm always consumed with her when we're not busy with our own schedules. "No. He doesn't care if I play in college as long as my major gets me into medical school and it doesn't interfere with my grades. If I can play by his rules until senior year, I'm planning to put in for the draft without him knowing. If I actually got picked, it wouldn't matter anymore. If I don't, then he'll never know and I'll continue forward with his plan. Gotta get a college ball spot first, though. None of it is easy or everyone would be doing it."

She rubs her hand along mine. "I've always believed with enough passion for something anything is possible. But what if he figures out your plan? Don't you have to start taking entrance exams and looking into medical schools for application requirements pretty early? Seems like a lot of work to do when you don't really plan on doing it."

I shrug. "It's not a bad backup plan, regardless. I've never heard of someone complaining about being a doctor. My parents have made a good living. At some point he'll have to get over it. If I actually got a shot at the NFL, I would be making my own money, so I wouldn't care what he thinks by that point. It's still a long way off."

Guilt spreads through me. "I feel like I'm making him out to be a bad guy. He's a good father and a great doctor, but he comes from a family of doctors, so he expects it to continue. It's a noble career choice—helping people. It's just not what I want to do. Somehow, my brothers and me got the athletic gene and a love for sports. All three of us want to go pro. Briar will have the hardest time; not that any of it is easy. The percentage of baseball players getting recruited every year is much less than football players. But it's good to have dreams, even if they don't come true. Sports is something we're good at and it makes us happy."

"You should tell him that. It doesn't matter what anyone else thinks. You're the one that has to live with the decision. As long as you're happy, screw everyone else. I've seen you play. As good as you are, maybe you'll get a scholarship and won't even need your dad to pay for school." This is the most I've ever confided in someone before. It's refreshing.

I kiss her on the cheek, because truthfully, I just want to. It's not because of anything she said. I love being around her. She isn't like most girls. How often do you find a girl that tells you to go big with your dreams? I'm positive if I had to let her go to achieve it, she'd walk away first. A lot of girls plot ways to get a ring and a baby—to tie a guy down. Especially one with money. Look at how Natalie panned out. The bitch was probably using the 'fake pregnancy' to buy her a little time, hoping I'd take her back and get sloppy and actually get her pregnant.

Not Kinzleigh, though. She wants to live big too, with dreams as high as the stars. "What was that for?" She turns and smiles at me as we ride along the fencerow, checking for bad posts or torn fence.

"For being you," I say. I mean it wholeheartedly. Pops comes into view, changing out a fence post. He mentioned on the phone a heifer got stuck last week. Cut her up pretty bad trying to get out.

"Who's that?" Pops is going to love her. He's always teasing me about needing a good country girl like Mims, my grandmother. I don't think he was counting on me falling for a piece of California. Thankfully, both of my grandparents on my dad's side are still alive and well. He likes to say he's as healthy as an ox. Makes me wonder where that phrase originated.

"That's my grandfather. We call him Pops," I say, closing in to where he is standing and digging up an existing wooden post in need of replacement. "I want you to meet him. He's important to me. Okay?"

"What if he doesn't like me?" I'm not sure there is a person on this planet that wouldn't like her.

I tightly squeeze her around the waist. With my chin resting on her shoulder, I say, "Baby, he's going to love you. Just wait and see."

"Well, well, look who finally decided to get away from that snooty subdivision and come back to the country. I thought you were starting to turn into a yuppie on me." I smile. Crazy old man. His new favorite show is Duck Dynasty. He doesn't watch much television, and when he does it's old westerns, but one day I brought it over and put it in the DVD player. From then on he was hooked. I'm almost positive if he could hang around with anyone, it would be Phil Robertson.

From the way Pops acts, you would never know he used to be one of the best family physicians around here. That's one thing I love about him. He didn't let money change him. You'd never know him and Mims are loaded by looking at them or being around them. He's the one that taught me how to save and invest money. He's the reason I could support myself and probably even Kinzleigh throughout college without having to work or dip into my trust fund Dad and Mom have put money in since the day we were born.

"Are you going to run that pie hole of yours or meet my girl?" I ask jokingly. Pops and I have a special kind of relationship. We joke, but I would never actually disrespect him.

He stabs the posthole tool into the ground and removes his glove as he walks toward us. If I had to compare the way he dresses and a physical appearance to someone, it would be George Strait. Even as old as he is, he has aged well, given the hard work he's put into this place.

When he reaches the side of the horse, he holds out his free hand to Kinzleigh after swatting me on the arm with the glove in his other hand. "Excuse the boy's bad manners, honey. I thought I taught him better than that." Kinzleigh laughs at his humor and it makes me feel good. "The name's John Gavin, but just call me Pops. That's what family calls me."

A look I've never seen from her shadows over her face. I'm not sure what to make of it. She looks like she's on the verge of crying from him treating her like part of the family, but she quickly dismisses it. "I'm Kinzleigh. It's nice to meet you, Pops."

"Well, Kinzleigh, I'm curious. How'd my boy here catch a girl as pretty as you? I'm impressed. I was starting to think he didn't have it in him," he quips as he winks at her.

She giggles as he openly picks me apart in front of her. I'm going to have to watch these two or they will be trying to embarrass me. "I'd be lying if I said he wasn't a catch himself, but I guess he knows his way around my heart. He knows all the right things to say."

She is looking at Pops, but I can see her blushing as she talks to him. Right now nothing can change my good mood listening to the two of them. I can't remove the grin that has found its way on my lips.

He looks at me and gives me an expression I know well—don't screw this up. He likes her. I can tell. He's very opinionated, and if he didn't, I would know immediately. Not that I was worried, but it warms my heart to know my family likes her. "A pretty girl and a personality. Looks like you hit a double whammy, Son. Maybe my preaching all these years wasn't a complete waste of breath."

I laugh at his bluntness. "Watch it, ole man. Don't forget who has to take care of you when you get old. We're about to go get on the tractor, Pops."

He nods and walks back to where he was when we got here. "Take her to meet your grandmother before you leave, boy. You hear me?"

I tip the bill of my ball cap, and reply. "Yes, sir."

Then I signal for Hendrix to take off toward the barn, leaving everything in the dust.

TWENTY-TWO

Kinzleigh

I wasn't expecting to meet his grandparents today, but now that I am, I'm thrilled. And what's even better—my anxiety is nowhere to be found. The way his grandfather treated me like family was heartwarming. His loving personality reminded me of the grandfather I lost. I miss Gramps. I could definitely see spending more time here, and I haven't even met his grandmother yet.

We arrive back at the barn and he lets Hendrix roam in the enclosed pen of grass behind it. I never thought I'd want to ride a horse. Coming from an urban area surrounded by nothing but sand and water, the only horseback riding you'll find is if you pay to ride at a stable, and there is usually a drive. Everything is so different here, so open. I could probably yell and the echo of my voice carry for miles.

Not far from the barn you can see another covered building that matches the exterior, but it's more open. It looks like its sole purpose is to keep equipment protected from the weather. Beneath the covering is a green and yellow tractor. He tugs me toward it in a sprint. "What are we doing?"

He looks back at me, but continues forward. "We have to haul some hay Pops just bought for the winter. The bales are too big to carry." Once we reach the tractor, he grabs the steering wheel and hauls himself up onto the yellow seat, before holding his hand out for me.

I look the tractor over, confused. I'm not sure where he expects me to sit. "What do you want me to do?"

He laughs, but then pats his thigh. "Sit with me."

It looks like a death trap on four huge wheels. What if I fall off? It's big overall, in my opinion, but the sitting area isn't all that big when you're talking two people. I feel the need to voice this concern out loud. It's not like I have that much experience with equipment. "What if I fall off or something? I wouldn't think that's safe or there'd be two seats."

He scoffs, and actually looks disgusted over the fact that I'm second-guessing him. "Trust me, yeah?"

Of course he's going to turn this into a trust thing. "You know I do."

His eyes flash. "Then get on and stop doing what you're doing. I see you rationalizing every possible thing that could happen in your head. Don't do that. You're going to drive yourself crazy. I would never let anything happen to you."

Finally accepting his hand, I place my foot on the floorboard area and step up onto the tractor. He pulls me onto his lap. "If you insist. You should be glad you look as yummy as you do today or I'd probably have declined your offer."

I can't lie. I thought his football uniform looked good on him, but that was before I was introduced to Wrangler. Remind me to thank the special creator for the tight goodness he invented. Boy does it do wonders for the Gluteus Maximus. What can I say; I'm a butt girl. Those paired with the fitted t-shirt and ball cap makes me want to take him in the woods and do naughty, naughty things to him.

"Yummy, huh? It's hot out," he purrs against my ear, seductively, and then I feel it—hard, bare skin rubbing against me. Sweat transferring to my shirt. Oh my heavens, he just took off his shirt. He fiddles with the shifter and then turns the key over, the engine of the tractor roaring to life.

I turn around to confirm he is, in fact, shirtless. My throat goes dry. I need a fan. Oh. My. Bloody. Hades. He is hot! I don't mean in the temperature sense either. He doesn't have an ounce of fat hiding his muscle and the boots and ball cap add the icing on the cake. The V of muscle that was on display last night is currently hidden by the sitting position he's in, beckoning my eyes to follow the arrow into the tight, dark jeans, so that I can see it again.

Do I want to follow the yellow brick road? Why yes, in fact, I do. I would love to experience the Emerald City that waits at the other side, full of bliss and pleasure. Each time I see him like this, I feel like someone hosed me down with pheromones.

Put a cork in it, Kinzleigh. This is the wrong time and place to be turned on. You're going to meet his grandmother soon, for goodness sakes!

I can feel the heat radiating from my cheeks, telling me I probably look like a tomato right now. I lightly slap my cheeks in an attempt to not look so obvious.

I clear my throat, trying to feign indifference. "Hot? I didn't notice. I'm fine. Are we going to get this party started?" My voice cracks toward the end.

Thank you, traitorous body. You just can't let me win once, can you?

He moves me from his thigh to the center of his lap, brushing my rear against his manhood. *Do not think dirty thoughts. Do not think dirty thoughts. Eyes on the grass ahead.*

I can feel his smile spreading as he brushes my hair to one side and kisses my neck. He puts the tractor in gear and backs up into the open field. I watch the muscles in his forearms move as he steers and shifts, which leads me to wonder if it's normal that I find this sexy. His biceps form rocks when he pulls back and I can feel the movement of his pectorals bouncing on my back.

The tractor has an attachment that looks like a large fork. I'm assuming that's the way he's going to haul the ginormous bales of hay scattered about at what I'm assuming was the drop off location. He controls the tractor until the fork slides underneath the bale and then he raises the hydraulic attachment so that it doesn't drag the ground.

Once loaded, he hauls the bale to one end of the large 'pole barn' I think he called it, and places it down so that it's covered from the weather but easily accessible when needed. I'm assuming we'll be doing this exact thing until all bales are lined up along this particular opening. Nothing else was being stored in this spot. Even with all the equipment underneath this thing there is plenty of space for more. It's the size of a house itself, minus the walls and filler.

I press back and settle in, letting the vibration of the engine and the rocking of the tractor each time it takes on weight become my beach. It may not be calming waves rolling in, but there is a certain calming effect to it if you let the sounds of the smoke stack on the tractor become your lullaby.

Several loads later he pulls the tractor back under the pole barn and parks it. When the engine silences, I hop down off the tractor and turn to watch as he does the same. I spot something and get an idea. There is a weathered baseball lying against one of the many poles that run down the center of the space where the roof pitch is. An odd place for a baseball, but I pick it up regardless.

Turning around, I toss it underhanded at Breyson's chest, as if it were a softball instead of a baseball. I was going to jokingly catch him off guard, but my plan quickly backfires when he catches it midair. "You're going to pay for that," he says as a smirk forms and his eyes glaze over.

I take off running through the field, laugh after laugh tumbling out of my mouth. I can hear him traipsing after me. I heighten my stride through the tall grass, running as fast as my short legs will allow. Halfway through the field, I turn to see how far back he is, but he's gone.

Where on earth did he go? Slowing my pace a little, I turn back to keep my eyes ahead and slam into him, falling backward. I scream in surprise when he pins me down and locks our lips, shushing me.

My eyes close at the heated contact. When his lips disappear, I open them. He looks me in the eyes. "You're playing with fire, baby. I'm not a good running back because of my looks. I will *always* catch you. By the way, making a good play is all about finding the opening."

"Noted, but you caught me a long time ago." I lock my legs around his waist, playing with the short hair on his head.

"Good. Let's go. I'm sure Pops has already told Mims to expect us." He stands, forcing me to break my hold and pulls me upright by my hand.

We walk through the field until a large house comes into view. It's a beautiful, white plantation style house with a wraparound porch and mint green shutters. Its high roof, with double doghouses hints at an upper floor.

The closer we get to the wooden door the more nervous I become. I try to exhale the anxiety building when Breyson stops, only letting me get a few steps ahead of him before halting me as well. Turning to face him, he pulls me into him and grasps my face in his hands. "What's wrong?" I ask, confused as to why he stopped.

"She's going to love you. Relax, baby. I don't like seeing you get worked up. You weren't like this with Pops. I promise you have nothing to worry about." Just hearing his voice is calming me down significantly.

"Okay." He kisses me and grabs my hand, interlocking our fingers. We begin walking once again, ascending the porch steps.

He opens the door and we walk inside. The house is more beautiful on the inside than out. The ceilings are high with beams running from one end to the other. It looks like something out of a magazine.

The floors are gray and look like they're made out of stained lumber versus pre-made floor planks. It's classy, but rustic. The walls are beige and the furniture appears to be made of a real leather—cattle hide maybe.

If the shoe fits . . .

We are on a cattle ranch.

The chandelier and the tabletop lamps look to be made out of some type of antlers. The coffee table is made of glass and wrought iron, and on top is a decorative piece with balls of cotton filling it. I glance around, noticing vases of more cotton stems littered throughout the room. The room is dressed to the nines with beautiful pieces of furniture and décor.

Never would have thought of cotton as pretty décor . . .

As we walk through the living room he calls out loud for her. "Mims. Where you at?"

We walk toward a kitchen that looks to be just as pristine and spotless as the rest of the house. As we come through the door, the cabinets are all ceiling height and painted white with a distressed style. The dropped hood has an edging that looks like rope. The appliances are stainless steel and the countertops a white marble with swirls of gray. "Breyson? Honey, is that you?"

She has the sweetest voice I've ever heard. It's soft and light. "Yeah, Mims, it's me and Kinzleigh."

She walks out of a door to the left of the bar. She is absolutely adorable. She isn't very tall and round in figure. In actuality, she is probably a little shorter than me, which is less than five-foot-two. Her hair is short, curled, and teased, like a vast percentage of the older female population. She has an apron over her clothes that reads: *Kiss the cook.*

Now that I see an item only those cooking would wear, I notice the smell lingering in the air. It smells delicious; like oatmeal and peanut butter.

"Oh good. I was waiting for you both. I'm making cookies. Are y'all hungry?" She walks closer to us and pulls Breyson in for a hug.

She then swats him on the butt and releases him from her hold. "Next time, don't wait so long before you come to see me. I'm not getting any younger, you know. You're not too old for me to you bend over my knee," she says teasingly, and it makes me melt.

He kisses her on the cheek. "Yes, ma'am. Smells good. You know I don't turn down my favorite cookies.

He looks at me, waving me closer. "Mims, this is my girlfriend, Kinzleigh."

She smiles before she even looks at me, and then pulls me in for a hug as well. It's not a forced awkward hug either. She really hugs me. A genuine hug. "It's a pleasure to meet you, Kinzleigh. You have a beautiful name."

She brings her voice down to a whisper outside of my ear, opposite of Breyson. "You must be a special girl for him to bring you home, honey. You're definitely the first."

She pulls back and winks at me. Butterflies swarm low in my belly. "It's lovely to meet you, Mrs. Abercrombie, and thank you. I'll be sure to tell my mother."

She waves her hand through the air. "Sweetie, call me Mims. I can't remember the last time someone called me by my last name. That makes me feel like we're handling business. This is family around here."

"Yes, ma'am," I say, copying Breyson. *Ma'am*—that very word sounds so strange. We don't do that in California. What seems to be a term of respect here is actually the opposite back home. I've heard it a few times from tourists, and every time it's met with agitation.

She turns back to Breyson, who is just standing there, watching the interaction. "Son, why don't you leave us girls to the kitchen. Surely, there is something outside you can be doing with Pops. He's getting older. Needs all the help he can get, though he'd never admit it. Kinzleigh and I can bond over preparing dinner. You'll both be staying, won't you?"

Breyson looks at me, silently asking if I'm okay with him leaving me here. I nod to assure him I'll be fine. "Okay, Mims. I have to clean out the stalls for the horses." He kisses me on the cheek. "See you in a bit?"

"Sure. I'll be here." He grabs a cookie from the freshly made batch cooling on the counter, stuffs it in his mouth, and heads back in the direction we came from earlier.

She grasps my hand, looking at my acrylic nails. I'm normally a natural girl, but Adalynn talked me into it during one of our girl dates. I'm still getting used to the tips even though I had them cut shorter so that I can function normally. "I hope you don't mind getting these hands a little dirty, sweetheart. Your nails are beautiful, but I would love to have your help."

"Absolutely. I'm not worried about messing them up. It was more of a friend's idea than mine. I may not be the best helper, though. My mom has shown me a little in the kitchen, but with her crazy schedule it's not a regular occurrence. Most of the time she just prefers to do it herself."

"Don't be silly. Every girl has to learn. You have to start somewhere. Cooking is an art that has to be mastered over time. Anyone who claims to be a perfect cook is full of it. Pops has eaten his fair share of burnt or tasteless food over the years. And then there are the mishaps that turn into the best recipes." I adore her.

She doesn't view me as the girl that comes from money or the girl that is spoiled and doesn't know how to do things for herself. She looks at me as she would anyone else—a clean canvas ready to be painted. His family is one of the humblest clans of people I've ever met.

An hour later, the food is all done. I have to say, I'm proud of myself. She taught me how to make homemade cornbread, and somehow I managed to do it without burning it. The menu is grilled pork chops, macaroni and cheese, green bean casserole, and cornbread. She made sweet tea to go with it and laughed when I crinkled my nose as she scooped and dumped many cups of sugar into the freshly boiled tea. Immediately followed was, "Honey, you haven't learned the south until you've had a glass of our famous sweet iced tea. It's a southern trademark. Try it, but if you don't like it that's okay too. You're probably better off without it anyway."

I did—try it that is. It was like drinking a glass of liquid diabetes. Southern sweet tea should come with a warning label. We settled on half and half . . .

She hands me a stack of plates to set the table. The size of the stack intimidates me a little. I don't remember seeing anyone else here. As I'm placing them around the table, the door flings open and a line of males in cowboy attire walks in, taking various seats around the table.

Breyson walks in last with a dirty face and clothes. The front of his hair is standing up from being wet with his sweat. I have never thought dirty looked good until now.

He walks toward the sink to wash up and someone begins talking. "Who's the fine kitchen help you have, Mims?" I turn around to a male about mid-twenties with a smirk on his face. He has reddish-brown hair peeping out of his cowboy hat and brown eyes. His skin is an olive complexion with a red hue to it, like permanent mild sunburn. I may not know much about boys, but I know *that* look, and I wish he would stop before Breyson does something crazy. He trails his eyes down my body.

"Tex, this is Kinzleigh, Breyson's girlfriend." Tex? That's a strange name. Mims walks over beside me, pointing to where I'll be sitting, which is right across from him. Great. "Kinzleigh, this is Tex. He's our hand from Texas, hence the name."

He is making me uncomfortable with the stares. I begin fiddling with my hands to occupy myself. "Breyson, huh? What you doing messing around with boys when a girl like you could have a real man."

He's cocky too, I see, and already grinding my nerves. This is the kind of guy I always stayed away from, for good reason. They're nothing but trouble. Changing women like t-shirts.

I used to watch friends get hurt by guys like him, because they gave them a little attention and threw a few compliments their way to get them in bed. When it was over, it was like they didn't exist or the guy was cruel to get rid of her, leaving a bruised ego and tears behind. I called it a mini depression.

"Knock it off, Tex." A pair of arms I recognize snake around my waist. "Don't let him bother you," he says lowly, but not that quietly. "He can only get girls by being an asshat. A flaw that works in his favor. It's the only thing he has going for him."

Tex clenches his jaw and moves forward, as if he's about to plunge at Breyson over the table. "You better be lucky I have some manners or we'd take this outside."

"Don't threaten me, Tex, unless you're prepared to back it up. I'm tired of your bad attitude toward everyone." Breyson stands up straight, as if he's waiting for the challenge.

Pops walks through the door. "Sit down, boys. Not on my property. Both of you know I don't condone fighting. If you still have that much testosterone you didn't work hard enough. Tex, you're one of the best hands I've got. Don't make me fire you over stupidity."

Pops takes a seat at the head of the table. Everyone but Breyson is already seated. Breyson points around the table, introducing me to each person, before finally sitting down himself. Pops, radiating power as he looks down the table, says, "Breyson, say grace."

Hats come off and heads bow. After quickly looking around, I follow suit. Everything goes quiet except for Breyson's voice as he prays over dinner—something I'm not used to.

"Amen," he says, and suddenly the middle of the table is swarmed by large hands as spoons are jerked and tossed and plates are filled with food in a hurried fashion. I've never seen anything like it. Mess hall—totally understand that phrase now.

The rest of dinner went by uneventful. Lots of eating. Not much talking. It was almost silent except for the metal forks scraping against the glass plates and ice clinking against the glasses. I'm assuming that's normal with tired, hungry men. I realized I do like southern food—again, all except the sweet tea.

Breyson stands at the door with his hand on the doorknob, ready to leave. Breyson's grandparents both hug me tightly. "You make him bring you back, you hear?"

Mims releases me and cups my face. "If you can't get him to bring you, just give me a call and I'll come get you myself. I could use a trip out of this house anyway." My body warms from her kindness.

Pops comes to stand beside her and places his arm around her shoulders. "I have a feeling we'll be seeing more of her, honey. Isn't that right, son?"

He looks at Breyson with a broad smile, causing Breyson to nod happily in response as he takes ahold of my hand. His grandparents are so cute together. It gives the world hope that there are actually happy endings to consist of growing old together. "Absolutely, Pops. We'll be back."

He leads me out the door, hand in hand. I wave back at them as we walk toward his truck. "Thank you for dinner," I say, before getting in Breyson's truck as he opens the door for me.

"Any time," I hear in return, just before he shuts it back, enclosing me in the dark cab of the truck. I lay my head against the headrest and smile. It's been a good day.

Breyson gets in the driver's side and cranks his truck, looking over at me with his big goofy grin still in place. "Thank you for coming with me."

I smile back. "It was a fun day. I'm the one that should be thanking you. Maybe we'll beat my parents home . . ." I hint, and that's all it takes before he puts the truck in drive.

When we pull into my driveway the lights are on, signaling my parents are home. "Want to come in?" I ask as he comes to a stop.

"I would, baby, but I'm filthy. Can I just call you later? I promised Braxton some bro time. He's been riding me lately. Seems he's feeling left out, because some hot blonde has taken up all my time in the recent months," he says in a way that makes my heart flutter.

"Okay." He reaches across the truck and trails his thumb across my bottom lip, before pulling me toward him. Closing our eyes at the same time, he kisses me. My whole body stills and I'm taken to my happy place— the place where thought escapes me. The place where nothing in the world exists for the amount of time his lips are pressed against mine. There is no bad, no ugly, just the beautiful dancing of his tongue with mine.

He pulls away. "It doesn't mean I won't miss you, though. Every time we're apart, my heart longs for yours. One day, Kinzleigh, houses won't separate us. Take it how you want, but the day will come eventually. I love you, girl."

You know, it's funny how fate works. Months ago, I would have freaked out completely at hearing something like that—something so permanent. People can change you, push you where you didn't intend to go.

This wasn't the path I wanted my life to take, but sometimes change happens whether we're ready for it or not. I hope I don't lose myself along the way. Fate dealt me a hand and I accepted it. I hope I don't end up on the losing end. "I love you too."

I get out of the car and turn toward him. "Breyson . . ."

"Yeah, baby," he says as if he has all the time in the world.

"Thanks for today. You took me out of my comfort zone, and it was fun."

"You're welcome, beautiful. They love you. Thank you for trusting me. Give me that and I'll give you the world." By the look in his eyes, I don't doubt it's true. "Goodnight, baby."

"Goodnight." I shut the door and walk toward my front door. As he pulls away, I kiss my palm and wave. "I'll miss you more," I whisper, more for myself than him. And then I breathe out, realizing how tranquil I feel. I'm in a calm place I've never known . . .

TWENTY-THREE

Kinzleigh

Sitting on my bed, I hold the two envelopes in my hand. One, I've been waiting on since the night I got home from Breyson's grandparents' and purchased online. The other completely fills me with anxiety. The return sender on the envelope reads: National Cheer Competition Association of America, NCCAA.

This one envelope holds the key to my future. It excites me and terrifies me all the same. If I am accepted, I get to travel the world this summer and throughout college to compete. It will give me the chance to explore new places. Meet new people. It opens up opportunities. Gives my resume strength. I will earn referrals. I don't know if I can open it.

You can do this, Kinzleigh. You are strong. It's just a letter.

A knock sounds on my door before it opens. Adalynn is standing on the other side in dark wash skinny jeans and brown, leather riding boots, with an olive-green tunic. The girl loves green, but I can see why. It's a beautiful color on her. I guess it's the red hair. "Hey, babe. Whatcha doing?"

Sometimes her southern accent still makes me laugh. Everything is so run together from talking fast, but drawn out at the same time. It seems like a contradiction.

She walks in and takes a seat on the edge of the bed, next to where I'm sitting with my legs crisscrossed, holding the two envelopes in my hand.

"Trying to decide if I want to open this envelope or not."

She looks down at the two in my hand. "What is it?"

"This one," I hold up the one I know contains Breyson's Christmas present, or part of it, "is Breyson's Super Bowl tickets. I had to pay out the ass for them through NFL On Location to ensure I got two *before* Christmas. It'll take me a while to replace that money, as in years, but it'll be worth it to see his face when he opens them. This other one," I hand the other out to her, "is my future."

She takes it from me and reads the sender's name aloud. "National Cheer Competition Association of America." Her eyes widen, realizing dawning. "Is this from your tryouts over the summer?"

I nod. "It will tell me if I've been selected or not. I'm terrified, because it only feels like one piece of paper. Don't you think it would be a thicker package if it were an acceptance letter? Usually rejection letters are short."

I close my eyes, trying to calm my nerves now running wild. "Stop doing that to yourself. Whatever is in this envelope doesn't define you. It may change your path, but it doesn't bring your journey to an end. Do you want me to open it?"

I nod, because honestly, I don't think my nerves can handle it.

She slides her finger beneath the seal, tearing it as she moves in a horizontal motion. Once completely broken, she removes the sheet of paper and unfolds it from the tri-folded state it's in. She reads in silence and it's only making me more anxious. "Would you tell me already? Give it to me straight. I'm becoming a nervous wreck over here!"

She clears her throat and begins reading aloud.

Dear Miss Baker,

We are pleased to inform you that you have been cordially invited to join our 2014 team after carefully reviewing your application and tryout video. You will receive an informational welcome packet after the New Year. Please be looking for this package as the company's annual meet and greet will be held at the end of February to introduce new team members. Thank you for your interest in NCCAA. We look forward to making you a part of this program.

Thank you,
Rachel Williams
President and CEO

I immediately stand and jump up and down in excitement, squealing my happiness in the highest possible octave. I cannot believe this. My dreams are coming true. Adalynn immediately hugs me, congratulating me. "Oh, my gosh, I have so much to do. I need to start training again as soon as possible. Wait! I need to find another trainer. I don't have much time. What do I even do after receiving this information? I get to see the world! Pinch me, this can't be real!"

Adalynn pinches me, hard. "Ouch! What was that for?"

"I'm just following orders," she says, and laughs as I roll my eyes. "All in good time, dear. You will do fine. Enjoy the holidays and then you can start all that hard work. Tell me more about these Super Bowl tickets. How much did those bad boys cost?"

"You don't want to know. I learned a lot shopping for Super Bowl tickets. And one is that the NFL strictly controls sales. Depending on how much you're willing to pay determines how early you get them. Since it's a surprise Christmas present I had to go directly through the source, like I told you before. I asked my dad for help, risking him thinking I'm crazy and telling me no. When I explained the circumstance he agreed to pay fifty percent of the ticket price as him and Mom's gift to Breyson if I opted out of going and let him take a *male* friend instead. He loves Breyson, but he'd probably pay anything to keep us out of sharing a hotel room this young." I smile as I remove the two tickets from the envelope, treating them like gold.

Now slightly bent from my previous spurt of excitement, I work to flatten the bend from my thumb, and then wave them in the air like a stack of hundreds fanned out. He is going to be shocked when he sees these.

She grabs them and looks at them, reading every word. "He is going to flip. You never told me what you decided. Just that your dad would help if you didn't," she says, still staring at them. "There are always ways around what Daddy says. I would know. Are you going?"

"No."

"But why? Do you know how many people get to go to Super Bowl?!" I want to laugh at the look of sheer terror on her face like I've lost my mind.

"Ryland is going with him. I've already made the hotel reservation and booked both flights. They don't see each other very often and last time they did Breyson spent a lot of it with me, so a trip away would be good for them. When I called Ryland he all but jumped through the phone at the opportunity. He even offered to pay for his flight and half of the room, but

I feel like it's rude to invite someone and make them pay. I'm good with my decision."

"I guess that's what counts. How exactly are you going to wrap that? It's not going to be a surprise if you just hand it to him like this," she says, looking genuinely confused.

I express a small laugh. "Well, I found a large gift card box and I'm going to fold up the flight and hotel confirmations and put them in the box and wrap that. I'm still deciding on the tickets. T-shirt boxes work, but I don't know if I want to do that yet. Besides, I got him a few small things to open too, as did Mom, so it won't be his only gift."

I love Christmas time. Always have. It's my favorite time of the year. Mom and I go all out on the tree and the decorations around the house. We've been going at it since the day after Thanksgiving. The house is covered and filled with lights, wreaths, garland, and tabletop decorations.

"Dang, girl. You're putting my gifts to shame. I hope Braxton doesn't compare." She releases a nervous laugh.

It's the week of Christmas and so many guests are scheduled to arrive today. It's hard to contain my excitement. I feel like I've had too many cups of eggnog and I hate that stuff. Konnor should be here any minute now. He's driving from Alabama.

Mom and Dad went to pick up Presley, Preston, Paxtyn, and their parents at the airport. I guarantee Paxtyn is only coming by force, if she hasn't found a way to back out by now. She has a very strong personality in comparison to the rest of her family, especially to be so young. Bratty is an understatement.

I take the tickets back from her. "What's the deal with you two anyway? Are you guys dating or not?"

Braxton and Adalynn have been inseparable since we went riding at Red Creek. She zones out and a smile stretches from ear to ear. She has this dreamy look on her face. "I was going to wait to tell you, but since you brought it up . . . Yes! We're a couple! I was fine being friends with benefits, hanging out occasionally, but he officially asked me to be his girlfriend after my birthday dinner at that yummy Italian restaurant with my parents. He got me a gift too." She pulls back her hair to reveal a pair of diamond stud earrings in her ears.

She is gleaming. I love seeing her like this. I immediately grab her and pull her into a bear hug, rocking side-to-side. "Adalynn, I am so happy for you guys! Congratulations!"

"I have some more good news since we're in an information celebratory mood." She pauses to look at me.

"Go on . . . spill!"

"Okay, well, you know how sometimes they have those modeling calls that come to places like a hotel conference room in various cities looking for people?" I nod, waiting for her to continue. "Well . . . I went to one like a month ago, not expecting anything to come of it, and they called me yesterday!" She screeches in excitement.

"Oh, my gosh! That's so awesome! What does that mean for you, exactly?" I cannot contain my excitement either. Things are looking up for both of us and nothing can spoil my good mood.

She takes a deep breath to calm down from our moments of jumping in the air like two kids. "I'm part of a modeling agency. Under contract and everything. They will get a financial cut of everything I make, but it will give me opportunities that I can't get by myself. I will build references, a portfolio. It would be smalltime jobs for now, like live manikin gigs, social media advertising for small businesses, shoots with self-employed photographers, smaller corporate shoots or last-minute replacements when a bigger model falls through."

Her eyes glaze over, like she's staring at a box full of assorted hot donuts. "If I do well, we could be talking big-time jobs, Kinzleigh. Things could happen for me—high-profile photo shoots, magazine covers, big brand advertisement, major department stores, and even fashion modeling for well-known designers. Runway modeling has always been my biggest dream like professional cheerleading is for you. Oh, my God! Could you imagine being part of *Fashion Week*. And the travel opportunities! We're talking Los Angeles, New York, Paris, and Rome. I can taste the culture. The possibilities are endless!"

The room is full of good vibes and happiness. It's great. "I have an idea," she says. "Since we both have all this good news, why don't we wait and tell everyone together at the clubhouse, night of the New Year's Eve Masquerade ball?"

The subdivision we live in was exactly as I expected. It's filled with the financially blessed. People of high stature live here. They have a clubhouse that hosts regular activities for the homeowners and their guests. Apparently, it is the place to live for the rich and famous that resides in this town. I've even heard through the grapevine of a Major League Baseball player that owns a house here.

Over the past few months, my mom and Adalynn's mom, Caroline Price, have kindled a friendship. Our dads work a lot, but they have met a few times. Her dad is the president of a large bank and her mom is an investment broker. With both of our mothers being businesswomen, they both clicked when they met.

Once Adalynn and I started getting close it became essential for them to meet. "I guess New Year's Eve would be as good a time as any to announce the information. It's only a couple of weeks away. Did you bring your presents, so we can wrap?"

"Yep, just outside the door. Hold on and I'll get them." She turns to walk toward my bedroom door and I go to the closet for mine. We decided to wrap together this year and make it a wrapping party. We went all out and got our paper and supplies from a paper company downtown to be different. Their options were so much classier than a local chain store, and much better quality.

Adalynn and Londyn took me in there for a bow making class with some of the girls from the squad a few nights ago and I fell in love with the wrapping paper and the endless ribbon options and the little crimped paper in all different colors. I felt like a kid in a candy shop. It's a little pricy for something people are going to tear up, but it adds a lot of character when they're all under the tree. The way I see it—perfect photo props for another year of memories. I get snap-happy during the holidays and end up with hundreds of photos.

Needless to say, a couple hundred dollars in I had to make myself stop picking things up. Londyn kept telling me I had a serious shopping addiction each time she swatted my hand away from the paper saying, and I quote, "Easy, girl. Back away from the paper before I shoot," while holding a bottle of body spray she drew from her purse like a pistol.

My return quip to her was holding my hands up in surrender, saying, "Oh, please, what are you going to do? Spritz me to death with your fruity body spray?"

Her response... "I aim to kill and don't miss. I will use force if necessary." I laugh out loud at the memory. Good times. I love my friends. They've brought me out of my shell more than anyone else did back in California. Maybe because southern people are different somehow. Not in a good or bad way, just different. We all have a lot of fun together, and it rarely involves things our parents wouldn't approve of, like alcohol.

"Why are you laughing?" I break from my reverie to Adalynn walking back into my room with an armful of stuff to wrap.

I had no idea I was even laughing out loud. That's a little embarrassing. If she didn't know me, she would probably think I was a weird kid. She's used to me zoning out by now. I tend to do it without thinking. "Just remembering the night of the bow wrapping class. It made me laugh."

"Awesomesauce! We act like we've been drinking when we all get together. Our silly meter tends to get cranked up to high." She laughs too, aloud, in a room with no other people. If walls could talk . . .

"Yes it does," I say, plopping down on the floor so that I can spread everything out in front of me. "Now come." She sits across from me and spreads her legs at my command, wasting no time before organizing all of her items.

I do something I've been dying too all day—turn on Christmas music. Because it's so much better when you can belt out the words with someone else than alone.

I look at the clock on my bedside table and realize we have been wrapping for two hours. Did we really have that much to wrap? The presents scattered all over my bedroom floor answers my question. When your list consists of parents, siblings, boyfriend, and friends, I suppose it grows quickly. As I'm tying the bow on the last gift, the door shuts downstairs.

Footsteps pound against the steps. Someone is running up the stairs. "Kinzleigh! You up here?"

I know that voice. One I've missed dearly. You don't realize how much someone makes an impact on your everyday life until they aren't in it. Konnor. My brother is finally home from school.

"Up here!" I shout back, hoping he will follow my voice to the right room. It's his first time to see our new house. For some unknown reason he didn't come home for thanksgiving. He has become the private one lately. And a little bit shady. We used to talk about everything. I feel like he's been distant lately.

"He sounds hot," Adalynn whispers as she combs her fingers through her hair. She's trying to primp before he makes it to the room. It'll be interesting to see her reaction when she sees him. Konnor has always had girls at his feet. He just never wanted them when he was with Sophia, but times have changed. Maybe Presley will finally get his attention.

The door opens and he takes in the two of us, as well as the presents littered all over the room. My eyes widen at the sight of him. Oh my . . .

"Which one is mine? You know I'm going to shake all the presents, so save them from getting crinkled and spill," he says, as a smirk plays out across his handsome face.

Konnor was always the one who couldn't wait for Christmas. Once, I caught him sneakily opening the paper at the corners to see what was on the inside, so now I have to hide his until Christmas morning. We always go big on each other for Christmas.

I can't take my eyes off his body. Not in a perverted way. I haven't seen him since summer, and when he left his body was a clean slate with the exception of two tattoos. Now he is covered in ink—what I can see anyway. I can't imagine the covered places being any different.

He glances at Adalynn in a way I've never seen him look at someone before. There is something dark about it. Konnor is just Konnor. He's always been the nice guy. The guy with a lot of friends. He laughed a lot. Found fun in anything. He didn't let things bother him. He was the life of the party. It was something I envied about him, because I was the shy one with anxiety and insecurities.

With Sophia, it was always love and passion. He adored her. Went to great lengths to make her happy. What I see now is gross. Something I never wanted to see on my brother. It's raw lust. His eyes sweep down her body, slowly, making me want to step in front of her to protect her. There is a fire in his eyes that scream one thing: sex. What on earth has he been doing? Can he even have all those tattoos on the football team?

"My sister has forgotten her manners. I'm Konnor, her brother, and you are?" His eyes are glued to Adalynn the entire time he speaks. She doesn't even look like she is breathing under his penetrative stare. I can't do anything but watch this weird interaction. This side of him is completely foreign to me.

"I'm Adalynn, the best friend." She manages to get the words out without stuttering; although, it seems like she had to work at it. He is wearing a cream-colored Henley with the sleeves pulled up to his elbows, revealing the tattoos covering his right arm. I'm assuming based on the right that the left isn't done, because there is a lot of visible clean skin. His jeans sit loosely on his hips. The more he talks, the more I notice something silver.

Standing, I walk over to him and grab his clean-shaven face in the clamp of my hand. "Konnor Aston Baker! What is in your mouth?"

He purses his lips at an attempt to hide it, but it's too late. "You got a tongue ring! What the heck, Konnor? I haven't seen you in months and you come home tatted and pierced? Why haven't you talked to me? How many tattoos do you have now?"

"You really want to do this here?" He looks back at Adalynn, whose eyes are dilated at my sudden outburst of anger.

"Adalynn, I'll be right back. K?" She nods and I push him out the door. "I need to show him his room anyway."

We get down the hall to his room and walk inside. I shut the door, trying to keep us from being heard. "What's going on? I thought you had to keep a clean image to be on a college football team. You're not messing up your chance for a scholarship are you? Why aren't you talking to me anymore about things? I thought we had no secrets with each other."

I poke my finger into his chest animatedly as I speak. To be truthful, I am scared, because this much change in such a short amount of time can't be good. I don't want him to end up looking like trash or back on drugs and alcohol as a coping mechanism for his pain. He's always been beautiful on the inside and out.

He wraps his arms around me and pulls me in for a hug. "I'm not going to do anything to mess up my spot on the team. I have more respect for Dad than that."

He lays his chin on top of my head and I hug him back, enjoying the moment of silence. I haven't hugged my brother in months. He feels like he's been working out more. "But don't be surprised if I'm not on it next year," he says, making my blood run cold. He's loved football for as long as I can remember.

"What?" I whisper, and look at him, almost in tears. "You love football."

"Things have changed. Change isn't always a bad thing. Football is not where I see my life going anymore. I've been talking to Dad about it since the semester started. He's supportive as long as I finish out my commitments this year. I'm a walk-on, so it doesn't change anything financially. I don't even play. I'm a benchwarmer. Something I haven't been in years. They won't miss me."

Moisture pools in the corners of my eyes. "You're scaring me."

He pulls me into his chest again. "I'm still the same Konnor as before, just a few shades darker. People change, Kinzleigh. It's just a matter of how and when. Sometimes life grips you by the neck and chokes you. I'm learning how to breathe with the vise around my neck. I survive the pain on the inside by inflicting it on the outside. Ink is my way to cope. Each time the needle punctures my skin, a little of the pain subsides. Not only that, but I like it. It's my body. You don't tell an artist how to paint his canvas. You can understand or you can fight me on it, but either way the results stay the same."

All of the anger I held before dissipates. He's right. I learned this with Breyson trying to tell me to change my Halloween costume. I had forgotten how much pain he has from Sophia. Now that I have Breyson, it's easier to understand than before. "I know. I'm sorry. It all just caught me off guard. I do understand, though, more so now than I did before. I wish I could take away the pain."

He pulls back and looks me in the eyes, the hint of a smirk present. "You always were the martyr, weren't you? Everyone has to face pain at some point, Sis. The key is to not let it destroy you."

His serious demeanor turns into a smile. "And besides, you don't have much room to talk. I got wind you went and got some ink of your own. I can't believe you did it without me. If I wasn't so excited to see that you permanently marked that virgin skin, I'd be mad. Let me see."

Ha! Virgin no longer applies to me, but for Breyson's safety, I'll keep that to myself. I pull the hem of my tunic up and the band of my leggings down just enough to reveal my tattoo. I wanted it in a place that was easy to cover if necessary.

He glances at it, reading the script that forms the heart, and crosses his arms over his chest as he looks back at me, a grin on his face. "You fell in love, didn't you?"

I don't even have to answer, because I can tell my face is blood red. "I'll be damned. I was starting to think I'd never see the day your stubborn ass fell in love. At least someone chiseled his way through that wall you had up. I'll have to commend him at the same time I threaten his life should he not treat you right," he says teasingly, and I slap his upper arm playfully.

"Shut up," I say, laughing. "Let me see all this hidden ink. I still can't believe you got a tongue ring."

He removes his shirt. "It serves a purpose." He winks after he says it.

"Ew. You're so gross! That was more information than I ever want to hear come out of your mouth." He holds his shirt crinkled in the fist of his hand. A look of vulnerability flashes across his face when I look him over. Maybe because we've always been so close and told each other everything, but this is something new. I never liked tattoos before I saw Breyson's, but looking at Konnor's allows me to see it in a new light. It looks like intricate artwork. Every piece is different, yet it's a collaboration too, all meant to work together.

He has a small piece of script under his left pectoral—trust. To most it's just a single word, but to him that one word means so much, because one person can destroy it forever.

He has one sleeve so far. The elaborate detail and variations of color is unbelievable. His tattoo artist has a lot of talent. "They look so real," I whisper in amazement.

"I take it you approve," he says, as I look each one over.

"Yeah, strangely, I do. They're beautiful. Let's go before Adalynn thinks we've been kidnapped. You can make yourself useful and help us take the presents downstairs to the tree," I say jokingly, bumping his shoulder with mine.

He puts his shirt back on and wraps his arm around the back of my shoulders, jerking me against his side. "She's a hot one."

"Don't even think about it. She's taken."

"Bummer," he says, before pulling me toward the door. It's going to take some getting used to this version of him . . .

TWENTY-FOUR

Kinzleigh

Adalynn excused herself thirty minutes after we finished arranging the presents at the bottom of the tree. She said something about meeting up with Braxton, but I know she's giving me and Konnor space to hang out since it's been a while.

"Want some hot cocoa? I made Grams' special mix." Every Christmas Grams was alive she made us hot cocoa from a mix she put together each year. She made them for Christmas gifts for distant friends also. Making it is fairly easy. You pour the different dry ingredients in the container of your choice and it comes out looking like one of the sand art things where each section is a different color.

She would always use the big glass jars for her Christmas gifts and top it off with small marshmallows. Between the flat lid and the screw on band, she added a cut square of decorative fabric and would then tie the directions around the neck of the jar with festive ribbon. She made many jar-filled boxes every year. She always believed everyone should have a Christmas gift, even if it's just something homemade.

To date, it's still the best hot chocolate I've ever had. I memorized the recipe the last Christmas she was with us. She had been sick for a long time and the cancer was finally consuming her. She was in so much pain and I knew that Christmas would be her last, even though I tried to deny it.

"You know I do. Who turns down Grams' hot chocolate? It wouldn't be Christmas without it. While you're doing that, I'm going to take my bag to my room," Konnor says, veering in a different direction.

Turning, I walk to the kitchen to make that special blend I've waited for all year. Placing the kettle of water on the cook top to warm it up, I turn on the eye. Two lanky arms snake around my neck and rest on top of my shoulders, a set of hands covering my eyes. "Did you miss me?"

Her voice comes out smooth as honey. Presley. Yes. I've missed my best friend. Turning the temperature to low, I turn around to face her.

What I didn't expect was for her to look the way she does. "Who are you and what have you done with my best friend?" She is drop-dead gorgeous. There is no other way to describe it.

Her hair looks a little darker—more of an espresso than a chocolate, falling to her breasts in big bouncy curls made from a curling rod. It's shinier than normal; making it obvious she got a gloss recently.

Her skin looks creamy like a porcelain doll, but not pale. She's wearing just enough eye shadow in colors of bronze and beige and gold to accentuate those big hypnotizing blue eyes and her lips are stained with a dark red lipstick instead of her usual pink.

Her low-cut sweater is the color of caramel, and her dark, tight designer jeans disappear into her UGG boots that match her sweater in color. She smells amazing.

She doesn't look like an eighteen-year-old. She looks like a woman. That brings me to wonder why. "What do you mean, sweetie? I look like I always do."

I raise my brow and point the spoon I'm holding in her direction. "Do I look like an idiot to you? You come in here smoking hot, and well beyond your normal beauty queen getup. This screams boy impression. Is there something you need to tell me?"

"Kinzleigh, where is that hot chocolate? Make an extra cup." Konnor walks in the kitchen with Preston close behind, but stops as soon as he sees Presley, causing Preston to rear end him.

"Dude! What the hell?" Preston tries to recover by stepping back.

"Presley." His lips are now pursed and his jaw steels, as if he's getting . . . angry?

"Konnor. It's good to see you. How have you been?" As Presley speaks, I turn to look at her. Her face says it all. I've never seen Presley with a longing look in her eyes, but right now she has it bad. She's never pined after a guy. She doesn't have to. She could have any guy she wants. Well, except for one.

"You look good. I guess you're eighteen now." He says it like that very sentence means everything. Say what? I turn to him eying her body, one part at a time. If it were possible to light someone on fire with a look, this would be it.

Am I missing something? Has he been waiting on her to turn eighteen? Are the feelings mutual and they just won't admit it? We've always been friends—all four of us. I have noticed him look her way a few times since she hit puberty, but right now he looks mad at clearly being attracted to her.

This is getting awkward. Konnor and Presley have never acted this way around each other. All I can do is look back and forth between them as they have some kind of stare off. Then I glance at Preston, who's wearing a smirk as if this isn't weird to him at all. "Yes. My birthday was in November. I never heard from you."

It just dawned on me like something hit me over the head. *Duh, Kinzleigh. You are such an idiot!* That's why she looks the way she does. Konnor is here.

Okay, well, we can't all just stand here. "Konnor, will you show Presley to the guest room across the hall from your room?"

Maybe they just need to talk it out. If this is about the stupid promise we made when we were kids, Konnor and I need to have a talk. He takes things way too seriously. If they like each other, they should explore the possibilities. No one would be better for Konnor than Presley. She has been in love with him since we were kids. I'm pretty naïve as far as all that goes, and even I picked up on it years ago.

"Sure," he says, and nods his head at the door, instructing her to follow.

As soon as they are out the door, I turn to Preston. "Is it me or was that a little too intense?"

He smiles, and I see the old Preston coming through, which makes me happy, because I was worried how this trip would go otherwise. I'm not sure if Breyson is going to be upset he's staying here, but he will just have to trust me. "Those two have some serious pent-up attraction for each other. It's been there forever. I don't know why they won't act on it. Everyone can see it but them."

At least I'm not the only one that notices it . . .

The kettle whistles, instructing me the water is hot. I remove it and pour it into the several mugs lined up on the counter I've already filled with the mix. Giving each a good stir, I hold out a mug to Preston and place the others on a tray to carry to the living room. I can hear Mom, Dad, and Presley's parents on the patio laughing and carrying on. "You up for a Christmas movie? Your choice."

"Only if you have *Home Alone*," he says, sipping his cocoa with a smile. "The original. None of that two and three shit."

"I should have known," I say, rolling my eyes. "You're so predictable." I throw a marshmallow, hitting him on the nose, and it bounces off into the mug, hitting the hot chocolate with a small splash, sending droplets of cocoa on his face. I splay my hand across my mouth, trying to hold in the laughter, but fail at the look of surprise on his face.

He sits his mug down. "You think that's funny, huh?" He steps toward me. I can tell he's plotting. What, I'm not sure. I back up and he plunges and grabs me, knocking me to the ground between his legs. "You want to know what happens when you challenge me? I retaliate."

He tickles me on the ribs, his fingers digging in. There is one way to make me cave and that's to tickle me. I hate to be tickled, because usually, the tickler is stronger than me and I can't get away. Konnor used to tickle me all the time when we were kids to get what he wanted.

I laugh and squirm, attempting to break free. I'm laughing so hard I can't breathe. I find an opening and bear crawl out of his hold to take off running through the house. I can hear him at my heels. I turn around to see how close. At the exact moment I look back, I run into something hard, falling backward on the hardwood floor, injuring my tailbone. "Ouch! That freaking hurt."

Preston comes to a screeching halt.

"What's going on, Kinzleigh?" When I realize it's not Preston, but Breyson, I look up. The expression marring his face makes me want to crawl in a hole and hide. He looks angry. And I don't mean like the night I fought back about the costume where he knew he ticked me off first, so when it came to Simon, his anger had dulled by his panic to fix our fight. This is pure hatred kind of anger.

He is staring daggers at Preston, but speaking to me. He works his jaw back and forth, a look to kill that's hard to miss. It's no secret he's not Preston's biggest fan. I don't know if he feels threatened by him or what, due to the fact that Preston and I have family history. "We were all four about to watch a Christmas movie in the living room. I was making the hot cocoa and we were just goofing off while waiting on Presley and Konnor to come back down. What are you doing here? I thought you couldn't come over tonight."

By the narrowing of his eyes and the deep expansion of his chest, I'm going to assume that was the wrong question to ask. He looks down at me. "If you would answer your phone you would know the plans changed."

This probably doesn't look good to an outsider. I know it's harmless and Preston knows it's harmless, because we've all four been close since we were born basically. There are no phases of my life that Preston and Presley aren't in—memories in abundance—but I could see how this might look bad to said boyfriend with jealousy issues.

"Sorry, my phone is in my room charging. I wasn't expecting to talk to you for a while. So . . . you get to stay after all?" I give him a fake cheesy grin as I stand to my feet, hoping to calm him down.

"He staying?" Well crap, it didn't work.

He's back to staring at Preston. I have a little bit of Déjà Vu going on from the pool party at Ryland's Jeep. "Of course he's staying here. Where else would he stay? He's like family."

"And right across from Kinzleigh's room. . . in case I get scared." I jerk my head in Preston's direction. He is grinning from ear to ear.

"Do you have to instigate him?! Jeez, Preston, do you want to die? Go put on the movie and we'll be there in a minute." I'm aggravated by his lack of maturity. He's the oldest one here and supposed to be the most mature, but he's acting like a child. Breyson is twice his size. He must be stupid, because Preston has never played a sport a day in his life. He only has muscle because he works out to keep up his sexy-boy image.

"Just thought he should know if he screws up, there is always someone waiting to take his place. Right. Across. The. Hall." He winks, but it's to be sarcastic. As he walks past Breyson, he shoves into him with his shoulder.

Breyson turns and pushes him from behind. "Breyson, stop! Do you want my dad to make you leave while they're here? They've been friends since before we were born. They're our guests. They won't be the ones to leave."

He stops as he processes the words coming out of my mouth. "Watch your back, asshole. No one messes with me and mine," he calls out in a harsh tone to Preston's retreating form.

"She's fair game until there's a ring on her left ring finger proving she's yours. You might want to remember that. Until then, she can always change her mind." When the last word exits Preston's mouth, he vanishes from the room.

Guys are exhausting. We're supposed to be in the Christmas spirit, not fighting. We have two weeks together and we're already off to a bad start. Presley and her family will be here until right after New Year's.

Breyson tenses, staring off in the direction Preston just went. "Why do you let him get to you? You know he's just trying to ruffle your feathers, and you let him win every time."

"He wants you. Do you not get that? How am I supposed to sleep for two weeks knowing he's across the hall half naked? How would you feel if you were in my shoes?" His voice is so soft, as if this is really bothering him. He won't even look at me.

"It doesn't matter what he wants, Breyson. He will never get it as long as I'm with you. Out of all the years I've known Preston, nothing has ever happened between us. If I wanted him things would have happened well before you came along . . . but it didn't. There is nothing for you to worry about." I wrap my arms around his waist from behind, resting my cheek against his back, feeling it expand with every breath.

I slip my hand beneath his shirt, knowing it'll make him relax. "I want you. My heart only belongs to one person. Stop worrying about every guy that may or may not have an adolescent crush on me. If my heart wants you there is no reason to give someone else a chance."

He turns around to face me and all the lines previously present from worry have disappeared. He wraps his arms around me. "I'm sorry. He makes me fucking crazy. I love you, Kinzleigh. I don't like people threatening our relationship, and it feels like someone constantly is. I'm continuously playing defense with us. I don't want some guy to come and steal you away from me. In my mind, he'll always be the one with the advantage, because he's known you longer. He has a part of you I never will—the past. It probably sounds stupid. Don't hold it against me."

I smile. He makes me feel special in ways he'll never understand. He makes me feel irreplaceable. "I won't. But that's never going to happen. Someone has to be unhappy to be stolen, and that's not the case with us. You make me happy. He may have my 'past' as you say, which he doesn't, not really. We never were anything other than friends. But you have my present and my future, and those are the only two that matter. I love *you*, Breyson, and no one else."

He kisses me, and finally smiles. "Okay. I'm not going to lie, I still don't like the fact that he's sleeping across from your room, but I trust you, even if I don't trust him. For you I'll try to deal with it. I don't want to drive a wedge in our relationship over something I can't control."

"That's why I love you—you trust me. We trust each other. There will always be a Natalie, a Simon, or a Preston in every relationship. We can't let it destroy our relationship. Now let's go watch some Christmas movies and drink cocoa." I rub my palm up his muscular stomach. "Maybe later we can sneak away and I'll show you just how much I love you."

The corners of his lips crawl toward his eyes. "That kind of ending I like."

For the first time since Grams died, I think I'm going to enjoy the holidays. I'm content with my life. Cheerleading is taking off, I have new friends as well as my old, and I have a great guy by my side that loves me.

Living with love in your heart isn't as bad as I once thought it would be. Maybe I can actually have love and happiness working together instead of against each other.

TWENTY-FIVE

A wave of excitement surges through my body and my eyes pop open. Christmas morning. I scratch off the sleep crust from the corners of my eyes and rub my hands over my face. *Christmas.* It finally occurs to me, and a smile spreads across my face.

Sitting up, I scratch through my matted hair and turn to place my feet on the floor. I press the home button on my iPhone for the time—five thirty. This happens to me every year, regardless of how late I stay up. My internal clock springs to life at the butt-crack of dawn on Christmas, so why should this year be any different? Oh . . . maybe because I'm eighteen and no longer a kid waiting on Santa!

Still, happiness and joy run through my veins. A side effect of Christmas.

I walk into my bathroom to wash my face and brush my teeth, before going in search of someone else with an overactive body clock. I open the door, bringing in the holiday spirit with my *Grinch* pajama pants and green tank, taking in the silence on the other side.

I bought the girls in the house matching pajamas. Trying to make the boys wear the matching reindeer pajamas I got them wasn't an easy task, but in the end, whining about making family memories prevailed. Luckily, daughters control daddies and daddies control sons. And I may have sworn to keep the photos off social media for mine and Presley's dads to agree.

I gave Konnor and Preston the tongue when they started whining about being less masculine should they wear anything with cartoon characters on them. When we take Christmas pictures I want us to look festive.

I stick my head out into the dark, quiet hall. I sigh. Guess I'm the only one awake, much to my disappointment. I may as well cook everyone breakfast if I'm going to be up this early. I walk down the hall to see if Presley is awake to keep me company in the wee hours of the morning. Usually, Presley is the early bird of the two. And if not, I'm prepared to wake her.

I walk up to her closed door and turn the doorknob quietly to ensure I don't wake anyone else in the house. It's still dark outside, so no light is coming through the window.

I stick my head through the crack and over the threshold. I spy movement, but I can't tell if she is awake or not. Opening the door wider, I tiptoe closer to the bed. I come to a stop when I get to the side, eyes widening now that my vision has adjusted to the dark again. Oh, my God. What, when, how plagues my mind. So many questions. A lot of confusion. So much scarring of my poor, innocent brain.

Konnor is lying in her bed in all his tattooed, naked glory, because the blankets have fallen off the end of the bed. Someone must have gotten wild last night. Seriously, does he have no respect for our parents? Or fear of Presley's dad? I've known the man all my life and he still intimidates me. Control. He operates on a lot of control. How else does one become as rich as him? Konnor could have at least put his clothes back on after, so if either of our parents walked in he could make something up about watching a movie and falling asleep. This—not good.

Presley—also naked—has her leg thrown over his manhood and her arm across his stomach. I press my palms together in prayer, silently thanking the stars he's covered. I don't think I can handle seeing my brother's sex tool. Some things you can't move past and that would be one. Instead, I get to look at Presley's rump since she's wrapped around his body with her head lying on his chest.

Why are you still standing here? Stop being creepy. How are you going to explain this if they wake up and see you standing over the bed staring? You don't want voyeur status.

Presley moves her leg, stirring in her sleep.

Please, stop moving. I'm sorry. I'll leave. Please don't show me any private parts.

I slowly and quietly back up toward the door. Once I get the door open after fumbling around for the knob in the dark, I pass through a crack only big enough for my body to fit. As I pull the door to, more stirring occurs, and then moaning starts. They cannot be serious! Thank God our parents' rooms are downstairs! They don't come up here, and maybe that's what they're banking on.

I'm thankful it's almost pitch-black in the room and hall, so they can't see the door. Putting my hand over my mouth to avoid being heard, I turn the knob as quietly as a mouse, until it's aligned with the frame, and I release the doorknob. The bed makes a ruckus and I run on my toes until I'm back in the safety of my room.

When I get inside, I quietly close my door and turn around. Preston is standing by my bed with his arms crossed over his bare chest. Startled, I fall into the door, throwing my hand over my chest. "Crap, Preston, what are you doing in here?"

"I could ask you the same," he says with a knowing smile on his face. He caught me doing something I didn't want to be caught doing. His hair is mussed, standing all over his head, and he's shirtless, wearing only his black reindeer pajama pants. "You're being shady. What are you running from?"

Should I tell him? It's kind of private. Oh, what the heck . . . If I'm going to be scarred after seeing that, then someone else should be too. "I. Just. Found." I inhale a hard breath between each word, attempting to catch my breath from trying not to get caught.

"You found what? Spit it out, woman. You're starting to worry me." He laces his hands on top of his head, making his muscles flex. Couldn't the boy have put a shirt on before he came in here? I'd be lying to deny that he's attractive. He's just not as hot as Breyson, but that could be based on the fact that I'm in love with him. It's a biased opinion. Still, love someone or not, it's human nature to look.

I hold up my index finger, signaling to give me a minute while I even my breathing out. "I woke up early, so I was planning to cook breakfast, but decided to go to Presley's room to see if she was awake and wanted to help."

I pause, dreading the return of this vision.

"Go on. I'm starting to get old here," he teases.

"Oh, shut up." I laugh. "Presley was . . . Well, Konnor was . . . They were naked! I was standing at the side of the bed, looking down at her body draped over his and the covers were on the floor. I couldn't believe what I was seeing, so I just stood there, and then they started stirring, so I hurried from the room. As I was trying to leave unnoticed, they started waking up for round . . . I don't even know what round it was!" I'm talking fast and rambling to the point that I can't breathe.

In the meantime, Preston is tightening his lips together, trying to muffle his laughter. "Why are you so calm? This is not funny! Our parents could walk in and then what is your dad going to do? I love my brother. I want him to live. You're her older brother. Don't you want to beat him up or something? For . . . you know. I can't even say it. But shouldn't you be mad? How do you know he's *not* deflowering your little sister?"

He walks over to me and grabs me by the shoulders, steering me toward the bed, and then pushes me into a sitting position on the edge. "A few things . . . For one, this has been building all week. I'm surprised they waited this long. Two, don't you think it'd be a little hypocritical for me to get mad at him for sleeping with my sister when I would sleep with his? He's not some random asshole. He's Konnor. There's a mutual family trust there. Three, Presley was *deflowered*—if that's what you want to call it—a long time ago. She's been with a lot worse. I don't like it, but it's her life. I'm not that kind of asshole. Someone hurts her I'll kill him, but when it's consensual I'm staying out of it."

He looks at me, his laughter no longer present. "And lastly, if I had to handpick someone for her to sleep with, it would be Konnor. He's one of my best friends and I know he's a good guy, regardless of how much he's hurting right now. He may not be ready for a relationship, which will hurt Presley, but she went into this warned. I talked to her after seeing them in the kitchen the day we got here. She chose to lay in his bed, or let him in hers, so she will have to deal with the repercussions, whatever that entails."

I stare off into space. He does make good points, but still, he doesn't have to be so calm. I as much as anyone know they would be good for each other, but that still doesn't make it easy to witness. "If you had seen what I saw, you wouldn't be this calm. They could have done it somewhere else! Do you really want to see your sister naked?"

He gives me with a look of disgust. "Hell no! Why would I want to see that shit?"

"Precisely, which is why you *can* be calm right now! I was this close," I say, holding my fingers apart to show a centimeter, before continuing, "to seeing his huh-huh. I had no forewarning of what I was walking into."

He bites his bottom lip, a smile on his face, and his brows dip between his eyes. "His huh-huh? Is that what you're calling it these days? Can you even say it, Kinzleigh? Or is that word too dirty for your vocabulary?"

What difference does it make what I call it? He's missing my entire point. "Yes. For your information, I can say it, I just choose not to."

"Say it and I'll leave you alone. I want to hear something dirty come out of your mouth. I need to know you have it in you." He moves closer to me, and suddenly, I remember that it's just the two of us in here . . . alone. I promised Breyson I wouldn't allow him in here without someone else present.

Holding out my hands, they slam against his chest, signifying he's way too close. "Come on, dirty boy. You can help me make breakfast. I don't feel like humoring your weird fantasy today. I reserve that for special occasions." I smile and turn to walk out of my bedroom, not checking to see if he's following behind me. Sheesh, what a morning, and the day has barely begun . . .

After consuming a large portion of scrambled eggs, toast, and ham, I finish off my juice and we all make our way to the Christmas tree for presents. I won't see Breyson until later today, since he is with his family as well.

I take a seat on the couch. Preston, Presley, and Konnor sit as well. Konnor and Presley keep eying each other as if they didn't finish getting each other out of their systems. They haven't been out of the bedroom more than half an hour or so.

Breyson and I can't be that bad. Can we? Surely not . . . no way. I am convinced we are not near that bad. I wonder where they are going to go from here. The way Presley keeps looking at him, there is no going back to the way they were. She looks like a girl in love. The kind of love you don't recover from. I hope he doesn't hurt her. I can't read him anymore. He looks completely void of any feeling. That scares me. He was always the passionate one. I really hope he hasn't become numb to emotions because of Sophia.

I'll have to focus on that later. I trust he won't hurt someone that is so important to not only us, but to Mom and Dad too. It's Christmas! And there are tons of presents under that tree, just waiting to be opened . . .

Christmas morning with my family has come and gone so fast. Wrapping paper is littered all over the floor and everyone is looking at everything they got. I need to shower and load everything in my car to go to Breyson's house.

My parents invited him here this morning to participate in the festivities, but today was a rare occasion at least once of his parents wasn't working at the hospital on a holiday, so he had to spend Christmas morning with them. He tried to convince me he was picking me up, but I have to stand my ground somewhere. My poor car is going to hate me if I don't drive it at least a couple times a week.

I walk to my closet in search of the perfect outfit, quickly settling on something that complements my hair and skin. I take it out to lay it out on my bed, ready to shower. Hot water is calling. I have too much to do and not much time to do it in. I want as much time with Breyson as I can get, and with guests, I'm already having to split my time.

I step out of the shower, steam enveloping me, scents of vanilla and spice to go with the holiday season swarming the room. Every inch of skin is smooth from a fresh shave. I go in search of my lotion when I see Presley sitting on my bed crying. Crying—something Presley doesn't do very often. And if I had to guess, it has something to do with Konnor. I clench my towel at my front, ensuring I'm covered. "Are you okay?"

She shakes her head and wipes underneath her eyes as the tears fall in a thick curtain down her face. I have never seen her cry like this. Tucking one side of the towel over the other to hold it on like a dress, I sit on the edge of the bed beside her and place my arm around her, resting my hand on the side of her head. I pull her toward me to rest it on my shoulder. "Tell me what's wrong."

She sniffles. "Kinzleigh, I'm sorry. I should go. I'm probably keeping you from Breyson. It's Christmas. I'm a stupid girl."

She is rambling and still crying. "Presley, shut up. You're my best friend. Breyson can wait. We're just opening presents. We have plenty of time for that. I see him daily. I don't see you much anymore. Tell me what's wrong. You're scaring me."

My shoulder is wet from her tears. "I made a mistake, Kinz. I don't know what to do. I couldn't help myself. In the moment I let my heart decide over my brain. I've ruined everything."

I exhale, knowing exactly what she's referring to. "Is this about Konnor?"

She nods and lifts her head. "How'd you know?"

Well, this is going to be a little embarrassing to admit. "I walked in your room this morning. I went to see if you were up, and because I didn't expect him to be there, I didn't knock. I managed to slip out when you two were starting another round," I say, embarrassed.

"I see. I screwed up. What have I done, Kinzleigh? I can't take it back. He doesn't want the same things I do. He said it was just sex. I said I could handle it. I've always been able to handle it. This shouldn't be different, but it is. I love him. I've loved him since I was a little kid, but to him I've always just been the best friend. He's everything I've ever wanted. And now that he finally noticed me, he's broken and damaged because of that stupid tramp. I swear I want to kill her."

"How do you know he doesn't want the same thing? You're not making sense. Just start from the beginning. I know Konnor better than anyone. Let me be the judge."

She blows out a breath, clearly gathering her thoughts. "The day we arrived, and he showed me my room, we were having casual small talk. Without thinking he kissed me on the cheek. He's done it a few times over the years, but this time it lingered, like he was considering what it'd be like to actually kiss me. Then, all of a sudden, he was apologizing and saying he shouldn't have done it. It hurt, but I understood. It didn't stop, though. The flirting and glances have been getting more frequent all week. Long story short, last night he wanted to watch a movie. I tried not to get excited. I really did. I couldn't help it, though, because he chose me to hang out with instead of waking up Preston."

She pauses briefly before continuing. "I'll admit, I started it by dropping my towel. He came to the bathroom as I was getting out of the shower. Then he followed me to my room . . . where my clothes were. At first it was innocent fun. I wanted to see his reaction, but the way he was looking at me changed everything. He commented on my body. Tension was thick. Then I put my clothes on. I wasn't expecting for it to go anywhere. He pulled me on his lap when the lights went out. Reaction became reflex. I got lost in the moment and things heated quickly. We kissed. Clothes came off. We hooked up. It escalated. Before either of us could really think of what we were *doing* it was already happening. Then it occurred to me that something I've wanted for years was happening, and I couldn't stop. I thought it would be fine, because we both know I'm not a virgin and certainly no saint. Casual sex is the only kind of sex I have."

She lowers her voice. "Something was different, though, Kinzleigh. With him, it was beautiful. It was hot. It was the greatest night of my existence. We connected on every possible level. He said things that don't get brought up during one-night stands. Things that are part of our history. I know he has to feel something too. We had sex three times. Each time it was different, but the second he left that room it was as if it never happened. He hasn't spoken to me since. He only looks at me briefly. When you came upstairs he left."

"Where did he go?"

She shrugs her shoulders. Her eyes are so blurred with tears it looks like a wall of water. Her blue eyes don't hold the sparkle they usually do. They look dull and jaded. Everyone that knows Presley knows she is a beautiful soul. Her personality is bubbly and spontaneous. She's carefree. She doesn't let anyone bring her down. She is one of the strongest people I know.

Presley can hide and show her emotions better than anyone. She keeps her feelings completely hidden unless she wants someone to see them, and then like a light switch turning on, you have a clear view of her inner self.

Those she trusts enough to see her for who she truly is are forever hooked. Girls want to be her friend and guys want her in any way they can have her. If I compared her to an object it would be a diamond: strong, luminescent, and rare. Seeing her broken over someone else makes me want to hurt him, my brother or not.

Her lips are quivering, and she isn't wearing a speck of makeup, which is rare for her. "I can't go back to just being his friend and loving him from afar. It would kill me to see him with someone else now. I love him so much. I will never love anyone else. I've tried, and that was before we kissed, had sex, and gave in to this thing that's been building for years. What do I do? I thought things would be better this morning than last night, but instead, they're worse. He's avoiding me."

I can usually pinpoint what Konnor is thinking, but since the breakup after Sophia cheated on him, he's unpredictable. I don't know who he's trying to protect—himself from more pain or her because he has trust issues.

I thought I'd have an answer, but I don't. "I don't know, Presley. Konnor is different now. You've seen the tattoos and piercings. Give me a few days to feel him out. Maybe I can talk to him and see what's going on in his head. You still have a week and the New Year's Eve party. I don't think you should let him go back to school without telling him how you feel, though. Maybe he's as confused as you are and trying to sort out his emotions. Konnor is the type of person that won't discuss an issue until he has it worked out in his head. Play it cool for a few days and see if it sorts itself out. If not, you need to talk to him at the party. It's a masked ball, so there will be plenty of time."

She nods and stands up. Standing with her, I give her a hug. "I hope I don't lose him, Kinzleigh. My heart will never be the same."

I hope they work it out, because I know exactly how she feels. Only time will tell . . .

TWENTY-SIX

Breyson

I look down at my watch impatiently. Where is she? She should have been here by now. My parents want her to open the gifts from them and then I have to take her to Pops' to show her the surprise that is waiting on her.

I don't see her coming up the drive. I pace the floor anxiously. I pull out my phone again for the fifteenth time in ten minutes with no texts and no missed calls. She should have been here thirty minutes ago. I've been waiting for today for what seems like a year. Her horse has been at Pops' for a week now.

I'm about to call her when I hear a car pull up in the driveway. Looking through the window, her black Range Rover comes to a stop. Finally. Next time I'm picking her up like I said I was going to do to start with. Girls' fashionably late nonsense is crap.

Making my way through the house, I meet her at the door with an armload of bags and wrapped boxes. "Hi," she says, as I open the door.

"Hi . . ." She looks beautiful; not that there's ever been a time she didn't blow me away. The girl got the best of everything in the gene pool. Those tight jeans make her ass especially grabbable. The brown leather riding boots hug her calves perfectly. Her bright red sweater conforms to her rack in a way that makes me want to take it off. Her hair is pulled to the side in the big curls I love. Beautiful. My girl. ". . . I was starting to think you were going to stand me up."

She crinkles her face like she is about to give me attitude. "Do you really think I would stand you up?"

"Nah, I guess not." I kiss her on the cheek, then on the lips. I've missed kissing her. We haven't had much alone time this week with her house being invaded by everyone, especially one I'd love to throw out on his ass. My jealousy over him being in the same house with the hottest girl on the planet overnight, knowing he wants her, is out of control.

She kisses me back with the same hunger and then breaks free, her lips now red from my assault. I guess I missed her more than I thought. "Babe, you know I could stand here and kiss you all day, but these presents are getting heavy."

"Shit, baby, I'm sorry. Give them to me. I didn't mean to be rude. I've just missed you." I take them from her hands and lead her into the living room where the tree is. She must have bought a present for everyone. I told her not to, but it doesn't surprise me that she did anyway. I'm ready to get this over with, so we can go.

"Mom, Dad, Kinzleigh's here," I shout across the house as I sit the presents down in front of the tree. Turning back to her, I pull her into my arms. "My brothers and sister aren't here right now, so you'll have to watch them open theirs later. Is that okay?"

"Sure, babe. I'm more excited about watching you open yours anyway." Her smile is weakening when she is excited about something. It's full force, revealing those bright white teeth, and thins her pouty lips, making me wonder what on earth she got me.

"Oh yeah? What'd you get me?" I can't keep my lips off of her. It's been too long since we've had private time. Every hormone in my body is out of control. One other part does not like the absence of her either. We've been having sex off and on for months. Some spans of time more than others, depending on schedules, parents, and when we can find a place alone since we both live at home, but regardless of how many times we have, I can't get enough.

"You'll never get it out of me. Presents are my favorite part. I love watching people open them, so I won't ruin the surprise. The only thing I'll tell you is I'm saving the best one for last. Since you have to take me somewhere for one of my presents, I'll give one of mine then." We need to get this show on the road. There is no way her present will top what I have waiting in that stall.

At the sound of footsteps walking across the floor, I pull her toward the couch. "Let's get started then . . ."

It took forever to open all of the presents, but it could have something to do with this rare amount of pent-up excitement I have. Before her nothing ever excited me this much. I don't know how to release it in increments.

My mother has a talent in shopping for a teenage girl apparently, because Kinzleigh got so much stuff, and every single thing she fell in love with. I was starting to get nervous she'd be over it by the time she got to mine. Mom loves the holidays, and the number of presents each person got confirms it.

Kinzleigh is surrounded and covered by things that range from purses to clothes and shoes to gift cards and more, between my parents and me. That wasn't their big gift, though, according to mom. "Brooks and I have one last gift. This one is for you and Breyson together, so he doesn't even know about this. It's part of your graduation present too," she says as she picks up a wrapped box behind dad's recliner.

Mom is grinning from ear to ear. I'm wondering what she could have gotten us that would have to be included as Christmas and graduation. That's extreme.

She sits the package down between me and Kinzleigh. It doesn't look that big. "You take one side and I take the other?" She nods and we both take a corner.

Once we get the wrapping paper completely torn away, the box underneath is just a cardboard shipping box. She really didn't want to give anything away I take it.

Reaching in my pocket, I pull out my pocketknife and fling open the blade. Point down I slide it along the tape line, slicing it open. Once the seal is broken, I close the knife and put it away.

Together we open the flaps to the box and look inside. There are two airline tickets and a confirmation for a three-room condo with everything all-inclusive, booked through their travel agent. Alongside it are two American Express gift cards with a note.

Breyson and Kinzleigh,

With the six of you about to go to college, and possibly different colleges at that, Brooks and I thought you all would like to take a trip together over the summer—a break from one school before starting another. We booked a fourteen-day stay for each of you to share a condo in the Florida Keys as you take a leap into adulthood and transition from high school to college. We love you all and are very proud of each and every one of you. The details are enclosed. The cards are to get everything you need prior to leaving. Use it on whatever you want. It is part of the gift. Each card is loaded with one thousand dollars. Cash for spending will be dispersed on the day of graduation, so do not keep the cards for the trip. This is something we chose to do. Merry Christmas and happy graduation! Thirteen years in the making. You've all earned it.

With love,

Mom and Dad

I don't know what to say. I'm speechless. Never in a million years would I have thought they would send the six of us on an all-expense paid vacation. My brothers and me, yes, but allowing and paying for our girlfriends to come too—unexpected. Not that Kinzleigh's parents are lacking financially, but the thought of them caring that much makes me forever indebted to them.

I go to stand and Kinzleigh beats me to it in a full on run toward my parents. She hugs my mom first, and based on the closeness, I can tell it's a genuine hug. Mom looks at me over Kinzleigh's shoulder and winks with a loving smile. I mouth, *thank you,* and make my way to hug them myself as she moves to my dad.

"I don't know what to say other than thank you. I'm overwhelmed with gratitude. You are amazing parents and I'm so fortunate to know you both, thanks to Breyson." I thought she was going to give my dad a sideways awkward hug, but I was wrong. She's hugging him the way I've seen her hug her own dad.

"You're welcome. Just keep that boy of mine happy and in line," he says in a low voice, but still loud enough for me to hear.

Knowing my parents love her as much as I do makes me ecstatic. So many guys have to deal with his girlfriend's parents hating him or vice versa, and I have been blessed to be excluded from that group.

My parents love her and hers love me, as well as getting along with each other. It gives me so much hope that this is just the beginning of an epic adventure. I hope the journey we're about to embark on is long and ends with forever, because she is the only heroine I want in my story.

TWENTY-SEVEN

Breyson

We pull up at Pops' ranch. I look over at her wearing one of those sleep masks I borrowed from my sister's room. Before we left the house, I made her put it on, so she wouldn't know where we were going until we got here. It's too easy to put two and two together.

As the truck comes to a halt and I shut down the engine, she looks over at me. Well, technically she turns her head. Her eyes are covered, and it makes me laugh. "Can I take this thing off now? You're lucky I don't get carsick. I won't take advantage of my sight after this ride. Not being able to see is brutal."

"Not a chance. I'll be the one to take things off of you, beautiful—on all counts. I'm coming around to get you. Don't you dare take off that mask. If you do there will be consequences. Understood?" Her face turns the color of crimson and she nods.

I still have to thank Adalynn for the time we've had since her little dirty dream. Who would have known underneath all that innocence is a little kink in the bed? We have tried a few things, but nothing major yet. Kind of hard when you're always looking over your shoulder during sex trying not to get caught. I have been researching, though, and have plans in the near future.

I still prefer making love to her, since I was never into that before, but

I would be worried I had lost my balls if I said I didn't enjoy the wild stuff too. By doing things with her I've never done with other girls, it makes me feel like I can give her something in return for her giving her virginity to me.

I've had wild sex—wild in the mind of a teenager anyway—because I was never interested in sweet stuff before her, but my imagination of wild then and the wild I'm discovering with her are two totally different things.

Teenagers don't know what they are doing in sex most of the time. Teenage boys only care about two things—where can I stick it until I come, and how many girls will let me stick it in. I can say that, because I was one of them, but not anymore. It's all about her. Now it's time to become adults, leaving all the other stuff behind.

Pulling open the door, I lift her out and carry her to the barn. "Breyson, I can walk. I'm not helpless. I already promised not to peek."

I kiss her on the lips to shush her. It always works when she starts rambling. The truth is, I like to do things for her. I like to spoil her. I just have to override her independence to do it.

Taking note of the small present she's holding in her hand for me, relief washes over me that it is nothing compared to what I got her. She already got me way too much stuff. I told her one gift, but she doesn't listen to a damn thing I say half the time. If I didn't love her so much she would drive me insane.

Setting her down on her feet in front of the stall, I turn to Hendrix and place my index finger over my lips for him to be quiet. It may sound crazy, but I would bet on anything the horse knows what I mean. He remains quiet, instead of his usual greeting of excitement when he sees me.

I place my thumb underneath the edge of the mask over her cheek and place my lips just outside her ear. "Merry Christmas, baby."

I remove the mask, and when she sees it she gasps. "Breyson!"

She squeals, and without notice tears begin streaming down her face. "It's beautiful! Oh, my gosh, it's too much!" Turning in my arms, she wraps her arms around my middle, squeezing me so hard I can barely breathe. And then she starts jumping, trying to take me with her, but I'm too heavy.

"She's yours. Now we can ride together." I will never tell her how much I spent on this horse, because she would probably kill me, bring me back to life, and kill me again. She's a solid black Arabian horse. Her coat looks like spun silk. "Look at her. Name her. Bond with her. We will ride in a bit after I show you your saddle."

"She's stunning, Breyson. What kind of horse is this?" Walking toward the stall, she extends her hand toward the horse.

"She's Arabian—a top end horse." I hope and pray she has no idea this is an expensive breed. I will always buy the best for her, but she doesn't have to know the details. "Do you know what you want to name her?"

"Divinity." The way she says it is reverent. "She is the most beautiful creature God has ever created. I will never forget this moment."

She walks closer to the gate and opens it. I'm a little nervous of how the horse will react, since they just met, but I try to let it go. "Hey, gorgeous. Come here, girl." The horse stands still and neighs.

Yeah, she has that effect on people doesn't she . . . I feel that way too.

"We're going to be best friends." Kinzleigh rubs Divinity's nose with the palm of her hand, and then lays her cheek against the flat bridge and moves her hand to the horse's neck, rubbing it.

It's unbelievable how the horse just stands there breathing, totally relaxed. Had she been scared this could've gone differently. It's said that animals have an extra sense humans lack. They can tell if they are in danger just from being around it. I stand still and watch her interact with her horse. This is what she does to me. She pulls me in and holds me to her, making me never want to look away.

Her white-blonde hair against the shiny black coat is stunning. This is why I went with a black horse. The contrast of her light and the horse's dark makes her stand out, and in turn, they are both beautiful without clashing with each other.

She is whispering to the horse, in what seems to be a conversation. It's so low I can't make out what she's saying. Walking closer, I reach out and pet Divinity. "You want to see your saddle?"

She finally lifts her head but continues to rub the horse's coat. "I would love to. Can she come see it too?"

I've already fitted the saddle on her and ridden her myself to make sure she was safe to ride being in a new place. I wasn't about to put my precious cargo on her back without knowing how she rides, but who am I to ruin her day and tell her that.

I've never told her no and I'm not about to start now. "Sure, baby, bring her out. I closed the main gate. If she decides to run there isn't many places she can go."

She follows behind me to the tack room and I open the door. On a saddle stand sits a pink and black zebra print saddle blanket and her black leather saddle with the seat done in the same pink and black zebra print to match the blanket. It's also trimmed with crystal accents. She throws her hands over her mouth as she takes it all in. "This is for me? It's perfect!"

I nod, a smile expanding, and she jumps up and down in an excited binge. Her calves are going to get a workout with all that jumping. My girl is an all-American princess. A shopping addict. A lover of pink. I had to get something that matched her personality and style.

Divinity sticks her head in the door beside Kinzleigh. I guess she wanted to see what all the excitement was about. "Isn't it beautiful, girl?" Divinity neighs in response. "When can we saddle her up?"

"Now if you want. I'm yours for the rest of the day. Do you want to try to ride by yourself or do you want me to ride with you? It's your choice." Her eyes say trouble.

"You ready to show him what we got, girl?" she asks Divinity as she scratches her neck lightly. Divinity stomps her foot and huffs. "Alone," she says as she looks back at me. "I need to learn how to ride her without you. I might want to ride sometime when you're busy."

She winks and blows me a kiss.

Hearing her wanting to do something on her own stings a little, but I know she needs her independence. It's what makes her thrive. If I take that away from her, I take away a vital piece of her—a part that makes her the girl I fell in love with. I will never be that guy.

Kinzleigh

I feel the wind against my face as Divinity runs through the field toward the back trails Breyson showed me. His grandfather lives in the small town of Sumrall, which has more countryside than where we live.

I love this horse. She is fast and it's exhilarating. Breyson is behind us, closing in on Hendrix. "Come on, girl, let's show them how fast you are." I heel her just enough to tell her to speed up and hold onto the reigns and saddle horn tightly as she increases speed.

There is freedom that comes with riding like this in a way I've never experienced before. Thinking back on how I misjudged this place before I moved here actually makes me feel like a horrible person. Most of the people I've met have been amazing. There is beauty and serenity to the surrounding nature here, making me love this place. Maybe, deep down, I was meant to be a country girl after all.

Coming to a stop in front of a small running creek, Breyson finally catches up to me. He looks a little worried at first, but as soon as he sees the smile across my face it melts away. "She's amazing, isn't she? And fast! That was incredible!"

He dismounts off of Hendrix and walks over to me, taking me by the hand. I extend my other hand, holding the small box that contains his present. "Come down. Let's give them a little water and rest for a minute."

Once he takes the box from me, I get off of Divinity. There is a large oak tree off to the side of the running creek. Pulling me toward the tree, he stops in front of it and sits on the grass, pulling me between his legs. "What made you stop here?"

He kisses me in the crook of my neck and it sends chills down my body. "I just thought it was pretty. It's wide open, but completely lined with trees, keeping it private from the outside world. I love this big tree."

"This is my favorite place. I used to come here all the time as a kid. If I needed to think or be alone for a while. Not far from here is a pond I haven't showed you yet. I used to fish in it for catfish or bass. I've never brought anyone else back here. This is my haven like the pier back in California was yours.

One day I'm going to build a house back here. Hopefully, to be a retreat from being on the road if I make it to the NFL, but either way, I will have it." I love when he lets a little bit of himself out, baring his soul. He's so intrigued with me and my wants I don't get a ton of insight into what makes Breyson the boy he is.

California seems like ages ago. It's funny how things work out. My heart doesn't hold the same love for California that it used to. Being here feels more like home. Maybe my desires are altering slightly.

I still want to be a professional cheerleader, but maybe it could be somewhere else. It seems a little dull if I have to experience it without the one I love. I turn in his arms and straddle him. His back is leaned against the tree. "What if that's not my haven anymore? What if I told you I found a new one? If I said I want this to be my haven, would you share?"

He grabs each side of my face and pulls me closer. "Do you mean that? I don't want you to just say something to make me happy. I understand that California is where you want to be and I'm okay with that. I accepted it when I fell in love with a California girl."

He closes his eyes for some reason.

"Will you look at me?" He opens them. They are glossy.

My heart is pounding. Adrenaline is rushing. "I've never meant anything more. I still want us to follow our dreams, but for the first time I want to make sure it's together. I'm willing to compromise now. I always wanted to cheer for the San Diego Chargers, but the want is not as strong anymore. As long as I get to cheer and you're by my side, I'll be happy. My future doesn't look so bright and sunny if I have to do it without you. Maybe there is a way we can be with the same team in college and for our career. If we want it bad enough, we can find a way."

One tear escapes his duct. Like he's done with me before, I catch it with my tongue and devour the saltiness that belongs to him. "Merry Christmas, baby. I love you, forever and always. Open your gift now."

He unwraps the gift and removes the contents from the box. As he reads the tickets, he looks up at me with so much love it's overwhelming. "You did this for me? I get to go to the Super Bowl? No one has ever done something like this for me."

"I did. I love you and I want you to be happy in a way that you've made me happy. You taught me happiness comes in so many things: give and take, compromise, selflessness, love, trust and respect, among other things. You've compromised your dreams to keep me in your life and I want to compromise my dreams to keep you in mine."

I kiss him softly. "I will always do everything I can to see you smile like you're smiling right now. It does things to my heart that I can't give up. I've already arranged everything. Ryland will meet you there. He deserves to go. This whole thing started because of him. If he hadn't moved to Laguna Beach, then you wouldn't have come to visit, and in turn we wouldn't have met. Then I wouldn't be living the amazing life I'm living. I wouldn't know love. I wouldn't be happy. He shared you with me when you came to visit. This is just a small way to say thank you that he brought us together, unconsciously or not."

"You're amazing." He crashes his lips into mine and the rest is utter perfection. I will never forget this tree as long as I live. It is a cornerstone for me—a turning of the page. I will no longer think about my own happiness first, but about his as well.

We made beautiful memories at the base of that tree—more than once. Then he marked it permanently with his pocketknife. A carving of a circle with our names in it and today's date—December twenty-fifth, two-thousand-and-thirteen. I asked why a circle and not a heart. His response was that a heart has start and stopping points, but a circle never ends . . .

just like our love.

My amazing man.

I'm so glad he never gave up in his quest for my heart. Now that I've finally let love in, the transformation amazes me more and more every day. I'm a happier person because of him. It's sad to know there are people that go through life without feeling this for another.

Living doesn't scare me like it used to—really living, that is. Before Breyson I was going through the motions, but not enjoying the activity. I wasn't feeling the goodness of life. This time, I'm going to enjoy every. last. second.

It's time to write my story . . .

TWENTY-EIGHT

Kinzleigh

Tonight is the New Year's Eve masked ball. Everyone who is anyone will be there. Presley, Adalynn, Londyn, and I went shopping for our dresses right after Christmas. Adalynn and Londyn have plastered themselves in my spacious room with me and Presley.

I used to be weird about so much girl time, because I kept to myself most of the time or was just with Presley, but now I wouldn't have it any other way. I think it has amazed Presley that I'm so open with other girls now. I'm almost positive she would kiss Breyson in thanks if need be.

Removing the protective plastic from over the dress, I then pull my dress off the hanger. It's a floor-length silver satin gown. The material is so thin a bra is not an option. The V neckline turns into wide satin straps that run over my shoulders, cross in the center of my back, and then reconnect with the front material on my ribcage. The entire back is open and forms the point of a diamond right above my butt. It's solid with no accents or pattern, because the design alone is enough to make it a bombshell. It has the slightest train in the back. My shoes are a tall pump stiletto, also in the same silver. My hair is tied in a knot beneath my right ear, stuck with crystal accent bobby pins.

I pull the thin material over my body, letting it fall into place. "Dayuum. You really have a way with putting the rest of us to shame," Adalynn says as she takes in my sexy little number.

I don't usually wear anything this revealing, but it's the start of a new year. Some things can change. It's time to stop worrying and start relaxing.

Like Adalynn has any room to talk in her thigh-length strapless black dress dusted with glitter and her silver stiletto pumps similar to mine. Her hair is swept over her right shoulder in a bundle, and in the back from her left ear to where the hair flows is pinned inward and lined with black satin flowers. It's a good thing the guys are on the taller side. The way Adalynn looks, her modeling career is going to take off. It's only a matter of time.

"I second that," Presley says. They do this every time we get together, and they are stunning. At this point I think it's just to give me a boost of confidence, especially when I'm branching out. They know how to make a girl feel like a princess.

Presley's dress consists of a glittery gold piece that has a sweetheart strapless neckline and is fitted down her body until it hits the bottom of her butt. On the left side, the fabric splits at her thigh, forming a knot with the fabric and reveals the rest of her left leg in its entirety. From the split, the fabric continues downward in an angle toward her right leg, and hits the floor at her right foot. She makes a statement with her dark red bootie pumps that match the stain of her lips. Her dark hair is in an elegant bun at the crown of her head.

"She always looks amazing. I wish I had that body. These girls can't go anywhere without a bra." This feels like Londyn on Halloween all over again. The girl has a rockin' body. I still don't get her comments about wanting mine.

She has on a champagne colored halter neckline dress, also dusted in a shimmering glitter. It wouldn't be New Year's Eve without some sparkle. Her dress fits snugly down her body and fans out like a mermaid's tail at her knees. She has her silky black hair is a classic twist on the back of her head, lined with a hairpiece that matches the colors in the dress. Her shoes are covered by the bottom hem of the dress, keeping the design hidden.

I've never been to a masquerade ball and I can't wait. Our face pieces are amazing, accentuating the dresses accordingly. We all focused on bold eyes and lips when perfecting our makeup, since half of our face will be covered.

"You guys are all crazy. Each and every one of you look beautiful. We all look so different, but gorgeous all the same."

We all finish off with a spritz of perfume when I hear my mom call up the stairs. "Limos are here!" Grabbing our matching clutch purses, we head downstairs.

We descend the stairs one by one. The guys are lined up at the bottom, waiting and watching. They each look stunning in their tuxedos. As my eyes lock on Breyson, his stare turns heated, but then he smiles as I get closer. The way we all coordinate is a practice for prom in a few short months. He is wearing a black tux and button-down shirt with a silver vest and tie. He looks amazing in formal wear. I've seen him in so many different looks and he wears each one better than any guy I've ever seen. The boy can't possibly get any finer, and he's all mine.

I scan over the rest of the guys beside him. They all look so handsome. Next to Breyson is his right-hand man, Braxton, of course, wearing a black tux with a white button-down and black vest and tie to match Adalynn's dress. Beside him is Briar, wearing a black tux with a white button-down and champagne-colored vest and tie. Last but not least is Konnor in a black tux, black button-down, and gold vest and tie to match Presley.

Love is in the air. A lot of sexual tension too. So thick you could slice it with a knife. I can even see a little of it in Konnor. He's trying to hide it, of course, by playing the casual date for Presley since everyone else is a couple, but it's there.

I can tell every time I catch him looking at Presley that he's fighting a war within himself. It sucks for both of them. I don't know how he's going to get past his trust issues, but if he doesn't he's going to live a life full of misery. He wants her, but I don't think he's going to let himself have her. I have a feeling in the pit of my stomach this is going to end badly.

We each take a hand as we come off the staircase. Breyson takes mine, helping me off the last step. "My lady, you look ravishing," he says, changing his voice to one of sophistication, but his smile gives him away, and it's hard to keep a straight face. He always makes the most serious times fun.

I laugh. "Are you ready to go?"

He leans in, his lips a breath from my ear. "You know it. I have plans for you, beautiful . . ."

The limo pulls up at the venue for the ball and the door is instantly opened for Breyson and I to exit the car by the security detail. He looks ever so professional with his black suit and the small wire running up his neck to the earpiece in his ear. I'm assuming the rest of it is under his jacket.

We give him our names as we exit the car, waiting momentarily as he scans the guest list and instructs us in the direction of the entrance where another member of security opens the rope to let us through.

We soon walk through the large, heavy doors into the massive open room. Everything is decorated beautifully. The room is decorated in a black, silver, and white color palette. The only overhead lights on are in the foyer and they are dimmed low to only be a guide. Once we come into the main area, the only lights on are the flickers of candlelight on each table and the white lights hung in various locations all over. It's like being under a galaxy of stars. I stop to take in the room. It's magnificent.

The room is speckled with large, round tables covered in black linen tablecloths. Each centerpiece is a martini glass vase filled with a clear gel that holds a black candle lit in the center with two unlit sparklers surrounding it. White plates have been placed perfectly on top of silver, round placemats, with flatware in an organized fashion. A black linen napkin is secured with a ring made out of small crystal stones and placed on top of the entire place setting. A silver place card at each setting marks the guest's assigned seat, written in a beautiful calligraphy.

There are white, sheer curtains secured from the center of the high ceiling that drapes down before coming back up to where it is attached at the corners of the room where the wall meets the ceiling. The same curtains run down the walls over white lights that shine through the sheer of the fabric. It reminds me of a waterfall reflecting light, kind of. This is only the work of a professional event planner.

Every face in the room is hiding behind a mask, all different shapes, sizes, and colors. The mystery of who is behind each one is exciting. Champagne flutes decorate the hands of many, tumblers in others that require a stronger drink. There is a DJ set up in the back of the large room and waiters are walking around in tuxedos with trays of bubbly, shimmering from the lights hitting the transparent liquid. A small bar is off in a corner, stocked with the best brands for the room of wealthy party guests.

Breyson leads me over to our table to sit. He removes his jacket and hangs it on the back of the chair. People are scattered around the room, mingling amongst the guests, some dancing in the center on the makeshift dance floor. "You want to dance?"

I look over at Breyson and almost kiss him due to the close proximity of his face to mine. "Sure."

He takes my hand and leads me to the dance floor. Braxton and Adalynn are already dancing to the soft music flowing through the room. It's a beautiful saxophone melody that I recognize as the one and only—*Kenny*

G. His music is unmistakable if you've ever heard him. My parents used to listen to it a lot and dance around the living room, hopelessly in love. It's soothing to the senses. Calming in nature.

Breyson places one hand on my waist and takes the other in his hand, placing his cheek next to mine as he begins leading us in a skilled rhythm. "I didn't know you could dance like this. Most people our age don't know how."

"I can't share all my secrets upfront." I can feel his smile against my cheek. "Then you would get bored."

I can't ever see that happening. I let him lead me around the dance floor as he explains. I love when the spotlight is on him for a while. What I do get bored of is talking about me. "My parents are old-fashioned. As we got older, Mom said we weren't taking out a girl unless we knew how to dance and behave properly according to her standards. She said one day we would need to know how to dance like this. I guess she was right." I can hear the smile in his voice as we get lost in each other, twirling around the dance floor in the soft glow of candlelight.

Dancing like this reminds me of when I was a small girl. I used to dance like this with my dad, standing on his feet, when he and my mom would dance in the living room. Me and my dad used to talk about taking ballroom dancing classes for fun as we listened to classic music or jazz. Times like those seem so long ago, but the memories are as strong as if it were yesterday.

The more we're together the more I realize how similar our upbringings are. "You look beautiful, Kinzleigh. Each time I see you, you stun me a little more. I care about you so much. One day we're going to look back on these memories when we're on the road or in a house—whatever we're doing at the time—remembering times like this, knowing that we made it. I hope you always know how much I love you."

"You're just trying to get laid," I tease. "You know you're going to get some. Stop being so nice." I like to pick with him when he gets all sweet and mushy. He's a jock on the outside and a sweetheart on the inside. It's like a surprise filling inside a donut. You'd never look at him and think he has such a good heart on the inside. His exterior is so manly and muscular, but when it comes to me he's a big teddy bear.

"Maybe I am." He laughs and splays the hand on my waist across the small of my back. "I'll tell you what I'd like to do though," he purrs into my ear.

"What's that?" I whisper, closing my eyes.

"Take you into a closet and hold you against the wall as I pull up that sexy dress you're wearing and slide inside that tight spot of yours that belongs to me. I want to do bad things to you with all of these people just a wall away. I want to see if you can keep quiet while I fuck you hard, knowing I'm the only one that ever has. You didn't wear a bra. Since I picked you up all I can think about is that thin fabric rubbing against your nipples. Do you know how hard that makes me?" I open my eyes.

His voice is low and husky. He's looking at me in a way that sends need for him straight to my thighs. He's no longer the sweet, love-making Breyson when he gets like this. He's the alpha Breyson, and I love it. I love the array of personas he has.

Oh dang.

My core clenches in want and I can feel dampness down low. Standing in the middle of this dance floor, among hundreds of people, he has me completely at his mercy. These are the things he continues to do to me— turns me from the shy and modest Kinzleigh to the girl that wants him to violate me in a public place. He knows exactly what he's doing. Time to change gears. It's time to role play. "No."

"So hard I have to work to hide it. I think you knew that dress would make me hard for you. You're teasing me. Do you know what happens when you tease me, Kinzleigh?"

I'm so turned on I can barely breathe without panting. He pulls me tighter, slamming me against him, knowing the excitement would show through the thin satin fabric of my dress. His nature has turned animalistic. I close my eyes again, trying to calm myself down before someone notices the look on my face. Instead, I moan at the hot breath against my ear. "You'll punish me?"

"Do you want me to punish you?" Yes. Yes, I do, if it means he's going to take me somewhere and do something forbidden. Knowing my parents wouldn't approve of such immoral behavior makes me want to do it more. I've been good all of my life. I want to be bad. I want to have sex with him in a closet where we could easily get caught.

Since he caught me having a sex dream, he catches me off guard with wild, crazy sex. Sometimes we try new things, and it's unbelievable. "Yes. I've been bad. I wore a revealing dress around eyes other than yours."

He digs his fingers into my side as we continue to dance. He whispers in my ear. "How do you want me to punish you, Kinzleigh?"

His voice alone has me on the verge of orgasming right here among all of these people. "I want you to spank me. I want you to use my body for your own benefit. I want you to make it so that it's hard not to scream."

He rubs his chest against mine. The added sensation on top of my already aroused state is only making it worse. "Do you want me to take you somewhere in the middle of this ball? Do you want to risk someone seeing me do those things to you? Tell me what you want."

"Yes. Right now. I'm ready for you. I need you. Please. I want you inside me." I'm on the verge of being embarrassed in front of all these people if he doesn't take me somewhere now.

"Again." He loves to hear me beg. I've learned it drives him a little crazy.

"Please, Breyson. I need you now. Please give me what I need. Please . . . punish me." Never in a million years would I have thought I'd be into trying anything remotely close to this.

He begins pulling me. I look around, thinking we're still in the middle of the dance floor, but we're actually on the edge. He danced us off to the side beside a hallway and I never even noticed. He's pulling me so fast I'm worried I'm going to trip on my stilettos. He stops at a door. I look around, hoping no one sees us go inside. I hope even more that it's not locked. There isn't a soul in sight.

Opening the door, he tugs me into a supply closet filled with tables and linens, among other things I can't see. It must have been unlocked from setting up the party. When he closes the door, he presses the lock on the knob. "You have me so turned on right now. I'm about to explode."

He kisses me roughly, biting and sucking on my lips. Pressing against me, I can feel how turned on he is. It increases my need for him as well. Grabbing ahold of my hand, he places it around his dick, only fabric separating the two. "Do you see what you do to me? Do you feel that? You're the only girl that does this to me. It's rock hard for you, and only you."

When he talks dirty like that it gets me ready every time . . .

Pushing me farther into the dark closet, he releases his hold on my lips and turns me around to face the opposite direction. "I'm going to spank you, Kinzleigh. I'm giving you what you want. I want to. This is your chance to back out. If you changed your mind tell me now."

I think about his words and a surge of adrenaline rushes through my body. It's frightening and exciting. Some dark place inside me wants to experience this. I know he would never hurt me. I know he's never done this with anyone else, and that alone makes it to where I couldn't say no if I wanted to. Trying new things together makes this sexier than I could have possibly imagined.

I shake my head for him to continue. "Hold on to that shelf in front of you." Doing as he says, I place my hands on the shelf and grip the edge tight. Then I bend forward.

Grabbing the fabric of my dress at my thighs, he begins crinkling it in his hands, raising it from the ground inch by inch, until the bottom reaches his fists. He slides it the rest of the way up, until I'm standing in my stilettos and thong, bare to him.

He rubs his hand over my right butt cheek, sliding his fingertip under the fabric of my underwear when he gets low, checking me. He growls and pulls away. The vacancy of his touch frustrates me as turned on as I am. I need this.

Before I can think of what to do next, his hand slams down onto my round bottom, making a slapping sound. It stings against my skin, but to my surprise, arouses me more. On reflex I clench the muscles between my legs. My panties get wetter and a moan slips from my lips. "You like that?"

"Yes." I can't lie. I don't know why I liked it. I feel dirty, but I want it again. As if he can read my mind . . .

Another slap comes, and then another. Between each, he lightly caresses the area with his fingertips. The mixture of sensations between a bite of pain followed by such a light tickle has me crazed.

He runs his fingertips underneath my panties again and yanks them hard, tearing them off as he touches the wetness pooled between my legs. This is the hottest thing we've ever done as long as we've been together.

I hear a zipper and then I can feel him poking my entrance, before he slides inside, filling me completely. He thrusts quickly and adjusts his angle. When he does, I feel him hit against my G-spot. I'm already so turned on I can feel the build inside.

He slides one hand under my dress and rubs up my stomach until he reaches my breast, squeezing it, keeping the other on my waist to hold my dress up. "Damn. You're so wet."

His dirty talk turns me on more. "You're mine, Kinzleigh," he says, as he bends over me whispering in my ear, never letting up. He continues to penetrate me, over and over again. It feels so good. Too good. "No one else gets to fuck you. Only mine. Forever. Say it."

"I'm. Only. Yours. Always." The words come out, pant after pant, as the pleasure consumes me. "I'm about to."

"Come on, baby. Show me how good I make you feel. I'm ready." He feels good like this. I can feel everything. It's amazing. It feels so good I can't think straight. He hits that spot a few more times, and everything slows down. My insides are pulsating around him, and I let the bliss take over. Grabbing his pants leg, I clench the fabric in my fist as I continue to spiral in the wave of pleasure that's consuming my body.

As I come down from the high, he stills, and lays his head on my back. "That was amazing," he says in a tired voice. "I love you, Kinzleigh. I love you so much it's insane. I will never be able to let you go. Don't ask me to."

"I love you too," I say, dreading letting go.

"We should go before someone comes looking for us."

"I wish we didn't have to."

"Me either," he says, "One day we won't restricted by parents and age."

He slides out and lowers my dress. I start looking for my panties when I realize they are torn and no longer wearable. I turn around as he is tucking his shirt in. He zips his trousers. "Looking for these?"

He holds up my panties with a grin on his face. I nod, biting my lip. "Looks like you're going commando for a while."

I smile. "Guess so, since someone left me with no other options."

He slips them into his pocket. "Come here, beautiful."

I walk closer to him and he places a hand on each side of my neck since I'm wearing a mask. I can only see his silhouette from the dark room now that my eyes have adjusted. "I love you. I mean it, Kinzleigh. What I feel for you is never replaceable. Where you go I go. Our hearts have grown together. They won't survive torn apart. Together forever, right? I'd rather die than live a second without you."

My heart swells when he talks like that. I fall in love with him a little more every day. I don't know if my heart can stand to love him any more than it already does, but it always surprises me. "Together forever. I promise."

We seal it with a kiss . . .

The rest of the night was fabulous. We talked and danced and ate. We mingled with our friends. Adalynn and I released our big news to everyone and we got congratulated together. The guys seemed happy for us and Breyson said we would have a proper celebration later when we're alone. Is it bad that I'm already counting down the minutes? I don't know what he's done to me, but I'll never be the same. Nothing ever gets old with him.

They just passed around champagne for when the clock strikes twelve. Our parents let us have one glass. It's eleven fifty-nine and everyone moves out onto the terrace, beginning the countdown. "Three, two, one . . . Happy New Year!" Everyone shouts in unison.

Fireworks start going off in the distance, making a spectacle across the sky, and the sparklers on the tables inside are burning down. The colors are magnificent. The sounds are memorable. I'll never forget this night for as long as I live.

Breyson grabs me and kisses me as we enter into a brand-new year. I wonder what it will hold. If it'll be better than last year . . .

Kisses occur all over the party, creating a domino effect. Everything blurs around the terrace, and the two of us stand under the midnight sky and live in the moment. Right now, no one else is present but us—me and my man.

It's the close of the best year of my life. I can't imagine the next one being any better, but I'm welcoming it with open arms. I have everything I've ever dreamed of and more. Nothing can go wrong, because everything is absolutely right.

TWENTY-NINE

FIVE WEEKS LATER . . .

I wake up to a rumble in my stomach. Sitting up quickly, I throw my hand over my mouth, hoping it will go away. I start to gag and jump out of bed. Making a mad dash for the bathroom, I barely make it to the toilet before I empty the contents of my stomach. After what feels like thirty minutes of hurling, the nausea subsides enough to leave the toilet bowl.

Today is not the day to have food poisoning. I am riding with Breyson's parents to drop him off at the airport for the Super Bowl tomorrow. It must have been something in Mom's chili last night. I told Breyson I didn't feel well after I ate it and I guess now it's taking its effect.

Walking over to my bathroom sink, I turn on the cold water and splash it over my face. I'm still queasy, but it's not as strong. I dig through my drawer until I find the Dramamine I keep for motion sickness. I wash it down with a small cup of water. I don't want to think about food, but maybe I could keep down some orange juice.

Returning to my bedroom, I remove a pair of slick shorts from my dresser drawer and pull them over my underwear, before walking downstairs. Mom is pressing the lever down on the toaster when I enter the kitchen. "Good morning. You want a bagel? I have your favorite: fat free strawberry cream cheese."

Just hearing about it makes my stomach churn.

"No, thanks. I'm not feeling great. I think last night's chili is disagreeing with me. I'm just going to have some juice."

I grab a glass from the cabinet and walk toward the refrigerator to remove the juice, pouring it into my glass. Mom walks over to me and places her palm on my forehead. "I'm sorry, sweetie. You don't feel hot. Maybe it's a bug. Do you need to stay home today instead of riding with Breyson?"

"No, I'll be fine. Besides, I won't get to see him for a couple of days. He won't fly back until Monday and I'll be at school all day. I took a Dramamine. It should start working soon and I'm sure it'll go away." I tilt my head back and drain the contents of the cup. Still thirsty, I pour another glass.

"Okay. Why don't you go relax in a hot bath? That always makes me feel better when my stomach is upset. Promise me you'll take it easy today?" She looks up from smearing the cream cheese across her bagel and the smell of it warm is starting to make me sick again.

I have to get out of here. I hate throwing up and I don't want to be hovering over the toilet again. My throat is already raw from the first time. "A bath sound good. Thanks," I say, scurrying off to get away from food.

I *did as Mom said and took* a hot bath. I even added some Epsom salt I keep for when my muscles are sore from training hard. It helped a lot in combination with the medicine. The nausea and vomiting have subsided. Thank goodness.

I look in the mirror and smear my gloss on my lips, before throwing it in my purse. It's cold out today. Has been all week. I'm not used to this weird wet cold here yet. It took forever to get cold, but once it finally did, it got *cold*.

I plop down on the edge of my bed and pull on my gray sweater boots over my leggings. My door opens and Breyson walks in. "Hey, beautiful. Are you ready?"

Walking over to where I sit, he bends forward and kisses me on the lips. "Hey, babe. Yeah, I'm almost ready. You excited about your trip?"

He sits on the edge and pulls me to straddle him. "I am. I'm not gonna lie, but it'd be so much better if you were coming. You sure you don't want to go? I can still call Ryland and tell him you're coming with me. It's not too late."

He pulls my earlobe in his mouth and begins kissing down my neck. I can't think. My hormones are raging, and he's barely touched me. "Breyson, I need you. Please."

He pulls his head back, a little stunned. He looks from the door to me, confused. "Baby."

"What?" I begin grinding on his lap, trying to get friction against my overly sensitized area.

"Are you okay?"

He hardens beneath me.

"What do you mean?"

Getting up, I walk to the door and lock it.

His eyes widen. "Your mom is downstairs. You know I'm not allowed in your room for long periods of time; especially not with the door shut. As much as I want to, I have a good thing going with your parents and I'm not looking to change it or piss them off."

Stopping before him, I push his shoulder, laying him down on the bed, and climb on top of him. I need him to quit being high and mighty right now. I need him inside me. I want him inside me. He shouldn't have started kissing me if he didn't want to have sex.

I don't know why I want it so bad. Maybe it's my hormones preparing for his upcoming absence. Maybe it's just because he looks incredibly hot right now. Whatever it is, I'm about to get it, with his approval or not. My mother rarely comes in my room. She calls me from the bottom of the stairs.

I unbutton his jeans, jerking them down in the front as hard as I can. "Shut up. I need you. Now. You're about to be gone. Please." I give him the pouty lip that always wins. He places his hands on his face and exhales, shaking his head. His mind and mouth may be trying to fight it, but his body is betraying him. I rub against him again. This time the only thing separating us is his briefs.

When he removes his hands, I can see in his eyes I've won. "Screw it. I can't tell you no. I don't know why I even try."

He flips me over and comes onto the bed, quickly working my leggings to my thighs—easy cover-up should someone get close. He walks forward on his knees, closing any space between us, and shoves his boxer-briefs down in the front enough to expose himself. "Be quiet, okay?" he whispers.

I bite my bottom lip and nod. His head presses against me, and then he rubs it up and down, wetting the tip. It's something he does almost every time, and I've come to like it. "Hold your legs back."

I wrap my arms around my legs, between my knees and thighs, holding them out of the way since I can't spread my legs on account of my leggings. My bottom lifts off the mattress about an inch when I tighten my hold, creating a slight angle.

He presses inside. I almost come off the bed. He pushes both of my legs down together to my right, twisting my body at my hips—legs to one side and body center. Nervous excitement fills me. We've never done it like this. He leans over me until his pelvis is flush with my bottom and he starts to move.

Pant after pant comes out. I'm quickly losing control. It feels too good. His hand splays over my top butt cheek, pushing up to open me more. He feels deeper like this. With every new thrust I get closer to orgasm.

Sweat breaks out on his forehead. A moan slips from my lips, but he captures it in his mouth just in time. Threading my fingers through his blond hair, I clench the strands, my other hand finding residence on the back of his thigh, wanting and needing him closer.

Each thrust is the perfect speed, a little hard mixed with a little soft, and there are no greater depths that it could go. I arch my back as my orgasm takes over my body, making me temporarily forget the sickness, the fact that he'll be gone, and that we're having sex with my parents downstairs. It's just us.

He stills, his fingers digging into my skin, and I know he's found release. We continue to kiss through the euphoria, not making a sound except for our breathing. There are no words to explain how good it feels when our skin is touching, our bodies are connected, and our lips are adjoined. It's hard to imagine this is what I was missing, but then again, I don't think sex with anyone else would have been like this.

The next two days are going to be excruciating. Maybe I should have been the one to go with him. Since I chose to stay, I have to tell him goodbye at the airport, and that never goes well with us. Airports have never been our thing.

THIRTY

Kinzleigh

Breyson is wearing a grin from ear to ear. Every time he looks at me it grows. I guess he's still enjoying the high from our little bedroom time earlier. It's amazing how much better it can be doing it with the risk of getting caught.

With the sighting of the first vacant spot after turning into the airport, his parents park the car, all of us filing out in a somewhat hurried fashion so that he has plenty of time without missing his flight. It is a pretty big airport.

We make it to our ending point in the airport—where we have to say our goodbyes, so that he can pass through security and head to the terminal to board. I stand back, trying to give his parents space to tell him bye.

A surge of nausea hits again, coming out of nowhere. Breathe. Deep breaths. Maybe it'll pass. I continue trying to breathe through it. I can feel the vomit crawling up my esophagus. Crap! Holding my palm over my mouth, I turn, looking for a trashcan. I spot one a little way behind me.

Taking off in a sprint, I make it to the trashcan in time to hurl, over and over again. Maybe Mom was right, and I do have some kind of virus. This is embarrassing. I wipe my mouth with the sleeve of my long sleeve tunic when Breyson comes running to where I am. Grabbing my face, he looks me in the eyes. "Baby, what's wrong? Are you sick? I can cancel the trip and stay here. Nothing is worth leaving you sick. Not even the Super Bowl."

"Don't be ridiculous."

His parents are standing right behind him with a concerned look on their faces. "Kinzleigh, are you okay?"

I nod, humiliated, hoping people all over this airport aren't staring at me. "I'm okay. I woke up with some kind of virus or food poisoning. I'm not sure which. Nothing a little time and Sprite won't fix." I look at Breyson again, staring into a pair of worried blue eyes. "You're worrying for no reason. I'll get some Saltine crackers. If I don't get better, I'll go see a doctor, okay? Don't cancel your trip. I'll be fine. I promise.

He doesn't look like he's buying it. I can tell he's battling getting on that plane. I look from him to his parents. They keep giving each other this weird look, as if they're communicating without words, because they don't want us to hear. It's making me uncomfortable.

Breyson's mom walks up to him and wraps her arm around his shoulders. "Honey, go enjoy yourself. I'm sure Kinzleigh wouldn't want to lose all that money she spent for you to go. I'll make sure she's all right. Your dad and I will be over here while you say your goodbyes."

They walk away, leaving us alone. "I can stay. I don't have to go, Kinzleigh. I can pay you back for the tickets. I don't like leaving you sick."

He pulls in to kiss me and I purse my lips. I love him, but there are lines I don't even cross. I refuse to kiss him with vomit breath. "Don't be silly. I'll be fine. Don't get too close, though. I don't want you to get it too."

"It's a little late for that . . ." He pulls me in for a hug and holds me tight. Wrapping my arms around his waist, I lay my cheek on his chest and inhale his scent. I love the way he smells.

It's a good thing I bought his brand of cologne to spray on my pillow at night while he's gone. "I'm going to miss you, Brey." A tear runs down my cheek, making me feel stupid. It's only two days for goodness sakes. This is ridiculous. If I can't be away from him now, how am I going to travel for competition? I need to learn how to distance myself. What is wrong with me?

He pulls back and kisses me down the center of my face. "I'm going to miss you more. I love you. I'll come over when I get back, okay?"

I laugh and push him away. "Go on. Get out of here. Have fun and take lots of pics for me, yeah?"

He begins backing toward the terminal. "Always, beautiful." Right before he disappears, he holds up his hand for me to see. My anklet is hanging from his fingertips. My heart melts. He kept it. Then I remember . . . "I love you too!" I shout back, and he vanishes inside the terminal.

"Be safe," I mumble to myself, and that's when the nausea comes back. Not again. Maybe I should go to the doctor.

We pull into Breyson's parents' house and his dad gets out, but doesn't kill the engine. I'm not sure what we're doing here. I figured they would take me home first. His mom changes to the driver's seat. "Kinzleigh . . . Why don't you come sit up front, okay? We're going for a ride."

"Okay. Where did you have in mind?" I change seats as instructed.

"We're going to have a little talk, woman to woman." I get a sinking feeling in the pit of my stomach. I feel like I'm getting in trouble for something, but I have no idea what. She pulls out of the drive, heading toward town.

We're both silent for a good ten minutes before she breaks the silence. "I'm going to say a few things, and I want you to take everything into consideration, okay?"

I nod, because I can't think of anything to say. I'm too nervous. "Kinzleigh, I've grown to love you like my own children. I think you're a great kid and I'm glad Breyson met you. I know I'm his mom, and this may seem awkward for you, but this conversation is between two women. You're eighteen now. I won't judge anything you say, and I want you to feel comfortable talking to me as if I'm your doctor. During the time we talk, try to forget I'm Breyson's mom."

I'm really confused. That is, until she turns into a clinic. One I recognize by the name listed on the sign. Obstetrics and Gynecology. My hands start shaking. My breaths become short, and my heart starts racing uncontrollably. She parks and kills the engine. "Trust me, okay? Let's go."

We exit the car and I follow her to the side entrance of the building where she uses her key code to get in. We walk up two flights of stairs and through a few doors into what I assume is her office. The building is dark and no one else is present. "Have a seat, honey."

She takes a seat behind her desk and I sit in one of the chairs in front of it. "I just want to ask you some questions for now. Okay?"

I cannot believe I'm here. I can't breathe and I'm freaking out. Why am I here? Then five little words answer it all. "When was your last period?"

My eyes go wide, and I swear my heart stopped beating. It was like someone hit me over the head with a common-sense stick. What scares me more than the question is the answer. I pull out my cell phone and can barely touch the right keys I'm shaking so hard. "December seventeenth was the first day of my last period, I think."

A lump forms in my throat as I answer the question. This cannot be happening. How did I not notice I missed a period? This is so unlike me.

Her face never alters like I expected it to. "How long are your cycles?" She places her arms on top of her desk.

I place my hands over my face and cry. I can't believe I was this stupid. "Twenty-eight days. I've never missed one." That answer opened the floodgates. I'm horrified. My boyfriend's mother is figuring all this out, because I was too stupid to.

She walks over and kneels in front of me, pulling me in her arms to comfort me as I start to panic. "Why don't we be sure before we jump to conclusions? It's the first weekend in February, so you only missed your January period. There are other reasons for a missed period. I'm going to get you to do a test for me, okay?"

"Okay." I look up at her and she stands. She leads me down a corridor into a bathroom and hands me a small, clear cup. I cannot believe my boyfriend's mom now knows without a shadow of doubt that we have sex. This is the most humiliating thing I've ever been through.

"I need you to urinate in this cup for me. Make sure you get enough of a sample that the test is accurate. When you get done, place the cup in the window. I'm going to go into the lab and get setup since it's an off day. When you're done, you can have a seat in my office and I'll meet you there."

I shut the door and do as she instructed. This doesn't feel real. Is it wrong to pray this is negative? First thing to do after this is over: get on birth control. I don't care what I have to do to hide it from my mom. I'll do it. I'll pay for it myself if I have to.

She doesn't believe in birth control, because she believes in abstinence, but she also doesn't believe in having a baby out of wedlock either. Not to mention, having a baby for me is not even an option. My cheerleading career is just starting to take off. That would ruin everything. I can't ever go through this again.

My knee begins bouncing from the nerves and my hands start sweating. I feel like I've been sitting here for an eternity. This is the most nerve-racking situation I've ever gotten myself into. My mother would kill me if she knew what I was doing right now. Not only do I know better, but also this will bring so much shame to my family. My mother is loving and caring, but also very set in her values. She has been beating me over the head with them since I was old enough to understand.

Breyson's mom finally returns to her office with a sheet of paper in her hand. Her face is void of all expression. She seems to have her poker face on, and I can't tell if that is a good or bad thing. I've gotten close to her since Breyson and I have been together, but not close enough to know all of her emotions. She sits down in her chair and looks at me. That's when I see it—pity.

Shit!

My eyes fill completely with tears and they pour out as the wall comes crashing down. "Honey, there is no easy way to say this. You're pregnant. The results are positive, and based on your period, I would say you probably conceived somewhere around New Years, putting you at . . ." She looks down at a desk calendar on her desk. ". . . Seven weeks, give or take. If the first day of your last period was December seventeenth and you have a twenty-eight-day cycle, you should be by the book. That timeline also makes sense with morning sickness."

I sit here, staring at her, barely processing what she is saying, and wondering why she isn't screaming at me, calling me names, and why she is calm. I'm anything but calm. Even being a doctor in this exact specialty, I would think it involving your own kids makes it different.

This is just a dream. This is just a dream. Wake up, Kinzleigh. Wake up!

"Kinzleigh. Honey. I know this is a lot to take in, but I need to know you're still with me." She walks in front of me and props against her desk, clenching the edge in her hands.

I blink and realize this isn't a dream. This is real. That thought shatters me completely. "I'm sorry. I didn't mean to. I swear I didn't. I'm so sorry. Please don't hate me."

I'm a blubbering mess and I can't see through the tears streaming down my face. I probably have mascara all over my cheeks. "You probably think I did this on purpose, or that I'm a whore. I'm so sorry. I should have been on birth control, but I didn't know how. My mom doesn't support birth control or premarital sex, so we used condoms . . ."

My eyes lose focus as I put two and two together. New Year's Eve flashes through my mind and the closet at the ball. It felt different, not because he changed condom brands, but because we had sex without one and he didn't pull out. And then he did it again this morning. I'm so stupid. We make each other stupid when we're caught up in the moment.

This is all my fault. We were lucky enough to get out of this mess that one time in the hospital, which makes it easier to do again. Letting it happen again is completely on me. I knew after that close call we needed to be more careful. This is my punishment for being such an idiot.

"... Most of the time," I whisper aloud. "I'm so sorry," I mumble placing my hands over my face to cover my shame.

"Kinzleigh." She grabs my wrists and pulls my hands away from my face. "Look at me."

I do as she says, but I can't hide the guilt and shame that is written all over my face. I haven't even begun to think about what this all really means. I'm still in a state of shock. "I could never think you were a whore, because you *both* made a mistake. I'll be honest. I'm not too thrilled about being a grandmother before my son graduates college or has a career. A baby *should* come after marriage. I wish he had been more responsible. I've been drilling all of them about safe sex since they were old enough for the birds and the bees talk."

She takes a calm, deep breath. "But it doesn't *always*. I do this for a living. I see way too many young girls in here, because they were not given the facts. Now you and Breyson will set an example for a lot of other kids on what *not* to do. It happens. You have great parents, Kinzleigh, and I'm not judging the way they parent, so don't misunderstand me, but I see this all the time. Parents are more worried about drilling in their kids' heads not to do it instead of what to do IF they're going to do it."

She pauses, thinking. "The truth is, in a perfect world, I would love for my kids to wait until they get married to have sex, but the reality of that is slim to none. Sex is more prevalent in relationships now than it's ever been. Kids need to know what to do to be safe and protected IF they are going to do it against their parents' advice. We can't be there to watch you twenty-four-seven. If a teenager wants to have sex, he or she is going to find a way. That's the nature of teenagers. I've been doing this a long time. I'd be willing to bet my paycheck that you were a virgin before you met my son. Am I right?"

I nod in response but can't say anything. "I suspected as much the night you first came over. That's why I was hovering. I know my son better than he thinks I do. I'm disappointed in you both, but I'm more disappointed in him, because he knew better. His father and I have talked with them all. I knew he wasn't innocent before you. I'm not stupid, but I'm glad he found you. You've settled him down significantly. You're a good girl, Kinzleigh, and I couldn't ask for anyone better for my son."

"I'm sorry," I repeat again, feeling the need to.

"What's done is done. There is no way to change it. We should look at the positive. If I have to be in this situation with my son, I'm glad he had enough wits about himself to pick a girl with values. It makes a mother proud. Everyone is entitled to make mistakes. Yours and his is a permanent one—one that I'm sure will change from a mistake to an unintentional accident later on down the road once it's here. A child is never a mistake, even if it's unplanned. If I didn't believe that with all of my heart, I wouldn't do this for a living."

She looks around on her desk as if she's searching for something. "Now that I've spoken to you as his mother and gotten all that off my chest, I'm speaking to you as a doctor. Prenatal care is important. I've delivered too many babies to young mothers that had none, because they were scared to tell anyone. You are the only thing protecting that baby. Good decisions start now. I want us to do an ultrasound and a pelvic exam. We can schedule your labs at your next visit when the clinic is open and I have staff. It's going to be uncomfortable since I'm guessing you've never had one before . . ."

She raises her brow and I shake my head to answer her question. "If you're uncomfortable with me doing either, I can refer you to one of my partners for a work-in, but since we're here already, it makes more sense to do them today to ensure everything looks normal. Either way, it's your choice. I understand if you'd rather your mom come with you."

This is too much to process in one day. What am I going to tell Breyson? Oh, my God. What am I going to tell my mother?! I can't think about any of that right now. I need to get this over with, so I can get out of here. This place is giving me anxiety. I need time to cope with all of this.

"Let's just get it over with. It can't possibly be any worse than my boyfriend's mom knowing we have sex and discovering I was pregnant before I did." I stand, and she wraps her arm around me and rubs her hand up and down my arm.

"No one will know until you're ready to tell someone, okay? Right now, I'm your doctor, not your boyfriend's mom. There is a doctor-patient confidentiality law I'm bound by even if I wanted to tell someone. I need you to remember that. Let's go see if we can get a heartbeat."

We walk into a small room with a table covered in a plastic paper beside a computer screen. She hands me a robe and paper blanket, instructing me to remove my bottoms in the connecting bathroom. "I will go ahead and just do your pelvic exam in here, so we don't use an extra room. Less for me to sanitize alone."

I sit on the edge of the table as she boots up the computer screen. While she's waiting, she takes a long stick looking device and covers it with a condom. "This is a vaginal ultrasound. The baby is too small to see with an abdominal one."

My nerves are running wild. She places my feet in the stirrups. "Scoot your bottom to the edge." I close my eyes, trying to think about something else. I feel uncomfortable and violated. "You're going to feel a little pressure."

In a split second, it enters my body.

Just breathe. Think happy thoughts. Think about Breyson.

Just like that, I'm taken there. Those beautiful blue eyes consume my mind, and his handsome face. I can hear her clicking keys on the keyboard as the device shifts from side to side inside me, but I tune it out. I don't want to look. I play our memories through my mind like a silent movie.

When I'm starting to relax, a whooshing sound fills the room, followed by a heartbeat, causing me to snap my eyes open. She turned on the overhead television screen for me to be able to see. I was in no way prepared for what was on that screen. It is a big black spot. It's not an exact shape of anything. Somewhere between a circle, an oval, and something else entirely. Inside it, on one segment of the large area, looks like a little peanut connected to one side. Right in the center of said peanut is a flittering dot. "Is that it?"

"That's it. It's small, but it's very much alive. Take good care of it." She begins pointing and explaining what each thing represents. I'm stunned. We made that. I don't know how I'm going to deal with all of this. I don't want to think about it right now, because I know I will get upset and it'll take away from this moment, but it's beautiful. "We were pretty close. Looks like you're due September twenty-third."

She hits some button, and then a printing sound occurs, before spitting out a strip of glossy paper. She hands me a strip of photos of what was just on the screen. I can't stop looking at it. This is our baby. What am I supposed to do? This changes everything. This wasn't supposed to happen . . .

Everything else passed reasonably fast. I laid there through the pelvic exam, trying to process everything, and once it was done I chose to wait outside while she cleaned everything up. I needed space.

I'm standing beside her SUV with an informational packet in one hand and my photos in the other. She sent me with a sample of prenatal vitamins to start and instructed me to take one every day. I'm supposed to come see her Monday for my blood work and to schedule a follow-up appointment four weeks out.

It's all starting to hit me. I feel overwhelmed. I'm only eighteen. And suddenly I'm a . . . mother? I need to go somewhere and think. Everything is happening too fast. Breyson isn't even here to help me through this. What if he hates me for this? I need to be alone. I need our tree. I want to go to Pops' ranch.

THIRTY-ONE

Kinzleigh

As soon as she dropped me off at my house, I jumped in my vehicle and headed in the direction of the ranch. I can't face my parents right now. I need time to myself. I need time to sort this out.

Once I pull in the long drive to the ranch, I park and head toward the barn. I didn't even tell them I was coming, but they told us anytime we wanted to come ride to treat it like our own. Without giving it any thought, I saddle up Divinity and climb on her back, taking off through the trees. It's cold out. The wind is whistling through the leaves, my cheeks freezing from the harshness of it hitting my skin. The winter has shown itself this month. I'm ready for spring.

Once I reach my destination, I release her to get some water and walk toward the large Oak tree that now holds our names. Running my fingers over the carving, the tears spill as the series of events comes flooding to the forefront of my mind, catching up with me.

I left everything at home. I never take off without my driver's license and phone, but I didn't want anyone to be able to reach me. I wonder what Breyson is doing. He said he was going to call once he landed. I'm sure I'll be back by then. I need to calm down. I can't talk to him like this. I refuse to mess up his trip. I'll have to deal with this on my own and figure out how to tell him when he gets back.

I sit at the base of the tree where we made love on Christmas Day. I'm torn inside. I can't be a mother. I'm too young. We both have dreams. This will ruin my cheerleading career. It says in the handbook that you can't have children and be in the NCCAA due to the strict schedule. I just got my welcome packet a few weeks ago. My first competition was this summer. Now, I'm going to be fat and pregnant.

This can't be happening to me. I've been waiting for this opportunity for years! We are just seniors in high school. What is everyone going to say when they find out I'm pregnant? What are we going to do about college? We can't end up with dead-end jobs to support a baby. This is not part of our plans! I need a plan! This cannot be the ending to our story. We just started.

Not able to hold the cries at bay anymore, I let them go. It's one of those ugly cries. The kind where you just need to scream and get it all out, and the kind you need to be completely alone for.

What about adoption? We can't be parents right now. It won't help me with the NCCAA, but at least I will still have a chance at college. I can cheer in college, and maybe still pro as well. Then there is Breyson. I won't ruin his career before it ever starts. I know him. He will give it all up and try to get some low paying job to support us while I go to college. I will not make him give everything up.

This is my fault. I should've been more responsible. Demanded we use a condom every time.

As the thought processes through my mind, I get a wave of nausea, as if the baby knew what I was considering. Bending over, I empty the contents of my stomach for the fourth time today. I haven't eaten anything now that I think about it. I have only had juice. I don't know how anything could be left in there to throw up. Once done, I lean against the tree with a raw throat. Who am I kidding? I would never be able to give mine and Breyson's baby away. I would never live through the guilt that someone else is raising my baby while I got a clean break on irresponsibility.

This isn't fair. How could I let this happen? I have never been this irresponsible in my entire life. How are we supposed to raise a baby? It takes money to raise a baby. You can't raise a baby off of love. I can't ask him to give up his football career and I won't. I'll have to figure something else out. I could never ask him to give his dreams up to support a baby and me. I'll have to give mine up. That thought breaks me completely in half.

Pulling my legs to my chest, I wrap my arms around them and lay my head on top of my knees. I'm giving myself one day to throw a pity party. Once I leave here, I leave here and pay for the consequences of my actions. I will do so without complaint. This is no one's fault but my own.

I don't know what I'm supposed to do now, but I'll figure it out. I'm exhausted from everything, mentally and physically—some of it from this hellacious day and some of it as side effects of my pregnant state.

My lips taste salty from the constant downpour of tears. The last thing that crosses my mind before the blackness consumes me is how much I wish Breyson were here, and then my body enters a sleep-induced state.

THIRTY-TWO

Breyson

We're midair and I already miss Kinzleigh. Aside from sleeping, we haven't been apart more than a few hours since the first day of school. I shouldn't have left her home sick while I come off for fun. Guilt consumes me whole. The second this plane lands I'm calling her. We've been in the air for a while now and everything has been smooth and peaceful.

I have a window seat. I look out at the setting sun. It's beautiful. The pinks and oranges of the horizon are stunning at this altitude. I wish Kinzleigh was here, sitting beside me, experiencing it with me. It will be nightfall soon. I can't wait to get off of this plane.

Reaching in my pocket, I pull out the one item I can't go anywhere without: her anklet. I'll never forget that day when she gave me her heart. I've kept it within reaching distance ever since—the anklet *and* the real thing.

It may seem stupid, but I enjoy being around her every day. I don't want space from her. She's my best friend. Kissing the heart of her anklet, I place it back in my pocket and reach in the opposite one, removing the black box. I've been waiting for the perfect time to give this to her but have yet to get that window of opportunity.

I open the box. Nestled inside is a small, round sapphire—the color of my eyes. A while back she made a comment that when she looks deep into my eyes it feels like I'm reading her soul. I want this to symbolize that. For her, my eyes are the window into my heart and soul. It's a promise that she is mine forever.

At Christmas, Preston said something that loops in my mind on a constant basis. It bothers me. He said she is fair game until there is a ring on her left finger. I claimed her right finger and her heart, now I want to claim her left. I know we're too young to get married, so this is just a promise of what's to come. I want her to be mine, forever.

On Valentine's Day I'm asking her to be mine for the rest of our lives. I love her, I need her, and I can't live without her. She can take that promise for whatever she wants. I just want it to exist. One day I'll swap this ring out for the final segment in our story—a diamond ring. Until then, this will do. She changed everything for me. Since her, everything has gone up.

I'll be on my knees for the rest of my life thanking God for her. I don't know how I was deserving of such an amazing girl, but I'll cherish her for the rest of our lives. I want to grow old with her. I want her to be the mother of my children. I want to show her the world, support her, and spoil her.

The brunette in the seat next to me stirs in her sleep, waking up. Closing the box, I slide it back in my pocket. "Hey, sexy. What you got there?" The girl is attractive and about my age, maybe even a year or so older. She must hate to fly, because she's been passed out drunk from the time we took off. I can smell it all over her.

"A gift for my girlfriend," I say, turning back to the window.

"Is this girlfriend serious?" She leans in closer in an attempt to rub her breasts on me. Since I'm by the window I can't go anywhere.

"Serious as it can be without papers," I say, hoping she will go back to what it was she was doing prior to trying to seduce me. Girls like her don't do anything for me anymore. It's hard to believe they ever did. That day seems like so long ago.

Obviously, my answer had the reverse effect. She places her hand on my thigh and tries to inch closer to my dick. "We could go to the bathroom. I've always wanted to join the mile-high club. She would never know. We could have our fun and go our separate ways at landing. I need something to relax me. I've never liked flying. It makes me nervous. I live in New York, but most of my dad's family lives in Alabama, so I have to fly a lot, although, not by choice."

The thought of cheating on Kinzleigh makes me sick. I would never hurt her like that over one orgasm, and if I had to guess by looking at this girl, I'd say she's been around the block a time or two. I'd have to be mentally insane to downgrade from Kinzleigh to her. Being between Kinzleigh's legs is the ultimate high. She is addictive on every level. She has the sweetest stuff there is. And no one's ever tasted it but me.

Grabbing her hand firmly, I remove it from the area next to my crotch. "Thanks, but no thanks. Like I said, I have a girlfriend. Being faithful to someone may not mean anything to you, but it means everything to me."

"Oh, come on. Every guy has a button to push him over the edge, I just need to find yours." She cannot be serious. Is she one of those girls? The type that can't handle being told no. They make it a game to get what they want, regardless of who it hurts in the process.

About to say something, a guy in a jacket walks by, eying us with a look to kill. His jacket is zipped, and he has his hands in the pockets. He looks from me to her and keeps walking toward the bathroom. That was creepy as fuck. "Hey, do you know that guy? He was looking at us weird."

She turns around, but it's the guy's retreating form. His face is turned away. "Don't think so. Now, where were we? Oh yes." Before I even know what she's doing, she grabs my crotch in her hand, causing me to jump. The surrounding passengers scream, and something hits me over the head. Everything goes black.

THIRTY-THREE

Breyson

My vision comes back, but my head is pounding. What just happened? I try to move my arms, but they don't budge. I look down to see why and I'm tied up. "What the fuck?" I attempt to look around. From the terrified looks on the surrounding passengers, something is very wrong.

Something hard presses into the back of my skull. "You trying to get my girl? She's mine. Only mine. I will have her no matter what it takes. And if I can't have her, no one will. You were hitting on the wrong girl, my friend." Hot breath seethes into my ear from behind. I am now fully aware of what is pressing into my head—the barrel of a gun.

How the fuck does someone get a gun on a plane after the terrorist attack on nine-eleven?

"Austin, please don't hurt him. He didn't do anything wrong. This is between you and me. No one has to get hurt. I'll come with you and never leave again. I promise, baby. Let the pilots land the plane and we'll get off . . . together." The girl sitting beside me whines every sentence, tied to her chair as well.

He starts pacing up and down the aisle. "Shut up, bitch. Haven't you done enough? I'm tired of you being a whore. Someone else always ends up hurt because you can't keep your legs closed. I already took care of that one piece of shit for fucking my girl." He laughs manically. "No one will *ever* find his body. I warned you last time."

He stops beside her and points the barrel of the pistol at her temple, before rubbing it harshly down her cheek, causing her to whimper. "Don't you know how much I love you, baby? No one else would do the things I do for you. I follow you. I watch you. I track you. I check your phone records. I know exactly who's around my kid. In your bed. You'll never get away from me. Do you know what I had to go through to stay protected for you going through security? It's never easy, but there's always a way, and for you, I'll do anything. I'd give my life for you. You always call my bluff. You want me to prove it? You want me to take down this plane and kill all of these innocent people to prove no one else will have you?"

She shakes her head as tears stream down her face. I don't know what I'm supposed to do. A man dressed in a military uniform attempts to barge toward him, but the psycho turns and shoots him in the chest before he is successful, causing the soldier to go down to the floor beside our seat.

My eyes widen as the blood pools underneath him in the aisle. Austin—she called him—scratches his head with the gun. "See what you made me do, Cheyenne? Because of you some kid will grow up without a daddy. You bring out the worst in me."

He bends down and roughly presses his lips to hers, before turning to the rest of the passengers. "Anybody else wanna be a hero? He got to die for his country and didn't even have to go to war." He seethes loud enough for everyone to hear.

Is this really happening right now? This has to be a bad dream. A fucked-up nightmare. I close my eyes and open them, hoping all of this will go away. It doesn't. Where are the pilots and the flight attendants? Don't they go through special training for this?

Everyone is terrified. There are people crying, people screaming out, while others stare off stunned. Kids are being rocked by their mothers. Prayers are being mumbled from mouths all over. Then it hits me. Kinzleigh . . .

Fuck this. This isn't how I'm going to die. I have someone to live for. We've barely had any time together. I can't give up without a fight. I've got to do something if we're going to get off this plane alive. I look around, studying my surroundings, attempting to form a strategy.

As if he knows what I'm thinking, the guy bends over my seat. "Don't try anything stupid, pretty boy, or you're next."

He looks at the girl next to me. "Don't cry, Cheyenne. You might mess up your makeup for the next guy you try to sweettalk into shoving his dick in you. I've given you plenty of chances to straighten up. You should have listened better. Remember, you did this to me. Back then, I wasn't good enough for you. Now, I'm the asshole you always wanted. Tell me, is it turning you on? Do I need to slap you around a little? Or is this enough of the excitement you need to thrive? You stupid bitch . . ."

Her face is soaked with tears. She shakes her head. "Please, Austin, I'll do anything. Let these people go. I'll remarry you like you asked. I made a mistake leaving. Please land this plane," she begs.

"What do you think I am? Stupid? Like I'm going to land this plane, so you can have me arrested and run off whoring around like you always do." He grabs her crotch and squeezes hard. What is wrong with this stupid prick? He's one sick fuck. He needs to be in an asylum.

She screams out in pain. He looks bored, as if he's not bothered by it at all. "I'm growing tired of your games, Cheyenne. You put a restraining order on me and tried to keep me away from my daughter. You think you're better than me? We're one in the same, baby. It'll be a cold day in Hell before you get her over me. She's better off with our parents than you."

He stares at her, as if he's thinking something over. "This plane is going down. All these people have you to thank for it. I may go to Hell for this, but you're going to bust the gates wide open right along beside me. Emma is better off without us. At least then she won't have a whoring mother or a jealous drugged-out father. Do you think this is the life I wanted for myself? For her? I'm giving her a chance at normalcy."

Everyone in the plane starts going crazy, panicking. My brain starts trying to rationalize everything. The sign was there. She was sick. I should have stayed. I promised I would never leave her. And now I could . . . die? I'm not ready to die. I have my whole life left. I've barely lived. I wasted so much time.

The girl then looks over at me and her demeanor is completely serious. "He's really that crazy. I'm so sorry. I wish I could change things. Just know that I'm sorry."

"Isn't that sweet. Are you starting to get a conscience, Cheyenne? After all this time? It's a shame you didn't have one before." This time when I look into his eyes, Satan himself is staring back. The evil is so thick you can feel it. He's made up his mind. He's going to kill us all.

They say when you're faced with death your whole life flashes before your eyes. Not for me. My past life isn't what's rolling in my head. What's looping in perfect color is the life I could've had. Marriage, kids, playing football, growing old in the country, and holding the hand of the girl I love when I take my last breath, peacefully in my sleep. The life I wanted with her.

I finally chose to live, and now it's being taken away from me. Her face will be the last thing I see when I take my last breath—those deep green, freckled eyes and that beautiful face. She is perfect to me. I wish I could have given her more. I wish I could have been her future. I was looking forward to seventy-two years with her when I woke up this morning and I didn't even get seventy-two hours.

Austin laughs sadistically and turns to the rest of the passengers. "Everyone gets one attempt at a goodbye before this plane goes down. Pilots are on strict orders. Say your prayers. You have about . . ." He looks at his watch. "Thirty minutes, and then the pilot up there is taking us down to the ground."

Everyone starts pulling out cell phones in a panic. The idiot can't tie a knot worth a shit, so I manage to get it loose enough to reach in my pocket for mine. He paces up and down the aisle again, glancing in each seat, making sure no one tries any foul play. I remove Kinzleigh's anklet and my cell phone.

Opening the camera, I switch it to video mode and hit record. Looking down I tell her goodbye . . . forever. "Hey, baby. I know you're going to be confused. I'll try to explain the best way I know how. I need you to listen to me, because I don't have much time. We've been held hostage. The plane is minutes away from going down. I love you, Kinzleigh, with all that I am. When you remember me, remember how much I loved you. No girl will ever compare. You're one of a kind."

A tear escapes and lands on the screen. The rope around my arms keeps my hands in my lap. "I should have stayed home."

I attempt to laugh to stop my tears, but it doesn't work. "Remember me, Kinzleigh. Remember the love we shared. If you forget, none of it will mean anything. In the short time I've known you, I've grown to love you more than I could ever explain. If I could choose dying today or going back to a time before I met you, I would choose to die, because the time I've spent with you has been amazing. You're the best thing that has ever happened to me. I have to break a promise, baby."

I fight to keep the tears at bay. It burns my eyes. I need to be strong for her, no matter how scared I am right now. "I know I said I would never leave you. If I had a choice I never would. Don't let this make you bitter. I can't die knowing you're miserable. My body will be gone, but I'll always be with you in your heart. Anytime you need me, I'll be there."

I can't hold it back anymore. The tears fall in a heavy curtain. "Kinzleigh, I'm sorry. I wanted to give you the world. I wanted more time with you, dammit."

I manage to get the ring free from my pocket and hold it in front of the phone. "I was going to give you this for Valentine's Day. I was going to give it to you in exchange for a promise that one day I could replace it with an engagement ring."

I swallow, trying to continue what I have left to say. "That promise is no longer possible, but I do need you to promise me something. Promise me you'll move on. Let yourself love again. You're worth it. Make some guy as happy as you've made me. I want you to follow your dreams, get married, and someday have kids. I know you're stubborn, but let someone take care of you. You're a special girl, Kinzleigh. Don't miss out on being happy and in love because of me."

I wipe my eyes on my shoulder, so that I can see. "No one will ever love you like I love you. We are soul mates, but it's my time to go. There is nothing we can do about that. You have so much love to give someone. Don't waste it. Don't make me die in vain. If I don't come back, know that I fought for you until I stopped breathing. One more thing and then I have to go."

I can already feel the plane becoming unsteady. "I want you to know you've made my life full. I meant everything I've ever said to you. You saved me. Thank you for trusting me with your heart. Tell my family I love them. Tell Ry not to feel guilty. And don't you dare carry this burden."

I raise her anklet over the phone. "I'll never let it go. I love you, beautiful girl." As the last syllable escapes my lips, I end the recording and message it to her, hoping and praying that it sends. If the universe is going to take everything from me, the least it can do is give her the message.

I may die today, but I'm not going down without a fight. I was forced to break one promise. I won't break another. If there is a way to get back to her, I'm going to find it. I need to find it. My sanity depends on it. I don't want to leave her with another man for all of eternity. I want to be her man. Selfishly I want it to be me. I sit silent for a moment and say a prayer.

God,

If today is the day I die, I have one request. Please watch over her. She's going to need it after she finds out. It took me a while to get here, but I know she loves me. I know she will be devastated. She will be depressed. She will blame herself. I need you to be her saving grace. Give her happiness and strength when she won't give it to herself. My life for hers. Keep her safe. Force her to move on. Make this my last request.

Amen.

I try to work myself out of the now loosened rope. Crying, sniffling, and praying is going on all around me. There has to be a way out of a situation like this. I find it hard to believe these planes don't come equipped with some way to survive after nine-eleven. Someone fucked-up somewhere. Flying is supposed to be safe now.

I turn toward Cheyenne. She is staring into space crying. She must realize I'm looking at her. I can feel the pain and heartache radiating off of her. Maybe she acts the way she does for a reason. Maybe it's a cover. It's sad she is leaving a daughter behind without a mother. No child should have to go through life not knowing her parents. I would fight blood and sweat until my body lay lifeless if I were a father.

The hijacker—the piece of shit not deserving to be called by his name—disappeared into the front of the plane. I assume heading for the cockpit. "How old is your daughter?"

She doesn't move an inch. "Two. She's not even old enough to remember me when I'm gone."

"I know it's none of my business, but what happened to him? Surely, you didn't willingly conceive a child with that psycho." I continue trying to maneuver my way out of this rope. I need to get free.

Her face saddens more, if that's even possible. "He wasn't always like this. We were high school sweethearts. If you had known him back then you wouldn't believe it's the same person. I got pregnant senior year. We got married after graduation. About a year ago I got pregnant with our son and we lost him right after we found out he was a boy. Austin always wanted a son. I slipped coming out of a store and hit my stomach when I fell. There was so much blood. It tore the placenta and he lost all of his fluid before I got to the hospital. They couldn't save him."

She cries harder. "They let us hold him after I gave birth. We were so sad. We coped differently. He snapped and blamed me, then got hooked on drugs. He would stay gone for nights at a time. Money was coming up missing. I'd find paraphernalia laying around the house. He was lying to coverup what he was doing. I got lonely and depressed. I was looking for attention to take my mind off what I lost and ended up in someone else's bed. He found out. That pushed him further. We tried to work it out, but it made him crazy. He became abusive and started stalking me, so I left for our daughter. That made things worse. I had to get a restraining order against him to protect us. I was scared. The last six months have been hell on earth. I'd bet my life he's high right now. The Austin I fell in love with wouldn't have hurt anyone, let alone kill innocent people."

I look out the window at the dark sky. We should have landed by now, but I'm guessing he made the pilots detour in a different direction if they are even still alive. Black ocean stretches for miles. I'm guessing we're somewhere off the east coast. It's hard to imagine that the man I just witnessed kill someone was ever a good person, but I guess events can drive a person to insanity. "You really love her, don't you?"

I look back at her. She has black smudging all over her face from wiping her tears. "So much I'd die willingly if I knew she would be able to move on happily, but knowing she won't, I'll fight to my death, trying to survive so I can get back to her. I won't give up without at least trying."

She nods. I can tell she's thinking. "I have an idea. It may work, and it may not, but I can't do it alone. I know now he's never going to stop. I'll do it if you'll promise me one thing, because I won't make it out to do it myself. Maybe this way I can make up for all the wrong I've done in God's eyes. By sacrificing myself to help all of these people survive."

I don't like the sound of any sacrificing. There has to be another way. "There has to be a way to help everyone. You shouldn't have to do that."

She shakes her head. "Listen to me. We're running out of time. I'm the only one that can persuade him. Are you going to help me or not?"

I don't know what other choice we have at this point. I nod. "If you can get the door open I'll push him out, but I'm going with him if I do, because we're thousands of feet in the air. I don't know much about plane mechanics, but I can imagine what kind of pressure we're talking about when the door opens." She pauses, a look of pure terror on her face.

She closes her eyes, already shaking. "I need you to record a message for me to my daughter and get it to my mom to put up for when she's old enough to hear it. I need her to know I love her. I need her to know I'd do anything to protect her. I may not have done everything right, but I never meant for her life to turn out this way. Can you do that for me? I'll give you all the information you need."

I nod, because I actually understand. We all have to make decisions or choose a path at some point in our lives. Sometimes they aren't the easiest or the prettiest. Sometimes they are final and fuckin' ugly, but either way you have to make a choice. "Good. Open your video camera. I'm ready. We have to hurry."

I fumble with my phone. My hands are shaky as I turn it on. I'm able to get one hand free after loosening the rope. I can hear him screaming at someone and a gunshot fire toward the front of the plane, closer to first class and the cockpit. Pressing record, she begins her videoconference. "My name is Cheyenne Cooper. I live with my mother, Helen Speights, and my daughter, Callea Cooper, at 65 Silent Night Lane in Almond, New York."

She pauses for a second. "Mom, I don't have much time to explain, so I'll leave it to this nice guy to fill you in on the details. I wanted to tell you goodbye. I'm not going to make it home. It has to do with Austin. My will and life insurance policy information, along with everything you need to take care of Callea, is in my safe under my bed. Thanks for suggesting I do one. Take care of Callea for me. When she's old enough, show her this message. I love you. Thank you for everything you've done for me."

She wipes her face and continues. This is the hardest thing I've ever watched, and I just saw someone murdered. Knowing you're about to die and anticipating it has to be far worse than it being unexpected. "Callea, I love you so much. When I recorded this, you were too little to understand. I hope you have grown into an amazing woman. You were the best thing that ever happened to me. Don't for one second think I regret having you. You made my life shine brighter. You changed me. I am so thankful for the two years I got to spend with you. You are the light where there is dark. I love you. Nana will take care of you. My only regret is that I missed seeing you grow up. I wanted to be there to see you graduate high school and college, to sit front row the day you walked down the aisle and to be by your side when you have babies of your own. I'll be there in spirit, okay. Me and your dad both love you unconditionally. I know you'll hear things, but don't blame him. He's sick, but he would do anything for you. Always love God, love people, and be kind. Never take anything for granted. Don't be sad. I'd rather it be me than you. Talk to me every day. I'll be listening. Your brother needs me now. I love you so much, baby. Goodbye."

I end the recording. She looks at me and asks, "What's your name?"

I clear my throat and wipe my wet eyes. Before I slip my phone in my pocket, I email the clip to myself, because even if I make it out, I highly doubt my phone will. "Breyson Abercrombie."

"I'm sorry we had to meet under these circumstances. Find the latch that opens the door while I distract him. When I get him there, open it. Once we're gone, close the door and get this damn plane grounded. Do not hesitate. Two lives are better than a plane full."

Austin comes barreling back down the aisle and stops beside us. "Are you ready to meet your maker, sweetheart?"

Her voice is shaky in his presence. She sounds weak where she just was strong. "I am. I want us to go together. Make love to me one last time before we go. Please. Will you let him go? No one should die tied to a chair. No more games. I'm sorry for everything. If I could go back I would've stayed home that day. I hurt too, you know. You weren't the only one that lost someone that day." For a split second, the guy's eyes soften, and he actually looks like he may have a soul after all.

I didn't think it was going to work, but he frees us from the rope that holds us to these chairs. He bends over, cups her face, and kisses her. The gun is stuck beneath the front band of his jeans. In some weird, demented way, I can see he loves her.

I have no idea why people do drugs if this is the crap they make you do. When he kisses down her neck, he lifts her off the chair and she looks down at me, mouthing to get ready. He walks her toward the bathroom and shuts the door once they're inside.

After the door is shut, I jump up and take off, looking for the door release. My stomach is in a ball of knots from the nerves. I'm not cut out for this hero bullshit. I don't like having to decide who lives and who dies.

I finally find the latch I'm looking for. A gunshot rings out, coming from the bathroom. The door flies open and Cheyenne runs toward the airplane door, topless, with the gun in her hand. He's following behind, also shirtless, with his pants undone, bleeding and holding his side. "Stupid bitch. Wait until I get to you. You're going to pay for that."

When she gets to the door, she screams. "Breyson, now!"

I pull the latch as two shots sound back to back—one in her chest and the other overhead into the side of the plane. She grabs him and they both get taken out by the gust of air that enters the pressurized plane. I quickly turn my head, unable to watch.

Before I can think, I close the door, but the mechanical alarm and lights are flashing. When he shot the plane, it must have hit something electrical. The pilot comes over the intercom for the first time since this shit started, stating all the instruments are out. Makes me wonder what the hell has been going on up there. They are flying blind . . .

The plane starts to descend at a rapid rate, taking a dive. This is it. We're going down. At least I will die knowing I tried. Screaming and panicking fills the cabin as the sky flies by the windows in a blur. This is my worst nightmare coming true.

Water comes into view. Searching around for anything I can use, I find some flares and grab them. Everyone knows if you go down into water, there's a better chance of survival than land. "Move to the back of the plane!"

All of the passengers swarm into the aisle, creating one hell of a clusterfuck, trying to fight gravity and move to the far back of the plane to prepare for when the nose breaks through the surface. We're falling almost completely vertical toward the black still water below.

I find something to hold onto and close my eyes as the sounds consume my mind, traumatizing me. This is it—the scariest moment of my life. I'm seconds away from dying. Kinzleigh's beautiful face and bright smile is the last image to flash through my mind.

When our lips touch in my mind, the throwing up from this morning reappears in my thoughts, and everything my mother has ever taught me hits me like a shoulder to the gut. I suddenly remember every single time we've had sex without me pulling out. The one that sticks out the most— New Year's Eve. She's not sick. She's fucking pregnant.

No. I have to live. For them.

The plane jars as it hits the water. It feels more like striking cement, causing it to fold up like a tin can. Without warning, everything goes dark.

THIRTY-FOUR

My eyes flutter open to the starry sky. My body is shaking. The temperature has dropped. I'm lying in the grass in front of mine and Breyson's Oak tree. I can't believe I fell asleep. It's nightfall. Crap!

Breyson has probably tried to call me by now. I don't even know what time it is, and after sleeping all this time, I'm still tired. This pregnancy fatigue is crap, and if this is only supposed to be the beginning, it's going to be a long year.

Divinity is standing beside me, as if she's been waiting on me to wake up. "Sorry, girl. I didn't mean to keep us here this long. Let's go back."

Standing, I walk over and mount her. Once ready, she takes off toward the barn. The wind is whistling through my ears. It's dark. There isn't a light on until we get to the barn. It's a little scarier out here at night. I can't see if anything is lurking around.

In a rush and freezing, I take off her saddle and walk her to her stall, closing the gate. "Thanks for today, girl. I needed it. Be back soon, okay?" She neighs, and I can hear the rhythm of her breathing. The February air is cold, making her breath visible under the moonlight.

I'm probably going to be sick from being out here so long only wearing a light jacket. I don't have anything to access the time until I get back to my

SUV, but the black color of the sky confirms it's getting late. Everyone is probably worried.

I run toward my Range Rover and climb in, starting the ignition. I crank the heat to high, waiting on the warm air to blow out. I shiver with the cold air hitting my face, leaving the ranch.

I need to talk to Breyson. I don't want him to be so worried he calls his mom in a panic, causing her to tell him about the baby. I don't want him to find out this way—miles away and on the phone.

Warm air assaults me. I almost close my eyes it feels so good. I shove my hand in front of the vent to thaw out my icy hands. It's making me sleepy. My body heats a few degrees at a time. Speeding down the highway, I get home ten minutes earlier than I normally do. Luckily, it was an off night for some law enforcement somewhere, because speeding I was definitely doing.

When I pull into my driveway, I can see Breyson's mom's car, as well as Konnor's. What is he doing here? Furthermore, what is she doing here? They've probably been looking for me. I should have taken my phone. I could have broken down, run out of gas, or who knows what else. What if his mom told them about the baby? She said she wouldn't, but that was before I took off. I'm not ready for my parents to know yet. I'm not sure if I'll ever be ready for their piercing eyes of judgment and disappointed hearts. Why do I make the dumbest decisions?

Shutting off the engine, I get out of my vehicle and walk slowly, trying to prepare for what I'm about to walk into. As I approach the front door, I exhale, trying to calm my nerves. I step inside to everyone gathered in the living room with solemn expressions. "Hey. I'm sorry if I worried everyone." I run my fingers through my hair, pulling out a dead leaf caught in a curl. "I needed some time to myself."

They all look at each other, then back at me, and that's when I realize Breyson's parents are crying. His mom is hysterical, and so is my mom. I may have them worried, but surely, it's not enough to cause all of this.

Konnor walks out of the kitchen as I close the door, and locks his eyes with mine. He hasn't looked at me this way since the night Grams died. "What's going on, Konnor? Why are you home?" My voice breaks, and his mom walks over to me and hugs me tightly.

My heart starts to race and the pace of my breathing increases, climbing to an uncontrollable rate. "You need to sit down. It's about Breyson."

Breyson? What does that mean? Breyson is in New York. I look around at everyone, my eyes locking with every seated pair. They are staring at me as if I'm about to go crazy, anticipating my reaction. "What do you mean? He should be in his hotel with Ryland by now. As a matter of fact, he's probably trying to call me as we speak. I need to get my phone."

"Kinzleigh, sit down," my dad says in a serious demeanor—one that I haven't heard since I was a kid. He never raises his voice at me.

I look back at Breyson's mom and realize something is wrong. My heart plummets to the pit of my stomach. I allow her to pull me to the couch where Dad turns on the television. It's already on the news. A reporter comes on the screen, an attractive young woman in about her mid-thirties, dressed for success.

She speaks. "Breaking news. Earlier this evening a code was called by a flight attendant on a plane from Alabama to New York, stating that the passengers were being held hostage by a man in his early twenties carrying a weapon. Gunfire was confirmed by the recorded outgoing call with air traffic control. The plane was forced to detour and went down off the east coast."

I stare at her, blinking, unmoving, unable to think about anything. "The Coast Guard is working to assess the wreckage and a search has been issued for any possible survivors. Currently, none have been reported. A full investigation is underway. A list has been compiled of confirmed passengers aboard the flight. Please stay tuned at the conclusion of this message if you know someone this may have affected. We have been informed the airline will be contacting families of those effected with further information as it is received."

Oh, God, no. Please don't let his name be on that list.

Tears build in my eyes and spill over, streaming down my face. My heart is about to beat out of my chest as the list scrolls up the television screen, and then my heart stops, my eyes locking on one single line and following it until it disappears.

Breyson Abercrombie—Hattiesburg, Mississippi

I stand to my feet, screaming and crying. "No. It's not him. It's someone else. There has to be a mistake. It's not him. He's in New York. Tons of people could have that name . . ."

"Kinzleigh!" Dad walks toward me. I take off in the direction of my room, climbing the stairs as fast as possible. I have to get to my phone. I'm going to prove this is just a mix up. I'm going to call him right now.

When I get to the top of the stairs, I run down the hall and barge through my door. Ripping my phone off the charger, I press the home button, lighting up the screen. A pending message from *Brey* shows across the screen. Holding up my phone at my dad standing in the doorframe, I scream, "See! A message. It's just a coincidence."

Tears are soaking my face. My dad looks at me with pity in his eyes. I open the message, instantly seeing his beautiful face. It's a video. I watch with what little piece of my heart is still beating and hanging on by a thread. I clench onto a tiny sliver of hope. I grab onto every word as if I'm going to have to recite what he says. My heart is aching, my eyes glued to him as he speaks. I love him more than myself. His eyes are red. He looks scared but trying to be strong. He always is. "Brey, no. Don't say it.

My eyes blur again, more tears spilling, the portal between the outside and in open. The bastard attempts to laugh at a time like this. "Remember me, Kinzleigh. I need you to remember the love we shared."

A tear hits the screen. He's looking down. Is he hiding? I need to wipe my eyes to see more clearly, but I can't turn away. I don't want to miss anything. He places a ring in front of the screen. It's gorgeous. I listen to every word as he spills his heart out on a damn video. As he tells me not to blame myself. As he begs me to move on. As he asks me to make him a promise. As he tells me to tell his family he loves them. As he says goodbye, because he knows he's going to die.

I cry harder, constantly swiping tears with the sleeve of my shirt, new ones replacing them. Every time I inhale my voice sounds from the surge of air hitting all at once. He raises my anklet over the phone. "I'll never let it go. I love you, beautiful girl."

The recording stops and so does my heart. I can't feel it beating anymore. My body goes numb. Sadness turns to anger. The only thing I can do is scream.

I scream and fall to the floor, throwing my phone at the wall, causing it to break into several pieces. "You can't do this to me! Don't leave me! Please. You promised! You made me love you. You said you wouldn't hurt me." My cries are quickly making my voice hoarse.

Everything is wet. I can't breathe. I don't want to at this point. I'm quickly suffocating in sadness and drowning in heartache. Head to the floor, I talk against the planks. "What am I supposed to do now? I can't live without you, Brey. How can you ask me to promise that? I will never love anyone else! I don't want to! I want to love you. Forever. Please come back. Please."

The few seconds of somber quickly returns to an emotional meltdown.

I sit back up on my knees. "I'll beg! Do you want me to beg? Huh?" I'm screaming at the ceiling, pulling at my hair so hard it should hurt, but I don't feel it.

I'm screaming so loud my voice is breaking into a strained whisper. "How am I supposed to raise your baby without you? This wasn't supposed to happen! I trusted you! How can you do this to me?"

I'm so distraught I don't even know who's in here, or who heard me. I don't care. I want my Brey back. I need him. There is no way I'll survive this. I'll never forgive myself for buying those tickets. I wish I had a do-over. I'd give anything for one.

My breathing is rapid and shallow. I can't catch my breath, but I can't stop screaming. I knew this would happen. He made me fall in love with him and then left me.

Konnor falls to his knees and wraps his arms around me. I hit him repeatedly with my balled-up fists as hard as I can, trying to get away, but he holds me anyway, becoming my punching bag. My chest cavity becomes heavy from the lack of oxygen. I can't see from all the tears in my eyes. I feel like I'm dying. But I know what's happening. I'm having a panic attack.

Panic turns into hyperventilating. I begin wheezing. The room starts fading out. I'm scared. My pulse is going crazy. I try to breathe, but it's as if the universe has gulped up all of the oxygen.

My world is blacking in, everything important disappearing. The last thing I remember is Konnor screaming, "Call nine-one-one! We need a fuckin' ambulance. She's turning blue."

twisting FATE

FATE SERIES BOOK THREE

ONE

Breyson

The nose of the plane tears through the still water similar to a baseball going through a sheet of glass at rapid speed. The multi-ton steel bird jars left and right, crumbling as it is forced through water as hard as cement. Bodies are flying everywhere in the cabin. I hold on for dear life as it all happens in a split second.

Blood is being sprayed as the life around me disintegrates on contact with the wall of the plane. It's like a horror film being played out in real life. The only thing I can't fathom is never seeing Kinzleigh's beautiful face again. I'm going to drown, or worse, become shark bait. I didn't get to kiss her one last time.

My head snaps backward and hits hard against the metal wall. A searing pain shoots through my body. I can feel something warm oozing down the back of my head and neck. I touch my fingers to it, and when I pull them back in front of me, they're covered in blood.

The front of the plane is quickly being purged through the water toward the bottom of the ocean. It gives you no time to think; only a second to react. This can't be the end of my life. I have to make it. I have to find a way. There is something I need to come back for. My soul is telling me to fight. She needs me.

This is it. It's time. I inhale, potentially taking my last breath. So many around me have already taken theirs, and the others are hanging on by a thread and ready to give up—ready to make peace with death. Me—I have something to go back to, and that makes the decision easy for me.

As quickly as the adrenaline races through my body, everything fades away but the dark water that surrounds me. Pitch-black—the color palette before me. I can't see anything.

Placing my arms out in front of me, I feel my way through the plane. My lungs are burning as I slowly exhale the only air in my body. I have to get out of here before gravity takes over and makes this my coffin, along with the others that are already dead.

Cold.

Smooth.

Glass.

Things that register underneath my fingertips. I back up slightly, touching a body—the pilot. Chills run down my arms and legs.

Don't think about it. Get the fuck out of here.

I place my arms on the armrests to hold my weight off of him. If this doesn't creep someone out, I don't know what will. I kick at the glass as hard as I can and as many times as I can, unsuccessful. There's too much water against the other side, making it like a block wall.

I look for something sharp that can puncture it. I will not die in here. I feel around until I find something metal, and with all my might I drive it against the glass. It crackles and spreads like a spider web. I kick at the weak spot again until it finally gives away. I can make out a short distance in front of me.

Gasping for air, I fight not to get taken under with the current as the shredded metal of the plane gets sucked under the water more rapidly with each passing second. I can't see from the black of the sky covering the horizon. The dark of night.

I can hardly breathe. Every time I try to come up for air, I get pulled underneath the water again. Too many people have lost their lives to the black hole that is the ocean floor, and it's trying to make me its next victim.

I somehow made it through the glass of the cockpit and away from the current created by the sinking metal. My lungs hurt from the lack of oxygen for extended periods, but I swim toward the surface for the last time. My muscles are so tired I can barely move, but I can't stop fighting. I need to find something to hold onto.

The sound of silence is deafening. The sudden peace is maddening. No cries for help or suffering. No sounds aside from the bubbling of the water as the plane sinks to the bottom of the ocean.

Something drifting in the water catches my attention. I swim in its direction. I can't make out what it is. My body is enduring too much exhaustion to care. Giving up would be easy. The pain has consumed my body. Surrendering my mind to death by letting the ocean take me would require no effort, but I can't. I have to keep going. I have to get back to her.

The gash in the back of my head is pounding with the beat of my heart, making me dizzy. My stomach churns, wanting to rid itself of everything filling it.

Finally reaching the floating remains in the water, I grab it and hold on for dear life. Maybe if I believe in my mind enough that I can get out of here it will really happen.

The water is cold, making me shake, but I would think it'd be colder to be February in New York. I didn't think of dying of hypothermia should I make it off that godforsaken plane. I encounter a sudden warmer spot. Maybe it's the adrenaline.

I have no idea where I am. I need food, water, and sleep, but looking out at the never-ending black water there is nothing in sight for miles. Is that a light? Whatever it is, it's off a good stretch in the distance. It looks like a small beam of light, but I can't be completely sure.

The closer it gets I notice a spotlight on what looks to be a small fishing vessel. I try to scream, but nothing comes out. Time has evaded me. I'm too tired from trying to stay afloat and dehydrated from being in the salty water.

I remember the flare I placed in my pocket before the plane went down. It's worth a try to see if it still works. Reaching down with what little bit of strength I have left, I try and keep myself balanced on the small makeshift float.

I'm shivering from being wet in the night air and my head is throbbing. My vision is starting to blur and everything in my mind is hazy. Something is wrong. My vision is blacking in, scaring me.

Pulling the flare out of my pocket, I hurry to set it off. I know my time is coming to an end. I can feel it. This is the part where I die. I'm scared. I'm scared of everything I'm about to leave behind. I always thought my death would be quick and painless, not having to anticipate it.

My eyes get heavy and a pair of speckled green eyes flash through my mind. "Breyson, I love you. Come back to us."

Like a cloud of smoke, it's gone. I tense and look around to see where the whisper was coming from. I recognize that voice, but the name escapes me. Why can't I think of her name?

"I'll never leave you," I call out into the onyx sky. "I promise. Wait for me."

My vision is fading quickly. The flare is set off, shooting into the sky, similar to fireworks. The beam of light in the distance scans back over me, but I'm already too far gone to do anything more.

I can't see anything but the face of a beautiful, familiar girl with perfect blonde curls and stunning green eyes. That face is unforgettable. I should know her, but I don't.

TWO

Kinzleigh

POST CRASH DAY ONE . . .

I think my tear ducts have officially been drained. I couldn't cry if I wanted to. My face is red and swollen from the constant flood of tears since I came out of the medicated state I was forcefully put in. I don't remember anything before I blacked out, but I couldn't breathe nor stop the tears.

If I thought I was heartless before, I was wrong. Now I know what it's like to be missing one of the most vital organs of the body—my heart. When I finished listening to that video message, my heart was no more. Call it what you want—dead, shattered, blackened, numb, absent, lifeless—I don't care, but it is forever gone.

Lying in this hospital bed only reminds me of that day after my seizure with him. The doctor said I experienced post-traumatic stress and went into a panic, causing my body to shut down in order to protect itself. I used to never call doctors quacks, but this time calls for something different. The nerve; to tell me I've experienced post-traumatic stress when the one and only person that I will ever love had to go through an actual trauma. No, what I experienced was cardiovascular death when it was ripped from the cavity of my body as he told me goodbye.

From what I've been told they had to medicate me in order to reduce my anxiety and keep stress down, so I don't miscarry our baby. What am I supposed to do? Now that I'm over the initial shock, I realize whose fault this actually is. It's not his fault at all; it's mine. I should've never bought those tickets. Had I not, he wouldn't have gotten on that plane. This is the reason I avoided relationships. They lead to love. Love leads to heartache.

My friends thought I was crazy to have the views I had with no prior cause but look at who was right. I have some kind of curse on me. Something bad happens to everyone I love unconditionally. First Grams and now Breyson. I can't let this happen again. I will never forgive myself. When he died, I died. My life will never again be whole. I will be miserable from this day forward. I've experienced true happiness, and that happiness is lying at the bottom of the ocean somewhere.

Bile rises from the pit of my stomach. Grabbing the trashcan beside my bed, I empty the contents of my stomach for what seems like the thousandth time. My throat is raw from the constant stomach acid traveling through my esophagus.

Breyson's mom told me I have a condition known as hyperemesis gravidarum, also known as severe morning sickness. I can't keep anything down, and what little bit I do is only because they prescribed me a nausea medicine they prescribe for cancer patients. I'm already losing weight between the pregnancy and his death. Breyson's mom is constantly trying to shovel food down my throat, but the thought of food physically makes me ill, baby or not.

A knock sounds at the door and it opens. That's the thing I hate about hospitals. What's the point in knocking if they are going to come in whether you want them to or not? "Hey, Sweetie. How are you holding up?" Breyson's mom walks in the room looking as bad as I do. You can see the pain written all over her face. She's hurting but trying to be strong. I can't imagine the thought of losing a child and I don't have a child . . . yet.

Placing the garbage can back on the floor, I fix the blanket laying over me. Swallowing hard to try and moisten my dry throat, I cry again. It hurts me to see his family because of the physical similarities, but of all of them, the only one I can't physically be around is Braxton. The last time he came to check on me I lost it, and by lost it, I mean completely flipped my shit. So they wouldn't overmedicate me in my newly pregnant state, they decided it was best if I didn't see him right now.

Will this ever get better? I can't avoid him forever. How am I supposed to look at Breyson's clone and remain in a normal mental state? Being around him is physically painful.

Wiping my eyes even though I know it won't do any good, I try to reply. "I've been better, but I'm alive. I think I would rather be dead, though, if I were brutally honest." The flow of tears increases from moderate to heavy. She sits on the hospital bed beside me as I turn on my side to make room. She begins rubbing my back in a motherly gesture.

"I know how you feel, even though the type of pain we're experiencing is different. I can see how much you love him, and as a mother it makes me happy to know he was loved. This is going to be hard to say, but as a medical professional I have obligations to my patients. First, I'm going to be his mother. I know my son, and over the last several months we've had a few heart-to-hearts that we never had before you came along. He had a lot of love in his heart for you. I believe with all of my heart you two would have been together forever had things not turned out this way. I owe you a thank you for molding him into the person he was when he left, but with that said, he wouldn't want to see you this way."

She swipes away her own tears. "I know it's hard, and it will take time, but for the baby's sake try and find a way to cope. It was unplanned, and I know you're young, but that baby is the only part of him we have left. Losing one is better than both, so do whatever is necessary to protect it. Find a way to eat. You're already losing weight and you still have a while to go before the second trimester is here. I know some of it is from the nausea, but a big part of it is from your emotions. A sudden drop in weight is never good for a fetus, especially since you're already so small."

I can't listen to this right now. I care about this baby, it would take a heartless person not to, but I care about Breyson more right now. How can someone ask me to try and not mourn his death? Let alone his own mother . . .

I know she's worried about the baby right now, and you can see the torment all over her face for her son, but I can't just pretend it didn't happen.

Tears stream down my face, clouding my vision. I want him back. I need him back. I can't function without him. I tried to avoid this, but I fell hard for him anyway, and now here I am. I'm sitting here in agony, needing him desperately. I have to get out of this hospital. I need to find a way to get him back. I want to talk to Beau.

She looks at me, clearly concerned. "Do you think you can hold down some soup? I'll go get you some."

I need to get her out of here. I'll do whatever it takes to bring him back, no matter how insane it sounds. "Sure, soup would be good. When can I leave? I want to go home."

I need to smell him. I need to be where I can feel him. This hospital is not the place I'm going to find him.

"I need to check the baby one more time and clear it with your Neurologist first, but after that you should be free to go once your discharge is done. We're going to monitor your anxiety. Stress releases hormones that can cause preterm labor, and at this stage that's something we want to avoid. I'll go get you something to eat and then we'll talk about getting you out of here. Okay?"

I hate to do this to her, because she is an amazing woman and has been nothing short of wonderful to me, but I have to get out of here. I nod and wipe my puffy tear-stained cheeks.

She stands and walks toward the door. As she places her hand over the handle, she looks back at me. "I know this is hard, and it's unfair, but somehow we will get through this. At some point we have to trust that God is in control, even when the outcome isn't what we want. I'm always here for you and hope you know I love you as if you were my own daughter. Just because," she clears her throat, "Breyson isn't here, that doesn't mean I want to see you any less than if he were." She swipes away the tear that falls down her face and exits the room.

I don't know where the tears consistently come from, because I can't cry anymore—wishful thinking I guess, because I can't stop them either. Sitting up, I throw my legs over the edge of the bed. As I stand, I grab onto the bed as the room spins with the wave of dizziness. Once it passes, I grab my duffle bag and pull out a pair of jeans, tee shirt, and a hoodie. I don't care if someone walks in. I change in the middle of the room to save time.

The ring Breyson bought me for my birthday lies on the table by the bed, so I grab it and slide it on my finger. Never again will I remove it for as long as I live, because it's all I have left. I can't get used to the small peanut living in my womb they keep calling my baby. On instinct, I place my hand over my flat belly. "I'll guard you with my life, baby."

Now fully dressed and free of IV lines and monitors, I place a ballcap on my head that one of the guys left in the room, so I don't look less like an escapee. Darting across the room in a hurry, I make it to the door uncaught. Opening it only a few inches, I peek my head out to check the hallway for hospital staff. When I see the coast is clear, I walk quickly to the elevator. Running would likely look suspicious. Thankfully, I make it undetected, already shoving my thumb against the down button several times.

And I have no car. Great.

Walking through the parking garage, I look around. Crap! I don't want to go back to that room. I'd be willing to do anything to avoid it. I can't handle being there right now. What I need is to put together a plan. "Kinzleigh?"

I turn in the direction of the familiar voice to see Simon standing with his hands in the pockets of his jeans. "Shouldn't you be . . . ya know . . . in the hospital? I was on my way to check on you."

Seeing a familiar face triggers an idea. "I can't be here anymore. I want to get away for a while. People are smothering me with the hovering. Will you take me somewhere?" If anyone could understand it would be Simon. He's been my friend since day one without the cattiness of being a girl. Adalynn or Londyn would carry me back to that room kicking and screaming if they had to, out of concern for my health.

He begins scratching the back of his head as he looks back and forth between me and the entrance of the hospital. *Don't even think about taking me back in there.* "I don't know, Kinzleigh. What if something happens to you because you left against medical advice? I don't want to be responsible for that. I care about what happens to you."

What is it about man-whore bad-boys that up and decide to be knights on white stallions around me? Do I wear some kind of sticker on my forehead that screams *damsel in distress*? It's getting annoying. I don't want to be treated any differently by guys than Adalynn or Presley. I don't need every guy that steps into my path to treat me as if I'm wife potential. They couldn't be more wrong. "I'm going with or without your help, Simon. You can take me, or I can find someone else, but make the choice. I need to go."

He lets out a breath and walks closer to me, before wrapping me in his arms. My face is being squished into the center of his chest. "I will take you. I'm just worried about you. I'm sorry you have to go through this. I'm always here if you need to talk to someone. You know that, right?"

He places his chin on top of my head and squeezes me tighter in his embrace. In one sense, I feel guilty, because of Breyson's issues with Simon, but in another, being with Simon is the first time I've relaxed since everything happened. Maybe it's because despite that one night at the Halloween party when Breyson and I got in a fight, our relationship is platonic.

Don't get me wrong, Simon is an attractive guy, but I don't feel about him the way he feels about me. I'm not interested in a casual hookup with him—a friend with benefits scenario. Simon sort of fills in Konnor's position as brother and protector since he's away at school and can't always be here when I need him.

"Yeah, I know. Let's go. I have something I need to do." He frees me from his hold and looks down at me like he's about to say something, but I interrupt his thought. "Promise me you won't judge?"

He works his top teeth over his bottom lip, as if he's slightly unsure of what he wants his answer to be, choosing not to say anything. Instead, he just takes my hand in his and begins walking through the parking lot.

We pull up at the cemetery that Breyson once told me Beau was buried at. I've never actually been here before, but this is something I feel like I need to do. My sanity depends on it. I don't know if Breyson being taken from me is some kind of punishment for something I've done, but I have to at least try to make it right.

My mom always said that we have to pay for our sins. Is this mine? I have dabbled in things this year that I've never done before, so it would make sense, but surely my sins wouldn't be consequential by his death. I've only slept with one person and been drunk one time. Shouldn't that be more of a slap on the hand?

"Why are we here, Kinzleigh? Should I be worried? You're not from the area and Breyson hasn't had a memorial service yet. Who could you possibly know that is buried out here?" Placing my hand on the door, I look over at him. He's staring off into the rows of headstones.

"It's fine. There is just something I need to do. Can you wait here? If you have questions, I will answer them later." I don't wait for his response before opening the door and stepping out, closing it behind me.

I walk down the pathway, slowly, so I can read the names as I pass. I don't know where his headstone is located, so I will have to search for it. One by one I read the names chiseled into the limestone and marble. I finally come to the one I'm looking for.

BEAU REEVES

JULY 10, 1992 - MARCH 8, 2010

You will never be forgotten

I stand directly in front of it. I'm not sure what to say since I've never met him before. I have faith that he can hear me, though. I need Breyson to come back to me. I need him like I need my lungs. The thought of carrying on in this life without him pains me. I feel like I'm internally bleeding, and without us linked together, it won't stop. I will mentally shut down without him—this I know.

I tried to tell him this would happen, that I would never come out of this if he left me. If I have to survive without him, I will be useless to the human race. Loving someone that hard and then it being jerked from underneath you without so much as a warning is a deadly shot to the heart.

"Hey, Beau." Tears build again. What a surprise. Sorrow has become my new constant mood. "I know you don't know me, but I wanted to talk to you. Perhaps I should start by introducing myself. I'm Kinzleigh—Breyson's Kinzleigh. He was in an accident, Beau, a bad one. I have no idea where he is or if he's okay, but I refuse to believe he's dead."

My tears are rolling off my cheeks and watering the grass below. I step closer to the headstone and fall to my knees. "I'm begging you to bring him home to me. There has to be something up there you can do. I'll do anything. No one knows but our parents, but I'm pregnant. He's going to be a father, and I can't raise this baby without a father. I'll give up cheerleading, school, even my own life if you'll just find a way to keep him alive. He's the best person I know, and I'm taking the blame for this. Will you talk to God for me? He needs another chance at life. You didn't get that option and I'm sorry. I wish I could change the outcome and give you your life back as well. His family shouldn't have to go through this again. From what Breyson told me, they went through enough with you. I will not believe he's dead until I see his body lying lifeless before me. I have to have more proof than someone's opinion. I need more time with him. I need to be able to tell him I love him one more time. If you'll bring him back, I'll let him go. I know I have some kind of curse on me. Everyone I love gets hurt. I'll stay away from him, but please, preserve his life, because I will never forgive myself if he dies. I promise to love him from afar and I don't break my promises."

I cover my face in my hands and let it out. I scream loud, releasing all of my frustration into the atmosphere. This isn't fair. I tried not to love someone. I spent years avoiding it; taking all means necessary to steer away from it. One time I fall and this is what I get—fate laughing in my face, proving me to be weak? "Is this what you wanted? Huh? To see me broken and ruined? Well, congratulations, you won! I need him. I need him more than I need to breathe. If you're going to take him then take me too. Please,

I'm begging you. Dying with him is easier than living without him."

The salty tears run inside my lips, touching my tongue. I can't see due to the stream of moisture pouring from my eyes, but I feel like someone is here with me. Then it's confirmed. "It doesn't get any easier, just so you know."

I don't recognize her voice. The air is cold, but I'm too numb to feel it. Wiping my eyes with the sleeve of my hoodie, I look beside me. It's a girl, standing, a few years older than me. She's beautiful, but tormented—that I can see. It's in her gray eyes. She has caramel-streaked hair, bronze skin, and she's petite like me. "Who are you?"

She is completely checked out of reality and zoned out in front of her. "Macie." *What the hell?* Everything Breyson told me floods back in. I didn't even know Beau and I already feel protective over him. Is this not the girl that potentially was the cause of his death?

"What are you doing here?" I'm not trying to be rude, but my hatred for cheaters always breaks the surface, whether I want it to or not.

"By the snippy tone in your voice I guess you must know who I am." She is still staring at the headstone in front of us with no personality in her voice. If I didn't know zombies were a figment of the imagination, I might believe they were real just by looking at her.

"It seems you've made a name for yourself, so yes, I know who you are. You didn't answer my question. What are you doing here?" She looks at me and automatically starts crying, as if I've turned on some kind of switch to her emotions.

"I would have thought the girl that tamed Breyson Abercrombie would be a little less judgmental than that. Lord knows Beau talked about it all the time—how he'd never settle down, even young. I guess it's to be expected, though, since I didn't make a case for myself. Didn't anyone ever teach you that things aren't always as they seem? Maybe you should tell yourself that next time you hear rumors flying." I'm a little stunned at the firecracker that just shot off from the girl I thought was soulless.

"What do you mean?" I need to keep her talking, because it's giving me a temporary break from the rain of tears that's been occurring for the past twenty-four hours. She walks past me and sits in the grass.

I watch her as she scoots closer to the headstone and sits with her back against it. She begins conversing as if I'm not even here. "Hey, Beau. I know it's been a while, but Talon has been keeping me busy. He looks just like you; more and more every day. He's starting to ask a lot of questions. Yesterday he asked me why all the little boys he sees have daddies but not him. It's getting harder to form an answer. He's still too young to understand, but I may bring him by. It's better than making something up. Mama keeps telling me I need to tell your parents about him, that he needs to know all of his family, but I can't. Don't hate me for it. I hope you understand my reasons. They all hate me, and wish it was me laying there instead of you. They never cared to learn the truth. I can't have our son around people that hate his mother. I won't put him in a toxic environment. Besides, even if I wanted to, I don't know where they are. You know I'm only in this hellhole of a city when I come to see you. I prefer to stay in my neck of the woods."

I listen to her talk to him, speechless. Her deep southern accent has me more intrigued than the average person I come across. Did she just say they have a son? I thought she cheated . . . "Anyway, I'll always love you, Beau. If I had it to do over again, I would've done it differently, but I guess I tell you that every time I come."

She's crying, and I actually feel guilty for assuming what everyone said was true. I can see how much she's hurting over this. It's evident that it's tarnishing her soul. Something isn't right. I'm never quick to judge someone, but I let my hatred for cheating get in the way of clear thinking—that there are two sides to every story. She looks at me with so much sorrow it hits me like a ton of bricks. "You want to know the real story now, or keep believing the version that everyone let snowball?"

The girl really sounds like she needs to talk to someone. Walking around with that much heartache can't be healthy, and didn't Breyson say it has been like three years since Beau died? That's a long time. She needs to let it out. It looks like it's eating away at her. "Yeah. I think I do."

Sitting back on my butt, I pull my knees up to my chest and hold them there with my arms. She begins rubbing the grass where his head probably lies six foot below. "I didn't cheat on him. I would never cheat on him." Her voice is low, barely above a whisper. Her eyes lock on mine, silently screaming for me to believe her, and for some reason, I do. I can't explain it, but I believe her. It's then that I know what she needs to move on—redemption.

"What about the so-called guy you were spotted with? Who was he?"

That was clearly her breaking point. She is now hysterical. "He was my childhood best friend. We've never done anything and that I swear. Beau knew who he was and was okay with us being together, because he knew we were nothing more than friends. He was like a brother to me. The problem was the guy that spotted us only knew me and not Dane. He assumed that we were lovers. If Beau wouldn't have had that wreck, he would have known as soon as he got to me that it was all a mistake. I haven't spoken to Dane since that night because of what happened. I not only lost the love of my life, but my best friend."

I feel horrible for her. It takes her a minute to catch her breath enough for her to continue. "I didn't go to that party because I was upset. I had just found out I was pregnant with Talon. It was my freshman year of college. Beau and I were partiers. We liked college life—it's why we became Greek. It was one stupid night when we both were wasted, and he didn't use a condom. We were always so careful, because we wanted to enjoy college. We loved each other and wanted forever together, but we didn't want to start off our lives with kids. We had plans to finish college and see the world first. I didn't take the morning after pill because I was on birth control. I didn't know that if you were taking antibiotics it counteracted the birth control, so it failed. Everything was ruined because of a normal infection most people get at some point several times over their lifetime."

This is the saddest thing I've ever heard. We are so much alike it's scary. She needs someone. Does she even have anyone? Does anyone know the truth, or has she been the martyr because of everyone's harsh judgment?

I go with my first reaction and move in closer to her. She has mascara smeared beneath her eyes. I take a seat beside her and grab her hand in mine. No one deserves to be alone in heartache. Everyone should have someone they can cry to when they need a shoulder. Maybe we can be that for each other.

A second passes and she lays her head on my shoulder, as if we've known each other forever. We cry together—me for Breyson and for the years of heartache she's gone through, and her for Beau and maybe because she is finally able to tell someone the truth. "I would never cheat on him," she repeats for the second time. "He was the love of my life. Still is. There has been no one since him. You have to believe me. I need someone to believe me."

I can only say one thing as we sit here and cry together— the only thing she needs to hear from me. "I believe you."

I don't know how long we've been sitting here in silence and I don't care. Sometimes you don't need words. Sometimes you just need to sit in the presence of someone else and meditate; to know they care enough to sit with you, not expecting an explanation. It is said that actions speak louder than words, and right now I'm giving that to her.

She finally breaks the silence but continues to lay her head on my shoulder. "You're pregnant, aren't you . . ."

"How did you know? Did you hear me talking to Beau?" I need to be more careful about blurting out that tidbit of information. I tend to not think when I'm distraught. That is something I'm not ready to reveal to the world yet. I already have enough people pitying me right now.

"It takes one to know one. I didn't get here until the end, so I missed it. I stay around, but in the shadows. I can't leave Beau. He's what keeps me here. We are from different towns, so I only come when I can. His parents left him. If I leave too, he has no one. I heard somewhere that a girl caught Breyson's heart. He's kind of known all over these parts. He's just one of those guys. Sociable. Mingles with people from every surrounding school. Every fixated girl wants to meet the one girl that got him past a party. He's broken a lot of hearts in the past. He doesn't know me—none of them do. They couldn't pick me out in a crowd, and if Beau didn't show me a photo I couldn't them. Even if he did, by now it's been so long I don't remember. Me and Beau never got to the meeting family part. We were too busy having fun at Mississippi State. Didn't come home unless we had to. I dropped out of school and moved home after he died."

She sighs and continues. "I'm sorry about Breyson. I wouldn't wish this life on anyone. It's lonely when someone takes your heart with him when he goes before you. It makes it even harder when you have to stare into the eyes of the one you lost every day and try not to break down. You better hope that baby looks like you to ease some of the pain. Talon looks just like Beau. Some days it takes every part of me and then some just to get out of bed and be his mother, because the pain consumes me still."

She lifts her head to look at me. "This kind of pain can't be smothered by drugs and alcohol. There is only one way to get rid of this kind of pain—a permanent ending."

"Why don't you just tell everyone the truth? You don't deserve to be viewed the way people are viewing you. How will you ever move on with your life if you don't come clean? Don't you want Talon to know Beau's family?" She shakes her head.

"I've never met Beau's family and don't want to. They made the decision to blame me on their own. It would only make Beau look bad. Then it would be that he was driving drunk without a cause. I can't do that to him. I would rather live my life knowing I'm viewed as a whore than for him to be up there shamed. All we have left when we go is our reputation. I won't ruin his. I will preserve it at any cost."

She really is a living martyr.

Now that everything is out in the open, one by one it hits me all over again: Breyson, our baby, cheerleading. My life is over. I was just starting to come to terms with having to sacrifice cheerleading, but I can't deal with sacrificing both him and cheerleading. "He can't be dead, Macie. I won't accept it. I never wanted to date someone in high school, let alone fall in love. We're too young. Everyone thought I was crazy, and likely annoying, but maybe I was the smart one. Then again, I think of our time together and I wouldn't trade a single day if it meant the outcome would still be the same. He rocked my world, changed it, and made it amazing. How do you go back to living an average life when you've had extraordinary?"

"Honestly, you take one day at a time. Anything you've ever heard about healing or grieving, forget it. There are no magic words or special potion to make everything okay. Time doesn't heal all wounds. You'll be lucky if you can stitch up the gaping hole that remains where your heart once was. Eventually, you'll be left with scar tissue. The only way I make it through the day is by telling myself that Talon needs me, because he already has to experience life without one parent. I can't take away the only one he has just because it would be easier to give up on life so I could be with Beau again." For once someone actually understands how I feel . . .

We continue to stare out into the cemetery and cry, time standing still, until Simon walks up, interrupting us. "Kinzleigh, are you okay? You've been out here for a while."

He comes closer and looks at me, and then at Macie. His jaw locks and anger mars his face. "Macie. What are you doing here? I thought you would be long gone by now. You know, living your happily ever after."

He looks back at me. "Kinzleigh, you don't want to hang around with people like her. You're better than that." My mouth is gaping. How can he be so heartless? I would have never taken Simon for a complete asshole.

"Simon! How can you say that someone? You don't even know what you're talking about." I'm disgusted at his hostility toward her. No one should be treated like a piece of trash.

"It's okay, Kinzleigh. I should get going, anyway." She stands to leave, but I pull on her hand.

"Wait, Macie. Friends? How can I get in touch with you?" Simon scowls. Does he really have the audacity to look like that?

She looks at Simon and back at me. "Sure, girl. I'll find you, okay?" I nod and release her hand. I have a feeling it may be a while, and that breaks me down further.

I watch her walk away, scared I'll never see her again. I silently vow that I will find her and help her. I don't know how yet, but I will find a way. She's dying for deliverance and that's what she is going to get. Everyone deserves to be freed from lifelong guilt. There is already so much pain and torment in the world as it is. There has to be a way for people like her to have a happily ever after—a second chance. It's always the selfless people that end up forever wallowing in misery. Someone needs to be her saving grace.

"You really don't know her, Kinzleigh. She isn't a good person." I look at Simon, unable to believe he is still going on about this.

"I am appalled at how judgmental you are being. Do you even know for sure or are you basing your opinions of her off what everyone else said, like I did?" Guilt etches in his facial features, but then my own words remind me that I can't be mad, because I did the same thing. "Words of the wise— don't judge someone based on what you hear. I've had enough for one day. Will you take me home?"

"Yeah, sure. I didn't mean to upset you, Kinzleigh. You know I care about you and just want to look out for you is all." I believe Simon cares about me, because he's spent a lot of time proving it, but I think he's hoping things will change between us now that Breyson isn't here. I will never feel that way about him or anyone else. I'm broken and unfixable. I'll never work right. I nod to get this conversation over with and begin walking to the car. I'm sure I'll have a lot of questions to answer after my disappearance.

We pull into the driveway of my house and my mom runs out the front door like a crazy person. This should be good. Now add being yelled at for acting stupid to my list today. He's been gone for barely any time and my life is already spiraling.

I'm about to get out of the car when Simon grabs my hand. "Kinzleigh, for what it's worth, I'm sorry you're having to go through this. I know it sucks losing someone you care about, but at some point, it'll get better. I'll always be here if you need someone to talk to. Just call me, okay?"

I know he means well, but I don't like to be pitied. The truth is he has no idea how this feels. He's never loved someone like I love Breyson and then lost that person in a split second with no forewarning. This feeling is something you can't describe to someone else. It's one of those things you have to experience firsthand to even begin to understand.

Feeling this way makes me wonder what kind of drugs the person was on that came up with the famous phrase—*It's better to have loved and lost than to have never loved at all.* I wonder if they ever had to experience loss, and if so, by death or just abandonment. That phrase might make more sense if I had more time with him, but a few short months isn't long enough.

"Yeah, thanks Simon. I'll talk to you later, okay?" He lets out a deep breath and nods his head.

Opening the door, I step outside and begin walking toward my very angry mother. She looks mentally and physically drained and her eyes are puffy like she's been crying. I slow my pace, not knowing what to expect.

The closer I come I recognize the terror on her face. It's the same look she had when Konnor was experimenting with drugs. "Hey, Mom. I'm sorry I left. I just couldn't be there anymore. I didn't mean to make you worry."

Her tears fall and she grabs me into a tight hug. "I was so worried about you. Don't ever do that to me again. Come on, let's get you to bed. You need to get some rest."

Sleep sounds amazing. My brain is exhausted. The best thing for an overworked mind is to escape into the land of dreams—the one place you can forget about all the bad in the world. Maybe if I go to sleep, I can see my blue-eyed boy again. Once my reality was like a dream, and now I'm escaping reality to turn to my dreams. It's strange how the tables can turn so quickly.

Walking into my room, I see something white peeking out from underneath my bed. I don't remember seeing that before. I come to the side and kneel down onto my hands and knees. Grabbing it in my hand, I tug it from beneath my bed and gasp when I realize what it is.

It's Breyson's undershirt from the last time we were together before we left for the airport. The memories of us making love right here on my bed trample my mind like a stampede. The last time it was just the two of us, before everything shattered around us and changed: the baby, the crash, and my episode.

The tears spill over as I clutch it to my chest. His scent, still present, floods my nostrils and the memories take over every facet of my mind. I'm bombarded with them hitting me full speed: the day we met on the beach, the first time we made love in my bed, and even my birthday when he told me he loved me, as well as the New Year's Eve ball when our crazed need for each other led to this pregnancy. My vision fogs, and the anxiety takes over.

In a state of distress, I remove all of my clothes except for my panties and pull his shirt over my head. I quickly pull back the covers and get in the unmade bed that we shared just before he left. For the first time since I woke up today, I let every memory run wild. If I don't let them then they will slip through my fingers like sand, and I can't let that happen.

I will have to learn to live in sorrow, because he deserves to be remembered for the amazing person that he was. "Why did you leave me, Breyson? I only asked you not to leave me. I can't live without you. If you wanted me to live without you then you shouldn't have made me fall in love with you. It's not fair for you to just love me and leave me. I want to come with you. Please take me with you."

I'm crying so hard I have to work to breath steadily. Why do bad things happen to good people? I don't understand. I need to understand. Just make me understand. I've never once in my life wanted to die. I've always had a great life, and then it was amplified when I met him, and cheerleading took off, but right now I don't care about any of it. I want to be with him, and the only way to be with him is to die.

I never understood suicidal people. For someone to be so sad that they'd rather not live. Honestly, I thought some of it was just exaggerated—an excuse for not living life to the fullest or giving yourself happiness. But in this moment, knowing I'll have to live sixty plus years without seeing his face or hearing him laugh—I understand.

They say a vast majority of good health is mental. Maybe that's true, because right now the pain is so immense, I physically feel like I'm shutting down. It's coursing through my body in a steady path, igniting like flame to gasoline. I feel like I'm burning alive while it continues to spread, devouring every inch of my flesh. As much as it hurts, I can't find the will to put out the fire; only to welcome the pain.

THREE

Leigh

When you have kids, they don't come with a handbook on how to raise them. No one prepares you for what it's like to see your children in this much pain. A mother doesn't want to watch her babies hurting. If I could, I would take away the heartache she is feeling, even if I had to go through it myself. I knew when she brought that boy home for the first time that he was the one. He was the boy she was going to marry. Call it a mother's intuition, I guess, but I knew. Then, to confirm it, he ended up living in the very place we moved.

I'm one of those people that believe everything happens for a reason, but it's times like these, as a human, I can't help but question why. She's a good kid. I've never had any problems out of her, and the one time she gives in and experiences high school a little, something like this hits her full speed.

I haven't even begun to process the information of her being pregnant. I thought I taught her better than that, but it's not my place to judge her mistakes. It's my job to love her through them. She will learn from it soon enough—nine months to be exact.

I am her support system, regardless of how much I want to scream and yell at her for not using her head. Kids are amazing, but they require a lot of love and money to raise them. It takes every bit of two parents to raise a baby, even though many single parents out there have done a phenomenal job alone. She's about to become one of them, and that breaks my heart. I don't know how to help her. I'm well anchored when it comes to sticky situations, but for the first time I'm clueless. I was happily married when both of my children were conceived. I'm *still* happily married to their father.

I sit on the couch trying to come up with some way to comfort her, to make her feel better, but I'm coming up short of ideas. I've never been through anything like this before. The phone starts to ring, and I almost let it go to the answering machine but decide against it. I pick up the cordless and answer, "Hello."

"Leigh, it's Ava. Is she home?" Panic fills her voice, and fatigue. She sounds exhausted. I can't imagine how she must be after losing a child, because I feel like *I've* lost a child, and Breyson wasn't even biologically mine. When your child loves someone, you start to love that person too. It comes a lot faster when it's a likable, respectful child.

"Yes, she's home. I haven't asked her where she's been yet. She didn't look good when Simon brought her home. I'm afraid to upset her with this pregnancy situation in the mix. How are you doing, Ava?"

She cries over the phone, sniffling. "I just received a call from the airline. They've searched the site where the plane went down and haven't found any survivors. They're doing what they can to recover everything, but they said it would take some time since it's an open investigation and would likely only find bodies. They advised me to begin making arrangements. My baby is really gone. I had a little bit of hope, but he's never coming back. I wanted to let you know so you can prepare Kinzleigh. I need to go." She disconnects the call, and I just stare out into space. This is what I was afraid of.

I might as well get this over with. It's not going to get any easier. Maybe she will begin to heal if she has closure. I stand and make my way to the staircase. It takes all of my strength to make it up the steps. No one ever wants to accept that their mate is gone. It's one of those things you deny until you die. Everyone wants the happily ever after, but this is real life. Not every story is a fairytale. You have to accept the good, the bad, and the ugly. I come to her door and hear her crying on the other side.

Easing the door open, I realize the lights are still on. When I walk inside her back is facing me. "Kinzleigh, I need to talk to you."

"Can. We. Talk. Later." She mutters and pauses between each word with a cry.

"No, honey, it can't wait." Walking across the room, I sit on the bed, placing my hand on her shoulder.

Turning over, she looks at me, and my heart stops beating at the sight of her. How can I do this to my child? "Breyson's mom just called and things don't look hopeful. They didn't find any survivors. They were told to start planning his memorial service. I'm sorry."

She looks at me, her face soaked with tears. Her lips quiver before she covers her face and screams over and over at the highest pitch she can make. "No! He's not dead. I refuse to believe he's dead. He's going to come back to me. You'll see."

"Kinzleigh, he's not coming back. I'm sorry. I know it's hard, but you need to heal, and you can't do that until you accept it and grieve." I'm trying so hard to be strong for her, but this is breaking my heart.

She screams in agony, tossing and turning in the bed. She is kicking like a child throwing a tantrum. I do the only thing I know to do, and that's to hug her, to be here for her. "Get out! I want to be alone. Leave me alone!"

I've never seen her like this. Not even when Ken's mother died, and I felt like we'd never get through that. It used to bother me that they were so close, feeling like I was failing as a mother that most times she would rather be at his parents' house, but I finally accepted it one day. They shared a connection I couldn't and didn't want to take away.

My eyes blur watching her, but I don't know what else to do other than give her some space. I walk quickly to the door and shut it behind me. Placing my back against the wood, I slide down until I'm sitting on the floor listening to her scream and curse and cry.

Placing my hands over my face, I cry silently as I witness my child die a little at the hands of love. She doesn't deserve this. Sometimes life can be cruelest to the people that deserve the best.

FOUR

Kinzleigh

I'm exhausted. I don't even want to get out of bed, but today is Breyson's memorial service. I force myself out and look at my small figure in the mirror. I've lost weight from the constant pregnancy sickness and not being able to eat from the depression. I have done nothing but lay in the bed in his oversized tee shirt. My hair is dirty, and I haven't showered since I got home from the hospital.

A knock sounds at my door and opens before I can respond. One look at me and a tear falls down Adalynn's face. I haven't spoken to her, or anyone else for that matter. "Why didn't you tell me?" One sentence, and I know exactly what she's referring to. "Don't shut me out, Kinzleigh. I can help you get through all of this, but only if you let me in."

I feel numb.

Everything she says goes in one ear and out the other. Nothing sticks. My energy is gone. I don't even have enough to shower, which is why I haven't. I feel like someone walked by, reached inside, and removed my soul from my body, leaving nothing but a shell. Tears have become an expectation on a regular basis. I don't try to wipe them away anymore.

I stare at her blankly, no expressions to give. She walks over to me and wraps me in her arms. Her black outfit matches my mood—dark. It's the symbolic color for death. "When did you find out?" she asks, not letting this go.

I don't want to think about the baby. I like pretending it's not there. "After we dropped Breyson off at the airport." I can't even say it without crying all over again. I still can't believe this has become my life. How am I supposed to go back to school or cheerleading like this? I'll never be happy again.

She tightens her hold around me. "I won't tell anyone until you're ready. You know I'll help you, right? You don't have to go through any of this alone. You're my best friend. You're family to me."

I know she expects the Kinzleigh she knows and loves to come back at some point, but that girl is long gone—a vapor in the wind. All I can do is recluse inside myself and try to hold on to what little bit of sanity I have left. "I'll help you get ready. You need a bath."

I have no choice but to let her lead me to the bathroom.

As embarrassing as it was to have someone help me bathe, I can't find the will to care. I guess times like these are when you discover who your true friends are.

I pull on my long, black maxi dress and a pair of sunglasses to hide my reddened eyes. I imagine to an outsider I look like I'm on drugs. Since I've been taking my nausea medication I don't get sick as often, but I can't eat much either. I'm getting thinner as the days go on and my clothes are getting big, but I don't want food. I'm doing good to get down one bowl of soup a day and that's only for the baby's sake.

We pull up at the cemetery and walk over to the new headstone beside Beau's with Breyson's name etched in the stone. A visitation service wasn't necessary since there is no body. I come to stand in front of the headstone and read the letters etched into the stone.

BREYSON PATRICK ABERCROMBIE

OCTOBER 2, 1995 - FEBRUARY 3, 2014

Forever remembered by the ones you love

The preacher starts his speech—one that he has given a million times I'm sure. It's sounds too practiced, and frankly, not good enough. I stare at the headstone in front of me, picturing my beautiful boy. I close my eyes and go to my happy place while the words and sadness flow around me.

Come back to me, Breyson. Let me feel you. If not in body, then in spirit. I need you to keep me going. I don't have the strength to do it myself.

The salty tears run down my face, underneath my shades.

I'm here, baby. I'm trying to get to you. Please don't give up on me. I need you to remember our love. I need you to keep going. Wait for me . . .

My eyes shoot open and the world spins around me like I'm going to pass out. It's finally happening. I'm having a mental breakdown, because I swear on everything, I feel like there is someone near me and I have never been one of those people that believe in ghosts. I'm a realist, but I promise on my life I heard Breyson's beautiful voice in my head.

The mind is a cruel thing. It has the ability to play tricks on us and make us hear and see things that aren't there. My subconscious wants him to be here so my mind has to be trying to ease the pain consuming me by giving me false hope.

But as crazy as it is, what if it were some kind of sign? Could it be? I've heard crazy stories about two mated souls having the ability to communicate with each another when they're apart, like twins separated at birth, but can still feel each other's pain and emotions subconsciously. What if it's real and I give up on him? What if me believing he's still alive actually keeps him alive? Can I find the will to hope that it could actually happen? It's a stretch, especially for me, and may make me crazier than I already am. The question I have to ask myself is would I rather live with the false hope that he could actually survive trying to get back to me or let him go just to avoid feeling crazy?

In one sense, I have to believe that supernatural is possible to believe in God. When you choose to believe in a higher power, you accept that the things seeming humanly impossible can actually happen if God wills them to.

Could his love for me bring him home? Could our baby bring him home? Could Beau bring him home? I know God can, but will he? Like an answer to my question I'm reminded of a piece of a bible verse. *Faith the size of a mustard seed can move mountains . . .*

I stand here with a war of questions going on in my mind as the memorial service comes and goes, not really listening. Everyone begins walking back to their cars, but I continue to stand here, staring straight ahead. "Are you ready to go, Sweetie?" Mom says.

"I'll be there in a few minutes, okay?" She nods and leaves me to myself.

I push my shades up on top of my head as the cars leave the cemetery behind, most of them never to return. But for people like me and Macie, this place becomes a second home.

I remove the piece of paper protected in plastic from the pocket of my white denim jacket and walk closer to the headstone. White is not a color often worn at a funeral, but I had to wear it since my black cotton dress is strapless and it's the middle of February.

Kneeling on my knees, I open the small Ziploc bag and remove one of the sonogram photos I was given when I found out I was pregnant. I look down at it, remembering that last day with him. "Hey, Brey. I didn't want to tell you this way, but I have no other option."

Uncontrollable tears spill from my eyes as I try to gather my thoughts. "I'm pregnant. I wanted to wait until you got back to tell you, so you could enjoy your trip, but I guess you never got there. I'm sorry. I didn't mean to get pregnant. I was going to take full responsibility and give up cheerleading, so you could keep your football dream, but that's no longer an option. You would've been a great football player and an even better dad. I know you would've stood by me, and that's why I was going to give it all up. I won't leave you here alone. I'll come back every day and visit. I hope you know how much I love you." Sliding the ultrasound photo back into the plastic bag, I seal it shut.

I dig my nails into the earth in front of the headstone, making a hole. I can't see in front of me, because my eyes are blurred from not wiping my eyes. I don't see the point, because they continue to fall, so it does nothing but make my skin raw. I don't know where the tears are coming from anymore. I don't drink enough.

"I want you to have this picture, Brey. It's our baby." I place the clear plastic bag containing the photo inside the hole before covering it back up. "Why'd you break your promise, Brey? I was counting on you to keep it, to prove me wrong. You were right about one thing—you've ruined me. I love you more than I love myself. More than anything in this world. I don't know why, but I'll try to wait for you. Show me you're still out there somewhere. I'm begging you, Brey. I'll beg all you want me to, but please get back to me."

That overwhelming feeling that I'm not alone returns. It makes the hairs on the back of my neck and arms stand up. I need to get a grip before I end up in one of those padded rooms by myself.

What's strange is that some of the pain dwindles for a moment. Like someone is protecting me, but I can't see them. I refuse to freak out. I believe in the existence of angels and demons, because I believe in God, but I can't bring myself to believe in ghosts or spirits being left behind when their bodies parish. I need to go back to bed. My mind is way out in left field. I'm upset and hurt, and my emotions are all over the place.

I stand for a moment, my hands covered in dirt, before I can make myself walk away. If I could pick one moment in my life and press rewind, I would go back to the night I bought those tickets and erase it, or even change my answer on the morning he asked me to go with him. Both ways bring us to the same outcome, dead or alive—together.

I walk closer to the headstone, bend down, and kiss the jagged stone. "Bye, Brey. Always remember you're my one and only. No one will ever replace you. You have my heart and soul, leaving my body as the only thing remaining to share with someone. Don't miss me too much up there."

I run my fingertips along the top and turn to leave, unsure of where I want to go from here . . .

My parents pull into the driveway of our house and come to a stop after easing into the open garage. I dart from the car and run toward my room without stopping. People—my family included—are the last ones I want to be around right now.

My clothes feel like they are strangling me. I need to get them off. Stripping down to nothing but my underwear, I pull back the cover and slide into bed. Grabbing the cologne from the bedside table, I spritz my pillow and wrap myself around the pillow, letting his scent take me back to another moment in time—a happier one. One I didn't have to pretend in . . .

FIVE

Kinzleigh

Lying here, thinking of him, and crying uncontrollably, wishing I could be in his arms, gives me a temporary escape mentally. I can feel the darkness swirling around me, pulling me toward it, begging me to give in.

I've always been a good girl. Never wanted to get into trouble. Breyson made me glad I was that kind of girl. He cherished me. I was everything to him. With him, there was no planning for the future like I've done all my life. When I was with him, I was content to live in the here and now. In life there are things that make us thrive—motivate us to be more than ordinary. Breyson was that for me.

I'm lost right now. My heart is missing, my brain is confused, and my soul is weeping because it's no longer in the presence of its mate. I've hit the ultimate bottom and I don't know how to climb out.

When you put a junkie in confinement without his drug of choice, he becomes volatile and will do anything to get more, even if it means hurting someone else to get that high one more time. But one more time turns into another and then another. There is no *one more time*. The drug is his master, his god. It's a codependency.

I'm the junkie and Breyson is my drug. My drug was taken from me. My body is going through withdrawals. I'm willing to do whatever it takes to replace the euphoria that he made me feel. My mind only processes one piece of information and shuts out the rest. I need something to replace the void, and nothing will stand in my way. That thought loops around on repeat until I can't think of anything else. It's a disease. I have to go find that replacement.

I throw off the covers and stand. I've been laying here in a daze for hours, afraid to go to sleep, terrified of what I may or may not see when I get to dreamland. I need to get out of here and do something to take my mind off of things. It's late and I'll have to sneak out, because Mom isn't going to welcome me taking off this late at night in my condition.

I pull on a pair of leggings, a tunic, and boots. I finish with my short denim jacket to keep me warm and grab my purse from my desk. Walking quietly to my bedroom door, I take a deep breath to relieve the nervous build-up in my gut. I've never snuck out of my house before. Turning the knob, I ease the door open and peek my head out.

The hallway is dark except for the night-light Mom keeps plugged in by the bathroom. I can hear my dad snoring, cluing me in that they are sound asleep. Mom's had to get used to Dad's snoring over the years, so she can sleep through anything. I'm good to go. I quietly shut my door, tiptoe down the hall and down the stairs to the front door.

When I get behind the wheel of my car, I sit in the dark silence for a moment. Where am I going to go? I really don't care at the moment. I start the engine and pull out of the driveway as slow as possible to avoid revving the engine and waking my parents.

I drive down the road, letting it guide me. Life is full of roads like the one in front of me. Some take you places you don't want to go and some end in happily ever afters. The only choice we're given is to trust it and follow. What are people like Macie and me supposed to do that end up on a dead end?

Not thinking, I turn into a tattoo parlor that's still open close to the local college campus. Removing my wallet from my purse, I pull the keys from the ignition and open the car door, stepping out. I robotically make my way toward the entrance. As I open the swinging glass door, the bell above the it chimes.

The last time I was in one of these shops, it was my birthday and I wanted to surprise Breyson. Unfortunately, I can't say the same for this trip. I shouldn't have been so quick to judge Konnor. Maybe he is right and the needle will relieve some of the pain. I need a filter.

The buildup of pain is like when electricity strikes something. It runs through the object like a portal, but it always has to have an exit. I need to find an exit before it destroys me. I can't house this much pain—a ground is a necessity. I look around at the posters on the wall that are covered in various premade designs.

Footsteps shuffling across the stained concrete floor draws my attention. A guy covered in tattoos comes walking toward the front counter. He's lean and attractive. His body is a masterpiece of design. He has chocolate brown hair. It's short, but spiked with gel, and his green eyes are outlined with a ring of brown. He has a mysterious vibe about him, like he hides skeletons of his own in his closet.

I watch him walk toward me, not saying anything. He has slightly gauged ears and an eyebrow ring. His jeans are loosely fitted and his band tee shirt hugs his sculpted torso. "Can I help you?" I turn back to the poster in front of me.

I can tell he is right behind me by the closeness in his voice. It's raspy like a singer from one of those metal bands Konnor listens to. From the looks of him, he probably belongs in a band. "I need a tattoo," I say, as I turn around to meet him eye-to-eye.

I don't waste any time. I'm here for one thing and one thing only. His eyes skim my body from top to bottom. When his face locks with mine he gasps, a look of torment and pain following immediately behind. If I didn't know any better, I would think he was looking at a ghost. I glance around me. He hesitates for a moment and then he breaks out in a forced smile.

"What'd you have in mind?" He appears to be in his early twenties, but no older than twenty-five. I think about what exactly it is that I want. He walks behind the counter and bends over, leaning on his forearms.

"I want a heart on my left ribcage being pierced by a commercial airplane. I want it to look realistic, and on the heart I want the initials B.A.P., the middle letter bigger than the rest for a last name. I want script above and below it—*My heart died with you. February 3, 2014.*"

His eyes change, meaning what I'm not sure, but I have a feeling it's that he gets it without having to ask anything else.

He stands upright and glances down at the tattoo that encircles his wrist. He rubs over the lettering. I'm not sure what it says from this distance, but it looks personal. When he looks back up, he doesn't look me in the eyes this time. Instead, he points his head in the direction of the back. "Come on. I think I can handle that."

I follow behind him through the doorway that leads to the tattoo stations lining each side of the room. It looks like we're the only two here. Given it's a weekend night, I'm sure most people my age and his are at the local bars and clubs, or even college parties. Lining each wall is built in stations with leather chairs that recline on demand. On the furthest wall is a black table covered in the same leather padding as the chairs, probably for tattoos that require lying flat.

He continues walking toward the table and stops. patting the top for me to sit, so I do. "I'll be right back."

He disappears through a doorway. The pain is building again. I feel like I'm drowning. No matter how much I try to stay afloat, the riptide pulls me under before I'm able to gasp for air.

After a few moments he returns with a bottle of amber liquid and a small glass. Sitting the glass on top of the table, he pours a small amount. "I don't usually tattoo someone that has consumed alcohol, because it thins the blood needed for clotting, but you look like you need this."

The torment is slowly eating me alive, causing me physical pain as it tries to burrow its way out of my body. Any amount of relief is better than none. Without thought, I grab the glass and press it to my lips, tilting my head back. I let the liquid fire run down the back of my throat, and then set the glass back on top of the leather. "Thanks."

"No problem. You ready to tattoo or do you need a minute? You don't really look like the kind of girl I normally see in here." He never breaks eye contact as he props his hip against the side of the table next to me. I choose to ignore his prior stereotypical comment.

"I'm ready," I say.

"Lay back and tuck your shirt underneath your bra. My name is Riggan, but my friends call me Rigg. What's yours?" I start to relax a little the more he talks, thanks to that shot of warm liquid running through my body and medicating my veins. I just now notice he has a lip ring as well—a loop through the right side of his bottom lip.

He crosses his arms in front of his chest, waiting for me to reply. He begins skimming his teeth over the ring by pulling his bottom lip into his mouth. "It's Kinzleigh."

"How old are you, Kinzleigh?"

"Eighteen." Lying flat against the table, I grab the hem of my tunic and pull it up my body, tucking it underneath the wiring of my bra.

He grabs a pair of black latex gloves from a box and pulls them on, then pops a new needle out of the plastic packaging and I watch as he sets up to ink my skin, everything robotic like he could do it in his sleep.

The buzzing of the gun fills my ears as he taps the pedal with his foot to load the first color. "You're not going to draw it on paper first and stencil it?"

This is different from the one I had done on my pelvis. That guy drew it on paper and tattooed over the transfer on my skin like a guide.

Now sitting on a rolling stool, he smirks at me, the cockiness evident. "I freehand, girl. It's more challenging. Anybody can trace. When you came to see me, you came to a pro—the best around. I'm usually available by appointment only, but for you I'm making an exception. I've been tattooing since I turned eighteen and drawing since I could pick up a pencil. I'm now twenty-four. You do the math. I don't trace anything. Ever."

That's nerve-racking, but luckily, I don't care right now. The needle is what I need, not the ink. I nod as he rolls closer to me with the tattoo gun. The various colors are sitting on a rolling tray beside his tattoo hand, the left one. You don't see left-handed people very often.

He touches my skin with the gun and I grit my teeth as I withstand the first puncture, followed by another. In this moment, I understand everything Konnor said. Each time the needle stabs my skin pain oozes out. I can breathe more easily as my skin is etched with color.

I stare at the ceiling, counting the squares as I bask in the relief of the pain exiting my body. A tear slides from the outward corner of my eye and runs down my face into my ear. I feel his eyes on me every few seconds, but I don't look at him.

The light hasn't returned, but the fog of darkness surrounding my soul thins a little, making life more bearable. I don't know how to live in darkness, but I'm sure I'll learn soon enough. The day he died all light was squandered, taking goodness with him. My soul is trapped at the bottom of the ocean with its other half, and the darkness of the ocean's depth is consuming me. I'm going to enjoy the few moments of peace I have while it lasts.

As soon as it began it ended. That's the way it seems. In reality, we've been here for hours. "It's finished." He cleans the area, then wipes the sensitive, red skin with a paper towel and rubs it down with petroleum jelly. He holds out his hand for mine. "You want to take a look?" Nodding, I take his hand and sit up in preparation to stand on my feet.

After getting steady on my feet, he leads me to a body-length mirror that hangs on the wall. I gasp as I look at the permanent piece of art on my skin. It's beautiful. The design begins with script right below my breast and continues halfway down my side. The bottom script stops at the level of where the navel is. He was right. The arrogance was deserved. He is talented beyond measure.

The whole piece looks three-dimensional. The way the plane is plunging through the heart, as if the muscle is really denting in. I'm speechless. "I love it." Tears spill as I take in every color, every line, and every letter. "How much do I owe you?"

I look up into the mirror, staring into his eyes through the reflection. He is standing behind me, shaking his head side-to-side. "This one's on the house."

"I want to pay you. Just tell me what I owe you. Please," I say in more of a begging manner.

"This is my shop. I decide who I charge and who I don't. I don't know what you're going through, but I have a pretty good guess. For what it's worth, I've been there. Losing someone is a bitch. I know it doesn't feel like it right now, but it gets easier as long as you accept it'll never completely go away. You have to learn to live with the pain. You'll have days where you relapse and want to die all over again. You have to learn to differentiate between the pain that's real and what your mind wants you to think is real. No one can help you. If you ever need to get out of your head, give me a call and we'll get a drink."

He pulls a business card out of his pocket and hands it to me. I take the card and remain silent, waiting for him to cover the tattoo with a paper towel and tape before making my way to the door, focusing on the sting every time my skin moves.

The second I exit, the pain hits me full force like a bus plowing into a body. It knocks the air from my lungs. There is only one place I want to be right now. My body makes the decision for me, as if it's possessed. I want to feel him, to sleep beside him, no matter how crazy it makes me. I'm starting to get used to the madness anyway.

There is only one place I know I'll feel him holding me while I sleep: his bed. His mom told me I was welcome to stay anytime I wanted, just to let her know. It's too late for that. I'll just have to sneak in, because I didn't plan it.

I turn off my headlights as I turn into the driveway. Security lights throughout the subdivision make it to where I can see what I'm doing, but I feel like I can't control my body. It's like an out-of-body experience. I don't know what is normal anymore.

It's late enough that anyone home is likely asleep. I'm not going to text any of them and risk waking them up. Once I shut off the engine, I get out of my car and close the door as quietly as possible, pushing it into place. Breyson told me once about a side window that isn't connected to the alarm system. He said his brothers and him cut the wire to disable it, so they could sneak out back when they had curfew.

Walking around the side of the house, I can only hope it is still unlocked. I get to the window and remove the screen from the outside, leaning it against the brick. Placing my fingers underneath the lip of the window, I push upward, inching the window open slowly, careful not to wake anyone. I stick my head inside to make sure the coast is clear before entering the house. All is dark and quiet, so I throw my leg over and climb inside.

I steady myself on my feet and look around at the empty room, holding my breath as I tiptoe my way across the floor to the staircase. When I reach the bottom, I step two at a time until I make it to the top. Thankfully, I don't hear any movement. I touch my hand to Breyson's doorknob and freeze. I haven't been in here since before he left, and I'm not sure how I'm going to react, but I can't back out now. I'm already here.

I close my eyes and try to remain calm, but it's not helping at all. It doesn't matter. I remain in a constant state of anxiety. Twisting the knob, I push the door open and walk in. Braxton's room is right down the hall and Briar's is across from his. Luckily, Breyson's is at the end of the hall by itself. Brylee's is downstairs along with their parents.

Carefully shutting the door, I take in the mostly dark room. The curtains from the window are open and the moonlight is shining through, allowing enough light in to see the bed and the area surrounding it.

Tears are already falling as I walk toward the unmade bed. I can smell the scent that is only his lingering in the air—a mixture of laundry detergent, soap, and deodorant. He always put on deodorant when he got out of the shower, wearing it to bed, so it always transferred to his sheets in his sleep, everything mixing together, giving it a smell that is only his.

It looks just like he would have left it when he woke up that morning. It wasn't in his nature to make his bed. He didn't see the point when no one came in his room and it was only going to end up unmade when he went to bed. I notice a picture on his nightstand that wasn't present the last time I came over. I sit on the edge of the bed and pick it up.

It's a closeup picture of him and me looking into each other's eyes. We're on the football field, dressed out in uniform, wrapped in each other's arms. I've never seen what we look like from an outside point of view before. His forehead is pressed against mine with my face in his hands. We look so in love I can't breathe looking at it. The gaping hole in my chest throbs as if someone just ripped the stitches open before the tear could heal.

I miss you so much, Brey. This isn't fair. We didn't have enough time together.

I don't know who took the photo, but it's stunning. The angle looks like it's coming from the bleachers. The nightstand beside the bed has two drawers. The top holds his boxers and the bottom his white undershirts. Removing one of each, I lay the frame down just long enough to change into his clothes before picking it back up. I hold it to my chest and lay down in his bed, pulling the covers over me. I feel content for the first time since that horrible day, and my mind is clear.

In hindsight, I shouldn't have consumed any alcohol knowing I'm pregnant, but I wasn't thinking about the baby. I don't know if you're even supposed to get tattoos while you're pregnant. I didn't think to ask. I didn't care, if I'm being honest. I hope I didn't do anything harmful. I've never done anything that stupid. Surely, one shot won't hurt it. I wasn't drunk. I need to stop being so selfish. Snuggling with the photo in my arms, I drift off to sleep.

SIX

Kinzleigh

White sand surrounds me, the granules conforming between my toes—a beach I've been on before. I recognize the familiarity everywhere, but I'm not sure why. Even something in the air feels familiar to me as I stand looking out at the clear water before me.

I'm wearing a white mono-kini, and as I glance down at myself, I have the strangest feeling of Déjà vu. The sun warms my shoulders and the breeze kisses my face. Why does it feel like I've been here before? I turn around to a bed sitting on the sand covered in white linen. Behind it is another small building. Farther down the beach is a beautiful villa built out into the water.

I look down at my left hand, confused by the beautiful square-cut diamond, and then it hits me. I dreamt of this place one night the week I met Breyson. Why am I here? Is this some kind of a sick joke my subconscious is trying to play on me? There is one way I will know this isn't real. I look down and search for the tattoo I had done earlier. It won't be there if this is something made up or a repeat of the same dream.

I stop breathing. My tattoo is there. The perfect piece of art on my ribcage is present, unlike the last time I had this dream, but what does this mean? I look down the beach, and the hole in my chest cavity begins to beat as if my heart has been revived. It has to be a mirage.

Breyson is standing in the sand looking at me with open arms like he's waiting on me to come to him. I don't even think. On instinct, I take off running toward him. I run down the stretch of beach as fast as my size six feet will move, causing my calves to burn.

After what seems like an eternity, I reach him and jump in his arms, gluing myself to him. Like he always does, he catches me and holds me underneath my butt. Tears stream down my face as I place my palms over his cheeks. "I've missed you. I've missed you so much. You left me. Please don't leave me again."

"I've missed you too, baby. I would never leave you by choice." He kisses me deeply and it's like we've been starved for each other. I moan as our tongues connect and I taste what I've been craving for days. He is everything to me. I lock my feet behind him, scared he will vanish into thin air.

He finally breaks the kiss once we're out of air, but I don't want him to. I don't need air as long as I have him. "When I said forever, I meant it, Kinzleigh. Look at your hand."

I look down at the gorgeous rock sitting perfectly on my ring finger. "What about it? Where did it come from?"

He removes one hand from my thigh—the left one—and then presses it against my cheek to wipe the tears freefalling. Cool metal chills my warm skin. Placing my right palm on the front of his hand, I bring it before me to inspect it. It's a silver wedding band encircling his ring finger. "We're married?"

"This is a dream, Kinzleigh. I'm as confused as you are. Our souls must be searching for one another. I can't be with you right now, but I'm trying to get to you. We're not married yet, but as soon as I can get back to you, I'll never leave your side again. You'll get sick of me before I leave you alone. I will marry you, Kinzleigh. I don't care what I have to sacrifice. I'll follow you wherever you want to go. I don't care that we're young. Our souls will always find each other just like that day on the beach, or when you moved to the same town. They won't stop until they're linked together forever. We're here, because they are fighting to connect again. You heard me at the cemetery, right?" I am completely insane, but right now I don't care. All I care about is the fact that he's here holding me and kissing me. It feels realer than anything else in my life at present.

"Yes, I heard you. Where are you, Brey? I need to know why I'm hearing you if you're dead. I have something to tell you. I'm pregnant. I don't want to raise our baby alone." Saying out loud that he's dead makes me kiss him again just to prove to myself he's real. It feels real, but if it's a dream I never want to wake up.

"I don't know where I am, baby, but I'll find you. I figured out you were pregnant right before the crash. The sudden sickness didn't make sense, and then it started fitting together like puzzle pieces. I should've stayed. I knew it then. You won't be alone. I'll make sure of it. Our baby will bring me home. My love for you will guide me. You're my life, Kinzleigh—always have been and always will be. When my life flashed before my eyes, all I saw was you. Te amo hermosa niña. Espérame—*I love you, beautiful girl. Wait for me.*" The second those beautiful words fall from his lips, they're against mine. I have no idea what it means.

Why is my Spanish class failing me when I actually need it? Since when does he know how to speak Spanish? I need to figure this out. I need to find my blue-eyed boy. I embed it to my memory to look up later.

"Make love to me, Breyson. I need to feel you. I need to know you're really here. Please . . ." The plea makes me sound desperate, but I don't care. I need him inside of me. I need it for my sanity. He carries me out into the clear water but never lets me go.

"I'll always give you what you want, Kinzleigh. I'm sorry I got you pregnant. We were pretty stupid about sex sometimes. I know this isn't what you wanted—what we wanted. We're young and didn't plan this, but of all the people it could've happened with, I'm glad it happened with you. I don't regret it. After a close call of being stuck with the wrong girl, I can't be upset about it happening with the right girl. Call me selfish, and a little bit crazy, but I like the idea of being tied to you permanently. You're carrying something that is mine. I'll always be a part of you." He lifts me into the air as if I weigh nothing and kisses my flat belly.

He begins removing my swimsuit with his free hand. Fluttering butterflies are occupying my stomach as he inches it down a little at a time. He kisses the side of my neck, the heat of our bodies mingling. My back arches, exposing more of my body to him.

Breyson is the only one that has this kind of power over me. The only one that weakens me with no more effort than a kiss. He sets me down in the water and I grab onto him in sheer terror of letting him go. "I need to remove your swimsuit, baby. I'm not going anywhere . . . yet." I whimper at the last word, but I stand on my feet anyway.

He hooks his hands onto the bottom half at my hips and finishes rolling my swimsuit down until it's gone. "I've missed the way you look naked."

He quickly removes the shorts he's wearing and lowers down on his knees in the water. I place my hands on his shoulders for support, wondering what he's doing. He kisses my stomach again and whispers something I can't make out. I feel alive for the first time in days.

We're not far enough out for the water to be deep. You can see straight through to the ocean floor. Shells and coral litter it as far as you can see. He sits back on his heels and pulls me down to sit on his lap. "I love you, Breyson, with all of my heart. You own every part of me: mind, body, and soul. You're the only person for me. I knew it before, but losing you confirms it."

He skims his hands up my back. I close my eyes, enjoying the way it feels in the warm water. Placing my breast in his mouth, he flicks his tongue over my nipple. That little bit of bliss puts me over the edge in euphoria. I've needed his touch. You don't realize how much you need something until it's gone.

He guides me over his tip and aligns at my entrance. "I love hearing you say things like that. We've come a long way from the two immature seventeen-year-olds we were that day on the beach. I know you're the one I want to experience my life with, Kinzleigh. People like us are lucky enough to find it early. *Show* me how much you love me. I'll hold onto it."

I want to stay this way forever. Our lips create a seal, and then he slips inside me. I can feel every inch as if it's real. How do you determine what's real and what's a dream when all the senses are part of it?

I've missed this—this internal connection. He guides me up and down as we kiss, breaths and moans exchanging. He goes slow, as if he's trying to draw it out.

He rocks me back and forth, knowing that will get me off. His mouth stays locked with mine, mingling and pulling at my lips. The sensation starts to build inside. Everything spasms down below. I want to stop and keep going at the same time. Pleasure courses through my body, making it difficult to focus on anything. He grips my waist and bears my body down against his pelvis as he gets off.

"Remember this, Kinzleigh. I'm coming for you. I need you to believe it's true. Me tengo que ir, por ahora—*I have to go for now*." Again, with the Spanish. I don't know what it means, and panic sets in. Why is he speaking to me in Spanish?

He pulls me off of his lap and I clench the skin on the back of his neck to keep him here. I don't understand what's happening. Reaching behind his neck, he breaks my hold and walks away from me, farther out into the ocean. "No!" I scream. "Don't leave me, Breyson. Please don't leave me."

I run after him, water splashing all around me as I wade through the water, but he's too fast. In a second, he's gone. Where did he go?

I release a high-pitched scream. It echoes into the atmosphere. I look around for him, already hysterical, but he's no longer here. No. This can't be happening to me again. I just got him back. It wasn't enough time. I need more time.

Everything around me is fading. I don't know what's happening. I don't want to go back. I need to find Breyson. "Breyson!" I scream as loud as I can, my voice scratching against my raw throat.

"Come back to me. Please, don't leave me again. I'm begging you to come back. Where are you? This isn't funny, Breyson!" I cough, shoving back the words trying to push their way out, my voice hoarse. I'm being repetitive, but I don't care. I need him to hear me. If he hears me, he'll come back. I know he will.

Something is holding me down, making it impossible to move, but I don't know what. "Shh, shh, shh. Kinzleigh, it's okay. Calm down. I got you."

My eyes open and Briar is laying behind me with his arms wrapped around my body, holding me to his chest. He's speaking low, in a calming tone. Sobs wrack my body as the realization occurs to me that it really was just a dream. "What did you see?"

"Is she okay?" Braxton's worried, fatigued voice comes from a short distance, but I can't see him. It sounds like he's beside the door, but he's staying out of my direct line of sight.

"Let me go back. I want to go back. Please, Briar, I need to find him. I have to know what he meant. He should've explained it to me. I don't get it!" I'm crying and kicking, but he continues to hold onto me even though he'll probably have bruises.

"Kinzleigh, it was just a dream. You're in his bed. Breyson isn't here. Tell me what you saw." He is calm, but I can tell by his tone he's upset. His voice is strained.

"It wasn't a dream. He was there. He said he was coming back for me. He kept saying things in Spanish. It was a clue. I need to know what it meant. If I go back to sleep, he'll find me again." The way he breathes out behind me, I can tell he doesn't believe me. He thinks I'm crazy, which is exactly the way I feel, but I can't give up. He asked me not to give up. I need to remember what he said, so I can put the clues together.

SEVEN

Breyson

Iopen my eyes to the beeping of a machine. Nothing looks familiar. I search my brain for any memory as to where I am or why I'm in a hospital bed but come up blank. Nothing stands out. I strain to remember the details of what would put me in a hospital. A fight? Could have been an attack. I squeeze my eyes shut, willing it to come forward. Black. Nothing. A void of information as if something is blocking my mind. Why can't I remember anything? I should start with basic information. Maybe I'm just tired. My name is . . . *Blank*. I'm from . . . *Zilch*. My address is . . . *Nada*.

Boom.

Boom.

Boom.

My heart is hitting against my chest with force. Hold up a second. Why can't I remember my fuckin' name, or my address, or my parents? I panic and look around for some clue as to what's going on. A hospital bracelet is wrapped around my wrist. Everything is written in Spanish. Why would it be written in Spanish? *Sin identificación —no identification.* Am I Spanish? No, that can't be right. My head is yelling in English. And I would know what the hell the words mean. I can only guess what one word is referring to, but I have no idea for sure. I must not have paid much attention in Spanish class.

My head is cloudy. When I touch the back of my skull my fingers meet a long strip of stitches, and the surrounding skin is sensitive. What happened to me? My heart is racing, causing the machine next to me to beep more frequently. I'm freaking out. I press inward on my temples with the tips of my fingers.

The hospital door opens, a middle-aged man walking through wearing a white lab coat. He's holding a metal clipboard and flipping through the pages attached to it—the doctor. He's tall, with black hair and bronze skin, dressed in slacks and a dressy shirt. I hope he can speak English, or else this is going to get awkward fast. Where am I? "I'm assuming you're probably confused, so I'm going to ask a few questions to see where you're at," he says as he looks up from the sheet of paper before him.

"I'm going to brief you first. My name is Dr. Samuel Rodriguez. I'm a Neurologist. You were found in the ocean unconscious, barely keeping afloat, by a local fisherman who brought you here for medical attention. We aren't sure how you got there or why since you didn't have any identification on you. We're assuming you were involved in some kind of boating accident, but you could have been drifting for a while, so we're unsure of where the wreckage would be. The only other thing we can think of is that someone hurt you and dumped you in the water, hoping you'd die there. By the time they found you, you had already lost a significant amount of blood. You endured blunt force trauma to the head, fracturing your skull and causing your brain to swell. We placed you in an induced coma to allow the swelling to decrease before we could assess the damage. That brings us to now—you conscious." He pauses for a moment, giving me a chance to process all of this information.

Boating accident? Do I own a boat? What kind of person would just leave me in the ocean to die, bleeding out? What if someone *was* trying to kill me? Oh, God. Why? What did I do to deserve that? Why can't I remember anything? I want to pound my head against a wall. When will I remember what happened? I have so many questions, but do I even want to know the answers at this point? If someone was aiming for me to be dead . . . "Where am I?"

He writes something on his clipboard and looks back up at me. "Spain." Spain? That sounds ludicrous. Did I live here? I could have been on vacation. That would mean someone is looking for me. "Tell me the last thing you remember."

I rub my hands over my face as I ponder. "It's okay if it takes you a while.

Try to let your brain process and see what comes back. Sometimes, all the brain needs is a trigger for a memory to return. I'll start with a few simple questions to see if it helps. What's your name?"

I blink at the question and the same panic from earlier returns. What is my name? My name is . . . Just like earlier, nothing. It's as if my mind has been erased. "I don't know," I say honestly.

He writes something down on that damn chart again. I feel like I'm in a psych ward. "It's okay if you don't know the answers right now. We are doing a basic evaluation so we can track change. The brain can be a tricky organ. Some things may come back quickly, some things may take a while, and some things may never come back. Prepare yourself for the worst outcome with a brain injury. Now, back to the questions. Do you know how old you are or what year you were born?" I think hard—really, I try—but again I come up with nothing.

I shake my head. I'm starting to get angry. He writes something for the third time. "Do you know where you're from?" I have a strong feeling it's not here, but where I have no idea. As I'm about to tell him no, a vision flashes through my mind, causing me to freeze. It's a girl, blonde, with bouncing curls. I close my eyes to focus. She is walking toward me. My heart picks up as it plays on. "What's wrong? Are you starting to remember something? What do you see?"

"A girl." She gets closer and I can see more of her features. Beautiful bright green eyes, a small nose, and full lips. She's beautiful.

"Do you know this girl?" I keep my eyes closed, scared the vision will slip away if I open them. I shake my head no. "That's okay. Keep letting your mind replay the memories." Is it a memory or just something my mind is making up?

Her silver gown sways as if she's dancing with me. Who is she? If I don't know her, I want to. She smiles as if she was complimented, and it takes my breath away. It's like watching a silent movie. She looks happy as she twirls around. It has to be me on the other side from the angle and proximity I'm watching it from. I pull her in closer, and when she looks up at me, I'm hooked. I have to know who she is. Someone that looks like that is unforgettable. "I know her . . . I have to know her," I whisper, as if I'm trying to convince myself.

I continue to watch as the memory plays, trying to find something to grasp onto. Hell, she could just be a figment of my imagination. One hand is propped on her waist and the other is holding her hand. I lean in and whisper something in her ear, and when I look up, she blushes and giggles.

This is cruel, but I can't stop the memory if I wanted to. She looks into my eyes and those green eyes cause something inside me to stir. I have to remember her, because I have a feeling she is important. Then, like a punch to the gut, I'm caught off guard when she says, "I love you."

It was no longer silent that time . . .

I get mad. I sling my hand against the tray of food beside me, sending it to the ground in my brief loss of control, food going everywhere. It's a good thing the doctor was standing on the other side of the bed. "Why can't I remember? How am I supposed to get back home if I can't remember who I am or where I'm from?"

I feel like screaming out my rage, but what good would it do? This is a nightmare. I take a mental note to rehash to myself the sequence of events so far: horrible accident, near death experience, rescued and brought to another country in which I am now stuck in, cannot remember anything of the previous said events and before.

"With a brain injury all we can do is wait it out. It takes time. There is no way to cure it or speed up the healing process. I'm not going to lie to you and give you false hope. The brain is unpredictable." Her face flashes through my mind again. Why is she the only thing coming back to me? What does that mean?

"Well, Doctor, then what is your medical determination and plan of care? I need to get out of here and go home." I know I'm being a smartass, but I don't care. He looks at the food scattered across the floor and back at me, before raising his brow. Yes, I know I had a lapse in good judgment, move on.

"I will keep you here for a while and monitor your condition. I cannot release you without any family to care for you until I know more of the outcome. You have retrograde amnesia. You have medial temporal lobe damage, but I want to do more tests now that the swelling has gone down. Get some rest and I'll have everything set up." Like I have any other option . . .

He walks to the door and touches the handle but looks back at me. "You're lucky to be alive. Things will be easier if you remember that. The amount of blood you lost—you could have died in the ocean. Had they not found you when they did, you would have."

Amnesia is not something I wanted to hear. I've never heard of anyone with amnesia come out with a good ending, but then again, I can't even remember my name, so what do I know . . .

How can this be better than dying, though? I am stuck in a hospital in a country I'm not familiar with and have no family or anyone that I know. I am completely alone. Even if I did know someone, I probably wouldn't remember him. What am I going to do if I don't regain my memory? Am I just supposed to stay here?

He pulls the door open with the clipboard of notes hanging by his side in his other hand. "Hey, Doc, what are the chances I will regain my memory? Give it to me straight."

From the serious demeanor on his face I'm going to guess the odds aren't in my favor. "It depends on your brain and how it heals. Every case is different. You may make a full recovery, you may only recover pieces of your prior life back but not all, or you may only get flashbacks here and there like with the girl, but no relevant information tied to them. There is also the possibility your life before the accident has been erased permanently and you will have to start over building new memories."

He then exits the room, leaving me to accept my new fate.

I place the heels of my hands on my forehead and grab at the hair on my head, pulling it in anger and frustration. I'd rather be dead than to never remember anything of my life. I could have had a great life—one I want to remember. Even if it was shitty, at least it was mine.

I want to get out of this bed, but I'm hooked to IV antibiotics, drips, pain medication, and wires for machines. I have to believe that when I can get out of this hospital something will strike a memory that I can grasp onto to find my way home.

EIGHT

Breyson

I've been in this damn hospital for a few weeks now and I feel like killing myself just to get out. I was given a tennis ball to relieve some of the tension. I've been through more tests than I can count. My medical status hasn't changed a single bit. None of my memories have returned except occasional flashbacks of that same girl. Each time it's something different, but I can never see myself in the visions. It's always like I'm looking through a window. It's the only thing that keeps me sane in this hellhole.

I want to find her, but I don't know how. She has to have answers. If I found her, I know I could piece back together the life I left behind. Where do people think I am? Did they give up looking for me? I'm probably just a photo on a missing persons poster by now, hanging on a board in a police station, lost with others.

Some days I get more than one flashback and some days I'm lucky to get one. The days I don't get any flashbacks are the days that inch by slowly, and they are mentally incapacitating. It's like my brain is trying hard to tell me something, but it's falling short every time.

Sitting on the edge of the bed, I bounce the ball against the floor. My stitches have been removed and the hair is beginning to grow back over the scar that has formed in their place. I can't take being in this tiny room any longer. I need to get out of here before I do something crazy, like hang myself. I feel fine aside from the fact that I remember nothing prior to waking up in this hospital. If I don't get discharged soon, I'm going to go mad.

I stand and walk toward the tiny window like I do several times a day. There isn't much of a view in terms of the hospital grounds, but at least it's something. Farther away, though, is enough to long to escape, even if just an hour.

Down below, past the busy intersection, where the sidewalk runs long and wide, people are packed in and scattered around the street market. Bright colors are visible from here. Fresh fruits look appetizing from the tables they sit on. Hats and purses hang from shop entrances. Smiles decorate the faces of the shoppers fingering through the hanging items for sale. What I wouldn't give to be some of them right now—free to do as I please.

As if my thoughts were voiced out loud, the door opens, and footsteps sound behind me. When I turn around it's the same doctor I've come to know pretty well. "Dr. Rodriguez."

"How are you feeling today, Son?" He calls me son, most likely, because he has no idea what my name is. I guess I should start thinking of a new name since I have no idea what mine is.

"The same way I always feel, Doc. You got any news for me today? I need good news." Another scan of my brain was taken earlier today to see if there have been any changes since the last one.

He walks over to me and places his hand on my shoulder. "Come sit down, Son." That doesn't sound good. In fact, it sounds horrible. That fatherly gesture that we need to have a talk is always a bad sign. I sigh and walk over to the bed I've become entirely too familiar with.

He takes a seat beside me as if we're about to have a heart-to-heart. We've developed this little relationship over the past few weeks. He stops by to visit regularly during his hospital hours, and even some when he's not scheduled to work. He feels bad I'm alone, even in my own head. I'm sure of it. He wouldn't come by during his off time for any other reason. "I'm going to say this, and we will discuss it when I finish. We will get it all out in the open first. Does that sound good?"

I nod. It's not like I have much of a choice since I have nowhere to go outside of my hole-in-the-wall room. "The scans are the same. There hasn't been a significant change since the first one. You're physically stable, so I can't keep you here anymore. Mentally, you may be lost, but physically, you can take care of yourself. Based on the anxious behavior every time I come in here, I'm sure you're ready to leave anyway. Medically speaking, you no longer need care, and like I explained to you from day one, I have no way of knowing whether your memory will come back or not. There is still a possibility that it could, but it's something that will be determined with time."

What the hell is he saying? What am I supposed to do, wander around like a homeless person? I don't think I believe in Karma, but I had to have done something pretty bad to end up like this. It would be tolerable if I had people I knew surrounding me to remind me of the things I don't remember. I feel like crying, or even ending it all. A mental breakdown is just beyond the horizon. What difference would it make anyway if everyone that knows me already thinks I'm dead? I've processed the thought of killing myself once or twice, but when I do is usually when I have the most flashbacks of . . . *her*. It's strange; like she is somehow keeping me here, forcing me to keep going.

"What am I supposed to do? I can't support myself. I have no money, no clothes, and no place to stay." I may be sick of this hospital, but at least it's a place to sleep and I have food to eat.

"I have no medical reason to keep you here any longer. The hospital advises against it. I like you. You seem like a good kid. I'm sorry you ended up in this situation. I want to help you. I have a proposition if you're open to it." He looks at me as if he asked me a question and is waiting for me to answer.

"Do I have a choice?" I search his face for emotion, but it's blank. He's old enough to be my father, which is why I'm guessing he has become somewhat attached to me.

"You always have a choice. No one can take away your freedom to choose. We can look at this objectively if you want. You come to a bridge you're going to have to cross if you want to get back home. The only thing between you and the other side is a cliff overlooking a high drop off. The bridge rocks and it's long. It looks scarier than it actually is. The only way to get to the other side is to hold onto the rope and walk across it. Every wooden plank that makes up the bridge is discovering who you are. Every clue is another step. You're lost right now, trying to figure out if the bridge even leads in the right direction. Carrying on a normal life may help you take the first step." I can kick and scream and throw a fit, but none of that will change the outcome.

The fact of the matter is, I'm stuck and he's willing to help me. "What's your proposition?"

"I'm glad you're openminded. I have a friend that breeds bulls for bull fighting. It's a popular sport here, like American football in the states. He is shorthanded right now and needs help. He provides a place to stay, three regular meals, and pay. I will help you get what you need to get started. If you stop trying so hard and let your brain heal naturally without pushing it, something may come back, or hopefully enough to get you where you belong. Worst case scenario, you make a new home." I run my fingers through my hair, making a mess of it. It doesn't sound that bad. If it gets me out of here, I'll do anything.

"Only if you let me pay you back for the clothes when I get my first paycheck. I don't want to be a charity case for anyone." He smirks, as if he almost expected me to offer it, and stands.

"I'm going to get you discharged. I will have a nurse bring you some scrubs until we can get you some clothes. He'll be expecting us soon, so we need to get going." He laughs and makes his way to the door.

"Expecting us? What if I had said no?"

"I figured you would see reason and say yes." His voice is laced with laughter as he walks through the door. I have grown to like him. I hope this isn't the last time I'll see him. He's the only sense of familiarity I have here. For the few minutes each time that he visits, I feel less alone, less like an orphan.

As I wait on a change of clothes I sit and wonder how my life is going to turn out. He's right. The only thing I can do is make the best of it and hope my memories come back. If I want it bad enough, I can achieve anything. This lost feeling is driving me crazy. I'm ready to feel like I have something to do that makes my life worth breathing the oxygen it takes to keep me alive.

I haven't had a flashback of her today, and right now I'd welcome it. I live for those brief flashbacks. I may not remember anything else in my life, but there is a reason my brain wants me to see her over and over. Most of the time it's just a look at her in one angle or another, but occasionally it's a memory without any names or relevant information. I know it's a memory trying to break free. It's like watching a damn movie of my life from the outside looking in, but on mute, and in brief clips cut from the whole reel. It's starting to piss me off, but I'm trying to give myself time, so I don't jinx myself and lose them altogether.

A nurse walks in and hands me a pair of scrubs to change into. I walk into the small bathroom to change out of this pathetic hospital gown. After shutting the door, I turn on the hot water of the shower, letting the steam fill the tiny room, and I step in. I place my palms against the wall and let the scorching hot water run down my body. It's hotter than it should be, but it's what I need right now. As the water rains down on my face from the top of my head, my mind wanders into the unknown.

It's her, but this time it's different than the other flashbacks. My mind is revealing more, and damn, she's naked. I'm in my own personal hell. Her body—I've never seen anything like it. She leans in, and in seconds, her lips are on mine.

I close my eyes and let myself watch, since none of it seems familiar. I feel like I'm invading someone's privacy, even though I can see my own hands roaming her beautiful body, touching her in places I wish I could really feel.

Her cheeks turn a light shade of red as the steam swirls around the large bathroom. My fingers are in her hair as I kiss her hungrily. It's fast and greedy like I'm addicted and can't get enough. I pull at her soft, full bottom lip and slide my tongue inside her mouth, parting her lips, to find hers in a game of hide and seek.

I close in on her, allowing her breasts to rub against my chest and her nipples instantly harden against my skin. Walking forward, I back her into the shower until she is standing underneath the water and close the door behind me. I never break the kiss as the water runs around our lips. Placing my fingertips on the side of her face, I trail down the silhouette of her body as I continue to devour her mouth. Grabbing her hands in mine I push her against the wall, pinning her hands above her head while I kiss down her neck.

My heart is pounding as I continue to watch, turned on to the point the skin of my dick is tight. I wish I could actually remember doing this instead of watching, but let it play on. They are now my lifeline. They keep me thriving.

I say something in her ear, just before her head rolls back against the wall in pleasure. Fuck, why can't I hear what's being said? That could be the key to everything. Grabbing underneath her ass I pick her up and prop her against the wall for support. Reaching between us with one hand I grab my dick and ease inside her. She grabs onto me to hold herself in place.

Her legs are bent and wrapped around me. She is lifting herself, pushing off my body, riding me in a standing position. God, I want to know what that feels like. I was a lucky son of a bitch. Her lips part and begin moving, but of course, I have no idea what she's saying. Her eyes are closed, but she lifts her head off the wall and opens them, looking directly into my eyes.

Staring into those green eyes seem familiar, but nothing comes to me. I want to feel her, and what it's like inside her. This is torture. I don't want to watch anymore. I want to experience it firsthand. This is like watching a homemade sex tape, but at least then you remember making it. I want to remember the way she sounds, the way she kisses, the way she tastes, and smells—her touch.

I continue to hold her waist to support her, but she is controlling the movements. Her mouth opens and her eyes close in ecstasy as she latches onto my lips with hers. Her movements slow down, so I take over the pace. She lets me as orgasms and bites my lip. She is hot when she comes. It doesn't take long after witnessing that in the vision that my movements halt as well. How am I ever going to live if I don't find her? I have to remember . . .

A knock sounds at the door and just like that, the vision vanishes back into the vault of my memory bank. "It's Dr. Rodriguez. I'm ready whenever you are." Now back in the present, I look down and realize my dick is still hard, a dull pain coursing through it. I can't deal with this shit right now. Maybe I need a cold shower instead. I shut off the water, before grabbing a towel and drying myself off. Wrapping it around me, I step out into the steam-filled room.

"I'll be out in five minutes," I call out, and listen as he steps away from the door. Placing my palms on the edge of the sink, I look at my reflection in the mirror. I see a boy, built for athletics, but nothing is familiar. It's like looking at a stranger. My soul inhabiting a foreign body. My slate is clean, but I don't want it to be. I bet most people don't have that thought, if given the chance to start over, righting every wrong.

I hang my head between my shoulders. This is my life now, so I might as well accept it and move on. I can't make myself remember, no matter how much I will it to happen, and unless someone from my past finds out I'm here, I have nothing to go on. I'm hanging in the balance, existing in the in-between.

NINE

Breyson

After purchasing me some clothes and toiletries as he promised, we pull onto a dirt road that winds left and right for about half a mile. He comes to a halt when we pull up at a property sitting on miles of open land.

Doc looks at me and then back at the road in front of him, letting me take in my surroundings. There is a large Spanish style house, making it impossible to see what lies in the back of the property. "I trust these people with my own kids. I would never leave you in the hands of someone I didn't trust. I know it's going to take a while for you to adjust, but I will check in on you every few days, okay?"

I look over at him as he glances between the driveway and me. The serious demeanor on his face tells me he means every word of what he says. If I want to get back home, I need to do whatever it takes to get there. "Okay."

When he kills the engine, we exit the car, making our way to the house. The door opens and a middle-aged woman with long, silky, black hair walks out onto the porch. She has a young boy trailing behind her. He looks to be about eight or nine. "Samuel, it's good to see you. I hope you are well. Is this the boy?"

I look over at Doc as he puts his arm over my shoulders, guiding me forward. "Yes, Maria, this is the one I was telling you about. Where is Antonio? I'd like to speak to him before I go." He continues pushing me forward until we reach the steps that lead to the porch. She's a very attractive woman, given her age. A comfortable vibe settles in my bones in her presence. I think I'll be okay here.

She smiles as we ascend the steps and walks over to give me a hug. I'm used to the heavy accent from being around Dr. Rodriguez and the hospital staff, so it's easier to decipher what she says. I'm just thankful people here speak English in a country that is not primary in the language.

She releases me but continues to rest her hands on the side of my shoulders in a motherly nature. "It's good to have you in our home. Any friend of Samuel's is a friend of ours. I want you to make yourself at home here. This is your home just as it is ours. Am I understood?"

I nod and respond, "Yes, ma'am."

In return she smiles bigger. "Good. My name is Maria Salvador, but I expect to be called Maria. Antonio is out back inspecting the cattle. He will show you around the property in the morning. It will be dark soon. You can spend the rest of the night familiarizing yourself with your living quarters." She looks beside her at the boy, who's quiet, and pulls him close. "This is my son, Marcus. He's been looking forward to meeting you since Samuel mentioned you might be interested in the position. You two will come to know each other quickly. It will be nice entertainment for him."

The boy takes me in and then regards his mother. "Do you want me to show him his room?"

"Yes, then you two can get acquainted. That would be great, actually. The food will be ready soon and I will call for both of you." He grins from ear-to-ear and waves his hand for me to follow him.

I pick up my one duffle bag of clothes and look at Doc. "I'll see you later then?"

He reaches in his pocket and pulls out a brand-new cell phone. "Oh, before I forget, this is for you while you're here. I'm only a tap away. Call me anytime you need me, and I will answer."

He hands it over to me, but I shake my head. "I can't accept that. You've done enough for me already."

Grabbing my hand, he places the cell phone in my palm and closes my fingers over it. "Son, I'm doing this more for myself than for you. Just take it and make the father in me feel better. You should always have a form of communication in case you need it."

Instead of arguing I take it. "Thank you for everything." He nods, and I turn to look at the boy waiting on me at the door. The excited look on his face eases the tension. I trail behind him into the house. I have a feeling I'm going to like this kid.

He guides me through the beautiful home decorated in orange, brown and cream colors. It's large and spacious. When we reach the back of the house we exit through a door onto a back patio, blades of grass coming up through the pavers. Occasionally, he looks over his shoulder to ensure I'm still following him. "You'll have your own place out here. Father built it for guests. He has another place for the workers, but my parents requested that you stay here."

I'm surprised by this level of hospitality, given they don't know me from a stranger on the street. "That's not necessary. I don't expect any special treatment. I'm fine with staying where the other employees stay," I tell him.

"No way. Dr. Rodriguez is a friend. My parents would be offended if you stayed out there." I continue to follow him until we reach a building that looks like a small version of the main house. This can't be a guest room. It's the size of a cottage. Bull fighting must be a bigger form of entertainment than I thought if he makes a living by raising cattle and selling them for sport. This place is nice, and I haven't even made it inside yet.

When we reach the door, he pulls a key from his pocket. Unlocking it, he opens the door. I take a look inside. It's exactly as I thought it was—a small house completely furnished. He walks inside and begins animatedly showing me where everything is. "The bedroom is in the back. You can find it when I leave. Mother says a bedroom is a person's private quarters," he says as he plops down on the sofa.

I drop my bag on the floor and sit on the opposite end. He's looking at me as if he wants to ask me questions but scared at the same time. I put him out of his misery by opening that door for him. "Is there something you want to know?"

His eyes widen at my forwardness. "Mother told me not to worry you with questions."

"It's okay. I don't mind. I may not be able to answer it, but you can ask." He looks as if he is unsure, but I guess his curiosity wins.

"Do you really not remember anything?" I shake my head. He remains quiet for a few seconds. "So, you don't have a name?"

"I imagine I do, but I don't know what it is."

"Well, we need to give you one then. You don't want to be known as *no name*." I can't help but laugh. Out of all the things he could ask, his worry of me not having a name was the most important. I knew I was going to like him.

"I do need a name. What did you have in mind?" I reach over and rub my palm over his jet-black hair, messing it up.

"Hey, don't mess up the hair," he says on a laugh. "It's your name. What do you want to be called? No one ever gets to pick their own name. You have to make it good." The kid has a good personality; I like that.

I lean back against the back of the sofa and extend my arms out to the side to rest on top. What do I want to be called? How do you just pick a name when there are so many? I should just pick the first name that comes to mind. "I like Bryce. You can call me that. What do you think?"

He rubs his chin as if there's an imaginary beard there. He's trying to act grown and wise. Then his face breaks and the seriousness disappears. "I like it. It's simple, but different, and not hard to say. You look like a Bryce."

I laugh again. "What does a 'Bryce' look like?"

"Like you. I don't know. You just do. I bet we will figure out what kind of stuff you like in no time. I think we should try different things, one at a time, to see if you remember anything. I did some research," he says, before pausing briefly in thought. "Okay, Mother did some research when I asked her if we could. She let me watch." There it is. I'm intrigued by how much time he's put into my condition. I've only known the kid about thirty minutes and already he feels like a little brother.

I try to keep the smirk off my face and remain serious, but it's harder than I thought. "Run it by me. I want to hear what you have in mind."

He scoots toward the middle of the couch and angles himself to face me. "Well, after Dr. Rodriguez came by to speak with Father and told him about your condition it got me thinking. I read somewhere that seeing or doing certain things from your past could spark a memory and bring it to the surface." He looks at me, as if he's expecting me to jump in and say something.

I hate to kill his optimism by being pessimistic, but my hopes of remembering were shattered while I was stuck in a hospital with nothing coming back. At this point, I'm just hoping to find some kind of clue to get back to where I came from. Getting my memories back is dead in the water. "You do realize there is a chance my memories may never come back, right?"

He gives me a *no crap* expression, as if I just said the dumbest thing he has ever heard. "You're not going to remember anything with that attitude, Bryce. As I was saying, I think that if we try different things maybe a memory will come back to you."

Where did that much spunk in such a young dude come from? "I'm not trying to sound arrogant, but why are you interested in helping me remember? What's in it for you? You don't even know me, kiddo."

He gives me a mischievous grin for the first time, and I sense a cocky side for kid his age. "Well, as you can see, there isn't that much to do around here. I don't have any siblings. I want to learn new things, like sports. Since my mother homeschools me, I don't get much playtime with other kids my age. I'll help you, and in turn you'll be helping me. I know you'll be helping my father during the day, but he won't make you work all week, so maybe on your off day or during your free time you can show me something new. I've seen those guys on TV that belong to a team. You look like them with all those muscles you have. We can try everything. Something has to work."

He's so animated when he starts talking about it that I can't stand the thought of letting him down. I don't believe my memory is coming back, but I can play along for his sake. "Okay. If this is something you really want to do, I'm down. When do you want to start and what's first on the list?"

He grins from ear-to-ear and stands quickly. I'm not sure what he has planned but seeing him this excited makes the day a little brighter in a world of gloom. He can't be older than ten. I should have asked. "I'm going to think about it and decide what's first. We start tomorrow after work if that's okay with you."

I don't respond immediately. His face falls as if he's afraid I'll back out. "Tomorrow is perfect. For now, what's on the agenda? I don't want to be a bad house guest my first night here."

He's back to wearing the smile he's had plastered on his face since we got in this house. "I'll come get you for dinner. You can do what you want until then. Mother does everything on a schedule, so mealtimes will always fall at the same time each day. You have about an hour. I'm going to plan for tomorrow. You should find everything you need in here. Are you okay by yourself for a while?"

"I think I can make do for a while. See you in a bit. Now go on and get to planning." I stand and mess up his hair again, before he laughs and takes off running out the door, trying to comb through the mess with his fingers.

I take a deep breath as I stand here alone. The silence is deafening. I liked it better with the kid in here, but I'll never admit it. Maybe it won't be so bad between me keeping him occupied and working. I don't like the idea of being left alone in my thoughts, or lack thereof.

I walk to the bedroom and set my bag on the bed, before spotting a set of sliding glass doors. The orange and pink in the horizon is visible through the door, confirming in color that the sun is setting. When I notice the chairs sitting vacant out on the small patio, I walk outside.

I sit in one of the chairs and stare off, listening to the sound of bulls blowing in the distance. It's beautiful here, but I feel like an orphan. I have no idea who my family is, where they are, or what they're doing. I want to know what they're like and if they're thinking of me. Have they moved on or do they have hope I'm wandering around lost somewhere?

Leaning forward and resting my elbows on my thighs, I fight to get a grip on my emotions. My eyes fill with tears as the questions race through my overwhelmed mind. I just wish I could remember something—anything. A tear is dispersed from the inner corner of my eye and runs down my nose, before falling to the ground. I'm so mad and alone I could scream. I'm not only alone physically, but also mentally. I want to know who did this to me. I'm stuck in a black hole with no way out.

What I wouldn't give for a memory right now—a human mind's basic response to experience. We take advantage of simple things. Things that seem useless until we're left without them. Who thinks of a life with no memories or inhabiting the earth with no identity? It's as if I don't exist. I'm a drifter in an unfamiliar place. No one is coming for me. I might as learn to live with my circumstance. This is my new life. My name is Bryce, and here is where my life begins. Who I was before is long gone.

We are who we make ourselves. It's time I stop feeling sorry for myself and learn to live, to be happy in some way. There is a kid counting on me. I won't let him down. My life as I once knew it is over, but his is just beginning really. Life is full of disappointment. I won't let it consume me and make me weak.

Just as I'm about to get up and clean up for dinner, an image flutters through my mind—*her*. She's walking down the stairs in a green and white dress with her hair fixed. She's impeccable. Every time I see her, my chest aches, and I can't figure out why. Like I always do, I soak it up, taking in every detail I can hold onto, until it vanishes, leaving my world grayer than it was before.

I can't help but wonder why it's *always* her. *Only* her. You hear about things like medical miracles or paranormal encounters, but you never hear much about the subconscious or the soul. It's one of the greatest unknowns. What kind of power does it hold? Can it resurface things that are buried so deep inside your mind won't let you unlock them?

I haven't had a single clue to anyone that may have been in my life but her. It's like there is something that I'm missing linking us together. Something fighting hard to keep her memory from getting completely lost. My mind may have a lock on my memories, but for every lock there is a key. It's all about finding the one that fits. Marcus could be the key. For the first time since I woke up in that hospital, an inkling of hope is there.

TEN

My life has become a recurring cycle of three things: wake up, visit the cemetery, go back to bed. In that exact order. It's been a month since Breyson's death, and the longest month of my entire life. I haven't been able to go to school since he left. Luckily, I've been so sick in this pregnancy I have a medical excuse not to go. I stay exhausted, because I wake up screaming every night from my dreams ending. In turn, I sleep more just to get pulled into a dream with him. If you didn't know my situation you would think I was bedridden with my pregnancy.

The only place I go is to the cemetery to talk to Breyson, but today that has to change. My parents are making me go to school, then I have to go to my doctor's appointment to check on the baby. To top it off, my parents are scheduling me an appointment with a Psychologist to try and help me cope. It's a waste really, because I'm not going. I tried to tell Mom it won't help, but she refuses to listen. She is grasping at straws to bring her baby back. Her baby is never coming back, just like Breyson is never coming back.

My alarm buzzes on the bedside table, reminding me of the hellacious day I have ahead of me. It's too soon. No one knows I'm pregnant except for mine and Breyson's family, and of course Adalynn.

I don't know how much longer I can keep it a secret now that I have to go back to school.

I walk into my bathroom to shower, turning on the hot water. I look down at my naked body. My belly is tight, and a slight bump has formed over my lower abdomen, like a hard pudge—nothing visible with clothes on, and even in a bikini wouldn't be associated with pregnancy since some girls have one naturally. It's still early, Mom said, when I brought it up with the whole returning to school idea, but I've lost weight, making what tiny protrusion is there more visible.

It reminds me that I've lost the person responsible for it, the most amazing boy. This baby is hidden beneath the surface for now, but at some point, even loose clothing won't hide this pregnancy. How much longer will it be until I have a round belly beneath my clothing for kids at school to gawk at? I don't know what I'm supposed to do about the morning sickness. Mom is supposed to talk to the principal. Not every class is by a bathroom and I refuse to throw up in front of my classmates. Whoever came up with that name was seriously misled, because I would give anything just to be sick in the morning. I have changed the name for mine to *all day* sickness. I've also been informed that mine may bleed over into the second and third trimester as severe as it is. *Great.*

As the thought crosses my mind a surge of nausea causes me to run to the toilet. I make it, but just as the acid burns my throat on its upward climb. When will this torture end? I have no idea how I'm supposed to sit in class all day if I can barely make it to the toilet a few feet away. If every woman had a pregnancy like this, I doubt there would be as many people in the world, because the chances of a second one would be slim. I don't have that to worry about, though. If I can just get through this pregnancy, this will be it for me. The thought of having sex with someone else disgusts me.

I don't think I will ever be able to stomach being touched by another man the way Breyson touched me. Once you've experienced sex with the man that captured your heart and is the keeper of your soul, everyone else falls short.

I went into losing my virginity with the mindset it was just an act— something everyone has to do at some point. It was more or less so I didn't have to carry it around—the infamous V-card. It was baggage I wanted to get rid of. I look back now and see how very wrong I was. I gave my virginity to someone that deserved it. I wasn't a married woman like I should have been, but at least it was with someone I loved, even if the love part came after the fact. I think my heart knew it all along. My mind had to catch up.

Maybe if I had started out with a meaningless relationship like Breyson was intended to be I would have seen things differently, but the man you love has the power to ruin you, to mark you as his whether he's here to claim it or not. My body will always be his, as well as everything else. I will never move on emotionally from him. I can learn to live with the pain over time, but I'll never be happy with anyone else, so there's no reason to try. I guess soul mates work that way. When one is lost, they both are.

When the nausea subsides enough to distance myself from the toilet, I step into the shower and enjoy the blanket of hot water, blistering me from the temperature. I need to hurry, but I don't know how. Everything in my life is moving at a snail's pace. Adalynn is taking me to school today. It's not in anyone's best interest for me to drive right now. In the state I'm in, I'm liable to run myself off a bridge or into a tree.

I pour my coconut shampoo into my hands and work it into a foamy lather, spreading it throughout my hair from root to tip. It's not what I've been using lately, but that's my little secret. I bought the same shampoo and body wash that Breyson used to use, but I have to go back into the real world now. Smelling like a man wouldn't be understandable to a normal member of society. As a matter of fact, it probably seems a little insane. Only I know that it helps keep his memory alive.

I finish bathing and shut the water off. Wrapping my towel around my wet body, I step out and brush my teeth at the sink. I want to go back to sleep and dream about him. I have no energy. All I want to do is lay in bed. How am I going to be a mother to someone? I don't know how to pull myself together to heal, let alone be a productive adult in the world. I'm stuck at the bottom of a pit with no way out.

I can't meet this baby's needs if I can't pick myself up from this emotional freefall I've been in since his disappearance. It might be time to start considering what is best for this baby. As quick as the thought appears, it disappears. It's the only thing left of Breyson, like his mother said. For that reason alone, I couldn't give this baby up if wanted to.

I pull on my black polo dress. School uniforms make my life a little easier. I need to steer away from all thought. I couldn't make a decision right now if I tried, much less a wise one. I comb through my hair and tousle the curls. It can dry on its own. I don't have the desire to impress anyone. The only person I ever cared about impressing was Breyson.

As I slide my shoes on my feet, my door opens. Adalynn walks inside and pulls me into her arms without a word. She's always been the caring and passionate one of the crew. "It's going to be okay. I promise. Everyone has been asking when you're coming back. We all miss you, Kinzleigh. The only way to heal is to continue living. I'm here to help you. You'll need this."

She hands me a new tube of waterproof mascara. She always thinks of everything. I need to remember to thank God for my friends. I will never take anyone for granted again.

"Thanks," I say as I take it from her. Looking in the mirror, I brush it on my eyelashes until the color is a bold black. I put on Grams' earrings and smear my tinted gloss over my lips. Picking up my book bag—which seems heavier than normal, even without books—I let out a deep breath and walk to the door.

As we pull into the school parking lot my chest tightens. It feels wrong to be here without him, like trespassing on private property. He was here before me. I can't just walk through those halls without him beside me. I came back too early. Who am I kidding? I can't do this. Panic overcomes me, and I feel short of breath. As I place my hand over the door handle, I begin to tremble, my body shaking uncontrollably. I have never been here without him.

Since I moved here it's been him and me. We were in our own little bubble before it got popped. I want it back. Adalynn takes my opposite hand. "It's okay to be scared, Kinzleigh. Let the fear drive you. Instead of being scared you can't live without him, fear you'll forget him if you don't learn to exist in the world you two lived in together. There is no rush. We can sit here for a while if you want to."

Adalynn is my best friend alongside Presley. She never puts herself first. She's one of the best people I know. I can't let her get a tardy because of me. I'm also keeping her from Braxton. I still can't be around him much. He is physically identical to Breyson. The real fear is that I'll embarrass myself somehow with him, even though their personalities are completely different. It's too soon. It hurts too much to look at him. I can hang around Londyn and Briar more, so she doesn't have to sacrifice her time with him. I can see how much they care about each other, and it makes me happy.

I think we often overlook what's right in front of us. I know I did until fate laughed at me, sending me into the very backyard of the boy I was trying to stay away from. As cruel as life can be, though, I wouldn't go back and change any of it.

I was given a taste of true love. That taste changed me forever. God humbled me. It's not okay to turn away love to avoid the risk of being hurt.

The risk is part of its appeal, I guess. It makes having it more beautiful. Being hurt sucks—that's no secret—but everyone needs a Breyson in their lives.

He loved me for who I am, and that love was unconditional. The love we shared was beautiful and rare. When I accepted that loving him was unavoidable and embraced it, the outcome was that I realized we had a love most people don't experience in a lifetime. I should be grateful that I was able to experience it at all, despite losing it.

I look down at our linked hands and then up at her face. "I'm ready. I can't promise I'll be able to walk with you and Braxton, but I think I can manage a day."

Just as I'm about to turn back for the door, I hear the one thing I'll never forget the sound of—his voice. "I'll be with you, baby. It's okay to be here. I'm with you always. I love you." My eyes widen, and chills run down my spine. I quiver, tears prickling my eyes.

"Why do you always do this to me? It's not fair. You know how hard it is for me to be away from you. I love you more; so much more," I say, playing the little game we used to always play when we said I love you or I miss you.

My heart is racing from the sound of his voice. It feels like it's missing until I hear him—my sexy southern comfort— in the accent that makes me weak in the knees. As soon as I feel or hear him, my heart revives itself, pounding against my chest as if it were never missing at all.

I open my eyes. I didn't realize they were even closed. Adalynn looks like she just saw a ghost. Her mouth is gaping, her eyes are wide, and her smooth, bronzed skin has paled. "Kinzleigh, talk to me. You're scaring me. Who are you talking to?"

Crap.

How am I supposed to explain this when I don't understand it? My crazy—the only thing it can be classified as when talking to people that are dead. I need to be locked away in an asylum to be alone in my unstable head. Next Beau will be talking to me, or Grams, and then I'll really be insane. "It's nothing. Can we go? I didn't get enough sleep last night. I'm sure I'm just delusional right now."

She narrows her eyes at me, as if she knows I'm lying, but to my surprise she lets it go. We walk toward the school entrance, and as we pass, the kids outside stare. The expressions they wear clearly reveal pity. They don't mask it at all. I'm now the little rich girl with the dead boyfriend.

Dread hits me like a freight train. I should consider homeschool. I can only imagine what people are going to say when they find out I'm pregnant at eighteen on top of everything. I'm not prepared for the whispers, the stares, the sympathy. I'll be a social outcast; good for nothing if I can't drink at parties and sleep around like a lot of the popular girls around here.

We walk inside, and I freeze. I can't pick up my feet, because I feel like they are weighted down with cinder blocks. I can see the exact spot I saw Breyson for the first time after I moved here—the first day of school. My lungs feel like I'm being anchored at the bottom of the ocean with no oxygen, constricted and unable to breathe. I will never make it through this day if I can't even get in the door.

"You okay, babe? Do you want to go back to the car?" Adalynn is staring at me as if I'm about to break. How did I become this lost girl? I was always so sure of myself, so strong and independent, yet here I am frail and crying constantly. I had finally found my place in the world and it was stolen from me.

I close my eyes and force deep breaths. The only way I'll be able to turn from the direction I'm heading is to concentrate on letting the air into my lungs. When I open them, I am the center of attention in a hallway filled with students.

My eyes fill with tears, but I refuse to let them fall. My hormones are already out of whack without the pain from the loss of my one true love. I want to go see Breyson. I don't think I can do this. I didn't give it enough time. The hair on my arms stand up and all the blood drains to my feet. I know one thing: I'm not alone.

I'm letting my mind control me. I've never been one of those people that believe in paranormal. I don't believe in ghosts and goblins or witchcraft. I believe that once you die your soul moves on to another place and there are only two options: Heaven or Hell. But what if the other person isn't dead? Could he really still be alive and trying to connect with me somehow? My heartbeat picks up and a small burst of air tickles the back of my neck, the way it always did when Breyson would stand behind me and whisper in my ear.

The air surrounding me becomes thick, as if someone is blocking it from circulation. I feel like someone is wrapped around me, holding me. As creepy as it is, it's also comforting. Why is this happening to me? How am I supposed to move on this way? I need a way to distance myself before my mind goes to a place it can't come back from.

I should strongly consider persuading my parents to let me homeschool.

With me being pregnant and depressed there is no reason for me to be here. Once I graduate, I'll move on to college somewhere and a change of scenery. It hurts too much to be here. "It's okay, baby. Trust me," a voice whispers; a voice I would still know even if I hadn't heard it in years.

My lips tremble and the tears fall. Teachers and students have stopped in the halls to stare at me as if I'm a nutcase—a character straight out of a psychiatrist's worse nightmare. Everyone is awaiting on my next move. I want to be left alone. High school is full of drama. What the hell do they expect from me?

Please stop talking to me, Breyson. You're making it harder on me. I feel crazy. Do you want me to be crazy? I shouldn't be hearing your voice. You're not here. You were taken from me. Please don't do this to me.

"Kinzleigh, talk to me. Do you need to leave?" I can hear Adalynn talking, but I seem to be stuck where I stand, as if my shoes are in wet tar. I'm lost in my mind. Until the nausea returns, reminding me that I forgot my medicine this morning. I can taste the acid in the back of my throat. My saliva is steadily increasing in volume. I gag, and just like that, my legs finally work. I run for the bathroom with my hand covering my mouth. I finally make it to the bathroom, the door hitting the wall from my hard shove, but the vomit soaking a section of my hand tells me I'm almost a minute too late. I burst into the stall, throwing up until all that is left are dry heaves, my eyes wet for a different reason this time.

I stand, pulling in air, and then grab a wad of toilet paper to clean myself up. I can't leave the confinement of this stall just yet, even with the lingering rancid smell. It's blocking me from the outside world. Against my will I break down as I press my backside against the door of the stall. I want it to end, all of it. I never asked for this. I would change places with anyone, including Breyson. No one will ever convince me that being the lover left behind isn't worse than all other parties effected by someone's death. Standing here wallowing isn't going to change anything either.

I push through the stall door to a vacant bathroom. I wash my hands and splash my cheeks with cold water. I'll have to get a juice from the drink machine. Maybe that will soothe my stomach. The holder dispenses a paper towel when I wave my hand in front of it. I dry my hands and am about to leave the girls' restroom when Natalie walks in—not a person I want to deal with right now. "You're pregnant, aren't you?"

Hasn't she tormented me enough? I shake my head, about to give her some lame virus excuse, but she interrupts. "You don't have to lie. It's obvious. Secrets like that don't stay secrets for long."

I toss the paper towel in the large, yellow trashcan. "What do you want, Natalie? You continue to torment me day in and day out, and I don't understand why. I have never in any way done anything to you. You're a bully. I'm sorry that things didn't work out the way you wanted them to, but it's not my fault he didn't choose you. Did you ever stop to think that I love him just like you do? I didn't let him have me trying to hurt you. I met him before I knew you even existed."

More tears cleanse my face, and for the first time in a while I feel like talking. "He told me about your 'pregnancy' before I moved here, so if you think for one second I did this on purpose, think again. He's the only guy I've slept with. I know you wanted this. For the life of me I can't imagine why. My life is ruined in more ways than one."

She stands there, watching my face swell from crying so hard. "This is your chance. Laugh it up. Bask in my misery. Neither of us have him. Does that make you happy? Does it make you feel like a better person to know that I'll be strapped down with a child to raise by myself? That the father of my unborn child and the love of my life is dead? He left before I found out. He died without knowing he's going to be a father. So, no, I most definitely didn't plan this. In fact, I tried to stay far away from it. If he were here you could ask him, but sometimes things don't work out the way we want them too. That's the way this sucky life works."

My voice is louder than it should be, and my throat is raw and sore from throwing up, a dull burn coating it. "Now, for the love of all things holy, will you grow up and get a life, so you can stop torturing me?"

I've been holding this in for a while with her, letting it build, and now it's time to let it all go. "You got what you wanted. If you can't have him no one can, right? Congratufuckinglations! You. Won." I don't think I've ever said that word, but right now, I think I have earned the right. As I stand here and talk about him the sorrow returns, making it hard to breathe, to think, to move. I don't even think waterproof mascara can stand up to this much moisture.

She moves closer to me, cornering me in the bathroom. On instinct, I step back and place my arms over my stomach, preparing for a hit. With her, you never know what to expect. Wouldn't be the first time she's tried to hurt me. My parents paid a hospital bill from it. This time I have something of Breyson's she can't take, even if she did have him.

Her eyes lower to my abdomen and she huffs. A scowl crosses her face, but she stops. "I'm not going to hurt you, Kinzleigh. I mean, for obvious reasons, you're not my favorite person, but I'm not a terrible person. I told you the drink was a joke to dirty up Breyson's perfect little blonde he couldn't take his eyes off of. Everyone does it. I didn't think it'd do anything but give you a high. I paid for it in community service hours. I just want to talk. Will you let me say what I need to say? Then, if you want, I will leave you alone."

I straighten. Her tone is laced with agitation, but sincere. I'm still weary. But she's right. She's not going to hurt me. Nothing she could do to me would hurt me worse than I already am. "Fine. What do you want to talk to me about? The bell already rung for first period and we're both late. Doesn't look good, considering . . ."

"I guess I deserve the hostility, given our track record." For the first time since I met her, her shoulders fall—surrender. "Look, Kinzleigh, I know you don't like me. I'm sorry. I can't take back what I've done."

Then the entitled princess starts to cry, and she's no longer standing tall, as if she's wearing a crooked crown. I never thought I'd see the day. "You're not the only one that loved him, you know. It's a blinding emotion. It makes you do things you'll regret. It makes you act out in ways you never would otherwise—like the fake pregnancy. I admit to it. He was pushing me away and I was grasping onto anything I could. I had my married cousin pee on a stick for me. I told her it was for a science project or she wouldn't have agreed to it. I don't know what I was thinking, or what I would've done had he stood by me and believed me with no question. I was biding more time till I could figure something out."

She pats at the salty liquid on her cheek, trying to keep her makeup intact. "But it didn't work. He was so angry. Angrier than I've ever seen him. It was a shot in the dark. He knew the chances were unlikely. He wouldn't have sex with me without a condom and he always pulled out. I tried . . . every time, so yes, I wanted what you have, but a baby wouldn't have made him love me. He's never looked at me like he looks at you. You're the one that made him careless, and that's what makes you different."

I draw in air, trying to calm down. It's not easy hearing about someone you love being with someone else that way, even when you knew he was prior to you. I only have him. "The way you feel about him, the way you're crying without him—imagine if some other girl got his attention and he chose her over you. I'm not making excuses for myself. I'm just trying to give you another point of view. Losing someone you love to someone else isn't easy to handle. It makes you desperate."

Why is she telling me this? "I never meant to hurt you, but in a way, I don't regret it, because it opened my eyes. Seeing how he reacted when he thought he might lose you cleared up any confusion I had. I will always love him, Kinzleigh, and that I can't change, but the only difference in you and me is you get his love returned. We can't control who we fall in love with. Breyson is hard not to love if you've spent any amount of time with him. You're the one that gets to keep him, even in his absence. I just wanted you to know how sorry I am for what I did to you. He really loved you. That baby in your womb proves it. I hope that you can accept my apology and we can start over."

She is crying as hard as I am. My back pressed against the wall, I slide down into a kneeling position. Even I know it takes a strong person to do what she just did. I place my hands over my face and let it out.

God, why was he taken from me? I don't understand. He didn't deserve to die.

"You want to get out of here?" I look up at her, breathing through the milder version of my sickness that never goes away. Do I want to leave with her? I might be crazy for this, but I don't think I'm ready to face everyone yet. When I took off to the bathroom Adalynn knew not to wait for me, because I don't want to make a big deal out of my nausea, hoping it would steer away rumors and assumptions. I guess I was wrong.

I know I shouldn't go with her, but I don't think she'll hurt me anymore. I'm going to trust her, even though I have every right not to. I nod, because I can't get out the words. "Come on, let's go."

Four words never sounded so good . . .

ELEVEN

Kinzleigh

It didn't take me being told twice before I jolted out the door and headed for the exit. On the trek through the parking lot, she caught up to me and ran ahead to show me to her car. Without hesitation, she unlocks the doors and sits in the driver's side, waiting for me to join her. We, as people, make hasty decisions looking for an easy way out when something is hard.

I realize that now that I'm sitting beside a girl I never thought I'd be sitting beside. The girl that's tried to embarrass me countless times, talked behind my back, and stopped at nothing to win back the only boy I will ever love. But things she said earlier lurk in my mind and I can't really blame her. For the longest time she saw me in the exact way I saw her—the villain.

In her mind I was the girl that took him from her. And the very thought of losing him to another girl is devastating. I'm not sure if I *could* watch him with someone else. I had never thought of it that way. It makes me sad. But I do love him. I have loved him since the start. We've both lost something. I wish there were some way to bring him back. I would do anything for Breyson, even if it meant giving him up for him to live. It's the only way I could let him go. I would bargain my happiness for his life any day.

I stare out the window at the passing blurs of green that indicate spring. It's days away from being here. An array of colors is slowly evolving from the departure of winter—a season that will haunt me for a long time. I feel so alone. More alone than I've ever felt in my life. Will the pain ever subside? I know it hasn't been long, but I can't imagine ever feeling better without him.

What happens to a person when their soul loses its mate? Does it slowly die until there is nothing left but the hollow shell of a person, or does it try to connect with another widowed soul? It could close off the wounded side like the sap of an injured tree. There are so many questions in this world that we can't answer on our own. If only I had a cheat sheet with all the answers . . .

"Where do you want to go?" she asks as she continues down the highway. I refuse to take her to our place. I may forgive her for what she did and sit next to a woman that's had sex with the boy I love, but I will not share our sacred place—our tree. Some things aren't meant to be shared. They are meant to be treasured in private.

To me, our place is like that movie *The Secret Garden* in comparison. I used to watch it at Grams' when I was a kid. They worked hard to keep it hidden from the outside world, scared it would no longer be just theirs— the place they went to escape.

The only other place I can think of that reminds me of him is the beach. It may not be the one we met at, but any beach will do. It's become a place of significance—ours and ours alone. "Do you guys have a beach close by?" I turn to look at her. A void look crosses her face.

"We do, but it's a bit of a drive. You up for it?" Anything is better than facing a school full of kids staring and snickering as if I am some alien from another planet.

I nod and look out the window. There isn't much to say, so I don't. I've never been a pretender. I'm not fake. If my face were a book it would be full of spoilers. I want to enjoy the peace and quiet. I don't know if it's safe to be alone in my thoughts, but I've decided I'd rather hear him and know that I'm just crazy than to not hear him at all. At this point, I should embrace the crazy and not avoid it.

I place my hand over my belly and can feel the small hard bump. It's a constant reminder of the love I had, as well as what's to come. What scares me is that I'll resent this baby, knowing I have to live without the one that helped create it. He would have been a good dad, even young. He loved me that much.

I brush the thought aside, because I can't deal with the what ifs right now.

I can only hold onto the things I know, and I know I'll never experience that kind of love again. Even if I was given the option, I don't want it. To move on with someone else means Breyson will be left behind and forgotten. I couldn't live with myself.

An hour and a half into the car ride, the strip of beach comes into view. Beautiful houses and condominiums line the left side of the highway. Natalie pulls off to the right side and kills the engine. Before I exit the car, I slip off my shoes. Luckily, it's one of those warm days right after a cold snap where mother nature isn't really sure what season she's going to be for the day.

The weather here is constantly back and forth during the winter months. One day it's warm and the next it's freezing. I step out of the car onto the sidewalk, looking out at the sand littered with sticks and occasional plastic. Bits and pieces of shells show through from where they were washed up. Wooden lounge chairs line the beach as far as the eye can see, freshly covered with the cushion from the lifeguard on duty. There is a putrid smell in the air, like fish. And the water is brown, much like the creeks I've been too back home. It's definitely no California beach, that's for sure. I let the sun warm my face, opening my eyes to the clear blue sky. It's a pretty day.

As if she senses the question in my mind, she says, "It's because of the barrier islands. If you've ever been far enough out to one of them the water is pretty just beyond it. The beach isn't what makes this place a tourist attraction, the casinos do. Hurricanes would be a lot worse without them, so they do serve a purpose, even though they make the water a lot less appealing."

Without a word, I walk along the gray sidewalk, stepping over the cracks, until I come to a short series of steps that lead to the sand. I descend, stepping down each one until I can feel the grainy sand between my toes.

I can sense her presence behind me, but she gives me space, and for that I'm thankful. When I get to the shoreline I stop. Seagulls are swarming overhead, squawking and scavenging for food. I close my eyes, instantly taken back to that night my parents told me we were moving. The night he kissed me for the first time. The water washes ashore and crashes against my bare ankles. My only complaint is that it's bright when I'd prefer the night. The breeze picks up and my hair flutters in the wind like the wings of a butterfly.

"Talk to me. I need to hear you, Brey." I whisper pleadingly into the air that's swirling around me. The times I don't feel him are the hardest times of all. I'm scared of what will happen when I don't feel him anymore. I wait, hoping I will hear him, see him, or sense him, but nothing happens.

Occasionally, I let the pain take over my body, because it reminds me that he was real. Now would be one of those times I'd welcome the pain. I allow all of my senses to take over but two—sight and taste. Keeping my eyes closed, I concentrate on the other three.

Sound. Waves breaking. Flapping wings. Tires rolling down the highway. A little girl's voice in the distance calling out to her mom. A barge horn goes off somewhere far out. Whispering wind.

Touch. Salt licks my face. Sea mist kisses my skin. Cold water blankets my feet—much too cool for swimming—causing a chill to sweep through my body. Crisp, clean air hugs me as it whirls in the atmosphere, keeping the temperature under control.

Smell. Putrid fishy perfume lingers still. The salt in the air burrows deep inside my nose with every inhale. Birds. The natural odor of their feathers is pushed around by the waddling and flapping they're doing. The hint of cooked seafood is starting to inhabit the area from the casino restaurants.

All things that still make up a tranquil place combined.

Sight and taste will always cause me pain. He's in everything I see, like where we've been, what we've done, but then he isn't. Certain memories require him to be present to activate, like the taste of his tongue, his skin, the way he looks just before he comes. The way his abs tighten and ripple when he's loving me. How he closes his eyes when he's kissing my body. The smile on his face when we're studying and he's watching me but doesn't think I notice.

I want to be able to look into his penetrating blue orbs that have a power over me no one else has. His eyes tell so many stories. They're kind. They're possessive. They're angry. They're always focused on me.

I want to taste his lips and his tongue as it connects with mine, wreaking havoc on my heart and mind. He is the one addiction I will never be able to break no matter how hard I try. Regardless of how much time goes by or how much help I get, the craving consumes the need to shake it. The memory of the high I was on when I was near him will keep me searching for the fix.

Salty moisture runs into the crevice of my mouth. I lick it, remembering the way his sweat coated his lips after he played a game, and deep down, though I'd never admit it, those salty kisses were my favorite.

He's never coming back, Kinzleigh. Say it. You need to come to terms with it before the darkness takes over and you can't find the light.

The beach is a peaceful place, and even though that will always be, it holds a deeper meaning for me. Had I not met Breyson that day I'd still be a cynical, immature little girl right now.

Breyson was my saving grace, my reality check to the broad world around me instead of the ridiculously small bubble I was living in. I know now, that every girl needs to be sprinkled with love, if only just once, because it has the power to heal the most tormented and tarnished souls. I wish I could have saved him the way he saved me. To pursue your dreams and goals is only meaningful if you have someone by your side to enjoy them with.

I back up and sit on the dry sand to try and make the best of this day. That's all I can do anymore. Natalie sits down beside me and we stare out at the choppy ocean as the waves roll in. For once, I allow myself to think of the bigger picture, which is something I haven't done. Pondering my future hasn't been a thought at all since he's been gone. I haven't considered what path I'll take now that Breyson won't be with me.

My dream was always to be an NFL cheerleader. I know they don't make a high enough salary to do it fulltime, but that's not why I wanted to be one. That didn't matter to me, because I knew I would go to college and get an education to pay the bills. I wanted to be an NFL cheerleader because cheerleading is something I enjoy. It was a way to travel to different places. My plan was to could do it on the side, because cheerleading is what I love. Just because I graduate doesn't mean I have to give it up. The point of a dream is to pursue something that makes you happy, not something that makes you rich.

Professional players are guys that got there because football is what they loved. You don't get into a profession like that because it's a high paying job. You get there because you're good. You have to devote years to practice, games, and schedules. To endure all of those things for most of your life there has to be a passion that motivates you. Going into something for the sake of getting rich takes away your perspective on the art of the game.

People laugh when they ask me what I want to pursue a career in and my response is NFL cheerleading. They don't take me seriously. What I never added was that I would do that on top of whatever I went to college for, just like the rest of them. I don't know what that something is yet, so why explain all that to someone that really doesn't care anyway? I have a starting goal and the rest will fall into place. I'm not an idiot. I know you have to have a realistic dream to be able to support yourself.

It doesn't matter now anyway. I'll have to give up that dream. You can't travel from city to city being a single parent. My only option is to amend my dream. In the beginning, I wanted to start my own cheerleading company when I was too old to be a cheerleader. I used to do it with my barbies all the time. I wanted to teach girls of all ages. I wanted to coach competition squads. I can still have that if I set my mind to it.

My dad is a successful entrepreneur, so I have the necessary resources to learn. I'll have to get a business degree if I want to be a business owner, so I have other options until I can obtain my dream. It's like building a Lego wall—one piece at a time. My parents always taught me that if there was a will for something there was a way to achieve it. It just may take longer now that I will have someone else added to the mix.

California is slipping farther away from me. I will have to stay close to my parents for college to get the necessary support I need to go to school with a baby. It's going to be hard, but it's my only option—the only one I'm giving myself. I will not give up the only piece of Breyson I have left. No matter how many times the thought crosses my mind, I won't take the easy way out.

Breyson and I were planning to go to a university together, but I can't leave the state when I'm going to have to have childcare and a place to stay. I refuse to burden my parents with my child. I won't be one of those teenage girls that gets pregnant and lives off of her parents, giving nothing up. I got myself into this mess. I will support this child one way or another. If I have to get a part-time job I will. Now they have online and night classes if I have to work during the day.

Natalie bumps my shoulder with hers. I didn't realize I was lost in my thoughts. "You want to talk about it? I'm a good listener. I promise not to judge or repeat anything."

I don't understand her at all. Generally, I like people until they've done something to give me a reason not to like them and not the other way around. "Why are you suddenly being nice to me?"

She drops her shoulders and holds her head in shame as she sifts the sand through her fingers. "Kinzleigh, the person I've been isn't who I am. I wouldn't have gotten Breyson otherwise. I am ashamed of what I did to you. Bad decisions shouldn't define my character forever. I'm not a mean person. I've never been intentionally cruel to others. I let jealousy, rage, and panic consume me. If I'm being honest, dating Breyson ruined me. When we were just friends that person you met would have never existed."

She keeps her eyes on the sand in her hand. "I used to be one of the guys, kind of. I went everywhere with them, especially Breyson. We had been friends for so long. One year he just seemed different. He started coming into his body. His confidence was high. I told myself I wouldn't let myself fall for him, because it would ruin everything we had together, but I did. Somewhere along the way I let him consume every part of me. In such a short amount of time I was losing myself. I started getting needy and bitchy when he would hang out with other girls. I called him more frequently to hang out. I noticed he was starting to back off a little and I thought I was losing him, so I seduced him. I knew he was protective over me getting hurt. He cared about my reputation with guys, so I did the one thing I knew would make him mine."

As hard as it is for me to hear this, I want more. I want to know that someone else was emotionally affected by Breyson the way I was, and that I'm not crazy to feel this way. Situations may be different, but love is still the same. "One night at a party I slipped the same thing I put in your drink in his beer. A lot of people were doing it for fun. They always bragged about how all you thought about was sex when you were high on it. My plan worked. We slept together that night and I pretended to be upset the next morning. We had been best friends for three years. School friends longer. I knew he would give me anything to make it right, given his reputation, so I asked him for exclusivity. He agreed to only sleep with me as long as nothing changed emotionally. That's the only reason I slipped that drug in your drink. It didn't hurt Breyson or people at my school, so I never imagined it would hurt you."

She looks up at me with so much regret in her eyes you can't mistake it. "Please, don't judge me. I loved him, Kinzleigh, but I was also an immature seventeen-year-old that didn't realize to be *in* love, the other person has to love you back. I guess you grow up a lot from junior to senior year, because you have to get ready to go out into the real world. I can't just make myself stop loving him, but one day I'll find someone that loves me back and it will replace the feelings I have for him. I'm really trying to move on. I'd like for us to be friends."

I'm not the only one with issues related to Breyson now. He had a tendency to hook people from the very beginning. I know I should lay our differences aside, but it makes it a little hard to trust someone when they have been so cruel in the past. Letting go is something I need to practice, starting with her. "Okay," I say, and turn back to look out at the water.

Boats out in the distance look like small specs.

We sit here in silence, enjoying the comfort of not being alone, both of us crying over the same boy we'll never get to see again. "What's it like?" she asks, her voice just above a whisper.

"What's what like?"

She pulls in her knees to her chest and wraps her arms around them. "To be loved by Breyson."

I wasn't expecting that. Honestly, I'm not even sure what to say. How do you answer that question? It seems so personal. I ponder for a moment on the question hanging out there. "Natalie, I don't know how it feels to be in your shoes. I'm sorry. It bothers me hearing that another woman is in love with the same person I am, but at the same time, I can't imagine how that must feel. I was fortunate when I fell in love that it was returned. To be loved by Breyson is unexplainable, and very personal. He makes you feel like you're the only girl. He's the best of every world. He loves wholeheartedly. Every day is a gift. When it ends, it breaks you. I realize now how blessed I was to find it and not have to settle with a stand-in. I hope you are able to that kind of love one day too, I really do."

We continue to relish in the previous silence as if that's the thing she needed to move on, to let him go. I wonder if we could learn to move on from Breyson together, but who knows what the future has in store. I don't bet on happy endings anymore.

Breyson is a hard person to move on from, but if this baby is going to have a chance at a happy life then I have to try. I've always been told things are easier in pairs, and friends are the backbone of a person. It's worth giving a shot.

I'm at rock bottom, so there's nowhere left to fall. I feel a little peace for the first time since Breyson left. The pain of his loss will never disappear, and I've come to terms with that, but if I can make it subside enough to function in life for someone that didn't ask to be brought into this world, that's the best I can hope for.

As if I flipped a switch and shut down some of the stress and depression I've been enduring, hunger strikes me for the first time since I found out I was pregnant. I wipe at my puffy, wet face to rid of the tears. Today I need to start trying to move on. As awkward as it is, I grab her hand in mine. "I think we can do this together, Natalie. In a way, we are going through the same thing. It takes one going through the same kind of pain to understand and help another. The only difference in me and you is you'll find love again one day. He was the person I was meant to be with, I'm sure of it, but that doesn't mean you don't hurt over his loss too. You did lose a best friend, after all. What do you say—stick together?"

She looks down at our linked hands, before her line of vision settles back on my face. She nods her head. Before I can even process what's happening, she grabs me and pulls me into a hug. "Thank you for giving me a chance. You won't regret it."

It's amazing to me that when you open your eyes to the world around you, you see things that you've been blind to the entire time. This whole time that I've been trying to cope with Breyson being taken from me, I never stopped to look around at the other people hurting from the same loss. It may be in a different way than me, but still hurting all the same.

Breyson had an effect on a lot of people, and his loss will linger for a long time to come. The only way to move forward is to be thankful for the time God gave us with him instead of questioning why he was taken.

"You want to get some food? I'm pretty hungry." She pulls away and stands but reaches down for my hand to help me up, and I take it.

I brush the sand from the back of my dress and we walk side-by-side toward the car. "Sure. Pregnant girl's gotta eat, right?"

She smiles, and I return it genuinely for the first time. It's a nice change. Today is a new day, and I'm going to try with everything in me to view it in a different light . . . for Breyson.

TWELVE

Breyson

I've been working for a solid month now. The money is good and they take care of me. I've had to learn the currency here. Antonio is teaching me a lot. He has shown me around the property and has been slowly teaching me the ways of breeding bullfighting cattle. He wants me to not only learn the aspects of breeding, but the culture behind it, and also the sport itself.

It's a lot to learn, and I still struggle with trying to remember everything, as I don't want to disappoint him. Family, honor, and respect are everything to them, and I don't want to fall short when they've been so good to me. This is how they make their livelihood. A big part of being successful in this business is having a reputation for breeding strong, aggressive bulls.

Bullfighting just started in March and will last until October. I have learned it is a very popular sport in this part of the world. Breeding the best fighting bulls is very important as a rancher, because if they don't pass the test to fight, males get slaughtered for meat and females are used for breeding until they are too old. Having to absorb loads of information about something you're not familiar with can get overwhelming. I haven't actually been to a fight yet, but they are supposed to take me in the coming weeks to show me how the hard work around here pays off.

The sun begins rising behind the clouds as I get out of bed to dress for a new day. The days are long, but I'm in a routine now, which makes it easier. I know what to expect, and that's more than I can say about anything else in my life right now. I walk in a sleep-induced state to the dresser in the corner of the small bedroom and open the drawer. I pull out a pair of dark blue denim jeans and a white tee shirt, my wardrobe six days a week. I pull the fitted tee on and it falls against my muscles.

Based on my size, it doesn't take a rocket scientist to know I must have been active in my former life. I had to have been some kind of athlete, but what I have no idea. My adopted family says that I can't be more than twenty. We have conversations about it from time to time.

Marcus keeps me busy in my time off doing *American activities* as he calls them. We have banned together and formed a brotherhood over the last month. He teaches me about Spanish culture and I teach him the things I can remember, which are only the things that are engrained into the habitual section of your brain. There aren't any memories attached to them. When shown an object I can remember what it is and its purpose, but nothing has sparked a personal memory to date. I asked him how he knew I was American, and he said the accent gives me away whether I remember it or not.

He seems to be doing his research, and each time he comes up with something new to try out on me. It started off small with things he could get his hands on around here. I get one full day off a week on Sunday, and I have time to myself at night after dinner. Marcus is usually waiting for me when I get off. We haven't gotten into anything big yet, but I am quickly earning trust with his family, so maybe this week we can get out and wander the streets of Spain. The boredom of being a recluse when I'm not working is starting to get to me. I can't learn anything holed up in a room.

The first thing he came up with was drawing and sketching on paper. It was quickly marked off the list. I was never meant to be an artist in this lifetime or the last. I wouldn't classify stick men and elementary house drawings art of any kind. He wanted to try painting and I dismissed it as fast as I could get no out of my mouth. If you can't draw, there is no way you can paint.

I don't envision my bulky and muscular frame as being the artist type. That may be stereotyping, since I don't know or remember any personally, but I blame it on the amnesia. No pun intended. I'm sure there are plenty beefy artists out there.

Next came music from an old acoustic guitar he found that belonged to someone in his family. That was a worse disaster than drawing. I'm almost positive as I strummed my fingers across the chords it sounded more like a drunk falling into it standing against a wall in a pitch-black room.

An artistic side of me doesn't exist. I keep telling him to move away from creative arts, but he is determined to try each thing for a week to ensure nothing is potentially missed by not being thorough. I may not remember who I am, but I know when it's time to move on. His persistence will payoff someday. I deal with it, because I could be doing this alone. Annoyance is better than loneliness.

As I recall the memories of that goofy kid it makes me laugh, but it's another workday for me, and time to get started. I step into my boots and cover my head with a hat to protect it from the sun.

I walk to the door, ready to get another day under my belt. I have bulls to breed, feed, and test. Duty calls. I have paychecks to make. I've already saved a nice cushion from my earnings and it's only been a month since I got here. Most of it is profit, since I have no expenses. Here goes. I open the door and step out into the cool morning breeze.

As I do every morning, I come into the barn and saddle up my quarter horse. He's a beauty, this one. He stands tall and proud—a stallion built for speed. My first morning here Antonio gave him to me. He said he was about to sell him, because he won't allow anyone here to ride him, making him useless. When I came into the barn and walked by each stall, he went crazy until I made it to his. Antonio told me his name is Rabia, meaning Rage in my language, and said, "This one has attitude."

He stood back and told me to feel him out, to see if he would let me work with him. He never moved as I saddled him up and mounted him. I'm assuming I have been on a horse before, because when I saddled him up it felt natural, as if I've done it a million times before. When I finished, he said, "Looks like you've found your horse. He's the strongest and fastest one here."

"Hey, boy. You ready to get some work done today?" I rub his neck and scratch his nose every morning after I've saddled him. He loves when I talk to him. We've developed a little bond, he and I. He likes the attention and I have someone to tell my deepest thoughts to without worrying of it being repeated since I know he doesn't understand. "Let's ride." I mount him and take off into the pasture.

The first stop is bringing the males in to breed the females in heat. Daily activities around here are pretty much repetitive. As I ride across the open field, a flashback occurs. They've been happening less as the days go on. I don't know if it's because work keeps me busy or if it's a sign they will eventually fade completely. I hope not the latter.

They always start out the same; rolling through my mind like the clouds in the sky. It starts with a single glance at her, slightly blurry at first, but then comes into focus, similar to the lens on a camera. The reaction is always the same—stop everything I'm doing to enjoy the show.

Her body is resting against mine—the same blonde hair, green-eyed girl it always is. Her curls are blowing in the wind. We're sitting on a horse. I keep my arms wrapped around her, looking at her from behind. It feels so real, as if I'm actually touching her instead of seeing it in my mind. Each time this happens I get a feeling that is never present otherwise. I love her, but how can you love a figment of your imagination? I wish I knew if she was real.

She lets go of the horn on the saddle and throws her arms above her head in the air. As much as her hair is blowing behind her, I know we're going fast. I tighten my grip, but she doesn't notice. She's lost in her own little world; free like a bird flying high. Her head falls back against my shoulder and we continue racing onward through a meadow. She looks happy, content. The sun is setting across the horizon and she bends her arms, lowering her hands into my hair.

I grasp onto every detail I can, in case I don't have another one for a while. Sometimes it ends abruptly without finishing the scene and sometimes it's so graphic I feel like I'm there. It's always on mute, though. I can't hear any words or sounds, except that one time when she said she loved me.

Surprising me, she places her left hand back on the horn of the saddle and throws her left leg over to the right side. What is she doing? My hand grips her hip, afraid she will fall off the running horse. As if the horse knew what she was doing, it slows to a trot. She takes her right leg and brings it in between our bodies before she releases it on my left side, now facing me. Damn . . . a closeup.

She smiles, as if she knows exactly how much of an effect she has on me. That smile could change the world, move mountains, and color a world of gray. My hands grip the reigns so tight the leather digs into my skin, but I can't help it. I clench my eyelids closed as the vision becomes high definition.

Please don't stop, please don't stop.

My hands automatically find her waist, pulling her closer to me. She places a palm on each side of my face and locks those bright green eyes with my blue ones. When she does, I'm paralyzed, unable to break free from the hold she has on me. My breathing picks up. I hold my breath in an attempt to keep quiet, as if that would allow me to hear something other than the silent movie playing in my mind.

I am completely zoned into my own head. I have no idea what is happening around me. I don't know where I am or what I'm doing, but I can't lose sight of her. I need to keep watching. If she can do this to me without being present, I can't imagine what it would be like if she were really here.

Please be real. I need you to be real.

Her eyes are astonishing, telling a story with each look. I need to learn how to read between the lines. She moves in closer and I swear my heart stops beating. No words come out, but I'm able to read her lips just before she joins her lips with mine—*together forever.*

Her soft lips touch mine and she slips away, leaving me sitting on the back of a horse in the middle of an open field at a dead halt.

Fuck.

I'm sick of this shit. I feel like pulling my hair out, screaming until something happens. Every single time, the vision gets better, then it slips away into the depths of my mind and I have no control over extracting them again. My mind cursed me. I fell in love with someone I can't touch except in my memories, and even then, it's limited. Antonio stops beside me on his horse. "Are you okay, Son? You look like you saw a ghost, no?"

I press inward on my skull with the heel of my hand, taking a deep breath to try and relieve some of the tension building. I pound one of my temples in frustration. "It's nothing. Just another vision of that girl. I don't know who she is, but she's the only memory I seem to get from who I was, and that's assuming she's even real. I don't get it. What's so special about her? Why can't I remember anyone else? What if my mind is creating her out of loneliness?"

He looks at me for a moment but doesn't say anything. That's how Antonio is. He doesn't riddle you with useless information. He remains quiet until something needs to be said, and I like that about him. When he does speak, it's wise, realistic, and keeps you coming back for more. "There are many things we question, but everything happens for a reason. Instead of asking why, embrace it when it comes. Our minds have a way of leading us if we let it. When it's ready to reveal everything to you it will. This could be it trying to heal from your injury. All good things come in time, Son. Patience is a virtue."

The man is wise. I know he's right, but that doesn't make it easier. Being lost is a horrible feeling to live with on a daily basis. I don't want to completely start over with a new life. I want the life I had back, no matter how good or bad it was. I'm zoning out again and my head is starting to throb around my scar. Staying focused is a problem since the accident.

At any given time, I become a recluse in my own mind and forget the things around me. Sometimes it's when I have a vision of her and sometimes it's when I'm doing nothing at all. "Do you need to take the day off?" he asks, pissing me off. I don't want to look like I can't do my job.

I need to figure out a way to get a grip on everything in my life. For some reason, I was dealt this life. I can't change the outcome, so I might as well quit wallowing and move on. "Nah, I'm fine. I need to work. I don't do well with extra time on my hands. What's first, boss?"

He looks at me for a moment, as if he's considering making me call it a day, but then shakes it off. "Come on, you're with me today. I'll have the other hand turn out the bulls. I don't want you around them if your head is bothering you. They are already aggressive creatures. Add females in heat and it's a recipe for disaster with you not feeling well. You're still healing, and that's fine, Son. Taking things slow doesn't show weakness. It doesn't mean you're less of an employee. I need to inseminate some of the older females. They only have a few more breeds left in them before I slaughter them for meat. You need to learn how to do it in the case that I can't be here."

He takes off ahead of me and I follow. I need to find things to do in my spare time besides staying cooped up around here. If I don't, things are only going to get worse for me. Maybe I can talk to them tonight about Marcus and I going into town and exploring. I need something to take my mind off the situation at hand, something to occupy my mind when I'm not working.

I need friends. Marcus has become my brother from another mother, but I need to find some kids my age to hang out with on occasion. People I can have adult conversation with. I have to watch what I say around Marcus, since he's just a kid. Being a bad example isn't in my nature. His mind is still developing, and he needs good examples in his life.

Now that the ideas are flowing, I think that's exactly what I'm going to do. I'm going to go out for a night in town. Alone . . .

THIRTEEN

Breyson

I'm adjusting my shirt in the mirror when Marcus comes barreling through the door. He has a smile plastered on his face until he sees the way I'm dressed. "Where are you going?"

"Out." I turn from the mirror and walk into the lounge area of the small cottage.

His face falls with disappointment. You can see it on his face. I come to stand before him. "Can I come? I bet Mom wouldn't care. She loves you like her own son. She trusts you. I know she does."

I mess his hair with my hand, because I know he can't stand it. "Not this time, little buddy. We can go out Sunday, yeah? I need to get away for a while. I have a lot on my mind, and you don't need to be out with me at night since I don't know the area yet."

I hate seeing him bummed, but there isn't anything I can do about it. I need some space. I can't deal with this depressed bullshit anymore. I need to find something or someone to take my mind off the things that are stressing me out. I want to find a way to release this anxiety and frustration that keeps building with no exit point or I'm literally going to explode. "It's because I'm a kid, isn't it?"

Shit.

"Come here, buddy," I say, grabbing him in the crook of my arm and then lead him to the couch. "Let's have a brotherly talk, okay?"

He nods and sits at the same time I do. "I'm a big kid, you know. I'm ten, so you don't have to treat me like a little kid. Give it to me straight, Bryce." I have to fight to hold back the laughter brewing over him trying to act grown. I can honestly say he's the ray of sunshine in the doom and gloom that I've become. Even though we don't share the same DNA, he's a brother by heart, which is all that matters.

I bend forward and rest my elbows on my thighs and he follows suit, copying me. It makes me smile to know that he looks up to me. I guess I do serve some kind of purpose. I need to remember that when I get down. I should be grateful that I have a family that cares about me and that I'm not out on the streets. They actually *feel* like family, and not just an employer. "You know you're my brother, right?"

He looks at me, a huge grin spreading across his face as he nods. "Well, sometimes brothers need a break from each other. It's not because they get tired of each other, but just to do their own things for a little while. I love our bro time, but I'm still older than you. I need to go do things that people my age do every once in a while. Does that make sense?"

He looks at the floor and imaginarily traces the tiles of the floor with his finger. I'm waiting for him to reply when he finally nods. "I wish I was older, so I could go with you," he says, and continues watching where his fingers move along the grout lines.

"Never wish that, Marcus. You have plenty of time to be a grown-up. Plus, it's not as great as you think it is. I wish I could remember being your age, but I haven't seen Dr. Rodriguez in a couple of weeks, and I have to make time for him too. He's done a lot for me, like bringing me to you, but he invited me to meet his family. He has a son around my age he wants me to meet. You wouldn't want me to be selfish with my time, would you?" I'm trying to find a way to explain to him in a way a ten-year-old would understand, without being crude.

He stops drawing the floor tiles and looks up at me. "Okay, I get it. I guess I'm being stingy. Tomorrow then?"

I called Dr. Rodriguez when I got off from work and told him I needed something to do to get away for a while and that I was getting really depressed. He said his son is home for the weekend from the university he attends and would be thrilled to take me out and show me around. He instructed me to come over for dinner to meet his wife and son. Since it's Saturday night and I don't have to work tomorrow, he told me I could stay over and he would bring me back tomorrow.

He should be here any minute now to pick me up. "You have my word. As soon as I get home, we'll do whatever you want. The day is yours." His smile comes back. I take it he's happy with my answer.

"Come on. Let's go find Mom. I need to tell her what I'm doing." I know she's not my mom, but since I got here, she has never once made me feel like an outsider. I watch the way she treats Marcus and she treats me the exact same. One night when everyone had gone to bed last week, she came out here to tell me good night. It was a little awkward at first, but she said she had something weighing down on her that she needed to tell me.

At first, I wasn't sure what to expect. I thought I had done something wrong, but I was completely off from what it actually was. She wanted me to know that she would never pressure me to call her anything other than what I felt comfortable with, but that I could call her 'Mom' if I wanted to. She wanted me to know that she would never try and replace my biological mother, whether I remember her or not, but that she knows how lost I feel right now. She became an orphan when her parents were killed in a car accident at a young age. She told me she knows how important it is to feel like you have a family and are loved by someone.

We talked for a while. She explained how she was lucky to get adopted by a family that loved her, and that just because we aren't from the same bloodline doesn't mean we aren't family. "Family is the people we choose to love and protect on a daily basis," she said. The longer we talked, the more I realized I would always be a part of this family, even if I didn't make a home here permanently. That night we developed a bond I'll never forget.

I was a little shocked by her forwardness, and I had to think on it for a little while. In the end, I concluded that just because she didn't give birth to me doesn't mean she's any less of a mother to me. Reproducing a child doesn't make someone a mother, love and nurture does. Having an adoptive family here has made everything more tolerable.

Marcus and I enter the main house. I look at him. "Hey, buddy, do you mind giving me a minute with Mom?" He shakes his head and turns in the direction of his room. "Mom," I call out, as I walk through the corridor into the kitchen.

"Aqui, hijo—*in here, son*," she says, and I follow her voice. I think sometimes she answers in Spanish out of habit from answering Marcus since they're bilingual. I'm picking up words here and there, but in no form am I fluent.

When I find her, she is folding a basket full of laundry. She looks up at me and smiles as I come into view. "You look nice. Are you going somewhere?"

I sit beside her and reach for a towel to help while I sit here, but she swats my hand before I can grab it. "Your work is outside, and that's enough. I can do this. Rest and talk to me."

She pats my thigh and goes back to folding. "I called Dr. Rodriguez."

She stops and looks at me, a look of concern quickly spreading across her face. "Dr. Rodriguez? Why? Are you okay?"

"Yeah, it's nothing like that. I've been down lately. I don't know." I start rubbing my hand over my hair on my forehead, pushing it into my eyes. It's starting to get longer, and I need a cut, but that's the last of my worries right now. It's curling out over my ears and at the nape of my neck. I sweep it to the side as I think of what to say, letting out a deep breath. "I had another vision of her today."

I finally told her about the visions the night she came and checked on me in my quarters. She told me something about her and it made me feel I owed her the same. She lays the bath towel back in the basket and turns toward me. "The blonde, yes?"

"Yeah . . . her. Antonio came up on me, frozen, sitting on Rage. I had zoned out to everything around me. I can't figure it out. Why her? Why is she the only one that I see? Nothing makes sense. The headaches are coming back and the zoning out is becoming a problem with work. What if I never get better? It's stressing me out and I need to get out and do something. I need to calm down. The loneliness is not helping anything either." I look down at the floor and rub my hands together anxiously.

She looks worried, and that reassures me that she cares. She scoots beside me and rubs her hand up and down my spine in a motherly way. "Cut yourself some slack. Your brain needs time to heal. It's probably trying to sort itself out. I do not imagine stress is adding a positive effect. Eventually, it will all fit together like a puzzle, and you will know what's real and what is fantasy. You know that the job is only here to help you, right? You are not an employee. We care about you. If you never worked for Antonio another day, this would still be your home."

I shake my head. I would never mooch off of them. They have been so good to me to offer their home, and they treat me as one of their own. She grabs my chin between her thumb and index finger, turning my head to face her. "Listen to me, Bryce."

The words roll off her tongue in her thick accent. "I know you have only been here a month, but I have come to love you as if I gave birth to you. This will always be your home. If you remembered who you were tomorrow and left here, I would expect you to come and see us sometime. I would miss you terribly, Antonio would miss you terribly, and Marcus would be devastated. Don't ever feel like you are just a laborer. Do you understand?"

I look in her chocolate brown eyes—the sincerity unmistakable—as they widen, waiting on a response from me. I haven't cried since the night I arrived and was overwhelmed with all the changes. Crying doesn't do anything but make you look like less of a man, but sometimes it's necessary to let yourself feel like a kid again. Occasionally, you just need the love of a mother. Right now, she's the only one I have, and that's enough.

Tears roll down my cheeks. I try to smother them, but it's long overdue. I blame it on my injury, but I know it's just from letting it build. I nod and wipe my eyes with my upper arm. "Te amo, hijo—*I love you, son*," she says, and pulls me in for a hug. She rocks slightly side to side. "Te amo, hijo," she repeats.

"I love you too, Mom. I love you too." As it comes out of my mouth, I realize how much I meant it. I'd be in a darker place if it weren't for them.

We sit idly for a few minutes, having one of those mother-son moments. The doorbell chimes, causing me to jump. "That's probably Dr. Rodriguez. He is taking me to his home for a meal and to introduce me to his son. He was going to show me around town and said I could stay the night with them. Is that okay?"

She stands but holds up her index finger at me. "One moment." I never considered that I may have rules to abide by since I'm living under their roof. We never discussed it. I've always just stayed around here when I'm not working. I start scratching the back of my head awkwardly. She yells toward Marcus's room on her way out. "Marcus, get the door!"

When she returns, she has a folded piece of paper in her hand. She holds it out for me to take. When my hand connects with hers to grab it, she doesn't let go. "I will have your phone number before you go. I won't have one of my own on the street without a way to reach you. Tell Diego to take you to the place written down. When you get there, ask for Big Sanchez. He will want to know who you are. It is imperative you repeat exactly as I tell you. *Maria Salvador, fiesta privada. Su hijo—Maria Salvador, private party. Her son.* He will take care of you from there."

She releases my hand, leaving the piece of paper in mine. I unfold it and read the handwriting scribbled in pen—*Descenso Rápido (Rapid Descent).*

That's an unusual name for a place. I have no idea where I'm going, but I don't question it. I trust her. I have to, or I wouldn't be sane. Trust goes a long way and is necessary in life. Without it, all would be lost.

Dr. Rodriguez comes into the room and stands in the doorway. "Maria, always good to see you." He looks at me. "You ready?"

"As I'll ever be." I slide the folded paper in the pocket of my jeans and hug her goodbye. I look at her one last time before I go. "I'll be home tomorrow. I promised to spend the day with Marcus."

She smiles and nods. "Be safe, Son."

I walk to the doorway where Dr. Rodriguez and Marcus are standing. I look at Marcus and mess up his hair like I always do. "Don't get into any trouble without me," I say, with a mischievous smirk on my face.

He laughs. "Me, trouble? Please." I nudge him and follow Dr. Rodriguez to his car sitting idle in the driveway. Tonight, I'm seeking peace of mind. I guess I'll find out if I get it.

FOURTEEN

Breyson

I met Diego and we immediately hit it off. He seems very similar to me. He's tall with short, black hair, and he's filled out like an athlete. He told me he's a soccer player, which is why he lives away at college instead of commuting. Dinner was uneventful, and I understand now why these two families are so close. They are both welcoming and kind.

I told him where Maria instructed us to go, and when I mentioned the name a huge grin spread across his face. When I asked why he looked like he was about to get laid, he told me it was a privately-owned salsa club for the elite of Spain. He said it's private invite only and it's discrete. He mentioned even with his dad being a well-known doctor he's never gotten in before, so he has no idea where the connection is with Maria, but that if you get invited you don't turn it down, because it's crawling with the most beautiful Spanish women around—the rich and famous singles hideout. I haven't seen it yet and already I'm excited.

We pull into an empty parking lot that doesn't look like the place he described. I look around. The buildings look like old abandoned warehouses. "Are you sure we're in the right place? I thought you said this was the elite of Spain. It looks like no one is even here."

"Oh, this is the right place, and from the stories I've heard I can't wait to get in. I told you it's discrete. You're not allowed to park near the building.

It draws too much attention. Never judge anything by its appearance." He shuts off the engine and we get out. I place my wallet in my front pocket instead of the back, because frankly, this place is a little sketchy. I could get jumped at any minute.

"If it's so discrete how do you know about it?" He is back to that shit-eating grin again. We round the car until we're standing at the hood.

"Let's just say I dated this girl once." The grin gives him away. Liar. "Okay, I'm lying. I banged this girl once. She belonged to a family coming from old money around here; a family you don't piss off, so her name will remain secret." I shake my head at his rambling and walk off. That was enough of an answer for me.

We walk across the street to the largest building on the row and come to a heavy steel door with a small rectangular slot at eye level. It opens, and a pair of eyes are on the other side. "Who are you and what do you want?"

A nervous tick occurs as I stare into a set of dark eyes, listening to his gruff voice. My stomach is in knots. Why do I feel like I'm about to pick up a shipment of drugs? I try to calm my raging nerves as I speak to the unknown man on the other side of the door. "I'm here to see Big Sanchez."

Immediately the door opens to a corridor. It's dark, and the paint is chipping off the concrete walls. The only light comes from the sconces hanging along the long hallway. If I wasn't creeped out before, I am now.

We step inside and the door slams behind us. I look at Diego. He doesn't look uneasy at all. Why is he so calm? We could be murdered here and our bodies would never be found.

Diego on my right, I turn to my left at the hulk looking guy wearing a black tee shirt and jeans with a pair of combat boots on. He has a silver chain around his neck for added effect. Nothing surrounds him but a stool and a bottle of water. I hope he gets paid well for this. He looks like he could fight off a lion.

"Follow me," he says, and leads us down the dim hallway. At the end he stops in front of a metal door and knocks. A buzzer goes off and a deadbolt slides open, signaling the door is unlocked. Do I even want to know the reason behind this much security for an office that sits in a place like this?

He turns the metal handle and inches the door forward. "Someone's here to see you, Sir," says the guard to the fat cat of a man sitting behind the large oak desk. He looks to be around Maria's age, and he has thick black hair against his bronze skin. He is large in frame, but not overweight. Smoke billows from his lips when he pulls the cigar away from his mouth.

Power is written all over his face.

He's wearing a suit. His fingers are covered in gold rings. "Leave us be, Tony." The door guard bows slightly and backs out of the room. How does Maria know a guy like this? He looks dangerous. His demeanor is serious, and his face is void of all emotion. "Come closer boys," he says and takes another drag from his cigar. I look at Diego and he just shrugs.

I swallow, and we step forward in unison. He leans back in his executive style chair and continues to watch us. "Who brings you to my part of the city?"

Now is the time to remember what Maria said and not fuck it up royally, or we may end up in a trash bin somewhere. "Maria Salvador, fiesta privada. Su hijo."

Something in his eyes flash, but I'm not sure what. It makes me want to ask her who he is when I get home, but if she wanted to tell me she would. I won't pry into her personal life. "So, Maria sent you, did she? How is she, boy?"

He's looking directly at me, and instantly, I know not to keep him waiting. I don't want any trouble. "She's good, Sir. I'm starting to wonder why she sent me here, though, to be honest."

He stands, and when I see his full size, my stomach drops to the floor. He's towering over me and I'm a fairly tall guy. He walks toward me and places his arm around my back like he's pulling me in for a sideways hug. He smells of cigars and spicy cologne. I want to crinkle my nose at the stench but refrain. "If Maria sent you to me you are important to her. Am I right?"

I nod, but don't speak, afraid of interrupting him in case he isn't finished. "Come," he says, and walks me to a glass wall to the right of his desk—the farthest from the door.

I look out, instantly realizing what this is. "They can't see you," he says, assuring me as I look out at the crowd. It's awkward to know he watches the guests, but I'm sure he has his reasons. It's a one-way window, like police interrogation rooms. I can see out, but no one can see in. My eyes widen as I watch what's going on.

It's nothing like I expected. The decor is a white and black color palette. It doesn't look like any salsa club I've ever pictured. There is a bar at the back in the shape of a horseshoe and the bartenders are wearing black slacks and crisp, white button-down shirts. There are white sofas scattered throughout the large area that stretches farther than the eye can see.

Beautiful girls are walking around with drink trays, wearing sexy dresses. The music is muted, but I can tell it's Latin. There is a dance floor in the center of the room and bodies are grinding and sweating to the beat of the music.

It's a mix between a gentleman's club and a salsa bar. "Do you like what you see?" he purrs close to me. I don't think I know how to dance like that, but it looks fun, as if they are letting their bodies do the talking. Feeling everything instead of saying it. It's very sexual, and it intrigues me. I can't pull my eyes away from the couples, so I nod.

"This is my life. I built this place for the elite, the supreme, the wealthiest of wealthy. It's a place for the people that devote many hours to their work. A place to let loose and enjoy a night filled with music, booze, and beautiful women when they don't have time to go find it themselves. They pay a hefty membership fee and I provide the rest. When they come here, they don't have to worry about the gold-digging whores. The members will not be bothered outside of these walls. Each girl I allow into this club goes through a screening process."

I continue to watch as I process what he's saying. "What type of club is this exactly?" There is a hallway in one corner of the room, but you cannot see beyond the entrance.

He smiles at me when I turn to face him. "It's whatever type of club you want it to be. There are only two rules here: consent and respect. I will not allow any man to disrespect the women I bring here, nor will they partake in any activities that aren't consensual. I do not run a brothel, but if two people want intimacy, I have places they can do privately. I bring people together and provide the tools for a good time, but that is all. What these people do after they meet is their business."

I understand what this place is, but there is one thing that I don't. "Why did Maria send me to you and how does she have elite status?" He looks out the window down below and links his hands together behind his back.

I glance at Diego. He is gleaming watching what is going on below us. I'm not even sure he is listening to the conversation. When I turn back to him, he speaks. "What I tell you in my office is in confidence and I expect it to remain that way. Am I clear?"

He waits until he has both of our attention and we nod for him to continue. "Maria and I go way back. We were lovers before she married. I loved her, but what we wanted were two separate things. I wanted a lavish lifestyle and a social nightlife, she wanted a family. She was going to give it up until her family found out and put a stop to it. They believe in arranged marriages and that is what she is in."

I can't believe what I'm hearing. Her family arranged her marriage to Antonio? As much as I like both of them, the thought of not being able to choose who I want to be with seems wrong. "Her family wanted her to be with a wealthy man; someone that could take care of her. I was nothing but a boy with dreams then. Now I'm one of the wealthiest men there is. I have clubs all over, but she keeps me here."

I completely misjudged him. Looking at him you would think he's a drug lord. Never would I have thought he was what he just described—a man longing for a taken woman. By the absence of a wedding band I would assume he never found another. He spends his life among parties. "Why did she send me here?"

He rubs his chin. "If Maria sent you to me it's because she knows I can help you. The question is, are you willing to take it?"

How can he help me?

Do I really want to know?

I couldn't be any worse off than I already am, so what do I have to lose? Absolutely nothing. I've already lost it all. "What do I have to do?"

The side of his mouth pulls up into a smirk. "Smart boy, I see. A man ready to better himself. I like that. You remind me of myself at your age. You will come work for me on Friday and Saturday night of every week until we change the agreement. You will be my assistant, doing whatever it is that I need you to. In return, I will compensate you immensely and you will have access to all of my resources. You will learn my culture, so you will better fit in when I need you, and that includes salsa dancing. I won't bother your schedule Monday through Thursday, but I expect you to make yourself available to me Friday and Saturday. Is there a problem with that?"

I usually work for Antonio through Saturday, but they both told me I didn't have to work every day. I don't want to back out on him, but Maria wouldn't have sent me here if there wasn't a reason. I don't know how he can help me, but the excitement takes over and that is all I need. It's an emotion I haven't had since I woke up in the hospital. I want more. I need more. It's the only way that I won't lose myself. I want to find it again. I said I'd do whatever it takes, and now I need to put it into action. I will still have weeknights and Sundays to spend with Marcus.

"It won't be a problem, Sir. I'll take the offer." He nods and walks back to his desk where he places his finger on a button.

"Tonight, you and your friend will be free to do as you please. Drinks are on me. Enjoy the girls. You will report to me at ten o'clock sharp the morning of next Friday. At that time, I will show you the staff entrance, but until then just do as you did today. That entrance is not to be given to outsiders," he says, and looks at Diego. I nod in understanding as he presses the button.

A girl comes over the speaker. "Mr. Sanchez, what can I do for you?"

"Angelique, come to my office, please."

"Yes, Sir. I'll be right there." He releases the button and takes a seat in his chair. A wooden door on the wall across from his desk opens and in walks a girl. She is smoking hot. My eyes widen as I take her in, undressing her with my eyes. She notices, but immediately turns to him as if she's afraid to be caught looking at me.

Waves of thick, black hair cascade down her back and her peach dress is tight against her small but curvy figure. It stops just below her ass at her thighs, allowing a full view of her long, slender legs. The color does wonders against her bronze skin. She has an amazing rack and the cleavage is peeping out of the neckline.

Damn.

Her lips are so plump that I can't help but to wonder how they taste. Those big brown eyes are lined with long, thick, black lashes. Her pumps scream *fuck me.*

I'd love to see them in the air as I plow into you.

I shake my head to remove the thought. "Angelique, this is . . ." He looks at me for an answer.

"Bryce."

"My new assistant. I want you to take the night off and show him a good time downstairs. Understood?" His face never falters as I look between the two of them. She looks between him and me, barely biting the corner of her lip.

Game on. I'm in. There's the sign I was looking for.

"Yes, sir."

"Good. You can go now," he says, dismissing all of us, and she walks back toward the door she came from. I need a drink; or a few. When I look at Diego, he is staring at her fine ass almost playing peek-a-boo with the hem of her dress.

We'll see who gets a piece of it first . . .

The three of us walk through a few offices and hallways before we come to an elevator. When we walk inside, I realize the back of the elevator is made of glass for viewing as it descends. She punches in a code on the inside keypad. The doors close and I enjoy the view as it descends. The name finally makes sense. We are going underground. By the lengthy elevator ride it must be pretty far down.

When the doors open Latin music floods inside, bouncing off my eardrums. I begin to relax as I take in my surroundings. People are clearly enjoying themselves. Angelique leads the way, I'm in the middle, and Diego is behind me. When we reach the bar, she nods at the bartender and stops, before turning around, mere inches from me.

Damn. I want to suck those lips.

She looks me over, heat flooding her cheeks.

That's right, girl. You know you want it . . .

Her breathing picks up. I can tell she is trying to say something. "When we are here, we are not employees. We become the members. It's one of the few rules. Mr. Sanchez calls this *the dungeon.* Sometimes he makes us come down and work undercover to make sure everyone is following the rules. He holds this place with high regard. Reputation is one of the most important things to him. He doesn't want clients knowing who works for him aside from the cantineros (*bartenders)* and the gorilas (*bouncers).* All private staff remain private. You have to blend in. What do you want to drink?"

I love listening to her talk. "That depends, sexy." I brush my thumb along her pouty, bottom lip and close the distance between us. "Are we drinking together? If so, tequila shots it is. I want to taste you."

Her breath hitches, and she nods, before turning around to the bartender. I look at Diego, who is now sitting at the bar with a leggy blonde between his legs, who's whispering something in his ear. I don't think I have to worry about him any longer . . .

"Dominic," she says loudly to get the bartender's attention. When he turns, she points between the three of us. "Abrir una pestaña (*Open a tab).* Six tequila shots." I grab her small waist in my hand and press against her backside. I want to feel the curves of her body.

Taking her hair in my hand, I brush it to one side like a curtain, revealing her neck. "I can't wait to see how this moves on the dance floor," I whisper into her ear and rub my front against her back. The bartender places the shots in front of us on the bar. She grabs a saltshaker and turns around. We are so close her flat stomach skims mine.

She grabs my hand and turns it palm up, those big brown eyes locking with mine, and then she brings it toward her face without looking away. Her tongue darts out to wet her lips. I want her. I bet her dark skin would look good naked against my light. She licks the inside of my wrist and sprinkles it with salt, before reaching for the shot and a lime wedge.

I know what she's about to do, and I'm ready for it when she lines up the waxy skin of the lime between my teeth, using my mouth as a vise. Placing my wrist at her lips, she licks the salt clean, presses the glass to her lips, and drops her head back, letting the liquid drain down her throat. She sinks her teeth into the lime between my lips. I catch a whiff of her perfume, sending me into a horny spiral.

I wrap my hand in her hair and pull her back, discarding the lime carcass. "I want the after shot," I say, closing the distance between us until our lips are sealed together. The switch has been flipped. The bitter tequila on her tongue has me ready for more.

I like the way it feels for our tongues to be tangled. I continue to twirl mine with hers, getting a sample of what's to come. My body is reacting to her. I walk forward until her back presses against the edge of the bar. I nip her lip with my teeth before releasing her. "It's my turn. I make the rules." My hands still wrapped in her hair, I pull her head back, exposing her neck.

I flatten my tongue against the blank space, wetting it, and trying to decide where I want it. She tastes good, but this isn't the right spot. The curves of her breasts are staring at me, giving me an idea. I grab the shot glass and press it between her cleavage, making it sit nice and tight. I bend forward, now eye level with her bronze chest. "Here's the spot I want. I lick it and sprinkle the salt, watching some of the grains fall to the floor around us and some stick.

The top curve of her right breast is ready for my tongue. I lick from one end of her breast to the other, transferring the salt to my tongue. Then I grab the rim of the shot glass between my teeth and free it from the confinement of her breasts, turning it back. The tequila burns the back of my throat. I bite the lime wedge and kiss her, sharing the remainder of the shot with her.

I'm hard and I've only been here fifteen minutes . . .

I grab a second shot and then a third. She watches me as I down the liquid, and then grabs her own, throwing it back. The tension is so thick I want to take her right here at this bar. I have no idea where it's coming from, but my body is in full fuckfest mode.

I down the last shot and the bartender replaces them with four new. A few more in and the alcohol is now coursing through my bloodstream, taking effect. My mind finally feels at ease. I don't have to think, and I like it. I don't want to have to think about anything tonight—from my actions to the consequences. Downing the final shot at the table, I whisper to her, "Dance with me."

She grabs my shirt in her fist and pulls me into her. My balance is unsteady, but I catch myself on the edge of the bar she is leaning against. She wraps one leg around mine and her heel rests on my calf. Her lips are so close to mine I can smell the alcohol on her breath. "Y luego llévame a la cama (*And then take me to bed*)."

I hope she speaks Spanish when she's screaming out my name. I don't understand what she's saying, but I love the way it sounds rolling off her tongue. I take her lips against mine, searching for her tongue. I roll mine softly against hers and then suck on her bottom lip. "Say something else. Keep it up and dancing won't be an option any longer."

"Eso es con lo que cuento, preciosa (*That's what I'm counting on, gorgeous*)." She kisses my neck and walks around me, taking my hand in hers. I'm so horny right now I may not make it to a bed. And I'm drunk, but I follow behind her as she pulls me out to the middle of the dance floor. Couples are drenched in sweat from dancing.

She pulls me in behind her, our bodies plastered together. It feels so good to touch someone like this. "I don't know how to dance like this. Will you teach me?"

She places my hands on her hips as she begins rolling her body against mine, and then leans her head back on my chest. "I will teach you whatever you want to learn. We will be seeing a lot of each other, yes?"

I can't concentrate on anything she's saying with her rubbing her ass against my dick. "Yeah, I guess we will. How old are you?" She doesn't look much older than me, but I really don't know how old I am. It's time to choose a number just like a name.

I sway my body in a slow rhythm but let her do most of the work. She lifts her arms and runs her slender fingers through my hair. "Twenty-four. How old are you?"

I can tell by the way she's moving neither of us are going to be here much longer. She is letting the music lead her body and it's hypnotic to watch. "Twenty-one."

She turns around. Lust is written all over her face. She wants me just as much as I want her. "Age is just a number, baby," she says, and kisses me, closing her lids lined in thick black lashes. She opens them. "I don't usually have sex with someone I just met, Bryce, but I like you, and I want you. Take me to bed. Hazme el amor *(Make love to me)*."

If I had any second thoughts before, the closing line in Spanish sealed the deal, and I don't even know what she said. I'm drunk and horny and I need a release my daily hell. "Where?"

Looking around, public displays of affection are normal here, but I want privacy. I have a lot of aggression built up, and her tight little body is fixing to be the one I take it out on. "Follow me, lover," she says, and leads me to the hallway I noticed earlier.

We come to the entrance and a bouncer is standing guard. "Necesito un cuarto *(I need a room)*," she says to him. He looks between the two of us and turns to the rack of keys behind him. Grabbing the one with a ten on it, he hands it to her and pulls back the curtain that's blocking the entrance.

I follow her down the long hallway until we come to the door marked with a ten. She slides the key in the slot and turns it, unlocking the door. We walk into the spacious room that houses a bed. The alcohol has taken over my brain, making me stupid, because the first thing I think to ask is, "Is it clean?"

She shuts the door and locks it. "Don't worry, babe. The sheets are changed between each guest and the room is sanitized. Mr. Sanchez is very tidy and clean."

She tugs my hand, pulling me in the direction of the bed. I make a quick glance around the room. In one area is a shelf lined with toys, new in the boxes. The bed is covered in white cotton linens similar to a hotel, but more expensive. Beside the bed is a bowl filled with condoms. At least I know I'm protected. She doesn't seem like a whore, but I don't know where she's been.

She stops when the back of her knees touches the edge of the mattress. My mind is numb. I can't think of anything but what's in front of me. I have to admit, she's the sexiest thing I've seen since I woke up here. "Kiss me," she says. She wraps her arms around my neck and plays with the hair that curls out at the nape of my neck.

Our lips meet. I place my hands on her ass, and what an ass she has. When I find the bottom hem of her dress, I pull it up slowly, revealing her body to me. Damn, it's better than I expected. I continue to kiss her as I unhook her bra and let it fall to the floor. I release my hold on her lips and take her in. Her golden skin is highlighted with a pair of black heels and an aqua, lace thong. "Undress me," I say, my eyes scanning the silhouette of her body.

She grabs the bottom of my polo and begins inching it up my torso until she reaches my underarms. I lift them above my head, allowing her to remove it. "Tu cuerpo es hermoso *(Your body is beautiful)*," she says, and kisses my chest. I grab her breasts in my hands, thumbing over her nipples while she unbuckles my belt, and then follows through with my jeans. I remove my shoes at the same time she inches my jeans and boxers over my butt, and they fall to the floor. She takes in my size, a flirty expression on her face.

"You like what you see?" She nods. I slide my hands underneath the waistband of her panties and turn her around. I want it rough. I dip my hand beneath the front panel and lower it until I feel the button nestled between her lips. I dip my finger inside her for lubrication. She's wet and ready. I spread it over her clit and rub in a circular motion to get her started. When she starts to moan, I inch down her panties with my other hand until they fall to the floor. "Keep the heels on."

I continue to stimulate her, wanting to hear that beautiful voice as she comes. I need her slick. Placing my hand between her shoulder blades, I push her down until she places her palms on the mattress in front of her. I'm so hard right now.

I release her to reach inside the bowl beside the bed and take out a condom. Tearing the package with my teeth, I remove the latex ring and toss the wrapper on the floor. I roll it on my dick until I'm covered. Grabbing my shaft, I position it at her sweet spot.

I thrust inside her, driving forward in a rough manner until completely inside. She moans, taking all of me. Fuck, that feels amazing. Grabbing her hips, I thrust slowly, allowing her to stretch around me, but quickly change pace once I'm coated in her arousal.

I'm going to assume I've done this enough in the past based on how naturally it comes—like riding a bike. She's wet, she's warm, and clenches every time my pelvis meets her skin. I increase speed, ramming it each time I pull out. I need to be deeper. Her black curls are resting on her back, tempting me. I can't help but to wrap them around my hand for support. "Damn, girl, you're wet."

I grab her shoulder in my other hand and continue. The faster and harder I go, the louder she screams—music to my ears. I feel like I could go for hours. It's probably the alcohol inhibiting my thoughts. I need a change. Pulling out, I get on the bed and pull her limber body on top of me until she's straddling me. "Ride me."

She grabs my dick in her hand and lowers herself down my shaft until she's seated on me. She grinds against me, as if she can't ride it hard enough. Wrapping her hand around my neck, she pulls me into a sitting position. "Mírame mientras monto *(Watch me while I ride)*." I really need to learn their language, but right now she could be saying *fuck you* and I wouldn't care.

She grabs onto the back of my neck for support and squats in a straddling position over me, standing on her heels. Her other hand is palm down on the mattress. She arches her back and begins pumping up and down, then starts rolling her body like she was doing on the dance floor.

She is spread open, teasing me to touch it. I reach between our bodies and press on her clit, causing her to scream out from the double stimulation. I rub and watch her face change as the pleasure consumes her. I close my eyes, enjoying the feeling taking over my body. I'm close. Grabbing her hip, I lift up and meet her thrust for thrust.

I pull out and turn, laying her on the bed. As I slip back inside, her eyes roll back in her head. "Follame *(Fuck me)*."

I place my hands on her hips, lifting her off the bed. Her feet are now flat. Kneeling, I pound into her at a fast pace, angling her slightly to hit the right spot. She screams out my name, an onslaught of words tumbling out; some I understand, and some are jumbled Spanish. I continue at a fast pace until I can feel her tightening around me, initiating my orgasm. When I feel that first spurt of my seed, I pull out and let myself finish.

I lay beside her, the alcohol overpowering my body. Sleep is coming more easily with every passing second. Just before I pass out, that beautiful voice fills my ears one more time. "Seras mia *(You'll be mine)*."

I don't know what it means, and I don't care. For the first time I have nothing on my mind: no pain, no visions, and no confusion. I found my escape from it all—her.

As everything fades, she scoots beside me and wraps herself around my body. For once, I'm not going to bed lonely. The darkness takes over as I pull her into my arms, and we both fall into a slumber . . . together.

FIFTEEN

Kinzleigh

The bell rings signaling the end of the day. I managed to make it through most of April without anyone at school discovering I'm pregnant. Natalie has kept her word by not telling anyone, but my belly is becoming more and more swollen. Being a small person doesn't help me hide it. My clothes are getting tighter and it's too warm to wear jackets and school hoodies. The one good thing is that I'm not as nauseous now as I was in the early weeks.

I stand from my desk in World Literature, but not before I look at Breyson's empty desk in front of me. No one's sat in it since he's been gone. I pick up my book bag from the floor and place it on my back. I'm doing better, but I still cry every day. It helps that I see him every night in my dreams. Those big blue eyes are always just as beautiful as the last time I saw them. I'm the last one out the door, as usual, when I notice Adalynn standing beside it. "Hey girl."

I don't like the look on her face. "Hey . . . what's up?" It gives her away that she's not with Braxton. Since football practice let up, they have been inseparable. She usually comes over at night after they've had their couple time.

"We need to talk." She has that look in her eyes, like I'm not going to like what she has to say. She means business. "People are starting to talk, Kinzleigh. Everyone around school is asking if you're pregnant. I think it's time you come out about it. With Breyson being gone rumors are spreading like wildfire. You don't want people to think someone else is the father. Briar has been suspended for the rest of the week for knocking a stupid prick out in Chemistry. He wouldn't shut up running his mouth about you. Now the baseball coach is pissed because he's the starting pitcher and has to miss a game. You know the boys are protective of you, but they refuse to say anything until you give them the green light. They know it's Breyson's, but they can't really do anything until it's out in the open."

I lean my head against the wall in defeat. This isn't what I wanted. I was just starting to make it through the school day without breaking down, and soon I'm going to be the center of drama once again. I don't really care what people think of me. I know how it looks with Breyson being gone, even though it's obvious if they would do the math. I can't do this right now.

Pushing off the wall with the bottom of my foot, I walk in the direction of the exit doors. I can fend for myself. I don't want anyone having to get involved in my personal affairs. Briar and Braxton shouldn't have to deal with my crap. "I'll talk to you later, Adalynn. I need some space to think."

I don't turn around to see if she is following me. I have more important things to do today. My life has become predictable. I have a schedule. I don't sway from the schedule. That is the way I cope with everything. It's time to visit Breyson.

I step outside and walk straight for my car. Most of the kids have already left campus. As I approach my Range Rover, I see one person that didn't dissipate with the rest of the student body: Simon. He's standing against my car door in his baseball uniform with his hands crossed over his chest. His eyes are narrowed at me and I can see him working his jaw from here. He should be on the field getting ready for tonight's game; one that Breyson should also be getting ready for since he played both sports.

"Hey, Simon. What are you doing here?" I unlock the doors with my remote and place my hand on the door handle to open it, but he doesn't move—not one inch. He just stands there staring at me as if his dog got ran over and I'm the number one suspect. "Are you okay?"

He eyes me from my head to my toes, stopping on my stomach. He walks away from my car a few feet. I can hear his cleats patter against the pavement. He stops and stares out at the road with his hands linked on top of his head. "Fuck!"

I remain standing here, stunned by his outburst. Was all that necessary? He yelled it loud enough for the entire baseball team to hear. He turns back around and walks straight for me, pinning me against the door of my car. "He got you pregnant?"

What do I say? He looks down at my stomach again. Is it really that noticeable? I thought I was doing a good job of hiding it. I follow his eyes to the protrusion around my midsection. It's at this very moment I realize just how noticeable it actually is. It's like a little basketball appeared overnight—not big, but big enough it's out of place on my normally flat midsection. Me not saying anything says everything. "How far along are you, Kinzleigh?"

Why does he sound mad? By the look on his face, short replies are best. "Four months."

Konnor wasn't this mad and he's my brother. Brothers are entitled to be angry when a guy knocks up his sister. "Stupid prick. He couldn't stand the thought of anyone else having a chance at you, could he? He had to go and knock you up to make sure of it. Do you realize how hard your life is going to be with a baby, Kinzleigh? What happened to cheerleading? What if y'all would have broken up? Then what? You still have to go to college."

Why do I feel like I'm being lectured by my father? Wait just one minute. What exactly is he accusing Breyson of? Is he implying Breyson got me pregnant on purpose? That's absurd! I admit I was a little naive when it came to sex due to my lack of experience. It's not like I really prepared for sex, but Breyson had dreams too. He didn't want to be strapped down with a baby, did he?

Kinzleigh! Do you actually think Breyson would do such a thing?!

"Simon, you've been one of my best friends since I moved here, and I've fought to remain your friend. I've even listened to your advice here and there, but you're about to cross a line. Once you cross it there is no coming back. Our friendship will end." He closes his eyes and wraps his arms around my neck, pulling me in for a hug.

I link my arms around his waist loosely, not knowing what else to do or say. This is awkward. "You're right. I shouldn't have reacted that way. I wasn't even going to say anything to you. It just came out when I noticed you actually looked pregnant. I was hoping it was just a rumor. I wanted to ask you something."

"What is it?"

He puts distance between us, but never completely releases me. "I wanted to know if you would do something for me, or with me. Shit, this isn't coming out right. Will you go with me to prom?"

Prom? I rub the side of my nose at the corner of my eye. That was not what I expected him to say. I have to give him a little credit. He is persistent. Why would he think I have any desire to go to prom? "I wasn't planning on going."

He closes his eyes and lets his head fall back, before letting out a sound of aggravation, and then he opens them again. "Kinzleigh, I know you're going to be upset about Breyson for a long time, but you can't just stop living your life. It may even help for you to be around friends. I promise I'm only asking as a friend. Come on, say you'll go. If you go and you're not having a good time I'll take you home. I promise."

"Simon, you could take any girl you want. Why do you want to waste your time worrying with me? Prom should be unforgettable. It's senior year. I will make your night miserable. I'm not a fun person to be around anymore."

"Go with me."

"Simon . . ."

"Kinzleigh, go with me. Please. I won't take no for an answer." Breathe in. Breathe out. It's times like these I wish I could be more like Presley. She always knows what to do in these situations. I miss her like crazy. She is always the life of the party, taking what she wants without being afraid.

Looking back, I realize how much of a bore I was. Maybe I should have hooked up with a guy that I didn't react to so much. I should have looked outside of my little cheer bubble and enjoyed myself more. How did Presley like being around me all those years? Now, I feel like I'm doomed. Somewhere deep inside, the girl Breyson brought out is hiding from the world, afraid of living without him. I want to move on, but I don't know how. "If I say yes, will you let me leave?"

His smile forms—the one that makes him the attractive boy he is. "Pick you up at seven?"

I roll my eyes. "Do I have a choice?" He slowly shakes his head. "I guess it's a date then. I mean . . . not a date, but a . . . I'll be ready at seven."

He closes in and kisses me on the cheek. "I'm glad I didn't have to go with plan B," he says, before he walks away.

I smile a little. "What was plan B?" He is already at a distance, causing me to yell.

He never stops walking. Instead, he turns and continues walking backward. "Doesn't matter. I got the answer I wanted." He smiles, and within seconds, he's gone.

Everyone keeps saying friends are what I need. We'll find out. Being alone doesn't seem to be doing any good. I feel wrong for trying to move on when Breyson can't. It doesn't seem fair. It's time to go talk to him. Maybe then I'll get my answer.

SIXTEEN

Kinzleigh

I pull up at the cemetery I've become familiar with. I'm here every day, and every day it's just as hard as the last. I shut off the engine to my black SUV and exit without taking any of my belongings. It's finally warm, and here I don't have to hide my stomach. I take off the jacket I leave zipped in an attempt to hide my pregnancy and lay it in the seat.

I weave through the many headstones until I come to the one I no longer have to look for. I've developed a form of OCD in my daily ritual, my routine the same every day. I read the name across the front and fix my hair, as if he can see me. I like to think he can, and I want to look presentable. There's a breeze out today and the sun is warm. "Hey, Brey. How is everything today?"

I walk closer to the headstone and sit with my back pressed against the stone. Leaning my head back, I let the sun heat my face and legs. "Everything is the same here. You aren't missing much. I think everyone is figuring out our little secret, though. I'm not ready for anyone to know, but I don't think I have a choice much longer. Adalynn said Briar got suspended. It's all because of me, and I don't know how to fix it. He can't play in tonight's game. I wish you were here to tell me what to do. You always knew. You were so sure of everything."

I do the same thing every day when I come here. I sit and have a one-way conversation with him. The truth is, I don't feel him as much as I did. I don't know what that means. The chill I used to get or the feeling that someone is near is mostly gone. I get it from time to time when I'm really upset, but the days that I do okay, it's rare. That thought alone makes me want to stay upset just to feel him, but I told myself I was going to move on for this baby.

I still dream of Breyson every night, but it's mostly memories of us together. I continue to wake up screaming each time they end, and each time I'm soaked in sweat. I've stayed in his bed a few times, but when I do the dreams are worse and more real. I couldn't keep waking up to Briar holding me in Breyson's bed, trying to comfort me. It's not fair to him, so I don't stay there anymore. I felt him crying a few times, but he tries to hide it. He's so different from Breyson and Braxton. He seems to be the nurturer of them all.

Braxton still tries to keep his distance, but I know I can't avoid him forever. I can tell it bothers him. I'm terrified that one day I'm going to forget he's not Breyson and do something stupid like kiss him. I would never forgive myself for doing something like that. The sad thing is, Adalynn would understand. This baby will probably look just like him and I won't ever be able to move on.

I sit here, lost in my own thoughts. "Simon asked me to prom. I don't want to go, but it's for the best. You know we're just friends. I know I don't owe you an explanation, but I still feel like I do. Why don't I feel you anymore, Brey? Is this your way of forcing me to move on? I can't do that. I won't. I need to feel you near me. I'll find out whether our baby is a boy or girl soon. I've been thinking about names but wanted to get your opinion."

I sit and wait, hoping to feel something, but instead I get nothing. Maybe if I keep going there will be some sign. "So far I've thought of a boy name. I like Bryce Patrick Abercrombie. I'm not sure of a girl name yet, but I still have time. Right now, I like Breycie, but that's as far as I've gotten. Either way, I want its name to mean something, to have a piece of you, even though you won't be a part of this baby's life."

I blow out, trying to keep the tears at bay. It usually doesn't work. I'd like to think he can still hear me. "Bryce Patrick Abercrombie," I say aloud. When I do, I feel a small flutter in my abdomen, startling me.

That was strange. I place my hand on my small bump of a belly and I feel it again. It felt like my stomach did a somersault. Was that the baby? I haven't felt anything before, still too small to make itself known. "Hey, baby. Is that you? Finally deciding to make me aware of your presence . . ."

I have one of those baby books at home. Breyson's mom told me to read it so I'll know what to expect, but I have only skimmed certain parts. It's a little frightening, to be honest, when it starts talking about problems and illnesses. I'm just now getting used to the idea of being pregnant. I don't need to worry about problems. I have enough anxiety as it is.

"Brey, I felt it—our baby." As the whisper escapes my lips, peacefulness envelops me. Finally, I feel something. I thought I was losing him. I let the calmness take over and the tear fall free. This is what I needed. I needed to know he is still watching over me. Call me crazy. I don't really care. I'll take him in whatever form I can get him.

I scoot along an imaginary line from the stone until I can lay on the grass, parallel to where the casket would be laying underneath if there were one. I rub the soft blades of grass through my fingers like I used to do with Breyson's hair.

Then, I look up at the sky, pretending I'm lying beside him. I always lose track of time when I'm here. Usually, I lock myself in my mind, thinking of him, or I talk for hours, reminiscing about us or telling him things I would if he were really lying beside me. At some point I will have to distance myself from this place, but I'm not ready for that day to come yet. I need a little more time with him first. Before long I will have someone else that needs me, and I will have to make my visits here sparse.

The day is passing quickly, like it always does. The sun is setting, and the swirls of orange and pink along the horizon are soothing. My eyes become heavy as the warm air blankets my body. Spring is here. "I love you, Brey, always have, always will. The fatigue sets in and my eyes fight to stay open, but in the end, sleep wins out and they fall closed.

SEVENTEEN

Kinzleigh

My eyes open to a rocking motion, and darkness, accompanied by the sound of crickets chirping and a breeze blowing my hair across my face. The only thing familiar is the hard body I'm resting against. My dream is calling for my return. I don't have time to register where I am before leaning my head against something firm layered with something soft.

"Brey . . . I knew you'd come back for me." I snuggle into the man-scented cotton shirt and allow sleep to consume me once again.

EIGHTEEN

Kinzleigh

I roll over under the plush comforter. The feathery pillow supports my head and a wave of male scent floods my nostrils as I stretch. It's not a smell I recognize. I must be still dreaming. "You okay?" The sound echoes around the room in a raspy voice I've heard before, reminding me of the night I got my tattoo. My eyes jolt open and I sit up in a panic.

I look around the unfamiliar room as my eyes come into focus. The walls are painted the color of charcoal and are the support for a collection of guitars. They range in size, shape and color, but are designed to be a stunning focal point. Against the wall to the left of me is a small desk, lined with a cup of freshly sharpened pencils and a bundle of notebooks. It's tidy and simple.

A chair sits in the corner with an amp and electric guitar resting on a stand beside it. You can definitely tell a musician lives here, which brings me back to my original reason for my sudden awareness in the world. Why did I hear Riggan's voice? I look around the bed covered in a solid black comforter, toward the foot, and there stands a body.

My eyes trail up that same lean, sculpted frame I saw that night in the tattoo shop. A pair of loose denim jeans and a red vintage tee shirt is what he is wearing. His hair is gelled in the same spiky fashion it was the first time I laid eyes on him. I can't see his shoes, but from the way he looks I'd guess Converse. This, or preppy, was the average guy at my school back in California.

He is standing before me with his tattooed arms crossed over his chest, scraping his top teeth over his bottom lip and lip ring. I narrow my eyes at him. "Why am I here, Riggan? How did I get here? What time is it? Where is my car?"

He cocks one eyebrow at me, as I sit here slightly out of breath and parched. "Are you going to give me time to actually answer your questions or keep firing them at me like paintballs?"

Smartass.

If it weren't for the smirk on his face, I might find it enjoyable to throw a shoe at him. "Enlighten me, please," I say sarcastically. I'm hungry, tired, and fighting these damn pregnancy hormones with no one here to relieve me of this horny state I'm in.

No one warned me of the crazy pregnancy side effects. I went from never wanting sex, to getting it regularly with the perfect person, to actually needing it—talk about whiplash. A guy's bed is the last place I need to be right now. On top of me being here alone with him, he is standing in front of me looking like a sexy rock god. Any girl would have to be blind not to notice how yummy he looks.

Snap out of it, Kinzleigh. You should be ashamed. What would Breyson think?

Without saying a word, he walks over to the chair in the corner of the room. There is a window next to it. He sits and raises it with one hand. As easy as the window lifted, I would assume he does this frequently. I'm still waiting on him to say something. He grabs the cigarette resting behind his left ear and reaches in his right pocket, pulling out a lighter.

He's so mysterious, and slightly broody. He carries around some kind of baggage, but what? I want to ask, but then I don't. Something is eating away at him. You don't have to have a lot of brains to figure that one out. He wears it on his face and it's in his body language. Now that I think about it, he mentioned at the tattoo parlor that he understood what I was going through.

He still hasn't said anything. Instead, he places the filter between his lips and lights the end until there is a bright orange bud. The paper burns back as he inhales. He holds the cigarette out the window as he pulls the smoke into his lungs—I assume from his chest expanding.

Occasionally, he looks over at me with that same look on his face, as if he's looking at a ghost. Each time he glances at me sitting in his bed, he takes a long drag from the cigarette, as if he desperately needs the nicotine. His hand is shaking each time he removes the cigarette from his lips, but he's trying to keep it out of my direct line of sight.

I can't do anything but sit here and stare at him. He intrigues me; not in the way I was with Breyson, but I want to get to know him, or even help him.

He stares blankly out the window into the black, starry sky. I can't tell what the view looks like from here. I don't know where here is. As he exhales, the cloud of smoke floats into the night air. "Riggan?"

He takes another drag before finally looking in my direction. He doesn't look me in the face for long, like it pains him to do so. His eyes are glassy, as if he is processing some kind of information. "I found you sleeping in front of a grave and brought you here. Your face was puffy like you'd been crying. I didn't want to wake you. You shouldn't be sleeping outside, Kinzleigh. There are crazy people out there, looking for someone like you to get their grimy hands on—someone trusting."

He stands from the chair and bends over out the window, resting his forearms on the window seal. "Are you okay? You can talk to me. It could help me as much as it could help you—to get out of my head for a while."

His voice is stern and strong. His jaw flexes back and forth. The paper on the cigarette burns rapidly each time he sucks on the filter. He doesn't speak, as if he needs that cigarette more than he needs to breathe.

When there is nothing left but the filter, he puts the cigarette out and flicks the bud out the window. Standing upright, he looks over at me. "Let's get out of here. There is a place I want to show you."

I look down at my uniform dress from school. I would imagine my hair is ratty and I need to brush my teeth. "Just tell me what's on your mind, Riggan. I'm not dressed to go anywhere."

He ignores what I said. Something is pestering his thoughts. "There are some clothes in the closet if you want to change. They should fit. I don't talk about my shit, so don't ask. I'm not one of those guys that sits around and pours his fucking heart out. I keep my shit buried for a good reason. I thought you would be one of those girls that don't ask questions because you have your own shit to deal with. Are you going to come with me or do you need to run home now because I'm an asshole?"

He crosses his arms over his chest and narrows his eyes at me, while playing with his black lip ring. Two words are running through my mind:

ass-hole. He wasn't lying about that.

Is it weird that I want to know more about him? I'm not used to being around this type of guy, and that draws me to him. He's different. For some reason, I only attract guys that act like I'm a rare breed of human and treat me like the little virginal Kinzleigh I was. I'm not that girl anymore. It's refreshing to be around someone that lives in darkness and welcomes it; someone that is okay with life being crappy. But I need to know what his expectations are before I go off with him. "Just friends?"

His eyes darken. "Sweetheart, if I wanted more than friends, I wouldn't waste my time hanging out. I don't do the boyfriend-girlfriend thing I'm sure you're used to."

His eyes then trail down my face and my torso. "The only relationship I'm interested in is the kind where we do one thing—fuck. Based on your current state I don't think we'll be going there. I may not have respect for myself anymore, but I still have respect for another guy's kid, and I'm not shoving my cock into anything housing one."

I blink at the bluntness just spat at me. What is his problem? Is this the same guy I met at the tattoo parlor? I should get up from this bed and stomp out of the room, demanding to be taken to my car, but something stops me. I remember the way Konnor changed after Sophia. He mentioned the pain gets so immense sometimes it becomes difficult to distinguish the good from the bad in its attempt to find an exit. In the process, he turns into a soulless creature not caring about the feelings of another. According to Konnor, pain distorts the way he views things.

Guys deal with pain different from girls. Could he be longing for someone to relieve him of the burdens he carries? Whatever his deal is, I want to know more. Some part of him beckons to be heard, whether he wants it or not. He needs someone. I can't be that one for myself, but I keep feeling like I can be it for someone else. It's not in my nature to leave him behind without even trying to understand him. "Fine," I say. "Show me where these clothes are."

He points his head in the direction of his closet. "I'll be waiting in the living room. Everything you need should be in there." He pulls a cellphone from his pocket and touches in various locations on the screen. "We need to leave in the next thirty minutes," he says, and turns for the bedroom door.

Once through the door, he shuts it and leaves me sitting in the middle of his large bed. I don't see why he couldn't at least tell me where we are going. Tossing back the comforter, I get out of bed and walk in the direction of the closet. It's filled with men's clothing on both sides of the walk-in closet. Most of it is dark, but there are little bouts of color mixed in. In the very back of the closet is a small section of women's clothing. Why does he have women's clothing in his closet? He just said he doesn't date, so I can't fathom him living with a woman he's just having sex with.

I'll just have to be silently curious. After his response earlier, I won't dare ask. I filter through the items hanging on the bar. They're fun and flashy, no doubt owned by someone young. The woman's style definitely differs from his—fashionista meets rock star. Each piece looks to be the right size, but I don't want to accentuate my belly. I settle on a flowy, turquoise and pink color block, racerback top, and a pair of white denim, cuffed, crop pants. I remove them from the rack and walk out of the closet, hoping they fit.

I slide the denim crops on over my butt first, and thankfully they fit, because my belly is higher in the front allowing them to button. The shirt is fitted in the back but hangs straight in the front. The loose material doesn't draw attention my protruding stomach. Whoever they belong to has taste.

I return to the closet in search of a pair of shoes. They're neatly lined up on the floor below the clothes. There are heels in every shape and color and a few pairs of flats. I settle on a pair of pink flats that match the shade in the top. I have no idea what my hair looks like and I have less-than-stellar breath. I walk out of the closet and notice a closed door next to it.

I turn the knob to see if it's locked and it opens. I enter into a small bathroom. It's plain with a black shower curtain and matching rugs, as well as accessories sitting on top of the sink.

The only wall decor hanging on the beige wall is an oversized framed poster. It's a large white guitar with what looks to be some kind of poem in black lettering. The whole thing is eye-catching, and I can't help but to read the words imprinted on the front.

The Musician in You
By: Abby Carter

The room was full the lights were low
Everyone inside was ready for the show
To them you were the God of rock
Living a small-town dream and climbing to the top
But to me you'll always be
The teenage boy that loved singing to me

You came out on that stage
And the crowd went into a craze
But when I saw you everyone else started to fade
You were the only one in the room
Baring your heart and soul was what you loved to do
That was just the musician living in you
Every time I watch you perform
For the slightest moment I feel forlorn
I'm terrified what will happen when you see
Just how exceptional you are compared to me
You are an addiction I crave
Forever in your hands my heart is enslaved
One day when your name is up in lights
Becoming the rock star that has all the girls in fights
Please remember the girl next door
That loved the boy you were before

I gasp as I finish the beautiful words flowing down the paper. It's beautiful, and so full of emotion it takes my breath away—to the point of having to sit on the toilet because my knees feel weak. Who is the girl that wrote that? You can feel her love rolling off the paper as you read it in your mind. She was terrified of being left behind by the one she loves, like I was for so long.

Why do I feel like something bad happened to her? It always seemed like the world was a bubbly, tranquil place, until something bad happened to me, and now I'm surrounded by death and despair. I want to know more about her. I'm broken from my endless thoughts with a knock on the door. "You ready?"

Crap. Was I even supposed to be in here?

"Just one sec." I jump up and tousle my curly blonde hair in the mirror. A bottle of mouthwash is sitting on the sink. I grab it. Twisting the top off, I pour a small amount of the liquid into my cupped hand and drink from it like a bowl. After a few seconds of swishing I spit it down the drain and rinse out the sink.

I open the door to Riggan leaning forward into the frame on the sides of his fists. He is working his jaw back and forth as he takes me in, slow and precise. His eyes darken as they glide down my small frame, and then they take on something else altogether, as if he's possessed. He looks like he has transformed into the ultimate predator and I am the prey. It's a little scary, if I'm being completely honest.

His face finally goes void. "I won't talk about it, so don't ask. I'll never talk about it." With that, he turns and walks away, leaving me standing in the doorway.

He knows I read it . . .

What just happened? Did he completely leave reality and go to some Riggan world inside his head that only he has access to? I don't think I've ever witnessed someone do that before. He looked like he could kill someone—under the control of something else. Whatever happened, he went to some dark place, and I need to know the trigger. I don't want to get caught in the line of fire next time it happens. Something about me is bothering him, but I don't know what.

For the first time since I met him, I'm terrified to see where this is going. I have a strong feeling he is dealing with demons that run deep, consuming his soul with guilt and regret. I want to know his story. I want to know why his soul is burning alive in his own body.

Each time he looks at me, it's like he's being doused with gasoline, making him burn hotter. He needs someone to save him. I'll do whatever I have to do to pull him from the pits of Hell. I just hope I don't get burned in the process.

NINETEEN

Kinzleigh

We pull into a place I don't recognize. It's in an older part of town than the main strip I've become familiar with. "Where are we?"

He shuts off the engine and looks over at me, but only briefly, triggering more questions. Every time he looks at me tonight, it's like he sees someone else, as if he wants to touch me but refrains. "A place I haven't been to in a really long time."

He's giving me no information tonight. I wish I knew what was going on in that head of his. He grabs a new pack of cigarettes he picked up at the local service station from the console and begins packing them on his left palm. I've never understood why people like to smoke. It stinks, and the one time I tried it back in middle school when Presley thought we were being cool, I found out it tasted horrible. I thought I was going to cough a lung right out of my throat.

He rolls the window down and tears the clear plastic off the box. I watch as he nervously removes the stick. His hands are shaking as he brings it between his lips. His eye contact never breaks as he stares at the building a few feet ahead.

Why would he bring you somewhere he's terrified to go?

I finally stop looking at him long enough to see where we are. He's not paying me any attention anyway. When I look at the small, quaint building,

I realize exactly why he looks like he does. Neon pink lettering brightens the exterior—*Abby's Spot.*

My eyes widen as the millions of questions race through my mind. The lighter sparks beside me and smoke starts to swirl around us in a clouded haze. I want to know what happened to her. "Are you okay?"

I don't know what else to say. He looks like a hollow corpse—similar to the way I feel living without Breyson. "I don't want to talk about it. I can't talk about it. I just need a minute."

He inhales the smoke, as if his mental stability depends on the chemicals entering his body. "Okay, I can wait."

I lean my head back on the headrest and close my eyes, letting my mind roam. There is so much sorrow in the world. It doesn't seem fair to the people that get taken, or the people left behind. What's the point of soul mates or lifelong partners if you don't get but a short amount of time together?

I'm not sure who has it worse, the people that go to a better place or the people left behind to cope with the absence of the one they lost. Look at people like Macie, Riggan, and me. It takes every ounce of strength just to breathe every day—forget happiness. Even if you move on, it feels like you're shorting yourself. How is it right to be with someone else when you can't give him or her your all?

Loving Breyson taught me to love hard or don't love at all. If you can't give someone all of you, then don't give him or her any part. I don't know what Riggan's story is, but I have a feeling he is striving just to stay alive. I wonder if people dealing with loss and pain are somehow wired to find each other—to make it easier to deal with by being with people going through the same. I know that since I've been broken, I've met more broken people than I've ever known in my entire life.

"Fuck!" I jump at the unexpected outburst as his fist smashes into the steering wheel. "I need to do this, but I don't think I can."

I don't know what else to do, so attempting to talk him down can't hurt. "I'll do it with you. You brought me here for a reason, yeah?"

The muscle in his jaw twitches back and forth as he stares at the lettering on the wall of the building. He doesn't seem like the type of guy who would get this worked up over a girl, but I am assuming there is something dark related to *this* girl. "Let's get this shit over with. This day is never going to get any easier."

We get out of his truck and walk toward the building. There is a line of people waiting at the door for entry. I cup his upper arm in my hand, stopping him. "I don't have my license."

"You don't need it as long as you're with me," he says, and continues forward. He looks like a man on a mission. Nothing can stop him or slow him down. From the outside, this doesn't look like the type of place someone like him would hang out in. It looks more like a sorority hangout—upscale and frilly.

Who am I to judge?

We get to the glass door and a large man is standing guard. He looks like a body builder. He is covered in muscle with broad shoulders. This guy could give the hulk a run for his money. He's wearing a pair of jeans and a black tee shirt with the company logo across his chest in the same pink as the signage. I'm surprised it even fits over his large frame.

"Well, well. Who do we have here? I thought I was going to get a call to come get your sorry ass out of prison before I saw you again. You've been on a roll. You too good for us around here now, Riggan?" When he speaks, it seems so harsh. What is his problem?

"Don't dig up my shit, Kane. I'm not in the mood to be pissed off today. I've been clean for 6 months now. Give it a rest and leave it buried," he says, balling his fists to his side.

Clean? As in . . .

I stand here awkwardly, looking back and forth between the two of them in the little stare off they seem to be having. Maybe I'm in over my head here. I don't want to be involved in any trouble.

Just when I'm about to walk back to the truck, the security guard holds out his hand at Riggan. "Truce? You know we just miss you around here. You're not the only one that lost someone, Bro."

My stomach sinks from that one word—*lost*.

I throw my hand up over my mouth as I unintentionally gasp out loud. I was two seconds too late. They both look over at me as my eyes moisten, and Kane develops that same look Riggan had earlier as he takes me in.

"Who is she?" His words come out short and choppy, as if trying to conceal emotion.

"Kinzleigh," Riggan replies. "She's just a friend. It's not what you think."

What is it with these two? This is the weirdest meeting I've ever been in. "That's all levels of fucked-up, Man. Fucked. Up."

What is he talking about? Can we just go in already?

"Leave. It. Buried. Kane." With that statement, Kane opens the door and steps to the side, letting us enter.

"Tell Amy it's on the house tonight. You're going to need it." He places his hand on the small of my back, guiding me in front of him. As we walk into the building, the first thing I notice is how classy it is, considering it's a bar. Potted trees sit in each corner of the room and the floor is white stone with a silver glitter embedded in the glossy topcoat.

There is a counter in the back with a girl wearing a sexy, short dress in hot pink. That must be the going color around here. Her bronzed cleavage is hanging out the neckline of her dress, and her thick, black hair is bouncing in curls down to the middle of her back. She has big, brown eyes and a smile plastered across the front of her face.

I wonder what it would feel like to be that happy again?

"Welcome to Abby's spot. IDs please." Even her voice sounds perky. Kill me now. She's gorgeous. I feel plain compared to a girl like that. I've never had that kind of sex appeal.

"Leslie, give them bands. Riggan is a friend of management. His guest is covered too. Give Amy a heads up, will you? These two are drinking on the house tonight," Kane calls out from across the room at the door.

She nods and pulls out two wristbands. "Of course." I'm about to say I won't be needing one, because I don't intend to drink, when Riggan shakes his head as I'm opening my mouth. Instead, I close it and let her wrap it around my small wrist.

A few more people come in the entry door, and Riggan nods for me to follow him through the door beside us. It opens up into a large open space. The bar is in the center of the building, forming an O. The place is packed with bodies from wall to wall. It's hard to describe this place. It's classy and girly, but it has a rock vibe. Sorority girl meets rock star? That's a strange combination, but then I remember how his closet looked the same. Coincidence? I think not . . .

There is a large opening in front for dancing, and a stage set up with band equipment. Round high-top tables are lined along the walls for sitting. The floor is the same stone as the entry, but the walls are filled with framed posters signed by various bands as well as guitars and other musical items decorating the wall.

"Pick somewhere to sit and I'll find you, okay? I'm going to the restroom. If the shot girl comes to the table, I want three shots of Jack." I nod, and he places a twenty in my hand, before he heads in a different direction.

I look around to find an empty table. There is a DJ booth sitting low-key in one of the corners of the room. The dance floor is full of sweating bodies grinding to the beat of the hip-hop music as the strobe lights bounce off the walls, matching the rhythm of the music.

Standing on my tiptoes, I finally spot an open table. I begin walking in its direction, squeezing my way through the crowd of people. I finally reach the vacant table and take a seat in the high chair. My anxiety is starting to rise. I don't do well in large crowds of unfamiliar people unless I have plenty of space.

"Can I get you something, sweetie?" I look over to the edge of the table and there is a tall, leggy brunette standing in a dress and heels similar to the girl at the front. They definitely don't hire ugly girls around here. I feel like I walked into a bar full of pageant girls.

When my eyes lock with hers she gasps. Why do I keep getting strange reactions here when people see me? I'm starting to get paranoid something is on my face. I shake it off, but maybe I need to make a bathroom break as soon as Riggan gets back. "Three shots of Jack, please."

"Are you kin to her?" My forehead wrinkles in confusion. Who is her?

"Who do you mean?" She looks uncomfortable. She glances side to side and then back at me. She is holding her round tray next to her ribs and her drink pad is laying on top. She puts the cap end of the pen between her teeth and then points it at the wall behind me. I turn to look at the wall to my left and stop breathing. I do mean literally. I can't breathe.

Hanging on the wall over the table is a framed picture of a girl in a coral, off-the-shoulder dress and tan cowgirl boots, leaning over an old-fashioned wooden fence. She is behind the fence looking straight at the camera. The background is a natural luscious green made by the grass and surrounding plant life. The leaves of a large oak tree drape over her, causing a shade. It's absolutely beautiful. Above the frame is the name of the girl in the photo.

There are two reasons for my sudden onset of labored breath and anxiety. The first being that the name residing on the wall is the one and only mysterious Abby Carter. The second, and main reason, is . . .

She. Looks. Just. Like. Me.

My hand goes over my mouth. The similarities between the two of us are uncanny. The only real differences are that her hair is straight where mine is curly, and she has baby blue eyes instead of bright green ones like me. I can't take my eyes away. We look like we could be sisters. I once heard that somewhere in the world we each have a doppelgänger, but I would have said it's a load of crap someone made up . . . until now. "What happened to her?"

I never look back at the cocktail waitress, but I have to know what happened to her. "It's not important," Riggan says, before she's able to answer, drawing my attention. His eyes are dilated, and he just stares at me. "Don't you have some shots to get, Sara?"

He doesn't sound happy. "Sure, Riggan. I'm sorry, I didn't know she was with you. It caught me off guard is all. We all miss . . ."

"Enough!" Did he really just shout at her? What the heck happened to him in the few minutes he was gone? She scampers off like a dog with its tail between its legs. It is now registering why everyone keeps looking at me like I've grown a third eyeball.

"Why are you being a dick? She didn't even do anything, Riggan. I don't remember you being this way when I met you at the tattoo shop." He pulls out a cigarette and drops the box on the table in front of him. Saying nothing, he lights it, inhales, and continues to stare at me.

The girl sets the shots down on the table without saying a word and turns to leave. He exhales, picks up shot glass number one, and presses it to his pink lips. Turning it back, he drains the contents and slams the glass back on the table. I watch as he does the same with glasses two and three.

Whatever. This is stupid.

I start to get up to leave when he grabs my hand. "Don't. Stay. I can't talk about it, Kinzleigh. I'm not looking for anything but a friend. In time, I'll try to tell you, but right now, I need someone that understands the need for companionship with silence. I'm sorry for being a prick. I'll work on it. But can you really blame me?" he says as he points at the girl on the wall. "It's a little difficult to look at you without things surfacing that have been buried for a long time."

I look down at his hand wrapped around mine, then back at his eyes. There is a plea in them, and instantly I sit back down. I don't want to be the pregnant girl in a bar, but how can you turn down someone begging you for help? What if I was the difference in someone choosing to live and die? That thought plagues my mind now that I've been brought into this world of darkness, only shades of black and gray present.

I know some of the thoughts that enter into a person's mind when grieving over the loss of a loved one—someone that owned every part of you. I know how important friends are during a time when you have so much pain and misery residing inside you the world seems like a cruel place.

"Okay, Riggan, I'll stay, but don't leave me in the dark anymore. If we're going to be friends, then you need to tell me these things. I understand there are things you can't talk about, but some things you can. This," I point to the photo on the wall that still looks like my long-lost twin, "is something you could have talked to me about."

For the first time since I've been here, he looks at the photo. I don't mean glance, but study, and the look on his face as he takes her in crushes me to watch. He looks like he's fighting something bigger than himself.

He turns back a few more shots. I'm starting to worry he's had too much. Each time he empties the glasses they are replaced with full ones. I have no idea where he's putting all of it. He's like a tank. He isn't saying much as he drowns himself in the numbing agent before him, so I people watch.

What else does a sober person do in a bar? The bar is full. Bodies linger against every wall, crack, and crevice. It's easy to recognize the wasted by the scenes of inappropriate groping on and off the dance floor.

"She died. A few years back." I'm now at full attention from his comment. I had that feeling but was hoping for a different outcome. When I turn to look at him, his forehead is resting on his wrist. "I can't talk about it anymore. It hurts too much. I need to keep it buried deep," he says, slurring a little as he talks, indicating he is already intoxicated. "If I don't, I'll drown from the guilt. I'll relapse. I won't make it."

I'm not sure what to say. Or what not to say. Do I ask questions? Do I act like I didn't hear anything at all? Do I try to comfort him? I battle the pros and cons of each in my mind and am about to say something when I don't get the chance.

"Riggan fuckin' Henley, is that you?" The voice is echoing as the person it belongs to gets closer. The guy is about mid-height and built. He clearly works out from the size of his arms. His canary yellow shirt fits snug against his muscular, tan frame, and his jeans hang low on his hips. He has a leather band snapped around his wrist, similar to the one Riggan wears, and a black studded belt.

You can hear him walking across the floor in his combat boots that were left unlaced. He has short, sandy-blond, spiky hair similar to Riggan's. You can tell it's gelled on top, and he also has an eyebrow ring. I take in his solid frame as he stops at the table and slaps Riggan on the back.

Riggan turns at the contact. I catch a hint of a smile as he notices who it is, but he quickly squanders it. "Maddox Burns. No shit, man. What the hell have you been up to? It's been a while."

They bump fists and the guy I don't know sits in the chairback stool on the other side of him after pulling a pair of drumsticks from his back pocket. He lays them on the table and his eyes set on me. "Who's she?"

I look into a pair of eyes the same shade as mine—vibrant, bright, and green. He doesn't sound too welcoming, much like the ones before him. Like he doesn't believe what he's seeing. This whole night was a bad idea.

"A friend. Maddox, this is Kinzleigh. Kinzleigh, Maddox." When he looks at my face again, he downs a shot and removes another cigarette from the pack, lighting it.

"No shit? The resemblance is insane, and you brought her here on the same . . ." He closes his eyes and shakes his head; I assume to clear it from the thoughts running rampant.

What's so special about today?

"What can I say, I thought it would be easier to deal." From the way he's sucking down that cigarette it doesn't look like he's dealing with whatever it is too well.

"Why haven't you been back here, man? You know you should have at least come on this day. It's been four years. You just left us all high and dry at our peak. Why don't you come back to the band? We need you. You don't have to torment yourself forever." I feel like I'm eavesdropping.

"I can't do that; more than that, I won't. That's final." He keeps his face blank as he stares at the photo in front of him, longing in his eyes.

"Maddox, get your ass on stage." We all turn around at the voice amplified over the speakers. It's a tall, slender guy with chocolate-brown hair on the longer side of short. It isn't long enough to bind, but it flips out over his ears. If he's muscular his muscles are hidden underneath his clothing. A guitar is hanging around his neck. He doesn't really fit the bill for a rock band with his preppy choice for clothing. Maybe I should stop stereotyping altogether.

They all look clean-cut but rough around the edges; light with a shade of dark. "Be right up," Maddox yells out and looks back at Riggan. "Come on. One night for old times' sake. You owe her that much, Riggan. Besides, you know Landon doesn't like to sing. We need our singer back, even if only for the importance tonight holds."

Riggan looks back and forth between the stage and the photo hanging on the wall, as if he's considering it, before he finally stands. "I'm giving you one night and then I'm locking it away, forever. I'm not that guy anymore. He was buried the day she was."

I'm a little stunned. He's a singer? I guess that part doesn't surprise me. I knew he had a voice that had to be worthy, but I never thought I'd hear it. "You good here?"

I nod, and he walks toward the stage with Maddox alongside him. When they climb the few steps to the top, he walks to the mic stand. "Hey," he says, and the girls go wild. They begin chanting his name and gathering on the floor as if we're at a concert; screaming like they're welcoming back their biggest fan. "Bear with me. It's been a while since I've been up here."

They only scream louder the more he speaks.

Maddox grabs a guitar off a stand in the back and brings it to Riggan. When he sees the beautiful, white, polished guitar, he looks taken aback. I recognize it from the poster. That tells me one thing—the guitar is his and the poster was specially made for him. The guitar is a color that represents purity, standing out. The shoulder strap is baby blue, along with the strings. It doesn't really go with the band in all its darkness represented by the members, but I have a feeling there is a story behind it.

Riggan looks as if he's afraid to touch it, but finally grasps it at the neck and removes it from Maddox's hand. He places his opposite hand under the bottom and turns it in a rotation to admire all sides. It's hard to see, but it looks like something is engraved in the back. Riggan looks at Maddox and he nods a silent answer to the question asked in code, turning to walk in the direction of the drums.

Riggan places the strap over his head, securing the guitar in place. He reaches in his pocket, removing something. As he places it to his lips, I can see it's a guitar pick. It's zebra print. That's an odd guitar pick for a guy to have. Kissing it, he says low, "Always for you, Abby. Rest in peace, baby. I'll always love you and miss you." He wasn't aiming to speak into the microphone, but it still picked up the words, and the crowd goes silent.

He strums it for a minute and turns a few knobs as he tunes the guitar. He looks across the crowd and then over at me, before he starts strumming a solo I actually recognize. *One* by Metallica. As the words start, I sit quietly and listen to his voice sing the opening line. "I can't remember anything. Can't tell if this is true or dream."

I have the weirdest feeling of Déjà vu as I watch him get lost in the lyrics. His voice is beautiful. The poem I read in the bathroom hits me full force, almost knocking the breath from my lungs. I feel exactly as she felt, minus the love for him. Everything is so raw: the crowd, the band, the music.

When he sings you can feel his connection to the music. He's lost in the lyrics, as if they hold a deeper meaning to him—his lifeline. He closes his eyes and sings from his soul. All of his emotions radiate from him as he sings each stanza. I can feel what he's feeling: sadness, guilt, anger, pain.

Watching him makes me think of Konnor. Since the incident with Sophia happened, I see him jotting things down in a notepad—lyrics representing the way he feels. I wonder if they would hit it off. Maybe I should take him to the tattoo parlor next time he comes home. Riggan did say he wanted to be friends.

The waitress from earlier walks over to the table and touches my arm to get my attention. "Can I get you anything to drink, sweetie?"

"Sprite, please." I can't take my eyes off of the performance. He's so talented as he plays the solos perfectly and on key. It's sad that he can't do this anymore. It's easy to see this is what those guys are made to do, but I know exactly how it feels to give up a dream—the one thing you're great at.

I've given up my dream to cheer. I'll be lucky if I get to open up the cheer company I want. I can't travel aside having a baby and full-time job. The reason I never wanted to settle down before was because I wouldn't have the time necessary for that life. You have to find a way to support yourself wanting to be a cheerleader in the NFL, since that doesn't pay the bills. I won't have that kind of time, because I'll be bouncing a baby on my knee.

I don't know how long I've been sitting here, but they have played through an entire list of songs. I've noticed the other band members gleaming from ear to ear as they watch him sing. It's like they've been waiting for this moment for a long time.

Riggan stops as he finishes the most recent song and looks into the crowd. "Guys, it's been fun, but this is last call and last song. This is the end. Enjoy it, and remember it, because it will be no more."

He looks down at the guitar and begins playing the final song—*Breaking Inside* by Shinedown. As he sings the song one particular line stands out. "You know there ain't no comin' back, when you're still carrying the past. You can't erase, separate."

I freeze. Like someone pulling the trigger to the gun aimed at my head. Everything I've worked so hard to move on from crashes down on top of me. The wall I've slowly built up to hold back the memories of Breyson and me, along with everything that has happened, just shattered, everything flooding out.

I can't do this.

I stand and run, weaving through the bodies, heading for the doors that lead outside. I can barely breathe, my lungs deflated. The tears pour down my face. I can't see where I'm going, but that doesn't stop me. "Kinzleigh," is called out over the speakers, Riggan saying my name.

I can't think of anything but running. This has always been an escape for me when nothing else worked. I tear through the glass doors, freeing myself from the confinement of this building. A gush of air chills my face. I can breathe a little easier, but not well enough.

"Kinzleigh! Wait up." I look behind me to see Riggan running out the door. "Kinzleigh, stop!" I never let up. I can't. When I get like this, I have to find an outlet for the anxiety. On top of everything else, I haven't felt or heard Breyson in a while. I'm not sure why, but I want it back. I need it back.

The horn of a car blasts through the night, sending a shockwave to my heart, and body crumpling against metal, that's the last thing I remember as pain slices and splinters through my body.

Baby. Our baby.

TWENTY

Breyson

A sudden pain slices through my chest that almost brings me to my knees. Placing my hand over my heart, I bend forward.

What the hell?

That feeling something bad is about to happen or has already happened hits me. As I'm feeding the livestock, the first thought that crosses my mind is Marcus. I don't worry about mounting my horse. I take off running toward the house as fast as my feet will take me.

Sweat pours from my pores and my boots are heavy, but I don't care. I can't fight the feeling in my gut that something is wrong. I thought everything was finally normal. I've been working at the ranch and I have opportunities at Rapid Descent with Big Sanchez. I haven't had any more visions, so I thought the night with Angelique was what I needed to release some of the stress and tension I've been putting on my brain.

I have no interest in taking things further with her. If I need a release and she's up for it I might take her to bed again, but nothing more. I hold more feelings for the girl in the visions than I do for Angelique, and I've slept with her, as well as developed a memory I can pull anytime I want.

I'm almost positive the girl in the visions is just a figment of my imagination anyway. It sucks too, because she is exceptionally remarkable. If only she *were* real . . . But that's the thing about wishing—in the end it's still just a wish.

I come charging through the front door screaming, "Marcus!" I look from room to room in a state of panic, but don't see him anywhere.

Where is he?

"Marcus!" Every bad situation imaginable is running through my head right now. He couldn't be more of a brother to me if we shared the same blood. I love that kid and would kill for him. I'm about to walk outside to the pool when he comes walking down the stairs.

"Bryce? What is it? I'm right here. Are you okay?" Relief floods my body as he comes into view, but that feeling in my gut hasn't gone away. What does it mean? It makes my stomach churn.

Dizziness fills my head. I must have gotten too hot. I'm not supposed to overexert myself. White light flashes through my mind, causing me to press on each side of my skull with my hands, blinding me from the life around me. My sight is locked on one shade. "Where's Mom?"

What's happening to me?

I feel like I'm going to vomit, and my head is pounding. I fall to my knees at the excruciating pain in my head. Ringing occurs in my ears. I scream out to Marcus, "Go get Mom!"

I growl with each pulse. The pain is almost unbearable. The only thing I can see is white, and then a spotlight beams down on something in the center of the room. I feel like I'm trapped in a horror film while a game is played on my mind.

My whole body is burning, making me want to rip my clothes off. I can't see anything, but I can hear Marcus's footsteps pound against the floor, fading out.

What's happening to my eyes? Why can't I fuckin' see?

Finally, something forms on the blank canvas in my mind—a bed with a body lying on top of it. A hospital. I would recognize one anywhere. I try to focus through the pain pumping through my veins with each beat of my heart.

Tightening my eyes shut, the picture becomes clear. A small body is hooked to machines and wires. I recognize who it belongs to. It knocks the breath clear out of my lungs. I fall forward on the palms of my hands. Those unforgettable blonde curls are matted, and her face is scraped up. Her eye is bruised and swollen, her lips cracked. The beautiful face I remember so well is altered into something that crushes me.

Please don't be dead. You can't be dead.

Someone in a white lab coat walks around to the monitor keeping track of vitals. She's talking to someone, but who I can't see. A nurse rolls in some kind of machine and stops beside the doctor. The doctor turns toward the girl in the bed and I can now see her side profile as she lifts the hospital gown, exposing skin.

That doctor seems familiar, like I've seen her before.

The pain is still immense, but more tolerable now that something else is requiring more of my focus. I want to know she's okay. The doctor was blocking the view, but she turns to pick something up off the cart and that's when I notice the girl's swollen stomach.

What the fuck?

The doctor squirts clear jelly on top of her bare stomach and touches some kind of wand connected to the rolling monitor in the center of the substance. She begins rolling it around all over the swollen area, confusing me until she turns the monitor, revealing a black screen. My heart rate speeds up when I see what's taking up space on the screen: a baby. It's tiny but moving.

What does this mean? What the hell does this mean?

"Bryce."

"Bryce."

"Bryce!"

I blink a few times and feel something moist trickle down my cheeks, clearing the vision as if it was never there. Maria is holding my face between her palms, swiping the wetness away with her thumbs. I didn't even realize I was back in an upright position, kneeling on my knees. "Está bien, hijo. Estoy aqui ahora. ¿Qué viste? *(It's okay, son. I'm here now. What did you see?)*"

"Baby." I recognize some of the words I've become familiar with, piecing the rest together. It takes every ounce of energy in my frozen state to get it across my lips.

I can't blink. I can't speak. I can only kneel, completely still. She squints back at my response as if she's as confused as I am. "Tell me what you saw."

My heart is pounding as if it's working overtime to pump the blood needed throughout my body. My eyes continue to release tears from the corner ducts. I feel like I'm being strangled each time I speak. Nothing comes from my lips but a gasp for air.

Pregnant. By who? What the hell happened to her?

I'm so confused, and that feeling in the pit of my stomach has eased a little with the disappearance of the vision. Once again, I'm back to the same unanswered question—is she real or make-believe? My beautiful girl is in a hospital. The worst thoughts come to mind: rape, abuse, attempted murder. I have so many questions. I need answers.

"The girl is pregnant." I take a deep breath. "And hurt." I can't say any more. It was all I could do to get that short sentence out of my mouth. Could she really be real? If she's real, does that mean she was mine? I have had some graphic visions, but I thought it was just my mind trying to heal. As the thought crosses my mind, my heart feels full, and aches like it's longing for her. My hand goes over my chest and rubs to relieve the pain.

Oh. Fuck. Me.

The realization makes my blood run cold. Anger surges through my body, igniting me. "Bryce? Tell me what's wrong." Standing to my feet, I back away from her. I'm so angry I don't need to be close to her right now. I don't want to hurt her. My jaw steels and my hands go for my hair, trying to keep from hitting something. "Bryce, talk to me."

She stands and walks toward me. "Stop."

Her eyes fall in a way that crushes me, but I can't risk hurting the people that I've come to love. I need to cool off, because I just figured out life is a motherfucking bitch. "Please don't shut me out. I want to help you." My hands are shaking. I look from her to Marcus and back to her. She gets it. "Marcus, go to your room for a little while. Okay? I need to talk to Bryce."

He looks worried, but I will preserve his innocence at all costs. He doesn't need anything else to worry about. He has been trying hard to help me get my memories back. He's a good kid, and right now I can't guarantee my language will be censored. "Okay, Mom."

He makes his way up the stairs and into his room before I turn back to look at her. By the look on her face, she is trying to figure out what it is that I've already figured out. To date, I've been selective in what I tell her about the visions. Some things your mother doesn't need to know, blood or not. I've skimmed over the details on the rated-R ones. I like to keep them to myself anyway, because I feel like they are private. They're one thing I don't have to share. I don't want anyone else to know her the way I know her in my dreams. "Tell me what's going on," she finally says.

I have no idea how to say this. I don't think there is an easy way, so I'll just put it out there. It's possible I'm insane and she'll admit me to a mental facility for observation. But I have a strong feeling that it's the truth, whether I know the details or not, and that scares the shit out of me. "I think I'm going to be a father."

I wait for her reaction. Her mouth drops slightly, but she remains calm. She dazes out as she looks at me. I'm not sure what's about to come out of her mouth, but I wait for it. Her big brown eyes gloss over, and then the tears that were filling them spill over. "Are you sure?"

Am I sure? Well no. I'm not sure of any damn thing anymore. I ponder the question anyway, allowing my mind to go back to some of the visions, all of which contain her. The angle is always the same, as if I'm behind a camera and she's in front of it. I think back on the way they make me feel, even knowing she could be a figment of my imagination. I'm in love with her. The emotional connection is so fierce I don't understand it. I'm not sure about much of anything, but of this, I'm sure. "Yes."

One word and my world lightens from black to gray. I don't know the details, but my heart and my soul are telling me I'm right. My brain just needs time to catch up. I do know this—I don't care what oceans I have to cross or what hurdles I have to jump, I will find out who she is and find her. I may not remember her name or where she is, but I believe she is the one for me, with all that I am.

"It's time we call Dr. Rodriguez. He may have some answers as to why you are having these kinds of visions." She looks hopeful, but this is something that is higher than science. I don't know why I'm having them, but I have to believe it's for a reason. Someone needs me. She needs me.

I'm quickly brought back to the matter at hand as I stand here trying to figure out *why* I'm having this epiphany, and that's not even the important part. I sling my hand across the top of the table that butts up to the wall, knocking over everything on top. Various shapes and colors of glass shatter against the hard floor. I should stay away from all objects when I'm mad. This has happened before.

I feel something wet run down my hand. When I look down, I see blood. A piece of the glass must have cut me during my tantrum. I don't even care. A little scratch doesn't hurt me as bad as knowing the girl I'm in love with is banged up and carrying my unborn child. What's worse is that I still don't know how to get to her or where she even is. I place my palms on top of the table and drop my head, chin to chest. "She's hurt, Mom. Someone hurt her bad. And the baby . . . What if? How am I supposed to know they're okay if I can't get to her?"

My heart is telling me I love her, but my brain is holding out on how much. It's choosing to only give me bits and pieces. It's a sick joke, really.

Am I trapped here until I learn some kind of major life lesson and then all of a sudden my mind will stop fucking around and give me my memories back? "I need to find her."

I think I'm trying to convince myself more than Mom. She walks over slowly and grabs my bleeding hand in her own. Wrapping it with a hand towel, she looks up at me. Her eyes make a promise as they lock with mine. "We will find her, Bryce."

I hope she's right, because I can't stomach to think that she's wrong . . .

TWENTY-ONE

I feel like I've been hit by a train. My eyes are glued shut and my whole face hurts. My hand is sweating and connected with another. I'm tired but confused. The beeping of a machine brings me into focus with reality.

Where am I?

I pry open my eyes. My throat is dry. I need water. I'm in the one place I can't seem to stay away from: a hospital. I look over to my left. Riggan is sleeping with his head on the mattress. The events of the night come back to me. I got upset at the bar and ran outside. The car. I don't remember much after seeing the car's headlights. It's all a haze in my head. Death is standing at my doorstep, yet again. I don't think I've ever felt like this. "Riggan."

My voice causes him to jolt awake. He looks at me, and instantly, I feel guilty. His eyes are red and bloodshot. He looks exhausted and upset. "Are you okay?"

"I'm sorry, Kinzleigh. I didn't get to you in time. I tried. I ran so fucking hard. I'm so sorry." His voice breaks. I'll admit it wasn't a walk in the park, but why is he sorry?

"Riggan, you didn't do anything. Stop being ridiculous."

Lines of confusion mar his face. "Why did you leave then?"

"That song reminded me of someone. It triggered some things I wasn't prepared for. It wasn't you. It was me."

"I shouldn't have had you there. You're pregnant for fuck's sake. I let my own demons consume me." That one word causes chills to run down my spine. *Pregnant.*

Oh, God, please let this baby be okay.

What is wrong with me? Am I so selfish that I don't think about this baby enough to protect it? I was only supposed to do one thing, and I can't even handle that. I look down at my belly as tears trickle down my face. Placing my hands on top of the growing bump, I do the only thing I can—pray.

> *Dear God,*
>
> *Please protect this baby. Let it be okay. I know I haven't done a very good job, but if you'll spare its life, I promise to do better. From here on out I will think of the baby first. I will put its needs in front of my own. This is the only piece of him I have left. Please, if you'll do this, consider it my last request.*
>
> *Amen.*

I open my eyes to Riggan eying my belly, inching his hand closer. "It's okay. You can touch it."

He looks unsure but rests his hand on my belly anyway. "Are you scared? You know . . . of being a teen mom."

I think over his question. Honestly, I haven't spent much time thinking about the baby. I had put it at the back of my mind, scared of where my thoughts would lead. Before, the only thing I'd considered is that my cheerleading career was over before it got started. I'm not sure if I will be able to cheer in college since down here fall classes start before I'm due to give birth. I'll be behind all of my friends a semester. Between studies and taking care of a baby, I won't have time for any extracurricular activities.

I begin thinking about all the money it's going to take to raise this baby. These are things I never considered until faced with the possibility of losing it. I don't want to be one of those girls that live off my parents. I should start looking for a part time job to save some money. I have enough to get started, but what about when it gets here? Diapers, food, and formula aren't cheap, and that doesn't include childcare for when I'm in school. I have no baby items either.

Attending UCLA in the fall is out. I was trying not to think about it, but it's coming quickly. Breyson had agreed to attend school there, because it's where I wanted to be, but I can't afford to live on my own, pay living expenses, and support another person.

I have to grow up. I'm maturing with age, and more frequently thinking of how hard it will be and how much I will have to sacrifice to be a young mother. There is still only one option—keep it. No matter what I have to do, I want this baby. I already know I'll never love anyone else the way I loved Breyson, but I'd rather have something left of him than nothing at all. I'm ready to answer the question. "Yes, I'm scared, but it's all I have left of the most amazing man I've ever known."

He looks at me as if he knows exactly what I mean, longing present in his eyes for the one he no longer has. He removes his hand and stands when a knock sounds on the door and opens. Breyson's mom and my mom walk in with a nurse behind them rolling some kind of cart. "I'm glad you're awake," Breyson's mom says as she walks to the other side of the bed, farthest from the door.

Riggan walks to the door, and for the first time I notice a cast on his lower arm and hand. He also has a slight limp when he walks.

What happened to him?

He stops and turns around as they set up the machine next to the bed. Mom is at my side, rubbing her hand over my hair as if she's scared to look away. "I'm glad you're okay," she says in a soothing tone.

I can't look away from Riggan. He stares back at me. There's something that I'm missing. "Will the baby be okay?" he asks the doctor, but never breaks eye contact with me. What is eating at his soul? The guilt is so strong that even I can feel it.

"We will know more soon," she says. "I will fill you in as soon as I know something."

He nods and walks out the door. As he disappears, a realization occurs. I need him, and I think he needs me just as much. We have a mutual connection. We share a common ground. I need repentance and he needs deliverance. The two of us will either save or destroy each other. I'm hoping for the former, but it's a risk I'm willing to take.

My hospital gown being lifted above my belly brings my attention back to the present. I grab onto the bed rails as my nerves get the better of me. "This may be a little cold. We have a warmer for it in the office." She squirts clear goo on my belly from the tube in her hand. "You took quite a hit. If it weren't for that boy, you and the baby would both be dead."

I gasp. It's sad and a little concerning that the thought of death doesn't scare me but excites me. If I died, I would get to be with Breyson again. That kind of love is dangerous. It drives people over the edge. It's the kind you don't come back from.

I stare at the ceiling as I realize just how crazy I've become. This isn't healthy, but I don't know how to fix myself. Mom swipes her finger up the side of my face, clearing a fallen tear. "It's okay to be scared."

If she knew of the things I was thinking she would be the one scared. Her daughter is daydreaming of how death would be better than life. I'm sure that's enough to admit me to the psych ward.

Something hard touches my belly and glides in different directions. After a few seconds, a swooshing sound fills the room, causing me to look at the monitor. It looks so different this time. Instead of a peanut, it looks like a baby. An alien baby, but a baby, nonetheless. The eye sockets are big, but the rest looks like a small baby. I can see a flutter on the screen where the heart is. But what's more, I can hear it.

My chest aches, and for the first time since Breyson died, my heart is trying to revive itself. Its small limbs are moving. Breyson's mom continues to move the wand in different areas to check everything, or so she says. I stare in awe, watching our baby as it moves inside of me. We created it together. "It's still a little early, but this is one time I'm pretty confident. Do you want to know the sex?"

My face hurts with movement, but I don't care. I smile as big as I can manage and nod my head. She moves the wand around for a minute and stops. The baby's legs come into focus. She points at the place between the spread. "Do you see that? Look right here," she says, pointing at the tiny extra add-on that looks more like a finger sticking out from the middle. "If I were to sit the baby on top of a glass table, you're looking up from below at the bottom. This is his penis. It's a boy."

A boy . . . just like the dream.

The night before I visited Breyson at the cemetery I had a dream. Sleep is the one place I get to be happy again. Most nights, I dream about my beautiful blue-eyed boy. They feel so real, as if my mind is showing me the life we never got to live. That dream almost broke me. It almost took my lungs from my body, leaving no option to breathe.

Brey and I were rocking on the front porch, my belly swollen out in front of me. The air was crisp, the sun warming my skin, and a cool breeze brushed against my face, sending my hair into a dance. It was the perfect fall day. I was staring out into the new flowerbed Breyson did for me, peaceful and happy from the bright colors alone.

He stood and moved in closer to me. "How's my son?" he asked and kneeled on his knees, so he was eye level with my round belly. He then placed both hands flat on my stomach and kissed my protruding belly button covered by my cotton maxi dress.

As soon as our son heard his daddy's voice he went to moving, causing a hard lump to form underneath Breyson's left hand. "He's good today— excited to hear his daddy, as usual. I think we need to re-evaluate the name situation, Brey. He needs a name."

He looked at me, his eyes smoldering and deep, penetrating into the depths of my soul. I always got lost in the aura that radiated from him, holding me to him. I'd come to realize in our time together that the greatest treasures are the simple things that make the heart light and the soul free. With him, I was living it. Life's meant to be lived to the fullest, to love and to be loved.

He smiled, making my heart skip a beat and my breaths shorten. It was difficult to breathe. "What do you think about Bryce? I know you wanted him to have my name, but he should have his own name. He's a part of me, but he's also a part of you. One thing we carry throughout life is our name. I want his to be strong, but also unique to him. But I live to make you happy. What about Bryce Patrick Abercrombie? We could spell Bryce with a Y instead of an I like your middle name is. That way he has a little bit of old, a little bit of new, a little bit of me and a little bit of you." He smiles at his little poem like he was proud he came up with it, and my heart burst.

How would I ever tell him no when he made points like these? He lived to please me, but what I loved is that he pleased me without always giving me my way. He knew how to handle me in a way no one else would. What he chose was absolutely perfect—same middle and last name, as well as initials, just a different first name. He even added something to include me.

I wrapped my arms around his neck and leaned forward in my rocking chair, resting my forehead against his. "When you put it like that, how could I refuse? You've always held the key to my heart, Brey. It's perfect."

A tear fell down my face in that moment on that porch, making me feel like a silly girl. Never missing a beat, he kissed it. "What's wrong?"

"I'm just happy is all. I love you, Brey. I want you forever." He leaned back with a cheesy grin on his face. "What?"

"I thought you might feel that way," he teased, before reaching in the pocket of his khaki shorts. I have always loved his lighthearted personality.

I laughed until he held out a little black box in the palm of his hand. For a moment, I forgot how to breathe. "Brey?"

"Shh. Don't say anything until I'm finished. I know we're young and we have our whole lives ahead of us. I've spent the last several months going back and forth in my head about this, but my heart won out. I knew your first thought would be that I'm only doing this because of him, but that's furthest thing from the truth. From the moment I laid eyes on you I knew you were different. I've loved you since that day I found you on the beach and I haven't stopped since. You are my everything. I won't be completely happy until I have you forever. I want you to be my wife. I want our son to know how much I love you. Marry me, Kinzleigh. Say you'll marry me," he begged, and then opened that small velvet box.

I gasped at the sight of what was nestled inside. It was the most beautiful diamond ring I'd ever seen. I'd known forever it would be the ultimate honor to wear Breyson's ring. My eyes were so full of tears I couldn't see anything but a blur. I blinked, letting them fall. "Yes. I'll marry you."

We both knew it was crazy to get married at eighteen in the current day and age, but a love like ours was a rarity in this world. Breyson was a gift you didn't give up. His love was a blessing. When God gave you a soul mate, you didn't take it for granted. You embraced it whether the timing was ideal or not. "Now kiss me."

He smiled from ear to ear as if I had handed him a million-dollar check. "Gladly," he whispered, and touched his lips to mine. He didn't kiss me rushed or greedily, he kissed me slow, cherishing me. I knew I'd make a lot of wrong decisions in my lifetime but marrying the love of my life was one that would always be right.

"Kinzleigh, did you hear what I said?" Breyson's mom's voice breaks through my thoughts, reminding me that it was just a dream. They always are . . . "Are you okay?"

Am I okay? No, I'm not. Why didn't I get my happily ever after? What did I do so wrong in life to be punished for a lifetime? Just once, I want my dream to seep into reality. "I miss him."

Bryce Patrick Abercrombie. That's your name, baby.

"Oh, honey, we all do," she says, and continues to point at the narrow area between my son's legs, moving on to something else. I've noticed she steers away from discussions of Breyson to keep her emotions in check, so I don't say anything else. "Everything looks okay, but I'm considering you a high-risk pregnancy from here on out. I want you to rest and take it easy. Stay off your feet. I'll give you an order to do all your schoolwork from home. I'm putting you on bedrest until your body heals. You don't need any extra stress on your body after a trauma. You both are lucky. This should be a wakeup call. You're the only thing this baby has for protection until he can survive on his own. Think about that."

I can't take my eyes off the baby on the screen. This is the first time since I found out I was pregnant that this baby and pregnancy feels real. It's all sinking in. He is my son and I'm his mother. He is my life now. The only connection between him and his father is me. I can't let Breyson die. I have to keep his memory alive for Bryce. Whatever I have to do to keep his best interests at heart I'll do, whether I'm happy or not. "Okay," I say, and this time I mean it wholeheartedly.

TWENTY-TWO

I sit here on my bed as I try to go over in my head exactly why I agreed to this. Maybe I should back out. I'm not ready for this. Will I ever be ready for this? It doesn't feel right. Every reason I try to come up with to cancel falls short. A night out of the house would be nice since it'll be the first time after my accident, but it seems like something always happens when I go somewhere. I long for the days when my life was almost perfect—to be able to go out and enjoy life freely. I can't go out now without some kind of major drama, or trauma. I have the worst luck out of anyone I know. It can only get better from here, because it can't possibly get any worse.

I look at my nightstand and reach out to grab my phone when I notice the picture sitting there; the same picture I found on Breyson's nightstand all those nights ago. I couldn't leave it behind. It was obviously special to him, and I wanted to be able to see what he saw each time he went to bed. "This was supposed to be something for us to do together, Brey."

You're talking to photos now, Kinzleigh? Yeah, you're a mental case in the works . . .

None of this means anything without him. Everything monumental that a person is supposed to do in high school only interested me when I was with Breyson. Without him, I don't want any of it, but I promised that I would move on, and moving on is what I have to do whether I like it or not.

Maybe, if I think it enough, I'll actually start to believe it.

My door opens and Adalynn walks in wearing a button-down shirt and shorts. She's carrying a hanger holding her dress under a plastic sheath in one hand and a tote bag in the opposite. "You look like hell."

I roll my eyes as she not-so-kindly states the obvious. The swelling is almost completely subsided, and the bruises are faded and discolored but still present. "You're right. Maybe I should just stay home," I say in a bland tone.

"Nice try, sweets, but you're going to have to do better than that. Luckily for you, I've had more modeling calls lately, which means I've learned some fabulous tips from the makeup artists. This one bag holds all of the magic to make that go away." Adalynn never takes no for an answer. Braxton doesn't have a chance.

I release a noise of frustration as she sets her things on my freshly made bed. The last formal I went to was the New Year's Eve ball with Breyson—the night I got pregnant. Now, here I sit, with a basketball size bump of a belly underneath my clothes. "Adalynn, I'm freaking pregnant. Why would anyone want to take me to prom? If it's out of guilt I'm really fine to just stay at home. Something bad always happens when I go out anyway."

"Stop fishing for compliments. You know you're one of the most beautiful girls I know, pregnant or not. Simon has been drooling over you since you moved here. It has nothing to do with you being pregnant. Besides, the boys will all be with us. We would never let anything happen to you, and you have a stunning new dress that deserves a night out on the town."

Why do I even argue with her?

"Fine, but I don't see how much fun I could possibly be. Everyone drinks on prom night and I'm stuck being pregnant." Placing my face in her hands, she kisses my forehead like the mother hen that she is.

"If my best friend can't drink, then I don't drink. You're not alone, Kinzleigh. That's what friends are for; to comfort each other in times of need and be there even when life is not full of glitter and sparkles. Friends 'til the end, yeah?" I swear she has an old soul. If I weren't a Christian, I would be certain reincarnation was a real thing and that hers came from a wise elderly woman, or maybe a philosopher.

I nod, and she turns and walks in the direction of my closet, disappearing inside. I hear hangers scrape against the rod for a short time and then it stops. When she walks out, she is holding my dress that we bought a couple of days ago when Mom took us shopping. Mom doesn't let me out of her sight since the car incident. I'm surprised she's even letting me go to prom without volunteering as a chaperone. I can't say that I blame her, though. I've put her through hell since Breyson died in my attempt to survive.

I still haven't gotten any real answers as to what happened the night of the accident. I've gone to the tattoo shop once or twice to talk to Riggan since I don't have his number, but he hasn't been there either time. I'm starting to think he's avoiding me, but I don't know why. He came in to say goodbye after we found out the baby was okay, and when he told me goodbye, I knew there was a possibility I wouldn't see him again based on the look he had. I wish I knew what was consuming his soul, eating him alive, and staining his conscience.

I take a deep breath, letting my thoughts run wild. They begin spreading like wildfire. I'm starting to think I was right all along. People always leave, especially when you need them the most.

The more I think about it the madder I get. I was conned into believing that things could be different for me, but they aren't. I was fine with my life; getting by. Sure, I wasn't really living, but at least I wasn't left with a gaping hole in my chest, wasting precious oxygen. Everyone leaves me. Grams left. Breyson left. Macie left. Now Riggan is gone. Why is it the people I need to stick by my side always disappoint me?

I'm not a violent person. Really, I'm not, but right now I want to hit something. I want to take out my anger on someone. Grams always said when you want to blame someone blame Satan, because the tragedy and pain in the world is always at the work of his hands. I hate him! He couldn't stand seeing me happy, so he made it to where we had to part ways. Now, Breyson is watching down on me from above and I have to live out this miserable life alone.

"Stop doing that."

"Excuse me?" I ask, confused.

"What you're doing in your head right now. I can see it. These emotions aren't part of your nature, so they are obvious when present. I don't know what's going on in your head right now but stop it. Whether it's guilt, regret, hatred, or shame, you're letting yourself lose the battle. Do you want to know what happens when you don't fight to win, Kinzleigh?"

I don't speak, because what I feel is really no one's damn business. If I want to hate myself then it's my own right. It doesn't matter what way you slice it, Breyson's death is partly my fault. It's my fault he left, it's my fault he got on that plane, and it's my fault I didn't go down in that cursed plane with him. I should have been there with him, fighting for my life beside him, and looking down on our loved ones next to him. Our souls are meant to stay together. They won't survive alone. The worst way to live is to live without your soul, carrying on in the form of a zombie or hollow shell—a carcass.

"I'm going to tell you whether you want to hear it or not. When you stop fighting and let darkness take over, it wins. When it wins there is no coming back. It takes you under, defeats you, and makes you want to stop living. When you start rationalizing that dying is better than living, you make decisions that not only affect you, but also the ones left behind that love you. Speaking from someone that knows that kind of pain, I'm telling you to think of everyone else and not just yourself." Did she really just accuse me of considering suicide?

What's scarier than the fact that the thoughts have crossed my mind briefly—very briefly—is that she somehow knows, and I haven't mentioned it to anyone. She always knows everything about anything. "What do you mean by *speaking from experience?*"

Something about the look on her face tells me I just opened a box that's been locked away for a long time. I don't like that look on her at all. "I had a brother once."

She pulls the plastic covering off the hanger. "I love this color on you." She removes it from the hanger and looks at me as if she didn't just point out an elephant in the room. "Well, off with it. At this pace we will miss prom all together."

Is she for real right now? How do you just say something like that and then act like you didn't say it at all? Am I supposed to forget she just said she *used* to have a brother? As in he's dead, missing, out of pocket, or disowned? What does that mean? "Adalynn . . . what do you mean *used to?*"

I tread lightly on the words as they pass through my lips, not knowing how she will react. I study her face for some kind of clue as to what is going on in her head. Her pupils decrease in diameter as her eyelids widen. She is staring off into space as if she is trying to re-bury something just uncovered. I should have just left it alone. She looks like she could be sick any second.

She shakes her head as she closes her eyes. "I can't," she whispers, and a single tear trickles down her cheek. A few seconds pass, and then, just like that, her demeanor changes.

"Let's get you dressed," she says as she wipes her face, and instantly she's back to smiling. There are more layers to Adalynn than I originally thought. It's crazy how so many times we're so absorbed in our own lives that we never stop to think there may be someone else that is battling a war within themselves and trying to stay afloat. Maybe we, as individuals, should look deeper in an effort to try and be there for someone else. I know I've been guilty too many times of only being concerned with myself and my problems. It's times like these I feel totally selfish.

"Okay," I say, and drop it all together. Maybe one day she will talk about it, but until then I will have to wait. The more time that passes I learn that some things are easier to bury deep than to have to deal with them. The only problem with that is that at some point it has to be dealt with or it will consume you. All skeletons are revealed at some point no matter how much you think they're hidden from the world.

I'm not as open with changing in front of people since my belly started protruding from my waistline. Luckily, I haven't had any stretch marks yet, but always being small and staying fit I'm suddenly a little self-conscious. I stand anyway and nervously remove my camisole.

As if she can sense my discomfort, her eyes never stray from my face. She helps place the dress over my head and pulls it down my body. My dress is a lavender one-shoulder number made of fitted satin over my breasts and flowing A-line in satin with an overlay of chiffon below by breasts to the floor. I bought it in hopes of making me look less pregnant. I haven't been at school for the last two weeks, because I've been ordered to stay in bed. I'm not complaining. The fewer stares the better.

"How are you holding up? I don't get much out of you anymore. You're trying to shut me out, aren't you?" I let the layers of material fall down my body, the hemline hitting the floor. She's right. I am shutting her out, unintentionally. My life is mostly a bubble of misery and I hate to be the rain of despair on someone else's happiness. She should get to enjoy being in love and the happiness that comes with it, not deal with sadness and anger all the time. "You're still my best friend, right?"

I would give anything to go back to the way things were. I miss being happy, I miss my friends, I miss being a kid and enjoying life—the life Breyson showed me I could have. No matter how much I try, though, I can't go back to that girl. I can't pretend that Breyson wasn't in my life. He was my one, my only. He's the one thing that I want now but can't have. No other wants will ever top that.

"Adalynn, you will always be my best friend. I'm just lost right now. I don't know if I will ever be happy again, but I'm trying. Maybe getting out of this school will change things. Maybe I should consider moving in with Presley to get a change of scenery after graduation, or even with Konnor at Alabama. I have a lot to figure out between now and then, but I can't be happy surrounded by everything that reminds me of him."

She says nothing more as she nods and reaches for her makeup bag. I sit on the bed and she begins painting my face in silence, concealing each bruise that remains, the reminder that I could've been closer to Breyson right now. My emotions stay in a constant frenzy as of late. One moment I want to be taken by death so I can be with my love at that very instant, but the next I feel guilty for having that thought because of Bryce. If I die, he dies, and I can't be responsible for his death too.

Each brush across my face is so light I barely notice that she's standing in front of me. My eyes remain closed. Every few seconds I feel a sweep of bristles across my eyelid followed by something cool and wet. The mixture of sensations makes me want to go to sleep. Instead, I let myself reel back to the New Year's Eve ball.

The moment I laid eyes on Breyson at the bottom of those stairs I knew that I would be forever his. He captured my heart and rode away with it, sealing my fate for eternity. I would give anything to be able to look into those blue eyes one more time; to be swept across the dance floor and be claimed by him. He always had a way of making me get lost in the moment, forgetting that we were in the middle of a crowd of people. Had I known how things were going to turn out I would have cherished every second with him instead of fighting it for so long.

From my first reaction to him I knew there was something different about him. I hate myself for being a spoiled brat and only thinking of myself. His soul was precious; one to grasp onto and never let go of. His kiss was enough to give me an emotional high, making my nerve endings pop off like fireworks each time he touched me. I want that feeling back. "I miss him, Adalynn." The admission comes out no louder than a whisper laced with a cry.

"I know, babe. It's okay to have moments of weakness, Kinzleigh. No one expects you to be strong all the time. When you find a love like you and Breyson had there is no other option but to break down when you lose your hold on it. The old saying goes—there's no shame in falling down, the shame is in not getting back up. Just remember that we love you, Kinzleigh, and we're always here to help you back up when you do."

Moments like these I'm reminded of how blessed I am. I've been through a lot of bad, but I haven't had to do it alone. For each rock I've stumbled on I've had someone there to catch me. I should thank God more for the beautiful people that I do have, because it's never promised that you won't lose them as well.

I should tell all of the people I love how I feel. If I've learned one thing, it's that the best way to live is as if it's the last day you'll see the people in your life. We never know when our time is up or theirs. "I love you, Adalynn. I'm not good with saying how I feel, but I do."

"I know you do. Actions always speak louder than words. I don't have to hear you say it to know you love me. I love you too. You'll always be my best friend, Kinzleigh Baker. You weren't only brought here for Breyson. I don't know why things happened the way they did, but I believe you will get your happy ending. We just have to wait and see what exactly that is. Come on, let me finish your hair and put my dress on. The boys will be here before long."

My nerves begin to get the best of me as I think about seeing Braxton for the first time in several weeks. I usually try to avoid him, and he doesn't push me. I need to bite the bullet and move on from this constant state of sorrow and pity for myself. I keep saying I'm going to do it, yet every time I take one step forward, I end up taking two steps back.

I look at myself in the mirror as Adalynn finishes getting herself ready. I can't believe the sight before me. You can't tell my face was covered in bruises and my belly is barely noticeable. For once, I feel beautiful without Breyson having to tell me. My hair is simple but elegant, teased and pinned at the crown of my head, my curls falling to the center of my back. Breyson liked my long curls. Tonight, I'll try to live for both of us; experience senior prom for him and I.

I look at Adalynn in her white dress that does wonders against the complexion of her skin. It's strapless with a sweetheart neckline that dips in the back into a point just above her butt. It actually reminds me of a heart from the neckline to the fabric in the back, like it would appear if she were standing in a hula-hoop but in the shape of a heart. The front is covered in a clear beading that sweeps in a pattern from the neckline to her waistline. The top is fitted snugly to her skin and then flows freely at the waistline to the ending at the floor. She looks like a bride.

I never thought I wanted to get married and now I find myself wishing I still had the option. Things can change so drastically in such a short amount of time. "Wow. You look beautiful," I say, still taking her in. Adalynn is one of the most beautiful people I know, inside and out; her and Presley both.

She brushes me off with a wave of her hand. "Beauty is in the eye of the beholder. You don't see how beautiful you are, sweets. You ready to do this? The walk down the stairs is the best part. It makes you feel like a princess for a mere moment in time, giving you a chance to experience being in a fairytale."

That might be true if my prince were standing at the bottom, but my fairytale has already ended. I slide on my open toe heels and dab on some lip gloss as a knock sounds at the door. It opens and Mom peeks her head inside. A huge smile unfolds on her face as she steps in and shuts the door. "The boys are here. You both look stunning." She walks over and lightly tousles the ends of my hair, brushing it over my shoulders. "Promise me you'll try and enjoy yourself for once. You deserve it."

"I'll try my best," I say, because it's the best answer I can give.

We walk toward the door and I pick up my handbag on the way. When I come to the top of the staircase I freeze. At the bottom, the boys are lined up just like they were the night of New Year's Eve. From right to left it's Braxton, then Briar with Londyn standing in front of him, and *Breyson?* I stare and blink repetitively, but nothing changes. He stares back at me, those blue eyes boring deep into my soul. My heart rate picks up and my breathing becomes unsteady.

"Breyson?" They begin looking at him confused, but I see what I see. He doesn't move an inch, just stares at me as if I'm the most beautiful girl in the room. His smile begins to form on his face, and for a moment, I can't breathe.

"Kinzleigh," he says and begins walking in my direction. He starts ascending the steps one at a time.

"Breyson," I whisper again. My eyes are locked on him, scared that at any second he will disappear.

He reaches the top of the stairs and stops before me. "Kinzleigh, it's Simon. I'm not Breyson. Are you okay?"

The exact moment he says his name his image morphs before me. It is Simon standing in front of me. My mind has deceived me. My eyes fill with tears as I realize my mistake, and I throw my hand over my mouth. "I'm so sorry."

I take a step back, but he grabs my wrist and pulls me toward him. Wrapping me in his arms, he whispers in my ear for only me to hear. "Don't sweat it. I promise it's fine, Kinzleigh. Do you hear me? It's okay."

I just publicly humiliated myself and I'm mortified. Why can't I just be normal for one damn second of the day? Is this some sick joke? Haven't I been through enough? I see him in my dreams, he consumes my thoughts every second of every day, and now I'm visualizing other people as him. When can I move on and start to pick up the pieces? "Let's go. The limo is waiting," he says, and takes my hand in his.

I need to get this night over with, so I can come back home. Suddenly, I have a bad feeling about tonight. I don't think things are going to go as smoothly as I originally thought. When things start off bad, they usually go downhill from there. We shall see just how far it descends.

TWENTY-THREE

Preston

My plans are going just as I had originally planned. Everything is falling into place nicely. I finished out my senior year at the end of December and I've been under Dad's wing since then learning the company. My grandfather is announcing his retirement and my dad's promotion, as well as welcoming me as CFO next month at the charity event he is hosting. I'm expected to attend, as well as bring a date, which brings me to my next series of events: Kinzleigh.

I told her I wouldn't come back until her graduation in two weeks, but I can't stand it anymore. I want her to come back with me the second her graduation ends, and I want her to have time to prepare. There is one minor bump in my plan that was unexpected—her pregnancy. I'm about to be a wealthy man and I've wanted her since I was a kid. That's one thing that hasn't changed. I'm willing to go to any means to get her.

It's a few months shy of being a year since I've had a girl in my bed, and it wasn't easy. I am a guy. I've kept my word since that day on our family yacht and focused on finishing school, but holding out is getting harder. I keep reminding myself that the wait for her is worth it.

My hand isn't doing the job anymore. I want to be inside her—only her. I want to experience those muscular legs wrapped around me while I slide inside that channel of warm, wet goodness. My cock gets hard just thinking about it.

I want her just as much today as I did the day I decided that one day she would be mine. I've put in the time to make it happen. I've spent years learning her desires, her likes and dislikes, and what makes her tick. All my hard work is hopefully about to pay off.

I lay here on a Saturday morning as I wait for my alarm clock to sound. I don't know why I have it. My body always awakens before 6AM—gym time. I sit up, rubbing my fingers through my short hair.

What to do? What to do?

A large sum of money is being deposited into my account today as my position acceptance bonus for following in my father's footsteps. There weren't many options for me growing up in a family empire that has been building for several generations. I guess it's a good thing I have strong business skills, because this path was expected of me, whether I wanted it or not.

I look around my room in my parents' house. This isn't good enough. It's time to grow up and be a man. I can't bring her here without a place to live.

I pick up my cell phone from the nightstand and check my messages: girls, girls, and more girls. They are always the same. Ready for a good time. They used to satisfy my needs, but my dick only wants one specific pussy. Until I get her, I'll never be satisfied. It's pointless to even waste my time.

Scrolling through my contacts, I touch the one I'm looking for. The phone rings twice before she picks up. "Preston? It's been a while. What's up? You want to meet up?" she says, her voice already changing.

Caroline is a girl I met at UC Berkeley. The last girl I fucked, actually. She was in school for real estate while I was getting my business degree. She's hot, and was a good lay for a while, but the only thing I noticed was a pretty face and blonde hair. I imagine someone else when I get off anyway, which is why I always turn girls around when I'm about to come. It makes it easier when I can't see their faces.

Standing, I walk toward my closet in search of clothes. "Nah, not for that anyway. I'm looking to buy a house and figured you could use the commission. You want the job?"

Shuffling sounds in the background. She must be changing locations. I hold the phone to my ear with my shoulder as I pull a pair of jeans off a hanger and pull them on, then take a bright-colored, pressed polo from another one. As I button my jeans, I slide my feet into a pair of brown, leather loafers. "Of course. What did you have in mind?"

Caroline came from a poor family. She was in school on a scholarship. I'm not a horrible guy. I don't just fuck and run. I'm friends with most of the girls I've hooked up with. When together I try and make friendly conversation, even if we're no longer in that hook-up phase.

Guys that use girls or give them false assumptions are douche bags. Why make a girl feel like a slut or used by leading her on and lying to her over and over again when you can come to an arrangement that benefits you both by being honest? I admire a girl that likes uncomplicated sex. It's the only type of sex I ever got involved with.

I was raised in a wealthy family, but my mother is all for helping the less fortunate. I'm giving her a chance instead of calling up my father's personal real estate agent that's in it for the lump piece of commission and nothing more.

I guess you could say I take after my mother in ways. If she satisfies me, I'll make her a well-known real estate agent in no time. "I need something a woman would like. I want you to think of your dream house and find me the top three. Set up a viewing for all three between midday and two o'clock. Call me in an hour with the details. Got it?"

"Sure, Preston. I have my laptop. I'm on my way now." I walk into my bathroom that me and Presley have always shared, about to hang up the phone, when I catch her voice. "Hey, Preston?"

"Yeah."

"Thanks for this," she says. I don't have time right now to get sentimental. I've made my decision. I'm going to talk to Kinzleigh tonight. It's unfortunate what happened to that Breyson guy, and this isn't how I wanted to make her mine, but I'm here to take care of her.

Kinzleigh needs me now more than ever, and maybe that's what will convince her to come, to give us a chance. I know she will love me in time. I've just never had the chance to make her fall. She needs a push to get there.

If I've learned anything about Kinzleigh Baker, it's that she's stubborn. Make her think she's in control and she'll do anything you want her to. It's not a bad thing, it's just how she operates. I always have and always will do anything for her.

"No problem. Talk to you soon," I say in response, and then disconnect the call. I have a lot to do today and that includes booking a flight to Mississippi.

TWENTY-FOUR

Kinzleigh

The limo pulls up at a large, beautiful building in the middle of the city—the venue the juniors chose for this year's prom. I've been silent since we left my house. I'm no longer in any kind of partying mood. I stay exhausted from the never-ending maze my mind keeps me in. It never stops reeling, not even for a second.

The limo comes to a halt and the blue neon shines through the tinted window. I stare at it, trying to get excited about being out with friends.

Who am I kidding? I can't do this . . .

"Are you okay?" I turn to look at Simon and I almost feel bad for him. This can't possibly be how he imagined spending his senior prom. I thought I could see all of these people, and blend into the crowd, but the truth is, I don't think I can.

As if he can sense the war within me, he continues. "It's just pictures, and then we will leave if you don't want to stay. We don't have to come back after we eat if you don't want to."

It's not like I can really back out unless I call someone to come get me. We all shared a limo. That would be awful for me to leave him hanging at his senior prom. I need to put on my big girl panties and deal with it. Maybe I'll be surprised once I get inside and actually have a decent time.

I take a deep breath as I see couples walking inside from all directions, the parking lot full of boys in tuxes and girls in dresses of all colors, cuts, and designs. As long as my mind doesn't take me back to the way *he* looked in one, I'll be okay. "I'm fine," I tell him. "We'll see how it goes."

We step out of the limo and walk toward the building.

Here goes . . .

Walking inside the entryway, we are led to the correct room reserved for our school's prom. As we enter, I'm consumed with something I never would have expected. As if things couldn't have already been bad enough by calling Simon by Breyson's name, now they are worse. The room has been transformed into a tropical oasis. Since I've been absent from school, I never thought to ask what the prom theme was this year. The lettering on the wall reads—*A Caribbean Affair*.

Fate hates me.

I try to keep breathing as I take everything in. The main lights are dimmed at the door and the rest are off, as if to represent the night. White lights are strung around the room to represent stars, and the walls are draped with black linens, assuming to be the dark horizon.

In one corner there is a virgin tiki bar. Tables fill the room covered with aqua-blue table linens. The centerpieces are vases filled with layers of sand, shells, and set in the middle are tea-light candles.

The place settings are white plates set on top of straw place mats, the rolled silverware on top varying in color by setting, each one of many different bright color options.

The chaperones are wearing white collared polos and khaki pants like the staff might wear at a tropical island resort.

Opposite from the tiki bar there is a photo backdrop for pictures with a photographer in place. It consists of a large section of contained sand with a thatch roof attached to the wall. The backdrop is a night view of the ocean, as if you're standing in front of the shoreline underneath a covering. Twinkling lights hang from the thatch roof, giving it a romantic feel.

One at a time, couples stand beneath it to have their pictures taken to capture the night forever. They each look happy. You can't tell the difference between the real couples and the ones just attending together.

I feel lightheaded and my skin flushed. I need to sit down. It reminds me too much of my first week with Breyson and the dream I've had set on a private island—not once, but twice.

I find the closest table and sit in an attempt to calm my nerves. It feels like I've been thrown into a real version of my dream, but the most important part is missing: Breyson.

Breathe. Just breathe. You can do this . . .

The song changes to a slower melody than it was before. All of the music I've heard since I've been here is some type of island music, like reggae. I know I heard Bob Marley at one point. The lyrics pull me in, commanding me to listen as if wanting to tell me a story. Each word feels like it was written for the week I met . . . *him.*

"You were California beautiful.
I was playin' everything but cool.
I can still hear that sound
Of every wave crashin' down"

The lyrics flow through my ears, pinning me to my chair. "Kinzleigh, are you okay? You don't look so good," Adalynn says, but I can't move. I can't do anything but listen to the song play as if I might miss something if I do.

"Who sings this?" I ask in a whisper, my lungs completely deprived of oxygen.

"Oh shit," she says. "I'm so sorry, Kinzleigh. It's a new song right now, but I never made the same connection you are until now."

"Who is it?" I choke out, my eyes filling with moisture.

"*19 You + Me* by Dan and Shay." I take back everything I originally thought. Fate doesn't hate me. It's trying to destroy me until there is nothing left.

Things I've been compressing for the past few months come back full force, as if that song was me pulling the trigger to my emotions.

I have an epiphany. I should have known it all along. I'm never going to move on as long as I'm here. There are too many reminders of the amazing life I had with the only person I'll ever be in love with. I'll continue to remember and want back the life that was ripped from me.

I don't know where I'll go, but I have to get out of here. I have to get out of this town. I could be a drifter—continue to go and hope I know where I need to be when I get there.

With nothing but time on my hands since I was ordered to stay home, I've completed all my work for the remainder of the year. There is only so much you can do in bed. I've done everything required for me to graduate.

My trust fund became accessible the day I turned eighteen. It's set with a monthly allowance that I can draw from if I need it. That money should keep me comfortable until I can figure out what I'm going to do. I don't need much anymore.

I could get a bus ticket and leave tonight when everyone goes to sleep. That's exactly what I'll do. I'll disappear and stop being a waste of space. I'm a burden to everyone that loves me.

All I need is a carry-on bag of clothes to get me by for now, until I find a place to start over, but I have to keep this a secret. I can't tell anyone I'm leaving, or they'll think I'm crazy and try to stop me.

It may be an insane idea, but it's the only thing that is going to help me. I know it in my gut. My parents would lock me up if they knew what I was attempting. But I have to start trusting my instincts. It's time to grow up.

This is the last option for Bryce and me. If he's going to have any chance of having a decent mother, I have to start from scratch and build us a new life. Search for happiness. People do it all the time, for many different reasons.

What I know is that I can't be here anymore. Everything in this town signifies my life with Breyson. There are no memories here before him. I have to find my inner strength for Bryce. I'm all he has. He already has to grow up without a father and that kills me more than anything. I don't want that life for any child, especially my own.

"Kinzleigh." I continue to plot my plan in my head, ignoring the voice somewhere, completely zoned out to anything else. "Kinzleigh!"

I come back to the present as the motion of a hand waves in front of my face. I look around, realizing that every one of my friends are staring at me as if I've gone completely nuts—maybe I have.

Simon is bent over in front of me with each hand resting on the cushion of the chair beside each outer thigh. I look at him, and then at each of them. I can see the sadness and pity written all over their faces—Braxton and Briar especially.

My eyes lock with Braxton's. I study his face for the first time since Breyson's accident. He looks the same as the person I long for day in and day out, but different in ways. The two are genetic clones but looking into his eyes feels like looking into the eyes of a stranger. That is the one clue that will always confirm Breyson is gone, even though his face is staring back at me.

Looking into Breyson's eyes was like looking into a window. There was an unspoken connection that we shared. One look and everything he felt for me or I felt for him was revealed to the other's soul. That kind of a connection only comes around once in life if you get the chance to experience it at all.

I may be young, but I'm not stupid. I should be happy he was put in my life for the time I had and make the best of the time I have left on this planet. One day I will see my beautiful, blue-eyed boy again. Until that day comes, I'm stuck.

Braxton's jaw hardens, as if he's unsure of what to say. Usually, I can't look at him at all. Maybe in knowing that tonight is the last night I'll see the replica of Breyson allows me to look at him in a different light. I want to memorize every feature one last time. Breyson will always be a part of my memory, but there is something different about seeing someone through the eyes versus recalling them from memory.

"I need to go," I say aloud, but speaking directly to Braxton, hoping he gets the hint. If anyone would understand it would be him. He has to wake up every day and look at his reflection in the mirror—a constant reminder of the brother he lost. He understands that no one else gets it, because the bond they shared was different than with anyone else. "Please don't follow me. I need time alone."

Simon stands as the last word exits my lips. "At least let me take you home, Kinzleigh."

"Don't worry about me. Enjoy your night and I'll see you guys tomorrow." I stand and walk in the direction of the door, not saying another word.

Deciding to leave gives me a little peace of mind. It feels right. Now, I just have to execute the plan. It's time to put things in motion. I'm ready to pick up the pieces of my shattered life and try to somehow put them back together. This is the only way I know how. This is the glue.

TWENTY-FIVE

Preston

Looking out the window of the first-class seat I'm sitting in, a nervous wave hits me. This is the moment I've been waiting for since the day I kissed Kinzleigh on our families' yacht. Nervousness is an emotion I haven't experienced since I was a kid. She is the one and only person that can bring that feeling out in me. The possibility that she could say no is what has me worried.

Kinzleigh has always been like a gypsy. You never know which direction she will go on something until she's there. It's one of the many things I love about her and the reason I've waited years to go after her, letting her mature. You don't get a girl forever if you get her too early.

I received a call from my banker right before I left, letting me know the house was a done deal. Coming from a wealthy family comes in handy during times like these. I have plenty of money in the bank and there is more where that comes from, but I'm still young and lack a long credit history except what my parents have made for me. I have those parents—the ones that add our names to credit cards to build each of us a line of credit.

Most guys my age aren't looking to settle down. The single ones are still partying and looking for the next girl to wet their dicks. The ones in relationships are trying to figure out a future, but I come from a family with a respectable reputation and I'm expected to carry it forward. I have a list of expectations to meet.

I've always known Kinzleigh would be the one I wanted to marry. We grew up together. It was a plan I made in my head when I was just a kid and that plan has never changed. Not even when she was with that Breyson guy.

I wasn't surprised he came into the picture. The surprise is that it didn't happen earlier with someone else. I've dated girls. I knew there would be guys along the way. It was luck that she wasn't interested in them for so long. But now, there is no one standing in my way. I'm making my move. I have all the means to make her happy. I've been working toward it for years.

That doesn't mean it'll be easy. Kinzleigh is not the type of girl to be swayed by money. She'll never be a trophy wife. She's headstrong, uncontrollable, and frustrating to any man with a swinging dick between his legs, but she's also beautiful, caring, and has a personality I fell in love with at a young age.

She's always going to do what she wants. And that's likely going to be something that involves pom poms. If she wants cheerleading, cheerleading is what she'll get. It's one of the only things I know for sure won't go away. She's been talking about it for too many years. I don't care what the hell she spends her days doing as long as by nightfall she's in my bed.

Everything is in play. Now, I just have to wait it out to see what the result is. Hopefully, by this time tomorrow we will be planning our life in California. If she agrees to this, it's going to take everything in me to come back for two weeks while I wait on her to graduate.

The problem with a break after a decision is that it gives a person time to think, to reason in their head, to change their mind. As soon as the offer on the house was accepted, I contacted an interior designer for a meeting. I want Kinzleigh with me during it.

I look at my watch. We should be landing in the next thirty minutes. I need to get off this plane. I'm getting anxious. I don't like the unknown. My life has been planned out since I was born. It's something I'm used to and has become something I need. I hate being taken by surprise. I've never been a spontaneous person. I could live by a schedule and be perfectly happy.

Locking my hands on the back of my head, I rest against the back of the seat and close my eyes to steady my breathing. *Get a fucking grip. Don't be a pussy. It's just Kinzleigh.*

That exact thought is why I feel this way. She holds the fucking key to my future, and I don't like losing that kind of control. I've always been in control of my own life and how I want to live. If she doesn't come back with me, I'll lose my fucking mind. All of my previous plans will have failed.

If I can't have her, I don't want anyone. No other girl will compare. They never do. Not a single girl to date has swayed my attention off her. I'll remain a bachelor and fuck my way through my spare time. She's the only girl I'll bring home and settle down with. It's her or no one.

The flight attendant comes over the speaker and announces that we're about to land. In less than two hours I'll know which direction I'll be heading.

Reaching in the pocket of my jeans, I pull out a stick of gum. I pop it in my mouth as we start to descend. After touching down a few times the plane rolls down the runway, before finally coming to a stop.

Next stop is the car rental and then I'll be on my way to Kinzleigh's house. I've prepared and memorized a speech. I have one shot at this. I highly doubt her parents will give me any problems if it's something she wants. Our parents have been unknowingly pushing us together for years. Her parents are actually the easy part.

Time steadily passing, I sign the necessary paperwork for the rental car and collect the keys. The sooner I get to that car the sooner I can be on my way to getting this over with. I glance at my watch for about the hundredth time while I wait on him to hand me back my credit card. "Thank you, Mr. Dunagin. Is there anything else I can help you with?"

"That'll be all. Thanks," I say, and turn from the middle-aged man standing on the other side of the counter. I walk at a quick pace until I get to the car assigned to me.

Holding down the button on the keyless remote, the alarm sounds, unlocking the car before me. She has one fine body. I run my fingertips along the black metal from back to front, until I reach the driver's side door of the black *Porsche 911*. She's sleek and built for speed. Under normal circumstances I'd enjoy her more, but for now I'm just going to have to see what she can do against the pavement. I have somewhere to be and the quicker I get there the better.

Halfway between the airport and Kinzleigh's house I booked the closest hotel. I could stay at her parents' house, but I want a place that we can talk alone. I'm prepared to do the manliest form of groveling if necessary. I won't be a pussy, because no woman wants a pussy of a man, but I will tell her how I feel. Anything she wants is hers. I'm a reasonable guy, and willing to bargain for what I want.

It's now dark out. I slow my speed on the highway as I read the various road signs to ensure I don't pass up the road they live on. It's a large subdivision and I've only been here once: Christmas. As I come up to the entrance, I veer off to the right and make my way in the direction of her house.

Once I reach her driveway, I make a right turn. A limo is sitting in the drive with the brake lights on. I wonder what it's doing here.

I ease up behind the garage and kill the engine of the car. I look out the window as the driver steps out and makes his way to the back, and then opens the door. He reaches his hand inside, grasping ahold of another—a smaller one.

A heel-covered foot exits, followed by a heap of purple fabric and the most beautiful girl I've ever seen. My heart begins to race when she looks at the car with a confused look on her face. The windows are tinted, disguising me.

Damn.

I've been away from her for four months and she still takes my breath away. That's something that has never changed. I've always had to take a second to gather myself before being around her, she just never knew it. To her we were just friends, but little did she know, she affected me in ways friends don't.

It's time to do this . . .

Opening the door, I step outside the footing and pull myself out. I step toward her and shut the door behind me. Her lips part slightly when she looks at me. I know that look well. She's surprised, but instead of the usual fire in her eyes she almost looks . . . relieved? My heart beats off rhythm at the thought that maybe she was hoping I'd come.

I make my way toward her at a steady pace. When I reach her, I stop. "Preston?"

Her voice gives her away. She is relieved, and more than that, she's upset. I hate seeing her upset. I would give an organ just to see her smile. "Yeah, Kinz. It's me. How have you been?"

I sound like a complete ass, but I'm not sure what else to say. I haven't talked to her since Christmas. It isn't because I didn't want to, but because I was trying to give her the space I promised, and then the whole accident happened with Breyson.

"What are you doing here? You aren't supposed to be here for another two weeks, right?" She's hurting, dammit. I hate seeing her in pain. She's worse than I thought she was going to be. I haven't seen her like this since Grams died—her grandmother.

Kinzleigh is normally a soft-spoken, free-spirited person, full of life and laughter. Sure, she's always been a little shy natured, and definitely weird around guys, but who was I to complain? That just meant it was better for me—no competition.

I didn't expect her to actually fall for that guy. I thought she was just finally experiencing life; things normal high school kids do. "I came to see you. Will you come talk to me for a while?"

Those green eyes that are normally the color of clover have faded to jade. She needs to get out of here, to have someone to worry about her for a change. Being here is killing her spirit. This place is destroying her.

She looks back and forth between her house and me as if she's trying to decide. "Okay. My parents weren't expecting me for a few hours anyway. Where do you want to go?"

"Wherever you want. I booked a hotel. It's quiet if you want to go there, or we could stay here and go out back to the pool. It's your choice. I just need to say what I came here to say."

She studies me in a way she's never studied me before. Our eyes remain locked, but she gives nothing away. She takes a deep breath. "Your hotel is fine. I don't really want to be here right now."

My heart stammers in my chest and I have to refrain from raising my hand over it. I hope to God I'm done running around with women. The one standing in front of me is the one I want.

We would be perfect for each other. She may not see it now, but she will in time. I'm a patient man when it comes to Kinzleigh Baker. Nothing or no one will stop me from getting her. She's the only one that can end my chase for her.

I close in and wrap my arms around her tiny frame. She encloses hers around my waist, resting her head against my chest. Inhaling, she releases a low sigh of contentment. Her belly brushes against mine and I tense for a moment. I would rather it be my child she's carrying, but it's something I have to accept if I want her. When you want someone, you can't pick and choose what you want of her. It's a package deal. It's all or nothing.

"Come on. Let's go." I turn and hold her in my arm next to my side, so I can guide her to the car. When we reach the passenger side door, I open it and help her in. I wait as she pulls the bottom of her dress in, making sure it doesn't get caught.

Closing the door, I rush to round the car to get in. This is my chance—my one and only. If I blow it, there won't be another. The pressure increases rapidly. I won't live with that option.

Don't fuck this up.

TWENTY-SIX

Preston

We reach the hotel and I pull up at valet—the only in the area with that service. Everything else is self-park. The doorman opens the door on Kinzleigh's side, helping her out.

I open the trunk of the car and grab my duffle bag, before meeting her in front of the hotel door. She begins fidgeting with her dress. I can tell she's uncomfortable. "You need something to wear?" I ask as I take her hand.

I halfway expect her to pull out of my grasp, but she doesn't. This gives me a little bit of hope for what is to come. Kinzleigh is usually straight forward, so this speaks volume. "I didn't bring anything. I can make do with what I'm wearing."

"You can wear something of mine. I have plenty. Okay?" I remember how good she looked that night in mine and Presley's bathroom in a tee shirt and boxers and the thought of it being mine sends a surge of excitement through me.

She looks at me as I open the door to the hotel, letting her enter first. "Are you sure? I'm not very comfortable, but I can deal with it until I get home."

I can't even believe she has to ask that. We've known each other forever. "Absolutely. What's mine is yours, Kinzleigh. Kind of always has been."

She blushes, her cheeks pink, and looks a little uncomfortable by my statement, but I want her to know. I want to be open. I meant it with every fiber of my being. I've waited a long time to be able to say how I feel to her. "Why don't you go sit down over there while I check in? Get off your feet. I know you're probably getting tired of standing in those shoes."

She nods and walks off in the direction of the seating area, located close to the registration desk. I watch her as she saunters forward, trying not to fall in the heels. She has me in a daze and she hasn't even done anything yet.

No girl has ever had my attention like Kinzleigh does. What's more is she never even noticed until I said something. That only makes me want her more. Most girls see money in conjunction with good looks, but not her. "Can I help you, Sir?"

I turn in the direction of the voice and realize I've stopped at the registration desk. My attention was elsewhere. It always is around her. When she walks in she claims the room. Some girls have that ability, and she's one of them. I've watched guys I know stumble and fall all over her since we all hit puberty.

"Checking in. I had a reservation under Preston Dunagin." She begins typing at her computer as I pull my wallet from the back pocket of my jeans. I open it and remove my credit card from the slot, waiting on her to finish.

"I see you have a one-night reservation for the presidential suit. Is that correct?"

I nod and hand her the credit card, then look back at Kinzleigh sitting in the chair. "You're all checked in. If you'll sign here, you can be on your way. Checkout is at eleven and here is your key card for the elevator and room. Your room will be the top floor and only accessible by the key swipe. Will there be anything else I can do for you tonight, Mr. Dunagin?"

I look back at the brunette behind the counter and shake my head. Signing the sheet of paper before me, I place my card back in my wallet and take the room key. "That'll be all. Thank you."

"Enjoy your stay," she says, and I head over to get Kinzleigh with my bag in hand.

I bend over the chair next to her ear and whisper. "Are you ready?" She jumps slightly and turns her head. Her lips are so close to mine I can feel her breath.

What I wouldn't give to kiss you right now . . .

She doesn't attempt to move away. Her eyes study mine as if she is lost in a thought. "Yes, I'm ready."

She goes to stand. On reflex I grab her arm in an attempt to help her. "Thanks," she says, and seems a little taken aback. It's hard to remember that Kinzleigh is so independent she doesn't like for people to help her do anything. Especially when I've always wanted to help her do everything.

We walk side by side until we reach the elevator. Once inside, I slide the key into the slot and we begin to ascend, the digital number rising with every passed floor. "What are you doing here?" she blurts out, catching me off guard.

When I look at her, she bites her lip. "It's just that I had kind of forgotten about that conversation we had with everything that's happened, and when I saw you it all came back to me, but I wasn't expecting you until graduation. Is everything okay with Presley?"

The elevator comes to a halt and the doors open. Placing my hand on the small of her back, I guide her out of the elevator into the massive open room. "I will tell you everything. Right now, I just want you to get comfortable. Are you hungry?"

She looks around as we both take in the large room. There is a bar and small kitchenette in the right corner of the room. A couch and television sits on the left-hand side of the room in a sitting area. A built-in desk and dining table complete the setup in another corner on the left. The colors are brown and gold—masculine, but classy.

As we walk through the short foyer into the openness of the room, I look around for the bedroom. "Yes. I haven't eaten dinner. Food would be good."

I spot a door beside the bar and open it. *There it is.* I turn and nod for her to follow me. We both walk inside, and I set the duffle bag on the bed. "Change into anything I brought, and I'll call for room service, okay? You need to eat, Kinzleigh. There are several tee shirts and a few pair of boxers in here. I'll leave you alone. Come out when you get ready."

A wave of her perfume filters through my nose as I inhale. She is rubbing the material of her dress between her thumb and index finger. I can't help myself. I want to touch her, to hold her, so I do something I know won't send her in a running panic.

Placing my palm cupped over her cheek, I kiss the other side. I can feel the warmth against my lips as the heat radiates from her skin. "I'll be waiting," I say next to her ear.

I'm about to pull away when she wraps her arms around me like she did back at her house, only this time tighter. I wrap my arms around her, enjoying the close contact.

She sniffles, as if she's crying but trying to hide it. I try to pull away to make sure she's okay, but she squeezes harder. The side of her face is buried in my shirt. "I've missed you, Preston. You're the closest thing I have to normalcy. Will you stay?"

My heart skips a beat hearing her say those words. I want to comfort her and take care of her. She may not love me the way I love her right now, but instant love with someone isn't always the case. With some couples, love grows. It sometimes starts as a friendship and transforms into something else. Other times, two people may not like each other at all in the beginning.

I don't believe in soul mates. I believe that love is a choice, and a gradual thing. I chose to love Kinzleigh Baker when I was young and have allowed that love to grow over the years.

I find it hard to believe each person has one other person in the world meant for them over an entire life span with all the bad things that happen. If it were true, there would be no way to move on for someone after the loss of a mate, because you would forever be broken. A heart may be breakable, but it can also mend itself over time.

"Of course, I'll stay. All you had to do was ask." I find the zipper to her dress and lower it, slowly, until it reaches the bottom. My heart pounds harder with every inch of skin revealed. If only I was behind her and not in front of her.

She's shaking underneath my touch as I peel the strap down her arm, letting the fabric fall to the floor between us. "I'm going to get you a shirt, okay?"

She nods and releases me. Stepping back, I take in her body. What guy would be able to resist? She's beautiful. Her cleavage forms mounds peeking out of the top of her strapless, black bra.

My eyes linger on her chest longer than I intended. They look bigger than I remember from seeing her in a swimsuit, but I also always saw them this way before she was pregnant.

My eyes scan down her body. Her belly is round and protruding from her hips, but not big. She still looks fit and toned aside from her firm bump of a belly. I pause on it, and she instantly crosses her arms over her stomach like she's trying to hide it. "You don't have to hide from me, Kinzleigh. I still think you're beautiful, even with that."

I unzip my duffle bag and remove a tee shirt, along with a pair of my boxers. I unfold the perfectly creased shirt and pull it over her head once

I get it past the pageant hair standing in the way. She puts her arms in the holes and it falls to her thighs. "I love you, Kinzleigh. I came back to tell you that I want you with me. Do you remember what I told you last summer?"

She bites the edge of her lip and nods. "I meant it. I know things are different now, but I still feel the same about you. I can help you if you'll let me. None of your original plans have to change. If cheerleading is what you want, then that's what you'll get. Or you can stay home when it's born. I'll help you raise the baby just like it's mine."

She's staring at me. Her eyes have always been one of her best features. When they're locked on yours it's hard to look away. "I know you don't love me like I love you, but give us a chance. One day, you may. Tonight, I'm just asking for right now."

I place my hand on her hip. "I can support you and the baby, put you through school, and give you a life you deserve. California is where your heart is. We can build a life together there. No one has to know the baby isn't mine if that's what you want to avoid questions. We've known each other our entire lives. Been friends the whole time. I'm done with college and starting my career. I bought a house. Come back to California. Just us. Move in with me."

I wait for a response. She stares at me, in thought, and the silence is deafening. The longer we stare at each other the more nervous I become.

She finally releases a breath and takes a seat on the edge of the bed, tears falling from her eyes. I'm not sure if those are good tears or bad. My stomach knots up. Upsetting her is the last thing I want to do.

Taking a seat beside her, I grab her hand in mine. I remain quiet, allowing her to process everything. I hate to see her cry. I die a little inside when she does.

I'm starting to think I made the wrong decision by coming here. Maybe she's just not ready, or over him enough to even try. She turns toward me, pulling her leg up on the bed. The movement causes me to look in her direction.

Don't look between her legs. Don't look between her legs.

We should have put my boxers on her first, because my dick is getting hard and now is neither the time nor the place. Never in a million years would I have thought I could be turned on by someone pregnant with another man's baby. "You know I do love you, right?"

I don't think I heard her correctly. "Well, no, Kinzleigh, I didn't know that."

She swipes her cheek. "Preston, you're one of my oldest friends. We grew up together. Experienced different ages together. I will always love you in ways, and I'm even attracted to you, but I can't love you as much as I love Breyson, or even in exactly the same way. I didn't choose to love him like I do. I just do. I didn't pick him to be that one for me either. Feeling that way about you would have been the easier choice. Dynamically, you and I would work better. But he stole my heart when it wasn't even up for grabs. Do you really want to be with someone that can't give you her whole heart?"

She pauses to let me think, to absorb every word, and I do. I think over the fact that I could find a girl who would love me, and only me. Someone that would be happy to give me her heart, with no competition, but I've thought on this since she started dating him and the answer remains the same.

Having some of her is better than none. I believe people can change, and that a person can move on from someone else when it doesn't work out. I have to. She may think she'll never love me that way, but there is always the possibility that she will.

I have to believe in that possibility, because the alternative will never be good enough. If I turn her away over pride, I will always live with the regret of *what if* in my mind. "Yeah. If it's you, Kinzleigh, I do."

"If I were going to be in a relationship with anyone else, I'd want it to be you, but you need to understand going in that I will never *stop* loving him. I can't. I've tried. It makes me more miserable."

She sighs. "The truth is, before you got here, I had already decided to leave. Had you come on time you would have missed me. I can't be surrounded by everything that reminds me of him anymore. If I'm going to have any chance at moving on, I have to get away from here."

She briefly looks down, but then her eyes return to mine. "I'll go with you, and even be in a relationship with you, as long as you can accept that and still want me. I do love you, Preston. I always have, in ways, and I always will. The four of us were pushed together throughout our lives—two boys and two girls, all close in age. I'm not stupid. I know Presley is in love with Konnor. And after what happened at Christmas, maybe he's been in love with her too. Now that I've finally admitted to myself that a person can't live without love, I recognize the feeling when it's there."

My heart beats in a weird rhythm each time she says those three words, regardless of how she means them. Love is love in any context.

I pull her hand toward me, telling her what I want. She stands on her knees on the mattress and closes the distance between us. To avoid her losing her balance, I place my other hand on her hip as she straddles me.

I wrap my hands in her curly, blonde hair, and pull her face to mine so I can look her in the eyes. There is one thing I need her to understand, so that she can at least try to move on. It's the only way we'll have a fair shot.

I press my forehead to hers and whisper an inch from her lips. "I'll never try to replace him, Kinz. It's okay to still love him. I just want you to love me too."

I want to kiss her, and I allow myself to. My lips brush against hers and she doesn't pull away. Instead, she kisses me back, as if she's missed doing this with someone. I slide my tongue through the crevice of her mouth in search of hers. She pushes it forward, and they mingle, tangling with one another in a sensual dance. Her taste is hypnotic and addictive, and unlike anything I've ever had. With each taste, each touch, I find myself wanting more of her.

She grinds against my hardened dick. The rhythm is enough to drive me mad. I've wanted her for so long my cock throbs with each contact from her. It's pressing hard against the denim of my jeans. She picks up the pace in her kiss from slow and steady to hunger and need.

She moans out in frustration. I can tell she needs to get off, but I don't want our first time to be in this damn hotel room like a bunch of high schoolers after prom. It would fit, since obviously, she went to prom, but I need more with her. I didn't come this far for a quick fuck.

I pull away from her and look her in the eyes. "You need to get off, Kinz?" I can tell she's irritated and slightly embarrassed. I like this side of her. I love seeing her turned on.

She nods her head. "It's these freaking hormones." She breathes out in aggravation. "I get turned on with very little effort at all. And I'm . . ." she trails off. I know what she was going to say. "Who would want me this way? It's cruel."

"I do. When I said I would take care of you, Kinzleigh, that meant all of your needs, including these. Tell me what you need from me. I want our first time to be in our own bed, but anything else, I'll do. I just have one question. When will you come back with me?" Her face is flushed, but she stops long enough to ponder the question.

"You're sure this is what you want? No regrets?" She's short of breath, but wraps her hands around my neck, combing her fingers through the bottom of my hairline.

"With all that I am."

"Tonight." The way she says it is so final it catches me off guard. I expected her to say after graduation, or even to give her long enough for her to pack her things and talk to her parents, but this makes me happy.

"What about your parents, and graduation?"

She growls out low. "Can we please discuss this later? I haven't been with anyone else in months and you kissed me. You started it. I can feel it pressed against me. It's torture."

Her straddled on top of me in panties and a tee shirt is my dream come true. I smile and fist her hair in my hand. "Anything you ask of me, consider it done."

Picking her up, I turn and sit her gently at the top of the bed, and then I crawl on. "I've waited years for this."

Resting on my knees between her legs, I grab the hem of her shirt and pull it over her head. I want to see all of her, though. Reaching behind her, I unclasp her bra and toss it beside me on the bed.

Fuck, she's beautiful.

I kiss her greedily, skimming my teeth along her bottom lip. I lay her back on the bed, so that I can have better access to her. Her breasts are full and in need of being sucked—nipples taut from her heightened state.

I cup my hand around her breast and rub the tip of my tongue over her nipple. Her skin is smooth and tastes amazing. Sucking her nipple into my mouth, I release it with a pop. She moans out, telling me she's ready for more, but then she confirms it. "Preston, please. Touch me."

Damn, I love hearing her say my name.

Sitting upright, I hook my index finger under her panties. She gets the hint and lifts off the bed, allowing me to pull them over her ass and slide them down her legs. She extends her legs and points her toes, making it easier for me to remove them. Her face is flushed to a shade of red. I want to know just how turned on she is right now.

I run the tips of my fingers up the inside of her leg until I reach the center. Her legs fall open. I can't take my eyes off her beautiful, pink pussy. It's glistening and wet, visible underneath the dim lights above the bed. I could nut from the sight of it. Instead, I dip my thumb inside, wanting to feel it; so hot and wet. I've never felt anything so amazing in my entire life.

As I pull out, I run the pad of my thumb up her slit and rub it in circles over her clit. I'm so turned on right now I feel like I could burst into flames from the heat coursing through me.

My eyes lock with hers as I continue to stimulate her, pleasure her, leaving my mark on her. "I want to taste you. Let me taste you," I mutter.

"Just don't stop. It feels so good. I need to get off. Please." I want to watch her beautiful face as she comes. I want to taste her cum on my tongue. I dip, spread, and swirl one last time as I lower my mouth to her sweet spot. I use the same rhythm as before, only this time with my tongue instead of thumb.

My senses are on overdrive. Her taste, her smell—it's all better than I imagined. Her pussy is one of those things that you only try once and you're completely hooked. Maybe the difference is that I was in love with her before I touched her this way. I dip my tongue inside her a few times to get another taste. When I run the tip along her folds she screams out. "Please, don't tease me."

It's time to show her what she will get every day if she wants it. There is one thing I know without a shadow of doubt that I'm good at, and that's going down on a girl. I flick the tip of my tongue over her clit in a steady rhythm, increasing the speed as her body tells me where she likes it. She grabs ahold of my hair and pulls. I suck her into my mouth and her legs close around my head. "I'm so close."

I begin flicking my tongue back and forth over her clit again, watching for the signs when she's starting to come. As her pelvis lifts off the mattress and her legs draw in, I exchange my tongue for my thumb and push my tongue inside her pussy.

She's coming.

I can feel the creamy warmth envelop my tongue as she tightens her muscles around it. Whispers of words slip from her lips. When her body lowers to the bed and her muscles relax, I pull out and swallow.

I know I will never tire of the way she tastes. I already want more. I've tried to imagine it for years, but nothing I ever imagined compared to the real thing.

Trailing kisses along her thigh and over her pelvis, she releases her hold on my hair and I sit up. Her face is red and damp from sweat. Her eyes are heavy. I love seeing her this way. I could spend the rest of my life just like this and be the happiest man alive. After tasting her like this, I'll do whatever it takes to keep her. "So, tonight, huh?"

She bites her bottom lip in her post-orgasmic state and points at my crotch. "Yeah, but don't you want me to take care of that first?" I look down and realize just how hard my dick is. It's throbbing for release, but I want her to know this is more than that for me.

"We have plenty of time," I say, and adjust my erection by pushing it down. I'm going to have blue balls from Hell, but she's worth it. "I have a house to show you. Don't we need to stop by your house and get a bag, so you can tell your parents?"

Within a second, she is shaking her head. "I'll call them from California. I don't want anything stopping me. I know what I want. Can we leave now?"

I have to admit, I don't like the idea of bailing on her parents, because they are like my own parents. I've known them since I was old enough to remember, and it feels wrong, but she's my priority now. If I have to call them tonight when she goes to sleep I will. "Okay. Go get cleaned up and I'll book the flight. I'll have you some clothes sent up from the gift shop downstairs and we'll order room service before we check out."

I bend down to kiss her. There is something erotic about her tasting her cum on my lips. I cup the back of her neck and enjoy the taste of her for a moment longer. She's all I care about now.

I'll forever be grateful that I decided to come earlier than I originally planned. I don't know what made her accept so easily this time, but I'll take it. I can't wait to start our lives together.

I release her lips. They are red and swollen from the heat of our kiss. It looks good on her. "Okay," she whispers.

"Take your time." I back up toward the bedroom door, taking her beautiful body in one last time, before I exit the room.

There are so many things to do and preparations to make. I smile for the first time after hooking up with a girl. Flirting is never needed once the deed is done. But she's not a girl I went after because the physical features were similar to another. She's *the girl*. And after all this time, she's going to be mine. For once, I'm actually looking forward to where my life is going.

TWENTY-SEVEN

Kinzleigh

Standing in the shower, I think back on the recent events. The hot water rains down over my sensitized skin. I can't believe I just hooked up with Preston. What the hell was I thinking? I was so upset I just wanted a distraction from my thoughts and these stupid pregnancy hormones are going to be the death of me. The combination is clearly a dangerous mix.

I have to admit, it was hot, and felt good, but right now I feel like I cheated on Breyson. He's the only man I've ever been with in that way until . . . *now.*

Oh, God. What have I done?

The guilt takes over my mind, body, and soul. What I thought might make me feel better does but doesn't. In a sense, I feel like I'm finally heading in the right direction of moving on, but at the same time, I feel guilty for even thinking that. Maybe I just need to let myself cry over him one last time.

The water is as hot as I can stand it, filling the room with steam. I feel so dirty, because I liked what he did to me. I never thought another man would touch me there. I don't know what to do with all of these emotions running through me. How am I supposed to feel? What's okay to feel? I'm so confused.

Pressing my back against the shower wall, I slide down into a squatting position. Tears build in my eyes and begin spilling over. Is it such a bad thing to want to be happy? I'm so sick of all this sadness. I want Breyson back, but there is nothing I can do to get him back. We don't always get what we want in life. I get that now.

I know I'm selfish in ways, but I want to try and build a new life for Bryce and me. He needs a normal, loving family, and not a single mother that can't give him the love he deserves because she's struggling to make ends meet.

I know Preston loves me and will take care of us. There isn't a doubt in my mind that he would make me happy, even if that happiness isn't equal to what I would have with Breyson. Our families are as close as any family could ever be. Preston and I date back to childhood, which means he's important to me. Breyson will always have my heart and my soul, but it's time to allow myself the chance to be happy again.

I can't be tormented and miserable for the rest of my life. I'll have to deal with the pain of losing the most important person I've ever met, but it's not about me anymore. It's about Bryce and what's good for him.

I am sure of one thing: I'm cursed. Every person I love whole-heartedly gets hurt, but that's another reason for me to take this opportunity. I couldn't control how I felt with Breyson, but I can with Preston. Sure, I meant it when I said I loved him, but he doesn't make my heart race or give me butterflies, nor does he have my emotions running wild at the sight of him.

Preston has been one of my best friends since I was a child. All four of us have been. It wasn't just Presley and me or Preston and Konnor. We were all friends. I may never love him like I loved Breyson, but I can control my outcome with him. As long as I continue to have control of my own emotions around Preston, which I do, there is no way he could end up hurt.

A well-known saying is that time heals all wounds. I would have never believed it before this day, because it hurts so bad to live without Breyson, but it being known by many has to count for something.

Maybe that's the point—the pain will never cease, only dull. It's possible I was expecting it to magically disappear, and that's an unrealistic expectation. Magic isn't real.

Something Preston said puts everything in perspective for me. *I don't want to replace him. I just want you to love me too.* Is that the secret to healing a broken heart? To be able to open your heart up to love at a greater multitude than one person?

I allow myself to ponder that thought. By knowing I love Preston too, I understand that you can love two people in different magnitudes, and in different ways. I suppose that we can make room for more than one person in our hearts. I will never love anyone with the magnitude that I loved Breyson, but I can try to heal from the loss him by allowing my heart to love another.

Like Preston said, just because someone is no longer in the picture, doesn't mean you have to replace them. Was I so scared of replacing Breyson that I built up anger and hatred toward everyone else? I suddenly feel as if a weight has been lifted from my shoulders. I'm growing as a person.

I think it's okay to forever hold onto the love and memory of someone you lost, as long as you don't let it consume you from living a normal life. People are going to come and go, and in times of despair we are going to fall.

Tonight, I'm allowing myself to fall, to cry, and to lay on the floor of the black pit I'm in. When I'm done, I'll get back up, brush myself off, and start living. I'm going to be strong and increase my pain tolerance. I can learn to live with the painful scar on my heart from where I fell for an amazing man—an irreplaceable one.

Bryce needs me, and even if I don't know why, there is a reason he was conceived. Every child is created by something higher than us. We have no control over the direction our lives will turn. I learned that the hard way. I thought I could draw out my own path and I was wrong. My fate is preplanned and the more I try to fight it the more it's going to destroy me. I feel like a puppet dangling from strings.

Placing my left hand over the tattoo that resides on my ribcage underneath my heart, I close my eyes and let the tears flow. I let myself miss him for another moment. "I love you, Breyson. I always will. I will miss you every day for the rest of my life," I whisper, as the water trickles down my face.

I cry for me, for Breyson, and for Bryce. We could've had a beautiful life together. We would have made an amazing family. I'm making myself a promise that I will try to be happy from this night forward. Breyson would want me to be happy.

I feel a flutter in my abdomen—my baby assuring me he's there. It's time to stop feeling sorry for myself over what I don't have and be thankful for the blessings that I do. It isn't my place to question the things I can't control, but to trust that no matter how much it hurts, there is a reason that it's supposed to be this way.

Until this point my thoughts have been repetitive, constantly cycling out to the point that I'm tired of them. I want to stop saying I'm going to do something and actually do it. I want a new series of thoughts. Out of sight out of mind, right? California could change everything around for me.

Standing, I finish my shower in a state of peace that I haven't had in a long time. Tomorrow will be a brighter day, a day for second chances.

TWENTY-EIGHT

Kinzleigh

The airport is lit up in lights. It's getting late and I'm tired, but I texted Mom letting her know I wouldn't be home tonight. I'll explain everything tomorrow. Right now, I just want to get away from here.

Preston brings the car to a halt and shuts off the engine. He looks over at me and takes my hand in his. It feels nice to be touched this way again. "Are you comfortable in that dress? We will go tomorrow and get you some clothes and things you need until I can add you to my account. I promise we'll get everything you need for the baby before it gets here. Okay?"

After I pulled myself together in the shower, Preston had room service waiting and a pink, cotton, maxi dress, along with some clean panties and a pair of flip flops. I'm just thankful it was a big enough hotel that they had a gift shop with adequate clothing. It fits perfectly and beats wearing that prom dress and heels.

By the time I got dressed I was starving. He ordered my favorite—a Philly steak and cheese po-boy with fries. I can't believe he's remembered all these years. I wonder how long he's truly felt this way about me. You have to make an effort to learn and remember all of someone's likes and dislikes, and that is something that goes beyond friendship.

I take a deep breath as we sit here in the parking lot of the airport. My parents are going to be heartbroken, but one day I hope they understand.

It makes me a little sad that I won't wake up in the same house with my parents anymore.

I look at Preston. He's wearing a look I've never noticed before. Maybe contentment, love, or happiness, or maybe all of the above. Before, arrogance and cockiness were a given where Preston was concerned. The change looks good on him. It makes him more attractive.

I like seeing him happy. In return, it makes me happy, and it's nice. It makes this decision easier. "Okay, Preston. The clothes are great. Thank you. You don't have to feel obligated to buy everything. That's not why I agreed to this. I have savings. At least I brought my purse."

He wraps his hand behind my neck and pulls me forward. His narrow lips lock with mine. I expect for him to deepen the kiss, but he breaks free. For whatever reason, he suddenly seems a little angry. "I said I wanted to take care of you, Kinzleigh—both of you. I meant it. I have the means to do so. This is what I want. Save your damn money for the baby a trust fund or whatever the hell you want to do with it, but you won't use it for necessities or wants as long as you're with me, and I hope that's a really long time."

Well, that stubborn Preston I've always known is still in there somewhere. I was starting to wonder with all that caring, selfless, sweet stuff he had going on. Preston has always had that dominant, controlling, alpha-male thing going on. He used to try to boss Presley and me around when we were kids. His dad is very similar.

"Fine, Preston . . . for now, but don't think we won't re-evaluate this conversation later. You know how I feel about that sort of thing. I want to pull my own weight." As if my words were a Christmas present, he smiles.

He leans in toward me, closing the distance between us, and stops next to my ear at the same time he laces his fingers on the backside of mine. "You can repay me in other ways, Kinzleigh. I've waited for this moment for a really long time; to call you mine."

He places the palm of my hand over the bulge at his crotch, his dick straining against his jeans. "Being inside of you by day's end for the rest of my life is the only payment I'll ever need. Think on that for a while. Now, let's go. We have a house to move into."

A surge of wetness soaks into my panties as he steps out of the car. I bang my head against the headrest. I could kill my treacherous body for being turned on. I never wanted sex before Breyson and my heart says I don't *want* it with anyone else, but my body and mind are deceiving me. How can my heart compete with my mind? The mind controls every organ, but the heart is a warrior, always fighting for what it wants regardless.

I need to figure out a way to deal with all the fighting going on inside me. I want sex. I like it. My mind says I want it and my body keeps hinting that I need it, but my heart makes me feel guilty for wanting it.

Sex is a natural, human need, right? I learned to like it being with Breyson, but having sex with another man while carrying Breyson's child feels wrong.

My door opens, and I realize I'm still sitting here lost in my own thoughts. Why should I be surprised? This is my life now. Mental conversations have become my normal. "You coming, Kinz?"

I grab my purse and rest one foot on the ground outside of the car. He holds out his hand and I take it, allowing him to pull me to a stand. "Yeah. I'm coming. I was just thinking, that's all."

He places his hands on each side of my face as I stand fully upright. "I promise I'll be good to you, Kinzleigh. I'll never step out on you. I know you still love him, but in time you'll see that we're right for each other. It's okay to let yourself love someone again. It doesn't make you a bad person. I know it'll take time. I'll help you through the bad days. I'll always be here for you, Kinzleigh, just like I always have been. No regrets?"

A small tear trickles down my cheek and he brushes it away with his thumb. I never really took the time to see it before, but he's a good person, and genuine. He's always taken care of me. I was blind to it before, but now, looking back on it, I see it.

I'm not sure why bad things have happened to me, but I can't help but to still be grateful for the things I've been given. I will miss Breyson terribly, but the fact that I still have a guy like Preston after me amazes me. There are so many girls out there that would give anything for a relationship with a guy like this and I've been granted it not once, but twice.

"No regrets," I whisper, and close my eyes as another tear exits my eye. "I do care for you, Preston, but I still miss him. I will always miss him."

He touches his lips to mine, silencing me, and then slips his tongue through my lips like he's asking me to dance. I give in and allow him to twirl his tongue with mine.

It feels so wrong and foreign kissing him, but it's the only thing that has been successful in keeping my mind off things that break me down. Sometimes the only thing left to do is surrender—free ourselves from the things that bind us.

He breaks free and locks his eyes with mine. "It's okay to miss him,

Kinzleigh. He's the first person you gave your heart to. We will get through it, okay. Together."

He will never understand that Breyson's not the first person I gave my heart to, but the only. I can't give away something to someone else that I no longer have in my possession. "Okay."

"Good. Let's go before we miss our flight."

TWENTY-NINE

The plane is mostly quiet, due to the time of night it is. It's peaceful sitting here in first class, looking out the window at the dark sky. I wonder what Breyson's last thought was. If he was scared. If he thought of me.

Stop.

I look over beside me to see that Preston is sleeping, along with a majority of the other passengers. With nothing to occupy my thoughts, they wander back to where they were previously going.

It's hard to process that I'm sitting in the last place Breyson was alive. I wish I could see what he saw, experience what he experienced. I didn't even get to tell him bye, or that I loved him. I should have told him more. I should have focused on the things that are important. My chances are gone.

I let myself do something I haven't done in months. I let myself remember him, our last moments, the video, and how much I love him. Staring blankly out the window, I weep. I'm not sure this will ever get easier. I don't understand why bad things happen to good people.

Always there when I need him, Bryce makes himself known inside my womb. The little flutters only become noticeable when I'm still, but always when I need him—when I'm lost over Breyson. "How do you always know when I need you?" I ask in a low whisper as I place my hand over my small, swollen belly.

Maybe Bryce was meant to be my saving grace in dealing with Breyson's death. *The lord giveth and the lord taketh away . . .*

If it weren't for his tiny but strong existence, I'm not sure I want to think of where I might be right now. I already love him beyond words and he isn't even here yet. I want to give him the best life that I can. I want him to know how much I love him, and how much Breyson would love him if he were here.

Tomorrow is going to be a new, better day. I have to believe it, so I repeat it to myself over and over as my eyes grow heavy under the dim light of the plane, exhaustion from my thoughts taking over.

Leaning against Preston's shoulder, I allow myself to drift off to a place I always see my beautiful blue-eyed boy—my dreams.

"Kinzleigh."

The world I've come to love is starting to fade. The green of the trees, the blue of the sky, and the running of a toddler in the backyard with the most amazing man I've ever met are blurring from where I stand on the front porch.

Breyson! Bryce! Where are you going?

I panic as they become a mirage in the distance. I take off running through the grass, the blades barely squishing between my toes before taking another step. Even though I'm running my heart out, they are still becoming farther away with each step I take.

"Kinzleigh, wake up."

I look around, trying to make sense of where I am and why they're missing. They were just here. My heart is pounding and the adrenaline is pumping through my veins, flooding my mind with panic.

Where are they? I run to their favorite hangout at mine and Breyson's tree. They always go there to have boy time. That has to be where they are.

The tree and the treehouse Breyson built Bryce last summer in that old oak tree comes into view. Without hesitation, I climb the net wall that leads to the entry as fast as I can. When I reach the top and see that it's empty, I go into a full panic mode.

The colors around me swirl together. What's happening? "Kinzleigh, we're here. Wake up." Something shaking my body startles me.

As my vision comes into focus, I realize I'm sitting inside of Preston's car in a driveway to a large, unfamiliar house. I recognize this neighborhood.

We made it to California. "Are you okay? You looked like you were having a nightmare."

If only he knew . . . Waking up is the nightmare.

"I'm fine," I say, wiping my sweaty palms on the fabric of my dress. "So, this is it?"

The house is large in size and the brick a neutral shade of beige. It's two stories with an attached garage. This looks bigger than my parents' old house.

The green grass is decorated with a sold sign. I didn't expect something of this size. I know Preston's parents are wealthy and that he would be making a generous salary once he took his place, but this is a lot more than I anticipated. Most couples start small and upsize when kids come into the mix. A house like this costs a fortune in California.

I can't do anything but stare at it as I place my hand on the door handle. "This is it. You ready to go see it?"

Think of Bryce. This is one time you can't do it alone. Put your pride behind you, Kinzleigh.

I put a smile on and look at him. "Absolutely. It's a beautiful house, but I would've been happy with anything. You didn't have to get something this big."

"The best deserves the best, Kinz. Besides, I'd be lying if I didn't admit that it was for me too," he says with a smirk on his face. "Come on."

I walk up to the door and place my hand on the door handle. I'm not sure I'm prepared to see the inside based on the beauty of the heavy, wooden door alone. It has to be a custom piece judging by the glass window.

Two arms envelop my waist and his hands rest over my protruding belly. I begin to feel a flutter from the contact. Bryce isn't big enough to be felt from the outside yet, but he's becoming very active; more active than usual during the day.

Why would he be more active with Preston's hands on my belly? Weird . . .

Preston kisses my neck and my nerves go crazy. It's not the same feelings I got with Breyson, but it's something. Definitely want and not repulsion.

My face heats and my hormones take over. His lips brush against the skin of my neck and stop just below the lobe of my ear. The number of hormones present when pregnant versus not is astounding.

On top of the raging hormones, the movements from Bryce are making me feel like I'm riding a rollercoaster. "Welcome home. From this day forward, I work for the three of us. You and that baby are my family now."

He takes his hands off my belly and the flutters immediately stop. *That is the strangest thing.*

He opens the door and we step inside a wide foyer with high ceilings. It takes my breath away and I haven't even seen it all. A tiny surge of excitement fills me as I picture us being on our own. We're not kids anymore. Maybe we'll be okay after all.

My life is changing at every turn. A few months ago, I was sure that Breyson and I would go to the same college. Maybe even get an apartment together along the way. Had things stayed the same, I'm sure we would be preparing to welcome our baby boy into the world come September. We would be a happy couple, and an even happier family of three.

I didn't anticipate being a mother at eighteen. I still feel like a child myself, but I've also learned that sometimes we have to accept the hand we're dealt. This isn't the vision I had for myself, but I think Preston and I can make it if we try.

I will always love Breyson in a way no one else can touch. I believe he was my soul mate. You can't deny it when you look back on the way everything happened. Stuff like that doesn't just happen coincidentally.

I've been broken and lost since his death, but there is one thing I've been wrong about. Broken things can be fixed. They may still have cracks or flaws, but with the right adhesive they can be mended. Sometimes they may even be more beautiful put back together than the original form.

For what it's worth, I know that Preston will love and take care of us. I believe it in my heart. Preston has been in my life for years. I'll even admit that I was wrong about him. Voluntarily taking on what he is—that's a selfless move. He's not arrogant at all. He's one of the humblest people I know.

I will always wish that things had turned out differently, because Breyson deserved to live whether we were together or not, but the world doesn't turn on wishing and hoping. Bad things happen. Tragedy strikes. Living in the past isn't going to bring Breyson back, or raise Bryce, nor will it make me happy. I will end up disappointed every time that the outcome can't be changed.

Bryce will never know Breyson physically, but he will know him through the stories I will share to keep his memory alive. Bryce needs a family, not a single mother. He needs a dad, like every boy, even if it isn't his biological one, and that's something I can't be for him. But I can give him a father that will love him just like Bryce is his own. For him, I will be happy. I will accept love from someone that loves me with open arms.

THIRTY

Breyson

It's the middle of July and my life remains the same. I've been in a pattern for months on end. During the week I help Antonio and on the weekend I'm at the club. I've been to a few bullfights with Antonio and Maria, but I stay pretty busy at the club, and I have to allot my extra time for Marcus.

Some might like the predictability that my life has become, but for me, it just pisses me off. Why, because it means I've spent more months of my life not knowing who I am or where I belong. I try not to complain, because I've been adopted into this family as if I'm one of their own, but the images in my head haunt me day in and day out.

After the day I had the vision of the pregnant girl, I can't eat, sleep, or think of anything but her. I can feel it down to my bones—she's pregnant with my child. Maria has been trying to think of a way for us to find out more about me, but to date we have yet to come up with anything, which brings me to my current whereabouts.

I'm standing at the entrance of the club. I never ask Big Sanchez for anything, but I feel like I've earned the right to ask for a favor. Word has it he has connections that run deep, and the power to get anything he wants. Today, I'm going to see if that's true.

I pull open the door and walk through the front office, no different than

I do every day. Angelique is sitting at her desk as I enter. A smile suddenly appears on her face as she takes me in, mentally undressing me with her eyes.

Fuck. I really don't want to deal with her today.

One night and several used condoms later and she won't stop. She comes on to me every time we are at work together—a closet here, a bathroom there, even company vehicles. It's getting old.

Everywhere I go she appears, making it a point to volunteer as my shadow. I was drunk, not thinking clearly, and she was hot. I haven't touched her since, but that doesn't stop her from trying. "Angelique," I say, nodding my head, so I can keep my hands in my pockets. The fewer limbs she can grasp onto the better. "Is he here?"

I stop in front of her desk but keep my distance. She licks her red-stained lips and stands. Her black dress looks as if it's painted on her body and stops at her thighs. Her breasts look like they could fall out of the rounded neckline with the slightest bend. I don't think the girl owns a single piece of clothing that would be considered conservative. It gets old, to be honest, nothing left to the imagination.

Her heels tap against the floor as she walks toward me. She's in heat and on the prowl. Removing my hand from my pocket, I scratch the back of my head as I look off in another direction.

Why in the hell did I fuck her?

This is awkward every damn time we're around each other, and it never gets easier. I couldn't have just taken the easy route and picked a guest to have a one-night stand with. I never do anything the easy way it seems. I'm starting to wonder if I have any sense.

"Hey, sexy. He's going to be awhile, but you're welcome to wait with me." She wraps her arms around my waist and I tense beneath her touch. This feels wrong compared to the last time. Guilt plagues my mind, but I'm unsure as to why.

Shit.

I look back at her. She has determination in her eyes. She's a woman used to getting what she wants and will stop at nothing to obtain it. "I've missed you, Bryce. I thought we had an agreement of sorts. You've left me waiting on you for months. Don't deny that the sex we had was amazing. You know you want more. Stop fighting it."

She runs her fingers up my shirt, over my tightened abs. That's the thing about being drunk—wasted would be a better term. You don't remember much of the act, just that it happened. "Look, Angelique . . ."

She places a finger from her free hand over my mouth, silencing me. She then pushes me backward until the back of my knees press against a chair. "Placer me (Dame placer)."

I'm still not sure as to why she chooses to say some phrases in Spanish when she knows I don't speak the language; at least, none aside from select phrases I've picked up from my family.

She places her palms on top of my shoulders and presses down, hinting she wants me to sit, so I do. This is going to be a losing battle for me. There is no point in arguing with her. She props one heel up on the seat of the chair beside my thigh, revealing that she isn't wearing panties.

Damn.

What the fuck am I supposed to do with that? A girl can't show a guy something like that and expect him to turn it down. It's not in our nature. We were designed for visual stimulation, and regardless of how much I deny it, I like what I see. And I haven't had sex since that night either. What would it hurt to have a little fun? I could be stuck here forever. Look at that wet pussy.

She wants you to touch it . . .

As if she can tell I'm thinking it over, she reaches over and turns the lock on the door beside us. She grabs my hand and places it on her smooth, tan thigh, guiding it up until it is cupping her mound. It's hot . . . and wet.

She brushes my finger between her folds and circles it in the wetness of her pussy. Her eyes lock with mine. "Siente lo que me haces (feel what you do to me)."

There is something about a hot Latin woman letting the Spanish roll off her tongue that's irresistible. My dick hardens at the feel of moisture running down my finger.

How the hell am I supposed to turn this down? It's not like I'm regularly having sex. The craving to bury myself inside her is building in my body. She is offering it up openly. She doesn't hide her want for this. I don't even have to work for it or make her meaningless promises. I have no reason to say no.

Fuck it . . .

I slide my finger inside, letting her pussy consume all of it. She clenches around it with each insertion and throws her head back in ecstasy, a moan escaping each time I push my finger inside and round it forward like a hook. I'm hitting her G-spot. I can feel it.

Each time I pull my finger out, I run it up the crevice and smear the wetness over her clit, slowly teasing and tormenting her. I place my opposite hand on the strap of her dress, pulling it down her arm. Her naked body is fine, if I remember correctly.

Her nipples harden to a point as I reveal each one at a time, while I continue to stimulate her. She is becoming needy, greedy, and loud. Grabbing her right breast in my left hand, I pull her to me, placing her nipple in my mouth, and I suck . . . hard.

I continue to rub slowly just to see how much she'll beg for it. It doesn't take long before she caps my hand with hers, controlling my pace. I let her. It's hot to watch.

I release her nipple, making a popping sound. I rub my finger up and down over her clit faster, causing her to let go with her own hand. I watch her face, waiting for the moment she comes. "Don't stop. I need to come," she says, and I can feel the amount of wetness increase. "Yes. Make me come, Bryce."

I increase my speed and change direction of the strokes. I want to see her overwhelmed. I insert the fingers from my free hand inside her pussy, so I can feel her when she clenches. It doesn't take long before I can feel her tighten around my left index and middle fingers. Her muscle pulsates for a few seconds as she vocalizes her orgasm.

She looks at me and licks her lips as I pull my fingers out of her body. They are covered in her cum. "You want more? You want to ride my dick?"

Her face is flushed a shade of pink. She nods. "You know I do, Bryce. I've been waiting months to have you inside me again."

I reach in my back pocket and pull a condom from my wallet. Handing her the small square, I tell her what she has to do to get it. "Show me how much you want it."

She bites her lip as she takes it from my grasp. Lowering her leg to the floor, she grabs the bottom hem of her dress and pulls it upward, over her head, baring herself to me. Slowly, she lowers to both knees in front of me.

Her bronze, naked body is beautiful against her black, silky hair cascading to her ribs. She knows exactly what she's doing, as her tiny fingers begin working at the button on my jeans. Sliding down my zipper, she grabs ahold of my dick in her manicured hand and pulls it free from the confinement of my briefs. "You have a beautiful cock," she says, and lowers her head to wrap her mouth around it. She swirls her tongue around the head and suctions as she takes me into her mouth, stopping at the back of her throat.

Damn, the girl can suck a dick.

She continues at a steady rhythm, but I need it faster, deeper. I fist her hair in my hand and push her head down, forcing her to take it deeper, causing her to gag a little. She doesn't stop. Instead, it's like I motivated her. She begins to bob faster, suck harder, taking me as deep as she can and she still isn't consuming all of me.

Leaning my head back against the wall, I close my eyes and enjoy the feel of her full lips around me. My mind wanders, and before I know it, I'm lost in my own head and zoned out.

Images form in my mind. It's been awhile since they have. I've had nothing since the vision of her in the hospital—the day I found out I possibly have a child out there somewhere, if it's all real.

It's an old Oak tree in what looks to be a field or a meadow. There is a pond with two horses taking a drink of water. I'm sitting on the ground, leaned against the tree in a position that is similar to the way I am now. It's then that I notice . . . *her.*

She's absolutely beautiful, and she's straddling me half-naked. Her top half is covered, but her bottom is bare. The color of her red sweater against her blonde hair is stunning. She is pumping up and down on me slowly, as if we're savoring the moment, and lost in each other. Looking at her, looking at me, I know that we were completely and unmistakably in love.

She has to be real, because no fantasy or dream could be this detailed or this good. Before I have time for any other thoughts, she says, "Breyson, I will always love you with all of my heart."

Startled, I buck forward, slamming my dick into the back of her throat. She releases me, gagging uncontrollably. "What the hell, Bryce?"

"What the fuck did you just say?"

"I said, what the hell—"

I cut her off mid-sentence. "Before that," I bark out. "What did you call me? What did you say?"

She crinkles her eyebrows, clearly confused. "I didn't say anything. Are you okay, Bryce? You look like you just saw a ghost."

I stand and shove my dick back into my jeans, quickly fastening them. "You didn't just call me . . . Breyson?"

She looks around the room. "Why would I call you that? Your name is Bryce. I don't know anyone named Breyson. What's wrong? You're starting to worry me."

I may have just found a piece to the puzzle. Thank God. It may not be much, but it's something. I came here for a reason. It isn't even my night to work. I let my damn hormones get in the way of the real reason I came here, to find out who I am, so I can find out if she's real or make-believe. I need to know whether she is a figment of my imagination, or if by some miracle, we're trying to find each other.

"I have to go."

"Are you fucking serious?" I don't know what she's so pissed about, considering she got off. If anyone should be pissed it should be me. I'm going to have to take care of the painful blue balls later, when my nuts are buried in my stomach.

I bend over to pick up her dress, handing it to her. "As a heart attack."

I walk around her and past her desk, opening the door that leads into Big Sanchez's office. It's against the rules to enter without calling first, but I need answers, and I need to know if he is the one to help me get them. I may pay for this, but it's something I have to do.

When I walk in, he has the phone up to his ear. He looks at me but continues talking. "Can you fax the monthly report to me? Something needs to be adjusted. I don't like the numbers I'm seeing."

He points at the chair in front of his desk and I sit. My stomach knotting confirms my nervousness. His demeanor has yet to change. "I expect it to be a priority. This is what I pay you for. If it doesn't get fixed you can find yourself another job. You're always replaceable. Get back to me in twenty-four hours."

Without another word he places the phone back on its receiver. He links his hands together and places them on the back of his head, leaning back in his chair. "It's your day off," he says in a clipped tone. "And you didn't tell me you were coming. I don't like unexpected guests."

If my nerves were starting to calm, they're not anymore. He looks like he could be a drug dealer and have me killed with one simple order. Whether he actually would or not is beside the point. If I didn't know he was a decent person deep down, I'd be scared shitless right now. "I was hoping for a favor. I need help." Before I even get the full sentence out of my mouth he leans forward, putting his arms on his desk.

"What with? Why didn't you just say so from the beginning?"

Maybe because you're the size of a wrestler and could kill me with one finger . . .

"Did Maria ever tell you why they adopted me?"

He studies me for a moment before he answers. "Maria and I haven't spoken in years. It's better that way. Things tend to get . . . *complicated* in the presence of one another. You came to me lost. I'm a simple man, and not one to meddle in someone else's affairs unless it is directly related to my business or me. If you want to come to me you will, in which I presume is what this unexpected meeting is about, so continue."

I run my hand through my hair as I think of how I'm going to get this all out. "Well . . . I was in some kind of an accident back in February. A fishing boat picked me up, close to dead, and brought me here, so I don't have many details. They think a plane or shipwreck. I have Amnesia. I don't have any recollection of anything prior to the accident: no name, birthday, where I'm from. I know nothing. My doctor kept me in the hospital as long as he could, hoping I would regain my memory, but so far, all I've had are a few visions here and there. Most of them don't include sound and they are of the same girl."

I take a deep breath, letting it linger in the air. "What is it you need my help with?"

I lock my eyes with his. I need him to know how serious I am. "At first, I thought she was just something my mind conjured up, but they get more specific with each vision. I need you to help me figure out who I am or where I'm from. There has to be a way. I can't stay in Spain for the rest of my life. Each day, it's like I'm trying to fill a void. I need to find the piece of the puzzle that's missing. I think she is to me what Maria is to you . . ."

He stands and walks around the desk toward the door. I turn to look at him in confusion. "Let's go. You can fill me in on the details on the way." With that vague response, he continues out the door.

Standing from the chair I'm sitting in, I follow him quickly in an attempt to catch up. We pass by Angelique, now dressed and sitting at her desk. She glares at me as we pass. "Angelique, hold my calls. I'll be out for the rest of the day. I don't want to be disturbed. Are we clear?" he asks as he pulls on his suit jacket from the coatrack standing beside the door.

I have no idea why, but I suddenly feel very guilty about our little rendezvous earlier and the night at the club. I feel like I cheated on someone. I get a sick feeling in the pit of my stomach the longer I look at her. I breathe in through my nose, trying to calm my nerves. I feel dirty, and I want the filth gone. "Yes, sir. I understand," she says, but is still glaring at me as if she wants to kill me.

He opens the door I previously entered when I arrived, and I follow behind him. I'm not sure where we're going or why, but I'm ready to find out. His reaction has piqued my interest. He could be my only key to the information I need to find out who I am whether my mind decides to work or not.

At this point, I don't care. I just want to find the girl that has invaded every facet of my mind and my dreams. Whether I have to make new memories or finally remember my old ones, I don't care, as long as I can find her. She's the void that I feel constantly. I know it. I will find her, no matter what it takes.

He leads me to a car awaiting our arrival outside. I'm not sure whether to keep my questions to myself or ask where it is we're going, because the curiosity is getting the best of me. He barks out orders in Spanish to the driver, and the car pulls out into the street, leaving the club behind.

Pulling his titanium phone from his jacket pocket, he keys something in and places it to his ear. Only a second passes before he speaks into the phone to the person on the other end of the line. "Expect me in an hour. I have a job for you." He silences to listen, but only a moment, before he continues. "Same place."

He replaces the phone in his pocket, and then he looks at me, as if he's choosing what he wants to say next. "Tell me everything you know, and I'll help you in any way I can."

THIRTY-ONE

Breyson

We pull up to a large building. It appears to be a lavish hotel or office space—a high-rise that extends into the sky. The driver pulls under the connected parking garage and follows the road until he reaches the top floor.

I reach for the door, but he stops me. "Don't ask him for any personal information. He won't give it to you for reasons you don't need to know. This is a business transaction, not a social meet. Keep that in mind and this will go a lot more smoothly."

I'm starting to wonder what I may have gotten myself into, since we had to pass through a security check to come onto this parking level. I signify that I understand and open the door. The rooftop parking lot is vacant, aside from one other car and a small helicopter.

Robotically, he begins walking toward an elevator to the adjacent building that is made of mirrors. Looking up at the distance between here and the top, I'm guessing it's a long ride.

Once inside the elevator, I realize it's a one-way window. It's only Big Sanchez and me ascending the side of the building. When I look at him, he is keying in a code on the keypad beside the doors.

The elevator starts to climb, giving you a view of the surrounding city. I don't think I'm afraid of heights, but this is a little scary. I plaster my back against the rear wall and try to only look straight ahead, taking deep breaths. It seems like an eternity before the elevator comes to a stop.

The wall behind me suddenly opens, causing me to stumble backward as I lose my footing. I didn't realize there were doors on both ends of the elevator.

He grabs my shirt to steady me. When I get my balance, I look at the space around me. It looks like an executive suite. The carpet is a milk chocolate color with mint green swirls and loops. The walls are done in textured wallpaper that matches the green in the carpet. At the opposite wall from where I stand, sits a crescent shaped desk in an espresso stained wood.

The lettering on the wall behind it reads, The Staton Agency. I'm not exactly sure what that means. "Mr. Sanchez," the petite brunette says from behind the counter with a smile like Miss America. "He's awaiting your arrival. You may continue to his office."

He acknowledges her and turns to a hallway that aligns horizontally with the same wall as her desk, but to the left-hand side of the large room. The hallway is long and dim in lighting.

As we reach the end, there is a large, heavy door made of chestnut. It looks expensive. There are no windows present or handles. What kind of door doesn't have handles? As we get to the end, a buzzer sounds, and the sliding of a bolt unlocks from the inside. The door opens freely, and we step inside.

When we get far enough inside to be clear of the doorway, the door shuts again and the lock slides back into place. The room is twice the size of the one we came from. The office is built of nothing but windows.

In the farthest corner sits a large desk. Even I can tell it cost a fortune. In the middle of the room is an area for seating, consisting of a couch and two chairs surrounding a round cast iron table. The corner opposite of the desk has a wet bar supporting decorative glass bottles filled with various colors of liquid. What kind of place is this?

The room is vacant. I thought someone was supposed to be waiting. I wonder where he is. There aren't many places to hide. The only solid wall is the one that holds the door we entered to the left-hand side.

A door at the farthest end becomes noticeable; although, it blends in with the wall. A man dressed in a perfectly pressed, designer suit emerges. His hair is short and combed to perfection. He has a beard, short to the face, and shaded the same color as his brown hair. His gray eyes look aged from the lines that extend beside the outside corners. He's taller than me, and a build that is medium in frame, but sculpted. Even in full clothing you can tell he's fit. It's in the way he carries himself. "Sanchez. Always a pleasure. What brings you in, my friend?"

He's . . . American?

Everyone I've met has the same accent; everyone except him. He talks just like me, but less drawn out. Excitement takes over, spreading throughout my body. I can barely breathe. I have no idea how he can help me, but I get the feeling that if anyone can, it'll be him. Why didn't I do this earlier?

Big Sanchez wraps his arm behind my back and squeezes the muscle between my shoulder and neck. "The boy needs your help. He's in a bit of a sticky situation, I guess you could say."

The man whom has yet to introduce himself adjusts the knot of his tie that is the same color as his eyes. He walks around his large desk and takes a seat in his chair. "Let's get down to business, shall we?"

Big Sanchez guides me to the two chairs that sit in front of the desk. I sit and wait as he opens a leather book holding a yellow, executive style notepad. He picks up a heavy, metal pen in his left hand and removes the top. I notice his finger is free from a ring, but a tan line is present, as if one was previously there.

I wonder what this guy's story is. He seems dry and void of any type of emotion—a permanent asshole. He looks at me after jotting down a few words. "Tell me everything you know. Any details omitted can be costly."

After what seems like hours and pages of paper he's written on, I get out the last detail. I told him every vision, every detail of her, the baby, and the name she called me back at the office. It nearly killed me to tell someone else what seemed like the most private moments, but if it helps me find her and where I belong, it's worth it. He recaps his pen and presses a button on his phone, then a female voice comes over the speaker. "Yes, sir?"

"Send in Juan."

"Right away, sir."

Not even a minute passes when the door opens and a male not much older than me walks in with a case in hand. Where the hell do these people come from? "Are we doing the standard kit, Mr. P?" he asks as he makes his way across the room.

That's a strange thing to be called.

"That will suffice, Juan. Make it a rush result."

I am thoroughly confused on what is going on. He places his case on the open corner of the desk and removes a pair of latex gloves, pulling them on his hands, only adding to my confusion.

I lean to the side, trying to see what is inside, but it just looks like a science kid's dream gift. It would be really great if someone felt the need to fill me in on what the hell is going on.

My eyes go wide as Juan pulls out a needle connected to a small rubber tubing that feeds into another glass tube on the opposite end of the needle. "It's nothing to panic over, boy," Mr. P tells me. "DNA tells a lot about a person. I need a few samples to be able to identify you. I'm not a magician."

"You need blood?"

"Among other things. Sit tight. You'll be out of that chair and on your way before you know it." He rounds the desk and begins walking in the direction of the bar. In a few short strides he arrives and starts pouring the bronze liquid in the glass beside it.

I watch as he chugs it back like it's the necessity he needs to make it through the day. What problems could this guy possibly have in his life that seem so bad he needs to drink at midday? The man is probably a billionaire, and he's slamming back liquor like water.

I'm so wrapped up in watching him drink that I fail to notice the rubber tie tightened around my bicep. "Form a fist," Juan says as he uncaps the needle. Doing as he says, I turn my head as he plunges the needle into the vein at my bend of my arm. It hurts no more than a brief sting, but for some reason the pain is worse if you watch the needle puncture your skin. I do like to watch as the blood drains from my arm into the test tube, though.

After the tube is full, he caps it and places a bandage over the small hole in my arm. Blood down. I wait for him to put away the sample to see what's next.

Juan runs a fine-tooth comb through my hair and my eyes wander to the mysterious man I know nothing about. I notice him staring vacantly out the window, still pouring the liquid down his throat like he's thirsty. I want to ask him questions but was already warned against it.

I feel like I've been pricked and prodded and placed under a microscope after being fingerprinted and had DNA samples taken from my hair, saliva, and blood. You'd think I was a criminal. "All finished, Mr. P," Juan says, as he places all of the sealed samples in a large envelope, making another seal, my guess so that they don't get compromised.

"Thank you, Juan. That'll be all for now." He walks back to his desk and picks up the envelope. He seems to be examining it, but then hands it back to Juan before he turns to leave the office. "Make it a stat case," he barks out, causing Juan to pick up his pace.

Big Sanchez stands from the chair beside me and I do the same. "I appreciate you seeing me on such short notice. We'll be in touch, I presume?" Their eyes lock for a moment before he responds.

"As always, Sanchez. You'll be hearing from me soon." As if on cue, he turns and leads me in the direction that we came when we arrived. This has been the strangest day, but for the first time since I woke up in the hospital bed four months ago, I have a little bit of hope.

I may never get my memory back, and that's something I can accept if I have a sense of belonging. I can't deny that I haven't been blessed with a great adoptive family, but there is something about knowing where you're supposed to be that fulfills you. That's something that you can't replace once lost.

I may not have my original memory anymore, but my soul tells me there is a girl that is grieving my absence—my only true mate. It doesn't take memory to know when your soul is trying to lead you.

Maybe I just need to learn to let it guide me and follow, instead of trying to force my brain to remember. It did get me here. Now, I must wait . . .

THIRTY-TWO

Kinzleigh

I wake up to the same boring routine every day. It's getting old. It's almost July. I've been here close to two months now and it isn't any easier than it was when I first arrived.

I still cry at some point during the day on a daily basis, but mostly when Preston is at work. I think it's the loneliness of being in this massive house all day by myself. Preston refuses to let me try and find a job. He uses the excuse that no one is going to hire a pregnant eighteen-year-old, but I know he is just trying to protect me. It makes me feel like a child.

The first week was okay, because I kept busy with all the people coming in to decorate and remodel parts of the house. Preston refuses to let me go in one of the rooms until it's finished. Everything was my choice except for his little pet project. Tonight is the night. We are going to dinner and then he's unveiling his big surprise. I have no idea what is so spectacular that I can't see it until it's finished.

I called my parents after I arrived to tell them the news. They weren't even that upset that I wanted to get away from everything, just that I felt the need to run away to do it. Maybe I did coward away, but no one will ever understand. They came to see me for the weekend after my arrival and had a talk with Preston. I think deep down Mom is beyond thrilled but trying not to show it. As long as someone's happy . . .

I called Adalynn and she was nothing short of angry. I didn't know she could use the words that came flying out of that sweet mouth. I tried to explain—really I did—but it was easier to take off and not have to say goodbye, and that's just something she will have to take my word on.

The last time I tried goodbye it didn't have a good ending. She ended up crying and said that she would fly out to see me when the baby was born. I think her and Braxton are getting ready to leave for college in August. I'm happy for them. They found happiness in each other—happiness that I used to have.

Staring at the ceiling like I do every morning, a hand begins rubbing my growing belly. "How are my two favorite people?" he asks in a raspy voice. Turning my head to the side to follow the sound, Preston is propped up on his elbow with a sleep-ridden smirk on his face.

It's early; barely light outside, but I can't sleep. I can never sleep, it seems, and sleep was something that always came so easy for me before, so I usually lay in our big king size bed and get lost in my thoughts until he wakes up.

I can't help but smile a little. Bryce isn't even his child, but no matter what, Preston always includes him as if he is. "We're good, just a little hungry. Do you want me to cook you breakfast before work?"

He wraps his arm around me, grabs my hip, and pulls me toward him as he lays flat on his back. Knowing what he wants, I throw my leg over him in a straddling position. He loves this, and I have no idea why. I feel like a fat cow this way. "It's Saturday, Kinz. I told you I'm not working on the weekend. They will be fine without me. That's my time with you—family time."

He trails his fingertips up my back and wraps his hand in my hair, pulling me down to his lips. He knows what kissing does to me. It's getting harder and harder to say no. We hook up, but I can't bring myself to have sex with him as long as I'm carrying Breyson's child. The idea makes me sick, even though the hormones are driving me crazy and I want to badly.

I am determined to enjoy my life somehow. I know I'll never experience sex like I had with Breyson again, so I might as well experience it casually with someone I trust: a friend.

His lips touch mine softly, but I need more. He's always gentle with me. I need him to stop being so damn caring all the time and kiss me like we're dying every once in a while. I break the kiss in frustration. "What's wrong?"

"Preston, I want you to be rough with me sometimes. I'm not a glass doll, or a child. I won't break, dammit. Can you stop being so sensitive all the time? Please . . ." I'm so mad I could cry. I hate being pregnant. My emotions are constantly changing. Maybe it's because Breyson was always the perfect balance of everything. He was soft when he needed to be soft and rough when I wanted it rough. He was completely freaking perfect.

Preston sits up and looks down at me. I'm staring into his chest, ashamed, until he roughly tugs on the locks of my hair, turning my face upward to look at his. "You want it rough?"

Is it weird that I want rough sex? I really wouldn't know. I have never been open about discussing sex with my friends, because I never had any input to give. I wasn't having sex. I was always the goody two shoes in everyone's eyes.

His voice takes on a sexy but harsh tone, and I think I just wet my panties. Closing my eyes, I nod my head. "Look at me."

I open them on command. "You don't have to be scared to tell me what you want, Kinzleigh. I just thought you liked things slow. I had no idea you were into anything else. This relationship is about give and take. It's my job to provide for you and make you happy. That happiness includes intimacy. I've wanted you for a long time. I sure as hell am not going to lose you now that I have you."

He crushes his lips to mine so hard it hurts, but I welcome it. I can't do anything slow and soft anymore without sadness consuming me.

Making love was something I experienced with Breyson; it was our thing, and it ended tragically and not by choice. I can't move on from him that way. Making love reminds me too much of Breyson. I need to limit myself to the familiarities of him if I'm going to have a chance at a happy life.

My body heats from the close contact. His tongue reaches for mine, searching to taste me. I allow it. This is what I need. He grabs the hem of his tee shirt I'm wearing and pulls it over my head. He breaks the kiss just before it comes off. "I love seeing my clothes on you." His eyes sweep over my body. First, my enlarged breasts, then my round stomach, and lastly, down as far as he can see. "You're the most beautiful girl I've ever seen."

He hardens beneath me and the feel of the tip touching my entrance sends a shockwave of desire through my body. It stands freely, because he's only wearing thin boxers, and I'm not putting any of my weight on him.

I let it push inside me as far as it will go with the fabric between us. It feels so good. Placing my nipple between his lips, he flicks the tip of his tongue over my sensitized center.

He runs his hand underneath the front of my panties and begins rubbing his thumb through the wetness, spreading it over my clit to lubricate it. He rubs it back and forth in a way he's learned gets me off. It doesn't take long, and I do. It never takes long, because I'm always sexually frustrated and constantly needing more.

Placing his thumb between his lips, he sucks it, tasting what he just did to me. "Do you want to fuck?" he asks. My cheeks ignite with heat as the filthy word passes through his lips.

I wish I was strong enough to not even consider saying yes, but I'm not. The thought of going through with it crosses my mind each time he asks. Sometimes I think that maybe it's the key to fully moving on. Breyson is the only man I've ever had sex with. Maybe it would sever my attachment to him if I could just break that bond. I look into his eyes as I battle with my own mind.

Should I? Should I not? Will it really hurt anything?

Each time I think I can be strong and go through with it. Like it does every time I sit in this predicament, I start to think of the last time I was with Breyson in my room on my bed and I falter. "I can't, Preston. I want to, but it'll have to wait until after Bryce is born."

Will it be any easier then? His face falls a little from the excitement that was building by my hesitation, but being the man that he is, he hides it. The man has the patience of a saint, making me feel extremely guilty for making him wait when he's given me all that he has.

I look down, now unable to look him in the eyes, but he takes my chin between his thumb and index finger, raising it to look at him. "Kinzleigh, you should know by now that I'm not just in this for sex. Don't get me wrong, I can't wait to have you that way, but for me it's more than that. I can wait. I'll always wait for you."

He reaches over to the bedside table beside him and opens the wooden drawer. I start to move off of his body, but he grabs my hip in the opposite hand, holding me still. Feeling around inside the contents of the drawer, he pulls something out, but I can't make out what it is. I never go in his drawer, but I don't think there is much in there—nothing important anyway.

I don't think anything of it when he looks me in the eyes. Whatever it is, he has it covered with his fist. Preston is a talker. He always has been, or at least with me he is. "I was going to wait until tonight to bring this up, but given the type of person you are, this is probably best."

My eyebrows wrinkle, verifying the state of confusion I'm now in. "What is it, Preston? Is something wrong?"

He shakes his head as he sits up with me still straddling his lap. "I wanted to take you out tonight because I have a few surprises for you; all of them to signify our future together. I guess now is as good as any to tell you. You never have been the kind of girl that likes surprises."

He's silent for a moment. Why does he look nervous? Preston isn't a nervous guy. He gets what he wants and has never had to be that way. "You realize how much I love you, right?"

Awkward . . .

"Yes, Preston. I think I get the gist of it. Why? Should I be worried?"

"No. Shit. This isn't how I planned this. Just hear me out, okay? Don't say anything until I'm finished. Please . . ."

I sarcastically hold up my hands in surrender. "Fine. Whatever it is, just tell me."

He's processing. "I know we've only technically been a couple for a couple of months, but you know it's just an added step to what we've always been. You know everything about me and I know everything about you. There are no surprises, no secrets. The two of us have always been an open book with each other."

His expression is soft, giving me no sign that I need to be concerned. "I know you've had a rough year. I get it. I understand that I'll never replace what you lost, but I also know that you're a strong person. You're the strongest one I know. You can withstand anything. I've never lied to you, Kinzleigh."

His thumb brushes over my skin. "I'll always support you in anything: a career, an education, a family . . . A relationship doesn't have to be perceived as the way you used to view it. It's a partnership, a friendship, and a compromise. I've never been in a relationship before you, and for good reason. I never liked the idea of giving someone else something that I wanted to be yours: my heart. Nothing has to change from what it's been. If you want to go to school in the fall, you can register anytime you want. If you want a career in cheerleading, I'll do anything in my power to make it happen. I want to give you the world, Kinzleigh. I just want one thing in exchange."

I don't know if I like the sound of where this conversation is headed. We don't get deep very often, because I just don't have it in me to think deeply anymore. With Breyson I gave it all I had: mind, body, heart, and soul.

Now, I want to live my life free from making decisions or having to think of what I want. I want to be a follower. Dreams don't come true. I know that now. "What are you asking?"

He opens his fist and my eyes go wide. I can't breathe, like I'm being strangled by an invisible set of hands. Am I ready for this? Can I even go through with it? "Marry me, Kinzleigh . . ."

My ears start ringing and my vision becomes distant and blurred. I feel like I'm sitting on a spinning merry-go-round watching the world speed by. A year ago, this was considered worse than death to me—the ultimate life-altering worst-case scenario.

Then Breyson came along and shook my world up, down, and all around. He made me see the good in falling in love, made me accept it, and even want it. When I heard those words, I wanted them to be from *his* mouth. I wanted to wear *his* ring. I wanted to mark myself as *his* forever.

The dream I had that week in California last year resurfaces. We were married . . . We were happy. Fate can be a hellacious thing. Sometimes, I think it's the work of the devil himself, tampering with the good in the world. My throat is dry and my heart feels like it's about to beat out of my chest.

But it's time to grow up. I'm having a baby. I'm going to be someone's mother. I've grown a lot over the last year, some for the better and some for the worst. There is one thing that I've learned: I'm cursed. Bad things happen to people that I love.

This knowledge could be good for me. There is one thing I know. I can control how much I love Preston. The way I feel about him isn't all-consuming. That's the best part of being with him. I can protect him from getting hurt.

Even if Breyson had come back, he's better off without me. I would have been forced to let him go. It was a promise I made that day at Beau's grave and promises made are always collected in due time.

Breyson and I loved each other too hard, too much. Our love for each other blinded us, making it impossible to steer clear of curve balls thrown at us. That kind of love gets you killed, because you aren't looking for it. It's no different than stumbling upon a snake hidden in the tall grass.

We were living a life behind rose-colored glasses, the two of us always in a constant state of bliss and perfection like nothing bad would ever happen. If we would have seen the world for the reality it is to begin with, maybe he'd still be here.

Loving Breyson was the worst and the best thing that's ever happened to me. It's the worst, because it's the reason for his death, and it's the best, because it made me a better person.

As overwhelming as this is, life isn't about me anymore. It's about Bryce. I'm not a kid anymore. I can't live on hopes and dreams. Cheer and travel are no longer the best thing for me. I can't have a career and cheer for the NFL and have a baby. A baby has needs, both financial and emotional. A baby needs a family—both a mother and a father. Breyson would want Bryce to be taken care of.

Fuck fate . . . I'm writing my own.

"Okay, Preston. I'll marry you . . ."

THIRTY-THREE

Kinzleigh

I stand here at the bathroom counter staring at the reflection of the large, round diamond on my left ring finger. It had to have cost a small fortune. "That ballsy twat! He actually went through with it? You said yes! What the hell, Kinzleigh? You can't even call your best friend after you accept a marriage proposal?"

I glance upward at the mirror. The sight behind me makes me smile. *Presley* . . . Standing in all her goddess glory. The girl is gorgeous. I don't know what my idiotic brother was thinking.

"Maybe I should be offended that I've been back in California for months and this is the first time I've been graced with your presence," I quip back in sarcasm.

"I guess you got me there. Call it even?"

I've always loved her bargaining strategy. Somehow, she makes it that nothing is ever one hundred percent her fault. It's either not or only fifty, no matter what the scenario.

"Depends . . . what'd you bring me back from Italy?" I'm still not sure what happened between Presley and my brother over New Year's, but whatever it was, wasn't good. I've never seen Presley as upset as she was when she left my house with Preston that night. I've wanted to ask several times, but then the accident happened, and I've been a zombie since.

"Only the best pair of heels money can buy." She is dangling a large, fancy gift bag from her index finger. "Although, judging from your current state, you won't be wearing them for a while. How is the bun in the oven?" I turn around as she starts walking toward me. The closer she gets, the more I notice that she's getting thinner. Presley is already thin . . .

She pulls me in for a hug and she feels thin as a rail and frail. It breaks my heart in two. What on earth happened over New Year's? I should have asked more questions. After that day in my room at my parents' house when she broke down, she never said much more, and then they went to the New Year's Eve ball together, so I assumed they worked it out. By the looks of her I was very, very wrong. I pull away, but don't let go of her.

"Bryce is fine, but we can talk about him later. How are you?" I lock eyes with her, so I can tell if she's lying. Immediately, she begins losing focus on me and trying to look anywhere but in my eyes. She's hiding something. I know she is.

"I'm fine. Why wouldn't I be?" Her pitch is higher than usual, like she's trying not to break, and this fake laugh comes out with the words. She's the worst liar I know.

"Presley." She looks around the room, still not looking at me. "Presley, look at me."

She hesitates at first, but finally looks at me. I can see it in her wet eyes— heartache. I know the feeling well. It finally makes sense why she's been in Italy for longer than planned. Presley's family always travels a lot in the summer, but Italy was her graduation trip, and it was never supposed to last more than a week. I have no idea what she's been doing since she's been back either. She didn't come see me before she left or as soon as she returned. I had no idea why, and now I feel so stupid . . .

"What happened between you and Konnor? Don't lie to me either, Presley." She starts to back out of my grasp. Her sun-kissed skin pales a little at hearing his name. She continues to walk backward in the direction of the bathroom door. I follow her, but it only causes her to speed up.

"Why would you think something happened? Has he said something?" She stops for a moment, like she may be a little hopeful.

"No. Tell me what happened."

She shakes her head and whispers so low I'm not sure I even heard what I thought she said correctly. "I hate him . . ."

Hate is the strongest word and shouldn't be used unless it's meant in the most absolute form. I narrow my eyes at her as she stands in the middle of Preston's and my room. This is the worst thing that could happen. This is not good at all. Presley is my best friend and Konnor is my brother. Our families are knit together too tight for something like this to happen. It's why I never wanted to be with Preston in the past.

"Presley . . ."

"Look, Kinzleigh, I need to go. I'll catch up with you later, okay? I just wanted to tell you everyone is getting together for that beach concert tomorrow night. It's kind of the last big thing before we all head off to college in a couple of weeks. I'm leaving California. I'm moving to Miami." She turns and walks toward the bedroom door in what seems like a rush to get away from me, from here.

Miami? What the hell is in Miami?

I panic. "Why are you going to Miami? I thought you were going to school at UCLA. We've planned it since we were kids." She stops as she places her hand on the doorknob, letting her shoulders drop.

My chest feels like it's being punctured with a steel blade. I'm losing everyone I care about. First, it was Breyson, and now it's Presley, the two most important people in my life. I thought she was going to be here to help me find happiness again. She has always kept me afloat, guided me through my adolescence, and taught me how to have fun.

When I moved to Mississippi, Adalynn took her place. I've never had to stand on my own before. What am I going to do now? I'm shy, meaning I cling to myself unless someone else pulls me out of my shell. My love for cheerleading made it worse, keeping me from getting out there and trying to live fully.

Now, I'm stuck without any of the things I know and love, learning to live a life without the things I let consume me before. I feel dizzy from the direction that my life has taken. There are too many changes coming at me too fast.

My eyes fill with tears as I lower myself to sit on the edge of the bed. I feel so alone. I thought we were going to school together. I know things changed when Brey was here, but he's gone now, except things aren't like they were before him. Me and Presley had all these plans and now she is moving on without me.

She looks back with her own set of tears present. "UCLA doesn't fit anymore. My reasons for going to school there no longer apply. I need to find my own way, Kinzleigh. If anyone could understand, it would be you. You had the chance to find yours and I let you. I know things have changed, but you know if Breyson were here you wouldn't be going either. No matter what, you'll always be my best friend, but I need you to let me go. I love you, Kinzleigh. You'll always be more like my sister than my friend, blood or not. I hope you show up tomorrow night. Once I leave, I don't know when I'll be back."

Without another word, she wipes her eyes and walks out the door, leaving me in the silence of my room. The panic worsens, and I begin shaking. Preston is all I have left, and he's going to be so busy making his name in the company I'll have nothing to occupy my thoughts.

That terrifies me. Being alone in my own head is never a good thing anymore. I haven't cried in a few weeks now, but that's about to change. I can't seem to hold it in. Screw it. I let them fall.

The door opens, and I look up to see Preston standing there. One look at me and he rushes to my side, dropping to his knees between my legs. "What's wrong? What the hell did she do to you, Kinz?"

"She's leaving." I blubber between sentences. "She's moving to Miami." He wipes the moisture that is drenching my cheeks. "Everyone is leaving me."

He grabs my face between his hands and kisses my wet lips. "Kinzleigh, look at me and listen carefully." I do as he says, still a crying mess. "I will never leave you, ever. That's a promise. Do you understand me?"

I nod my head and he stands, pulling me off the bed. "Come on. It's time for some good news. I like to see you smile. Right now, I need to see the happy Kinzleigh that I know is in there wanting to come out. Are you ready or do you need a minute? Our reservation for dinner is soon."

In the short time that Presley has been here I forgot Preston was taking me out tonight to celebrate—what I'm not sure. He won't tell me, and the suspense had me excited until Presley dropped a bomb on me. "Give me a few minutes to touch up my makeup and I'll be ready. I'll meet you downstairs."

He takes my left hand and brings it to his lips, kissing just below the large diamond on my ring finger. "Sure, baby. Anything for my fiancé." I can feel the smile form with his lips pressed against my skin. I'll be okay.

He turns and walks back to the door, pulling it shut as he exits. I read something a while back that hit home for me. Happiness isn't something that we find, but something that we choose, and the only person that can truly make us happy is ourselves. That thought gives me some peace of mind. I'm choosing to be happy.

THIRTY-FOUR

Kinzleigh

Dinner was a nice turn to what could have been a bad day. We ate at a small Italian restaurant in town that was tranquil and quiet. It was a place I had never been to and a drive, but Preston was adamant about me trying their food. He was convinced I've never had Italian food that was as authentic as this place. He told me an Italian family opened it years ago, but it's become one of the best restaurants around, even though they don't believe in paid advertisement. 'The food speaks for itself, and a happy customer is a lifelong customer'—that's their motto.

I must admit, he was right, and I am in the physical state to prove it. I think my stomach grew, and not as a result of Bryce getting bigger. I couldn't eat anything more if I tried.

Right now, I want nothing more than to curl up on the couch and watch a movie while Preston rubs my feet, our usual Saturday night ritual, but apparently, dinner was not my surprise, so I must continue through the food coma I feel like I'm in. He looks too excited to do anything else. Who knows what he has up his sleeve.

He pulls his car into the vacant parking lot of a large brick building. There is no sign on the building to tell me where we are. It's located in a nice part of town, but I've never been here before. "Preston, where are we?"

He turns into the parking spot in front of the glass door located at the front of the building and kills the engine. The smile present on his face is contagious, and I have no idea why.

It's one of those smiles that take up the entire bottom half of a person's face, and when you look at them you can't help but to smile in a way that mirrors theirs. "That, sexy, is a surprise. You'll just have to wait and see. Wait here. I'll come around and get you."

He steps out of the car and makes his way around the front of the car in a sprint. Pulling the door open, he reaches inside for my hand. Placing one foot outside on the ground, I use his hand for leverage and stand. He guides me to the door and pulls a key from his pocket. When he slides it in the lock and turns, it works.

He has a key?

He opens the door and links his fingers with mine. Walking inside, he pulls me along with him. As we cross over the threshold, he flips a switch to the right-hand side of the doorframe.

Spotlights come on above a high, half-moon shaped counter with built-in shelving in the wall behind it. The floors are marble, and the rest of the room is empty. "What is this place? Is the company opening another office?"

He is still grinning from ear to ear and starts shaking his head. "No. It's yours."

Huh? I must be hearing things. "I'm sorry, what did you just say?"

He laughs. I really don't see what is so funny. "You're cute when you're confused. It used to be a business, but they had to file bankruptcy. Always a plus when buying property. Quick, cheap sale. Come on, there's something I want to show you."

We walk through the empty room toward the back wall. On each side of the high counter there is an open doorway. As we walk through one of them, my breath catches at the sight before me.

I take in my surroundings, slowly scanning each thing in the room. It's a wide-open space with high ceilings. It's filled with mats, trampolines, harnesses, and everything I could possibly imagine for tumbling. It's a cheerleader's dream in here. It's also cruel. Why would he do this to me? He knows I have to give up that dream.

The tears begin to fall. I thought I had buried that dream when I found out I was pregnant, but seeing all of this today tells me otherwise. I turn and look at him with tears streaming down my face. "Why would you do this to me? You know I can't cheer anymore."

He pulls me into a hug and brushes my hair over my shoulder. Leaning in, he kisses me, and when he looks in my eyes I can see there is no malicious intent. His eyes are still smiling even with it absent on his lips. If he didn't do it to be cruel then why would he bring me here?

"Do you remember when you were twelve and you stayed over at the house after you got back from your first big cheerleading competition? I think it was the one where the squad won first place for the first time at a national event?" I have no idea why this is relevant, but obviously he has some point to make. I nod, still a little confused, especially that he even remembers that kind of stuff.

"Do you remember coming to my room to watch a movie because you were so excited you couldn't sleep, and Presley fell asleep before you for once?" Again, I nod.

"Well, I remember everything about that night. I remember it was the first time you totally stunned me. It was the first time I wanted you the way a man wants a woman and not the way a boy that wants a girl. That night you were so excited all you could do was talk nonstop. Being a fifteen-year-old boy, I didn't care anything about cheerleading, but I was drawn to you and how animated you were. All I could do was listen." He looks me in the eyes, as if he can't look away. For once, I realize just how long Preston has been in the background.

I can't speak. I want to hear what else he has to say. "You said something that stuck with me. You told me that one day you wanted to open your own cheerleading company and share your love for cheerleading with girls that were as passionate about it as you were. You have a gift, Kinzleigh. You found the one thing that makes you happy and that's worth fighting for. You may not be able to cheer in a squad right now, but pregnancy doesn't last forever. You still have options later. No matter which path you take, you shouldn't give up your dream just because you have to amend it. I have the means to help you make it come true. This place is yours. Anything you need that isn't already here, just say the word and it will be."

I'm at a loss for words. He has done more for me than I can even begin to comprehend. I knew Preston loved me that night in the hotel room, but I never stopped to think of how long or to what degree that love measured.

We've always been friends. I thought it was just convenient for him to love me, though, because we've always been around each other. I never even fathomed that he could genuinely love me for me. I don't feel deserving of this kind of love once, much less twice. My hope is that one day I can love him as much as he loves me.

"Say something," he says, looking deep into my eyes. "If it's not what you want, we can do something different. I just thought . . ."

"It's amazing, Preston. It's . . . Why are you so good to me? You could have any girl you want at the drop of a hat, with no baggage. Someone that could quickly give you her whole heart. Why me? Why wait?"

He breaks out into a smile and rubs his thumb along my cheekbone. "That's easy. I'm good to you because I want you. I've wanted you since we were kids. I would go to any lengths to make you happy. I love you and I want to spend my life with you. I don't give you things expecting anything in return aside from you, baggage and all. You don't give up on something you want just because it's difficult to obtain. You keep at it, like I've done with you. I will treasure you until the end."

His words bring tears to my eyes, but a different kind this time—tears of joy and not sorrow. I feel blessed knowing this is the kind of man I can spend my time with, even if he's still in second place.

Breyson will always be my first and my only one true love, my soul mate. I'll always love him the most, but to have a guy that loves me unconditionally, one that will take on loving a child that isn't his, voluntarily, to raise it as his own—that's a real man. When I look at him now, it's a look of admiration.

I wrap my arms around his neck and twirl my fingers in his hair. Pulling him down closer to my face, I grin. "You know I don't know a thing about business, Mr. Dunagin. Whatever will I do with my own company?"

He bites the edge of his lip at the sound of my teasing tone and nuzzles the tip of his nose along my jawline until it stops at my ear. "It's a good thing you're marrying an expert in the trade, Mrs. Dunagin to be. I think you'll be fine."

His voice is soft and seductive, making me hate my body right now. He kisses the lobe of my ear and begins pulling me in the direction that we came. "I have one more thing to show you."

THIRTY-FIVE

We're standing at the front door to our house as he unlocks the door and turns off the alarm system. "Preston, you don't have to do anything else for me. You've done enough."

"Let me spoil you," he says, as he pulls me inside and shuts the door, locking it behind him. "Besides, this one isn't really for you anyway."

He has a cheesy grin on his face like he's proud of himself. *Not really for you*. What does that mean?

He grabs me behind the legs and back, cradling me. It takes me by surprise, causing me to yelp and grab him tightly behind the neck. "What are you doing? Put me down. I'm heavy."

He raises a brow at me as if I just said something stupid. "I think I can handle it."

Kissing me on the cheek, he walks up the stairs one by one. When he reaches the top, he continues down the hall. I thought he was going to take me to bed until he stops in front of the door I haven't been allowed to go in. I assumed he was renovating it into an office to stay close even though the room downstairs would be more private.

Setting me down, I notice a bow tied around the door that was not there before we left. I would know, because this door has to be passed in order to get downstairs. My curiosity is quickly elevating.

He stands behind me and places each palm over my eyes like a blindfold. "I've been working on this for a while. I hope you like it, baby. Keep your eyes closed," he says in a whisper outside my ear, and then one hand leaves my face.

I hear the door open and I can feel his body pressed against mine from behind. "I got you, baby. Walk inside." I do as he says and put one foot in front of the other. I have no idea where I am going or what I'm in for, but his vacant hand returns to my eye to make sure I'm not peeking.

It feels like forever, but that could be because I'm walking at a snail's pace. He finally stops, causing me to stop with him. "This is only the beginning for us, for our family."

He drops one hand at a time and I open my eyes. I gasp at the beautiful sight before me. My mind is overwhelmed with emotions from the night's events. Nothing could have prepared me for everything he has done. My eyes take in everything from the ceiling to the floor. It's more than I could have ever dreamed of.

I turn in his arms and link my hands behind his neck. I pull him down to kiss his lips. I can't explain the way I feel right now. My heart is full of some form of love. When our lips break free, I look him in the eyes. "You designed a nursery?"

He searches my eyes with his own. "I did. Well, I helped design it. The interior designer did most of it. I just gave her the approval on each decision. Do you like it?"

"It's perfect, Preston." I smile and take it in again. The color of the walls is a cornflower blue. It's not the traditional baby blue one would normally see for a boy's nursery, but that's what makes it more beautiful.

The crown molding is thick and painted ivory as well as the baseboards. The furniture is the same antique white to match. The crib is placed inside a nook of built-in shelving that is stocked with books and baby decor.

I walk over and run my hand along the railing of the beautiful wooden crib. The bedding is made of white linen with a sailboat theme that is carried throughout the room. I continue to familiarize myself with the room. There are French doors on one wall that I open. It's a closet packed with hanging clothes, all with the tags still on them. The floor is lined with pairs upon pairs of shoes.

I close the closet back and walk over to the other wall across from the crib. In one corner sets a large wooden armoire that matches the rest of the furniture, including the changing table against the wall next to it. When I open the doors, folded clothes fill it from one end to the other. The drawers below the doors hold socks, hats, and blankets.

What catches my attention most of all is the gliding white recliner with the matching ottoman. It rests in the center of the room atop the large area rug of several masculine colors, including the blue in the walls that spans over the hardwood floor. I can't stop myself from sitting in it. It's as comfortable as it looks.

My emotions are running wild. I'm trying to take everything in, but it's hard to keep from breaking down. I never asked him to do this, but the fact that he did makes my heart grow—the same heart that I thought was completely dead.

Placing my hand on my belly, I look at him. He's staring at me, his face void of all emotion. I've probably freaked him out with my constant state of emotional breakdowns today.

"What made you pick sailboats?" I ask, as I begin gliding back and forth, peace instantly washing over me from the soothing motion.

"It reminded me of the summers on our family yacht. Some of my fondest memories are of those summers. I lived for those summers. Every memory I hold onto are the memories with you. You'll always be the girl I couldn't let go, Kinzleigh. What better life to have than a life spent with the girl you grew up with? I want Bryce to have that kind of an example. Even though I didn't help conceive him, I want him to feel as if he's mine. I want him to know he's wanted. I may not be his father, but I want to be his dad. Every child deserves to have the best kind of family; the family like we had. Our relationship may not be conventional, but we have a history that most people wouldn't understand. I would do anything for you and for Bryce. I give you my word."

Here comes the flood. That was the key that unlocked the gate I've been trying to keep closed. In all of the bad there is a little bit of good trying to shine through.

My life may not have turned out the way I wanted it to, but when I look around it's still pretty damn amazing. I tend to forget that I'm one of the luckiest girls alive. I found a love that most would kill for, even if only for a short time, and to then get to spend a lifetime with a man that loves me unconditionally.

Life is about living in the moment and not wishing for the things we don't have. I learned that with Breyson. I will always be grateful that I was blessed to know such an extraordinary person.

I was on a path of selfishness and loneliness, but he changed that. He showed me that life is empty without love. I wish I could have shared the rest of my life with him, but whatever the reason, God had other plans.

"I'm glad you came back for me," I say, as he closes the space between us. The longer we're together, the more I realize that Preston is my only option to recover. He's my only chance at breaking my addiction to Breyson.

That addiction is no longer good for me, and unless I sever it, I'll spend the rest of my life going down a road of destruction, trying to find something in comparison.

It takes a strong and patient person to stand by an addict, to love them even though they love the addiction more. I call myself an addict, because when I originally went through withdrawals from Breyson's absence, the hallucinations started. I was out of my mind. I was so distraught that I thought they were real, but as time continues to pass, I know that simply isn't the case.

I've always been taught that God will never put on you more than you can handle, and that what doesn't kill you only makes you stronger. Maybe the sequence of events was to teach me to find my own inner strength.

I'll never really know. As much as I want to, it isn't my place to question God. I'm proud of myself. Slowly but surely, I'm picking up the pieces that were shattered when I lost Breyson.

Preston places one arm under my bent knees and the other behind my back, picking me up like before. "I'll never give up on the possibility of us unless you send me away. I'll always be yours. I'm taking my woman to bed."

THIRTY-SIX

Kinzleigh

I wake up to kisses being showered all over me. Placing my arms above my head, I stretch and sit up. His happy assault on my body continues. He grabs the sheets and the comforter in his hand and tosses them back, revealing my body in all of its pregnant glory.

I sleep in nothing but a camisole and panties lately. I was twenty-five weeks pregnant Tuesday. The baby bump and the California heat don't mix. I still have the rest of July, August, and most of September to go before my due date. I'm not sure I'll survive.

Throwing his leg over mine, he straddles me, but doesn't put any weight on my body. Placing each hand on the headboard behind my head, he kisses the top of each swollen breast.

The one positive I've found to pregnancy: an awesome rack. When he raises his head just above my lips with a smirk present, I cover my mouth as I speak to avoid the inevitable morning breath. "What's gotten into you? Why are you in such a good mood?"

He laughs and pries my hand away from my mouth. I tighten my lips shut when he kisses me. I'm glad he is amused, but bad breath is self-explanatory. It has bad in the title for a reason. "I love you for your bad breath and all," he says in a teasing tone.

"Shut up!" I shout in laughter and slap his shoulder. "I never knew you had such weird fetishes. I must say, I'm stunned. I thought you were a high-maintenance pretty boy."

He grabs my wrists and pins them above my head. Grabbing my top lip between his teeth, he skims the skin and releases it with a pop. "The only pretty thing about me is the way I will look with you on top of me as I make you come."

My face floods with heat at the filth that exits his perfect, professional mouth. "You like when I talk dirty to you, huh?" *Yes. Yes, I do.* "Do you want me to make you come all over my tongue?"

I can feel my panties getting wetter with each word. It's becoming difficult to sit still in this position. He switches my wrists from both hands into one and runs the tips of his fingertips down my body until they rest at the crotch of my panties. "Is that pussy hot for me?"

Oh . . . "Yes."

He dips his finger beneath the seam of my underwear, pulling them to the side, and then runs the tip barely inside, teasing me, before running it up through my folds. "Do you want it? Do you want me to make you come?"

My breathing deepens and becomes more sporadic. "Yes," I whisper, and I close my eyes at his touch. He slides one finger inside until all that is visible is his hand. His motion is slow and steady, tormenting me. It's enough to drive a girl mad.

Releasing my hands, he backs down my legs, taking my panties with him. He doesn't even wait for me to lift myself. He does it for me. Putting his finger in his mouth, he sucks until it's clean. "I want you on my tongue."

He clenches the hem of my camisole and pulls it over my head to remove it. "I actually love your body like this." Taking my hand in his, he lays flat on his back and pulls me toward him. "Straddle my face."

That statement alone is enough to make a girl blush. I'm ashamed at how turned on hearing dirty things makes me. I blame it on the fact that I'm carrying a boy and maybe it's the testosterone.

I do as he says and grab ahold of the headboard in front of me. He spreads me apart and dips his tongue inside, swirling it around, before tracing me with his tongue until he stops on the magical spot.

I tighten my hold on the headboard. He places one hand on my hip for added support and the other he starts the same torturous assault on my body he was just doing, but with added stimulation back and forth with his tongue.

The mixture of sensations is too much. I'm not going to last long at all.

To top it off, he picks up speed with his tongue, rotating between flicking and sucking. I bite my tongue to keep from screaming out like I want to, creating a smothered moan.

The euphoria of how good it feels is becoming the focal point in my mind. I can't think of anything else.

Without thought, I begin rocking just enough that he hardens his tongue to give me the control. Everything tightens as I feel the pulsating begin to consume my body.

I rock harder, until the waves of pleasure take over and everything feels like it's in slow motion. I reach down and grab his hair, pulling it as I savor the feeling.

When it's over, the bundle of nerves is sensitive from my orgasm. For the first time, I want more. I *need* more.

He's an unselfish man, constantly meeting my needs and never expecting anything in return. He never pushes me to go all the way. This time, I want to be the one to make him come. I scoot down his body until I reach his knees, kissing the chiseled muscles along the way.

His black boxer briefs are tight from his arousal. I wonder if it's weird that I like seeing him hard, especially since I don't like the way I look right now. It makes me still feel sexy even though I don't feel petite anymore. My body has always been my absolute form of self-confidence, and now my figure has been compromised.

I hook my fingers underneath the gray band of his briefs, pulling the front outward to allow his erection to spring free. He lifts himself off the bed enough for me to work them over his butt.

I continue to scoot down his long legs until I get his underwear completely off. He is completely naked. His eyes are heavy and his bottom lip is clamped between his teeth as he watches me undress him.

I look him over. It's the first time I've really looked at him completely bare like this. He's thick. I'm not sure I'll be any good at this, but here goes.

I grab the bottom of his shaft in my hand, holding it still as I bend down and place my lips around it. I swirl my tongue over the slit of his head, tasting the bead of cum at the end. It's salty, but not as bad as I expected.

He grabs my long hair in his hand, fisting it, and he moans. "You have no idea how long I've pictured you like this."

For some reason, that information motivates me to keep going. It turns me on more, so I widen my mouth and relax my jaw to allow myself to take him deeper. I start slowly to adjust and force myself to breathe through my nose. I can feel it touch the back of my throat and I stop. The more I relax, the more it starts to feel natural. I suction around it and allow my saliva to wet it as I back off. "Fuck, Kinzleigh."

I get more comfortable with each praise that comes from his lips. He pulls on my hair more the harder I suck, so I quicken my pace. He bucks his hips forward, slamming his head at the back of my throat.

I gag not expecting it but am able to control myself by controlling my breathing through my nose. "I'm sorry, Kinzleigh. I didn't mean to. I've wanted this for so long, and it's better than I ever imagined it would be. You can stop if you need to," he says in a quick outburst, although by the sound of his labored words he doesn't really want me to.

His arousal has the opposite effect of making me want to stop. I look up at him as I reach the head, flicking my tongue on the dip underneath the tip.

His eyes roll back in his head. "Damn, I want to come so bad. I'm almost there." I continue, getting more comfortable as I go, and he begins tugging hard on my hair. "Kinzleigh, stop, I'm about to blow."

Instead of stopping, I take him as deep as I can, sucking as hard as I can. I don't want to stop. I want to know how it feels for him to completely release. I want his approval.

As I begin releasing him from my mouth inch by inch, his dick starts pulsating in my mouth, excreting a warm, salty substance in spurts. It's thick and wet on my tongue, filling my mouth. When it stops, giving me no more, I release him from my mouth.

I can't swallow. I won't. I think I'll gag. As if he knows exactly what I'm thinking, he hands me a cup of water from the bedside table. "Here, baby. Spit it in here."

He has a smirk as big as California spread across his face. I take it and dispense his cum into the cup. "I'm glad you find this amusing," I say teasingly.

"Hey, I'm high right now. It comes with the territory. That was amazing." He sits up, meeting me eye to eye. Touching his lips to mine, he slides his tongue inside, and brushes it against mine, swirling the two together.

The taste is foreign to me. It seems gross to think about, but it's strangely a turn-on to know my taste is on his tongue and his mine.

He releases me on a moan. "At least I can mix myself with you one way. I can't wait to connect my body with yours. I've been thinking."

"About . . ."

"A few things. First thing is that I know you want to wait until the baby is born to have sex. Since we are waiting, why don't we just do this right and wait until after we get married? I've waited this long already, I can wait longer. I want to start our lives together right. I want you to be the last girl I ever take to bed, Kinzleigh."

For the people that don't know him, that's a big step for Preston. I've seen him with the most beautiful girls hanging on his arm, dying for a chance to be more than his entertainment for the evening. He liked sex and wasn't ashamed of it.

I've heard him with my own ears tell girls that all they would ever get from him was a good time; some on more than one occasion and some not so much. I always thought he just liked being a playboy, but knowing what I know now, I know it's because of me.

I'm the only girl he ever let close to him emotionally. I always thought it was just because the four of us were forced together on a constant basis and it came with the territory of our parents being close, but now, maybe I was wrong. Maybe it was something more all along.

Oh. My. Gosh. Why did I never see this before?

"Preston, why did you always date blondes?"

"I've never dated anyone other than you. That's kind of irrelevant from the topic at hand, don't you think? Will you please answer my question? I don't really want to talk about other girls."

"I'll answer your question when you answer mine. You know what I mean. Why were all the girls I ever saw you with blonde?" I feel like such an idiot that I never noticed before. I think the ones I can remember even had light eyes . . .

My eyes feel like saucers right now. Maybe I'm just dreaming this up, because no girl has that kind of effect on a guy, right? No way . . . It can't be.

His jaw steels and he looks at me so hard it makes me want to squirm away terrified. "Do you really want to know? Once you have that knowledge you can never give it back. Don't ask questions you don't want the cold-hard truth to."

Do I really want to know? My heart starts frantically beating. I feel like a schoolgirl with a new crush, wondering if he has a crush too. The kind of adrenaline rush where you want to prove to all the other girls that you're the one he wants, as if it gives you a boost of confidence to know that girl is you. Why do I feel this way? I've never in my entire life felt this way.

"Yes. I think I *need* to know . . ."

"It was the closest thing to you." He pauses like he is gathering his thoughts. "You were the only girl I had any interest in. I didn't understand it then, so I didn't try. You were the only girl I had any real connection with. You were what I wanted physically, but you were also three years younger than me, and I knew after talking to someone older that if we got together young, chances were, it wouldn't last. That was not an option for me, so I waited. I waited for you to experience high school. I waited for you to experience dating, so you would see that we had something a lot of people don't: friendship. I didn't like it, but I had an ulterior motive that trumped my need to be jealous. It was an added bonus that you actually didn't take an interest in dating. Well, until . . . that guy."

He takes a deep breath, but never breaks eye contact with me. "Even though I had all that in mind, I'm still a guy. I still have raging hormones and a natural need to have sex, just as every other guy on this planet does. I couldn't have you then, so I took other girls to bed. When I lost my virginity, it was the first girl that took an interest in me sexually and she was nothing like you. I was fifteen and thought sex was just sex, and who it was with didn't matter."

He brushes my long hair over my shoulder. I have no idea where this is going, but I know I want to hear the rest. "Despite my age and in inexperience, I couldn't get off . . ."

Did he just say what I think he said? That was not at all what I was expecting. My mouth is apparently gaping, because he jumps in to continue. "At first. Not that we knew what we were doing at that age, but it's kind of a known thing that a guy's first time doesn't take more than five minutes. She knew I was a virgin and about thirty minutes in, started acting pissed off."

"I don't understand how this is relevant to the original question," I say when he doesn't immediately continue.

"I'm getting to it. The next part is a little embarrassing to admit. I made her turn around, so I didn't have to see her face and could close my eyes without her noticing. After I closed my eyes, I imagined you. That was all it took for me. From that point on I only bedded blondes. It made things easier and less obvious. It's much easier to pretend you have a type than explain a specific person."

I'm not sure if this is supposed to creep me out, but it's one of the most flattering things I've ever heard. I don't even know how to respond. "One more thing. I feel like I need to say this. I know you've been through a lot, Kinzleigh. I know that guy meant a lot to you. It was an unexpected thing and killed me that I almost lost you to him. It devastated me more to see you hurt. I'll always have your best interests at heart. I could've dealt with being heartbroken to know you were happy, but as hard as it is to understand, every event that occurs leads us to where we are supposed to be."

Life is cruel. Why? Because it gives you people; hands them to you on a silver platter to love and grow attached to, forming a bond that can't easily be broken. And then, as if trying to teach you some big life lesson, it revokes them.

What's even crueler is that I'm handed someone else after that's been with me all along, and everything he is saying makes complete sense, but I don't want it to. That means it was plotted out all along for Breyson to die, for me to be heartbroken, and for Preston to be the one I'm supposed to end up with.

That makes no sense at all. Breyson is my soul mate. You only have one soul mate. How can that be true? If he was my soul mate, then how is this where I'm supposed to be?

It dawns on me—the memory of an English project my junior year. We were given an assignment to read a book and dissect it, to break down its meaning in the form of a term paper. The point was to open ourselves up to a new perspective, but to practice formal writing.

My assigned book was *Eat, Pray, Love* by Elizabeth Gilbert. I remember an excerpt about what a soul mate was and its role. Basically, in summary, it was that your soul mate is a mirror of our own—a perfect fit in another person. It talked about how your soul mate only came into your life briefly to tear down your walls and to reveal layers about yourself that you didn't know you had; to change you. It seemed silly then, but now . . .

The things that it said were exactly what Breyson was to me; so much so that it's scary when looking at them in comparison. Could he have been sent to me by a higher power to wake me up from the person that I was and the person that I was on the path to becoming? It seems paranormal, but weirder things happen all the time. There are so many things about life we don't understand.

I'm done trying to figure out the question of why. It's like running around in circles. It's exhausting, and you end up exactly where you started.

Preston is still looking at me, saying nothing more. If Breyson was sent to me to show me the kind of life I was missing by living the way I was, then it worked. I can't go back to the person I was before I met him. I want to live in love and happiness. "Okay. We can wait until we're married. When do you want to get married?"

He smiles—a rare, earth-shattering smile. "December."

"What's so special about December?"

"Bryce will be here and it'll be long enough after you deliver that we can properly enjoy our honeymoon," he says, matter of fact. Of course, his business side comes out.

"Okay. December it is."

He kisses me, and I can feel him harden beneath me again. "You've made me a happy man. The company is hosting an event at the end of August. It's to announce a buy-in for some land overseas. Dad wants to expand globally and we're starting with a resort in Greece. I have to be present to oversee groundbreaking in December. We can honeymoon there with Bryce and we'll be back in January for the opening of your cheerleading studio. The renovations are already confirmed with a start date, and you can supervise it until we leave."

Why do I get the feeling I'm not going to like the rest of this conversation? "What exactly are you asking?"

"It's similar to the charity event we had a couple of weeks ago, but this one is going to be bigger with more people. I'm starting to pop up in the magazines as one of the most eligible bachelors because of my age and family's business reputation. I want the world to know I'm a taken man. I want to announce our engagement at the event."

The bomb has been dropped. He knows I hate charity events or large masses of money-hungry people. I will never be a trophy wife and he knows this. "Preston," I whine. "You know I hate attending stuff like that. All those people make me nervous."

Tugging my hair downward, he bares my neck to him, and then licks from my collarbone to the lobe of my ear. A moan unintentionally escapes my lips. "You'll be fine. I promise I won't leave you and I'll make it worth your while."

"I don't know . . ."

As if he won't take no for an answer, he places his thumb in his mouth and sucks. He then places the wet pad over my clit and begins rubbing in a circular motion. It feels so good I can't think straight. "I'll do whatever it takes until you agree. A satiated woman is a happy woman. I can be very convincing," he says seductively.

"Yes," I say as he brings me to the edge. "Right there."

I can feel his smile pressed against my neck as he delivers the orgasm I needed. "I knew you'd see it my way." He kisses me on the lips as he throws his legs over the side of the bed. "Just remember you said yes. No backing out. It's always been our most absolute rule."

Crap. I should have known . . .

The one rule we made up when we all used to play together and conjure up daredevil schemes to occupy our time as kids in the summer. I was the reluctant one and would always agree in the heat of the moment and then try to back out when the worry set in of what I had agreed to.

I was also one of those kids that didn't like to break the rules either, so he figured out a way around it by making a list of game rules to keep me from backing out at the last minute, and stupid me never even caught on until I was older.

"You ass." I laugh and try to push him backward by pressing on his chest, but he already has a tight hold from behind.

He stands with me in his arms, pregnant and all. I wrap my legs around his waist, scared he'll drop me. "Hey, don't hate just because my plan worked."

"Where are we going?"

"To make out in the hot, steamy shower. I seem to remember a concert on the beach mentioned in passing yesterday." I rub my fingers through the back of his hair. I'm finally starting to feel a little of the excitement that has been absent for some time now.

THIRTY-SEVEN

Kinzleigh

My stomach growls uncontrollably. I shouldn't wait so long to eat between meals. After finally getting over the whole pregnancy sickness thing, I don't want it back.

It's a little after lunch, and having a shower makes me feel better. Wrapping the fluffy, white towel around my body, I tuck it and begin walking out of the bathroom and across the bedroom, toward the stairs.

I stop when I reach the door. Preston is sitting on the bed with his laptop and phone in front of him, as well as papers scattered all around him. "I'm going to make me some lunch. Do you want any?"

"Sure," he says, and looks at me. "I have to work for an hour or so and then we can go. I didn't figure you wanted to be there all day anyway. Is that okay?"

The beach event is supposed to be an all-day thing. There will be several bands that perform well into the night, some I know and some I don't. I have no desire to be there until the evening when it starts to cool off. Pregnancy and heat do not mesh well, and besides, the thought of wearing a swimsuit disgusts me.

"That's fine. I'm sure I can find stuff to do. Mom shipped some more boxes I need to unpack. I'll leave you to it." I open the door and he calls out my name as I walk down the hall a few feet.

"Hey, Kinzleigh." I peek my head back inside the door. "What do you think of me converting the basement into an office for when I need to work at home? I can be home with you more that way. I'd rather save the bedrooms in case we ever need them. Did you have any plans for it?"

"It's all yours, babe. I never go down there. You don't have to ask. This is your house."

"It's our house," he retorts. "Everything that is mine is equally yours."

I roll my eyes. "Whatever you say. Lunch will be ready in about thirty minutes. Come down when you're ready."

I disappear down the hall and run my fingers through my wet hair as I descend the stairs. Walking into the kitchen, I make my way to the pantry. I pull out random things that may or may not go together. I guess I'm going to have to learn to improve my cooking skills. If not, we are going to starve or get fat from eating out.

Setting the various packaging on the counter, I remember the chicken breasts in the freezer. I guess chicken salad sandwiches will suffice. As I open the freezer door, the doorbell chimes.

Who could that be?

It rings three more times before I'm able to make it to the front door. Of course, someone decides to visit the one time I don't put on clothes. Looking down at my body, I make sure all the inappropriate parts are covered. I crack the door just enough for me to stick my head out, immediately surprised. I was in no way prepared for who is standing on the other side.

"Macie?"

"Hey, Kinzleigh." She looks around and then back at me. "May I come in?"

"Of course." I use the door as a shield and open it, keeping my body covered. She steps inside and her eyes go wide as she takes in our house. I shut the door and clutch the towel in my hand, afraid it may come untucked. "Are you okay?"

She is carrying a duffel bag strapped to her body. "I know I should have called first, but the only people that I knew had your number hate me. The truth is, I needed to get away for a few days. I didn't know where. I went to the cemetery to tell Beau I wouldn't be back for a while and I thought of you."

She looks a little embarrassed. "I found out where you lived and went by your house. Your mom was there and told me where to find you. I guess I could've gotten your number from her. I'm sorry. Maybe I should go."

She turns around and takes a step toward the door. If she leaves now, I may never see her again. She looks as awful now as she did the day I saw her at his grave. "Macie, wait . . ." I grab her arm, stopping her. "You can stay here for as long as you need."

The look in her eyes is one that says a weight has been lifted from her shoulders. You can tell just by looking at her that she has been living in agony since he died. It makes me realize how much Preston has helped me to slowly let go of Breyson, making the pain of missing him more bearable.

I've learned that when you truly love someone and lose them, you'll never totally rid of the pain, but it's how you learn to carry on living with the pain that makes the difference.

She doesn't have anyone in her life like Preston, Adalynn, Braxton, Briar, or Londyn. She's completely alone. Everyone has judged her and left her to wallow in guilt and sorrow on a daily basis.

I don't know how I can help her, but I will spend every second that I can trying. "You're coming with us tonight. You need a night to be free with no exploitation from the people around you. No one knows you here. No one will pass judgment for who you were or who you will become. They will only know you for who you allow yourself to be right now."

She blinks, and a tear is expelled from her eye. "Teach me how to be someone else. Please." The begging in her tone breaks my heart. It's evident that she is dying inside.

"Of course, I will teach you," I say in the most absolute way I know how. "Me and you are a lot alike in ways. We should stick together."

THIRTY-EIGHT

Kinzleigh

I come bursting through the bedroom door, slamming it behind me. Clenching my towel in my fist, I lean my head against the bedroom door.

Preston is walking around the room in a pair of faded denim jeans with the band of his boxer briefs peeping out of the top. He's rubbing his hand through his hair as he speaks into the phone held up to his ear with the opposite hand.

For some reason, this image is sexy.

Think, Kinzleigh, think.

He glances at me standing against the door and stops. "Finish briefing me later. Something suddenly came up." He slides the phone in his pocket and walks toward me. "Why do you look like you've seen a ghost? Are you hurt?"

"I'm probably about to drop a bomb on you," I say nervously. I should have asked before I volunteered to let her stay. It's good manners, and also a sense of respect to others living in the house. I give him my best fake smile in hopes that he doesn't get mad.

"Go on . . ."

He looks amused. That's a good start. "Well . . . it's kind of funny, really. I was in the kitchen deciding what was for lunch and the doorbell rang, so

I went to see who it was."

"You answered the door in that?" he asks, interrupting me. Of all the questions he could have asked that's the first thing he thought of. Men—they are all the same.

"I was limited in options. That's beside the point. Anyway, when I opened the door it was someone from home, as in my parents' current place of home. That someone is going through a rough time, like me, but she doesn't have anyone to help her through it like I do with you." Maybe if I just get it all out, he won't think about it. "I told her she could stay with us for a while," I blurt out.

I close my eyes as the last syllable escapes my lips. A moment later, I peek out of one. He's biting his lip with a smile breaking through. Clearly, he's trying not to laugh. Fully opening my eyes, I push off the door. "What's so funny?"

"Did you really think I was going to be mad?" He closes the distance between us and stops in front of me.

"Yes. I realized, after the fact, that I probably should have ran it by you first." He inches his face closer to mine.

"When are you going to get it through that thick skull of yours that what's mine is yours . . . and vice versa," he purrs, and closes his hand around the tucked towel above my breasts.

He tugs, releasing the fold between the two and the towel falls to the floor in a pile. He grabs a breast in each hand and walks me backward until I'm back against the door with a soft thud. "You're wearing my ring, Kinzleigh Baker, and soon you'll take my name. Anything I have is yours. All I want in exchange is to call you mine, forever."

My breathing picks up from his touch. He has to stop saying things like that. I like hearing it a little too much. It's strange to be honest. "So, she can stay?" I don't know why I asked. I suppose to occupy my mind.

He runs his hands down the sides of my body and snakes them around until he's cupping my butt. He kisses below the lobe of my ear and traces the tip of his tongue down the length of my neck. "If you want her to stay, she stays."

How is it that he can turn me on at the drop of a few words and touches to my body? It has to be the pregnancy hormones.

I have the strangest feeling. It's one of those feelings that takes over your body and controls your limbs. Grabbing the back of his neck, I pull his lips to mine. I need to feel the heat of his kiss. I want to feel his skin against mine. What does this mean?

His hand descends until it reaches my thigh. He picks up my right leg and wraps it around his waist. I can't get as close as I want to because of my stomach. It's not enough. I deepen the kiss and it becomes a hunger that I can't feed; a thirst that I can't quench. I have no idea what is wrong with me, but I can't stop. I don't want to stop. I want him to take me to bed . . . I think I'm ready.

"Preston," I moan in shortened breaths as I release my lips from his.

"Tell me what you need."

"Make love to me."

As if I just released a monster, he picks me up and turns for the large unmade bed. His kiss is rushed and needy. "Are you sure? I thought we were going to wait. We really need to wait . . ." His words and his actions say two different things.

I have no idea why, but I'm completely sure. I don't understand these feelings. I've only loved one man and those feelings were different, and many things in one: uncontrollable, life-altering, earth-shattering, even deadly, but this . . . This is different.

These feelings get stronger every day. They grow like a plant instead of hitting you like a freight train at full speed. These are heightened in his presence and dull when he's absent, whereas with Breyson, it was always constant and amplified. We were always at full throttle with each other. Why is that? I can't love two people, can I? Is it possible to love two people in different ways? "Yes. I'm sure."

"You have no idea how long I've waited to hear you say that. Damn." Placing his knee on the bed, he lays me down in the center.

He's standing at the side of the bed, looking at me, as he unbuttons his jeans. His eyes are burning into mine, never leaving their sight on me. From my peripheral vision, he hooks his thumbs under the band of his briefs and lowers his jeans and underwear in unison to the floor, before stepping out of them completely.

He's rock-hard. Picking up my foot, he places it to his lips and kisses the inside of my ankle gently. "I've visualized this day so many times. I love you, Kinzleigh. I always have and always will."

Placing my foot flat on the bed, he grabs underneath my knees and spreads me open. He then rests on his bent knees on the bed and closes the distance between our bodies, caressing his hands from my knees to the crease next to my most intimate place.

His touch is light enough to send my need for him into overdrive, but hard enough I feel every brush. "I love you too, Preston." My voice takes on a needy whisper and I didn't even mean to say it aloud.

His breath catches. It's the first time I've actually said it as a lover's term of endearment and not in a friendly manner during a conversation like the night in the hotel room.

I haven't thought much of it. It just came out of nowhere. I can't take it back and I'm not sure I want to. I miss having love and being in love. Is that so wrong? It is kind of soon, but do we really get to pick and choose when it happens or with whom?

He places one hand on the bed to hold his weight and the other on the side of my stomach, alongside my ribcage where my tattoo resides. He lowers his lips to mine, and I can feel the tip of his dick touching my entrance.

It ignites a desire in me that I haven't felt in months. I need this. I need a pleasure that will blanket every inch of me, inside and out. I need freedom from the pain left by the absence of the only man that has ever claimed me this way.

Someone else doesn't have to understand it. I'm not asking for understanding. Judgement comes easy when a person doesn't walk in the same shoes as the person they're judging. It's surprising what a person will do to eliminate the constant nagging of the hole in your chest.

Wrapping my legs around his waist, I dig my heels into his butt, trying to pull him closer. "Do you want it, baby?" he asks, as he releases the hold on my lips.

Our faces are so close that I can feel his breath when he speaks, warming my already heated lips. "Yes," I tell him. One word is about to change everything.

I thought Breyson would be my one and only, but assumptions get you exactly where I am today—a different plan entirely. I haven't wanted this since Breyson and I never thought I would again, but for some unknown reason, I want it with Preston.

He aligns himself, ready to enter, when something painful shoots through my side. "Ouch," I say. It wasn't enough to cause alarm, but it was enough to take my breath away and catch me off guard.

His eyes widen. "Was that the baby?"

I'm a little confused. "Was what the baby?"

"You don't feel that? Right here under my hand." When I actually pay attention, I do feel Bryce move underneath his hand. I think that's the first time someone other than me has felt him—movement from the outside. It's why his question threw me for a loop.

"You can feel him?" A cheesy grin spreads across his face. Bryce moves again. When he does a pain shoots through my leg, leaving a numbing sensation. It's enough to make me squint my eyes until they're closed and scrunch my face. It feels like a pinched nerve or something.

"Kinzleigh, maybe we should wait until after your doctor appointment to have sex. I don't think any form of pain is supposed to be a good thing. Those looks aren't good for a guy's ego. Are you okay? What's wrong?"

I open my eyes as I realize the direction he's heading. "No, I'm fine. It's fine. It just caught me off guard. I'm ready." I try to pull him closer to me.

He shakes his head as he bites back a smile. "As much as it kills me to tell you no after wanting this for so long with you, the baby is more important. I don't want to do anything that could hurt you or him. I don't think it's going to kill us to wait one more week. You do have another checkup next week, right?"

"You have got to be freaking kidding me. Please tell me you are. Preston, no. I'm fine, really. I want it. I want this with you. Just put it in already. Come on. You've been building me up since that night in the hotel before I came back with you. Hooking up isn't doing it anymore. I want sex." I know I'm whining, even begging, but I don't care. When I make a decision, I usually stick to it. I want this.

"It's just a week, baby. Once we make sure it's nothing then we will have sex five times a day if you want. I just don't want to do anything that could hurt you. Come on, you can introduce me to our house guest."

I'm sexually frustrated. I want him to know how aggravated I am right now. It may be childish, but so be it. Guys get to act pissy when they don't get laid. I think girls should have the same right.

He leans down to kiss me, but I turn my head. "Don't be like that," he says.

I push on his chest. I want up. I'm the one pregnant. What entitles him to make this decision solely? Shouldn't I be the one to decide what is okay for my body and what isn't?

He is getting pissed, but I don't care. Instead of saying something like I thought he was, he gets up. I sit up and stand from the bed in a hurry, but my leg gives out on me. The same leg that had the shooting pain.

I start to fall but he grabs my arm. "Dammit, Kinzleigh, chill out.

Something isn't right. I know you're mad but get over it. Fuck, sometimes your health is more important than your damn pride."

I don't like to be talked to like a child. It triggers my bitch nerve like a spark. I try to pull from his grasp, but he tightens his hold. "Sit down, Kinzleigh. You can be mad at me whenever you can walk without the possibility of falling and hurting yourself or the baby."

I release my frustration verbally, and like a child, throw a tantrum. I want to rebel, but instead, I sit on the edge of the bed like he says. I hate how mad I feel right now. To avoid the tears I can feel coming, I place the heels of my hands over my eyes. He begins rubbing in a circular motion up my legs. "Kinzleigh, look at me."

My eyes are starting to sting. I have no idea why I'm so mad. Maybe from being shut down the one time I actually wanted to go through with scx, or maybe it's just these stupid pregnancy hormones.

I don't recall a time ever being told no when I wanted to have sex with Breyson once we got past the hurdle of waiting in the beginning of him wanting to prove we were more. He never could tell me no. I always had that control with him in the bedroom, and I liked it.

As much as I want to sit here and pout, I open my eyes and look at him. He's kneeling between my legs. I can't deny how sexy this visual is—him naked and on his knees between my legs. "I can assure you that I want to have sex a hell of a lot more than you do. I've waited for this exact moment for years, but I'm not going to let my dick make a decision that could have consequences. I don't know anything about pregnancy. Maybe I'm being brash, but I'd rather be safe than sorry. You and this baby mean everything to me whether you believe it or not, and the thought of something happening to either of you does not sit well with me. If you don't want to wait until your appointment, we can call the doctor first thing in the morning. Okay?"

He does have a good point. It's a little humiliating. My short temper always gets the best of me. "Okay. I read something about the baby sitting on the sciatic nerve awhile back. Maybe that's what it is."

He softly kisses my lips and stands. "Come on. Let's get dressed and go downstairs. We're being rude staying locked up here anyway."

Holding out his hand for me, I take it, and he never lets go the entire time I walk to the closet. I dress for the beach party in the comfort of sand-colored linen pants and a pink tee shirt.

I slide on my flip-flops while I wait on Preston to finish dressing in shorts and a polo. Once he fills his pockets with his wallet and keys, we both go downstairs.

The day has definitely taken an interesting turn, and now I'm not sure what to expect. I haven't seen hardly any of my friends from school yet, and now I'm very pregnant.

On top of that, I have a new friend in the mix that I have to show a good time. With her, everything counts right now, and she needs me. She wouldn't have come here if she wasn't desperately seeking help.

Tonight, I'll have to act less like an eighteen-year-old girl that's tired from pregnancy and more like the eighteen-year-old I should be.

Macie turns to look back from the couch that she is sitting on as we reach the bottom of the stairs. She looks from me to Preston, and when she does her eyes grow round in shape. It doesn't even faze me. Preston gets that kind of look from everyone, especially girls.

Well, everyone except me. For some reason, it never affected me the way it does everyone else, but I've also known him my entire life. He has this powerful aura around him that draws people; he always has. I guess it has something to do with coming from one of the wealthiest families around.

She stands as we round the couch and wipes her hands down her denim skirt. She straightens her posture and holds out her hand in front of her. "I'm Macie. It's nice to meet you," she says nervously.

Preston walks forward from the place we are currently standing and wraps his arm around her shoulders in a sideways hug. "Handshakes are for business deals and acquaintances. If you're a friend of Kinzleigh's, you're a friend of mine. You're welcome to stay here as long as you'd like. Utilize the amenities as if you live here."

His hospitality is surprising, yet I don't know why. Everything Preston does is surprising. He turns to look at me as he releases her from the friendly embrace. "I'm going to finish up some calls about the basement. Show her to her room and then we'll eat out on the way to the concert. Sound good?"

"Sure. Come on, Macie. I'll show you to the lower level guest room, unless you want to be on the upper level in a guest room close to us. This one will give you more privacy, though." Preston takes that as his cue to excuse himself in the direction of the basement.

"I'm not a picky houseguest. Anything you have is probably nicer than what I'm used to. Talon and I share a room at my mom's." Share a room? Sometimes I forget how fortunate I am. I've never had to share a room before. Actually, it's the complete opposite. I could've had multiple rooms had I wanted them.

"Why do you have to share a room?" I ask out of curiosity. I walk through the kitchen in the direction of the hallway that leads to the largest bedroom aside from the master suite.

She is following close behind me from the sound of her footsteps on the tile floor. "We live in a small, three-bedroom, wood-frame house, and my brother still lives at home. After I got pregnant and Beau died, I was forced to move back home, because dead-end jobs don't pay enough to get our own place when having to feed and clothe another person."

I feel really bad for her. We're in the same situation, but then we're not. I have family that can afford to help me out if I need it and that doesn't even include Preston. I've never had to go without anything. I stop at the door to her room. "What about school?"

She closes her eyes briefly before she answers. "My mom couldn't afford to pay for my school. I was on an honors scholarship. A requirement to keep the scholarship was to reside on campus in the dorms and keep up good grades. I can't live in a dorm with a baby, so I had to drop out. I haven't had the funds to go back and my mom can't work because of a back disability she incurred when she was a nurse. I have to work two jobs just to help out with the bills. She helps me with my son, though. I work at a clothing store during the day and a twenty-four-hour gym at night. I've always wanted to own my own boutique, but it doesn't look like that's ever going to happen, and I've accepted it."

I can tell she longs for a better life but doesn't have a way to attain it. "What about your dad?"

"I never met him. My mom won't tell me who he is, because he has a family. She used to be a travel nurse and had a short-term affair with one of the attending physicians. I was the result. He wanted her to abort me. She wanted to keep me. My brother's father raised me until he was killed in an offshore accident. He worked on an oil rig in the gulf." She is clenching her bag as if she's getting uncomfortable with this conversation. My curiosity wants to know more about her, but maybe it's best to let it go.

"Well, tonight that Macie gets a break. Tonight, you can be anyone you want to be. Bury all of the things you wish you could forget and be free until you have to go back home. How long do you have until you have to go back home?" I ease the door open, waiting on her to answer.

"My mom and brother volunteered to take care of Talon for one week when I mentioned getting away. I think they're hoping I'll find happiness somewhere, but it'll never happen." I nod, knowing exactly what she means, and walk inside the large room.

The bedroom has a king size bed sitting in the center of the room. It's decorated in gray and lilac colors with touches of ivory in sporadic locations such as the throw pillows. The furniture sits perfectly nestled in various places around the room, empty and ready for use.

The on-suite bathroom has never been used and the walk-in closet is filled with boxes of my clothes that Mom shipped to me. I put them in here until I lose this pregnancy weight. There is no reason to take up our closet space when I can't fit in them right now.

Actually, I have an idea. "Macie, when is the last time you fixed yourself up?" She's absolutely gorgeous with her long, brown hair with its natural hints of caramel, gray eyes, and perfect complexion, not to mention her body, but I'm more so just confirming what I think.

"It was the last frat party I went to with Beau—the night before I found out I was pregnant with Talon." I look at the ceiling as I figure out the math in my head.

"I see," I say, trying not to make a big deal about it. The fact that she has lived like a zombie for over four years has me silently panicking on the inside.

How is she still alive after mourning for that long? I can understand never loving anyone to that depth again, because I'm there, but to never have the longing to be in the presence of a man again after experiencing love at that magnitude is hard to imagine.

The thing about loving someone the way I imagine that she loved Beau, or me with Breyson, is that it marks you. It leaves scars on your mind known as memories. Each time you recall one you long to have it back with someone, even if small in comparison to the first time around.

Love is an unforgettable emotion. No matter how hard you try, it's unavoidable at some point. I tried to run from it, but it catches you, hooks you, and then moves on to the next victim. When the high fades or gets taken from you, you can't help but to go looking for it in someone else.

Love is one of only a few things that makes the world continue to turn. If that weren't the case, no one would remarry or move on. Isn't it said somewhere that love and happiness go hand in hand? If that's the case, then will the permanent absence of one lead to the other?

The loneliness of Breyson being gone destroyed my ability to love and kept me in a miserable state. It wasn't until I allowed myself to feel something for Preston that some of the happiness returned, and in turn made it possible for me to love again.

If she doesn't choose to find the possibility of happiness, will her ability to love be impaired? Will she have to learn to let go of Beau before she can be happy again, or will it take someone pushing her in that direction? I'm going to assume the latter, because clearly, the former isn't going to happen if left up to her. "Go in the bathroom and get cleaned up. Relax. Take some 'you' time. I have the perfect outfit for you to wear tonight and I'm sure you want a hot shower after coming all the way from Mississippi, or even a long bath."

"Okay." She walks into the bathroom but stops inside the door. "Hey, Kinzleigh . . ." I glance at her, but I am still a little lost in my own thoughts. "Thank you for letting me stay. I've been drowning for a while."

She shuts the door, leaving me with that vital piece of information. That word—drowning—says so much more than I think she intended. She's searching for someone to save her, and she came to me.

THIRTY-NINE

Kinzleigh

We arrive at the beach just as the sun is setting. It's packed with cars and bodies are scattered everywhere. I look back at Macie in the backseat. She's even more beautiful than I imagined she would be. It's like polishing a raw diamond. You know the beauty is there, but it needs a little work to be brought up to its full potential.

Her hair falls in loose waves from being curled and the black, off the shoulder top accentuates her petite frame. The short, white, denim shorts elongate her legs and brings out the bronze hues in her skin. Her body is to die for, and every time I've seen her, she has it covered with loose clothing.

The gold dusted on her eyelids makes her gray eyes pop without overdoing it. Her makeup is light with a little bit of eyeliner, mascara, and clear gloss. She looks like she's about to hurl.

When Preston kills the engine to the car his eyes meet mine. "Will you give us a minute?"

"Sure. I'll be standing at the front waiting." He opens the door and leaves us alone.

"Are you okay?" I ask when I know he's out of earshot.

Her eyes are scanning the crowd. "I think so. It's just been a long time since I've been around people this way. I work an hour away from home so no one knows who I am, and I'm only there to work."

"You're a long way from home. No one will know you here. First thing's first. What do you want your name to be?" If she is going to totally let loose, it might as well be all or nothing. Even though it's not likely, I've learned that you never know when you're going to run into someone, regardless of how far you are from home. I know, I moved to the same school as Breyson once.

Her eyebrows dip like she's thinking. "Lauren," she says. "It's my middle name. No one hardly knows my middle name." She closes her eyes and repeats it as if she's trying to convince herself. "I'm ready," she whispers, and opens her eyes. "I'm ready," she repeats, more sternly this time.

I may even be as nervous as she is. I don't think anyone knows that I'm pregnant, let alone that it's not Preston's, and I don't know how everyone will react. We might be holding onto each other if this doesn't go well. "It's like getting used to cold water. We just have to go all in at once. No dipping the toes in."

As we step out of the car, we meet Preston at the hood. He cups his hand on the back of my neck and pulls me close to him where no one else can hear. "Have you decided what you want to tell everyone? It's you and me 'til the end. If you want to keep down questions, we can tell everyone he's mine. You are wearing my ring. No one has to know the truth but us. It's none of their damn business."

It seems so wrong to lie. I feel like it's cutting Breyson out of the one thing that is and will always be his, but I don't want to rehash my life events and open old wounds over and over again. I've finally gotten to a point since Breyson died that I'm starting to move on and be happy. I don't want to break down again by letting my thoughts run wild. "We can tell them he's yours if you want."

He kisses my lips, but only a light brush; I would imagine to avoid making Macie feel awkward. "Not much longer and you're all mine . . . forever. Both of you. I can't wait." I return a small smile and we all begin walking toward the beach.

As we weave through bodies, I glance down the beach from left to right. The mixed colors painting the sky still light up the beach—the last step before nightfall.

The ocean is filled with surfers that haven't given up for the day and a few people in waist-deep water. Blankets and coolers are scattered all over the beach and layered with people sitting and lying.

A short distance down the strip of sand I can see a stage set up with people clothed in something other than swimsuits surrounding it. That's where we need to be. "Preston, down there," I say, and point in the direction I want to go.

As we get closer, I can hear music playing. It's not a band I'm familiar with, but they sound good. I think the bands are supposed to change every half-hour of so until the early hours of the morning.

We stop at the back of the crowd to listen to the band currently playing. I scan the crowd for Presley. She said she was going to be here. "Kinzleigh? Preston? Do my eyes deceive me or is this shit real?"

That voice was not the first one I wanted to hear. As a matter of fact, it's not one I care to hear at all. She used to be my friend, or at least I thought, until she acted like a complete bitch at Presley's pool party last summer. The slur in her tone of overdone excitement tells me she's drunk. She's that girl that you avoid when she's drunk, because all she does is stir up drama. "Hey, Lexi."

She bounces in our direction as she weaves through the bodies in close proximity, clearing her path. "Well, well. I guess it is true. You two finally quit lying to yourselves and gave in. It's about time. Everyone else saw it. I don't know why you didn't, Kinzleigh. There never was or will be a more perfect couple than you two."

Her voice sends chills up my spine. It drips of sarcasm. What happened to her? She seems so bitter. She wraps her arms around me, pulling me into an awkward hug. "We have missed you around here. You can take the girl out of California, but not California out of the girl. I knew it was a matter of time until you came back. You always were Hollywood at heart. Wait a minute," she says, and cups her hands over my shoulders, putting distance between us.

She looks down at my stomach and over at Preston. "You don't waste any time, do you? Was this your insurance policy for keeping little miss perfect?"

"Knock it off, Lexi." I can hear the annoyance in his tone. Everyone is used to this kind of behavior when it comes to her. She's jealous of everyone that has more than her. Her parents are comfortable, but not rich.

I grab her wrist with my left hand to remove it from my body, but she stops me with her other hand. "You have to be fucking kidding me."

She is looking at the ring on my left finger. I had forgotten it was even there. "You did it on purpose, didn't you? This was part of your grand scheme in becoming a professional cheerleader, wasn't it? Your security blanket to keep a perfect lifestyle on a tiny salary, so you wouldn't have to find a job to pay the bills when Daddy's money ran dry."

I've never been more humiliated in my life. I look at Macie, who looks mortified, and over at Preston, who's glaring like he's about to murder her.

Because she is letting the alcohol flow through her veins and alter her brain, she doesn't stop there. She looks at Preston as she speaks this time. "At least when me and you were fucking, I had the decency to use birth control, so you didn't have a bastard child in a family that thrives on a perfect reputation, but then you were always extra careful with the rest of us."

She looks from Preston back to me. "I didn't get as much time as the rest of them, because I'm not *blonde* like you. I got one time with him and then he moved on to girls that he could easily pretend were you in his mind. Did he tell you that, sweet girl? How someone else does all the work of getting him up but he *comes* calling out your name? Not all of us can be the perfect, innocent little Kinzleigh Baker."

I slap her, hard. I didn't plan it. It just happened. It was like a reflex when I heard her say those things, especially about my child. I won't tolerate anyone calling him a bastard. He was created in love, and I don't owe anyone an explanation, but no one talks about my family that way.

I may have to answer to God for conceiving my child outside of marriage, but my child doesn't deserve to be spoken of that way when it isn't his fault. Breyson deserves more than that.

Wait a minute. It just clicked. I look at Preston, and he doesn't look happy. In fact, the look on his face as he looks at her is terrifying. If she was looking at him instead of boring a hole in my head, she would likely back off. "Is she the one you lost your virginity to?"

His eyes relax a little when he looks me in the eyes. Guilt takes the place of his anger. Maybe because of what happened between her, Breyson, and me at Presley's pool party last year. I don't understand what I did to her. "It was a long time ago, Kinzleigh," he says in a hushed tone.

Why does this girl have to be involved with every guy I actually begin to have deep feelings for? I remember the words that came from Preston's mouth. *When I lost my virginity, it was the first girl that took an interest in me sexually and she was nothing like you.*

Has she been plotting some kind of evil revenge on me since the beginning? I feel so hurt right now. I have done nothing to deserve her hatred. I look back and she is holding the side of her face in a stunned manner.

She moves closer to me in a way to intimidate someone. "How does it feel to know you get my seconds for once? Hand-me-downs don't feel so good, do they?"

I narrow my eyes in anger. It's sad really. Maybe she's gone crazy. I'm about to just tell her the truth when someone speaks behind me. "I advise you to walk the fuck away, Lexi. When you mess with Kinzleigh, you mess with my family. I protect what's mine. You're about to place yourself in a man's shoes. Are you sure you want to do that?"

My eyes blur just before I close them. I haven't heard that voice in so long. It's like a trigger to things that have been locked away lately, but it's also like coming home. *Ryland.*

FORTY

Kinzleigh

Lexi stares behind me and begins backing away. "Fine. I said my peace. I just did what the rest of the girls around here have wanted to do but didn't have the backbone to do it."

She turns and walks away, leaving me to remain in the pool of embarrassment she threw me in. The band is still playing, but the sea of people that surround us are staring as if it's the most interesting thing that's happened all night.

I hate drama. I always have and always will. It's the one reason I'm glad high school is over. The sad thing is, people like Lexi will probably never change.

"Kinzleigh, are you okay?" A hand rests on top of my shoulder from behind. My shoulders fall. I can't explain what hearing his voice does to me. He's the closest thing I have left to Breyson, because he's where it all began.

I haven't seen Ryland in a year. I don't know what to expect when I turn around. Anything could happen with my emotions.

I pivot until I'm standing face-to-face with Ryland. He's wearing a swimsuit with water beads all over his body. He looks fitter than I remember. He no longer looks like a high school kid. He's starting to look like a man.

My eyes lock with his and that's when I recognize it—hurt. His demeanor is completely off. Ryland was always the fun loving, goofy kid. That was what drew you to him as a friend. He liked to have fun and he didn't care what anyone else thought. The serious vibe he is giving off is just . . . wrong. I don't like it.

"I'm okay. How are you? It's been a while . . ." For a second, I'm taken back to that week last summer of the four of us hanging out at his pool house. It seems like so long ago, yet it also seems like just yesterday. It's funny how that works.

He pulls me in for a hug against his damp chest. I assume he's been surfing. "Why don't we go someplace we can talk."

"Okay," I say, and can feel Preston getting closer. I remember that we aren't alone. We can't talk openly here. It's weird, but it feels like Breyson is something we share—our secret, even though he's not a secret at all.

I'm ashamed that I never thought to call and check on him. Braxton and Briar had each other, but who did Ryland have? Has he been dealing with Breyson's death alone? They were so close. I feel selfish that all I worried about was my own suffering and misery.

"She's not leaving my side," Preston says, stepping in closer.

"Do I need to give y'all some privacy?" Macie's voice finally brings me back to the present. Crap, I forgot she was here. I'm being rude. Everything that has just happened has me in a tailspin.

Ryland and I look at her at the same time. I guess her southern accent sticks out in California. It's one you don't hear that often.

"And you are?" he asks as he scans her body. The look in his eyes is one of pure male hunger and lust. I've seen that look before. It was the way Breyson used to look at me.

Hold the phone. Why is this just now occurring to me? This could have been really awkward. How do they not know each other? I look between the two of them as they stare at each other. What do I do? Oh, my gosh. I have no idea what to do. This completely goes against the grain of the original plan. "This is . . ." I'm stumbling over my words. "Well, she's . . ."

"I'm Lauren." She holds out her hand at Ryland. "I'm just a friend Kinzleigh met along the way. I came to visit for a few days."

A cocky smirk unfolds on his face. He takes hold of her small hand in his. "My friends call me Ry. It's always good to hear an accent from my neck of the woods."

This is the strangest thing I've ever been involved in. It's like knowing something top secret but being scared to voice it aloud to someone else.

"I thought she was . . ." My head whips in Preston's direction as the words tumble out of his mouth, like I'm trying to catch a falling vase before it shatters. This information could be disastrous. It may be wrong to keep it to myself, but that's something I'll have to live with. She doesn't need anything else thrown at her right now.

"She is staying for a week, babe. *Lauren* is here until next Sunday." I hope he catches the emphasis on her name as I stare daggers at him. Preston is clearly confused but refrains from saying anything more.

They are still staring at each other. "Want me to show you around, Lauren? I'm sure Kinzleigh doesn't mind if I borrow you for a while. I'll return you later."

Macie is starting to blush, or maybe it's the heat. I have an eerie feeling about this. Should I make up some excuse to get her to stay?

I'm putting something together, but when I see the smile on Macie's face it all comes crashing down. It's the first time I've ever seen her smile. Maybe it's wrong to let her go off blind with Beau's brother and him with Beau's girlfriend, but it's not in me to take away the one ounce of happiness I've seen on her. What can possibly happen in one night anyway?

Macie looks at me as if she's waiting for my opinion. "It's okay. Go have fun. You deserve it," I say, with a small smile of encouragement. "Ry will take care of you."

Her smile gets a little more pronounced. I keep thinking every second that they are together this big, invisible elephant in the room is going to show itself, but it doesn't. More questions definitely need to be asked before she goes back home.

He begins pulling her away from the crowd when I yell, "Do I need to wait for her or are you bringing her to our house?"

"I'll get her home. Text me the address. Don't wait up." The turn of events has me dizzy. I'm not in the mood to hear the bands anymore. I haven't even seen Presley, and usually she makes herself known wherever she goes. Where is she?

"Oh, Kinzleigh," he calls out as he continues walking, but now backward. "We still need to talk. I'll call you and we'll meet up."

In no more time than it took me to nod, I watch their retreating forms disappear into the crowd of people. Preston turns me to face him. "I'm sorry about Lexi. I don't know what her problem is, but I never expected her to act like that. If I had known anything like that was going to happen, I would've told you who it was. I didn't think that mattered at the time."

For what it's worth, he looks a little worried. That makes it a little better. I'm actually surprised I didn't have a panic attack. It seems like they are getting better and less frequent as time goes by. I'm finally able to control them again. "It's fine. It's not your fault. I never asked for a name anyway."

I stare off unintentionally. "What's on your mind?" He twirls a lock of my hair around his finger as his eyes settle on my lips.

I look up at him from underneath my lashes as I wrap my arms around his waist. My arms are stretched, because of my protruding stomach getting in the way between us. "I was just thinking. I don't really want to stay here anymore. Do you want to go see a movie? We could even stop for ice cream on the way home."

He kisses the middle of my forehead and brushes the tip of his nose down mine. "Sounds like a brilliant idea. I'm always up for anything when it comes to spending time with you."

Linking my hand in his, we walk hand-in-hand down the beach in the direction of where we parked. It's a summer night, but something in the air shifts. I can't explain it. The only thing I can compare it to is when you can sense a storm coming. It's a strange feeling, and one that leaves me uneasy.

I look over at Preston, but he looks completely at peace. I can't help but to think that something is about to happen. The water is calm, though, and everyone in passing is laughing and having a good time.

Maybe I'm letting Lexi's poisonous attitude get to me. I just need a change of scenery and everything will go back to the way it was, because nothing in my life is ever normal.

FORTY-ONE

Kinzleigh

The garage opens and Preston drives the car inside. It's late, but for some reason I'm not tired like I usually am.

The automatic light comes on as the garage door closes back into place. He grabs the grocery bag full of our favorite ice cream and we exit the car.

I stand at the door of the house, waiting on him to unlock it. "Go change into some comfortable clothes and I'll bring up our ice cream, okay?"

"Okay." I leave him to disable the alarm. Walking into the bedroom, I open the drawer full of my pajamas and begin shuffling through its contents. It's probably the only clothes I have unpacked in our bedroom from the stuff Mom shipped.

Something white peeking out from the bottom catches my attention. I'm not known to be the most organized person. My sleep clothes are just dumped in my drawer instead of being folded.

I grab ahold of it and pull it through the mound of clothes buried on top of it. When I get it out, I realize what it is, and my hearts plummets to my stomach.

It's Breyson's shirt that I've slept in on many occasions since his death, and it's never been washed, at least, I don't think it has.

I hold the fabric to my nose and breathe in, letting the fragrance permeate. I can still smell his cologne; although faint, it's still there.

As the scent lingers in the depths of my nostrils, the memory comes back of that day in my room where he left it, before we left for the airport. It's crazy how that happens—one familiar smell and memories you've worked hard to keep suppressed for your sanity are unlocked with no effort at all.

"You can wear it if you want to." His voice startles me, making me jump. I throw it back in the drawer and look in the mirror. Preston is standing just inside the door with two bowls full of ice cream.

I slide off my linen pants and toss them in the hamper. "I don't know how that got in there. I guess Mom found it in my room and sent it with the rest of my pajamas," I say, my words coming out jumbled together.

He walks toward me and sets the bowls down on top of the dresser. "Kinzleigh, you don't have to hide things from me. It's okay to still be sad sometimes when a memory resurfaces or you find something that reminds you of someone you loved. I've seen you do it with Grams throughout the years since her passing, and this is no different."

He grabs the bottom hem of my tee shirt and pulls it over my head. In one motion, he reaches behind me and unclasps my bra as he searches my eyes. "I told you when you came here with me that I knew you would have bad days, and that I would help you through them. Do I like that you loved someone before me, no, but can it happen, yes. If I didn't believe wholeheartedly that the heart can love more than once, I wouldn't have asked you to be mine."

He hooks his fingers under the straps that rest on my shoulders, pulling them down my arms until my bra falls to the floor. "If you want to wear it, then wear it. If it helps you on the days you miss him, then I'm okay with it. Selflessness is part of loving someone."

Reaching in the drawer, he pulls the shirt back out and places it over my head. All I can do is stare at the man before me as I place my arms in the appropriate holes, letting the shirt fall. It's snugger than the last time I wore it, but still fits loosely. "I'm just asking you to be open with me. Let me in. Don't hide things from me or lie to me. We're a team. When you hurt, I hurt, and when you're happy, I'm happy. Got it?"

With every passing day he tugs on my heartstrings more than the day before. I've always loved Preston as a friend, but it's quickly turning into something so much more.

I guess there is something to be said about a person that takes time to be your friend first and has the patience to stand by you even when you're mourning the loss of someone else.

He leans in and kisses me. "Come on, let's go watch movies and stuff ourselves full of ice cream before it melts. We can share and have two flavors instead of one."

He holds up his fingers to emphasize two with a big grin on his face. It makes me laugh. "Who said I wanted to share my rainbow sherbet?"

I grab my bowl off of the dresser and back away. He knows I'm teasing, but not by the expression on my face. I've always had an expert poker face when I needed one, as my dad would say—never giving anything away.

He picks up his bowl of mint chocolate chip and begins moving forward like an animal getting ready to pounce. "I can make you share."

He has a heated look in his eyes. Oh . . . my.

I dip my spoon in the bowl and scoop out a spoonful. Placing it in my mouth, I turn it face down on my tongue and seductively inch the spoon out, wiping it clean.

I close my eyes, savoring the cold as it melts, and moan as the fruity flavored ice cream coats my tongue. "Mmm."

When I open them, he is standing right in front of me, face almost touching mine. I didn't even hear him walking. He tilts his head to the side an inch and closes his lips on mine.

I haven't even had a chance to swallow the ice cream when he slips his tongue between the split of my lips. His tongue skims mine, playing in the cold liquid remaining in my mouth.

A throaty groan sounds as he grabs my breast through the fabric of the shirt. He pulls free, breaking the connection between the two of us. My breathing has turned heavy.

He licks his lips, making me want more. "I know what you're doing. It's not going to work. You're the sexiest damn woman I've ever laid my eyes on and my dick will probably hate me, but luckily, I pride myself on being a strong guy. When I say I want something, I don't stop until I get it. I'm patient. I won't bury myself inside you until after your doctor's appointment."

My mouth drops slightly. That cocky little bastard. I knew he was still buried somewhere down in there under all that caring and sweetness.

He shoves his spoonful of mint chocolate chip ice cream in my mouth. I close my lips around it, and he pulls the clean spoon from my mouth, before he kisses me on the edge of the lips. "See, sharing isn't so bad," he says, and walks to the bed, continuing to eat his ice cream.

What exactly just happened here? I'm really not even sure. Did I just get played in my own game? Damn him. I need to work harder, because I'm seriously lacking a much-needed skill.

I turn around to him sitting in the middle of the bed pigging out on his ice cream. He is staring straight ahead at the television that he hasn't even powered on yet. His lips are pursed together tightly between bites.

He knows I'm at a disadvantage and the little twerp thinks it's funny. It's hard not to find the humor in the situation. I guess I did set myself up for that.

The smile I'm trying really hard to hold back breaks free and I start to laugh; a laugh that quickly becomes uncontrollable. It's the hardest I've laughed in a really long time.

Apparently, it's contagious as well, because he almost spits ice cream when he bursts into laughter after me. I find my flip flop on the floor beside me and pick it up.

I throw it at him. It catches him off guard, causing him to have to swat in front of his face to knock it off its course to his nose. I laugh harder.

Suddenly, I stop cold and my eyes widen in surprise. I can feel my cheeks heating from embarrassment. He jumps up when he takes in my expression. "Kinzleigh, what's wrong?"

I hold up my hand in a stop position, hoping he won't come any farther. He doesn't get the memo. I back away. I want to crawl under a rock and die. If I could just get to the bathroom, maybe he won't notice. My panties are saturated, but I don't feel anything trickling down my leg. "It's nothing. Just don't come any closer."

I'm trying to come up with any excuse to get him out of here. "Kinzleigh, tell me what's wrong. You're scaring me. Is the baby okay?"

He continues stalking toward me. I run into something hard—the bathroom door. He grabs it before I can, keeping me from opening it. "I'm fine, Preston. We're both fine. Can I please have some privacy?"

He looks down when I inadvertently tug on the hem of the tee shirt and press my legs together. "Baby, why are you embarrassed? It's just me. It's normal. I read it in that book."

I look up at the ceiling as I try to keep the tears of humiliation from falling. I've never had a problem holding my bladder before. "You're a guy, Preston. I freaking peed on myself! How is that normal?" My tone continues to rise in pitch with each word.

"The bigger the baby gets, the more it will press against your organs, which includes your bladder, baby. It's fine. We've known each other our whole lives. Do you really think that's going to gross me out and suddenly make me change my mind?" I cannot believe we are standing here having this conversation, and at almost nineteen years old, I've peed in my underwear. If my panties are going to be wet, it should at least be from pleasure.

How is he always such a know-it-all? "Wait, what book?"

"That pregnancy book in the drawer by the bed." My eyebrows dip. I don't remember buying any pregnancy books. It's because *I* haven't . . .

The tear I was holding back defeats me and escapes. He is holding me hostage. One hand is holding onto the doorframe and the other is still residing on the doorknob. The answer is silently lingering between us, but I want confirmation. "You've been reading a baby book?"

He shrugs his shoulders as if this is not a big deal at all. "I like to be knowledgeable. We're about to have a baby, so I figured I needed to be prepared if anything happened. That way I can be calm if you're worried."

This is the biggest of bigs, and it makes my heart expand even more. All of the embarrassment I previously felt subsides, and a little more of the man that he truly is becomes revealed. What does it say about a man that reads a baby book for a woman carrying a child he didn't even conceive, especially when *I* haven't even read one?

I'm in complete awe of him. My eyes lock with his and I can't move them. I don't want to. I study them, trying to figure out why he's so good to me. "You're an amazing guy, Preston. Why me, when you could have anyone? No matter what you tell me, I still don't understand."

He releases the doorframe and cups the lower portion of my face in his hand. The softness in his touch becomes a need as he rubs his fingers along the curves of my lips. "Because no one else is my Kinzleigh. I want you and need you. That need runs deep to my core, and I don't care who knows it. Come on, let me bathe you. I want to take care of you."

Opening the door, he steps forward, inching me inside. He closes it behind us. The look in his eyes as he stares at me is more of a demand than a gesture. I don't argue.

This is what he needs. There isn't an ounce of lust in his eyes. "I want to have a life with you aside from sex. I want to be the man you can depend on and come to for anything. Let me take care of you."

He is staring at me, waiting for my approval. "Okay."

Without looking away, he turns on the water and begins filling the large tub. He allows himself to look away, but only long enough to add bubble bath and calming crystals. There are enough things lining the tub for comfort, soothing, and relaxation to last a year, but I have yet to use any of it.

As the tub fills, he grabs the hem of my shirt and pulls it over my head. I can't look anywhere else but at the man before me. I guess maybe it's curiosity of how it feels to let someone care for you this way. I've always been completely independent except for right after Brey died. I was dependent for completely different reasons. It was necessary, not voluntary.

He hooks his index finger under the inside waistband of my panties and slides them down my legs slowly, squatting as he forces them to descend. When they reach the floor, I rest my hands on his shoulders for support and step out.

He stands and guides me to the step of the tub, where I enter and sit down. I continue to watch him as he takes a seat on the side of the tub. "Relax, baby. I got you."

I lean against the back porcelain and slide down until I'm completely covered by the bubbly water, drenching my curls. The tub is set in a nook that gives it a sense of a hideaway.

He reaches over and grabs the remote, turning the main lights of the bathroom off and bringing the spotlights above the tub to a dim. He presses a few more buttons and soft jazz music begins to play through the speakers.

I have to admit this is nice. The hot water on my body is quickly easing my tension. The aroma of the bath scents opens my mind and allows me to think.

I close my eyes as he runs his hand through the water. I can't help but to think about Macie and all she has been through. I wish there was someone to help her. I've never had a problem with family or money. I have no idea how it feels being her.

As our conversation from earlier passes through my mind, an idea sparks. If I had stayed in Mississippi, surrounded by Breyson, I wouldn't be where I am today. It was leaving behind everything that reminded me of him that helped me to move forward without him.

Sure, California is where we met, but our life together was in Mississippi. Maybe what she needs is a clean break from it all. "Hey, Preston . . ."

I open my eyes to him squirting body wash on a loofah. He reaches in the water and picks up my foot closest to him, and rubs it from my toes up my leg, leaving suds in its wake. "What?"

I'm not sure how he is going to respond to this. I never ask him about anything related to work. "Would you be willing to hire Macie?"

He continues bathing me, but this time he looks at me. "Why?"

One word. I'm not sure that's a good start to the direction of this conversation. "I think it would help her to get a fresh start somewhere, but I don't see her leaving unless she has a justified reason. She's been through a lot; things worse than you or I have ever been through."

I lose my nerve halfway through. "Maybe it's stupid. I'm sorry. I shouldn't have asked and put that kind of pressure on you."

He's gazing at me with an intense stare. I'm starting to regret bringing up such an idea until he finally responds. "Consider it done. We will sit down and make her an offer before she leaves."

I'm a little stunned, to be honest. It was just a thought. I'm not sure that I expected him to agree, truthfully. "Are you sure? I don't want you to feel obligated to do something just because I asked you. It wasn't really my place to get in your business affairs."

He sets my washed leg back in the water and starts on my arm. "Actually, I've been looking for a personal assistant for a while now. I was about to pull the male applications, because every female I've interviewed so far comes across like they are looking for more than a job. This way we're both happy. You help out a friend and I get an assistant that is there to do a job and nothing else. The pay will be worth it, and I'll supply a place to live as well as childcare if she's available to travel. She is required to go where I go."

I don't know if she will go for it or not, but I guess there is no loss in asking, even if she doesn't accept the offer. I want to help someone the way I've been helped through the loss of Breyson.

I can't imagine where I would be right now if Preston hadn't come back for me. Also, I still feel at fault for Breyson's death. If I spend my life trying to help others, maybe I can get some peace in my soul for the guilt that is always there. "Thank you, Preston. It means a lot."

"I only have one condition." I don't like that phrase at all. Usually, it means he wants something that I'm not going to like, so he bargains for it with something that I really want. It's bribery.

I give him a pouty face; the same one I used to use on Brey. His serious expression never changes. Sometimes, I forget how different they really are.

Brey, how I wish you were here . . .

"What is it?" With Preston, there is never a hint as to what is going on it that mind of his. He is good at blocking his emotions from being readable.

"I know you want to have sex, and I want to worse, but . . ." There's that magical word—*but*. "I know I keep going back and forth, because I like to make you happy, and when you get in those raging pregnancy hormonal states it's the hottest thing I've ever seen, but I at least want to wait until after we announce our engagement. If you don't want to wait until we get married in December, I'll compromise."

I like the sound of compromise, because it shows maturity, and not someone on a power trip. He pauses briefly, but I don't say a word. "After the party, we'll go away for a few days to Barbados or somewhere. I just want it to be special, Kinzleigh. I've waited years for the chance to be your man. You're different to me than any other girl. I want the first time we make love to be after I've proven to the world that you're going to be my wife. I've made my decision."

He drops the loofah in the water and begins massaging the bottom of my water-wrinkled foot. His deep voice is relaxing. "I want us to spend more time getting to know each other as a couple, so when that time comes our connection is so deep it becomes a part of the intimacy as well, and not just a fuck because your hormones are crazy. I know you've only been with one person and it was meaningful to you because you loved him. I'll never try to replace that, but I've never had that with anyone, and I want it with you. Can you understand that?"

It's always hard when he brings up Breyson, but it's something that I'll have to get used to. My heart still hurts each time I think of my beautiful, blue-eyed boy and how much I miss him.

I've come to terms with the fact that the pain will never subside no matter how much or how fast I'm able to move on with someone else, but I guess that's part of true love. Like a limb removed from your body, you have to relearn how to live with its absence.

There is always a way to go on living, but it's a life-altering change. I'm still hoping that the connection of coming together in intimacy with Preston will drown out the constant, nagging pain in my mind, heart, and soul for Breyson.

When I think of the baby inside my womb that was created by another man, though, I'm still hesitant, no matter how much I want to take that next step with him. When I sit and think about it not in the heat of the moment, I have mixed emotions.

Maybe I need to talk to someone else that understands. It's a huge decision, and one that I don't need to take lightly. Once it happens, there is no going back. It's irreversible—final. "Okay, Preston. We will wait."

FORTY-TWO

Kinzleigh

I toss and turn in bed. The only light in the room is the numbers of the clock on the bedside table. I thought I would be fast asleep after my bath, but I've only been asleep for a couple of hours and now I'm wide-awake.

Preston's arm is wrapped around me and his body is pressed against mine from behind. I'm getting hot. He must have forgotten to turn the air down before bed.

Grabbing his hand, I gently lay it to rest on his side. He doesn't budge, so I turn back the thick comforter and sit up on the edge of the bed.

As quietly as possible, I stand and walk toward the door on my tiptoes. I feel like a little kid trying to sneak out without waking my parents. When I look back Preston is still sleeping peacefully.

I slowly twist the doorknob and crack the door open. When it doesn't make a sound, I continue to open it far enough I can walk out. I pull the door closed at a snail's pace, hoping not to wake him since he has to be up early for work.

The hallway is dark and quiet. I wonder if Macie ever came home. I texted Ryland the address before bed and told him where the extra key was located, but I never got a reply. I'm not sure whether to be relieved or worried.

I turn on the hallway light long enough to turn the temperature down until the air kicks on throughout the house. I have no idea what I'm going to do in the wee hours, but I'm not tired enough to go back to bed.

The rumbling of my stomach as I make my way down the stairs directs me to the kitchen for a snack. I don't know what I want, but I'm craving something salty after eating that ice cream earlier.

I walk across the cold tile of the kitchen in the direction of the food pantry. I begin rummaging through it, looking for some chips. I know they're in here somewhere. I find what I'm looking for and grab the bag.

As I'm pouring a bowl full of chips, I hear the side door open and hushed giggles. I stay where I am, because she has to come through the kitchen to get to her room. I stand perfectly still, and when I hear a husky voice followed by another laugh, I know she isn't alone. Their voices are thick with lust. I don't need confirmation to know what happened.

What the hell have I done?

My anxiety starts to pick up as the thoughts of them having sex run wild through my mind. My doctors have warned me about keeping it under control while I'm pregnant. I try to tune out the voices and close my eyes.

Breathe in. Breathe out. Repeat.

It takes a few minutes, but I manage to talk myself down from the spiral of emotions that were starting to take place. I'm probably overreacting. I doubt she slept with him. They just met. Maybe they're just flirting. He will leave and she'll never see him again. Neither of them has to know who the other is.

The door shuts and I hear footsteps. They are getting closer to me with each step. She walks through the kitchen and the sight causes me to drop the plastic bowl of chips in my hand.

She jumps at the sound of the bowl hitting the tile floor. "Kinzleigh? What are you doing up so late? Did I wake you?"

I can feel my face heating, but I can't speak, not yet anyway. "You slept with him, didn't you?" Based on what she's wearing, I know the answer.

No girl comes home wearing Ryland Reeves' boxers unless they were physically removed from his body like a token or trophy. Every girl in school wanted the blond surfer with dimples and a body to die for, and that was proof they got him for a little while. I know that much from Presley.

"What have I done?" I whisper aloud accidentally. I didn't mean for her to hear, but it slipped.

She rushes over to me and grabs me by the shoulders. "Kinzleigh, it isn't your fault. I'm an adult. I make my own decisions. There is just something about him that I can't place. I haven't been with a man since Beau, but I wanted this. Don't you dare blame yourself."

The look in her eyes kills me. It's the effect of a night in the sack with Ryland Reeves. I know that look, because I've seen it on girls before. She likes him. Like really likes him. The only person I know that's been with him that didn't wear it was Presley, because they are one in the same. I'm not sure they aren't still hooking up, honestly. "Macie, we need to talk."

What exactly do I tell her? I can't tell her she just had sex with her dead boyfriend's brother. That's a for sure way for someone to end up in the middle of a mental breakdown. But I can't let her fall for Ryland either. That would be the epitome of stupid. Just like Presley, he doesn't commit.

I'm not cut out for this sort of thing. How did this happen? I begin pacing back and forth behind the counter, crunching the chips under my feet, before hitting myself on the forehead with the heel of my hand.

"What do you need to talk to me about? You wanted me to have fun, so I did. What's the problem?" Her voice is low but agitated.

'What is the problem', she says . . .

If only you knew, little bird.

There is no easy way to do this. Anything I tell her is for her own good, even though both are bad. Just go with the lesser of the two evils.

I stop, standing over the heap of crushed chips that are now scattered across the floor. The aroma of salt and vinegar is filling my nose, making me salivate. I stare down at my mess. What a waste. Those would have been good.

Focus, Kinzleigh, focus!

"Macie," I whine. "It's not that. I did, I do, want you to have fun. Just with anyone except . . . Ry. He's not the kind of guy that a girl like you wants to get involved with. He's dangerous to someone like you."

I continue in my well-worn path of chip crumbles, ignoring the stabbing sensation on the bottom of my feet from some of the sharp edges, letting my arms flail as I speak. My mind isn't working right now, because my mouth has taken control. "He . . . well he . . . Just trust me, okay?"

"What do you mean, 'a girl like me'?" Oh, boy. There's that tone. None of this is coming out right. My mouth opens to try and rectify where this conversation is being steered, but she cuts me off. "A girl that is broken? Is that what kind of girl you mean? Or a girl that lives a pathetic, lonely life, because she's undeserving of anything more? That's it, isn't it? I'm not good enough for your friends, am I, because of my past? Don't worry, in a few days I'll be back in Mississippi with a few good memories that may ease some of the self-loathing misery the poor southern girl is stuck with permanently. It's the card I drew in life, right?"

Tears are streaming down her face. I've pulled the trigger to a gun I didn't even know I was holding. I'm stunned. How do I fix this? "That's not what I meant at all," I say, barely above a whisper as I stare into her pain-stricken eyes. "Please . . . let me explain."

I take a step forward, but she takes a step back. She doesn't want to be near me right now. "Tomorrow."

She managed to get the one word out in between breaths. I feel like I'm watching her drown while I'm sitting in the boat with no paddle. I let her go, saying nothing more. I messed up.

I watch her disappear down the hallway. Maybe I was in over my head. I shouldn't have said anything. What would it really have hurt to think she just slept with a stranger? She's right—she'll go back home in a few days. I just want to help her.

But really, how does a person save someone else from drowning that is barely keeping their own head above water? The odds aren't great, but we come out alive together or we drown together. No one left behind.

FORTY-THREE

Kinzleigh

I couldn't sleep at all last night. All I can think about is Macie. Things have been rocky since that night in the kitchen. She's avoided me like a plague. She comes home after I'm in my room for the night and is gone before I wake. I've seen Ryland's truck picking her up and dropping her off a few times over the last week.

It's been lonely. Preston has been working extra hours at the office getting ready for the new project release event where we will announce our engagement. I wanted to get to know Macie better, but instead, I ruined it.

Today she is leaving to go back to Mississippi. Preston is going to offer her a job before she does. I was confident when I first asked him to do it, but now, I'm not so sure.

I stand over the stove cooking scrambled eggs and ham, lost in thought, when two arms snake around me from behind. The smell of soap and cologne mixes in the air. A clean-shaven cheek rests against mine before he kisses my cheek.

"Good morning," he says in a deep voice. His hands rest on my round stomach and his breath tickles the skin against my neck as he trails kisses down it, giving me chill bumps. "There is something strangely erotic about you barefoot and pregnant standing at the stove."

I turn off the heated eye and turn in his arms. He is fully dressed in black suit pants and an aqua long sleeve shirt with a patterned tie in both colors. I grab the knot of his tie and tighten it into place. "It's hard to get used to you wearing suits. I'm surprised your dad hasn't made you shorten your hair even more."

Preston has always had hair longer than his dad's taste prefers. It's still short in the back and around the sides, but he keeps the top longer. It falls long enough to bypass his eyebrows if he doesn't brush it back, and that's only been recently. It's another thing that attributes to his model-like features.

"He isn't going to bite the hand the helps feed him," he says in a cocky but teasing tone, followed by a smirk. "Business plans have tripled since I started, and projects are scheduled on the books to keep us busy for at least the next five years."

"You know what happens when you get too cocky. You fall on your ass," I quip back teasingly.

"Cockiness is a must in this business. At work, I'm a Grade-A asshole, but it's what keeps us on top. I never want you to see the man I have to be when I'm there."

I wonder if that's what Dad was always referring to when he said similar things. He told us all the time that he left work at work and home at home. Do all self-employed business owners have two different personalities? That sounds exhausting. "What—"

"Am I interrupting?" We both turn as Macie walks into the kitchen in her pajamas. It's the first time she's spoken to me since that night.

"Not at all. I was just making breakfast. I'm sure you're hungry. Sit and I'll make you a plate." She nods and pulls out a stool at the bar. I remove a clean plate from the cabinet and add a scoop of eggs and a piece of ham.

She stands and walks over to the refrigerator at the same time I set her plate in front of her on the bar. "Are you looking for something?"

Preston removes a coffee mug and pours it full of black coffee. "Do you have any ketchup?"

Preston and I look at each other as he takes a sip from his cup, both thinking the same thing. We look at her in unison and he places his cup on the top of the bar. "It's in the door, but why do you want ketchup?"

"For my eggs," she says, and instantly my face gives away what that sounds like to me. She laughs as she pulls the bottle out of the door and walks back to her seat. "I get that reaction to a lot of the food preferences I have."

As if the sheer thought of what she is going to do with that ketchup isn't bad enough, she opens the cap and squeezes it in a zigzag formation over the top of her scrambled eggs.

I would imagine I have a look of horror and disgust written all over my face. Without saying anything, I reach in the drawer and take a fork. I hand it to her. She looks amused by my reaction. "Don't knock it 'til you try it."

I get an odd feeling that means more than trying various and weird combinations of food. I may need to cross-examine that phrase and reiterate it at a later time when we're alone. "Have you enjoyed your stay, Macie?"

Preston's voice reminds me there are more important topics at hand right now. He looks at his watch, meaning he's running short on time. "It's been great and much-needed. Thank y'all for allowing me to stay here. I'll be out of your way in a few hours," she says as she picks up her glass of juice.

"That's actually what we wanted to talk to you about," he says.

She sets her glass back down and looks between the two of us. "What do you mean? Is there a problem?"

Preston doesn't waste any time before he picks up right where he left off. "I don't know how much Kinzleigh has told you about me, but my family has established a very wealthy business investing in real estate across the country, and now in the process of expanding internationally. I don't have the time to give you the full rundown, but the gist is that we develop the land that we purchase and manage it ourselves or resell it once it's complete for a profit, among other things that are irrelevant at this time. I've been in the process of looking for a personal assistant for a while. Kinzleigh mentioned you might be interested in the position and spoke highly of you. She thinks that you would be a good candidate."

Her eyes widen as she sets down her fork. "Are you serious?"

He reaches in his pocket and pulls out a folded piece of paper. "I never joke about business. The position comes with perks. The company will provide housing for a certain time period since it will require you to move, absorb moving expenses, you will be given a company vehicle for the time of your employment, and childcare will be arranged in exchange for twenty-four-hour availability. Travel is a requirement. You will be with me at all times unless I instruct you otherwise."

He places the folded piece of paper on the counter in front of him and slides it to the other side. "This is starting salary. Raise evaluation will take place after the ninety days probation period and all other benefits will be discussed upon acceptance of the offer."

She picks up the piece of paper in her small hands. Preston continues to sip on his coffee while he waits. When she opens the sheet of paper and scans the details her mouth drops. Her eyes begin to gloss over when she looks at him. "That's more in one month than I currently make in a year. Is this correct?"

He clears his throat. "I don't make mistakes when it comes to numbers. But you can't compare Mississippi part-time wages to California full-time with a reputable company. It's nowhere close in bracket. Don't take it lightly, though. A personal assistant isn't an easy job. You'll be at my every beck and call. This is no job you've ever done, and there is a lot you will have to learn. Chances are you won't like me as a boss, but you'll respect me. I was raised to take care of good employees. It's a hectic schedule, and should you commit, you'll be well compensated. Prove your worth and it will only increase."

Preston places his hand back in the pocket of his pants, letting the information linger in the air. I've never been involved in a business deal before. I almost feel like I'm intruding.

She looks down at the piece of paper again. "When would I have to be moved here and ready to start?"

He places his empty cup in the sink and walks over to the barstool next to her, grabbing his jacket from where it's hanging on the back. "You are required to be moved in and ready to work the Monday before the charity event in August. It's the last Monday of the month. That gives you a little under two months to make preparations and get settled; familiarize yourself with the area. Your residence is move-in ready."

She looks a little overwhelmed. I notice her grab for a necklace that is hanging beneath her shirt and close her eyes. I've never noticed it before.

When she opens her eyes, she looks between her enclosed fist and the paper in her opposite hand. It occurs to me that she said she is still living in that town because of Beau being buried there. She doesn't want to leave him with his parents here. I'm not sure she even knows where his parents moved. Maybe she needs time to think it over.

Before I can say something to try and alleviate her being put on the spot, she answers, "I'll take it." She looks up and straightens her shoulders. "I would like to accept the offer."

He shakes his jacket out that is hooked on his fingers and rounds the bar, walking in my direction. "Good. Then it's settled. I'll get your number from Kinzleigh and she will give you mine. I have to get going, but I'll be in touch."

He grabs my chin between his thumb and index finger, drawing me closer to his lips. He kisses me so softly I can barely feel it. "A car will pick both of you up in two hours. He will have instructions on where to go and a key to her house. Go shopping and spend some money. You've been in this house too long. A company event is coming up the two of you need dresses for. You have your card. Use it."

I nod and he takes a few steps in the direction of the garage. He stops beside Macie. "Clear your schedule for today and cancel your flight. Kinzleigh will take care of everything you need for the party and you can leave it at your house. An acceptance bonus and wardrobe allowance will be deposited into your bank account, so make sure you give Kinzleigh the details to forward to me. You will reflect me and my family's company. I expect you to dress like it. Business formal is the dress code. As of today, you work for me. You will be compensated biweekly on the same schedule as all the other employees. Sever your contracts with previous employers."

He looks down at his watch again. "The car will have you at the company jet at six o'clock sharp. I'm giving you this break to inform your family, move, and get you and your son settled here, in your home, with necessary arrangements, so you are ready to work at the deadline already set. No alternate agreements will be made. The itinerary between now and your start date is up to you. Decide the date you want to be picked up and let me know. I will make arrangements for movers and the flight to be there promptly and on schedule. Use your time wisely."

Without another word, he exits the room. The two of us stand here speechless with our mouths gaping. I've never seen this side of Preston before. What just happened? Does some magical business witch get summoned when a member of his family takes their place in the famous 'Dunagin Empire' to bestow assertiveness and power upon them?

He's barely out of college for crying out loud. I thought that came with age, not wealth. I should know by now that nothing is ever as we think it is anyway. "I guess that's our cue to get ready," I say, and glance over at her.

She looks like a terrified bunny in the middle of a lion's den. I can't say that I blame her. I was raised around those people and I still am not used to it, especially not on Preston. I think he's right. I don't want to know what he's like at work. "I guess so," she responds quietly.

We both exit in opposite directions. Maybe I'll get the chance to talk to her, after all. I need someone's advice on Preston and I and a baby that I'm incubating that doesn't come from his seed.

I'm confused, and I need an opinion from someone on the outside looking in. Someone that can put it in perspective for me. I don't want to be viewed as a tramp or whore, but the fact remains that Breyson isn't here, and he's never coming back.

I need someone that has stepped over that line and been with a man sexually after her one and only is no longer an option.

FORTY-FOUR

Kinzleigh

The doorbell chimes. The car must be here. I slip on my flip flops. Comfort is more important at this size than cuteness. A cotton maxi dress and flip flops will have to do. I know what happens when I go shopping and I don't want my feet to hate me later. I spritz myself with perfume before grabbing my purse.

Macie is standing at the door when I make it to the bottom of the stairs. She gives me a small smile as I set the alarm and then we walk out the door together.

The driver holds the back door open, allowing us to enter. Macie gets in first. "Miss Baker, I hope you are well today," he says, tipping his hat with his free hand.

"I am. Thank you for asking, Bernard." Preston made him my permanent chauffeur for the time being; something to do with me moving further along in my pregnancy and not wanting me to be alone, but I think there are other undisclosed reasons.

It was annoying at first, but I'm starting to enjoy not having to drive. Once on the seat, I slide over, allowing Bernard to close the door. Macie and I sit in an awkward silence as the driver gets behind the wheel and pulls out of the driveway.

"I'm sorry," we both blurt out in unison. "Me too!" we shout again together. The synced response causes us both to laugh.

"You go first," she says, nudging me playfully.

I'll try this one more time. Hopefully, I don't screw it up again. "I'm not great with words but give me a chance and I'll try to explain." When she nods, I gather my thoughts. "Ry is a great guy as long as you're just in the friend zone. He's kind of cynical when it comes to being in a relationship. Trust me, it takes one to know one. He's only interested in girls for one thing and doesn't hide it, which was the opposite of me. I slept with no one and he sleeps with anyone that draws his attention."

She doesn't look upset, so I keep going. "It's none of my business what you do in your life. I know you're an adult. If you want the same thing, I have no problem, but I know and understand what you've been through. I was only trying to protect you because I've seen girls at my school start hooking up with him, thinking they could handle the whole 'friends with benefits' thing, and then they fall hard for him. He's a very likable person. When a girl gets that way, he cuts it off, every single time, and he can sense it a mile away."

She stares straight ahead, nodding to acknowledge that she heard me. "It was nothing. We were just having fun. He made me feel things that I haven't felt in . . ." She closes her eyes and her voice lowers to a whisper. "A long time. I knew I was going back home, but I've been miserable for so long that I just wanted to hold onto that feeling for a little while. Does that make sense?"

Her mouth says it's nothing, but her eyes tell another story. There is more to it than what she's giving away, but I don't comment. Instead, I think back on how miserable I was back in Mississippi.

Everything around me was a constant reminder of the time Breyson and I shared and the love we had for each other. Everywhere I went and everything I saw brought back the memories, and it felt like my heart was rupturing all over again. I don't think I would have ever been able to move on there, just as she hasn't.

Each person has a switch that snaps them out of the trance they fall into when something unfortunate happens in their life. When we are lost, we want to be found. We want to find that one way out of the maze that we keep wandering around in.

Preston was my out. He was one piece of happiness that existed before I met Breyson, so when he reached into the water as I was drowning, I grabbed on and held on. His investment in me instead of giving up has helped me to find happiness again. That happiness from having a friend that cared about me has turned into love. "I think I understand."

A few seconds pass between us, and houses come and go as we continue down the street. "It's because of you, you know."

I look over at her, unsure of what she means. "Me letting myself have a night to remember is because of you. Watching you and Preston. I've always lived with this guilt that because I lived and he died, I should live in misery, but you proved me wrong."

"How? I didn't do anything."

"Oh, but you did. When I found out you moved to California, I was angry. I was angry because I was still stuck there carrying the burden of his death and you were moving on. I came here to see why you could so easily move on after Breyson's death but I couldn't from Beau's."

She looks out the window, but she continues talking. "When I got here, I watched you. I realized that you were hurting just like me, but the difference was you were coping while I was burying. We can't control tragic circumstances in life, no matter what the situation is or how much we hurt as a result from it. You and Preston have shown me that love is more of a verb and not a noun. Losing one person you love doesn't have to be final, meaning you lost your only shot. I may not ever love someone again like I loved Beau, but if I can at least try to make each day better than the one before, I've accomplished greatness."

She grabs ahold of that necklace that she keeps tucked beneath her shirt again. "You got all that from me?"

I guess we are our own worst critics, because I didn't think I was fairing that well. She nods. "It's why I let him take me to bed, and it's also the reason I took the job. I wanted to see if being with another man the way I was last with Beau would help me to let him go. I want to work toward being happy again. My mind has been my enemy for so long that I finally just surrendered."

We are so much alike. "Did it work?"

My heart rate picks up a little as I wait on the answer to the question I've been asking since I moved back to California. "So much so that I almost feel a different kind of guilt."

Instantly, a tear spills out of her eye. "The weight gone is foreign, but I finally feel like I can breathe. It was almost too much to bear. Don't feel guilty for what you have with Preston. Embrace it. Whatever you can do to free yourself from the chains that bind you, do it. No one should be incarcerated forever. It won't bring them back."

We do have one difference. She's already given birth to her child. "Do you think it would be wrong to sleep with Preston while carrying Breyson's child? Be honest, woman to woman. I won't get angry. I need unbiased advice."

She wipes her fingers underneath her eye to check for eyeliner smudges. "Honestly, if Breyson was alive and the two of you just broke up, then yes, I would see something wrong with it. Out of respect, it wouldn't be appropriate to have sex with one man while the father of your child has no say in your actions even though you're carrying his child. The health of the child is also at risk with bringing in another partner. But you and Breyson didn't break up, Kinzleigh."

She grabs my hand. "He died and he's never coming back. You're also in a committed, monogamous relationship with someone you trust. Sex isn't going to harm that baby over sex with Preston any more than it would if you were having sex with Breyson. The baby is deep in your womb, above your cervix, which is closed until you get closer to delivery. Having sex with your fiancé is normal, pregnant or not. It's not a health choice, it's an ethical one. It's no one's business but your own. No one will know unless you tell them. People believe what they want to believe anyway, regardless of whether it's the truth, even if you *didn't* do it."

She does have a good point. I guess I just needed to hear it from someone else. I've always been drilled by my parents that a person's reputation is everything, and once it's ruined you can never get it back. I need to stop worrying about so much, I suppose. "Macie, can I ask you a question?"

"Anything."

We're getting close to our destination based on our surroundings as I glance out the window. "Why won't you come clean about what happened? You know, about what happened with that guy. Why do you have to suffer when you did nothing wrong? Don't you think Talon will start asking questions about Beau's family?"

As a subdivision comes into view, I remember when Preston's family's company was developing it, because he and I lost in a game of truth or dare. An all-night sleepover in the half-done house was the result. We weren't supposed to be here, and Konnor and Presley always chose things they knew made me uncomfortable when making bets and playing games. I never did like to break rules until . . . Breyson.

Her silence tells me she's obviously thinking. Unconsciously, I look up at the sky, wondering if he can see me right now. If he could, would he be happy I'm moving on or sad? The thought plagues me. I guess I'll never know.

"Because it's my cross to bear," she says. "It's not going to change anything. Doesn't mean they'd believe me if I did. They could demand a paternity test and make things worse, regardless of the result, and I'm not doing that to my son. It's easier for people to point the blame at someone else than to face the fact that they were wrong and missed out on time with their grandson. I don't care what people think of me. The only person's opinion that matters already knows the truth, because he knows and sees all. We all have to answer for our actions one day, and as long as he knows that I didn't cheat on Beau, then let them pass their judgments."

The car comes to a halt, but I can tell she has something more to say. "The truth is, Beau made a mistake by getting behind the wheel that night. He had been drinking, and he let his emotions and the gossip of someone else alter his judgment. We never drank and drive. It was our one absolute rule. Had he called me or vice versa, he'd still be alive today and Talon would have his father, but people are imperfect beings. I would rather everyone think that Beau made that judgment call for a just cause than to shame him. Every action shows someone's character, and his was beautiful. I will endure what I have to in order to keep it flawless. That's a consequence of loving someone."

She allows a small smile to slip through before hiding it away. The world needs more people like Macie. As much as she's been through, and I only know a small portion of it, she is genuine. Most people are fake and self-absorbed, like I was at one time, but she carries on instead of blaming the world for her problems. It makes me happy to help her in any way I can, because she truly deserves it.

The driver opens the door beside Macie, and she gasps, drawing me back into the present. When I look over at her, she is staring at the house through the open door and steps out to get a better view.

I follow behind her. As I stand, Bernard places a key in my hand with a smile on his face. He's an older gentleman, around the age of my father. "This is where I'm staying?"

Bernard winks at me before I look at her. She looks like she is about to cry but trying to hold it back. I walk closer to her with the key in hand. "It's not where you're staying . . ." I look her in the eyes as her face straightens out. "It's where you live."

She wraps her arms around my neck, hugging me tightly. "Thank you, Kinzleigh. I will forever be indebted to you for everything you've done for me. I've never lived in anything this nice. I'll never let you down."

The house is quaint and smaller than the ones they build now, but still a larger size as far as houses are concerned. It was designed to look like a beach style version of a cottage. It's one of the bigger ones on the street.

The house is one story but has four bedrooms, and there is a small studio apartment for guests that sits above a separate garage. There is a built-in pool on the back side, because the company doesn't build houses without them anymore.

Buyers in California want outdoor living, because you rarely get big yards. I actually think this one was the show house, which means it's never been lived in and is fully furnished for staging already.

I pry her off of me, so she can see my face. "Macie, you don't owe me anything. Someone recently told me that every event leads us to where we are supposed to be. I know the sequence of events leading to the finale aren't always pleasant or easy, and sometimes they sure as hell don't seem fair or make sense, but we have to have faith there is a purpose for them. We may not know why yet, but you are meant to be in California."

I dangle the key in the air from my middle finger at eye level. "Go look at your new house," I tell her. I can't help but feel the excitement as I take in her expression. "Welcome to the homeowners' club."

Her eyes enlarge, giving away her stunned state. "Wait, I own this house? I thought I was just renting it while I'm an employee."

I nod my head and my smile broadens. "Maybe lease to own, but it's yours. You and Preston will work out the details."

Preston sent me a message letting me know that the transfer of title was already in process. I don't know all the legalities, but I know the company probably gets some kind of tax write-off or something. They'll likely just take a small portion from each check to pay back the company. I don't really know or care.

His company wouldn't be as big and successful as it is if there wasn't some perk to it. It probably works out on paper with the way her income is recorded or something. Whatever it is, I know it's legit and legal, so I trust him. He's very good at business. He always has been. "It's yours. Now go. We have a lot to do before your flight."

She takes the key from my fingers and walks down the walkway to the front door. I stand back for a minute, watching her until she disappears inside. It makes my heart happy to be a part of helping those less fortunate than me.

It gives me an idea for the cheer company that I want to run by Preston later. I think I have found my niche in the world. I love cheerleading, and even though my dream was altered a little from the original plan, I think it's better than before.

The driver returned to the car to give us some privacy. I stand at the edge of the walkway perfectly still. Hearing a sound across the street, I turn to look. It's a little boy around the age of seven throwing a football with his dad. His mom is bouncing a baby girl on her knee from where she's sitting as she watches them.

The laughter of the little boy as he catches the pass and takes off running fills the air. The man glances across the street at me as I watch them, and for a second, he looks like Breyson. He continues playing with his son, ignoring my gaze, and a vision flashes in my mind of it being the two of us and a mini version combined.

I place my hands on my belly and look up at the sky. It appears to be a brighter shade of blue and the clouds seem whiter than they usually do. The sun feels like a spotlight shining down on my face, warming me. "Such a beautiful day."

Bryce moves at the sound of my voice. "I am who I am because of you, Brey. I'm a better person today, because I was given the chance to know and love you. I'll never forget that. Know that I will always love you no matter what. You will always be the man I loved first and the hardest. I may love him too, but he'll never replace my love for you."

FORTY-FIVE

The crowd goes wild with every puncture through the bulls hide. I stand, leaning forward over the railing as I watch. No matter how many times the fighter sticks him, he keeps enduring. It doesn't make a difference how much it hurts or how many times he sways, he refuses to die. He's stubborn and won't give up without a fight. Even though he's an animal, he shows honor to his breed by standing until his death. It shows his strength.

I'm starting to think I'll be stuck here forever. August is almost over and I still haven't heard anything about the results. Maybe my expectations were unrealistic, but I was thinking it would take like a week. I shouldn't complain, though, since I have an income and a place to call home for now.

I have a sinking feeling in my gut. They've become more frequent as time passes. It's like I'm on a deadline and I have no idea what that deadline is or what happens if I miss it. It's this weird feeling that you're losing something or that it's slowly slipping out of your grasp, and your instant reflex is to tighten your hold.

There is something I'm missing. September is nearing quickly, and these uneasy feelings are daily at this point. The visions are also becoming less frequent. Things are changing, and I don't know what that means. I was thinking it was my brain's way of bringing back my memory and now

I'm not so sure.

A nervous twitch occurs as the queasiness consumes my body. The bile begins inching up my throat, as if I'm close to vomiting. What the hell is wrong with me? I tighten my hold on the rail in front of me as I breathe steadily, trying to make the nausea subside. Something isn't right. I close my eyes when I start to get dizzy. Maybe today is important, but my mind can't place it.

I tighten my eyelids shut and an image emerges in my mind. It's hazy at first, but it clears. It looks like Catholic Church, maybe, but I can't be sure. It's massive and it appears to have been decorated for some type of event. Like I've learned since I've started having these episodes, I continue to let it play in hopes that I get more information, like the name drop last time.

All the seats are filled from wall to wall. A line of guys dressed out in tuxedos make their way toward what appears to be an alter and a priest. I try to focus on the faces, but the only one that looks vaguely familiar is the one in the front wearing the white vest and tie over the black button down. He stops in front and the rest of them take formation behind him.

One by one, girls walk down the aisle, each holding a bouquet of flowers. Out of them, two look familiar—a redhead and a brunette. A sense of Déjà vu overwhelms me as their faces come into view. I'm starting to think this is just some bullshit my mind has concocted until everyone that was sitting, stands.

The ceiling-high doors in the back swing out until they are completely open. I feel like I'm in the other end of the room, because I can't see anything. When I finally get a view of who it is, I stop breathing. What the fuck is this? This feels wrong. This has to be some twisted game my mind is playing with me.

It's the blonde from all of my visions. She's walking between two middle-aged adults. She resembles the man, but her eyes are the same color as the woman's. I'm assuming it's her parents. She's beautiful. Damn, she is beautiful. I can't move my eyes from her long enough to take in anything around her.

The fitted, off the shoulder, lace dress is the color of ivory and hugs her small figure until it hits below her calf where it branches out into a train. Her blonde hair is pulled to the side in a bundle of curls and her full lips are stained red. Aside from her lips, her makeup isn't heavy. When she smiles my heart stops beating.

I turn to see who she's smiling at and it's the familiar guy from earlier. He returns the smile tenfold. An urge to kill sparks in my veins. Stupid prick. I want to physically alter that smile. When I look back at her, I notice the huge elephant in the room that I didn't notice before. Fucking hell.

The dark-haired woman beside her is carrying a baby. The way she is carrying him, his back and head are resting against her chest. She has one arm over his chest and the other under his bottom, as if she's showing him to the world. He's asleep or so it seems. He looks like he's young, but he's old enough to have noticeable features.

The more I look at him . . .

Hell to the motherfucking no! No, no, no, no, no.

I look between the three of them again and the vision starts to fade. Tears sting my eyes as a previous vision was just confirmed. I don't know what kind of paranormal shit is going on in my mind, but there is no way in hell I'm letting the woman of my dreams marry another man, and I sure as fuck am not going to sit around and let him raise my son. I can see it all over his face. He looks just like me.

I get jarred backward as the bull slams into the wall I'm leaning on. It brings me out of my head. I can't sit around anymore waiting on something to happen on its own. I have to do something myself. A thought occurs to me. What if I'm too late? I have no sense of time. Rage and anger envelop me. I grab my hair and pull as hard as I can.

The fighter stabs another spear in the bull's side, next to his heart. He staggers a few times from left to right before he finally gives up the fight and falls to his death. The crowd around me goes wild with excitement.

Metaphorically speaking, I take more from it than some sport and representation of skill. I'm the bull right now, and if I lose her, death will be the end result. I've sat back and tried to wait patiently on my brain to heal. It had its chance. I'm taking matters into my own hands. I'm wasting away without her in my life, and I don't even remember what that life with her was like.

I may die a lonely man, but it sure as hell won't be because I didn't fight. Nah, fuck that. The best things in life are worth fighting for. If my kid is walking around calling someone else Daddy, it's going to be because my body has turned to dust. He better enjoy getting to touch her now, because I'm taking back what's mine.

I take off running in a sprint when I hear my name called out. "Bryce, wait up."

Marcus.

"I have something I need to take care of. I'll catch you at home, Buddy."

I never look back. I can't. I've made up my mind.

I increase speed from a sprint to a full-out run. In a few seconds flat, I reach the exit doors. As I do, my phone starts to ring. I reach in my pocket as I allow my breathing to slow from its heightened state. The number is unfamiliar. "Hello."

"Look across the street." I do as he says, but I don't see anything out of the ordinary. "Do you see that cafe?"

"Yes."

"Walk to it. When you see the hostess, your keyword is viper. She'll take it from there. I'll be waiting." The line goes dead. I look around, but still see nothing. I take a step in the direction of the cafe, but it all feels cryptic. I consider turning back, but then I remember the way she looked walking down an aisle with the wrong person at the other end. My heart rate picks up rapidly, as if I never stopped running.

I've heard that love makes you stupid, but if stupid gets me back to her I'll take it. My memories can go to Hell. I'll make new ones. I don't need memories to know that I'm in love with her. I know how my body reacts just from a dream, and reality is so much better.

My heart overturns my brain and my feet continue to move forward. Before I know it, I'm walking faster than I expected. It doesn't take long before I arrive at the entry door. I open it and walk in. A young woman is standing at a hostess podium. "Can I help you?"

I look around at the mostly empty restaurant. "Viper," I say in a hushed tone.

She looks at me, sudden awareness clouding around her. "Follow me."

Turning, she walks toward the back and through the kitchen doors. It's like a maze weaving in and out of the tight spaces. With every foot forward, stares burn through me. I have no idea where we are going.

At the back of the kitchen, a door comes into view. She pulls a key from her pocket and unlocks it, and when she opens the door, she steps to the side. "When you get to the bottom, further instructions will be given."

This is the weirdest shit I've been through yet. The steps are made of wood, and they creak. The only light is the single bulb hanging from the ceiling, midway from the door to the bottom. I descend slowly, unsure of what I've gotten myself into.

When I reach the bottom, a light shines from a room in the corner. The clinking of coins and the male voices conversing in Spanish give me a hint as to what I'm walking into.

I follow the light. When I reach the entry, my expectations are confirmed.

It's an underground poker ring. "I see you decided to come," he says.

It's *him*—the guy I've been putting all of my hope into for answers. He's sitting among a table of men in the dreary room with a cigar resting between his teeth. Smoke permeates the room. "Mr. P, do you have good news for me?"

He looks me in the eyes, sizing me up. I'm tired of games. I just want to get what I came to him for and leave. There is something about him that's off, but I can't put my finger on it.

His cheeks sink inward as he puffs on the end of the cigar. Smoke billows from his lips as he speaks. "I may have some information of interest, but I'm a man of trade. I did something for you, and if you want it, you'll do something for me. I'm a fair and simple man. Are you interested or not?"

I don't have a good feeling about this. Usually, the best form of advice is to listen to your gut. Mine is throwing up red flags, but the benefits of what I'll get if I do this outweigh the risks.

And from the looks of him, he's smart and careful. There's no doubt in my mind that he has what information I need to get back to her. I just need to play by his rules to get it. "What do I have to do?"

"Smart boy. You know what you want and you'll do anything to get it. You'll succeed in life." He stands. "Let's take this to my office. My business doesn't get handled out in the open."

I watch the other men as I follow him toward the only other door in the room. None of them ever look up from the cards in their hands. It's as if they haven't heard a word he's said. That means one thing—he's dangerous.

As I follow him into the office, he shuts the door behind me. "Take a seat."

His tone is clipped and the command in it is intimidating. I do as he says and sit in the chair that faces the large Oak desk. He walks around it and sits opposite of me in his large, black, leather chair. He then leans back and props his elbow on the arm, his middle finger resting above his top lip.

The silence is awkward. He pulls out a desk drawer with the opposite hand and removes a large, eight by eleven letter size, yellow envelope. It doesn't look thick, but my nerves are going crazy. "Everything you need to know about your identity is in this."

He slaps it face down on the desk and slides it across the clean surface, stopping directly in front of me, but he never picks up his hand. "What's the catch?"

One side of his mouth arches and he leans forward. Lowering his voice to just above a whisper, he starts with, "You'll be going to the United States of America. For reasons that will remain disclosed, I can no longer reside in the States. I need you to make a delivery for me. One job and then you forget you ever met me. Got it?"

The thought of why he's been banned or exiled from an entire country makes me queasy. Most likely, it's to avoid capture for something really bad. I'm not sure I want to be involved in something of that nature. There is a risk of getting caught and punished for something I didn't even do. I consider backing out and running in the other direction, back to where I came from, but my eye catches sight of the envelope in front of me.

That one envelope holds the key to my freedom; the golden ticket I've been looking for. If I turn it down now, I may not find another way back home. When I first met Dr. Rodriguez, he told me I had to find the bridge from here to home, and that bridge was my memories. A bridge takes time to cross. Boats are faster. "Where do I have to go and what do I have to deliver?"

He lifts his hand, leaving the envelope lying before me, transferring ownership. "Rule number one, don't ask questions. The less you know, the less likely you'll fuck up and create problems that I have to fix. Leave the details for me. Your plane leaves in three days. Meet Big Sanchez at sundown on Friday, back side of the club. A car will be waiting, so don't be late. Further instructions will be given at takeoff. You're dismissed."

I'm officially creeped-out. I don't think twice before grabbing the envelope and standing, quickly grabbing for the door handle, but stop at the sound of his voice. "Oh, and Breyson."

It's the first time I've heard that name directed at me aloud. It's strange to hear, but oddly, I get a sense of familiarity as the syllables pass through my ear. I remain facing the door, waiting for him to say what he has to say. "Don't even think about fucking me over. The price to pay will be vast, and I will find you. Never mistake my kindness for a weakness."

My hands shake uncontrollably. I open the door and scurry toward the stairs. The thought plays on repeat with each step I take. In three days, I'll be on my way back to my life, back to her.

I'm not sure what to expect when I get there, but I'll be damned if I'm going to just let her go. My mind might have taken a hiatus, but I would walk through Hell for her. I can feel it all the way down to my core. I can feel the connection like a current of electricity buzzing in my veins.

She just needs to see me and she'll feel it too. Soul mates overpower all else. That guy won't stand a chance.

FORTY-SIX

I run through the door of the guesthouse and grab my duffle bag. In a hurry opening it, the drawer comes completely free of the dresser it sits in. I dump the contents of each one on the center of the bed.

The only thing I can think of is getting back home. I've been here for almost seven months, wandering around like a lost soul. I'm not wasting another second of my life. I had a run in with death and I beat it, but there is no guarantee it won't come knocking on my door again.

I shove various items of clothing into the bag. When there is nothing left, I zip up the bag and drop it on the floor beside the bed. The envelope is still lying in the place I left it when I entered. Picking it up, I turn it over to the sealed side. I tear it along the glue seam.

The top now open, the edge of the contents inside are revealed. I place my hand around it and sit on the foot of the bed as I slide the stack of papers out of the envelope. My stomach feels like it's twisting in knots. I attempt to calm my nerves with deep breaths.

The stack of papers is now face up in front of me. The first one reads, *Certificate of live birth*—copy. The name on the front is Breyson Patrick Abercrombie. Date of birth is October 2, 1995, making me almost nineteen.

I continue reading the information, going down line by line. With each one giving me back my identity, the emotion in my chest thickens. Mother's name, Father's name, the list goes on and on. My eyes fill with tears, because for the first time since I've been here, I have a sense of belonging.

I lay that page face down and continue to skim through the various pages. It's all here: social security information, address, phone numbers, and health records. He found everything. With the turn of each page more information is revealed.

What I didn't expect to see was a news article—***Plane crash off the east coast. No survivors found.***

None of the information triggers a memory. It's like reading about someone else's life. I read the article that follows and scan each name that was listed as an on-board passenger.

Mine stands out on the piece of paper. Everyone really does think I'm dead. This is the weirdest feeling. It's like being able to witness what happens after your own death.

I place it to the side and another article catches my attention. This time it's from a local paper. ***Memorial service for local senior held at 10AM.***

The first line under the photo of the headstone catches my attention. ***Star running back of local high school involved in hostage plane incident on the way to New York for Super Bowl ends in fatality***.

I don't think I can stomach to read any more. How do you even go back after something like that? No wonder no one was looking for me. People have probably moved on and forgotten about me by now.

Maybe I should just stay here, start a new life, and let them continue on. It seems almost cruel to just show up after having to deal with that kind of tragedy.

I almost put down the stack of papers, but something takes over and pushes me to continue looking. I can't explain it, but it's like something physically takes over my body and turns to the next page. More articles, but this time the heading isn't about me.

Pregnant girlfriend of deceased football player hit by car, hospitalizing both in critical condition.

How the fuck is this possible? How did I have a vision of this when it happened? I check the date in disbelief. I calculate back in my mind to that day and it adds up. Does this mean every vision I've had is true? If that's the case, how do I decipher what is past, present, and future? I move the paper and something falls from between the pages.

Setting down the papers beside me, I reach down and pick it up. It's a bundle of about five photographs scattered by my foot. The first one is of the two of us standing on a football field, dressed out in uniform.

My helmet is lying upside down as if it landed where I dropped it. I look sweaty as if right after a game. We're standing face to face, wrapped in each other's arms. I don't know who would've taken that picture, but we're consumed with each other.

Damn, my heart hurts. She's beautiful . . .

I shuffle to the next photo. The next one is the two of us again, standing side by side. I recognize the silver dress from one of the first visions I had. We look happy. How did I get lucky enough to have a girl like that by my side?

Again, I change to the next one. This one I must have taken. She's standing up against the front of a beautiful, black horse. They are both standing in the grass. Based on the clothing she has on, it's winter. She doesn't know I'm taking the picture. Her fingers are wrapped up in the horse's mane as if she's feeling the texture. The other hand is scratching the flat surface between its eyes, and she has a smile a mile wide.

I fall backward on the bed with the photos in my hand. How can you miss someone so much that you don't even remember? Without her it feels like a part of me is missing. The longer I stare at every feature, the blurrier my vision becomes. I blink to clear it and the tears drain over my cheekbone and into my ear.

My visions didn't do her justice. My mind may not remember, but my heart does, and the absence of her is killing me. Maybe that's why my memories are locked away; an attempt for my mind to protect me from heartache.

I flip to the next photograph. It's her in a long, black dress, kneeling in front of a headstone. I feel a familiar pull toward the location, though I don't know why. The photo is a closeup shot. Whoever took it must have been close to her, because I can see my name engraved on the headstone.

Tears are streaming down her puffy face in the reflection of the glossy stone. I don't like seeing her like that. It causes me physical pain to see her hurt, even in only a photograph. I wonder how she felt, how she still feels. She probably thought I left her.

I get to the last picture. Nothing could've prepared me for it. Seeing her with him creates a pain that is worse than dying. There is a stabbing sensation in my chest, because she actually has a smile on her face. She looks good. If I had to choose between the previous look on her and this one, I'd choose this one.

I'm not going to lie, the thought of him touching her sends my blood boiling, but I can't blame him either. Look at her. Just looking at her triggers emotions I haven't felt in the six months I've been here.

I can't tell where they are, but the photo looks like it's more of an invasion of privacy than a staged picture. He is standing behind her in front of a mirror, slightly bent over with his chin resting over her shoulder. His hands are flat against her round, pregnant belly, and they are both smiling in the mirror.

A part of me wants to rip his limbs clean from his body for touching what's mine while I'm here and at a disadvantage, but another part of me wants to shake his hand when I get her back for putting a smile on her face when I wasn't there to. That part makes me want to thank him for taking care of her. I'll try to let it go that he's standing in my place now, but that's all about to change.

I am claiming what's mine. I had her first. It's evident by the baby she's carrying in her womb. He may think he's claiming her right now, but I will always be her last.

The thought of him making her body his makes the bile rise to my throat. I toss the photos on the bed in a heated mood. My fists begin clenching uncontrollably with the urge to hit something.

The right to judge is not yours when the stain of the same sin is on your hands.

Fuck. I may not have the right to be pissed because of what I did with Angelique, but I don't have to like it. I want to be the one touching her the way he's touching her.

How am I supposed to sit back for three days when I know he's probably having his way with her? I need to find something to occupy my time. A knock sounds at the door as I stand, ready to go busy myself. "Bryce? Are you in here?"

The small trampling of footsteps tells me he's looking for me. "In here, Marcus." He comes through the door carrying a ball. "What's up, buddy?"

"I was just thinking we could try something else. You look like you're having one of those days again." If I wasn't so ready to get back home right now, I would find the humor in this situation.

Occasionally, he comes up with some new thing for us to try to get my memories back. I was starting to think he finally gave up, but I guess I was wrong. It does give me something to do.

"What do you have this time? We've already played baseball and basketball with no results. Do you really think this is going to work?" I say as I raise my brow in a sarcastic notion.

He's holding a ball in one hand with his small fingers lined up over the white laces on it, and he's hitting against the rubber with the other hand. "Those don't look as cool as this one, though. I got this one in town with Mom the other day. I had to agree to extra chores to get it, but how could I pass this up? She said it's called a football. It doesn't look anything like our footballs. We kick those. But then she said it's an American football. It's going to be different this time. I just know it."

"You think this one's going to work, huh? What makes you so sure?" I've learned to just go with his shenanigans. If it puts a smile on his face, who am I to rain on his parade?

I walk over and stop beside him, mussing his hair with the palm of my hand. It aggravates the shit out of him, but his love for me keeps him from saying anything derogatory about it. He swats at my hand. "I have a good feeling. Today is the day."

His confidence is hard not to catch, but I stopped getting my hopes up a long time ago. "Okay, then. Lead the way."

I follow him to his favorite spot in the yard. I stop while he continues to increase the distance between us. He continues to move forward pretty far out. I doubt he can even throw it that far, but I'll let him give it a try.

He readies himself and takes position to throw. When he does, the ball soars in a spiraling motion through the air. I sprint backward as I calculate the distance in my head. Damn, the boy can throw. I never saw that one coming. I jump up to catch the pass and when the ball touches my skin it's like a drape was pulled back.

One by one the memories sift through my mind as if someone is holding down the forward button on a digital camera photo roll. My mind processes each memory as if it's been lost and is finally filing them away where they belong. All of the information he gave me now registers in my mind.

I remember everything: my family, my friends, and *her*. My beautiful girl has finally come back to my memories in a way that I can actually remember every damn second we were together. "Kinzleigh . . ."

I feel like the air has been sucked from my lungs. No longer paying attention, I land on my back with the ball in hand. The thud of the hard ground beneath me proves that the wind has been knocked out of me.

Curling up in a fetal position, I roll over onto my knees and forearms, trying to catch my breath.

They've been absent for so long I want to browse through each chapter in my mind just to prove to myself they are really real. One memory in particular stands out—the day I left for New York in the airport when we were saying goodbye.

I remember how she was acting in her room that day before we left, and then when she kept throwing up. Oh, for the love of God. I push up onto my knees in a kneeling position. She was pregnant then. My mother taught me better than that. She's a fucking OBGYN for crying out loud. How could I not have seen it then?

I left her alone and sick. I left her to deal with finding out she was pregnant without me there. She had dreams and goals for her life. What the hell have I done? What kind of future are we going to have now?

Then it dawns on me.

I slept with another woman. The thought brings immediate tears to my eyes and a sick feeling in the pit of my stomach. I promised I would never take another woman to bed. I had the perfect one, and my mind tried to tell me she was real, but instead of believing it, I went out and tried to dissolve it. I feel like I've cheated on her.

That's not even the worst part. What if she doesn't forgive me? I have to come clean. I don't want another man taking care of the most precious thing to me, nor raising my child.

I calculate back. If she didn't start getting sick until February, then she can't be due until at least next month. I always thought Mom's ramblings about her day job were worthless information, but right now they may be the key to everything.

I stand and run back toward my room where I came from. I can hear Marcus following closely behind, but I don't have time to explain. "Bryce, are you okay? What's wrong?"

"Go get Mom, Marcus. Please, buddy." I continue running as fast as I can through the yard. I may not have room to judge that Kinzleigh is with another guy, but I swear on everything, if it's the one I think it is I will blow the fuck up.

Tearing through the door, I run to the photos I was staring at earlier. I'm pretty sure I know who I saw, but I want to be totally sure. I move around the scattered photos looking for the one I want. When I come to it, my blood is boiling. "Son of a bitch."

I sling the photo across the room as far as the light piece of paper will go. I begin pacing across the floor. I want to pull my hair out and scratch my skin off. I was partially okay with a man, because she isn't aware that I'm even alive, and I told her in that damn video that I sent to move on, but I didn't expect it to be Preston.

I place my palms flat against the edging of the dresser. My jaw begins working back and forth. My eyes are so full of anger and hatred that they hurt. The pain in my heart is agonizing. How do I compete with the best friend? I bet me being out of the picture was all just a bonus in his plan.

Out of rage, I sling my arm across the top of the dresser, sending everything that rests on top flying in the air. I used to not worry about him so much when we were together, because I knew that Kinzleigh was all mine and she loved me. It wasn't a secret that we were meant to be together.

What scares the hell out of me is that she's had time to be with him, time to develop feelings and let the ones she had for me fade. Three days could be three days too late. I have to get another flight. I have to leave tonight.

Pulling out my cell phone, I call back the number from earlier. It only rings one time before he answers. "This better be good, Breyson. I'm busy."

The guy really is kind of creepy. I have no idea how he got all of the photos that he did, because going back through them, I realize that some of them came from my room. The thought of someone being in my family's home gives me the chills. "I need an earlier flight. I'll do whatever you need me to do. Three days is too long."

The line becomes silent for a few seconds. "A car will pick you up in two hours. Be ready. I don't wait."

"Thank you," I say, but the line goes dead as the words come out of my mouth. I slide the cell phone back in my pocket and look around the room. I have most of the things I need.

"Bryce, are you okay?" Mom comes running in the room with a terrified expression. I didn't even think of how I was going to break this to her. She's been the only mother I've had for almost seven months. Never once did she treat me as anything but her child. I'm really going to miss my family. She may not be blood, but she's just as much family as my own.

"Mom, my real name is Breyson, and I'm going back home. There is someone there worth fighting for. I have to try before I lose her forever." Her hand immediately covers her mouth as she gasps.

I gather the photos behind me and walk over in her direction. I place them in her hands as her eyes pool with moisture. "True love is worth fighting for, Mom. When you know that person is the only one in existence for you, you go after them. Who gives a damn what anyone else thinks?"

I bore into her eyes so she can understand what I mean. I've never had the conversation with her about that first night at the club with Big Sanchez. I've never told her I know that they were so much more than friends. No one should have to give up the one person that means the most to them to make someone else happy, or out of fear. "Late is better than never."

She grabs me in a hug and squeezes me tightly. "When do you leave?"

"Tonight."

She places her palms on each side of my face. "You'll always be my son no matter where you are. We're going to miss you. Come back and see me when you've retrieved her heart and bring her with you. I want to meet her."

She blinks the tears away with no shame. "Yes, ma'am. I'll never forget my family. Will you help me pack?"

"I thought you'd never ask."

It's said that where a person has been and what he's gone through makes him the person he's going to be. I believe that. I may have been thrown a major curve ball, but it'll only make me cherish the things that I have more when I get them back.

FORTY-SEVEN

Breyson

The car is due to arrive in ten minutes. My bags are packed and I'm more than ready to get out of here. On another note, seeing Maria's face causes me a bit of an emotional setback. I can tell she really is going to miss me, and that speaks volumes.

I'm standing at the door with the three of them lined up before me. Antonio walks up to me first and places his hand on my shoulder. "Son, you know you're always welcome here. I want you to remember that, and anytime you want to get away, just come here and you have a place to stay."

Antonio is more of a non-verbal person. He keeps to himself, but only speaks when necessary. He doesn't show his emotions very often, so we've never gotten real personal. "I'll be back. I'm not sure if I have ever told you, but I want to thank you for giving me a place to stay when I had nowhere else to go, and for giving me a job."

He squeezes my shoulder and his jaw muscle begins flexing back and forth. He takes a minute to speak before he clears his throat. "It may have started as a job, but that was just the key that brought you here. It has turned into so much more. This is your home and we are your family. Never forget that."

Maria comes forward almost in a sprint and wraps her arms around me. I return the embrace. "Don't keep your adoptive mother waiting too long before you come back, okay?" she whispers in a whine next to my ear between sniffles.

"I won't. I promise. I love you, Mom." When the words come out of my mouth her crying becomes a little heavier. She lets go and kisses my cheek.

"I love you too, Son. Take care of yourself. You have my number, yes?" I nod. "Use it. I want to hear from you at least once a week. Will you do that?" I nod again and look at Marcus standing back.

He is staring off into space, zoned out. I wave him over. "Come here, buddy." He walks toward me and stops beside Maria. I kneel down to his level and gather my thoughts briefly before speaking. I remember something that I've held onto. It had no meaning until earlier today.

I reach into my pocket and pull out a silver anklet. A couple of months ago I went to see Dr. Rodriguez for one of our weekly chats. Usually, we met in town for lunch or I went to his home for dinner.

One night when I was over, we got to talking about the accident. I began asking questions that were plaguing my mind. *Why didn't anyone report the wreckage or me being found to discover my whereabouts or identity?* Another nagging thought was my lack of identity when I was found.

Sitting on the couch that night, he told me everything he knew. He was on call and a local fisherman came in screaming in a panic. Apparently, by the time they got to me, most of the wreckage except for what I was holding onto had already sunk to the bottom of the ocean. Since I clearly wasn't from Spain, they didn't know who to report me missing to, and I had lost a lot of blood from the gash on my head. The only thing the officials could come up with was that during the accident my belongings fell free from my body—all except one thing.

He had excused himself to his office. I had no idea what he was doing, but he brought back a small plastic bag holding this silver anklet. Hanging from it was a small silver heart with an engraving of initials on it. He told me that he held on to it for me, and in the process of everything had forgotten about it. He told me that when they took my clothes off of my body it was in the toe section of my shoe. He figured it was important if it was there, because it was the only thing on me.

Since that night, I've carried it with me at all times. It was the only thing I had left of who I was. Today, I remember exactly where it came from. I remember the words that came from Kinzleigh's mouth on the night of homecoming when she gave me her heart.

It's a treasure to me, but the real treasure is her. I don't need a piece of jewelry to remind me of that. Her heart is buried deep inside me, connected to mine. It's time to let it go to someone that I know will take care of it forever. "Do you see this?"

He nods as I dangle it in front of him. "This belonged to someone very special to me. She gave it to me on the night she gave me her heart. It's someone that I love very much. Someone I need to go back and find, because she needs me. One day, when you're grown, a very lucky lady will give you her heart, and you'll do anything it takes to keep it."

He is looking at me as if I'm his hero. "I wouldn't remember who I was if it hadn't of been for you. When I had no hope, you kept striving for more. You were persistent and that's a rare quality to find; never lose it. I'll be gone for a while, but you'll always be one of my brothers and I love you very much. I want you to have this."

I open his small hand and lay it in his palm before closing it into a fist. "Will you take care of this for me?" He looks down at his fist and when he looks back at me, he begins smiling from ear to ear.

He nods, and the excitement shows in his movements. "I won't let you down, Bryce, I mean Breyson. You can count on me."

"Good. I knew I could." I pull his small body to mine and give him a hug before I stand. I grab my duffle bag in my hand and turn to open the front door. I can see headlights coming down the road, signaling it's time to go.

I look back one more time at the people that have been my family for over six months. I don't know where I would be right now if it hadn't been for them. I would probably be on the streets doing only God knows what to get by. They took a chance on me without knowing anything about me, and for that I'll be eternally grateful. "I'll see you soon."

I walk out the door, taking that promise with me—a promise that I will return with the girl of my dreams in my arms. I also made a promise that I would never leave her. It's time to prove that I keep my promises no matter what.

I was taught from the time I was old enough to understand that a man's word is all he has. I've spent my life trying to live up to the values that my family instilled in me. Come hell or high water, I will be the man she needs. Death can come knocking at my door, but until it defeats me, I will fight tooth and nail for my family, starting with Kinzleigh.

FORTY-EIGHT

Breyson

We pull up to a private airstrip about twenty miles out. It's night, and all of the lights on the plane and runway are lit up. When I step out of the back of the car, the flashbacks of that night consume my mind, sending a cold chill all the way to my bones.

My breathing picks up as each scene plays through my mind. I feel like I can't breathe from the anxiety of the plane crash and the events that led to it. How am I supposed to get on this plane?

My chest constricts from the panic that is setting in. I bend forward to try and calm down. Mr. P comes out of nowhere and holds out his hand. "Here, take this."

A small pill lays flat on his palm. Without thought, I take it and toss it in my mouth. "What is it?"

"Something that will calm you down. Post-traumatic stress can be a bitch. It'll get better with time. You ready to do this?" That statement brings me back to the present. I have no choice but to get on that plane.

"Tell me what I have to do." I hope and pray to God that I don't have to do anything illegal. With a guy like him, I have no idea what to expect. He tilts his head in the direction of the private plane and walks toward the stairway.

I follow until we get aboard. The plane is top of the line and clearly expensive. I wonder how on earth he has so much money. I'm not going to ask, though. I don't think I want to know the answer.

He takes a seat in one of the leather chairs and points at the opposite for me to sit. I do as instructed. He performs a waving motion over his head. The flight attendant brings a thick envelope and he takes it. He lays it on the wooden, round table between us and slides it closer to me. "I need you to deliver this to my wife."

That sentence stunned me. His wife? He's married? I think back on that day that I saw him in his office and the tan line of a wedding band was present on his ring finger. "Where is she?"

"New York." That state holds so much more meaning than the two words it takes to say. I guess it's Fate taking me there, because I have other promises that I have to keep.

The night of the plane crash, Cheyenne only asked for one thing in exchange for her life to be sacrificed should I come out alive. That one thing was to deliver something to her mother and daughter. When I get to New York, I will hope and pray I can find that video. A part of me wants to watch it and a part of me doesn't.

"She lives there?" I ask. I have no idea what his reaction will be. He seems like a very private man.

He studies me for a moment. "I'm going to add you to a circle of trust that I never open to anyone. Ask me why I'm doing it now and I couldn't tell you. My job requires me to never form any type of personal attachments to anyone. It's a job that requires lives to be taken, and I'm the one that takes them." My eyes widen in sheer terror at that sentence.

He's a fucking hitman? My stomach feels like a massive ball of knots. How did I get involved with someone that commits murder for a living? "Before you freak out, let me clarify something. People come to me when they need someone taken care of, but I only terminate bad people. A scenario would be this: your daughter gets raped and left to die. You want the perpetrator to get what he deserves, right?"

As odd as it sounds, I nod. "Bad people in the world deserve to die. You can call it a form of natural selection if you want. I never take the life of someone that doesn't deserve it. I make a lot of money doing what I do, but what got me here was when someone wronged my family. That scenario I previously stated was my daughter twenty years ago. That bastard raped her when she was walking home from a friend's house one night and left her lying in the street to bleed to death from the slit he cut on her throat to keep her from screaming."

He gets a hard look in his eyes as he tells me this. Why in the hell is he telling me this? "She was thirteen fucking years old. She may have been conceived when I was in college and had nothing, but she was my baby. I was only thirty-three at the time, but I was old enough to plot his murder once I found him. I had the honor of looking in his eyes as I told him who I was and watched him die."

I cannot believe I'm having this conversation with someone. The people and things you hear about in this world that make it ugly and scary are really out there hiding in the shadows. "Why are you telling me this?"

"Because, you are the only person that has personal ties between Spain and the United States. I may need you on occasion. I'll never ask you to do anything illegal, but until I can bring my wife here, I need a way to get things or information to her. Back then, I was emotionally tied to the job and got sloppy. I'm much smarter now. When the sorry bastard was reported missing, I was a person of interest. As a result, they searched my home, and the token I took to remind me he got what he deserved appeared, and I had to flee."

He becomes quiet when part of the staff passes down the aisle. When they are out of earshot, he continues. "Word of mouth brings me clients, but I can't come back to the states often, and until government officials stop watching over my wife, I can't bring her here. Luckily, my son is not tied to me. I like it that way. It keeps him safe. I will never contact you unless I need you for a job, and should you agree, I'll compensate you well and provide you and your family protection should you need it."

My head feels like it's spinning from this entire conversation. I don't know whether to laugh or cry at the irony of the things that I encounter in one lifetime. I feel like I'm mentally insane for even considering his offer.

The fact of the matter is that I can't say I wouldn't do the same if something that horrific happened to my child or Kinzleigh. We are all human, and we are born with an instinct to protect what's ours. When a man fails to protect his family, he has nothing else. That is the ultimate and most absolute form of failure.

I have to think about my family. I haven't met my child yet, but I already know I would walk to the ends of the earth for it. "Nothing illegal, right? I would just be a delivery boy of sort on occasions?"

"Yes."

"Okay." I'd likely agree to anything to ensure my loved ones are protected.

He did say he only harms bad people. As moral and decent people, we must band together sometimes to keep values alive. Do I agree with what he does? No. Do I feel like he's playing God when he shouldn't be? Yes. Do I understand why he considers what he does plausible? Absolutely.

We all would kill for the people that matter to us the most, as well as die for them. I guess he considers what he does a way to help the people of the world that can't do it themselves. I can't say if only taking the lives of guilty people pardons him from the pits of Hell, because it's not my place to judge. Something like that is between him and God alone.

He stands from his chair and lays a notepad sized piece of paper face down on top of the envelope. "The address is listed. All you have to do is show up at the door and state the line I have written. When she lets you in, give her the package and exit through the back of the house. A car and an envelope will be waiting for you. Call me when it's done."

He walks down the aisle in the direction of the exit, but then he stops. "Oh, and Breyson, I trust that this information will never leave your lips. You are bound to silence for as long as you live. Breaking that agreement is costly—a life for a life. Please don't make me make that call."

He exits the plane, leaving me alone with that open-ended thought. Never in my life would I have imagined myself in the place that I am. What happened to living a normal life? I turn the piece of paper over and read the line I was given—*Phillip sent me with a message. I have a delivery.*

Phillip? Is that what Mr. P stands for? Instructions come from the flight attendant that we are about to take off. I fasten my seatbelt and lay my head back against the headrest. Only two stops and a plane ride between each until I see my beautiful girl again. I wonder what she will look like when I see her in person.

I place my hand over the ache in my chest. Without her I feel like a piece of me is missing. If I ever get her back in my arms, I don't think I'll physically be able to leave her again. Knowing I wasn't there with her while she experienced the pregnancy as she carried our child nearly kills me. I want to experience everything with her, but I guess what matters the most is that I'm on my way back.

I remember telling her one night that I would give her the world if I could. I may not be able to give her the world, but I'll do everything in my power to keep her happy and make her dreams come true.

FORTY-NINE

Breyson

I place my foot on the pavement. I can hear the busy streets of New York all around me. I got to my destination six months too late. This is so much different than country life back home. Kinzleigh would probably like it here. Maybe I'll bring her back someday. I can't wait to experience the rest of my life with her by my side.

I look up at the building before me. According to the driver, this is the address listed on the piece of paper. It's a huge skyrise that extends for miles. I walk forward in its direction. When I reach the door, a member of staff opens it, allowing me to enter. I walk inside to a massive lobby made of creams and golds.

I ask for the location of the elevator and he points me in the direction I need to go. Once I arrive, I press the up button and wait for the door to open, and then shortly after, I step inside and punch in the code on the elevator to take me to the top floor. I don't even want to know how much living in a place like this cost. The door shuts as I enter the last digit and it ascends.

After what feels like forever, the elevator chimes, signaling the arrival on the appropriate floor. I exit into a short hallway that leads to a large hardwood door. I have no idea what is going to be on the other side. Nerves are beginning to get the best of me. I take a deep breath and bring my fist to eye level but not touching the door.

Don't be a pussy. Just do it.

I bring my fist down to connect with wood and repeat it twice but no more. I wait. The sound of heels hitting against the floor get louder with each step. The door opens to a woman that looks younger than him, but not by much. She has aged gracefully and looks polished. She fits the image of what I would expect from someone that lives in a place like this, located in the heart of Manhattan.

"Can I help you?" She looks around and back at me as if she's puzzled. I now realize that a code is required to even get to this floor, so I recite the line from the paper exactly as it was written.

Her face changes into an expression of surprise. She backs up, opening the door farther, allowing me to enter. "Come in."

I stop in the foyer and unzip my duffle bag, removing the envelope, and hand it to her. She looks at it, silently studying it. When she looks back at me her eyes are glossed over. "How is he?"

I answer the best way I know how. "He seemed okay . . ."

"It's been a year since my last package, in case you were wondering. You seemed a little confused." She turns and walks away. I'm not sure what to do. Do I follow or just stand here? I choose the latter. A few feet ahead she stops and looks back. "Come on. You look like you need a good meal and I could use the company. Leave your bag at the door."

She continues walking, and this time, I follow her. I come through the door that opens into a large kitchen. It doesn't take long for me to catch up to her. Wearing six-inch heels and a pencil skirt doesn't leave much room for walking.

I sit at one of the stools behind the bar while she pulls ingredients from the refrigerator. She places a pan on the cooktop and begins combining ingredients into a bowl. It's easy to see that she's making an omelet. "It's a meeting place," she says, as she whisks the eggs in the bowl.

"Excuse me?"

"The package. It's instructions for a place to meet. I never know when they're coming or where the meeting place will be. The length of stay is always different. I live for those packages." I can tell from the break in her voice that she's about to cry. I have to admit this is a little awkward, given the fact that I just met her five minutes ago. Obviously, she has things she keeps buried deep and needs to get them out.

I'm not sure what to say, so I say the first thing that comes to mind. "I don't know much about either of you, but I know that he wants you with him. That much he made very clear in our conversation before I came here.

As an eighteen-year-old, I may not have a long history of wisdom, but I know that if you love someone you stick with them no matter what. In the end, late is better than never."

She has whisked those eggs beyond the necessary timeframe. If she keeps going, the heat produced from her constant stirring may very well scramble the eggs with no stove necessary.

She stops what she's doing and finally looks up at me for the first time since she started beating the eggs to a liquid disaster. "You know, that's the first time anyone has cared enough to tell me to stay. The only person that knows anything continuously tells me to leave. She doesn't get it, and likely never will. It takes someone that has experienced that kind of love for another to understand. You're going to make a very lucky girl happy."

I tap my fingers on top of the bar as I process everything she said. "You're right about everything but one thing. She's not the lucky one, I am. I don't know what God was thinking when he gave me her, but I will be at his mercy forever, and on my knees in gratitude. When the two of us are together it's like the stars align and our hearts sync together. She's the reason I wake up every day, and the reason I push to be a better man. Eighteen or eighty-eight, I'll always feel the same. Having her by my side every day for the rest of my life is the greatest blessing of them all."

She pours the egg mixture into the hot pan. A small smile forms. Every second I waste is another second I don't get to spend with Kinzleigh, and I still have another stop to make before I can fly back home. "If it's okay with you, ma'am, I'll eat and be on my way. I have someone that needs me, and I've been away from her long enough. I hope you don't mind."

"Of course. It's nice to be hopeful for once. Young love is motivational. My only piece of advice is when life happens don't lose that love you two have for each other. Instead, channel it and let it drive you for more, so when you get my age and look back, you love each other more in the present than in the past, instead of the opposite."

"I'll make a mental note. If we make it through the curve balls that we've already been thrown, we'll make it through anything." When I say if, that's what I mean. As I sit here, I remember a very specific catch phrase that Preston said last Christmas—*until there is a ring on her left finger proving she's yours, she can always change her mind.*

I grow more nervous with every passing moment. I can't lose her. If I do, I won't survive. I stayed alive for her. If I can't have her, I have nothing to live for.

FIFTY

Breyson

I walk down the busy streets of New York, lost in my own head. There was a car waiting in the garage when we went down the private elevator and an envelope that held a large sum of money lying on the seat. I gave the driver a pickup destination once I made the call of confirmation, as promised. I need some space right now and being in the backseat of an enclosed car is not going to do it.

I pull the cell phone from my pocket. I insisted leaving it in Spain, but they wouldn't have it until I was able to get another phone in The States. I have no idea where I'm going, but hopefully the walk and fresh air will help me to clear my head. The only thing ever running through my mind is Kinzleigh. It's either a curse or a blessing; I have yet to determine which.

I can see what looks like a park ahead. Benches are scattered throughout. When I arrive to the closest one, I sit and stare off into the distance. I have no idea what I'm even going to say or do when I get to her. Should I plan it all out or just wing it?

I lay the phone on my lap. Reflexively, I lace my fingers together on top of my head and lean against the back of the bench, looking up at the branches that extend out above me. Speckles of blue peek through the gaps between each leaf. The sun shines down in a pattern. "Daddy, I want to fly. Make me fly. I want to be a bird." The pipsqueak sound of the voice catches my attention.

I look out before me and see a family. The woman is blonde and petite, but with a curvy figure similar to Kinzleigh. The man is taller with a muscular build and darker hair. Neither looks older than thirty. The little boy has dirty-blond hair, cut short enough it stands up in the front on its own. He can't be more than five and reminds me of the way I looked as a kid.

The little boy is running toward the man with his hands high in the air. "Please, Daddy. Make me fly. I want to fly like you."

The man picks him up with both hands, laying him flat. He runs, making his son soar through the air. The small boy is holding his arms out like a set of wings. For some reason, I can't take my eyes away. His laughter as he flies through the air sends chills down my spine. I shake as I watch the three of them.

I turn my eyes to the blonde woman. She is standing to the side watching them and clapping her hands as she shouts, "Yay! Look at you go. You're flying so high." The smile on her face is enough to send anyone into a state of nirvana.

Tears sting my eyes. That family should be us. We shouldn't have to go through all this bullshit to be together. I press inward on my eyes to halt the tears from spilling. I just need a fix. I need one dose of the drug I've done without for so long. I need to hear her voice.

I look down at the phone in my lap and pick it up. I pull up the phone app. One by one, I type in the digits that form her number. I stare at it with my thumb over the call button. I battle with the choice in my head. My heart overpowers my brain, and I touch the green button, placing it to my ear.

It rings three times and picks up. I can hear giggling in the background. "Preston, stop. That tickles. Okay, okay, truce." I can hear shuffling in the background for a second. "Hello?"

I can't breathe. The tear I was holding back falls at the sound of her voice. "Hello, who's there?" I can't describe the feeling I have right now. In every vision over the past six months I've gone over and over in my head the different possibilities of what she sounds like. When my memories came back, I thought I knew. The pain in my chest amplifies and triples. "If you're not going to answer then don't call me, creep."

The call disconnects and everything I was holding in breaks free. I cry. It's one of those cries that a man is only entitled to once or twice in his lifetime. "God, I need her." I'm at my breaking point. I don't know what I was expecting, but hearing her laugh and play with another man was my rock bottom.

I lean forward, placing my forearms on my thighs. Tears drip off the tip of my nose. I'm at a loss. The feeling in my heart and soul isn't a good one. She's slipping away from me—the one thing I never thought could happen. I pull the photo out of my pocket that I brought with me, the one of the two of us on the football field.

Can separation make someone fall out of love with another? A thought occurs to me that didn't before. What if she chooses him? I continue to stare at the photo. Something is pushing me to keep going regardless.

I don't have a clue why, but sorrow and pain turn into jealousy and rage. Fuck him if he thinks he's getting her. I'm going after my family. The sooner I get done here, the sooner I can reclaim what's mine. We're meant to be together, and no matter what fire we have to walk through to get there, love conquers all.

Abercrombie boys don't back down, and we sure as hell don't go down without a fight. One of us is going to lose, and when it comes to Kinzleigh Baker, it isn't going to be me. Let the battle begin.

FIFTY-ONE

Breyson

I shuffle through countless emails as I search for the one I'm looking for. I sit in the back seat of the car I've been provided with to utilize for as long as I need. One more stop and I'll be free and homebound. If I play my cards right, I should be landing by tonight. The shock of what all has happened is starting to subside and I feel drained.

Email after email, I look for the only one of my concern. I finally find it and open the email from the folder it's in. I'm not sure that I'm emotionally prepared to witness this from the outside looking in. Either way, it has to be done. Tapping the file, I wait for the clip to load.

I sit with my back against the seat and my feet pressed firmly on the floor of the car. The video clip plays back. With each second that I watch, the memories get stronger in my mind from what they were before I got on the plane from Spain. I want to turn it off, but I can't. I want to see what Kinzleigh saw.

The one thing I didn't consider when I recorded and sent it was her anxiety. It almost makes me feel guilty knowing I put her through that. And all while she was pregnant with my child. It still hasn't completely registered that I'm going to be a father this young. I guess I really do get careless when it comes to her. I wonder if it's a boy or a girl and who it'll look like. I hope her.

The video ends. I feel weak and nauseated. I have no idea why I made it out alive when so many people lost their lives. I should have died along with them. I don't see how it was fair, but I guess it's not my place to question it either. I've always been taught that everything happens for a reason, whether good or bad. There is nothing a person can do to change that.

I give myself a moment to gather myself mentally before watching the second video. Pressing the play button, I immerse myself as it plays through. Watching it a second time is so much more brutal than witnessing it firsthand. I'm not sure if it's because I didn't know Kinzleigh was pregnant at the time and now I do, but my heart feels like it's being ripped from my chest cavity as she speaks to her daughter.

No young child should be left behind without parents. It's an unnatural and unfair part of life; another part of the ugly in the world. To me, it's no different than a parent having to bury a child. No one should have to go through that shit, especially when there are so many bad people in the world that deserve to die.

The video ends at the same time a road sign labeled *Silent Knight Lane* comes into view. It's time to do this. I just hope I don't add stress to someone. The car pulls in the driveway to the house labeled with the correct number and stops in front of the closed garage.

The sooner you get this over with, the sooner you can be on your way home. She needs you. Your baby needs you.

I don't wait for the driver to exit before I open the door and get out. I walk down the sidewalk to the entryway. Once I approach the door, it opens, and a woman is standing on the other side.

As I take in her features, it hits an emotional barrier that I built on the way over like a wrecking ball, breaking it down. She looks just like the girl in the video clip, only older. "Can I help you?"

I place my hands in the pockets of my shorts. "Are you Helen Speights?"

She looks around as if someone is going to pop out of the bushes with a camera. "Who wants to know?"

"My name is Breyson Abercrombie. I was in the plane crash with your daughter, Cheyenne. I have something for you and Callea." I'm almost afraid to speak in a loud voice due to fear of putting her in to cardiac arrest.

Her eyes immediately pool with tears and they fall one after the other. Sadness used to freak me out, but now it's become an almost constant state of mind.

She swipes the tears and moves to the side, allowing me to enter her home. "Please excuse the mess. I wasn't expecting company. Toddlers can be messy." She tries to hide her sorrow with a laugh, but it's strained.

I stand inside the foyer as she closes the door. Toys are scattered from one end to the other and the house is quiet. The toddler in question seems to be absent from this picture.

She starts picking up toys, filling her arms with them, but I touch her shoulder lightly to stop her. "Please don't do that on my account. It really doesn't bother me. I'm only here because I made a promise to someone."

She leaves them in a pile and stands. The pain in her eyes is enough to bring a grown man to his knees. I can only imagine what she must feel like, what my parents must feel like, or any parent losing a child must feel like. Nothing would ever be the same after that. I saw that firsthand with Cheyenne and the soulless creature that died with blood-stained hands.

I haven't even met my kid yet and the thought that something could have happened when Kinzleigh was hit by a car makes my blood run cold. The only reason I haven't thought about it is because of the recent photo I got in the package from Mr. P. showing me she was still pregnant. Her belly was round to almost a fully pregnant state.

"Follow me to the sitting room." She walks forward and I follow behind, taking in the portraits hanging on the walls. They are all of Cheyenne at different stages of life. The only thing that's off from the way I saw her are the smiles present on her face in every photo.

She is glowing in every picture, especially the last one, where she's lying in a hospital bed holding a baby with a large grin stretched from ear to ear. The man beside her looks nothing like the man that was the cause of her death. He is holding the baby's small hand with his index finger and staring at her with so much love it's clearly evident. They say misery loves company, and in their case, I guess it's true.

I didn't realize I had stopped to stare until she appears behind me. "That was the happiest day of her life. She loved that baby and would've died for her. I'm proud of her." She strains to get each word out.

I answer with the phrase that I know she will understand without having to drive the details of that day into her mind. "I know. I witnessed it." She gasps and searches my eyes with her own. "You have every right to be proud."

Additional tears fall from the corners of her aged eyes. The funny thing about tears, I've discovered, is that when they are shed, a part of you feels better. There is something about crying that relieves the heart and soul from the burdens of pain they carry from time to time. Some may see it as a form of weakness, including me at one time, but that's not the case at all. It takes a strong person to allow that much emotion to roam freely, because in abundance it's a lot to bear.

She leads me into the sitting room and I sit across from her on the love seat. She stares blankly across the room. "I need to tell you why I'm here," I tell her.

She comes back into the present and I continue. "The night of the crash we knew we were going to die. I need you to know that Cheyenne did not die in vain. She's a heroine. She sacrificed herself hoping to spare a life—lives. She sacrificed herself to protect her daughter from a dangerous man. In the short time I knew her, it was clear how much she loved her. She realized it was never going to stop, I believe, and made a permanent decision before more people got hurt. I don't know why God decided to spare me while the rest of them died, but to spare even one life is the greatest honor a person can die with. I'll do everything in my power to ensure the world knows what really happened that night."

I can tell I've resurfaced emotions she's worked hard to suppress; most likely trying to be strong for a little girl that doesn't understand. "Cheyenne only had one request. To say goodbye and make sure that I got it to you should I make it out alive. It's taken me awhile to get here, but I made it." Pulling the phone from my pocket, I ready the file for playback and hand it to her. She takes it and stares at it for a moment before mashing play. I listen to the audio as she watches the clip.

It isn't any easier to hear the third time around. She cries hysterically as it plays on. It takes everything in me to hold back the tears trying to force their way out as I witness her watch her daughter say goodbye in the last moments of her life. Watching her mourn the loss of her child is by far one of the hardest things I've had to do in my eighteen years of life.

Not knowing what else to do, I stand and walk over to her. As the video ends, she drops the phone to the floor and covers her face with her hands as she sobs uncontrollably, like she's been holding this in since she was notified of the accident.

Sitting down next to her, I wrap my arms around her. She is small compared to my muscular frame, allowing me to envelop her easily. She doesn't pull away as she continues to release the pent-up anger and sadness that has been locked away inside her.

I'm not sure how long I've been sitting here holding her, but the small footsteps and voice in the background captures my attention. "Nana, why are you crying?"

I release her from my hold and look over to the little girl standing in the doorway. She's rubbing her eyes, making it obvious she just woke up from a nap.

My eyes lock on her, memorizing her. She has long brown hair that falls just below her shoulders. It's mostly straight, but her baby curls at the ends are still present. Her skin is smooth but kissed by the sun, creating a bronze hue.

The little girl looks like an even mix of her parents, but her blue eyes are big and the focal feature of her face. She's holding a ragdoll that is half her size. The way she talks so well, I would guess she's already turned three.

Cheyenne's mom wipes her face with the collar of her shirt, trying to erase the evidence of her breakdown. "Sometimes grownups get sad too. Come here, Callea."

The small girl walks toward the sofa clenching tight onto her doll. It looks old and ratty, but she is holding it tight to her little body. If I had to guess, I'd bet it was Cheyenne's. She stops in front of me as if she is puzzling something together in her tiny mind. "Did my mommy send you?"

I put my finger in my ear and wiggle it. Obviously, I'm hearing things. "What did you say?"

"Did my mommy send you from Heaven? She went to live in Heaven for a little while, but I have to stay with Nana until I get big. I can't go there yet." The hairs on the back of my neck stand up.

"Your mommy did send me, but I haven't been to Heaven. Did your nana tell you about Heaven?" I have no idea what the reaction of Cheyenne's mom is to all of this, because I can't look away from the big, bright eyes in front of me.

She walks closer and raises her arms—including the doll—for me to pick her up. I place my hands underneath her arms, lifting her, and place her on my lap. "Nana told me that Mommy went to live with Jesus in Heaven, but sometimes when I go to sleep, Mommy visits me. She said a nice man was coming to see Nana, but to keep it a secret until he comes."

I feel like I'm going to throw up. Maybe my mind is shutting down from all of the emotions and stress of the day. Clearly, I'm hallucinating and hearing things. I try to ask her a simple question to check back into reality. "Do you miss your mommy?"

"I miss her when it's a sunny day. Sometimes, she tells me important things." Maybe, if I just play along, I'll feel less like a person that has mentally snapped.

I look over to my side and Cheyenne's mom looks like she's seen a ghost. Callea places her small palm on my forehead, turning my attention back to her. "What kinds of things does she tell you?"

"She said to take care of Nana until you came with the present. She said it would be a long time, because you were sick." As she says the word long, she expands her arms out to her sides to show me her version of the measurement on a scale. She then places her palm back on my forehead like she's checking for fever. "Do you feel better?"

I am completely and inevitably mind-fucked. If you put a mirror under my nose right now it would likely be clean, because I can't breathe. I sit here, staring at her, ignoring the pain in my chest from the lack of oxygen. I've never been one to believe in ghosts or spirits returning after death in an alternate form, but I've always heard that children have a sixth sense.

I feel like I'm in the middle of that MTV show and Ashton Kutcher is going to jump out stating it's all a prank. But who the hell would be able to make this shit up? I have entered into fucked-up-ville, and my life has become the crazy shit writers dream up to put in a fictional book. People would pay big money to read about this shit, and I'm stuck living it against my will.

Why can't I return to normal for once? Where did I make a wrong turn? I want a do-over; any time after Kinzleigh and I got together. Somewhere I jumped on the carousel of crazy and I want off.

My head is spinning. All I want is to be back in a love bubble with Kinzleigh. I wish I could erase getting on the plane that day, but each decision changes the outcome of the future, for better or for worse. That's something I will think about now, before I wish to change things of the past.

I'm currently in a state of mind that excuses me from any crazy talk that may occur from here on out. "I do feel better," I tell her. "But I won't feel great until I get back home. I've been gone for a long time. I'm homesick. I have to go see someone very important to me, but I promised your mommy that I would stop by and tell you something first. If I tell you, will you remember it forever?"

I'm not sure what I'm going to say, but I think about that little boy in the park. She nods but remains oddly quiet for a toddler. "When your mommy and I were flying high in the sky, like birds, she had to fly extra-high to

Heaven for a little while like your nana told you, but she had to go quickly and didn't get a chance to give you a goodbye kiss first."

She settles on my lap and hugs her doll to the front of her body with a curious expression, as if I'm telling a story. I've never been that comfortable around small kids. It's a rather difficult task to try and explain a complex scenario to a mind that is not able to process it in its entirety. "She was really sad that she couldn't tell you bye, so she sent me to give you a message. It's top secret until you become a big girl, and then Nana will tell you the story again." My voice lowers to a whisper to prove my point. "Can you keep it a secret?"

Her eyes light up and she gives me a cheesy grin, showing a mouthful of baby teeth. She nods continuously while wiggling on my lap, and a high-pitched squeal escapes. "I'm the bestest secret keeper ever! I pinky promise."

She holds out her tiny pinky for me to link mine with hers. It takes everything in me not to break down right now. I thought it was hard with Cheyenne's mother, but this is worse, multiplied by a hundred. I can feel my eyes moistening, but I refuse to let them fall.

My heart cannot physically take this. I feel like I'm lying to her, because I know that she is going to grow up without a mother. She is going to grow up and realize that her mother is never coming back, and that Heaven is only a place you visit permanently. It's a one-way ride.

The innocence of a child is something worth preserving at all costs. I'm learning that now, as I sit and watch her face conform to every word that comes from my mouth. Even the strongest of men would fall to their knees to avoid having to do this to a child.

It reminds me of the things that my sister needs my mother for, like prom, getting married, and having babies. When I'm reminded that she is going to be forced to grow up without her mother, it makes me want to fall on my knees and beg God to let me trade places with Cheyenne.

I was selfish before, but the truth is, Kinzleigh can live without me. A child can live without its father more easily than without its mother. I won't deny that they are both crucially imperative to a full life, but if having to choose one or the other, a child needs its mother.

How her father could make the decision that his child is better off without them is selfish, and most likely the reason he will burn eternally if he didn't repent before he took his last breath. He played God when it wasn't his place, altering his daughter's life forever.

Because knowing her now, I see how precious she is. "I had a feeling you would be an expert secret keeper. Your mom wanted me to tell you how much she misses you, and that she will be counting the days until she can see you again. She said to always mind Nana and to be extra nice, because she will be watching you."

I rub my chin, as if I'm trying to remember if I left out anything. My arm is around her to keep her from falling off. She snuggles into my chest as she waits for me to finish. On the exterior I'm putting on a happy face, but on the inside, I'm unraveling. I'll never understand the ugly things of the world. They should lurk in the shadows, but instead, they invade the light, breeding more darkness.

I snap my fingers. "Oh yeah. She said she loves you to the moon and back, to infinity and beyond, and forever and ever. She told me to make sure you know how important it is that you remember. Do you promise with all your heart that you won't forget?" As I say the word heart, I touch my index finger to its location on her tiny body.

"I'll lock it up and throw away the key," she says with laughter in her voice. I can't stay here any longer. If I do, I'm going to wither away and die before I get to Kinzleigh. If I don't get to her, all this will become a waste and what Cheyenne did will be meaningless.

I sit her down on her feet in front of me. "Good. It's time for me to go now. How about you go play with your doll and give me one minute to tell Nana something, okay?"

"K," she says in a singsong voice. "It's time for Dolly's nap." I watch as she disappears down the hall. I think I understand the meaning of little girls having grown men wrapped around their fingers.

I look over at Cheyenne's mother, and her face is drenched in tears she's no longer trying to hide. "I'd like to forward the clip to you and then I'll be on my way. If I give you the phone, can you type in the email address?"

She nods, but she's still staring off blankly. I reach down and pick up the phone from the floor in front of her and ready the file to be forwarded. Giving it over to her, she looks down and types for a minute before handing it back to me.

Checking it over, I send it and stand, sliding the phone safely back in my pocket as I look down at her. She looks like a petrified statue, no longer able to function. "Are you sure you're going to be okay? I don't want to leave you like this."

For the first time since I started talking to her, she looks at me. "I'll be okay. I just need a few minutes to myself. Thank you for what you did. We are strangers to you. You didn't have to come here before you went home, but you did, and I'll always be thankful. It gives me closure, and I can finally lay her to rest. Go home to your family. I can tell you that they are struggling, and that's the place you need to be." She goes back to staring blankly, and I take that as my cue to excuse myself.

I get to the car still parked in the driveway and seat myself in the back. The window is down, giving me direct access to the driver. "I need the next flight out."

Without another word, I raise the glass to give myself privacy. As soon as it's up, the dam breaks. A man can only be strong for so long before he can't take anymore. The aftermath of what I just had to endure is worse than I ever imagined it would be.

I sit here and cry like a fucking baby, unashamed. My heart is shattered into a million pieces. I've seen life in the form that no one wants to witness it. I've traveled the road of tragedy from end to end.

Right now, I'm mentally walking down a rundown street in a dark alley where the grime and filth reside. The stench is enough to burn the hair in your nose. This is where the monsters thrive; the bloodsucking demons that hide in the darkness for a passerby to come through so they can leech on and destroy the good, allowing evil to permeate and multiply. Here, you fight it or become it. I'll fight to remember and hold onto the good, because I sure as hell am not becoming a host.

FIFTY-TWO

Breyson

The car pulls up at the airstrip and the plane is already waiting. I yawn and stretch when it comes to a stop. The exhaustion must have taken over, pulling me into a slumber. I'm one step closer to my final destination. The door opens and I slide across the seat, exiting the car.

The driver holds out my duffel bag and I accept it. "Mr. Abercrombie, it's been a pleasure. I hope you enjoy your flight." He reaches in the interior pocket of his suit, pulling out the envelope of money I tried to return to him when I found it. "Mr. P. left specific orders to make sure you received this and kept it. Please take it."

I'm tired and not in the mood to argue, so I do. "Thank you, but it's really not necessary."

He smiles and tips his hat. "There will be a car waiting for your arrival. Where shall I confirm the pickup?"

"Miss—" I start thinking about the photos and the phone call. I recall information stored away from the past. "Fucking bastard."

"Excuse me, sir?" I didn't realize I voiced that aloud.

"Sorry, the pickup will be in California; as close to Laguna Beach as possible." I cannot believe he took her back to California. Of course, he lured her back to his stomping ground. How could I have even thought they would be in Mississippi?

"I'll make the arrangements." He closes the door behind me and returns to the car as I get on that death trap of a plane for the second time. I'm going to get the girl or die trying.

FIFTY-THREE

The limo pulls up to the venue that is hosting the event for Preston's company. I hate attending things like this. I feel like I stick out and I get awkward around so many people. Preston is turning into a very important person, and that alone makes me nervous. It means I have to pay close attention to the things I do, because cameras will be everywhere.

The thought has my nerves running wild, heating like coils throughout my body. I hate big crowds. I close my eyes and breathe to calm my anxiety. Two warm hands take residence on my face, covering my cheeks. His breath tickles my lips as he speaks in a low, sexy voice. "Do you trust me?"

A shiver runs down my body and I whisper in return, "Yes."

"Open your eyes." I do as he says and stare into his. "You have nothing to be nervous about. People always love you. I'll never leave your side, not even for a second. Tonight, I will tell the world you will soon be my wife, and as soon as I can get away, we will leave for the weekend. Are you sure you're ready for sex? I can still wait if you want to."

My cheeks flush as the smell of mint lingers between us. I've thought about it over and over as I examined the consequences from every possible angle. The answer remains the same. I'm ready to take this next step with him. We'll be married by Christmas.

Sex is the only other barrier we have to cross, and it's not going to get easier for me. I had something a lot of people don't. I lost my virginity and got the love of a lifetime with it. I got to experience the most amazing relationship alongside the only man I've ever been with. The only way to move past this hurdle is to just saddle up that horse and ride it, literally, as well as figuratively. "Yes, I'm sure. I want to do it, Preston."

The guilt that I'm betraying Breyson still surfaces on a regular basis, but I'm learning to channel it so that it doesn't consume me. He's dead and there is nothing I can do to change that. No matter how much I wish I could will him back, I can't. I don't have to forget Breyson to move on, but I do have to make room in my heart for someone else.

Like Macie said, Preston is my fiancé, not some random hook-up. Sex is part of a relationship with someone, and it's a part that I miss. No matter how many times my hormones take over and I just want to scream, *do it already*, there is still a part of me that holds back when my heart steps in front of the marathon my mind is trying to run.

I've been spending a lot of time with Macie and Talon since they moved here a month ago, and she continues to assure me that my feelings of guilt are normal. She tells me repeatedly that time is the only thing that will allow those feelings to fade.

Being around Talon is giving me a comfort around kids that I've never had before. He's a really good kid. He's older, but I'm actually starting to look forward to Bryce arriving.

Macie volunteered to help me at the cheerleading company until she begins work with Preston, so I don't have to do as much heavy lifting, and I must say, it's coming along better than I anticipated. I'm so thrilled with everything that I've decided to start classes for Business Administration and Marketing in the spring.

I refuse to be dead weight in this marriage, regardless of how much money Preston makes. It isn't in me to sit around and do nothing, relying on him and everyone else to do what I could be doing. I want to be an asset to my company and not just a coach. I have goals of where I want to take it and it requires brains and skill to get there.

Preston kisses my lips and his breathing picks up slightly. He moves one hand to my very round belly and Bryce begins moving at the sound of his voice. "Can you believe he's going to be here in a few short weeks?"

A knot forms underneath his hand and moves. Preston smiles from ear to ear as he looks me in the eyes. "That's so cool. I can't believe he can hear what we're saying." He looks so proud that you'd never know it wasn't his child.

I have mixed emotions about the matter. In one sense, it breaks my heart that Breyson isn't here to witness Bryce's growth and the birth of his child. He won't get to watch him grow and thrive or learn new things. In another light, I'm thankful that blood doesn't matter to Preston, because it takes a special person to look past the biological aspect of a child and still feel as if that child is a part of them whether genetics match or not.

Our moms hosted a shower awhile back that brought up a topic of conversation that night in bed. He asked what last name I was giving the baby. I guess I had never thought of it before it was asked.

I haven't had much contact with Breyson's family since I moved back; there isn't much to say. His mom calls about once a week to check on me, but it's a little awkward since I'm in a relationship and living with another man.

Preston gave me the option of giving Bryce his last name to keep our names all the same and to keep us out of the media. He assured me that he would always look at Bryce as his own, and this was his way to prove it. He also made it clear that he would never try to push Breyson's name or role in Bryce's life out of the way. He left the decision for me to make and said he would support me either way.

I've thought about it hard.

I decided that I'm sticking with Abercrombie. He was conceived an Abercrombie and he will forever be an Abercrombie. If the media wants to drag our names through the mud for a good story then so be it, but I just don't have it in me to take that away from Breyson. Bryce will always be Breyson's son, and when the time is right, he will know who his biological father is. It is not my intention to forget Breyson, but to lay him to rest and attempt to live a reasonably happy life.

I return Preston's smile. "It has gone by fast, hasn't it? I'm just ready to meet him."

I don't get the last word out of my mouth good and he lays one on me. He kisses me deeply and packed with meaning behind it. Every time he intertwines our tongues slow and steady, circling them in a hypnotic, enticing rhythm, I know he's having an emotional moment. I've learned things about him I never knew before. I suppose that's just part of being with someone on a near constant basis.

He lets go and slowly opens his eyes. He looks peaceful. "I love you, Kinzleigh. I can't wait to call you my wife."

"I love you too, crazy boy, but what was that for?" I wipe the shiny lip gloss off of his lips with my thumb.

"I just had an odd sense of urgency to say it. I don't know, I'm just ready to make you mine. The sooner I get that other ring on your finger, the sooner I'll stop worrying about you changing your mind." He attempts to cover his insecurity with a laugh.

I stop wiping and look him in the eyes. Preston has never been insecure before. Why is he now? I choose not to bring attention to it. Maybe it's just an emotional night for him, because after it's over everything will be public. "Don't be silly. I wouldn't have said yes if that were a possibility. Come on or we're going to be late for *your* event."

As we exit the car, my black chiffon dress falls to my feet. It's one shoulder and the top hem is lined with black, satin roses. I had to get something that fit loose over my belly without making me look bigger than the cow I feel like I am. My hair is done in an elegant side bun and I'll never reveal I'm wearing flats with a formal gown, but I wouldn't be caught dead in heels right now.

Preston holds out his arm for me and I take it. We walk together toward the stairs, and I can already see members of the security detail checking names of guests off the list. When they take in Preston, the rope is immediately pulled to the side, letting us through.

We enter the building and make our way into the large ballroom. Hundreds of guests are waiting. I feel like my clothes are constricting around my body and eyes everywhere are boring into me. I can barely breathe. Why did I agree to this? The urge to turn around and run overwhelms me, but I know I'd never stop until I got back home.

I need to do something to take my mind off of all the wealthy and significant people that surround me, most likely judging me just as Lexi did at the beach. I never really stopped to think how this looks for a girl like me with a guy like Preston.

People approach us. I have no idea who most of these people are and what their role is in the company. Should I have asked all of these questions before? Do I keep quiet or attempt to speak and risk embarrassing him?

1, 2, 3, 4, 5, 6, 7, 8 . . .

I feel a light squeeze on my hand as Preston talks about things that I don't understand with the man in front of him. Am I freaking out that obviously or has he just learned my bad habits? Whatever the case is, it's oddly calming.

The past couple of hours has consisted of meet and greets to every possible important businessman here, and I'm getting tired. I'm not used to so much standing in a given time period, and I feel like my feet are starting to swell.

As if he knows what I'm thinking, he leans next to my ear. "We're about to go, okay?" I nod, and he leads me toward the front of the room in the direction of a mic stand. He lets go of my hand and removes the wireless mic from the stand it sits in.

I stand nervously as he taps the top, making sure it's turned on. He doesn't look nervous at all. I guess some people are just born to be in the spotlight. "Can I have everyone's attention please? There were two reasons we set up this event tonight. The first is to announce that *Dunagin Properties and Development* has decided for the time since we opened our doors to expand from one of the fastest growing national companies and begin developing property globally."

Everyone around the room begins clapping. His eyes scan the room as if he's addressing each person individually. "The first project will break ground in December—a resort on the beaches of Greece, and completion is scheduled for next summer."

Everyone begins talking around the room and his eyes lock with mine. The microphone never leaves his lips. "If I could hold everyone's attention for a few more moments I'll leave you to mingle for the rest of the evening."

The room silences once again. "I brought a very special guest with me tonight that some of you have already been introduced to. Kinzleigh, I just want you to know that the past several months with you have been the happiest months of my life. Not a day goes by that I'm not thankful you agreed to take a step past friendship into courtship with me. You've been my friend for as long as I can remember. Our families have a bond unlike any other. I knew from a young age that I felt differently about you than any other girl, and it's continued to build over the years. I've never been happier than when I was able to call you my girlfriend, but nothing will compare to the day I can call you my wife. Thank you for agreeing to marry me and making me the happiest man alive. I'm madly in love with you. I love you, Kinzleigh Baker."

Tears fall from my eyes as I listen to the words come from his mouth. His grin spreads and his eyes light up. "I just wanted everyone to know that I asked her to marry me, and she said yes."

Everyone around the room claps, and I can see camera flashes in my peripheral vision, but my focus never leaves him. That was nothing like I expected it to be. He hands off the mic to someone beside him and begins walking toward me. He stops only inches away and wraps his arms around me. "It's official, Mrs. Dunagin to be. No turning back now."

His smile is contagious. "No turning back," I repeat, and he closes in to kiss me. If you had asked me seven or eight months ago what I predicted in my future, this wasn't it. Preston wasn't the man standing before me, giving a speech that he loves me in front of hundreds of people to prove that he's proud to marry me.

The truth is, Breyson was the man that I thought would be before me pledging his love. I thought the ring on my finger would have belonged to him. I thought I would grow old with Breyson by my side as we sat on our porch in the country and watched our grandchildren run and play in the yard. The person I imagined at the end of the aisle when I repeated my vows was him, but life doesn't always happen the way we want or expect it to.

We each walk a path in life, but that path is rarely straight. They are made with twists and turns, some worn, and some grown up from lack of footsteps. Others have obstacles in the way that you have to break through.

Regardless of what a person's path looks like, it's custom built from everything that happens between events and choices. Sometimes unforeseen circumstances make us veer in a direction we weren't expecting. Even if it leads to a dead end, there is always a loophole, a way to keep going.

My dead end was when Breyson died in that plane accident, but my loophole was Preston. "Are you ready for your weekend getaway, beautiful?"

I've chosen to take the detour and continue walking, instead of standing at the dead end, stuck forever. "As ready as I'll ever be."

FIFTY-FOUR

Kinzleigh

The elevator chimes and Preston takes my hand, leading me into the car. The doors close and I'm caught off guard as he pins me against the wall, slamming his lips to mine. I can feel the heat behind his kiss. His neediness shows each time his tongue collides with mine. He searches my mouth from east to west, leaving a piece of himself in each possible place. "I can't wait to be inside you," he says, as his warm breath kisses my lips, breaking for only a moment.

He sucks my bottom lip into his as if he's starving for more. He narrows his tongue and runs it along my jawline, sending a jolt of need throughout my body. Adrenaline is coursing through my veins. I can feel the increased blood flow pumping with each beat of my heart.

His lips touch the lobe of my ear. "I'm going to watch you while you come." My reaction to the filthy things coming from his lips is to tilt my head to reveal more of my neck. I haven't felt a need like this in a long time.

He places the tips of his fingers on my shoulder and traces the top of my arm, leaving chills where they've been. I press my legs together as the muscles begin clenching down below, needing to be filled.

This time doesn't compare to the previous times we've hooked up. They've become sparser recently, because he wanted to wait until this night, and things were getting more heated each time. I'm finally ready to give him myself.

The elevator car comes to a stop and the door slides open. He separates himself from me with a cocky grin in place. My cheeks feel hot, telling me they have morphed into a shade of red. We have arrived at the top floor, the king of suites. I haven't even been inside and I can already tell it's going to be unbelievable.

He backs up in the doorway to hold the doors open. His eyes slowly scan my body, making me feel as if I'm standing before him naked. It's a bit intimidating. He holds out his hand palm up, asking for mine. I place mine on top and let him lead me out of the elevator to the room door. He places the key card in the slot to unlock it.

He allows me to enter first. As I take in my surroundings, I'm beginning to get nervous. Red rose petals are scattered along the dark, hardwood floor, beginning at the door and continue down the entryway hall. Soft music is playing throughout the room and the lights are dim. I smell a subtle aroma in the room that reminds of lavender. He obviously had this setup ahead of time.

Everything is starting to set in. I have only been with one man in this way, and that was almost seven months ago. I'm terrified I am going to be thinking about Breyson while I'm with Preston. I think I just need a minute to get myself together.

The door clicks shut. I turn to Preston easing up to me. "Are you okay? You can still change your mind? I want your mind to be clear when we do. I want to be the only one you're thinking about."

"I'm fine. I'm just a little nervous now that it's actually here. It's been a while. You know I've only been with one person, Preston, and even though I thought it started out casually, I was wrong. I've never been with someone sexually that I didn't also feel something for emotionally. I think I was just lying to myself. This is a big step for me. I may have thought I wanted it before, but the reality is, I wasn't ready . . . until now. After tonight, I know I want to do this . . . with you." I wrap my arms around his waist, pulling him closer to me.

His hands remain in the pockets of his pants, but his eyes speak volume. He has something on his mind, but he's not going to tell me yet. He's going to think it through until the words are aligned in his head just as he wants them, so he doesn't say the wrong thing. "Will you give me a minute?" I ask.

"Of course. Take your time. I'm still waiting on our luggage to come up and then it's just the two of us . . . alone."

I let go and follow the petals across the floor. I'm going to guess they lead to the bedroom, and in turn, I will find the bathroom. I feel like Dorothy following the yellow brick road. I watch each step until the petals disappear underneath a door. I look up, and I'm standing right in front of it. I open the door. When I walk inside the view takes my breath away.

A large king-sized bed sits in the middle of the room, covered in fluffy white linens. Hues of sea-green speckle the room, reminding me of the water. The rose petals continue through the room and end spread all over the bed. The lights in here are also dim, but the flickering of candles capture my attention.

The French doors of the balcony are opened to my left and the sheer, white curtains are blowing with the breeze. It's dark outside, but I can hear the waves of the ocean washing against the shore. It's as perfect as it could possibly be.

Instead of walking to the bathroom as I planned, I take the opposite direction to the balcony. There is something about the water and the beach that has always been appeasing to my nerves and anxiety. I look down and a couple catches my attention, standing in each other's arms at the edge of the water. They look like they are lost in nirvana with each other.

An ache forms in my chest; one that I've done well suppressing for a while. I remember the week that was Brey and me. I'll always miss him terribly. Not a day goes by that I don't think about him in one sense or another. Just because I'm choosing to live, doesn't mean that I love him any less today than I did the day I said goodbye to him at the airport.

I look up at the dark sky. It's the perfect shade of onyx. All of the stars are shining brightly, and if you look close enough, they appear to twinkle in the rhythm of a song. The breeze blows against my face, taking the fallen strands of my hair into flight.

The pain of losing him will never go away, but I need to numb it as much as possible. A tear I wasn't expecting falls free. "Breyson, you were my first, and I thought you would be my last. Please forgive me for what I'm about to do. I'm sorry," I whisper, allowing my voice to be carried away with the wind.

A pair of lips touch the nape of my neck and kiss their way across the top of my bare shoulder. "You miss him, don't you?" My heart stops. How do I answer that? I remain silent. The zipper to my dress descends. My breathing becomes unsteady. "It's okay, Kinzleigh. I don't get jealous anymore."

I turn to face him. "What do you mean?"

He places his hand against my cheek. "At first, I felt territorial when his name was brought up or when my mind reminded me you've loved someone else, but then I realized it was good for me. It taught me that when you allow yourself to open up with someone, you fall hard, and you stay true to that person and always do right by him. The heart is the purest part of a person. The mind can deceive us, lie to us, and mislead us, but the heart cannot. There is enough room for both of us in yours, and by knowing how much you love him, I know you mean it when you tell me you love me."

He moves his hand into my hair and pulls the pins free until it falls in waves down my back. "I know I'm not as pure as you sexually, but intimately, I am. When I give myself to you, it's in a way I've never given myself to anyone. It means more to me that you've only had sex with someone you care deeply for, because in turn, I know that when we do this, you feel strongly for me. I know we aren't each other's first, but I want us to be each other's last."

He grabs the fabric over my one shoulder and peels it down my arm until the dress is low enough it will willingly fall to the floor in a pile at my feet. I nod, at a loss for words. I try to even out my breathing as I place my hands on the front of his shoulders. Sliding them over the curve, his jacket falls over them and I push the sleeves down his arms. Grabbing it in his hands, he folds it and tosses it on the chair inside the door.

Not wearing a bra, I am standing in my flats and panties before him. Everything else is bare. One by one, I unbutton his shirt, my eyes following my hands. I can feel his eyes on me as I bare his torso.

When his shirt is laying in a wrinkled mess on the floor, he removes his shoes, now standing in only a pair of suit pants. Tangling his hand in the back of my hair, he pulls me into a kiss.

My eyes close, letting him rid my mind of all thought. I allow myself to escape into a different frame of mind. I don't want to think, only feel.

He turns us around until my back is facing the bed, and walks forward, toward it. The back of my knees meets with the mattress and I sit, making him bend to still be able to keep his lips attached to mine. His hand now cupped behind my head, he guides me backward until I'm lying flat on my back.

He releases me and unbuckles his belt, then undoes the button on his pants. Lowering his pants and boxers, he bares himself. Grabbing my hips in his hands, he slides my underwear off in one swift motion. My shoes fall to the floor, creating a soft thud.

I prop up on my elbows and scoot upward until I'm lying completely on the mattress. He follows me until he's over me completely, looking down. Lowering his face to mine, he kisses me, making love to me with his mouth. My belly prevents his body from being aligned with mine, but he makes do. Sliding his arm underneath my back, he flips us over. He's muscular, but his build is lean, He's much stronger than he appears, though.

He pulls me into a straddling position on top of him and scoots against the headboard, so we are facing each other in a seated position without offsetting my balance. His hard shaft is lying under me, between my legs, further enhancing my need. Our breathing staggered and our faces both flushed, we allow ourselves to get lost in each other's kiss.

He breaks the kiss, but I clutch his hair in my hands, pulling him back for more. "Wait, Kinzleigh."

I stop, aggravated, and look at him. I let him know, aloud, in a low growl, just how frustrated I am. He's already gotten me in the mood and ready to go. Talk time is over. "What?"

He kisses my breast, calming my annoyance a few degrees. I can't help the grinding motion that occurs with the temptation of what is between my legs. He smiles, and both of our eyes become heavy, but he doesn't attempt to keep going. I surrender and stop, so he can get out whatever it is he needs to say. "I just wanted to say this before we went all the way. I didn't bring any condoms, because of obvious reasons."

He looks down at my stomach, briefly, and continues. "I know that we've hooked up some, but I wanted to tell you I got tested after our talk on the yacht last summer, and again before I came back for you. I've never had sex without a rubber, but I wanted to be sure. I'm clean. I told you I wouldn't sleep with another woman until I had an answer from you, and I kept my word. I haven't been with a girl aside from you in over a year, and that's the truth. I want to feel you in a way I've never felt a girl. I want to feel you bare."

This hasn't been a topic of conversation to date, and I didn't ever think of this. I've been with Breyson bare, but I don't recall a time it was ever really discussed; it just happened.

I reason in my head. We are getting married and I'm already pregnant, but I'm pregnant. The two perspectives of the same thing alternately leave me in the middle. I have a solution. "Just don't come in me until after the baby is born, okay?"

I may be willing to do what I'm about to do, but there are just some lines I won't cross. Those two things are not going to mix by fault. It would be different if I was carrying Preston's kid—created by *his* sperm.

He smiles and fists my curls in his left hand, pulling me closer to him like he can't get enough. His right hand dips down below, resting against my sweet spot. He messages lightly with his thumb, enough to send me into a blissful state of euphoria as I arch my back needing more.

Untangling his hand from my hair, he traces down the seam of my back until it is cupped over my butt. The muscles in his arm flex as he lifts me off of his body. He stops the pleasure he's inflicting on me and I whine.

I shift the weight from my shins to my knees, creating a larger space between the two of us, and look down as he grabs the base of his shaft. The head is positioned at my entrance but not touching.

Now that I've taken the weight from him, he moves the opposite hand to my hip and lowers me to the height he wants me. His head is pressed against me, ready for entry, and the sudden desire to lower myself is consuming my mind.

He rubs his head up and down between my folds, creating an aura in my body that is intoxicating. "Damn, you're so wet. Do you want it?"

It's been months since I've felt this feeling, and the added hormones don't help. "Yes."

He positions his dick back at my opening and pulls me down, entering me slowly, groaning until he is completely buried inside of me. "That feels so good," he says, positioning both hands on my hips, but then he holds me still so that I can't move.

"What's wrong?" I ask.

"Give me a minute. It feels better than I expected it to." I clench the muscle between my legs, the soft throbbing making me want to ride him. He needs to start moving or something. "Shit, Kinzleigh. You're going to make me come if you keep doing that. You're already tight without squeezing my dick."

I take matters into my own hands. Just sitting here isn't going to cut it. I've waited too long for this. He's inside me now. There's no turning back.

Placing my hands on his chest, I push him back, hinting I want him flat against the mattress. He pushes down the length of the bed with me on top of him, so that he can. Lacing my fingers with his, I pin them above his head to give me leverage as I rock back and forth. Luckily, I find the spot I need on the first try.

I squeeze his hands, each hit against that perfect spot feeling better than the one before. My orgasm builds with each thrust back and forth. I can't control the moaning. "I'm about to come."

I close my eyes and enjoy the ride. The feelings blossom like a rose, beginning as a small bud and blooming into a mind-blowing orgasm. I lock my lips with his to silence the cry that wants to escape.

When the wave of pleasure subsides, I pull back and open my eyes. Preston's mouth is slightly gaping. "Damn, Kinzleigh. That was the hottest thing I've ever seen." A throaty groan escapes in between sentences. "You're so wet. It's running down me."

I've stirred some kind of animal inside him. He rolls me over and grabs my ankles, pulling them into the air as he gets balanced on his knees, resting a heel on each shoulder. He begins thrusting slow and deep, watching my face conform with each one.

I grab the pillow in my hands and hold on. The smirk and fire in his eyes confirms he's just getting started. He continues a slow rhythm, torturing me. "You like using my body to come? You like getting yourself off on me?"

He grinds his hips in a circular motion, causing my eyes to roll back in my head. "Yes," I breathe out.

"You want it rough? Is slow not good enough? Does my girl want dirty sex?" He slides out slowly and completely, knowing exactly what he's doing to me.

That is exactly what I want. I want something that won't remind me of sex with Breyson. I want something different; something my mind won't be able to compare. I want to be in an alternate state of mind. I have never wanted to channel my pain and heartache through sex before, but right now, I want to let the pleasure consume me. I want to forget everything but this moment, even if only for one brief pause in time.

For the first time in my entire life I understand girls like Presley. I understand the need to try and let the one who possesses you completely go by getting under someone else. Sometimes, the only way to cope with the reality of living in Hell on earth is to find a mental distraction . . . like sex. Sex creates a world that can take away the thought process, numb the pain, and replace the happiness that was taken from you with a synthetic version.

I love Preston, but I don't want him to make love to me the way Breyson made love to me. Instead, I want him to treat me like a dirty whore. I want him to hurt my body while still making it feel good. That is only and absolute way that I can ensure I won't think of *Breyson* during sex with Preston.

"Give it to me hard. I want to feel you as deep as possible. I want you to hurt me." He spreads my legs wide, forming a V in the air, and then leans forward and picks up pace using my ankles to balance himself.

He pulls out and rams it in over and over. With each thrust my body scoots one inch closer to the headboard. My body is shaking, but it's not enough. My head is clear, but I'm still mentally here. "Harder."

He pulls out and lowers my legs to the side. Sweat is beading across his forehead. "Turn over. Get on all fours. You want naughty tonight, then I'll give it to you. Anything for you, baby. You want me to fuck you like an animal? I can do that. We have the rest of our lives to make love."

The filth excreting from his mouth turns me on more than it should. I shouldn't like this, but I do. I've always been the good girl, strived to be perfect, and it's gotten me nowhere but down a road of heartache and lost in the land of crushed dreams.

I want to be bad. I want to be taken someplace other than where I am, because where I am feels good, but it also feels wrong. Guilt is starting to chase me.

I quickly take position on my hands and knees as he aligns behind me. He places his hands on my hips and wastes no time before he shoves forward and thrusts his dick inside me as hard as he can, slamming his pelvis against my bottom.

He's so far inside me from this angle that it took my breath away. He pulls out and does it again, harder. I cry out. "Do you want me to stop? Slow down? Go softer?"

I clench the sheets in my fists. It hurts, but it also feels good. It's hard to explain. There is a pinch of pain, but I want more. I can't think about anything. My focus is on the pain when I accept the thrust and the pleasure when it retracts. My concentration is locked on trying to endure his length. It's bittersweet. "No," I whisper. "Don't stop."

Grunts come from him as he quickens his pace. I dig my toes into the sheets each time he thrusts harder. He moves one hand up to grab my shoulder for support and reaches around my body with the other, rubbing me down below. The extra stimulation is what I need to take me over the edge, to take me into oblivion.

I'm numb inside; aching and sore between my legs from the assault on my body. I don't know how many more times he enters me, but he finally pulls out and catches his semen in his fist.

I stand from the bed and walk to the bathroom to get him a towel. His eyes are heavy when I hand it to him. The smile on his face tells me he's happy, but tired, and shortly he'll be out cold. "That was amazing, baby. Was it what you expected?"

He's not even paying attention to what he's saying. He's walking around on cloud nine and slightly delusional from exhaustion. I need to be alone for a little while, and by the looks of him, he'll be asleep in about five minutes. "Of course. It was better." I lie.

I kiss him on the lips as he takes the hand towel to wipe himself clean, immediately getting under the covers after throwing the soiled linen on the floor. "I'm going to take a quick bath to unwind. Don't wait up. I'll be in bed shortly. You know I've been having a harder time sleeping the past few days. The warm water relaxes me."

"Are you sure? I can wait up if you want." He's already starting to doze off. He can barely hold his eyes open. I reach down and pick up his boxer briefs, tossing them to him. He picks them up and pulls them up his body, before rolling on his stomach.

"I'm sure. Don't be silly. I won't be long and then I'll come to bed."

I walk to the bathroom and make it to the door when he mumbles, "Kinzleigh . . ." I stop. "I love you."

My eyes fill with tears. "I love you too, Preston."

Like a zombie, I walk to the large Jacuzzi tub and start the warm water. I step inside and sit, letting the water fill the tub around me. Everything that was being suppressed breaks free. I do the opposite of what I wanted to do—cry.

I cry because it wasn't what I expected. It isn't the sex I'm referring to. The sex was as good as sex can be, I guess. If you think about it, all sex is pretty much the same, or at least in my case. I don't have much to compare, but you either know how to do it or you don't. You don't need an instruction manual to partake in it. What I mean is, the emotions that Preston and I share during sex are nothing like when Breyson and I did it, and at this point I don't know if that will ever change.

I knew from the first time Breyson and I slept together I would be forever ruined when it came to guys. In my heart, I love Preston, but I'm not consumed by him. I could be happy with Preston forever, but not as happy as I would be with Breyson. He was right when he said he'd be marrying his friend, because he is my friend. I've grown to love him in a way I never would have imagined, but I love Breyson more.

I went into this blindsided and naive. You can't experience name brands and then buy generic, expecting it to be exactly the same. Something is always going to be different, no matter how similar they are. When you experience the best there is from the beginning, it sets you up for failure should you ever lose it.

I miss him so much. I have no idea why my heart hates me this much. I've tried everything, and just when I take one step forward, something knocks me two steps back.

I'm tired of being heartbroken. I'm tired of knowing that no matter how much Preston loves me or how much I actually love him in return, it'll never be good enough. Something is always there to remind me that Breyson is the one my heart and soul yearns for. If he's so right for me then why isn't he here? It's the epitome of cruel.

FIFTY-FIVE

The small beam of light through the window wakes me up. I rub my eyes, trying to focus. The sun is rising, signaling the start of a new day—a very important day. I get to finally look into the most beautiful green eyes I've ever seen. The only problem is, I have no idea where to find her. It's not like I can just call her and tell her this shit over the phone.

I scrub my hands over my face in an attempt to wake up. I look around the private cabin of the plane, plotting. I'm going to have to think outside the box to find her. She could be anywhere.

If I were Kinzleigh, where would I be?

I don't know how I fell asleep in the same type of metal canister that almost killed me. Mental exhaustion triumphs fear I suppose.

I fall back against the pillow and stare at the ceiling. I could go see Ryland. He may flip his shit, but if I had to guess, he knows where to find her. I should just show up and pretend I'm a couple months late for my annual summer stay. A good joke always softens a serious situation. I have a car ride to think over how I'm going to do this.

I jump out of bed and search the small room for my duffle bag. I remove a clean pair of clothes and quickly change. The less time I waste, the more time I have to see her. Who knows what screw-ups could go down in between.

I sit on the edge of the bed and pull on my sneakers. Shoving all of my belongings back into the bag, I pull my ball cap on my head and exit the cabin, walking toward the front of the plane.

With one thing on my mind, I don't waste time looking for the flight attendant. If I had to guess, the car is already waiting outside. Making my way down the steps, I see the car near the plane. It's never felt so good to be on California soil.

I take off in a sprint toward the car. The driver notices me closing in quickly and opens the door, attempting to get out. "Not necessary, sir. I need you to drive." I open the backdoor and toss my bag on the seat, before sliding inside.

Back in the driver's seat, he turns to look at me. "Good morning. My instructions are to take you anywhere you want to go. Where will it be first?"

"112 Seagull Cove. Laguna Beach." He faces the front and starts the car. Waiting is going to be hellacious, but I've made it this far. I can't stop now. I prop my elbow on the door and watch out the window as everything familiar passes by. It's amazing how you can go without seeing something for so long and one look at it brings back all the memories stored away.

He pulls into a driveway I haven't seen in over a year. I see Ryland's vehicles parked, but the others are absent. When the driver comes to a stop, I open the door. "Will you wait here? I may need you after this."

"Of course. Take your time." I draw in a deep breath and put one foot on the pavement, pulling up on the doorframe.

I walk toward the back of the house where the pool house is at a steady pace. Ryland rounds the corner at the gate, so I lean against the hood of his truck. He's carrying a surfboard under his arm and looking down at his cell phone as he walks, not paying attention. "You're still at it I see. When are you going to put that surfboard down and play a real sport?"

I've teased him about his love for surfing since he discovered he could ride a wave. I mostly rag him about it because I'm not any good. It's hard as shit and he makes it look so easy. The guy will be competing in major heats around the world in no time if he keeps it up, but I'm not going to tell him that. His ego is too big already.

He looks up and stops mid-step. I can't stop the smirk from forming as I watch his face contort from his confusion. He looks around, and then down at himself, as if he's not sure what he's looking at. It may be wrong, but I'd be lying if I didn't admit this is a little fun. "You didn't think I was going to miss my weekly summer visit, did you? Late is better than never. Isn't that how the saying goes?"

He stands there staring at me like he's looking at a ghost. I should have known this wasn't going to be easy. Even though my two brothers and I are triplets, all sharing the same womb, Braxton and I are identical twins—split from the same fertilized egg and sharing one birth sack—while Briar was a separate fertilized egg all together and had his own space. Briar looks nothing like us.

Braxton and I may look just alike, but if you hang around us on a daily basis you can tell us apart. Braxton and Ryland were never that close, because he was closer to Beau. Ryland has always been able to tell us apart. It's just going to take more for him to believe it.

There is one thing that no one knows except Ryland and me. Ryland's dad has always had a love for fishing most wouldn't understand. He's the guy that plans a fishing trip twice a year and even competes in local competitions. If that doesn't tell you anything, he loves to watch Bass Masters on television, and he has a shrine in his mancave devoted to all of the pro fishermen he's met along the way.

One of his most prized possessions was a fishing lure he got signed by his favorite fisherman. He kept it inside a small, clear box. Ryland and I used to look at it all the time. Once, when we were kids, we thought it would bring us luck to fish with it in the lake by our houses. We were sure we would have a bucketful of fish by the day's end. We were wrong.

We lost the lure.

Ryland threw out his line and got a bite on the other end. It was a big one by the pull on the pole. We weren't very big at the time, so it took both of us to reel it in. We got it all the way to the bank before it broke the line and took the lure with it. Today, that lure would have been worth thousands, but it's hooked in the mouth of that fish somewhere at the bottom of the lake.

When Uncle Joe found out it was missing, he was pissed. We swore we would never tell anyone it was us. He blamed it on Beau anyway, so we figured if someone had already paid for the crime, what's the point? Uncle Joe moped around for two weeks after that. We haven't discussed it since. "You look like you see a ghost. I expected a little more excitement over my return. I got to thinking. Do you think Uncle Joe ever figured out it was us that took his prized fishing lure?"

He drops everything he's holding in his hands, his phone hitting the pavement. I just now notice the luggage stacked neatly by his truck, like it's waiting to be loaded. It finally dawns on me—he's about to start college. "Breyson?"

He doesn't move. He doesn't speak. I've never seen Ryland so quiet. "Yeah, Ry, it's me."

"I . . . I . . . I thought you were . . . dead," he stammers. I can see how this would be a little awkward. Hell, I wouldn't believe it either if the shoes were on the other feet.

I rub my hand over the top of my head like a brush. "It's kind of a funny story . . ."

If I don't find the humor in this situation the opposite will occur. I refuse to breakdown again. I've had enough breakdowns to last me a lifetime. "Let's just say I took an involuntary leave of absence." I laugh, thinking he will do the same. I was wrong.

Instead, his face turns angry. "What the fuck, Breyson? Where the hell have you been? Do you know what people have gone through over the last six months? You actually have the audacity to laugh. This isn't fucking funny. I feel like I'm one step from losing my goddamn mind."

I've never seen Ryland cry. At Beau's funeral he looked like a hollow shell, as if his emotions had been stripped from his body. When you looked in his eyes there was nothing there. It took a year for his personality to come back, and he and Beau weren't that close. Right now, his eyes are filled to the brim without the tears actually spilling over. The part that doesn't sit well with me is that he acts like I planned all this shit. He has no idea what I've been through.

My temper flares. "You know what? Fuck you, Ryland. Do I know what y'all have been through? What about what I've been through? You want to know what I've dealt with the past six months? I'll tell you. I witnessed a girl sacrifice herself for people she didn't know, leaving a child behind with no mother. I had to anticipate my death as a hunk of steel fell from the air into shark-infested water with no way out, and bleeding on top of it. Then woke up in a country where I knew no one, including myself. I was stranded with no memory. The only connection I had to anyone was my dreams, not knowing if the girl I'm in love with was real or not. I wandered around for months trying to formulate an existence with no foundation but my body. And not one fucking person was looking for me!"

I push off the hood of the truck. I'm worked up now. I typically hold things in. I let them build until I detonate like a bomb with a long fuse. "If you think everyone else has had it bad, think again. Try figuring out your girl is pregnant with your kid through some paranormal bullshit your mind concocted. Imagine feeling like a foster child in a family that didn't have to take you in but did."

The tears are stinging my eyes. "Have you heard enough yet? I'm not finished. Imagine knowing the love of your life is out there in the world somewhere, alone, carrying your child, and you can't get to her. It's a helpless feeling. Try gaining your memories back only to know that you were the only survivor in something so tragic it's almost unbearable. I should have died with all of those people. Carry that burden for the rest of your life and then come at me."

I walk in his direction until we're face to face. The first tear I've ever seen him shed falls down his face. I lower my tone from yelling to just above a whisper. My jaw twitches. "Of all the things I've been through, you want to know which part is the worst? Imagine finding out the mysterious girl you've dreamed about for months is not only carrying your baby, but also moving on with another guy, and there is nothing you can do about it, because you're thousands of miles away. Then, when you are finally able to remember, you find out the guy is the very one that's been after her for years. Does it sound like a soap opera yet? Try fucking living it. I am done with the bullshit. I came here for Kinzleigh. Where is she?"

My teeth are gritted together, anger rolling off of me. He takes a few steps back, but I have no idea why. "Breyson, a lot of shit has happened since you've been gone. I'm not sure you want to know where she is."

I follow him. He's not going to give me some shady answer without an explanation. "Where is she, Ryland?"

He takes a deep breath, and then gives me a pathetic expression. Pity is written all over his face. What could be so bad that he is suddenly feeling sorry for me now after dropping multiple bombs on him earlier?

"Follow me," he says, as he picks up the cell phone he previously dropped and walks through the gate. I trail behind him until we make it to the pool house.

I close the door behind me. It looks the same as the last time I was here, but also different. It's lived in. He doesn't say anything as he walks to the bar, grabbing the rolled newspaper. He holds it out in front of me. "This was released this morning."

I yank it out of his hand and unroll it, studying the front page. It hurts far worse than anything I've endured in my life to date, and probably ever will. Kinzleigh and Preston made the front page of the paper. They are dressed formally, looking into each other's eyes with smiles on their faces. The headline rips my heart from my chest.

Most eligible bachelor announces engagement.

A near death experience was nothing compared to this. I knew they were together, but I didn't know they were that serious. Why am I surprised? I know he'd do anything to get her. He's made that clear before. My head is pounding from anger. She's slipping from my fingers and it's killing me.

She may be engaged, but she isn't married yet. I came here knowing I'd have to fight for her and that's what I'm going to do. I won't just stand by and watch her marry another man and take my kid. If he wants her, he can pry her from my cold, dead fingers. "Where is she, Ryland?"

I stare at the woman I love, letting myself get angrier. The best wars are fought with emotion. When personal ties drive you, you fight harder and endure more than you normally would. You find a strength inside you didn't know you had. It's no different than a ballplayer playing for a deceased teammate. There is an underlying motive that empowers you. "I don't know where she is. Presley left for Miami a few hours ago. I doubt she answers."

Wrong answer.

I look up, more serious than I have ever been about anything in my entire life. "Find her. Now!" I bark out the order through clenched teeth. I'll beat it out of the little shit if I have to—I've done it before. We are close enough we can beat the hell out of each other and then stand and shake hands. He knows when I'm serious and when I'm joking.

He nods and does something on his cell phone. Placing it to his ear, he waits. "Hey, Lauren. I need to know where Kinzleigh is." He pauses and looks at me. "Something important came up."

He walks over to the bar and jots something down on a piece of paper. Who is Lauren? I've never heard Kinzleigh mention that name. Whoever it is isn't important. I only care about one thing—her location. He finishes the call and slides his phone in the pocket of his swim trunks.

I walk over to him and hold out my hand. He looks nervous. "Are you sure you want to do this? Don't do anything stupid, Breyson. She's carrying your son. Bryce is due next month—three weeks to be exact. She doesn't need any added stress. Kinzleigh has been through enough already."

I place my hand over my heart, letting the words sink in. It's a boy . . . I'm going to have a son. I had a feeling from the visions, but nothing was real until now. I close my eyes, the tears I've been holding back now falling free. I repeat his name in my mind, making sure to memorize it. "Wait, what did you call him?"

"Bryce. His name is Bryce Patrick Abercrombie . . . after you. That's what she named the baby. She's been through a lot, Breyson. I know you're upset, but the Kinzleigh you see in that photo compared to the Kinzleigh she was before he went back and got her are two totally different people. You wouldn't even recognize her if you had seen the girl she was a few months ago. I don't like seeing them together any more than you do, but he pulled her out of the fire when no one else could, including your brothers. He deserves a little respect. All I'm saying is to think about that when you show up like Rambo and let your jealousy take control."

My knees weaken. I lower myself onto the barstool, feeling like I'm about to pass out. At every turn something proves that we belong together. There is an inner connection attempting to pull us back together. She named our son the very name I went by in Spain. Could it be coincidence? Yes. Do I think it is? No.

My hands are shaking and my pulse is erratic. I'll do anything to get her back. I'll chase her to the end of the earth. I would rope the moon or catch a star if that's what she wanted. I need to remind her she's supposed to be with me. There are too many signs that point us together.

"Will you take me to her? Please. I need to see her. It's been too long." I look him in the eyes. "I can't lose her, Ry."

"Yeah, man. Of course, I will."

She is still mine. She has to be. I have to believe that when she sees me everything will be right in world again. We're meant to be together . . . forever. The alternative is not an option for me.

FIFTY-SIX

Breyson

I've had enough traveling. When this is all over, I'm not going anywhere for a long time. Ryland pulls into a large resort that sits on the beach. At least they didn't go out of the state for whatever this little getaway is supposed to represent. I don't even want to think about what I'm about to walk into. My mind is starting to sway, and the thought is making me sick.

Shut it down, Breyson. Shut. It. Down.

He stops and kills the engine. I look over at him when he places his hand on my shoulder and hands me a slip of paper with the opposite hand. "You're going to need this. It has the room number on it, because they asked for a 'do not disturb' to be added to their room at the front desk, so they aren't allowed to give out any information. Whatever you tell them, you didn't get this information from Lauren. She works for Preston and is one of Kinzleigh's best friends. She has no idea why I asked for this information. Her job could be at stake if Preston finds out she gave out his private information without his consent. I'll stay here until you're done."

I take the piece of paper and step out of his truck. When I read the room and floor number, I raise my head and look into the sky at the building before me—top floor. Here goes nothing.

Call it excitement, or buildup, but the most important girl in the world to me is a few floors away. It doesn't take me long to make it to the elevator.

In fact, I'm pretty sure to the average passerby I probably looked like a blur.

I pace in the elevator car as it ascends. It feels like it's going one mile per hour. I watch the digital numbers above the door rise as it bypasses each floor. "Come on."

It feels like an eternity when the door finally opens on the top floor. I walk to the door and place my fist up to knock on the door but stop. This is it. This is the moment I've waited for almost seven months now. I knock on the door and wait. Nothing. I knock again, louder this time. I finally hear someone stirring. The soft footsteps tell me it's Kinzleigh.

She opens the door and it takes all that I have not to grab her up in my arms. Damn. She's beautiful. Her curly blonde hair is sticking out in every direction and she has a scowl on her face from being woken. She always did hate for someone to wake her up. The small slits that are her eyes are trying to focus. She hasn't completely made out my features yet.

My eyes run down her tiny body. She's wearing a pink tee shirt. No surprise there, it's her favorite color. It's tight around her belly where my son is growing. Seeing it in reality is so much different than in a photo. I can't believe I've missed this. I will not break down right now. This isn't the time nor the place. Her legs are still gorgeous. Short but muscular and made to be wrapped around me.

"Hey, Kinz. How have you been?" I probably sound like an idiot right now, but I don't care. I want to hear her voice. She balls up her fists and rubs her eyes. When she has them fully open, her face changes into something I don't like. I know the look in those deep green eyes. I don't like to see her in pain, especially not when looking at me.

She looks behind her and steps outside in the hall, shutting the door quietly. We are completely alone. Her lips are better than I remember. What comes out of them, though, hurts me. "Braxton, what are you doing here?"

She thinks I'm my identical twin brother. I never even thought of that. I have no idea how to deal with this. "I'm here for you."

She is zoned out, staring at me. Her eyes scan each feature on my face as if she's studying them. She doesn't even realize she's doing it, or that I'm watching her do it. Her eyes aren't as bright as they were when I left. She looks like she's missing something vital. It's killing me to watch her long for me. She is so obvious anyone would know it. I realize how right Ryland was. If my beautiful girl looks like this now, what did she look like six months ago? "Kinzleigh."

She shakes her head. "I'm sorry. I'm just tired. I had a late night. Not sleeping well these days," she says as she lays her hands on opposite sides of her belly. "Why are you here, Braxton? Is Adalynn okay?"

Not being able to touch her is torture. I want her. God knows I do. I want her forever. I have since the day I laid my eyes on her. I want our baby. I want a life together. I don't care how young we are. There is always a way to make it work. I catch a glimpse of the diamond on her finger and it fuels my anger.

I take a step closer to her. "Kinzleigh, it's me, Breyson."

Her eyes glaze over. She slaps me across the face. It stings, but I don't budge. She places her hand over her mouth, surprised by her own response. The tears run down her face, staining her cheeks.

My skin is burning, the blood bubbling just below it, but if it relieves some of the pain she's holding inside, I'll gladly deal with it. She removes her hand and her lips are quivering. "I'm so sorry. It's just that . . . you know that . . . you know how much I miss him. You know why I can't be around you, Braxton. Please go."

She turns to leave and I grab her hand, pulling her to me. I place my palms on her face so I can be sure she's looking at me. "Do you remember what I always told you, beautiful girl? I told you I'd never leave you. I told you I'd always find you, 'til death do us part. I meant it, Kinzleigh. I'll cross any barrier, I'll swim any distance, and I'll fight any battle to make it back to you. I've already survived a plane crash and amnesia; I think I can handle anything."

She looks like a deer caught in headlights. I have her attention, so I keep going. "I remember every kiss, every time I made love to you, and every time you told me you loved me. We were made for each other, Kinz. I know that when I wanted to give up, you kept me going. There are a lot of things I can't explain, but I can explain that your soul and my soul are designed to fit together. If you don't believe it's me, ask me anything that only I would know."

She doesn't say anything. It's clear she's confused, hurt, and maybe even angry. "You don't have anything to say? I'll say it for you. You want me to name the best things that have ever happened to me? Let's move through time. The first time I ever saw you on the beach you took my breath away. I knew you were different. The first time I kissed you on the pier you hooked me. The first time I made love to you in your bed, you ruined me."

I wipe the tears that are soaking her face. "The first time you left me instead of taking me to the airport, you changed me. The first time you came after me, you caught me. That week last summer was the best week of firsts in my life, but that's only the beginning. When you trusted me enough to be mine, you made me realize how much I needed to try in order to keep you."

She looks like she's barely breathing. "You gave me your heart on Homecoming and I'm here to take it back. You marked your body for me on your birthday and I'm taking that back too. You promised me forever by our tree at Christmas and forever starts today. You conceived my baby at the start of a new year that signified our love for one another, and planned or not, it was meant to be."

I pin her against the door. "I should have stayed home instead of leaving on the day you were sick. I didn't put it together that you were pregnant. If I had followed my gut and took care of you, we wouldn't have wasted so much time apart. I always have and always will be yours, Kinzleigh. I would do anything for you. You own my heart. Even when we're apart, ultimately, we are connected. When I was gone, somehow my mind still dreamt of you and kept you alive in my memory when everything else slept. When I didn't know my name, I chose Bryce, just as you chose it for our son."

She gasps, and her green eyes sparkle a little. "You want to know if it's really me, then there is only one way to find out."

I lean forward and press my lips to hers. When I do, everything feels like it shifts back into alignment for the first time since I woke up in the hospital back in February. No one will ever be able to convince me that we aren't meant for each other.

I take my time kissing her, re-familiarizing myself with her and savoring her. This moment makes everything that I had to go through worth it. I didn't expect for life to throw a major curveball when I boarded that plane, but sometimes you have to alter your swing, because the hit may be worth it.

FIFTY-SEVEN

The world around me fades away. His kiss, and only his kiss, does this to me. He places me in a trance each time we're together. I thought I was crazy—completely insane—and I still could be, but I'm drowning in my own tears from listening to his quick version of our life story.

Finally, I've left Hell and entered into Heaven. I haven't touched these lips in so long. Without a thought, I tangle my hands into his hair and stand on my tiptoes to fully reach him. He runs his hands up and down my body in frenzy. I can feel his need to claim my body pressed against me.

What am I doing?

I pull away from him and look back at the hotel room door. The man I agreed to marry is inside. I got so emotional about him showing up out of nowhere that I didn't even consider I'm not single. What am I supposed to do now? I'm reminded of what I did last night. I slept with another guy.

Oh God, I slept with someone else and he's alive.

I place my hands over my face in shame. I look him in the eyes with so much guilt I almost can't breathe. Panic is starting to set in. How do I explain any of this? "Kinzleigh, what's wrong?"

"I can't do this," I whisper. My entire body feels like it is going to lock down. "I'm not alone."

"I gathered that much. Come back with me. Ryland is downstairs. I'm here to stay. We can be a family." I start crying to the point of it becoming verbal. Every word he says comes at my heart like a serrated edge knife. I've done the one thing that is unforgivable.

"I can't." My breaths are coming out in pants and my throat is hurting.

"You can't be fucking serious. You're not going to stay with him. Did you not hear anything I just said? I'm not leaving here without you."

I can feel a panic attack starting. I have to tell him. I'll never be able to live with myself if I don't tell him. "I slept with him."

He stops and presses into the doorframe that he's holding onto. "I don't care, Kinzleigh. It would be a little shitty for me to be mad when I was allegedly pronounced dead. I figured when I came here that you had been with him. I've been with someone too. It was a few months back when I was confused, depressed, and not sure how to decipher fantasy from reality. I had amnesia, so I didn't know who you were, and I was drunk. I swear to you it'll never happen again for as long as I live."

I only cry harder. It doesn't make it any easier to know that we're equal. I'm torn, stuck in quicksand and rapidly sinking. I didn't ask for any of this. "I didn't sleep with him until last night . . . after we announced our engagement."

He is staring at me with a blank expression. I'm not sure what he's going to say. He looks mad and hurt, but not as upset as I would've previously imagined he would be in this situation. "Do you love him?"

My heart falls to the pit of my stomach as the question lingers in the air between us. No matter what I say, someone is going to get hurt in this situation. I never wanted to love someone else, but I do. I love two people. The depth in which I love them each are different, but still, both are love.

Breyson and I lose ourselves in one another. The love that we feel for each other is uncontrollable—a dangerous intoxication. No one will ever love Breyson like I love Breyson, but no one will curse him like I curse him either.

Everything since I met him hits me like a tidal wave. I continue fighting for air as I consider what I have to do to save him. I'm taken back to February by my mind, with thoughts that never stop. I remember going to the cemetery when I went to talk to Beau—where I met Macie.

A certain promise was made. I promised before God and everyone that lies to rest there, that if Breyson's life was spared, I would let him go. I would let him live.

Being in love with me guarantees that I will be in love with him, and in turn be the cause of his death somehow. It's already happened once. I don't know why, but each person I love with no holds barred ends up hurt. Maybe because I was so critical of love in the prior years of my life, or maybe because I was selfish and the consequence is to never reap the benefit of an unselfish love—true love.

God knows how much I love him, how much I want him, and how much I need him, but the one word emphasized is *I*. It's not about me anymore. Being with me is not what's best for *him*. He's spent the last half-year away from everything he loves. He deserves a shot at happiness, a chance to do something he loves like play football. He may think this is what he wants now, but he'll see that he's better off without me.

For the first time in my life I'm going to be completely unselfish for him and for Bryce. I'm not giving myself what I want. If I stay with Preston, I know Breyson can experience being a college student with nothing holding him back, and Bryce will be financially taken care of with a roof over his head. After this, I'm going to want to crawl in a hole and die, but it's something I have to do. I have to let him go.

"Yes, Breyson, I do love him, but I love you too. In your absence I made a promise to him that I'm going to keep." The look in his eyes is making me wither inside. My body is aching from a lack of necessary oxygen as I take short, irregular breaths. I want to completely break down, but I have to be strong. He'll never let me go if he can see how I really feel. I have to find a strength I've never found inside myself before. I have to be strong for both of us.

His face moves closer to mine, almost kissing me. "I call bullshit. You don't want to be with him. You're just scared. You know you want to be with me. For once let your stubbornness rest."

His breath is tickling my lips and my body is reacting to his. I fist my hands at my sides to keep them from wrapping around him. I have to lie. I have to hurt him. It's the only way he'll believe me and move on.

"This is what I want. I want to stay with him. I'm about to have a baby, Breyson. A baby needs food, constant clothing and care, as well as diapers. All of those things require money. He can provide a roof over our heads and put food on the table. You haven't even finished high school. I won't be the reason you have to miss out on any more of your life. I want you to go to college and play football. I want you to experience the life you've missed out on because of me. I've already given up my dream to cheer in the NFL after college to raise Bryce. I won't allow you to give up yours too. I've made my decision, so don't try and change my mind."

I open the door and begin backing inside. I can't hold this in much longer. I need to get away from him. "Don't do this," he whispers. I count in my head to try and even out my breathing.

I shield myself with the door as if it's going to give me protection from my own breaking heart. I'll never forgive myself for doing this to him, but as Macie referenced, that's my cross to bear. "Goodbye, Breyson. I'll always love you."

I close the door, shutting out the only person I'll ever love above all else. The tears I was able to hold back for a matter of minutes breaks through the barrier and descends rapidly in a thick curtain. I turn and place my back to the door, sliding down to the floor in hysterics.

"Are you okay?" Preston asks. He is standing before me with his arms crossed over his chest. He looks void of emotion, robotic.

"You know?" I ask him the question even though I know the answer. I can see it by the expression he's wearing.

"I've been standing here awhile. It woke me up when you weren't in bed and I realized it's been too long for a trip to the bathroom." He squats so he can be eye level with me. "I saw everything, including the way you kissed him back when he kissed you. There is only one thing I need to know. Are you going to go back to him?"

I'm wheezing between breaths. My head is pounding from the shortage of oxygen and the pain in my chest is unbearable. He wipes my tear-drenched face with the back of his hand. I can imagine this is his worst nightmare. "No. I made a promise to you. When I put on this ring, and accepted your proposal, I promised you the rest of my life, and I'm going to keep it. I love him, but I also love you. This is what's best for all of us. No matter which way this goes, someone is going to get hurt. It's just harder than I would have ever imagined."

He kisses me, knowing Breyson's lips were just there. It doesn't feel the same. It doesn't take me to another world. It doesn't make my heart beat uncontrollably or make me feel like I can conquer the world.

When Preston kisses me, it only makes my heart mildly flutter. It only numbs my mind briefly from thought. His kiss makes me happy, but it doesn't alter my universe like when Breyson kisses me. That's the reason I know I can be with him and he won't get hurt. Every sense and emotion are controllable, and that's the justification of my choice.

I will defeat my curse by not giving in to the choice it wants me to make. I will gladly accept forever without him to know that my hands are not stained by the death of someone I love.

"Breathe for me. I'll help you through the pain," he says, as he pulls me to my feet. "You'll always be my favorite girl no matter what or who you choose, but I'm glad you chose me."

FIFTY-EIGHT

Breyson

What? She blames herself for what happened? If she thinks I'm going to give up that easily she has another thing fucking coming. Nothing ever worth having comes easily.

That doesn't make hearing her say she's going to be with another man any easier. It hurts like hell. The only thing keeping me from turning into a caveman right now and throwing her over my shoulder to carry her out of here is the fact that I know it won't have the desired result and she is very much pregnant with my kid.

I didn't fall in love with an easy woman. Her stubbornness drives me insane, but I've studied her. I know how to read her emotions and expressions. I vested time in her for a reason. I know she's lying. It's written all over her face.

I need to remind her that we can't live without each other. She actually thinks I'm going to be happier without her. Has she completely left her brain somewhere? I don't give a shit about football if she isn't there to watch me.

I bang my fist against the frame of the door. Pushing off, I begin pacing back and forth in front of it. I can still hear her crying on the other side. I need to formulate some kind of plan. I sure as shit am not leaving her in a hotel room with him. I can't be mad that she's *been* with another man, but that was before, and this is now. I'm back. I do not share. She will be mine again, she just doesn't believe it yet.

Something isn't sitting right with one of the things she said. Why is she worried about money for the baby? I have plenty of money invested, and I added her as the sole beneficiary should something happen to me. My grandparents' attorney was supposed to be processing everything when I left.

As soon as I get back home, I'm going to figure out what the hell happened for her to have to be taken care of by someone aside from me. Regardless, it isn't going to change anything now. She'll probably think I'm making it all up. I'm going to have to win her back another way.

I don't hear anything on the other side of the door anymore. My mind is going crazy with the possibilities of what they could be doing on the other side. I can't stand the thought of him having her again. I know he's never going to give her up willingly. Once you've had Kinzleigh you don't let her go. I know, I've had her, and I outran death to get back to her.

I bang on the door. "Kinzleigh, let me in."

I don't hear anything. The silence is deafening, and my mind is wandering to places and playing out scenes that it shouldn't be. I'm liable to kill someone. I continue to bang on the door, only louder this time. "Open the door, Kinzleigh."

It finally opens, and this time it's Preston standing on the other side. He's standing in nothing but a damn pair of boxers. "Look, Breyson, I know you've probably been through a lot, and I like you, but she said you need to go. You're upsetting her, and it's not good for the baby. I think we'll both agree we don't like to see her hurt. I'll make sure you know when he's on the way."

I laugh sarcastically. "Says the bastard that's been trying to steal my woman since the day I claimed her." I step into his personal space. I don't know what came over me, but suddenly, I'm pissed. I guess it makes a difference when you see the tool that is trying to stick his dick in the girl that is incubating your child. I don't know about spoiled rich boys, but country boys find that disrespectful.

"Back off, Breyson." I push him backward, and he stumbles through the door. Kinzleigh is sitting on the bed holding her stomach with her face still covered in tears. Not paying attention, I'm caught off guard when he shoves me back. "I said back off. You don't get it, do you? You're only hurting her more."

Right now, I'm not thinking about anything but the seed planted in my mind. I've dwelled on it, and it has already begun to grow, taking over like a weed. All I see right now is red and the prick standing in front of me. I gain my footing and close in on him. "Breyson, please leave," Kinzleigh whines behind him.

That only triggers me. Once I've drifted into this depth of anger, there is no turning back until I release the adrenaline built up in my muscles.

I stand face to face with him. My jaw flexes back and forth as I grit my teeth, and I seethe the words as I lock my eyes with his. "You acted like a man when you fucked my girl while she was pregnant with my kid, you can be a man and face me now. Let me tell you something, Motherfucker. I don't know what kind of ethics you believe in, but down south, in the eyes of a real man, that's no different than spitting in his face or screwing his wife. You may have thought I was dead, but you could have at least waited until she wasn't carrying my son to get your dick wet."

He takes a step closer. Good. At least I know she isn't with a bitch-boy. He's going to man up to his actions. He's cut, but he's still smaller than me. "Don't start something you don't want to finish."

"Stop, Breyson! It wasn't his idea. It was mine. If you want to blame someone, blame me!" she yells.

I'm still not listening. Right now, I don't really care whose idea it was. He made that decision and now he can face it. If he were a real man, he would have put his foot down out of respect for someone else, instead of thinking of himself. I bet if the roles were reversed, his view on the matter would be different.

I'm getting an itch I need to scratch. Too much anger and adrenaline has built up at this point. The fact that he is staring back at me with what appears to be a very slight smirk may have something to do with it.

I step forward at the same time my right fist comes up in a hook and slams against the left side of his jaw. Spit goes flying out of his mouth as he stumbles a little.

The tension released as I hit him was euphoric, taking me to an out of body state. All I can see is him having sex with her. I punch him with my left fist, followed by my right. My limbs are now swinging on repeat. With each hit, I feel a little bit better.

He bends forward and runs into me with his shoulder, pushing me back toward the wall until I slam into it. "Stop!" Kinzleigh's screaming is the only thing that registers. "I think my water just broke."

It doesn't take that smart of a person to halt when they hear that sentence. I look at her, and she is holding the bottom side of her belly with her legs spread shoulder width apart over a liquid puddle quickly absorbing into the carpet. Her face is red and puffy from crying and some of her blonde curls are stuck to her cheeks. We both stand, shoulder to shoulder, looking at her.

My mood immediately changes from anger to worry. Only one thing now processes, making me feel like a dumbass. Ryland said she wasn't due for about three more weeks. Without further thought, I rush over to her. I'm scared out of my mind, but I'll never show it. "Where are your clothes? I'll get them and then take you to the hospital."

"Like hell you are. I think you've done enough." Preston is carrying her bag in his hand and lays it flat on the bed, unzipping it.

"It's my kid, Preston. Try and stop me."

A high-pitched scream comes from Kinzleigh's mouth, silencing us both. "Would you two shut up? You're both acting like children. I'm the one that is going to decide who is taking me and it's neither of you. If either of you want to be there for the birth of this baby, then you can ride together and fix your shit. I'm riding with Ryland. I dare either of you to stop me."

She walks over to her bag and grabs a pair of clothes to change into. I don't know what to say. I don't think I've ever heard her cuss, nor do I remember her having that fiery of an attitude. It's like Halloween night on steroids. I'm a little stunned to be honest.

We both stand here and watch her as she stomps toward a door on the other side of the room. She stops halfway and doubles over, as if in pain. I start to move in her direction, as does Preston. When we get close, she holds out her hand, stopping us. "Don't touch me." Her voice sounds pained. "If either of you love me, you'll call Ryland and tell him to come help me."

I watch her, helplessly, as she tries to straighten up and waddle to the bathroom. "Fuck!" I press inward on my forehead with the heels of my hands. I'm about to be a father and instead of acting like a man I'm letting my temper control me like a boy. I feel like banging my head against a brick wall. I refuse to miss the birth of my son because I was acting like an ass.

I fish my phone out of my pocket and unlock the screen. I dial Ryland's number from memory and press call. Two rings and he answers the phone. "What's up?"

"I need you to come up and get Kinzleigh. She's in labor." I hold my breath and wait for the question I know is coming.

"Dude, what the hell? What did you do to her?" I can hear the truck door slam in my ear. "I knew better than to do this shit. Breyson, I told you not to fuck with her."

He continues to mumble line after line of things that are not going to change the situation at hand. I'm really not in the mood, but because I don't want to rev up my temper any more, I listen to him ramble and bitch like a little girl. "Just hurry up," I say, and hang up the call.

I look at Preston and he's staring daggers at me. I return the gesture. "Are we going to do this? We might as well go ahead and get it over with."

"Look, I'm sorry if you feel that us being together disrespected you, but you weren't here, Breyson. You didn't have to see her in the state she was in. I mentioned waiting until we got married. She didn't want to. I'd love to see if you could tell her no when you've had to watch her drown in pain and misery. So yeah, I caved and gave her what she wanted in an attempt to make her happy. I wasn't thinking of what *Breyson* would want, I was thinking of a way to help her stop thinking of you long enough to put a damn smile on her face. Whether you like it or not, we both love her. One of us is going to lose. There is nothing we can do about it. That's the result of falling in love with the same girl. You can make this difficult on her if you want to, but I'm going to be with her until she takes my ring off of her finger and tells me she wants me to leave."

He walks past me to the suitcase with his hand on his jaw, as if he's realigning it. I won't lose. I can't. It's not in me to carry on living without her, but he's also right. There is only room for one of us in her life in the way we both want to be. We are going to have to fight for her heart. Whoever wins it over, wins her. This is going to be a battle fought with love, not muscle. Bring it on.

FIFTY-NINE

Kinzleigh

I clutch onto the rail of the hospital bed with each contraction. It feels like a menstrual cramp times one hundred. If I close my eyes and breathe through it, I can handle it.

The hospital door opens and a girl that doesn't look much older than me walks in. "Hi. I just need to get registration and insurance information."

Preston is sitting on one side of the bed and Breyson on the other. They cannot both be seriously staying in here the whole time. This is awkward. Preston stands. "I got it." He leans down and kisses me on the forehead. "I'll be right back."

I don't want to look at Breyson right now. I don't think I can. Thankfully, I don't have to, because the doctor walks in. She's a young blonde, maybe mid-thirties, in a pair of royal blue scrubs. She couldn't have been an attending but a few years. I hope she's here to bring me some pain medication, because I've been here for two hours and my contractions are getting more intense and closer together. She hasn't checked me since I came in and was at three centimeters.

The machine beside me monitoring the baby and the pattern of the contractions beeps every few seconds. The low swooshing sound originating from the heart rate monitor strapped on my stomach reminds me that there is a living being inside of me.

The doctor pulls on a pair of latex gloves and stands at the end of the bed. I grit my teeth as another contraction starts. "I'm going to check you and see if you're dilated enough for an epidural."

I nod and look at the ceiling as she puts one hand on my inner thigh to keep me from closing my legs and the other disappears under the sheets. If I wasn't in so much pain this would be really awkward. I'll never get used to this for as long as I live. "Mmmmm."

I look at the doctor's face. I don't like wordless answers. It's usually not a good thing. I'm hesitant to ask, but I do anyway. "What's wrong?"

Breyson grabs my hand in his. I pretend I don't notice, but I do, and I choose to ignore the fact that it is calming me. "You're dilated too far to get an epidural. You're already at eight centimeters. You'll likely be ready to push in thirty minutes."

Each time a contraction starts, the pain is my complete focus, and some last longer than others. "You've got to be kidding. Please tell me you're joking. I cannot push this baby out without any medication."

The thought is bringing back the anxiety that I recently got rid of when they gave me a shot of Stadol to dull the pain. It's a worthless drug really. It makes you feel drunk and you can still feel the pain.

"You can and you will. You have no choice. It's too late to give you an epidural. Most first-time mothers don't progress this quickly. I'll be back to check you in a little bit, and we should be ready to meet your baby by then." She smiles, and it's enough to make me cringe. I'm glad someone is bouncy and in a good mood, because it sure isn't me.

"How do you feel?" I look at Breyson, who's sitting as close to me as he can get.

"I've been better," I tell him, looking him in the eyes. He always did have the most beautiful blue eyes. You look at them once and you get lost in their depth. I've discovered you can read a lot about a person by looking into their eyes. The eyes are the only part of a person that can't lie.

He places his hand on my belly. "We're going to be parents today. Strange huh?"

"Yes, I suppose it is." He squeezes my hand, and I'll never admit it, but everything feels right in the world. Right now, I finally understand that phrase, by whom I don't know—*It's better to have loved and lost than never to have loved at all.*

This moment is beautiful. He's beautiful. I'll never trade a single second of our time together, because a fraction of time with him is better than the life I would have had if I had never met him. "I've missed you, Kinzleigh. Not a day went by that I didn't dream of you or think of you. I couldn't have picked a better mother for my child. It's time for us to grow up, just a little earlier than we would have originally planned."

I close my eyes as I let his voice soothe me. I'm not strong when I'm around him. You can't lasso your heart when it's already soaring high in the sky. You might as well sit back and just let it fly.

I open my eyes and I can feel them filling, blurring the sight in front of me. "I've missed you too. God knows I've wished for this day so many times since you've been gone. No matter what happens, know that I'll always love you, Brey. Never doubt that."

"Then don't give up on us. Don't take the easy way out. I may not be able to give you the stars, but I can try my best. I'll never let you or Bryce do without. I'm just asking you to trust me." If only he knew how much I wanted to, but that's just it. Giving in to him would be the easy way. Letting him go is the hardest thing I'll ever have to do, but it's a price I'll pay for him being alive.

I don't know how I have any tears left, but I do. It seems I always do when they are shed for him. "Breyson . . ."

The door opens and the nurse comes in this time. We never look away from each other. It's as if time stands still. He does that thing he is so good at, where he connects our souls through the windows that are our eyes.

I allow my soul to intertwine with his, to enjoy the feeling as they dance together while our bodies sit in silence. Our hearts are synced, beating in the same rhythm. I'm giving myself one more night to love him freely, to let myself feel him in the most intimate way there is. This way is far more intimate than sex will ever be.

After tonight, I have to set him free. It'll never get any easier. He is my ultimate and only weakness. I'll send him away with all of my love. He's the only one that's really ever had it completely anyway. I never notice when the nurse checks me. "It's time to push. Call the doctor."

Preston comes back in the room with the labor and nursery staff. "Are you both staying?" the doctor asks as she walks in the room, suiting up for delivery.

The two of them look at each other. "Preston, I'm asking you to give me this. I'm asking you to set our differences aside for a day and wait outside. I'm asking you to be a man and willingly let me have this moment to witness the birth of my son, privately. We may have to share her right now, but some things are not to be shared. One day you'll understand."

Preston looks at me and back at Breyson. "Okay, Breyson. I'll give you that." He looks at me one last time. "I'll be with Ryland in the waiting room if you need me."

Then he turns and leaves the two of us alone to bring our son into the world. After today, so many things will change.

SIXTY

Breyson

I could lose everything after today. I heard it in her voice when I asked her not to give up on us. She's decided in her mind she isn't going to change her answer. For whatever reason, she thinks I'm better off without her. I won't walk away easily, but I have to live with the possibility that when this is all said and done, I may have to if I can't get her back.

I'm not one to beg, but I was prepared to beg Preston to give me this. I need this to hold onto. "Take a deep breath and push, push, push. Come on, Kinzleigh, hold it. I need a big one this time. I can see the head."

Kinzleigh screams in agony and grits her teeth each time she carries out the instructions the doctor voices aloud. Her face turns red each time she pushes. I hold her leg back with my left forearm, hand wrapped around her calf, and allow her to use my right hand as a stress toy like the doctor instructed.

"One more push and the head will be out. Great job, honey. Give me another push just like the last one." Kinzleigh looks exhausted, but she is also the strongest girl I know. "Dad, are you ready to meet your baby? Look down here." I glance between Kinzleigh's legs, my eyes widening a little. I've never seen anything like it. "Kinzleigh, chin on chest and bear down like you're going to do a crunch. Ready, deep breath, and push."

I watch as she pushes his head out. It's full of blond, wet hair. I wipe my moist eyes on my shirt with my shoulder. "Give it a break and then one more push." The doctor suctions his mouth out as if she's done this a million times. "One final push, Kinzleigh. Let's get this baby out."

The doctor pulls on his head at the same time she pushes, working the shoulders out. In one swift motion, the rest of his body comes out, and she cradles him on her arm, almost like a football, clearing his airway. "It's a boy!"

Kinzleigh lays her head back in relief.

I can't describe the way it feels to watch the woman I've completely fallen in love with give birth to my child. It's a moment I'll never forget as long as I live. I thought I had experienced the best in life when I met her, but I was wrong. This is it. Life doesn't get any better than this. Something changed in me when I laid my eyes on him. I don't know what or why, but it feels like everything is falling into place.

I look at Kinzleigh and I can tell she feels the same way I do. When he starts to cry, I smile, and so does she. It's a sound I'll never forget. She looks more beautiful right now—flushed and covered in sweat—than I've ever seen her.

I don't know how long she'll fight us before she gives in, but I'll wait patiently until she does. This isn't something you give up on. Your family is something you give your all for.

The doctor clamps off the umbilical cord and gives me a pair of scissors to cut it, and I do. I can't believe we made him. It may have been the wrong timing since we are just now out of high school and unmarried, but at the same time, it feels like he couldn't have come at a more perfect time.

The doctor lays him on top of Kinzleigh's stomach and continues wiping him off. That cry is the most beautiful thing I've ever heard. Any man that doesn't cry at least a tear when he hears his baby take its first breaths of air isn't a man. Knowing you helped create something like this is overwhelming, no matter what age you are.

The tech picks him up and carries him to the incubator after letting Kinzleigh bond with him. I follow, unable to look away, and wanting to make sure he's okay. While they weigh him and clean him up, I pull out my phone and take a picture, capturing a moment of time. The scale reads six pounds and 2 ounces. Even a few weeks early, he's perfect.

The tech hands him to me all bundled up in a blanket with a cap on his head. I take him and hold him in my arms as close to me as I can. He feels so breakable. He looks up at me with his little gray eyes, and my heart feels like it's going to burst in my chest. "Hey, Buddy. I'm your daddy. I love you." I kiss his forehead and walk over to Kinzleigh. She's watching us, crying.

I lay him in her arms. "You did good, beautiful. He's perfect. This feeling is indescribable." I place one arm around hers that is holding Bryce and the other on her face. I don't care what the consequences are. I bend over and kiss the mother of my child. "I love you, Kinzleigh Berlyn Baker. I don't know why you're so scared, but I'll win you back. I'm here to stay. You may give up on us, but I won't. I'll take care of you both, Kinzleigh. I'll die for you and him. I'm not asking you to take my word for it. I'll prove it day in and day out until you accept that we belong to each other. Know that I'm not walking away from this. Walking away is for cowards. Staying and fighting for what you want is what makes heroes. One day, I'm going to be yours."

lasting
FATE
FATE SERIES BOOK FOUR

ONE

Breyson

What little bit of hope I had was squandered today, but no matter how much I want to give up, I can't. I won't. Watching that car pull away with my girl and my son, without me, was the hardest thing I've ever had to do. I thought being away from them was hard—not knowing about their existence or mine—but I was wrong. That was easy compared to this. At least then there was the possibility that it was all a dream. This, I know, is not.

I've spent the last twenty-four hours getting to know my son—holding him in my arms and bonding with him. I got down on my knees and begged her not to make the decision she did today. There is some underlying reason scaring her. Ask me what the fuck it is and I couldn't tell you. We both know two people couldn't be more meant for each other than us if it were drawn out across the sky with the stars. Kinzleigh is one of the most readable people I know, or at least when it comes to me, but she isn't giving in. The stubborn girl is convinced that I need to go live a life without her or with someone else.

The thought of another girl physically makes me ill. I even told her so, but she still looked me in the eyes and told me her decision remained the same. She's leaving with Preston, and come December she's marrying him. She lied to me today. For the first time in our entire relationship she looked me dead in the eyes and lied to me. She's never lied to me. When I asked why she was choosing him, she told me that in the absence of me she fell for him. She asked me to let her go.

"Fuck," I yell, not caring who's around me. I begin pulling my hair, jerking harder with each increment of distance that grows between us. What the hell was I supposed to say to that? No longer seeing the car in my line of vision, I begin to panic. It's building rapidly and I need to free it—the anxiety and adrenaline spreading like fire throughout my body.

I find my victim in the light pole behind me as I take out my anger and frustration. With each swing I feel a little better. I don't care how bad it hurts. My heart hurts worse than any physical pain I could inflict on my skin and bones. You could skin the hide from my body, break every bone inside, or remove my limbs one by one, but the pain wouldn't compare to the ache in my chest. I've never felt like this.

When my arms won't physically move anymore, I drop to my knees as the tears stream down my face. My knuckles are bloody and look like they've been through a meat grinder. The pain jolts through my body with every beat of my heart. I lean back on my heels and look up at the sky. I'm so mad and hurt, but mostly confused.

I only want to know one thing: why? "What more do I have to do to prove that I love her? Is this some kind of test? Tell me what I have to do to get her back and I'll do it. We have a kid! Please, God, just tell me what I have to do. Name the price and I'll pay it!"

Yelling at God isn't going to do anything, but I'm desperate. I probably look crazy, or shit, even like a pussy, but I don't care. I just lost the only girl that has my heart and son, all within five minutes. I need the answer key to all these questions.

I've never had girl problems, and now I'm clueless as to how to fix this. Something has to make her break. I know she wants me, wants us, and wants our family. I have to figure out what is standing in the way so I can destroy it.

A hand touches the top of my shoulder. "Come on, Man. You don't want to be this guy. You aren't going to win her back in the parking lot of the family birthplace. She's made her decision and right now you can't change it. We'll find another way. Maybe it's time you went back home for a while. Your family needs to know you're alive."

Ryland hasn't left the hospital since we got here. I guess I should be grateful, because he's my only way out of this place. He's barely raising his voice, as if he's scared I'm going to go crazy and end up AWOL again. "I'm not leaving with my girl and my son here. I won't be across the country while another man takes my place as his father. Our family didn't raise us that way. I'm staying here until I get her back; win them back. I will convince her."

"Brey."

"Drop it, Ryland. What the hell is wrong with you?" My tone is angry, but I can't help it.

"I know what she's scared of." I turn in the direction of the voice carrying through the parking lot. It's a petite girl with long, brown hair, and gray eyes. She looks around my age or maybe even a few years older.

"Who are you?" I bark out.

"Lauren, her best friend. I can help you break down her walls, but you have to be willing to do what I say or it won't work." Something in her eyes looks familiar, but I can't place it. It's probably just one of those weird things where someone looks familiar even though you have no clue who they are. What have I got to lose at this point?

"Tell me what you know."

She takes the first step in my direction, her heels tapping against the pavement. She looks too young to be dressed in the expensive office attire she's dressed in. It finally rings a bell. She's the one Ryland was talking to on the phone; the girl that works for Preston. If she works for Preston, then why would she be willing to help me?

She stops a few feet away, looking down at me. "For starters, you need to get up and be the man she fell in love with. Wallowing and sorrow never get the girl; fighting does." Her accent matches mine. I don't know why, but I feel like I should know her.

"Lauren . . ." Ryland loops his arm around mine, helping me to my feet. My energy has been depleted from taking out my wrath on the pole. The pole won based on the bloody pulp my knuckles have become. "How have you been?" I look over at Ryland, wondering about the strange tone in his voice. My brows line for a moment and I wipe my face with the bottom fabric of my shirt.

He has his hands in his pockets. Is he nervous? What the fuck? "Hey, Rye. I've been good, just busy." Rye? When did he start getting people to call him by his childhood nickname again? We all do it, because we've been calling him that for years, but I don't know who she is. I don't have time to analyze this shit right now. I'll have to figure out what is going on with him later.

He's usually a cocky, but lovable, ass when it comes to girls. The furthest he makes it with a girl emotionally is asking her name and relationship status before he shoves his dick inside her. Right now, the look in his eyes and the tone in his voice are telling me something about her has him piqued; a longing present to make her his, but I don't think he's figured that out yet.

Back to the topic at hand. I'm getting distracted. "Are you two going to stand here and act awkward after what I'm sure was a late night rendezvous in the sack, or are you going to give me some useful information so I can leave you two to deal with whatever the fuck is going on here?"

She looks back at me, her eyes now widened a little more than they were before. I can't explain the attitude I have when I'm at odds with Kinzleigh, but it's not controllable. I'm a dick. I'll admit it. Anyone that's ever loved someone would understand the need to get things moving at the pace of a hare and not a tortoise. "For one, you can get your ass in gear and fulfill the promises you make to her instead of reciting them."

"What the hell is your problem?" I may be acting like an ass, but I have good reason. She, however, does not. Each day without Kinzleigh is a day I miss out on loving her and watching my son grow. I've missed out on enough already.

She exhales. "Look, Breyson, I've gotten close to Kinzleigh over the last month and she's talked to me. I know what will get her back to you, but you're going to have to trust me. That trust is going to require you being absent for a little while."

"Like hell I am. I'm not going to just give up on her. How is that going to prove I'm fulfilling my promises to them?" This girl wants me to trust her? I don't even know her.

Ryland places the back side of his hand against my bicep, getting my attention. "Brey, maybe you should hear her out. Kinzleigh trusts her, and you really don't have any other options. Your way is obviously not working at the moment. Would you rather be absent temporarily or permanently? You don't want to drive her away for good."

I close my eyes, trying to calm my raging nerves. The throbbing pain in my hands tells me I can't get mad again. Talking to her hasn't helped, pledging my love to her hasn't helped, and begging her has left me begging alone. Listening wouldn't be the worst thing I've tried so far. "You have five minutes to make your case, then I'm going after her."

"She thinks loving you is cursing you, marking your soul for death to collect. Words won't win her back. She is convinced that if she allows herself to love you again, you'll soon be dead. It all has to do with the plane accident. When you disappeared, she bargained with God; her happiness for your life. When you showed back up, to her, that was the toll being collected, and she paid the price by leaving you for him." The look in her eyes turns to sadness.

"That's the stupidest shit I've ever heard. How is what happened her fault at all? I can't even see logical reasoning behind that. Besides, that doesn't make sense, because she said she loves him, so how is that any different?" I cannot believe I'm hearing this crap. It's completely ridiculous.

She begins shaking her head. "She loves him because he's been there for her, supported her, and loved her even when she didn't love him, but she's *in love* with you. The heart can love over and over again, and in many depths and forms, but the soul can only belong to one, and hers belongs to you. With everything that's happened she believes in supernatural and spiritual more so now than ever before. The price for your life spared is happiness, and someone has to pay it. Unless it's sacrificed by one's heart that truly loves her, the curse remains and she pays the price. It may sound like a bunch of stupid bullshit to you, and I admit it's farfetched, but she actually believes it."

None of this is making any damn sense. It sounds like something straight out of a paranormal folktale, or some kind of weird voodoo curse, or magical spell. I can't believe I'm actually listening to this shit. "What exactly are you telling me to do?"

"As much as you don't like it, Preston loves her. I've witnessed it firsthand. She makes him happy, and he would do anything for her and Bryce. According to what she has led herself to believe, I figure it would mean if he willingly sacrifices his own happiness, hers is free, and she can love the one whom she chooses. The debt has to be paid by someone. A girl will do anything for the one she loves, and that includes letting him go. She's made up her mind. Unless you can change it, the only thing that can push y'all back together is fate or God almighty himself."

I'm getting aggravated with all of the riddles. Maybe I've gotten stupid with my head injury, but she is not telling me a damn thing that is believable. "Okay, let's just say for sake of argument that I'm going along with all of this bullshit, which is what it is, by the way. What makes you think Preston "Rich-boy" Dunagin is ever going to let her go? We all know that isn't going to happen. He's already said he would never be the one to walk away from her, so we're at a standstill. Besides, I find it hard to believe Kinzleigh told you all of this. I love her with everything that I am, but she's never been a deep thinker or philosophical type person."

She finally starts to smirk a little, as if I'm not getting the big hint to the joke lingering in the air. "She didn't. She told me the basics and I figured out the rest. She's not that hard to read if you pay attention. She's pretty deep when she wants to be. With her, it's all about reading between the lines. As I said before, your soul belongs to hers and vice versa. I can't say that I buy it, but if you choose to believe in soul mates then there is only one way a soul will let the other move on without it: death. You're back; therefore, neither of you will be able to function happily without the connection to the other. Since you never died, your souls never split, making it impossible for hers to collide with another. Mated souls that part won't be apart for long. Misery they will bestow until they find where they belong. Soul mates are one of those things you either completely believe in or not at all. There is no in between."

Back to the fucking riddles again. I feel like driving my head through a brick wall. If I feel like I'm standing in a pile of bull shit, then why am I still standing here listening? I should just walk away and do things my way. Why aren't my feet moving?

"So you just expect me to sit back and do nothing, hoping she will magically appear at my doorstep? No one gets anywhere sitting on the sidelines. I'm sorry, but I've always been taught to get in the game and play. I can't do it. I can't live on wishing and hoping. It's not in me to stand behind the line and settle for second string while someone else plays the game, getting their hands dirty." She is back to shaking her head again.

"Have you listened to anything she said while you've been back? If she came back to you today, where would you live? How would you pay bills, buy food, and provide simple necessities? You haven't finished high school, you don't have a job, and you're not living the dream that you told Kinzleigh you had. A woman becomes a mother when she feels the baby move inside her womb, but a man becomes a father when he meets his child for the first time. Right now, Preston has a lead on you. He can provide for her and a baby, you can't. He sure as hell won't let her go if you can't support her, no matter how much she's hurting. Part of loving someone is to provide for them. What are you doing to prove that their *needs* are what you're after and not your *wants?* Patience is a virtue, and sometimes in life you have to look at the big picture and not the short distance in front of you."

I'm trying to process all of this and formulate some comeback as to why all of this sounds like the biggest load of crap I've ever heard, but I'm honestly coming up with nothing. "I don't want to be without her. I don't want to go a day without seeing her and our son. I want forever." I'm so lost in my thoughts that I didn't mean to verbalize the last one.

"Then I suggest you let it drive you to put a plan in motion. She won't come back to you if you give up your dream on account of Bryce. You're going to have to continue on as if you never got on that plane and you graduated high school. You're going to have to be a college student and a grown up at the same time to get her back. She needs to know you can support her and have your dream as well, even if in a lesser form than the original plan, just as she has. Then, and only then, will you get her back." She looks at the silver watch on her wrist. "I have to go. Duty calls. Best of luck to you, Breyson. This time, I hope you get the girl."

What does that even mean, *this time?* She turns and walks off, as if this was all some big dream. Too bad it isn't. It's my life. My head is pounding from the buildup of anxiety and stress getting to me. I want to kick and scream; throw a tantrum in the middle of the floor like a toddler to get my way, but reality isn't that way at all. If I could demand for her to come back I would, but she will only hate me that way. I won't take away her free will, even if the result doesn't lean in my favor.

Leaning against the metal pole that is now stained with my blood, I dissect each piece of information she gave me versus the way I know Kinzleigh is. No matter how many different ways you dice it the ending result is the same. Everything she said is rightfully true. I have plenty of money invested, but Kinzleigh never has been and never will be one swayed by money as bribery. Everyone that knows her history with Preston knows she isn't that way. Forever is a process and it's going to take some work to get there.

If I were honest with myself, I could've figured this out on my own. I'm reminded of something my dad used to tell me when I got frustrated over playing a bad game or losing. *Those that set a goal and put in the time and effort it takes to get there will earn the victory in the end. The ones that work hard in life get the payoff.* Most of the time he was probably referring to medical school, but he used it in multiple scenarios and I always applied it to football. I suppose this is no different. I went into this knowing I was going to have to fight. I might as well start to do something about it. The father of time is pissing me off right now.

"Where do you want to go?" I refocus my eyes on Ryland as he closes in some of the distance between us.

"Book us a flight. It's time to make my comeback and formulate a plan. You're coming with me. I'm not getting on another damn plane by myself for a while. I need to speak with my attorney. Kinzleigh should have been cut a check when they pronounced me dead. I don't know what happened, and it doesn't matter now, but until I figure out a career, I need to find a place to live and start acting like a man. I can't bring a family home to live with Mom and Dad. It's going to take money for all that. It's time to cash in on my trust fund and that money I've been investing for years."

I push off the pole, not giving him any time to say anything. "We're going back home. Someone is holding on to something that is mine and I intend to get it back, no matter what I have to do. I need you with me to do this, to face everyone. Can you be my wingman?"

"Sure, Brey. I'll always be your wingman. I'm offended you even have to ask. Honestly, I don't understand the feelings you have for Kinzleigh, but I can tell they're real. I'll do anything you need if it helps you get her back." I nod my head and begin walking in the direction of his truck a few rows over.

I've made the decision to try and live without her for a little while, but actually enduring it day in and day out until I get her back is going to be the hard part. It almost killed me when I wasn't sure she was real. Now that I've spent the last two days with her, survival is going to be the next step above impossible. The faster I get all of this done, the faster I can get her back and we can begin our lives together . . .

TWO

Breyson

We pull up at my house in the rental vehicle. All vehicles seem to be present except for Moms and mine, leaving me to assume she's at work and maybe they sold mine. "Are you ready to do this?"

I look over at Ryland in the driver's seat and he looks a little pale, his knuckles turning white from the grip he has on the steering wheel. If anyone should be nervous about doing this, it should be me. I have no idea how this is going to go. With Kinzleigh, I got slapped and then left. I don't know if she's in an emotional state of shock or lying to me, because frankly she wasn't herself when she told me goodbye. She acted more like a soulless person. In the time since I reappeared, she has built up a wall to her emotions; emotions I used to be able to read like a book.

"As ready as I'm going to be," I say in return as I open the door to the truck and get out, walking to the front.

I stand in front of the truck, looking at the house before me. It doesn't feel like home anymore. I feel like I'm walking into a stranger's house. The truth is, I don't belong here anymore. Where I belong is with the beautiful blonde girl in California. Where she is, is where I belong, whether it's here or there. I feel just as lost here as I did in Spain, because she's not with me. I guess that's what happens when your soul is connected with another, but they remain absent from one another. As crazy as I want to think Lauren sounds, I'm starting to think she's right . . . about everything.

Is it that crazy to believe in soul mates, especially with the extreme and bizarre things the two of us have been through? I'll be honest, when I think of my age and how fast we fell for each other it seems crazy to me, but then I imagine myself walking away, and then I really feel like a damn lunatic. That shit alone is enough to beat someone to death over.

That conversation from earlier is branded in my mind, pushing me forward. I have to do this. I have to bring her back to me. It's simple. We belong together. After so much misery and heartache we should get a fucking break.

The front door appears faster than I thought it would. I guess my heart is steering my limbs this time.

I hear Ryland step up behind me as I place my hand on the doorknob. "Do you want me to wait out here?"

"Hell no. I need you with me. I need someone to be a buffer for some of the emotional overkill. One person can only bear so much. I was at my limit when Kinzleigh left with our son; when she left without me." I look beside me where he is now standing. He nods but doesn't say anything more. He doesn't need to. He knows what I need from him right now. Ryland and I have always been more like brothers than cousins. It's why we're so close.

I push the door open. The house is unusually quiet for everyone to be home. It's the first red flag. I walk inside and close the door. I still hear nothing. When I look over at Ryland, he has the same look on his face: worry. "Mom, Dad, Braxton, Briar, Brylee!" I call out as loud as possible. Where the hell is everyone?

I begin searching all of the rooms in the lower floor of the house but find nothing. "You look outside and I'll look upstairs," I say to Ryland and sprint up the stairs to the second floor. It finally dawns on me that maybe Mom wasn't at work, and maybe they all went somewhere together. Maybe they didn't sell my truck and my brothers drove it.

I get to the top of the stairs and the strangest feeling overtakes me. Without thought my feet begin walking in the direction of my room. I have no idea why, but I don't question the bad feeling I have in my gut, more so now than before; I've learned not to. When I get to the door, I notice it's cracked, so I push it open.

The sight before me cuts off my air like a rope around my neck, leaving me unable to breathe. "Ryland!" I manage to scream out his name as the tears fall without any effort. "Fuck, Mom." I run over to her limp body lying on my bed. The panic consuming me is nothing I've ever experienced before.

Her hand is hanging off the bed with a pill bottle loosely enclosed inside. Pills are scattered across the floor below it. I've never seen her this way. I get to her side and wrap my arms around her. I'm crying hysterically as I pick up her limp body, unsure of what to do. "Mom, please wake up. Fuck!"

I push her eyelids open and her eyes are rolled in the back of her head. Her breathing is barely noticeable. "Ryland!" I can barely get his name out of my mouth from the anxiety and adrenaline coursing through my body. I've never seen her so weak. She's always been a strong woman. I should have come sooner.

I finally hear Ryland running up the stairs and he barrels through my bedroom door. His eyes widen to the size of saucers as he takes in what is laying across my lap. I feel her pulse and it's still there, but faint. My heart feels like it's to the point of bursting in two. "Call a fucking ambulance!" I scream.

He pulls out his phone with shaky hands and dials the number. I'm not even listening to him talk as I rock back and forth with my mother in my arms like a baby. "What the hell were you thinking, Mom? Please don't die. Dammit, wake up." I begin frantically slapping her face in an attempt to get some kind of response out of her. She's a doctor for fuck's sake. She knows what that shit does. How long has she been like this? Why would they leave her alone in this condition? Signs are always there if you pay attention.

"Ava, we're home." I can hear my dad calling out her name from the front door. He's talking to someone calmly, as if nothing is even happening. I get mad. Ryland is spitting out my address into the phone for the dispatcher. I'm two seconds away from driving her myself.

I stand with her in my arms and run through the bedroom door, Ryland following closely behind. They're standing at the bottom of the stairs but look up when they hear my footsteps as I descend from the upper floor. It's Dad and Braxton standing next to Briar. I'm not sure where Brylee is.

Braxton drops the cell phone he's holding in his hand and I can hear the screen shatter against the tile floor. Every one of them looks like they've seen a ghost. They aren't speaking, or even acknowledging Mom is hanging onto her life by a thread in my arms. "Are y'all just going to stand there or fucking help me so she doesn't die?"

They are blinking and rubbing their eyes as if they're trying to figure out if I'm a mirage. I get how odd this is, but there are more important matters at hand. I finally got my existence and family back. I am not losing them now. "Breyson?" Braxton is the first one to speak, but it comes out like a question instead of a statement.

"Yeah, Brax, it's me. Snap out of it. Mom needs help." His mouth falls toward the floor, and Dad takes off in a sprint across the room. His physician reflexes must have finally kicked in. It's more of a blur, but suddenly he's standing in front of me, holding my face between his hands.

"Son . . . you're here? Where the hell have you been?" His voice is no louder than a whisper. A tear falls down his aged face as he searches my eyes for answers to all the questions in his mind. I can't recall a time I've ever seen Dad cry. If I have, I don't remember. The men in my family aren't criers.

It kills me to see them so hurt, which brings me back to the present. "Dad, can we please talk about this later? Mom is messed up . . . I think she took pills."

As if he is just now realizing she's even in the room he looks down. "Oh, God. Ava, what have you done?" He grabs her from my arms into his own. "Please, baby, wake up. He's back. Come back to me."

He kisses her on the lips and anything whole left inside of me shatters. I've never seen Dad so panicky. He's the most laidback person of anyone I know, even in disastrous situations, but this could be his ruin. I now understand an increment of what it's like to feel like you're losing your heart and soul.

I stare down at my mother. Her lips are starting to turn blue. "Where are the fucking paramedics?" In a state of panic, I scream. As the last word exits my mouth, I hear the sirens sound outside the door. My heart is beating out of my chest. I've worked too hard to get back here to start losing the ones I love. No matter what I have to do, I will find happiness and normalcy again. If this is the work of Satan, he can go fuck himself.

I sit in the chair of the hospital's emergency waiting area, my attempt at waiting patiently as they pump my mother's stomach. How did all of this happen? The woman I knew was so sure of everything, and now she's trying to kill herself? Why? She believes in saving people, not killing them.

Dad sits in the chair next to me. Braxton and Briar went to the cafeteria to get something to eat since we can't see her yet. Brylee is at a friend's house, but Dad told her to stay there for now. I lean forward, placing my forearms on top of my thighs and look down at the floor. I'm so worried I can't think straight. The woman I've lived with for eighteen years could die.

Dad stands and takes a knee in front of me, grabbing me by the back of the neck with both hands. I look up at him with tears in my eyes. His expression matches mine. I can see the muscle in his jaw working back and forth as he tries to gather his thoughts. It's been a long time since I've looked my father in the eyes. "It's good to have you home, Son." He's trying so hard not to break down in front of me, but he's failing miserably. His wet cheeks are the first that gives him away.

He pulls me in with force, crushing my face into his broad chest. It takes a lot of humility to bring a grown man to his knees, especially one of his stature. He begins to weep outside of my ear.

This is one of those moments you don't have very often with a parent. For some reason they are always trying to act ten-foot-tall and bulletproof in front of their kids. "Where have you been, Son?"

He sounds out of breath and weak. It's unfamiliarity with him. He lets me go and backs up enough to look at me, continuing to hold the back of my neck and the side of my face in his hands as he studies every feature on my face, no doubt double checking to make sure he's not crazy. I stare back. It feels good to see someone that looks like me. It reassures me I'm where I belong. I'm not an orphan after all. "Where you been?" he whispers, repeating himself.

"For now, know that I was in the closest place I could get to home," I say in response, not ready to elaborate. It's not much of an answer, but it's all I've got. There is no way to explain where I've been to someone that hasn't experienced it. He nods and stands to take the seat beside me. There is one thing Dad has always been good at and that's to let something go when he knows you don't want to talk about it any further.

I continue to stare straight ahead at the passing nurses and doctors, carrying on as if there aren't people in this hospital holding onto their lifeline with all they have. Dad puts his arm around me and squeezes my shoulder in his right hand. "She hasn't been well since we found out you were in an accident. A few months ago, it got worse. She took a leave at work and stayed in bed constantly. She started having nightmares; screaming your name. She was dying on the inside with every waking day. I didn't know what else to do."

He looks over at me. "I thought she was getting better. I never knew she would do something like this." His matching blue eyes are faded and worn out. "You were actually in a plane accident, right? This wasn't all for nothing?" Anyone else would wonder how he has the audacity to ask a question like that, but I can see how much they are hurting and how the thought could pass through someone's mind I would just run off. It happens to people all the time.

That night starts replaying in my mind, reminding me of what I went through and what I somehow survived. I nod and my eyes lose focus. "Yeah, I was, but I don't think I'm ready to talk about it yet. I've got too much on my mind right now with Mom and Kinzleigh; my son."

"You know?" He looks at me with a confused expression. I suppose the situation would seem strange to an outsider. It's still strange to me.

"Yes. I know. I was there when he was born." I place my hands over my face, trying not to cry again, but I seem to be having a hard time getting my heart and brain to agree. My mind is trying to be strong, but my heart is in mourning. As the vision of that car pulling away with the two most important people to me resurfaces, I break down.

Most guys my age probably wouldn't give a shit. Hell, some of them would see this as an easy way out, but not me. When you find the girl that consumes you, completes you, and captivates you, nothing else matters. Football used to be my dream, but now my dream is a life with her. Dreams are worth fighting for. A life in love is better than a life filled with booze, sex, and partying. No one is prepared to be a parent at eighteen, but you have to play the game with the cards you're dealt.

In hindsight, I would have been more careful, because this is going to affect both of our lives, but I would rather give up my football dream and work for a living if it means I can have my family together. If you're going to fuck carelessly, you have to be prepared for the consequences.

Kinzleigh is the only girl I was careless with. My family raised me to take responsibility for my actions, whether it was something I wanted or not. Any boy can conceive a kid, but only a man stays and raises it. The alternative—the option she's giving me—is not going to work for me. I need her.

"If you went there before you came here, then, where is she?" he asks, knowing we were inseparable. I want that year back plus some. Everything bombards me like a tidal wave crashing against my body.

"She left me." There is no way to feel like a man right now. Every time I take a step toward the light, the fucking darkness follows me, smoldering it. It cuts off my circulation, my air supply. The only thing in existence that can defeat this feeling is her. Her absence can ruin me. I will armor up. I will win.

"Dad, I need your help." It's time to start asking for help; something I try to rarely do. Things are bigger than me right now that have to be done if I'm going to win her back, starting with a place to live. I've never known Kinzleigh to go back on her word.

"Anything, Son. What is it?"

"I need help getting back on my feet. I need to finish high school so I can go to college. I need to figure how to live on my own. I have a kid now. I won't stop until she's mine again. I won't live with half of me missing. I need to know how to cash in on my investment accounts and my trust fund until I can find a job. Kinzleigh should have already been the primary beneficiary, but according to her she's staying because he can support them. I need to find out what happened with my attorney. Her warped view that I would be happier without her is horse shit, but the other is a legitimate reason that needs to be rectified as soon as possible."

I look up at him from the floor. It pisses me off to ask for help, because we've always been taught independence, but it's something I'll have to get over . . . for now. "Consider it done as soon as we get your mom out of here, okay?" I nod and lean my head back against the wall behind me.

"Abercrombie family?" My head snaps forward and a tall, slender man with a pair of scrubs is standing at the entrance to the waiting area. I jump to my feet at the same time as Dad.

We come to a stop in front of him. "Brooks," he says, addressing my father. He releases a breath before he continues in a hushed tone. "She's going to be fine, but I'm going to have to keep her on suicide watch for a while before I can discharge her. It's a state requirement. There is nothing I can do to get around it, fellow physician or not. I will do everything I can to keep her admittance discrete. This could ruin her reputation to practice medicine at this hospital. She's a damn good doctor. Something like that would be a huge misfortune."

Dad looks a little sick. I'm guessing this is the first time since we brought her in that he's thought of this from a career aspect. Mom has always loved her job. She said bringing babies into this world was her calling, and something she's wanted to do since she was old enough to have a dream. "What's the damage?" Dad asks. "She's been through enough with the . . . death." He pauses and looks at me briefly. "Or accident of our son. This isn't like her. She's been in mourning for over six months. She can't lose anything else important to her."

"I'm going to be honest, Brooks. She's probably going to have to see a Psychiatrist on the books before she can practice again. You're going to have to see the hospital administrator to know what the course of action will be, but someone has to sign off that she's mentally capable of treating patients. She's sleeping right now, but you can go in. She needs to rest and remain stress free. She needs medicine, but you're going to have to administer it now that she's abused it. She swallowed a lot of pills. If you wouldn't have gotten to her when you did, she would be dead right now."

Dad places his hands in the pockets of his khakis. His shoulders slump. He's thinking, and probably praying. Above all else, he's stressing. I can hear it in his breathing. "I'm going to leave you two alone. You know where to find me if you need me. I'm here for the next eight hours."

"Thanks, Michael," Dad says, and the doctor turns and leaves. Dad pulls one hand free from his pocket and begins massaging left and right across his forehead, hard enough to redden it in color. He takes the other hand out and covers his face with his hands, shaking his head from side to side.

"Dad, it'll be okay. I'm sure with a little bit of time everything will be fine." I rest my hand on his shoulder, not knowing what else to do. He turns and pulls me into a hug, squeezing me tight. I tense. The muscle-to-muscle contact is a little weird, to be honest. I haven't hugged Dad like this in years. When a boy hits puberty he doesn't do the *guy-hugging* thing anymore. I pat his back awkwardly.

"I may not have told you enough, Son, but I love you. I know I'm not very good with voicing the way I feel, but you kids are everything to me. When you were gone a piece of me was missing. I won't lose my son again. Whatever you need to bring Kinzleigh back here, it's yours." He sniffs once and lets go, never giving me a chance to respond. "Come on. You need to be there when your mother wakes up."

We're all standing in the room listening to nothing but the beeping of the machines. Everyone has been quiet the majority of the time we've been here. There's a strange awkwardness between my brothers and me. I'm hoping it's something that will fade over time. We've always been close and now I feel like an outsider. Maybe they're in shock. They haven't said more than five words since they walked in the house earlier today.

Mom stirs on the hospital bed, causing everyone to freeze. My heart begins to race. I don't know what to expect when she wakes up. Maybe this isn't a good idea. I don't want to put her into cardiac or respiratory arrest when she sees Braxton and I side by side. Every other time I was alone, making everyone think I was Braxton.

I stand here frozen, waging back and forth in my mind on the right decision. Her eyes slowly open and I take a step back, only to run into Braxton. He places his hand over my shoulder, halting me. "Come on, Brother. We've all been living in Hell since you've been gone. It's been long enough." Finally, he speaks, aside from verifying that I'm in fact real and not a ghost. "I don't know what to say, because it probably won't improve your mindset from where you've been or what you've been through, but know that not a day went by where we didn't think of you and miss you. You're my brother, best friend, and partner in crime. I'm glad you're back. It's just a little bit of a shell shock is all."

Mom starts looking around and I allow him to steer me toward the foot of her bed. She looks around the room, confused. When her eyes end on the two of us in front of her, what she says causes me to shut down. "Am I in heaven?"

She looks at Braxton first, long enough to differentiate which one is which like she always does, and then me. "Breyson," she whispers, as tears develop and begin to fall. "I found you." Her voice is scratchy and hoarse; from the procedure I'm sure. She looks like she's in pain when she moves from the squinting.

Damn.

My legs develop a mind of their own and rush to the side of her bed, my hands grabbing her face as I sit on the edge beside her. She appears a little out of it, but I need her to understand. There is no holding back tears when you hear something like that, man or not. I've never been a pussy, but I'll be damned if it doesn't have an effect on my heart when I hear my mother say something like that. "Mom, listen to me. I'm not dead and you're not dead. We're all very much alive. I'm here, and I'll never leave again."

She stares at me, not saying a word. I can see by the way her eyes scan side-to-side that she's trying to determine if she's living in reality or fantasy. I wrap my arms around her frail body and pull her against me, crashing her face into my chest. She tenses at first, but then relaxes and wraps her arms around me, clutching my shirt in her fists. She begins to sob, and I let her. You want to know why? Because knowing that your life meant something to someone else makes you feel valued. When you feel like an orphan for almost seven months, it's nice to be missed.

I never look away from the wall behind her, because that means I'll have to distance myself from her and I can't bear to do that to her. I can hear the door open and close, leaving nothing but silence. I can feel that we're alone. My dad and brothers stepped outside to give us privacy. The wetness from her tears soaks through my shirt. I sense that she needs to get this out. She squeezes me tighter and I do her.

I've never seen her this emotional, and it makes my heart ache. I feel guilty that I didn't try harder to find a way back before. I shouldn't have let this much time lapse. It's ruined so many lives; even my own if I don't get Kinzleigh back. I feel like such a fuck-up right now. "I'm sorry, Mom." The words make her cry harder. She is gasping for breath from crying so hard.

I don't know what else to say. I'm terrified to speak at the possibility of making this worse than it already is. I do what I do best when I can't find the right words—something I always did with Kinzleigh. I hold her, letting her feel my presence and know that I'm here.

"Not. Your. Fault," she says, trying to catch her breath between words.

"It feels like it," I respond. "Why would you try to hurt yourself, Mom?"

She doesn't immediately respond. Her breathing evens out slightly, but it's still irregular. She sighs against the dip in my chest. "I don't know how to explain," she finally says, her voice muffled against my shirt.

"Try," I say sternly. "I need to know you won't try this again. Attempting to kill yourself isn't a joke. This is so unlike you." Moving my hands to her shoulders, I try to put space between us, but it only makes her tighten her hold.

"I'll explain, but I need to hold you right now. When a mother thinks one of her kids is dead a piece of her dies as well. Can you give me that for a while? I know you've always been stubborn and not big on affection, but I need this." She nestles her ear to the spot where my heart beats below my exterior. With each heartbeat her breathing regulates as if it's the medication she needs to calm down.

"Okay, Mom. I can do that. I need to know what you were thinking." The image of her lying almost lifeless on my bed with an empty pill bottle in hand will be forever a memory. I have enough tragic memories floating around up there right now without adding more. It's time for some good or my mind is going to explode.

She begins speaking in a monotone dialogue similar to a narrator or golf announcer on television. "I was sad at first, heartbroken really, but I was getting by. Kinzleigh's pregnancy kept me occupied for a while, but when she left things took a turn for the worst."

She stops momentarily, as if she accidentally told a secret that was supposed to be kept. It's weird how my heart and mind are completely in sync with everything related to Kinzleigh, because automatically, I know why she stopped talking. "I know about my son. He's beautiful."

She digs her fingernails into my back, causing pressure points of pain as they pierce the skin. I breathe through it. She's not going to ask what she wants to know. Instead, she continues. "What I was focusing my energy on was that baby—the only part of you I had left. I suppose, secretly, I was hoping he would look like you so that when I looked at him and he smiled, it was like you were smiling down on me from Heaven through him."

She pauses briefly, taking every word into consideration. I think I know why. She doesn't want me angry with Kinzleigh over something she says. "When she left it was like you were really gone. I was alone. I can't blame her, Breyson. Kinzleigh was in a very bad state when she was here. That boy is, or was, good for her at the time. When I talk to her now, she doesn't seem dead inside. She has a little bit of that spark back—the part of her that makes everyone love her."

She looks up at me for the first time since I sat down, putting distance between us. "I'll admit she isn't the same person she was when you left, but it's expected for someone her age that's been through more pain and sudden change in a year than most experience in their entire lives. Y'all were crazy about each other, and it's clear to anyone around you two. I'll never understand why your connection to her is so strong at such a young age, but I can see it."

Yeah, to everyone but the person that matters. I wish someone would tell Kinzleigh that.

"A couple months ago the depression was starting to consume me. I couldn't even get out of bed. Your father made me an appointment with a colleague. I started taking an antidepressant and anxiety medication. I got a call this morning from Kinzleigh's mother that Bryce was born and she was flying back to California for a few days. She wanted to know if I wanted to come with her. I wanted to, I did, but everything started closing in on me. All I could process was that you missed the birth of your son, that you wouldn't get to watch him grow up, and that I couldn't experience my son bonding with my grandchild the first and most important week of a father's life. Everything was crashing down around me."

She looks as if it's painful for her to speak. "You don't have to talk if it hurts you. You've said enough."

She shakes her head. "I need to get this out. I need you to understand."

She lays her head back on my chest as if she needs to be touching me while she finishes telling me. I can feel fresh tears on my already damp shirt. "When I got off the phone I ran to your truck. I went to your tombstone first. I wanted you to know you were a father now. My mind broke down and nothing made sense. I started thinking you were just lost, and somehow, I could find you. It sounds crazy, but I felt like you weren't dead. I told myself I was distraught, and my nerves were sparking like fireworks, so I ran home. I knew I wasn't in the state of mind to drive or someone could be killed, so I locked your truck and left it there."

Her voice lowers to almost a whisper from the hoarse state it's in, and her tone saddens. "When I got home, I was hysterical and drenched in sweat. I remembered how I used to find Kinzleigh in your bed when she was having a hard time coping that day. You could always tell which days were worse than others, because on the bad days she woke up everyone in the house screaming in her sleep, and Briar would have to hold her until she calmed down. The good days I would find her the next morning wrapped around your pillow in your clothes. I thought I would see if it helped me the way it helped her, so I went and got my medicine from the cabinet before walking to your room."

She stops talking and sniffles a few times, catching her breath from talking nonstop without inhaling between sentences. I'm trying my best to focus on her and only her, but it's becoming a little more difficult now that she brought up Kinzleigh again. It's hard not to visualize the image of her waking up in terrors now forming in my mind.

The thought of her in pain kills me. It makes me want to throw everything down and say fuck it; fly back to California and throw her stubborn ass over my shoulder, bring her back, and make love to her every morning and every night until I prove to her she was wrong. I don't know how many people in the world are as crazy in love with someone as I am about her, but I know it has to be rare. I'd be an idiot to let her go.

She's been mine since the day I laid eyes on her on that beach and she'll be mine until the day I die. I'm going crazy without her. The more time I waste, the more time I'm away from her. I need to talk to Braxton and Briar about these nightmares and sleepovers in my bed. I want to know more.

"It didn't help. The sadness consumed me. I panicked and took a pill. It didn't help either. I took another and another until most of the bottle was gone. I wasn't trying to die." I'm broken from my thoughts as those last few sentences are voiced out loud by my mom. "I just wanted a temporary break."

I haven't been back in the country but a few days and already my to-do list is long. Standing in the airport that cold day in February, I never imagined the destruction left behind after that plane took off. Not only do I need to get my life back, but everyone else's too. "You'll never have to go through that again, Mom. I promise."

I zone out as I continue to hold her, making up for lost time. In time I want to tell my family everything I've gone through. I want to tell them that even though I was gone, I was also taken care of by an amazing family. I want to share the events of that night and what I've been doing over the last six months, but now is not the time. There are too many things that need to be mended right now, starting with my heart. I can't concentrate on anything with half of it across the damn country.

"Breyson . . ."

"Yeah?"

"If you've seen Bryce, I'm assuming you made a detour to California first, so where is Kinzleigh and the baby?" I can hear the longing in her voice. She probably misses Kinzleigh almost as much as I do, not to mention the grandchild she has yet to meet. My parents are family-oriented people, and whether I'm eighteen or twenty-eight they aren't just going to forget their own blood as if he doesn't exist; even if Kinzleigh and I never got back together—we are—she just doesn't know it yet.

"She stayed with Preston in California." Even saying his name leaves a bad taste in my mouth, giving me the urge to spit. It's hard to like the guy when he has something that belongs to me. He's been after her since before I left. I tried to remain calm, but the hurricane is about to begin. I'm giving him a little more time to hand over what's mine, and then I'm going to start tearing shit up.

"Why?"

It's a simple question. Do I even know the real answer? I'd like to think that I do, but really, I don't. Maybe because it's the stupidest shit I've ever heard, yet I have to go along with it, because what other option do I have?

My temper wants to flare each time I think about her living with another guy, making me want to rip him apart limb by motherfucking limb.

One thought.

That's all it takes and I can feel the rage begin to rise. I don't know how

I thought I was going to do this. Lauren said to give it time and get my life in order, but I don't think that's going to work for me.

Fuck.

"Hell, I don't know. She thinks I'm better off without her. She has some warped idea that what happened to me is her fault—that and I don't have a place for us to live. She agreed to marry him, Mom. She's not going to fucking marry someone else. I will ever more, fuck his rich-boy, preppy-ass shit up. He didn't see half of what I'm capable of in that hotel room." My next sentence comes out muffled as she raises her head and slaps her hand over my mouth.

Her eyes grow wide. That was the key to drying up her tears. The only thing remaining is dampness left behind from the previous ones. "Breyson Patrick Abercrombie, you may talk that way around your friends, but I am still your mother. I do not want to hear that filth, is that clear?" She removes her hand, allowing me to respond. A simple nod won't suffice.

"Yes, ma'am." Her tone says she's serious. She raised three boys and she knows how to get her point across when she feels disrespected as a woman. One thing I've learned over the years: do not piss off Ava Abercrombie. No one wants to see her wrath. The woman is scary when she wants to be. I never thought of this before, but maybe that's where I get my temper. Dad is more laidback like Briar.

"Good, now we can discuss this like adults. Besides, if you're going to raise a child, as I expect you are . . ." she says as she raises one brow, "then you need to control your tongue. Have you ever heard your father or I curse like that in front any of you kids?"

Here goes the lecture.

I drop my head into the hand of my arm resting on the inner side of my knee. "No, ma'am," I say in a bored, drug out tone.

"I know how girls work. She will come around, honey. She's just confused right now, I'm sure. Everything will fall into place. You know your father and I will help you in any way we can. No one expects you to have it all together in these circumstances. You've been gone . . ." Her octave raises and she jerks my head upward to look at her. "Oh my gosh, where exactly have you been?"

"Mom, I'll tell you at some point, but right now I'm not in the mental state to do so. I would appreciate it if we could keep to some type of normalcy until I'm ready to elaborate on the last six months, almost seven now. Every detail doesn't have to be rehashed." Her eyes narrow slightly as if she's about to scold me for talking back, but then she sighs and drops the subject.

"Fine. I guess I can understand. I know you didn't come back to everything being the same as when you left, but everything will work out the way it's supposed to. You have to believe that, baby. Your dad and I always taught you that sometimes you have to sacrifice things to get what you want. It may take some time, but in the end, it'll pay off. If you love her the way I think you do, then you're going to have to be her support, her backbone. Don't push too hard or you'll push her away."

She begins running her long fingers through my hair like she used to when I was a kid. It's already time for a haircut again. She looks like she's floating on cloud nine the more we talk. "My babies are growing up so fast. I can't believe y'all are in college. I know you're behind, but don't worry, we'll get you caught up."

She looks down from watching her fingers comb through my blonde hair. I feel it sticking out all over my head. "I do want you to remember something when you get discouraged. Can you do that?"

My eyes close from the hypnotic feel of her fingertips brushing against my scalp, making me want to fall asleep. I nod. "Things always get worse before they get better. If you don't give up, you'll win her back. Love conquers all other things. Never let anyone tell you that true love doesn't exist, because it does. It's more real than most of the things you'll encounter, but you have to remember it's forever. You two have it. When you're at your wits end, remember your heart will always win. Occasionally, it just lets the mind lead for a little while to make it a fair game. When you get her back, make sure you never let the love you have for her die."

I open my eyes and look at her, speechless. It's hard to believe that just came from the mouth of my mother; the woman that's always been serious and reserved when it comes to relationships and emotions, aside from saying I love you like all mothers do. My mouth drops a little, causing her to laugh. Based on the frown lines appearing around her mouth, I'm guessing it's been a while since she has.

"What? Don't look so surprised. Your mother is a hopeless romantic, believe it or not. I have to keep some things to myself," she says and winks at me.

I place my hand over my heart. I think I just realized why my dad loves my mother so much. She's one of those people you fall a little more in love with as time goes by. I've known her for almost nineteen years and I just realized today I love her a little more than yesterday. Is that possible with a parent? "I want to hear more," I whisper.

"Later," she says and kisses my forehead. "You know, you get your passionate, loving nature from me. It just took the right person to bring it to the surface, but it's been in there hiding all along. Go call Kinzleigh. You have to start somewhere, and I want to know about my grandchild."

I continue to sit here for a minute, going over the instructions in my head. I didn't think of something as simple as calling her. Will she talk to me? "Go on, get moving. I expect an update and a picture when you get back."

I stand and walk to the door. "Oh, and Breyson . . ." I turn to look at her one last time before exiting. "I love you."

"I love you too, Mom. Thanks." I leave the room in search of somewhere quiet. I have a girl to get back.

THREE

Preston

I pull into the drive and notice the garage is open. I've told Kinzleigh to keep it shut. It's a nice area, but that doesn't mean we don't get strays from time to time looking for easy access to steal. Kinzleigh's mom should be here soon to help her with the baby for a few days. Maybe she's already here. I could use her help so I can get some work done. I'm swamped with projects and a new baby is more work than I thought it'd be. I try to give Kinzleigh a break when I get home, but I have a ton of work to catch up on from doing so.

Pulling under the garage door, I park and kill the engine. I grab my briefcase and step out of my beamer. It's been a long day. I'm ready to unwind. I completely understand now why my father has always been a scotch drinker.

I grab the knot of my tie and pull, loosening it from the noose it's becoming around my neck. When I get to the door my heart plummets to my stomach. It's cracked open, but it doesn't seem tampered with. It's not like Kinzleigh to be so careless. My first thought is that someone has broken in somehow. I push it open and walk inside. "Hello?"

I drop my bag at the door and pick up pace when I hear Bryce screaming at the top of his lungs. A fear I've never known races through my body. What if she's hurt? "Kinzleigh," I call out throughout the house. I get no response. When I make it to the living room Bryce is lying in his bassinet screaming, and Kinzleigh is lying on the couch staring off into space like a zombie, ignoring him.

His face is blood red like he's been crying for a while. I reach over and pick him up, pulling him to my chest. "Hey, buddy. Shh, shh, shh. It's okay," I say as I rock him. It's not helping. He's obviously hungry or wet. Hell, I don't know. I've never had a baby before, and I'm a guy. I would get cranky if I was hungry. Kinzleigh is breastfeeding, so I don't know what I'm supposed to do about it.

"Kinzleigh, when is the last time you fed him? Didn't the nurse say he has to be fed every two hours?" I look over at her, still attempting to calm him down. My ears are stinging from his constant crying, putting my nerves on edge. I can't think. She hasn't even acknowledged I'm in the room. "Kinzleigh, what the fuck?" The only response I get from her are tears that fall from the corner of her eye and trickle down her nose before dropping onto the leather of the sofa.

"I can't," is all she says, and goes back to staring off into space. What the hell does that even mean, she can't? She was feeding him fine when I left.

"You can't or won't? What happened to you? Are you sick?" He is still screaming, so I reach in the bassinet and grab his pacifier, hoping it calms him a little until I can figure out what the hell I'm supposed to do now.

"I can't," she says again. She's not even looking at him. I begin walking toward her in an attempt to see what's wrong and get her to feed him. She closes her eyes before I get there. "Please don't. I can't hold him. Please, take him somewhere else. Please . . ." I don't understand. She was fine when I left for work. I try to give him his pacifier. We don't have any formula, because she wanted to feed him naturally. How does everything change so drastically in twelve hours?

He takes it for a second before he figures out nothing is coming out of it and spits it back out, now mad as hell. I can't deal with this shit right now. I'm worried about her, because she's not acting right, but I have to get him calmed down first. Pulling out my phone from the pocket of my slacks, I hit one of the contacts in my immediate access list. It rings for a minute before the line picks up. "Preston? It's seven thirty and the sitter just left. Do I need to call her back? Is that Bryce? Is he okay?"

Her voice is drowned out from his crying. I walk out of the room with the phone up to my ear. "Hey, Macie. I need your help. It's an emergency. It's about Kinzleigh. You can bring Talon, but I need you to come to the house.”

“Anything, Preston. Is she okay? What’s wrong?”

I peek my head back in the door. She’s still lying on the couch in the exact same position she was in when I left. She is still staring at the wall blankly, no emotion registering on her face. “I don’t think so. I came home and Bryce was screaming in his bassinet. She’s just lying on the couch in a vegetative state. She won’t hold him. I have no idea when she’s fed him last. Can you bring some formula?”

She sighs. “I think I know what’s wrong with her. I’ll be right there. Give me fifteen minutes.” She doesn’t wait for an answer before disconnecting the call. I slide the phone back in my pocket and begin bouncing him in my arms slightly while I pat his back. His tiny head is resting against my cheek.

“It’s okay, buddy. We’ll get your mom fixed, okay? Don’t worry. She must have a reason for letting you cry; she has to. You’ll love her. I have my entire life. She’s hard not to love.” His cry is dying down, from the exhaustion I’m sure, but not stopping completely. I stand in the doorway watching her. I’ve never in my entire life seen her like this, not even when her grandmother died. It’s like her soul has been sucked from her body, leaving nothing but a hollow woman lying in this big house.

I’m scared to know what that means. I need to talk to Macie. She’s a girl; knows what girls think. I have a feeling I’m losing her. And we just got started. I’ve never been in love with a girl like I’m in love with Kinzleigh, and I never will be again, but I can’t stand seeing her like this. What’s the good in loving someone if they don’t love you back in the same way?

If this is going to be what she becomes then I’ll have to make another choice; one that is going to forever destroy me. I won’t trap her. We were happy before he came back, but things have changed. I won’t watch her disintegrate and become lifeless to preserve my own happiness.

The realization occurs that if she doesn’t get better, I may have to let her go. Watching her lay there as if she’s alive, but dead, is killing me inside. I’ve never been an emotional guy until I went back to Mississippi that night and saw her the way I did, wandering around lost and shutting down. Something changed in me that night. From that point forward it wasn’t about me, but her. I’ve been trying to live that way ever since. I’m no longer a college kid. I’m a man. Now, I’ve learned that when you love someone you do what’s best for her, even if it isn’t what’s best for you.

I want to walk over to her right now, but I have to take care of Bryce first. I made a promise to love and care for both of them. I’m going to keep that promise for as long as I can. Right now I'm scared, and I don't know how long I'm going to get to hold onto what has become my family. Just because this child doesn't share my blood, he still has a piece of my heart.

Bryce finally cried himself to sleep, but he won't be asleep long. Macie should be here soon. I can tell his diaper needs to be changed anyway from the soggy mess it has become.

I stare at the girl that captured my heart from the time I was just a kid. I've really grown into a man from then to now. I rub my thumb back and forth on Bryce's head, above his ear. "I need to leave you for a minute, but I promise I'll come take care of you," I whisper into the air in her direction. "I love you, Kinzleigh."

My eyes fill to the brim with tears, but I close my lids before they have the chance to fall. It's destroying me on the inside seeing her in so much pain, but she doesn't have room in her life for someone that can't contain his emotions.

I kiss the top of his head. His baby smell fills my nostrils. "I love you also, buddy." I hold him close to me and begin walking in the direction of the stairs, toward his room. I'm going to savor every moment with the two of them. My brain wants me to believe that I still have them forever, but my heart is preparing me for the worst.

It doesn't seem fair for a person to fall in love with someone that will in time give their heart to another. It's wrong, and it's also why I don't believe in soul mates. If I did and they were, then I wouldn't have fallen for Kinzleigh, but I did . . .

After changing his diaper, I sit in the rocker and start to rock him back and forth. Macie walks in with a bottle made in one hand. She takes one look at me and gets a saddened look in her eyes; more like a look of pity. "You've gotten attached to him, haven't you?"

"Yeah." I'm not one of those guys that talks about my emotions. I prefer to keep to myself. I'm a loner. Revealing parts of yourself to others sets you up for gossip and judgment. Coming from a family in the media that was something you didn't do. Kinzleigh is the only person I've ever let in.

"I hope I'm not overstepping any boundaries, because I really like you as a boss and a person, but you know there is only one way to fix her, right?" I continue rocking back and forth, staring at the wall before me. I want to know, but at the same time I don't. I'm not sure I want to know the answer, because I think I already do.

"What's that?"

"Preston, you can't fight soul mates. I know you love her, and I really believe she loves you in return, but she's meant for him. I was skeptical to believe it at first, seeing her with you, but his return has changed everything. Her soul is fighting her, mourning for its other half. A doctor is going to tell you it's postpartum depression, but we both know what's really wrong with her."

I'm getting mad. Things were going great before he came back. I'm not going to be an asshole and say I wish he would've died, because I don't, but she's the only girl I've ever wanted. That should count for something.

"So, you think I should just hand her over to him? What kind of man hands over the only thing he wants in life. I've only ever loved her . . ."

"I'm saying you should set her free. Then, the right decision will be made. She made you a promise, and I don't think she's going to break it, but if she keeps going like she is downstairs, her heart may break it for her. Her soul is turning against her; rebelling until she gives it what it wants. As silly as it sounds, I really believe someone can die of a broken heart. Would you rather keep her alive and well or allow her to suffer slowly? If you really love her, prove it, and free her from the ring that binds her. Selflessness is the ultimate sacrifice in love."

I look down at the bundle in my arms. I can't let them go yet. I need more time. She could still get better. She has to get better. I'm trying to convince myself, but it's not working. Bryce wakes up crying. "Here, give him to me. Talon is watching television in the spare room downstairs. Go tend to her. She needs someone. She looks horrible."

I stand and hand him to her. I watch her sit in the chair and stick the bottle in his mouth, but I can't quit looking at him. "Preston . . ." I glance up at her. "We'll be fine. I've raised one baby. Go on." I nod and follow instructions, leaving the room. When I get to where Kinzleigh is, she looks worse than she did before. It feels like someone has a hold on my heart and squeezing as hard as they can until it becomes lifeless.

I get to her and squat down so that I'm at her level. "Kinzleigh," I whisper. Her eyes are so void of life and emotion that I'm not sure she even heard me. She doesn't look at me. It's as if she's dead.

Fuck it. I can't take this anymore.

I slide my arms underneath her and lift her, pulling her against my chest. "I'll do whatever I have to do to fix you, Kinz. I promise." I walk her upstairs and into our bathroom, sitting her on the toilet. She slumps slightly but holds herself up.

"Lift your arms." She does as I say. I remove her shirt and she lowers them back down. I unclasp her bra and remove that too. She is now sitting in just her underwear.

I unbutton my shirt and let it fall to the floor. Grabbing the collar of my undershirt, I pull it over my head and toss it down on the other one, forming a pile. I work quickly to unfasten my belt and pants, letting them drop to the floor as well. Stepping out of my shoes and pants in unison, I kick them to the side. Wrapping my arms around her waist, I pick her up and she wraps her legs around me, and then lays her head against my chest.

I walk over to the large, round tub and step in. Reaching forward and down, I turn the nozzle and adjust the settings until the water is warm, letting it run.

I sit down as the bathtub fills with water, with her in my lap. My eyes fill with moisture again, but this time I let them fall. I've never seen anyone like this, unable to function. My heart is breaking; shattering is a more appropriate word. The only things at the forefront of my mind are the things Macie said. I hold her wrapped in my arms and silently cry, because it doesn't seem fair.

My heart is trying to convince my mind that it's wrong, duking it out on what's best for her. I don't want to let her go. I want to love her each and every day for the rest of my life. I want to give her the world, and be her world, but after seeing the way she reacted to him at the hotel that day and seeing her when she told him goodbye, and looking at her now, my mind is overpowering my heart. I'm fighting a losing battle. It's clear that what I want and what she wants are two different things.

I could hold onto her if I wanted, but my love for her guilts me and won't let me do this to her. I feel like I'm being stabbed in the heart over what I have to do. I'll never be the same after this. I'll never give my heart to another woman. When I do this, I'm defying everything I was taught by giving in. I'm sacrificing my happiness for hers.

When her and Bryce go, my heart goes with them. Not only will I become the same bachelor I was before, but worse. The difference between before and after is that now there will be no possibility of getting what I want. All rules will be thrown out. Something has to fill the void that will be left behind.

After holding her in the bathtub with no rush to get out and trying to convince myself to go back on my decision, I bathed her and gave her some sleeping medicine from the bathroom cabinet.

I place her on the bed and pull the covers over her. It doesn't take her long before her eyes begin to roll in the back of her head and her lids close.

Her cell phone on the nightstand starts to ring. I notice it's an unsaved number. It doesn't even look like a United States format. Trying not to wake her, I answer the call. "Hello."

The line is silent. "Can I talk to Kinzleigh?"

I look down at her. She is sleeping and looks peaceful for the first time since I got home from work. I'm not waking her. Besides, I'm about to give her to the bastard anyway; he can let me have a few more hours. "Now is not a good time," I say in a clipped tone.

"Are we really going to play it this way?" he breathes out while I walk out of the room, quietly shutting the door. I move far enough away she can't hear me if she wakes.

I need him to stop calling, because what I have to do has to be done in person and I don't need him to worry Kinzleigh until this is done. "She doesn't want to see you, Breyson. Please stop calling." I disconnect the call and throw the phone at the wall, leaving a crack in the sheetrock and a now shattered phone lying on the floor.

I run my hands through my hair and rest against the wall, sliding down until I'm sitting on the floor. Leaning my head back I close my eyes. "I'm taking it you're going to let her go?"

I open my eyes to Macie walking down the hall in my direction. "I don't want to. I feel like I'm not fighting for her if I let her go, and she's the one girl that's actually worth it."

"I get why you would feel that way, but in actuality she'll love you more for letting her go one day. I know you don't feel this way now, but at some point in the future you'll meet your one, and you'll understand what she's going through. The heart can love over and over, but the soul can only fit together with one other soul, and right now hers is taken." She takes a seat against the wall beside me.

I begin shaking my head at her. "You're wrong about that. There will be no others for me. I gave the whole love thing one shot. If I ever dabble in companionship after this, it will be for the sole purpose of sex."

She gives me a half smile and we sit here in the quiet of the hallway. I'm going to hate myself after this; I already do. "I need you to do me a favor."

"Sure, Preston. What is it?" I can see from my peripheral vision. She looks over at me, but I continue to stare straight ahead.

"I need you to take care of Kinzleigh and Bryce for a couple of days.

I love her, and under normal circumstances I'm sure she'd be a great mother, but I don't think she's capable of caring for him right now. I would never forgive myself if I left and something happened to either of them, but especially him, knowing she isn't well. There's someone I have to go see, and I prefer to do it alone." Call it being a caveman, an alpha, an asshole, whatever you want, but I will not give her to him unless I know they are both taken care of, financially and emotionally.

"Hey, you know you guys are like family to me. I would do anything for y'all. I really hate that things can't work out for you. Love triangles shouldn't exist. Someone is always on the losing end."

For what it's worth, she actually looks like she's stuck in the middle of the battlefield, not knowing which side to pull for.

"Someone always gets the girl though, right? That's all that matters. Otherwise, this would all be for nothing." I stand. I might as well get this over with. I have a bag to pack and a flight to book. "I'll leave you everything you need."

I begin walking back to the bedroom but stop at the door. I don't look back as I speak. "Macie, I don't know your story and I probably never will, but I'm pretty good at reading people. I just have one question. Does the pain in your chest of losing someone you love ever go away?"

"Never," she responds in more of a whisper behind me.

"I didn't think so." That spot in my chest that holds the one organ I can't live without—according to science—just flatlined.

FOUR

Breyson

"Son of a bitch!" I scream and throw the phone through the parking lot as far as it will fly. I can feel the rage starting to build in my core. It's heating and spreading throughout my body like a fire, consuming my oxygen. I haven't felt this kind of anger in a really long time. I need to get out of here and away from people. What kind of sorry-ass man won't let me talk to her? We have a child together. There should be some kind of mutual respect there.

I fucking hate his guts. I want to kill him. I want to rip his heart from his chest, just as he has mine.

There's only one place I can go when I get like this, one place that has always allowed me to blow off steam when I'm at the point of no return with my anger. I begin jogging. I can get there by foot. Actually, I prefer this method to a vehicle. I have to burn off some of this rage and the only way to do so is to work it off.

I put one foot in front of the other, my pace increasing from a sprint to a full out run. With each thought that invades my mind I push harder, drive myself faster. I'm starting to sweat, soaking my fitted gray shirt. It's weighing me down like the memories in my mind. I need to unload. The heat in August and September are no different than July in the south.

Reaching for the bottom hem of my tee shirt, I pull it up my torso and over my body. I tuck one end of it under the waistband of my jeans and continue running along the side of the highway. My feet are digging into the grass with each stride.

Coach used to make us do this when training for a new season. It's a long stretch, but my subdivision and high school are straight ahead. He thought if we got used to running a long distance of grass, then the distance of the football field would come easily. He was one of those coaches more into strength and endurance training than size.

As if I'm not angry enough, the last time we were together begins to play in my mind. What I wouldn't give to touch her one more time, to feel her, and to make love to her. I swear, if I ever get the chance, I will make it last. I would imprint every detail of her to memory as if it were my only chance. Every inch of her body will always be burned into my mind. One look into those green eyes and my heart is reconciled with its owner. One touch and my soul returns home; the only place it belongs.

I can see my subdivision entrance come into view. I'm burning up and short of breath from the distance I've just run. I've made it this far. I can't stop now. The sooner I get there, the sooner I can release some of this anger that I'm housing. I'm livid. The way I feel right now is unexplainable to any other human being unless he's been there.

Loving someone in every form possible, but not able to hold her, kiss her, and make love to her is excruciating. Knowing you have a son but can't hold him anytime you want could possibly drive someone mad. It is beyond me how anyone could just forget they have a child, as she expects me to do, because I just found out about mine, and already, he consumes my world.

I close my eyes, trying to shake off the thoughts and photos that are lurking in every facet of my mind. Her body always did do things to me that no other girl's did. Kinzleigh is the type of girl that destroys you for better or for worse. I wanted her yesterday, I want her today, and I sure as hell will want her tomorrow. Her presence and absence will forever wreak havoc on my heart.

I can see the pool house from where I stand. I turn, leaving the street for my driveway. I'm almost there. Looking under the doormat, I unlock the door with the spare key. I barge through the door. I don't even remove the key from the lock.

I stop abruptly, placing my hands on my knees in an attempt to catch my breath. My abs tighten with each breath exhaled. I look around the room, scanning for what I'm looking for. When I find it, I stand and walk in that direction, picking up the gloves on my way. I extend my neck in each direction, loosening it, until I hear the pop I'm waiting for. I cover both hands, because the way I'm feeling right now I'm going to need it.

Once my knuckles are completely protected, I swing my arms, stretching my shoulder joints. I inhale deeply, letting the rage fully consume my body, drowning out all conscious thought, except for one. I need to make someone pay for the shitstorm going on in my head. I allow my mind to go to the one place no normal man would go. I formulate the image of him touching her, putting his lips on her body, and experiencing her in a way that was only meant for me, taking what's mine as his own. Like a chain it binds me, but also sets me free.

I swing, my fist making contact with the bag. Like a drug, I begin to feel the high. Pulling back, I drive it again, climbing the high. I need more, so I begin swinging with both arms, one after the other, and as hard as I can. My arms burn, but I don't let that stop me. Instead, I picture the bag being Preston and I get a second wind. I scream out in rage. When I close my jaw, I bite down on the inside of my cheek. I can taste blood, but I don't stop. Instead, I let it pool.

I can no longer feel my arms. They feel foreign on my body—dead weight. I still have my legs. I make the switch to the lower half of my body. Dad made us take MMA classes when we were younger. The movements are now like a reflex. I channel the anger to steer them, making them effective, swift, and right on target. Blood is draining from the corner of my mouth as it fills.

Tears begin to exude from the ducts, trying to rid my body of some of the rage poisoning me. I get déjà vu as a set of hands enclose around my biceps, squeezing. One command is all I hear. "Breyson, stop."

Braxton.

I fall into the bag, hugging it, and heaving. I cry from the rage flowing through my veins. Before I got on that plane, anger was the only time I ever shed a tear, and that was rare. I was in this frame of mind last time because of her, and I'm here now because of her. I've never let Braxton see me cry. I don't have enough energy left to be embarrassed. He clutches the back of my neck in one hand, pulling me backward. "I got you, bro. I got you," he repeats.

When I turn around, he envelops me in a hug. It's a little awkward, but nothing aside from brotherly. My arms remain by my side, and I lightly punch his sides. It's all I have left. Everything else has dissipated, leaving me drained. "I need her. I fucking need her and she won't talk to me. I want to see my son. This is not how I wanted this to go. He's just as much mine as he is hers. I have a right to see him!" I scream out.

He squeezes the back of my neck hard. With his opposite hand over my shoulder, he pushes me backward, creating a space between us. He's looking at me, man to man, and he appears mad. He lightly smacks me on the cheek. "I said I got you. Do you think I'm going to let someone keep a member of our family away from us? Hell no. Whether it's her keeping him away or Preston, it won't last long. You know how we are about family. Fight or die trying, right? Nothing and no one stands in the way."

I close my eyes and nod, acknowledging everything he says. I begin clenching my fists, itching to go at it again, but refuse. I need to cool off. I need to get some sleep, because come tomorrow I'm going to see my attorney about that damn money in question. "Is Mom good?"

He nods. "She's sleeping. What you need from me?"

"I need to be alone right now, but I do need you to do something for me." I pull the gloves off my hands, waiting on him to commit.

"Anything. You know that."

"Will you go to Pops' house? I need you to break the news without giving him a heart attack. I haven't had a good track record so far with confronting people since my return. I need him with me tomorrow. I don't know what I'm doing, and I have one chance to try and not fuck this up." I look up at him as I finish asking the question.

He lets go of me and begins backing away. "You know I'd do anything you need me to. You're my brother. Consider it done. I'll stop by when I head out for school. I just have to pack my bag." I stand here watching him. I nod. He turns and opens the door, stepping outside, and leaving me with my thoughts once again. Me deep in thought inside my head is never a good thing these days.

My body is covered with sweat, reminding me of the lapse in mental stability I had. I walk over to the doors that lead into our pool house. I can see the pool through the glass. The sun is starting to set, but the radiance against the water is inviting. I think I might.

Opening the door, I can feel the Mississippi heat baking my skin. I reach down and pop the button of my jeans through the slit and slide down the zipper. I hook my thumbs under the waistband and pull them down until they drop to my feet. I step out, remaining in nothing but my boxers.

I walk to the edge of the deep end and dive in, breaking through the cool, still water. I come back up through the surface, instantly cooling a few degrees as the water envelops me. Without thought, I swim to the right corner of the deep end, grabbing the concrete edge in my hands. It wasn't planned, but sure enough as I stare at the two sides meeting in this very corner, I'm reminded of the night at Ryland's pool house; the night I had her in a corner matching this one, wrapped around my waist as I enjoyed the feel of her wet body against mine, sucking the droplets of water from her full lips.

I close my eyes. I refuse to become angry again. That isn't going to change the outcome of anything. Instead, I'm going to live through my memories for a little while and enjoy them. I'd rather have them than to go back to the time in which I didn't. If this ends badly, losing her physically is something I'll have to live with, but I don't want to go another day where I can't remember the love we experienced. At least the memories are mine and no one else's.

If I concentrate hard enough, I can almost see the blushing of her cheeks and feel her breath against my lips. I remember the way her shirt clung to her breasts, showing the outline but nothing more. I almost lost it like a damn virgin getting his first piece of action when she pressed herself against me. That one week was the best week of my life, because I met the girl that forever changed me. Blonde hair and green eyes never looked so good until I laid my eyes on Kinzleigh Baker.

I shake my head to clear the thoughts. I'm going to bed. The sooner I go to sleep, the sooner I wake up and start climbing out of this nightmare. Placing my hands flat on the concrete, I hoist myself up until my body is free from the water. This whole situation is bullshit anyway.

I walk toward the pool house, grabbing my jeans on the way. I don't feel like sleeping in my room tonight. After seeing Mom in it earlier the way she was, I'm not sure if I'll ever be able to again. I don't intend on living here much longer anyway. My brothers and I always kept spare clothes in there for when we came in late.

I open the door and a burst of air hits me, causing chill bumps to emerge. I shut the door behind me, and sprint in the direction of the bathroom. I'm now freezing. I quickly step in the shower and stand under the hot water until I warm up.

I'm mentally exhausted from today's events; so much so that I don't feel like standing here. I soap up my washcloth and hurriedly lather my body. It takes ten minutes tops before I'm getting out and drying off.

As I rub the towel over my hair, ridding of the excess moisture, the smell of my soap lingers, settling in my nostrils as I inhale. I've missed the smells of home. It's weird how associated smells are linked with memory and familiarity. My eyes are starting to get heavy. I wrap the towel around my waist after drying the water from my body.

When I get to the dresser, I remove a pair of boxer-briefs and pull them on, discarding the towel in the process. Three strides are what it takes and I'm falling face first onto the bed. I barely have time to get beneath the covers before my eyes are closing, dragging me into a realm that is currently better than my reality; a world where I have her . . . again.

A banging sound occurs, waking me up. Shit, I feel like I've been hit by a truck. I rub the heels of my hands over my eyes, trying to focus. Looking over at the nightstand I can see green digital numbers, but it takes a few seconds before I can make them out: 3AM. Who in the hell would be here at this time? It gets louder with every second that passes.

"Hold on a second," I holler out, aggravated.

Swinging my legs over the side of the bed, I stand and quickly grab a pair of sweatpants from the dresser, along with a white tee shirt. The loud banging continues.

"I'm coming, fuck!" When I get to the door and open it, I wasn't expecting what is standing on the other side, or should I say who.

Preston.

"What the hell are you doing here?" After the day I've had, I'd love nothing more than to knock him out. He's standing with his hands in the pockets of his jeans and I'm suddenly aware of this situation. I begin looking around for her.

"She's not here." His voice comes out a little short. I look at him face to face now that I'm fully awake. He looks like shit. His hair is messy and sticking out as if he's had his fingers through it a million times.

"Where is she? Is she okay?" I'm starting to get a little panicked. I don't know why else he would be here if something wasn't wrong.

"She's not hurt . . ." He never said she was fine or well, just not hurt. I don't know how I should take that. It could mean a variety of things, with her or Bryce.

Why is he here then? He's got the one thing we both want. Come to think of it . . .

I take a step forward, invading his personal space. "I really should beat the shit out of you right now. You have a lot of nerve showing up here, at *my* house. You've taken enough from me . . . Don't you think? You had your chance with her for years, but you just had to wait until I got her, didn't you?"

He doesn't back down. He actually looks a little bored. "Are you going to keep up the Rambo act or do you actually want to get down to business? We can take this outside and fight it out if you want or you can sheathe your sword of testosterone and talk to me like a man. I have something I need to discuss with you in regard to something we both want but only one can have. If you want her back, I suggest you listen to what I have to say."

"You're here about Kinzleigh?"

"Yes, I thought that was obvious, but there are a few things that need to be laid out on the table if you want me to hand her over to you, because I won't until they are. And right now, she's wearing *my* ring."

My heart skips at the words that just came from his mouth. I feel like someone has raped me of my oxygen. I work hard to catch my breath. There has to be a catch, or either I'm dreaming one. It's hard for me to believe he's just going to give her away without putting up a fight. We both know he wants her. "What's the catch?"

He exhales as if he's at the end of his rope and ready to let go. "Breyson, there is no fucking catch. When are you going to realize it's not about you or me, but about her? Do you think I want to be here doing this? Did it ever occur to you that maybe someone else could love her the way you love her? Fuck, are we going to do this or not? Let your bad boy image rest for a while. We both know your hands have been in just as many panties as mine. Stop acting like you're better for her than me. I'm grown and getting too old for high school shit."

Without another word I open the door the rest of the way and step aside. I never looked at it that way before. I know someone else could love her. I just never wanted them to.

I nod for him to come inside. "Yeah, sure, Preston. Come in. I guess we're going to have to do this at some point."

He walks inside and I close the door. This is going to end badly for someone. I guess it's time for one of us to surrender, because one is going to lose. You can't fight the inevitable.

If he's comparing the way he loves her to the way I love her, then one of us is in for a long road of misery . . .

FIVE

Preston

I stand inside the room wondering why the hell I'm about to do this, but then I remember the way she looked when I came home from work yesterday. I have no choice. She loved him intimately before she did me. I found out the hard way that timing really is everything. I missed my chance by a week last summer and I'll pay for it for the rest of my life.

I've lost her emotionally since his return. The state she's in right now isn't good for anyone, so here I am, feeling like I'm facing my own death.

If you love someone, set her free . . .

Placing my hands on the back of the sofa, I lean forward slightly, letting my head fall. My heart is beating unsteadily. What I'm about to do cannot be undone. My chest is aching uncontrollably. I've never experienced anything like this in my entire life. This will annihilate me. I want to make sure he's going to treat her like the amazing woman that she is. I need to know she will never go without. I need to know he's going to love her and only her every damn second of every day for the rest of her life. Then, and only then, will I let her go.

I stand fully and turn to face him. He's standing with his arms crossed in front of his chest. "I want to know what your intentions are with her if you were to get her back," I blurt out. There is no reason to beat around the bush. I came here for one reason and one reason only.

"What's it to you?" The prick is really starting to get on my nerves. I'm so fucking sick of his attitude. He's not the only one with something to lose. I get he has to act cocky to ensure his balls are still there, but at some point, you grow up and realize that real men don't act like that. He needs to step over the line from the boy in high school to the family man, because that's what he's going to have to be for her and for Bryce.

"Because I fucking love her, that's what it is to me, and I've known her a hell of a lot longer than you. I'm not giving her up if you're going to hurt her at any point in this lifetime!" My blood is starting to boil and I'm pushing my fingers in his chest. I'm sure it's a little of my broken heart taking it out on everyone else.

He stands there staring daggers at me, then looks down at my hand before I remove it. If he wants to get mad I welcome it. She's my priority, not him. I will not watch her exist like she was when I left ever again.

I'm already mad. I might as well get out everything I came here to say. "You think you're the only one that could take care of her, love her, and protect her? Well, I hate to burst your little jock bubble, but you're not. You may not like me and that's fine. Rightly, I don't give a shit, but dammit, you're the one she wants. I know I can support her and Bryce. I know I can love her and only her for the rest of my life. I know I could raise him as if he were my own blood, because I already feel like he is. You seem to forget I was here picking up the pieces when you were gone. I know I can protect her from being hurt physically . . ."

My eyes are starting to sting. I'm beginning to wither and fucking die inside. I wasn't emotionally prepared for this like I thought I was. They fill, blurring my direct line of vision from me to him. My brown lashes feel damp as they touch with each blink.

My voice comes out strained. "But I can't protect her emotionally. I can't protect what isn't mine. Dammit, the truth is, her heart belongs to you. Do I understand why? Hell no. But it is what it is, and there's nothing I can do about it. I've lived in denial over it since I made my move to make her mine, but I was too late. I wish like hell I could erase that week you came to California, but I can't. I was always selfish before and I wish to God I could be now, because if I was, I could hold onto her, but I can't spend another day watching her deteriorate emotionally like she did yesterday. I'm not a monster."

I take a moment to gather my thoughts. His face softens a little from arrogance to relief, an emotion I wish I could wear right now instead of pain and heartache. I bore my eyes into his. I want to make myself very clear. "So, I'm going to ask you again. What are your intentions? Is getting her back some kind of attempt to prove your manhood or are you completely and irrevocably in love with her? If you can't give me the assurance I need, then maybe I was a fool for coming here and you don't deserve her. Her heart is the purest of pure and she deserves the best. One way or another she's going to get it. The only way I can live the rest of my life without her by my side is to know she is going to live a life full of highs instead of lows, and because I love her, I'm going to free her from her promise to me. I'm going to walk away, but not a damn second before you answer my questions so that I'll know I'm making the right decision."

He relaxes his stance once I step off my soapbox and rubs his hands over his face. I can hear him breathing, but he remains quiet. When he looks at me this time there is something in his eyes that has never been present when looking at me before: respect. "You really do love her, don't you?" His voice saddens at the question. He knows the answer. I don't have to confirm it, but I will.

"With every cell in my body. The truth is, I always have. My time with her has been incredible. My heart will be destroyed when this ends, but it's a consequence I'm willing to take if it means hers will heal. She's been through enough sadness. It's time for her to be happy for a while." I can already feel my control on my emotions being revoked.

"Preston, this is a feeling I wouldn't wish on anyone. The kind of heartache caused when you fall in love with a girl and then lose her is the worst pain. I was willing to fight you for her; win her outright. You have no idea how much I respect you as a man for coming here, for talking to me face to face when I know your pride doesn't welcome it, and for willingly bowing out when I can see it's about to kill you. I wish I had that kind of strength, but I don't. I've wanted her since the day I met her and it's only increased since. My heart and soul won't allow me to let her go. My intentions are forever. If I'm honest, they have been since we met. The only way I can live is with her by my side. She's the reason I made it back to begin with."

That's a good start, but that doesn't pay the bills. "Where are you going to live, Breyson? How are you going to feed the three of you? Have you thought of those things? She's not in a place mentally or physically to work right now, and to be honest, she shouldn't have to. She should be caring for an infant and going to school if that's what she wants, but you're going to have to sacrifice the things you want and provide for them; that's what a man does. It's the reason I waited so long to be with her. She wasn't ready for long term back then. I'm not trying to offend or downgrade you, but I've finished college and have a damn good paying job. I can provide for them. I just need to know that if I transfer their care to you, you can handle it."

"I have plenty of money invested, Preston. It's the one thing my family did right. I just have to withdraw it. I was planning to start the process today. I'm perfectly capable of taking care of her. I'll figure out a living arrangement as soon as I work out the finances. I have means to work until I find something more permanent, but I should be well set if it takes a while. I would never let her go without; either of them." He walks to the back of the couch beside me and lays his fisted knuckles on top of it. Turning his head to the side to face me, he continues. "Are you really going to let her go without a fight?"

I'm leaning against the couch, my butt pressed to it. I look at him. I may be willing to let her go, but he also needs to know what he's up against should she decide to stay. "I am. There is only one exception. There is one way you won't get her back. Should that happen, you have to let her go, let her live. Are you prepared to do so?"

His jaw begins to twitch. I know he doesn't like the thought, but neither do I. "What's your exception?" He holds up his fingers in quotation marks.

"Should she *choose* to stay, I'm not going to make her leave. I'm only giving her an out, free of guilt, if she *wants* it. Neither of us can make the choice for her. Her free will should remain intact no matter what either of us wants." He needs to understand we aren't kids anymore. We aren't competing over a toy, but a person. The heart of another should be handled with care.

He stands there for a moment, zoned into his own head. He looks like he's processing everything I've said. "Yeah, okay. Fine. If she chooses to stay without being conditioned I'll leave her alone, but I can't forget I have a son. I will be in his life if I have to move to California to do so."

Now that we have all of that out of the way and he's brought up the living situation, we have one more issue to address, one more thing to lay on the table. "Are you willing to stay in California if that's where she wants to live? I bought her a studio to start a cheerleading company. It's hers. I don't want it back."

He begins rubbing the top of his hair. I can be an overwhelming guy at times, but usually over things important to me. "If I buy you out, what do you want for it?"

"I don't want your money. It was a gift. I don't take back things that were gifts, regardless of who she chooses to be with. Our history goes back much further than our relationship. She is free to do with it as she pleases, even if she moves back here with you. There is only one thing I want from you. I'm asking you man to man, person to person, because it's something that I can't have without you being open to it."

I'm usually more of a demanding my way type guy, because I learned from the best—my father. I don't have problems getting what I want, but this is something that I have to respect him on. Now that I'm here, I could imagine how I would feel if the situation were reversed.

"What is it? I'm not going to agree until I know what it is." I assumed that would be his response, because it's what I would have said. We're more alike than I care to admit aloud.

"I still want to be a part of their lives, especially Bryce. It'll take a while before I can really control my feelings enough to be around Kinzleigh and see you two together, but we were friends before this and friends I want to remain. If she's with you I will never cross that line, as I would expect the same if flipped. Us and our families go back too far. It's really best if we're on good terms." He pushes off the sofa and walks backward.

I can tell he's not happy about it. His jaw is working overtime and he's pacing back and forth with his hands interlaced on top of his head. He begins mumbling to himself. I remain calm. What I'm asking for is worth it to me to be a man about the whole situation. He finally stops. "I need you to answer one question before I actually consider this."

"I'm listening."

"I get it with Kinzleigh. I don't like it, but I get it. Why Bryce? He's not yours. If you aren't with her then why would you want to be involved? Wouldn't you rather be free from something that would tie you down like a child? It's not one of those things you can go back and forth on. Kids don't understand if you just come and go. They get attached. Are you trying to replace me by getting close to him in hopes Kinzleigh will come back to you on her own?"

Now, I'm just insulted. I've been more than logical and understanding about everything that I do, including this.

Actually, it pisses me off, considering he was of the same caliber of male in the Pre-Kinzleigh period. A man-whore is what we both were. There is no reason to deny it. When you learn what it feels like to stick your dick in things it becomes somewhat addictive. It was a part of who we were before we gave it up for sappy lovesick shit. Besides, I have a younger sister. I remember how she was when we were younger. Paxtyn was glued to Presley and I both. We were her heroes, even though she's only a few years younger than Presley.

"Nice. You really want to hit below the belt with assumptions like you know me? I've been nothing but respectful toward you since you showed up at our hotel room. The truth is I've been in his life longer than you if you want to get technical. You may consider me an asshole for bringing up things you couldn't control, but there it is."

I'm not trying to be a dick, but I don't like when people insult or downgrade me based on who I was before, or who they think I am. He's no better than me. He could have left it at why.

The best method to avoid doubt and confusion is full disclosure. "I get that he isn't mine biologically. He'll never look like me—big deal. But that doesn't mean I wasn't there when you couldn't be. I am the one that felt him move when she was pregnant. I am the one that spent hours outside of work learning how to prepare for a baby. I am the one that has financially supported him to this point. I am the one that comes home from work since he was born and takes care of him to give Kinzleigh a break, even if only a few days."

He is standing still in front of me. His eyes look like they on the verge of spilling with tears. Right now, we are in a mutual no judgment zone. I feel like an asshole, but I'm simply trying to prove I'm not an evil person. People change. I am not trying to plot against him. If I were interested in anything other than their wellbeing, I wouldn't be here talking to him.

I lower my tone. Fuck, I feel like such a prick right now, even though I shouldn't. "Whether it's been days, months, or years, I've grown attached to him. I love him as if he were my own. I'm just trying to make you understand that I want a relationship with him as much as you. You are his father, I get that, and I will never overstep my boundary or try to replace you. You can tell him I'm his uncle, or whatever the hell you want. It's your call. I'm just asking you to let me be a part of his life. I'm giving up the girl I'm in love with, because she loved you first. I'm only asking that you not make me completely give him up as well."

He's staring off at the wall behind me, lost in thought. I have no idea what he's thinking or what he's going to say. "This is so fucked up," he mumbles underneath his breath. He looks at me. "On my terms? No barging in and trying to control everything with your power plays, right?"

I hold up my right hand. "You have my word. That means everything in my family."

He takes a deep breath. "Fine, but the first time you try the drop-in game, you're out. I'll get over our issues and consider you family for Kinzleigh and Bryce. I'll even try to set aside my jealousy of knowing you've been with her in a way I wish you hadn't, but you better fucking remember that family is for life. You want to be family you stay around for the long haul. Don't hurt *our* family."

I nod and look down at my watch. If I'm going to try and get back before Kinzleigh notices I'm gone, then I need to get going. I would rather explain everything once D-day arrives and he's ready to collect. I begin walking forward, toward the door. There is something I need to make very clear.

I stop next to him, our shoulders touching each other, but facing different directions. "If I had any intention of hurting either of them, I would've deleted your call from the call history when I answered the phone and never discussed you again, but instead I'm here, sacrificing my wants to make her happy. Make sure you practice what you preach, because I'll always be waiting in case you fuck up. Know their value. Second chances only come around once in a lifetime. If you hurt them, I will recover what I set free."

I'm not trying to cause any more problems, but everything needs to be laid out in the open. Excuses and ignorance can be costly, and most of the times are. Nothing but silence momentarily fills the air. "What time should I expect you?"

"Tomorrow or maybe later today. It depends. I need to take care of a few things that can't wait." I nod and continue walking my path to the door. Grabbing the knob, I turn and pull it open. "Preston?"

"Yeah," I say, but never look back.

"How is she? How is Bryce? I want to be prepared." There is no way to prepare oneself for the image he's about to see.

I close my eyes and try to breathe through the pain of what it looked like seeing her like that. There are no words that can properly describe the way it feels. "Bryce is fine. Kinzleigh . . . well, she's going to need some tender love and care. Envision her like a classic car. When you're looking at a rusty body and an engine that doesn't run right, it doesn't stop you from investing time and money, because you remember the way she looked brand new, and how she'll be even more beautiful when she's restored."

"She's really that bad?" he asks as I take a step out the door.

"I wouldn't waste any time if I were you. We'll be waiting." I continue out the door, shutting it behind me. I did what I came to do. I just need to keep my game face on for a little while longer and then I can lock all of this away inside my own safe, never to be opened again. The worst part is yet to come; the part where I let her go. When she leaves with him, and when she takes Bryce, everything in my world will come crashing down.

SIX

Breyson

I'm in complete shock over what just happened. Is this real or is this a dream? I slap my face a few times. The sting that registers after each hit tells me it is very much real. My heart begins to race. No later than tomorrow she could be on her way home where she belongs. She may have been born in California, but she's a southern girl at heart.

I can't help the excitement coursing through my veins. It's hard not to worry this is a set up, but he seemed genuine enough. If it were, it would never happen again when he witnessed the wrath that would come.

The only worry I still have is her refusing to give in. I have to believe that she has learned by now we are meant to be together. There is no reason to fight it.

Kinzleigh is also the most stubborn person I know. She chose him once. Will she do it again? It's plain and simple. I'll have to make her see it my way. The option to fail does not exist. She can't possibly turn me away.

He said himself that she isn't well. That thought becomes poison in my mind. I don't like the thought of her being ill, especially because we aren't together. If this doesn't prove that us being apart is wrong, then I don't know what will.

It can't be past four in the morning. There is no way I can go back to sleep right now. What am I supposed to do until I talk to Braxton about his meeting with Pops? He's probably sleeping in his dorm right now. I can't just sit here twiddling my fucking thumbs when I have so much to do today.

I have to figure out finances and living arrangements before packing a bag for California. The thought of getting on a plane still leaves me queasy, but bringing them home is the most important thing and that's what keeps me going.

At the rate I'm pacing across the floor I'm sure to leave a wear pattern in the rug. Screw this; I can't wait any longer. Pops is always up early to get started working at daylight. The drive will fill some of the time. Braxton promised he would make him aware that I was alive and home. I'm going to talk to him. I need to start getting everything worked out, so I will have everything ready when I return with them. No matter what, they will come back with me. That, or I remain there. I will not go another day without them in my life.

Rushing back to the bedroom area, I make my way to the closet that holds extra clothes for my brothers and me. We all wear the same size, so we keep this area stocked with clothes we may need. It keeps us from having to go in the house, especially if we don't want to wake Mom and Dad. From the bottom hanger I remove a pair of faded jeans and switch them out with the sweatpants I'm currently wearing. The first shirt I notice is the one I grab from the bar on top: a black polo. Quickly, I pull it over my head.

Last, but not least, I slide on a pair of shoes that lie at the bottom of the closet. One thing I didn't consider: no wallet. I had to get a temporary ID in California to be able to get on the plane with Ryland, but I don't remember what I did with it.

How am I going to withdraw any funds without a photo ID? I guess I'll have to go get a new one, yet again. My to-do list is growing at a rapid rate. Pops has access to withdraw from my investment accounts since he's the one that helped me set them up years ago when I was a kid, but I have to have Mom or Dad to transfer or withdraw from my trust fund since they started it. Without them I only have access to partial withdrawals until I'm twenty-one.

Since it'll probably take time to cash in on my investment accounts, it's all I have left until I get back from California. I'm sure I have access to my checking account, but with no ID I'm stuck. I don't have time for this shit. I would have never imagined leaving the state would end up causing so much havoc on my life. How the hell do you reverse death?

I'm just going to have to call Dad once I get to Pops' house. There are no other options. I have to have money. I have no cell, because I broke the one I had on the pavement, no wallet, and not much more than the clothes on my back unless I go in my room and wake everyone who's home.

Walking to the door, I grab the first set of keys hanging on the hook beside it. I don't even look to see which vehicle it's for as I walk out the door in the direction of the garage.

When I get to the garage doors, I look down and notice the key ring. It's Kinzleigh's set to my truck. I know this by the keychain she had made especially for it. It's a silver heart that looks similar to the charm on the anklet she gave me Homecoming night. One side is marked with diamond-like crystals and the other side has our initials engraved in the middle with the phrase, *two hearts beating wildly,* flowing in a circle around them. She put her own spin on my idea. She had it made after I carved almost the same thing in that old Oak tree out at Pops' ranch—our Oak tree.

My heart starts beating harder and it becomes painful, as if someone is trying to rip it apart with the recognition of the words in my mind. I get a sinking feeling in my stomach. She really isn't okay. I can feel it. "Kinzleigh, why do you have to be so hardheaded?" I rub over the etching in the metal, taking a deep breath.

So close, yet so far away . . .

I notice my truck in the driveway. Someone must have brought it home, because Mom said she left it. It's still so strange to have some of the things I thought I lost forever. I will rebuild my life one thing at a time, starting with the most important.

I sit in the driveway of Pops' house, nervous to go inside. My life has become the epitome of complicated. It feels like I don't exist. I'm just wandering around in a world that is going on without me, lost. When life is passing by around me, I'm at a standstill. I've never been one of those people that let complications stand in my way. There is no reason to start now.

I pull the door handle toward me and push open the door of my truck. I step out and immediately feel the breeze blowing across my face. It's nice out today. The sky is clear and the palette consists of greens with a fall mix of red, orange, and yellow. I miss the tranquility that I feel each time I'm here.

I look at the garage and see a head of teased curls walking beside the vehicle parked underneath. Immediately I smile. "Can I help you?" she yells before my truck and I become visible to her. My heart always warms a little in the presence of Mims. She's one of those people known to have a pure heart.

"I don't know, can you?" I laugh at my sarcasm. One of the most common southern English mistakes is using *can I* instead of *may I*. It was always a problem for me—one in which she corrected constantly—which is why it's funny hearing it come from her.

She locks me in her sights and stops at the edge of the open garage. She places her hand over her mouth and begins to weep. I rush over to her, throwing my arms around her four-foot-eleven frame. I always did tower over her from the time I hit puberty. "Shh, don't cry, Mims. I didn't plan to barge in unexpected like this. I know I should've called to warn you, but the only phone I had is shattered in the parking lot of the hospital."

She locks her arms around my waist and squeezes tight. "Breyson, you have no idea how happy everyone is that you're alive." She pulls away and places her aged hands on my cheeks. "Let me look at you," she says as wet tears trail down her wrinkled skin. "Yep, it's you," she says in relief. "Come on, dear. There is someone waiting for you."

She grabs my hand and leads me inside. I close my eyes briefly as I take in the smell of her house. It's strange how each person's home has a distinct smell, unique to its owner. I come into the kitchen and Pops is sitting at the farm table by the windows. He's staring out at the barn, eating his breakfast in a mechanical rhythm as if he's lost in thought.

Mims clears her throat. "John Gavin. There is someone here you want to see." He sets down the piece of fried bacon he is holding and looks over to where we stand.

Immediately he stands, pushing his chair back across the tile floor. He brushes his hands over his Wrangler jeans, removing any grease or food particles that may be on the surface. Walking toward me, he grabs the back of my neck in one hand and lightly slaps my cheek with the other. His eyes look softer than the usual hardness they hold. He's a man that harnesses his emotions inside, only revealing them from time to time. "Son, it's good to have you home. This is the place where you belong."

I'm starting to get overwhelmed by the emotion in the room. "Pops, I need your help."

"Let's take this somewhere else. A man's business is better to be kept in private. Besides, I know someone else you need to see," he says, and winks before turning in the direction of the door, grabbing his cowboy hat off the table. I follow closely behind from the house to the opening of the barn. I now know exactly who we're going to see: Hendrix.

I come into view and immediately he begins to go crazy inside the stall, shoving the gate with his head. He wants to be released. He wants to be ridden. "Hey, boy. Not today, okay, but I promise I'll be back soon. I have someone I need to bring home first."

I pet his head and I can hear rhythmic exhales coming from behind me. It's too deep to be human. I know exactly who it is. I turn to the black mare, standing in the stall behind me. She's the most beautiful horse I've ever seen, fitting perfectly with the most beautiful girl. I walk over to her and begin rubbing up her nose, between her eyes. She isn't making any great attempt to move. There is sadness in her dark eyes that I don't remember being present last time I saw her.

"You miss her, don't you, girl?" Her head dips slightly as the words escape me. "Don't worry, I'll bring her home. I promise."

"She's been like that for a while. Kinzleigh stopped coming here after the news was released about the plane accident. I don't think she could bear being around this place. I can't say that I blame her. This was an escape for the two of you, wasn't it?" I continue petting Divinity, attempting to cheer her up. It doesn't seem to be working. If anyone can understand, it's me.

Kinzleigh leaves a mark on people. She's sweet and caring, but bashful. She's guarded, but when she lets you in, she's the most loving person you'll ever meet. Sometimes, it takes pushing her out of her shell, but when she moves into a comfort zone, she's fun to be around. She inches into your heart and embeds herself without even trying. "Yeah, it was. It still is. That old Oak tree will always be ours."

"I spoke with your daddy. I think I know why you're here. Saddle her up. There is something I want to show you. I'll ride Hendrix. They need to get out of here anyway." I turn around and he's already leading Hendrix out of the gate. When Pops wants to talk about something, it's usually for good reason. Right now, I need all the help I can get.

"Yes, Sir." I open the gate and lead the black beaut out of her stall in the direction of the tack room. I stop at the tie down post just outside of the barn entry and tie her to it with a lead rope to keep her from running off.

When I walk into the room with the saddles, the first one I see is Kinzleigh's. I run the tips of my fingers over it, remembering Christmas Day when I gave it to her. I hope and pray she makes this easy, but I am willing to beg if I have to. I need her, and if it takes living in California I'm prepared to do so, but this is where we belong.

I move on, grabbing my saddle from the stand and quickly saddle Divinity. Placing my left foot in the stirrup, I grab each end of the saddle and mount her. Pops is already seated on Hendrix and waiting for me. He takes off through the open field towards the back of the property line. "Come on, girl," I say as I heel her, following behind. I know exactly where he's going: our spot. I didn't realize how much I've missed this, riding in the country with the breeze blowing across my face. It's peaceful.

It doesn't take long when we come out of the path that runs through a wooded area, opening into the back field. It's miles of open pasture with lush green grass. I can see our Oak tree and the pond. When Divinity catches it in her vision, she takes off running at full speed. I bear down into the saddle and lean forward, allowing the wind to blow over me.

Divinity passes Hendrix as she rushes toward the tree and the pond. She didn't act like this last time Kinzleigh and I rode together. She continues running wide open until she reaches the huge Oak and digs her hoofs into the grass, halting herself.

I have to firmly press my weight down into the stirrups to avoid flying headfirst over the horse. I get off once she stops. "Divinity, what the hell?" I place my hands on my hips as I work to catch my breath. She hangs her head slightly and moves past me as if I'm not even here. My brows furrow as I turn to watch her in confusion. She continues to the front of the tree where mine and Kinzleigh's names are carved into the bark. Am I really seeing what I think I'm seeing? How strange.

She places her nose against the hollowed lines in the wood, pressing directly in the middle of the circle. She begins to slow down her rhythm of breathing. A few seconds lapse and she kneels, then lies on the spot in front of the tree in the same spot Kinzleigh and I have spent so many days and nights. You don't see a horse laying very often, especially fully saddled. It's as if she is mourning the loss of her owner, her best friend. "Well I'll be," Pops says from behind me.

I turn and he's already released Hendrix to get a drink of water at the pond. He's standing next to me, but slightly behind, watching the entire ordeal. "Have you ever seen anything like this?" I ask, glancing back over to her.

"I've been ranching since I was just a boy. I've seen a fair share of things in my day, but this is a first. I don't have many of those anymore at my age, but one thing to always remember about an animal is that they're never predictable. They know a lot more than you will ever think. Their senses are impeccable." He closes in on me and puts his arm around me from behind, resting his hand on my opposite shoulder.

"Come on, Son. Let's give her some space. Miracles and things out of the ordinary happen every day. One is standing right beside me. It's not our place to second-guess the things that can happen at the hand of God and his creatures, but only to enjoy them and know that they are real. I'm sure stranger things have happened."

I allow him to lead me back toward the open pasture. It's just now that I notice wooden stakes in various places not far from the Oak tree. I look over at him as he stares out over the clearing. "What's this?"

He repositions the cowboy hat sitting on top of his head. "This is where your house will be in a few months." I stick my index finger in my ear like a cork and wiggle it around. Surely, I'm hearing things.

"What do you mean it's where my house will be? I don't know anything about a house." He looks at me as if I just asked the dumbest question on the planet.

"When Braxton came over yesterday, he filled me in on everything going on. A man needs a place for his family to lay their heads at night. I called in a long overdue favor and the property lines have already been surveyed. The builders will start construction Monday. I had to pull a few strings on such short notice, but let's just say being a good doctor for over twenty years pays off."

I begin shaking my head as I look back and forth between him and the staked off area of florescent orange tape.

"You and Dad have always drilled it in my head to work for everything I have, and to never accept handouts. I can't accept this Pops. I will have to find another way. I have money, I just have to go through the necessary steps to get it." I squat down, placing my forearms on my thighs, playing with the longer strands of grass.

He hooks his thumbs in the pockets of his jeans, still staring out in front of him. "Breyson, no one said anything about a handout. If I did that it would show you that I don't care about you, because then I wouldn't be teaching you ways to become a man of worth and value. In order to become a decent man, you have to know the quality of working by the sweat of your brow. This is simply a loan. It's just coming from me instead of a bank."

He starts stomping the grass under his feet with the bottom of his boot.

"You will work to provide for your family, and you will make your mortgage payments to me and Mims. You've always loved this place, and Mims and I are getting older. We won't be around forever. This land needs to belong to someone with the heart that understands its beauty for the way God made it, and not someone just interested in subdivisions and shopping malls. It would also be nice to have your help around here from time to time, but I don't want you giving up school and football. Where there is a will there is a way, Son. I will continue to pay you to work for me while you're in school, as I always have."

He turns toward me and squats so that we're eye level. "Family helps family when they're in need. I have instilled that in your father and I've instilled it in all of you boys. There is no shame in asking for help when you need it, as long as you accept it and strive to stand back up on your own two feet. Then, you pay it forward to someone else. I have lived that way all my life and look how much I've been blessed. Just look around you. You worry about your family first and everything else will work itself out. When your priorities are right, Son, God will help you with the rest."

I begin shaking my head again. "I have to have somewhere to bring them now. I can't wait months. I have to be able to afford a place now."

He cups his callused hand around the back of my neck, drawing my attention. "You want to know the beauty of always doing business with the same person?"

I nod. "After the news of the accident went viral, I received a call from our attorney. He said you called him about transferring the primary recipient on all of your accounts from your dad to Kinzleigh, but you never made it in to sign the paperwork before the accident. Since you were just a kid that basically lived with me in the summer when the accounts were opened, I was the joint account holder. I've already had everything processed. Most of the money is sitting in an account set up for Kinzleigh and Bryce, and the rest is sitting in cash inside the safe."

He looks me in the eyes to make sure I'm listening. "I wasn't going to keep the full amount in cash. Both of you are too young to have easy access to that amount of money and are both still learning the responsibility of managing it. Your parents have always paid the way for both of you. I wasn't going to give her the rest until she turned twenty-one. What's in cash is enough to live comfortably for any person for that amount of time. Neither will do without. No eighteen-year-old needs access to that kind of money in a lump some, because once it's gone there is no way to get it back.

Mims and I were already planning a trip to California to take her the cash when the baby arrived, but the plans have clearly changed. Take what you need to get by for now, and then we will figure out everything else when you're not in a panic and your family is standing next to you, so you can think without your head being in a fog."

It seems too good to be true. I'm so used to everything going badly I'm almost afraid to hope that I could finally be getting a break. It makes me want to look over my shoulder in expectation that I'm about to get smoked upside the head by a ball soaring through the air.

As if he can see the thoughts running wild in my mind, he saves me from having to respond. "As far as living arrangements until the house is built, coincidentally, I had a tenant move out of my rental property down the road. You can stay there until the house is finished, and then I'll list it for rent. It'll give you some time to get all of the finances organized, develop a routine, and to get your identity back. You need to figure out school. There has to be some kind of option, because of your special circumstances. This ranch will be yours one day, but never do I want you to feel pressured to follow in your father's footsteps or mine. Follow your heart where it leads you. If it's football, play football, but either way a man needs an education. I want you to stop worrying until you bring your family home. Am I clear?"

My eyes begin to blur and I quickly turn away. Pops is the last person I want to cry in front of. He's a hard man; always has been. "Son, look at me."

I do as he says, trying to blink the moisture away. "Even the strongest men have to break down occasionally. It's the only way to cleanse the soul and keep moving forward. As long as you do it in the company of yourself or to the woman God put by your side, there is no reason to be embarrassed."

He stands and I do the same. "Thanks, Pops. I won't let you down."

One side of his mouth pulls up into a half smile and he lightly smacks my back. "I know you won't, Son, and that's why I'm helping you. Come on, you have a family to bring home. There's no reason to wait longer than you have to."

It finally feels like some of that darkness is being broken with a ray of sunshine. I hope it lasts, because I'm tired of living and breathing under constant rain and thunder—a blackened sky. I'm ready to prosper in the heightened state of the day. When the sun goes down at the day's end, I want to know I have the woman I love to accompany me through each night and the beautiful son we created even though he wasn't planned. That is the only thing in life that I care about from now through the rest of my life.

SEVEN

Preston

I stand in the doorway with my hands in my pockets, watching her sleep. According to Macie that's all she does. I haven't been home long, but I can't move from the location I'm standing in. My time with her has come to an end and I feel like I'm holding on by a thread. "Breyson," she mumbles in her sleep and turns over, kicking under the covers while clenching the comforter. "Don't leave me."

A drop of moisture trickles down the line of my nose and settles on my bottom lip. I know I've made the right decision for her, but the pain in my chest causes me to second-guess myself. My heart wants to murder me by surrendering itself to the other side and my brain is screaming asshole. I need to talk to her, to tell her everything is okay, but I can't bear to wake her, so I do the next best thing.

I walk into the room and around the foot of the bed until I'm standing on the other side. There is a decorative chair in the corner that I pull over to the edge of the bed. I take a seat and grasp her hand in mine. She is the most beautiful girl I've ever seen. Her breathing is even and her features are relaxed, giving her a look of peacefulness and contentment.

I begin rubbing my thumb over the back of her hand, watching her sleep. She begins to move and stretch, fluttering her eyelids until her freckled green eyes are staring at me. "Preston, what are you doing? Is Bryce okay?"

My heart picks up speed hearing her sound an octave above dead, even though she still doesn't sound like herself.

"Hey, Kinz. He's fine. I just need to talk to you for a minute. I have something important to tell you." She pulls her hand free and places her palms flat against the mattress, pushing herself into a sitting position and scooting against the headboard.

"What is it?"

"Kinz, I'm letting you go. Your heart doesn't want to be here; it doesn't want me." Her face takes on a saddened look and that kills me even more. My eyes cloud, but I clear them, because I'll never make it out otherwise. This is best for her. I clear my throat, trying to contain my emotions.

"Preston . . ."

"Let me finish. I know you love me, I do, but you're not *in* love with me. My love for you blinded me, causing me to overlook the most important thing: what your heart wanted."

I lean forward, placing my forearms to my thighs. I look down at the sheets so I can say this. "I will always love you, Kinz. You will always be the girl I chose first, the girl I'd do anything for. I want you to know not a day will go by that my heart won't falter when I think of you or Bryce, but your heart is bound to another, and that's the one thing I can't control. I tried."

I look up and tears are streaming down her face. I hate seeing her cry. It's always been my kryptonite. She changes position onto her knees at the edge of the bed, so she can be closer to me. "Preston, stop being crazy. I made you a promise and I'm not breaking it. That means something . . ."

I place my hand on the side of her face as I stand. "I know you won't, beautiful. That's why I am. I'm walking away from you, Kinzleigh, but I want you to know it's the fucking hardest thing I've ever had to do."

Her eyes turn downcast, no longer holding any emotions back, but I tilt her face to look back at me. "Hey, you can't fight fate, right? Isn't that what this is; giving in to what's supposed to be the outcome? We can't control our destiny. It will catch up with us at some point, so I might as well just surrender now before I'm in any deeper, yeah?"

Everything I say is a lie, but it's the only way to make her let go and stop being miserable. I don't believe the words coming out of my own mouth but making it into a joke is the only way to keep my sanity intact. I will always control my own life. No one or nothing controls me.

"Preston, I'm sorry. I'll do better by you. I've been a shitty fiancé. Don't do this. I love you. You're the one I chose." She is fisting my shirt in her hand, attempting to pull me to her. I want to give in. I want to hold her and tell her I'll be here forever, but that's the selfish thing to do. I promised her I'd always do what's best for her and this isn't it. She'll always be half alive as long as he's here.

I press my lips to hers one last time and allow myself one final taste. She kisses me back, but I stop. I look deep into those clover green eyes, pointing out her speckles to distract me. "You could never be a shitty anything. You deserve happiness, Kinz, and I will stop at nothing to give it to you, even when it comes to sacrificing my own. I have to go out of town for a while, but I'm sure you'll be gone when I return."

I begin to pull away and she clings on tighter. "Preston . . . stop." Her voice is drained and distraught. I have to get out of here before I revoke everything I just worked so hard to do. "Bye, Kinz. I love you. I always have, and I always will. Go back to him. Don't make me do this in vain."

I grab her by the wrists, shucking her hands from my clothing. I turn and walk quickly to the door. Her crying gets louder the further I get. "Don't leave me! Please, don't leave me," she screams over and over. I sprint down the stairs, passing Macie with Bryce in her arms. I stop, but only briefly.

"Are you okay?" she asks.

"I'm not, but I will be," I respond honestly. "Breyson will be here later today or at the latest tomorrow. Stay with her until she leaves, then I will give you your next assignment. Call me when it's done."

She nods, knowing I won't talk about it from this point forward. I will bear my own shit. I look down at Bryce. His gray eyes are open. I rub my palm over his thin layer of blonde hair and kiss his forehead. "Hey, buddy. I'll be gone for a little while. You're going to be with your daddy and mommy. They need some time with you together. When the dust settles, Uncle Preston will come see you, okay?"

He starts to whine at the sound of my voice; a voice he's become familiar with. I want to pick him up, to make him understand that I'm not leaving him, and that it's killing me to give away what is my family, but I have to leave until I can get my shit together. Then, I will come for him and spend the rest of my life making up for the time I was gone, even if I have to make a biweekly fly in to Mississippi for the weekend. He is and will always be my little man.

I look up at Macie one last time before I go. "Take care of my little man, got it?" She nods again and I walk in the direction of the door, leaving everything I want in life behind. I am done for. No more relationships. This was it for me. I gave it a try and got burned. My heart is ripped in two and forever that way it will stay, to remind me that although the time I had was beautiful, it didn't last.

I've already arranged everything at the office. I'm heading to Greece early. It's time to move on. It's going to take time to move on from her, and something I will have to do away from here. I just wish I didn't feel like a corpse inside.

First stop on my list—a bar. I need something and that something needs to be strong. I need to drown the way I feel inside. Hearing her beg has gutted me. That vision is not going to be easy to bury.

EIGHT

Kinzleigh

I feel like I'm hyperventilating. I can't breathe. I'm the worst possible person in the world. I can't get anything right no matter how hard I try. What kind of person loves two men? No matter which direction I choose someone gets hurt. Knowing I am hurting either of them hurts me in return. I have no idea how I got in this situation. I have never once in my life seen Preston like I just saw him.

I consider everything he said. What does he mean he's letting me go? I don't understand and it's making me panic. I already chose. I chose him. Now where am I supposed to go? I can't just waltz up to Breyson's door and expect him to want me back. I chose another man over him. That doesn't even include the fact that I told myself and everyone else I would let him go live a full and happy life, free from the burden of me. I always make such a mess of things.

It's been at least twenty minutes and Preston hasn't come back. I thought he would come back. He's not coming back. If I do know anything about Preston, it's that when he makes a decision he sticks with it. I sit back on the bed, pulling my knees to my chest with my arms wrapped around them. My face is soaked, but it doesn't stop the tears from coming.

I stare off at the wall in front of me, beginning to zone out like I have been since I left Breyson standing at the hospital. I can't describe it. I feel as if I'm alive, but completely out of touch with reality. All I want to do is sleep and withdraw into myself. I don't even notice most of the time that Macie is here caring for my child—the child I can't bear to touch. Each time I look at his face I see Breyson. Every day he looks more and more like him. I'm not sure I'll ever be able to if his eyes turn blue as well.

My mind is turning against me and my heart is dying slowly, suffering, and beating slower with each breath. The pain is so immense that I almost can't bear it. My soul feels like it's leaving my body like a vapor in the wind. I thought this would be easy, but now I'm so far gone I don't know how to fix myself. I feel like I'm falling into a dark hole, and any minute the opening is going to close, forever trapping me inside.

I wanted to give Breyson back everything he's lost since February. I wanted him to live a full life, but instead I've become a horrible mother and an even worse person.

A knock sounds at my door. I don't answer. I can't take care of him. I can't hold him. I don't even want to look at him. Another knock sounds, but I remain quiet. "Kinz, it's me, Macie. May I come in? Bryce is asleep in his crib."

I release the breath I wasn't even aware I was holding and begin to relax. The fact this behavior isn't scaring me should be setting off alarms mentally, but nothing registers.

I watch as the handle slowly turns and the door inches open. I tighten the hold around my legs and rest my chin on the crevice formed between my knees. The first thing I notice is a section of long, brown, wavy hair that falls through the crack of the door, followed by a head.

Macie looks at the bed. I'm sure to see if I'm asleep. When she notices me awake, she walks the rest of the way inside. "Do you want to talk about it?"

I shake my head as she walks in the direction of the bed. "You'd be surprised at how much it may help. You forget that I've been where you are."

"What, a horrible mother? A heartless person? A stupid teenager in love with two different men? I don't think so, Macie. Last time I checked you were a pretty damn good mother, still mourning the loss of one man that has been gone for five years." My words are clipped, making me feel like an even worse person.

"You're sick, Kinzleigh. You aren't a bad mother at all, but you do need help. This is something you can't defeat on your own. Everything has built up on you all at once and your hormone levels have gotten messed up." She sits on the bed and wraps her hand around the back of mine.

I can't blame being a bad person on a mental sickness. That's crazy. I've somehow gotten myself into this mess, falling deeper and deeper with every given day. "That has nothing to do with loving and wanting two men. That has nothing to do with the fact I can't even look at my baby. I should want him! Why don't I want him?" I ask, now whispering instead of screaming. I begin crying again as the words come out of my mouth.

"You're sick," she says again. "It takes one that's experienced it to recognize the symptoms in someone else. It's not you that doesn't want Bryce it's your brain tricking you, because it's confused. As for the other situation, I think you love Preston more because he took care of you when you were down, and you became attached to him since y'all were always close. If you ask me you're only in love with Breyson and you just need to be reminded, but hey, I'm just an outsider looking in.

Why is everyone telling me they know what is wrong with me and what is best for me? No one knows, not even me. What's best for two people doesn't always intertwine. Even if I thought I was good for Breyson, he wouldn't take me back now anyway. I just want to be by myself right now. "I'm sorry, Macie. I need to go. I have to go."

I stand and run toward the door, never looking back. I'm so sick of everyone acting as if they know what I'm going through. No one knows how this feels. I just lost my best friend of almost nineteen years and the love of my life is across the country, because I'm too stupid to let myself have him. I have a baby that I can't even look at because every time I do, I feel like I'm being stabbed in the heart.

The thought of not wanting anything to do with my own baby just causes me to cry harder. I want to want him, but I don't. Maybe I wasn't prepared for this. I can't do it. He isn't going to thrive with me. I wasn't made to be a mother. Maybe I should give him to Breyson and just disappear. That would be best for everyone.

I'm running so fast that I trip on one of the steps and go tumbling down the staircase, landing at the bottom. A shooting pain starts in my ankle. I hear Macie walking down the hallway, so I get up and hobble in pain until I reach the garage door.

The keys to my new BMW SUV are hanging on the key ring beside the door. It was a baby and engagement gift since my parents haven't transported my Range Rover yet. I grab them in a hurry and continue to the car barefooted. I can barely see in front of me with the tears pouring out of my eyes.

I shouldn't be driving in this condition, but I can't find the will to care. The only person that could get hurt is me. My life doesn't really matter. Honestly, people would probably be better off without me. I've become nothing but a complication to everyone.

I get behind the wheel and shut the door, pressing the button on the garage remote clipped on my sun visor. Before a single thought can pass through my mind, I back out and leave everything I've known since May in the rearview mirror. I have no idea where I'm going to go, but anywhere will suffice.

I press harder on the gas to increase speed. There is something freeing about being alone on the road; no one present to hear your deepest thoughts but yourself, and most importantly, the pavement doesn't judge you. The only thing it cares about is having a little company from time to time.

I don't ask any questions. I'm not capable of thinking right now. Instead, I allow my heart to guide me in the direction it wants to go. The mind can be deceiving, but the heart is incapable of lying. It may not give you the answer you want, but it's always the answer it's supposed to be.

I turn down road after road, not knowing where I'm going, but sure to find the place I'm meant to be soon enough. A strange sensation consumes my body; a feeling like I got that night at the bonfire on the beach prior to Breyson showing up out of the blue. It's as if something is shifting around me, or stars falling into alignment. I can't explain why, but something is about to happen. I'm not sure whether to welcome it or hide and hope it doesn't find me.

I shut off the engine and where I am comes into focus. I guess I'm long overdue for a visit. My subconscious knows more than my brain. It guided me here of all places. I step out of my car and a sense of déjà vu takes over, only a year plus later. The September breeze blows around me, whispering in my ear. The ocean holds so many secrets, yet it never gets full.

It's quiet, only a few morning takers; mostly surfers resembling specs out a few hundred feet from the shoreline, but most people like it down the stretch of beach to my right. This place was always my humble abode away from home.

The pier looks the same as it always does, tranquil and welcoming. Each time I come here I can almost hear it calling my name. My last visit here changed my life, starting with my first real kiss from the only boy to ever steal my heart. He still hasn't given it back. Even if I could recoup it, I don't think I would. I'd rather him keep it; that just verifies it was real.

I shut and lock the doors; never taking my eyes away from the long stretch of wood that creates the pier. My feet start to move along the sidewalk before the texture changes to loose sand squishing between my toes. It's still cool from the night air. I continue to move forward as if being on that pier is a necessity for survival. It's always been a place to calm me when my nerves decided to go haywire. My calves begin to burn as my feet pummel their way through the sand.

I finally reach the first step of the pier. Placing my hand on the rail I trail my hand over it, taking in the rough texture of the wood caused by years of rain and heat bearing down on it. I take a deep breath before lifting one foot and placing it on the step. Then, I follow it with the other. Before I realize it I'm standing completely on top of the pier.

I look to the end. The color palette is gray, white, and blue laid out for miles. There is no ending in sight. I take my time, putting one foot in front of the other. It's been so long since I've been here, and the last memory is hitting me like a football player tackling me, running full speed.

My oxygen is depleting and my lips begin to tingle. I remember that night as if it were yesterday. The memories of Breyson and I are always so vivid, as if I'm living it all over again with each memory that comes forward from the reel they are stored on in my mind.

I reach the end of the pier and sit on the edge, hanging my legs over the side. They still don't reach the water. I let myself remember the night on the pier when Breyson kissed me for the first time. I close my eyes and place my fingers on my lips, remembering the way they felt pressed against his. He will always be the only person to own me. I have always been his, but he's no longer mine. It's too late. I let him go and that will always be my biggest regret, but if it keeps him happy then I'll learn to live with it.

The breeze picks up and my hair sways in the wind. I get the oddest sensation. It's as if I'm not alone, but then again, I'm crazy as of late. I'll probably be that way for the rest of my life.

I can see seagulls flying overhead, making noise as they soar through the sky. I wonder what it would be like to have an aerial view of everything like a bird does. Would it change your perspective of things to watch things from above?

The memories are evoking emotions that I thought I laid to rest, but I was wrong. My chest is killing me. My mind is in a haze to everything but

Breyson. It doesn't take long for the cleansing process to occur, pouring out through my tear ducts. With each tear I cry an ounce of pain deteriorates, but then is replaced with a new wound. If I could physically see my heart right now, I imagine there would be a lot of scarring. "Breyson, if I knew then what I know now . . ."

"Would you change it?"

My eyes widen at the sound of the southern voice I'll never grow tired of hearing. You know, the brain is a cruel organ. I've discovered this on so many occasions. Do you embrace the hallucinations or do you pretend you never heard them and hope they go away?

No matter how many times I answer this question I always react the same. I embrace them, because the alternative is to forget, and I don't want to forget. "No," I whisper into the air. "I wouldn't change a single second with you."

"Then turn around."

That voice again, deep and low, makes me quake upon hearing it. I have no idea why, but I follow instructions. I pull my legs up onto the pier and make a one-eighty-degree turn. What I see steals the very air from my lungs as if someone is holding me by the throat, squeezing as hard as they can.

"Breyson, what are you doing here?" I'm trying to sound strong, but my voice is being treacherous.

"I came to take you home where you belong." He remains standing where he is, waiting for a response.

"What makes you think I want to go back? I told you, I chose. You're better off without me." My voice cracks as the words exit. My heart doesn't want them said aloud, but my mind is steering my tongue.

"I call bullshit. Stop fighting us, Kinz. You know we're meant to be together. One way or another we will be together, dead or alive." He inches forward, slowly, as if I'm an abused, abandoned animal, scared I'll run away. Maybe I'm tired of running.

I release a long, steady breath, relaxing some of the tension I've been carrying since February. I'm exhausted from burdens I've been bearing in his absence. "You don't want to be with someone like me. I'm different. I can't even be a good mother to our baby, Breyson. I've barely held him since he was born."

Tears are soaking my face. He sits down beside me, wraps his arm around my waist from behind, and scoops me into his arms, pulling me to straddle his lap. "I'm not the person you left behind. Something is wrong with me," I whisper and try to look away, ashamed.

He turns my face so that I have no choice but to look him in the eyes. Those blue eyes are smoldering, dominating, and unforgettable. They lock on you and you're doomed. You get lost in their depth without even realizing you're hooked. My heart feels like it's soaring just by touching him. "It's because we are supposed to raise him together," he says, brushing my wet hair off of my face.

He swipes his thumb over my bottom lip as he bores into me, reading all of my secrets without my consent. He's the only one that has ever had that capability, the ability to read into my soul just by looking into my eyes. Chill bumps sprout all over my skin with each touch from him.

"Your soul belongs to me, Kinzleigh, as mine does to you. Fate mated them together. If you try to fight what's meant to be, you'll always lose. You're sick because your soul is yearning for its mate. The person you are is in here," he says, pointing to where my heart resides below the surface.

"Why should I believe that? That would be too easy."

"It is easy. Why do you keep fighting what God placed together? Didn't your parents teach you that everything happens for a reason, good or bad? How do you feel right now? How does this make you feel?" He touches his lips to mine, and a rush floods through my body.

My body begins heating and a tingling sensation tickles my lips. His tongue slides through the crevice between my lips and brushes against mine. That's all it takes and I'm completely lost in a world I've been locked out of for so long. The metal cuff that has had my heart under lock breaks free. I feel like I'm high, but I haven't consumed any drugs.

My heart has a mind of its own. Without any further ado, my fingers thread through the back of his hair, and I kiss him back. I can't describe the emotions taking control of my body. An unexpected moan escapes my lips and I hear a throaty groan in return. In one swift motion he turns me so that my back is lying on the very pier this happened on two summers ago.

My legs instantly wrap around his waist. I want him so badly right now I would allow it right here in the open if I hadn't just given birth to a baby.

My tears have changed from sadness to surrender. I want him, I need him, and in this moment, I know without a shadow of doubt I can't live without him. I've already tried. I may be a little hesitant to believe soul mates have as much control as he says, but one thing is for sure, and that's the fact that we always end up back together.

He breaks the kiss and the loss of contact burns inside. He wipes the tears in a constant rain down my face. "Say you'll be mine, Kinzleigh. Tell me you'll stop fighting us and come back home where you know you're meant to be. I will do anything to support my family. As long as you're with me I will never let you or our son go without. I will sacrifice anything to provide for both of you. I've already figured out a place to stay. I just need to fill it with my family. You are and will always be the love of my life. I don't care what hurdles stand in our way; we can jump them as long as we do it together. I'm enough of a man that I'll beg if that's what you need, but don't make me live without my family anymore. I can't do it, and more importantly, I won't. I've never lied to you and I don't intend to start now."

He rubs his rough hand up my leg and underneath my shirt, baring my stomach. It makes me slightly uncomfortable just having had a baby and not being completely back to my old size, but the fact that he's touching me and my need for it drowns out self-conscious thoughts.

He bends down and kisses beside my belly button and comes back up to ensure I'm looking into his eyes. "I love you, Kinzleigh, with all that I am. You gave me your heart standing behind the field house. When I promised you I would take care of it that meant forever. What happened to me was *not* your fault. Give me forever; that's all I'm asking."

My heart sends a shooting pain throughout my chest cavity, as if warning me not to make the wrong choice. I'm giving in. I can't deny him anything anymore, not even myself. I tried to walk away from him once; I'm not strong enough to do it twice. If there is some kind of curse on me then I'll just have to outsmart it. Coexisting in a world together, but apart, is no longer an option. I will die of a broken heart before I can survive without him.

"My heart has always been yours, Breyson, even before I told you so, and I've never taken it back."

The flood of emotion pours out, hindering my ability to speak. "I tried to walk away from you, to give you a better life in an attempt to replace what you lost, but it's wearing me down. I'm exhausted. The truth is, the love I feel for you is unexplainable. I can't eat, sleep, or function being apart from you. The only thing left is to give in to my heart's only desire or allow it to destroy me slowly. For as long as you want me, I'll be yours."

He's holding his weight above me. With one free hand he grips my chin between his thumb and index finger, tilting my head slightly so he can study me as he does when he tells me something important. "Forever with you is what I need, Kinzleigh."

My eyes close at the sound of that word. I've dreamt so many times of hearing it come out of his mouth. I'm not sure in what context he means it right now, but taking into consideration he is not presenting me with a ring, I'm going to assume that he means in more of a metaphorical sense instead of literal. I don't care. I'll take him in whatever way I can have him. "Okay, but under one condition," I whisper, and open my eyes.

For the first time since he left the airport back in February, I feel like my heart is pulling itself together, mending the open wounds that have been bleeding. "Anything, just name it, and it's yours."

"I'll come back and never walk away again as long as you don't give up football. If you sacrifice your dream, I'll sacrifice my heart, and that's a promise." I've never been more serious of anything in my life. I will not let him give up his lifelong dream to provide for us. We can do this together or not at all.

"I can't promise something I have no control over, but I'll try my best. We can sail to our dreams together and that's all that matters. I will always fight for you, for us, and for our family with whatever means necessary. I've never been a quitter. Giving up isn't in my blood."

That's the last thing he says before his lips crash to mine.

We made out on that pier for well over an hour. I guess you can say we were making up for lost time. Breyson Abercrombie has always been it for me—my man.

When you find the person whose soul was carved out to fit your own, it's hard to stay away. I'm done living a life in sadness. I had happiness once, before it was taken from me, and I can already tell I'm on the road to recovery.

There are times I think life can be cruel by the things that Breyson and I have endured just to end up together, but I have learned a humility I have never before had. Life is too short to settle for less than what you want.

The best piece of advice is to treasure each day with someone, because come tomorrow they could vanish. Today, I'm starting my forever. I just pray with everything in me this time it lasts . . .

NINE

Breyson

We waltz into the house Kinzleigh has called home for the past few months. The monstrous size, I'll admit, is a little intimidating. Knowing this lifestyle is what I'm up against is difficult to swallow. I hope she doesn't freak out with financial hardship and run back to Preston. I finally got her back. I almost didn't survive losing her the first time. Losing her a second, I wouldn't have a chance.

I owe Preston everything for putting his pride aside and bowing out, leaving her in my care. It's not something I was prepared to do. I can tell Kinzleigh has a long road ahead of being back to herself, but I'll do everything in my power to bring that girl back to the surface. I know she's hiding in there somewhere.

This is the second time I've been to this house today. The first time was to pick up Kinzleigh, only to be told by Lauren that she ran off to think. From the conversation that Preston and I had I was worried to think of her being on her own. I didn't have anything to give me a hint as to where I should look, so I went with my gut. I know where I would go if I wanted to get away from everything: the place that started it all.

On a whim I bailed and went to the pier, the first amazing memory we had after I met her. When I saw her at the other end, I was terrified. Honestly, I was expecting to have to beg and plead for longer, but based on the way she looked, she's worn down. I feel the same way.

One thing I've learned is that without question we are meant to be together. If we weren't then we would have both moved on by now. Kinzleigh and I were premeditated and planned for each other before we ever set foot into this world, and of that I'm certain. I believe it just as much as I believe in God.

I shut the massive wooden door as we walk into the entryway but never let go of her hand. I'd kill to see her smile again the way she used to. I pull her toward me, wrapping her in my arms. "I'm going to bring you back, Kinzleigh. Do you hear me? I'll make you happy again."

I kiss her lips softly, cleansing the salty tears from her mouth. I'm sick and fucking tired of seeing her cry. It kills me inside.

"I don't know what's wrong with me. I want to be happy I just don't feel it. It's hard to be hopeful when something always swoops in and tries to rip us apart, Breyson. Do you get that? Why is it so wrong for us to be together?"

I feel like I'm being gutted as her voice gets screechy with every sentence. "Shh, shh, shh. Stop crying."

I wipe her face with my thumbs and tilt her head so that I can see deep into her eyes, making the black speckles more noticeable. "I can't tell you where we'll be in a week, month, or a year, but I can tell you this: I will walk through Hell, barefooted and tenfold, before I will let anything come between us again. You are my world, Kinzleigh, and you always have been. We will make it, baby. Will you trust me?"

She searches my eyes with her own, her lips quivering. She nods, barely even noticeable, but I can feel it since my hands are holding her cheeks. "The moving truck should be here within the hour. For now, I need you to pack enough to fly with for you and Bryce. I'll never leave your side again."

I run my fingers along her neck, across her bare shoulders, and down her arms. She is wearing a tank, leaving her chest and arms bare. Her skin is smooth, making me want to remove every stitch of clothing from her body, tangling with her in a bed that is ours, and only ours. I haven't seen that body in so long, but that's about to change.

I take her small hand in mine and lead her into the open family room. As soon as our footsteps begin trampling over the wood, Bryce starts to cry. Hearing him cry stirs something inside of me that I can't ignore. That's my son, our son. Lauren stands from the couch, but I hold out my hand, stopping her. "Thank you for everything you've done, but we'll take it from here. This is something we need to do alone."

She nods and turns for the patio doors. "I'll give you two some time alone." Opening them, she exits, leaving us by ourselves.

I look at Kinzleigh. She is staring off, zoned out, as if she can't even hear him crying. She's worse than I thought. I walk toward the staircase in the direction of his cry, pulling her alongside me. "Breyson, maybe I should wait here."

I stop as I place my foot on the first step and turn my head back to look at her. She looks like a terrified pup that was separated from its mother. "No, Kinzleigh. You'll be a great mother. We certainly didn't plan him, but now that he's here I want him. We are going to learn this together. Trust me, yeah?" She nods and I continue up the stairs.

His cry changes from a whine to a piercing scream, causing my heart rate to pick up. The past few nights I've spent dreaming of being able to come to him when he cries. I've been absent from his life more than I want to be. I pick up pace, pulling Kinzleigh along with me. Her short legs start to slip on the stairs and she falls on her shins, but she quickly gathers herself and trudges along after me.

We come to a door marked with the initials BAP hanging on the front in navy lettering, the A in the center bigger than the first and middle name. It still seems surreal that we thought of the same first name oceans apart. If I hadn't been witnessing everything between us firsthand, I'd think I was crazy. I'm just thankful she didn't give him Preston's last name. I don't know if I would've been able to handle it. We may be young, but I come from a family that doesn't tolerate conceiving a child and not providing for it. I had sex with her and helped conceive him, I'll father him.

Pushing open the door I walk inside, and as I take in the room I feel like I've been hit at full frontal by a tidal wave. There are things I didn't consider until now, as I briefly take in the room. Preston really was being honest with me.

The whole nursery is done in a nautical theme. I know without a shadow of doubt this wasn't the work of Kinzleigh, and even though it completely kills me that I didn't get to be the one here for this, I can't even be mad at the guy, not anymore anyway. He stood in my place without anyone asking him to when I couldn't. Then, in the same respect, returned her unselfishly.

Only a real man would do something like that, and it's now that I realize how much respect I have for him. Before, I agreed to it, but only now do I whole-heartedly accept what it is he asked me for. If Preston wants to be in my son's life, then that's what he'll get. So far, he's been just as much of a father to Bryce as me. It's not blood that makes someone a daddy but being involved.

We arrive at the crib and I look inside. A little bundle dressed in brown and green is kicking and wailing as he flails his tiny arms straight out above him. The only time I've been able to hold him was that short time at the hospital. My eyes moisten as I take in the small baby I helped create. I silently make a promise to myself that no matter what I have to do or give up, neither of them will ever want for anything.

I reach inside, scooping my hands underneath his head and bottom just like the nurse taught me. I lift him off the mattress and bring him to my chest. He's still crying. I turn around and Kinzleigh is standing by the rocker in the middle of the room, petrified. "Do you think he's hungry?"

She begins biting her nails and shrugs her shoulders. "Maybe."

"How do you feed him?"

She looks away from me, almost as if she's ashamed. I notice her eyes filling with wetness and I walk over to her, attempting to bounce him on my way. "Kinzleigh, look at me."

She does as I ask, and I can see the guilt all over her face. She falls into the rocker and places her hands over her face. I squat with him in my arms so that I'm level in height with her and remove her hands from her face with one of mine. "I was nursing him, but the last time I remember trying, I looked down at him and all I could see was you. I couldn't do it. I had forgotten until now, but I couldn't feed our own baby, so I let him go hungry. I couldn't look at him or hold him. I just left him crying in a wet diaper with nothing to eat, because he reminded me of what I couldn't have. I couldn't move and my whole body ached. If Preston had not of come home and taken care of him, what could have happened?"

She is now bawling in front of me. "Don't you see what kind of person I've become? I don't deserve him. I put him down and neglected him. If I can't care for him and don't want to hold him, then I shouldn't have him in my life at all. What's wrong with me?"

They are both crying hysterically. I feel so helpless, but that's not what she needs from me. This is the time to be a man and think like one. It's time to put aside boyhood and step into manhood. "Everyone makes mistakes, Kinzleigh. You've gone through a lot and I've gone through a lot. It's only natural that Bryce will experience the debris from some of it. Don't let the decisions of yesterday define who you are today or tomorrow. What's important is that you recognize the problem and fix it."

I kiss the top of Bryce's head and scoot in-between Kinzleigh's legs. I grab her chin between my index finger and thumb, pulling her toward me enough that my lips touch hers. "I'm here now. We are back together, so our hearts can begin to heal. He is ours to take care of and look after. We loved each other enough to get carried away with sex. He's our responsibility together, equally. Feed our son," I say, and lay him in her arms.

I can feel her shaking. "What if I don't have any milk left? I haven't tried to pump or feed him in over twenty-four hours. I don't know what I'm doing."

"Kinzleigh, just try. We can learn *together*. There's only one way out: forward. I need you to take the first step with me. If it doesn't work, then we will figure out the alternative. You chose to feed him this way, so try." I kiss her lips one more time, teasing her a little with my tongue to relax her. I can feel the tension in her body start to dwindle and I release her lips. "I believe in you. I believe in us. We've never been parents before, so we aren't going to be perfect at it. We have to learn. That's part of growing up."

I look down and Bryce is rooting against her shirt, reflexively looking for food. It's amazing to see the survival instincts that a baby is born with. She is watching him and her breaths are coming out short and quick. I place my hands at the bottom hem of her red tank and begin easing it up her body. She holds him with one hand while I pull the shirt over the opposite and then exchange until all that is left is to remove it over her head completely, and I do.

My eyes never leave hers as I reach behind her and undo the clasp on her bra, releasing her engorged breasts. Her cheeks are becoming a red hue to match her shirt. "Feed our son," I say again. I rake my fingers around her until my hand is cupped around her breast, waiting on her to meet me halfway. She is holding him loosely in her arms, resting on her lap. I continue to stare into her eyes but catch a glimpse from my peripheral vision.

Her hold on him tightens and her arms slide back, toward her body. His face becomes flush with her skin and he feels around until his mouth finds her nipple. My opposite hand rests on her cheek and I begin rubbing her T-zone area with my thumb to comfort her. She closes her eyes and a solemn tear escapes, making its way to reside elsewhere. One releases from my own eye, accompanying hers. She and I are always a pair, no matter what the situation is. Who knows where those two teardrops will end up, but they'll be together, a piece of her and a piece of me.

"Breyson . . ."

"What, beautiful?"

"I love you. I've never needed anything like I need you. I don't care how many times the sun rises or sets as long as I'm watching it with you. I don't care whether we're rich or poor, as long as I'm with you. I don't care if we live on a beachfront property or in an open field, as long as I live with you. Nothing has meaning to me if I can't experience it with you. Don't you see? My heart will always belong . . . *to you.*" Her voice is faint, but there is more meaning behind it than if she were screaming it from a rooftop.

I crash my lips to hers, not able to do anything more. My heart feels like it's about to explode. I break free, but press my forehead to hers, looking into her eyes. "I love you too, Kinz. Not a fucking day goes by that my love for you doesn't quadruple in magnitude. There is love, and then there is epic love, love at its greatest degree. You and I were forever meant to be. I hope now you realize that, so we never have to stand at this fork again."

I finally break eye contact with her and look down. There is nothing more beautiful than watching your woman nurse your son, providing his food supply, and nurturing him to contentment and satisfaction. This, among other things, is one of the greatest treasures in life. A life without love is no life at all. You may have to fall in the darkest pit to figure it out, but when you're looking back from the other side, it's totally worth it all.

My eyes catch the ink residing on her ribcage, ink that was absent when I left. My jaw steels as I take it in. I'm at a loss for words. It's beautiful, even though it brings back a few memories better left buried. I can't help but to run my fingers over the parts not covered by Bryce's feet, admiring the variations in color. It destroys me to imagine what she was going through thinking I was dead. Not only does the plane piercing her heart gut me completely, but also the words, *my heart died with you,* finishes me.

"When did you get this?"

"Not long after the accident. It was one of my worst days." My eyes fill with tears as I trace my initials on her skin. Knowing you have someone that loves you enough to tattoo a memorial piece permanently on her body, covering that amount of space, is indescribable. I want to entwine us in every possible way. I want to make her my wife, but not this way. I need the assurance of forever. No more chancing us being apart.

"You'll never have to go through that kind of pain again, beautiful. I'm sorry. If I could take it back I would in a heartbeat, no questions asked."

Maybe there was some kind of lesson in humility that we were supposed to be taught by having to endure all of this, but only one thing matters. "We were given a second chance, for whatever reason, and now it's up to us to make it count."

This was always the place I loved to be, right here looking into the eyes of the woman that was made for me. Before her I was on the path to destruction, fucking every girl that would fall in bed with me, partying, and living a meaningless life. It's always surreal to imagine feeling this way about someone when you're just out of high school, but instead of questioning it I'm going to embrace it.

The love that she radiates when in my presence is enough to knock a grown man over. I have no idea why I've been gifted such an amazing woman. I know that almost losing her is enough to keep me from ever experiencing that again. Each time I look into her green eyes she bares a little more of what's inside to me. Nothing in my entire life has ever felt more mine than her. There is no way to explain it to another human being. It's something you have to be granted access to—a soul mate.

Everything I ever thought I wanted in life means nothing anymore unless she is by my side to experience it with me. I could be handed everything money could buy, or be given the opportunity to experience every dream I've ever had, like football, but to receive it alone would be a disappointment instead.

Looking back, it's hard to believe two stupid seventeen-year-olds would find what we found in each other. We knew so little then, but now, a year plus later we have a map for a future. Next month, the two of us will be nineteen. We have a lot to figure out, but at the same time we've figured out the most important part, and that is the plot to our story, that we need each other. The rest is mere details along the way.

"What are you thinking about?" she asks.

"When you think of me what comes to mind?" I have an idea of what I want to get her for her birthday in barely over a month. It's sudden and people may think I'm crazy, but also it feels like it's been too long. I know what I want in life. I just need to know she wants the same. There are two places in this world that mean the most to us: that old oak tree and that pier. I need a way to permanently link them to our story, a lifelong memory after all of the bad to create a happily ever after. I think I have the perfect plan in mind.

She's holding Bryce like a football, cradled to her body. She switches him to her other breast and then looks at me. I take her left hand in mine, rubbing my fingers over her ring finger. It's no longer holding another man's ring. Only one ring belongs on her finger, and that's mine. I will never lose her to another man again. Of that, I am certain.

She looks down at our hands, but then back at me. "Why do you ask?"

The beauty of her is astounding. I can't wait to hold her body, touch it, and kiss all over it, taking it and enjoying it as mine. I want to look into her eyes, as I become the last man she'll ever be with sexually. I get what Dad was trying to tell me that night in the pool house when I was messed up about Kinzleigh before she moved here.

Monogamy is a beautiful thing. To have sex with someone because you love her over and over again is not even comparable to anything else. I want to learn her body inside and out, her likes and dislikes for years to come. If I ever had any thought that I wanted another woman, in which I didn't, Angelique confirmed that Kinzleigh is enough for me in every possible way. I may only be eighteen, but I don't need to sleep with a list full of women to prove my manhood or to live a full life. I've been there and done that, and trust me, it's not all it's made out to be.

I pull her hand up to kiss the back. "I just want to know."

She studies me briefly, as if she is pondering the question. "Do you want the honest answer?"

That question frightens me a little. I'm starting to regret asking, but I'd rather know. "Yes, I think I do. An honest answer is always the best answer."

She stands and walks over to the crib, laying Bryce inside. He's now sleeping peacefully, the opposite of when we arrived. She walks back over and kneels before me. I'm trying not to look at her half naked body, but it's getting harder now that nothing is in the way. She grabs the bottom hem of my shirt and begins pulling it up my body. Reflexively I raise my arms, allowing her to remove it. "What are you doing?"

"Shh. I'm about to answer your question, but I want to feel your skin while I do. I haven't seen your body in so long." She tosses my shirt aside and wraps her hands around me, resting them flush with my back, pulling my body to hers. Her breasts press against my chest and my dick hardens against my jeans. She kisses my collar bone and runs her hands down the waist of my jeans, stopping at the top of my butt, her favorite place. "I've missed this," she says against my skin.

Everything about her stuns me; it always has. I can never get enough of her. There is no way I can ever walk away from her or forget her, not even with fucking amnesia. My brain knew it and my heart knew it. "You're the most beautiful woman I've ever seen, Kinzleigh, and you're all I'll ever need. I will never want anyone else whether we are together or not."

She presses her index finger to my lips, hushing me. "I thought I was the one that was supposed to be talking." I can't help but to grin. Finally, a piece of the woman I fell in love with is trying so hard to break free. She smiles back at me, though small, but still a smile, nonetheless. "I know you like to run those beautiful lips, but maybe it's time I pour my heart out since you're so good at it."

She moves in closer to my face and my breathing becomes heightened just thinking of kissing her. "You want to know what comes to mind when I think of you? Here goes . . . I think of the cocky but beautiful blue-eyed boy I met on the beach, the very one that had me in a state of confusion and weak at the knees. When I think of you, I remember the boy that took my breath away on the pier the night you first kissed me. When I think of you, I think of the boy that consumed my mind enough I gave myself to him on my very bed."

I can already tell this is about to consume every facet of my mind. "Breyson, when I think of you, I think of the one I was led to when I ended up in the same town as you. When I think of you, I think of the one that captured my heart, rocked my world, changed it, and made it extraordinary. You didn't give up on me, on us, even when I tried to force it on you, and that speaks volumes. In church one Sunday they made us watch this movie called Fireproof and one line came back to me when you showed up at that pier. The man in the movie said, *you don't leave your partner in a fire.* No matter how stubborn I am or how stupid I'm acting you've never left me. You've always stood by my side."

I watch as a tear falls down her face. She's never been one to go over the top to express her feelings. This is a huge step for her. "When I think of you, I picture the man I want to marry and the father of my kids, my lifelong partner. I know what it's like to live without you, and I never want to experience that hell again. Breyson, you are my best friend, soul mate, lover, and hopefully someday husband. I never foresaw this life until you came along, but now, when I look at you, I see nothing less than forever."

I suck in a breath and hold it. I take her face in my hands and pull it closer to me. "You have no idea how much I needed to hear that." My lips crush against hers, pulling her bottom lip into my mouth. I can't get enough of her. Everything of her drives me wild: her scent, her touch, and her taste. Everything is like an aphrodisiac. The only problem is that her body is under lock and key for six weeks total after our son was born.

I need to touch her in some form. I need to know that I still please her like I used to. We were always great together from talking all the way to the bedroom. There has never been two people that fit together better than Kinzleigh and I.

I haven't touched her aside from kissing since the day I left on that fucking plane. I wasn't the last man to touch her and that thought drives me mad. I try not to think about it, but I can't help it. I need to remedy it quickly.

I place my hands over her shorts, cupping her ass through the cotton. I squeeze and align her body against mine; the only thing separating us physically is the bulge of my dick in its hardened state. A moan slips between her full lips unconsciously. It's enough to give me consent to push her further. I pick her up off the floor enough that she wraps her legs around me, the benefit of me being so much taller than her.

I continue to kiss, suck, and lick her as I lay her on her back on top of the floor. She arches her back as I trail my tongue along her jawline, sucking the lobe of her ear into my mouth. She always liked me sucking her ear lobe. It was like a start button to rev up her sexual engine. As expected, she tilts her head to the side, giving me better access to her neck, the seam to her body.

I kiss in a path, starting at the cohesion of her neck and jaw, traveling down to the top of her shoulder. I back up slightly until my face is level with the piece of artwork that will forever remain on her body; a mural devoted to me. I kiss the point of contact between the plane and where it pierces the heart. Her stomach constricts at a rapid pace, showing that her rate of breathing is getting faster the lower I get.

I never look up. Instead, I continue familiarizing myself with the body I have dreamed of for months on end. She tenses when I reach her stomach. She's small, so she only carried baby weight in her stomach. She's already back to her size, just a little softer. To me, she's more beautiful than before, because she's been incubating something that belongs to me for the past nine months, making her body adjusted for me.

I reach up and cup her breast, rubbing my thumb over her pebbled nipple, relaxing her. I finally reach the pink ink that stretches across her pelvis, just above the elastic band of her shorts. I hold my weight with my knees and thighs to free my other hand, placing it under the band. I can feel her heart rate pounding through her pulse. "Breyson, I can't yet."

I pop my head up at her. "We're not going to have sex, baby. I just need to touch you. I want to take back what you gave me."

"It's not that," she says, and her cheeks start to turn a shade of pink. "You don't understand. You don't want to be down there yet. Will you just come back up here? I can make you feel good."

She places her fingers in her mouth and begins nibbling at the tips as if she's nervous. "You're bleeding," I state. I may be a guy, but my mother is an Obstetrician and we were required to take Health Freshman year. A woman's body is not as foreign to a man as most would like to think; especially not with one he loves.

She nods, but I don't care. Blood is draining from the furthest point of origin and I'm going for the closest. I don't even have to remove her shorts for where I'm going. I just want to taste her, and then I'll be happy. I can get her off with my finger. There is one reason I want to taste her, because I never have. Not in that spot at least.

I was never interested in going down on a woman before Kinzleigh. My parents drilled in my head to protect myself from disease before her and I got together. I always used a condom, so I sure as hell wasn't putting my mouth down there. Then, when we got together, I was so hyped up on the fact that she was a virgin all I wanted was to stick my dick inside her. Plus, Kinzleigh is shy when it comes to sex, or she was. We experimented, but it was mostly with different styles of sex. "I don't care, Kinzleigh. I stopped caring about stuff with you a long time ago."

I grab the waistband of her shorts and begin to pull them down in the front when she grabs my hair in her fist. "Breyson, you don't have to do that. Really, it's okay." She's never told me no before. Something tells me this isn't about her bleeding. She knows I haven't gone down on anyone before. When it was brought up, neither had she . . .

"He went down on you, didn't he?" I have no right to be mad, but the look on my face must be stating otherwise, because her lips start quivering and her eyes begin churning out tears at a rapid rate. I don't even need the answer verbally. Her reaction gives me the confirmation I need.

"I'm so sorry," she says. Her voice sounds completely distraught. The look on her face says she's vulnerable. Does it piss me off that he got one of her firsts? Hell yeah. Do I want to think about it? Fuck no. Why do I ask some of the stupidest questions known to mankind? You never ask questions unless you're prepared for the answer.

I feel guilty. Of course, I would, it's Kinzleigh. I just got her back. I sure as fuck am not going to lose her over my raging jealousy. I said I was letting it all go and that's what I'm going to do. This is such a mood killer. I take a second to clear the toxins excreting into my mind. She tries to close her legs, but I stop her. Grabbing a knee in each hand I push them open as far as they will go.

I place my thumb in my mouth and suck, moistening it. I dip my hand into her shorts until I can feel her clit underneath my thumb. I begin to massage in a circular motion. She grabs the rug in her fists, her breathing picking up. She attempts to close her legs again, but for a different reason this time. I block them with my shoulders. My jaw muscle begins to twitch back and forth as my teeth exert pressure against each other. I'm promising myself that after this anything to do with her and Preston will be laid to rest.

I look her in the eyes. She's biting her bottom lip. Her face is still soaked with more tears flowing to keep it that way. "I don't care where you've been while I was gone, Kinz, as long as there are no others from this point forward. I will be the last man to touch, see, or enter right here. This is, and forevermore, belongs to me. This is mine. Are we clear?"

"Yes," she moans out in a breathy voice. "You're the only one I'll ever want. No one does to me what you do to me. That I promise." I press down just enough that when I rub it drives her wild.

"Good, remember that, because I don't give away my things. Once mine, always mine. You are the most important thing I've ever had. That alone means I'll guard you with my life. There is one more thing I need. I need to watch you come apart at my hands. I haven't needed many things, but this I need." Her eyes start to roll back in her head as I continue ravaging her body with pleasure. It will be my goal to cause an ever-fucking-massacre on her mind, body, and soul. I will consume Kinzleigh Baker. She better get ready, because Breyson Abercrombie is about to leave a mark.

I continue to feel her tense below me. I know she's getting close. I don't want her to come this way, so I stop. "Breyson, please, don't stop. It feels so good. It's been too long. I want you to touch me." She always knew how much I liked to hear her beg. It's one of those things I can't explain, but it turns on a switch making me crazy—a sexual mad-hatter.

I pull out my hand enough to grasp the band in each hand on her hips, pulling her shorts down just enough to reveal the place I need to see. "Tell me how much you've missed me touching you."

"The absence of you obliterates me, in all context. I need your touch to survive, just as much as I need you alive. Please, don't stop. I've dreamed of this day since the day you left." Bloody hell. I feel like an animal about to feast on my prey. I kiss the pink ink, licking in a horizontal line along the font.

This is something I've dreamed about since I left. She has no fucking idea. I will have no mercy on her body ever again. I need to remember each time I touch her that tomorrow is no guarantee. The only way I'll ever live from now on is as if it's my last.

I run two thumbs down her lips and spread them apart, revealing the spot I know is throbbing for contact. I place my tongue at the bottom and swipe up her slowly, torturing her.

On reflex she bucks her hips closer to my face. She lets out a whine. I narrow the tip of my tongue, hardening it into a point. It's time I remind her who owns her in every possible way. I place my tongue centered over her clit and begin flicking up and down, slowly at first, then increasing speed. She fists my hair, adding to my crazed state, furthering my assault. Her taste is driving me wild, addicting me. I place my lips over the small, sensitive button and suck, causing her to scream out before slapping her hand over her mouth.

That's my girl.

She's exactly where I want her. I look up when she begins to tighten her muscles, knowing she's about to come. I want to watch the face of the woman I love when nothing but pleasure consumes her. I want to engrain it in my memory. Never again will I take being able to memorize and recall something on command for granted.

She arches her back as I go back to flicking in a rapid motion. I can feel her orgasm building, because she's squeezing my head with her legs. I never let up as I hear her moan out and halt all movement, letting her ride out her orgasm. It's the most beautiful thing I've ever watched.

When it's over, I neatly pull her shorts back in place. My dick is throbbing for release, but I ignore it. I lift to my knees and kiss her, allowing her to taste the mixture of us, as I did. She grabs my dick through my jeans before I even register what she's doing.

Damn, it feels good.

I want to sink inside her, but I have no choice but to wait. I've waited this long, what's a few more weeks? "I can suck you off," she says, and I feel like I could blow my load just by hearing such a filthy phrase exit her pure lips. I consider it, but Bryce interrupts my thoughts as he begins to cry, reminding me that it's no longer just the two of us, but three.

"Another time," I say, rubbing my thumb across her cheek. "Today was about you. We have the rest of our lives for you to worry about me."

I kiss her again, not able to resist those beautiful, full lips. I can't explain it, but when I kiss her it's no longer ordinary, but extraordinary. My heart feels so full that it consumes all of my oxygen to sustain it. "I'll get Bryce. You start packing. Let's go home."

She smiles when I say the last word: *home*. That does have a nice ring to it. I stand to my feet when she speaks. "Breyson?"

"What, beautiful girl?"

"I love you. Always have; always will. Don't think for a second that I ever stopped loving you, because it's not possible. I've tried. I was meant to be yours. I was born to love you." I bite my tongue to inflict pain. It's better than crying. Maybe now that we're moving forward I can get my balls back and stop feeling so emotional. So many emotions are a little degrading to a man, but never will I tire of hearing that she loves me. It keeps me going.

"I know that now. I just needed to be reminded. You're it for me, Kinzleigh. This: you, me, him, us, it's all I'll ever need. Nothing in this world could ever make me happy if you're not a part of it. I need you to always remember that. When times get hard, when I piss you off, or when you start to question if we moved too fast, remember that this is what life is all about. We've both confirmed through other people that we're meant to be together. Young or old, fate chose me to be your mate and you mine. It's only right that we always stand side by side."

She closes her eyes and I turn to Bryce whining in his crib. I reach down and pick him up, bringing him to rest against my chest, underneath my chin. I walk over to the visible changing table in the room and lay him across it, preparing to change his diaper, or at least try.

These two people are what I would die for if I had to. Nothing is, or will ever be, more important than them. The most important thing in life is to never give up on the things you want most. Never turn your back on the woman meant for you. If I would have given up another man would be calling her his wife and trying to raise my son. Time can be a friend as well as an enemy, and because I kept pushing for her, I'm now taking them home. My family.

TEN

Kinzleigh

We've been back in Mississippi close to a week now. It's strange to think that my life has changed so dramatically in such a short amount of time. That day I packed what I could fit in my largest suitcases and had the movers pack up everything else that belonged to me. They delivered it to our home two days later.

I stand in the small house we are renting from his grandfather, still full of moving boxes. It may not be but a tenth of the size that I'm used to living in, but it's ours, and that's all that matters. Looking back at my life, I realize how different I am today than I was. I'm a much more thankful person as well as a better one. I have realized exactly how valuable people are that you care about. This was almost the worst year of my life, but there is still time to make up for it, and that's exactly what I intend to do.

Bryce starts to cry, signaling it's time for him to eat. I smile and begin walking down the hall toward his room. As soon as we returned Breyson had me consult with a colleague of his mother about my depression. She confirmed that along with a large percentage of new moms, I'm struggling with postpartum depression. She made it clear that I'm not alone and that there is a way to fight it, so now I take medicine that is safe for breastfeeding mothers. Each day is a little brighter and better than the one before.

I walk in his room, actually enjoying the sound of his cry, because it means I hear it. Only a very short time ago I couldn't say that. "Hey, buddy, Mommy is here."

At the sound of my voice his cry quietens down. I reach over the railing of his crib and tickle his tummy, making him smile, or what I call a smile. He's too young to be sure. "What did your daddy dress you in today, huh? Is that a deer on your onesie?" Bryce's mouth broadens as much as he can open it, and it melts my heart.

Breyson has done so much to help with Bryce that I actually feel bad. I try to do more, but he claims he's making up for lost time. I don't even try to argue. What kind of person would? The man has lost enough without trying to take more. We've been back barely any amount of time and already he's trying to southernize our son. It's adorable. His onesie has a buck on the front with the catch phrase, *Daddy's little hunter*.

Grabbing Bryce underneath his arms, I pick him up and cradle him in my arms. He looks more and more like Breyson each day as his features continue to develop. It was confirmed when we took Bryce to meet the rest of his family and his mom pulled out Breyson's baby photos. The resemblance is unreal, even with Bryce being a newborn. Bryce's eyes are still in question, because they haven't changed yet.

Immediately Bryce starts rooting, looking for food. I can't be any more thankful that in my lapse of mental health my milk didn't dry up. Nursing him has formed a bond I can't explain to someone that hasn't experienced it for herself. This is something only I can give him. "Okay, little boy, I know you're hungry."

I sit in the rocking chair in the corner of his room, preparing to feed him. Once he begins eating, I take in his room. It's finally finished. Breyson has been working on it since we got here when he isn't working with Pops at the ranch or figuring out options for school, which is usually in the evening and well into the night. I try to help when I can, but he doesn't let me do much. It's cute.

I rub Bryce's cheek with my thumb. "I don't think you're going to be able to escape it, buddy. I hope you like football, because you were born and bred to play. Based on your room I would say that your daddy is already planning it. I will admit you get it honest from both sides. Football is in your blood."

"Damn right it is." I hear the voice that will always give me butterflies and make me weak at the knees. I can't help but to slightly laugh at his abruptness, though I try to hold it in.

I look up to the most beautiful sight in the world. Most people spend thousands of dollars to travel for views like this, but I somehow get to wake up to it every morning and go to sleep next to it at night. He's leaned up against the doorframe with his arms crossed over his chest, looking sexier than ever. Holy crap!

"You know what is does to me seeing you in Wranglers and boots, Mr. Abercrombie." His white tee shirt is fitted over his muscles and because of his stance his biceps are flexed.

He pushes off the doorframe with a huge smirk on his face.

Now is not the time to get hot and bothered, Kinzleigh!

He walks across the room, stopping in front of me. My eyes are level with his crotch. My cheeks start to heat. You would think by now that I wouldn't get this bashful around him, but I'm assuming this will be the case forever. "And here I thought you just wanted me for my personality," he teases.

I visually scan up his body and he's slowly pulling his shirt up, revealing his sculpted stomach, and toying with me.

Like Dad always said when nervous, just visualize him naked. No, no, no. Bad idea. Bad idea. Stop it!

I'm screaming at myself mentally, trying to get *that* picture out of my head. That just amplified the way I feel, not reversed it.

He reaches his chest and removes his shirt all the way. His stomach is glistening with sweat.

Damn.

He grabs my only free hand that is currently clutched onto the arm of the chair, placing it against his abs. He tightens his stomach, making them more defined. My face feels like it's on fire. He slides my hand along the ridges, downward, toward the waistband of his jeans.

Breathe. Just breathe . . .

He pushes my hand under the waistband of his jeans, slowly, but continuously. "The way I make you feel when I'm wearing Wranglers, boots, and walking around shirtless, is only an eighth of the way you make me feel on your worst day. When you wake up with messy hair, morning breath, and not a speck of makeup, you still have me hard as a fucking rock, and don't you ever forget it," he says in a husky voice as he cups my hand over his shaft, hardened and ready to go.

I close my eyes. This no-sex thing is so not fair, considering the circumstances. How do you avoid getting turned on when the love of your life says things like that? It's not possible. It also doesn't help that it's been over half a year since he's made love to me! That's like a century when you feel the way I feel about him.

I remove my hand from his pants. My mood has just become volatile. I don't look at him as I change Bryce to the other side to finish eating. "It's not fair to tease me, Breyson. Why is waiting not hard for you? Is it because you're more experienced?"

I feel like such a mood sucker, but in times like these when I feel like I'm on edge and ready to jump and he's calm and collected, I'm completely out of my league. Sex probably isn't that big of a deal to someone that's had it anytime they wanted for years.

When Bryce is situated I look up to find him bent forward with his face directly in line with mine, but in a mirror image. "Baby, as soon as we hit the six-week mark you won't ever have a chance to ask that question again. It takes every ounce of strength in my body to keep from attacking you like an animal, but the thought of hurting you is enough to keep my hormones in check."

He presses his lips to mine and like a junkie getting a fix all the previous worry vanishes. I'll never get used to the way I feel when he kisses me. It's like walking through the twilight zone.

He breaks free sooner than he normally does. "Kinzleigh, I may be more experienced in some things than you, but looking back in hindsight, I would take it all back if I had known I was going to end up with you. No amount of experience in the entire world could have prepared me for making love for the first time. Everything prior to you was meaningless, and it wasn't even enjoyable now that I know what the term becoming one actually means. The emotional connection we shared when we had sex was indescribable and that was before we had to live thinking we lost each other. Imagining what it will feel like after experiencing the loss of you, possibly forever, makes waiting one of the hardest things I've ever done alongside all of the others that also involve you . . ."

I feel so stupid now. Why do I have to be such a whiney girl? I don't know what happened to my confidence. Maybe experiencing pregnancy and childbirth was one of the causes, but I feel like it has dissipated. He looks down at Bryce as if he's thinking about something. Meanwhile, I stare at him. It's hard not to.

He looks back up at me. When he starts to speak his tone softens. "If you ever second-guess how you affect me or how I feel about you, look at him. He wouldn't be here if I didn't get completely lost in you, unable to process anything else. We complete each other, Kinzleigh. When you feel, I feel. When we're together the world is in alignment and it's as if no one else exists. No word that exists in the human language comes close to properly defining how I feel about you."

My heart is no longer a solid or continuous force. It has transpired into a wild, liquid chemical, so potent that it has to be handled with care. I keep falling deeper and deeper into the Breyson hole. "I feel like we've lost so much time," I say breathlessly.

"Oh, but baby, we gained so much more than we lost." I'm completely done for. I reach behind his neck, cupping my hand around it, and pull him in to kiss me. I need more. I always will need more from him, because nothing is ever enough.

Bryce releases me and starts making little noises. We both break the kiss at the same time and look down to him staring up at us with a small smile on his face.

Breyson picks him up with a grin from ear to ear. "I missed you, little buddy. I think Hendrix is going to love you, just wait and see. You ready to go see Grandma and Grandpa while Mommy and I go to the football game tonight? It's time for Daddy to take Mommy on a date. It's long overdue, so Grandma is going to watch you. I know she said she's too young to be called Grandma, but I think it'd be funny if you just stuck with it. Gigi sounds funny. What is a Gigi anyway?"

Breyson is walking around the room talking to Bryce as if no one is listening. I can't do anything but sit here in this chair and watch in complete awe. How did I get this lucky? I heard somewhere that you fall more in love with someone once he becomes the father of your child, and in this moment, I would have to completely agree. Nothing this world could ever offer would compare to this, not even a life spent professionally cheerleading.

We pull into the parking lot of the school. I can see the field lights overhead in the distance from Breyson's truck as he parks. Being in this truck gives me déjà vu. It seems like just yesterday, yet it seems like an eternity since we were just two high school kids making out in his truck. Now, we're just out of high school, living together, and parents to one beautiful little boy.

We have no idea what we're doing and it's going to be one bumpy ride, but I wouldn't have it any other way. I can only thank God each and every day that he spared Breyson's life. Now, I get to spend the rest of my life with the man that owns my heart and my son doesn't have to grow up without his father.

My nerves are starting to get the best of me. I haven't been to school since I ran out of prom, left with Preston, and never looked back. "Are you sure you're ready to do this," I ask.

I look over at Breyson and he's squeezing the life out of the steering wheel, looking straight ahead through the windshield. "We don't have to go in there, Breyson. We can just go to a movie or something. Give yourself more time."

I grab his hand in mine, lacing them as he releases his hold on the steering wheel. IIe looks at the two connected, and then up at me. "It's time I face the crowd. I got a second chance to live, to have my girl, and to build a life. I'm not going to hide anymore. I'm just nervous how everyone is going to act around me, that's all."

He kisses my left hand and I notice his eyesight linger on my ring finger longer than normal. There are so many things to say, yet I don't know how. I want to apologize for giving up on us when I went back with Preston. I want to scream that I'll never accept an offer of forever with anyone else but him. I want to promise him that he is my beginning, middle, and end— my forever. I get lost in my thoughts and don't have a clue what to say. I know they are roaming around in my mind, but I can never execute them properly.

I start to open my mouth when he cuts me off. "You look beautiful tonight. I know I forgot to tell you when we left the house because we were getting Bryce ready, but you always stun me speechless; you always have, but now when I look at you it's hard to breathe for long periods of time."

I don't know what to say, because it's hard to believe I still have that effect on him. "You still find me beautiful even though I have stretch marks and baby weight? You can tell me the truth. I know my body looks different."

"You want the truth, huh?"

My nerves just amplified, but I want to know. I nod, now too nervous to verbalize my answer. He exits his truck and walks around the front until he's standing at my door, opening it. Grabbing my hand, he helps me out and guides me to the tailgate, lowers it, and lifts me until I'm sitting on the edge of it.

He places each hand palm down on the outer edge of my thighs. The cold front coming through makes it chilly enough to wear my short denim jacket. Breyson is bent forward, looking down at my thighs. I have no idea what is going to come out of his mouth, but I'm going over and over in my head the absolute worst. What finally exits, though, I never saw coming.

He looks up at me, his blue eyes honing in on my green ones, commanding me to listen. "You're more beautiful to me now than you were the first time I laid eyes on you in that bikini on the beach. Your body is sexier to me than any other woman I've ever set my sight on. Truth? Those few marks across your stomach verify that my baby had a place to grow. That baby weight proves that you helped create a miracle. Your new curves are evidence that you gave birth to our son. One look at you and I'm no less turned on than I ever was before. I want you more now than I ever have."

I can't speak. Nothing I say could even come close to explaining how I feel right now. I've been down about my body and if he would still find me as attractive as he did before he left. I know he loves me, and I didn't expect him to ever verbalize it because of that love and Bryce, but a girl still wonders in the back of her mind.

It's important for a girl to feel sexy for her man. Guys don't understand. His body is still chiseled to perfection, not undergoing any change at all, and there will always be a line of beautiful women ready to replace me. When he left, I was physically fit and every muscle was visible in a feminine way since I was an athlete, but it's changed. Even once the baby weight is gone it won't be as good as it once was.

He kisses me on the lips lightly, smiling against mine. "Let's go watch Oak Grove run the other team in the ground, shall we?"

I smile back. "I thought you'd never ask," I say and hop off the tailgate. He wraps his arm around my shoulders, holding me pressed to his side. This is where I feel like I belong; like several pieces cut from the same cloth, but only two fit together seamlessly. You can try your damnedest to make any two match up, but there is only one that was cut out to form against the other one perfectly.

The wind is blowing my hair, sending chills down my body. I start to shake a little, and Breyson nestles me closer as we arrive at the ticket booth. "Two please," he says to the woman inside the box as he hands her the money.

He looks over at me. "Are you cold? I may have a blanket in the truck. Do you want me to check?"

"This is all the warmth I need." He grins from ear to ear and everything in my world fades away but him. My heart stops beating and I feel lightheaded. His smile is contagious.

He takes the tickets and we walk through the gate in unison. Luckily, Oak Grove is a big school, so I can only feel a percentage of eyes on us as we walk through the crowd. Most are lost in their own lives.

The ones that stop us in our pursuit to the stadium are classmates and people that know Breyson or his parents, I assume. I stand silently as they hug or give Breyson some form of welcome home gesture. None are long for fear of making him feel awkward I'm sure. Breyson just smiles and says thank you, continuing on our way to the final destination.

We finally arrive to the stairs that lead up the bleachers and climb them one by one. I scan the faces in the crowd, looking for Adalynn. She agreed to come home from school for the weekend. I still can't believe they've all started college.

It's going to be sad not having them here, but that's all part of growing up. I won't lie and say that I'm not the slightest bit envious, because I always planned for the day of leaving for some top of the line college, but I have Breyson to stay with me and that keeps me from ever being sad again. At least they are going together. Braxton and Adalynn are at LSU where Braxton got a football scholarship and Briar and Londyn are at Georgia for him to play baseball. I hope they both find what Breyson and I found in one another, but at least they are on the right path.

"Kinzleigh! Over here," Adalynn screams from the middle section. I look up and she's waving her hand in the air with a look of excitement written all over her face.

"Looks like I'm not the only one that missed you," Breyson says in my ear by my side. "I guess it's back to sharing you again, isn't it? That was short lived."

I look at him and smile. "Never again. I'm all yours. Forever," I say for only him to hear. It started as a joke, but means so much more and he knows it.

His eyes deepen in color as he processes what I said. He releases me from his side to make room for two lanes of traffic on the bleachers but rests his hands on my shoulders from behind me.

We climb the bleachers, making our way toward her. Adalynn comes barreling out of her row as we reach her level, attacking me with a hug. "My bestie is back! Where is my nephew? I've stayed away to give Breyson his time, but I'm getting impatient. You better be glad I didn't skip school and come back early when I found out you were back home. I need baby love."

"He's with Breyson's parents. He hasn't had his shots yet. Breyson works during the day, so you're free to come by and see him before you leave for school." It's almost time for kickoff.

"Absolutely. I'll be there." Adalynn turns and makes her way back down the row with Breyson and I following closely behind.

We sit, waiting patiently for the coin toss when Breyson's football coach begins walking onto the field with a microphone in his hand, stopping centerfield at the fifty-yard line. Breyson is holding my hand in his lap, watching. I can see the longing in his eyes. His misses playing and that breaks my heart.

I told Breyson to go to the local university and see if there are any options for him to play football, but he continues to change the subject, saying he can just wait and we will go together in the spring. I feel like there is something he isn't telling me, because there has to be an option to redshirt for a year or something. He's the best running back around.

Our school gave him a deal, because of his circumstances. They are allowing him to take his same classes from senior year, picking up where he left off in February only they are condensing the material of three months into a week at twelve hours a day. It will consist of core curriculum mandatory by the state to graduate. Once complete he can then take his final exams. Upon passing he will receive his high school diploma. He starts on Monday.

He's staring at the players on the sideline when the coach begins talking through the microphone, his voice amplified through the speakers. "Can I have everyone's attention please?"

The crowd silences waiting for him to speak. "Earlier this year we lost one of our senior players from last season, our first string running back, in a tragic accident for many people; one that shook up our community."

I look at Breyson and his eyes are wide, slightly glossed over as if he's trying to shove back his emotions. We still haven't discussed that night. I'm waiting for him to come to me freely.

He squeezes my hand, but never takes his eyes off the coach. "I'm not sure of the details for his extended absence, but I have never been more pleased to announce that by the grace of God, Breyson Abercrombie is alive and well, sitting in our stands for the first game of the season."

The crowd begins to stand around us, clapping and cheering, screaming out his name. He looks slightly overwhelmed, but I don't know what to do, so I wrap my free hand over his bicep, rubbing up and down his arm. "Breyson, tonight your teammates are playing for you."

That's the last thing the coach says before walking off the field. The crowd is still going wild when the team captains take their position for the toss-up. Breyson looks anything but okay right now. Actually, he looks like he's holding on by a thread emotionally.

The toss up confirms that we get the ball first. Breyson leans forward resting his forearms on his thighs, holding my hand between his palms as if he's scared to let me go. I can't deny that it makes me happy. I guess that comes with going for months without being able to touch him at all.

I sit here lost in my own thoughts. It's funny that one year ago I was such a selfish person. Looking at the cheerleaders on the sidelines doesn't hold the same flame that it used to. Would I still like to cheer? Absolutely. Would I still give up anything for it? Hell no. I have a lot of things to figure out for myself such as where to go from here, the cheer company, and my career path, but one thing I've learned is to prioritize.

My child and Breyson come first. I have four years of college ahead. If I get to cheer one season of college football, then I'll have accomplished a massive goal. Right now, I would rather put my wants on the back-burner and give Breyson his dream.

Breyson is watching and shouting as Oak Grove scores a touchdown. I squeeze his hand to get his attention when the two-point conversion is good. He looks at me. "Talk to me. Why won't you go to the university about football? Classes have barely started. It hasn't even been long enough to really work out schedule changes. I'm sure there are options for late registration. You know you're good enough. Don't shut me out. When you do that, we are losing each other."

I unveil myself, knowing he can read me like an open book, not barring any emotions from him. His eyes are smoldering. He takes a deep breath, relaxing himself. "It doesn't matter, Kinzleigh. I won't lose you. We're in this together. Why is it fair for me to go after a dream when you aren't? Maybe it's just not meant for me to play."

I narrow my eyes. He is bullshitting on so many levels right now, which is pissing me off. There is something he's not telling me. "Don't lie to me. For one, you are not going to lose me, ever, whether you play football or not, if it's out of your control. Two, your entire world is football. If you expect me to believe that you're giving up this easily then you must think

I'm stupid. I told you once that I won't let you give up your dream for me and Bryce, so you better start talking."

He pulls his bottom lip between his teeth, trying to keep a serious face. I was always laughable when on a tangent, until we were apart. I was kind of enjoying being taken seriously, but I guess it is funny thinking of my five-foot-two petite frame throwing a tantrum up next to him.

"Nothing ever gets past you, does it?" He laughs, no longer able to hold back. "You always were feisty," he whispers next to my ear. "I can't wait until I can re-familiarize myself on just how much."

Oh, dear. He's trying to change the subject by seducing me. He always had that power over me. Damn him.

Think bottles, diapers, and babies. Oh my. Good one, Kinzleigh. You're now becoming a corny reciter of Wizard of Oz lingo.

Not this time. "Don't change the subject," I say, feigning my most serious tone.

He finally becomes serious. "Fine. Whenever Bryce was born you told me that you wouldn't even consider coming back until I went after football, so immediately before I went to California for you, I went to talk to the coach at the local university. I was surprised he would even meet with me on late notice. Coincidentally, they were having late open tryouts for second and third string walk-ons shortly after I got there for some reason, so I gave it a shot. It was a long stretch since I don't have my diploma or GED yet, but I explained my situation and the coach told me to show up anyway and if I got through maybe we could work something out with admissions."

"Why didn't you just say so? What happened?"

"I didn't tell anyone. I was grasping at everything I could to try to get you back. I went to the tryout and they said they would contact me if I got a position. The season is starting and there's a ton of people waiting in line for any football opportunity, so I'm assuming I didn't get it. I'm just a kid that was good in high school with unfortunate circumstances and no way to advance. If they wanted me, they would have called me by now, but you're wrong about one thing. I still love football, but football is no longer my world, you and Bryce are."

The crowd is going crazy around us as Oak Grove scores another touchdown, but we are so lost in each other we never look away. He rubs his thumb over my left ring finger as I've noticed him doing a few times before. "There's always next year. I'll try again."

There is sadness in his voice that kills me. I feel like someone is gripping my heart in their fist, killing me slowly. There has to be another way. I will not accept that this is the end. Breyson is the best person I know. He's completely unselfish and he deserves the world. I don't care what it takes to give it to him; I'll do it.

Breyson turns into our driveway. It's getting late. When we went by to pick up Bryce we visited with his parents for a while. Oak Grove won 36-13. Watching Breyson replay the game for his dad warmed my heart. "Hey, baby, will you check the mail? I forgot today. I've already put in a mail forward with the post office, so we could have mail."

He stops at the end of the driveway and puts the truck in park. He has held my hand the entire night, always my left one. I want to ask questions, but I choose to leave it alone. Something is on his mind.

He kisses my hand before releasing it. "I'll be right back."

I use the overhead light while the door is open to check on Bryce. He's sleeping peacefully. Breyson gets back in the truck and immediately I register that something is wrong. "Are you okay? What is it?"

He hands me an envelope and I take it. "This has the college's logo on it. Open it." I try to hand it back to him, but he shakes his head.

"I can't. Will you do it? Please." I flip it over and slide my finger underneath the seam, opening the flap. Removing the folded sheet of paper from the envelope, I unfold it. I read the print and look at him. He looks like he's going to throw up.

"You're on the team," I say, barely able to speak, because I'm on the verge of tears I'm so happy for him.

"Are you serious? What else does it say?"

A tear rolls down my face. I try to squander it with a laugh, but it's a little too late. I can tell he's trying not to get excited and that's what makes it harder not to cry. God knows I would do anything for this man. "It says for you to contact admissions first thing Monday morning to get admitted to the school officially, and then report to the coach's office Monday afternoon at half past three for a meeting. It's signed by the athletic department. It's legit."

"I got in?" he says to me, avoiding emotion, as if he's having a hard time believing it.

"You deserve this, Brey. It's okay to be emotional or excited. It may not be first string or a paid scholarship to your first-choice school, but I believe in you. You've defeated so many odds already. You'll be playing in no time at all. We will do whatever we have to do to make this work."

He looks back at Bryce's car seat, then at me. "I don't know, Kinzleigh. What if I can't juggle it all? What if our high school won't let me push back the diploma tutoring a day to go to the university? They are already making an exception for me. Then, there is no guarantee the university will even let me in classes late. You and him come first. I will provide for you both before I do anything for me. How is this even fair if it works out? What about you? I can't take it. I wouldn't be able to live with myself."

I shake my head. He's so stubborn. I turn in my seat to face him. "Breyson, we don't even need money right now. We have more than enough to live well over comfortable for years. I have my own trust fund to help contribute, remember? We will have graduated and be working fulltime jobs before we have to worry. You only work to feel like a man. You can do this and you will. I don't need designer things or a top of the line house, not anymore. You're the only thing that matters to me; you and Bryce."

The dam breaks and I can't hold back my emotions. I'm finally finding the words that I want to say. "I'm sorry that I gave up on you being alive. The signs were there, but I didn't believe in us enough to believe they were real. I'm sorry that I let someone else have what has always been yours. I thought I was doing what was best with the situation at hand."

I'm crying and babbling.

"But most of all, I'm sorry that I let my fear get in the way of picking up where we left off when you came back for me. You've never given up on me, or us. I've always been the one to give up prematurely. You've always put me and my dreams first. This time let me put you first. I don't want to leave Bryce with a sitter right now anyway. I'll start school in January as planned. This is really what I want. I promise."

His eyes are filled to the brim. He's not blinking, but the tears fall anyway. He moves across the truck as much as the center console will allow and wraps his hands in my hair, placing his forehead and nose to mine. Our lips are enough distance apart to allow us to speak freely. "How did I get lucky with you, Kinzleigh? Why did you give me a shot when you would make any man the happiest man alive?"

"Each soul is made in pairs and separated once created. Its only purpose is to exist and search until it finds its mate. There is no luck involved. Ours just fought a little harder to ensure they didn't have to coexist an eternity apart.”

As if acting on reflex he kisses me, just as I knew he would, only reassuring me that my theory isn't a theory, but the truth. I love this man with all that I am. For as long as we both shall live, we will have no end, just like that circle around our names in that old Oak tree.

He breaks free from the kiss. “Please don't ever leave me.”

“Never,” I say. “I cannot live without my heart.”

ELEVEN

Breyson

OCTOBER . . .

The alarm on my phone sounds, waking me up. Today is Kinzleigh's birthday. I've been thinking about it since I got her back. Last year she gave me something to remember it by, something I'll never forget for as long as I live. It was the most permanent thing you can do to show your love for someone. She tattooed the date she gave me her virginity on her body. Not only once has she given me a tribute on her body, but twice: one a good memory and the other bad.

There is only one thing that could top it and that is to do the one thing I've wanted to do for what seems like forever. Some people will think we're crazy, others will say we're stupid, but to me it's the only thing missing. The only way to live a full life is to live not giving a damn what anyone else thinks.

Here's the thing. Kinzleigh Baker has been my entire world since the day I laid my eyes on her. The two of us have been through the most fucked-up circumstances together, yet here we are still just as crazy about each other as the day we finally acknowledged the feelings and admitted them openly.

I will never be fully satisfied until Kinzleigh is completely and utterly mine in every possible way there is. I've already marked her body, won her heart, and claimed her soul. We even share a child together. Our lives are connected in every way, almost. The only thing left is a legally binding contract that says she's mine and replaces her last name.

Today is the day that I ask Kinzleigh Baker to be my wife.

The Monday after that first football game I went and spoke with the school, both of them. My high school agreed to push my start back a day, but I had to go that following Saturday to finish, which was fine. The dean of admissions is granting me late semester entry because of my situation, but I have to catch up any prior work assigned to make it fair. It's probably for political purposes to make the school look good, but whatever. I guess you could say it's an—*I'm sorry you were in a fucked-up situation, so here's an apology from the city since it's a local college.*

I was required to complete my high school curriculum prior to start and bring something signed by my principal to signify completion until I received the hard copy of my diploma and final transcript.

The coach of the football team had watched some of my football videos and wanted me even though it's a second-string position, which also helped my admissions case. Where no one else has pull, the athletic department does. He couldn't guarantee me any playing time and I'm not on scholarship, but I don't care. It's better than nothing.

I'm finally getting my life back. Everything is falling into place. I'm even doing well in all of my classes. Pops has given me a job that pays well with an easily adjustable schedule, we have enough money in the bank to take care of our needs plus some without my income from the ranch, and we're still able to achieve our dreams even though they've been slightly altered. I would say we're pretty fucking blessed.

I have the perfect plan for this evening. My mind has been driving me crazy plotting it out. I have the best surprise for Kinzleigh and keeping it a secret hasn't been easy with her wanting to see her horse. Bryce has helped keep her away some, though not much. Pops has been taking care of everything just as he said he would. She thinks this little house is what we're going to live in forever, but when I say I'll try my best to give her the world, I mean it.

The foundation is poured and the frame is up for the house, including the roof. Pops is taking care of the basic structure and house plans, and Kinzleigh gets to pick out everything for the inside. By then it won't be a surprise anymore. The only thing I care about is the look on her face when she sees our house being built in front of our Oak tree.

The first order of business is to go pick out the ring. Kinzleigh thinks

I have to work today since I stay busy with football and classes at the university, not to mention homework and studying. It cuts down on the time I can help out on the ranch since I'm a fulltime student, so I told her Mims and Pops were throwing her a birthday bash and cooking us dinner because they wanted to see Bryce.

Little does she know it's just a ploy to get her to our tree. Mims and Pops are going to watch Bryce for the whole thing. I can't wait to get that ring on her finger.

I roll over, draping my arm over her, pulling her to my chest. She makes a noise in her sleep and starts to rub her ass on my dick.

Fuck me. It's been too long for this shit. Today she is all mine. She's finally been cleared for sex, and though a little early, I'm diving in headfirst—the smaller of the two. As much as I want it now, I'm making myself wait until tonight. My dick is going to go on strike if I don't give him some action soon, but I refuse to jack off. I'm waiting for Kinzleigh, and plus, once you've had the best, everything else falls short and isn't even worth it. I can actually confirm that's true now, even though I wish I could take back what happened in Spain.

Kinzleigh stops squirming when she feels my erection poking her in the ass. That's what she gets. I place my hand flat against her belly, pressing her back closer against my front, letting her know exactly how much I want her right now.

I place my lips to her left ear. "Happy birthday, baby. Nineteen is going to be good to you." She moans slightly and tries to turn over, but I hold her still. "Starting now."

I want a piece of her. I want to watch her come, reminding me that I can still affect her in a way no one else can. Closing my lips over the lobe of her ear, I suck, flicking my tongue back and forth as I slide my hand down her stomach, dipping underneath her panties.

"Are you wet for me, baby?"

She arches her back, giving me better access to her pussy. "Yes," she breathes.

"Do you want me to make you come for your birthday?"

She reaches back and clenches my hair in her fist as I continue downward. I can already feel the heat without even touching it.

That's my girl . . .

"Please, Breyson. Make me come. I need you to touch me." Dammit, her asking for it gets me every time. It turns me on like nothing else.

Touching the tip of my index finger to her opening, I rub her wetness in circles, expanding it up through her folds until I reach that perfect little spot; that spot I'm craving to taste.

Since the first day I got a taste, I'm hooked. I want more.

I start out slow, rubbing in circles, and allowing my finger to become familiar with her clit, searching for the exact spot that makes her crazy. "Is that where you like it, baby? Do you like my finger on your clit?"

She moans and throws her leg back over mine, spreading wider for me. Her voice becomes higher in octave, giving me the green light to speed up. I change direction from circles to up and down, quickening my pace. "Please don't stop. I'm about to come."

"That's it, baby. Come for me." Her voice becomes louder, her breathing sparser. She tightens the muscles in her legs and begins to jerk her hips. "I fucking love watching you come."

She pulls my hair so hard that it hurts, but it only turns me on more. My dick is so hard I feel like it's going to explode.

She starts to relax, signaling the end of her orgasm. I remove my hand and she releases the hold on my hair, turning over to face me. She's staring at me with a lazy smile and softened eyes.

I place my finger in my mouth and suck it clean while she's watching me. "Your taste has become my drug. I crave it, love it, and get a high I've never known when I get it. Next time it's going to be my tongue."

Her cheeks start to flush. "So . . . how's your morning so far?" I ask with a cocky grin, no doubt changing the mood.

She tightens her lips together, trying not to laugh, but the smile in her eyes gives her away. "That good, huh?"

She playfully hits me in the shoulder as she bursts out in laughter. "Shut up," she squeals jokingly.

"You shouldn't have done that," I say and roll on top of her, trapping her beneath me.

She looks up at me through her eyelashes. "Oh yeah? What are you going to do about it?"

I push up from my forearms, shifting all my weight onto my knees, now straddling her in my boxer-briefs. She is slowly sweeping her eyes down my stomach, so I know she's not paying attention. Perfect.

"This . . ." I swiftly move my fingers to her ribcage and begin tickling her. She hates to be tickled.

"Brey—stop. Pleeeease," she draws out in laughter, having a hard time breathing. Her laugh is getting louder and more prominent, the laugh that makes my heart soar. "I swear no more hitting. Stop . . . I can't take it!" She is kicking and turning underneath me, but I'm stronger.

She's laughing so hard she can barely breathe. In her attempt to intake air she snorts, making me laugh in return. "Truce. I surrender. Just stop. You win!" she stammers between breaths.

She's arching and twisting, trying to get away from me. Her neck becomes exposed, the veins more noticeable because of her straining to breathe and talk.

Damn, she's beautiful.

Bryce starts to cry through the monitor. His room is directly across from ours, so I'm sure our laughing woke him up. Altering the position of my hands from the claws they're in, I clamp them around her narrow sides and bend forward.

I kiss the jugular vein protruding from her neck and beating with the pulse of her heart. She becomes limp under my touch as I swipe my tongue up her neck, tracing it to her ear. "Nothing makes me happier than to hear you surrender to me," I whisper. "I'll get him. Stay in bed. It's your birthday."

I throw my leg over her and stand from our bed. Bryce is getting pissed off from having to wait. I guess the apple really doesn't fall far from the tree. He may be just an infant, but the boy has a temper already. I grab a tee shirt from the dresser drawer on the way to his room. As I walk through his door his cry becomes lethal to a person's ears.

"Hey," I say as I bend over the crib, propping my crossed arms on top of the front railing. "Is that necessary, little buddy? I know what you want—trust me, I want it too—but that is not going to make getting it any faster."

He starts kicking his little legs at the sound of my voice. He's still whiney, but he's lowered his octave. I reach in and pick him up, cradling him so I can look at his face. Bringing him closer, I kiss his head.

I will never be able to properly express how much I love him already. He may have been an accident, but he will never be a mistake. To be able to look into the eyes of another person, knowing you created them from something so minute to this tiny human being that thrives and grows each day is such a miracle. This is my son, someone I'm responsible for, and someone to teach and take care of.

His changing table is nearby, filled with everything I need. I try really hard to help Kinzleigh do things for him no matter how busy I get. I realized being stuck in a foreign place with no family or friends, and not knowing anything about who I was, time can be your worst enemy. For six months I missed everything important to me. Never again will I miss anything if I can help it.

My entire life I've spent wishing I were older because of football. Playing college football and getting drafted after was everything I lived for and dreamed of, hurrying the hands of time, but now I realize exactly how precious time is. I missed a lot, but I could have missed so much more.

Now, I have all the time in the world to play football. As much as I want to play, if I never played another day, I'd still be happy, because I have them.

I lay him down and stick his pacifier in his mouth to soothe him until Kinzleigh feeds him. Holding the tabs of his diaper, I pause. "Don't get any bright ideas, buddy. It goes in the diaper not on Daddy. Do we have a mutual understanding?"

His arms are flailing back and forth and his legs are sticking up in the air. I know he's too little to understand what I'm saying, but I like to think he does anyway. Besides, I'm still making up for lost time. He didn't get to hear my voice before he was born.

Two arms wrap around my waist from behind. "The secret is to open the diaper and when the air hits him close it to be sure he doesn't have to pee again. Don't ask me why but take my word for it. Trial. And. Error."

The vision I'm picturing in my head right now is priceless. I can see it now—Kinzleigh screaming and ducking because he has no control over his boy parts yet. He's barely over a month old and already making Daddy proud. I look at Bryce, who is looking at us. "You tee-teed on Mommy, didn't you? Awesome! I have a partner in crime already."

"Don't get any ideas. I'm outnumbered."

I do as she said and sure enough Bryce pees again. I can't do anything but laugh. Kinzleigh presses her face in the center of my back, smelling my tee shirt. I finish changing Bryce's diaper and pick him up. I turn in her arms to face her. "Are you okay?"

"What do you mean?"

"Weren't you just smelling my shirt? Does it stink?"

Her eyes widen as if she's been caught with her hand in the cookie jar before dinner. Her mouth falls open slightly. "It's nothing," she says.

"Talk to me. It's never nothing."

"It's just something I used to do when you were—"

"Dead?"

She starts twirling her hair around her finger. "Yes. After the memorial service I found the tee shirt you were wearing that last day we were together . . . you know, in my room."

"You mean my undershirt?"

"Yes. It was shoved under the edge of my bed. Anyway, it was covered in your scent. It was the only thing that could comfort me. I guess I formed a habit. It's stu—"

I place my index finger of my free hand over her lips, hushing her. "Nothing is ever stupid. It makes me feel better knowing how much you missed me, how much you hurt because I was gone. I know I haven't told you anything about my time away, but I will when I can. Just know that when I look back at both situations, you had it so much worse than me. Trying to survive in a world without the other half of you, knowing there is a huge part of you missing, and being forced to move on alone doesn't even compare to forgetting it all."

She closes her eyes, pauses, and opens them again. "I have something for you. It's part of your birthday present. Since you never want to celebrate yours because of it being close to mine, I decided I would wait until today."

"I told you not to get me anything. I have everything I want."

She rolls her eyes. "Like I'm not going to get you a birthday present. You might as well let that one go. You will always have something on special days. That's what you do when you love someone. You go out of your way to make them feel special, especially on their most important days."

She turns and walks out of Bryce's room, but I follow her across the hall into our bedroom. She stops beside her side of the bed, opening the drawer of her nightstand. I can't tell what she removed, because obviously she didn't want me to see it.

When she turns to face me, she places her hands along with the item behind her back and comes to stand in front of me. She looks like she is rehearsing something in her head. I'm not sure whether I should be worried or excited. "Here goes," she whispers, clearly nervous, but why I have no idea.

"Promise me you won't laugh at me?"

My eyebrows dip in my new state of confusion. "I would never laugh at you, Kinzleigh, but only with you. There is a difference."

"Do you remember that silver anklet I gave you on homecoming?"

Of course, she has to bring up something I gave away. I know she would understand the circumstances, but I haven't told her about my other family yet. "Yes . . . you gave me your heart. Why?"

"Well, back then I looked at it like we had two separate hearts, in two separate bodies, able to survive on their own. When you . . . didn't come back, I realized that we don't have two separate hearts. We share one. Living with the thought of you being gone forever almost destroyed me, because it needs the other half to continue beating. It wasn't until you came back that I felt alive again. I was surviving, not thriving."

She pulls a medium sized, black, velvet box out from behind her back; a box made for jewelry. I'm not sure I understand what she's giving me.

She holds the box on one palm and opens the top with the other hand. It's a necklace box. On the inside lies two small chain necklaces made of silver with a unisex charm dangling from each end, half of a heart. Both sides align perfectly when placing them together. I've never been a guy to wear jewelry, but it's meaningful, and what makes it more so is that she bought it because of its significance.

She pulls one of the two from the box that holds it and looks up at me. "This side of the heart symbolizes me. My initials are engraved on the top, and set inside the silver is my birthstone, pink."

She flips the heart over as I lightly bounce Bryce in my arms and continues. "There is half of a statement engraved on the back side of each. Yours says, *when we come together*, and beneath it has Bryce's initials with his birthstone set in the middle of the loop of the P."

She sits the box on the edge of the bed and walks closer to me, unclasping the two ends of the chain. "Breyson, you are the keeper of my heart, or my half, perhaps. I've known it was yours from the time you barged into my life and claimed it. Paired with any other heart my body recognizes it as foreign matter, a toxin to me, and fights to reject it, but as long as I have yours it continues to beat, keeping me alive."

She reaches up and wraps each end around my neck, hooking them together. Damn, I love this woman with all that I am. "What's the other one look like?"

"It symbolizes you—your initials, opal for the birthstone. It also has Bryce's initials on the back to match mine." She says it nonchalantly while she puts hers on, as if it's no big deal, but it's the biggest deal. She couldn't have gotten a more perfect gift.

"But what does the sentence on the back read in its entirety when you put each half of the heart together?"

"When we come together, our hearts beat as one." The woman can gut me with one sentence.

"Come here," I command.

She walks over to me, placing her index finger inside Bryce's hand. I grab her chin between my thumb and index fingers, touching my lips to hers. She has the softest lips. Her lips hold the power to medicate open wounds. "Thank you for the gift. It's perfect. I love you, Kinzleigh."

"I love you too, baby."

A knock sounds at the door, breaking up our perfect moment. That should be Adalynn. She's surprising Kinzleigh with a few hours of shopping and doing whatever it is girls do while I go talk to Kinzleigh's dad, asking him for her hand in marriage. Adalynn is under direct orders not to be late or it will mess up all of my plans for the evening.

"I wonder who that could be. Are you expecting someone?"

I shrug my shoulders. That way I don't have to verbally lie. "Will you get it? I'll change Bryce's clothes and then you can feed him. I'm surprised he's waited this long without screaming."

"Looks like you have a daddy's boy," she says and winks as she turns to walk out the door.

I look down at Bryce, cradling him like a football on my left arm. He's sucking on his pacifier, looking back at me with his left arm slightly dangling as if he doesn't have a care in the world. "We're going to make a good team, little buddy. You want to pal around with Daddy today? You have to stay with Nana while I pick up Mommy's ring, but the rest of the time is boys' day, just the two of us."

I walk over to his dresser and pull out a pair of jeans that are tiny. I can't even believe they make denim jeans so small. "What else do we have in here? I better make you look nice or Mommy will have my head."

His closet doors are next to the dresser, filled to capacity with clothes. I've discovered exactly how much women like to shop, especially when they're bored at home all day. If I come home to any more packages, I'm going to have to hide Kinzleigh's laptop and her bankcard or our bank account is going to quickly dwindle.

I open the doors and stand in the doorway, looking at the array of colors hanging on the bar. Bryce makes a noise when he exhales. "Yeah, buddy, I feel the same way. At least we're in agreement. Your closet is scary. Who needs this many clothes?"

This isn't as easy of a task as I thought. I can hear Adalynn and Kinzleigh walking down the hallway, getting closer to the door. I just now realize that I'm still wearing boxer-briefs and a white tee shirt. I'm standing here worried about getting Bryce ready to go and I'm not even dressed.

Shit . . .

The door swings open before I can make a plan and in walks the two of them. On instinct, my free hand along with Bryce's jeans goes over my crotch area in an attempt to cover myself.

Both of them halt; the laughing stops and everything gets really awkward. The room becomes silent as we all three stand here looking from one person to another. Why the hell did I have to hook up with so many girls? "Adalynn . . ."

"Hey, Breyson."

"I don't mean to sound like a dick, but could you get out . . . please."

"Oh, right. I'll just wait in the living room." She looks at Kinzleigh. "Bring me that baby. I want to hold him."

"Sure, I'll bring him in just a second," Kinzleigh says as Adalynn walks out of the room, but never takes her eyes off of me.

"I . . . um . . . forgot you were not dressed. She said she wants to go shopping for my birthday and take me out for lunch, her treat. It's not a big deal, though. I should probably just stay here with Bryce since you have to work. I'll go tell her now." She turns to walk toward the door.

"Kinzleigh, stop."

She turns around, placing her sleeve-covered fist up to her lips. "Are you going to let me speak? Or are you going to ramble without letting me get a word in?"

"Sorry. Go ahead."

"I have an easy day today and there is something your dad needs my help with. Pack Bryce's diaper bag and take my truck or ride with Adalynn since your car has the car seat. It's your birthday. You stay in this house all week. Running to Wal-Mart is not getting out. Go have fun. You've been pumping and freezing milk for bottles, right?"

She nods.

"Then we will be fine. Your parents can watch Bryce while I run to the ranch. We're supposed to be at Mims and Pops' house by seven. Meet me back here at six thirty, okay?"

"Are you sure?" She stands there as if she's thinking about something. "What do you have to help my dad do?"

"I think he wanted help moving something." She narrows her eyes like she knows I'm lying, but then shrugs as if she bought it. "Yes, I'm sure. Go have fun."

I walk toward her and extend my arm out to hand her Bryce. "Here, you can pick out his clothes. That closet is no place for a man. I'm going to take a shower."

I kiss her on the lips as she takes our son. Now it's time to make preparations for tonight, the night to begin the process of making her my wife.

TWELVE

Breyson

My phone rings as I turn into Kinzleigh's parents' house. I quickly glance at the screen while slowing my pace. Braxton's number pops up on the screen. He's helping me get everything set up at the ranch while I do everything else. "Hello?"

"Dude, what if this shit is not how you want it? I really don't want to live with that kind of pressure."

"Braxton, you don't even have that many items on the to-do list. What's the problem?"

"I don't know. I'm not romantic. You're the one that has turned into a love-struck pussy. My idea of romance is roses and a box of chocolates. Here you are, wanting lights and candles and rose petals. I'm out of my league here."

"I have an idea. Why don't you just take your dick out of the equation and see what ideas you come up with. You might surprise yourself. There is more to making a girl happy than seeing how many times in a day you can get her off. They do like a little romance occasionally. If this is the kind of attitude you have all the time, then I don't know how Adalynn puts up with you."

"Why do you always have to bust my balls, Breyson?"

"Because you'll thank me for it one day. I've explained to you what to do. As soon as I get done, I'll be there. This is my only proposal. I have one chance to get it right. Don't fuck this up for me. Someday you're going to be calling me for this shit."

"Whatever. Fine. Just hurry up. I can't promise this is going to be pretty."

"One chance, Braxton. This is the shit women dream about their whole life. They all want the epic proposal they can tell a million times until they're old and gray. Do. Not. Fuck. This. Up. I'm depending on you. I don't ask you for much."

He breathes into the phone. "Yeah. Okay, man. I get it. You know I'll always have your back. See you soon?"

"Yeah, see you soon."

I am now sitting in the driveway, parked behind the garage. My stomach feels like I'm about to be dropped off a three-hundred-foot rollercoaster ride at seventy miles per hour. Being raised in the south comes with certain traditions that you can't escape. One is asking your girl's father for her hand in marriage. Normally, it's supposed to come before you knock up his daughter, but I've never been good at following rules. I just hope he doesn't hold it against me.

No one has ever told me what you do if the man says no. It's just assumed he says yes. Now I'm even more nervous. We're young, and with that comes the speech that we don't have a clue what we're doing and we're acting like foolish teenagers. I take a deep breath and open the door. There's only one way to find out.

I open the back door and remove Bryce's carrier from the base. He's awake, looking at me and sucking his pacifier. "I'm about to ask Pawpaw if I can marry your mother. Wish me luck. I might need you as my wingman."

He continues staring at me and sucking his pacifier as if my future is not in the hands of his grandfather. "You're supposed to be calming me down, buddy. This affects you too, you know. Your parents need to be married. Your mother needs to share our last name. It's just not right otherwise."

He drops his pacifier from his mouth and is pulling his mouth up, trying to smile. "Is Daddy being nervous funny to you?" My voice is teasing and he takes notice, waving his arms in the air before he starts cooing.

We make it to the door and I knock. I stand impatiently as the footsteps on the other side get louder. The door opens and Kinzleigh's mom is standing on the other side. She takes one look at me, and then down at the carrier in my hand and smiles. "How are two of my favorite boys?"

She steps to the side, letting us enter. As I walk inside, she grabs me, pulling me into a hug. "I have a feeling I know why you're here. Just remember, eye contact and speak clearly. If he knows you're nervous he'll eat you alive."

She pulls away and grabs the carrier out of my hand, winking as she walks further into the house. I shut the door. My heart is pounding out of my chest at the realization that it's becoming more real. Who came up with this rule anyway? She's the one I want to marry, not her dad.

I follow her mom inside. She places Bryce's carrier on the island in the kitchen and begins unbuckling his car seat while she's talking in baby talk. "Did you come to see Nana? Nana has been missing you, sweet boy."

I set the diaper bag down beside his carrier. She looks over at me as she picks up Bryce, pulling him out of his car seat. She cradles him in her arms and begins patting him on the butt and rocking from side to side. I'm standing here, staring at the two of them.

"Breyson, don't be nervous. We both love you as if you're already our son." She looks down at Bryce and back up at me. "If he hasn't killed you by now, you're golden," she says with a smile on her face. "Just remember, he did this once, and one day if you two have a daughter, some poor boy will have to do it with you."

That's a scary thought. If I have a daughter, I'm not letting her within ten feet of a guy like I was. God knew I couldn't handle a girl. "Where is he?"

"In the den reading the news. Go ahead. Bryce and I will be just fine." It's time to do this. Today is a day I don't have time to waste.

I walk through the doorway from the kitchen into the den, where I immediately see Kinzleigh's dad sitting in his recliner buried under a stack of Sunday papers with NASCAR playing on the television.

He looks up at the same time he lowers the book of newspaper he has spread out in front of him. "Breyson. What do I owe the pleasure? You said you had something important you wanted to talk to me about?"

His tone is void of any emotion. I can't tell if he knows why I'm here or if he's intrigued as to why I'm here without Kinzleigh. I make my way further into the room and round the couch, sitting on the end closest to him. "Yes, Sir. I did, I do."

He stares at me briefly before he folds up the paper and lays it on the side table by his chair. He picks up the television remote and mutes the sound on the television. "Okay, I'm listening. Lay it on me."

You would think from the nerves sparking in my stomach that I'm terrified of the man, but we're actually pretty close. "Well, Sir, it's about Kinzleigh . . ."

"Go on . . ."

I take a deep breath, preparing myself for the speech that I've recited over and over again in my head, hoping it comes out exactly as I have rehearsed. I clear my throat and wipe my sweaty palms down my jeans, trying to dry them off.

"I want you to know that she is an amazing girl; the best, and I couldn't envision my life with anyone else. You and your wife have done a phenomenal job raising such a beautiful person, inside and out. Honestly, I don't deserve her, but for some reason she loves me, making me the luckiest man in the world. That girl is everything to me, Sir. I know we're young, but I love her with everything that I am. I feel the need to tell you how sorry I am that I made things more complicated by impregnating her prior to this conversation, but if I had to choose someone to be the mother of my child it would always be her. I was raised by parents that taught me the importance of family. Even though he is not the basis of this decision I still want Bryce to be raised by both of his parents under wedlock. I'm here because I want to ask you for her hand in marriage."

I feel a sense of relief wash over me by getting those words off my chest, but the most important part is yet to come. I still need his blessing. It's good manners. He starts rubbing his hand back and forth over the nape of his neck, deep in thought. I remain silent, giving him the opportunity of letting my request sink in.

"Breyson, Son, I appreciate you coming here and asking me, but you know she's my only little girl . . ."

That sentence sounds like a no is coming. My stomach is starting to knot up again. "Yes, Sir."

He studies me. I feel like I could throw up right now. "Follow me," he says, and stands.

I do the same and follow him toward the staircase. We begin to climb one step at a time. I haven't been up here since the day I left for the airport. The layout is similar to the way their house in California was, but different.

We reach the top of the stairs and turn in the opposite direction of the bedrooms, the side with only one door. I've never been in that door before.

He opens it and walks in, holding it open until I enter. It's an office. The back wall is a bookshelf, filled with books. I wouldn't have taken him for a reader.

He walks around the desk and sits in the large leather chair that sits in front of the bookshelf behind the large Oak desk. "Have a seat, Son."

I have no idea why we're here, but I do as I'm told. He spins in the chair and begins scanning through the books on the shelf that stands the same height as him in a sitting position. He removes one and turns back around, handing it to me. It's a photo album labeled 'Kinzleigh'.

I look back and forth between him and the book. "Go ahead, open it."

I open the book and the first photograph is Kinzleigh's mom in the hospital holding her, along with him and Konnor, who was only a toddler at the time. I flip through the pages, each one with photographs of her a little older than the one before. The book tells the story of her entire life summarized. She's beautiful; she always has been, and she looks happy in every one.

When I look up he has a remote in his hand, pointing it to a TV behind me on the wall. "I had a feeling this was the reason you were coming to talk to me, so I put this in. I want you to see something."

I turn around as the sound of a home video starts playing. He must have skipped ahead, because it's not the beginning. Her mom must be recording, because he's sitting on the twin-size bed with Kinzleigh. The room is pink and sparkly, but everything visible is something related to a princess.

They are both sitting against the headboard with a big book spread out in their laps. Kinzleigh looks about five, with the same platinum curls and green eyes she has now. I can't take my eyes away.

He's reading what sounds like the end of a fairytale by the way he mentions the prince and the princess getting married and living happily ever after. I'm starting to wonder why he's showing me this until Kinzleigh opens her mouth and starts talking. "Daddy, will I marry a prince?"

I'm glued to the conversation that takes place between the two of them, starting with his response.

"One day, baby girl, when you're grown, you'll marry someone so much better than a prince."

"Like what, Daddy?"

"Well, see, a prince is only in fairytales, which is only a story that daddies and mommies read to their little girls. A fairytale has to end, but one day when you get big, you'll meet a boy that makes you smile, kind of like Daddy, but this boy will ask you if he can have your heart. Do you know how I call you my princess, because I love you?"

"Because I'm pretty like a princess?"

He laughs. "Yes, because you're pretty like a princess, but also because I love you and you're special. One day a boy is going to love you in a different way than Daddy. He will come ask me if he can marry you like the princess in the book. If he comes and asks Daddy if he can make you his princess, then you know he's your prince."

"Then I get to wear a big fluffy dress to marry my prince?"

I'm assuming after that it's a lost cause, because he just goes along with it. I'm speechless, staring at the now paused screen. "Breyson."

I turn around not knowing what to say, but he doesn't expect me to. "This was your test and you passed with flying colors. I know you love her, but there are so many boys out there that lose respect, becoming selfish. One day you may have a daughter and you'll understand that she's your little girl. It's hard enough to let her go when you *give* her away to a deserving man, but it's another thing entirely to have one think he's entitled simply because he wants her. By you coming here it shows your character and that you will put her before yourself."

He places his forearms on the desk and finishes his thought. "I do wish that you two would have at least been more careful and finished school before you strapped yourselves with a baby, but it's done. There is no reason to ever look back and wish things a different way. He's a beautiful baby, and now he's made a place in everyone's heart. She is my only little girl, Breyson. I will do anything to protect her, but because I know that there is something different between you two, I'll give you my blessing in marrying her. She is my heart. Treat her like the princess that she is and never take her for granted. Don't make me regret this. Are we clear?"

In this moment I feel relieved. I have one step behind me, but still another to go. "Yes, Sir. I give you my word."

"Good. Now go on. You have a proposal to make."

I stand and walk to the door, opening it, but I stop. "Oh, Mr. Baker . . . Thank you for trusting me enough to give me a chance. She's changed me, made me into a man I'm proud to be."

Without another word I continue out the door. One more stop and it's go time. I sprint down the stairs and quickly make my way through the living room. Kinzleigh's mom is feeding Bryce in the recliner. "I take it you're on your way to propose by that smile across your face?"

I didn't even know I was smiling. "Yes, ma'am. Will you watch Bryce long enough for me to go get her ring? He's not supposed to be out yet. I'll be back as soon as I'm done. Kinzleigh is shopping for her birthday."

"Sure, honey. Take your time. We will be just fine."

"Thanks, Mrs. Baker."

I never stop walking in the sprint for Kinzleigh's vehicle. The longer I wait, the more rushed I will be. Picking out the ring is one of the most important parts; the semblance of forever.

THIRTEEN

Kinzleigh

It's half past six and Adalynn just pulled in to drop me off back at our house so I can ride with Breyson to Mims and Pops' house for our birthday bash. Breyson doesn't appear to be here yet. Strange. He's always on time.

I unbuckle my seatbelt and grab my purse. The car is loaded down with bags from our retail therapy around town. It's been forever since I've had a day to be a teenager. It was really nice to just let loose and be free. I probably spent more money than I should have, but I couldn't help myself.

Adalynn steps out of the car at the same time I do, grabbing bags from the back seat. She walks with me to the door. I pull Breyson's keys from my purse and enter the correct one into the lock, opening the door. She walks in directly behind me, sitting the bags along the wall by the doorway.

I look at her and she has tears in her eyes. "What's wrong? Are you okay?"

She pokes her middle fingers in each corner, trying to stop them before they fall. "I'm going to miss you, Kinzleigh. I've been missing you since you left back in May. I have to hit the road with Braxton in an hour to head back to school, but if you're ever free for a weekend you should come to Baton Rouge. It's a different world there."

It just dawned on me that after today neither she nor Londyn will be back for a while. They only came back for the weekend to celebrate our birthday. My girl crew will be non-existent once again. I left them and now they're leaving me. It hurts a lot worse when it's you being left behind. "I'm going to miss you too, Adalynn. You have been the most amazing friend to me since I moved here."

She holds out her arms and a tear rolls down her cheek. "Come here."

I walk over to her and hug her. My mind takes me back to that day I moved here. I was so mad at my parents for uprooting us and moving us clear across the country, but it turns out that it was the best thing to ever happen to me. I was sitting on the patio, staring out at the pool when Adalynn barged into my life without a care in the world, and she's made her place in my heart since.

It's funny how some of the most amazing friends can come from unexpected circumstances, and in those times when you're at a low in your life from things going on that you have no control over. That's what happened to me. I was a control freak that had my control taken away from me, sending me into a meltdown, but I learned sometimes that is the most amazing thing that could happen.

When you have a chance to let loose and enjoy life, your spirit is set free. My parents freed me from a life of bondage in my own chains, giving me the chance to really live. For that, I'll always be grateful. Back then I was a selfish teenager void of any love, but the girl I am today is so full of love my heart feels like it could burst from overfill.

She squeezes me as tight as she can, and I find myself tearing up as well. Goodbyes are always the worst parts of life. "I never expected that gloomy blonde by the pool to become my best friend, but yet here you are. You're a beautiful person, Kinzleigh Baker. I saw it that day and it radiates even brighter today. Never let anyone steal your shine, babe, even in the absence of me. I'm so glad you got your happily ever after, because seeing you hurt was the hardest thing I've ever had to watch with a friend. I was helpless in so many ways. It's why I let you go to California and didn't bother you, but that doesn't mean that I didn't love you, because I did, and I still do. Now you're here, and happy. I know I won't be here but know that you'll always be my sister. I promise to call you every day. I love you, Kinzleigh. Make Breyson take care of you for me or I swear I'll come back and bestow my wrath on him."

I laugh in the midst of my tears. "I love you too. You know you're my best friend. I don't have to tell you. Now go before you're late."

I push her back, hinting for her to leave. "Okay, okay. I'm going."

She walks to the door and pulls her sunglasses down from where they rest on top of her red hair. "Darlin', you better give that baby a kiss from Aunt Adalynn."

Her southern accent always gets thicker when her emotions are heightened, and I absolutely adore it. I nod with a huge smile on my face. When I moved here I had so many stereotypes about southern people. Coming from the west coast I thought I was doomed and headed for cow fields in the middle of rednecks, but I was so wrong. Television ruins us, making us believe things are different than what they really are.

My main piece of advice to anyone about life would be to ignore the stereotypes, because what you could be missing out on if you don't is an amazing life with extraordinary people.

She realizes why I'm smiling so big. "Shut up. I don't want to hear about my country accent. Okay, I'm really going this time."

"I wasn't going to say a word. It's amazing," I tease. "Be careful on the road!" The last syllable exits as she shuts the door.

I'm standing in the now empty house not knowing what to do with myself. It's too quiet. Where is Breyson? After what happened in February, timing will be everything. If he's late I will be paranoid. There is nothing I can do about that.

My cell phone starts ringing, causing me to jump. When I see Breyson's name and photo pop up on the screen my heart calms down. "Hey. Where are you?"

"Hey, beautiful. I'm still at the ranch. I got caught up with one of the cattle. Can you just meet me here? Bryce is already with Mims and Pops. He's fine."

"Sure. It's too quiet here anyway. I don't like it. It makes me nervous."

"So, you don't mind living with two boys? It's bound to get rowdy at some point."

"I wouldn't have it any other way. I'll be there in ten minutes. I love you."

"I love you too. Be careful."

"Okay, baby. See you soon."

I disconnect the call and drop my phone in my purse as I head for the door, grabbing Breyson's keys in my hand along the way and locking the door behind me. Eighteen started as a good year but quickly went to Hell in a hand basket. I'm praying with everything I am that nineteen is a better

year.

I park Breyson's truck beside the big Magnolia tree in Mims' yard, next to the house and my Range Rover. I'm a little behind schedule with Adalynn saying goodbye, but it doesn't look like anyone is even here. I thought it was supposed to be a bash.

The sun is starting to go down, but it's still light outside. I knock on the door and it immediately opens. Mims is standing on the other side holding Bryce. "Hi, Mims."

"Hey, Kinzleigh. Come in, honey. You know you don't have to knock."

I walk inside and into the kitchen. "Do you need me to get Bryce? Where is Breyson?"

"He's fine, honey. We're bonding. Breyson instructed me to send you to the barn. He said someone wants to see you."

My eyebrows dip, but then I think of Divinity and I get excited. I haven't seen her in so long. "You're sure he's okay? I don't want him to be a burden."

"Go on. It's been a long time since you've been here. Now that you both are settled in the house, I expect regular visits."

It doesn't take her telling me twice and I'm nodding and out the door, running for the barn. I can see the barn light already on. I stop, but only long enough to open the gate and close it behind me.

"Breyson!" I shout out as I come into the main doorway. Hendrix is missing, but Divinity is completely saddled for me, tied to the post. She tries to pull from the post to get to me when she hears my voice.

"Hey, girl. I've missed you," I say as I come into reaching distance. I place my palm on her nose, running it up into her hairline. She breathes in a steady rhythm, standing still under my touch.

"I bet you thought I left you, didn't you, girl? I'm so sorry. I'll never leave you again." I trail my fingers down her neck and along her side when I notice a folded piece of card stock tied to a piece of twine, hanging from the horn of the saddle. "What's this?"

I remove it from the saddle and open it. It's a note.

Kinzleigh,

Meet me at our spot. Your prince will be waiting.

Love,
Breyson

I hold it to my chest, trying not to get too mushy. That is so romantic. This is one of those things you put in your hope chest to keep forever.

I untie and mount Divinity, instructing her to go. On the first command she takes off in the direction of our tree. I've forgotten how much of a rush it is to ride like this. Nothing holds you back. It's just you and the wind in your hair.

We make it through the section of trees that opens up into the field on the back of the property. My mouth drops open when Divinity comes into the clearing. Breyson has the Oak tree lit up with white lights wrapping the branches. He's sitting on Hendrix beside it, waiting for me.

Immediately my hand goes over my mouth and Divinity slows to a walk. I can even see a blanket spread out beneath it with a picnic basket. I can't take my eyes off of him. Hendrix inches forward, our eyes never leaving one another.

"Miss Baker, I was instructed to take special care of you. Rumor has it today is your birthday," he says as he comes up beside me, completely serious.

I have the biggest grin on my face right now. Role-playing used to be our thing. I feign the best southern accent I can muster. "Why yes, Mr. Abercrombie, it is. What do you have planned for me?"

He grabs my hand and the horses make a circle as if we're dancing horseback. "I thought we could dance. We're long overdue."

"But there's no music."

The horses stop and he gets off of Hendrix before helping me down by my waist. "Oh, but Miss Baker, I'll always ensure there's music for dancing."

On point, music starts playing. I have no idea where it's even coming from. He is smiling as if he's outdone himself. It's that award-winning smile that could kill a girl's heart upon looking at it for too long. He holds his hand out and does a southern boy's version of a prince's curtsy. "May I have this dance?"

I feel like I'm in a fairytale and I've been made a princess for a night. My chest is hurting from the amount of love that my heart holds for him. He weakens me, but he also gives me strength. "I'll always save a dance for you," I say, and take his hand.

He pulls me into his arms and twirls me around beside our tree. He pulls me close, resting one hand over mine, and the other on my lower back. We begin swaying to the music. It reminds me of the night at the New Year's Eve ball. "I can't believe you did all of this for my birthday. I didn't know you were so romantic."

"You make me a lot of things I never was before."

We continue to dance in each other's arms, enjoying the beauty of the sun setting, now making the lights on our tree stand out more with the sun going down. "Do you think this will ever go away?" I ask.

"What?"

"This feeling I have inside. The one where I feel so overwhelmed that I want to laugh and cry simultaneously, because the overflow of love and happiness needs a point of exit or my heart is going to explode."

His cheek is pressed to mine. The tips of grass are starting to blow with the breeze, brushing against our legs. "I think if it was going to it would have at least dwindled by now. I feel the same way. It's weird, isn't it? Feeling this way about someone so young."

"I most certainly think we defy the norm, yes."

"Promise me we will never be normal," he says. "No matter what we have to endure to make it, promise we will never stop fighting for each other. Sometimes life is going to suck, sometimes it will try to rip us to shreds, but we can never let it win. Promise me."

His voice is so soft, but still holds that masculine tone. This moment is so surreal that I want to pinch myself just to see if it's real. I feel like I'm about to wake up and realize it's all just a dream. "I promise. If we made it through the last eight months, we can make it through anything."

"There's something else I want to show you."

I put some distance between us so I can see his face. I raise a brow. "There's more?"

"Never underestimate what I can do, Miss Baker. The best is yet to come." He pulls a handkerchief from the pocket of his jeans and puts it over my eyes, tying it in the back. "This is your last year to be a teenager. I have to make it count."

Last time he blindfolded me like this I was surprised with a horse. I can only imagine what he has up his sleeve. I can't see a thing. He reaches around my waist with one arm and around the back of my knees with the other, picking me up. Immediately my arms link around his neck. "You always did spoil me, Mr. Abercrombie."

He starts walking, to where I have no idea. "I always told you I'd try to give you the world."

"But you already do . . ."

He sets me down and places his hands over my shoulders, stopping me from moving any further than where I stand. "I want to say something before I let you see anything. I don't know why I was given the chance to have a girl like you, because you really deserve so much better than anything I'll ever be, but I'm not going to question it anymore. The guy I've become since I met you actually makes me proud to claim. I'm a better person because of you. With you by my side I'll only continue to be a better man. There are no limits to what I'm capable of when it comes to you, starting with this . . ."

He removes my blindfold and what stands before me literally steals my oxygen. I know that sounds crazy, but I am finding it hard to inhale. My arms are behind me, holding him on each side of his butt, now clenching his jeans in my fists. I'm in shock.

Standing before me is the outside of a house, completed with a frame, full roof, and the outer walls surrounded by stacks of brick ready to complete the exterior. "What is this?" I whisper, because it's all I can get out without choking.

"Our house."

I turn in his arms. "You're building us a house? How? When? Is this real?"

"It's been in process since I came to California. They assured us it'd be ready to move in by Christmas at the latest." I feel faint.

He moves in front of me, taking my hand in his. "Come on, let's go see it."

I'm having trouble putting one foot in front of the other, but somehow my limbs begin to move. The closer we get to the doorway I notice the path lit up by candles.

He places his hands on my waist and helps me into the house, stepping up himself once I'm inside. I can't believe how big it is. Don't get me wrong, it's nothing on the scale of massive, but it makes the house we live in now look tiny. It's perfect. I would choose this with Breyson versus a house like Preston's any day of the week.

Rose petals are scattered along the path made of candles, sparking my curiosity of what's at the end. Breyson takes me by the hand, leading me. The inner walls are still supporting beams, making it hard to really picture the ending result, so I don't try. I'm more interested in what's at the end of his little setup.

I listen as he explains what each room is along the way. He turns before we get to the last room, now facing me. "This is our room," he says, moving to the side.

I walk past him, astounded by what I see. He must have spent hours doing this. The room is set up with a king size bed, fully dressed in white, and surrounded with candles along the floor. White lights are running along the top beam, lighting up the room. I'm not even going to ask how he's powering them. Breyson will always find a way.

In the middle of the bed is a section of red rose petals just like the ones scattered throughout the house but sitting on top of the pile is a small, square box. There are only two things that could come in a box of that size, and based on our surroundings, I'm going to say it's not earrings.

I can no longer control my emotions. Everything around me has sent them into overdrive. I turn around and I'm staring at his beautiful, bare chest, just like I was that day I met him on the beach. I look up and he has a smile on his face. "Happy birthday, Princess."

"You did all of this just for my birthday?"

The tears are streaming down my face one after the other. I'm not even ashamed. He places a hand on each cheek, looking into my eyes. "It's the most important day. The day that represents you being born will always be the best day, because it confirmed I would have you in my life. That's worth going all out for."

"I don't know what to say." I scan his eyes, trying to find my words.

He places his hands on the hem of my dress, pulling it up my body until he removes it completely, leaving me standing in underwear and cowgirl boots. "That's okay, because I have more to say, but first I want you naked.

He reaches behind me, unhooking the clasp of my bra. He pulls the straps off of my shoulders, letting it fall to the floor. He closes in, pressing his lips to mine. I'm so ready for this man to take me that I could scream. Each time he kisses me I get so lost anything could be happening around me and I wouldn't know.

He runs his hands from the center of my back over my butt, but underneath my panties, pushing them down as he continues downward. They fall to the floor at the same time he lifts me by the thighs. His taste is sending me into a hormonal frenzy.

I wrap my legs around his waist as he lays me on the center of the bed, placing his hands beside me on the mattress. He releases his lips from mine. "Breyson, please don't stop. We've waited long enough. I need you this way. Please. You know I'll beg."

He looks me in the eyes, balancing his weight on top of me on his forearms beside my shoulders. He runs his fingers through my curls. "You know you would never really have to beg me, right? I like it, but sex will never be something you have to ask for. I love sex with you more than you will ever like it with me, but before we do there is something I want to say."

That phrase makes me nervous, but I have no idea why. "Okay."

He stands at the foot of the bed, but never veers his eyes off of me. I watch as he unbuttons his jeans and slides them down his legs, stepping out of them. With every second that I have to wait I'm becoming more nervous, as if it's our first time. In a way it is. The one thing we will have this time that we didn't have our first time is knowing without a shadow of doubt that we love each other, completely and solely, and we'll be intertwined with each other so tight that it's as if we're one.

He removes his boxer-briefs, slowly, as if he wants to study my reaction. I feel like my skin should be turning red from the heat I feel inside. I look down. His dick is fully hardened and ready to go. I can't take my eyes off of him, but that's no surprise. He consumes me, and he always has.

He takes ahold of one foot at a time, removing my boots. He places one knee on the bed, then the other, and crawls back toward me. He slides one arm underneath my back and reaches behind my head with the other. In one motion he turns, pulling me on top of him. I'm trying not to focus on his dick poking at my entrance.

He rubs his thumb along my bottom lip. "I'm going to get mushy, but it's unavoidable so don't hold it against my manhood, okay?"

I smile. It doesn't matter how mushy Breyson gets, he'd still reek of manliness and ooze sex appeal. The man is an ocean of testosterone. "I'll try," I tease.

"Kinzleigh, I never cared about commitment until I met you. Some can use the excuse they are scared, but not me. I just didn't want anything to do with a serious relationship. It didn't appeal to me. When I met you, though, something was different. At first, I thought it was because you didn't cling onto me like most girls did, making it easy. I thought once we had sex it would go away. It wasn't until I left California that I realized it was so much more. I was going crazy, but then you showed up at school and everything just clicked into place. I was in denial for a while that it was love at our age, but you changed my mind pretty quickly. With each passing day I fell more in love with you, but what made me absolutely sure that I can't live without you was almost losing you. I can't live in this world without you by my side, Kinzleigh. I've tried. I can't explain the connection we have and I'm not going to try. Once, I told you I was going to ruin you, but that's not true. It's you that has ruined me. You own my heart, you consume my mind, and you are completely irreplaceable. We share a child together; one we both love and would do anything for. As long we have each other we can conquer the world. You own me completely, but there is one thing missing for me to own you in return."

He opens his palm between us, holding that little black box. I stare at it wide-eyed. He opens it with the other hand. Sitting in the slit is a very familiar diamond shining brightly from the light reflecting off of it. In this second of time I've never been surer that we are connected in more ways than I will ever understand. It's the same diamond I've visualized in not one dream, but two.

I look up at him with tear-filled eyes. "Marry me, Kinzleigh. I want to be your Prince, the one that makes your dreams come true. Say you'll be mine, forever. I want to be the one standing at the end, waiting on you to walk in the room in your fluffy white dress. The next time I make love to you I want to make love to my fiancé."

I take a breath as he says those words. He watched the video. That's the only way he could know something like that. A whole new set of emotions floods through me as I picture him asking my dad if he can marry me.

I never wanted to be in the place that I am until I met Breyson. We're alike in that sense. Before him I didn't want to be married or have kids. I wasn't content unless I was chasing a dream or cheerleading, but that was before. Now, I admire the relationship my parents have and the one my grandparents had. I guess that's what happens when you find the boy that changes you, and makes you see the world in color instead of black and white.

I place my left hand out in front of me, spreading my fingers apart. "You have always been my prince, Breyson Abercrombie. When I envision myself getting to dress up like a princess for the ball, you'll always be the one waiting as I come down the stairs. I love you with everything I am, and anything short of forever is not long enough. Nothing will make me happier than to be your wife."

He flashes that boyish grin I fell in love with that summer on the beach and removes the ring from the little box it's nestled in, before sliding it on my left ring finger; the one closest to my heart. It's the perfect fit, just like everything else between us.

I look at the large, square diamond sitting perfectly on my finger and look up at him with a smile that matches his. "Make love to me. I've waited long enough . . ."

FOURTEEN

Breyson

She doesn't have to ask twice. I've been waiting for this day for too long. I want to look in her eyes as I make love to her. I grab her hair in my hand, cupping the back of her head. I need to taste her again.

I press my lips to hers, hungry for her. I've never wanted anything as much as I want her. I suck her bottom lip between mine, skimming my teeth over her skin. She moans and starts grinding against me. Damn . . . she's so wet.

She slides her tongue in my mouth and I'm completely done for. I probably won't even last long. It's going to be the most embarrassing shit ever. I need to get her off before I even attempt sliding my dick inside that tight, moist place, warming my cock to fucking perfection. I need to think about something else.

I place the pad of my thumb over her pussy, dipping it inside. She tightens her muscles and I swear I feel like I could blow already. I'm wound up so tight I could burst.

Her wetness is oozing out, coating my thumb. "Fuck, baby, you're so wet."

I slide my thumb up through her folds, lubricating her clit. Her head rolls backward, her curly hair cascading down her back. It's longer than it's ever been, the ends meeting the small of her back. Her eyes are closed and she bites her bottom lip as I trail my tongue down her neck. She's so fucking hot. She has no idea just how much.

I exert pressure on her clit, rubbing up and down. She looks like she's consumed with ecstasy, but she's still grinding her pussy on top of my dick, spreading her wetness along my shaft. It feels fucking insane. "You want my dick, baby?"

She places her hands on my shoulders. I rub her faster, causing her to halt her movements. She opens her eyes. "Yes. I want you inside me. I need it," she breathes.

"Come for me and you can have it. It's all yours, baby. Only yours."

I increase speed again. She whimpers and her eyes begin to lose focus. She's about to come. She begins to moan but crashes her lips to mine in an attempt to smother it.

What I thought was wet was nothing compared to what's running down on my cock. I can't stand it anymore. I want in. I continue to kiss her roughly as I cup my hand over her ass and flip us over. She's lying on her back, her legs wrapped around my waist and pulling me toward her.

Bryce crosses my mind. I want to be in her bare, but we need to be more responsible. "Wait," I say against her lips. I'm trying to get my breathing under control. She looks worried, as if she's done something wrong.

Fuck, that's not my intention.

"I just need to ask you something. Are you on birth control? I don't want to use a condom, but I have one if I need it."

She bites the side of her lip and nods her head. "Yes, I had an IUD put in. It's good for five years unless I have it removed before. I love Bryce, but I think it's way too soon to even think of another one." I can't help but to smile at her last sentence, because even though she is completely right, it's the point of planning a future together that has me on cloud nine constantly. This is really real, her and I . . . for the rest of our lives.

I kiss her again, because I never get tired of it. Aligning my dick at her entrance, I push inside . . . and fuck if it isn't the best feeling known in existence. Dammit, she's so tight, which seems weird considering what childbirth looks like.

I thrust until I'm as far as I can go and stop. As anxious as I am to have her this way, I can't bring myself to rush. It's been too long since I've gotten to have all of her. I suppose when you live with the possibility of never getting something again it changes your perspective, and you just want to savor it when you get it.

I slowdown in the way that I kiss her, letting our tongues mingle, memorize, and express what we can't with words. I pull out slowly, but just before disconnecting completely I thrust back inside, pushing as deep as I can go.

She places her hands on my hips, pulling me toward her with each thrust, as if she can't get me close enough. She has each heel hooked behind me, on the inside of my legs. Her tongue plays with mine at the perfect rhythm, alternating between lightly sucking, teasing, and nibbling.

She is moaning against my mouth, her breathing climbing the longer we kiss. Placing my hand on her hip, I pull her toward me, creating an angle. I can tell the difference by the wall the head of my dick is hitting each time I bury myself inside her.

She begins arching her back, pulling her lips free as her head extends further into the pillow, elongating her neck. I keep a steady rhythm, but make the depth of insertion harder, slamming against her G-spot, and causing her to cry out. It only feeds my need.

I bite the lobe of her ear and trace the point of my tongue down her neck. It's too hot, wet, and tight. Each time I'm as deep in her as I can go, she tightens her muscles and squeezes my dick. I can't hold out any longer. I'm about to come. I'm trying to hold it, but it's starting to hurt, so I speed up.

I look her in the eyes. I can tell she's about to come, but I want to watch her when she does. I want to wait on her. I'll always wait for her. This girl is my addiction, my drug, and my life. Anything I have is hers. "Come with me," I whisper.

"I'm about to."

Her mouth drops slightly, and she digs her nails into my skin at the moment she tightens around me, signaling she's letting go. Her eyes become glassy as if she's high. One last thrust and my dick starts to pulse, my cum spurting inside her. I'm no longer able to move.

We both relax but continue to stare at each other. The head of my dick is sensitive from my release and beginning to tickle, but I don't want to pull out yet. I'm not ready to, so I ignore it.

A tear drops from each outer corner of her eye and trails down her cheekbones. "What's wrong?"

"I love you, Breyson. I've missed this. I've missed you. So damn much. We're bringing each other out of the dark, but in our absence I've learned to cherish the simple things. My heart is more content now than it's ever been. Even on my worst day there is no more sadness. The beauty of living in the bad—you hold on when you find the good. I can't wait to start our forever. I can't wait to take your name."

Her emotions have obviously been tampered with, sending her spiraling into a full-on happy cry. If she wasn't laughing in the midst of her tears, I'd be worried. "Baby . . . I'm here. I'll always be here, from this day forward."

It's difficult not to laugh. I kiss her from her forehead to her chin, and then each cheek. "I've missed you too. More than you will ever know."

The girl that swore she'd never love anyone is crazy in love with me, and I take pride in knowing it. The best feeling in the world is knowing the person you're completely in love with is also in love with you. This feeling I carry on a daily basis is rarer than gold, and worth protecting. "I love you, Kinzleigh."

I pull out and lay beside her on my back. She turns on her side and lays her head on my chest, throwing her top leg over mine. She starts to draw circles on my chest with her left index finger, both of us lying here silent and just enjoying the company of each other. I have to remember to check the time, because everyone will be at Mims and Pops' house for her surprise party soon. I told her it was a birthday bash with just my parents and grandparents, but everyone will be here.

My brothers and the girls didn't really leave to go back to school earlier, but I didn't want Kinzleigh to suspect anything when they have a drive. They are sacrificing sleep and being tired in their first classes of the day tomorrow so they can be here for the surprise before they go. It's sort of our engagement party as well. Everyone was in on the surprise except her. I'm dying to see the look on her face.

Then, if it's not too late, I'm going to bring her back to our blanket I've made under the tree for a little while, just the two of us, since we're pressed for time now. It will be dark by then and the white lights should light up the pond enough to see. This is her day and I want her to remember it forever.

Chill bumps start to sprout beneath my fingers as I rub up and down her arm. "Breyson . . ."

She pulls me from my thoughts. "What, beautiful?"

"What made you pick this ring?"

I look over at her and she is still tracing circles on my chest, staring at the diamond on her finger. That's a weird question. "It just stuck out. Why? Do you not like it?"

The air is starting to turn cold. She's cold. I can tell from her shaking. I reach underneath us and pull the comforter down, lifting us until I can pull it over us. She sits up, covering herself with the blanket, but looks back at me.

"It's perfect. Truth. In fact, it's so perfect that two dreams I've had I was wearing this exact ring. I don't remember telling you about them. That's why I'm asking . . ."

Her cheeks are flushed as if she's in a panic. She looks at the ring and back at me. "Tell me I told you about them and I just don't remember. There is no way you picked out the exact ring. It's just not possible."

Maybe she's not shaking from the temperature. Her chest rising and falling at a rapid rate says she's breathing in short, quick bursts. I stare at her, blinking, now more confused than ever. I'm sure my face shows it. I'm lying with one arm propping up my head and I take her hand with the other. "Come lay back down. Why are you panicking? Talk to me."

"Just tell me you knew somehow . . ."

I sit up. "Knew about what? Kinzleigh, what's wrong? What are you talking about? I don't know anything about a dream. Lay back down and we'll talk."

She's back to crying. Why the hell is she crying? I'm starting to worry. I was not anticipating this emotion today. I am about to say something, but then she grabs me by the face and pulls me into a kiss so hard we almost smack noses. Thankfully, my reflexes were faster.

She's already getting me aroused again. I've always been like that with Kinzleigh. It doesn't matter that we just had sex. She can kiss me once and I'm ready to go.

She throws one leg over me, now straddling me. I can already tell she's ready to go as her wet pussy touches my now fully erect cock. She is acting as if she's sexually starved, taking control, and lowering herself on me completely.

A throaty groan is the effect of the way my hormones are raging. I'm so horny right now I can't breathe, but I need to know more. "Kin—fuck," I breathe, forgetting everything, including my own name as she bounces up and down on my dick, squeezing each time she comes up.

Fuck it.

I grab her ass in each hand, squeezing. She pushes my chest as hard as she can, pressing me flat against the mattress. Where is this coming from? This is hot as fuck. All I know is I like it, a lot.

She interlaces each hand with mine, holding them down above my head.

Leaning forward slightly, she begins to ride me, rocking back and forth. She closes her eyes as she uses my body for her benefit. I swear on my life a minute of hitting against that spot deep in her pussy and she's coming on top of me. It's the most amazing thing I've ever seen.

I lay here and watch her ride out her orgasm, about to blow my load once again. She opens her eyes as she sits straight up, placing my hands on her breasts. She gives me a mischievous grin. "It's my turn to make you come."

Shit . . .

I watch her push up and down on my dick, slowly at first, but I can tell shit is about to get real, and I'm so fucking ready.

She begins to increase speed. I watch her as she leans back, grabbing the top of my legs for leverage, also creating an amazing view.

She rolls her hips as she rides me, fast and hard. I squeeze her nipples between my thumb and index fingers, causing her to clamp down on me. "I'm not going to last if you keep doing that," I say, my voice deepening.

"That's what I'm counting on," she breathes, but never lets up. She clamps down again as she sits down all the way and I'm done for. It feels too good. Everything stacks up in my mind, from the angle and what it feels like inside, to the look on her face, and her body from this view.

I grab her hips in my hands and hold her down, her skin flush with mine as I come inside her for the second time within thirty minutes. I'm fighting to catch my breath and I didn't even do anything to exert myself physically.

With a smile on her face she tries to get off, but I hold her still. "You're going to take it all, beautiful."

She relaxes and presses her chest to mine as she trails kisses along my shoulder. "Kinzleigh . . ."

"Hmmmm?"

"Where the fuck have you been hiding that?"

"It's you. You make me crazy that way. I can never get enough no matter how many times I get you . . . and then, when I find out just how intimately you know me inside, how connected and in tune to each other we really are, it sets off triggers and I transform into this needy, completely mad woman," she says, still kissing all over my body as if she's still not finished having her way with me.

At this rate we will be alternating between making love and fucking all night. It actually sounds like the best plan, but I know everyone is waiting. I'm still curious about these dreams, but it'll have to wait until later when we come back to our tree.

I grab her hair in my fist, pulling it back so that I can see her face. I place my index finger over her pouty bottom lip, drawing down her chin and the front of her neck. I place a single kiss in the dip where her neck and collarbones meet. "As much as I would love to stay here all night, my plans have only begun. Your birthday isn't over yet. I have something else to show you, then we will come back here to wind down and pick up where we left off before the night is over."

"There's more?" She moans, lightly swaying with me still inside her. "You've done too much. I don't deserve all of this."

I've created a monster, a really hot one. I'm still semi-erect from before. If she gets me ready again, we will never leave. I pick her up, removing myself from her, and swiftly change positions, laying her on her back with me on top of her.

She gives me a pouty face. "Can't we just stay here and get lost in each other? That's what I want for my birthday. Please . . ."

That is the one face that could get her out of murder and she knows it. Under ordinary circumstances I'd give in, but it's not just about us. There are several people giving up other things to be a part of this. I smirk. "Not a chance. As tempting as that is, beautiful, I won't let you sway my plans, not today. Try again tomorrow," I say, and nip her bottom lip."

I get off the bed in search of my clothes. She props up on her elbows, watching me. "It's your fault, you know."

My face is plastered with a cocky grin. "Why's that?"

"If you want me to be able to function in everyday society you really shouldn't look so sexy. Don't blame me if I have to have my fix several times throughout the day when you're the one that gave me the drug that hooked me. Just saying . . ."

"Come," I state.

"You have to be touching me to do that."

I laugh and point to the space in front of me. "Here."

She bites her bottom lip and pushes off the bed, walking toward me. "Just so we're clear, as long as I'm your only dealer I will feed your addiction anytime you start to crave, because it feeds mine too."

I kiss her, wanting more, but deny myself. "Get dressed. It's your birthday and we have so much more to do."

I pull my shirt over my head, now fully dressed, and start blowing out the candles spread throughout the house while she dresses. We're finally getting somewhere. I don't need to burn it down in my first attempt at real—my balls are lost—mushy romance. I won't lie, being a guy, I had to dig deep for this, but the look on her face makes it completely worth it. Guys aren't wired to naturally come up with all of this romantic shit. It takes work.

I finish blowing out the candles as she is pulling her boots on her feet. I love seeing her in a pair of cowgirl boots. I smile and hold out my hand for her to take mine. "Come on, birthday girl. Mims and Pops are probably waiting."

FIFTEEN

Kinzleigh

I feel like I went to sleep and woke up in the middle of a fairytale. I look around at everything he's done as he leads me out of the house, our house. The house, our tree, and the solitude of it being in the middle of nature with nothing or no one to bother you makes it as if I'm living a dream and he really is my real-life prince.

The lights are making everything look magical as the darkness takes over. The white twinkling lights against the onyx backdrop is beautiful. "I still can't believe you did all of this," I say as we walk toward the horses standing close to the lights eating grass. "This is by far the best birthday a girl could ever have, even in her dreams."

He places his arm around me, pulling me to his side. He kisses my temple. "That makes me happy, baby. There is nothing I wouldn't do for you. Are you hungry?"

"I could eat," I say. We walk up to Hendrix and Divinity and part ways.

"Stay close to me, okay?"

He should know better. It's been forever since we've ridden together. I won't let his protectiveness stop me from riding uninhibited. I want to feel the wind in my hair. "Sure."

"Kinzleigh . . . promise me."

Is he for real right now? I sneak my left hand behind my back and cross my fingers. I know Breyson, and he will make me ride with him if I don't. Men . . . you can't live with them and you can't live without them. Holding up my right hand, I say, "Scouts honor."

He's going to be pissed when he finds out, but if he hasn't figured out my loophole by now that's not my problem. My promise is void; I don't care how elementary and childish it is. "Good."

I turn, placing my hands on the horn and the back of the saddle, and then insert my left foot in the stirrup. I pull myself up and throw my leg over, adjusting myself in the saddle. Breyson looks at me as if he can tell I'm up to something, but he doesn't say anything.

Once he mounts Hendrix, he pulls on the reigns for him to turn toward the wooded path in the opposite direction. I do the same and ride up beside him. We both ride together at a walk. I can't stand it anymore. Divinity is faster than Hendrix and I miss our races horseback.

I pat Divinity above her front leg on the side he can't see. A huge grin is spreading across my face as the adrenaline begins pumping through my body with each beat of my heart. "Race you to the barn!" I shout, challenging him, and then heel Divinity to take off.

"Kinzleigh, dammit." I can hear him commanding Hendrix behind me. I bend forward, letting the wind roll off my back.

It's hard to see in front of me, but I can see the outline of the trees and hear her hoofs trampling against the ground. I can hear Hendrix, but it's muted, so I must be a good stretch ahead. There is no other feeling like this. It releases every amount of stress that you have stored.

I can see the light of the barn as she comes into the pasture. I peek behind me and no longer see Breyson. I'm going to win. My heart is beating so fast it's hard to breathe slow and steady. The constant high-speed keeps my adrenaline spiking every time I think it's starting to decrease.

I tighten my hold on the reigns as the front of the barn gets close and I dig my boots into the stirrups, preparing for an abrupt halt. I pull back on the reigns and she stops. I still don't hear Breyson. I dismount Divinity as quickly as I can and run her to her stall, leading her inside. I'll unsaddle her later.

Instead of going back out the front I decide to go out the back of the barn to miss Breyson. "Bye girl. I'll be back in a little while."

I run out the back and round the barn, passing between the barn and the building that stores the tractors and equipment. There is no light, but I know that it's an open space. I look from side to side but keep running.

In a split second I'm caught off guard with something grabbing me from behind, causing me to scream. A hand goes over my mouth, hushing me. I can't see anything from the lack of light. I get shoved front first against the side of the barn and the furious voice starts whispering next to my ear. "You want adrenaline, baby?"

His voice calms me, but then I hear a zipper, and my nerves start going wild. I can hear the anger and worry in his voice. "You want to find out what that does to me? Spread your legs and put your palms on the wall."

I do as he says. Normally, I would argue, and he would let me, but he has his boundaries. That boundary is my safety or what's best for me, and I just crossed it. I knew what I was doing, and I knew he would be mad.

He's been working on this ranch since he was a kid. He's told me some scary stories of the woods. I am just hardheaded and chose to ignore them. Instead of causing a fight he's going to fuck me selfishly so he can touch me, but still show me he's angry. I know him well enough to know what's coming.

He pulls my dress up and slides my panties down to my thighs. His voice is seething. He doesn't like riding at night because of animals in the woods that can easily spook the horses. Being so far in the country and having so much open land brings them out, especially with cattle.

He runs his finger through my folds, causing me to close my eyes. I try to turn my head, but he keeps it still. He's stern, but not hurting me. "First, I lose sight of you and every possible scenario plays in my head. Everything is black around me and I'm worried if you're okay. There are no rules in the woods, Kinzleigh. Animals don't have emotions. They don't have guilt after a kill. Everything is instinct. When they get hungry, they eat. They were created to prey."

He still has one hand over my mouth. He cups his hand over my mound with the other, pulling me back to give him better access. I know what he's getting ready to do, and I want him to.

He releases his hold on me down below and aligns himself at my entrance. He rubs his head in circles, lubricating it. "Do you not remember how easy it is to be taken from me? One mishap and everything between us vanishes. You want me to play out a scenario?"

I nod, knowing that's what he wants. "Divinity steps in a deep hole and goes down, pulling you down with her. She loses balance on the way down and falls on her side," he says, as he slams into me as hard as he can. "Breaking your leg under her weight in the process."

I won't lie, it hurt, but this is a pain I want. Breyson has always been big for me and today is the first day we've had sex since February. My body will have to readjust and he knows it. This is a pain I need, because it's a pain inflicted *by* him and not *because* of him.

He doesn't give my body time to welcome the invasion before he starts thrusting in and out, hard. "A bobcat is ready to eat and hears you scream in distress, drawing his attention."

He finally releases my mouth, only to place both hands on my hips for more control on my body. He lifts me slightly, making his head hit deeper and harder against my walls. I bite my tongue to avoid whining. "You're unarmed, scared, and now slow because of an injury, giving him an advantage." His voice is uneven from the variations of speaking and breathing while slamming inside of me.

With each addition to the story his thrusts become rougher and harder, letting his emotions steer him. "You're the smaller of the two, so he goes after you first, thinking it'll be an easy kill, and he's successful, because you have no way to protect yourself. You're the weaker one. He was built to kill and you weren't."

He slows his pace a little. "I will always have your best interests at heart, baby, but I need you to listen and trust me, because there are times when I know more than you." He stills, emptying himself inside me. I can feel the light pulsations inside.

He moves one hand up my body, underneath my dress, stopping on my breast and pulling me back against him. His lips are right outside my ear. "Don't do that to me again, Kinzleigh. Never leave me deaf and blind when it comes to you, because in one split second . . ." He pulls out of me, leaving me to deal with his sudden absence. "You're gone. Then Bryce and I are left without you. It may never happen, but we both know how things can turn bad quickly. I can't live without you again. Prevention is better than consequence."

He pulls my panties up my legs and lowers my dress back in place. I turn around and he kisses me briefly. "Do you understand now?"

I nod. It's dark, but when I really look at him, I can still make out the features on his face. "I'm sorry. I didn't think about anything like that."

"You never do. You do things on a whim, and although sometimes it makes me crazy, I love that about you, which is why I told you." He smiles. I can see his white teeth.

"How did you get ahead of me?" Now that I'm able to stop and think I'm curious. I would have seen him if he had passed me.

He places his hands on my cheeks. "First rule when trying to be sly: never show your hand. I can read you better than you can read yourself. Plus, you can't outsmart the player that made the rules. I know this land like the back of my hand. There are shortcuts everywhere."

"You knew? Why didn't you say anything?"

"Because I know now that life is too short to bitch and pick fights over petty things. You were stubborn when I met you and you'll be stubborn until the day you die. I will never try to change anything about you. Together, all of your quirks and qualities made me fall in love with you. My job as your man, in protecting you, will be to discretely outsmart you," he says with a cocky grin.

I can't help it. I laugh. Everyone knows I'm stubborn, including myself. If I didn't see the humor in the situation we would constantly fight. I'm a strong-willed woman. It takes a certain type of man to be able to handle me. The best part of Breyson is that he's hard when he needs to be hard and soft otherwise—never an asshole. He can love me for who I am but put his foot down when I'm taking things too far. He completes me. His qualities and his heart make him irreplaceable. I will never again let him go.

He releases me and pulls up his pants, fastening them. That is one sexy view. He fixes his clothes and releases a low laugh. "Seriously, they are going to think we got mauled by a bear or something. Let's go, beautiful. The boys have to catch up for a while, because I'm not even close to being done with you."

I take his arm in mine and walk beside him this time. Sometimes I just have to be reminded that he's my partner, and that means my place is beside him, not in front of or behind.

SIXTEEN

Kinzleigh

We walk through the yard from the barn to the house. The lights are visible through the windows, but everything seems quiet. I have no idea what time it is. I'm starting to feel guilty for leaving Bryce so long.

Breyson takes my left hand in his right, playing with the ring that now takes up occupancy there. "Mims, we're back," he shouts, as if someone could really hear him. We're outside. Is he scared we're going to sneak up on them and scare them?

We climb up the steps to the deck that is built onto the back patio. He places his hand on the doorknob and looks at me. "Always you and me?"

"Forever," I say.

He opens the door and leads me through the kitchen toward the stairs of the finished basement. I thought he said we were eating. Why is he going to the basement? The lights don't even appear to be on.

He starts down the stairs and I pull on his hand to question him. He looks me in the eyes and says two words that hold so much power. "Trust me."

I nod and descend the stairs with him. We reach the door and he opens it with his free hand. I can't see a thing. "Flip the light switch, baby. It's on your side."

I feel up the wall until I reach the switch and flip it up. The lights come on and voices all shout in unison. "Surprise!"

Startled, I almost jump out of my skin as confetti goes flying around the room. My hand goes over my mouth as I take in the room full of people. Everyone we know is standing is here. Pink and black balloons are scattered throughout the room, along with presents and I even spot a cake.

I look at Breyson with tears in my eyes. "You did this all for me?"

Our eyes lock. "Happy birthday, baby. Not only is it your birthday party, but also our engagement party, because . . ." He raises our linked hands in the air showing off my ring, and then increases the loudness of his voice. "She said yes!"

Everyone around the room starts clapping and shouting. I scan them briefly, but the one I can't take my eyes off of is Breyson. He looks so happy and is grinning from ear to ear. It squeezes my heart and makes it warm to see him like this, especially over something as simple as me.

"My little sister is getting married, huh?" A voice I haven't heard in so long pulls me out of my love-struck state.

I turn in the direction of the voice. Konnor is standing a few feet in front of me. He looks different, but the same. He looks more like he was pulled out of a rock band than a top ranked football team. "Konnor . . ." I whisper. "You came."

He smiles and opens his arms. "I wouldn't miss this for the world."

I look at Breyson and he releases my hand, signaling for me to go to him. Without another thought I take off in a sprint. Once I reach him I jump into his arms, clenching my arms tight around his neck. He twirls me around in his hold, squeezing me just as tight in return.

Konnor never came to California the entire time I was there. I don't think he could. Too much happened to him there. I haven't seen him since before I left with Preston. To be honest, I'm not sure what he's been up to. Since the situation with Presley happened, he's been distant, always coming up with an excuse as to why he can't come home for this and that, or that he's busy with school and football.

I feel like two very important people to me are hurting when they don't have to be. I wish for once Konnor could put the situation with Sophia behind him, because he's missing out on something, or someone perhaps, that I know he wants. If I wasn't so happy and surprised to see him here, I would question him, but his presence is the most important thing to me right now.

Konnor and I have always been close, but one thing I've learned as I age is that people have to sort out their own problems. Getting involved in someone else's affairs drives them further away and it usually doesn't change the outcome. "I've missed you. Please don't stay away from me for so long again."

"I know, baby girl. I've just been sorting my shit. I'm sorry. You'll always be my favorite girl though."

In our little reunion I've forgotten that we're in the middle of a crowd of people. "How long are you staying?" I ask as he sets me down.

He looks at me. "Tomorrow night I go back, after I spend the day with you. Anything you want to do, name it, and it's yours."

It's not the answer I wanted, but I'll take it. I notice some new tattoos that weren't present the last time I saw him. He's still standing close enough no one else can hear. "About the ink . . . I get it. I didn't before, but I do now."

His eyes change for a moment. I can see the hurt in them, but then he clears it, covering it with a smirk. "You got another piece, didn't you?"

I nod, glancing at Breyson from the corner of my eye. "It's fairly large," I state.

"Show me tomorrow?"

"Of course."

Bryce starts crying. Believe it or not I've missed his cry in the short time I've been gone. It reminds me of the amazing little person that I was given. "There's someone I want you to meet," I say, and grab his hand, pulling him toward the cry.

"We'll be right back," I turn and shout to Breyson, who is now talking to Braxton. I pull Konnor through the crowd, stopping when someone congratulates me or tells me happy birthday. I don't want to ignore everyone, but it's been too long since I've seen my only brother. Besides, everyone here knows each other, so they are already mingling.

The basement is completely finished and made as a guest space. There is a large open area filled with a sectional and wall-mounted television, and a small kitchen. In the back there is a short hall that leads to a full bathroom and a bedroom big enough for furniture and walking space.

I open the bedroom door and Bryce is in his Pack n' Play in the corner, closest to the door. I turn on the light and walk over to him. "Hey, buddy. Mommy is here."

I pick up his pacifier lying beside him and put it in his mouth before picking him up. Unable to help it, I kiss his chubby little cheek, holding my beautiful bundle in my arms. "There's someone I want you to meet," I whisper against his small face.

When I turn around Konnor is standing against the doorframe with his arms crossed over his chest and his eyes wide. He looks terrified, and here I thought I was the one scared of babies. It makes me smile seeing the one that's always had it together a little frayed. "You want to hold him?"

He tenses a little. "Uh . . . that's okay. I can just look."

"Konnor, it's okay. You're not going to hurt him. They are not as fragile as they seem. You can sit if it makes you feel better."

He continues looking at me and runs his hand over his black hair as if he's thinking. He finally walks into the room and takes a seat on the edge of the bed. "Okay, bring me my nephew."

My smile broadens. I walk close enough that I can lay Bryce in his arms. Konnor looks stiff. "Just relax. He can sense when you're uncomfortable."

"Well he would be a smart kid, because I am uncomfortable. My experience with little people is limited." I laugh. I've missed him more than I realized.

I take a seat beside him, rubbing Bryce's head. "The only thing you really have to remember is to support his head and his bottom in unison since he doesn't have that kind of control yet. The rest you learn with time."

"Is it weird?" he asks.

"Is what weird?"

"Being a mom, getting married, and us being grown. We're not kids anymore."

He looks up at me. "I know I haven't been around much, but I'll try harder. I've just been dealing with a lot of shit. I'm glad things are working out for you, though. I was worried about you, but you finally look happy. Preston is my best friend and I hate to see him hurt, but Breyson is a good guy; better than I thought. I guess the heart has a funny way of getting what it wants."

I have a feeling that last sentence doesn't only apply to me. "What happened between you and Presley?"

I notice his jaw steel at the sound of her name. I told myself I wasn't going to ask, but we've always been straightforward with each other. There is no reason to change now. "What are you talking about?"

"I know you slept with her, Konnor. Don't lie to me; you never have."

"Did she tell you that?"

"No." My face flushes remembering last Christmas morning. "I accidentally walked in on the aftermath and possibly the beginning of round two.”

I hang my head in shame and close my eyes. No matter who I’m telling, it never gets any less embarrassing. I saw more of my brother that morning than I ever wanted to see.

I peek through one eye and he is silently laughing. In fact, it starts to become verbal the longer I sit here. “What’s so funny?”

“I’m visualizing how horrified you must have looked. You were a prude when it came to anything sexual back then, no offense. I’ve got to give credit to Breyson. I don’t know how the hell he broke your shell when so many failed, but I’m glad he did.” He is totally teasing me. What an ass.

My mouth is hanging to the floor it feels like. I hit him on the back of the head. “Ouch. What was that for?”

“That’s what you get. I was holding out for the best and I’m so glad I did. It was totally worth it.” His mouth turns into one of disgust. Maybe next time he won’t mock me and I won’t have to resort to physical violence and implanting pictures in his mind of his sister that he doesn’t want.

“On a serious note, though, what happened with you and Presley?”

“It should have never happened. It was a mistake.”

“Konnor, do you really expect me to believe that?”

“We both know it shouldn’t have happened. It’s fine. Just let it go.”

I narrow my eyes at him. I’m getting angry. “Really? Because it sure didn’t look like ‘it’s fine’ when I saw her last. She isn’t the same. She was my best friend and now she’s distant. Why is that, Konnor?”

He sighs and looks down at Bryce. “Kinzleigh, Presley deserves better than me. She deserves a guy that hasn’t been tainted. Sophia ruined me. I will never love a girl again. I had to force Presley to see it, so that I could protect her . . . from me.”

“What did you do?” I whisper. “Please, Konnor, tell me you didn’t hurt her.”

“All you need to know is that I did what was best for her by making her see the asshole that I really am. I’m not the guy she thinks she has a crush on anymore. Leave it alone, Kinzleigh. As much as I love you, this is one situation you don’t need to stick your nose in.”

My heart is aching. The look on her face that day in my room, her moving to Miami, and her not being here for my birthday which is something she’s never missed, it’s all building and killing me. She’s my best friend. What has he done? The worst part is that I can tell he wants her. One mention of her name and it takes all he has to keep everything hidden, but the eyes don't lie.

I want to kick and scream, to demand for him to tell me what he did, but for some strange reason I think I already know. If I'm right, that is the ultimate betrayal, the one thing you can't undo. I think that is what he's counting on . . .

A knock sounds at the door and it opens. Breyson peeps inside. "Baby, you're missing your own party."

He looks between Konnor and me. "Is everything okay?"

As much as I love my brother, I can't be around him right now. I know that he was hurt, but sometimes that's part of life. We all get hurt at one point or another. I even get living lost for a little while, and doing things you wouldn't normally do, but there is no excuse for intentionally hurting people that you have loved and cared about your entire life.

In life we have a choice. We can choose to be like the haters or to go against them. He's letting the people like Sophia win by becoming just like her. Presley didn't do anything wrong besides loving a boy that is trying to get revenge on love, and all because he got his heart ripped out. The problem is that love is the most powerful emotion there is; it's pure. Revenge is a quality of the weak and it'll never win.

I stand and take Bryce out of his arms. "Yeah, everything is okay." I never take my eyes off of Konnor. "I'll always love you, Konnor, but I don't approve of the person that you're becoming. I really hope you get your shit together before it's too late. I miss the passionate person that you were. Someone can only steal from you if you let *her*. Maybe you should think about that."

I turn and walk toward Breyson, passing him. I can hear him say something to Konnor, but I don't stick around to listen. Now, more so than ever, I'm worried about Presley . . .

Breyson lifts me by the waist, putting me on Divinity. He mounts her and sits in the saddle behind me, pulling me to sit halfway on the saddle and halfway on his lap. She's the bigger of the two horses, so he chose to ride her.

The party was a success. This is by far the best birthday a girl could wish for. What could be better than having the boy you're hopelessly in love with ask you to ride into forever with him, a healthy baby boy, a path laid out for success, and family by your side? Not. A. Damn. Thing.

Not long after our talk Konnor said he needed to be alone for a while and that he would see me tomorrow, kissed me on the cheek, and left. I don't even know where to start with him. I never would have foreseen him becoming this person. He's always been the one with a solid head on his shoulders, and not to mention the biggest heart.

"What's bothering you, beautiful?"

I cannot let him ruin my perfect day. I will not. Like he said, we're grown. He has to fight his own battles just like I did. I didn't like anyone trying to tell me how to live. He'll either fly or he'll fall on his face. The choice has to be left to him.

I lay my head back against Breyson's shoulder, holding the flashlight until we make it back to our tree for a little while to cap the night off. Bryce is sleeping soundly back at Mims'. There wasn't a chance Breyson was letting us ride separately after earlier. That's okay with me. This is so much better.

Divinity begins walking through the pasture, toward the path that runs through the wooded area. "Nothing that needs to be dealt with today," I say.

"Did you enjoy your birthday?"

"It was epic."

"Good."

"No, really. It was amazing. Thank you for today. I've lived and breathed sadness for so long. I needed a day like today. I'm glad we got a second chance at this. No allotment of time with you will ever be enough, but I'll settle for a lifetime."

He has his arms around me, securing me from falling, and holding onto the reigns. "You know, every time that I think I can't love you any more, I do. It's as if my heart is on a tangent of proving that I am wrong over and over again. I'll never grow tired of hearing how you feel, Kinzleigh. Promise me you'll never stop. After spending half a year apart, I need to hear it every day."

"I promise. With all that I am. You'll always know how I feel about you, because now I know how precious time is. If anything were to ever happen to me, I don't want you to question how I felt about you."

He remains silent for a moment as we ride, now through the thick stretch of pines. "I won't. If you go, I go. There are no other options."

We ride the rest of the way in silence, pondering anything and everything.

Sometimes I find myself wondering what he's thinking, because I'm in awe of him.

We finally make it through the clearing to our tree. The stars are burning bright, mapped out across the sky. Breyson gets off first and helps me down. Wrapping his arm around me, he leads me to the blanket he has made. He lays down, patting the blanket for me to join him, so I do.

The leaves of the tree are spaced enough that you can look at the sky and enjoy it. He pulls me closer into his arms. "You know what this reminds me of?" I ask.

"That night at my house after the game," he states.

"Yeah. It seems so long ago."

"But it also feels like yesterday."

I have to agree with him there. It's strange how that works. We lay here, nestled in each other's arms, and enjoying the cool wind blowing across our faces. I had to wear a hoodie with the cooler weather tonight.

I often find myself wondering meaningless things, things that have no justification for being answered, but merely a result of the brain being at a peaceful standstill. Like right now, as I look at each twinkling star just like I have so many nights before. Does each one serve a purpose? Why is each new star created? Could it be that each one represents a person; there to guide its assigned member to the places in life they're destined to be? I know each person has a path, but what happens when human nature detours off the predetermined path? Is there some kind of invisible force, like a star, that bumps us back onto the right path? Surely, God put them there for something other than to glimmer in the night.

Breyson begins playing with my ring by twirling it back and forth on my finger, now pulling me out of my thoughts. "Will you tell me about the dreams? I want to know."

Honestly, I had forgotten about that until now. How do I really explain them? When I look back on them, they seem crazy, but crazier things have happened. Can paranormal circumstances really exist?

"Do you remember everything about that week you spent in California?"

"Yes. I'll never forget it . . ."

"Well, the night that me and Presley came over to watch movies, you know, when you and I took a dip in the pool . . ." I squeeze my legs together as those visions become active in my mind. "That was also the first night Preston kind of hit on me . . ."

I wait, not sure if I should have left that small piece of information out.

He tightens his hold around me, pressing me closer to his side. "When you were wearing my clothes?"

"Yes," I say, treading lightly.

"Did he kiss you?"

I think on that topic. Did he kiss me? No, he didn't, not that night anyway. Then, it dawns on me . . . I did let him kiss me on the yacht. Does that count? I'm starting to slightly panic. "When?" My voice is a whisper, now scared to tell him.

As if he can sense my mood change, he rolls over on top of me, holding his weight above me. "I was referring to that night specifically, but now I'm curious to any of that week."

I can see his eyes deepen under the white lights. They do so when his emotions start to spike, such as when he's angry or upset. "Only the day of the pool party after the whole Lexi thing happened."

He doesn't say anything. He just lies above me, holding my attention. I'm starting to worry. Maybe I should have mentioned this earlier. I never thought it was relevant, to be honest. I had actually forgotten about it. That is what happens in the presence of Breyson. I forget all other things.

The silence is getting to me. "Breyson, I'm sorry. We weren't like we are now. Besides, it really wasn't like you think."

"I just want to know one thing. I'm not going to live in the past. We will never move on if I do. I've accepted that Preston will always be a part of our lives as much as I don't like certain aspects. I can't be mad anyway. I did allow Lexi to kiss me after that, but only to embarrass her. I didn't let her enter my mouth. It wasn't a proud moment, but I was pissed off. You had just stormed out of my life and I knew it was a significant loss then even though I had just met you."

"What do you want to know?"

"Was there ever a point when you wanted him more than you wanted me? I want honesty, no matter what the answer is."

Is he serious? I thought that was completely clear. It hurts me to know that question would even cross his mind. "Never," I say with everything in me. "There was never one single second that I wanted anyone more than you, nor was there a moment when I missed you less than the one before. Even when you were gone you were still here with me."

He rubs the back of his hand over my cheek and along my lips, becoming familiar with the softness. "I know what you mean."

He presses his lips to me so soft that I can barely tell they're against mine. He positions on his forearms and knees so that he can continue to look into my eyes. "Now, I want to know about those dreams."

My insides become vapor at the sound of his voice. When you feel this strongly for someone there is no going back. "That night I stayed with Presley after the pool house I had the first one."

I close my eyes so that I can properly describe it. Breyson has a way of making me forget what I was thinking or what I wanted to say just by looking into his eyes. He controls me in a way that I want to be controlled. "We were standing on a beach; just the two of us. I remember it was so vivid that it felt real. I could even tell that it was warm out, but not too hot, and the breeze was blowing. The water was crystal clear, bearing all its secrets for the viewer."

"What were we doing?"

"First, we were just standing in the bright white sand at the shoreline. I was wearing a white swimsuit. You came up behind me and wrapped your arms around me. We were wearing wedding bands." My voice lowers. "Mine was the exact ring I'm wearing now. Every detail is the same. You picked me up and when you turned around is when I noticed a white canopy bed in the sand. The linens were white and sheer, blowing in the breeze. You carried me over and laid me down, then took your shorts off and got in the bed. I remember you slowly removed my swimsuit. The detail was incredible. It was almost as if I could actually feel it, like I was really there. Right before you pushed inside me, I called you my husband."

I open my eyes and he is looking directly into mine. "That's why I went running. I panicked. I had just met you, only kissed you a couple of times, and there I was having dreams about a honeymoon. It freaked me out. Then, as if it wasn't weird enough, you pulled up."

A grin starts turning up on his face. "You were dreaming about me naked, huh? And having sexy dreams about me . . . Interesting."

I playfully slap him on the shoulder. "This is not the time to make jokes. It was weird, right? I mean, you didn't do anything like that . . ."

He bites his bottom lip, trying to keep his smile from spreading.

Guilty, guilty, guilty!

"Did you?"

"Something . . . like that."

Oh, no he's not. He is not getting out of this. One embarrassing story for another. "Tell me."

He slides his hand under my back and rotates us until I'm straddling him. He runs his hands down my body, stopping on my butt. I can feel him hardening underneath me. It's starting to look like we are going to be at this all night. I'm not complaining. I never want to go another day without him. When he makes love to me it fills a physical void. When we got back together the emotional one became permanently fixed.

"Do you really want to know?"

"Yes."

"The day I met you on the beach . . ."

I can feel his erection getting more prominent as he goes on.

"I sort of relieved myself in Ryland's shower that evening thinking of you. You had my hormones going crazy. Let's just say it had been a really long time since I had done that."

What do I do? I burst out laughing. I'm talking can hardly breathe laughing so hard. Why? Well, the irony really. Back then I probably would have turned into a tomato had I known that information, but now, it's so flattering coming from a guy as sexy as Breyson. I'm really not exaggerating. He's that hot.

I make a line down the center of my face with my hands in a praying position. "You think that's funny, huh?"

"I'm. Sorry. I . . ."

Still laughing, he bucks upward, pressing his hardness into me.

All laughter halts.

With me only wearing a dress I can feel it even more than if I were wearing jeans. Shamelessly, I begin rubbing against it. "You want it?"

Oh, damn. I love when he talks to me like that. Maybe it has something to do with his accent and his deep voice combined, but it does crazy things to me.

"Yes."

"Tell me about the second dream first."

"Can it wait until later?"

"No."

Talk about a sexy time mood kill. I look down at him from the aroused state I was quickly climbing to. I huff. Yes, like a child not getting her way. "Fine."

"I think I need to know more than I want to."

Well, when you put it that way . . .

"It was when you were gone. That day was one of my worst days. I did some things I'm not proud of, because I was pregnant, and I knew it."

The air chills talking about. It takes me back to a dark time in my life. "Like what?"

I'm staring straight ahead in the dark. "Well, I had been crying all day. I could barely eat or function. It was the day of your memorial service. I can't explain it. I felt you there. You were speaking to me, telling me to wait for you. I was breaking down mentally. I told you I was pregnant that day, standing at your headstone. I even buried an ultrasound photo. I came home and found your shirt peeking out from under my bed."

It always hurts me to remember those days, even with him here beneath me. I was living in a world void of color. It takes no effort to shed a tear going back to that time in my life. "I remember my clothes feeling like they were suffocating me. I stripped down into nothing and put your shirt on. I got in bed and let every memory of you flood through me. I cried until I fell asleep. I woke up in the middle of the night and had to leave. I couldn't bear to be in there anymore, so I snuck out."

I feel him tighten his hold on my hips. "I got in my car and just drove. I ended up at one of the tattoo shops close to the university. That's when I met Riggan."

"Who's Riggan?"

His voice spiked. Jealousy.

"He's the one that did my tattoo. He could tell when I told him what I wanted that I was going through something. He also could tell because he had gone through it too, I found out later. We had that in common. He gave me a shot of liquor. I didn't tell him I was pregnant. It didn't matter to me then. The pain and you mattered more. Riggan is also the one that saved me from the car; the reason Bryce and I are both here. I was with him that night, but that's a story for another day."

I look down. Breyson looks like he's slightly zoned. "Anyway, after I got the tattoo I went to your house. Your mom told me I could stay anytime I wanted. I remembered the window that stayed unlocked, so I snuck in. I walked into your room and found that photo on your nightstand of us. I put on your clothes and then laid with that photo in my arms until I fell asleep. That's when the dream came. We were on that same beach, but this time it was different . . ."

I watch him swallow; his Adam's apple bobs up and down. "This time I started out . . . alone. I thought it was just a cruel remake of the first dream, because I was in the same swimsuit, but my tattoo was present, my new one. You were walking down the stretch of beach. All I could think was there you were, just as real as you could ever be. You stopped and held out your arms. I took off running as fast as I could and jumped in your arms. You felt just as real as you looked."

My tears are streaming now, present whether I want them there or not. "Those damn wedding bands were present again. You walked me out into the water and made love to me." I close my eyes. "It felt so real. It was the realist thing in my life then. The weird thing about it though was that you kept saying things to me in Spanish. I couldn't figure it out. Then, you walked away from me. You left me there, in the shallow of that water, alone. You walked further into the ocean and vanished before my eyes. I screamed and ran after you, but you were gone. I remember waking up to Briar holding me. I kept telling him I needed to know what you said in Spanish, because it had to be some kind of clue, but I think everyone thought I was crazy."

Breyson looks like he's seen a ghost. He finally begins to blink when I don't say anything else. He sits up quickly, grabbing my face in his hands. "I was in Spain. That's why it was Spanish, baby. I was in Spain. Oh my God, baby, I was in Spain." He keeps repeating it to himself over and over.

Breyson has never told me anything about his time away. He said he was still trying to process everything and then with trying to get me back he just wanted to savor the good for a while before he started digging back into the dark places of his mind, but that he promised when he could he would tell me. I want to know more, but I'm okay with waiting.

I lived in darkness long enough that we can just resurface a few at a time. I would rather spend the majority of our days living in the good. I can't explain some of the things that have happened in our lives, but it's time to lay the past to rest.

He removes my hoodie and pulls my dress up, removing it too. "I need you, beautiful. Right now, all I need is you."

He places his lips to mine. What Breyson wants Breyson will get. Now I live to please him. That's what you do when you love someone. You do everything you can to make their wishes come true . . . and so I will, underneath our lit tree with the company of the moon and stars.

SEVENTEEN

Kinzleigh

A knock sounds at the door, waking me. "Go away," I mumble. Breyson and I stayed out at our tree late, rotating between talking and making love until the wee hours of the morning. I'm so tired that when Bryce woke up to eat, I picked him up, gave him what he wanted, and got back in bed with him. I figured he would fall asleep at some point.

The knock sounds again. I sit up, trying to focus my eyes. Breyson has already left for the day. Bryce is still sleeping. I place pillows around him as a precaution and get out of bed. There goes that knocking again. "I'm coming, I'm coming." I grumble as I walk down the hall.

I get to the door and open it. A hand holding a coffee shop cup comes toward me. "I brought a peace offering."

It's kind of hard to stay mad at him. I take the coffee. "You're still not off the hook, but this is a start in the right direction. You still remember how to talk to me early in the morning. What is it with all you early risers? Haven't you ever heard of sleeping past eight?"

I smell it: white chocolate mocha. Yes, he definitely remembered my favorite. "I don't sleep much anymore. Not by choice."

I take a sip, letting the warm tasty goodness swarm my mouth. I want to ask him questions, but last time that didn't turn out too well.

Last night's talk with Breyson got me thinking about someone I haven't thought of in a while: Riggan. I want to find him. The tattoo shop is the first place I'm starting.

I step to the side and allow him to enter. He walks in looking around the room. I might as well get right to it. "There is something I want you to help me with today."

He turns around to face me. "Yeah, what's that?"

"I want to find someone that's important to me. His name is Riggan. Actually, I think you'd like him. You two have a lot in common. Last time I saw him he was going through a lot and being around me didn't help, so I want to make sure he's okay."

He lifts a brow. "Breyson is going to be okay with you hunting down some guy?"

"I'll call him before we leave, plus, you'll be with me. Are you up for a scavenger hunt of sorts?"

"Sure . . . I guess. Who's Riggan anyway?"

"The one that did this," I say as I pull up my shirt to the bottom of my bra.

"Holy shit. That's a big piece." He walks closer and bends over, taking it in. "Damn, that's some good ink. I wouldn't mind having him do one on me."

"He freehanded it," I say as I lower my shirt.

He stands. "No shit?"

"I swear. I was a little worried at first, but when he was tattooing he seemed like he had it all together. Each time after that he was withdrawn into himself; like the barrier that was up while he had a tattoo gun in his hand was crumbling. After he left the hospital from my accident, I could tell he was off. I don't want him blaming himself just because I was with him. I tried to check on him a few times before I left with Preston, but I think he's avoiding me. The few times I went in the tattoo shop to ask about him no one had seen him, supposedly. There are things that I know, so either he's avoiding me or everyone he tattoos with is telling me the truth and he's not doing well. I really hope it's not the latter, but I have a bad feeling in my gut."

He is looking at me, rubbing his hand through his short, black hair. "Okay, but if we're going to do this then you need to leave Bryce with Mom. She's home today. From the way it sounds we will be going places not okay for an infant."

He's right. I had not thought all the details through, but this is something

I feel that I need to do. After everything that happened, I want to find him. Something that bodyguard at Abby's spot said is really bothering me. "Okay. Let me get him and myself ready. Will you call Mom? You can watch TV if you want."

"Sure."

I turn and walk back into the bedroom, now anxious. I have no idea what will happen or if I'll be prepared for what I'll find, but you don't give up on people just because they're in a dark place. That's when they need someone the most . . .

"It's that tattoo shop right there," I say, pointing at the overhead sign on the building to my right.

He pulls into the parking lot and finds an open spot in front of the door. I barely wait for him to kill the engine before I'm stepping out of the car and running for the door.

I walk inside. Everything looks exactly as it did. The front counter is vacant. I walk past it and through the door to the back. Each chair is filled with a client. The artist closest to the door looks up from the large back piece he's doing on a girl that can't be much older than me. It looks like feathery wings. He's lean with a Mohawk, spiked with red tips on his brown hair. The only space clear of tattoos, that I can see, is the frontal of his face. Normally, that many tattoos would creep me out, but somehow it fits him, or maybe it's because I've become fond of tattoos. "Can I help you?" he asks.

Konnor walks up beside me. "I'm looking for Riggan. Is he here?"

The guy looks over at the artist in the spot beside him, as if he's verifying what to say. The beefy guy beside him nods. "Riggan had to take a leave. We're not sure when he'll be back."

I need more information than that. "He did a piece on me several months ago. My brother wanted another and liked mine, so he was going to use Riggan. Do you know where I could find him?"

"He didn't say. Just said he needed a break and left." The guy looks at Konnor and gives him a head nod since his hands are sheathed in latex. "What's up, man? I'm Kye. One of us has an opening in a few hours if you want to come back."

This is not going how I planned, but with Konnor being smart like he always is, he saves it. "Cool. We have a few things to do. We may stop back by."

A head pops up from the back chair. "Kinzleigh, right?"

My eyes immediately follow the voice. His face is familiar, but why is not coming to me. Where do I know that spiky, sandy-blonde hair? You can tell he's built because of the tee shirt he's wearing that has been almost shredded. The sleeves are cut off and half of the side underneath the arms. He's sitting in the chair getting an arm piece. "Yes . . ."

That moment when someone knows you and you can't remember their name, but you don't want to admit you don't remember them so you don't offend them—yeah, that's me right now.

He laughs, clearly amused by my lack of memory. "It's Maddox. Maddox Burns. I met you at Abby's Spot. I was the sexy drummer," he says, winking at me.

My eyes widen as I finally remember who he is. He doesn't look like the rock boy right now. He actually looks completely normal, and he's dressed like Breyson and his friends dress when they work out.

I realize I'm still standing here staring at him. "Oh yeah, sorry, you just look different. I didn't recognize you."

"What do you want with Riggan?"

"I just want to make sure he's okay. I consider him a friend."

He looks at me for a minute before he says something to the tattoo artist at work on his shoulder piece. "Hey, Justin, can you give me a second?"

"Sure, I could use a smoke." He sets the tattoo gun down on the sanitized tray that holds the ink and removes his gloves before walking outside.

"Come here," Maddox says as he glances around the room. I do as he says and walk across the room to where he sits.

He starts talking in a low voice that only Konnor and I can hear. "Since Abby died, Riggan goes off the deep end from time to time when he can't cope. He depends on other things to do it for him. We thought he had finally got his shit together when he started working here, but after that night at Abby's and what happened with you, he snapped. I think it brought back old memories. We've all tried to check on him, but it does no good. I'll give you the last address he was spending a lot of time at. He will be at his apartment or there most likely, but there are no guarantees."

He pulls out his cell phone and looks at me. "Give me your number and I'll text it to you. That way you'll have my number if you need any help."

I call out my number one digit at a time, watching as he keys it in his phone. When he looks up, I feel mine vibrate, signaling I received a text. "Thanks, Maddox. I appreciate it."

I start to back away when he stops me. "Oh, and Kinzleigh . . ."

"Yeah?"

"Don't be surprised at what you find. The Riggan you met was the version that had his life together. This one, well, the picture won't be as pretty."

My stomach nose-dives to the floor. Now, I want to find him more than ever. I nod, unable to speak for fear of what else he might say. I take off in a dash for the car, not stopping until I'm sitting in the passenger seat.

Konnor is a few seconds behind me. He shuts the driver's side door and looks over at me. "Are you sure you want to do this, Kinzleigh? You have no idea what you're getting yourself into."

"But you do, right?"

His jaw steels as if I just slapped him in the face. I didn't mean it that way. I'm just worried. "Konnor, I didn't mean anything by that other than you've been around people involved with drugs. I swear that's all . . ."

"It's fine. Why apologize? I did try some things for a while, so it's true. The difference is I was trying it with other rich kids, so I didn't have to deal with any of the dirty or filthy shit that comes with true drug addicts. I'm with you, I just want to make sure you want to do this."

"I need to do this," I say. "We could be the difference in life or death, slavery or freedom . . ." I take a deep breath. "He saved me once. It's time I return the favor."

Konnor's look softens at the words that come from my mouth. One bad decision can change a person's life, altering it forever. I know that now. If I can help someone I will.

"Tell me where to go," he says and begins backing out of the parking lot.

We stopped by Riggan's apartment first. It was locked. We knocked for a good ten minutes with no response. Knocking was being modest. It was more like banging. I listened closely for a grumble, footsteps, yelling, something, but got nothing. His neighbor—a middle-aged woman—opened her door finally and said he hasn't been home in a few weeks.

A dead end . . .

Here we are, at the address that Maddox gave us. It's a house down one of the avenues not far from the shop. It's a small lot with a yard that hasn't been cut in a while. The paint is chipping off the wood and there is a green porch light that is still on. Why green I have no idea.

Konnor walks closely beside me as we ascend the porch steps. The boards creak a little as we bear weight on them, giving away their age. I begin knocking on the door, waiting for someone to answer. I stand here for a few minutes when we finally hear someone walking through the house.

The door opens and a girl answers. She's tall and slender, skinnier than me, with a bad blonde coloring job and open sores on her arms and face from picking. She looks like she could be pretty if she didn't look so run down. She squints her eyes as she looks at us both. "Can I help you?"

"I'm looking for Riggan. Is he here?"

She glances at Konnor and smiles as she rakes her eyes down his body. It gives me the creeps. "Sure," she says. "He's in the back room. You can go back."

She moves to the side, opening the door further. I walk in as close to the doorframe as possible, avoiding touching her. She watches me as I pass. "He's going to love seeing you. He has this thing for blondes."

My nose scrunches as I look at her, but obviously I wasn't discreet at all.

She starts laughing. "Not me. Riggan is my half-brother." She holds out her hand. "I'm Lily."

I'm hesitant to touch her, but it's just bad manners not to shake her hand. I don't know much about drug addiction, but if I was going to assume, I would say she is definitely on something. I touch the edge of her fingers with mine, trying to be polite.

I look at Konnor. I can tell he's thinking the same thing. I release her hand from mine. "Riggan is down the hall, last room to the right."

I begin walking through the room. There are empty soda cans and pizza boxes lying on the bar, but other than that this little old house is unusually spotless.

I turn to walk down the hallway and everything is quiet. I'm getting nervous. I make it to the last door and place my hand on the knob. I'm not sure if I should knock or barge in.

"Riggan," I call out to the closed door.

No answer.

"Riggan." This time I say it a little louder.

I turn the doorknob and find that it's unlocked. I push the door enough to crack it open. I hear nothing, so I push it open further. What I see once it's wide open breaks my heart.

Riggan is sitting on the floor with his back against the full-size bed and his head slumped down. His legs are bent and his knees lateral with his chest. He's resting his arms on his knees. He has a pipe in one hand and a lighter in the other.

I rush over and kneel on my knees in front of him. On the floor beside him is a small photo, unfolded, with wear lines like it's been carried in a wallet for a long time. It's her, Abby, lying on the bed in cotton shorts and a tee shirt with a textbook and notebook in front of her, biting on the cap of a pen. Her hair is piled on top of her head and she's not wearing any makeup, but she has a huge grin on her face as if the photographer is talking to her. I recognize the room is Riggan's bedroom, in the same gray and black tones as it is currently.

There is such a sadness knowing she is dead. She didn't get a second chance like my Brey. She looked happy. It makes you wonder what she thought the day she woke up on her last.

Next to the photo is a small bag with the remains of a crystallized substance inside. I look at him again. He hasn't even moved. "Riggan," I say, as I lightly shake his shoulder. "Wake up."

"Riggan." I shake him harder.

He jumps but lifts his head. He looks at me, but his eyes aren't focused. By the way his eyes look I would guess he hasn't slept much in a couple of days. "Riggan," I whisper. "What are you doing?"

His eyes are dilated. "Abby?" His eyes are filling with moisture.

I take his hand and remove the pipe, putting it on the bedside table, followed by the lighter. This is a time when you want to scream that life isn't fair, but it wouldn't do any good. I just hope one day he can lay her to rest enough to move on. Would it be too much to hope that he gets another chance at love?

He's watching me. I can tell he's high. It doesn't take a genius to see it. "No, Riggan. It's Kinzleigh." I think this is the only time in my existence that I've ever hated telling someone my name.

"Where is Abby?"

What the hell am I supposed to say to that? He's clearly not coherent. I cannot and will not tell him something with that amount of sensitivity. "I don't know, Riggan." I lie.

"But you look just like her," he says. "Are you trying to play a trick on me, Abby?"

I will not cry. I will not cry. I will not cry.

"Riggan, you need help. I want to help you."

He grabs me by the waist, trying to pull me toward him. "Come here, baby. Do that thing you used to always do."

I'm trying to pull away, but he is stronger than me. "Riggan, it's me, Kinzleigh. Remember you did a tattoo for me and then we went to Abby's spot. You saved me from being run over by a car. Do you remember?"

He stills and looks at me. I'm starting to think he is finally focusing back to reality when he looks down at my left ring finger. "What the fuck is this, Abby? Huh? It was one fight. One fight and you're giving up on us? You said you liked my music, and that you'd always support me, but yet you refuse to go with me? You can write anywhere. I won't take that away from you. Let's talk this out. I need you with me."

I'm at a complete loss for words. Is he lost in something that actually happened? "Riggan, I'm not Abby." I walk closer to him on my knees, trying to get his attention. I grab his face in my hands. "Are you listening to me? I'm not Abby. I'm Kinzleigh. Look at my eyes. What color are they?"

"Green," he whispers.

"What color are Abby's?"

"Blue."

"You need help, Riggan. You can't keep living like this. People love you. Do you think Abby would want you to live like this?"

His face contorts into one of anger and he starts screaming. "Abby loved me! She only wanted one thing and I couldn't even give her that. I fucked up the only thing I truly cared about. Now she's dead because of me! I killed her! Are you happy? I'll admit it. I killed her. Why shouldn't I live like this? I'm the one that should be dead!"

He places his hand under the mattress and pulls out a pistol. My eyes go wide as I catch sight of it. A wave of terror runs through me that I've never known. He places it to his temple with his finger on the trigger. "I need her. I fucking need her. There is only one way to get her back . . ."

"Riggan, please don't." I grab his wrist, but he's pressing the barrel into his skull. Tears are flooding from my eyes in panic. "Don't do this . . ."

"I love you, Abby. Please forgive me."

I close my eyes, still trying to pull the gun from his hand. The only thing I can think is that someone is about to die . . . and I can't stop it.

"What the fuck, Kinzleigh?" I hear two familiar voices scream out those four little words in unison when the gun goes off.

My eyes flutter open to the touch of two hands on my face. Breyson is leaning over me with tears in his eyes. "Am I dead?"

"For fuck's sake, Kinzleigh, you almost gave me a heart attack. Next time you want to be a superhero could you at least wait until I can keep my eyes on you? Did that six months apart really mean so little to you that you would risk it again? Dammit!" He's breathing heavily.

Nope, I'm not dead, but I'm about to wish I were. He's pissed. Last night was about a tenth of what he is right now. He is seething, which means it's about to detonate. I want to know what exactly just happened, but I'm scared to ask.

I'm lying on the floor and can only see the ceiling above me. As morbid as it sounds, I don't see any blood spatter. Does that mean everyone is okay?

Breyson grabs me by the hands, pulling me up into a sitting position. He wraps his arms around me, squeezing tightly. "I can't lose you again, Kinzleigh. What were you doing? I'm calling the cops."

"No!"

He leans back, scrunching his brows like I've really lost my mind. "He will either hate me or thank me. Call the local hospital and tell them he's a threat to himself or others. They are required to take him. He doesn't belong in a jail cell. He belongs in a rehab facility, Breyson. You say you can't lose me again, well there is something I need to show you . . ."

I pull free from him. Konnor and Riggan are absent from the room, and the gun is laying against the wall. I don't see any blood in the room and immediately I feel relieved.

The photo is still lying on the floor. I reach over to pick it up and lean back to Breyson. I hand it to him. "This is what's wrong with him. This is what I discovered while you were gone. He needs to lay her to rest, Breyson. He isn't out to hurt anyone. His mind is tainted with guilt. I don't know all the details but being in a cell with criminals isn't what he needs."

He opens it. I can tell when he realizes what he's looking at, because I can see him adjust the focus of his eyes as if he's seeing things. I did the same thing that night in Abby's spot.

He looks up at me and he pulls me into his arms, against him. "I'm just glad you're okay. Who is she and why does she look like your clone?"

"She's his Kinzleigh," I say. "Abby Carter *was* her name."

"What do you mean was?"

"She died a few years back. He's not dangerous he's broken. He saved me, Breyson, and he saved Bryce. I want to save him."

He exhales, knowing he's lost this battle. "Okay, Kinzleigh. If this is what you want, I'll back you one hundred percent, but only if you promise me one thing."

"Anything . . ."

"Promise me you won't try to do anything like this unless I'm with you. I don't care where I am you will always come first, but a vague text won't cut it. We're a team, remember?"

The scent of his shirt invades my nose, intoxicating me. "Okay. I'm sorry. Next time I'll wait for you."

"Good."

He continues to hold me. "Breyson . . ."

"Hmmm?"

"What just happened, exactly?"

"When I got here Konnor was pacing and mumbling that you've been back here a while. We took off when we heard that guy yell. All we could see as we got to the door was a gun. I grabbed you and Konnor knocked the gun away just as it fired. I think it went through the ceiling."

"Oh . . . one more question."

"What?"

"How did you know I was here?"

"I was changing classes when I saw your text. I called Konnor and he filled me in and said something seemed sketchy. I wasn't far, so I came over here immediately. I didn't have a good feeling."

Of course, he didn't. Breyson is always in tune with everything that involves me. Why would I be surprised now? I guess it's time to get used to the fact that he will always be my knight in shining armor. There is something comforting in knowing that.

EIGHTEEN

Kinzleigh

It's still hard to believe Breyson is a college football player. Every time there is a game and I see him standing on the sidelines I could jump up and down I'm so happy for him. He may not get any playing time, but he deserves this. He's worked his butt off in school and in practice. Tonight is game night and like every other game we are all going out to support him whether he plays a second or not.

Bryce had his shots this week, but I'm still not comfortable taking him out in a crowd of that size, so Mims and Pops volunteered to stay behind and watch him.

Breyson had to be there with the team, so I'll be riding with my parents there and then back with him. I look in the mirror at myself. It's ironic his school colors ended up being the same as they were in high school, only he has changed from a warrior to an eagle. I smile as I look at my reflection in the mirror.

Breyson had me a jersey made to match his. He always was big about marking me with his number when it came to football. He gave it to me after his first dressed-out game. His instructions were that it had to be worn at every game so all the college guys would know I was taken. The thought causes me to roll my eyes with a smile. As if the large diamond on my finger doesn't say that already.

I tousle my curls in the mirror after applying my lip-gloss, the finishing touch of my makeup. A small noise sounds from Bryce's mouth. I look at him through the mirror. He's sitting in the middle of mine and Breyson's bed in his carrier, flailing his arms back and forth while staring at me.

"What do you think, little boy? Does Mommy look good enough for Daddy?" At the sound of my voice he begins to smile. I've been working my butt off at home during the day with a couple different workout DVDs until I can get back in a gym and it's paying off. I'm finally back in my pre-pregnancy jeans and more comfortable in my own skin now that I'm toning up.

A knock sounds at the front door. "Guess who's here? I bet it's Nana," I say in a singsong voice to Bryce. I turn and put his diaper bag strap on my shoulder before picking up his carrier in both hands.

We walk down the hall until we're in the kitchen, heading for the front door. I place the handle of his carrier on my arm and balance the weight on my thigh so I can free up a hand to open the door.

"We're ready," I say as I open the door, only it's not my parents. I don't recognize the person standing on the other side. She's definitely beautiful, exotic kind of. Her hair is long and silky black, curled in bouncing waves. She has perky boobs peeking out of a low-cut shirt. She has a small but curvy frame fit into skinny jeans and leather riding boots. Her yellow shirt against her bronze skin would make any girl jealous. She's also accented in diamonds, stating she's not hurting for money either.

"Can I help you?"

She smiles, but it's not a polite smile. It's the smile girls use when they clearly think they are better than you, and also the one that says they are in no way here to befriend you, but to take something that is yours.

"I'm here to see Breyson," she says.

My heart halts in my chest. Please tell me she's not who I think she is. I am willing to beg. Sometimes you just know without a shadow of a doubt that something is a particular way even though you hope you're wrong. Her accent tells me I'm right, but with everything I am I want to be wrong.

"Who are you?"

Her smile spreads, turning into a malicious grin. She runs her fingers through her long, bouncing curls as an act of confidence. She looks down at Bryce and back up at me. "I'm Angelique. I thought I'd surprise him with a visit, maybe to *catch up,*" she says, emphasizing the last two words, hinting at what she really means. "My plane from Spain just landed an hour ago.

Is he here?"

No matter how secure you feel in your relationship or how much your man loves you, one look at a girl like her and knowing he's been with her sexually sends it all crashing down.

She starts looking over my shoulder as if she's waiting on him to walk out. My eyes fill with tears. I will not let her see me cry. I will not let her get to me. I take a deep breath. If I ever had a poker face now is the time to use it.

"He's not here. You need to leave. I'm sorry you wasted a trip, but it's best if you go back to where you came from. He doesn't want you here. If Breyson wanted to be with you he wouldn't have come back."

"Maybe you should let him make that decision," she quips. "The truth may surprise you."

"He already did when he slid this ring on my finger." She's really pissing me off.

Her stare turns into one of hatred. "That baby doesn't even look like him. Are you sure it's his?"

"Get the hell off my property. Don't stand on my doorstep insulting me. Breyson knows damn well this is his child and you have no idea what you're even talking about. Breyson isn't here and his location isn't your concern. He's taken. Go find someone else. No one likes a home-wrecker."

I start to slam the door when she catches it, holding it open. I notice her reading the school name across the front of my jersey. I want to scream. Why is it that every time my life starts moving in the right direction something has to knock me over and laugh in my face? I get that my life isn't perfect and it never will be, but dammit I wish everyone would leave Breyson and me alone. I swear the universe hates me.

"Sweetie, men are predictable. All it takes is planting the right seed. I came back to make him mine, and I'm not leaving until I get what I came for." She winks at me, ensuring that I hate her even more. "See you tonight," she says, and turns to leave.

I look down at Bryce now sleeping. I shut the door and set his carrier down on the floor. Pressing my back to the door, I slide down and break down, no longer able to hold the tears back. I feel so childish, but what if he does leave me? I have put him through hell so many times. What if he decides I wasn't worth it and chooses to be with her instead? I was so sure he would never choose anyone else, but there is always that possibility.

My nerves are attacking my stomach, making me sick. I start to gag, quickly run to the nearest trashcan, and empty my stomach of the previously consumed meal. I throw up until I can't throw up anymore. Grabbing a paper towel from the roll on the kitchen counter, I wipe my mouth. I catch sight of my engagement ring and something clicks that has never clicked before.

I don't care what it takes, Breyson is mine. Somewhere along the way I lost my confidence. I became this scared little girl afraid to stand up for the things that I want. It's time to stop letting life trample all over me. If she wants to fight over him then the bitch can bring it on. I have the advantage. I'm his fiancé.

The first step is fixing the mess I've made of my face. I need to step up my game. Maybe I'll surprise him with an overnight stay after the game, just the two of us. The more I linger on that thought, the more perfect the idea becomes. I have the perfect plan, but I need Mom involved to pull it off.

I fix my makeup, making my eyes smoky instead of the natural earth shades that they were before. I amplify my eyelashes with the mascara I reserve for special occasions. The shit is that expensive, but it's totally worth it. I walk over to my jewelry box and pull out my diamond studs, changing out my silver hoops with them.

Grabbing ahold of the necklace that matches Breyson's, I kiss the half heart. "I'm counting on you to trump everything else," I mumble. Neither of us has taken them off since we put them on. I also remove my silver watch and place it on my left wrist.

Looking in the mirror I still feel plain. I look at my watch. I have some time before my parents get here, and Bryce is still sleeping in his carrier that is now back in the middle of our bed.

It's going to be obvious that I'm letting her get to me if I straighten my hair now, and besides, Breyson likes it better curly. I remember the way he looked at me the day I walked down the stairs that week in California when Mom did my hair in a low ball of curls. I don't have time to wait on Mom to do the small braid at the front, so I'll omit it. It won't take me long.

I insert the last pin and spray it in place with hairspray. I look down at my black converse shoes. They are comfortable, but they no longer go with the rest of me. The jersey can be dressy or casual, but my hair and makeup says I'm dolling up.

I walk over to our closet and glance through all of my shoes. I have a pair of wedges that are comfortable, but will I look stupid wearing shoes like that to a football game? I've never dressed up for a football game. I've always been a cheerleader or dressed for comfort when we went to college and NFL games.

Screw it. It's worth it. Breyson said we would be close to the student section, and I remember how some of the sorority girls dress. I pick them up and walk back over to my bed, changing shoes. Luckily, I painted my toenails yesterday.

Just as I finish by spraying myself with perfume, I hear a knock at the door. I really hope it's my parents this time. I don't think I can handle any more surprises. I might as well go make sure before I pick up Bryce again.

When I get to the door and open it, I'm relieved to see Mom standing on the other side. "Hey, honey, are you ready?"

"Almost. There is something I want to do. In fact, I need this. Will you help me? It's kind of big and I am really sorry it's late notice, but something unexpected happened."

Mom lights up with a smile. "Sure, baby, what is it?" she asks in a chirpy voice, confirming that she's in as good of a mood as she looks.

I'm just now realizing why. I never have been one to ask her for help or want to have those special talks of boys and friends, nor have I made a huge effort to do those mother/daughter things that most normal girls enjoy.

I've always been a brat really; stuck in my own little self-absorbed cheerleading bubble. The few times we've talked or done things were because she initiated it, and I dreaded every second. It's kind of sad. I'll never get that do-over in life. Being a mom myself has opened my eyes to a lot of things that matter, like a real relationship with your parents being one.

Starting tonight I'm changing that. One of these days I'm going to look back and my mother won't be here to do things with anymore. I need to take advantage of every second now while I have the chance or I'm going to regret it. "Tell Dad to kill the engine. It's going to take a while. We may even miss kickoff."

She signals something to Dad and starts to walk inside. I move back to let her enter. She takes one look at me and can tell something is different. I've never once dressed this way for sports.

She nods at me and wraps her arm around my shoulders. "Tell me about it. We have time. I'll help you any way I can."

I hope she can, because fighting over a boy is something I'm completely out of my league on. Girls can be evil, and I don't know what Angelique has up her sleeve. A girl used to getting what she wants can be lethal to any relationship. I've witnessed that with my own eyes. I know Mom can help me arrange the other.

NINETEEN

Breyson

I'm sitting in front of my locker, suited up. I have no idea why I'm even nervous. I'm only a bench warmer. I probably won't see any play time this entire season. I haven't so far. I've never been happier to be a bench warmer though. I've worked my ass off for it. At least I'm part of the team. Maybe now I can relax.

"Yo, Brey, you all right? You look like shit." Fisher sits on the bench beside me but facing the opposite direction. He's the first-string quarterback. We hit it off when I started coming to practice. He came from Arkansas when he was offered a full ride. The guy is pretty cool. He's the closest thing I have now that my brothers are gone all the time. I don't really see anyone from high school anymore. Most are in school and scattered, went off to work, or we just no longer have anything in common because they stay out drinking and partying, something I'm no longer interested in.

"Yeah, I'm just nervous for some reason. I have no idea why. You would think this is my first time to dress out. I never got nervous over football when I started every game, and now I'm not even playing and feel like I could throw up." Fisher is tall and built but lean like me. He has the same dirty-blonde hair, but his is a little longer and flips at the ends. He has darker features than me like his eyes and skin.

"Maybe that means you'll get some play time then. Sometimes our gut knows more than our mind does. You got a girl coming, man?"

"Yeah. My whole family will be here. I tried to talk them out of it, but I guess when you have abnormal circumstances, they don't want to miss anything. You?"

I have told Fisher bits and pieces of what happened over the last month. It kind of comes with the territory when the starting quarterback notices at practice you're better than second string and wants to know why you're a walk-on instead of getting a full ride somewhere.

"Nah," he says. "I had a girlfriend back home, but we weren't that serious. Just having fun really. I told myself when I moved here, I'd concentrate on football and school. Haven't dated anyone since I been here. Where I'm from if you have any aspirations in life you don't seriously date anyone. I'm from a small town, the kind where the locals know everything about everyone and work at the same few places. Becoming serious in high school for most people traps them there. Both of us wanted out, so we had a mutual goal in mind. That kept either of us from getting hearts in our eyes if that makes sense. She went out west after graduation, one of those girls chasing an acting dream. It's almost laughable, because her chances are so slim in making it, but she was cool and it was a mutual breakup, so whatever makes her happy. I just do me."

I like Fisher. He's really laidback and unlike a lot of the guys here, he isn't an ass kisser. He's genuine and he's here because he loves the game, willing to play whether he gets drafted or calls it quits after he graduates. He isn't just chasing big dollar signs. He enjoys life along the way.

"You haven't had a string of girls following you around since you're the starting quarterback? Isn't that the benefit for quarterbacks?" I ask jokingly.

"I must admit I've had some pretty nice offers, but none that really interested me." He laughs as I raise my brow.

"I guess you want the long explanation based on that facial expression, huh?"

"You know it," I say.

He's looking straight ahead, tapping his cleat against the concrete floor. "Shit, I don't know, man. I love sex, don't get me wrong, but I kind of like to be into the girl first. I don't really know how to explain it. When I say I'm from a small town, I mean like really small. There weren't that many girls to choose from really, and most of the guys didn't want to just pass them around between each other. Besides, there wasn't much to do. Most people threw parties in fields for fun. The next town over was a drive so you only did it to shop or go to games, etc."

He looks at me and laughs. "It sounds stupid, doesn't it? I guess I was just kind of shocked when I came here and girls started throwing themselves at me. I liked having to work for it, to be honest. It made getting the goods that much better. I'm not pleading my case, am I?"

I grin. "Actually, I get it. I found one of those girls once."

"Really? What happened to her?"

"I asked her to marry me," I say proudly. "I was a wild one once, and then I discovered the girls you have to work for are usually the ones that bring you to your knees."

"No shit. I feel you there."

Coach walks in the locker room, his voice echoing throughout the room. "Let's go guys. It's game time. Get your asses in gear." He starts clapping his hands together with the clipboard under his arm.

Everyone starts slamming lockers and walking in some version of a line toward the tunnel. "I guess it's go time," Fisher says as he stands and slaps me on the back. "Don't be nervous. You never know; if we get enough points on the board Coach may put you in to give first string a rest. I got your back. I'll try to get you some playtime. If so, you got this. I've seen you in practice. A bench is not your place. The field is where you should be, and I obviously need some help on the field. What we're doing isn't working. We need some wins. You just need a chance to redeem yourself from the shit you were pushed in at the worst possible time when it comes to football."

"Thanks, Fisher."

I can hear a whistle bounce off the walls, increasing the volume. "Abercrombie. Austin. Tunnel, now, or both of you will be on the bench."

Fisher starts jogging toward the tunnel with his helmet in his hand. I stand and do the same. "Coming, Coach," I say as I pick up my helmet.

I run through the locker room toward the tunnel to catch up with the rest of the team, putting on my helmet along the way. Everyone is waiting to run out. It's still surreal being here now. In high school it was a sure thing in my mind, but now second string makes me as happy as first, because I could have lost the opportunity for it all.

I follow the rest of the team as they make the sprint across the field to the sidelines. The size of college stadiums makes high school look tiny.

Once I get to my spot, I immediately start looking for Kinzleigh in the section I got her tickets for. I find my parents almost immediately, but she isn't there. She knows the game is about to start, so where is she? She could have just been running late and got held up in traffic—parking is a bitch on game day—but knowing Kinzleigh's ability to get herself into trouble my first thought is to worry.

I need to brush it off. She probably has a reason for being late. It was probably something with Bryce and I'm just being paranoid. I turn back around to pay attention to what is happening on the field. Our team wins the toss up and we choose to kick off. I watch as special teams take their places on the field, ready to start.

"Hey, Breyson. Looking sexy, baby!"

Chills run down my spine as I hear the shout coming from behind me. I would know that accent and voice anywhere. I've heard it in the most intimate ways. This has to be some kind of fucked-up dream.

"Breyson!"

That voice again. Do I turn around or pretend I didn't hear it? "Ah, dude, is that your woman? You were holding back, man. Damn, you didn't say she was exotic."

I look at Fisher beside me, waiting for the ball to change hands. Special teams are already off the field and defensive line is on. I close my eyes. This shit cannot be happening. Please tell me someone is screwing with my head.

At the risk of being crazy I turn around to confirm my worst nightmare is coming to life. As sure as I am that the sky is blue, Angelique Madden— the queen of seduction—is standing in the first row of the stadium.

Fuck, fuck, fuck!

"Are you going to go say hey before Coach hears her and bitches out about the distraction? She is still standing there yelling your name. Wave or something. Don't leave your girl hanging."

I lace my fingers together, resting my hands on the top of my helmet. My heart is racing at what feels like ninety miles per hour.

Still glancing at Angelique in shock, I notice Kinzleigh walk up and stop behind her, but far enough to the side I can see her. She's the most beautiful girl I've ever seen, and that's not just because she's mine. She really is gorgeous, especially the way she looks tonight.

I watch her eye Angelique. The look on her face is killing me. I want to walk over to her, to kiss her, and to give her some kind of an explanation as to who that girl staring at me is, but from the look on her face I think she already knows.

My eyes are connected with Kinzleigh's. I want her to read my lips. I want her to know that there is nothing this woman could do to pull me away from her. I want her to know that she is my past, present, and my future. Angelique was just a bad dream that I wish I could erase. Without looking at Fisher I say, "That's not my girl. The blonde behind her is. The one in front was a mistake . . ."

"Damn, man, you need to fix that shit. Offense is going out. That's my cue."

I never break contact with Kinzleigh as Fisher runs out on the field. I can't. Why is Angelique still standing there? Damn, what is she even doing here? How the hell did she even know where I would be? I made it clear we were nothing. Even before I could remember . . .

"Good luck, baby. I'll be waiting for you . . . Like old times," she purrs and winks, turning to find her seat in the stadium. She couldn't have gotten seats this close to the players. The only reason I can get them is because I'm a player. She eyes Kinzleigh with a smirk on her face as she struts by her.

Kinzleigh crosses her arms across her chest as if she's uncomfortable. Her eyes are starting to reflect under the stadium lights as if they're filling with tears. She's trying not to cry. I can tell from her stance that she's intimidated, even at this distance. Dammit, she shouldn't be. Kinzleigh will always outshine every other girl in my eyes.

She tries to smile, but it's fake. I hate seeing her upset. She turns and begins walking up the steps that lead higher into the stadium. "Kinzleigh!" I call out.

She stops and looks at me mid step. "I love you. Always. Don't forget, okay?" I'm waiting for a response; anything to tell me we're okay. The crowd starts screaming, but I don't care. She's what I care about.

"It looks like Matthew Huff is going to run it all the way down the field. Could this be a touchdown? He's wide open," says the sports announcer over the speakers.

I'm still looking at Kinzleigh, but the crowd starts to become quiet. "I know," she mouths.

The announcer begins speaking again. "Player is down. He took a shoulder directly into the knee before he went down at the five-yard line."

I turn around to see what is going on. Matt is lying on the field holding his hands around his knee as the trainers run out onto the field with the coaches.

They are all hovered over him, making it difficult to see anything. They pull Matt up and the crowd starts clapping as he hobbles off the field with the trainers, not bearing any weight on the injured leg. "Abercrombie!"

I turn at the sound of Coach's voice. He waves me over. I run in front of the line to where he stands. "Yeah, Coach?"

"Matt is out for the remainder of the game. He may have torn his ACL, but they will have to get him checked out. Here's your chance. Put some points on the board."

He gives me the play and pats me on the butt, dismissing me. I'm having a hard time processing everything, because it's all happening so fast. I hate that he's hurt, but I can't believe I'm actually going to get to play for a game.

I look up at Kinzleigh and she must have figured out what is going on, because that smile that has been absent is right back on her face as she looks back at me. That's the one that could motivate me to run marathons.

I place my fingertips to my mouth and point to her, sending a kiss. She places a fist to her heart and begins walking to her seat next to our parents. I take off running onto the field, ready to give it all I've got. The game is calling me. This is my chance to prove I'm made to do this, and that I belong on this field. I'm supposed to play football. It's time to go big or go home.

TWENTY

Breyson

I'm sweating. The other team is good, but I keep treading right along with them. Their offense is steadily putting points on the board, but so are we.

The score is tied with less than a minute in the final quarter. We have the ball, which gives us a slight advantage. We have the option to kick a field goal, but I want to run the ball. This may be my only night to play. I've always played taking the risky option and it's gotten me pretty far, so there is no reason to stop now.

The line takes position, ready to run the play. I take in the location of the defense, looking for any holes. Fisher acts like he's about to throw the ball in the opening to an open receiver, but I run up beside him and he passes it off to me. I cradle the ball and take off running. I can see the end zone. I just need to get the ball across that line.

A player comes at me and I spin around as he jumps, dodging him, but barely. I keep going, shoving into another player with my shoulder knocking him out of the way. I make it to the five-yard line and a player twice my size grabs me by the waist trying to get me down.

Fuck, he's heavy. I won't go down without a fight. I lock my legs and dig my cleats into the grass, exerting all of my weight into my center core, trying to keep my balance. He pulls harder, but I continue to push forward, dragging him with me.

The crowd is going wild. I'm getting weak: three yards, two, one . . .

A surge of adrenaline sparks and a growl escapes, causing me to bend forward and drive that last yard as the buzzer of the timer sounds. "Touchdown Eagles!"

I drop in the end zone, expended of all my energy. I look up at Fisher holding out his hand for me and I take it. I stand to the rest of the team now gathered around, all patting me on the back and chest bumping me.

The one thing that could make this moment perfect is Kinzleigh. "I'll be back!" I holler out and take off in a sprint across the field.

I pass the coach, headed for the field exit, removing my helmet. "Breyson, where you going?"

"I'll be right back, Coach. There's something I need to do real quick."

"Hurry up and get in the locker room," he yells.

"Sure thing, Coach."

Fans are exiting the stadium, making it crowded. I run, weaving in and out of bodies, looking for her. As I read each section label on the cement walls, someone grabs my jersey, pulling me from the side. I look over and Angelique is walking alongside me. She's really starting to piss me off. She has no reason to be here.

"What do you want, Angelique?"

"I thought that was obvious . . ."

"I'm with someone. You need to go back to Spain. There is nothing here for you; at least not if you're here for me."

"You're making a mistake. I'm better for you than her. We could go far together," she says, still trying to pull me to her. We are at a standstill on the concrete, the flow of bodies detouring around us.

She places her hands around my waist, trying to brush her breasts on me. I grab her wrists, prying them from my body. "That's where you're wrong, Angelique. No one is better for me than her. Meeting you was during a period of my life that should have never happened. Don't you get that? I'm finally getting my life back. I won't lose it again, especially over someone that means nothing to me."

She narrows her eyes slightly. "So you're saying those times you took me to bed and fucked me for hours on end meant nothing to you? I don't believe you . . ."

"Believe what you want. I don't really give a shit, but at least get it right; it was only one night. I'm not trying to be a dick, but if you care about me at all, then leave. There is someone out there for you, but I'm not it. You shouldn't have come here."

The spark in her eyes should tell me she isn't going to take a hint that easily. She holds up her hands in surrender and I release her wrists from my hold. She goes for the crotch of my pants. "I just need to remind you. Let me . . ."

As soon as she says it, she gets pulled backward by the hair, causing her hands to immediately go for it. She falls to the ground in her loss of balance. "Back up off my man, bitch!"

Kinzleigh is standing just over her normal five-foot height, bent forward, and looking down at Angelique on the ground, pointing her left index finger at her. Her diamond ring is catching beams of light and making it shine. "Listen, you little home-wreckin' whore. He told you he didn't want you. You were a meaningless quest to get him off when he didn't even know his own name. Don't be that needy, desperate girl. It's not attractive. Accept that it was a fling and move on. His heart is here or he wouldn't have come back when he got his memories back. We share a child together and we're engaged. I'm going to tell you this one time only, and if I see your pretty little tan face around my fiancé again, you will regret it."

She walks closer to her from the distance she was previously standing. I can do nothing but stand here and hide my arousal with my hands and helmet. There is something extremely hot about your girl willing to fight over you. Kinzleigh doesn't look done talking. "I may have appeared to be a shy doormat when you came to my house earlier, but every girl is capable of crazy, and I'm not afraid to let mine loose. When it comes to holding onto my man when someone else is trying to steal him and is important to me, I will let the crazy ride, every time. Do not mistake my tender heart as a weakness, because girl you're messing with my life, and I know now that is worth fighting for."

Kinzleigh stands straight from the slightly bent position she was in. "Now go on and find you someone else; preferably single if you don't want that pretty face altered by some other pissed off girl."

Angelique stands and brushes off the back of her jeans. She looks at me as if she's waiting for me to side with her. I'm trying really hard not to laugh. I shrug my shoulders. "What she said . . ."

Angelique huffs and walks past us, moving in the same direction of the remaining fans still exiting the game. Kinzleigh's back is facing me. She drops her fingers and turns around. "Breyson, I'm sorr—"

"That was so fucking hot," I blurt out, cutting her off.

She dips her eyebrows. "What?"

I walk closer to her, minimizing the distance between us. "Jealousy increases your hotness factor by ten points, and you're already at a ten. Watching you bring the claws out for me has me so turned on I could take you right here in the wide open of this stadium."

Her cheeks start to tint with a rose shade. "You are?"

When I'm close enough to her that no one can see me, I remove my helmet from its position in front of my crotch and place my free hand at the small of her back, pulling her against me. "Hell yeah, I am. If I didn't have to be in the locker room like five minutes ago, I'd stay true to my word and take you into the nearest corner, pull those jeans to your thighs, and bend you over while I show you just how much that turned me on."

She closes her eyes and wraps her arms around my waist. "You better stop talking to me like that or you're going to miss your player meeting in the locker room. I'm actually thinking dirty enough thoughts I would probably let you take me in a corner. You know what it does to me when I see you dressed out in uniform."

She releases me and opens her eyes, stepping back. Placing her hands on my shoulder pads she motions for me to turn around. Knowing she can't physically turn me around I play along, turning in a one-hundred-eighty-degree turn. She walks closer to my backside.

"You know you just broke the team's losing streak, right?"

"Me, among others," I say.

"That may be, Mr. Abercrombie, but I believe it was you that scored the winning touchdown."

"You saw that, huh?" I smile. She is not helping my current state of arousal to decrease before I have to walk in a locker room full of males and probably one pissed off coach because I'm late. Right this second, though, I can't find the will to care, even though I know I'll regret it later.

"Mmmm hmmm. Do you know what that means for you, Abercrombie?" She calls me by my last name when playing with me.

She wraps her arms around me from behind. Most of the people are gone around us. Her hands slip under the waist of my pants. Her fingertips are brushing across my clean-shaven pubic area, coming close to my dick, but never touching. It's driving me fucking insane. I want her touching it. "No, but if it has anything to do with what you're doing, I'm ready to find out. Why don't you enlighten me?"

She pulls her hands free and I'm ready to jump her. "Tonight. I have a surprise for you. Meet me at the end of the tunnel. I'll be the girl waiting for her hot fiancé."

She releases me completely and slaps me on the ass before walking past me, never looking back. I smile as I watch her retreating form. Who would have thought the shy blonde at the beach that never said an unkind word would become the firecracker she is today. The girl can wind me up so tight I feel like I could snap. The best part of it all is that she's mine.

I take off running toward the locker room. Coach is going to fucking kill me. Angelique just had to show up and start all of that shit. I'm supposed to be with the team right now. I only went to give Kinzleigh a kiss and I didn't even get that. That's what Kinzleigh does to me, though. I get so lost in her that everything else becomes irrelevant no matter how important it is.

As I come into the locker room everyone has already scattered off to the showers. Shit, I missed the end of game meeting. Not good.

Fisher walks by with a towel around his waist, freshly showered. "Coach wants you in his office," he says as he stops at his locker, opening it.

That nervous feeling I had earlier comes back full force. What if he kicks me off the team? Dammit, I need to quit acting so self-centered. This isn't high school anymore.

I walk back to his office and he's shuffling through paperwork. "You wanted to see me, Coach?" I walk inside as he looks up.

"Shut the door, Son."

Fuck!

The hardness and edge to his voice doesn't sound good. I turn to shut the door, now shaking from what he's about to say. I stand with my back against the door, propping my foot up against it. I'm clenching the face guard of my helmet in my fist.

Coach is around mid-forties, light brown hair and pale blue eyes. He's a medium build, slightly aged around the eyes, and soft around the midsection, but otherwise in pretty good shape. He wears a gold sports ring on one hand. I'm not sure if it's a handed down family heirloom or his personally.

"Where were you?" He looks at me, leans back in his chair, and links his fingers on the back of his head.

"There was something I had to straighten out that occurred at kickoff. Sorry, Coach, it won't happen again."

"You bet your ass it won't. When you're here you're on my time. I'm not your babysitter, I'm not your daddy, and I'm not your friend, I'm your coach. I have to think about everyone on this team, so in a sense I'm like your boss. What you did after the game was completely unacceptable. We go on the field as a team and exit as a team. We come back here to go over things while they're fresh. Once I dismiss the team you have plenty of time to deal with girlfriends and any other personal mishaps. What do you think would happen if you pulled a stunt like that in the NFL?"

He looks at me in a brief pause, but not long enough for me to formulate an answer.

"They could sever your contract or penalize you in one way or another; that's what they would do. Why? Because there is a never-ending list of players behind you waiting to take your place; ones would follow the rules and prioritize accordingly."

He leans forward and places his forearms on his desk. "You're here, Breyson, because I took a chance on you. I know your high school coach well and I trust his judgment. He never asks me to recruit his players, but with you he called in a favor and personally brought me a game tape. I vouched for you, because I feel like you can bring a lot to this team, but it wasn't easy. I had to go before the athletic department and plead your case for a multitude of reasons. I went out on a limb already, but I don't play favorites. I won't keep you here just because you're a good player. You still have to earn your place just like everyone else on the team. And pulling shit like that definitely won't get you a scholarship later."

"I understand, Coach. You're right. I'm sorry. It won't happen again." I feel like I'm being repetitive, but deep down I'm freaking out.

"Good. Now, come sit down. There is something else we need to talk about."

Shit, what now?

I do as instructed and sit in one of the two chairs in front of his desk. "What is it, Coach?"

"I just got word from the trainer that Matt is going to be out for the rest of the season. He tore his ACL and is going to have to undergo surgery to fix it. I'm moving you to first string for the remainder of the season. Right now, I can't make any decisions further than that."

I stare at him.

Shock.

That's what I'm in. An ACL injury isn't something to be happy of, but this is giving me a shot to play. I feel like I'm sitting in a dream. Am I really going to be starting every game? Holy shit. I'm trying to contain my excitement, but it's getting harder the longer I sit here. I can't wait to tell Kinzleigh. "Do I have any objections?"

"No, Sir. Thank you for this opportunity, Coach."

"Good. I know you aren't on any form of scholarship right now and I can't make any promises this season, because most of the budget is probably maxed, but I'll get with the athletic department and see if there is anything we can do next year. Maybe we can at least work out a partial. I'll get with you on it when I know more. For now, you are dismissed."

I stand, ready to hurry up and shower so I can get out of here. I rush to the door and grab the handle. "Oh, Breyson."

I turn, still holding the door handle in my grasp. "Keep playing like you played tonight and I guarantee you won't have any problems getting another starting spot come next season. Your ability to think out of the box under pressure and take risks will carry you places. I can tell you have the heart for the game, and that alone makes all the difference."

"Thanks, Coach," I say and head out the door. I need to hurry. I have a girl waiting on me . . .

TWENTY-ONE

Kinzleigh

I can do this. I can do this. There is nothing to be nervous about. It's only Breyson.

I pace back and forth at the opening of the tunnel, waiting on him to exit. Mom called and made all of the arrangements while I packed our bags. I was surprised to find out once I got to talk with Mom that she had the problem of another woman trying to interfere once before my parents got married. I should have given her a chance a long time ago.

After Breyson left I went to change. I want to look my best. I put on a sexy bra and panty set that match, along with sheer stockings that hook to my panties for added sex appeal. Now that I'm finally comfortable in my own body I decided to be a little risqué with my choice of outfit. I went with a hot pink, long sleeve, cotton dress that stops mid-thigh, but fitted all the way down and a low-cut scoop neck in the front, revealing the necklace I have yet to take off as well as the amazing post pregnancy breastfeeding cleavage. I never had boobs to brag about until I got pregnant, but I have to say the size is a plus, and they have yet to decrease. Maybe they will become a permanent fixture.

It's a dress Mom bought last winter when she had to go back to California for a high-profile case. She always brings me back outfits that are to die for when she goes away on business. The woman has impeccable taste, but I always stuck them in the back of my closet, afraid to get out of my comfort zone.

The heels of my black booties are tapping against the concrete from my nerves. I finally put on the shoes Presley brought me from Italy. I've never dressed like this in front of Breyson, or ever, for that matter. I've never been confident enough to pull it off. That was always Presley. I never had the boobs for it either until Bryce changed that.

Mom agreed to keep him so Breyson and I could have a weekend together away from home. I've been storing milk since he was born and I packed my pump to keep it up while I'm away. I hate to leave him, but I never want us to get away from having time as a couple, even though we're young parents. It was another thing Mom and I talked about. She explained how imperative it really is to make time for each other in the midst of kids and busy lives, and that it is the foundation for the temptations that will arise during a marriage, especially if either of us are successful in our careers. The thought that Angelique is only the beginning starts another whole ball of nerves. I hope that I'm always enough for him.

I look down at my watch. Breyson always does this to me no matter how long we are together. He always gives me a stomach full of butterflies and leaves me breathless. I hope I don't screw this up. I've never planned a romantic getaway before. I want this weekend to be perfect, especially after tonight with him getting to play.

I can hear footsteps coming through the tunnel. This is it. I take my place in the middle of the tunnel at the end, holding a red, long-stemmed rose. He walks into the light and my heart stops like it always does when I see him for the first time. He's wearing a navy polo with a hot pink, brand logo stitched on the left chest to match my dress. His jeans are a faded blue, contrasting against the dark of his shirt, and fit perfectly over his sculpted legs. He even gelled his hair. He's beautiful.

He stops when he sees me. The look he gives me as his eyes scan down my body has my heart doing somersaults. I know I made the right decision based on the heated look in his eyes. That look makes a girl feel like she can conquer the world.

He places his right hand over his heart. "What's this?"

Just breathe. Speak slowly. Eye to eye contact. You got this.

"I've come to take you away, Abercrombie. I decided I'd like to keep you to myself for a couple of days."

He smirks and steps toward me so slowly it's making my nerves continue to tangle into a knot. I'm trying to even out my breathing with each step he takes. I feel like my hands are shaking, wrapped around the stem of the rose. Why am I always on an uneven playing field with him?

He stops two steps from touching me. "Where is it that you're taking me, Baker?

I extend my hand, holding out the single rose. I smile, suddenly getting a surge of boldness. "That's for me to know and you to find out. What do you say; do you want to go?"

He takes the rose from my hand. His eyes deepen to a darker shade of blue. His smile enlarges as he weaves the stem through his fingers. He places his hands on my hips, rubbing them over my waist, toward my back until they are resting on each butt cheek. He squeezes. "Baby, take me anywhere you want to go and I'll follow."

He picks me up as if I weigh nothing and I wrap my legs around his waist. He kisses my neck and instantly my eyes close, enjoying the feel of his lips against my skin. I don't pay attention to where he is going, only noticing that he is moving his legs.

My upper back becomes pressed against cool, hard concrete; the tunnel wall I'm guessing. His lips begin to make a path down my neck toward my cleavage. The closer he gets to the soft bulges peeking out of my neckline, the wetter the trail becomes, now feeling his tongue gliding along my skin. "You look so damn hot, baby. Did you dress up just to take me out?"

He nips the soft skin just above my neckline, causing me to squeeze my legs tighter around his waist. I feel one hand slip off my backside and reconnect on my knee. My hands link behind his neck for extra support. "I wanted to look sexy for you. I wanted this weekend to be special. I've never gotten to do anything like this for you. I want to keep you happy."

I can feel his erection pressing between my legs but confined inside his jeans. I feel ashamed that I want him inside me, even in such a public place. I need him. Everything with Angelique has me on edge. Luckily, we haven't seen anyone passing by.

He lifts his head to look at me. "You could dress like this or in a pair of sweats and you would be sexy to me, but I won't deny that you have me salivating right now. Here I was prepared to take you out and you've already one-upped me."

He presses his lips to mine and everything running wild inside calms down. My hands move into the bottom of his hairline as my tongue slides inside of his mouth first. I'm needy right now and want confirmation that it's still only me on his mind. All girls do it from time to time when another woman barges into the picture. They would be lying if they said otherwise.

He runs his hand up the length of my leg, coming in contact with the straps that connect my stockings to my panties. I hear a throaty groan, but he doesn't stop. Right now, he has all the access he needs with my short dress hiked up to my hips. I want him to take it this time. I need him to be a sex-driven man right now.

He slides his thumb underneath the edging of my panties as he reaches the end of my leg. The light brushing of the pad of his thumb over my outer fold is driving me crazy. I moan and he presses me harder against the wall, repositioning himself to hold my weight in his opposite arm comfortably.

He presses into me with his thumb as we continue to kiss. It feels so good, but I need more. He breaks free, breathing heavily. "Damn, you're wet. You want it, baby?"

"Breyson, please . . ."

"Tell me what you want, baby."

"I want you inside me."

He looks around us to see if anyone is around. The tunnel is dark. The only light shining in is one of the beams from the field lights barely peeking inside the entry to the tunnel. "Here, out in the open? Not that I'm complaining, it's hot, but you are never this bold and always modest. The closest we came was a dark closet on New Year's Eve that resulted in our son. What's going on? Talk to me."

I do not want to go into this conversation with him. There are some things that girls need to keep buried deep down into their chests of self-conscious moments. "Just forget it. It's nothing. Come on, let's go."

Breyson repositions his hand between my legs, exchanging his thumb for his index and middle fingers, slipping them inside in unison. I claw my nails down the back of his neck as I close my eyes. "I never said I didn't want it. In fact, I want it really bad. I just want you to tell me what you're thinking. Don't keep things from me. Not even if you think I don't want to hear them."

He slides his fingers in and out, continuing at a steady rhythm. He rubs his thumb up through my folds, rotating his hand in a rocking motion. Each time he pulls his fingers out his thumb rubs from back to front over my clit and then back down as he slips them back in. "It's stupid," I say, barely able to concentrate while he's doing that. "Please don't make me tell you."

"Tell me and then I'll fuck you against this wall." I cannot believe I'm about to resort to bribery, but I want him. I'll always want him no matter what it takes.

I look him in the eyes as he continues tormenting me with pleasure. He doesn't even act like he's straining to hold me up. I hate myself for asking this question, but I need to know. It's going to plague my mind if I don't. I know he loves me, but the recent unexpected visitor is nestling her unwelcome self in my mind. "Will you be honest? Even if it isn't what I want the answer to be?"

I study his eyes, knowing that the eyes can't lie. They are the window to the deepest places of a person; places not visible to the naked eye. "I've always told you the truth."

I take a deep breath. Here goes. "Is there any micro molecule of any kind inside you that still wants her? Will you ever look back on this day, knowing you had the chance to have her, and regret choosing me? I need to make sure that I will be enough for you . . . forever."

His eyes soften a little. He holds me wrapped around him against the wall with his body but releases his hold on my butt and I hear a zipper being unzipped. He grabs one of my hands from behind his neck and places it around his shaft. "Do you feel how hard you make me? Not an increment of my dick is ever soft around you. I have to give it everything I have to contain myself and keep it under control when I'm with you. That's not just now, baby. It's been that way since I met you, and it's not just sexual. I'm hard as a fucking rock not only because you're hot as hell, but also because of the way I feel emotionally about you. Those thoughts you are having, I've had them too. It's like poison taking over your body. It's excruciating and consumes every part of you, making it hard to concentrate on anything else. It's toxic to your mental health. If I can take them away from you I will."

He places his hand under my thigh to support me, pulls his fingers on the other hand free from me, and places them in his mouth as he sucks them clean. "I wish I could take back what happened when we were apart, but I can't. I didn't know who I was or that this life was real. I never developed feelings for someone else, though, even then. There is not a cell in my body that has or will ever want someone besides you."

He reaches down and places his hand over mine, moves my panties to the side with his fingers of the hand holding my thigh, and guides his erection between my legs. We both let go as he aligns the head at my entrance, never looking away from each other. With both hands placed under my thighs, he positions me and pulls me closer at the same time he thrusts inside.

I moan as he fills me completely, and in every possible way. He thrusts in and out at a steady pace, taking his time. "Baby, you will always be more than enough for me. You complete me. Forever is what I was counting on when I asked you to be my wife. No one else will ever fit together like we do. No one else will ever love or need you as much as me. I will spend the rest of my life showing you that you are the only one I want and need."

Those thoughts I was having—gone. Sometimes I feel stupid for thinking the things I do from time to time, but without making me feel more insecure over petty things, he reassures me.

He reaches between us and begins rubbing his thumb over my clit again, but faster this time. This time he's doing it in a constant fast motion. He does it this way when he wants me to get off, because he won't last. I can already feel it building from my emotions being all over the place. This is what I needed from him: to show me that I still have the same effect on him no matter how many beautiful women want him.

I clutch his hair in both hands behind his neck and smash my lips to his as my orgasm takes over. Like a roller coaster making it to the top after the climb, from here it's a free-fall, and though it doesn't last very long, it's the biggest rush to the bottom.

He quickens his thrusts as I squeeze between my legs. I can feel the small vibrations inside me as he comes. He stops once he's expended it all. He kisses me over and over again all over my face. We both start laughing. Right now, I feel completely high, because of my addiction standing before me, continuing to give me my fix.

Footsteps are shuffling on the concrete. With each one someone is getting closer, and I'm bare from the waist down. Breyson looks down the tunnel. "Shit. We need to go. That may be Coach."

He pulls out of me and I unlock my feet from behind his waist. He sets me down on the ground and I pull my dress back in place while he adjusts himself back into his jeans and zips them. I start patting myself, making sure I'm covered.

Breyson wraps his arm around my shoulders. "Come on, beautiful. I'm ready to see this surprise you have planned."

Oh, right. I totally forgot about that in our little spurt of naughtiness inside the football tunnel. I look at my watch. We still have time to catch our flight, but we don't have any time to waste now. A wave of excitement hits me as I begin to think of all the different scenarios of our little getaway, and he isn't expecting a thing . . .

TWENTY-TWO

Kinzleigh

Mom was able to work out all of the details. Breyson has no idea where we're going, because I've never brought him here. I noticed he looked a little pale when we were on the plane. I want to ask him questions so bad, but I don't want to trigger anything that could hurt him. He's been through so much already. I would never ask him to fly had he not done it a few times trying to bring Bryce and I back to Mississippi. I won't ever make him do it alone. I'm not sure my heart could handle it anyway.

Isn't that the way to defeat a fear? To keep doing what scares you over and over . . . I won't pretend to know. From now on, it will always be the two of us.

The cab pulls into the harbor. Mom also took care of getting someone to captain the boat. Dad has taught me a few things, but I wouldn't feel comfortable navigating a boat of its size by myself and I have no idea if Breyson knows how. I keep calling it a boat. It's a yacht. There is a difference.

Even if he did know how I wouldn't ask. After all, it is supposed to be a surprise. I want us to enjoy ourselves. I'm not sure when we'll be able to do something like this again.

"Where are we?"

I look over at Breyson, sitting beside me with my hand in his. "Somewhere

I haven't been in a while, but it's something I've always loved, and I want to share it with you."

He grabs my face between his hands and kisses me gently, making everything in my world feel perfect. "If it's something you love I know I'll love it too."

Swoon. For a jock he has a way with words I'll never understand.

I hand the driver a wad of cash and open the door. "Come on, let's get our bags."

He opens the trunk as we exit the cab. I reach in to get my bag when Breyson stops me. "Let me."

"Are you sure? I can hold it. It's not that heavy."

"Baby, I'm your man. I'm supposed to do things like this for you. That's the way things are supposed to be. It's a little thing, but it's an important thing."

And that's one reason in a bowl of many why I love you . . .

I step back, allowing him to get our luggage. He closes the trunk and the driver leaves us standing in the quiet tranquility of the harbor. He looks around, taking everything in. His eyes are widening as he notices the large yachts docked here.

I start to smile. Dad used to always tell me that the only toy a man needs to be happy is a boat. They went in together with Presley's family so they could get one double the size but half the expense. We were almost always together anyway, so it made sense. "You ready, big guy?"

He looks at me with a cheesy grin. "If we're going on one of those then hell yes."

I can't wait to show him which one is ours. If a person doesn't have a love for the water, it's because they haven't been with people that are experienced boaters. It's very calming. You're in a completely different world when you're out in the ocean. There are no schedules, no watches, and no rushing. You get completely lost in a world of leisure and relaxation.

We finally make it to the dock that has our boat at the end of it. I stop and hold out my hand for his. We walk to the end and stop at the last boat. *A family affair* is what they decided to name it when they bought it many years ago. We were just kids at the time.

I look over at Breyson. He's staring out in front of him. "Are you ready?"

He's grinning from ear to ear. "This is your family's boat? I was thinking like a small party boat, maybe even something with a small cabin, but this? Holy shit, Kinzleigh, this is huge."

I laugh a little. Breyson's family has money, so I don't know why he's surprised. My parents don't usually advertise their wealth. Sure, we have nice things, but aside from major purchases that are also necessities they don't live lavishly. This is their biggest splurge that I can remember over my entire life. We don't have multiple unnecessary cars or houses and they didn't talk of buying crazy things like planes and islands. My family isn't like that. My dad was raised to work for what he has, to provide for his family, and to live comfortably, but nothing more.

My family's business started out small with my grandfather and has really grown over the years. It hasn't always been as big as it is now. Since my dad started working right out of school with my grandfather, he was able to learn it from the bottom up; then when my grandfather retired and he took over it really took off, or so my dad always said.

It's really no different than Preston and Presley's family's business. Even putting aside that factor, both of our mothers are highly recommended and sought after attorneys, bringing in a nice salary themselves. My parents are not only humble, but also private. Neither my brother nor I know what my parents make and we probably never will.

"It's definitely not small," I say as I wink at him. "You going to help me on it or are we going to gawk at it all night?"

"Oh, right, sorry." He lightly tosses the bags on the deck and steps across. I take a deep breath as he gets balanced and turned around. I hate this part. Don't ask me why. The wobble and dip from one hard surface to another makes me uneasy. Maybe the possibility of falling, I don't know.

He holds his hand out for me and I take it, trying not to look at the dark water below as I step across. Once I get my balance I move away from the edge. "So . . . we get this all to ourselves for the entire weekend?"

I can see the naughtiness in his eyes and it has me excited. I won't even lie to myself. I nod. "Well, ourselves and the captain, but he will stay in his quarters. There are plenty of places for us to have . . . privacy," I say with a mischievous grin starting to form.

"Miss Baker, Mr. Abercrombie, are the two of you ready to go?" The captain comes on deck, interrupting our moment. He's around my parents' age and he's the one they will hire if they want someone else to navigate, so I'm at ease with him. I've been around him for years.

"Hi, Paul. Yes, I believe we're ready. I hope you've been well." I raise my brow at him and place my hands on my hips. "And stop with the formality. You know to call me Kinzleigh. I'm like your adopted niece," I say teasingly.

He smiles. "I've been well, Kinzleigh, thank you for asking. Give me about fifteen minutes and we will be on our way."

I nod as he bows out. I turn back to Breyson. "Come on, baby. Let me give you a proper tour, starting with the bedroom."

He picks up our bags. "So, where exactly are we going?"

"Somewhere no one will bother us. You probably won't have cell service, though. I hope that won't be a problem." I start to bite my bottom lip in my moment of seductive sarcasm.

He walks closer to me, stopping just outside my ear. "I think I like the idea of being trapped at sea with you and no way for anyone to reach us. That gives me more time to devour your body with no interruptions," he whispers huskily.

I can feel my face heating. He stands upright where our faces are mirroring each other, becoming serious. "But . . . what if there is an emergency with Bryce? How will they get in touch with us?"

"We are in modern times." I laugh. "We have Wi-Fi through an auto-positioning satellite. I wouldn't leave Bryce with no way to make sure he's okay."

"I wasn't saying you would, baby. I was just wondering for myself." He places his hand on the back of my thigh, sliding it upward and under my skirt. The sensation of his fingertips moving along my skin, toward the middle of my legs, is making my hormones instantly spike. He grabs my butt as he closes in on me. "Now show me that bedroom or I will rip that dress off right here on this deck."

He doesn't have to tell me twice. I turn and lead him in the direction that I want to go. For the next forty-eight hours I'm going to lose myself in him, escaping into our bubble before we have to go back to the real world.

We lay in this king-sized bed tangled up in each other's naked body and the sheets. Breyson is combing his fingers through my hair with one hand and rubbing his other hand up and down my thigh. I can smell his cologne as I lay here with my head on his chest, playing with his blonde happy trail. We're lying in a silent peace, coming down from the high we always create in each other.

We started leaving the dock around the time we walked in the bedroom and started making out uncontrollably. Maybe it was the rush of being here, on this big boat, or maybe it's just that no matter how many times we have each other it's never enough. Feeling this way about him scares me to death, but it also keeps me coming back for more. "I love you, Breyson."

"I love you, Kinzleigh."

"I would have never in a million years seen this coming that summer. Now, I can't wait to be your wife. I'm ready to make our vows to each other."

He continues rubbing up my thigh as if he's completely at ease. "Me either, but it was the best thing that ever happened to me, even considering all the shit that happened between then and now."

He pauses. "If you could go back, would you change anything? Anything at all . . ."

I think about that for a minute. Would I change anything? I try to think deeply. Considering all options, there is only one. "Only one thing . . ."

"What is it? Tell me the truth."

"That day on my bed when you asked me if I wanted to go with you instead of Ryland and I said no; instead, I would have said yes and I would have gotten on that plane with you."

He shifts, placing my head on the mattress so that he can look down at me, still running the tips of his fingers up and down my bare thigh. He looks me in the eyes, studying my deepest thoughts. I always feel more naked than actually being without clothes when he does this. There is no hiding from Breyson, because he is the only one that can see straight through me.

"Even knowing you could have died along with all of those other people? And Bryce? He wouldn't exist. What happened to me wasn't normal, Kinzleigh. I should have died with everyone else. It wasn't fair that I got a second chance and none of them did."

He has so much guilt in his voice that it breaks my heart in half, but I'm not holding back my feelings anymore, ever again. I never know if death will come knocking at either of our doors when we're not looking, separating us once again. I will tell him how I feel every single day for the rest of my life.

"Yes," I say. "I can't explain why you were standing on the beach that day or why you found me on the pier that night. I have no idea why I never once turned my head when a guy tried to flirt with me, yet I gave you my virginity the same week I met you. When I think of how rare it is that I moved to the same town as you it makes me feel crazy. I will never understand why I deserve to feel the love that I have for you or why you love me as much as you show me, but now that I have it, I can't fathom a life without you. I tried it, Breyson, I did. It's not worth going on apart. I used to be afraid of dying, but when I thought you were dead, I dreamed of dying too."

"Again, what about Bryce? You can still say that knowing that you were pregnant?"

I place my hands on his face, tracing the outline of his eyes. "I love Bryce with everything that I am. Now that he's here I can't even think of a moment without him in it, but he wasn't here then. I didn't know he existed, so taking him out of the picture leaves you and me. I would have packed my bag, I would have boarded that plane, and I would have gone down into the ocean with you. It's you and me always, baby. From now until the end you're stuck with me. We live together or we die together."

My beautiful blue-eyed boy stares at me silently. I'm not sure if he's really that surprised or if he is gathering his thoughts for a lecture I have coming on why what I said isn't smart. I know it's a selfish way of thinking, but it is what it is. I can't help that Breyson changed me from an epic failure at love to a self-sacrificing woman over the man I fell in love with.

Looking back, I remember learning about some of the famous couples in school: Bonnie and Clyde, Romeo and Juliet, among others. Their stories are all different, but their endings are the same. They found the person that they couldn't survive without, so they chose not to. Before, I thought they were crazy, but now, I admire them, because they did the one thing most can't: they defeated death by succumbing to it instead of running from it because of their love for each other.

I'm not finished saying what's weighing on my heart. I tread lightly, not wanting to turn this weekend into a memorial on things that need to be laid to rest, but sometimes a person just needs to be reminded of the things they can't see because they are being blinded with guilt. It's one of the strongest emotions next to hatred and love; all very different things, but most of the time they go hand in hand.

"Breyson, there are things in life we can't explain. Bad things happen to good people, good things happen to bad people, and some people are given second chances, whether bad or good. The point is—it's not our place to question them, because even if we don't understand them, it's what was meant to be. I can't begin to understand how deep our connection is or why some of the things happened to us that did, but at some point, I stopped asking why and how, and accepted what is. I didn't die back at homecoming, you didn't die in that plane crash, and Bryce and I didn't die in the car accident. It wasn't our time to die, baby. Stop blaming yourself for surviving and thank God that Bryce doesn't have to grow up without ever having the chance to know his father, because you're a person worth knowing. I thank God every night and every morning that I have another day to call you mine."

"Marry me."

I'm suddenly confused. I thought that's what he was asking when he put the diamond on my finger.

"Didn't I already agree to that?"

He shakes his head, but his expression remains serious. "Marry me."

Again, he's repeating something I've already said yes to, or so I thought. I look down at my left finger to ensure the large, beautiful diamond is in fact there. Unless I'm suddenly seeing a mirage, it's there. Okay, I'll play along. "Okay . . ."

His smile breaks free, starting small, but steadily growing in size. "Why do I get the feeling I was the victim of trickery, Abercrombie?"

"Because you were," he says nonchalantly and shamelessly.

"And what was I tricked into?"

"Marrying me this weekend."

My eyes become very large, but definitely a mismatch to the rather broad grin across the bottom half of my face. "You do know my mother will kill me, right? I finally started asking for her mother/daughter help and I think she's excited about planning a wedding. Shouldn't I feel guilty, because for some reason I don't . . ."

"No, baby, we can still have a wedding. I'm not trying to take that tradition away from you. That is a girl thing I'm not going anywhere near. Besides, I do want to be the one waiting at the altar for you with everyone there to witness it, but I also want to marry you, just the two of us, now. Weddings are just symbolism for the act of marriage, but the union takes place before God. We don't need an audience for that; just a preacher."

I study his expression for a minute, trying to decide if he's for real or if this is a joke, but I know Breyson. He doesn't joke about something this serious, especially not with me. He's trying not to show his excitement in case I say no, but there is no hiding that kind of happiness. That's the kind that blinds darkness.

My heart feels jittery and my nerves are sending sparks of electricity all over my body. For a long time, I thought it was just that everything was so new and because of my inexperience with dating, but two years later and after being with someone else along the way, I still get these sensations with him and only him.

I'm totally going to agree to this insanity . . . and I'm going to love every second of it. Breyson and I aren't a normal couple and we never have been, so why start acting like one now? We're young, but our relationship is like ten years advanced in maturity; it has been from the beginning.

"Tell me when and where . . ."

There's that smile responsible for the palpitations and the shortness of breath. One day it's going to send me into cardiac arrest. My stomach is completely in knots from the monstrosity of internal mess that Breyson causes with that one single smile. Anyone that turns down that beautiful look is soulless.

"Monday before we go home. We can stay a few more hours. I'll take the day off from school. I just have to be there for practice, and I can't miss study hall. I want it to be the one place that started it all: the pier. Then, we go home married, you plan a wedding, and I plan a surprise honeymoon. All you have to do is tell me when, and you and your mom can go crazy. What do you think?"

I think I would do anything you asked me to, you amazing man.

"It sounds like a date, Abercrombie. I think I even have the perfect dress for the occasion."

My smile most likely matches his. In a few short hours I can forever call him mine. It may be sudden, but at the same time it feels like it's been forever. The irony . . .

"You've made me one happy man, and now I'm going to fuck you all over this yacht, princess."

Maybe so . . . but not as happy as you've made me. Yes, please! You are totally going to fuck me all over this yacht and I'm going to let you . . .

He lays his lips against mine at the same time his hand slides between my legs, ready for the next round. I'm just glad this time we're already naked.

TWENTY-THREE

Breyson

I begin to wake up from the deep sleep I was in. I stretch like I do every morning and rub my hand down my stomach. I roll over to hold Kinzleigh, but she isn't there. Her spot is empty, but still warm. We had a late night last night, but a memorable one. That girl is everything and so much more. Instead of tiring of her, each day I love her more than the day before, as crazy as that sounds. I always think my love for her has topped out, but then I surprise myself.

The room is quiet. I stand from the bed and walk to the bathroom, but she isn't there. I guess I'll just have to look. I find my bag lying on the floor by the door. Maybe there are some shorts in there. I grab it and place it on the edge of the bed, unzip it, and begin digging through the contents. I find a pair of my football shorts and pull them on.

Seconds later, I walk through the interior of the boat, looking in each room along the way, but still don't see her. Where is she?

As I walk by a window in the main living space, I notice her standing on the deck at the railing. Her curly blonde hair is blowing behind her with the breeze. She's bent over the railing in a black, silk nightie that stops just below her ass, and she's looking out at the water with her face angled so that I can see her side profile. I wish I had a camera right now. Actually . . .

I run back to the bedroom and pick up my phone, turning on the camera.

When I get back, she's in the same stance she was in previously. Her expression is peaceful, and she has a slight smile across her face. Knowing I helped put it there makes my day better, hell, my life.

I snap a few photos and slide my phone into the pocket of my shorts. I'm getting those printed. Sliding the door open I walk out onto the deck. Her head turns at the sound and her smile enlarges. "You're up."

"You weren't in bed. What are you doing out here?"

I walk up behind her and place my arms on each side of her, resting my hands on the railing beside her arms. When the breeze creates a vacant place on her neck, I kiss her soft skin.

"Couldn't sleep. I didn't want to wake you. You looked like you were sleeping good."

I place my hand on the front of her thigh, sliding it underneath her nightie. "You better be glad we're anchored out in the middle of the ocean away from roaming eyes or else I wouldn't be okay with you dressed like you are. This is for my enjoyment only," I say, running my hand completely up her body, stopping on her breast. Her nipples are hard.

"How can you still want it after last night? You aren't tired of me for one day yet?" Her breathing is picking up as she speaks, causing her words to come out uneven.

If only she knew . . .

I press my front to her back. The shorts are a mesh material. They hide nothing in terms of manhood. My now erect dick is pressed firmly against the crack of her ass, only covered by the thin silk. "Do I feel like I'm tired of you? I could have you on the hour, every hour, seven days a week and still never tire of being inside you. Do you understand?"

She lays her head against my shoulder as I rub my thumb over her nipple. "You could have me twenty-four times a day and I wouldn't deny you one single time. During the last twelve hours we could sleep in between. Waking up that way will never stem a complaint."

I could stay like this with you every single day and never go back to reality . . .

"Breyson, touch me, please . . ."

"Have you changed your mind about what we discussed last night?"

"About marrying you before we go home?"

"Yes."

"No. I won't. I want this as much as you do."

I think I'm finally ready to tell Kinzleigh what happened those six months I was gone. I don't like digging into that dark time of my life, but I don't want to go into a marriage with any secrets.

I want to form our covenant alone and in a place that means a lot to us. I wanted to make that pier and Oak tree two memorable places. I had the Oak tree in my proposal, and I'll marry her on that pier. We're in California, so it worked out perfectly.

Kinzleigh can take a year to plan a wedding for all I care, because I'll still be able to call her my wife. I do, however, want her to meet the people that I consider my second family, and to do that she has to know the full story.

I contact what I call my adopted mother and brother once a week as Maria asked me to, but usually when I'm alone at work since I haven't really gone into great detail about them yet. I want them at my wedding no matter what I have to do to get them there.

There is also one more thing I want to do. I made the decision last night when I was buried deep inside her. I want to wait until she's my wife to make love to her again. Have we been sexually active since we met? Yes, but I want to stop having sex with her as my fiancé and start making love to her as my wife. Two days may not seem like a lot, but when you love someone as much as I love Kinzleigh and that's one way you actually show it, it feels like an eternity.

I move my hand from her breast to her hips and turn her around so that I can look at her. Once she is facing me, I lean her back against the rail. "Good. I will make love to you again as soon as you are my wife in the eyes of God."

She looks at me. "Are you serious?"

I remove one hand from her side, pulling it out from under her nightie, and I brush her curls over her shoulder. "I am serious. I'd like to try and do things somewhat right, even if we haven't so far. It's only two days and we will be glad we did."

I kiss the outline of her lips, savoring the fullness of them. "I want to spend today and tomorrow studying everything about each other. It's time I told you about everything that happened in my absence and I want to know more about what I missed in your life. You said a lot of things last night that made perfect sense. It's time to lay everything that happened to rest so that when we become one in every possible way, there is nothing left to hold us back. When we step forward as husband and wife, I want it to be a new start. Since I've been back, we've studied each other's bodies like a road map, but I don't want to ever look back and there be something that I don't know about you. I want to know everything. *I do* is equal to forever, baby."

She is staring into my eyes. Those green irises are like a wonder of the world. I've never been lost before in anything, except when I'm with her. I can look into her eyes and all thought ceases. I can kiss her and everything that I'm dealing with unravels. There is no greater place to be than next to her.

She smiles so big that it lights up her eyes, causing my heart to falter from the multitude of emotion that it evokes. I'm guessing I must have said something right, though I'm not sure what. "I love to see you smile."

She wraps her hands around my waist and squeezes as hard as she can. "I'm glad I make you happy, because you'll have me for the rest of your life. I want to be the person you confide in. You're my best friend and I want to be yours. You sure do know your way to a girl's heart, Brey."

"I only want to know the way to one and that's yours."

I tilt her head and kiss her, but this time it's with a different goal in mind. I don't kiss her to arouse her, but to communicate with her from my heart to hers.

I break free before it turns heated fast. It's not something I can help with her. Her cheeks are in the beginning shades of pink already. "The day is yours, beautiful girl. What do you want to do first? Let's have some fun. We will get down to the talking tonight."

She continues to hold on to me, looking up at me with her chin against the center of my chest. "We could take a dip. The water probably feels nice."

I look over her head and the rail at the water down below. I'm getting a panicky feeling at the thought of getting back in the ocean. The truth is I've gotten on a plane again multiple times even though it still gives me slight anxiety, though I will never admit it to Kinzleigh.

There is no doubt going down on that plane was scary, but in your mind it's instant. The second you hit that water you know you're done for. There is a totally different fear in having to float around exhausted, being bait for whatever hungry animal is swimming around below that you can't see; waiting for your death slowly. If there are shark attacks close to shore, then we are in their territory out here, and a lot slower than them.

I need to stop being a pussy and just do it, but what if something does happen and I freeze, not able to protect her? I'm getting mad. I've never been scared of anything in my life. I mean what are the odds we would actually become shark food today, but then again what are the odds you'll board a plane and end up in a plane crash? Slim, but oh yeah, I was that slim percentage!

"Brey."

I look down and Kinzleigh looks worried. "Huh? I'm sorry, did you say something?"

"Talk to me," she says, and a tear trickles down the right side of her face. "What did I say? I'm sorry."

I'm confused. Her lips are starting to quiver. Why is she crying? I swipe it away with my fingertips. "What do you mean, beautiful? You didn't say anything."

One tear turns into more. Shit, what did I do? "Kinzleigh, what's wrong?"

"Tell me what I said that upset you."

"What are you talking about? You didn't say anything that upset me."

She looks down at her arm and I follow her line of vision. It's just now that I realize I'm digging my fingernails into her flesh. "Fuck, baby, I'm sorry."

I let go and inspect it. My fingernails aren't long, but they're long enough that you can see the four crescent shapes forming a single line in the skin over her tricep, from my index to my pinky nail. How did I not notice I was hurting her?

I pull her into me, placing my cheek on top of her head. "Kinzleigh, I am so sorry."

"You went total zombie on me. I've never seen you zone out like that. Seeing you withdraw into your head like that crushed me. Don't shut me out anymore. You said you would tell me things."

Her voice cracks. She's really upset. I'm such a fucking dumbass sometimes. "It's the water. I don't think I can get in the ocean yet. The plane thing is still scary, but I have made myself do it enough that I can get through it. The first few times I had no choice, but with this I keep remembering that night, floating around alone, and thinking I was about to die from exhaustion and drowning or become shark bait; whichever came first. I was going over the chances in my mind, but I can't protect you in there if something did happen, because I'm too much of a pussy to be a man. I would turn into a scared little boy, and because of that I can't go in there."

She pulls away from me and looks up at me. Her cheeks are stained with her tears. "I think we need to have this talk now. Everything else can come later. You always start with the bad and end with the good, that way the happy things are the last to cross your mind."

She grabs my hand and leads me across the deck, back to the doors. I follow her through the main area and back into the bedroom until she walks through the bathroom door. There is a large garden tub. She reaches down and turns on the water, feeling it until it's at the correct temperature.

As it begins to fill with water, she pours what looks like bubble bath under the faucet of running water, transforming it into a soapy mixture. She stands before me and pulls her nightie over her head, leaving her completely nude. At the sight of her I automatically start to adjust myself. "It's only a bath. I won't push for us to have sex until after we get married, but I think this conversation calls for nerve therapy and a bath is the cure."

I nod and she takes a step closer to me. She grabs the waistband of my shorts and briefs, pulls them out and then down until they fall the rest of the way to the floor. We've showered together, but never taken a bath together. I'm not a bath kind of guy. I don't like the idea of soaking in my own filth or my junk free-floating, but strangely, the thought of doing it with her is enticing.

She steps in first and I follow behind. The water is almost too hot to sit in, but bearable. She sits against one end and me at the other. I grab her foot and begin massaging it in my hand to deter me from having to speak.

"Would you rather talk and me listen or me ask questions and you answer?"

"You ask and I'll answer." Maybe it's easier this way. I can focus on her as I answer instead of getting lost in that maze inside my head.

"What exactly happened on that plane?"

Her voice is almost a whisper and her cheeks are still damp. The sooner I get this over with, the sooner we can leave this behind and never revisit it.

"There was this girl in the seat next to me on the plane. I was looking down at a promise ring I had bought you for Valentine's Day when she hit on me. I turned her down. I think she had been drinking anyway. The girl seemed like she had problems. This guy passed by looking at me as if he wanted to kill me, but I brushed it off. The next thing I noticed I had blacked out."

Her eyes look like they are refilling with new tears. I thought we were done with crying. I don't like seeing Kinzleigh cry. I never have. "Why did you black out?"

"I think he hit me on the back of the head. When I woke up, he had bound us to the seats we were sitting in. He acted like we were hooking up and I didn't even know her. After that everything happened so fast, but yet slow at the same time. The guy had to be completely strung out on drugs. He pulled out a gun and started talking about how he was bringing the plane down. He shot someone, Kinzleigh. I watched him murder someone in cold blood as if it didn't faze him at all."

"But why?"

My vision is starting to blur as if I'm losing focus, slipping into my mind. The things he said, the looks on faces, the panic, it's all beginning to hit me.

One word. "Her."

"What did she do?"

I fight to stay focused on her beautiful face. "She told me they were high school sweethearts. She got pregnant with a little girl and they got married. They were an ideal couple until she miscarried their second child, his son. Instead of turning to professional help to cope or coping through each other they both used outside sources. He blamed her and turned to drugs, and she felt guilty and found attention in other men."

"He killed all of those people leaving parents without children and children without parents, including his own, all because of an unfortunate accident that was no one's fault?"

"Something like that. I think he just snapped somewhere through it all. The guy seriously had checked out mentally . . . but the crazy thing was I could actually see in some twisted way that he loved her enough to do anything to keep her, no matter how crazy it seemed to everyone else. I will never know what was going on in his mind, but he almost acted like he was doing what was best; everyone else just got caught in the crossfire. I guess that is what drugs do for your mental state. You start thinking crazy shit."

I continue rubbing the bottom of her foot. Her pink toenails are covered in bubbles. I kiss the pad of each toe. I've always loved her feet and I usually hate feet. They are weird and dirty, but hers are cute and tiny. I'm getting sidetracked.

"Anyway, the rest happened fast. We both made a video. I sent one to you and promised to send the other to her mother for her daughter. She said it was never going to stop if she didn't end it. Each time he did something it escalated from the time before, so she seduced him into going to the bathroom in an effort to get the gun. The plan was to take him down and try to get control of everything, but it backfired a little. She shot him, but not in a place that would take him out."

I close my eyes. "They came running down the aisle. He got the gun back at the same time she told me to open the door. He ended up shooting something electrical, causing a malfunction in the plane. It was all for nothing. Do you see why I feel so guilty? I should have done more. I should have tried to get the gun myself instead of standing by while a girl with a toddler at home sacrificed her life trying to save others."

I open my eyes to look at her. "All I could think about was getting back home to you," I whisper. "Something inside kept driving me to fight, but I should have done more. I didn't want to be a superhero, but I feel like the villain."

She pulls her foot out of my hand and changes position to her hands and knees, moving toward me. She straddles my lap and places her hands on my face. "Don't ever feel like the villain." She kisses me with her naked body on top of mine, making it a lot harder to deny myself of her.

Her lips are so soft. I clench her hair in my fists, pulling her closer to me. She stops kissing me and pulls her lips free from mine; separating the two of us enough she can look into my eyes. "Listen to me."

I wrap my arms around her waist, not wanting to let go. In my arms is the only place she ever needs to be. "The two of us have always been mature for our age, or at least since we met, maturing our relationship that much more. Most teenagers don't love someone like we love each other. We are the minority. Most our age don't see past the fun and partying. The need and desire to love one person generally comes later in life when it's the next step."

She lightly kisses my lips again. "Along the way we were forced to be adults faster than most. Bryce came into our little package deal, so our maturity level increased from what it already was. Instead of being supported by our parents we now have to support ourselves plus one. Somewhere in the midst of everything you've forgotten that we're still just kids. I know you want to be a man, and even at nineteen you are more of a man than some thirty-year-olds, but you were eighteen when you were on that plane, Breyson. Once in a while it's okay to act your age. You were scared and had never experienced anything like that before. Cut yourself some damn slack."

She's come so far since that gorgeous, skittish girl I stumbled upon wearing a little bikini on that hot summer day at the beach. She was just a girl then, but now she is an amazing woman. I'm a lucky guy and damn proud to call her mine.

I smirk. Her outbursts here and there always get me in a playful mood, because they are usually unexpected and come at a time when you need them the most. "Have I told you I love you lately?"

She returns my grin. "Maybe not in the last five minutes."

"I do. More than you will ever know."

"I love you more, Brey."

"Impossible."

"That's a matter of opinion, Abercrombie."

"Nope. It's a fact. I'm older, which makes me wiser, and I said so."

"You have two days on me, Abercrombie. I would hardly classify that as older."

"You like my name?"

"Abercrombie? I guess . . ."

"Well, you can have it."

Her smile triples in size, making everything previously wrong in the world right. "Gladly," she says and leans in to kiss me, but stops just before my lips. "You always were the best gift giver."

It's taking all of my control not to bury myself inside her. It would be so easy with her in this position. Kinzleigh consumes my entire life and that's something that will never change.

I find a loofa and some body wash on the edge of the bathtub. I grab it and squirt the creamy soap onto the loofa. "When do you want to have a wedding?" I ask, as I start smearing the soap all over her body, forming a lather.

"Well, it depends on what you think of the venue."

I raise my brow. Does any guy care about that? I didn't know my opinion would actually matter. I thought my job was to pick out a tux and be there when and where I'm told. "You're actually asking my opinion?"

"I'm offended. Of course, I'm asking your opinion! It's your wedding too."

I start rubbing the loofa in circles over her nipple. The rough material must feel good, because she arches her back, pushing into it further. She is so hot when she's aroused.

"I didn't know guys had anything to do with wedding planning. Where did you have in mind?"

She smiles. "I want a barn wedding."

That is something I never expected to come out of her mouth. Kinzleigh was born and raised in California. She will always be a Cali girl at heart and that's okay. I love everything about her. I was prepared to become a permanent resident if she wouldn't come back with me, but for her to start showing signs of a southern belle breaking through is a surprise.

"You're an only daughter and your family has money, so your mom has probably been budgeting for a massive wedding since you were born and you want a wedding at a barn? Are you feeling okay?"

She laughs and takes the loofa from me, squirting more soap on it. She's covered in suds, but damn if she doesn't look sexy. "I guess that is to be expected."

She starts at the bottom of my neck, bathing me as I did with her. "If you think that's what I want—"

"Actually, it is what I want. It's ironic really. When I first came here, I'll admit that I was devastated to leave California, but now I feel like I'm where I'm meant to be. I don't want just any barn wedding. I want *the* barn wedding at the only barn that means anything to me. The west is what I know, but the south is where my heart lies."

She never ceases to amaze me. "It's perfect. When?"

"End of March? It'll give me long enough to let Mom plan a wedding and it should be warming back up. It'll also leave more options open for honeymoon planning."

I've got the honeymoon covered. I want to find this place in her dreams. I've asked her things from time to time, hinting around to get an idea without her suspecting anything.

"Okay. I don't care who you invite or how many as long as you make room for four extra people."

"Sure, baby. Who is it?"

"My family."

She stops lathering my chest but continues to look down. I suspect she will be confused, but I'm not sure of any other way to just say it. After all, that's what they are to me.

She looks up. Her brows are dipped in the center as if she's trying to figure out what I mean. "You don't think I would include your family at our wedding?"

She actually looks upset. I grab her face between my hands and pull her toward me. "No baby, that's not what I mean. I meant my family in Spain . . ."

Her eyes instantly gloss with tears at the realization that we've only covered half of the big question mark that was my absence. That was only the beginning. It's going to be a long bath, but I promised I would tell her everything and I'm not going to leave out a single detail.

TWENTY-FOUR

Kinzleigh

I stand in front of the mirror looking at myself. My cream-colored, spaghetti strap, satin dress falls perfectly against my tan skin all the way to the floor. I found the dress a few weeks ago and bought it. I figured it would come in use for something. The only reason I brought it with me was because Mom told me I could plan a romantic dinner for Breyson and I Saturday night and get all dressed up. She went digging through my closet, pulled it out, and said rule number one to keeping your guy happy was to never stop dressing up for him, then placed it neatly in my suitcase.

I twirl slowly. I feel pretty. My long blonde curls hang down my back the way Breyson likes them. My makeup is done in various shades of beige and gold, shimmering in the light. I can't wait until he sees me. I suppose Mom is right. Knowing your man is proud to stand by your side because he thinks you're beautiful always makes a girl feel good.

We arrived back at the dock last night so we could meet with a preacher first thing this morning. We found one that would marry us on short notice after a brief meeting with him, and then Breyson and I went to the nearest jeweler for wedding bands.

I'm still trying to digest everything he told me about those six months he was away. It's a lot to take in, but it makes me feel better to know he wasn't alone for the time he was gone. We sat in that bathtub until the water was cold and our skin was wrinkled, talking about everything that happened after that crash. We laughed, we cried, and we held each other.

He told me about his family on the ranch that treated him like he was a part of their family from the time he arrived. It's strange how close the similarities are between his family in Spain and his real family, but I guess that also makes it bittersweet when you're in a new place, lost, and with no one familiar.

What broke my heart the most out of everything was when he described his loss of memory. To imagine that we could have lived a lifetime apart if his memory didn't return shatters me completely inside. There was no way for me to know he was alive and trapped somewhere. I'd like to think in such modern times someone would have notified the U.S. government somehow, but for whatever the reason, it didn't work out that way. I will always be thankful each and every day that his memory returned, especially before I married another man.

Breyson told me he talks to his adopted mother and brother once a week. I hate that he couldn't tell me before, but now that I know the dark spots, I can understand him not wanting to elaborate. I didn't experience any of what he's described and it's scary to me.

He wants them to come stay with us in our new house the week before the wedding if possible, so as soon as we announce the date he's going to call them with the news and book the flight. I'm nervous to meet them, but I'm also anxious to meet the people that are so important to him, especially knowing they took care of him when no one else could, even though he was a stranger to them.

Saturday and Sunday during the day we did nothing but lay around relaxing in the sunshine and talking, relearning each other with no interruptions of football, babies, work, or life in general. We spent time focusing on each other. Honestly, it was nice. It reminded me of a time that is long gone now.

Saturday night after sunset we came inside starving. My parents have someone that cleans and keeps the kitchen stocked before we take out the boat. All we have to do is call ahead and everything is waiting for us. I shuffled through the contents in the kitchen and found the ingredients to make Dad's mostly homemade spaghetti. It was something he used to let me help him make as a child.

While we were waiting on the food to cook, I found my parents' wine collection. Collecting wine has become a hobby for them over the years.

Occasionally Mom and Dad would sneak off to Napa Valley for the weekend. They've been collecting their entire marriage. We never went on vacation without them bringing back a bottle of wine: Italy, France, England, you name the place and we probably have a bottle made there.

It's actually an interesting hobby when you think of opening a bottle that is twenty plus years old. It gives me an idea for part of Breyson's wedding present. Thinking of this only being the beginning of a long future together is an excitement in itself.

That night I decided on a sweet, white wine. We opened it, poured a glass, and made wedding plans. I can't wait until I get to start putting it into action. I was never interested in a wedding before Breyson, but now I find myself becoming more excited each time we talk about it.

After dinner we played a game of poker with the set my parents had put up in the cabinets. Breyson won . . . because I let him. The truth is I'm pretty damn good at poker. When your mother pulls late hours and you don't have a sister, you find things to do that are neutral to gender. It was something I used to do with Dad and Konnor. I've been playing for years, but I didn't have the heart to tell Breyson when he found the set and assumed I couldn't play, so I played along. His need and excitement to teach me triumphed my need to win, but isn't that what girls do for their men?

I smile as I think about the look on his face when he was teaching me to play Texas hold 'em. His grin as he explained the rules was too cute to interrupt. When he *won,* he threw his cards on the table and jumped up, throwing his hands in the air and chanting that he won. All I could do was laugh and shrug my shoulders over being defeated. What girl would ruin that moment for her guy? That would be cruel . . .

Sunday night we watched a movie and decided to write our own vows, so I locked myself away in this very bedroom and he stayed in the living quarters.

A knock sounds on the bedroom door. I feel like I have butterflies flying around in my stomach. I think writing and reciting my own vows to him is more nerve racking than if we were to repeat the preacher, but it'll mean more as well. "Kinzleigh, baby, are you ready? The cab is here."

I take a deep breath and throw my makeup back in my makeup bag. I spray myself with perfume and throw it inside as well. "Yes, I'm ready. You can come in."

Breyson hasn't seen this dress. I kept it a secret when I bought it because I didn't know what I was going to use it for at the time, but it fits the whole wedding thing. I have been stuck away in this room for over an hour getting ready, not letting him enter.

I watch through the mirror as he opens the door. I always lose all sense of real time when I see him. He grins as he takes me in. I will never get tired of seeing that look on his face when he looks at me. I always feel so ordinary compared to him.

He walks inside looking sexier than ever. He's gelled the front of his hair up and he's wearing a pair of khaki pants with a pair of brown, leather flip flops and a white, long-sleeved button-down with the sleeves rolled up just below his elbows. The top two buttons are unbuttoned, accentuating his defined chest.

Damn, I really couldn't have packed better if I had planned this.

I turn around as he stops in the center of the room, now standing with his hands in his pockets. He is the sexiest man alive. No one will ever come close in comparison to him. He's also my best friend.

His eyes lock with mine and then slowly rake down my body as if he's slowly undressing me in his mind, planning the whole event mentally of what he's going to do to me later. "How do I look?" I hold out my hands and twirl once for him.

"Incredible."

One word and I feel like royalty. The way he says it is so final, as if it takes no thought at all. Breyson has a way of making me sound like the most beautiful girl in the world. It's overwhelming. I never want this feeling he gives me to end.

He starts walking toward me, stopping barely a foot away. "Every time I lay my eyes on you, you captivate me. It places me in a temporary trance, rendering me speechless until I'm able to catch my breath. That is the absolute truth."

I wonder how normal it is to feel this strongly about someone. It seems too intense to be real, but at the same time I constantly crave it. He says things like that and my heart melts into a liquid substance. Like molten lava it has to wait until cooled to transform back into a solid form.

"You have no idea how much I love you, Breyson."

"If it's anywhere close to the way I feel about you I have a pretty good idea." Putty in his hands is where I stay. "You ready to marry me, Kinzleigh Baker?"

"I've been ready."

He takes my hand and grabs my bag off of the bed. We walk to the door of the bedroom. Nothing I've ever wanted has been as absolute as this, not even cheerleading . . .

TWENTY-FIVE

Breyson

I shake my hands out trying to expel the nervous energy. In an hour I'll be a married man. Not only will I be married, but also, I'll be married to the girl of my dreams and the mother of my child. This is something I've wanted for a while. I know we're young and there are several things in my future that I'm unsure of, but this isn't one of them. The two of us will make it. Failure is not an option here. Divorce will never be a discussion when referring to She or I as a couple.

I stick my hands in my pockets, trying to stop moving. The preacher has watched me pace back and forth since we got to the end of his pier. "Son, you going to be okay?"

"Just ready to get started, Sir. I don't want her to back out. I think I just need to see her walking toward me."

When we got here Kinzleigh went to the changing house to freshen up, or so she said. I don't know what she could possibly be doing. She just got ready for crying out loud.

Shit, I've turned into a whipped pussy. Is it okay to think curse words and crude humor in front of a preacher? He doesn't know I'm thinking it, right? Fuck! Dammit, shut the hell up.

I slap my hands over my face. I don't know what has happened to me. I can't think straight. He places his hand on my shoulder. "She'll be here.

Women aren't on time unless they're late by our watch. Learn that now and you'll have a much easier life."

"Yes, Sir. I guess you're right."

The preacher that's marrying us is an older man in his sixties with white hair. We had to meet with him for a minimum of thirty minutes before he would agree to marry us. He said we had to pass his marital questionnaire before he would proceed. It was mostly questions about why we wanted to get married and different scenarios of what could happen in a marriage and how we would respond. Then, he opened the bible and read to us what God's expectations were in regard to marriage. I listened to every word. I don't want to ever be taken from her again or vice versa.

I'm assuming we passed with flying colors, because he told us what time to meet him here and sent us to the courthouse to apply for a marriage license. Now, here we are, waiting, and I'm a nervous wreck.

"It makes my heart happy to still see love as strong as this in couples, especially of your age. A lot has changed since I married my wife."

"We're definitely not the average couple, that's for sure, but I really do love her. There are no words appropriate enough to describe it properly. I may only be nineteen, but I don't feel it. Age is just a number anyway. I need her next to me. The way I look at it is that I get to enjoy her and love her longer."

"As long as you remember your own words and to keep God in the center of your relationship, you'll be fine. Life won't always be easy, but you never stop fighting for each other."

I turn and look down the pier. Kinzleigh is standing at the opposite end directly in front of me. My nerves instantly calm. This is one of those mental photos I'll never forget, and I love being on this side of the lens. She's stunning. This is the best idea I've ever had.

"I intend to, Sir. Until the day I stop breathing, I'll always fight for her. That's a promise."

She takes a step forward and then another until she's walking slowly down the pier, coming toward me. It's the perfect day. It's still warm, but not hot, and there's a slight breeze blowing her dress and her curls, making the view from here remarkable.

I'm staring at her, and her at me. I know I have a cheesy-ass grin on my face, but I don't care. She's one of the only two things I care about now. This right here is what makes life worth living. She's smiling so hard a dip forms in her cheeks, almost resembling dimples.

She stops in front of me, finally.

"Hi," I say.

"Hi," she says in return.

I hold out my hand for her and she takes it. I rub my thumb over her knuckles as she walks to stand facing me in front of the preacher. I can't take my eyes off of her, and I don't want to.

"I know we discussed that the two of you didn't want a traditional ceremony, but I'd like to say a few words and then we will get started. I will keep it simple as you both asked. Is that all right?"

I nod and she follows behind me doing the same.

"Good. I want to start off with a short prayer. Bow your heads."

We do as the preacher asks, but I continue to rub the tops of her hands, both placed in mine.

"Dear Heavenly Father,

We have come before you today as the ultimate counselor to ask for your grace in the holy matrimony of Kinzleigh and Breyson. They understand the importance of this covenant and that it is a lifelong commitment, and also that it is not to be taken lightly. They are here today asking that you lay to rest each self and bring them together as one from this day forward, and for as long as they both shall live. We ask this of you, Lord.

In your name we pray,

Amen."

I open my eyes and Kinzleigh is already pulling away to dab the corners of hers with a handkerchief.

"Kinzleigh, Breyson, do you both understand fully why you're here?"

I nod to her and at the same time we answer. "We do."

"Do you understand that you are asking to enter into a lifelong covenant with each other; one that is not meant to be broken for any reason aside from death?"

"We do."

"Do you understand that under this covenant you are leaving your parents and becoming one with each other?"

"We do."

"Do you understand that as husband and wife it is your job to love, honor, and remain faithful to each other in sickness and in health for all the days of your lives?"

"We do."

"Do you understand that it is your duty to provide and care for each other, as well as any children that are gifted to you for all the days of your lives?"

"We do."

"Good. Now you can recite your vows. Breyson, we will start with you. Do you have Kinzleigh's ring?"

I pull the small, white gold band from my right pocket that's frosted with round diamonds across the top, showing it to him in my palm.

"Place it on the edge of her finger, recite your vows, and when you finish, slide it in place."

I look back at Kinzleigh. This is the moment I've been waiting for since I knew she was going to one day become my wife. Today is that day.

"Kinzleigh, from the first day I met you I knew there was something different about you. From the beginning you bewitched me when I was in your presence. Before you, I was on a path to destruction and heading for a life of emptiness, but you changed me. I would have never in a million years thought I was going to meet my wife at seventeen, but yet here we are. I stand here today with so much love in my heart for you that I can't even begin to measure it, but know that each and every day it only increases in magnitude. I know that we're young, and that we're only just starting on our journey through life, but I promise to always love and protect you no matter what crosses our path. I have watched you transform into the most amazing and strongest woman I know. I'm honored to call you my wife and I'm so glad that you chose to love me. I know there will be times when we may struggle in some way or another, there will be times when I make you mad, and there will be times when you want to give up, but I'm begging that you don't. I promise to always be your driving force when you have none, to support you in everything you do, and to love you through every circumstance. You own every part of me. No matter what anyone says you are my soul mate, Kinzleigh, my best friend, and the love of my life. Like that circle around our names on our tree and this band I'm about to place on your finger, my love for you will never end."

I slide the band down her left ring finger, leaving it in the place it will stay forever. "With this ring, I thee wed."

Tears begin falling from her eyes as she continues to scan mine. I want to kiss her so bad. This and the birth of my son are the two greatest days of my life.

TWENTY-SIX

Kinzleigh

I was not prepared for how his vows would make me feel. I'm temporarily stunned. I'm so glad I finally stopped fighting us. There was never a moment that I doubted he was the one for me, but the fact that I almost let him go is a tragedy; a mistake I'll never make again.

I'll remember those words forever. I've locked them away in the safe that is my heart and will forever be the keeper of the key.

I'm an emotional mess already and I haven't even started my vows to him.

"Kinzleigh, do you have your ring?"

I look at the preacher and let go of Breyson's hand long enough to remove the titanium band wrapped around my thumb. I chose one of the strongest metals, because to me it represents our love for each other. It can withstand anything, and it's not penetrable by an outside force.

Taking his left hand, I slide it on the edge of his finger and look him in the eyes.

"Breyson, you are the most amazing man I've ever met. You have strength about you that I can't explain, because I've never seen it before in anyone else. You're rough when you need to be, but then you know when to be gentle. Since the beginning you've put up with more crap from me than most guys would. I started off as a selfish person, but without knowing, you have guided me to become a woman that I'm proud of. I never thought that by giving you a chance I would find the love of a lifetime, but I'm so glad I did. Giving you my heart was the best decision I've ever made. Not only have you taken care of it, but also, you've guarded it with your life, literally. I trust you implicitly. Today I'm making a promise to you that I will guard yours with the same respect that you have mine. I know things will get tough at times, I know there are a lot of things we have left to learn in life, and I know there will be things that try to tear us apart, but I want you to know that no matter what and from this day forward I'll never again give up on us. With one look into the depths of my eyes you can read my deepest secrets. My love for you overwhelms me at times, but it keeps me alive. You are an addiction I never want to fight. I vow to you that I will always put your needs before my own no matter what they are. The only thing I see in my future is a life with you, because that's the only part that matters. The best part of knowing that you love me is that you'll never stop. I want you to know that not only will I never walk away from you, but also that I can't. You are the best thing that's ever happened to me, and not only have you given me the greatest love I've ever known and a road leading to a lifetime of true love ahead, but also you gave me an amazing little boy. You are my best friend, the other half of my heart, and only mate. I feel worthy that you chose me to be your wife. You are someone that is worth loving with the greatest amount of effort forever. I love you with a fierceness I can't explain."

I push the ring down his finger, setting it in place. "With this ring, I thee wed."

"It is with the power vested in me and with God as my witness that I now pronounce you husband and wife. Breyson, you may kiss your bride."

Breyson's face matches mine; starting as a tear-stained mess to the huge smiles we are now wearing.

"And this, Mrs. Abercrombie, is what I've been waiting for . . ."

He pushes his hands into my hair, leaning into me. His lips touch mine, and that amazing little tingle returns. Things I used to never notice or things that scared me are now my primary focus. The simple things are sometimes the most important things.

This is the most beautiful moment there could ever be. I meant every word and then some. I love this man with all that I am. I will never stop loving him. Some things aren't meant to have an end, but only a continuous flow. Like our love, like that amazing circle he carved in our tree, and like the beautiful bands that now wrap around our left ring fingers, all are symbolizing the beginning of an amazing life to come . . .

TWENTY-SEVEN

I make it to practice just in time. I dropped Kinzleigh off at her parents' house and came straight here. I offered to drive her and Bryce back home, but she said she wanted to spend some time with her mom and to start making wedding arrangements. It should all be downhill from here. I got what I wanted.

"What put that big-ass grin on your face?"

I look over at Fisher as he puts on his helmet, standing beside me on the sidelines. Coach is doing some shit on the field with defensive line, giving us a few minutes before we have to take the field.

"I got hitched."

"No shit? When?"

"This morning."

"Damn, Son, you work fast."

I shrug. "You know what they say. When you find the one you want, you better put a ring on it before someone else does, so I did. We went to California for the weekend. It was the place we met, so it just felt right."

"Well, congratulations. When do I get to meet her?"

Actually, that's a brilliant idea. I feel guilty, because all Kinzleigh does is stay home with Bryce all day. Sure, she goes shopping occasionally, but all of her friends are now gone off to college. She's already postponed college and cheerleading. I've met a few friends since I got on the team and through my classes, but I don't like to talk about them much for fear of upsetting her.

I slap him on the back, lightly shoving him forward. "Why didn't you mention that earlier, dipshit?"

"What the hell?"

"That's the best idea you've had yet. Don't you know girls?"

He raises his brow. "Didn't we have this conversation already? Besides, what does me knowing girls have to do with meeting yours?"

"Do I really have to explain?"

He looks out at the field and back at me, pulling his helmet up to clear his face, but never completely removing it from his head. "Yes, but make it quick."

I shake my head. "I knocked her up, so for the time being she pretty much stays at home all day with our son. She's not originally from here, so her few friends have left for school. Maybe if she meets some girls our age it'll be easier for her to start school in the spring. Didn't you say you were in a fraternity now? That's easy access to the college female population, right?"

"Ah, I get it. Yeah, I am. I figured it was an easy way to meet people in a new place, and actually, Thursday night we are having a costume party since Friday is Halloween. I could introduce her to a few people. Thursday nights the houses are packed. You guys should come. Frat row. Biggest house on the left. You can't miss it. You should have enough time to get a costume between now and then. It doesn't liven up 'til around ten."

"Where's my offensive line? Get your asses out here!"

He pulls his helmet back in place and inserts his mouth guard. I follow behind him onto the field to take position for the play. I don't care much to go to a party, and I hate to be away from Bryce for another night so soon, because I feel like we are dumping him off on our parents, but if it helps Kinzleigh meet some new friends it'll be worth it. She needs to have a girl to talk to when I'm not around.

I'm sweating from a hard practice as we walk into the field house to shower and leave. I open my locker and pull out my cell phone, hitting Kinzleigh's number. It only rings once before she picks up.

"Hey, baby."

"Hey, where are you at?"

"I'm still at Mom and Dad's house talking wedding stuff. Why?"

"Do you want to come meet me in town?"

I hear Bryce in the background making noises. It's funny how much I miss such a little person.

"Sure, but what for?"

"There's a guy on the team that's become one of my friends. I've mentioned him a couple of times. I think you'd like him and he wants to meet you, so we're going to a costume party Thursday night, but we have to get costumes. I figured you could meet me at that place across from campus and then we can get a bite to eat after we find something. What do you think?"

"You want to go to a party? Like at school? With other people our age?"

She is stuttering and forgetting what she's trying to say. She only does that when she's nervous. I've never been able to figure out why she's so shy and awkward around big groups of people as gorgeous and friendly as she is. There are girls that don't look half as good as her with a plain personality and they can be complete bitches; stuck up to most people that come in contact with them. I've only met a few people that didn't like her, and it was all jealousy.

When Kinzleigh gets like this you have to push her or she will lock down in her comfort bubble. "I do. I think it will be fun. I'll even get Mom to watch Bryce. Aren't you going to be starting school in January? I think it would be good to start meeting people now so when you start classes you'll already know some students in case our schedules don't work out exactly right."

She takes a deep breath into the phone. "Okay. If it's something you want to do. I don't know if there will be a costume that I'll feel comfortable in, though. I've been working my butt off, but my body didn't transform back exactly like it was before I got pregnant, even though I'm back in my old size."

"That's because it's more beautiful now than it was before. You have a few more curves, but nothing more. I want you to look and feel sexy, but not like last year. You're my wife. Some things I like to selfishly keep for myself. I don't want drunk frat guys gawking at you. My temper is short when it comes to you and you know this. I can handle short, and maybe even somewhat low-cut, but if it's not too much to ask, keep the midsection covered please.”

“Okay. I wanted to find Bryce a costume anyway, so I can sit with Mom and give out candy to the neighborhood kids. Where do you want to meet?”

“That small house across from campus on the service road has them. It’s the only yellow house on the street. You can’t miss it. I’m about to shower and then I’ll head over. We should get there around the same time if you leave now.”

“Okay. I love you.”

I will never get tired of hearing those three little words from her. I always thought they were overrated and overused until they were used in the correct context.

“I love you too, beautiful. Be careful, okay?”

“Okay, bye.”

I listen as the line goes dead. That last phrase will probably be one I use too often. The world becomes a scary place when you have people that you’re terrified of losing. I could lose it all; hell, I already have once, but I could recover from the loss of anything except them.

I place my phone back inside my locker and grab my shower bag. It’s time to go meet my wife . . .

TWENTY-EIGHT

Kinzleigh

I shut off the engine to my car and look around. I don't see Breyson's truck yet. I cannot believe he wants to go to a party where I will know no one. I feel like I have done exceptional with keeping my anxiety under control for quite some time, but this has it on edge. I know I need to find new friends, but I didn't give much thought to how that would happen. I can't just expect it to happen for me.

I grab my purse and keys, opening my door. I step out and walk to the back door to lift Bryce's carrier from the base. I might as well start looking around while I'm waiting for Breyson.

I lock the doors and walk toward the store entry, causing the bell above the door to chime as I open it.

"Hey, darlin'. Is there something I can help you find?"

I haven't heard an accent quite that thick in a while; not since Adalynn left. I follow the sound of the voice until I spot the person it belongs to.

It's a girl around my age. She has the same platinum blonde hair falling straight to the middle of her back, but her skin is darker, as if she tans. She's wearing a pair of tight jeans and cowgirl boots with a neon pink tee shirt that has the store name and logo on it.

She's beautiful, but the first thing I notice about her is the color of her eyes. They are light, but the color is hard to decipher. I'm not sure if they fall in the blue family or the green, because they aren't absolute in either. My guess is they change color. The way her makeup is done to perfection makes them stand out even more.

She's squatted in front of a shelf unloading the contents of a cardboard box. She smiles at me, showing off a pair of dimples, and stands. "I have to say, I don't normally get female lookers, but I'm flattered nonetheless."

She waves me inside. "Come on in, sweetie. I promise not to bite . . . too hard." She winks.

I like her. I don't know why, but she makes me feel comfortable . . . except for the fact that I'm standing inside the door staring at her like an idiot.

Awesome, Kinzleigh. You're off to a good start so far.

"Oh, sorry. I was trying to think if I forgot anything. You know that feeling you get when it feels like you're missing something." I lie. "I'm looking for a few Halloween costumes."

She scans me entirely. Her smile never breaks. I'm guessing she wears it often. "I think I can find something for you. You got a name, darlin'?"

"Kinzleigh Ba—I mean Abercrombie."

"Well, okay then. Kinzleigh, I'm Karsyn. Are you thinking sexy, knock his socks off, or something to wear with the little one on your hip?"

I laugh. I actually laugh within five minutes of meeting someone. I can't help it. She seems so carefree and nice. I've never been so comfortable with someone I don't know. Normally I'd be colored with embarrassment.

"That a girl. I knew we would loosen you up eventually. I'm going to guess by that ring on your finger we might need to settle somewhere in the middle. Follow me to the back. I think I have a few things."

I follow her toward the two doors with a curtain hanging in each doorway but pulled to the side revealing they are dressing rooms. "You can set little bit down on the bench while we get you a few things to try on. I'm sure your arm is getting tired and I'm the only one here, so I keep the back locked. The front door will sound if anyone comes in."

I walk in the small, square room and set the carrier down along with my purse. Her heels are tapping against the hardwood floor with each step, the sounds confirming it's an old house that's been converted. I follow her to the section of the store completely devoted to the array of costumes hanging from racks and the large wall. "Your eyes are really pretty. What color are they?"

She grabs the metal pole used to get items out of reach from the hook it hangs on. She is holding it like a staff. "What color are they not would be a better question. Some call them blue and some call them green, other days they are somewhere in between. It depends on what day you catch me on. They change colors depending on the colors close by like my clothes and eye shadow. They never go real deep of any one shade, though. They stay a light hue."

She is back to looking at the costumes on the wall. I'm not sure why, but I want to know more about her.

"Do you go to school across the street?"

"Second year; sophomore. You?"

"I'm starting in January. My husband does, though. He is on the football team. He's the one that suggested we go to this costume party Thursday night."

"Oh, you're going to the one on frat row? Well, why didn't you say something? My sorority is little sister of sorts to the fraternity throwing it."

"Really?" I suddenly get a big smile on my face. "I was kind of nervous. Breyson is good at meeting new people. Me—not so much. I'm more reserved upfront. I'm not originally from here and all of the people I became friends with senior year have left for college."

"It's your lucky day then." She winks playfully, pulling up one side of her mouth to make it more pronounced. "You'll know someone now and you weren't even trying. Besides, I had a friendship opening and I think you just landed the spot. What do you say, friends?"

"I think that's an awesome idea." Already a huge weight has been lifted from my shoulders. She is steadily pulling down costumes and hanging them on the rack nearby. "Are you a cheerleader by any chance?" I got lucky once today, maybe I will twice.

"Hell no," she says, but never looks at me. "Generally speaking—no offense—they're too cliquish for me. The ones from high school thought they were better than everyone else and entitled to every damn thing, especially the football players, even if they were already taken."

That statement reminds me of Lexi. "Sounds like you've had a bad experience and I know the type of people you're talking about, but we aren't all like that."

"I like you, Kinzleigh, and I believe you, but since you aren't from here, I'll give you a free pass. Other than you I'm going to stay away from cheerleaders and football players. They deserve each other. I got burned once by someone, I won't a second time. I'll stick to my horses. No matter what, they're always loyal."

I think I like her even more than before. She doesn't have to elaborate further. She's said enough that anyone could put two and two together. People suck sometimes. The good people get the shitty hand most of the time, while the bad people come out smelling like roses. It's a wonder there are even still nice people in the world. You can tell even without knowing her that she has a pure heart. Those make the best friends.

"Are you from here?"

"Not directly, but not all that far away. I'm from the outskirts I guess you could say. My family owns a ranch in a small town, but located in the country. Anything and everything aside from the gas station and local grocery store requires a drive."

She pulls down one more costume and gathers them all in one hand, replacing the pole back on the hook it came from. "I think I know which one will be the winner, but a girl has to have options. Go try them on and let me know when you have the first one on. I'll look and see what we have for half pint over there."

I take them out of her hand and turn for the dressing room. "Oh, Karsyn, I'm going to need one for Breyson too."

"They are all made to be couple costumes. We find your best and then he has his. The woman makes the man look good, not the other way around. That's basic female fact number one. Now go."

In the midst of trying on all the costumes she gave me I can't find any I like. I feel like they're too revealing or too overused every Halloween. I pull the last one off the hanger and pull it on my body. I don't expect it to work, but once I get it on, and look in the mirror I'm in love.

"Kinzleigh, are you in there?"

"Just a minute."

I twirl in the mirror as I look at the white Spartan dress. It has a halter neckline and drapes like a sheet. The top half of the dress is slit all the way down to the naval, but in a classy way, still covering both breasts and the midsection. The material is held firmly in place by the two gold bands that run horizontally across the torso: one under the breasts and the other just above the pelvis. According to the picture with the costume, it comes with an armband and disc earrings in the same bronzed gold as the dress bands.

I open the curtain to Breyson standing on the other side, and Karsyn beside him with a knowing grin. She winks. I'm not sure why until I look back at Breyson with his mouth hanging open as he follows the contours of my body with his eyes.

"I knew that would be the one."

"We'll take it." Breyson follows behind her previous comment without taking his eyes off of me. He makes me feel like the sexiest woman alive with no effort on his part at all.

"Even though you haven't seen what you'll be wearing?"

Karsyn is standing next to Breyson, but slightly behind him. I glance back over at her and she has a huge mischievous grin across her face.

I finally start to envision what a Spartan man wears, or at least based off of that television show I've seen. I instantly pull my bottom lip between my teeth and bite down to try and keep from laughing. I have no idea if Breyson will wear it, but damn will he probably look sexy if he does.

He looks back and forth between Karsyn and me. "Wait, what exactly do you call this?"

I'm about to open my mouth when Karsyn holds up the male version of the costume. "A Spartan."

She pushes the hanger into his chest. "Get to changing, cutie. Your woman has found the one. Better keep her happy."

He looks back at me. "I can find something else if you don't want to wear that."

He scans my costume once more. "Hell no. If it means you're wearing that I'll wear anything." He flashes that grin that makes my panties moist. "I'm enough of a man that I can handle it." He winks, making me want to pull him into this dressing room and have my way with him.

He disappears into the dressing room and I look back at Karsyn. She is trying not to laugh. I can tell by the glossy sheen coating her eyes and the tight smile across her lips. I shake my head. She has no idea that Breyson isn't scared to do anything. He knows what kind of body he has. She just challenged him.

"I cannot believe men used to wear this shit." Breyson's mumbles start coming out from behind that curtain one by one.

Bryce is still sleeping in his carrier, not making a sound. I walk further into the store where Karsyn is standing and turn to face the two dressing rooms just as she is.

The curtain to the other dressing room finally opens and Breyson remains standing in the doorway with one arm against the frame.

"Holy shit." Karsyn's thick accent comes out with no hint of laughter remaining behind it.

"Yep. He has that effect on people."

"That is one fine specimen of a man you have. I hope you realize no one that has ever tried that costume on has pulled it off. That's why it is always so funny, but him . . . damn girl, you are lucky you get to go home to that every night. No wonder you have a baby." She is talking with no shame in her voice and no effort to remain unheard.

I allow my eyes to enjoy the sight before me slowly. He's wearing a bronzed gold facemask that only reveals his eyes and mouth. His cape is connected over one shoulder with a small version of the shield he has clipped to his waist. The cape covers one half of his chest and one shoulder in front and then drapes down in the back. His sculpted stomach is bare, and his waist is covered with a brown, leather waistband that forms the top of the Chiton, or what we would classify as a knee-length skirt. The sandal wraps up each leg, past his muscular calf, and he is holding a long sword.

I sigh. "Yes, I know. The effect of looking at him never dulls over time either."

We are standing here talking as if he's not directly across from me, staring at me with a grin on his face. Is it slightly embarrassing that we are both gaping at him shamelessly? Yes, but when you somehow catch a guy that looks like that you come to terms with the fact you'll always be gawking. Am I jealous someone else is ogling him too? No, because I'm the one that gets to take him home, and usually the ones that verbally gawk in the girl's presence mean no harm anyway. It's more of a compliment instead.

"I never knew a guy in a skirt would land that kind of a reaction out of women."

"Not *a* guy, baby, *you* in a skirt would land that kind of reaction."

"Is this the one we're going with?"

"I think it is. We may be finding that corner after all." I allow my eyes to rake down his body. I'm now ready for that amazing session I've waited two days for.

His eyes turn heated, his pupils changing in size.

"Whoa, whoa, whoa. This is an AB conversation and I'm going to C my way out of it. Too much info guys. Meet me at the counter whenever you're ready to check out."

I never look away from Breyson, but I can hear Karsyn's boots fading as she walks across the floor.

"Come here," he commands.

I walk over to him, stopping a few inches away. I want to touch him, and I want to undress him, but most of all I want to ride him. I want to rock his world and alter his universe the way he has mine. "Yes."

"You like what you see?"

"You know I do."

"You still want to go eat or do you want drive thru so I can take you home and show you what I want to do to you right now?"

"Well, that depends. Does it have something to do with stripping me naked?"

He grabs my hand in his. "Where's Bryce?"

I glance in the next dressing room to him still sleeping. "He's sleeping. I fed him right before we left."

He pulls me into the dressing room and shuts the curtain. He backs me against the wall and places my hand on his hard erection. "Do you really have to ask?"

He makes me feel like a sex-crazed addict. "I want to go home. I don't need food to survive. I need your touch, your kiss, and your love. The rest is optional."

"Go change. I'm taking you home and I'm going to spend the rest of the night making love to my wife . . ."

If that's what he says, then that's what it will be. He steps back to let me pass, smacking me on the butt as I do. "This is one time I need you to hurry."

I rush back to my own dressing room and change quite possibly faster than I ever have. You would think my sexual want for him would have faded by now, but it's only gotten stronger with time. Every time he offers his body to me, I feel like a beggar waiting for him to throw me a crumb. It's slightly pathetic the way falling in love with someone can make you feel. There is no magic cool button like a hairdryer when I'm around him. My emotions feel like they are constantly on repeat since his return, but I'll admit that I would gladly take this form of repeat than the sadness it was before.

As I'm getting my shirt back on, he opens the curtain and picks up Bryce's carrier in one hand. With the other, he touches my cheek and leans in to kiss me. He always kisses me goodbye now. "I'll take him in my truck. Pay for the costumes and meet me at home. I'll run through and get us something to eat. Be waiting for me, preferably naked."

Only Breyson can say something like that and have you rushing to follow through. I gather my costume as he exits with our son. "Hey, you still have your base to the car seat, right?"

"Always, baby. It never comes out of my truck." He continues to walk forward as if he's on a mission with a deadline. I watch his retreating form all the way to the door. The man has a beautiful backside.

With both costumes in hand I walk to the register. Karsyn is sitting on a stool with a magazine open in front of her face. "You ready, little mama?"

Her personality is definitely unforgettable. "I am. Did you find an infant costume?"

"I did. It's a surprise, though. No peeking until you get home. I think you'll like it."

She rings up the items and bags them. I hand her my card to pay for it. "How will I get in touch with you?"

She slides the register receipt across the counter. Scribbled across the top in a big, bubbly handwriting is the name Karsyn Davies and her number. "I got you covered, little mama. Now, I know you're dying to set me up with the most perfect guy ever, so I'll add a disclaimer. My number is for your use only, and although you probably have the most amazing and hottest single guy friend ever, I'm not the least bit interested. Sorry, not sorry. No offense to you personally. It happens all the time, so I go ahead and get it out of the way before it's a thought."

I pick up the receipt and fold it in half, placing it in my wallet with my card. She hands me the bag and I take it, walking for the door. "See you Thursday?"

"I'll be the one in white," she says and winks. I take it she does it a lot in good humor. I think we will be great friends. For now, it's time to go enjoy my man . . .

TWENTY-NINE

Kinzleigh

A hand with a ring finger wrapped in a metal band dips between my breasts and underneath the strip of fabric at the front of my dress, cupping over my right breast. He rubs my nipple between two fingers, hardening it. The gentle pulling is making me crazy. I look up from the eye shadow palette in my hand to Breyson smiling in the mirror.

"Have I told you lately that you're beautiful?"

"Yes, but I don't mind hearing it again. Like your favorite song some things are worth repeating over and over. Those amazing little compliments are becoming a vital part of me."

His other hand snakes around my waist, pulling me against him. He's hard and ready, pressed against me. "You ready to get it?"

He knows I love when he talks dirty to me. My cheeks start to heat. "Where's Bryce?"

"Mom already picked him up. She had to drop something off for Mims, so she was already coming out here. Saves us from having to make a stop and gives us some *alone* time before we have to leave. I need to mark my territory before I have to watch guys drooling all over you. I want my scent covering you, repelling them. I want to plant my seed inside of you, consuming your thoughts for hours on end. I want you to still feel me even in my absence. For that, I need you thoroughly fucked and satisfied."

I lay my head against his bare chest. He's standing in only his trunk briefs that he will wear beneath his costume. His hair is still wet, fresh from a shower, and the smell that's emanating from his body is hypnotizing. "No one will be drooling over me. I don't know why you assume everyone will find me irresistible. In fact, to everyone but you I'm just an ordinary girl. I still haven't figured out why you do."

He moves his hand off my breast and already I want him to put it back. He runs it down my front until both hands are clenching material at thigh level. He starts inching my white dress up slowly, moving his face directly next to mine so that our reflections are level in the mirror.

He begins to whisper. "That's where you're wrong, beautiful. You are anything but ordinary. I'm about to show you just how powerful you are when I make you watch me in this mirror as I sink inside you and come apart completely. You will forever be and always have been my undoing, peeling me back layer by layer until you've stripped me completely bare, each and every time I'm with you."

So have you . . .

He hikes the skirt of my dress up to my waist, revealing the white lacy thong beneath. "Hands on the dresser," he commands. "And hold the dress."

Oh, my hell, I love when he gets bossy. I chunk the makeup into my makeup bag and do as he says. He places both hands underneath the waistband of my underwear at my hips, lightly trailing them around to my pelvis before continuing downward. He runs his middle finger through my folds, over the opening, wetting the tip of his finger and bringing it back up to my clit.

I close my eyes. "Look at me. I want you to watch."

He continues to rub up and down in a steady motion, almost as if he's matching the rhythm to music playing. My muscles contract uncontrollably, wanting to be filled by him.

He hooks the index finger of his free hand on the V section of my thong that lies above the crack of my butt, pulling the band over my round cheeks and down to my thighs. I'm so wet it's uncomfortable, yet he never stops rubbing my clit, making me crazy. "Reach back and pull my briefs down, then go back to your current position."

My breathing hitches from the excitement. The past few days between his busy schedule and both of us trying to care for Bryce we've become domesticated quickly, falling into a repetitive pattern of sex in bed before falling into a sleep-induced coma. Not that I would complain, it's still amazing. With his work schedule at the ranch and schoolwork, on top of football, he still makes time for Bryce and me. Our sex life has just become more of a ritual instead of the spontaneous way it used to be, but I guess that's part of marriage and babies.

I reach back and cup my hands on his waist, dipping them underneath the elastic band. The feel of his smooth skin as I push it over his firm butt is only exciting me further. Don't ask me why, but I've always loved his ass. Once I get the band below his rounded backside, I trail my hands around to the front, brushing against the length of his shaft as I move my hand upward to pull the front of his underwear out and away from the head, allowing his erection to spring free from the confinement of his underwear as its hardened position rests against his pelvis.

Once he is fully bared I push his briefs in a line down his center, tracing back down his length, and ending with his testicles in one hand, wrapping the opposite around his dick. He sucks in air and runs his finger down my folds roughly, inserting it into my opening, and shoves it as deep as he can get it. I moan. I can't control it. It feels too good.

"You better be ready for it, baby, because you're about to get it."

I nod against his chest and rub my fisted hand up and down his dick. I love the way it feels in my small hand. He takes a step back with a throaty groan as I start circling my thumb over his head, spreading the pre-cum around. "Hands back on the dresser and bend forward. Now."

I do as he says in anticipation for the way it feels on first entry. It's like getting that first taste of junk food after you've fasted from it for weeks. Your hunger for it is enough to drive you insane, but it's not near as overwhelming as when you actually taste and feel the texture against your tongue.

I bend forward with my hands clenched on each side of the dresser but remain watching him in the mirror; standing tall behind me as I bare myself to him completely, giving him the access he needs.

He pulls his finger out of me, but leaves it lingering over my clit as he aligns his head at my entrance with his free hand. He takes his time, circling the head in the wetness that is steadily increasing in amount, toying with me. I've never been so damn ready for him to screw me. I feel like I could scream from the void he's leaving me with.

He makes no effort to relieve me of the raging hormones that are consuming my bloodstream. I even press my ass further into the hard tip he's teasing me with. He's already stimulated my clit at such a slow, mechanical rhythm in an effort to keep me from coming that I'm sexually frustrated.

I can't stand it any longer. "Breyson! For the love of my mental health would you please fuck me already!"

At the very second I get the last word out he slams into me, burying himself completely. It's as if I've finally scratched an itch that has been pestering the shit out of me. It's such a relief.

He grabs me by the shoulder and leans forward at a dead standstill. "I was waiting on you to ask, baby."

He straightens his stance, thrusting slowly at first while he begins rubbing my clit again. I'm so lost in a world of fantasy that I can't think of anything but how good he feels inside me, and his hands touching me in the most intimate way possible.

The more he gets used to the rhythm of the two opposing directions going at the same time, he begins thrusting harder and faster. The mixture of sensations is almost too much to handle, making me back up into him more, as well as clenching tighter on the dresser with the sensitivity increasing underneath his finger. My eyes start to close.

"Watch me. I want you to see what you do to me." I arch my back as he deepens his thrusts and moans start escaping from my mouth one by one, uncontrollably. With each arch of my back I bare myself to him more. The angle is causing him to hit against something inside, only fueling the orgasm that is building. With each hit it hurts, but it also feels amazing: a painful pleasure.

I look at him through the reflection, memorizing how he looks in the light. Each time he thrusts, his abs contract and his jaw steels. His eyes are heavy and each time he slides inside this low grunt sounds. It's the sexiest view I've ever seen. *He's* the sexiest man I've ever seen, and he's completely aroused. There is no misinterpreting with a look like that. The best part of it all is that I'm the one that makes him this way.

He lets go of my shoulder and grabs the back half of my hair that is hanging down my back. He tugs, pulling me into a standing position. He kisses down my neck. "Fuck, you're beautiful. I want to watch you come, but not in the mirror."

He pulls out of me and turns me around so fast I don't even have time to process what's happening before he picks me up and slams me on the dresser. My dress is waded up at my waist.

He bends forward and places my feet flat on top of the dresser, spreading my legs as far apart as they will go. He places his tongue against my clit in a point and begins flicking up and down on the sensitized and swollen button. Without thinking I slam my head against the mirror, but he never stops. My orgasm has built up and stopped so many times I'm ready to come. "Breyson, I'm about to come."

He never lets up this time. Everything is pounding and blurring around me. I grab his hair in my fist as my orgasm starts to take over my body, consuming every facet of my mind, and making the world around me slow down. My clit becomes overly sensitive, needing a break. "Breyson, stop I can't take it anymore. I want you back inside me."

He stands, pulling my legs to wrap around his waist. He kisses me at the same time he thrusts inside me. I can taste myself on his lips. His hands are cupped around my thighs, squeezing with each thrust. He picks up my bottom, tilting it, and hitting that amazing spot inside. His tongue slips through my lips looking for mine. Our tongues entwine, our lips weaving together. I could kiss him for hours.

I can feel another orgasm, but different this time. I don't usually get two orgasms in one sexual experience, even though they are totally different kinds. It happens occasionally, but not very often. My mind is completely clear and consumed by him simultaneously. He releases my lips. "I'm not going to last much longer. Are you almost there? I want you to come with me; always together."

What he doesn't know is I will always be ready when he asks, because he only asks when he knows I'm about to get off. He knows his way around my body like the back of his hand. The clenching of muscles between my legs is confirmation. "I'm ready . . . now."

Everything is reeling in slow motion. My core muscles are all tightening but feel relaxed at the same time. My toes curl as I ride out my orgasm, my mind completely lost somewhere between reality and nirvana. He presses into me once more and locks his lips with mine as he lets his seed spurt inside me.

I can feel the light pulsations as he finishes his release. He talks against my lips and between kisses. "I love you, Kinzleigh. I love you so fucking much. Don't ever leave me." His voice sounds almost like a dry cry; a plea.

I tighten my legs around his waist, not ready for him to disconnect from me just yet. I love the feel of us together. I could stay like this for hours, locked up and tangled into each other. I run my index finger from the center of his forehead, down his nose, and over his lips, outlining the center of his body until stopping on his chest. "My silly, beautiful, blue-eyed husband. Me marrying you was me signing a contract of forever with you. It was also you taking complete ownership of me. When will you figure out the things that scare you are the same things that terrify me? I could never leave the man that keeps my heart beating. You may love me, but what you forget is that my love for you in return is infinite."

He smiles and that is the greatest compliment a person could receive. The ability to make someone smile whole-heartedly is priceless.

"Sometimes a guy just needs reassurance." He picks up my left hand and brings the back to his lips, kissing it. He places his thumb over the center diamond of my engagement ring. "I'm counting on this as my insurance policy for you. As long as you're wearing it I'm covered."

I smirk. "The only way it's parting from my body is with the limb that holds it."

His smile brightens. "You ready to go to this party?"

"As long as I'm with you I'm ready for anything, Brey . . ."

"You're the greatest wife a man could ask for. You really are. Come on, beautiful. Help me put this horrible man skirt on."

He exits my body and already I feel the void becoming present once again. If I could stay home with him like this all hours of the day, I would. Our bubble is always better than the world going on around us.

THIRTY

Breyson

I cannot believe they got me to wear this damn costume. My competitive nature wouldn't let me back down and now I'm going to pay for it with the embarrassment of walking around in public in a skirt.

Each time I look at Kinzleigh and see how beautiful she is, I forget all of the embarrassment. The top of her hair is all teased when I prefer it natural, but she's still unbelievably stunning. Whether she's painted in makeup like she is now or completely bare of it she is the hottest girl I've ever met. I don't tell people that just because she's mine. The first time I ever saw her she was completely bare of makeup with her hair piled on top of her head, and I was just as hung up then as I am now.

I open the passenger door to my truck, parked in a parking lot over from frat row. There are cars everywhere. I hold out my hand for her to step down from the truck. There is a breeze out, but luckily the cold front has already passed or I would be freezing in what is basically a loincloth.

She places both feet on the side step and then lowers herself onto the ground. I raise her hand in the air and spin her around. She smiles, slightly blushing as she looks from side to side. "When did you turn into this big romantic? You've always been good to me, but you have bypassed sweet Breyson and brought out the big guns."

"When I realized I almost lost you and got a second chance. They usually only come around once. Plus, you make me this way. Do you realize other than small things we've never fought or stayed mad at each other for long?"

I wrap my arm around her and follow behind another couple in a costume, assuming they're going to the same place we are. She shrugs her shoulders. "I've never really thought about it. We just have a lot in common I suppose."

"Yeah, we do, but that's something worth taking care of. I get that we're not most couples. In fact, we're probably the opposite of most couples. A vast majority of the population isn't married at nineteen, especially not if they're in college. We may be in the minority, but we're going to be one of the few that make it, regardless of where we end up in the future."

"You're right. I never want us to change. This works for us, you know?"

I kiss her on the cheek as we come into the yard already littered with red plastic cups. "I know, baby."

We walk down the front sidewalk toward the door. "Breyson. Over here."

I turn to Fisher standing in a small group in front of the house but off to the side. "Sup, man? What the hell are you supposed to be?"

I detour us in his direction, never releasing her from my side. He's wearing a pair of black slacks, a bowtie with no shirt, and cuffs around his wrists. He places one hand behind his head and the other on his crouch. He then starts rolling his hips in a way a male college student shouldn't know how. "I'm Magic Mike, dude. Is it not fucking obvious?"

Kinzleigh laughs and chimes in. "I knew what you were. It is most definitely obvious if you've ever seen the movie."

He breaks from the small group he's in and walks toward us, draping his arm around her on top of mine. "Sometimes you have to watch him. I think he's been hit out on the field too many times, knocking a few screws loose. Are you sure you want to be married to a guy like that?" He winks and she laughs again, showing that she's comfortable. I knew I liked the guy for some reason.

"Hey. Get off my woman."

He slaps me on the back of the head. "Guys wearing skirts don't get to demand things. I don't care how cool you think you are."

I draw my plastic sword, placing the point at his throat jokingly. "I'm a warrior. Get it right."

He surrenders his hands. "Fine. Put that shit away before you injure yourself." He laughs and holds out his hand for Kinzleigh. "I'm Fisher. You must be Kinzleigh."

She flashes a proud smile at him already knowing her name. "How did you know?"

Fisher takes a step and puts his arm around my neck, bearing his weight on me. "I wish I could say it was because I'm that good at guessing, but your man here doesn't shut up about you. I'm surprised we actually get any practicing done. Since I'm your new favorite person you can do me a favor. Tell him to tone that shit down, will ya? He's making the rest of us guys look bad. You and I need to form a central alliance against him and find his balls. I know they're down there somewhere."

I laugh and shove him playfully. "Shut that shit up. I'm not that bad. You make me sound like a pussy."

"Hey, you said it not me."

Kinzleigh is actually laughing out loud. I look at her with a smile on my face. "Are you agreeing with him? Don't forget who you're going home with."

She shakes her head with a big smile spread across the bottom half of her face. "Are you guys always like this?"

"You see he's a royal pain in my ass," I say.

"You can blow smoke up her ass if you want to, Breyson, but you know your college football days would not be enjoyable without me present. You need me. The sooner you come to terms with it, the sooner you can move on."

"I like him. It sounds like you have someone to keep you in line."

Fisher grabs Kinzleigh in his other arm, pulling her next to his other side. "You hear that, Breyson? I told you I'm a likable guy . . ."

"Kinzleigh?"

We all three turn in the direction of that voice. It's the girl from the costume store walking up the sidewalk. Her and Kinzleigh acted friendly, but I'm not sure I even caught her name.

Kinzleigh slips out of Fisher's arm and walks over to meet her. "Hey girl. I love the costume."

I'm assuming by the large set of feathery, white wings on her back she is supposed to be the purest of guardians; an angel. The girl is wearing a short, skintight, white dress with flowing sleeves and it's lowcut in the front with cleavage spilling out. The white appears brighter against her tanned skin, and she's wearing a set of white heels to match. The only color on her entire body is the silver shimmer in her makeup, her pink lips, and her light eyes.

"I was just about to go inside to meet some friends. Want to come with? I can introduce you . . ."

"Um . . ."

Kinzleigh turns around to glance at me. "Breyson, you remember Karsyn, right? From the costume shop . . ."

I don't want her to leave my side, but I told myself I was going to give her a chance to branch out and meet people. It's crazy, but I feel like Kinzleigh has been the one to make all of the sacrifices. She's the one that put off school and has given up all her cheerleading plans since she found out she was pregnant, starting with the competition squad she was supposed to be on last year. I can't help but to feel responsible. After all, I'm the one going to school and also getting to play football. It's time to give her some slack on the rope I'm holding.

I'm about to speak when Fisher releases me and walks toward her. He holds out his hand in front of him, waiting for Karsyn to take it. "I'm Fisher," he says.

She takes the edge of his hand as if she's only doing it out of good manners. What's funny is I've seen how the cheerleaders act around him. They all want to sink their teeth into him, but it doesn't faze him at all. I was starting to get a little worried that he is either secretly in a relationship or he has another underlying issue, because no red-blooded, single, heterosexual male would turn down every girl to cross his path.

I shake my head at the unfamiliar gesture of him actually appearing interested in a member of the opposite sex.

"Karsyn." She gives him a half, fake smile and looks back at Kinzleigh as she links her hands together, clearly not wanting him to reach for it again.

"Are you Greek?"

"Yep." She points to the keychain holding the Greek lettering she represents on her key ring. "You?"

"No shit? Phi Mu, huh?" He points to the lettering that labels the house in front of us. "I guess we'll be seeing a lot of each other then."

I have no idea what any of that means. I always just assumed fraternities and sororities were an easy option for drinking underage.

"I wouldn't count on it," she returns and looks at me. "So, are you going to let your girl come with me for a little bit?"

"Sure." I look at Kinzleigh. "Go have fun. You have your cell, right?"

She nods.

"Good. I'll find you in a bit."

Karsyn links her arm around Kinzleigh's and begins pulling her toward the door where she disappears. I can only imagine the drunk frat boys that will be hitting on her, but I cannot let my jealousy get out of control. I will not have a redo of our last Halloween party. Even if I don't trust them, I trust her, and that's enough.

I'm staring at the door in thought. Fisher punches me in the arm. I look at him. "What the hell was that for, asshole?"

"Dude, who was that? Why didn't you tell me about her? I thought we were friends . . ."

"Calm the fuck down. I just met her. I didn't get her name until the exact second you did when it came out of Kinzleigh's mouth. Even if I did, why would it matter? It never crossed my mind that you might actually be interested when you haven't shown any prior interest in girls. I'd be willing to bet you've barely gotten laid since you started college, and now suddenly, I'm supposed to be promoting pussy for you? Cut me some slack. I'm not a mind reader."

"Whatever, Man. Hook me up."

"What do I look like? Why can you not hook yourself up? Are you doubting your womanizing skills?"

"What part of 'I'm from a small town with limited options did you not comprehend'? It's not like I have an infinite amount of experience. That girl is slightly out of my league, quarterback or not."

"Okay, first off, that's bullshit. No girl is ever out of your league. That's a sorry excuse some guy came up with because he failed miserably. You just have to be different than what they're used to. You only think of her that way because she's not falling all over you like every other girl that sees you as the hot starting quarterback. Learn how to read between the lines. Those girls use guys like you to increase their social status without actually getting to know you. That girl in there is probably just a girl some asshole ran through like a tornado. Maybe you should gain her trust first. Work for it. You wanted a chase, now you got it."

"You got all of that by just learning her name? Where did you learn so much about girls? You're married at nineteen."

"When I stopped running after random pussy, I learned a lot."

"Okay, fine, but your girl is friends with her. Get me a window."

I shake my head at him and laugh. I wonder if I was this bad to Ryland that summer I first met Kinzleigh. I guess it's time to pay it forward. "I'll see what I can do, but you owe me, and don't think I'll forget when it's time to pay up."

"I'll gladly pay up. Come on let's go get a beer. We aren't going to stand out here all night."

That sounds like a plan to me. I want to see if I can find Kinzleigh. Maybe it'll give this goofball another chance to talk to Karsyn.

It's seems to always be the blondes that hook you at first sight. It's like they have this imaginary pull, leaving us guys in a state of confusion and wanting more, but not understanding why. Look at that Riggan guy for example. He's in rehab over his. Who knows if he'll ever come out really *alive* . . . One girl—the right girl—has the ability to cause mass destruction on a man. That kind of debris takes years to recover from.

THIRTY-ONE

Kinzleigh

I follow Karsyn through the crowd. Music is blaring throughout the room. It's been a long time since I've been to a party. I almost feel out of place. Maybe it's because I'm not a student and while all of these people are carefree, I have a baby at home. Leaving him behind to come to something like this leaves me feeling guilty.

Karsyn places her mouth close to my ear. "Do you want a drink?"

She turns her head so I can do the same since you can't hear otherwise. "I can't I'm nursing."

"Of course. So, have you applied for spring semester yet?"

We come into the room lined with several kegs among other forms of alcohol. "Karsyn! I knew you'd come see me."

A guy is standing by one of the kegs, resting his forearm on a high-top table full of red plastic cups that match the ones littering the lawn. He is clearly sampling while he works from the slur in his speech. He's the standard prep or jock, wearing a wrinkle free button-down advertising an expensive brand logo I recognize well on the left chest. His hair is short, black, and gelled. He's cute, but because of his baby face he's nothing for a girl to drool over. He doesn't really strike me as a football player, though, with his lean frame, no muscles or bulk anywhere to be seen. I wonder if this is her boyfriend. That Fisher guy seemed smitten by her and he was ten times cuter than this guy.

"Of course, I'm going to come see you. You're the one serving the alcohol." You can hear the sarcastic dry humor in her voice, but she appears to be totally serious, making me want to laugh. She is a real firecracker. She smiles and winks, but I recognize it as a friendly gesture and not one present with a crush.

He smiles at her and shows off a set of dimples, making him cuter than my original presumption. He lays his right hand over the location of his heart. "Always a heartbreaker, Karsyn. When are you going to give in to me and let me take you on a date?"

"Come on, Luke, you know I don't date. Don't be silly. Besides, that would just make our totally awesome friendship awkward when it doesn't work out. How about a Bud Light?"

I'm envious of her witty personality. Sometimes I feel like mine is dull because of my shy nature, but somehow, I still end up being friends with outgoing people. It's strange, honestly.

"Who's your friend?"

"This is Kinzleigh," she says. She looks at me as she takes the cup that he recently filled to the brim with beer. "Kinzleigh, this is Luke. We share the same major, so we met in class first semester, but somehow, we have been in three classes together since. How does that continue to happen at a school of this size, Luke?"

She turns her head back to him and takes a sip of beer at the same time she says his name, dripping with sarcasm. He winks at me and shrugs his shoulders with a huge grin smeared across his face. "No idea. I guess we just keep picking the same times when we make our schedules. Two great minds think alike. Isn't that what they say?"

I place my hand over my mouth, trying not to laugh at him blatantly admitting he looks at her schedule before making his own.

She shakes her head at him and rolls her eyes. "You have no shame, do you? Come on, Kinzleigh. Let's go circulate. I'm sure Luke here has a keg to manage."

I follow behind her as she walks off. He calls out from behind us. "Those who take risks are the ones that will succeed. See you around, Karsyn."

He's a little annoying, but oddly, it's kind of cute. "Not in this lifetime," she mumbles and then reaches back to grab my hand.

We weave through the crowd, Karsyn in front of me. I have no idea where we are going, but I'm going to have fun tonight if it's the last thing I do. I try really hard to be a responsible mother for Bryce, so I never get out and do anything. Once in a while, I suppose, we can both be kids for a few hours.

Karsyn downs her glass of beer and pulls us both into the middle of the dance floor next to a group of girls. I assume she knows them based on their reaction as we close in next to them. A hip-hop beat comes over the speaker system and the dance floor becomes packed with people.

Karsyn throws her hands in the air and starts singing at the song at the top of her lungs. She has a strong voice, but one that is enjoyable to listen to. I'm standing here watching all of them, not yet feeling that bold for the lack of alcohol in my system.

She grabs my hands in hers, pulling me closer to her. "Dance with me!"

What the heck . . . Why not . . . I don't know any of these people here. I probably won't ever see them again. I allow her to pull my hands over our heads and we both start swaying our hips to the music. I've never been a great dancer aside from cheerleading routines, but I give it my best shot. Free styling was never one of my strong points. I roll my hips to the best of my ability and allow her to twirl me around. I'm starting to relax and enjoy myself. This is fun.

The song changes and this time I start to sing along with her. Those who know me know that I'm no singer, but the music is so loud and with the constant flow of alcohol from cup to mouth no one is paying attention anyway. It's mostly couples grinding against each other, preparing for the epic proportions of bodily fluids that will be exchanged later. Then there are also a few cliques of girls like Karsyn and me. That's as far as the eye can see aside from the loft overhead where I assume are bedrooms.

Karsyn dances around me until she's behind me dancing back to back. With my arms raised in the air I sway them side-to-side in a rhythm opposite to the motion of my hips, brushing against Karsyn's backside.

I glance up and catch a glimpse of Breyson with a red cup in his hand, leaning forward with his forearms on top of the rail, watching me. He winks at me, making my heart rate speed up. I blow him a kiss and he opens his free hand to catch it, and then closes his fist with a smile on his face.

Out of nowhere Angelique comes up behind him and puts her grubby little paws on his waist, running them up his bare back. My heart stops completely. I feel like I'm going to throw up. Breyson's eyebrows dip as if he's slightly confused.

That's because the only person supposed to be touching you that way is down here!

I'm beginning to panic. She's watching me. She knows I can see her, and even worse, she has a dirty grin on her face. Her hands slide to the front and start to descend as if she's going for his crotch, but he grabs them and slings them off, standing upright to turn around.

You know what, I'm sick of this shit. Breyson and I have withstood a lot of fire and we're still standing strong. When something is important to you, you fight for it, no matter what that entails. It may require stepping out of your comfort zone, but at some point, you have to stand up for yourself or people will trample all over you. Girls can be backstabbing and cruel. This is something I will have to fight constantly if I'm going to support Breyson's dream to play in the NFL.

I look at Karsyn. "I'll be right back."

I storm forward, pushing my way through the crowd looking for the stairs. I find them and grab the railing, ascending the steps so fast my thighs are burning. I am no longer thinking about anything but the tramp that has her hands on my husband. All I can see is a haze of red.

Breyson can't even see me as I reach the top, because he is saying something to her. Her hand goes for his arm and I grab it, twisting it as hard as I can as I jerk it backward. She screams and starts to turn toward me, but I never let up. I want her to feel an increment of the pain I feel when I uncontrollably envision him sticking his dick inside her every time I have to see her face.

"You stupid whore. I told you next time you showed your face around here I was going to make sure it was your last. But you can't stand it, can you? Why can't you leave us alone and go find your own man? This one is taken."

She shoves me backward trying to free her hand from my hold. "How do you even know he really wants you? Have you asked him since there became options? Did it ever occur to you that maybe he's only with you because he knocked you up and is making an effort to remain a good guy? Maybe I can make him happier than you."

She just pressed detonate. Before her words may have made me unsure and self-conscious, but not now. After someone proves his love for you over and over, you actually start to believe it. Breyson *tells* me how much he loves me constantly, and more than that, he *shows* me. I trust him with every part of me, because he *earned* it. A rock wall doesn't crumble by someone firing a few stones at it with a slingshot.

I barrel toward her, pushing her against the wall with my hands. I grab her black hair in one hand and slap her across the cheek with the other as hard as I can. It's like my body has taken over and put my brain in time out. I've never held so much rage for another human being, not even the night I slapped Lexi and she said some nasty things as well. This woman, though, has experienced him in the most intimate way and is also trying to take him from me.

I pull her hair in my hand harder, jerking her head to the side, and clench my teeth together. "I know he wants me because he asked me to marry him, you selfish little twit. He's had every opportunity to back out and live a life with someone else, even after you showed up, but you know what? He still asked me to marry him and followed through with it. I'm going to tell you something else too. If anything regarding my son exits from your mouth again, a slap will be the least of your worries, because when I get finished with you, you will wish you were dead. My son may have been unplanned, but that doesn't make him any less special. You may look at me with pity in your eyes, but you're the one I feel sorry for. Instead of finding your own happy ending you have to prey on a married man. Understand one thing, bitch; no one will make him happier than me."

My breathing is rapid and short as I work to catch up from the lack of air intake while I was all but spitting in her face. I hate to resort to violence of any kind and I don't condone it, but there is always an exception to almost every rule, and she deserved it. I don't care who you are or what the situation is, once someone is in a relationship they are off limits, especially if they have entered into the sanctity of marriage. There are no excuses otherwise.

Her eyes fill with tears. For the first time since I met the evil, heartless female she actually looks remorseful. She looks from me to Breyson and begins talking, her Spanish accent thick. "You're married to her now? What she says is true?"

"I tried to explain, but you wouldn't let me get a word in. You have a good side, Angelique, I've seen it, but somewhere since then you've lost it. For the last time, there is someone meant for you, but that someone isn't me. What we had was just a fling during a time I was lost, literally. My place is here, with her."

I totally forgot he was even standing there. I can feel him step behind me, placing his hands gently on my arms. "Let her go, baby. I think she gets the point now."

I didn't realize I was still holding onto her hair, and I grabbed her shirt in my fist at some point during my rage. He pulls me toward him, creating a space between Angelique and I. Breyson is my therapy. He's my match when I need fire and my water when I get too hot.

She looks at me. "I'm sorry. I need to go." Two short sentences and she is running down the stairs. I instantly relax, knowing she is further in distance from the most important part of my life.

"I'm so fucking sorry, baby," he whispers in my ear. "I had no idea she was still here. I'm sorry."

I close my eyes and a tear falls down my cheek, probably from the adrenaline coursing through my body. My emotions are freefalling from the roller coaster they just went on. I trust Breyson and I meant what I said, but there is one question I have that I didn't consider before. I will ask it once and it will never arise again.

I turn around to face him. I look in his eyes, instigating an emotional connection. He places his hands on each side of my face as if he's about to kiss me. "There is something I need to ask you. I need you to be honest with me no matter what the answer is. Whether it hurts me or not I want the truth."

He looks slightly worried, but nods. "Okay."

"If you get drafted into the NFL you're going to have a lot of women putting you in similar situations or worse. I won't get to be with you all the time. Will you be strong enough to withstand the temptation and stay true to me forever? I know we haven't gone without sex for long periods of time since we've been together, but in the case we have no choice, can you endure it and wait for me? Can you always be faithful to me no matter what?"

He backs me against the wall, pinning me against it. "There are no other options. I don't need sex, Kinzleigh, what I need is a life with you. I don't want sex with anyone but you. You're my wife, meaning you are my only. I will never cheat on you for any reason, famous or not."

A sense of relief washes over me. That's all I need to know. He meant it. I can feel it in my heart. "Can we go home? I just want to cuddle with you."

He pulls me into a tight hug, squeezing me hard. "That's the best idea I've heard all night."

He kisses me on the top of the head. I have grown to love his sweet gestures. A life with Breyson is an amazing journey. Every day you get little sprinkles of sugar to make it sweeter. It's one thing you look forward to for the rest of your life.

THIRTY-TWO

Breyson

DECEMBER . . .

"Breyson, wake up. It's Christmas and it's snowing!" The soft but excited whisper blows into my ear. I pretend I'm asleep, knowing what's coming next. Kinzleigh has been in an exceptionally good mood since we moved in the new house at the beginning of this month. We are officially homeowners. It turned out so much better than I expected. She's been like a kid on crack candy with Christmas decorations ever since.

The mattress dips underneath me, jousting me every time she comes down from jumping up and down on the bed. "Breyson, it's time to see what Santa brought."

I barely peek through my closed eyelashes as her face falls. She plops down into a straddling position on top of me, landing right where I want her. She begins shaking my shoulder. "Breyson. Come on, get up. It's our first Christmas as a married couple and Bryce's first Christmas."

I open my eyes at the same time my face transforms, now looking like The Grinch. "Got ya." Grabbing her by the ribs, I flip us over and start tickling her.

Tickling is the one thing she hates, but I love it, because I get to hear that rare, uninhibited laugh that is better than any morning coffee. I do this every morning when she wakes me up for work before school and she continues to fall for it. That makes the score even, thus, anger is not allowed.

She is kicking and screaming, bucking wildly underneath me, but I never let up. That amazing little laugh is right around the corner. "Breyson! Stahhhhp! I give up."

Nope, not yet . . .

"You know what I want."

I dig my fingers into her sides deeper, working my fingers faster into her skin. She is now laughing so hard she can't breathe; that perfect laugh. Beautiful. She is tossing and turning, lightly punching my forearms. "O-kay . . . Please. I. Can't. Breathe."

Now that my morning addiction has been fed, I stop and lightly kiss her lips, getting out of bed. "Morning, baby."

She sits up, trying to catch her breath, narrowing her eyes and pretending to be mad, but the smile on her face gives her away. "You know I don't like to be tickled."

Her bare legs are peeking out of the oversized tee shirt she is wearing— my shirt. She wears one every night to bed. We wash more of my clothes than hers, but I don't say anything because I like seeing her in my shirts. "Yet you continue to fall for it. Besides, I like to hear your laugh. It sets me up for a good day. You wouldn't want me to get out of routine and flunk in class or mess up at practice, would you?"

She scoots to the edge of the bed, preparing to get up. I place a hand flat on the bed to each side of her. She looks at me. "Well, when you put it that way, I sound like such an asshole."

"I knew you'd see it my way."

Bryce starts crying, signaling it's mealtime. The boy is getting to be a chunk now that he's started eating baby food. He loves it. Kinzleigh's face falls. "How are you feeling? You all right?"

"No. I feel guilty."

Kinzleigh decided this would be her last week to breastfeed. After New Year's we are switching him to formula. She is starting school in a few weeks and it's just easier with our school schedules, plus she is starting to train for cheerleading tryouts in hopes she makes the squad next season.

"Hey, you have nothing to feel guilty about. You have given it to him for four months. I'm proud of you. Even if you choose to stay home with our kids later, you still need to go to school and get a degree for you or you'll regret it. You don't have to miss out on this phase of your life just because we have a kid in the mix."

She smiles. "Why are you always right?"

"I'm not. I just skip the stage of panic, so I come to the conclusion faster than you."

I kiss her, lingering on her lips. They are soft and taste like our mint toothpaste. I smile against her mouth, suck her bottom lip between mine, and release it. "Have you been kissing Santa, Mrs. Abercrombie?"

Her cheeks flush and she places her fingers over her lips. "Maybe. I heard he's really hot this year. I couldn't risk having bad breath, you know . . . just in case."

I want to show her just how hot she makes me, but Bryce increases the pitch of his cry. Duty calls. "I'll get him. Meet me in front of the Christmas tree. I have a feeling Santa left you something awesome."

Her smile lights up the room. If I didn't know any better, I would think she was a kid, but the biggest present of them all is waiting in the barn. It's really for Bryce, but it's something that will grow with him. Neither of them can do more than look at each other for a couple of years, but I started a tradition with Divinity last Christmas and I figured each of them should have their own horse. I did growing up. Pops always said a horse is a man's best friend. A horse will always stand by its owner once that bond is established, so I thought if they grew up together it would be a deeper connection.

Pops has been in ranching his entire life. He has contacts he has acquired over the years. He knows a few breeders, so he made a call. We lucked out because one of them had a colt that would be ready to leave his mother right before Christmas. We made the trip and picked him up last week.

Keeping Kinzleigh out of the barn has not been an easy task. The woman loves her horse. I swear she was meant to be from the country. The only reason she didn't go against my request is because she has been busy getting things ready to start school for spring semester.

We started the process of looking for a sitter to keep Bryce Monday through Friday during school hours and our parents are going to help out for practices and her training if we're both unavailable. Kinzleigh is steering that wagon. She will pick the best candidate for the job.

Kinzleigh and Karsyn have become glued at the hip. She's over frequently and has helped Kinzleigh a lot since my schedule is so busy between work, school, and football. She even introduced her to a couple of girls in her sorority that are on the cheerleading squad this year. They have filled her in on the tryout schedule and process for next season. Some of the guilt fades now that she is working toward getting her life back on track. I believe we can still be good parents and go after our dreams.

Since that first game I played in, I've started every game. Coach kept his word. We were barely putting points on the board before I started and since then have only lost one game. I'd like to say it's all because of me, but Fisher and I make a good team, plus I get along with all of the other players. Maybe we can turn this team around from the losing record they've had and put the school back on the radar for recruiting.

It's really true when you hear a win is a team effort. Also, when you think you've completely lost out on the opportunity to play and you've wanted to since you were old enough to throw a ball, you tend to find a passion you never knew you had, and that in turn makes me play better.

Kinzleigh's mom was a little upset when we told her we eloped after our return, but her faith in me was restored once Kinzleigh told her that we were still having a wedding and asked her to help plan it. Kinzleigh explained that with all we have been through it was something we needed to do alone. The big shot attorney actually cried and hugged us both.

Her mom is really nice, but from what Kinzleigh has told me she is brutal in court. I think she's even been helping Mom with the whole accidental overdose situation at the hospital. Mom's been seeing someone, but has not been cleared by the hospital administration to practice until she finishes the program that they required of her with a licensed hospital psychiatrist. Once she goes back to the clinic there will be a period in which her plan of care will have to be evaluated on every patient to ensure her mental state is well enough to practice safely. It has something to do with malpractice prevention.

Kinzleigh and her mom have been going crazy with wedding details since we got back from our little weekend wedding getaway. Apparently in a girls' world four months to plan a wedding is like a week in real time. They are in full panic mode. I don't even step foot in the spare bedroom, especially after Kinzleigh had to devote some time to us getting moved in here.

The plan is to get married the first weekend in March. It will be at the barn like Kinzleigh wanted, but they are building a large gazebo on a section of wooded land between the barn and our house for the reception, and then after it can be used for whatever else. It's actually really nice. The wedding preparations are another reason it's been hard to keep Kinzleigh out of the barn, so I had to let her mom in on the surprise to help me out.

I stand upright and reach for a pair of sweatpants. Kinzleigh jumps up from the bed and bolts for the hallway. I walk into Bryce's room at the same time Kinzleigh's footsteps are trampling against the hardwood floor. Bryce is so mad his face is turning red as he cries.

I reach into his crib and pick him up underneath his arms, raising him slightly above my head. "Good morning, little buddy. Are you ready to see what Santa brought you? You have no idea what Daddy is even talking about do you?" I ask in a baby voice as I lay him on the changing table to change his diaper.

It only takes me a few seconds to change him. I've got diaper changing down to an art. I pick him up and place him beside my ribs on my arm like a football. It's the kid's favorite spot. Don't ask me why, because it looks really uncomfortable, but every time I put him there, he chills out as if he's lounging and content. It doesn't matter whether he's hungry, wet, or just moody.

I walk to his closet and reach under the stack of neatly folded blankets for one of Kinzleigh's presents. It's small, so I didn't want to put it under the tree making it obvious. I hid it here, because she put all of his blankets on the top shelf until it was cold enough for the extra ones. She hasn't touched them since they were put up there, because she has to get a chair or have me reach up to get whatever she needs. Short people and high things don't mix well, but it's good for me. They make great hiding places.

Grabbing the small box, I hear her voice. "Breyson! You're slower than Christmas. Would you come on already?"

"Someone's impatient." I look down at Bryce and smile as I mumble the sentence. He just stares at me, returning his toothless baby smile. I love this kid. He's the greatest thing ever. You really couldn't ask for a better baby. He only cries when he needs something, and generally, if you pick him up and talk to him, he will calm down for a little while until you get it. He has the most easy-going temperament.

Placing the small box in my pocket, I walk through the hallway and into the large, open living room. The ceilings are high, so Kinzleigh got the twelve-foot tree she had to have. That bad boy was a bitch to put together, but it definitely makes for a better Christmas. I guess for something that only rolls around once a year you might as well go big.

I look in the direction of the tree and my eyes widen as they stop on Kinzleigh. Fucking hell, she is hot. I adjust my semi, trying to keep it from getting any harder with my son in my arms. "Where was that outfit last night?"

She is standing in the corner of the room by the fireplace, positioned in front of the tree with her hands pressed together, rubbing them against each other. She is wearing a hot pink Santa hat trimmed in white and decorated with small rhinestones over her long, curly hair. The only form of clothing she is wearing is what looks like a velvet bra in the same pink shade and a short, velvet, hot pink skirt also lined in white fur along the bottom hem, exactly like the hat. All three pieces of material are covered in some kind of rhinestones, giving off a reflective light.

You can tell her training is paying off by the light sculpting of abs in the beginning stages down her stomach. Her face is bare of makeup except for the hot pink lipstick on her lips. My eyes burn into her as they trace down the seam of her body, memorizing every inch of the way she looks in this very moment. This is the best damn Christmas I've ever had.

I can't help but smile when I get to the white furry slippers on her tiny feet. She goes for Santa's sexy mistress until you get to her feet where she mixes it up with Legally Blonde's version of comfort. That's my baby, my wife, and the girl that undeniably stole my heart. Even dressing down she is completely prissy. God, I love her.

She smiles at me, most likely because I'm standing in the middle of the room staring. Every day with her gets better than the day before. I'm not exaggerating. It really does.

"It was a surprise. I'm Santa's helper. Sit in the present opening chair. I want to watch you open yours and Bryce's gifts. I even invested in a video camera for us, since this is our first big event as a family," she says, pointing to the video camera mounted on a tripod behind the couch. She has it angled at the chair she has beside the tree. When did she set all this up? I haven't been gone that long.

"Damn woman. How am I supposed to concentrate with you wearing that? Are you trying to drive me insane? You better watch your backside when you bend over to pick up the presents. I will not be held accountable for my actions if a finger disappears or I lose control over a hand."

She puts her hands on her hips and sticks her leg out to the side, tapping her fuzzy slipper-covered foot against the floor. I have to bite my tongue to keep from making a dirty comment. That sexy woman is going to be the death of me.

She points at the baby swing she has sitting in the middle of the floor facing the tree. She has been putting it there a lot since we put the tree up the day after Thanksgiving. Bryce likes to stare at the twinkling colored lights. "Baby. Swing. I'm going to get our hot chocolate I made from Grams' famous mix while you so kindly build a fire. It's snowing on Christmas! We have to have a fire. They go together. How on earth we got lucky with snow on Christmas Day I have no idea, but I'm taking full advantage. I'll turn down the heat so it doesn't get too hot, and I'll bring back a bottle so he can eat while you open your presents. Until then his pacifier is in the swing."

She says nothing more and walks toward the kitchen, swaying as she passes, causing me to grunt a little. I feel like a deer in rut needing to mark her. I watch her ass all the way into the kitchen where she disappears out of sight. There is no adjusting myself now. I have an erect dick to deal with and a fully awake infant, leaving no way to properly make it go away until it gives up from not getting any. It won't be anytime soon either with her wearing that.

"You're putting that back on when innocent eyes are not present and entering into dreamland," I shout loud enough for her to hear me.

"As long as it ends up back on the floor," she yells in return. Damn, she was made for me. It doesn't matter how crazy of a scheme I could come up with. She would do it. I don't think she has ever denied me anything.

I look down at Bryce not making a peep, but now that we're quiet, I can hear his breathing. "Little man, you heard the boss. You have to get in your swing. I know you like your spot, but Daddy is not making Mommy mad. I'll have to pay for it later and that's not happening. One day you'll understand. Us men have to look out for each other."

I move my feet from the spot I'm standing in and walk to his swing, lay him inside, and fasten the straps. I turn it on, letting it begin the rocking process. Christmas music starts playing through the built-in speakers. It sounds like the Chipmunks to be exact, making me laugh. Again, only Kinzleigh.

"I'll be right back, buddy." He's already staring at the lights on the tree in a peaceful contentment. I walk across the room to the front door and step outside onto the porch. The wind blowing across my bare chest causes chill bumps to form. "Shit, it's cold."

All of the greenish-brown grass is covered in a thin layer of white. We rarely get snow here and for it to actually stick is rarer. I guess the meteorologist actually got it right this year. I've heard it's supposed to snow and then didn't so many times I don't even listen to it anymore.

I was going to ride them to the barn on the four-wheeler later, but I'm not getting Bryce out in this. I'll have to start my truck in a little while to let it warm up.

When we built the house, we went ahead and put a large building in the back for my four-wheeler and guy stuff. Kinzleigh got free rein on the house. All I wanted was a mancave for my stuff that don't belong in a family household and a place to store things I accumulate over the years. I don't imagine a west coast girl going for deer heads hanging on the wall of the living room, so I made it easy for both of us to save an argument. Mancave. Problem solved. The pool goes in the ground this spring. There was no point in doing it in the winter.

I look out in front of me at the view. I can't believe we were blessed with so much at such a young age. Thank God for hardworking parents with values. Had Pops not taught me the importance of saving and investing money at a time I didn't need it for myself and Dad's work ethic that we needed to learn responsibility, I wouldn't be here.

Kinzleigh and I would have probably ended up as dropouts, working dead-end jobs and barely making ends meet in some rundown house or economy-priced apartment, but instead we are blessed to have come from such good families. It's a luxury not many have. Not all people get this kind of ending. The things that were instilled in me I want to pass on to my kids.

I cross my arms over my chest from the chill in the air. Even with it being cold all I can do is stand here and relax. It's nice to have a break from school and football. I've been going nonstop since I showed up from Spain.

Things are finally on my side. I am married to the girl of my dreams, we have a beautiful son, we live in a nice house, and I have one semester of college under my belt, not to mention getting to play football when I thought my chances passed me by. My life is pretty fucking great.

The door opens and I turn around. Kinzleigh is standing behind the door with her head peeking out. "Are you okay? You've been out here for a while and it's freezing."

"Yeah, sorry baby. I was just enjoying the view." I'm consumed with a rush of emotions from my previous thoughts. "I love you, Kinzleigh. I know our life hasn't been perfect, but it's getting pretty damn close. I'm really glad you married me."

"I love you too, baby." She pauses. "Should I be worried?"

"No. I just needed to say it. I was feeling sentimental, I guess."

"Okay. We better get started. We have a lot of stops today. Your parents' house at lunch and mine at dinner. Then, I was thinking we could come back here for Christmas movies next to the Christmas tree and maybe even a little sexy time in front of the fire. What do you think?"

She flashes a cheesy grin at me. I laugh and walk to the woodpile sitting on the drying rack by the door, grabbing an armful of logs. "Sounds like an amazing Christmas night. You know I'm always down for sexy time with you, no matter where it is."

I get to the door and she opens it, letting me pass. It's time to build my woman a fire. I'm always striving to make her happy, because in return it makes me happy.

After a few attempts, the fire is finally breathing in the fireplace, steadily building into a large flame. I stand, waiting for my next set of instructions from the hot-as-hell naughty elf by the tree. "What next?"

Bryce is laying in his swing with a bottle propped on a cushion to hold it up. "Your chair and hot chocolate are waiting."

I sit in the chair as instructed and watch as Kinzleigh bends over, now shuffling through the never-ending presents packed beneath the tree. I have no idea why we have so many presents. I don't need anything and Bryce isn't old enough to enjoy presents.

I grab my mug of hot chocolate and tilt my head, trying to see underneath her skirt. She starts to stand upright and I notice a black thong. Things are getting a tad bit difficult.

"Here it is," she says. The box she holds up is wrapped in black wrapping paper. It isn't big, but she looks like she is about to burst to give it to me, so it makes me more excited to open it.

She holds out her hand with the present lying in her palm. "I know you said you didn't want to go overboard on presents between the two of us this year because you wanted to save it for our honeymoon, but there was something I wanted to do for you. It wasn't really something I could wrap, so I had an idea to give you something to open."

She takes a deep breath, as if she's nervous. "It's something you wanted, but I've watched you put it off over and over again because there is always this or that. You've given me so much that I wanted to give something back to you, something that is only yours. Here, just open it. I'm rambling."

I take the box and pat my thigh. "Will you sit with me while I open it?"

She walks closer and sits on my leg, wrapping her arm around my neck. I slide my fingers underneath the fold and tear the paper until the box is all that's left. I pull off the lid and inside sits two silver keys on a Browning keychain. I didn't even know she knew what the Browning logo was. "What does it open?"

She has a sly grin on her face. She stands and grabs two jackets off the couch that I didn't notice before, handing one to me. "Put this on."

I pull the hoodie over my head and watch as she puts on her puffy, white jacket, zipping it all the way up the front. "Hold on to that key. I'll be right back."

She disappears in the direction of the laundry room and comes back with Bryce's stroller and a pair of his pants. "Will you pick him up?"

I stand from the chair and walk to his swing, turning it off. I do as she asks, pulling the empty bottle from his mouth and moving the cushion to get him out. Holding him to my chest she slides his pants over his bare legs and his onesie-covered bottom. It's long sleeves already, but she wraps a blanket over him in my arms. "Lay him in the stroller if you don't mind while I get his pacifier."

I pat his back until he burps and lay him down flat in the stroller. She sticks his pacifier in his mouth and pulls a hat on his head to rest on top of his ears, then lays an additional blanket over his front. "Okay, we're ready. Come on. Your boots are by the back door. You can just put those on."

Without another word she takes off in that direction, never looking behind to see if I'm following. I have to sprint to catch up to her. I discovered the first week I met her that she is fast for such a short person when she wants to be, and that is still seen to be true. The door is cracked from where she recently went out. I step in my boots and pull them on in a hurry before running after her.

"Kinzleigh, wait up. What's the rush?"

"You want your Christmas present, don't you?"

"You are my Christmas present . . ."

"No need for the romantic banter. You're already getting laid tonight."

"I wasn't trying to get laid. Hey, why are we going to the shed? Nothing is in there except the four-wheeler."

She stops abruptly at the entrance and I almost run into her. "Or is it? Pick a door and then you'll see which lock the key will fit in."

She pushes open the door to the main part of the shed. There are only two doors inside. One is a small tool room with a workspace and the other is upstairs to what at some point will be my mancave. "So, this is a scavenger hunt of sorts?"

"Something like that." She slaps me on the butt. "Now go."

I walk inside and take in my surroundings, but nothing looks different. I walk toward the steep set of stairs to the upper floor. It's not done yet, so I don't see how anything could be up there, but it's the bigger of the two spaces. They haven't even finished the floor yet.

Regardless of what I think, I climb the steps with the keys in my hand. When I reach the top, I slide the key inside and turn it. It unlocks. I open the door and let it swing open, now in complete shock as I see what is laid out before me. "Merry Christmas, baby. You deserve it."

I turn around and she's standing behind me holding Bryce to her chest. I grab her face in my hands and slam my lips against hers so hard I wouldn't be surprised if I left a bruise. "Baby, what the fuck? When did you do this? You shouldn't have. It's too much."

"Breyson, I love you, but shut up. You are the most giving person I know and you never expect anything in return. I did this just as much for me as for you. Your reaction made it totally worth it. For once relax and be on the receiving end."

"I love you, woman. You are the most amazing person I know. Just wait until later."

"I'll be counting on it."

I turn and step inside the door. I cannot believe she finished my room. Holy shit. It's so much better than I envisioned it.

The floor is wood, but it's gray stained two by twelve plywood boards giving it a rustic edge. The sheetrock has been painted khaki and immediately on my right side—the wall next to the door—is a rack for pool sticks. In front of it stands a pool table with black felt. On my left—opposite of the way the door swings—is a short countertop holding a microwave and sink, and beside it is a refrigerator in black. I walk further inside and against the back wall to my right is a black, leather sofa that sits directly across from a built-in entertainment center holding what has to be a seventy-inch television, a game system, and a speaker system.

This is unreal. The coffee table and the end tables on each side of the couch are a cast iron base with a glass top. In the furthest corner of the room beside the only window outside is a camouflage rocking recliner, but that's not really what blows me away.

The room is a man's dream, but what gets me the most is the attention to detail scattered throughout the room. The lamps and chandelier are made from deer antlers with beige, twill shades. Light switch covers, picture frames, and wall décor are all done in a hunting or camp theme. She has framed pictures hanging around the room of hunting trips over the years with Pops, Dad, and my brothers. I didn't know she had even seen any of these photos. All of my mounted deer heads are also hanging throughout the room in a neat fashion.

The picture that stands out the most is the one on the end table. It's of me and Kinzleigh squatted, side by side, holding up the head of a buck by the antlers: her first kill. The ritual is to smear blood of your first kill somewhere on you; maybe for good luck, I am unsure of the reason. I had spread the deer's blood on her cheeks and thought she was going to throw up, but my little city girl pulled through and actually got excited when she stopped thinking about the blood and realized she actually killed a deer.

The photo was taken a month ago. I had begged Kinzleigh to go hunting with me when rifle hunting opened for deer season. She turned her nose up at first, but I wanted to be the first and only person to take her. I want to always make new memories with her.

She finally agreed to go, so I gave her basic instructions on how to use a gun and took her to my tree stand at the back section of pops' property. We sat there for about thirty minutes before that buck walked out into the opening—one of the many food plots Pops always plants before season. My heart was pounding. I helped her hold and stabilize the rifle, then told her to try aiming behind the shoulder so the bullet would penetrate straight through the heart, but she did the rest. She set her scope and pulled the trigger all by herself, laying it down with one round.

I pick up the frame as I remember how excited she was. The head and cape are at the taxidermist now getting mounted as a surprise for her.

When I saw her walk out of the bedroom that morning fully dressed in Camouflage, I thought I was going to come on myself. It doesn't matter what she wears she's beautiful. "I know it's your mancave—no girls only rule and all—but I just thought it fit. You can take it out if you don't want it in here."

She can't be serious. I can barely speak from what I've seen already. I look up at her standing off to the side giving me space. "It's perfect and it's staying. This right here is the best part out of all of it. I always want you present in everything. Don't ever forget it."

I don't know why, but I'm tearing up a little as I look around. No one has ever done something this thoughtful for me. I never expected something like this from her. It's the most perfect and unselfish gift she could have gotten me, but that's Kinzleigh, though. That's who she is.

A lot of girls would bitch about a guy wanting a little bit of space to himself. A guy grows up with sports, hunting, and fishing, among other things. He's raised to be tough and to embrace the testosterone, but then he meets that one girl that he can't live without and marries her, getting thrown into a woman's world and completely pushing aside all of those manly things he's always had. Most of the time guys try not to complain, but only hope for a small space he can go when he needs to surround himself with those manly things for a little while.

I brought it up to Kinzleigh one time, treading lightly so I didn't hurt her feelings. Instead of bitching about it and asking unnecessary questions she praised it, constantly asking how it was coming along when I added it to the plan of the building. She gets it, because she gets me. I'm the one that kept putting it off because I felt guilty for asking for it.

Two steps and I'm standing in front of her, cupping the back of her head. "I swear on everything, Kinzleigh, if you ever leave me, I won't survive. It hurts to think of us ever being apart again. I need you like I need my damn heart. I love you. Do you understand? I love you with everything that I am. I can't explain it, but you have made me the man that I am. Your love has given me worth and made my life valuable."

That emotional buildup surfaces, expelling a tear. At least I'm not crying as hard as she is. "I will never leave you, baby. Ever. Our love is infinite. I will be with you for the rest of my life."

I press my lips to hers, kissing her with a need to express myself. She tries to pull away, but I can't. My feelings are overwhelming me, trapped inside my body. I need a ground. I need something to be my outlet, releasing some of it from within. "Baby," she mumbles against my lips.

I part my lips from hers. "Can it wait?"

"You have one more gift."

"On top of all this?"

She nods. "There are two keys . . ."

I turn around and there are two doors on the opposite end of the entertainment center. One is a small bathroom and the other a small walk in closet. I choose the closet.

I turn the doorknob and pull open the door. All of my hunting clothes and gear occupy the hanging space, but against the wall inside is a fireproof gun safe. These things are like a thousand dollars or more. I've always wanted one, but never bought one. It's huge and weighs a ton. I clench my teeth, trying to pull myself together.

"Open it," she says, as if this isn't even the present.

I look at her. Her eyes are so clear, holding purity in them. "What did you do?"

"I get to stun you for once. Nothing more, nothing less." I shake my head from side to side, barely able to contain the feelings that I'm harboring inside. My hands are shaking, but I have no idea why. Maybe it's from not knowing what's on the other side of that door.

I insert the other key and turn it to unlock the door. I push down the handle and pull the door back to open it, and that's when I see the letters carved into the wood, causing me to slam the door and take a step back. I clench my hair in my fist. "Fucking shit. Is that what I think it is?"

Tears are streaming down my face, but it's because of the history behind what's resting inside that safe. One late-night storytelling session at Mims and Pops' house and Kinzleigh recovers a family heirloom from it. My face feels splotchy. I can't even open the door. "It's okay, baby. You can wait if you want."

I press my hands against the edges of the black safe, staring at the gold brand logo on the safe door. I've heard this story since I was a little kid. It was always Pops' biggest regret in life. His dad, my great grandfather, had this rifle: a Remington 30-06. He lived on this very land that Pops lives on today. Back then they were poor, so it was his most prized possession, used to ranch this land and feed his family. He carved his initials in the stock. Since Pops is John Gavin Abercrombie Jr., he was senior with the same initials, JGA.

When he was older he got terminally ill and gave the gun to Pops. Pops was still in medical school when he died, living off of the bare essentials. My great grandfather died with nothing but this land that meant so much to him. Pops wasn't making any money yet, so he had to sell everything he could just to give him a proper burial, one being the gun. On top of that he had to keep the land up and the cattle fed until he finished school.

The only thing Pops' dad asked him for on his deathbed was to keep the land in the family, because one day it would be worth something. To this day Pops has every single original acre plus some. The number count I last knew of was two thousand acres, give or take.

When Pops' career took off, he went and searched for the gun, but had no luck in finding it. I have always wanted to look for it, but it's only ever been a thought that was quickly dismissed. After all, that was like thirty plus years ago. How in the hell a nineteen-year-old girl found it I have no idea.

There is no way that is the same gun. In disbelief, I open the door again and grab ahold of the barrel, pulling it out. The wood is dull, showing its age. I run my hands down it, admiring it. The initials JGA are carved in a jagged instead of smooth texture, verifying it was carved with a pocketknife instead of machine. I turn it over, thinking any second it's going to vanish and this is all a dream.

I look at Kinzleigh. "Has Pops seen this?" She's crying, still holding Bryce, and watching me. She nods. "How?"

I can't say anything else, but she fills in the sentence. "One day when you were at school I went and talked to Pops after that night we were over and he told me that story. I couldn't think of anything else. I had to get all of the photos to frame for in here from him and your Mom, so I got him to tell me everything he remembered about selling it. I won't lie. I got Mom to help me. Somehow she was able to track down the name of the original buyer and found a contact for his family since he passed away several years ago. They really weren't far. They lived around the Petal area. Anyway, I called and spoke to his wife first. When I started asking questions, she handed the phone to her husband. He told me to stop by and gave me the address, so I did. It was in the possession of the original buyer's grandson. His dad inherited it and had recently passed away, but he had no use for it. He was about to have an estate auction and it was one of the items he was planning to sell. I was prepared to pay him anything for it, but when I told him the story and showed him the name on my license, he said he would never feel right selling me something that belonged in the family and gave it to me. He was a really nice man, maybe a little older than your dad. He told me his grandfather was a picker of sorts, always buying junk, and his dad never got rid of anything after he acquired all of his grandfather's belongs when he passed, so he didn't think it was anything special to hold onto."

I run my fingertips over the initials. "I can never top this." I cannot believe she did this. I don't even know what to say. Just when I think she can't surprise me anymore, she does, always keeping me on my toes.

"I don't want you to try. I didn't do this to show off or to outdo you. I saw something that was important when I watched your face as he told that story. What's important to you is important to me. A gift from the heart is the most valuable of them all. You can't put a price tag on this reaction. Seeing you today from my point of view is priceless and will embed itself in my mental photo album forever."

This is one of the many reasons I love her. She is one of a kind and she's all mine.

I place the gun back in the safe and lock it, placing the key ring in my pocket. "Thank you . . . for everything. This is the best Christmas I've ever had, and you made it special in every way. I will never forget this, Kinzleigh."

I wrap my arm around her shoulders, leading her toward the door. "It's my turn to watch you open your present, but first we need warm clothes for where we're going."

THIRTY-THREE

Kinzleigh

I put on a top, a pair of skinny jeans, flats, and a hoodie. Bryce is sleeping in his car seat in the backseat of Breyson's truck as we drive through the field to the barn. We pass the Gazebo that is being built for the wedding. It's going to be beautiful. It's a little extreme to build something like that on personal property, but with the money my parents are saving on a venue it's worth it and we can use it for birthdays, family gatherings, or just to picnic in the future. This will always be our home, so to us it adds value. Where some have photos only of their special day, I will have the entire venue plus the photos to admire when feeling sentimental.

"Looks like they have the foundation and pathway poured. Now they just have to build onto it. Are you excited to dance with me at our wedding?"

"As long as I get the first one." He winks. I love dancing with Breyson. He's the most amazing dancer. I remember the first time he showed me his real dancing skills at the New Year's Eve ball. I was blown away that an eighteen-year-old could dance like that.

Most kids our age don't get past the whole 'guy holds girl by the waist and girl wraps her arms around his neck, swaying in a robotic side-to-side motion' type of dancing. Not with Breyson.

Dancing with Breyson is an art. When I'm in his arms on the dance floor no one else exists. He holds my hand and the small of my back, either gliding me around the floor with precision or simply remaining within a box around us. The only way I can even begin to describe it is when Cinderella is dancing with the Prince at the ball, twirling in the midst of everyone but not realizing they are present, because she's completely lost in the arms of the man she loves from first sight.

I somewhat knew what I was doing from dancing with the older generation as a child, my dad, but Breyson has a grace and confidence about him. It makes you feel magical in a world that has left romance behind, making you feel even more special.

We pull up at the barn, directly in front of the entrance to keep the truck in view. The snow starts to fall again, calling for you to touch it. He puts the truck in park and turns the heat down to the minimum level on fan and warm but not hot in temperature, so Bryce doesn't get too hot.

I jump out before he can say anything. The only time I've been around snow is the year my parents took us skiing in Colorado when I was fourteen. I run out in the open and start twirling around with my arms straight out to my sides. As each snowflake hits my warm skin it melts, leaving behind a small water droplet in its place.

His truck door shuts and I can hear his boots squishing against the icy snow stuck to the ground. It's not the powdery snow I've been around out west. This is more like ice or slush, but the white landscape is still beautiful. "You know, you kind of look like a lost angel."

He has my attention. I start fluttering my arms, enjoying the cool air against my skin and drifting specs of white falling through the air. "Oh yeah? What do you mean by lost?"

"I mean Angels are supposed to be pure right, constantly at the hand of God? Imagine if one got lost on earth for a little while in the midst of humanity. Don't you think it'd be like a blind man gaining his vision? They know the things that are here, but the experience of it is new. I'd picture them looking like you just looked, as if they've found something never before seen and unfamiliar even though you know it exists."

I laugh. My beautiful blue-eyed boy is getting deep. "I guess you could look at it like that. I have only been around snow once. I like it. We traveled abroad or to warm climates usually. Mom hates the cold and Dad loves Mom, so you understand why."

I tilt my head back, now looking up at the sky. It's clear, making the white flakes more visible. I twirl again, enjoying something different than constant heat. Who knows when it will snow here again? It could be years from what Breyson has told me. He said he was a kid last time it snowed like this.

A hand links with mine. Breyson pulls me against him and wraps his arms around me, looking down to meet my eyes. "So, you've never made a snowman?"

I look up at him. His serious demeanor is just as beautiful as when he wears a smile. I shake my head. "I've always wanted to when I watch Christmas movies, but I've never been anywhere for a white Christmas."

He smiles and kisses the tip of my cold nose. His chilled lips brush against my skin, drawing a line from my nose to my ear. "We will have to rectify that. I like being your first. I think I may start making a list and checking it twice. I want you to experience everything the world has to offer. We have our entire lives to make that happen."

The roughness of his voice always drives my heart wild. "But first I want to show you something. This present is more for Bryce, but since he's not old enough to enjoy it yet I wanted it to be a surprise for you."

I've learned not to try and guess Breyson's surprises. I end up being wrong every time. Surprises are definitely his thing. He always blows me away. Who knows what he has up his sleeve for the honeymoon. I suddenly get a wave of nervousness. "Okay. Let me peek in on Bryce first."

I open the door to ensure fabric doesn't cover Bryce's airways and that he's not too warm. He's sleeping soundly and sucking on his pacifier. Closing the door quietly, I take the hand that Breyson now has extended out for me, letting him lead me into the barn.

Just before he gets to the end stalls for Divinity and Hendrix, he stops at the one that stays empty. I look inside and throw my hand over my mouth. In the corner on a bed of hay is a reddish-brown colt looking straight at me. "You bought him his own horse! It's the cutest thing I've ever seen! Can I pet it?"

I can't hide the excitement in my voice. I was overwhelmed when he got me Divinity last year, but knowing this is for our child is on a completely different level. Breyson has that knowing smile on his face; the look saying he knows he did good and it's inflating his ego a little. "What do you think?"

"Was my screaming not enough of a clue?"

I start jumping up and down in place, clapping my hands together. "Open the gate, Brey. I want to pet it. It's so little."

"This is his first separation from his mother. He's going to need some extra love. Are you up for it? I know you have a lot going on with school coming up, the wedding, and Bryce.”

“Yes!” I squeal, completely unashamed. “When is he rideable?”

“Not for a couple of years. Every person needs their own horse, though. All of our kids will have one. That’s why I bought a colt instead of an adult horse. By the time he’s rideable we can sit Bryce on his back and walk alongside the horse holding onto the two of them at the same time. They can learn together.”

My heart is about burst at the seams. He has his hand on the gate, ready to open it. I kiss him. “You’re the most thoughtful person I know. Bryce is lucky to have a father like you. You never stray from the person that you are and I love that about you.”

“Baby, I’m open to follow you anywhere. We can live in the city or we can live in the country, even somewhere in between, but the south is where my roots are. I want our kids to know where they come from. This will always be our home, even if only half the year. This is where we first built a life together. I never want to forget that.”

When I think there isn’t room in my heart to love him any more, it grows. He is the thing that makes my world continue to turn. I know that no matter what trials and tribulations we go through, we can always come out on the other side as long as we continue to face them together.

“I love this place too, baby. I know I wasn’t born here and there are still things I will have to learn, but that’s a part of our journey that I look forward to. Just as you like to be the first to show me a new experience, I love to experience it for the first time with you. This isn’t where I’m from, but it feels like more of a home to me than any other place has.”

He opens the gate and we walk inside the stall. The colt stands as we enter. I slow my pace to avoid him feeling threatened. I hold my hand out and slowly walk forward until I am in arm’s reach of his fur. “Hey, little boy. It’s okay. I’m just going to give you some love.”

I touch his mane, combing my fingers through it. He stands there, staring at me and breathing. A horse breathing is the most relaxing sound. It’s a steady rhythm, never changing pace. The mother inside me already wants to take him in and give him love. It’s sad to imagine being taken from your mother at a young age. Animal or not, he’s just a baby.

I never thought I was cut out to be a mother, but now I can’t imagine my life any other way. It truly changes something inside of you I can’t explain. You no longer care about yourself, but your child. It’s strange looking back on the shallow person I was not all that long ago. I was a bud that summer

I met Breyson; not developed or beautiful, but he has given me food and nurture, helping me to blossom into a beautiful rose, opening a layer at a time.

I press my cheek against his neck, rubbing my hand along his back. "What are you going to name him?"

This is so similar to last Christmas, but better. "I don't know." I never look back at Breyson. I pull my head back to look at the small horse instead. "What do you want to be called, baby boy?"

For a moment I let my mind roam, tossing out possibilities. I try to think of something that Bryce could say easily when he starts talking, but still represents something meaningful in our family.

Bryce is our little love child. He wasn't planned, but he is the result of the fierce love that Breyson and I have for each other. We both share a love for football. Mine started with the game I told Breyson about on the pier the night I found out I was moving here: the San Diego Chargers game for Konnor's eighth birthday. Both of us met in California and the blue the team represents reminds me of Breyson's eyes. "How about Diego? Do you like that . . . Diego?" He nuzzles his nose against my other hand. "I'm taking that as a yes."

I turn and look at Breyson. He is standing before me with a deep look in his eyes, holding an open jewelry box. Sitting nestled inside are a pair of earrings. The center stone is large and round cut, sizing about the diameter of the tip of my pinky finger. They are deep blue in color—I'm guessing sapphires—and outlined with a surrounding strand of small glistening diamonds. "As you did with Bryce you couldn't have picked a better name. I'm not sure if I told you, but Dr. Rodriguez's son's name was Diego, my friend. I think it's perfect."

I place my hands over my nose and mouth, completely stunned, as I look at the most beautiful set of earrings I've ever seen. When I think I understand our emotional connection another curveball is thrown our way, leaving me confused yet again. As if I didn't cry enough watching Breyson with his Christmas gift my eyes are filling with tears, sure to make me a blubbering mess within minutes.

I cup my hand around his and the box, brushing my thumb over the two gems inside. "They're beautiful. I don't know what to say."

He starts talking. "When I decided I was buying this horse I had to tell your mom so she could help me keep you out of here with all the wedding planning going on. I was trying to get ideas for what to buy you for

Christmas, since every time I ask you feel the need to tell me all you want for Christmas is me, which you already have."

He raises his brow at me. Okay yes, I remember saying that, but I wasn't being facetious. I meant it. The little things are more important when you've had to go without them for a while. "Somewhere in the mix she started telling me that for good luck in a marriage a bride must wear something old, something new, something borrowed, and something blue on her wedding day. Since we haven't had the best run with good luck in the past I figured it wouldn't hurt to go with tradition, and I wanted some of it to be from me so that each time you put it on I will cross your mind. Here is your something new and your something blue."

Yep, the blubbering mess is well on its way. What woman needs extravagant romantic gestures when you have a man like this? I don't need fantasy; I need reality. This is real life romance. I wrap my arms around his neck and jump in his arms. He catches me like he always does, and we kiss, because that's what we do. We don't have to say thank you in a million different ways. We show instead of tell.

This is my story, being written day by day. You only have one chance to get it right. Unlike a book, in life there is no backspace key or eraser to change it. You can only flip through the pages of what has already happened and continue forward. Everything recorded is permanent. When I flip back through the story of our lives, I want to know that ours is good enough to read over and over.

I look in those beautiful blue irises in front of me. "Take me to your truck, Abercrombie. I want to make out like two hormonal teenagers until we're disturbed by the bundle in the back."

He grins, showing off that unforgettable smile. "I thought you'd never ask."

THIRTY-FOUR

FEBRUARY …

Iwalk in Psychology class and sit in my usual seat. It feels surreal to be back in school. I never in a million years thought I would miss schoolwork, but I did. I think it's more that I wasn't doing anything with my life than the actual work. I've always wanted to hold my own weight in our relationship. Now that I have a career path it's like a weight has been lifted from my shoulders.

I decided that I want to stick to business. I still want to continue with a cheerleading company. I started school last month as a Business Administration major with a minor in marketing.

Right after Christmas Macie called me about the building that Preston purchased for me. She said that the title is ready to hand over with my name on it; the documents just need to be signed. One signature and I am legally the owner. I tried to back out, because I feel guilty accepting something like that since Preston and I aren't together anymore, but she told me she was under strict orders to make sure that I took it. It wasn't negotiable.

I was stuck with a decision to make. I'm here and the building is in California. I could sell it, but I feel worse about cashing in a gift for a profit than taking it and making it successful. Making it a success is the best way to thank someone, and in a few years, I'll have a business degree.

Breyson and I talked about it one night before bed. We both came to an agreement that I could hire someone to manage it full-time and the two of us fly up when our schedules allow, overseeing things until we see where things go with it. With us both working enough to save most of the money still put up, we can swing it.

We pay Pops a monthly mortgage payment for the house out of the money we have from Breyson's accounts and my trust fund. It's no different than a bank loan minus the interest. We will pay it off faster and it's cheaper. We pay utilities and necessities with money we make working part time.

Breyson still works on the ranch when not occupied with school or football. The cheerleading program I was training with not far from where our parents live in Oak Grove liked my skill level in tumbling and asked if I would be interested in coaching a few classes a week for the younger girls. They would pay me and allow me to continue training for free since I would be an employee. The distance from our parents works out to drop Bryce off when I have a class.

I accepted the offer, because it helps out to have an extra income and this is what I want to do with my life, so it gives me experience. I would have been stupid to turn it down.

Breyson and I were going to hire a sitter to watch Bryce during the day while we are in school, but Mims wouldn't allow it. She told us that she doesn't have anything else to do with her days and it would save us money we didn't need to spend. Then she went on and on about germs and sickness and that she needed to bond with her first and only great grandson, because she wouldn't be around forever. I've learned you don't argue with Mims. She is set in her ways and I absolutely adore her. It's a win both ways. I know Bryce is taken care of, it saves on childcare, and she gets her way.

The upcoming months are going to be pretty busy between Breyson and I. We both have things coming up for next football season, tryouts for me, we have the wedding and honeymoon during spring break next month, and in the midst of all that we have to keep up our grades and finish out finals in May.

This summer we are spending two of the only three-week break Breyson gets from school and football in California to open and get everything sorted for the cheerleading company. We agreed to make it a tradition to always spend at least a week during each summer in California since that's where everything started between us, so we rented a beach house and we're officially introducing Bryce to the beach. I can't believe he will be over halfway to one then. Time is going by so fast with him.

If all of that isn't a busy enough schedule, hopefully we will be starting training and practices to get ready for next football season. If everything works out the way we hope, Breyson will be the starting running back next season and I will get to watch, but this time on the sidelines as a college cheerleader. I never thought I'd miss wearing black and gold after high school, but I'd give anything to be wearing those colors again, because that would mean I made the squad.

Karsyn walks in and plops down in the seat beside me. This semester I was able to get a couple of classes with Breyson and one with Karsyn since we are all still taking basic courses. Somehow, I even ended up in a class with Fisher. Considering the size of this campus I'm going to assume a certain hot, blue-eyed football player had something to do with that instead of blaming it on coincidence, but I can't prove it and he will take it to the grave.

I shake my head, thinking about the overprotective man that I love. I'm taking advantage of it, though, because once basics are done, Breyson and Karsyn will be in totally different classes related to their major and I'll be studying alone or in a different group.

Psychology 110 is a course required for every major, so it's in an auditorium style classroom with about one hundred students, give or take. I look at Karsyn and laugh as I take in what she's dressed in. "Late night?"

We chose the eight o'clock class on Tuesday and Thursday. Okay, well I did. I have too much to do in my day not to get started early. She looks down at herself and back at me. "What, this? Don't get me wrong, your ass wanting to take the 8AM class is fucking insane, but no, I didn't just roll out of bed and come to class. I dress for comfort. Every time I see a freshman girl dressed up for class like she is going to the club I want to scream *you are an epic failure to society.*"

I'm laughing out loud to the point that it's embarrassing. People are staring at me, but I can't help it. One would have to understand Karsyn. She curses like a sailor, has no filter, and is as country as they come. She never cares what other people think and I love that about her.

The outfit that has me almost in tears is a pair of black sweatpants with Batman written down the leg in yellow and tucked in her trusty cowgirl boots, a long sleeve fitted white tee shirt with a matching camisole visible underneath from the thin material, and a black infinity scarf wrapped around her neck. Her white-blonde hair hangs straight in a ponytail with a pair of aviator shades resting on top of her head and her makeup is done to perfection, as it always is. It's like she woke up and smacked together three different people into one outfit. What's even funnier, is strangely, the girl can pull it off.

"Have I told you I love you today? I will haunt you if you ever stop being my friend. Love stalking is not beneath me." I say it jokingly, but I actually mean it. I have never met another girl quite like Karsyn. She keeps you in a constant good mood, making you laugh at all hours of the day with no effort at all.

"Awe, I love you too, sweet cheeks." She holds up her right hand as if she's about to swear on a bible. "Full disclaimer: I am giving you permission; love stalking is perfectly acceptable, and in most cases, encouraged. We will be twinksters 'til the end, my female version of a soul mate. Two peas in a pod, you and I."

She looks around like she's making sure the professor isn't waiting to start class, and then glances at her watch. "Okay, time to get down to business. I have approximately five minutes to give this presentation."

I raise my brow at her word choice. "Presentation?"

"Yes." She takes a deep breath, dramatizing it completely. "What are you doing this weekend?"

I think. If there was something I was supposed to be doing it's not coming to me. "Planning a wedding? Actually, I need to ask you something."

She cups her hand over my mouth, shushing me. "Yes, pumpkin, I would be honored to be a bridesmaid, but that conversation will have to be postponed. This is on a time restriction . . . and no you are not fucking wedding planning. What did I tell you? You do not want to become Bridezilla. All I hear about is wedding planning. I love you, but no. Just no. Good God, woman, you're already married for Pete's sake. We are going to have some fun. I need you, Batgirl."

I tighten my lips in a narrow line as she removes her hand slowly, trying not to laugh out loud again. How on earth she finishes my sentences who knows. I can't be that predictable. "What, O' important one?"

"I am riding in the rodeo this weekend. It's a little over an hour from here, in Jackson. It's the big one around these parts that they have every February. I want you to come with. They have several different showings that I have to ride in over the course of the weekend, but once I'm done, I can sit with you. They have a dance on Saturday night—beer, boots, and boys. How can you resist? Ok, maybe the boys are for me."

A rodeo? I've never been to a rodeo. "I don't know . . . we have a lot going on right now. We have two trips planned already. I don't know if Breyson will want to spend the money."

"Let me see your phone. Make it snappy."

I remove it from my purse that is sitting in my lap and hand it to her. "What for?"

"Hold all questions until the end. Passcode?"

"1005."

I watch curiously as she navigates around my phone with ease. She places it to her ear. "Breyson, Karsyn. Quick question. I want Kinzleigh to come to the Dixie National Rodeo this weekend. I think she needs a break from all the wedding stuff before her brain fries. I already have a room booked and you can even bring a friend so that you aren't tagging along third wheel. What do you say? Are you going to let her go?"

Her eyebrows dip. "Um . . ."

She glances at me. "Have you ever been to a rodeo? What kind of a question is that?" she mumbles into the phone. "Who hasn't been to a rodeo?"

"I haven't." Of course, he's going to make this about his list of my firsts that he's responsible for.

"What the fuck?" She is gawking at me. Literally, I could pick her chin up off the floor. "Please tell me you're going to go after hearing that shit. As a true southern belle, I cannot allow a friend to continue living here knowing she has never been to a rodeo. That would be completely unacceptable."

"Watch your language, Miss Davies, and put the cell phone away. Class is starting." The professor walks down the adjacent aisle in her tight pencil skirt and matching jacket, her heels tapping against the floor. She wears her hair pulled back in a tight bun every day. She's not very friendly and acts uptight. The woman probably needs to get laid. I don't curse often, but it doesn't bother me to hear. This is college. I'm sure most everyone in this room does.

"After classes adjourn. Gotta go, bye."

She tosses the phone in my purse. "Looks like he agrees that you should definitely try your boots out in the purpose they were invented for and not just a fashion statement, love bug. Get ready. This weekend you're going to forget about responsibility and have fun. You'll thank me later."

She winks and turns to face the front as if none of that just happened. What could be so special about a rodeo? I shake my head and pull out my notebook, ready to take lecture notes. I guess I'm about to find out . . .

THIRTY-FIVE

Breyson

"Y ou ready to roll out?" I look over at the sound of Fisher's voice. He is walking out of his dorm building with a duffel bag.

"Damn, dude, it's about time. What the hell were you doing in there? You take longer to get ready than my wife and she has to get two people ready." I stand from the bench I've been occupying as he passes, flipping me off.

The smell of cologne passes through the air as I follow behind him. I look down at my shoes and shake my head. Someone's got the Karsyn itch. It's really kind of funny to see someone else look this bad. I guess it's a lot different seeing it on someone else.

I open the door to my truck and climb inside. Fisher tosses his bag in the backseat and sits in the passenger seat. "Where are we picking up the girls?"

"You mean where are we picking up Karsyn?"

"Dude, are you going to continue to bust my balls? I think she's hot, so what? Lots of girls are hot."

"Yes, because someone other than me finally has that look in their eyes. I've earned the right to bust your balls."

"What look? You got married at nineteen, boy. There is no comparison to the look I have and the look that you have."

Yeah right. He may be referring to the look I have now, but I remember how it started. He has the look. It takes one to know one. "You'll see."

I back out of the parking lot and start down the street. "They are actually at the sorority house. Kinzleigh rode with me today since we were leaving right after school. Our clothes are in the back. Karsyn is packing her stuff. Her dad agreed to haul her horse so she's riding with us. I think he takes cattle or something up there anyway. I wasn't really listening."

He not so discreetly looks at his cell phone and starts biting on his thumbnail, further proving my point. "Hey, why don't you live on frat row if Karsyn lives in a house?"

"A spot hasn't opened up yet. Seniority gets rooms first and I'm in the football dorm anyway. You live off campus or you'd be there too."

I pull into the street lined with sorority housing and find a parking spot available. I pull out my phone to call Kinzleigh. She answers on second ring.

"Hey, baby. Are you here?"

"We're outside."

"Okay. We'll be out in a minute."

"See you then."

I disconnect the call and sit here, waiting on females. I wonder how many men around the world are patiently waiting on a girl right now.

I lay my head against the headrest and close my eyes as the heat from the heater blows against my face. I cannot believe I didn't think of a rodeo to add to the list. In all the time we've been together a rodeo never crossed my mind. I need to get my head in the game if I'm going to make a bucket list. I never want there to be something she hasn't experienced, or more importantly, that we haven't experienced together.

"Damn."

I open my eyes and look at Fisher following his sudden outburst. His eyes are bulging out at whatever he's staring at straight ahead. Directing my eyes to his line of vision, I see exactly what he's staring at.

"I would say that's an accurate description."

I'm sure he's looking at Karsyn, but the one I'm looking at is the one beside her. They are dressed similar and they could pull off being sisters. Kinzleigh is wearing a pair of tight, bootcut jeans and black, pointed toe boots with a turquoise pattern. Her top is long sleeved, black, and hanging off the shoulder, revealing her creamy white skin, and her necklace that matches mine is hanging over it.

"Are you thinking what I'm thinking?"

"Most likely." It doesn't take that smart of a person to assume what he's thinking, because I constantly stay in that frame of mind with Kinzleigh.

I can't take my eyes off of her. She wore her hair down and curly just how I like it. The length has grown over the months, ending at the small of her back. It looks like her makeup is more dramatic than she usually wears it. Her eyes are bolder than they usually are. The gray and black smoky thing she has going on makes the green in her eyes more prominent, and her plump lips are stained a fire engine red.

We both open our doors at the same time, stepping out of the truck as they reach the edge of the sidewalk that runs in front of parking. I round the truck and grab Kinzleigh by the waist, pulling her into me.

I back up to the driver's side of the truck to give us some privacy. Pressing her up against the door of the truck I scrape my hand along the contour of her body, stopping on her ass covered by the tight denim jeans. "If we weren't in public right now, I'd strip you bare and fuck you against the side of this truck."

She looks out from under her long eyelashes, thicker from the makeup. Her perfume is toxic to my control, causing it to slip. "And I would let you."

"You look beautiful."

I trail one hand down to her thigh and lift her leg to hook around my waist, placing my hand back over her ass when she keeps it there. I continue to look at her, not able to look away. Without thought my other hand runs up her side, taking position cupped on her breast.

What does me in is when I press my erection against her, the top two of her front teeth scrape lightly against her full bottom lip. The bright white against the red has me raging with arousal. It's the sexiest thing I've ever seen. "Are you ever going to stop turning me on to the point of embarrassment? Do you think I'll ever be able to look at you without wanting to take you in the very spot I sight you in? Will I ever be able to put my hands on you without my insides turning into an inferno?"

She tilts her head back as I press into her further, placing her red lips so close they are almost touching mine, and slightly puckered as if she's about to kiss me. She stares at me bright eyed, blinking slowly as she stares into my eyes. "I hope not, because that would be a tragedy."

If I didn't think she could get any sexier she just did. I grab her by the thighs and pick her up until she's higher than me, looking down. Her hands are resting on my shoulders. I spin her around, holding onto her tightly.

"Don't ever change."

"I won't. What you see is what you get."

"That's what I'm counting on."

I want to kiss her so bad, and I still might. Whether I am sporting smeared red lipstick or not is to be determined.

"Hell no! If I have to watch that, I should at least be drunk. Y'all, I hate to break up this never-ending love fest that you two always have going on, but I'm getting bored. I don't need to witness another second of your sexcapades or I might scream. Can we go? We still have an hour drive." Add in the mouth of Karsyn and my dick is no longer in a hardened state. Nope, it's completely soft.

I slightly shake my head at Kinzleigh and we both laugh at the same time. I set her down and she adjusts her top that has ridden up from picking her up. "Let's ride."

"Kinzleigh, you're sitting in the back with me. This is a girls' weekend, we're just letting boys be in it."

If I hadn't come to know Karsyn that statement might piss me off, but the girl is hardcore and funny as hell. I would probably pay a lot of money to be a fly on the wall if Fisher could ever get past the man-hater walls she has up, so I choose not to say anything at all. Instead, I'll check my hot wife out in the rearview mirror.

THIRTY-SIX

Kinzleigh

We checked in our hotel as soon as we arrived and grabbed dinner at one of the local restaurants. I've caught Fisher glancing at Karsyn off and on since we left. I might have caught her looking once, but I can't be sure. The girl has a poker face like I've never seen before. You can never tell what she is thinking.

"Kinzleigh, do you want to go ahead and walk over with me? I have to get changed and get my horse ready so I can get in my lineup before the show starts." Our hotel is just across the street from the coliseum, but I hate to just bail on Breyson.

I look at him, but as usual he knows what I'm thinking without me having to say anything. "Go ahead. I have to shower anyway. We'll meet you there?"

He gives me a half smile. He seems a little disappointed, but he'll never admit it. The truth is I've never really had a single friend since we've been together before. Shortly after Adalynn and I became friends she started a thing with Braxton. Londyn has been with Briar since I met her and they have been my only real friends since me and Breyson started dating, so it's always kind of been him and me against the world.

My relationship with Presley has been almost non-existent since last New Year's. She agreed to be part of my wedding party, but things just aren't the same. Something is off with her and I can't put my finger on it. I really could kill Konnor sometimes.

"Okay," I say. Karsyn hands him two tickets and walks to the door of our room, opening it. I grab my jacket from the chair and pull it on, removing my hair from underneath the collar.

I follow her outside, walking in the direction of the large dome building across the street. "So . . . what do you think of Fisher? He's really outgoing like you are."

She shrugs. "He seems quiet to me."

"This is the quietest I've ever seen him."

"He's a football player, isn't he?"

I roll my eyes. "Yes, so?"

"So . . . I don't date football players. You know this. Besides, I need my man to be a tad bit livelier. You know, someone that can keep up with me."

I link my arm in hers. "Describe him."

"Who?"

"Your dream guy."

"I quit dreaming long ago, Darlin'. Dreaming ends in disaster. Me, I don't need a Mister right. Mister right now suits me just fine. Assholes are what I prefer; the emotionally detached."

She sounds like the total opposite extreme of what I was Pre-Breyson. "Are you ever going to tell me about him?"

"Who, sweetie?"

"The one that broke your heart."

"Not much to tell. The dumb bastard slept with his spirit girl. Why they invented that stupid shit I'll never know. I knew what spirit girls did behind closed doors, but I thought I was avoiding it because he loved me. Firsthand, I realized I was wrong. I got burned by the fire once, I won't go near it again."

She pulls back the fence so that we can walk under it. "But you loved him?"

"Something like that, but it wasn't like your little white picket fence relationship. It didn't matter, though. It never does. Most men think with their cocks primarily, and the ones that learn it gets them nowhere become taken quickly." She looks at me, and winks, referring to Breyson.

"What happened to him?"

"Oh, you know, he knocked her up and was forced by his parents to marry her. They live somewhere in a rundown single-wide trailer. He works in a local factory and she does nails at a small salon. Neither of them have a pot to piss in. They got what they deserved. One day when he has the balls to admit he fucked up I'll have the pleasure of telling him to stick it where the sun doesn't shine, because I sure as hell don't need him."

She pulls out a pack of cigarettes from her purse and packs them on the heel of her hand. Removing one from the box, she lights it. "You smoke?"

"Sometimes. It depends on my mood. Right now, it's going downhill fast." She inhales and blows out a puff of smoke, mixing with the fog that is expelled each time we breathe into the cold air. I bundle up into my jacket as we continue to walk across the pavement, now halfway to the coliseum.

"One more question and I'll drop it."

She looks at me while she continues to puff on the cigarette. It looks foreign on her, like it doesn't belong. "You're relentless." She turns her head and blows out the smoke she's holding in her lungs before looking back at me. "Shoot."

"How can you decipher the good guys from the bad guys if you don't let any close to you?"

"That's the beauty of not wanting either, peaches. I only need a man for one thing. When I need my occasional fix there is always someone happy to oblige. Until then, I keep them at a safe distance." She loves pet names I've discovered, churning them out in a rotation so she never gets bored.

I wonder if this is how I always sounded. No wonder Presley was always trying to set me up back then. I want to scream at her to follow the light, but I know it won't do any good. Something, or someone, perhaps, will break her. Until then, I'll just inconspicuously drop hints about a certain someone that has his eyes on her. Plant a seed, water it, sit back and watch it grow.

We finally make it to the section reserved for the horse trailers and trucks. There are people scattered everywhere in wranglers, button-downs, and cowboy hats. Some even have numbers pinned to the back of them. Karsyn looks at me. "You want to know what revs my engine up?"

I can't wait to hear this. "There is really no telling with you . . ."

She stops and throws down the cigarette bud, putting out the orange glow with the section of her boot that covers the ball of her foot. Our arms are still linked together, standing side by side. "You see that guy over there by the red pickup? The one that doesn't have a trailer because he doesn't need a horse."

I look in the direction she is discretely pointing in. "The guy standing next to the truck bed with his forearms resting over the side next to the toolbox?"

"That would be him . . ."

"What's so special about him? I can barely see his profile, much less his face."

"It's not because of the distance from him to us. It's because you don't study the beautiful physical attributes of the male population. Look at his hindquarters covered in that tight pair of Wranglers. On one side he has a glove tucked in his back pocket while the other has a snuff ring worn in the denim. Do you see it?"

I cannot believe I'm looking at another man's butt. I feel like I'm cheating even though there are no sexual thoughts being tossed around in my mind. "Yeah, so?"

"The glove is to avoid rope burn and the ring is the result of the can that resides there constantly, holding the tobacco he needs in his bloodstream to calm the adrenaline he will have after his ride. Watch his cocky stance against the side of the truck as he talks to the other guy that's leaned over the tailgate; his friendly competition."

"Okay . . . you're still not telling me anything."

"That, my little blonde bunny, is a bull rider. That is what gives me lady-wood. He's built to be tough and born to compete for the longest ride. Total asshole, but amazing in bed. Tonight, that one's all mine. You're about to find out why I continued to be involved with rodeo after high school. I didn't want to continue barrel-racing full time, because it consumes every weekend and I'm a science major for the purpose of veterinary school. It's too much travel to make decent money at it unless it's a career choice. The schedule is too complex to do it and for me to go to school at the same time. I had to choose, and my love is for animals, so I chose school. It's a more permanent way to get the same outcome. Occasionally, I go to close rodeos and just run the flags around the arena with the other show girls, ride barrel, or both. Dad is big in the equine shows anyway, so it usually works out. People are always looking to buy horses at a rodeo. He wants me riding barrel tonight, so I guess I'm doing both."

"So, you're going to sleep with someone that you have never met before? How do you avoid emotional attachment? Isn't that kind of, I don't know, scary? You don't know where he's been."

"Do I hear judgment in your tone, shortcake?"

"No! I would never judge you. I'm just trying to understand. I've only been with two people; one I knew all my life and the other, the one I gave my virginity to, I married."

"Welcome to world of rodeo. This is where the rowdy boys stay—the cowboys. They bleed and sweat getting ready for that eight second ride. They are wild, rough, and ready to rumble under the sheets, but nothing more. They are bred to be heartbreakers. Everyone knows you don't fall in love with a cowboy. Emotional attachments are mental. If you want a piece of that you shut down your mind. You don't ask questions. Like them you ride, get off, and do it all over again. You may get bucked off the first time, but the rush keeps you coming back for more."

She starts to move forward, pulling me with her. "My trailer is just over here. I have to get ready and get my horse. This is the side of me you haven't seen yet. This is my first love."

The way she talks about it has my excitement peaking. Not the whole cowboy thing, but the show itself. It sounds so different than anything I've ever been involved with. I'm ready to see what this rodeo is all about.

Karsyn walks out of the horse trailer. She looks flashy and dolled up in her rodeo attire. It's almost like a country version of a beauty pageant. The sparkles, the vivid colors, and the eccentric fashion are eye-catching.

Her denim jeans are a dark blue with a rhinestone pattern on the back pockets. She's wearing a turquoise, long-sleeved button-down tucked into her tight jeans. She is showing off leather chaps over her jeans that are black in color with a turquoise pattern like my boots and matching tassels hanging from the outer edging. Even her boots and hat match in solid black.

She walks past me toward her horse that is tied to the back of the trailer. Even the horse is full of color and dressed out for the occasion. She's just as beautiful; a buttercup color Palomino with turquoise ankle wraps and a matching saddle. Everything on that horse is made for show; the gear is catching light and making it sparkle like diamonds when it moves. It's completely different than the type of reigns and gear I've seen at the ranch. "Is it safe to assume this is your favorite color?"

"Among a few others," she says, now brushing out the mane. "Didn't you notice, sweets? I have a very colorful personality and my wardrobe usually matches. Who the hell am I kidding? I'm a damn lunatic, but I would consider myself fun. Anyway, I buy rodeo gear like some girls buy shoes and handbags. My horse is always decked out in reflection to my outfit and spoiled. After all, she is the one that does all the work.”

Since Breyson bought Divinity for me I’ve formed a love for horses I never knew I had. They are the most beautiful creatures. Learning about them has become a hobby. Each one is beautiful in its own way no matter their pattern or color, size or sex.

I walk toward them. “What’s her name?”

“This is Lucy. Before you ask, yes, it’s because of the television show. It was my mom’s favorite. I was told we used to watch it together when I couldn’t sleep at night, even though I wasn’t old enough to understand it, and apparently that’s the name I chose for her when she was born—probably because it was easier to say. Later, when I was much older, I had an undying love for the ditzy redhead married to the sexy Cuban that I had a total crush on. Don’t judge.”

I hold up my hands in front of me. “I wasn’t going to say a thing. I like it. It suits her. The story behind it gives her character. Do you mind if I pet her?”

She is holding onto the reigns. “I’ll give you something even better. Come get on. You can ride her to my lineup. She’s friendly and she really likes girls. We have enough time that I can show you behind the scenes, the gut of the rodeo, and then bring you back to the main entrance. The boys should be here by then.”

I won’t lie. I’m really excited. The grin on my face probably reflects the way I feel on the inside. I reach out and pet her, letting her get familiar with me. “Hello, Lucy. It’s nice to meet you.” I always find myself talking to horses like I’m talking to a person. It may be crazy, but Divinity seems to like it.

I grab her saddle and mount her. Sitting on top of her like this makes me feel like a beauty queen, which is totally different than leisure riding. I can see why Karsyn has developed a passion for horse fashion. It gives me an idea for the wedding. “This look fits you.”

“If I ride Divinity in the wedding will you help me doll her up like this? Maybe even the other horses for the bridesmaids? I wouldn’t really know what I was doing.”

She flashes a smile, petting Lucy on the nose. “You hear that, Luce? We’ve rubbed off on her. You want to be in a wedding?” Lucy starts rubbing her nose up and down Karsyn’s hand. It looks like she’s saying yes, but based on Karsyn’s hand no longer moving to pet her, I’m guessing she taught it to her as a trick. "What Lucy wants, Lucy gets." She winks. "We would be honored to help you become a beautiful bride, Darlin'."

She turns and starts walking toward the back of the coliseum, leading Lucy through trailers and other horses standing around. She makes it a point to walk right by the red truck she pointed out earlier.

The cowboy is still standing in the same position. As we pass, she discretely holds her arm out to the right of her, letting her fingertips brush across his lower back, not much higher than his butt. She is bold. I don't know why I'm surprised anymore.

He turns around like he's about to say something until his gray eyes slowly take in her body. "I'm sorry, Darlin', I didn't see you there." She has a seductive smile on her face. This is flirting I'm not used to. Even with Presley it was natural. This is more like predator and prey; only he's the prey. It seems backward.

I watch the interaction, not saying a word. It's like a soap opera. In her defense, the guy is cute. I have no idea how she picked him out so quickly. His hat covers his head, but the bottom hair peeking out the back looks black, and definitely short. He smiles at her, showing off a set of dimples that matches hers. The way his eyes naturally squint is kind of sexy. "That's okay, sweetheart. You ride barrel?"

"Not usually, but I am tonight," she says in passing. "Good luck." She gives him the famous Karsyn wink and continues like he didn't catch her attention at all.

"What's your name?" He calls out the question as the distance increases.

"Karsyn." She never looks back as she responds. She obviously knows exactly what she's doing.

When we get out of earshot the curiosity is killing me. "You're not going to ask his name? I thought you said you were going to hook up with him."

"Watch and learn, peaches."

"Hey, Karsyn."

We both turn around at the same time. It's the cowboy.

"What's up, babe?"

"You watch bull riding?"

"Depends . . . why do you ask?"

She has a straight face, no emotion showing through. He holds out his hand as if he wants a handshake. I remember Breyson doing that not all that long ago. Instead of looking at him like he's crazy she takes it. A smile breaks free, but I'm not sure why.

"I'm Clint. I ride well with an audience. You think you can help me out with that?"

She pulls her hand back, but it forms into a fist. "I'll see what I can work out, Clint."

She takes a few steps back, pulling us along with her before turning around, leaving him standing in the same spot he was just in. I'm completely lost at what just happened; maybe because I never had to do any of this. It seems like too much work to me.

As we walk onto the red dirt ground from the pavement we were just walking on, people become more scattered. I can see other flag girls all gathered in a group horseback. I'm only assuming they are flag girls based on the flags they are holding next to them that are sitting in a stand hooked to the saddle. Most are sponsor flags.

I realize we are at the back of the arena. I can see the gates in front of us that allow entry. To each side are different stalls with their own gates. I study my surroundings, noticing a chute that spurs from a pen of bulls. It's like a different world back here. "What was that?"

She hands me a small folded up piece of paper as she ties Lucy to a holding bar. Holding it in my hand as I grab the horn of the saddle, I push up on the stirrups and throw my leg over, jumping down. I open it and notice a messy handwriting.

I'd like to see more of you, gorgeous girl. Find me later . . .
You know where.
-Clint

"That's supposed to work?" I laugh. "It seems so elementary."

"I love your innocence, peaches. You should hold onto it forever. You are a rare edition, love, but yes, it works. That is my invitation into those fine-ass jeans. It's not supposed to be calculus." She holds out her hand for the note. I hand it back to her.

We both know by Colbie Caillat and Gavin DeGraw starts to play—my ringtone for Breyson. One song speaks so much volume when you put it in play aside the two of us and everything that's happened throughout our relationship.

Since Breyson and I got married I've become an emotional sap, watching and reading every romance imaginable. Having a hobby is kind of nice, but the amount of money I spend on the general arts of the public—books, music, and movies—has gotten out of hand. It could have something to do with all the free time I had staying at home with a newborn.

My most recent find—*Safe Haven* by Nicholas Sparks—left me a crying mess as that song started to play on the movie. I was already pulling from the tissue box from the story itself, but then I heard that, and I was doomed. First thing I did: download it from iTunes. It's been his ringtone ever since.

I pull out my phone, now looking at the picture that is saved under his contact detail. It's a photo of the day we got married on the pier. Breyson got the preacher to take a picture of him standing behind me at the end of the pier with his arms wrapped around me. We wanted to have a picture of the actual wedding day, but that's not the photo I saved.

When we were on the plane flying back home, I was going through the photos I took of us on the boat when I found one that I didn't take or know anything about. Next to the photo the minister took was a candid shot. The two of us were standing at the end of the pier. It was right after we posed for the picture. I had turned around to give Breyson a hug. After he wrapped his arms around my waist, he picked me up high enough he could look up at me. I felt so tiny looking down at him and wrapped in his arms.

I guess we had gotten lost in each other, forgetting about the minister, because my hands were resting on his cheeks and we were looking into each other's eyes, smiling. The sun was behind the clouds enough that the background light looks tranquil. A photo I didn't know about is now my favorite one. I haven't even been away from him long and I already miss him.

"Where are you?" I ask, answering the call.

"Turn around."

I do and Breyson is standing a few feet back. I instantly smile at his outfit. He is always the master of surprises. I'm constantly on my toes with him, never knowing what he's going to do next.

I smile, but never disconnect the call. "There's this really sexy guy here. I think I may ask for his digits."

"Oh yeah? What does he look like?"

"Hmmm. Well, he's kind of tall, has short, dirty-blond hair, blue eyes to die for, and a smile that makes my heart feel like it could fly. I might even be thinking about him naked."

We remain standing apart but staring at each other as we talk in the phone.

"He sounds hot."

"Oh, he is. You should see what he's wearing right now. A pair of tight jeans that do wonders for his ass, a long-sleeved shirt that hugs his chest, a ball cap, and a pair of cowboy boots."

Breyson never dresses in boots and Wranglers unless he's on the ranch. He was raised country, but he's not a cowboy. I've always called him my southern prep, because you'd never know he dressed like this if you haven't seen him at Pops'. He never wears any form of a hat other than a ball cap, and when he does it's usually when it's summer and hot, but him in a ball cap and boots is my absolute weakness. This . . . is all for me.

"That's funny, I think I just saw him."

"Do you think he'd talk to me?"

"I think he'd do a whole lot more than talk to you if given the chance. Word is he's been crushing on you for a while."

It's getting harder to keep the grin to a minimal.

"Do me a favor, will you?"

"What's that, beautiful?"

"Tell him to come kiss me."

We lower our phones at the same time, never breaking eye contact. He slides his in his jean pocket and starts walking toward me. I can't think. This is the sexiest man on the planet and he's totally and irreversibly mine. This man has completely stolen my heart.

He stops in front of me and places his hand on the side of my neck. I wrap my hand around his wrist, waiting for it.

"Finally . . . Next time, don't make a man wait so long."

He lays his lips on mine and that tingle that will never get old starts to spread across my lips. I believe that lips have memory. Kissing is a standard act, but each person does it slightly different. It doesn't matter whether it's been twelve hours or seven months since we last indulged in it, because every time our lips touch, they pick up right where we last left off.

THIRTY-SEVEN

Kinzleigh

Breyson, Fisher, and I are finally sitting in our seats ready for the rodeo to start. Breyson reaches over and grabs my hand, pulling it to rest on his thigh. I look around the large coliseum. The ceiling is in the shape of a dome and there is a bowl of seating around the center arena that is made of red dirt.

Each time I glance at Fisher he's looking at the gate. If I had to guess he's looking for a certain someone. It's kind of sad really, knowing what she's going to do with that Clint guy and Fisher is here wanting her attention, but not outwardly admitting it. The guy really isn't that bad. I've gotten to know him in the Speech class we have together. He's really easy going, but he has a goofy personality about him, constantly making people laugh.

I wish Karsyn would let herself get to know him, but she is a free spirit not wanting to be tamed. If Fisher wants to catch her he's got his work cut out for him, but I get an inkling that he doesn't give up that easily on something he wants.

The lights go off and a male's voice starts talking through the speaker. A spotlight comes on, shining down on the gate that leads into the arena. It's an older man on a horse holding a microphone in one hand. He's talking about rodeo, an opening introduction of sorts.

The big screen television comes on showing a short trailer with cowboys and cattle. The announcer asks that everyone bow their heads for a short prayer and he prays, asking for safety on all of the people involved in the show. At the prayer's end he announces for everyone to stand for the national anthem at the same time an American flag appears on the screen.

As we stand Breyson pulls me closer to him, tucking me underneath his arm. I wrap my arm around his lower back. This is my spot, my nook; I fit perfectly in it, my height against his. I place my right hand over my heart as the female voice starts singing.

Whoever it is singing has a set of lungs. The national anthem isn't something everyone can pull off, because it's nothing but vocal. There is no music to hide behind. There is something about that voice, though, that sounds familiar.

I start looking around to see where it's coming from. I finally see another spotlight shining down in the corner beside the bull riders, not far from the gate. My mouth drops when I realize it's Karsyn. Holy crap, her voice is amazing. I remembered at the Halloween party hearing it some, but I never knew it was like that.

I slap Breyson in the stomach with the palm of my hand, requesting his attention. He has his ball cap over his heart as she sings; the only reason he had to remove his arm from around me. He lowers his head, making his ear level with my mouth. "That's Karsyn singing. Check it out . . . in the corner."

He nods and looks where I direct him. I notice him nudge Fisher and point with his head to where she is standing holding a microphone.

She finishes up the anthem and runs through the gate. After a few seconds, fireworks go off from the center of the arena. I can hear hooves trampling against the dirt in a steady rhythm. The overhead lights come on to the flag girls rushing through the gate, carrying the flags they are representing horseback.

Every girl is carrying a different flag, mostly sponsors of the rodeo. A few I notice are Wrangler, Justin boots, and Dodge. Each horse runs in a single file line around the circle one full lap, letting all horses enter the arena.

Karsyn comes in last, on Lucy, holding the American flag. They each stop in their designated formation as the announcer comes through the middle, still talking and giving everyone permission to be seated. My adrenaline is already starting to spike. I wonder what it would be like sitting on one of those horses like that.

The older man announces a list of different details, mostly boring stuff, but I guess it has to do with the different parties that helped put on the event. Out of nowhere a clown enters into the arena making jokes. I laugh. I can't help it. Something that so many people are terrified of is walking around in huge shorts with suspenders covering a bright yellow shirt. The two continue in a humorous bicker before the announcer calls the start of the rodeo and the flag girls take off in a full run, exiting the arena.

Breyson leans over the arm of the fold out seat to whisper in my ear. "Are you ready for the fun to start?"

I never cease to amaze myself at the things I find fun; new things that I still discover on a daily basis, thanks to mostly Breyson and of course others. I have no idea what to expect, but I'm ready to find out. "Yes! What comes first?"

He places his arm over the back of the chair. I love when he attempts to get closer to me. I never imagined I'd like public displays of affection, but with Breyson I do. I welcome every touch, every embrace, and every kiss I can get from him. After two years he still turns my insides out and constantly makes me feel like I'm going on the triple loop of a roller coaster.

His lips touch my ear, sending chills all over my body. "I love being here with you, watching you try new things. Your excitement makes me feel like I'm trying them for the first time all over again. I never want to stop courting you, even when we're old and gray."

My eyes close. He always says the most romantic things at the most unexpected times, making it even better. All my life I've seen girls with the misconstrued idea of what romance is. Romance isn't over the top dates or epic proposals, it's the realistic proportions of your man doing whatever and it still makes your heart feel like it's going to dance right out of your chest.

I don't need the Eiffel Tower in June or the Alps in December to feel like I'm being romanced. I need for my husband to tell me that he never wants to stop courting me. I need to dance in our backyard under the stars. I need to sit by his side with his arm around me while he whispers sweet nothings in my ear. That is the definition of real-life romance, and I'm one of the luckiest women in the world because I have it.

I lay the side of my head against his mouth and pretend for a moment that we're not in the middle of hundreds of people watching a man ride a bucking horse. Right now, I want to enjoy that it's just the two of us in a sea of people we'll never see again. "Have I told you lately that I'm the luckiest girl in the world?"

He alters his position so that he's holding up my head with his forehead, freeing his lips. "Tell me why . . ."

"The complexity of my emotions by the simple things."

"That was deep."

He cups his hand on my arm and pulls me into him. He starts lightly rubbing up and down the length of my upper arm while the world is continuing around us.

"You captivate me with little to no effort at all. You say things sometimes as if you don't even have to think about them, like they are just existing in your mind and waiting for the right moment to be released. You always make me feel special. I mean, what happened to you? You were the cocky jock that everyone wanted and I was just the shy, distant girl that turned your head. How did that turn you into this amazing person most don't get the chance to meet in their lifetime, but I get to have you every day?"

"I fell in love with my muse is all . . ."

The most perfect answer in a matter of nine words, and I'm going to sit here and meditate on it while I watch a rodeo with my husband, because this is what you do when you're in love. You enjoy each other's company without distractions of things that don't matter, always keeping each other first no matter what. He is my better half and my best friend.

THIRTY-EIGHT

WEDDING DAY . . .

The men got booted out of the house. We ended up at Mims and Pops' house to get ready for the wedding. My bride and her maids are at our house. I'm not sure who invented the rule that I'm not supposed to see her before the wedding. I have a feeling it was a woman, though. No man would come up with something so ridiculous. I don't like it, not one bit.

I'm standing at the dresser mirror looking at myself. It's been a long time since I've worn a tux. After all, I didn't make it to my senior prom. Kinzleigh went with beige since it's outdoors and rustic style. I cannot wait to see what she looks like.

Braxton places his hands on my shoulders from behind me. "My little brother is growing up so fast. Slow down, Son, you're making me feel old."

I raise my brow. His exceedingly cocky attitude never fails; even toned down a notch since him and Adalynn started dating. "That whole three-minute difference is really starting to make you an old man. I can already see a few grays."

He closes in on the distance from his head to the mirror, shuffling around the blonde hairs on his head. "No the hell I don't. Shut the fuck up."

I smile and shake my head. He's so predictable. "I don't know how

Adalynn puts up with you and your self-absorbed tendencies."

"She has no complaints . . . in *any* department."

"Dude, way too much information. I don't want to hear that shit."

I walk to the edge of the bed and sit down, leaving him to himself to sort out his conceited issues. He's my brother, my best friend, and I love him, but how we split from the same exact DNA I will never understand. If you don't know us you can't tell us apart, but our personalities, though overall similar, are completely different.

Fisher takes a seat beside me. Even though I've only known him since the start of school last fall, he's become a best friend. When Kinzleigh told me to choose my groomsmen I didn't even have to think about it, he was already chosen. "You ready to do this?"

"You are aware I'm already married, right?"

I start putting on my shoes. All I will be lacking is the jacket for the finishing touch. "Yes, but now it's going to be for everyone to witness. It makes it more real, you know, so are you ready?"

"More than anything I've ever been ready for before. I've known since she showed up at school senior year that I wasn't going to be able to walk away from her again. The context in which I want her is forever, infinite, never ending. We claimed ownership over each other a long time ago. This is merely a show . . ."

"You know your soul is really aged for the physical years your body has been on this earth, right? I don't believe in reincarnation, but sometimes you say things that make it hard not to wonder. I thought I was in the minority by not wanting to sleep with every girl willing to spread her legs, but you make even me look bad."

I laugh. It's not all that often that Fisher gets serious. Really and truly the guy jokes nonstop. His personality is laidback and fun. He keeps things light instead of constantly being weighted down with heavy topics of conversation, but that's why he has so many friends. I've lost most of mine by not following the crowd. Being married at nineteen puts a damper on things, but an endless friends list is overrated. I'd rather have six true friends than a ton of meaningless ones anyway.

Hell, even Preston is included in that list. He's become a close friend and I never thought I'd say that. He kept his word. He's called several times over the past few months to check on Bryce, never overstepping his boundaries. Out of respect, he calls me instead of Kinzleigh. That alone established a trust I didn't think I'd ever have, considering the things that have happened, so I finally told him he has my permission to contact her occasionally to check on her as long as he doesn't break my trust.

The crazy thing is that I trust Preston as much as I trust my brothers around my wife, even knowing he loves her and has slept with her, but he's earned it. He's here and he volunteered to hold Bryce during the ceremony. He took a week leave to come down for the wedding. He's here for a few days to spend time with Bryce, so Kinzleigh and I agreed to let him keep Bryce while we're gone on our honeymoon if he wants. We made the offer last night at the rehearsal dinner, and without a second to think on it he agreed. Besides the fact that he's earned my trust, I trust Kinzleigh implicitly.

I set my foot on the floor, linking my hands over my lap. "Nah, I just found a girl at a young age that turned my head, and then she inadvertently stole my heart. I figured I better make it permanent before some other strapping lad comes along and tries to steal her away and she realizes I'm not as spectacular as she thinks I am."

Most of the time Fisher has a smile on his face, especially when I try to joke first. The only time I've ever seen him down was after the rodeo when Karsyn stumbled in the hotel room in the middle of the night with a post-fucked look. Down might not even be the appropriate word. He actually looked like he wanted to rip someone to shreds and I have never seen him with an ounce of violent anger, not even on the field.

"You still twisted up about Karsyn?"

He looks out in the distance, slightly zoning out. "Hey, if she wants to go fuck some lame cowboy that doesn't care about anything but dipping his wick all the power to her. I don't give a shit."

I know he was up with her for a while that night. The light coming in the door when she arrived woke me up for a minute, before I quickly passed out again. He's not even looking at me, so I study his face. His hands are fisted on his thighs and his jaw muscle is working overtime. His lips start to move, but no words exit. He's mumbling something silently to himself.

Shit . . .

I slap my hand over his shoulder and squeeze. He looks at me. "What?"

My cheeks pull back, forming a straight line out of my lips. "My man, if you want her then go get her. Like I told you before, be the one that's different. Be bold. You only live once. You wanted a chase, remember? Put on your running shoes and go after her. Generally speaking, the ones that take the most work are the ones that are worth it; the ones you'll never release once you catch. Just remember . . . it doesn't matter where she's gone before you, but only where she refrains from going after you . . .”

He places the heel of his hand against his forehead, rubbing his hair from side to side. “Fuck, I don’t know. It just seems like she hasn’t really looked my way. It’s a little hard on my ego.”

“Things aren’t always as they seem, buddy. Everyone knows that.”

The door bursts open and in walks Ryland and Konnor. Konnor is holding a guitar case and Ryland a bottle of champagne; both fully dressed to match the rest of the groomsmen. Kinzleigh chose coral and turquoise as the wedding colors. We all are wearing beige tuxedos, but my vest and tie are white to match the bride and theirs are rotating between the two colors: three in turquoise and two in coral.

“The west coast country boy has arrived! Who missed me?” I look up at Ryland holding his arms above his head in a V, clutching the bottle of champagne by the neck. He has almost shaved his head. Those blonde curls he had—gone. Now, without the bleaching of the sun, it’s the color of mine. He looks older.

He wasn’t here for rehearsal, because he was at a surfing competition yesterday and couldn’t get a flight until last night. All I can do is shake my head and laugh. Ryland is one of those guys you shouldn’t try to explain in words. The guy is a fucking nut, but the bastard is loyal. “It’s about time my best man showed up.”

“Hey, watch your mouth, lover boy. I made it before the ceremony. That makes me early . . . and I brought the booze. You don’t even have to say thank you.”

“If you aren’t here to crash the wedding. Your motive is yet to be determined. As far as the booze, there is a fountain full of that stuff under the gazebo. Try again . . .”

He looks at Braxton. “Do you think the bride would notice if I used it as a weapon instead of a gift? No one would notice he was gone. You could even stand in his place, twin.”

“Fuck that. I’m not getting hitched. The bride may be hot and all, but that’s asking too much.”

I stand and walk over to Ryland, grabbing the bottle of champagne from his long, narrow fingers and give him a man hug. “I’m just busting your balls. I’m glad you made it safely.”

He gives me a stop sign with his hand. “I bear gifts.”

“I thought I was supposed to be the one giving gifts,” I say. “Why didn’t someone clue me in? I could’ve saved a ton of money on your ass.”

He looks at me as if I'm the biggest idiot on the planet. "You don't come to a wedding without a wedding gift, dick. What the hell is wrong with you? Even I knew that and I stay away from weddings. The thought of clingy girls at weddings gives me hives. When you throw that garter aim away from me, that's all I'm saying. Me being here speaks volumes. Don't say I never did anything for you."

"You are a disgrace, Reeves. Just for that I hope it hits you in the face and you get attacked by single women." He forms a look of disgust on his face. If there were a phobia for commitment, I would diagnose Ryland with it. "Lay it on me. Where's my present?"

He pulls two envelopes from his jacket pocket, handing me the larger of the two. It looks like a card. "This one isn't from me. This goes with the bottle you already took. It's from the bride. By the way, she's smoking hot today." He winks as I take the card from his hand. Is it bad that I'm slightly jealous he saw her before me?

I pull the card from the unsealed envelope it's in, opening it. It's a note written in Kinzleigh's handwriting.

Breyson,

I know that we have already stepped into marriage together, but I still want to do this traditionally. When we were on my parents' yacht I had an idea. Every year that we are together I want to collect a bottle of wine or champagne born that year, so that when we are looking back fifty years from now we can see how far we have come together. Each bottle will signify a year that we have been married. I love you more than I could ever explain and I will always be the luckiest girl in the world for being blessed with a husband like you. We will make it. One day we're going to stand in the middle of our wine cellar and confirm that sometimes love is all you need. The bottle that you are holding was born in the year 2014 at a vineyard in Napa Valley, California, the state we met and also married. Since we actually married in October I got a bottle from that year. I'll meet you at the altar. I'll be in white.

-Kinzleigh

She continues to surprise me each and every day. She still takes my breath away and leaves me speechless after all this time. It seems like we've been together forever, yet it still feels new. When she took my heart, she grabbed ahold of it and never let go. It reminds me of that song by Chris Young, *Old Love Feels New.*

I look up at Ryland and he hands me the smaller envelope. I open it and lying inside are two airline tickets to Vegas and a hotel reservation for October of 2016, the week of Kinzleigh's twenty-first birthday as well as mine. Only Ryland . . .

"Twenty-first birthday in Vegas? Don't you think it's a little early for that? That's over a year away. I don't know what I'm going to be doing then."

"If you expected romantic you should know better. I missed that gene. Everyone should see Vegas. Take Kinzleigh to Vegas, get her drunk, and have your way with her. That is spice, my man. You do not plan Vegas around your life, you plan your life around Vegas." He starts tapping his temple with his index finger. "Fucking genius."

And you're a fucking nut.

I hit myself in the face with the envelope, shaking my head in shame. Where did his parents go wrong? He's a damn idiot, but he's my best friend. I introduce the two additions to Fisher as I did with my brothers last night.

I look at Konnor and shake his hand. "What's up, man? What's with the guitar?"

"A surprise I've been planning for Kinzleigh."

I nod and the door opens again. Mom peeks her head in. "Sweetie, your brother is back from the airport. They're here."

A rush of nerves hit me full force. Maria said they couldn't get here earlier because of passport issues, but thankfully they were able to make it in time for the wedding. Briar and Dad went to pick them up this morning. Kinzleigh wanted the ceremony to be late afternoon, so the reception could be from sunset into the night. I haven't seen them since I said goodbye back at the start of fall.

I walk to the door and follow Mom outside where Dad is pulling up in Moms vehicle. All four doors open and they step out. My emotions hit me like a freight train as I see them exit the vehicle. Antonio, Maria, Marcus, and Dr. Rodriguez are all setting foot on American soil . . . for me.

My eyes begin to fill. Marcus comes running at me first. "Breyson, Breyson, we're here!" It's crazy how much he's grown since I last saw him.

I squat down to his level and hold out my arms as the amazing kid that is like a brother to me runs into them, closing them around him. "It's about time, buddy."

I squeeze him tight, not realizing how much I missed the kid. I release him to look him in the face and ruffle his hair like I always did. He narrows his eyes at me and swats my hand away. "Hey, don't mess up the do. There might be girls here. I have to look my best." He leans in and puts his hand in a line beside his mouth, the back facing his lips as if he's telling a secret away from someone's line of vision. "Mom's words, not mine."

I laugh. "I've missed you, kiddo."

He never even acknowledges my comment. He just continues as if I didn't even say anything. "Where is she? When do I get to meet her? I have something for her."

"You do? I can take you to her if you want to meet her. We still have time." I have never cared about rules, so there is no reason to start now. This is more important than not seeing the bride before the ceremony. Nothing about our life is traditional.

His eyes light up and he looks back at the rest of them. "We're going to see the pretty bride, Mom. See you later."

"Hold up, buddy. I think they should come too. Don't you?"

He pulls up one side of his face in a crinkled scrunch, as if he's too cool to hang out his parents. Oh boy . . . "Ugh . . . I guess they can come." Never thought I would long to hear an accent like that until now, being away from them.

I stand and place my hand on his outer shoulder, walking toward them with him to my side. Maria starts to step forward before anyone else. She throws her arms around me and hugs me hard. "Te extrañé, hijo (I've missed you, Son)."

"I've missed you too, Mom." I don't attempt to let go of the hold I have around her waist. I don't speak Spanish fluently, but being around it so long I learned enough to recognize certain phrases.

I owe these people so much. They are the reason I had a place to go, they are the reason I kept my chin up when I had no hope, and they are the reason I found my way back home. She whispers in my ear. "I want to meet my daughter-in-law and my grandson. I want to meet everyone important to you."

A family is the best thing that we are given in life. A family is what molds you. Not only was I gifted one family, but two. In a twisted way what happened was good for me, because in the end I got back out of it tenfold what I went in with, and maybe that is what Fate was trying to show me. There is always an unexpected surprise around every corner, whether good or bad. "That can definitely be arranged."

I move down the line greeting the other two. Antonio grabs me behind the neck and pulls me in for a hug, patting me on the back with the other hand. "Congratulations, Son."

Dr. Rodriguez hugs me as well. "Looks like you found your way home just fine."

"Thanks to all of you," I say.

I turn around and my mom is a blubbering mess standing in my dad's arms. Briar must have gone inside to get ready. "Mom, Dad, for all intents and purposes this is my adoptive family. These are the people that took me in, provided for me, and helped me get better, both mentally and physically. They are also the same people that helped me find my way back home."

My mom doesn't waste any time before she all but runs in the direction of Maria, pulling her into a hug. She whispers something in her ear that no one else can hear. Maria looks at me with tears in her eyes and a smile on her face. This is my family . . .

Kinzleigh

I stand in the full-length mirror I have hung on my bedroom closet, looking at myself. I have no idea why I'm nervous. I'm already married for Heaven's sake. It could be the fact that everyone we know is here and I'll be at the center of all the staring eyes. "Looking divine, peaches. Beau-ti-ful . . ."

Karsyn places her hands on my bare shoulders. Thank goodness it's warm out today. I smile at her. When getting a compliment from Karsyn you actually believe it, because she's not the kind of person to just throw them out there.

"Did I get my vision right?"

"Sweetie pie, sugar drop, and honey bun, this looks awesome. I love your mind. The two of us put it together beautifully. You're going to knock his socks off. The boots are the best part." She winks and kisses my cheek.

When I started thinking about my dress, I had this idea. It was a stretch and a little eccentric, but I went with it. I wanted princess versus cowgirl, the mix that makes up who I am since I met Breyson. I tossed out the idea to Karsyn and Mom over lunch one day to see how crazy I was, and they actually liked it, so we had it custom made.

My dress is strapless and made of a sweetheart, corset top in white with a lace overlay. At my hips it blossoms out like a ball gown, making my waist look tiny. This is where I mixed it up. In the front it stops just above my knees but continues to get longer as the bottom hem rounds my legs and cascades into a short train in the back. I wanted the front to be short enough to show off my cowgirl boots, but I didn't want a tea length dress like the bridesmaids' dresses. I wanted the Cinderella look, but altered to fit our country backdrop.

My hair is in a messy ball of curls to the side, behind my right ear. Rhinestone studded bobby pins were dispersed to shine when catching light. I chose to omit a veil all together. I let Karsyn do my makeup and she didn't disappoint me. She left it in neutral shades for my eyes, but bold, making my green eyes stand out. The most dramatic point is my bright red lips stained with smudge-proof lipstick and the sapphire earrings that Breyson got me for Christmas.

Karsyn grabs my left hand, removing my engagement ring, and then moves it to my right ring finger. The rest of the girls are still getting ready in the other room, leaving just the two of us.

She starts to look me over like a painter admiring his masterpiece, checking for any finishing touches needing to be made. It seems like she's trying to process something, because she never looks me in the eyes.

"I have something I need to tell you."

"Okay . . ."

"You're my only friend here."

"No, I'm not." Where on earth did that come from? She is the single most random person I know.

She rolls her eyes. "Must I explain everything, peaches? That phrase is starting to sound like a broken record."

She begins brushing her hands over my shoulders as if she's removing dust or lint, clearly to distract her. "I have several people that associate with me, but they are not my friends. I was taught to always be nice to everyone without letting people trample all over you. They are only people that coincide next to me on a daily basis, occasionally needing an ear to listen while they practice speaking. I don't generally get along with girls. I'm just different that way, I guess. Maybe it was growing up without a mother."

She sighs. "I tend to befriend guys, leaving out the bullshit that comes with females. A girl burned me and I swore I would never trust another. I've been that way ever since. But then there you were. You walked into the store and there was something about you that told me I should be your friend, that I needed you in my life."

She smiles. "I know I am a pain in the ass ninety percent of the time, but you deal with it. I don't verbalize my feelings much. Most of the time I don't even evaluate them myself, because they scare me. I missed out on the part in life where a girl has a mother to turn to and gets nurtured by her. Most girls learn at an early age how to decipher feelings and what actions they go with. How to come back from pain. Emotions confuse me. I don't know how to sort them out well. Mine just kind of get tangled up in each other. They're stuck on repeat. I know I haven't spoken of my home life much. There are many things I'll reveal over time. My dad is a rancher, though different from Breyson. We own a breeding farm. With that comes a lot of responsibility. He did the best he could to raise me alone."

I have a feeling she's going to be fixing makeup soon. She starts tapping her index finger over her lips, precisely choosing what words will come next.

"What I'm trying to say is, I may not always be the best friend when you need me to be, but I will try. If I do something wrong like laugh at you when I'm supposed to cry with you, I may need you to give me a little love slap and teach me what I'm supposed to do. You're my best friend. I think I love you, peaches. Like for real hearts and candy kind of love. I want this womance to work between us. Sisters from another mother, right?"

I start laughing and crying simultaneously. I'm not sure how. I didn't even know that was possible. When in need of a word Karsyn will make up her own. She is the perfect swirled product of sweet and sour, never too much of either. Only Karsyn could come up with some of the things she does. I throw my arms around her bare shoulders. "That was the greatest best friend love pledge I've ever heard. We will carry on this womance forever. I promise."

"Oh, I have something for you; two things actually. I'm going to give you mine first."

She walks over to her bag and grabs a black velvet box. "Breyson gave you your something new and something blue, so I wanted to give you something borrowed."

She opens the box and what lies inside are a set of pearls—a necklace. I place my hand over my mouth, stunned. They're beautiful. "These were my mother's. My dad gave them to her on their wedding day. She left them to me. They are very special to me, as are you. They've been in this box since she died. I can't bring myself to wear them, because nothing has been worthy enough, but this is. You and Breyson share something really special, Darlin'. These are as real as they come, and I think they deserve to be worn once in a while."

She removes them from the cushion they rest on, holding them out in a line. "They're beautiful. I'd be honored to wear them."

"Turn around, Kinzleigh."

That's the first time she's called me by my real name in longer than I can remember. It makes this moment sacred. I turn around and she picks them up over my head, sitting them on my chest. Automatically, my hand goes to touch them as she hooks the ends on the back of my neck.

When she finishes, I look back in the mirror, admiring them. She grabs her phone off the dresser. "I'm starting a photo album of important things for my hope chest. Will you take a picture with me?"

I'm trying really hard not to get emotional, but this is a sentimental moment. As we grow, some friends come and go, while others nestle in and stay around for the long haul. I don't know what will happen with Adalynn, Presley, Macie, and Londyn. I can only hope that we all remain close with them moving off and finding their own way, but I can tell that Karsyn is one of those that you find somewhere along the way and she never leaves.

"Like you even have to ask."

I walk toward the center of the room to give us more space and wrap my arm around her waist from behind, hers mirroring mine. I place my other hand flat against her abdomen and look at the screen as she holds it out in front of us, making this moment permanent to file away in the pages of our story. "One, two, three . . ."

I smile for the camera as she touches the little button to snap the photo. Friends are like angels. They are always watching over you, even if from afar, and they are always by your side when you need them. It doesn't matter if they have to drop what they're doing to get there. Everywhere you turn in life there are little gifts from God to get you through life. It's up to us to recognize them when they come.

"Okay, I promised I would give you Breyson's gift." She lays her phone back down in the spot she picked it up from and shuffles through her bag.

She pulls out a shoebox and hands it to me. "This is your wedding gift."

I take it from her and remove the lid. Inside lies a frame holding a photo of me. It's of the day I was standing on the yacht looking out at the water. It was the morning after Breyson mentioned us getting married. I woke up and couldn't bear to wake him. My emotions were going wild to the point that I couldn't sleep. I look like I'm in complete peace. I'm happy in that photo.

Lying underneath it is another frame, but smaller. It's the day Bryce was born. I'm in a hospital bed holding Bryce with Breyson by my side. I can't even explain the looks on our faces. You can tell that we were longing for each other but fighting it. It completely breaks my heart seeing it from the outside looking in.

Last, but not least, are a jewelry box and a card. I open the jewelry box first. It's a silver bracelet with a heart shaped locket and engraved on the front are the words, *my heart belongs to you.* I open it. On one side are our initials as a couple; Breyson's first on the left, mine on the right, and our last initial in the center. On the other is the date we got married on the pier.

Tears are streaming down my face and I haven't even opened the card. I take a deep breath, trying to gather myself. Breyson always outdoes himself. His gifts are always with so much thought. I open the card and written on the pages in his handwriting is a note.

> *Kinzleigh, my love . . .*
>
> *I know you're probably a little confused by the gifts, so I wanted to explain. First, I'll explain the one of us, our family. I will never forget that day for as long as I live. That is the day that we welcomed our son into the world. It was a bittersweet day for me, because even though I couldn't have you, I had a piece of you in him. That is the day I made a promise to myself that I was going to get you back. What lies in this picture, Kinzleigh, is my life; the two of you. I will gladly sacrifice mine to ensure the two of you have yours. The photo of you on the yacht was to show you how I see you through my eyes. When I saw you like that my heart stopped beating for a moment. There will never be a day that I don't look at you and see the most beautiful woman in the world, because to me you are. When you wonder if you're enough for me, look at this photo. You exceed everything I ever thought I deserved*

in a lifetime. I am beyond blessed to call you my life partner and my wife. I love you.

-Breyson

I look at Karsyn. I can imagine my makeup is turning into a hot mess right now. I'm depending on the term waterproof to prove it right now. I hold out the jewelry box to Karsyn. "Will you put it on me?"

"Of course, I will, shortcake. You don't even have to ask." She walks closer to me and removes the bracelet from the box, hooking it back around my left wrist, closest to my heart.

A knock sounds at the door and Karsyn walks over to open it. "What are you doing here? Shoo, you cannot see her before the wedding."

"Breyson? Is everything okay?" I set the shoebox on the edge of the dresser.

"I have someone that wants to meet you. Can you come out?"

Karsyn looks back at me and I nod. She shrugs. "Okay, but don't say I didn't do my maid of honor duties."

She opens the door further and points her finger in Breyson's face. "I'm warning you now, no kissing the bride until the preacher says so. I don't care if you're hot and I don't care if you're bigger. These boots on my feet are not only there for looks. I know how to use them."

She walks out the door. "See you in a few minutes, peaches." The real name was short-lived. I'm back to being called everything under the category of fruit and desert.

Breyson holds out his hand for me to take his. "Who is it?"

He smiles. "Hello to you too. You look beautiful. It's someone that's heard a lot about you."

He leads me into our living room and I stop when I see them. I don't have to think. I know exactly who they are. "Kinzleigh, this is my family from Spain."

I don't know how much more my heart can take today. I'm overwhelmed with emotions being evoked from all different sides. I hold up my hand in an awkward wave, not knowing what else to do. "Hi. It's nice to finally meet you all . . ."

Breyson continues to pull me closer. The little boy walks forward and holds out his hand. "I'm Marcus, the little brother." He's so cute and animated. I have a feeling this one never meets a stranger. I look down. He really isn't that much shorter than me.

I take his small hand in mine and shake it. "Hi, Marcus. You sure are cute like Breyson."

"Please. He gets it from me. Don't let him fool you." Everyone laughs at the same time. He's adorable. He doesn't even seem to notice the difference in physical appearance, even at his young age—their dark skin and hair and eyes, to Breyson's light everything. That makes me love him a little more, because family isn't about skin color, but about love. It makes my heart feel better knowing these are the kind of people Breyson was around.

I look at Breyson and he has a proud smile on his face. I can tell he's attached to them. I look back at Marcus. "Well, Marcus. Did you keep him out of trouble for me when he was away?"

"For sure. He was on his best behavior. Scouts honor," he says, holding up his hand. "You're really pretty. How'd he end up with someone like you? Are you sure you chose the right brother?"

I start laughing, but this time harder. I love his little personality. Breyson throws his arm around him, pulling him away from me and toward him. "Hey, little buddy, I love you, but those are fighting words. Eyes off my woman."

The woman walks over and wraps her arms around me unexpectedly. "I'm Maria. It's nice to finally meet you after hearing so much about you."

"It's nice to meet you as well. Thank you for taking such good care of him. I will always be grateful for all of you."

I hug each and every one of them as they introduce themselves. It's surreal that all of this is happening, but I'm really glad I can finally put closure to an array of questions I had in my mind of the time Breyson was away. I feel like we can finally move forward and build a life together, both including the important people along the way.

"Kinzleigh, I brought something for you." I turn around as Marcus is pulling from Breyson's grasp and walking toward me.

"You did? That was so thoughtful." I'm expecting a small wedding gift or something homemade.

He reaches in his pocket and pulls something out in his fist. When he opens his little hand, I almost lose it. My silver anklet that I gave Breyson is lying on his small palm. He picks it up out of his hand, allowing it to dangle from his fingers.

"When my brother left, I was sad, because he's my only brother. He took time to play with me and teach me things. The night he left he gave me this to hold onto and keep safe. He told me you gave him your heart, but that he didn't need this one anymore, because your heart was inside his heart. He told me he had to go, because he had to come find you or you'd be heartbroken. He gave me this to remember him by, but I don't want to just remember him. This belongs to you. I want you to have it back. The only thing I want is for you to promise you'll keep him in my life. I want to see my brother again."

I'm thanking the Heavens that Karsyn used waterproof makeup, because I've completely turned into an emotional wreck. Tears are spilling out one after another with no effort at all. With each passing day my heart grows, strengthening me, but with that comes feeling more. With feeling more, every emotion experienced is more consuming and more prominent. There is no hiding it.

I bend down and get on my knees in front of him. I grab his hands in mine with him still holding the anklet. "Marcus, you have my word that you will at least see your brother once a year. I hope it's more, but if not, that I promise. I would never take him away from you. There is enough of him to share. Those important to Breyson are important to me. I am very thankful to you for keeping my favorite anklet safe. My grandmother gave this to me a long time ago and you saved the day by bringing it back to me. Do you want to know why?"

He bores his brown eyes into my green ones, listening. "Why?"

"Because a bride has to have certain things to get married and I was missing something old, but now I have it because of you."

He grins from ear to ear as if he just won the lottery. "Will you be the one to put it on me?"

He nods and I hold out my right wrist while he unhooks it, wraps it around, and hooks it back again. I look up at Breyson and he has tears in his eyes. I smile at him when he mouths, *thank you*. What he doesn't realize is that he shouldn't be thanking me. I'm the one that should be thanking him. He has opened my heart and in turn allowed me to love so fiercely that it's something you can't ever explain to someone else. They have to experience it for themselves. It's time to put our pasts behind us and move forward, because the people in front of us are part of our future.

THIRTY-NINE

Breyson

I walk to the barn entry with my groomsmen walking beside me. I barely recognize the place. There are white lights everywhere: in trees, trimming the barn, and mixed in twigs on the altar in the doorway of the barn. White chairs filled with people we know are in two sections, split on each side of the aisle that runs down the center. Everything around me is decorated to draw attention to the rustic feel of the barn and the woods instead of taking away from it.

The minister we've known all our life is standing at the altar waiting to get started. We take our positions and wait patiently. My nerves are getting worked up. We are legally married already, but we got married alone. This time everyone will be watching. That's not the part that has me nervous. I've been wanting to publicly mark her with my name and ring for what seems like forever, but this means we're one step closer to the honeymoon I've been working on for months.

Soft music is playing around us. I have no idea where Kinzleigh is going to be coming from. She won't tell me anything, but if it has anything to do with the way she looked earlier, my jaw is going to drop. It took all of my willpower not to kiss her when I saw her at the house. Every time I see her, she is more beautiful than she was the last.

I keep looking at Mims' house across the pasture, thinking she's going to come from there, but it should be time to start. The music changes to another song and everyone becomes silent, turning their heads toward the woods.

Ryland nudges me and I look at him. He points to the wood line that goes to our house. I follow his finger and notice the bridesmaids coming out in a timed manner horseback. Londyn is already halfway across the passing on one of Pops' horses. Each girl's dress is matched in color to the groomsman she is with, all strapless and knee length with boots.

Coming out of the opening is Lauren. Each horse is one of our several mares, and each is fully dressed out to match with the wedding theme. I watch each come through the field, waiting for the one that will make my heart stop.

Following Lauren is Adalynn, then Presley, and finally Karsyn on her own horse. My stomach is twisted in so many knots I feel like I can't breathe. This wasn't part of the rehearsal last night. I had no idea she was going to use horses. She must have gotten Pops' help with that. Every step is on time with the music playing.

The song that starts playing next I instantly recognize. When Kinzleigh discovered it, she made me listen to it the second I walked through the door. Literally, I opened the door and she started screaming, *I found our song!* I shouldn't be surprised she made it our wedding song. I think it's even my ringtone on her phone. In her defense, she was spot on with saying it was a reflection of us, so I don't mind that she chose it—*We both know* by Colbie Caillat and Gavin DeGraw.

Divinity comes out of the wood line when the passing is clear. The girls are all sitting horseback on the opposite side of us, turned, so they can watch Kinzleigh. My heart falters at the sight of her. It is by far the most beautiful way I've ever seen her. The silky, black coat against the white of her dress makes her stand out. The train of her dress is fanned out over Divinity's backside, making her look like a princess.

Everyone stands as she comes across the pasture. My eyes are glued to her. The feeling going on inside of me is consuming me. The lyrics of the song, the beauty of her, and knowing that I got the girl is almost too much to bear. She is proof that if you want something bad enough you can obtain it, you may just have to work overtime for it.

She gets to the end of the aisle and her dad helps her off Divinity. Her eyes lock with mine and they stray no more.

Come to me, baby.

She smiles and her dad walks her down the aisle, stopping in front of us. As far as I'm concerned there are no others in the room but her.

I love you, I mouth.

She mouths it back to me. The preacher makes a short introduction and then starts. "Who gives this woman to this man?"

"Her mother and I do," her dad responds, and then kisses her on the cheek before laying her hand in mine and taking his seat next to her mother. She steps under our altar as the preacher gives his speech.

This is a moment when I want us completely open to each other. I want her to look into my eyes and me hers, knowing there will never be another for either of us. We are each other's forever. We have fought to get here, and we have fought for each other. As long as we always remember that no matter what trials and tribulation we face, we stick it out and hold onto our love for one another, nothing else matters.

Today, we make history . . .

FORTY

Kinzleigh

"Ladies and gentlemen, I now pronounce to you Mr. and Mrs. Breyson Abercrombie. Son, you may now kiss your bride."

Breyson gives me that panty-dropping smile and places his hand flat on my lower back, pulling me into him. "The part I've been waiting for since I saw you earlier."

He rests his other hand on the side of my neck and presses his lips into mine. He deepens the kiss, sliding his tongue through the crack of my lips as if we're all alone. It feels like we are. I close my eyes and let my tongue dance with his. He dips me backward, making me feel like a princess yet again.

A whistle sounds and then another, following into a domino effect between groomsmen. "Save some for the honeymoon!" The sound of Braxton's voice shouts through the air, causing both of us to laugh against each other's lips.

He stands upright, pulling me with him. Grabbing my hand in his, he raises both of them between us in the air and starts running down the aisle toward Divinity with me in tow as everyone stands. He helps me up and gets on behind me, instructing her to go.

Divinity takes off towards the wood line where the gazebo was built, all set up for the reception. I have always loved riding horseback with Breyson.

He has his arms by my sides, holding onto the reigns. He's not as close to me as he normally is, because my dress is in the way. Oh, how I wish I could tear it off right now . . .

"I'm so happy right now," he says next to my ear.

He's about to be happier. "Go home first. We have to give everyone time to get to the gazebo. We're supposed to come in last. We can walk there."

"Okay. What do we do in the meantime?"

"Use your imagination. We have about fifteen minutes."

He heels Divinity to make her go faster, the house now appearing. As we get to the front yard, he pulls on the reigns for her to stop. He doesn't even wait for her to completely stop before he's jumping off.

He holds his hand up for me, helping me down. I have to take off running to avoid falling as he runs to the front door. At least I'm not wearing heels. He turns around as we get on the porch and crushes his lips to mine, pulling my body into his. His breathing is quickening, showing his need.

His kiss is rushed and rough, making me crazy. The adrenaline in knowing we're on a crunch for time makes it even better. Opening the door, he backs us inside and shuts it behind us. He turns us back around and slams my back into the door, continuing to kiss me.

He presses his body against mine as he rubs his hands up and down my body in frenzy, looking for an opening in a multitude of fabric. I reach down, immediately finding the button of his pants, undoing them, followed by the zipper.

I un-tuck his button-down shirt from his trousers and slide my hands under the band of his pants and briefs in unison, working them over his butt and erection, letting them fall to his thighs. He continues to lick and suck, twirl and taste, fueling my hunger for him more.

I wrap one leg around his, pulling him closer. Placing the palm of my hands over the backs of his, I guide them down my body, instructing him on where to go. When I touch his hands to the bare part of my knees, I run them underneath the skirt until he's just outside my panties. "Touch me."

He rubs his fingers over the outside of my panties, feeling the shape of my most private parts. "Tell me who this belongs to."

Oh, damn. He has that tone; that sexy deepening of his voice he does when he transforms into this alpha male role. "You."

He places his hand down the front of my panties, rubbing me from top to bottom, not stopping on any one place. "How long does it belong to me?"

"Forever."

He presses his finger harder against me and runs it up and into my folds. "You want it?"

"Yes. Please. We're running out of time."

He hooks his free hand around my leg and wraps it around his waist. Letting go, I keep it there. He pulls my panties to the side with one hand and rubs the head of his dick in circles over my opening, lubricating it to enter. He has to squat a little to get it in being in this position. "You're wet for me, baby."

"I'm always wet for you."

He pushes inside me, standing straighter as he buries himself deep. He grabs my thighs and picks me up, holding me against the front door. I lock both legs around his waist and link my hands behind his neck. "And I'm always hard for you."

He balances most of my weight on one arm and starts rubbing my clit with the other hand as he thrusts in and out. He doesn't waste his time teasing. He's doing this to make me come. He rubs the pad of his thumb up and down over my clit in a fast motion, never letting up. It's starting to get sensitive, building for an orgasm.

I lay my head back against the door. I'm unable to move from the sensation of him thrusting in and out at the same time he's rubbing my clit. He licks up the length of my neck, stopping just outside my ear. "Come for me, baby."

"Don't stop. I'm almost there."

He continues, rubbing faster. I grab his hair in my fist, pulling it as he brings me to the climb, about to free-fall. As my orgasm starts, I crush my lips to his, wanting to taste him while I come. My world slows down, enjoying the feel of him sliding back and forth inside me while I ride out my orgasm. I begin to contract around his dick, squeezing him. He moans against my lips and his thrusts start to slow, eventually coming to a complete stop.

He releases my lips and lays his forehead against the door beside my head, both of us breathing heavily. "I'll never get tired of this."

"Me either," I say, running my fingers through the hair on the back of his head. "No matter how many times or how many different ways, it never gets old. To this day, you still throw my heart off beat just like the first day I saw you. I just want you to know."

He looks at me, rubbing his thumb over my bottom lip. "You're so good to me. I'm glad there is no more darkness. I love the light. We made it to the light, baby. We got our happy ending."

Hearing him talk in that low tone makes my stomach flip. I will do anything to make him happy. We're close to two years in and he still has me twitterpated. This summer will mark two years exactly since I met him and it's been the best two years of my life, even counting the bad parts, because the good parts are so amazing that it makes up for the not so good.

I smile against his thumb. "And looking back, it was worth the bumpy ride to get here. Take me to our reception, baby. I want to dance with you at our wedding."

We walk along the pathway that leads to the gazebo when I hear it. "Everyone rise and welcome Mr. and Mrs. Breyson Abercrombie."

The guests are all piled under the gazebo as we walk in. Breyson and I walk in hand-in-hand as everyone claps. It's so surreal. Everything.

The DJ starts playing a slow song and Breyson walks us into the middle of the dance floor. He places one hand on the small of my back and the other hand in mine. He pulls me into him as the words start playing in the song. *These are the days* by Van Morrison.

"May I have this dance?"

"I'll always dance with you."

He lays his cheek against mine and starts to sway to the music, allowing me to get lost in his world . . . again. The mix of the sweet harmony in the song while dancing with the love of my life takes me into my happy place. When I'm in his arms I drift off into this world where it's just the two of us. Time does not exist in this world. It's just him and I, infinitely.

He twirls me around and pulls me back to him. "I like this song," he says. "This is how I feel when I'm with you."

"Me too. Promise me this will never change. I know we've talked about this, but maybe it's the wedding making me extra emotional. I want this to work. I want us to be permanent. We're young, so we're going to have to try harder than most. Promise we will never get too busy for each other. When we have careers or hectic schedules, even kids running wild, promise me that before we go to bed, you'll always dance with me in our living room, because these are the things I can't live without. I don't need anything else, but I do need you to love me. The little things are the only things I will ever need."

He kisses me on the cheek as he dances with me in his arms. "I promise on my life."

As the song ends my dad walks up to us. "May I step in?"

Breyson looks at him and gives him my hand. "Yes, Sir."

Another song comes on—*The way you look tonight* by Frank Sinatra. Dad holds my hand in his beginning our father, daughter dance. "It's been a while, Dad."

"Too long." It's different dancing with Dad. It brings back a lot of memories growing up of when I used to stand on his feet before bed and let him lead me around the living room to the classics like this. It was our time, and because of it I still have a love for old love songs.

"Are you happy? Is this for sure what you want?" I lay my head against his chest as we lightly sway to the music, not making any attempt to go anywhere.

"I've never been happier or surer of anything in my life. I get it now."

"What's that, sweetheart?"

"The relationship that you and Mom have. I never got it before, but now I do. It seems like staying married is the minority in current day and time. It's scary. What did you guys do to make it so long?"

"Oh, I don't know. I guess we realized that marriage would always take work. If you're not willing to work at it then there is no reason to start it at all. You'll be fine, baby girl. Always remember he comes before yourself and you'll be okay."

No one has a greater dad than me. I may be a little partial to him, because he's mine, but he's worthy of an award in my book. I would be devastated if anything ever happened to either of my parents, but I've always been a daddy's girl.

As the song wraps up, I can hear the echo of the microphone. "Baby girl, I've been working on a surprise for you. Congratulations to you and Breyson, my new brother-in-law. Breyson, you better take care of her."

"I'll meet you under the tent, baby girl. They are serving the food. I'm sure the guests are hungry. Take your time." He kisses my temple then turns and walks to exit the gazebo where the tent covered in white lights sits adjacent.

I'm barely paying attention, because of that voice. I instantly smile and look to the end of the gazebo all lit up in lights. My eyes go wide at what is standing there. How the—

When?

My hands go over my mouth. He got him here. I never even asked, but Konnor got Riggan here. Maddox and the whole band are set up to play at the end of the room. Konnor and Riggan are both standing side by side, each with a guitar in hand behind a microphone.

I look at each of them, but Maddox must be the only one that understands my confusion. He just smiles from behind the drums and winks at me. I want to cry. Riggan actually looks okay. The last time I saw him he was being driven away by my brother to a drug rehab facility. I have so many questions. I tried to see him, but he refused to see anyone, or so I thought.

Konnor looks at Riggan and he nods. They both start strumming the guitar simultaneously. It's not a song I recognize, but I'm drawn to the two of them.

A tear rolls down my face and Breyson's arm wraps around me as they start to sing. Oh my word, he wrote a song for me. The chorus is what gets me . . .

Once broken, but then was found
The one meant for you was able to turn you around
The path you're on is headed dream bound
You let love in and I'm so damn proud
Wear your happiness like a crown

They sound amazing together. My heart is beating hard throughout the entire song. I have no idea how this happened, but I'm glad it did. The beat is a light rock melody and they look like the stage is exactly where they're supposed to be.

I notice Presley from the corner of my eye. She's been staring daggers at Konnor all night, but right now even she's lost watching them. That's how good they are. I'm shocked. I knew Riggan could sing from that night at *Abby's Spot*, and I knew Konnor had been dabbling some in writing and learning how to play, but I never would have imagined this.

They finish the song and place their guitars in the stands. I never think. All I can do is run to both of them. I jump in Riggan's arms first, wrapping my arms around his neck. "I'm glad you're okay. Please don't ever do that to me again. You're a friend to me. I need you in my life."

His breathing is even. He doesn't say anything. Maybe it's too soon to bring up what happened. I don't want him to snap. He stands here, hugging me back. "I'm sorry. It just got to be too much. First her, but then you got hurt and it was completely my fault. I couldn't handle both of you."

He brings his voice down to a whisper. "You look so much like her it hurts. I don't know how to fix the hole in my chest, but I'm trying. Your brother came to see me in rehab a few times and started playing with me. The music helps me, but I feel guilty. I feel like I'm doing wrong by playing again."

I never look at him. I remain with my lips just outside his ear. "You want to know what I think? Just don't hate me, okay?"

I can feel the muscles in his jaw moving back and forth, before halting. "Okay."

"I read that poem on your bathroom wall that she wrote. She loved you, Riggan. She saw something special in you when you played. I could feel the emotions rolling off the page as I read them. If music is something you love, then continue. Abby knew how good you were and she still fell in love with you. Don't make her death be in vain by giving up a talent that she believed in. She would want you to play."

"She would have liked you. It may take me a little while to come around, but I'm getting there. Your brother has kind of become my sponsor. Go back to your wedding, Kinzleigh. We can talk about sad stuff later. Tonight is a night for happy."

He sets me down on my feet. I know he's right. There is a tent full of guests to mingle with and entertain, but I'm going to keep my eyes on him.

I move to Konnor and throw my arms around his neck. "Thank you for my surprise. I love it. Why have you been hiding that from me?"

"I was just playing around. It was the best wedding gift I could come up with. Everything else was lame."

"Stop being modest. That was awesome. Now I'll expect a song at every birthday and Christmas."

"I wouldn't get your hopes up, baby girl."

Most of the older guests have already sat down in the tent with a plate of food. I let him go and hip-hop music starts playing over the speakers.

Karsyn grabs the microphone and places it next to her lips. "Kinzleigh, enough of the mushy stuff. I'm starting to get the creeps. You know I have a limit and it was reached when you locked lips with your hot husband at the altar. Now it's time for fun, so get your butt on the dance floor." She points. "Now."

I laugh as the vulgar lyrics start playing and back up toward the middle. She downs the contents of the clear punch cup in her hand and sets it down along with the microphone. Someone's been sneaking around the champagne fountain. "Only if you come with," I say.

She starts moving her head to the rhythm of the music as she walks toward me. Next come the hand motions. I'm never going to get out of this. She continues to stalk toward me with a huge grin on her face. She reaches where I'm standing and when a certain beat catches, she starts pumping her arms and hips at me in a squat.

I shake my head at her, trying not to laugh. "I can't dance!"

She puts her hand at her ear pretending she can't hear me. She turns around and starts shaking her butt toward me, rolling her hips with the music.

I look around the room. Everyone is in the tent socializing and eating except for the wedding party around me, now dancing. Adalynn is grinding on Braxton, Londyn on Briar, and even Macie on Ryland. I notice Presley dancing with Fisher. Hmmm. That's weird. Instead of glancing at everyone else, screw it.

Karsyn turns around and notices me trying to dance. If it's not a cheerleading routine or slow dancing, there are only two words that describe my dancing skills. They suck. She should remember from the Halloween party. A continuous rotation of rap songs is playing, but this one is slower. I try moving my arms first. Karsyn places her hands on my hips, guiding me in the way I'm supposed to be rolling. A few tries and I'm starting to get the hang of it.

Konnor walks up behind Karsyn and grabs her hips, starting to grind his front on her backside. This seems so backward, knowing Fisher likes Karsyn and Presley's feelings over Konnor. A pair of hands snakes around my waist from behind, and a set of lips move forward beside my ear. "Follow me, baby."

Breyson aligns his body with mine. He runs his fingertips up my sides. I raise my arms, allowing him to trace up my body. I bend my arms behind his head, touching him. He places one hand on my hip and the other flat on my belly. What he does next I am totally not ready for.

He begins rolling his hips behind me, thrusting into me, but making my body match the rhythm of his. I had no idea he could dance like this. This is like sex without actually having sex, and it's extremely hot. I watch Karsyn basically having dry sex with Konnor, bent over in front of him, rolling her ass in his crotch to the music.

Karsyn looks at me and winks. Why I have no idea. Breyson pulls away and the song changes to, *I'm in love with a stripper* by T-pain.

A chair touches the back of my knees and Breyson pushes me into a sitting position. "Hell yeah, brother. Give it to her!"

I look over at Braxton, confused, until I see Breyson round the chair. I'm not sure what he's doing until he starts slowly removing his tuxedo jacket, tossing it to the side. "Break her in, Brey. Whoop, whoop!" My mouth drops at Karsyn instigating this.

He's still rolling and thrusting his hips to the song, now slowly unbuttoning his vest as he closes in on me. Oh my hell. I can feel my face flushing ten shades of red. He slides his vest off and tosses it in my lap with a smile on his face. He knows exactly what this is doing to me.

I'm clutching onto the sides of the chair. He's now halfway done loosening the knot on his tie. He pulls it over his head and places it over mine. The tuxedo rental store is not getting this tie back. I'll buy it. It now has sentimental value.

Damn, he's so sexy.

He pulls the shirt from his pants, freeing it. He starts unbuttoning the buttons one at a time, from the bottom up, until it's completely open. Each time he rolls his hips his abs tighten, forming ridges up his stomach.

He places his hands on the back of the chair for leverage and leans forward, barely leaving any space between us. He grinds his body in a roll, starting from his chest and ends brushing his crotch against me. His *hard* crotch, might I add. I am so turned on right now. I cannot believe my husband is giving me a lap dance in front of all our friends.

"Welcome to the first day of the rest of your life."

Nothing is ever dull with an Abercrombie boy. If this is the kind of things I have to look forward to, bring it. I'm ready.

I grab his hips, stilling him. Leaning forward, I stick out the tip of my tongue, and swipe it up the center of his stomach. When I look at him, he is staring at me, his eyes heating and darkening. He's ready to fuck. The shy girl is gone. I can play too.

Game on.

I smirk and wink like Karsyn always does. "Bring it on, Abercrombie. Bring. It. On."

FORTY-ONE

Breyson

"When are you going to tell me where we're going?"

I look over at her in the passenger seat of her Range Rover. She is rubbing her hands raw in her lap, clearly nervous. I take her hand in mine and pull it to my lips, kiss the back of her hand, and lay the two connected on the center console.

"When we get there."

She narrows her eyes at me and puckers her lips as if she could possibly be mad. I haven't been working on this surprise for months to ruin it now. Throughout our relationship strange connections have happened between Kinzleigh and I, things I can't explain. For whatever reasons we're always so in tune with each other that we experience almost paranormal type thoughts, like my dreams when I was away and hers. They could just be the brain's way of coping or they could be the work of God, who knows, but I've decided to embrace it and just go with the idea that it's because we were handpicked for each other.

I spent weeks searching images on the web for a beach that looks like the dream she described. The one I found may not be exact, but it's pretty damn close, and it has private sections available. For the next week I have her all to myself.

All in all, I would say today has been a success. The reception was fun.

I really liked seeing Kinzleigh let loose and have fun. As much as I hate to say it, because she takes some of my time away from Kinzleigh, Karsyn has been good for her. She seems to relax her and open her up, helping her not to be so uptight. I always thought Presley and Adalynn helped her, but even they didn't have the effect Karsyn has.

We went through all the wedding festivities after I gave Kinzleigh a lap dance that I had actually been planning for a while. I figured it would throw her off, but the look on her face was priceless. Karsyn calling her out to dance to hip-hop music was all part of the plan. It was a damn great one too, because dirty dancing with her was better than I thought it would be.

The night was filled with cake, photos, dancing, champagne, and finally sliding that garter from her thigh after she threw the bouquet. We're now here riding in this car to the airport. The cans dragging on the pavement behind us are proof.

"You're stubborn, Abercrombie."

"That may be, beautiful, but all in good reason, and it sounds like the pot is calling the kettle black. Don't you think?"

"Point taken."

I pull in the nearest gas station with a carwash to get the shaving cream off of her car before we leave it parked at the airport. I stop at the pump and look at her. "You want to go inside and get us a drink and a carwash code while I cut the cans off the back?"

"Sure, what do you want?"

"Water is fine. We should try to sleep on the plane. It's late and it's a long flight."

"Okay. I'll be right back."

We both exit the car at the same time, and I watch her backside as she walks in. She's wearing skintight jeans with frilly rhinestones on the back pockets, a lowcut, long-sleeved shirt, and her boots. Those jeans do wonders for her ass. I asked where she got them and she shot me a dumbfounded look and told me they were called *Miss Me* jeans. I have no idea why, because I will not miss them when I roll them off of her.

She disappears inside the service station and I reach in my pocket for my pocketknife as I walk to the back of her car. I laugh as I look at the disaster of a job my brothers and the rest of our wedding party did on her car.

Opening my pocketknife, I slide the blade into the condom stuck to the back window, remove it, and toss it in the trash: one down and about ten to go.

When the car is free of all sexual supplies and I've cut the strings from the back, throwing the cans in the trash, I get back in the vehicle with Kinzleigh. She hands me the slip of paper with the three-digit code.

Taking it, I start the car and drive to the tunnel, punching in the code on the keypad. As I pull in and stop with the buzzer, Kinzleigh grabs my hand and places it into the neckline of her shirt, cupping her breast underneath her bra. I look at her with a grin on my face and then glance down at my hand.

"Want to have car sex? We have condoms," she says as she fans out a few condom packets in her other hand. "We could pretend we're still in high school and just left prom. You can take advantage of me and send me home after curfew."

She has a cheesy grin on her face and starts lifting her eyebrows up and down. I have to bite my tongue so hard I can taste blood in an attempt to keep a serious face. I know my eyes are deceiving me, but I can at least try.

"Baby, if we have car sex, I'm not using a condom. It's all or nothing with you. Ya know, the perks of marriage." I wink, knowing damn well we quit using condoms long before we were married. "I want to feel the hot and wet goodness coating my cock as you sit on it."

Her cheeks flush. I'm still the pro at role-playing. This will never change. Men are built to be perverts. You accept it and move on, living happily with your dirty thoughts that occur about every two and a half seconds. It's when you try to fight it that you have problems.

"Now Brey, what if you get me pregnant? Then what on earth will we do? We can't have a baby in high school." She starts rubbing my hand around on her plump, round breast. My dick was already semi-hard and now it's growing.

"It's too late to worry about that. I've already checked that one off the list, sweetheart."

She lowers her hands to the button of her jeans, undoing them. Her thumbs hook under the waistband and she starts to push them down along with her panties, baring her bottom half inch by inch. I squeeze her boob. I can't help it. It's sitting under my hand, tempting me.

Her nipple hardens underneath it, making me salivate. I want it in my mouth. I look behind us out the rearview mirror. It's almost midnight and the service station is clear except for the attendant inside. We had to exit off the interstate to find a gas station, so it's in a wooded area about halfway to New Orleans.

Her windows are tinted, and the carwash is spraying foam all over the car. She completely removes her pants and boots, standing on her knees in the seat of the car. "Drop 'em, Abercrombie. I'm letting you in."

My breathing is heavy. I can't move. She has her pussy all but staring at me in the face. She removes my hand from her shirt and places it over her mound, my fingers outside of her wet entrance.

Holy shit . . .

She picks her leg up, resting her foot on the console beside the gear shifter, opening herself up to me. I can only sit here like this is the first time I've been seduced by a woman and have no fucking idea what I'm supposed to do. You'd think I didn't know how to use my dick, the very organ that's been my best friend since I discovered it.

She has her hand placed on the outside of mine, controlling it like a puppet master controls a puppet. She presses my fingers inward, slightly dipping them inside of her. I bite my bottom lip between my teeth. "You wanted to feel the hot and wet while I sit on you, so drop 'em."

I swallow, my mouth now thick. My fingers finally start to work on their own, pressing inside deeper. Damn, I want in. "Unbutton me."

I thrust upward, giving her better access to the button on my jeans. She wastes no time unbuttoning and unzipping them. I remove my hand to shove my jeans and briefs down to my thighs. I'm hard as a rock. I'm taller, so the seat is already slid back enough to give her room.

"Show me how much you want it, beautiful. It's all yours. Ride me. I want you to get yourself off."

She climbs over the center and straddles my lap. I place my hands on her thighs as she takes my shaft in her hand and positions it at her entrance. She sits down, allowing me to sink inside of her. I grunt at the feeling of her wrapped around me. It's so wet and I haven't even kissed her.

The carwash sign is lighting up, telling us to drive forward, but I'm not going anywhere. She starts to rock back and forth. The head of my dick is hitting something hard, making it hard not to come. I'm trying to think of something, anything, to hold out until she gets hers.

She grabs my hands and runs them up her flat stomach, guiding them in the direction of her breasts. She loves them to be touched during sex. The underwire of her bra goes up as my hands reach them, cupping each one.

Her head leans back and she starts to squeeze my dick. *Fuck.* I start rubbing her nipples with my thumbs. Her back is arched and she's resting her hands on my knees, picking up pace.

Football, baseball, algebra—don't think of the way it feels.

I'm thinking of the way it feels.

I can feel the tug in my balls. I can't hold out anymore. It feels too good. And maybe some of it is that we're in public and it would be easy to get caught. "Baby, I can't hold it much longer. Are you about to come?"

"I'm ready. Come with me."

Thank fuck.

At the beginning of her orgasm her face contorts into a beautiful, erotic pose. I can feel the first spurt of my seed releasing inside her and then another. I squeeze her boobs, hard, letting her ride out her orgasm.

When she's done, she starts to get off, but I hold her here. I just need to sit like this for a second. The sensitivity of my head after release won't allow it for long, but until I can't stand it anymore, I want to sit here connected together so I can look into her eyes. "Stay."

She wraps her arms around my neck and kisses me on the lips. "I love you, Breyson."

"I love you too, Kinzleigh. I really do."

"You should be able to sleep on the plane just fine now. Take me on my honeymoon, husband. I'm ready for our first official vacation together."

I kiss her one more time. "Anything for you, beautiful."

FORTY-TWO

Kinzleigh

We had to take a commercial plane first and then once we arrived at the airport we had to get on another smaller aircraft until we reached a port for a taxi boat to our final destination. I have no idea what he's planning, but I'm really freaking excited. I'm sitting between Breyson's legs, leaning up against his body and watching the clear water wash up against the side of the boat. An island comes into view as we ride through the sunshine.

I pull my shades up on my head to get a better look at it and I become breathless, instantly knowing what this is. I recognize it from my dreams . . .

At the airport we changed clothes due to the significant difference in climate. Back home it's still cool at night, but here it's a permanent warm all year round, the rays from the sun kissing my face and hugging my shoulders. The sky is the perfect shade of baby blue, white clouds effortlessly ornamented to create a beautiful balance of light colors.

My dress is white, strapless, and fitted at the top, the skirt flowing, dancing with the slightest breeze. Breyson is wearing a white linen button down shirt with the sleeves rolled up to his elbows and a pair of khaki shorts, his brown leather sandals offsetting the light in the best way.

The boat pulls up at the hut that was built out from the shoreline to let us off. It has a roof made with a material that resembles straw, giving it more character. It's private, but not at all small. The water is clear and washing against the brown wooden posts that disappear into the seafloor below. I look back at Breyson with tears in my eyes. "How did you find this place?"

"You can find anything on the web, baby." The cool breeze blows my hair across my face and he brushes it away with the tips of his fingers. "Come on. I want to see where we're staying for the next week."

We both stand and he gathers our bags from the boat. Placing them on the dock, he helps me out of the boat and then follows behind me. It's beautiful here. I'm so emotional. The place that helped me cope when he was gone is now real.

I run my fingers along the wood railing of the pier, the dark stain more beautiful under my creamy skin, and walk toward the entry of the thatch hut; also where the pier branches out into a long one that stretches across the water to the shore in the distance, depositing into the white sand. It feels like we live out in the middle of the ocean.

I turn to Breyson and hold out my hand as the boat backs up to leave. He's standing with his hands in his pockets, watching me. "Leave the bags. Come into the water with me. This is something I need to do."

He starts walking with the one request, never asking me questions of why, but simply giving in to my desires. That is one thing I love about him. He doesn't need an explanation for everything. He's simply content with making me happy.

He grabs my hand and follows me down the pier, remaining silent as we walk hand in hand. At the end of the pier I slip out of my flip flips and leave them lying there, as does Breyson. We always seem to end up at the beach. It's our place in this world. The locations may be different, but still, a beach is where we belong.

My toes sink into the warm, white sand, squishing between my toes. Breyson pulls back on my hand, halting me. I look back. "What's wrong?"

He places one arm on my waist and the other behind my knees, scooping me into his arms. I place my arms around his neck. "What's this for?"

I smile.

"I'm going to carry you over the threshold, Mrs. Abercrombie."

"Don't we need a door for that?"

"Not when we can make our own. I've learned that the water is a different world from the shore and the shoreline is the portal between the two. That's the only door I need."

I don't say anything. I let him carry me into the clear water. He wades through the water until he's thigh deep and sets me down. The water is warm, soaking me to my waist. A soft breeze continues to blow, taking my hair in its grasp. "Dance with me," he says, not really a question, but more of a statement.

"There's no music."

"It doesn't matter. We can make our own. There's no one here to judge us. I get you all to myself for a week: no interruptions of friends, school, football, or caring for someone else. This week it's back to where it all began—us. I want to dance with my wife."

I wrap my arms around his neck, but this time he holds me by the waist, pulling me into him, and we dance. I slide my arms down to rest on his shoulders, a more relaxed position, and lay my head on his chest, listening to the rhythm of his heart beating. "Just for the record, I don't care what anyone else thinks. Your opinion of me is the only one that matters. You're my number one."

He lays his cheek on the top of my head and continues to sway, barely moving in the water. "That's probably a good thing, because to most people we likely seem crazy."

I laugh. He's right. Perhaps we are crazy, but that's okay. If we're crazy, then being normal is boring. I'll take crazy any day. "What do you want to do while we're here?"

"Whatever you want to do, beautiful."

"That's not the answer I was looking for, babe. Everyone knows you never agree to things without reading the tiny disclaimer in small print. What if I told you I'd be your sex slave for a day if you would help me murder someone?"

"I'd do it, help you hide the body, and then say what the hell did we just do, run off to another country, and live happily ever after with you."

"You're hopeless, Abercrombie."

"So I've been told. It must be your body. It hypnotizes me. That makes it all your fault."

I raise my head and look at him. He looks down at me. "What?"

"Gosh, I love you." I put my hands on his face. "Kiss me, you amazing man."

He presses his lips to mine and kisses me, following through by sliding his tongue against mine. I reach up to unbutton his shirt, starting with the top, and slowly descending until I get to the last one. I push each side over his shoulder, sliding the shirt down his arms. He stops kissing me, now watching me as I kiss each pectoral. "What are you doing?" he asks.

"Making my dreams a reality. We're alone. Let's make a memory."

He reaches behind me to grab ahold of my zipper and slowly slides it down the length of my back. He peels the top of my dress down to my waist, baring my upper half completely. The dress was tight enough I didn't need a bra. "You're beautiful like this. I want you naked all the time. You aren't wearing any clothes this week."

"You're in luck. I'm on my honeymoon. My husband is really hot, so he has a way of getting what he wants."

He grins at me. "Will you tell me if I do it different than in the dream?"

"Yes, but we have all week to get it right, so kiss me." He bends forward and lays his lips on mine, kissing me softer than he has in a really long time. The movement is so slow and intricate it's mesmerizing.

He places his hands on my thighs and picks me up, skimming me against his body, our skin creating friction. I wrap my legs around his waist and look down at him. "Make love to me, Breyson. I want to add one more secret to the many that already exist here . . ."

FORTY-THREE

Breyson

A FEW DAYS LATER ...

I roll over and kiss her stomach. The weather is warm and we've been laying on a large blanket in the sand for about thirty minutes now. "What are you doing?"

She looks over at me. She's wearing sunglasses and a beach hat. I always thought those hats were for old women, but somehow, she makes it sexy. "I'm reading. Are you getting bored?"

"I was just wondering. Do you still read that sexy stuff you used to read sometimes?" I prop up on my forearms and start sifting the sand through my fingers.

She pulls her shades down her nose and looks at me with a grin. "Why do you ask? Do you like that I may or may not read sexy books?"

I shrug my shoulders. I wonder if I'll sound like a douche if I say yes. I remember some really hot times that resulted from her reading books. *Fuck it*. Sometimes I feel like I've lost my balls anyway during the times when I turn into a sappy, love-struck bastard. "Maybe."

She sets her iPad down on her beach bag. "Oh, yeah? Why?"

"A certain closet in public that resulted in our son and a hot, steamy shower after a dirty dream come to mind. I'm also wondering if that little late-night rendezvous in the car a few nights ago had something to do with what you're reading."

"Hmm . . . So you like my random outbursts of wanting to be fucked in strange places?"

I love hearing filthy language come out of that clean mouth of hers. It fuels my fire. "Yes."

There is no reason to lie. I'm a guy. It's a title I'm proud of. Men are animals; when it comes to sex anyway. I will wear that badge proudly. "You keep saying dirty things and you're going to be wearing sand in some uncomfortable places."

She sits up and then stands. "Where are you going?" I roll over on my back and prop myself up again. She takes off her hat and tosses it down on her spot. With me laying and her standing she looks like she is towering over me.

She is wearing a strapless, black and pink bikini covered in white polka dots. "When I was a kid Mom and Dad used to take us to the beach every weekend for a couple of hours. We used to play flag football and it was fun. I haven't played in a long time. I miss it."

She reaches behind her and then removes her top. My eyes go wide. She throws it down beside her hat and reaches into her bag, pulling out a football. "What do you say, Abercrombie, are you up for a game? This time I don't want to play flag, though. Let's shake it up and play tackle. Can you handle tackling a girl?"

I think I just came a little. She is tossing the football from hand to hand with a smirk on her face.

Damn, I love you, woman.

I jump up and she takes a step back. "If you're the offense, I think I can handle it."

She starts walking backward. "Game on. Just remember, I was raised in a die-hard football family. I play to win."

She turns and starts prancing off, drawing attention to that beautiful round ass. I remove my trunks and shout. "Why don't we turn it up another notch!"

She turns around and stops, as she looks at me, completely nude. I point at her bikini bottoms. "Drop your panties, Mrs. Abercrombie."

She swipes her tongue over her upper teeth. "All right." She throws the ball through the air and I catch it. Beautiful throw. I knew I loved her for a reason. This is going to be fun.

She hooks her thumbs under the side strings, pushing them down and stepping out of them. She wads them up and throws them at me. I catch them too. She's watching me, so I place them up to my nose. Her mouth opens. Dropping them on the blanket I start to walk forward. "You can throw first," I say, and throw her the ball.

She catches it at the same time I get to where she is standing. I slap her on the ass, causing her to squeal. "If you can get me down, baby, you can have anything you want."

"Anything?"

"Anything."

"Challenge accepted."

I point out the end zones. "Here's the way we're going to do this. I'm going to start at your end zone, the furthest point away from mine. I want you to pass me the ball from mine and I'll run it out. If you can get me down before I reach the goal line you get anything you want and you get the ball, but if I make a touchdown then I get what I want. Deal?"

She is staring at my crotch. That spot always did draw her attention, starting that night at Ryland's pool house when she appeared at the door. "Deal," she says.

We split, moving to our designated side. Her body is hard not to look at, but when it comes to football and getting what I want, I have amazing focus. I take my stance, waiting for her to pass me the ball. She pulls her arm back and throws it toward me. I catch it and cradle the ball. We take off running at the same time.

Holy shit, her boobs are bouncing as she runs.

I take the right side and so does she, attempting to block me. I spin to the left, but the girl has fast reflexes. She wasn't lying. She's good. I don't want to barrel through her, because I'm twice her size. If I get around her, she'll never catch me.

I'm about to go back to the right when she reaches out and grabs my balls in her hand. My reflex as a guy is to protect them with my life and it causes me to stumble, diving face first and almost eating sand, but I catch myself with my hands. She bursts out in laughter as I stand back to my feet. "That was dirty."

She has a grin on her face. "Hey, I never said I was going to play fair."

"Some might call that cheating."

"You said I had to get you down. You never once specified how. There is always a loophole, Abercrombie. I can't help that I think outside the box." She actually forms a box with her hand movements as she speaks.

I throw the football down in the sand and take a step forward. There is not an ounce of laughter on my face. Her eyes enlarge slightly. She knows what's coming, because she turns and takes off running. I even give her a few seconds head start running down the strip of beach before I take off after her. I'm a running back. I'm trained to run, and fast. There is no way in hell she will ever outrun me.

I take off, my strides double in size. It doesn't take me long to catch her and pass her, turning around and stopping in front of her. I grab her waist and pick her up, throwing her over my shoulder. She screams and starts slapping me on the butt as I start walking. "Breyson, put me down!"

I slap hers harder, most likely leaving a handprint. I take off in a sprint toward the water. "Breyson, no."

"Hold your breath, beautiful. You're going in whether you like it or not." I can feel the warm water on my feet as I enter. The water slows me down a little, but not much. When I get deep enough, I pull her off my shoulder and into a cradling position in my arms. I sling her back to get momentum and throw her in the water.

I wait for her to break the surface from underneath the water. She stands upright, wiping her hands over her face and through her hair. "Now you can say we skinny-dipped on our honeymoon," I say, one side of my mouth pulled into a smirk.

She wades through the water, coming toward me. The look on her face says she has something up her sleeve. She grabs her breasts in her hands, pressing them together. I bite my bottom lip. Watching her touch herself has my dick hardening instantly from the chub I was already sporting.

She stops in front of me and grabs my erection in her hand. She starts fisting her hand up and down in the water. My breathing picks up. "Saddle up, Abercrombie. I'm about to ride. I want you on your knees."

Fucking hell.

She's bossy and I love it. Just when I think I can figure her out she mixes it up, never letting things become boring. One thing I love is watching her come out of her shell. We've grown a lot as individuals since we met, and also as a couple. It makes our relationship that much more special. With her . . . I look forward to the future instead of dreading it.

FORTY-FOUR

JULY . . . CALIFORNIA

I watch the two people I adore the most in this world run across the sand as I sit on my lounger with a permanent grin etched on my face. Breyson is holding Bryce in the air in his hands, flying him like a plane. He squeals. "Fly, Da-da."

I can't believe he'll be one at the end of August. One more month and his infant days are over. This year has really flown by. It saddens me, because I feel like Bryce is doing things early. Mom comments all the time about how smart he is. I didn't start walking until my first birthday, she said, and was slower to talk. He's been saying 'da-da' for a while, but since Breyson started flying him through the air on a daily basis, he picked up that word too.

After we got back from our honeymoon, things really took off. Cheerleading tryouts came and went and everything for football is set for Breyson.

We both finished the semester with good grades and I took off the summer to spend time with Bryce and every moment I can with Breyson since he has certain requirements with football. I received good news a couple of months ago. My training paid off and I made the cheerleading squad. Starting in the fall, Breyson and I both get to suit up for every game.

We're both moving toward our dreams one step at a time.

Breyson finally decided on a major. He went with Kinesiology, the study of human movement. It kind of goes hand in hand with sports anyway. I'm so happy for him, more so than myself.

Our baby boy started walking earlier this month and now he can't stay still. Crawling wasn't good enough for him, I guess, because that phase didn't last long. He's so much like Breyson it's scary, and he tries to mimic everything he does. It's adorable.

From his looks all the way to his personality, he's a mini Breyson. I swear all I did was incubate him. The only things he got from me were my green eyes and upfront shy nature, but once he warms up, all Breyson.

This is our first family vacation. It was more business, because I had to come sign the papers for the cheerleading company and make a decision on what I was going to do with it. I decided that I was going to offer Andy, my old coach, a partnership, splitting the company down the middle with fifty percent ownership each. He's the best around here and I want him with me. I also need someone that can be here fulltime and someone I can trust. I will always love California, but our home and school is in Mississippi, as well as our families.

Last night Breyson and I went to my old gym and made him the offer. I think he was in shock at first, but he gladly accepted. I've always liked Andy and I think he'll take the company further than I would have ever imagined. He just never had the investment opportunity until now to branch out on his own.

I look out at the shoreline where the two men in my life are. Breyson is squatting down, whispering something to Bryce. He holds out his little arms and starts toddling toward me. "Mama, Mama."

He melts my heart.

Breyson is standing behind him gleaming. It's hard not to be proud of such an amazing thing, whether you planned it or not. These two are what I live for.

I stand and start walking to meet him halfway. He loses his balance in the sand and falls, now crying. Breyson takes off running as if he's about to fall off a ledge. It's just a little sand. He's the most amazing father anyone could ask for, and that's strange considering his age, but Breyson's always been mature.

We both reach him at the same time, but Breyson grabs him first, turning him in his arms. "You okay, buddy?"

I grab his hand and brush off the sand stuck to it. Talking in my baby voice I start talking to him. "Tell Daddy to quit being silly. Little boys are tough, especially if you're going to play football like Daddy."

Bryce stops crying and starts laughing and clapping his hands together, squealing with excitement. "Ball, ball."

I smile. I never thought I'd be a good boy mom.

"He's a keeper, Mom. He's going to be a football star. I can feel it already."

"Not if you keep babying him, Abercrombie. He's a male and he's yours. A few scratches are good for him. If he's going to survive in our families, he has to grow thick skin. You know how Braxton and Ryland are, and Briar won't always be around to protect him from their jokes."

Bryce holds out his arms for me, which is a rare thing when Breyson has him. My baby is all Daddy's boy. I grab him and throw him in the air, catching him instantly, and pull him down just above my face. "Isn't that right, buddy?"

He grabs my lips in his hand, clawing them. I place him on my hip and grab his hand, moving it. I start smooching him all over his face and neck, causing him to laugh. I love hearing his baby laugh.

I look at Breyson. He looks serious as he watches me with Bryce, but then starts to speak. "Is it bad that I'm not ready for him to grow up?"

"No. I think every good parent feels that way. It just means we're doing something right."

He smiles, a heated gleam in his eyes. "Better watch out, Mama, give it a few more years and I may keep you knocked-up."

My temperature rises, and I know my face is flushed. He's never said anything like that before. Sure, the thought of more kind of lingered between us, one day, but he's never mentioned a time frame or made it verbal really. I confirm we're on the same page with, "I'd like that."

Bryce starts wiggling, wanting down, and breaking the moment. He barely wants to be held since he learned to walk. There was a very short period of him crawling. I don't think he liked the rubbing against his knees. It seems like right after he started crawling he started pulling up on everything and trying to walk.

I stand him on the sand and hold his hand. Breyson grabs the other one and we start walking him toward the edge of the water to let him dip his feet in. Along the way he pulls his feet up, swinging from our hands like we've done before. It's his favorite thing to do, and once he starts you can barely get him to stop. I always worry he's going to pull an arm out of socket, but I have come to find that kids are tougher than you think.

Breyson leans in over him to kiss me. I meet him halfway.

"I love you, Kinzleigh."

"And I love you, Breyson. I always will."

Everything that lies ahead is pointing to a bright future. Just when you think things are perfect everything can spin out of control, so the key is to never take for granted the good things. We had an amazing start and a bumpy middle, but I have a feeling we'll have a strong finish.

EPILOGUE

DECEMBER ... FOUR YEARS LATER ...

I'm standing on the sidelines with the rest of the cheerleaders. The game is about to start. I stretch, along with the rest of the girls on the squad. "Kinzleigh, let's go. Time to line up," Jessica says and tosses me my pompoms.

I catch them and start running across the field toward the football tunnel. Half the squad stands on one side while the rest of us stand on the other.

I take my position, waiting, as the cleat sounds get closer to the exit. You can hear the players pumping themselves up by hollering back and forth to each other. I still get nervous before this part. Don't ask why. I guess, because it still seems surreal that things happened the way they did. As the coach starts to emerge the players dressed out in blue and gold take off running out of the tunnel, and onto the field.

I watch each one pass, searching for the jersey marked with the number forty-four. They are running so fast it's always hard to pinpoint, but it never fails that he finds me first. He pulls up his helmet just before he reaches me and briefly kisses me on the lips. "Win us a ballgame, baby."

"Anything for you, beautiful." Breyson pulls down his helmet and keeps running with the rest of the players.

Breyson played for the Golden Eagles all four years of college, each year getting better than the one before. Him and Fisher completely transformed the statistics for the team, putting them back on the map for NFL scouts. The school went from barely winning any games to barely losing. Once I made the cheerleading squad that first year, I did every year after. I put my mind toward a goal and achieved it, making me proud of myself.

Senior year was the best year of them all, though, for two different reasons. The biggest surprise came right before graduation when Breyson got the call that he was being drafted with the San Diego Chargers. He had worked so hard between putting in for the draft and going to the trainings for it, such as the NFL Combine. He actually broke down and cried not even a second after he got the call that spring, and now, here we are.

Breyson encouraged me to tryout for the cheerleading squad once I was finished with school. It was a stretch, but I gave it a shot and actually made it. We had to deal with issues that arose like the 'no fraternization policy' in force, but somehow between contract negotiations and the fact that we were already married before, we were able to make it work to some degree. I'm not going to tryout after this year. I'm going to put all of the focus on my family and my company. I had a dream and I made it happen. That's what matters.

I still feel like I'm living in a dream and can't make myself wake up, because I didn't have any high hopes of actually making it. Becoming an NFL cheerleader used to be my number one goal, but not anymore. Breyson getting his dream was, and he did. Me getting on the squad of the same team was the mega bonus if there ever was one. And after this year, I will file it away in our memories and become one of the wives in the skybox supporting her husband.

Andy has done a phenomenal job with the company and it's my primary career focus, but it will never be more important than my family. Cheerleading in the NFL has been a hobby, since I will be at every game for Breyson anyway. When I walk away I'll never look back.

I graduated with a double major in *Business Administration* and *Entertainers and Performers,* as well as a minor in Marketing. I could have stuck solely to *Entertainers and Performers,* but I wanted to have an education backing me to help me make the company a success. It's done so well over the past few years, though, that we are already looking to expand in the spring.

The squad rushes to our place on the sidelines, getting ready for kickoff.

I look up into the front row of the stadium to my favorite people.

"Hey, Mom!" I look up at Bryce waving in his seat beside his Uncle Preston. He's wearing his Chargers jersey with his daddy's number—Breyson's miniature twin. He just turned five a few months back. That boy is my entire world and he is possibly the sweetest person I've ever met. I'm not just saying that because he's my own. He has a huge heart.

Preston has been actively involved in his life since our wedding. He comes down every chance he gets and even keeps him for a few days here and there for a 'boys' weekend' as they call it. It was a little awkward at first, but Breyson and Preston are actually really close now. We were able to completely put the past behind us.

The whirlwind of things that have happened with all of our friends over the years has kept the drama rolling in, but somehow it always ends the way it's supposed to end. At least we have all remained close.

"Go Chargers! Hi, Mom! Someone is missing you." I smile, trying not to laugh at *Go Chargers* coming out of her mouth. Usually she's wearing much different colors, and a certain someone I know wouldn't be impressed. Karsyn is holding my Kennedi Brianne on her hip, all decked out in her team gear to match Bryce, but with an added blue and gold bow clipped to her headband. She is standing in front of their seat next to the wall separating the stadium from the field.

Kennedi was our Christmas present last year. She was our one chance to experience planning a baby. Breyson didn't get to experience my pregnancy with Bryce, and when he started believing that he had a chance at the pros he wanted to start trying for another one so he could experience it all. I rarely deny Breyson what he wants. He doesn't ask for much, so I went and had my IUD removed and she was conceived two months later.

I wave at my two amazing little minions. I'm not sure if there are any more kids in our future, but right now we are content with the two precious gifts that we have. The rest we'll see with time.

Kennedi's first birthday party is later tonight. Karsyn has been helping me plan it. Since the day of my wedding when she pledged her girl love to me, we have been inseparable, and that hasn't changed yet. Sometimes you stumble upon the people that will be forever at your side. That's what happened with Breyson and with Karsyn. The day I met her I never imagined this kind of friendship would blossom in the midst of her crazy, erratic personality, but today she is my best friend, sister of the heart, and my children's Godmother. It wasn't even a question. She was the only person that crossed my mind when Breyson and I discussed it.

"I love you guys!" When I say it, I'm referring to all of them, because I do. I turn and watch the kickoff.

This is my life. It's not perfect and sometimes it's hectic, but it's mine. Breyson and I both had a dream and we didn't let anything stand in our way of achieving it. No dream is unreachable if you want it bad enough. The two of us are proof, because we made it. The dreams we had as kids are a reality today. The only difference is that we found someone to experience our dreams with instead of experiencing them alone.

In the beginning, we never wanted this life—either of us—but through finding each other we realized just how special a family is. Our kids are a result of how much we love each other, a combination of each other. I have more love in my heart today than I ever thought possible, and I wouldn't trade it for anything in the world.

Breyson

I grab the small, pink cake off the bar after lighting the number one candle in the center. Everyone is waiting in the dining room, so we can sing happy birthday to Kennedi; one of only two girls that's ever stolen my heart.

When I got drafted Kinzleigh and I bought a house here, so we're here during season and back home when I'm off. We got our country and we got our California. It couldn't have worked out more perfect than it did. We're one of the few people that can have our cake and eat it too.

I walk through the doorway toward Kennedi's highchair that is covered in balloons tied to the legs. Karsyn and Preston were the only ones that could make it on short notice since they came to the game for babysitting duty. We have a rotation going between all available parties between our families, and it works for us. We don't want a nanny raising our kids if we can help it. Things are a little harder when everyone lives within flying distance instead of driving. Preston is the closest person to us residentially, but he travels a lot. I'm sure Mims will have a late birthday party for Kennedi with the whole family once we're back home long enough.

Fisher is still my best friend, but he plays for another team, so during season we rarely see each other. I'm glad to see him so happy with his life right now. The guy didn't have it easy in some ways, but everything panned out and ended with things on his side.

Everyone starts singing *happy birthday* as I walk across the room.

Kennedi is beating her hands on the tray of the highchair. She's beautiful, combining the best mixture of Kinzleigh and I, but she did get my eyes, and I like to think it's because she came straight from my heart. She doesn't take after one of us in particular like Bryce does me. Every time I look at her, I get a consuming emotion of pride running through my veins. I feel like she's my do-over for what I missed with Bryce, and she'll always have a little extra special place in my heart for it.

"Daddy, can I help her blow out the candle?" Bryce is standing in a chair on one side of her and Kinzleigh on the other. That boy is my sidekick. You couldn't have picked a better kid if you could write the features on a list and have it custom made. He is loving, and always asking to help do anything we need him to. He's only five and he's smart, not to mention the most tenderhearted child you'll ever meet. He's reserved up front like Kinzleigh, but once he gets to know you, he'll consume your heart with his funny personality.

Kennedi is wired a little more like me. She never meets a stranger even though she can barely talk. She never cries when someone holds her that she doesn't know, and she's loud. God is the child loud. Put her down and she is gone like a bolt of lightning. Not being able to walk didn't stop her any. She figured out a way to speed crawl. It's funny to watch. And she'll walk holding on to things, but the only thing she seems scared of was letting go until about a couple of weeks ago. We're in for it now that there's nothing holding her back.

The girl is going to be the death of me with her erratic and wild personality. One second I'm having to get on to her for getting in things she isn't supposed to be in, and then she gives me that look like I just stole her cake and I'm a goner. She wants Kinzleigh when she's hurt or whiney, but come bedtime she's a daddy's girl, in my lap ready to be rocked and read to.

During the day you would think Bryce and Kennedi are two unrelated kids in regard to personality, like night and day, but every morning for the past two weeks when I wake up, she's in his bed. Kinzleigh and I had no idea how she kept getting there because she's still in a crib, and then one night we stayed up to watch her on the video monitor.

As soon as we left the room she stood up and threw her favorite blanket over her crib rail to the floor and looked around, making sure no one would catch her. She then threw one leg over the crib followed by the other, letting herself fall. She was using her diaper as her cushion to break the fall. Thank God the bedrooms are carpet. If it wasn't so damn funny I would've spanked her to keep her from doing it again out of worry she'd hurt herself. After she got up, she ran to Bryce's room, her diaper keeping her from being quiet, and stopped on the side of his bed. She isn't tall enough to climb up on her own. She was pulling out her pacifier and swatting him with it at the same she was saying, "Bubba." It only took her saying it twice and he sat up and helped her in the bed, then they both laid down together and went back to sleep. They had formed a routine, obviously.

Kinzleigh and I haven't had the heart to bring it up, because it's better seeing them that way. I love my kids with all my heart. There isn't a day that goes by that I have any regrets of the path my life has taken. There is nothing I wish I had done that I didn't, and there is never a day that my love for my wife doesn't grow more than the day before. The two of us defeated the odds and we will continue to do so. We keep each other first, never keep secrets from one another, and if it would hurt each other we don't do it. That has made our relationship stronger than it's ever been.

We finish singing and I set the cake down. Kinzleigh grabs Kennedi's hands before they grab the flame of the candle. I shake my head. She tried. "Sure, buddy. You can help her blow it out. On the count of three: one, two, three . . ."

He blows the candle, putting out the flame. Everyone claps as I remove the wax candle. "I want a picture before she demolishes the cake. Breyson get in. I want a family picture."

"If you want to have a permanent photo of my face, Karsyn, all you have to do is ask. Don't volunteer my kids. I'll happily pose for you."

She rolls her eyes. Karsyn has been around long enough she's family. She's like that lost puppy that shows up at your doorstep and you kind of fall in love with her, even though she's broken and scarred. She's become like an adopted sister over the years. "Don't kid yourself, Breybear. Only Kinzleigh wants that and none of us have any idea why . . . Love you," she says in a singsong voice making a cheesy grin. "Besides, I have something much better to look at waiting for me at home. Now, hurry up before she dives face first into the cake and you mess up my photo album for this year."

I move over to Bryce and grab him in my arms, holding him diagonal in front of me. "Smile for the camera, buddy." She counts to three and snaps the picture.

"Okay, now you three move. I want to see what the girl has got. Kennedi, remember what Aunt Karsyn told you. It's all or nothing. You only get to do this once. I'm recording it."

Preston throws a cheese puff and hits her in the back of the head. "Hey! Cut it out, P. What was that for?"

"She's one. Like she knows what any of that means. She'd probably eat a bowl of dirt if you set it in front of her."

"You're just jealous because she loves me more than you. Get over it, P. You're no longer the favorite. Girls always stick together. Don't be upset, you still have Bryce. For some reason he thinks you're cool."

This is my family. They are goofy and most of the time they are fucking insane, but they are constant. They are always there when you need them. They would do anything for us and for my kids. Family sticks by your side no matter what and will come running when you need them, blood or not. I'd give my life for any of them.

Kennedi squeals very loud in a high pitch tone. "Okay, I'm letting her go or you can deal with her wrath," Kinzleigh says. As soon as she does, Kennedi slams her hands in the cake, squishing it between her fingers. She must like the texture, because for a moment she doesn't attempt to eat any. She just sits there squeezing it, letting it mush between her fingers and laughing as if it's the greatest thing in the world. She is the greatest thing in the world; all three of them are.

She grabs a handful and smashes it against her mouth, covering herself with pink icing and chocolate cake. She is obviously sucking on it based on the dramatic sucking motion her lips are doing. I'm standing in front of her watching her make a massacre out of a perfectly good cake. She slams both hands back down, grabbing cake in both hands. She acts like she is about to eat more when she slings it all over Karsyn and me.

I swipe my cheek, covering my fingers in the gooey concoction. She is laughing and still shoving cake in her mouth as Karsyn and I look at each other and burst out laughing. Kinzleigh is already bent over out of breath. I suppose that's what you get when you're in the war zone of a one-year-old with free rein over food.

There is no telling what I look like, but as long as she is having fun that's all that matters. This is what my life has become. I laugh more now than I ever have in my entire life. It's full of ups and downs, sacrifices and blessings, sometimes it's hard and sometimes it's the easiest thing in the world, but it's a life I wouldn't trade for anything in the world. I don't think a man really starts living until he has kids, because you finally learn what being selfless really is. It's the hardest, but most rewarding job in the world.

I walk toward my cake-covered angel as Kinzleigh removes the tray. "Okay, beautiful, I think it's time to clean you up. You've had enough messy stuff for one day." I pick her up under the arms and raise her over my head, wiggling her in the air. "You're going to be my little troublemaker, aren't you?" She lays her palms on my face, smearing it around, now fully covering me with cake.

I put her on my hip, visibly able to see cake on the tip of my nose. I look at Kinzleigh. "Yep. I'd say we have our hands full, Mom."

I turn and walk in the direction of the bathroom, passing Preston along the way. "That's a good look for you, man."

"Not a word, Preston, or you're next."

I look down at Kennedi asleep in my arms. Karsyn and Preston left about an hour ago. Bryce fell asleep on the couch watching his favorite movie, favorite for now anyway. I stand and walk Kennedi to her crib, laying her inside: one down, one to go.

I pick Bryce up and take him to his own bed, turning off the lights and television along the way. I lay him down and cover him up as he turns on his side. I kiss his temple. "Goodnight, buddy."

The house is now quiet. It's time to find my woman. I grab the monitors on the way to the sliding glass doors. Kinzleigh is sitting outside in our swing looking out at the city. For a country boy I have to admit, you can't beat this kind of view. It's a totally different world than back home. Having the option for both is a dream come true.

I stop at the door before opening it. Sometimes I still like to watch her when she doesn't know I'm here. It's one of those calming things that you can't explain, reflecting back on the one that makes your world turn, and the beginning of the amazing life that you were given.

I grab the remote to the surround sound, turning it on, and slide the door open. She looks back at me as our playlist starts to play, her shoulder length hair blowing in the breeze. She cut it after Kennedi was born, because it was easier with two kids. I didn't care as long as it was still in the loose, blonde curls I've always had a weakness for. "Kids asleep?" she asks.

I hold up the monitors. "Yeah."

"Good. I need you to myself for a little while."

I walk to the swing and put the monitors on the patio table. She is sitting with her feet laid out across the swing. I pick them up and sit down, laying them across my lap. She shakes her head. "Not close enough."

She rotates herself in the opposite direction. I open my arm for her to snuggle in her nook. "Are you tired?"

"A little," I say, "but I'm not too tired for this."

"You never are. You played a good game."

I start to swing with her snuggled up beside me, looking out at San Diego all lit up. I kiss her head. "Thanks, baby. As long as you're proud of me that's all that matters."

"Thanks for helping me with the kids. You do a lot even though you stay busy with the team. You're my rock."

"We're a team. There is no I or U in team. It doesn't matter how tired I am, I should never stop helping you. You're my partner and I'll never leave you alone to do anything."

She grabs my opposite hand resting in my lap, linking it with the back of hers. "I still feel like I hit the jackpot with you, even after all these years."

"That's funny, because I feel like I'm the lucky one."

The song we danced to at our wedding starts to play. "It seems like that night was so long ago, but it also seems like just yesterday."

"That's because every day together is an adventure. It makes the time pass by faster. It's one of those bittersweet things I guess."

She sits up and stands from the swing, turning to face me. I stop swinging, thinking she's ready to go in when she reaches up the bottom of her dress and pulls her panties down her legs. "You want to have a quickie and pass out? They should be out for a while."

She props her leg on the swing and places my hand on her thigh. It takes no effort. My cock is already hard. Years in and she still has me just as hard as the first time. Sex with a woman you love is like a fine wine. It only gets better with time.

I rub my hand up her leg and look at her. "Baby, I am ready for sex with you anytime."

I mean it. I will never deny or decline her offers. She's everything to me— my very reason for breathing. Marriage is give and take; it's compromise. More than that, I still want her every time she asks. I love her and that's still a way I show it. We're in this for the long haul, for the rest of our lives.

ACKNOWLEDGMENTS

There are so many people to thank, but that would take up pages. First and foremost I want to thank my amazing boyfriend, Patrick, for being my backbone and such a huge support, and also for understanding when I have to take time out of my schedule to write. I talk about my characters as if they are real people, and instead of getting annoyed you sit there and nod, letting me ramble. There are times that I get stressed or strap myself out because I can't say no, but you are always there to keep me going and to keep me sane. I love you more than you will ever know and I am so blessed to have you as a permanent fixture in my life. Your support and encouragement means more to me than you'll ever know.

Writing was never something I dreamed of like most writers, but a fellow writer and amazing friend, Victoria Ashley, took a leap of faith and told me to give writing a try. I did, and now I feel like it's where I belong. I still feel like I owe her the moon for introducing me to this amazing life. Victoria, you will always have a special place in my heart that no one can touch. I know you are getting busier with your own writing career and some days we barely say two words to each other, but know that I'm always thinking of you. It is amazing the feeling that I get seeing your writing career take off, knowing I found you with the beginning, Wake Up Call. You are one of my best friends and always will be. You are an amazing person. You really are. There are no words to explain how much of a friend you've been since the very beginning when being a writer was not even a thought. Thank you for being an amazing friend and advisor. I'm so glad that I found you. I love you, girlie.

Books have been important to me for two years now and storytelling for one. I get completely lost in the characters as I transfer the story from mind to manuscript. They have become my babies and I hope it shows in my writing. This has been the greatest journey I could have ever hoped for and I hope it continues for years to come.

Jessica Grover, my editor, thank you for branching out and contacting me as a reader. Not only did I find my editor, but also a very special friend. I will never be able to put into words the amount of gratitude I have for you. No matter how crazy and hectic your own schedule is you take the time to help me sift through countless words day in and day out to better the story for the readers. I absolutely love your crazy, sporadic personality. You have helped to bring me out of my shell more than you truly know. Never change, my dear. You have a beautiful heart and you will be in mine forever. You have a lot to bring to the table in contributing to the creation of what goes on in my mind. I think you know this based on the tears I've shed for book trailers. Thank you for crying right along with me at the close of Breyson and Kinzleigh's story. Not once did you judge or say they aren't real. Instead, you shared my heartbreak as if we both just lost an amazing friend, mourning their end. Thank you for purchasing Accepted and being a creeper on social media to find me. I assure you, I gained so much more than you. Know that I love you, my amazing friend.

Elizabeth Thiele, my personal assistant, you are also an amazing friend I found along the way. You keep me motivated by your reactions and responses as the story is being written. I know that you have a busy schedule and yet you continue to spend hours at a time promoting me and helping me in any way that I need. I appreciate everything you do and will do everything in my power to always show you. You are a twinkling star in my sky. Keep being the amazing person that you are. As an author and as a friend, I am very lucky to know you. You do a lot for me.

Heidi Sturgess, my lovely friend and beta reader, there are no words to place you in a category. You, my lady, are a truly amazing person inside and out. You have no idea how I look while reading those amazing Heidi emails regarding your thoughts for each chapter. You are that lucky penny that one stumbles upon somewhere in their life, not expecting what it will bring at all. Never ever change the person that you are. You are a valuable person. I hold you very close to my heart. Even though I've never met you, you are a treasured friend. I'm very thankful to have you in my corner. I love that we can get lost in a world of fiction with no judgments, no feeling crazy, but completely understanding one another. Thank you for giving my writing a chance.

Stephanie Phillips, my gem, I would never forget my first girl love. One comment thread about copyrighting is the irony to such an amazing friend. You have no idea how thankful I am for you my sweet, amazing person. Watching you grow as a writer has given me a sense of pride I never thought I could have. It's a beautiful thing. You mean so much to me, and even though you are thousands of miles away I feel like you are so close. One day we will get to see each other in person instead of our amazing FaceTime chats, but until then, know how important you are to me. You have been with me since I published book one and you will be with me 'til the end.

Hetty Whitmore Rasmussen, my promoter and friend, I haven't known you for long either, but you have been the sweetest person. I have no idea how Victoria found you, but that's just an addition to the list of things I will always be thankful to Victoria for. Thank you for everything you've done for me.

Clarise Tan, my cover designer, you are an amazing artist. You always take my vision for a cover and exceed my expectations, helping to bring my characters to life. I'm so glad Victoria sent me your way, because I can't imagine a better person to do my covers. You have also become a great friend.

To each and every one of you, I specifically tried to make each of you feel special as you have made me feel over the months, but as a whole know that I love EACH and EVERY one of you. You continue to give me an amazing amount of support. I could write page for page on what I love about you all, but it would take all day. All of you are important to me in ways you will never understand. I can only try to tell you over and over so you will have an increment of the way I feel when you make me feel special.

It doesn't matter if I become successful or stay a small time Indie just telling stories because they are screaming to be told, you all will be with me 'til the end. I will always make time for you, because you guys were with me from the beginning. Thank you for being amazing people and never ever change who you are. As a group you guys are my rare gems that cannot be assigned a price. That's how valuable you are. I'm not one for getting sappy, but know that I meant every word.

There are others as well that have recently become special to me, and if you're reading this you know who you are. Even though I didn't specify each and every person know you are no less important.

Love you guys!

Never let romance die, because it is something that should live in the hearts of everyone.

If you are a blogger, know that you are a tremendous help to authors. Every promotion helps to continue writing. We may not say it enough, but this would not be possible without y'all, so from my heart, thank you.

ALSO BY CHARISSE SPIERS:

Accepted Fate (Fate, #1)

Changing Fate (Fate, #2)

Twisting Fate (Fate, #3)

Lasting Fate (Fate, #4)

Chasing Fate (Fate, #5)

Fated for You (Fate, #6)

Fated For Me (Fate, #7)

Fate By Forgiveness (Fate, #8)

Finding Fate (Fate, #9)

Gifted Fate (Fate, #10)

Alluring Fate (Fate, #11)

Fight For You (A Broken Soul Novel)

Marked (Shadows in the Dark, #1)

Love and War: Volume One (Shadows in the Dark, #2)

Love and War: Volume Two (Shadows in the Dark, #3)

Sex Sessions: Uncut (Camera Tales, #1)

Sex Sessions: After the Cut (Camera Tales, #2)

Sex Sessions: Passionate Consequences (Camera Tales, #3)

Sex Sessions: Bundle (Uncut and After the Cut with bonus content)

ABOUT THE AUTHOR

I found books when I was going through a hard time in life. They became my means of escape when things got bad. I realized quickly how much I loved to take a backseat to someone else's life and watch the journey unfold. That began my journey with books in November of 2012. I constantly had a book open on my Kindle app. Never in a million years would I have imagined myself as a writer, because I never thought I was creative enough. I'm living proof that things will fall into place when they're meant to be. People will make their way into our lives when we don't expect it, setting the path for what we are meant to do. Never give up on people. Never stop taking a chance on others. Someone took a chance on trusting me with her work when she didn't know me from a stranger on the street and gave me the opportunity of a lifetime as our relationship progressed, which led me to editing and writing as well. This is my dream I never knew I had. As soon as I sat down and gave writing a shot, it was like the floodgates opened. Now, I am lost in a world of fiction in my head, new characters constantly screaming for their stories to be told. Continue to dream and to go for them. No one ever found happiness by sitting on the sidelines. Sometimes we have to take risks and put ourselves out there. Thank you for all of your support, and may there be many books to come. XOXO- C

Stay up to date on release info

www.charissespiers.com

charissespiersbooks@gmail.com